TRAITORS & PATRIOTS

A NOVEL OF THE AMERICAN CIVIL WAR

Book One of THE BATTLE CRY OF FREEDOM TRILOGY

by

RYAN McCARVILL

R
RETROSPECTIVE PUBLISHING

RETROSPECTIVE PUBLISHING

ISBN:
978-1-7778861-0-3 (Book)
978-1-7778861-1-0 (Electronic Book)

Editor: Laura McFarlane
Book Cover and Interior Design: Andrew Davis
Map Illustrations: Theodor Jurma

To Ida,
and to Mom and Dad

Map
OF THE STATES AND TERRITORIES OF THE
United States of America
C. 1859
WASHINGTON TERRITORY
OREGON
CALIFORNIA
UTAH TERRITORY
NEW MEXICO TERRITORY
NEBRASKA TERRITORY
UNORGANIZED TERRITORY
KANSAS TERRITORY
INDIAN TERRITORY
TEXAS
MINNESOTA
IOWA
MISSOURI
ARKANSAS
LOUISIANA
WISCONSIN
ILLINOIS
MICHIGAN
INDIANA
OHIO
KENTUCKY
TENNESSEE
MISSISSIPPI
ALABAMA
GEORGIA
FLORIDA
SOUTH CAROLINA
NORTH CAROLINA
VIRGINIA
Richmond
Charleston
PENNSYLVANIA
NEW YORK
NEW HAMPSHIRE
VERMONT
MAINE
MASSACHUSETTS
RHODE ISLAND
CONNECTICUT
NEW JERSEY
DELAWARE
MARYLAND
DISTRICT OF COLUMBIA
NORTH
SOUTH
EAST
WEST

A Map of
NORTHERN VIRGINIA
& MARYLAND
and Surrounding States
c. 1860
MARYLAND
Potomac River
Martinsburg
Harper's Ferry
BALTIMORE & OHIO R
MAYFAIR
Winchester
Kernstown
Allegheny Range
WASHINGTON
Leesburg
Moorefield
Strasburg
Valley
Shenandoah River
Front Royal
Shenandoah
MANASSAS GAP RR
Alexandria
Manassas
Junction
Mt. Jackson
ORANGE & ALEXANDRIA RR
Potomac River
Culpepper CH
Aquia Creek Sta.
Harrisonburg
Fredericksburg
Cross Keys
Port Republic
Rappahannock River
Gordonsville
VIRGINIA CENTRAL RR
Staunton
Waynesboro
Fredericks Hall Sta.
Beaver Dam Sta.
Charlottesville
RICHMOND & FREDERICKSBURG RR
Hanover Junction
Hanover CH
VIRGINIA
Chickahominy River
James River
RICHMOND
ORANGE & ALEXANDRIA RR
RICHMOND & DANVILLE RR
Appomattox River
Petersburg
Lynchburg
SOUTH SIDE RR

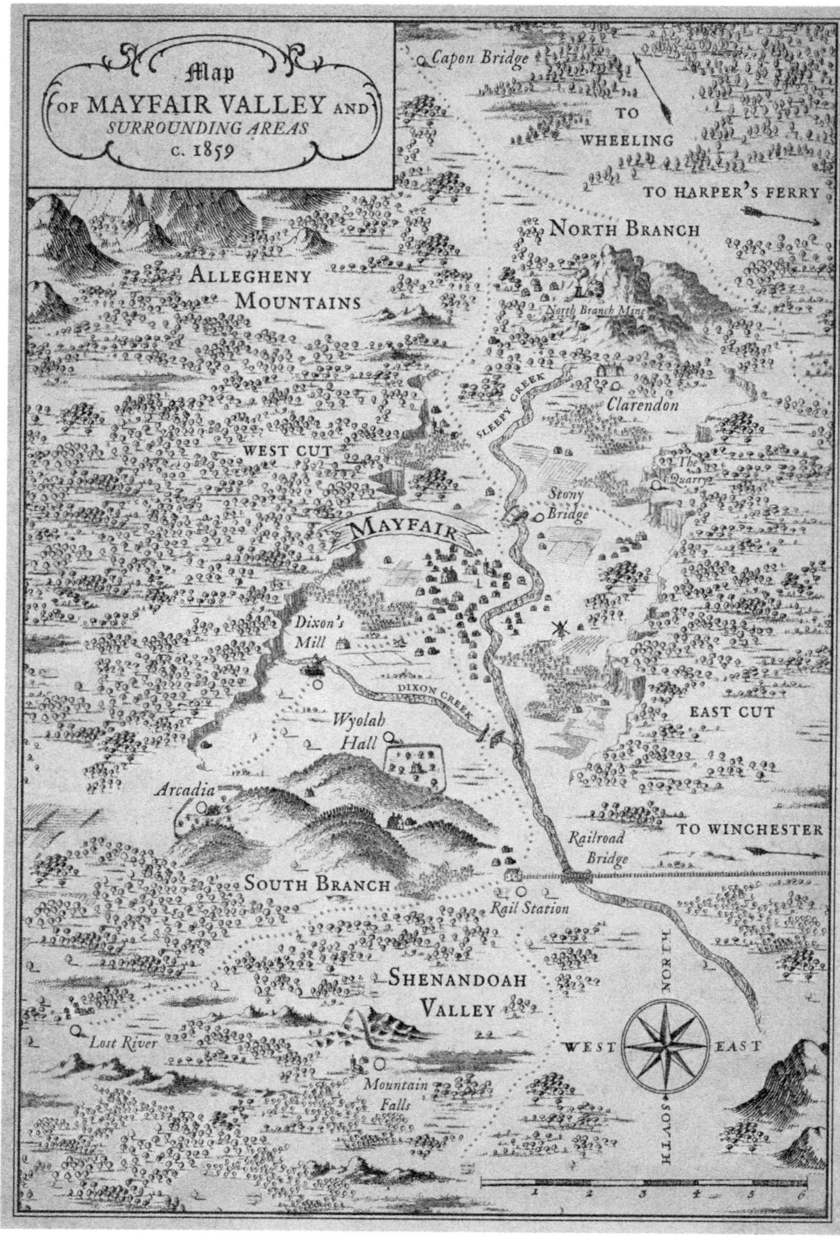
Map
of MAYFAIR VALLEY and
SURROUNDING AREAS
c. 1859
Capon Bridge
TO
WHEELING
TO HARPER'S FERRY
NORTH BRANCH
ALLEGHENY
MOUNTAINS
North Branch Mine
SLEEPY CREEK
Clarendon
WEST CUT
The Quarry
Stony
Bridge
MAYFAIR
Dixon's
Mill
DIXON CREEK
Wyolah
Hall
EAST CUT
Arcadia
TO WINCHESTER
Railroad
Bridge
SOUTH BRANCH
Rail Station
SHENANDOAH
VALLEY
NORTH
WEST
EAST
SOUTH
Lost River
Mountain
Falls
1
2
3
4
5
6

October 18, 1859

Sleep evades me again, and for that I suppose I'm thankful. While I am awake, my mind's eye can reproduce only vague and hazy vignettes of that horrible day. They are no less disturbing, but at least I can distract myself with the duties of living. It's only after I drift off to sleep that the fragmented terrors take hold of me, dragging me down some dark, subconscious hole like a host of soulless wights.

I have faith, strained and doubtful as it might be, that nightmares can be defeated with pen and paper. I've tried and failed, time and again, to capture the essence of that one nightmare in particular. Sometimes when I wake up, the world around me seems not to have changed since what Mama calls THE BAD TIMES *— what some other folks call* THE GOOD OLD TIMES.

It's been said that there is no dawn for the negro slave. For the slave it is all night, forever. My dream, however, always begins with the brightest sunshine.

I remember color, as if waking up. A warm, lush redness fills my vision: the summer sun peered through closed eyelids. I hear the sound of my own joyous laughter — a child's laughter — in my ears. My eyes open and a searing white sun looks back at me.

Don't look straight at the sun. Mama told me that countless times, just as she commanded me to never look the Colonel, our master, in the eye.

In this moment, I was happy to watch the sun winking through the broad green leaves of a beech tree, to feel creamy drops of color burning into my vision. From on high, a leaf detached from its stem and floated down to rest on the bridge of my nose. It tickled me there and made me laugh, and as I peered through tiny holes in the leaf's veiny flesh I imagined myself as a caterpillar having a picnic.

And then, somewhere in the distance, the plantation bell rang.

I turned my head and the leaf fell from my face. I wondered for a brief moment whether I'd imagined the bell sound, but I hadn't. The plantation bell had rung; other folks had heard it too, for there came over the whole company of field hands working nearby a deathly hush. Folks froze mid-step, and they turned to each other as veils of fear came down over their eyes. Who would be the first to turn and answer the bell's call?

The bell rang a second time. Before the third knell sounded, the whole mass of people fell into step toward the willow grove behind the house we called Clarendon, or simply the 'big-house.' In those days, Clarendon was the largest plantation in the Mayfair Valley. Today it's something very different. But on the hottest summer days, when I hear the faint sound of whips across the Valley, it does not take much to imagine myself back in the old days when Colonel Thomas Spencer was the greatest planter in the wider Shenandoah.

I found myself moving with the field hands toward the back of the big-house. Looking toward the veranda wrapping around the first storey, I saw that it was Miss Sarah pulling the rope of the plantation bell. She stood shaded from the glare of the late afternoon sun. I remember seeing the bouquet of wildflowers I had picked for Miss Sarah earlier that day. She still held them in her white-gloved hands, and even while ringing the bell she brought the flowers up to her dainty nose.

I knew Miss Sarah Carter, beautiful and raven-haired, as a great teller of tales. (I should mention she was the Colonel's niece, and like a daughter to him, and no doubt his favorite.) On Sunday afternoons she would gather all the servants' children and read them Bible stories. Sometimes the real old folks, retired from the house and fields, would sit down and listen too. Miss Sarah's stories were often about Christ the Savior, but she also told stories of ordained heroes conquering great nations of infidel sinners, and of courageous saints who brought the word of God to dark-skinned heathens. Always, the hero of the story was accompanied by a faithful servant who obeyed his master in life and death.

As we passed around the house, one of the Colonel's men stepped up to the plantation bell and took the ringing rope from Miss Sarah, and he thrashed it again and again while cursing us aloud. This inspired all the folks to pick up their feet and run. The sudden pounding of feet frightened me, but I could only watch helplessly as the crowd overtook me.

"Ben!"

Mama's voice. Turning, I saw Mama standing outside our cabin with her hand outstretched.

"Come here, child — quick! Massa Colonel's callin."

I pushed through the crowd and ran to her. Mama clicked her tongue and muttered about the state of my undress. I was completely naked, for I had already outgrown the linen shirt and trousers given to me back in the spring. Each of Clarendon's servant families received a clothing allowance only once a year, and this caused Mama to lament my regular growth spurts.

Of course, naked children were not a strange sight, especially in the summer. Many boys and girls my age (I was four or five then, if my birth year can be trusted), and even some much older, walked about the woods and fields of Clarendon without clothes and always without shoes. Sometimes the children were naked even through the cold winter months, though usually a fever took these unfortunate souls before the next spring arrived. This possibility seemed to worry Mama greatly, for she would often speak about it with Daddy each night after dark.

Mama took my hand. The sun beat down upon us as we neared the grove. No longer did it seem such a happy and innocent orb of light, but a pale leering eye turning a mocking glare upon the shuffling mass of black faces.

I looked up at Mama and saw her broad, kerchief-covered head scanning back and forth. These days I cannot help but see her face as older than it really had been back then. Mama is beautiful even now, but in those days she was the most radiant being I knew — more enchanting than even Miss Sarah, whose beauty was startling though somehow unreal

Mama pulled hard on my arm so that I would keep step with her long legs. She walked stiffly, limping along with a grimace set on her lips, the way some women walked when they were about to have a baby.

"Are you okay, Mama?"

"Hush, child. Where you been at all day?"

"I was playin, Mama. I picked flowers for Miss Sarah and her friend. Miss Sarah's friend made a waxed boat for me, Mama. He sent it down the brook."

"Which friend? That Mr. Roscoe?"

"I don't know, Mama."

"He's a kind man, that Mr. Roscoe. And he's the Colonel's guest, so he's to be treated proper. I don't want you botherin him none. You hear?"

"Yes, Mama."

Somehow, I could tell Mama's mind was somewhere else. Somewhere bad. Her head kept jerking back and forth, as if she was looking for something, or someone. It was only now that I saw that Mama's lip had been split open. One eye was red and swollen. To write such words even now makes my heart ache. In the dream, and in my memory, I looked upon these injuries with a child's bland curiosity.

"You hurt, Mama. You bleedin."

"Never you mind that, child."

Some of the other mothers around us began to sing. Their voices were low and sorrowful, and they seemed to share in a great, unified sadness. Some of the older children joined in, their own voices high and warbling. I listened as the people sang, and I can hear their voices even now, so many years later:

As I went down in the valley to pray,
Studying about that good old way;
You shall wear the starry crown,
Good Lord, show me the way

We rounded the house and entered the vast lawn that looked over rolling hills and fields of golden wheat and white cotton stretching to the walls of the Mayfair Valley beyond. The summit of the North Branch, the larger of the Valley's twin mountains, loomed overhead. I heard more voices on the breeze: deep, dark voices resonating with great power.

An old woman looked around at the growing assembly with dawning horror. "Massa Colonel called all the out-farm niggers," she said. She turned her eyes, yellow with cataracts, up toward the cloudless sky. "Be merciful, oh Lord. Oh Jesus Lord, be merciful..."

"Shut up, Auntie," a young woman muttered. She was eyeing the Colonel's men with growing anxiety. "You bring all wrath down on us!"

"The Colonel called all the out-farms together but once before," the old woman said. "I seen my sister's boy butchered for pickin apples from the Colonel's orchard."

Another woman clicked her tongue. "Pshaw! Massa Colonel wouldn't dare. Lashings and knifings is one thing, but we's too valuable for him to kill us."

"Hush!" the young woman hissed. She covered her infant daughter's ears with her hands. "What's wrong with y'all, spinnin such dark yarns?"

"They ain't yarns, children," the old woman replied. "You see for youself soon enough."

We turned into the grove, where twin willow trees stood together like the proscenium of some natural theatre. And standing motionless all around there waited a solemn congregation of the plantation's young men, what the Colonel's men called 'bulls,' and among them were the girls and women who had no husbands or children. I looked upon these strong youths with great awe. It was my dream back then to work the fields when I became older. I wished to become a worker just like Daddy.

The great congregation of field hands shifted at last, and like the Red Sea they parted for the mothers and children to enter the circle and bear witness in the shade of the willow trees.

The people looked all around themselves with wide eyes and slack jaws. Most had never seen all of Clarendon's servants gathered in one place before. For a time, the congregation had the appearance of a family reunion. Friends, cousins, old flames and acquaintances who lived on opposite ends of the estate, all met in a general hubbub. Every conversation contained imaginative theories as to why so many of Clarendon's hands had been called together.

Within the circle stood Colonel Spencer with his men, all of them armed with whips, muskets, and pistols. The Colonel's men hurried about brandishing their weapons, some of them holding snapping dogs on rope leashes. The men ordered the people to step forward and keep silent, or else.

I saw then, upon a patch of red clay, the crumpled form of a naked man. His exposed back, which should have been covered with dark brown skin like that of his trembling arms, torso, and legs, was instead open, slicked red, and running with blood and white marrow. All down his spine the flesh had been stripped in ragged furrows by whips. Looking closer, I realized that nothing of the man's shoulders remained except white blades protruding from the running red, the exposed bone and dangling sinews baking under the sun.

And then…Lord. Then the bleeding man looked up and turned his bruised face to the crowd.

It was Daddy.

A strangled cry escaped Mama's throat before she silenced herself and snatched me up and tried to force my head under the covers of her skirt. I pushed back, scratching and screaming, but now Mama crouched down and buried my face against her bosom and hushed me. I could feel her own tears dripping hot on the top of my head. Twisting, I wriggled away so that I could look out at the world once more. I glared up at the white sun overhead, hating it, refusing to look away no matter how much the light burned.

"Now hear this!"

It was the Colonel. I turned my head and strained to see. The Colonel's face had never been a visage of kindness, but today he wore a vengeful sneer that caused me to tremble. Mama had turned away from the sight completely, tears still running from her eyes, and she mumbled the words of some song while several women around us placed their outstretched hands upon Mama's head and murmured low incantations.

The Colonel pointed at Daddy, who shivered in a growing pool of blood.

"This beast before you lifted his hand against the sacred temple of a white man's body," the Colonel said, projecting in a voice loud enough for all five hundred hands to hear. "He tells me he

was compelled to strike my men because they had taken his wife into the woods to be...corrected."

The Colonel looked back toward Clarendon and lifted his chin.

"Look here, girls!"

All heads turned to follow the Colonel's gaze. The Colonel's family was assembled in the shade of the veranda. The five Spencer daughters were lined up to watch the proceedings, but their eyes were cast down. Miss Sarah stood with them. Beside Miss Sarah was a handsome man in his early middle age whom I instantly recognized as her betrothed and my erstwhile playmate. John Roscoe was his name. Rumor suggested he was poor white trash from beyond the Valley borders, come to usurp the Colonel of his riches. As far as I was concerned, he was the only man who ever looked at us negroes with anything one might call compassion.

"Now look here," the Colonel called to his family. "Look this here Joby in the face. Someday, when you have property of your own, you must learn to remain strong while you correct them. Remember that you are not beating a man."

The Spencer daughters then looked upon Daddy's crumpled form, and one by one their gazes hardened to stone. Meanwhile I could not take my eyes off Miss Sarah, who in my childish estimation was the living proof that fairy tales of beautiful princesses were all true. But why, why wasn't Miss Sarah doing anything to help Daddy? How could she, who professed to love all of Clarendon's servants as children, merely stand back as one of her beloved was tortured under the sun? Why could she not step forward, even if she had to stand alone, to beg for the Colonel's mercy? Why would she not stop him?!

And Mr. Roscoe. His compassion had faded, and now he wore an expression of solemn curiosity, of dark, morbid fascination. He looked upon the assembled hands as if we were a colony of black ants, and he a naturalist.

"I'm inclined, and well within my rights," the Colonel said, "to cancel next month's food rations and let you-all starve for thirty days and nights. Maybe then we'll see how many of you lash out at my boys like wild animals."

All at once, hundreds of voices erupted in a terrible uproar:

"Be merciful, Massa Colonel!"

"Pray for us, Massa, we know not what we does!"

"Punish him, Massa Colonel! Punish that damn nigger and spare my children!"

Without a word, the Colonel drew an aged flintlock pistol and fired a shot in the air. The people screamed and drew back, and all their commotion ceased. Breathless, I watched the tiny gust of gunsmoke rise and fade against the azure sky.

"Now," the Colonel said. "I'm a good master, ain't I?"

Hundreds of voices, mine not among them, answered in unison: "Yes, Massa Colonel."

"And I'm a merciful, Christian master, ain't I?"

"Yes, Massa Colonel."

"And surely the whole bunch shouldn't be thrown out just because of one rotten apple?"

"Yes, Massa Colonel."

"Now I'll tell you-all what I'm going to do," the Colonel said. "I'm going to give you-all your

rations next month. I know in my heart that even while this mutt was acting out, the rest of you were hard at work."

A collective sigh went up from the crowd, punctuated by fervent cries: "God bless you, Massa Colonel!"

And now the Colonel beckoned loudly for a young man, who strode forward with a set of iron shears in his hands.

"But an example must be made," the Colonel called. "A dog won't bite if he can't bark, and he won't bark if he can't bite. Go ahead, Tobias."

The young man named Tobias stooped over Daddy and brought the yawning, rusty shears low. Suddenly, miraculously, Daddy's strength returned. He cried out and pushed himself up, and once finally on his feet he clutched at the Colonel's throat. I remember seeing the Colonel's eyes bulge wide even as Daddy's narrowed with hatred and vindication. For a long, breathless moment, all eyes watched with shock as black choked the life from white.

But suddenly a punch sent Daddy flying, and then three of the Colonel's men pinned Daddy down. Daddy screamed — I hear his screams echoing even now — and in order to drag him off the Colonel they tore at the loose strands of lacerated flesh that hung from his open back. Then the man named Tobias kicked Daddy's legs open and brought the scraping shears down.

The horrible screaming began, like the sound of a screeching newborn under a surgeon's knife. Mama tried to cover my eyes and pull me away, but I fought against her. I had to see.

I remember seeing the laughing faces of the Colonel's men and hating them. I remember the feeling of shock at seeing dark delight on other black faces, who gazed upon the scene with all the bloodlust of a crowd of Romans. I remember opening my own mouth to scream, to fill the air with my infant rage and somehow share in Daddy's pain.

When it was over, my eyes fell on Daddy. He was sobbing and clutching at the dirt. I thought to cry out to him, but for whatever reason I remained silent. I wonder to this day what might have happened should I have called his attention. Would he have seen Mama and I through the dripping blood that stung his vision? Would he have recognized us within the crowd? Would I have shared with my father just one final look, however brief it might have been; a loving gaze of goodbye, a silent farewell to treasure in my heart. Might I have shared such a moment with my father, if only I'd had the courage to speak up?

Maybe. But I didn't speak up. I remained silent then, as I remain silent today. Lord knows, I have no hope that any eyes but my own will ever light upon these scratchings on this paper.

And always, without fail, blackness consumes me before my voice can usher forth. By that, I mean that my dream abruptly ends there. The candle of memory is snuffed out before I can speak, before I can so much as scream.

I awake; my sheets are soaked and I am shivering in the dark. Stricken with shock, I touch a hand to my open mouth. I realize I screamed after all — I cried out in my sleep.

If only the horror of that day was just a mere nightmare. How happy would I be to writhe in terror, knowing that all the brutalities I witnessed were only figments of my imagination. But it was all real, right down to the scraping sound of those horrible, rust-bitten shears.

Turning, I peer across the darkened pantry and see Mama asleep in her cot. She is still sleeping, snoring, and peaceful. And she is old, and the realization yet deepens that I am no longer a small child. I am a man, twenty-seven years old, twenty-two years free, but still bound to the grounds of Clarendon as if nothing had changed. Mama and I serve a different family now, and the Roscoes pay us a wage for our services. All the other servants are gone — freed long ago, after the Colonel gave the deed of Clarendon to John Roscoe. Daddy is gone too, sold the day after his maiming, to which plantation in which county of which state, I haven't the slightest idea. Years of searching have yielded no leads, for the Colonel kept no bill of sale.

But still ringing in my ears, I can hear hundreds of voices cheering as the rusty shears snap and grind. I hear the cheering voices drown out Daddy's screams. Many times I've wondered what that cheering had meant, for it was my own people who had cheered for Daddy's mutilation.

Had the people cheered in a desperate effort to reassure the Colonel that they were good and trustworthy servants, and that they were eternally grateful for their master's leniency? Had they cheered to warn other would-be rebels of what fate awaited those who threatened the plantation's fragile peace? I've even considered that they, with their collective spirit starved and degraded over so many nameless generations, cheered for their brother's castration as some kind of gruesome entertainment — a brief respite, however cruel and insane, from the whips that would too soon start a-cracking once more.

That nightmare is a quarter-century old now, a specter that continues to invade my dreams without warning or pattern, and never have I been able to conquer it. Once or twice I've mentioned this dream to Mama, but she simply turns away and refuses to speak about it. But to her it's not just a dream, but a shared memory. And I know this memory still lingers in her own mind, for there are some nights where she herself will awake screaming and sobbing. What wretches we are, Mama and I.

So here I now sit, writing these reflections by the light of a single candle within Clarendon's great library. The sky beyond the windows is still dark, the late October night without deep and foreboding. For a moment I imagine the sound of heavy footsteps in the darkness, and in my mind's eye I can see a great army on the march, their faces lit by torches burning like meteors streaming across a clear night sky.

But as I strain to listen, a dissenting voice tells me the only earthly sound to be heard is the creaking of this old house we call Clarendon. Outside, the plantation fields are empty and overgrown, the slave cabins rotting, the overseers long gone to ply their ghastly trade elsewhere. Only the willows remain in the grove near the garden, and the long columns of beech trees lining the clay road that opens to the Mayfair Valley and the wider Shenandoah and the world beyond. The Colonel is gone, and so are his slaves, and Daddy too. Gone like whispers on the night wind.

Only the dark of night remains, and I sense that dawn will be a long time coming. Awake and bleary-eyed, and with darkness pressing in from all sides, I sit here and wonder with creeping dread whether a new day will come at all.

For the slave it is all night, forever.

And there it is again: the sound of marching boots. If this be a dream, I will gladly take this one over any depiction of that nightmarish day in the grove. Presently I hear the great ghostly army on the move once more. Boots heavy, boots quick. An army of night, tramping by torchlight toward — where? I do not know.

But I hope, and it is my only hope in this dark and silent hour, that following close behind that phantom vanguard are the first shades of a new day which shall cast away all shadows, the stretching fingers of a coming dawn's shining light.

I

A HOUSE DIVIDED

October – December 1859

Oh! I wish I was in the land of cotton
Good times there are not forgotten
Look away! Look away! Look away, Dixieland!

"Dixie" by Daniel Decatur Emmett

Chapter I
CRUCIBLE

The soldiers came by torchlight.

They marched groggy and bleary-eyed down the darkened country road to the village of Harper's Ferry. Each man shouldered a rifled musket, loaded and primed, and each carried a blazing torch to ward off the creeping night. Their staccatoed breaths misted in the frigid predawn air.

The young lieutenant at the head of the company pressed his horse. Though the horse was a sickly nag confiscated from a local farm, the lieutenant rode her high in the saddle like he was old Washington himself. He saw the world through shifting green-gray eyes drawn into slits of quick judgment and contempt for any sign of inferiority that might shade the aura of his own youthful ambition and promise. His cheeks were drawn, clean-shaven, and he had a head of sandy hair trimmed tightly around overlarge ears. He had long legs, booted to the knee and thick with saddle muscles.

The marching men whispered rumors of what lay ahead at Harper's Ferry. A slave uprising was the favorite theory. Word held that a gang of renegade slaves had overpowered their masters, slashed their throats, stolen their weapons, and barricaded themselves somewhere in the town. Another rumor, dispelled by most of the soldiers as 'pure and utter *flam*', suggested the slaves were being led by white abolitionists.

"*Yankee* abolitionists," one of the soldiers corrected, as if there was any debate.

The young lieutenant was not one to believe idle rumors, but he did believe the official orders printed on the telegram in his pocket.

To the officer in command:
Lead your men south across Potomac River by way of Maryland Heights. Await my arrival by train at five o'clock instant.

Col. R.E. Lee

The lieutenant did not know Colonel Lee per se, but he certainly knew the name. The Lees were one of the oldest and greatest families in Virginia. They had fought alongside Washington in the Revolution and helped build the Union's capital. When he was still a boy, the young lieutenant had visited the famous Lee plantation at Arlington across the river from Washington City. Robert Lee was of course one of the Union's most famous and revered officers. Years ago, he had even served as the superintendent at the Military Academy at West Point, a place the young lieutenant knew quite well.

Lee's message sounded rather vague, innocuous. The young lieutenant soured at the thought that this might be some kind of roundabout exercise, some silly war game like the ones cadets played back at the Point.

The company rounded a bend in the river, and he saw the dim lights of Harper's Ferry. There were tiny orbs of light dancing in the black like fireflies. But then came the pops of gunfire — bright flashes of light sparking before the darkness sucked them up — and the vision became clear.

Harper's Ferry was under attack.

The lieutenant drew his sword and turned his horse. The stamping men behind him staggered to a halt, their tunnel vision broken, and they looked up at him as they caught their breath.

The lieutenant pointed his sword forward. "By doubles, double time."

The company sergeant stepped up and echoed in a thick Irish brogue: "Doubles, lads, and double time!"

The lieutenant turned and spurred his nag forward, and she let out a ragged whinny before pounding down the mountain trail toward a bridge spanning the river. Man and horse bounded the bridge and covered the ground to the town limits before the rest of the company had fully made it down the mountain.

Riding toward a pool of light from a gas lamp — still evidently a rare thing in these mountain towns — the lieutenant turned his head and saw several dark shapes materialize in the gloom. They were Virginia militia, scared and shivering.

There had been no need for much of an army for almost a decade now, not since the Mexican War. Local defense was therefore delegated to volunteer companies whose training involved little more than how to shoot a musket, and sometimes not even that much. Tonight on the platform, some of the militiamen sauntering about were still wearing their pajamas under heavy coats.

One of the figures called, "W-Who goes there?"

The lieutenant rode into the light. "Point that shotgun somewhere else. I'm white and Christian."

Another voice sounded, "Thank God," and a sickly face emerged from the gloom. "I'm the captain here."

The lieutenant sat his horse. "Are you commissioned, Captain?"

The militia captain blinked. "The way you ask that question makes me think I ought to be, son."

The answer was no. The lieutenant studied the silent streets. A church tower loomed over the whole of Harper's Ferry, its steeple illuminated in some ghostly light. Somewhere far off, a dog barked.

"What's the situation here? I heard gunfire across the river."

The militia captain stared back at him and scratched his chin. He was very old, with a long sinewy neck built like a celery stalk. His eyes bulged and his fat lips were turned outward, giving him the singular appearance of a gasping trout with a man's body. "All I am is honest, so I'll tell you I ain't commissioned. I'm the village smith. Boys started callin me 'Captain' when we started. Joke, really."

The lieutenant nodded stiffly. The man might be a captain of a sort, but he was still only civilian militia. Therefore, he was subject to the lieutenant's orders.

"I'd like a report on the situation."

"Just hold on a minute," the militia captain said. "I need to know who I'm talking to."

"Lieutenant Jonathan Jacob Roscoe," the lieutenant replied. "Until Colonel Lee arrives, I'm the commanding officer here."

The captain shrugged. "Sure, fella."

"Your report?"

"Oh, right." The militia captain nodded vaguely across town. "They were holed up in the armory until just now. They broke in there and stole some weapons. They tried to make a break for it, but we chased em into the fire-engine house yonder."

The lieutenant listened for gunfire and heard none. For now, Harper's Ferry was quiet. "How many men do you have under your command, Captain?"

The militia captain squinted at him. "I dunno how many we got. Hunderd? More comin every hour from all over. We's all volunteers."

The lieutenant nodded distractedly. He had hoped this news would help him relax, but the knot in his chest only wound tighter. Until Colonel Lee arrived, he was now in command of over *two hundred men* counting the militia and his own company. They were looking to him for direction, for leadership — and what if the bullets started flying this instant? A tiny worm called doubt gnawed at the lieutenant's brain, reminding him he was just twenty years old and that he sported scraggly blonde hairs on his upper lip where he knew there should be a mustache by now. His horse, sensing something amiss, shied away and tore at the reins.

The lieutenant was suddenly aware the militia captain was watching him closely. Taking stock of him, sizing him up. Maybe remembering his face.

"Just how old are you, son?"

Grunting, the lieutenant steadied his horse with a savage tug at the reins. He steeled his spine and looked past the militia captain toward the town. "Enough chat," the lieutenant said. "Take me to get a look at the enemy, Captain."

"The enemy?" the militia captain scoffed. "One of them idiots is my cousin."

The militiamen laughed.

The lieutenant turned and watched as his company of soldiers — pudgy lung-hackers to the man — finally staggered across the bridge from the Maryland side and collapsed in a heap before him. His ears perked to the sound of a rumbling engine. Turning back, he spied an open-air rail station across a mud yard. A slowing train rolled in from the north side of town and finally rumbled to a halt at the station. The train announced itself with a belch of ashen steam and a banshee shriek.

Colonel Lee had arrived.

The lieutenant dismounted and pushed the reins into the hands of the nearest militiaman and strode toward the platform. Ascending the platform steps, the lieutenant cupped his frozen hands and blew hot breath into them and wrung them together. All the while, the gears of his mind whirred with sour realizations. No sooner had he accepted the burden of command, no sooner had he cut the doubtful knot in his chest clean through, but that a superior officer had come to supersede him.

Why, the young lieutenant had just been getting warmed up.

❧

Except Jonathan Jacob Roscoe was certainly no lieutenant — not yet anyway.

'JJ' was still a Firstie, or senior cadet, in his final year at West Point; his graduation was set for next June. And he had only a vague idea why a company of soldiers had been sent tramping through the Appalachian foothills in the middle of the night. Were anyone else to ask JJ Roscoe then and there how a West Point cadet had come to lead a company of regulars, he would not have been able to say exactly why.

He could, however, say how. Not twelve hours before, JJ was seated in the last carriage on the last Baltimore & Ohio Railroad train leaving Washington that night. He was travelling home to Virginia on furlough, the first he'd taken in nearly four years. He had not returned home since he left it, not for summer nor Thanksgiving nor even Christmas. Whenever he wrote to his father about the possibility of coming home for such events, he received pleasant and doting explanations why it was better that he spend the holidays focused on his studies.

But now, at Father's request, JJ was finally on his way back home.

The letter had indeed come as a surprise. More surprising, perhaps, was the manner in which the letter was delivered: directly into JJ's hand by none other than Colonel Beauregard, the Superintendent of West Point. At first, JJ wondered whether he had been called into Beauregard's office to hear some terrible news about his family.

"Nothing unseemly about it, Roscoe," the colonel had assured him with a diplomatic smile. "Just pack your bags and see the sergeant outside for your train ticket. And please say hello to your father for me. Tell JR I look forward to seeing him next time I'm in Washington."

It was no surprise to JJ that Beauregard knew his father. John Roscoe was a senior, highly respected member of the United States Senate. 'JR' (JJ was always proud to go by his initials, just like Father) was an immensely popular figure who seemed to know everyone; certainly everyone seemed to know him. Being a senator from Virginia, long the arbitrating spirit between the Republican-leaning North and the Democrat-dominated South, Father was considered by some to be a likely candidate for president in 1860. Father routinely denied such claims, but JJ sometimes wondered what it would be like to be not just the son of a senator, but a president. *The* president.

For now, being the son of a senator exposed JJ to enough scrutiny at the Point. He knew how the other cadets (and even some of the instructors) whispered about his family, and about his relationship with his father in particular. Somehow, word had gotten around that JJ had only joined the Academy to flee disgrace back home. Despite JJ's best efforts at denying these stories, the rumors persisted.

During the long journey from West Point down to Washington, JJ read Father's most recent letter over and over. He chewed on one line in particular.

You are to come home to receive news of the Roscoe family legacy, and your rightful place.

Just a few words that meant so much. JJ would graduate next spring, and after that he would be a bonafide officer in the United States Army. A soldier could go far in the Republic, as long as there was a war to be fought. Why, a soldier could even become president, just like Andrew Jackson or Zachary Taylor.

But these days the United States had appetite for war, busy as the states were with digging canals, laying telegraph wires, building railroads, and exterminating savages out on the western plains. Of course there were many points of contention between the Northern states and the Southern states that were starting to boil over, such as the debate over the future of the institution of slavery.

Many people in the North — making up some three-fifths of the Union's population — were rather indifferent to the idea of negroes in chains. The 'peculiar institution' was as far away in their minds as Han China. After all, what did slavery have to do with life on a small farm near Bangor, Maine or out on the cattle plains near Mason City, Iowa? Most folks didn't approve of the concept on basic principle, citing moral or religious reasons, but any open calls for the immediate emancipation of slaves were reserved for only a tiny minority of abolitionist activists.

Meanwhile, it was the opinion of many others (mostly Southerners, but a fair share of Northerners too) that for the Federal government to outlaw one kind of property ownership was an act of tyranny no different than old King George's taxation without representation. Americans had fought and died for their liberty, hadn't they? And didn't the Constitution maintain a rule for counting slaves as three-fifths of a person for census purposes? The institution of slavery was an *American* institution, a Christian institution, and the Union was better off with a trusted system that kept the white and black races from tearing out each other's throats — which they would surely do, many claimed, were there no means of keeping them separate.

While at West Point, JJ had listened to a great many political debates between his fellow Southern cadets and their Northern counterparts. There were other sore spots between the sections, mostly regarding the passing of recent tariffs and customs laws, of which the vast majority favored Northern industrialists at the expense of Southern producers. Animosity between the two sections was at fever pitch, with some newspaper pundits even claiming that the 'other side' were no longer Americans at all but some kind of degenerate civilization. Of course, no one except the lunatics in state asylums believed the states would settle their differences by going to war. In a world of absolute monarchs and tyrannical despots and untamed lands ravaged by endless tribal warfare, the United States was one of only a handful of democracies that existed. Civil war was therefore out of the question, for what cause could possibly be worth the cost of peace, progress, and democracy?

This was all to say, a soldier's career options were severely limited in peacetime. This was why Father's letter excited JJ so much. Very likely, Father being the brilliant man he was, a decision had been made to match JJ's talents for planning and leadership and decision-making — all evident even from a young age — with a position more fitting for a young man of great ambition.

Father was calling JJ home to take over the Roscoe family enterprise.

JJ spent much of his journey south daydreaming about his new life as President of the North Branch Mining Company. This was the coal mining enterprise Father had begun so many years ago, long before JJ and his siblings were born. What so many other men had called a dirty job Father deemed a shining opportunity. America was swiftly becoming a land of steam engines, and someone had to feed the insatiable iron beasts. But always there was a larger goal in mind.

Even as a young child, JJ strategized with Father about the Roscoe family's legacy. First they would nurture the growth of a single coal mine, then a cluster of them along a strip of the Blue Ridge mountains. After that, they would build a railroad company with a fleet of trains fueled by Roscoe coal. And after that, Father's ambition was to build *the* railroad — the much-anticipated transcontinental line that would stretch from the Atlantic to the Pacific.

"After all," Father often said, "it's one thing to be known as just another rich man. It's another thing entirely to be known for conquering an entire continent. Once we've joined East and West, there will be no more North and South. There will be no more sections of squabbling states. There will only be the *United States*, no longer a loose confederacy but a single nation bound by steel."

Father's dream was JJ's too, and in his mind's eye he saw rail cars racing back and forth between New York and San Francisco, all of them branded with the name *ROSCOE* in giant white letters. With such power as the railroad might provide, who needed to occupy the damn White House?

But there was only one problem — and it was a big one — that stuck in JJ's throat during his entire journey southward. Before JJ could continue his work with Father, he knew that he had to face the people of the Mayfair Valley again. He'd have to confront once and for all the horrible humiliation that had made him flee from his home like a thief in the night. He'd have to stand tall against those looks of revulsion and disgust on the faces of his neighbors, against all that mocking laughter from those he'd once called friends. And he'd have to somehow come to terms with the fact that he had fallen prey to such grotesque, sinful temptation.

Worst of all, JJ knew he would have to beg forgiveness of Father, and of his family too, for turning the Roscoe name into a laughingstock.

The train kept rolling southward. The closer JJ got to home, the more anxious he felt.

Father had news to impart about the Roscoe family legacy. But what would it be like to speak with Father again? Would his mother embrace him? And JJ's siblings, would they welcome him with love, or had their minds been poisoned against him? Did all those letters they sent to him over the years conceal their true feelings, feelings of disgust and disappointment? During his time in New York, JJ had often wondered whether his family maybe considered him some kind of, well...some kind of *enemy*.

But every time JJ looked at Father's letter—

Your rightful place

—he felt the stirrings of hope. Maybe, after four years of exile from home (a *necessary* exile, JJ knew, for what else could Father have done to save his family's reputation?), it was finally time to come back and rebuild. Time to start anew. And so, again and again, JJ read those same words:

Your rightful place.

Your rightful place.

Your rightful—

A whistle shrieked. JJ was jolted awake as the rumbling engines shuddered and died.

The train had stopped.

JJ sat up in his seat. It was very dark out, probably close to midnight or just after. The car was nearly empty. But just now, he watched as dozens of armed men in blue uniforms scrambled aboard the train and occupied the seats all around him. They were all talking excitedly amongst themselves about escaped slaves, abolitionist traitors, and the end of the civilized world.

One of the soldiers, a sneering thug with a cloudy left eye, approached slowly and stared down at JJ.

"Get up and get lost," the soldier said gruffly. He hauled JJ up by his shirt collar and pushed him to the back of the carriage.

Stunned, JJ gave no protest. He was wearing civilian clothes and had no way to prove he was an officer in training. And in any case, it didn't matter — an officer in training was still lesser in rank than a private soldier. JJ sulked to the back of the carriage. He could feel the eyes of haughty soldiers and other passengers peeling his skin back layer by layer, exposing the raw red flesh underneath. He slumped down on a bench at the very back of the train.

The train whistled again and the engine rumbled to life, and the carriage shuddered and began to roll forward. At that moment, a heavy man with chevrons on his sleeves leaped aboard, gasping. The company sergeant announced in a thick Irish brogue that he was now acting commander of the expedition, since no able-bodied officers were available to lead the men. The only officer who *had* been able-bodied and available was now laid up at the barracks infirmary, and despite the Irishman's best attempt at a euphemism, it was clear the officer was shitting himself bloody with dysentery. The enlisted men snickered and lay back to lounge and smoke cigars.

JJ's mind raced. Was there really no officer in command of these laggards? To his eye, the soldiers were bound for policing action somewhere — the fact that each man carried a rifled musket suggested as much. If there was to be a fight, even the dim possibility of one, then the men *needed* an officer. Coming mostly from lower class or immigrant backgrounds, private soldiers were lazy and corruptible by nature, or so JJ's instructors had explained. In order to perform their duties properly, the men needed a leader with tact and bold vision.

JJ stood up. Soldiering was not meant to be done at a classroom desk. As he walked back up the aisle, he thought of boys younger than he who had led saber charges during the Revolution, or who were now fighting the Sioux and Comanches out west. This, JJ knew, was his chance to show his quality. But thinking back on this moment much later on, he could not remember how he felt just before he seized the horns of fate. It was as if he sat outside himself, watching the whole thing as a detached observer, as he heard himself say:

"First Sergeant? I will lead you and these men."

At once, all heads in the carriage turned to look at him. JJ quivered with hesitation for but a moment before he stiffened and set his face with grim composure. He marched down the carriage aisle like he was on the parade ground at the Point. He halted exactly a foot before the first sergeant.

The sergeant looked JJ up and down with a measure of scrutiny. "Yer a leftenant, darlin?"

"*Lieu*-tenant," JJ corrected. After a moment he added, "*Sir*."

The sergeant blinked. "Yer a *lieu*tenant, *sir*?"

"Indeed I am. Lieutenant Roscoe."

When the sergeant merely cocked a bushy eyebrow, JJ went on. "I've just returned from active duty at Fort Jay, New York." He glared at the men around, ensuring they looked away before he did. "I may not be an officer of your company nor your regiment, but as ranking officer here it's my sworn duty to take command." He turned back at last to the sergeant. "Now if you'll quit gawking at me, I'd like a report on the situation."

If the sergeant saw through JJ's ruse, he did not let on. In fact he seemed immeasurably grateful the burden of command had been lifted from his shoulders. He fished a telegram out of his pocket and handed it to JJ.

"That's all there is, Lieutenant, darlin."

JJ pocketed the dispatch. "I'll be needing a uniform, a sidearm, and a saber."

The sergeant's mouth worked in silence for a moment. "Ye mean ye didn't bring em down from New York with ye, Lieutenant?"

JJ offered the first lie he could think of. "I was at a party in Washington tonight." Feeling the eyes of the soldiers hot on his neck, he advanced closer to the sergeant until he nearly stood on the man's boots. His voice sounded stronger than he felt. "Now if you're through interrogating a commissioned officer of the United States, *Sergeant*, let's see about that uniform and sidearm."

The sergeant's hands went to his belt. There was a moment of furious unbuckling until the sergeant unwrapped his belt, complete with pistol and saber. "Take me weapons, sir. One of the boys can give you his uniform." He turned to the nearest man and snapped his fingers. "Miller, strip down."

"No," JJ said. He turned and walked up the aisle and stopped beside his old seat. He looked down at the sneering soldier with the cloudy eye, who had watched JJ assume command with a steadily drooping spirit.

"On your feet," JJ ordered.

The man stood. He was a full head taller than JJ, but his neck was craned down in fear and his shoulders were slumped in shame. He gave JJ a pleading look. JJ assumed a stony, unblinking stare. He'd spent the last four years perfecting this look in the mirror.

"This man is about my size," JJ said. "I'll take his uniform."

The sergeant nodded. "Aye, sir. It's a fit match."

Yawning militiamen shuffled about the station platform at Harper's Ferry. They carried shotguns, their grandfathers' muskets, spades, and a collection of clubs. A young boy of fifteen stood ready to assault the gates of Hell itself with a crude pitchfork grasped in thin, girlish fingers. JJ shook his head and sighed.

Shadowy figures climbed down from the inbound train from Arlington. Two gentlemen passengers in regal clothes stepped down from the head carriage. The first gentleman was short but boasted great, bushy whiskers and a flamboyant riding hat stuck with a huge red feather. Feeling the chill of the night air, the feathered gentleman turned and offered his coat to the second man. This second gentleman was older and taller and wore locks of silver hair and a snowy white beard. He walked slowly, but with dignified purpose.

JJ's sharp eye considered the elegant man's gray suit, which was something of a sore thumb in this part of Virginia. He guessed the man had just abandoned a grand dinner party to catch the first train to Harper's Ferry.

JJ offered a smart salute. "Colonel Robert Lee, I presume."

Colonel Lee returned the salute with a veteran's simplicity. "And you are?"

"Lieutenant Jonathan Roscoe at your service, sir."

Lee nodded, slow and graceful. The old man exuded a refined, patrician air. "Allow me to introduce my second-in-command…"

The feathered gentleman beside Lee extended his hand. "Lieutenant J-E-B Stuart. Call me Jeb."

JJ took Stuart's hand, but his chest tightened with jealousy. Jeb Stuart wasn't much older than JJ, but Stuart exuded the cavalier attitude of a cavalryman. There was something in the man's eyes that JJ immediately detested — maybe because Lee had identified the man as *second-in-command*. What, then, did that make JJ himself? A superfluous functionary?

"My, that's quite a grip on you," Stuart said, hiding a grimace.

JJ let go and smiled. "Pleasure to meet you, Lieutenant Stuart."

Colonel Lee sniffed the cool morning air. "Forgive our casual dress, Lieutenant Roscoe." His voice was level and warm, smooth like malted brandy. "Mr. Stuart and I were at a dinner party at my Arlington residence this evening. I received a telegram with orders from President Buchanan to assume command at Harper's Ferry post-haste. Why we're all here *exactly*, I'm still not sure."

"I have an idea, sir," JJ said. "The local militia say there are abolitionist rebels locked up somewhere in town. They have hostages, sir."

Lee did not respond, but JJ knew the old man had heard him. Lee stepped to the edge of the platform and watched as the company of soldiers filed into the village. His measured gaze noted every bootstep and arm swing. Lee turned to JJ and said, "You lead a fine unit, Lieutenant Roscoe."

JJ nodded graciously. "Thank you, sir."

"Did you encounter resistance along the bridge?"

"None, sir, but the rail line was cut. We disembarked and made the rest of the journey on foot."

Lee surveyed the militiamen gathered around. "Who is in command here?"

The old militia captain stepped forward. "That'd be me, fella."

JJ turned on the militia captain. "*I am, sir,*" he corrected.

The captain gasped like a trout. The words seemed foreign to him. "I am, *sir*."

"Thank you for mustering, Captain," Lee said. "You and your boys have done Virginia a fine service. You may all return home now."

The militia captain raised a contrarian finger. "Fella? Uh — *sir?* Me and the boys here. We ain't gonna leave without seein these sons of bitches brought in or brought down. They killed our neighbors, good folk all."

Lee shook his head. "It will be bloody work."

The captain held firm. "This here's our land, Colonel. These here our homes, our families. And these bastards — these bastards think they can just come down and take all that away from us? I won't stand for it, nosir. None of us will — right, boys?"

There was a chorus of agreement from the militiamen.

Lee surveyed the men. "It is your right to defend your homes," he said. "And I suppose many hands make light work." He nodded slowly. "Very well, Captain. I will assume leadership of these enlisted men. Your own volunteers report to you, but *you* report to me."

The captain nodded vigorously. "Yessir. Thank you, sir." He looked sidelong at JJ and offered an acknowledging smile, apparently pleased that he was catching on to military affairs so quickly.

Lee turned toward the heart of the village. "Let's see about dealing with these people."

JJ turned to his sergeant. "Bring up some horses for these gentlemen."

The officers mounted up. The militia captain led Lee's horse by the reins and the great company of soldiers and militiamen started through town.

"They're shacked up in the fire engine house, sir," the militia captain explained. "Other side of town."

Lee nodded. "Renegade negroes, as I understand."

"Nosir. Whites, mostly. Coupla runaway darkies with em, mind."

"White?" It was the first time Lee sounded at all surprised.

"Yessir. They come across the river from Maryland two nights ago. They break into the armory downstreet, to get weapons for some kind of rebellion. With the darkies and all? But we get wise to it and come out to see what's the commotion. They open fire, murder four. We shot a couple of them in turn, but we figure there's round a dozen still in the engine house. They got hostages. We know that because their leader step out, says his name is John Brown the Redeemer and says he's gonna send all the slavers to burn in Hell for their sins. Says he wants freedom for the darkies." Here, the captain threw up his hands and laughed. "And the goddamn darkies don't want nothin to do with em! A freedman fella what works with the railroad tried to raise the alarm, so they shot him down cold. Warn't a bad darkie neither, so I'm told."

They entered Harper's Ferry as dawn approached from the east. JJ noted the tiny spider webs in the grass all sparkling with the night's frost. Winter was on the way, but thankfully the branches of the trees were still shrouded with golden leaves. The town was one of pleasant brick homes nestled in the mountains where the Shenandoah River met the Potomac. JJ imagined all walks of people milling about on their day's business. The place reminded him very much of his own hometown farther west. But except for the armed men prowling the streets in gloomy silence, Harper's Ferry appeared as a ghost town.

JJ stole an admiring glance at Colonel Lee. The man had a magnetism about him, an aura of strength and brilliance. JJ knew all the stories of Lee's brilliance at Contreras and Vera Cruz years ago, back when the colonel's beard had been black instead of white. Lee rode tall in the saddle and always had. He was said to be, and seeing him now JJ could heartily confirm he was, the personification of victory.

Lee said, "So you are from Virginia, Lieutenant."

"I am, sir. Mayfair."

Lee looked ahead. "I don't know it."

"You may know my father, sir. John Roscoe, United States Senator." After a brief pause, JJ chanced to add: "He's a Democrat."

Lee nodded curtly. "*Roscoe*. Of course. He's the coal man trying to build some railroad across the western wastes, isn't he?"

JJ blushed. "That would be him, sir."

Lee shrugged. "Well, it's certainly ambitious."

"Ah!" Jeb Stuart cried. "So you're a Valley man, eh?" He flashed a wide grin.

JJ's skin crawled. Stuart's desire for attention seemed too intentional to call him charismatic. He had a peacock feather stuck in his hat, for God's sake. Lee, on the other hand — Lee's charisma was instinctual, effortless, even if a little patronizing.

"Good whiskey in the Riverlands," Stuart said.

"I live more in the mountains, matter of fact," JJ said, directing his response to Lee exclusively. "Mayfair is a valley of its own, and a back door right into the heart of the Shenandoah to be sure." JJ straightened in the saddle. "Why, Colonel, I believe your own father took the pass through Mayfair to whip a brigade of Hessians during the Revolution. Battle of Capon Bridge, August '76. My grandfather served under your father as a drummer boy. He said your father was a great man and..."

JJ's voice faded as he watched Lee's eyes cloud with disinterest. He felt a knot tighten in his stomach. What could he possibly say that would impress a man like Lee?

It was not long before Stuart went off again. "I'm a Piedmont man myself," he said. "It's as Georgia as Virginia gets. Beautiful country. Horses, women, all beautiful. And we've got the best-behaved negroes in the whole solid Southland."

JJ turned to bore holes in the man's skull with his eyes, but Mr. Peacock kept jawing. "You-all ought to give your negroes some rose gardens to trim up here in the mountains," Stuart explained. "Keeps them busy. And a bunch of busy black hands is a su-premely su-blime sight."

Darkness fled west as the light of the coming day spread out in the eastern sky. In the gray murk of the new morning, rays of candlelight winked out from windows as the townsfolk, their eyes rimmed red from an anxious and sleepless night, pulled their curtains back and opened their shutters to peer out at the soldiers marching to their rescue.

"Will you return to Mayfair when we are finished here, Lieutenant?" Lee asked.

"Yes, sir," JJ said. "I was actually en route home to see my family."

"And a sweetheart, surely?" Stuart asked with a grin.

JJ worked his jaw. "Er...no. No sweetheart." He added, rather unconvincingly: "Not yet, anyway."

Stuart laughed. "Then I pity you, Lieutenant. I really do."

JJ gritted his teeth. He didn't need anything from this damn clown, and certainly not his *pity*.

Lee calmly scanned the rows of houses and storefronts. "Home and family. These are the things worth fighting for, gentlemen."

Stuart flashed another grin. "A few medals and headlines couldn't hurt either." He winked at JJ. "Those'll help on the sweetheart front, Lieutenant."

JJ forced a smile and said nothing.

In the chilly predawn, two hundred men moved to surround the fire engine shelter in the center of town. It was a small brick warehouse lined with three white doors, each large enough for a wheeled fire engine to pass through. The masonry was pocked with chipped bullet holes and the doors had been splintered by gunfire. The broken glass in the shattered windows was stained black with smoke. The area around the engine house was still, like a photograph, and from within there was nothing but eerie silence.

Lee stared at the engine house. He looked first at Stuart, then JJ.

"Gentlemen, it seems we are confronted with an insane degenerate who is the leader of a mob of fanatics. It is possible he may have even coerced the negroes in his party to commit violence against their will, such is their servile nature. We must kill the fanatics and spare the negroes if we can, for I'm sure their benefactors will want their property returned to them, unspoiled."

Stuart responded to this last remark with an assured nod.

JJ gazed upon the still engine house with a quiet foreboding. Up to now, he'd never fired a shot in anger. He wasn't even a particularly good marksman, based on his results on the Point's firing range. And now he was going to be part of an all-out firefight?

But, hell, of course he was. Fighting was what he was here to do. And it's what he *would* do.

"This lunatic Brown has so far succeeded because he is skilled in the trade of terror," Lee said. The old man looked all around at the drawn faces of the soldiers and militia standing at the ready. "And the Union certainly is terrorized, I can assure you of that. Every newspaper across the country is printing this story for the morning edition. But we, gentlemen, are here to give this story a happy ending."

JJ and the others nodded. Just then, the shining sun broke over Harper's Ferry.

Lee said: "And so, gentlemen. Let us begin."

❧

All at once, blasting gunfire shattered the still morning air.

Standing ready with the soldiers, JJ's nostrils stung with the gusting stench of gunpowder. Up ahead, the shadowy faces of rebel defenders peered out from the engine house. The rebels poked their shotguns out from the broken windows to return fire, but the hail of musket balls suppressed them.

A shrill ring punctuated the gunfire as JJ drew his gleaming saber.

"*With me* — Let's go!"

The soldiers charged with throaty cheers. They closed in and slammed their shoulders against the brick walls of the house, some crouching for cover under the open windows. JJ stepped up beside the main door as two soldiers pounded on the splintered wood with sledgehammers.

From inside came the sounds of muffled voices screaming and cursing and boots clomping on the hard floor. One defender, a young white man with blazing eyes, appeared in an open window to fire down on the soldiers crouched low, but a whining bullet clove his head in two and he fell back into the shadows.

From inside, a man bellowed: "Deny God's will and I shall deny ye salvation!"

The doors exploded from a shotgun blast and the two soldiers with sledgehammers went down screaming and clutching ragged limbs. The other soldiers drew back in fear.

The sledgehammers were useless. They would be all day trying to break the door down, and JJ knew Brown's rebels, fresh from raiding the armory, likely had enough ammunition inside to fight off an entire regiment.

The gunsmoke cleared a little and JJ could see the village around him again. He spied a wooden ladder resting against the side of a half-painted house. Abandoned cans of whitewash lay open on their sides, the gravel around them stained with spilled paint.

JJ barked at his men to follow. They hurried across the street to retrieve the ladder. On their return, Brown's rebels appeared in the windows and were again sent down by suppressing fire by the combined might of the soldiers and militiamen. The blasting gunfire tapered off as JJ and his men rushed the main door.

From inside, the same bellowing voice sounded as before: "You are my hammer and weapon of war. With you I break nations in pieces. With you I destroy kingdoms!"

JJ and his men heaved together and drove the heavy ladder against the door. There was a sharp crack and the door groaned under the impact, but still it held firm. Men screamed and swore oaths at them from inside. The soldiers staggered back, their hands stinging and bruised. JJ ignored the vicious splinters in his hands and called for another charge. The men heaved, grunting and sweating under the ladder's weight, and together they rushed the door again. This time they smote the door and tore it from its hinges.

JJ was first through the fractured space, with other soldiers scrambling behind. The rebels, brandishing their weapons in the thick smoke, braced against the attack with fingers quivering on triggers and faces contorted with fear and rage. Even through the smoke JJ saw the terror in their eyes, the sickening realization that they were being called to reap the horror they had sown all through their long, murderous night. JJ despised them.

For a split second, he thought they might stand down and surrender. But then a giant, barrel-chested man crouched low and bellowed, "Behold a pale horse, and it's rider's name was Death!"

The giant charged. JJ brought his saber down with all his strength upon the man's head. The man ducked and evaded the blade's edge, but JJ brought the flat side down on the back of the man's neck with great force. The man toppled bleeding from the blow, but he twisted round and fired his shotgun one last time. The soldier beside JJ — it was the Irish sergeant — crashed to the ground with a gaping gutshot.

A cry went up for the hostages to get down. Then, a terrific series of thunderclaps split the air and JJ fell blinded by a sudden gust of smoke.

After a moment, JJ staggered upright again. He was covered in blood, dust, and black soot. He could hear only a shrill ringing in his ears and realized he would be deaf for a time — perhaps a long time. Warm blood oozed from his ears and ran down his neck. He wiped the snot running from his nostrils and peered through the clearing smoke.

A living corpse shuffled through the smoke, making right for JJ. Lacerated flesh hung from his bones where the shrapnel of balls and bullets had ripped and chipped at his body. Yet still the corpse staggered on, a crude hatchet in hand, and his terror-stricken eyes — the only part of him that seemed yet human — were fixed on JJ. From the corpse's throat came a bloodcurdling scream.

JJ turned. Feeling the world pulse in lucid slow motion, as if everything had become a dream, he leveled his saber and thrust at the advancing corpse. The blade passed through the undead thing like a hot knife through butter, until suddenly the blade shuddered and would go no further.

JJ pulled the saber back, but it would not budge — *stuck*. Ready to leap back lest the corpse swing the hatchet down, JJ looked up. But the corpse's living eyes were fading to lifeless gray, and at last every part of the sad creature was finally, truly dead. Then came the heavy weight as the body fell, with JJ's saber still protruding from the chest like a pork skewer.

As the smoke cleared, JJ stood staring down at the body. He realized that, just minutes ago, the body had been a living, breathing man. But no. Looking closer, JJ saw a dead boy at his feet, no older than he was.

JJ paced about the engine house. The walls were chipped with buckshot. Most of the rebels lay dead and riddled with shot, or else crumpled and reeling on the floor in bloody agony. Six unscathed rebels, including one wide-eyed runaway slave, cowered in the corner as captives. JJ's men advanced, picking their steps over the dead, and they struck the survivors down with the butts of their muskets. A breathless corporal, blood trickling into his eye, reported to JJ. "We've recovered the hostages, Lieutenant. All accounted for, all well."

JJ nodded to the man, but his eyes were fixed on the saber that stuck out from the dead boy's chest. Reaching down, he hauled until the notched blade came free again. He unbuttoned a pocket and pulled out a spotted handkerchief. He ran the kerchief over the bloody blade until it shone again.

JJ stepped over the dead boy and approached the wounded giant who had first attacked him. The man was old and wore a great gray beard that was spattered with blood. Barely conscious, the old man clutched a wooden cross and murmured, "A time to love, and a time to hate. A time for war, and a time for peace..." Now he looked up at JJ with glistening eyes and a saintly calm. "Freedom under God."

JJ watched the man with detached curiosity. Slowly, he knelt down and looked into the man's bleary eyes for a long, unbroken moment.

Coughing, with an outstretched hand reaching for something, the man muttered, "Freedom under God..."

JJ saw the man's goal: a pistol on the ground nearby. He picked up the pistol and held it just out of the man's reach. He looked into the old man's eyes once more. "Are you the one they call John Brown?"

Empty-handed, the man's saintly calm became red-faced rage. He slammed a fist into the dust and blood on the floor. "No...no...*no*..."

"Identify yourself," JJ said sharply. "Are you John Brown?"

Across the engine house, a young man shouted, "Don't tell him nothin, Pa!"

"*Shut up*," a soldier snarled, and he cracked the butt of his musket against the kid's mouth.

With newfound strength, the old man lifted himself up on his elbows. Quivering, he looked up into JJ's eyes with seething hatred. "My name is John Brown, servant of the Lord." He stretched out and spat on JJ's boots. "In the name of Jesus Christ, they must be...free..."

The man's eyes rolled back in his head, and he went limp.

After a brief moment of silence, several soldiers standing nearby burst out laughing. For his part, JJ stood up and stared down at the crumpled figure. JJ nodded curtly to two soldiers nearby, and their laughter was cut short. Presently they stepped forward and hauled the wounded Brown to his feet.

"Wake up," JJ said, slapping the man's cheeks.

Brown groaned, consciousness nearing the surface, but he slipped away again.

"Stand him up," JJ ordered. "Come on, stand him up straight."

The soldiers held Brown upright. JJ clasped Brown's jaw with a vice grip and squeezed, and the pressure forced the old man's fluttering eyes open wide.

"I said *wake up*. Ah, and there he is, our Lord's servant. John Brown: you are hereby under arrest pending charges for treason against the United States of America. May God have mercy on your soul."

Chapter 2

MOTHER BAILEY'S QUIETING SYRUP

Mae Jane led the young doctor up the grand staircase. "Lady Isabella ain't slept in three days," she said. "Her forehead's boilin hot one minute, clam-cold the next. I surely don't know what to make of it."

The young doctor mumbled, "Of course you don't."

"What's that, Doctor, sir?"

"Nothing. You're a woman after all, not to mention a...well, anyway. Where is she?"

"This way, sir."

She hurried down the sunlit second-floor corridor toward Clarendon's east wing. Turning her head, she saw Dr. Harper lingering far behind. He did not seem in the least concerned about haste; rather, he was busy inspecting the oil paintings that lined the walls.

"These are exquisite," the young doctor marveled, adjusting the half-moon spectacles on the bridge of his nose. "I had no idea Clarendon featured such works. This is by Cole, isn't it? *The Course of Empire.*"

Mae Jane swallowed her deep concern for Lady Isabella, which tread the waters just above panic. She offered the most pleasant smile she could manage.

"Maybe so, sir. I ain't much schooled in the arts, fine or otherwise."

"No, I wouldn't think a slave would be."

Mae Jane smiled. "Oh, I ain't a slave, Doctor, sir. I'm a freedman. My name's *Freeman*, see, and—"

Harper cleared his throat and waited for her to say something more important.

Behind a well-sculpted mask of politeness, Mae Jane's eyes dimmed with sincere distaste. This was always the way. Any time she spoke alone with a white man, their eyes tended to glaze over just like Harper's had just now, their verbal communication reduced to grunts, groans, and heavy sighs.

She reminded herself to be patient. She'd known many men like Dr. Harper in her long years, and she knew how to deal with them. Still, the dealing never got any easier, especially now that she wasn't just a 'darkie' and not just a 'wench', but had grown to become an *old* darkie wench.

"If you'll follow me, please, Doctor. The Lady of Clarendon is very sick."

Harper made to follow, but he halted again. "But the cycle is incomplete," he said, complaining to Mae Jane as if she ought to know or care what the hell he was talking about. The young doctor pointed at the wall. "There are only four paintings here, beginning with the empire's humble agrarian origins in *Savage State* and ending with the industrial-scale blood and fire of *Destruction*. See? The imperial city is tearing itself apart, brother against brother. But the fifth piece is missing. Here there ought to be *Desolation*: the scene of the great empire's lonely extinction, the return to a state of nature, where weeds sprout upon the ruins of civilization. Without a proper coda, the whole work is left without an ending."

Mae Jane sighed under her breath. "All I know is, thems is Mr. John's — I mean Senator Roscoe's favorite paintins. Maybe he prefers to leave the ending unknown, like a mystery. Maybe there's still room for a happy ending."

Harper laughed. "That's a stupid idea."

Mae Jane's patience had vanished, though a thin smile remained. She pushed it wider and broader until she felt the edges of her mouth twitch. "Will you *please* follow me, Doctor, sir?"

She managed to bring Harper to the east wing study without further delay. Putting a hand on the knob, she squeezed and lifted up against the door. This quieted the latch and the door opened silently. It had been many years since Mae Jane had learned this trick. She still had the scar on her forehead from when the Lady threw a bottle at her head for opening the study door too loudly.

The looming entrance to the study was shapeless and black, and beyond it there seemed to be nothing but a blank abyss. At the door, Dr. Harper paused and peered into the gloom.

"In quickly," Mae Jane urged. "The light hurts the Lady's eyes."

Darkness enveloped them as Mae Jane closed the door. Standing within the study, one would never know it was seven o'clock in the morning on a bright October day. Mae Jane fumbled in the dark, and her eyes caught something dark moving amidst the wreckage. Harper saw it too, and he sucked in a fearful breath. Mae Jane blushed with embarrassment. Rats again.

Mae Jane finally succeeded in lighting a kerosene lamp. The lamp cast a brave pool of light against the inky blackness. The space was barricaded with stacks of books, old junk, and piles of discarded evening dresses, bodices, and corsets. Upon a long sofa lay a dark shape that began to move and moan.

Mae Jane stepped up to the writhing form and said, "Lady Isabella, may I present—"

The shape on the sofa gave a hideous, bellowing groan of protest.

Quieter now, Mae Jane said, "...Dr. Ira Harper." She turned and looked at Dr. Harper, who seemed to be searching for a possible excuse for abandoning the whole situation before he waded too far into it.

"Doctor, sir? May I present Lady Isabella Spencer."

Presently, the shape on the sofa rolled over and became a woman. Seeing the state of her mistress, Mae Jane's heart sank. Isabella was pale, her dress soaked through with cold sweat, her lips blue and trembling and cracked from dehydration. She'd once been beautiful: quick-witted, vivacious, the belle of every society ball. Now she was a gray-haired, emaciated shadow who rarely ventured beyond the study's four walls, not even to spend time with her own children.

Harper swallowed and approached the sofa. He looked around for a space to set his doctor's bag, and Mae Jane stepped up to clear a table of dust-covered books. Harper mumbled a vague thank-you and proceeded to fish through his bag for a stethoscope.

"Mrs. Roscoe. Mrs. Roscoe, is it?"

Isabella groaned a meager, unintelligible reply.

"Mrs. Roscoe, I'm going to examine you now. I'm going to put my hands on you, in and around the vicinity of your breasts. This is a strictly scientific procedure, Mrs. Roscoe. Do you understand?"

There came another mumble, which the young doctor took as a consenting *yes*. He knelt down beside the sofa and examined Isabella, whose body was drenched in sweat.

Mae Jane went about lighting small candles, and slowly more of the space was revealed. Years ago, back when Clarendon had belonged to the Spencer family, this study had been the office of Colonel Thomas Spencer — *Massa Colonel*, as Mae Jane remembered. Little about the room had changed since those forgotten years. Even the newly installed curtains, designed to block out all traces of light, had absorbed the sour odor of the old man's cigars. There were several hundred dresses and gowns in a rainbow of colors strewn throughout the study. They were heaped over chairs, piled on the rug, and knotted together in a cloth tower upon the Colonel's writing desk. An ancient coat tree in the corner had long ago splintered under the crushing weight of sixty ballroom gowns. Lady Isabella considered herself a private collector of fine fashion, with an emphasis on the word *private*; precisely none of the gowns had ever been worn in public, but more arrived by courier every day.

Dominating the room was a monstrous oil portrait of the powder-wigged war hero himself: Thomas Spencer, known to all simply as *the Colonel*. The Colonel stood with his long-dead wife Anna, and the couple was flanked by a team of handsome foxhounds. The white plantation house called Clarendon gleamed like Camelot in the background.

The Colonel had been the kind of man who desired only sons and was cursed to have only daughters. Small portraits of the Colonel's five daughters lined the borders of the larger painting, with each girl's name written in fine cursive letters below her likeness. The last name, below a portrait of a pudgy young girl, was ISABELLA.

The rest of the study was covered with paintings of other members of the Spencer family, most of them dead and gone now. The place was like a museum for the family, or maybe it was more like a shrine.

Dr. Harper moved a stethoscope across Isabella's chest and squinted behind his spectacles, his thick blonde mustache tick-tocking as he swished his mouth back and forth. The young doctor removed the stethoscope and looked up at Mae Jane.

"The rate of Mrs. Roscoe's resting pulse has quickened since her last examination — to an alarming rate, I should add."

Suddenly lucid, Isabella rose up snapped her fingers against the tip of the young doctor's nose. "Speak to *me*, boy," she growled with surprising strength and coherence. "*She* is not your patient."

White-faced and trembling, Dr. Harper bowed to Isabella. "Forgive me, ma'am. The rate of your pulse is, well, it's rather disconcerting, ma'am. I don't say that lightly, either. It could be a sign of various ailments, any one of which I'd consider serious."

"What about my fever?" Isabella asked.

"You don't have a fever. Not just yet, at least."

Isabella's face was slicked with sweat. She glared at the young doctor with bleary, red-rimmed eyes, indignant and doubtful. "*Excuse me?*"

Mae Jane stepped forward. "There's hookworm in the Valley, Doctor, sir. Our Thomas, one of his school chums came down with it, so he says. Maybe he—"

Harper laughed and shook his head. "You women. Always drawing your own conclusions." He looked at each of them in turn with a condescension that was far beyond his years. Mae Jane joined Isabella in glaring back at him. Blushing, the young doctor breathed a heavy sigh. "In any case, Mrs. Roscoe doesn't—"

"*Lady Spencer*."

"Lady Spencer doesn't have a rash. She has no abdominal pain—"

"My body aches all over..."

"—or intestinal cramps." Harper reached out and pressed his fingers down on Isabella's abdomen in a methodical pattern. "Do you have blood in your stool?"

"What?"

"Have you noticed—"

"That's none of your concern, *boy*."

Trying to hide his exasperation, Harper turned to Mae Jane for the answer. Mae Jane shook her head, no.

Nodding, Harper stood up and found a nearby chair. "It's not a hookworm," he said, sitting down again. "In fact, it's nothing that's invaded Mrs. Ros — Lady Spencer's body. Rather, I think the issue is what she *isn't* taking in."

Mae Jane swallowed. "What does that mean, Doctor?"

"He means that my body is in distress because I haven't had my medicine," Isabella said.

Harper offered a nod of agreement. "As a matter of fact, yes."

Isabella stared daggers at the doctor. "*Then why won't you give it to me?*"

Then, her meager energy spent, Isabella collapsed back on the sofa and groaned miserably.

Mae Jane looked at the young doctor. "It's been a long while, sir. The Lady's been unwell a long while. Your daddy must have explained her condition to you before."

"That old fart Franklin ran out of my medicine over a month ago," Isabella said. "What good is a store if the proprietor can't keep the shelves stocked? I've had to dilute my prescription with water just to make it last, but I tell you *it's not enough*."

Mae Jane picked her way across the cramped study to the huge writing desk that dominated its center. From the desk, Mae Jane picked up a tall brown bottle that was nearly empty. The label on it read SRIGLEY'S SEDATIVE SOLUTION. She offered the bottle to Harper, and he studied the label in the candlelight.

Meanwhile, Mae Jane studied Isabella. She was a long-limbed woman and very thin, with wrists thinner than poplar twigs. Her hair had turned gray long before it was fashionable or fair for a woman her age, but it had once been that beautiful sand color which Mae Jane so adored. The deep wrinkles and purplish bags under her eyes suggested she was well beyond sixty, though Mae Jane knew the woman was still in her forties. In fact, Isabella and Mae Jane were the same age, sharing the same birthday (though Mae Jane, not knowing the *actual* day or year of her birth, suspected she was in fact several years older). They'd grown up together as bosom companions, Isabella holding the leash while Mae Jane learned to live with the prickly rope collar around her neck. As youths, Mae Jane had witnessed the growing Isabella eclipse all the other Spencer sisters in both beauty and grace, attracting all sorts of suitors.

But that had all been a long time ago. Some twenty years had passed since Isabella Spencer became, officially, Isabella Roscoe, and none of those years had been kind to her. In recent time, Isabella had taken to calling herself a Spencer once more, maybe to try and recapture the spirit of the old times.

"I never seen her like this before," Mae Jane said. "She ain't never been this bad. You sure she don't have a fever, Doctor?"

Harper stared at Isabella, as if the longer he looked suffering in the eye the less it would disturb him. "She needs water," he said. "Hydration and rest. Get her out of those damned clothes and draw her a nice, hot bath. Fresh clothes, more hydration. And sustenance, for God's sake. Soup, bread, anything she'll take down. When she sweats, bathe and dress her again."

"For how long?"

Harper shrugged. "As long as it takes." He wagged the empty bottle under Mae Jane's nose. "Continue giving her this, and she'll only become further enslaved to it."

Isabella, only half-conscious now, murmured one word: "Srigley's..."

Harper peered down at her over his spectacles. "Complete abstinence is what your body needs, ma'am."

Isabella's eyes slowly opened again. Turning her head with a grimace, she glared at Harper. "Don't tell me what I need, boy. I've been suffering the same disease of the soul since before you were even born. Your father always gave me my medicine. He knew what I *needed* as well as you think you do."

The mention of the young doctor's father shook away his pretentious airs. With drooping shoulders Harper said, "Lady Spencer, I am doing my utmost to provide good care. I'm sure my father did the same in his time, God rest his soul, but now it's just me."

Isabella snorted. "*Good care?* Just which Harper boy are you anyway? You're not the God-cursed sodomite, are you?"

Harper blushed a deep, furious red. "I shouldn't dignify that question with an answer," he said stiffly.

"Hm. But you *will* answer me, Doctor."

"*I'm not him,*" Harper snapped. There was sweat on the young doctor's brow, and his half-moon spectacles fogged with steam. "That was my brother Richard. And you don't have to worry about him anymore. He's...he's..."

"I don't care in the least about him," Isabella replied, her voice cold. "We were discussing *my* woes, were we not?"

Mae Jane hung her head. This was the Lady's way. One moment she could be charming, her bright and sensual eyes thrilling any man or woman who looked upon them. The next she could lash out like a murderous wild animal, without an ounce of mercy in her heart.

Harper opened his journal — not really his, Mae Jane saw, but his father's — and thumbed through it. "Here," he said. "She's been taking daily doses of laudanum for seventeen years. *Seventeen years.*" Shocked, he looked up at Mae Jane. "Do you know what something like that does to a woman's body chemistry, Mrs...?"

"Freeman."

"Do you know what that does to a woman's body chemistry, Mrs. Freeman?"

"I bet you fixin to tell me, Doctor."

"I didn't think you'd know. But simply put, the Lady Spencer who started on her medicine nearly twenty years ago isn't the Lady Spencer here and now. Laudanum, of course, is an opiate; it instantly relieves an anxious body and soothes a worried mind with feelings of intense euphoria. But when the effects subside, as they always do, spiritual anxiety returns with a vengeance. And so the only way to maintain bliss is to increase the dosage amount, as well as dosage cadence. Wouldn't *you* want to feel absolutely wonderful all the time? Perhaps any of us would. Well, if you decide bliss is your goal, your body will surely help you get it. Lady Spencer's internal systems have been transformed over time — trained, if you will — with every organ doing its part to soak up every last drop from every bottle. But there comes the cost. Her entire body now has but one singular focus, which is to consume and process her *medicine*. It has become as critical to her living functions as air and water. As such, without the expected dosage, the body's systems become severely distressed."

Mae Jane understood the stark seriousness of the situation, even without the doctor's explanation. In the last six months, ever since she started on the latest and greatest of laudanum products called Srigley's, Isabella had become less and less, well, *recognizable*. No longer did the Lady eat. She slept in fits, often waking up screaming. Twice she'd nearly set Clarendon on fire when, in a sluggish stupor, she knocked a candle onto the floor and forgotten about it. It had become habit for Mae Jane, upon approaching the closed door of the east wing study, to steel herself for the possibility that she might walk in to find Lady Isabella dead.

Mae Jane wet the rag again and wrung it and placed it upon Isabella's forehead, cooing softly all the while. Though she could not believe she was uttering the words, she said, "Can't we give her just a little, Doctor? If a lot ain't so good for her, then maybe a little will—"

"She said it herself," the young doctor replied. "Mr. Franklin won't carry Srigley's in his store any longer. And if I may, I commend him for it. Srigley's is poison."

Here, Mae Jane forgot the subservient humility expected of her. "Well if *I* may, Doctor, don't be too sure Mr. Franklin won't ever carry it again. Lady Isabella's been a fine customer to him all these years. A fine customer indeed. When he understands the Lady's need, maybe he'll stock it again."

"He won't," Harper said flatly. "Not with the tariff that Congress just placed on it. They passed a new bill up in Washington, the snakes. Tinctures and medicines of all kinds — they're double, triple the cost of just a year ago. They might be made with Southern ingredients, but they're bottled in Northern factories. And we all know how the Yankees idolize their profit margins..."

Mae Jane shook her head. "I don't know nothin about Yankees," she said. "I don't know nothin about most everything. But I do know Mr. John — Senator Roscoe, I mean. I know there ain't no price he wouldn't pay to get his wife the medicine she needs."

Harper seemed to consider this point. "I'm sure you're right," he said at last. "But the issue is obtaining Srigley's in the first place. Such tinctures aren't to be found anywhere, not even in Richmond. There's a black market sprung up, though I'm sure the Senator wouldn't be interested in stooping that low."

Mae Jane pushed greasy strands of wet hair from Isabella's face. "Well, I can't speak for the Senator..."

Isabella opened her eyes suddenly, as if snapping awake from a terrible dream. "And you can't speak for me either, Mae Jane." Her fluttering eyes rolled until they landed on Harper. "I *must* have my medicine, Doctor. Whatever the cost, I must have it."

Harper's mustache swished. He was deep in thought. "I will have to consult your husband," he said at last. He stood up and made ready to leave. "The Senator will have the final decision about any changes to your treatment and—"

"*NO!*"

Isabella clutched at the young doctor briefly, but her strength evaporated once again. She put her trembling hands to her face. "I mean — what I mean is, my husband has delegated decisions regarding my personal health to Mae Jane here, and ultimately to myself." She looked up and offered a crooked attempt at a smile. Through yellow teeth she said, "Isn't that rather progressive of him, Doctor?"

Harper grimaced. "Progressive, possibly. Advisable? That's another matter."

"Yes, quite progressive," Isabella said with a shaky smile. "And we spare no expense, Doctor. Like Mae Jane said, the Senator wants the very best for his darling wife."

"Indeed." Harper took a deep, resigned breath. "Very well," he said at last, and he scratched a few notes in his journal. "I will speak with some colleagues in Baltimore. They may be able to help source a six- to twelve-months' supply of Mother Bailey's."

Isabella flashed her yellow smile again, but this time the desperation in her eyes was undeniable. She released a hysterical laugh that gave Mae Jane goosebumps. "But, Doctor, I don't know whether you're teasing me or not." Her false smile suddenly vanished, and now her face took on a monstrous, black-eyed intensity. "Tell me you're not teasing me, Doctor. I said I want *Srigley's Sedative Solution*, and only Srigley's will do."

Harper pulled at his shirt collar and cleared his throat. Unable to look at the quaking Isabella, he instead directed his answer to Mae Jane. "Srigley's Sedative is clearly ineffective in relieving Lady Spencer's particular case of melancholy," he said. "And it may in fact be disrupting her constitution's ability to fight off an actual fever, should one afflict her. I would like to experiment with a new tincture. One that is much more potent."

Isabella's eyes gleamed hungrily, but her voice remained noncommittal. "*More* potent?"

Mae Jane heard all this with a draining spirit. She had in fact hoped that Dr. Harper would stand firm and deny Lady Isabella her medicine — *any* sort of medicine. She had postured for Isabella only to remain within her good graces. But in fact she had hoped that, after a difficult period of adjustment, Isabella would finally emerge from the poisonous fog that had encased her mind and body for so many years. Now, it seemed Isabella would not clear the fog but merely plunge herself into something deeper and more destructive.

"Mother Bailey's Quieting Syrup," Harper said. "I've read the research that it cures *horses* of their anxiety, which is to say quite a lot about its potency." Now he wagged a finger and frowned, as if warning a child. "For yourself, it will be one spoonful twice daily. Anything more is extremely dangerous. I don't want to receive a call from Miss Freeland here and have her tell me you've taken ill from overindulgence. Laudanum is a mood-enriching elixir, not a libation."

At first, Isabella looked as if she was ready to knock the young doctor bloody. But then, upon watching Harper scribble a prescription into his notebook and tear the strip out, Isabella draped herself in gracious adoration.

"I understand, Doctor," the Lady of Clarendon said, assuming the sweet, sultry voice of her youth. "You're a good man, Dr. Harper. A *fine* man, indeed. Thank you ever so much."

Isabella reached up and squeezed the young doctor's weak and bony hand. As she did, she skillfully worked the prescription into her own grasp. Mae Jane couldn't help but smile. As a younger woman, Isabella Spencer had always known how to get what she wanted from a man. Even battered by years of ill health, the belle of yesterday's ball was somehow still able to captivate the young doctor as if he was a clueless suitor.

"I should note," Harper said, "that Mr. Franklin *does* carry Mother Bailey's in his store. You might be able to purchase a bottle or two until a larger shipment arrives from Baltimore. I surely hope Mother B's brings you great relief."

Isabella offered a charming smile. "I'll be sure to let you know if it does, Doctor." Her smile vanished and she dropped his hand, evidently finished with him, and she proceeded to roll over and go to sleep.

There came a knock at the door, and then it opened. Turning her head, Mae Jane saw standing in the doorway a beautiful girl with ivory skin and sunburnt freckles. The morning light outside cast streams of quicksilver through her raven hair. The girl carried a bowl and washcloth.

"Oh, pardon me," the girl said sheepishly. "I didn't know we had visitors. I…I heard Cousin Isabella might have a fever, so I brought some cold, refreshing water."

Isabella scoffed, and Sarah shrank back.

Mae Jane, for her part, smiled at Sarah. Blessed girl. "Come in, Sarah, come in, child."

"*And close the damn door*!" Isabella roared from the couch. "The light. The *light*!"

Sarah hurried inside and closed the door, and there was candlelit darkness once more. Dr. Harper shot up from his chair and ran his fingers through his hair, blushing.

"Hello, Sarah — *Miss Roscoe*, I mean."

Mae Jane took the bucket and cloth from Sarah, who offered the doctor a friendly though rather distracted smile.

"Hello, Doctor," Sarah said.

Harper's hopeful grin stretched from ear to ear. "You must remember me, don't you? Ira. I'm—"

"Richard's younger brother, yes," Sarah said, her smile straining a little. "Of course I remember you, Ira. It's been…well, some time."

"Indeed it has. You've been away?"

"Richmond. I attend a girl's school there. It's very proper."

"*Very proper*," a voice mocked; it was Lady Isabella, speaking from the couch.

Sarah grimaced, but only briefly; otherwise she maintained a pleasant disposition. And Harper, he was absolutely smitten. Of course, Sarah Roscoe had that effect on most men, young and old.

"Daddy — that is, my father — has called me back home to…well, I don't exactly know for what reason."

"We's happy to have her back," Mae Jane said with a warm smile. Kneeling on the floor, she soaked the washcloth and then wrung it, and she laid it upon Isabella's brow. Soothed by the cool wet touch of the cloth, Isabella sighed.

"Is there anything I might help with?" Sarah asked.

Mae Jane shook her head. "No, child. We's got it all covered here. You run along now. Ben's in the kitchens whippin up breakfast."

"I beg your pardon, Mae Jane, but I can't find Ben anywhere. And Tom and Bayard, they're…well, they're crawling on the walls, so to speak."

Mae Jane heaved an exasperated sigh. Typical Ben, shirking his household duties once again. "Laws, that boy…"

Sarah laughed. "I'm sure he's only worming his way into a book somewhere."

Isabella pushed the wet cloth away from her face and glared at Mae Jane. "That fat-lipped luggard could use a correction or three," she muttered. "Clarendon still has its whipping post, you know. It's about the only thing left over from the good times. You ought to take him there, Mae Jane, and show your boy how things *used* to be around here."

Dr. Harper let out a dark-humored chuckle that made Mae Jane want to jab her fingers in his eyes.

Sarah, meanwhile, was shocked. "That's a terrible thing to say…"

Hearing this, Harper's laugh vanished, and the young doctor assumed the righteous indignance of a parson. "I must say I'm inclined to agree with your daughter, Lady Spencer."

Isabella scowled at him. "She's not my *daughter*, idiot."

"Hush," Mae Jane said, replacing the wet cloth.

Sarah was kinder in her explanation to the young doctor. "My mother was Sarah *Carter*, Daddy's first wife and the Lady's first cousin. She died a long time ago while giving birth to me. Daddy and Cousin Isabella married soon after and—"

"And *nothing*," Isabella snapped. "It was all a ruse to acquire the deed to my father's house. My beloved husband didn't want a wife — he wanted *Clarendon*. Now it's the Spencer estate no longer, but the Roscoe dunghill."

Mae Jane clicked her tongue. "Now, Bella, we know you don't mean that . . ."

"No doubt you've seen the sorry state of the place, Doctor," Isabella went on. "Fields choked with weeds. Creepers and vines taking over. The mansion is disrepair, the whole place ugly and sickly. But that's what happens when you don't have enough niggers to keep the place. That's what happens when you spit in the face of tradition and *set them all free* on a whim. And for what? So my beloved husband can call himself a progressive Southerner."

A stiff silence hung in the rancid air of the study. For a long moment, no one moved.

Mae Jane drew a deep, self-calming breath. "We understand, Bella. *I* understand. You ain't feelin so good today, and there ain't nothin wrong with feelin bad now and then."

"I'd feel better if only I could get some damn peace and quiet," Isabella growled.

Another silence. Mae Jane turned to Sarah and the young doctor, who both understood the meaning in her look.

"Well then," Harper said, gathering his things, "I suppose I should be off." He looked immensely relieved at the prospect of escape.

Sarah curtsied toward Isabella, and then she and the young doctor retreated to the door. Mae Jane stood up, one leg at a time, her knees creaking. Just as Mae Jane turned to leave, however, Isabella reached out and clutched her hand.

"Wait," Isabella said. "I want to talk to the orphan."

Mae Jane looked toward the door, where Sarah stood watching. Mae Jane could read the silent pain on the girl's face at the word *orphan*. At least Isabella hadn't called Sarah her favorite insult, 'the Carter bitch.'

With a dignified air, Sarah approached the sofa again and stood before Isabella.

Isabella produced Harper's prescription, and she thrust the yellow paper into the air. "Go into town this morning," she said, "and fetch my medicine for me."

With a formal bow, Sarah stepped forward. "Of course, dear Cousin."

As Sarah reached for the paper, Isabella held it firm. She glared up at Sarah with hateful eyes. "I see how you look at me, stupid girl. You pity me, don't you? Yes, you actually *pity* me! You think yourself so beautiful, pure, and ageless. Do you feel sorry for me for growing old, girl? Well, you will learn soon enough. This life is not all dances and barbecues and handsome boys coming to call."

Sarah hung her head and waited for the diatribe to end. Mae Jane wanted to step forward and pull the girl away, but she remained rooted to her spot on the floor.

"It will *all* end," Isabella went on, "and much too quickly. A woman is a shooting star in the night, shining brilliantly but once — and then winking out." She reached up and touched the sallow skin of her own cheek. Her voice was thick, slurring and sluggish from the effects of her medicine. "A woman's beauty is a painful thing, for no sooner does it blossom than it begins its slow decay to a sagging yellow death." Her eyes suddenly hardened to stone. "*Remember it*, girl. Soon enough not even a mulatto will want you for sport."

Sarah fought back tears. "I wish to go now," she said, trembling.

"Then *go*, orphan."

Sarah fled. White light poured into the study as Dr. Harper opened the door and stepped hastily outside. Sarah followed quickly, slamming the door behind her, and the loud *thud* caused Isabella to groan with pain.

Still standing in the murky darkness, Mae Jane fought the urge to rush up and haul Isabella upright and slap her once, twice, three times across the face, and *hard*. She'd give the woman something to groan about, all right.

Mae Jane went to the door. "I'll send Benny to fetch you at suppertime," she said stiffly.

"Why?" Isabella whined. "Why can't I eat in here? I always eat in here."

Mae Jane bit her tongue until the urge to shout had passed. "Because Mr. John's comin home today," she replied. "You husband's comin home after a long while away. It'd be nice for the two of you to make an appearance together. For the children."

Isabella moaned and rolled over. "I gave *the children* life. I gave them everything I have. And what do *the children* ever do for me? What does anyone ever give to me?"

On another day, Mae Jane might have stayed to listen, to console, to provide some words of comfort. But today, with Isabella being as she was, Mae Jane hadn't the slightest interest in lingering one minute longer than her duty required. Instead she went to the door, and she was just starting to turn the knob when—

"Mae Jane?"

She stopped. Turning, Mae Jane looked into the darkened study one final time. Lady Isabella lay under the sickly light of a tallow candle.

Isabella said, in a voice vulnerable and girlish: "I love you, sister."

Swallowing, Mae Jane offered the refrain, repeated since they were little girls: "I love you, sister."

Then Mae Jane turned and shut the door behind her, squeezing and lifting to ensure the latch closed without a sound.

Chapter 3
THE ORPHAN

STILL TREMBLING FROM HER ENCOUNTER with *that woman* (her private name for Cousin Isabella), Sarah Roscoe did her best to oblige Dr. Ira Harper as he fumbled his way through an invitation for 'coffee and polite conversation' sometime very soon.

"We'll be chaperoned, of course," he said.

With her ears still hot and ringing from the word *orphan*, Sarah bit her tongue and offered the man — *boy*; he was a year younger than the twins, for pity's sake — a sorrowful shake of her head. "I'm afraid I'll be preoccupied, unfortunately."

"But I haven't said which day yet."

Sarah searched for a means of escape. Her mind was sharper than most people gave her credit for, and she found the answer quite quickly. "I'll be returning to school in Richmond any day now," she explained. "Daddy is coming home today from Washington, and he expressly wanted to see me, which is why I'm here. But of course, I'll have to return to my studies in just a few days. You can understand, Ira, I'm sure."

It was a white lie sprinkled with truth, but in fact it was all rather yellow. Poor Ira Harper seemed to guess at this too, though he had no grounds to object.

"Well," he said, deflated. "Maybe someday, then."

"Maybe someday!" Sarah agreed, beaming.

Finally, she succeeded in guiding him across the threshold such that she could shut the door and be rid of him. God be gracious, what an exhausting morning it had been so far. She lingered behind the dark safety of the door for several long moments before she slunk over to a window and peeled back the curtains there, and looking out she saw the young doctor mount his horse and ride down the estate's clay path toward the main road beyond. Watching the boy astride his horse, Sarah had to admit that he bore a striking resemblance to his older brother Richard…

But no, Sarah would not think of Richard Harper. She would not think about her former beau this morning, not today, not ever again for that matter. He'd *hurt* her a long time ago, and that was that, no more to be said. It was water gone under the bridge — gone under a very great many bridges, in fact. And besides—

Orphan.

Oh, Lord. How evil that old witch was, and frustrating too, the way she could infect Sarah's thoughts without needing to be present. It was like a demonic spirit called Cousin Isabella followed Sarah everywhere, trailing after her like a noxious cloud…

Orphan.

Sarah went upstairs to finish her daily toilet. She lamented being seen by someone outside the family in such an unkempt state. The desire to bring fresh water to *that woman* had been an instinct of good will, a Christian impulse, but what good had it done? Cousin Isabella was a rank sort of sponge that soaked up only hatred and bile, and not even the golden smile of the Christ Child could thaw that old shrunken heart.

Entering her bedroom, Sarah confirmed that all her things had remained untouched and in place as she had left them. Tom had a vulgar habit of sneaking into her room and rummaging through her things just to annoy her. She was also keenly aware that Jem had taken to pacing through her room by times, pausing now and then to spray a mist of her perfume or inspect feminine objects like earrings and powder brushes — not out of any interest in Sarah of course, but to find clues to help answer his fumbling curiosities about the fairer sex.

She sat down before her vanity and picked up her hairbrush.

Taking up a hairbrush, she ran it through her long hair and idly hummed an old lullaby. Rays of sunlight filtering in through the window felt warm on her skin, and a sense of calm returned.

"Of course Ira Harper would want to have 'coffee and polite conversation' with you," she whispered to her reflection. "Of course Sam Hanley would write to Daddy asking for your hand. Of course that man in Richmond — do you remember how *that man* in Richmond stopped in the street and looked at you? Of course he might become obsessed, make countless inquiries, and journey all over the world in a quest to find you. Of course he might, his *look* said it all! And of course, even if that man doesn't find his way to you, the right suitor will, sooner or later."

But why *of course*? And what did *sooner or later* really mean? Was she really as arresting, as much of a 'catch' (to use the latest term out of Richmond), as she thought?

Not everything about Sarah's appearance was to her liking. Far from it, actually. Her eyes were an enchanting emerald green, especially when the bright light of day shone on them, but she considered them set too far apart. She felt her neck was too long, her eyelashes too sparse, and she often wore large hats to hide her dreadful elephant ears. She deemed her hair, night black against her porcelain skin, coarse and ugly — nothing at all like the 'Roscoe hair' the rest of her family enjoyed: silken, lush locks the color of sand. Her skin was pale to the point of looking sickly, and her nose and cheeks were pocked with dark red freckles which she cursed as her greatest defect. Leaning forward, Sarah analyzed her reflection for wrinkles around her eyes and cautiously touched her jaw to test the perkiness of her flesh, ever fearful of the 'turkey neck' that had already afflicted her dear friend Mary Beth Merrick.

Sarah did not spend so much time before the mirror out of vanity, or at least that's what she told herself. A girl — a *woman,* she corrected — had to look presentable at all times, even in her own house. Why, a young gentleman could come calling at the door at any moment, just like the case with Ira Harper.

And, oh, what if that handsome stranger from Richmond might chance upon the doorstep? Banish the thought! Now she was just being silly.

Slowly, Sarah turned her head back and forth to study how the morning light accentuated the contours of her face. If she was pleased with anything about herself, it was the shape of her face. Not wide and fat like some girls, and not vulpine either, but with a pleasant point in her chin offset by a plush jawline, with cheekbones that were prominent but not conspicuous. It was her mother's face.

Turning away from the vanity, Sarah looked toward the portrait of her mother hanging on the nearby wall. The oil paint was faded and flecked, but still there was a vision of a dark-haired beauty. It was Mother, also named Sarah. Mother had still been an unwed Carter when this portrait was made, dated 1835, and the artist had captured her bright and youthful face flushed with life and hope.

Sarah knew Mother's story quite well, for as a young girl she had asked incessantly about her. Mother's branch of the Carter family had been one of the most powerful families in Virginia some two hundred years earlier. But in Mother's time, her father squandered the family fortune, and the Carter children were forced to live with distant relations. That's how Sarah Carter ended up in Mayfair of all places, living here at Clarendon with Colonel Spencer and his brood of beautiful daughters.

But Sarah Carter, it was said, outshone all the Spencer girls when she made her debut before Mayfair society. No wonder Cousin Isabella was jealous; she was a creature of envy, just like some wicked stepmother from some crude fairytale!

Sarah Carter attracted no shortage of fine suitors, but it was a handsome stranger (hailing from exactly where, nobody knew) who won her heart when he came to the Valley. Sarah Carter became Sarah Roscoe, but no sooner had married life begun than it ended in heartbreak. Mother died on the birthing bed, and the unnamed girl she'd brought into the world was named Sarah in her honor.

Orphan.

Sarah looked at her reflection once more. Except she wasn't an orphan. She had Daddy. Well, whenever he was home, at least. Daddy was elected to the Senate soon after Mother died, and he was gone for what seemed like several years. Sarah learned of Daddy only from the letters he mailed home from Washington, the ones misted in his musky cologne. She smiled as a memory came to mind, one of seeing Daddy for the very first time. He picked her up and swung her around, and she knew that she was his world the same as he was hers.

About that same time Sarah was reunited with Daddy, he proposed to and married Cousin Isabella (she'd only been sixteen or so then). The twins were born the next year.

Daddy never spent much time at home. And so, Sarah had grown up wandering the wide halls of Clarendon. Cousin Isabella was no sort of mother, not to her and not even to her own children. Colonel Spencer had been ancient, and though he was a kindly man so far as Sarah knew, he died when she was still quite young. Cousin Isabella wore black for her father's funeral and never took it off.

A woman is a shooting star in the night, shining brilliantly but once — and then winking out.

Was that really true? Sarah had been shining for twenty-three years now (soon to be twenty-four). She was already considered ancient for a debutante, and well aware of the cruel nickname the other girls in the Valley had coined for her: *Spinster Sarah*. But this sorry state of affairs had nothing to do with Sarah's lack of charm or grace. Love had been cruel, with disappointments and heartbreaks around every corner.

Heartbreaks, like what had happened with Richard Harper...

Like what happened between Richard and *JJ*...

But no matter. Mother had outshone the Spencer girls, each of them more beautiful than the last. So would Sarah outshine the latest batch of pretty faces. The Claiborne family's annual Harvest Festival ball — happening *tonight*, as a matter of fact — would be Sarah's opportunity to really turn heads, to gather around her as many adoring young gentlemen as she could.

Though she faced stiff competition, Sarah was confident that 1859 was the year in which she would receive a proposal of marriage from an irresistible bachelor. (She was not yet open to the idea of marrying a middle-aged widower, although she supposed such a match would offer certain advantages.)

Humming a lullaby, Sarah looked down at Mother's old engagement ring on her finger (on her right hand, of course). Father had given the ring to an infant Sarah after Mother died, intending for Sarah to wear it whenever she became engaged one day.

Gently, Sarah pulled the ring off and examined it in the morning light. She moved the ring to her left hand, to the tip of her ring finger, and there she paused. It was bad luck to go any further, and so she let her imagination run. She pictured a set of large, warm hands — rough but not *rough* like the hands of a commoner, and not dainty like a nancy-boy's hands either — caressing hers, sliding the ring into its proper place.

Yes, this year would finally be *the* year. The year when Sarah could finally leave sad old Clarendon, could finally walk beyond the looming shadow of *that woman*. The year when Sarah could start her own family, one in which she felt a true sense of belonging. A family that *looked* like she did, at least.

Feeling as satisfied as she decided she could be in her appearance, Sarah set her brush down on her vanity. She stood up, checked herself a final time in the mirror, and turned away. She kissed the tips of her fingers and gently touched Mother's portrait, a daily ritual that gave her peace of mind. Someday, when she moved into her own house with her own husband and her own family, Sarah decided she would bring Mother with her.

Leaving her room, Sarah descended the broad, spiraling grand staircase to the first floor. She paused in the grand foyer (what the family sometimes called the 'puppy ballroom') and imagined what the space might look like festooned with ribbons and wedding ornaments. She imagined what she looked like, descending the steps like a queen in a glimmering white dress.

She traced a path through the long hallways. There were a dozen or more parlors and sitting rooms that had gone unoccupied for many years now, with furniture covered in white sheets. A huge ballroom stood cold, dark, and empty. It was difficult to remember the place as it used to be: bright, glittering with a thousand candles, and packed wall-to-wall with guests from Mayfair and well beyond. Clarendon had once been a vibrant place, the social center of Mayfair, but it hadn't been like that since, well...

Not since JJ left home.

Sarah made her way toward the library. Back when Clarendon was built, which to Sarah might have been a thousand years ago, the library had been the original ballroom. Nowadays the dance floor was carpeted, and cluttered with chairs and sofas and armchairs perched in pools of light that came streaming in from the windows. The walls were lined with bookshelves housing thousands of books, most of which had never been read. A massive fireplace dominated the room's center, a great hearth in which a full-grown man could stand up straight. Mounted above the fireplace was a collection of stuffed deer heads: a twelve-pointer, a twenty-eight pointer, and a thirty-six — so named, Sarah understood, by counting the tips of their antlers. Resting below the heads was Colonel Spencer's saber, pistols, and his prized long rifle: the weapons with which he had earned his fame as a hero in Andrew Jackson's army.

Or something like that, anyway. Sarah had never paid much attention to history, and especially not the history of the Spencer family. And Daddy's family, the Roscoes, had no history at all. Daddy had no siblings, no cousins to speak of, and his parents had died when he was a young boy. Standing in the library, Sarah felt that she stood in a museum, a shrine to a man and time as far removed as Caesar's

Rome. And Sarah was of the firm opinion that museums were decidedly boring and stuffy places.

Within the library, a young black man looked up from Father's huge work desk, which was covered with books and papers. He beamed when he saw Sarah approach.

"Good morning, Miss Sarah."

"Good morning, Ben," Sarah said, returning his smile. "How many times must I say it, you don't have to call me *miss*. Certainly not when we're here at home. You know your mother's looking for you? It seems you've shirked your breakfast duties."

Ben sat up with a start. With a look of dismay, he looked to the grandfather clock across the vast room. "Oh, *laws*," he moaned. "I couldn't sleep, so I sat down to work awhile. I didn't realize how much time had passed—"

"It's fine," Sarah laughed. "Mae Jane's in the kitchens now, I suspect."

Ben stood up and straightened his simple bowtie, which was always crooked no matter how much he fussed with it. "I should go help Mama. I should—"

"Just you linger a moment," Sarah said. She put her hands out and touched his chest. It was a simple gesture, intended only to keep him from barreling her over, but the effect was that both of them were struck dumb for a long moment. They stared at each other, watching each other, maybe waiting for the other to move. Suddenly, Sarah withdrew her hands as if she'd touched something hot. Turning, she nodded officially to the papers strewn across the desk.

"What are you working on?"

Ben cleared his throat and set upon the books and papers as if someone else had dumped them there and he'd only just discovered them. "Oh, nothing," he said. "It's nothing really."

Sarah laughed. "Organizing Daddy's mail again, are you?"

Ben's embarrassment lifted then, and he permitted himself to laugh too. "It never seems to end," he said. "How your father gets anything done with so many people trying to bend his ear, I'll never understand."

"It's because he drops all the busywork on *you*, Ben."

He shrugged and laughed again. "I suppose you're right. But in any case, I'm shirking my secretarial duties just now. I'm working on a...well, what you might call a personal project."

"What's it about?"

Ben's timidness returned. "I've been having these...dreams, of late. Nightmares."

"Oh! I'm sorry..."

"It's fine," he said quickly. "It's completely fine. It's just...well, I thought that maybe by writing them down, I could make sense of them. Disarm them, somehow. They're only dreams after all."

"I heard once that dreams are distant memories from other lives we've lived,"

Sarah said wistfully. "Isn't that so sublimely romantic?"

Ben shrugged and looked down at his papers. "I suppose so," he murmured, becoming suddenly morose. But when he looked up at her again, he smiled. "I once dreamed I was flying through the air. Do you think I was a bird in a past life?"

Sarah laughed. Looking at Ben, she forgot about Cousin Isabella and the dank dreariness of Clarendon. Ben's eyes were large and soft, windows to a gentle soul. And there was no mistaking that he was utterly captivated by her, and his unwavering attention never ceased to make her spirits soar. So apparent was his awe whenever they were together, that Sarah had long ago learned to depend on Ben's adoration as a means of overcoming her own loneliness. And if she was being honest, a small part of her likewise held him in great and giddy esteem. One only had to look at Ben once to admire his square jaw, his broad shoulders that pulled against the hand-me-down suit that was two sizes too small.

"Your bowtie never sits straight," she said, and she reached out to fix it.

Ben was a few years older than Sarah, and her oldest friend. Ben had once been a slave to the Colonel, but after the old man retired and Daddy freed all of Clarendon's slaves, Ben had remained on the estate with his mother Mae Jane to serve as footman and housemaid, respectively. In recent time, Daddy had begun to groom Ben as his advisor on all things legal and political. But years ago, before her brothers were born, Sarah and Ben were faithful playmates.

Sarah could still remember wandering Clarendon's towering hallways together with Ben. Without an army of slaves to care for the place, the huge mansion appeared to Sarah as some kind of abandoned castle from a fairy tale. She and Ben would lose themselves in the maze of rooms and corridors littered with covered furniture. It was through Ben that Sarah had learned the important details of her mother's life — what few details Ben knew, anyway. When neither Father nor anyone else seemed interested in sharing their memories of Mother, Ben told Sarah all he remembered about the beautiful 'Miss Sarah.'

Satisfied with the state of Ben's bowtie, Sarah stepped back. "There. That's better." Now she nodded at Ben's sprawling books and letters. "It certainly looks like you've been dreaming quite a lot lately."

Ben laughed. "Oh. Well, *this* is something a little different. Certainly it's not something you'd be interested in hearing about. Even less than my silly dreams."

"You can tell me, Ben. I can't promise I'll understand a word of what you say, but you can tell me whatever is on your mind."

"Well," Ben said, "if you really want to know, I wrote a letter to the Supreme Court."

Sarah nodded slowly. "...I see."

"I'll never send it, of course," Ben added. "I guess you might call it an effort of argumentation. A Socratic exercise."

Sarah wandered along the rows of bookshelves. "What's it about?"

"Well, in short, it's about the Dred Scott case."

Sarah turned and looked at him, and she saw that his bowtie had already gone crooked. "That dratted thing," she said, and she hurried forward to correct it. As she fussed, she said, "You see? I haven't the slightest idea just what you're talking about. Stop being so stiff. Just relax."

Ben stood frozen, his head held high. "Two years ago, a slave sued for his freedom. So far as I can tell, it was the first and only time a negro went before the Supreme Court — his attorneys did, anyway. The case focused on the Missouri Compromise line." Ben paused. "You know about the Missouri Compromise?"

Sarah pursed her lips and shook her head.

"Well," Ben said with a laugh, "let me start there. The Compromise is a continental boundary that Congress drew some forty years ago. From the southern border of Missouri all the way to the Pacific, all states south of the line are to remain open to slavery's expansion. All states north of the line will be free-soil states. Congress drew the line many years before you and I were born, in order to avoid civil war between the Northern states and Southern states. About ten years ago, your father helped shape a new compromise that reaffirmed those policies."

With a sigh, Sarah untied Ben's bowtie and slipped it out from his collar and set to work on it. "Well, I suppose that all makes good enough sense to me."

"It worked for a while, you're right," Ben said. "Now enter Dred Scott. He claimed that because his master took him into unorganized territory *north* of the Missouri Compromise, that his status as a slave eroded over time."

Sarah stepped close to Ben once more, such that their noses almost touched. She could see that his pulse throbbing in his neck had quickened. She draped the ends of the bowtie around his neck and retied it, the way it ought to look. Ben was very aware of her closeness; his eyes kept darting toward the door.

"What?" she said. "Nobody is going to see us here, Ben."

"It's just—"

"It's just me and you," she said. "But regarding your Dred Whoever, his doesn't sound like a very strong case. If a man takes his horse from Virginia to New Hampshire it's still a horse, and it's still owned by the same man. Nothing has changed."

"Yes," Ben said. "But what if horses were outlawed in New Hampshire? Or what if New Hampshire wasn't a state at all, but a wild land? Scott was taken out into the Western Territories, which have no laws to speak of. Maybe if his master had taken him south of the line, his case would be moot. But since he was north of the line—"

"Straight!" she said, victorious. She stepped back to admire her work.

Ben laughed and patted the bow. "I'm indebted to you, m'lady."

"Don't you dare touch that, or you'll ruin it. Now, what were you saying?"

"Just that Dred Scott's status of a slave was one of the main questions of the case.

If a slave leaves the borders of the Union and settles there in a wild territory, is he still bound by the Union's laws?"

"Well, there are some laws that are universal," Sarah said. "They transcend borders. Like marriage, for instance. Or the commandment against murder."

Ben shrugged. "Or perhaps the universal evil of slavery? What some call the 'peculiar institution' is illegal in almost every other civilized nation on the planet. Even 'degenerate' Mexico outlawed slavery back in the '20s, and ten years ago we went to war with Mexico so that we could — big surprise — cede more land for slave plantations. This ignores, of course, that slavery is outlawed in most states of the *United States*, and has been for decades now. So why should the laws of just one state or section apply in perpetuity to *all* the unorganized lands beyond the national border?"

Sarah shook her head. "Oh, Ben, all this hurts my head. You know they taught us in school that women aren't supposed to think about politics. Our minds weren't designed to think of such matters."

"I'd say you're doing just fine," Ben said. "Anyway, to make a long story short: Dred Scott lost the case."

Sarah nodded. "I see. And so, what, you think you can overturn it?"

"No," Ben said. He blushed and shook his head. "Of course not. After all, part of the Court's ruling held that negroes are not now, and never will be, American citizens. That means we don't have a right to our day in court." Ben sighed. "As I said, it's only an exercise, and maybe not a very good one. But I wanted to challenge the Chief Justice's assertion that slaves could be held in bondage north of the Missouri Compromise line. If that were true, then that means the Supreme Court just nullified the one thing preventing slavery's expansion all over the Union."

Sarah let out a long breath. "That all sounds rather serious."

Ben nodded. "It could be."

"So if you're not going to mail your letter, then you're just going to tuck it away somewhere?"

Ben shrugged. "I thought maybe I'd let your father read it. If it resonates with him, perhaps he could share the idea with his colleagues in Congress. Or maybe someone would publish it in the editorial column of a newspaper." His eyes brightened. "That's how someone small can effect real change, by transferring ideas from the printed word into peoples' hearts. If enough people start talking about an idea, then the politicians will *have* to listen. They'll be compelled to do something." After another moment's consideration, Ben shook his head and laughed at himself. "But who am I kidding? Nobody is going to listen to a negro's wailings about matters he doesn't even understand."

"That sounds like your mother talking, not you," Sarah said. "Ben, if I were you I frankly don't know what I would do. Bury my head in the sand, maybe. Stay out of it, keep to my own affairs. But that's never been you."

Here, Sarah's attention fixed on a stone bust of Colonel Spencer that sat on the desk. It was a hideous memorial, and it looked nothing like the man, but somehow Sarah was fond of looking at it. She had few memories of the Colonel (she'd been only a toddler when he died), but the old man had always been kind to her. One time, after Lady Isabella had been particularly cruel, Sarah remembered receiving a pretty doll from the Colonel. While she stroked the doll's hair, completely in love, the Colonel quietly explained to her that while Sarah and most children were delivered to their parents by a white stork, Isabella had been dropped from on high by a ghastly magpie. That story always made Sarah feel better when she remembered it.

With a smile on her lips, Sarah looked up at Ben. She saw that his neck was corded with tension, his eyes fixed in a hateful stare directed at the Colonel's stone visage.

"Ben, is everything all right?"

The shrill knelling of Mae Jane's breakfast bell shattered the stillness of the moment. All of a sudden, the big house was alive with the patter and pounding of feet.

Ben seemed thankful for the distraction. Turning his head to the ceiling, he said, "Here they come."

They left the library and passed into the grand foyer. They were just in time to see young Tom, twelve years old, bound to the floor from seven steps up, nearly breaking his neck in the attempt.

"Watch yourself!" Sarah cried, her heart in her throat.

Tom ignored her and ran on to the dining room. His dozy, faithful retriever Tipper was close behind, waddling hurriedly after his boy and the promise of breakfast scraps.

Little Bayard, the youngest at eight, was next down the stairs. Bayard had been born 'funny' (that was Mae Jane's word for it), and Father often talked about sending the boy to live in an asylum downstate. Cousin Isabella, however, would have none of it, and Bayard remained at home in the Valley.

Bayard had fully descended the stairs before he paused and, seeking to imitate Tom, rushed back up the first two steps before turning and jumping them. He landed awkwardly but leaped up again. He raced toward the dining room with a broad grin and a gurgling, triumphant laugh.

Sarah turned to Ben and they laughed together. She caught herself admiring Ben again, noting the depth in his eyes. She tilted her head down and stared up at him. "You'll be joining us for breakfast, won't you, Ben?"

Ben seemed to read something in her posture, in her expression, for he flushed and smiled from ear to ear. "First I should help Mama," he said. "And then, well, I'd be delighted." With that, he turned toward the dining room.

Sarah lingered in place a moment longer. Her giddy enchantment with Ben suddenly darkened with practical realizations. She knew she had to dismiss any romantic inclinations where Ben Freeman was concerned. Besides, despite his looks and good character, the reality was that Ben was a negro. 'Freedman' or not, Ben would never fit in with proper Mayfair society. Rather, proper Mayfair society had no room for him. It didn't matter that Ben was Daddy's trusted confidante, nor that Ben was better educated than most of the Valley's white gentry. It didn't matter that Ben was an aspiring lawyer either, an impossible dream considering his heritage. Ben was *black,* and as far as anyone in Mayfair or Virginia or the rest of the Union was concerned, he would never be anything more than that.

However — and for Sarah there was always a however — she was still without a husband, without a home and family of her own. And shouldn't that mean she could go on admiring Ben, and tease him even, without shame? Shouldn't that mean she could straighten his bowtie whenever she wanted? And besides, it really was a lovely feeling to be adored by someone. Surely Ben himself had to know it was all innocent play.

"One more thing, Ben."

He turned and waited. "Yes, Miss Sarah?"

For a moment she felt a tinge of guilt, for she saw the eager expectation on his face. The moment, brief as it was, soon passed. "I wonder whether you might drive me into town this morning," she said. "It's auction day, and I'm hoping my dress finally arrived from Richmond. In any case, I have an order to pick up for *that wom*...I mean, for Cousin Isabella. She's made me her errand-girl today."

Ben smiled and nodded. "Of course I'll drive you. Don't forget, your father's train arrives this afternoon. If we leave soon we'll have a few hours to spare in town. I can get the coach ready now, if you'd like."

Sarah walked up to Ben and squeezed his hand. The mere touch sent a shiver down her spine, and she reminded herself again: *innocent play.*

"Breakfast first," she said, beaming. "Afterward, a coach ride would be ever so fine, Ben. Ever so fine indeed."

Chapter 4

JACOB'S LADDER

It was the last Friday of the month, which meant it was auction day. And being the last Friday of October, that meant it was also time for the Mayfair Valley Harvest Festival. With a grim statue of Thomas Jefferson watching over the town's main square, the farmers and artisans of the Valley assembled carts and stalls packed with goods and wares.

The 1859 harvest, the old folks said, was the richest and most plentiful in two generations. Business prospects for the coming year looked very promising indeed. Here today, the charge of *the sale* electrified the air.

And best of all, that very night, the people of Mayfair and the surrounding villages would gather for a barbecue social hosted by the eminent Clay Claiborne of Wyolah Hall. The Claibornes' annual ball and barbecue was expected to be, without fail and as always, a gathering of special magnificence.

Of course, the troubling news from Harper's Ferry found its way into every conversation one way or another. Facts were few and rumors abounded, but the sentiment was unshakeable. What happened at Harper's Ferry was not just another attempt by self-righteous Northerners to steal away Southern slaves in the night. And it was different than any backwater shootouts way off in Kansas, a place as distant to Mayfair folks as Imperial Russia. No, this was something new and deeply troubling:

John Brown and his deranged followers had planned a coordinated *attack* on the Commonwealth of Virginia. What was more, their intention was to inspire slave uprisings across the entire South, from Maryland to Texas. Brown's very purpose, in his own words in a letter published by the *Mayfair First Witness,* was to encourage slaves to kill their masters and take up arms in a titanic struggle against white rule.

As Ben Freeman meandered between market stalls, he heard the phrase "Thank God for R.E. Lee!" repeated more times than he could count. Ben had long ago learned to maintain strict silence and not linger too long when listening in to white folks talking together. He busied himself by idly examining fruits and ears of corn, picking out a few here and there and handing change over to scowling farmers who demanded he set the money on the table so the coins could be washed. All the while, Ben listened to the babbling voices of the Mayfair Valley.

Surely, folks said, an attack on the South was an attack on the entire Union? Surely even the most ardent abolitionist in Boston would understand that such an act of terror perpetrated against Americans in any state meant it was an attack on *all* Americans, on *all* the United States? Indeed, Brown promised retribution — and a race war.

Race war. Ben couldn't help but smile at that, though his smile held little humor. The 'race war' was a warped, apocalyptic vision that even the Roscoes whispered of from time to time. Of course, everyone knew the story of St. Domingue, where Haitian slaves had revolted against their French overlords and slaughtered countless white families. Here in Virginia there had been slave uprisings too, but none of them had amounted to much. Still, folks in Mayfair were seemingly obsessed with the idea that, sooner or later, the slaves would realize they outnumbered whites in the Valley four-to-one. Some of the First Families (the richest plantation owners, who could trace their roots back to Virginia's founding), had even built underground bunkers stockpiled with food and weapons, where they could wait out the apocalypse. It would not take much, Ben feared, for a spark to become a wildfire. And though Ben couldn't speak to the character of all Mayfair folks, he at least knew the Roscoes were good people, even if a little naive and self-centered. (At the very least, they didn't have a bunker.) Nevertheless, history was full of stories of good people getting swept up in the winds of war.

No matter what people thought of slavery, the Mayfair folks insisted, there were good and innocent people lying dead in Harper's Ferry. They had wives, husbands, children. So it all raised the question: would those holier-than-thou Yankee abolitionists condemn the massacre — a massacre carried out by fanatics of their own political persuasion — or would they twist it into just another anti-South tirade? To politicize such a senseless attack, folks said, would be most deplorable.

John Brown and his surviving followers had been arrested, but there remained a hundred questions that demanded answers. There remained the foul, festering smell of panic in the air. Surely President Buchanan, calling himself a friend of the South, must *do something*. If Buchanan would not do something, then Congress must enact emergency measures to prevent future attacks. And if the Federal government in Washington would not do anything, well, Virginians would protect their own. The State legislature would take matters into its own hands.

"Well there's at least one thing of which I'm certain," a man declared. "After all that's happened, life can't just *go on*."

But as the town marketplace became more congested and the prospects of two-for-ones sales piqued curiosities, despair over the Harper's Ferry tragedy was soon displaced by the frenzy of good old fashioned American commerce.

To Ben's eye, Mayfair was quintessentially Southern. The town might as well be a microcosm of the South, for that matter. With its houses and storefronts of brick and painted board, it thought highly of itself as a placed soon destined to become a city (though except for auction days the wagon-rutted streets were usually half empty). Mayfair was sterile, yet decrepit. It was rich, yet poor. On the Branches and along the Cuts, proud plantation houses glared down on the shacks of sharecroppers below. The Valley itself was beautiful in all seasons, and except for the occasional slave lynching it was a peaceful place too. Mayfair was indeed a paradise if one had wealth and social connections. It was hell to have neither, and most folks had neither.

Ben watched as farmers paraded lean holsteins and squat pigs through the square. There was a good deal of excitement when a red fox slipped around ankles and stepping feet to snatch a fat hen from a chicken stall. Alerted to the commotion, onlookers staggered around in confusion as the fox made good its escape. The owner of the hen shouldered a pheasant rifle, called a stout warning for the crowd to scatter, and pulled the trigger. Ben's heart leapt as the rifle exploded in a gust of smoke. The fox and its squawking prey had disappeared in a misty red cloud of fur and feathers.

The chicken farmer who had done the shooting took off his hat and spat brown tobacco juice. "Better dead than with the devil."

There were mixed emotions from the crowd. Some cheered, some groaned, and others, mostly children, sobbed uncontrollably. Within moments two black men in ragged clothes were sent to pick up the fox carcass and carry it into the woods. Out of sight, out of mind. Events resumed their normal happiness.

Ben checked his pocket watch, a gift from Senator Roscoe. It was getting on to noon already, and the Senator's train would soon arrive at the station. Standing on his tip-toes, Ben gazed over the crowd for some sign of Sarah. Spying the steps of the county courthouse under looming pillars, Ben decided the courthouse would make a good vantage point.

As Ben cut a path against the grain of the crowd, a man pushed bodily against him and gained the courthouse steps first. With a leaping bound and twirl, the man wheeled about to face the crowd.

"*Bondsmen*!" the man shouted, and he repeated this cry as heads slowly turned to acknowledge him. "I need twenty bondsmen for the Delta market!"

The man was dark-skinned, but not so dark-skinned that he could not still brand himself a white man. He wore a pencil-thin mustache and had a peculiar accent. Ben guessed the man was from Louisiana, but he needed no guessing to know the man was a slave trader.

For auction day in Mayfair was not just an occasion to showcase crops and animal livestock. In one corner of the square stood several rows of people in chains. They wore simple drab clothes, for the wearing of colors or any expression of individuality was strictly forbidden by their masters. They withered under the October sun, which thanks to Virginia's Indian summer was still strong enough to kill. Their eyes were cast down and they spoke little, managing only hoarse whispers to their neighbors when the overseers were not looking or listening.

Ben watched the people closely. Mothers were permitted to hold their children, but wives could not hold their husbands and young men could not touch their sweethearts. Back on the plantations they were permitted to breed, for this was the only means of population growth and control since the overseas slave trade had been outlawed long ago. But the idea of one slave *loving* another or having a *family* was absurd. It was, as some in Mayfair suggested, like having a family of sheepdogs. The puppies were born either for work or sale. Any intimacy between the mother and father was merely a means to an end. Why should Africans be any different?

The trader bellowed louder: "Cash for slaves! *Cash for slaves*!"

A leather riding crop shot into the sky. The white-gloved hand that held the crop belonged to burly Clay Claiborne, who grinned at the trader from under the flat brow of a Panama hat. "I've got twenty coloreds for sale, sir."

A gasp went up from the crowd. *Twenty*!

Claiborne towered above the crowd in a dazzling cream-colored suit. He was built like a bull with a large, jovial face and a wide jaw. He wore his silver hair long and curly but kept his cheeks clean-shaven. Claiborne was a learned man of ambition: tobacco planter, historian, and a physician to boot. Not only was he richest man in the Valley, but 'good ol Clay' was also the best-loved man in the Mayfair Valley, if only because so many folks aspired to be like him. His offer of twenty slaves *for cash* was met with applause and looks of admiration, and not a few looks of envy.

The Louisiana trader clapped his hands with joy and barked at his assistant to fetch the transfer papers.

Claiborne was famous, not just in Mayfair but all across the South, for his best-selling treatise on slave care. "I propose to every entrepreneurial gentleman a new way of keeping both pigs and negroes out of mischief," the treatise noted in one section. "Give each slave one or two piglets every spring to tend and feed throughout the rest of the year. At slaughtering time, half the butchered hog shall go to you, the master. The other half shall go to the servant. This is an efficient way to fatten swine that requires little to no white labor or oversight. And besides, it is contrary to negro nature to run away and leave a fat pig."

Claiborne and the trader crossed the town square together to inspect the people in chains. Lesser planters followed behind in a gaggle, eager to bend the trader's ear. Perhaps the esteemed gentleman trader could buy one of *their* slaves?

Auction day was a time when men were most easily seduced by their dreams and ambitions. Poor subsistence farmers, aspiring to become part of the slave-owning gentry, cautiously inquired the trader about the price of a young bull negro.

"Please, gentlemen, in due time," the trader said to the scavengers. "I'll now inspect Mr. Claiborne's bondsmen. If I find them to be satisfactory, as I'm sure they will be, I'll buy them and take them with me to New Orleans. In that case, my purse will be closed to all other business. But don't despair. There's yet more cotton to be picked along the Delta, and more hands are needed to work the fields. You'll have many more like me venturing up here to buy your stock. But for today, I know this: every gentleman in the Deep South knows if a slave has a Claiborne brand on his arm, it's worth its weight in gold."

Claiborne beamed, his cheeks bright red and joyful. "Much obliged," the big man said with a tip of his hat. "You honor me, sir. Truly."

Taking his place under the shadow of one of the courthouse's imposing Ionic columns, Ben's eyes followed the excitable group of planters, traders, and desperate would-be planters and traders. Though he had ascended the steps to search for Sarah in the crowd, he pulled a small notebook and pencil from his breast pocket. It was a habit of his, learned from Jem Roscoe, to record his observations whenever the mood struck. Leaning against the column, Ben began to jot down notes detailing what he saw.

Ben's gaze fell on the rows of slaves drooping in the baking heat. An overseer hollered something and clapped his hands and the slaves stiffened to rapt attention. Ben noted that the boys of the local militia couldn't have performed with such precision, especially while beaten and malnourished. And the slaves would have moved still faster and tighter with a whip behind them of course, but considering there were white women and children milling about the town square, the whips had been graciously left behind at the plantation.

"Claiborne's selling *twenty* darkies?" a voice scoffed.

Ben flinched. The voice was startlingly close. Listening, and looking past the tall column beside him, Ben guessed there were two men standing just on the other side. Ben thought to move away, that being the polite thing to do — the safest thing too. But he thought against it and stayed where he was, and after a time he even leaned back and peered around the back of the pillar. Though Ben squinted at two silhouettes against the midmorning sun, he could still make something of their features and expressions.

"Look at em all," the second man said, nodding at the would-be buyers and sellers. "Yammerin for a piece of the action like a bunch of fuckin Yankees."

The first man spat a clean stream of chewing tobacco. "A fool and his money are soon parted. Those idiots would buy a bull for a thousand dollars today, and by nightfall some damn Quaker will have smuggled them off to Canada."

The second man spat too, but tobacco erupted from his mouth like a spewing geyser.

"Watch it, Horace!"

"Sorry, Boss." The man named Horace wiped his mouth. "Shit, I should have gotten into negras when I had the chance. Ain't the case that a regular man can afford one no more."

"It's not worth your trouble now," the first man explained. "More darkies means more mouths to feed, bodies to clothe, but no guarantees the gin will crank out any more cotton. Meanwhile, half the *new money* planters in Mayfair have leached their soil. You see those poor fools down there? They're desperate, desperate because they feel every bump in the road and think it's rock bottom. But they're right to be scared. The Yankees have set up all those foreigner farms way out in the northwest — picture it: millions of acres filled with Germans and Polacks — and soon enough they won't need Southern goods. By the time we're old and gray, Horace, Virginia won't be the Union's breadbasket any longer. But in the meantime there's still money to be made along the Gulf shores, as that trader just said. It's warm and wet there, and there's plenty of land left. What's more, down in Louisiana you don't have abolitionists camped across the river waiting to steal your investment from under your nose."

"My brother works at Poplar Forest down in Bedford County," the man named Horace said. "He said they had ten slaves play dead when a fever struck the plantation. Preacher took the coffins away, but not to the graves. He put them on a train to Cleveland. Negras escaped in goddamn coffins!"

The first man shook his head. "The abolitionists are getting bolder. And why not? There's no one stepping up to stop them. Virginia has become nothing more than a bleeding border of their influence. There's no money for real *planting* here anymore. And if New Orleans or Atlanta is going to pay a thousand dollars or more for a prime buck? I tell you, Horace, Virginia's true cash crop isn't cotton, it's *darkies*. Claiborne may be a terrible spendthrift, but the old fellow certainly knows how to earn the fortunes he squanders."

Obscured by the column, Ben watched the crowd beyond but listened to nothing except the two men talking. He turned his head to study them. The first man was in his late twenties. He was the Statue of David made mortal, with a strong chiseled jaw and golden skin. But instead of walking naked with a sling, this David wore fine boots and a pale yellow suit and carried a riding crop with a dull blade attached to the end. The man's companion, the man named Horace, was squat and ugly.

"Claiborne needs the money," the first man said.

"I doubt it, Boss. Reckon Claiborne could buy most of the Valley if he wanted."

"No," the first man said with a slow shake of his head. "His debts are killing him. It's simple mathematics, Horace. Claiborne has always had more creditors than any other man in Mayfair. And with how the Northern wind is blowing, those creditors are starting to call."

"How do you know that?"

The answer was matter of fact. "I make it my business to know everything about my competitors." Now the young man grinned. "If you really want in the game, you could buy one from me, Horace. I'll give you a friendship price. Certainly you could afford a bitch." When Horace demurred, the young man went on: "It's simple. Fuck her whenever you like, and produce your own workforce." The young man shrugged. "Your wife won't mind, will she? You could say you're doing it for the good of the family. Every roll in the hay is an investment in your future."

Horace laughed and clutched his stomach.

The young man laughed with him. Turning his head, he caught sight of Ben behind the column above them and turned around. Ben thought to move away, but it was too late.

The young man nudged his companion, who was still in stitches. Then he elbowed Horace in the gut to shut him up. Horace looked up, confused, and turned his head. His bright, cackling joy clouded upon seeing Ben standing apart from them.

Horace snarled, "The hell you starin at, boy?"

Ben kept his eyes on the crowd. He placed his pencil in the folds of his notebook and closed it, and he tucked the notebook in the crook of his arm. He pulled out a battered cigar case — another gift from the Senator — and a box of matches. He lit a thin cigar and studied the people milling about. He tried to look nonchalant, but nervous sweat beaded on his brow.

Horace pressed him. "Who you belong to? Best run off to massa."

Ben tapped ashes from his cigar and turned to face the two men. He saw himself through their eyes: six feet and broad-shouldered, a black man in a dark suit he could not have possibly afforded on his own; his hair coarse and cut close to his scalp; large features, eyes wide and shining. His left ear was overlarge, and his right would have been the same if not for the missing lobe where a knife had cut it off. The jagged remnant was blistered with scar tissue.

Ben watched the two men and felt fear creep into his heart. Seeing their wolfish grins, it took everything for him not to turn and run. He knew by the way they looked at him that they knew he wouldn't flee. Still grinning, the two men walked over until they stood next to him.

Horace growled, "You gonna answer me, boy? I asked you a question."

Ben dropped his cigar on the ground. He considered kicking the man in the crotch to buy some time to escape. But what he would do about the other man, Ben hadn't decided yet. Looking at the young gentleman again, noting his rippling bulk under his suit, Ben decided against violence.

Ben tightened his lips and forced them up and wide, forming as out of molasses a smile that was courteous but not patronizing, meek but which did not draw attention to itself. A smile that would not offend a white man. It was a smile Mama had taught him, and one that was so well-practiced it sometimes felt genuine.

"I beg your pardon, gentlemen," Ben said. "I don't want any trouble."

With that, Ben turned to go. The young man rushed forward and cut him off.

"Who said anything about trouble?" the young man said. He placed his hand against Ben's chest. "What would really give you trouble is if we took issue with a nigger hanging around a county courthouse without proper supervision. So answer my friend's question: who owns you, blackie?"

The answer to that question was simple. *No one*. Nobody owned him, for God's sake. Nobody fucking owned him because he was *free*, and because owning a human being was—

Ben took a breath and tried to relax his shoulders. Despite his best efforts to hide his feelings behind his mask, the young man's eyes lit up.

"I know you," the young man said. "Why yes, you're Big John Roscoe's little pet."

The man ran his fingers along the seams of Ben's fine dark suit. It was a hand-me-down from the twins, and many years out of fashion, but of good cloth and well-tailored. Certainly it was not the kind of garb any other black man in Mayfair might wear.

"Yes," the young man said. "Your name is Ben Something-or-other. You're Roscoe's butler."

"His secretary," Ben said.

The young man laughed. "Ah! In that case, Horace is my grand vizier." Now he extended his hand with a smile. The smile was warm, but the man's lips were tense and white. "Henry Cutler," the man said. "It's a sincere pleasure, good sir."

Ben finally recognized the man. "Henry Cutler. You're the Judge's son."

"Correction: the Judge is *my* father." Henry Cutler smiled and indicated his welcoming hand.

Hesitating a moment, Ben took it.

In an instant, Henry's grasp tightened like a vice. Ben felt sudden pain and heard the sickening crunch of bones in his hand. His strength drained away as needles shot up his arm and hot sweat burst on his forehead. Henry's warm smile remained, and though his grip was strong there was no sign of strain on his face, not even the pumping outline of his pulse. Henry's eyes dripped curdled hatred, but his voice was airy and pleasant:

"Nigger in white man's clothes. What an absolute disgrace."

Straining, looking into Henry Cutler's smile, Ben imagined maggots crawling just behind those shocking white teeth.

Seeing the notebook tucked under Ben's incapacitated arm, Henry reached out and snatched it. "And look, Horace," Henry said, waving the notebook aloft. "This boy wants the world to know he's literate. How about that? A nigger who can read."

Ben's eyes narrowed and his body tensed. He clenched his other fist and made ready to strike, even if only to buy time for an escape. He would deal with the consequences later.

"Go ahead," Henry said, with a cold gleam in his eyes. "Go ahead and hit me, boy. See what happens to you."

While Henry couldn't have known, Ben was dangerously close to taking him up on that offer. But then a voice in Ben's mind spoke up. It wasn't his voice, but that of Senator Roscoe, the man who had been like a father to him since he was a boy.

Nothing good may happen before its proper time.

It was one of John Roscoe's favorite sayings, intended to counsel patience. Just as often the phrase aggravated Ben, for it seemed to call for apathy, a resigning shrug of the shoulders. And in the face of a man like Henry Cutler, such advice was almost useless.

Somehow, the Senator's voice distracted Ben long enough that he thought twice about what would happen to him after striking a white man. Henry was right. Even if Ben escaped the town square, which was unlikely, he would be hunted down and strung up, maimed and tortured until he died, and his body would be discarded in a place where Mama could never find it. Right now he didn't give a damn about what happened to him — he'd try to take as many bastards with him as he could — but the thought of a dejected, disconsolate Mama gave Ben the strength to unclench his fist.

But he wasn't going to give up without some kind of show of defiance. Smiling against the bone-crushing pain in his hand, Ben looked directly at Henry and said, "Pinching another man's book? It's a pity you haven't graduated beyond schoolyard games, Mr. Cutler."

In answer, Henry hocked and spat. A gob of brown tobacco juice hit Ben's eye and sent him reeling. Horace burst out laughing.

Henry finally released his vice grip and brought out a handkerchief to dab the corners of his mouth. "Smug one, this," he seethed. "You know, you ought to visit Arcadia sometime. I'll show you the games I like to play with uppity fellows like you." He passed the stolen notebook over to Horace. "In the meantime, maybe I'll just keep this. The inner workings of the negroid mind might make for some interesting reading."

"Careful," Ben warned. "There are a few big words in there that might give you trouble."

Henry turned back on Ben with a snarl, but suddenly a sweet voice called out from below.

"*Ben*! There you are. Come along, Ben!"

The three men looked down into the square. A young woman in a floppy hat waved at them from the crowd. Even from this distance, and in the midst of a great crowd, her beauty still caught and fixed the eye. Petite, with long raven hair and freckles dotting a sunburnt nose.

Sarah Roscoe.

Suddenly infatuated, Henry breathed a heavy sigh. He could not take his eyes off Sarah.

"Well now," he whispered to Ben. "Is that the Senator's daughter? Last I saw her she was just a child." Henry's smile brightened. "My, my, she's blossomed into a real Georgia peach."

Ben shuddered with anger. Sensing the change in him, Henry grinned.

From below, Sarah waved at Ben and called for him again. Without a word, Ben tore free from Henry's grasp and started down the steps in a hurry.

"Stop there!" Henry called.

Ben wasn't sure why he turned back, but he did. Standing tall, he watched as Henry snatched the notebook from Horace and descended the courthouse steps. With a smile, Henry offered the notebook back to Ben.

After a moment's hesitation, Ben reached out and took the notebook. Henry held it firm.

"Careful, nigger," Henry whispered. "Your fancy clothes might be clean, but those darkie thoughts in your head..." He clicked his tongue and nodded toward Sarah. "I can only imagine what a big strapping boy like you would do to a dainty little cunny like hers." He looked up and waved at Sarah with a bright smile, as if he and Ben were simply wrapping up a polite conversation. "Just like I can imagine what those mitts of yours would do to me if I made you real *mad*. But I suppose you'll never find out about any of those things, will you?"

Ben tugged at the notebook. Henry held it firm.

"*Will you?*"

Ben strained to pull the notebook free. Finally, Henry let it go and laughed.

"Of course, you can write about them. Write anything you want in that little book, but it will never come true."

Ben swallowed hard and tried to stop shaking. He smiled at Henry, intending for it to be defiant but managing only that same humble smile he had perfected through so many years of deferring to whites.

Henry's eyes, which had narrowed to dagger points, widened a little and turned black with disgust. "Not much sport, are you?" He tore at the velvet cravat from around his throat and pushed it against Ben's chest. "Keep it," he said, pointing at the tobacco juice dribbling down Ben's cheek. "For God's sake, boy, clean yourself up."

❧

When Ben finally reached Sarah, she tried to take his arm.

"Escort me, would you, Ben? Oh look at you, you're a mess!"

Ben stepped away from her. "Apologies, Miss Sarah. I...I had an accident."

He looked down at the cravat drooping from his open hand. His face was still covered in tobacco juice, so he cleaned himself with the cravat. It was not long until the scent of Henry Cutler's perfume sickened him, and he imagined Henry laughing at him from some distance away. Ben dropped the cravat on the ground and left it there for unknowing feet to trample.

"Ben? Please." She reached out and took his arm. "I keep getting jostled by the crowd."

Ben flinched. Sarah's touch sent needles of electricity up his arm and down his spine, but he felt a sudden flush of embarrassment. Looking around, he saw scowls and cold glares directed at them. An old woman pointed at them with a shocked expression. Ben could read the woman's thoughts as one might read a telegraph: *A young white woman, and Senator Roscoe's virgin daughter no less, hanging off the arm of a bull negro?* Ben felt hot sweat pooling under his collar.

"Please, Miss Sarah," he murmured. "Not in such a public place."

"Whatever do you mean?" Sarah said playfully.

"You know exactly what I mean," Ben said. "A white woman and a black...Miss Sarah, it's just not proper."

She laughed. "Since when do you care about me being proper, *Mister* Freeman?"

He stiffened and looked away from her. "I care about you very much, in fact—about you *being proper*, I mean. Your reputation reflects upon your father. Therefore, I care very much."

Sarah's smile vanished and she stared at him, incredulous. She withdrew her arm from his and adjusted her hat on her head. "Very well then," she said coolly. "You'd think I was playing the part of the crazed strumpet."

Ben sighed and shook his head. "That's not what I mean. I just—"

"Come along, *Mr.* Freeman," Sarah said with a sniff. "You may carry my shopping bags."

Morose, Ben followed behind. "Yes, Miss Sarah."

They meandered through the open marketplace, heading in the direction of the general store down the street. Sarah wore a billowing pink muslin dress with wide hoop skirts that was hopelessly impractical for a day at the market, but it certainly caught people's attention. She wore a basque fitted so high and tight that her breasts nearly spilled out of it. Ben was acutely aware of men staring at Sarah's chest even as they walked arm-in-arm with their wives and sweethearts.

Sarah, it seemed, was also aware of this attention. Too aware, in fact. She fluttered her eyelashes and flashed a dazzling white smile. Passing gentlemen raised their hats to her while their disapproving women hurried their men along.

They stopped several times while Sarah chatted with young bachelors who kissed her hand in a show of flattery, and with older men who were already married but kissed her hand all the same. To every man she met Sarah presented an adoring, eyelash-flapping character. The men, for their part, leered at Sarah with lecherous gazes. The men regarded Ben, if they regarded him at all, with the mild contempt reserved for rodents. Ben's irritation steadily grew so he bit on his tongue to distract himself with pain. After a short while, he realized his tongue was bleeding.

Sarah bid her most recent admirer good day with a teasing remark. Ben watched as the young man turned and carried on with his day, looking as if he walked on clouds. Meanwhile, the dark clouds in Ben's mind were ready to split open. He felt a headache coming on, and wanted more than anything to get back home.

"Ben, did you know Sam Hanley wrote to Daddy a few weeks ago asking for my hand?"

"Oh?"

"*Oh* indeed," she said with a mischievous smile. Suddenly her smile disappeared, and she turned on him. "Wait. You *knew?*"

Ben shrugged. "Your father is too busy to read every letter mailed to him. Especially when he spends so much time in Washington."

Sarah rolled her eyes. "How typical." She moved along the stalls, investigating merchandise and nodding graciously to eager merchants. "Then you must also know Daddy's response," she said, and dark glee returned to her voice. "Daddy's going to turn poor Sam down of course, bless his heart. Cousins or not, the Hanleys don't have much money, and the little they do have is *new*." She pronounced the last word like a child spitting out some kind of bitter food.

"Isn't that a shame."

"Don't be coy, Benjamin."

"I'm not trying to be coy," he explained. "I just think you deserve better."

She smiled. They walked side by side now. It seemed Sarah had warmed to him again, and for whatever inexplicable reason, that made Ben walk with an extra bounce in his step.

"Who was that man you were speaking with?" Sarah asked. "Back at the courthouse."

The bounce in Ben's step flattened. "No one," he said. After a moment, he begrudgingly added, "Judge Cutler's son."

"Henry Cutler?" she exclaimed. Intense curiosity colored her reaction. "But I thought he'd moved to Mississippi. Helping out on his uncle's plantation, as I understood it."

Ben said flatly, "I suppose he's back."

Sarah smiled then, and Ben couldn't be sure what her smile was supposed to mean. She turned and looked back toward the courthouse. "Oh, there he is. The southern sun seems to have done him well. He looks rather charming, doesn't he?"

Ben refused to look back. Glowering, he instead looked up at the distant ridges bordering the Valley. Henry Cutler, charming? Yes. As a snake.

"I can't say I'm particularly fond of him."

"Jealous, are you, Mr. Freeman?"

"Virtue over charm," Ben replied. "That is the quality which your father said would mark the appropriate suitor."

Sarah's spirit cooled to him once more. "Oh indeed? Thank you for the timely reminder, *Father*."

They passed beyond the market and ventured down the main street toward Dance & Franklin's, the general store.

"A man like Henry Cutler would make a wonderful husband," Sarah said, evidently still thinking about suitors. "Don't you think, Ben? Being the Judge's son and all, he must be very intelligent. He's handsome, certainly. And surely he would have to be—"

"—Rich?"

"Wealth doesn't matter to me," Sarah said. "What matters is his family. The Cutlers are pious, respectable. They seem perfectly happy and functional, and their home at Arcadia bustles like a small city. I wish I could say the same for our family at Clarendon. What was it you said, Ben? *Virtue over charm?* I should think the Cutlers have plenty of virtue to go around."

Ben searched his pockets for his cigar case. He needed to smoke whenever his mind raced, and it was running full tilt just now.

"I heard Henry had relations with a negro girl on his uncle's plantation," Ben said. "People say that's why he's returned. His uncle found out and sent him back. Sold the girl too — and sold their lovechild separately as punishment."

Sarah turned on Ben with rare but no less biting anger. "You shouldn't take to such nasty rumors," she said sternly. "That's an ugly, *ugly* thing to say about a man."

But what about the slave girl and her child? That was what Ben wished to say. Instead he looked down and murmured, "You're right, Miss Sarah. That's an unfounded rumor, and I apologize."

Sarah heaved a loud sigh. Wheeling around at the helm of her wide-turning dress, she moaned, "In any case, I have to marry *someone*." She said what followed to the world at large, to God if He could hear it. "I'll be twenty-four next year. *Twenty-four*. To call such an age *ancient* is no longer a case of being facetious." Her face brightened a moment later and she went on her tiptoes to peer over the crowd. "Oh, I wonder if Percy Claiborne is here today..."

Ben finally managed to light a match and then his cigar. He was eager to change the conversation. "Did you get everything on your shopping list?"

"Not everything," she said. "That woman wishes me to pick up more medicine."

That was what Sarah called Lady Isabella when she and Ben were alone. *That woman*.

Soon they were at the door of Dance & Franklin's General Store. A young slave boy stood out on the veranda with a stack of fresh *Mayfair First Witness* papers at his feet. He waved about and shouted, "Negroes and Yankees attack Harper's Ferry!" He glanced sidelong at Ben for a brief moment. "Negroes and Yankees attack Harper's Ferry!"

Ben opened the front door for Sarah, and she breezed past.

Turning, she waited for him. "Aren't you coming in?"

Ben shook his head. "It's not, well..."

"What?" She looked at him, a laughing smile forming on her lips, her eyes confused and bemused and maybe even a little pitiful. "Because it's not *proper?*"

Stuttering, Ben said, "Sarah, you know I can't...you know that I'm not allowed—"

"*Negroes and Yankees attack Harper's Ferry*!" came the newsboy's incessant cry.

Ben fished for change in his pocket and offered some of the boy. "One copy, please."

The boy passed a newspaper over. He and Ben regarded each other for a long, quiet moment. The boy was fearful, and perhaps a little ashamed. But there was a dare-you defiance in him too, and he regarded Ben's manner and fine clothes with the peculiar expression of frank disdain that only children can exhibit so well. With that, the boy turned and resumed his hollering:

"*Harper's Ferry attacked! Read all about it!*"

"I know you are family," Sarah said to Ben. She reached out and grabbed his elbow and pulled him toward the door. "Now stop standing there and follow me."

Ben laughed and, tucking the newspaper under his other arm, went inside with Sarah.

Inside the general store, Ben was struck by an overwhelming potpourri: a scent of sawdust and mothballs, together with bags of grain and chicken feed. A long, battered counter ran the length of the store. Across the narrow aisle the sun slashed down on heavy bags of flour, sugar, and animal feed. Dust particles floated and danced in the beams of light. Scattered around the room was all manner of furniture, tools, saddles and stirrups, parts for plows and cotton gins. Nailed up on crossbeams like voodoo idols were tin coffee cups, horseshoes, spoons and spatulas, cooking pots, and gas lanterns, old and new. Foodstuffs and medicines lined the shelves behind the counter, and far to the back were two racks of clothing with a hand-lettered sign above that read DON'T LOSE YOUR SHIRT — SAVE WITH MAYFAIR FIRST BANK.

"Excuse me!"

Ben saw the ancient shopkeeper gawking at them through spectacles thick as mason jars. The shopkeeper shut the catalogue he was perusing and advanced down the counter, wispy white curls bouncing atop a balding head. His eyes narrowed with scrutiny when he saw Sarah. "Excuse me, Miss..." He was the kind of man who saw a person a hundred times but never remembered their name, or else pretended not to.

"Good morning, Mr. Franklin. I'm Sarah Roscoe here to pick up a prescription for Lady Isabella Spencer."

The shopkeeper's answer was to point a long, bony finger at Ben. "Your boy can't be in here, Miss. I gotta mind the store, and if he's in the store I gotta mind his hands instead. I can't rightly do both at the same time, if you understand me."

Movement through the window behind them caught Ben's eye. Turning, he saw the newsboy peering in at the scene through the window.

Sarah looked at Ben, then looked back at the shopkeeper. She smiled at the old man with glistening doe eyes, her old standard. Instead of feeling frustration, Ben bit his lip to keep himself from laughing.

Sarah ran a finger along the counter. "I suppose you're right, Mr. Franklin. I do apologize, and sincerely so. But seeing as I am here for just one thing..."

She took out her coin purse with white-gloved fingers and set it on the counter. "A prescription for my stepmother — my *cousin* — as mentioned. If we conclude our business post-haste, why, Mr. Freeman and I will be out of your hair in no time." Her smile brightened. "Then you can go back to minding the store."

Her charm was intoxicating, but the shopkeeper maintained a cold sobriety and placed both fists on the counter. "I ain't turnin my back on a coon what standin in my store, Miss. He ain't allowed to be in here. Beg your pardon, but that's the way it is. What, you live under a rock and don't know the law?"

Ben scowled at the old man. Before he realized what he was doing, he blurted: "I won't have you insult Miss Roscoe, sir."

The shopkeeper slapped the counter with a ringed hand and snarled: "Quit your backtalk, you uppity bastard. G'won now, out of my store!"

"*Please*, gentlemen," Sarah said, still maintaining a smiling composure. "There's really no need for such a distasteful encounter. Mightn't I merely trouble you for Lady Spencer's order, Mr. Franklin?"

A tin bell sounded with a short, dull clang. Ben's eyes landed on the grimy bell nailed to a beam over the counter and followed the white yarn stringing across the ceiling to the back where it disappeared through a large screw hole cut into the frame of a closed door.

"That's a customer," the shopkeeper grunted. The old man reached for a notepad and tapped it several times as if deciphering a message, then picked up a paper bag from the counter and checked the items inside. Now he closed the bag up and handed it over the counter.

Ben saw that the shopkeeper held the bag out to him.

"Yeah, you. G'won and take it, boy."

Ben rooted himself to his spot.

Sarah turned to him and offered an encouraging nod. "It's all right, Ben. This is Mr. Franklin's peace offering, yes?"

The shopkeeper muttered under his breath.

Slowly, Ben went to the counter and took the paper bag. The shopkeeper pointed a quivering finger toward the back door. "Through there," he said. To make a point, he added, "That door's where folks send their coloreds for pickups. Them ones know to wait outside."

Feeling the shopkeeper's eyes hot on the back of his head, Ben made for the door. Behind him he heard Sarah saying, "Now, could you open that purse yourself and take out the correct change, Mr. Franklin? I myself find the handling of money rather abhorrent. Maybe not *abhorrent*, but certainly distasteful. Don't you think?"

"Can't say I'm inclined to agree, Miss."

The door groaned as Ben opened it.

"And don't come back in that way!" the shopkeeper shouted. "You walk round to the front and stand on the street until your lady comes out. You hear me, boy?"

Ben considered slamming the door behind him, and perhaps he would try to split the door with all the force he could muster. It was a response that, while decidedly petty, seemed justified. But Ben knew that whatever someone like him could justify was apt to be vilified by the townsfolk — the shopkeeper Franklin and all the others. And whatever or *whomever* Mayfair folks vilified, they maimed or killed. It was as simple as that. Ben was not sure if Sarah would ever understand. Sometimes he was not sure if she *wanted* to understand the reality of—

"*You hear me, boy?*"

Ben turned back and said in a hushed voice, "Yessir, Mr. Franklin, sir."

He hated himself for responding like that to the old bastard. But meekness meant survival. *Speak only when spoken to* — that phrase had always held a different meaning for Ben Freeman, and certainly it did for many other people too. Such lamblike docility seemed to be an affront to human dignity. Thinking back on all the countless times he'd been yielding and submissive was enough to make Ben nauseous. Just once, he wanted to use his tongue against the smug bastards who lorded over him. Indeed he spent a good deal of time fantasizing about all the clever and cutting things he'd say to the men and women who bullied him, who rejected him, who pretended he did not exist. But maybe using one's tongue wasn't quite as important as keeping it.

Stepping out into the light, Ben's lungs took in a breath of fresh air. The drone of people in the town square sounded very far away. Ben looked upon an outhouse squatting in a patch of dirt, and beyond it lay an intricate mess of rotting picket fences and overgrown yards filled with old farm junk. Farther ahead, a dirt path snaked up into the foothills of the South Branch.

Ben spied movement around a thick patch of chest-high weeds. He stepped out into the yard and saw a black man in rags rubbing a yellow dog on the belly. The dog's tongue was out and its eyes had rolled back in its head. The man was laughing softly to himself, cooing at the dog, calling her a great girl, great girl.

Sensing he was being watched, the man in rags turned his head. His eyes traced up from Ben's shining shoes, fine black trousers, pristine waistcoat and starched shirt. The eyes widened with surprise when they saw Ben's face. The man in rags stood suddenly erect and took off his misshapen hat. He took a hasty step back, and the dog yelped when he accidentally stepped on her tail.

"Sorry, girl," the man in rags said to the dog. He turned quickly to Ben. "And sorry to *you*, mister. Sorry, *sir*, I mean. I shoulda stayed by the door. I know I shoulda. I just seen this here pup and she a happy thing. Very sorry, sir."

Ben stared at the man. Now here was a picture. A black man in rags standing opposite a black man in a tailored suit. It was the joke Ben had endured all his life from whites and blacks alike, and here it was presented to him plain as day, and this time he couldn't pretend he didn't see it.

Maybe Sarah wasn't the only one who didn't want to understand the way things really were in Mayfair. Ben had known the truth of it all, a long time ago, but maybe he had forgotten it. Time, in its passing, had a way of eroding memory like water washed away grains of sand. But this man in rags before him still lived the truth, the truth that waited up that mountain path yonder, toward the slave plantations on the South Branch. The man wore that suffering truth in the deep wrinkles etched on his face, and in the scars that ran along his forearms and hands. Ben knew there had to be more scars underneath the rags.

Ben removed his hat and nodded to the man. "No need to be sorry," he said. "Was it you who rang Franklin's doorbell?"

"Uh-huh. I mean, yes, *sir*."

"What's your name?"

"Moses."

"Moses what?"

"Ain't got no name but Moses."

Ben studied the man further. Around his neck Moses wore a silver chain with a silver cross, a peculiar ornament for a man in bondage. Upon the cross was the crude visage of a saint.

Moses, noticing how Ben's eyes lingered, grasped the cross in his hand. "It's Saint Anthony," he said. "Gift from a French priest what passed through the Valley some years ago." He added defensively, instinctively, "Massa knows about it. He let me keep it. It ain't worth nothin, nothin above sentiment."

Ben nodded and smiled, unsure of what to say. He offered the paper bag Franklin had given to him. "Here. That's for your, your..."

"Marse Cutler, yes, sir. Thank you, sir."

Ben gestured back at the screen door. "Then I suppose old Franklin will just credit it to your, uhm...to Judge Cutler's account."

Moses smiled a broad smile full of rotten teeth. "Thank you, sir. God bless you, sir."

"Good day," Ben said.

When Moses turned to go, Ben noticed the man had a tattoo on the back of his neck, just below the hairline where his silver chain was slung. It signified he belonged to so-and-so of such-and-such plantation. It was a human cattle brand, and one Ben knew instantly.

"Clarendon."

The word stopped Moses in his tracks. Slowly, he turned around and stared at Ben.

Ben stepped forward. "Colonel Thomas Spencer. He was your former master, yes?"

When Moses offered no response beyond a blank, vaguely apprehensive stare, Ben turned around. He reached up to his starched collar and pulled it down to reveal the back of his neck. There, inked into Ben's skin, was a brand much the same as what Moses wore. Except Ben's brand was deformed and misshapen. It was elongated from many growth spurts, for Colonel Spencer's seal had been burned into his skin when he was just two years old.

Moses nodded slowly. "Clarendon," he echoed, his voice barely above a whisper. He looked Ben up and down once more, as if seeing him for the first time. "You still they nigger?" Moses asked. "I mean, you still a Clarendon nigger?"

Ben couldn't help but smile, though there wasn't much humor behind it. "According to them, I am," he said, gesturing vaguely toward the town center. "And according to some of our own folks, I still am. What I really am is a freedman."

Moses tested the word on his tongue. "Freedman." He squinted at Ben with intense skepticism. "You a freedman from *Clarendon?*"

Ben nodded. "The new master — John Roscoe — he manumitted all of Colonel Spencer's slaves. Some five hundred of them were unshackled, just like that. My mama and I, we stayed behind to work for John Roscoe and his family. But the others? They all scattered every which way. That was twenty years ago now."

Moses looked up into the sky, now down at the ground, maybe trying to add up the years in his head. He got only so far before he sighed and shrugged. "Can't fathom it," he said. "But I knew John Roscoe. I seen him with the Colonel. Youngish man. Liked to eat. Seen him get fatter by the day."

Ben laughed. "You recall him right." But very quickly Ben's laugh faded, and his smile too. If this man Moses remembered Senator Roscoe, that meant he was a slave at Clarendon at the same time as Ben, who had been just a child back then. And if Moses knew the Senator, that meant the Colonel had sold Moses to the Cutlers just shortly before the old man died. It was only after the Colonel's death that the Senator freed all of Clarendon's slaves. Moses had missed his chance at freedom by no more than a year, and maybe a few months. Maybe just a few weeks.

Moses too appeared stunned by this slow-coming awareness. Finally, he seemed to emerge from a fog that had gripped his mind. "I should hurry on home," he said, slurring his words as if drunk. "Mistress be wonderin where I is." Tripping over himself, Moses backpedaled toward the slopes of the South Branch. Bowing incessantly, he murmured, "Good day to you, sir. Good day to you."

"Good day," Ben called. He was sorry to see the man go. He thought to follow Moses and walk with him awhile. Maybe Moses had had family back at Clarendon, a wife and children who had been scattered to the wind before or after the great manumission. Maybe there was a chance Ben could help Moses find his family, maybe find some way to—

But Moses had already disappeared.

Turning down the alley, Ben looked over and saw the stray yellow dog wagging her tail. She fell to the ground and showed him her belly, which was swollen with sores. Ben was overcome with disgust, but then he took a closer look. The dog was a reject — just like him, and just like Moses too. Kneeling, Ben carefully rubbed and scratched the dog's belly, careful to avoid the sores. He laughed when the dog's tongue lolled out of her mouth and she panted with pleasure.

A vision of the slave Moses lingered in Ben's mind. Maybe it was the dawning realization that petting a diseased dog might have been the greatest happiness Moses had known in a long time, and now that Ben had interrupted him with a bag of goods from Dance & Franklin's it was back to the numbing horror of Judge Cutler's fields and the stinging whips.

The dog sat up suddenly, and Ben retracted his hand in case she had a mind to bite. But no, the dog was listening for something, a distant sound floating toward them on the wind. Turning his head, Ben thought he could hear it too:

Drums. Drums and squealing pipes, and the voices of a hundred men singing as one.

Ben patted the stray dog a final time and stood up. "That'd be Jem," he said aloud.

❧

The crowd gathered in the town square flocked to greet the militiamen. Ben rejoined Sarah in the street outside Dance & Franklin's, and together they looked upon the approaching parade.

The 'soldiers' were led by Clay Claiborne's son Percy, who rode astride a proud white horse in Napoleonic style, hand in his jacket's breast pocket, a blood red cape custom-made in New Orleans (that was said to have cost more than all the other men's uniforms combined) billowing behind him.

The boys wore a mismatched array of hand-me-down muskets and shotguns, and they wore blue forage caps with peaks embroidered with gold thread. Some had discarded the caps in favor of wide-brimmed slouch hats or Revolution-era tricorn relics passed down from veteran grandfathers. Out of uniform they were farmers, blacksmiths, bakers, coal miners, millers, bartenders, bookkeepers, lawyers, and lumbermen. The finest-dressed among them were the sons of wealthy planters.

"I don't see him," Sarah said. "I don't see Jem. Do you see him?"

Ben shook his head. "Maybe he's already gone home to Clarendon?"

"And skip the parade?" Sarah exclaimed. "His head is too big to miss out on this."

"There he is," Ben said, and he pointed.

Sarah called, "Jem! Oh, *Jem*!"

Bringing up the rear atop a dancing Greenbrier, Jem turned his head, his blue-gray eyes reflecting the joy of the cheering crowd. Jem pulled off his forage cap with a dramatic sweep of his arm, and a lazy tangle of dusty hair fell around his face. His broad smile glittered behind locks of hair, stretching wider as the crowd roared with renewed energy. He broke ranks with the militiamen and hurried toward them.

"You're back at last!" Sarah said.

Jem picked Sarah up and twirled her around. Sarah screamed and slapped Jem's shoulder until he set her down laughing. Next he turned and shook hands with Ben. "Good to see you, old boy," Jem said. "It feels like an age, doesn't it?"

Ben grinned. "I count just two days. And it smells like you've spent most of that time drinking."

Jem laughed. "Has it been that long? I was ready to march on Boston."

"Hurry up and join us," Sarah said. "We're riding to the station to pick up Daddy."

This announcement caused Jem's smile to fade. "Father's home?"

"Of course," Sarah said. "His train comes in at noon. Did you forget again?"

Ben watched as Jem's eyes clouded with a quiet, dawning terror. Ben had his guesses as to why Jem might balk at the idea of seeing his father, but he had no intention of prying.

"I can't go," Jem insisted. He turned and scanned the crowd, as if searching for someone. "There's…there's someone I'm looking—"

"Places to go, people to see," Sarah finished. She shook her head. "No, Jeremiah. As your elder, I command you to ride to the station with us."

"Dear sister, you *command* me?"

"Daddy would be disappointed if you weren't there to greet him. This might be the only time he comes home all year."

A dark thought crossed Ben's mind just then. It might be the *last* time John Roscoe came home. The Senator had been diagnosed with tuberculosis over a year ago. The latest word from Washington was that the old man's condition had severely worsened, and he now needed a cane to remain mobile. Even the slightest effort caused the old man to wheeze and feel faint.

Pouting, Sarah lifted up the package intended for Lady Spencer. "Oh, Ben, this is too heavy for me."

"What's Mother ordered now?" Jem asked. "Anything for me?"

"Medicine," Sarah said.

Jem gave a wry smile. "Ah, I see."

Ben took the package into his arms. To Jem he said, "Maybe you could tell us about your little camping trip on the way to the station."

"Not much to tell," Jem replied. "Clay Claiborne railed about duty and honor, and about politics. How abolitionists are the devil and our God-given rights are under threat and all that."

Ben nodded toward the slaves lined up in the square. "Well, it seems his God-given rights are still intact."

Jem laughed. "I was happiest when the shooting started. I shot a rabbit in the dark, you know."

"My hero!" Sarah teased. "Come. Whoever it is you want to see, you'll see them tonight at Wyolah Hall."

Jem looked yet uncertain. Just then, a little girl pushed to the front of the crowd and offered Jem a bouquet of lemon queens. Jem brightened and thanked the girl, and then he handed the flowers around to the other militiamen with a halloo.

"*Dixie*!" one of the boys cried. "Let's sing *Dixie* for them, soldiers!"

A great cheer went up. And then, all together, the militiamen chorused in one voice:

I wish I was in Dixie — Hooray! Hooray!
In Dixieland I'll take my stand
To live and die in Dixie
Away, away, away down south in Dixie!

The song might have gone on like that, but suddenly there came an ear-splitting scream.

A deafening silence fell over the town square. Cheerful voices died in stricken throats and pumping arms drooped as hundreds of heads turned toward the source of the scream. The quiet was again pierced by shrieks of fear and rage from tiny lungs.

Ben's eyes fell upon the Louisiana slave trader, who carried a small black girl over his shoulder. The girl writhed and bucked and screamed. The trader, his face red with embarrassment, only held the girl tighter and doubled his pace. The girl reached out in desperation for her mother, who was still chained to the line of Clay Claiborne's slaves. The mother, who to Ben's eye was barely a woman herself, stood with her head bowed in shame. A two-year-old boy clutched at her legs.

Sarah turned to Ben and said in a low voice, "I don't understand."

Ben understood it perfectly. "The girl's been sold."

Clay Claiborne, always aware of public perception, tried to make the best of the situation. He followed behind the trader speaking to the writhing little girl in a hushed, loving tone. But his attempts at soothing the girl only made her shriek louder.

At last the trader heaved the little girl onto a waiting wagon, where nineteen other slaves sat in chains with their heads hung low. Ben suspected the wagon was bound for the coast, maybe to Newport or even Washington, where a waiting steamer would transport the twenty Claiborne slaves, along with untold thousands of others from plantations all over Virginia, down to the bustling slave markets in New Orleans.

Before she could be shackled, the little girl kicked the trader in the jaw and tried to clamber over the side of the wagon and run. The trader caught the girl by the leg and wound up, intending to thrash the little body against the side of the wagon. Claiborne lunged and stayed the man's hand, and he shook his head. They exchanged low murmurs and eventually the trader nodded irritably. The trader barked at a young woman chained in the wagon, and this woman wrapped her arms around the screaming girl and held her down while the trader chained them together.

Now the exasperated trader, relieved at last, shook hands with Claiborne. He hopped aboard the wagon and his assistant slashed at the reins, and the two horses pulling the wagon started off down the road.

The little girl stood up. In vain she reached out to her mother one last time, but the young slave woman pulled her down again and buried the child's head in her bosom. The surrogate looked with fearful, trembling eyes at her young husband, who could only turn away and massage a blister on his foot.

Back in the square, the little girl's mother was overcome with despair and dropped to her knees. Her little boy sobbed, screamed, and beat his fists against her body. Other slaves moved in quickly to pick them up and stand them straight lest they further embarrass their master in front of such a watchful crowd.

The head overseer shot forward and pried the boy from his mother's arms. In so doing, he yanked the little boy's arm from its socket. The boy shrieked and the crowd let out a great gasp of shock. The overseer, feeling hot eyes of disgust from the watching crowd, turned to his employer for direction.

Claiborne, nose and cheeks red with humiliation, clapped his hands twice. "That's enough, Johnny. Get em home."

The overseer nodded and whistled sharply. Like a trained army, the slaves turned and shuffled into a soldierly formation that might have inspired creeping envy among the militiamen.

The mother, meanwhile, scooped up her broken baby boy and turned her back on the wagon that carried her daughter away. Watching the heartbroken mother trudging forward with her child in her arms, Ben was overcome with sadness and rage. He saw on the young woman's face the guise of his own mother, and the little boy in her arms might have been Ben himself.

The mother did not look back at the departing wagon. Instead, she began to sing in a trembling voice:

We are climbing Jacob's Ladder
Soldiers of the cross, brothers, sisters, all
Every round goes higher, higher

And what had begun as a single, quivering voice soon became a chorus of deep, vibrant voices singing as one. As they walked down the road together, the slaves sang:

Sinners do you love your Jesus?
If you love him, why not serve him?
Rise, shine, give God the glory
We are climbing higher…higher…

The slaves' voices rang clear and deep, and a great hush fell over the people of Mayfair as they and their toy soldiers stopped to listen.

But they did not listen long.

Sensing the happy, prideful joy of their victorious parade ebbing away, Percy Claiborne and a handful of militiamen turned their heads to the heavens and sang *Dixie* anew — this time louder:

Oh! I wish I was in the land of cotton
Good times there are not forgotten
Look away! Look away! Look away, Dixieland!

It was a challenge to the slaves' voices. More white voices joined them, young and old, this time with renewed purpose and determination.

Ben turned his head and saw that Jem Roscoe sang as loudly as the others, and though Jem's voice was not vengeful like the others a spirit of defiance still burst from him with zealous energy. Sarah was not singing as she did not know the words to the song, but she was smiling at the apparent joy of the moment. Looking around, Ben saw the same humble pleasure on the faces that surrounded him.

Jem dug his elbow into Sarah's side and sang into her ear, and Sarah laughed and finally joined in as best she could. The entire town of Mayfair sang as one voice, and for a brief time the rival songs clashed in the air until the overwhelming power of *Dixie* finally stamped *Jacob's Ladder* down into the dust. The deep, soulful voices of the slaves wavered and at last fell silent.

And as those voices faded, so too did all sound from Ben Freeman's ears. He felt himself suddenly deaf and mute. Looking out at the slaves marching away up the side of the South Branch, Ben felt his suit itching him in countless places. He wanted more than anything to tear away his tie and starched collar, to bare for the people of Mayfair the skin they so abhorred. His suit was no different than the rags on the slaves' backs, or maybe it was worse: a clown suit. He felt the brand on his neck burn and blister as if the searing iron had been freshly touched to his flesh.

"Shall we go, Ben?" Sarah asked over the commotion. Her voice sounded distant and alien. "Daddy's train will be here soon."

His head still swimming in a sludge of semi-consciousness, Ben nodded limply. Yes. Yes, it was time to go.

Turning away, Ben trudged toward the Roscoes' coach. As he crossed the square, he stared down the long road leading back to the shallow slopes of the South Branch. The slaves marched away, back to their plantation home, their bare feet kicking up dust. With none daring to sing another note, the only sound they made now was the dull rattling of their rusty chains scraping along the red dirt road.

Chapter 5
THE PATRIARCH

Mayfair's train station, the first built in the northwestern mountain counties, was less than a year old. The knotted lumber planks that made up the station platform still held that pungent fresh-cut pine smell. The smell of pine trees reminded Jem of gin, though he knew it ought to be the other way around.

Seeing the slow approach of Father's train, watching it float hearse-like over a bed of steam, Jem felt an inexplicable dread rising within him. His desire for a drink suddenly became a desperate, all-consuming need.

Jem turned to Sarah and Ben, but they were not looking at the train but rather all around them. The station was crowded with ragged, gaunt-eyed folks who wandered the platform in a ceaseless shuffle.

"There's more going than coming," Ben observed.

Jem looked around. "How do you know?"

"Look at their trunks," Sarah said quietly, her voice barely heard above the bustle. "They're taking whatever they can carry with them."

Jem felt Sarah go tense as a young family in rags passed nearby. She sniffed and grimaced, as if detecting a foul stench. One of the children turned her head and regarded them all with a blank stare. As the family kept on, Sarah shook her head with an uncomprehending awe tinged with frustration.

"I wish they wouldn't always *stare* at you like that," she said, waving a fan. "It makes you feel...well, it makes you feel awful for no reason."

Times had been tough all over. Though some in the Valley had experienced a bumper crop (mostly the wealthy planters who owned slaves and huge tracts of land), many others lost their shirts when blight came to the Valley in August. Credits were mounting also for the RRC (that was the Roscoe Railroad Company, in which Jem served as acting company president). In order to stave off financial collapse, due in no small part to his father's constant siphoning of company funds to pay for his political ambitions, Jem had been forced to make some tough decisions.

He looked into the sullen eyes of some of those tough decisions just now. He could see in their eyes a hundred cutting questions, questions that he sometimes asked himself when he lay sleepless in bed. Couldn't he have done something more to prevent all those firings? Shouldn't he have *known* that a disaster of some kind might rear its head at any moment? Shouldn't he have planned for any and all possibilities? What was a *boy* doing running a coal mine anyway?

And that was only one of the many bitter ironies related to the RRC. The Roscoe 'Railroad' Company had no railroad to speak of (something that Father insisted he was coming, and very soon), but it did have a coal mine atop the North Branch Mountain. It was Jem's responsibility to oversee operations at the mine, and he did this to the best of his ability. Still, he yearned to do something else, to *be* somewhere else, and he awoke most days with the hope that his twin brother JJ had finally returned from New York to assume command. If JJ came back — *when* he came back — Jem would be free to pursue his own path. But lately, Jem started to wonder whether his hope was really a delusion.

Iron wheels hissed, and the screeching of the train's brakes grew so loud that Jem clutched his aching head and groaned. A banshee shriek followed a final death-gasp from the train's steam-whistle, and then the violence was mercifully over. The train gave a great rumbling sigh, and then went silent.

No sign of life emerged. All life on the platform, however, mobbed the train in a rush. Throngs of ragged people jostled for position at the narrow, wrought-iron step ladders. They peered up at the closed-curtained windows of the luxury cars (reserved for first class travelers) with great curiosity and not a little jealousy. Dog-faced conductors stepped down and ordered those pushing forward to make way for disembarking passengers.

All at once, the train came to life like a black beetle fluttering its wings. Doors were thrown open and eager, fortune-seeking men from Somewhere, Kentucky and Anyplace, Maryland stepped down into the crowd of erstwhile Mayfair folk. The departing crowd stepped back and regarded these newcomers — in a way, their *replacements* — with mixed airs of envy and empathy.

Just now, Jem saw a quivering cane press down on the station platform. The cane was followed by a pair of black shoes that gleamed like new despite the heavy red dust that hung in the air. The shoes shuffled forward. The clacking cane pressed down, bowed, and sprang up, the cycle repeating itself again and again.

Senator John Roscoe was not so old, but old enough to earn the description. Looking at Father now, Jem realized that much of the man's great weight, the mighty paunch he carried that had earned him the nickname 'Big JR', had all but disappeared. Father's skin was pale and drawn, stretched taut in some places and hanging loose and shapeless in others, like the work of an incompetent taxidermist. His heavy suit hung from his shrunken form like a nightgown. He hacked into a handkerchief and winced with each cough, as if with each attempt at clearing his throat he was jabbed with a piece of pointed iron.

For a moment, Jem tried to convince himself that he looked upon a different man. This could not be *the* legendary John Roscoe, the industrialist with six patents to his name and who had served in the United States Senate since the presidency of Andrew Jackson. This could not be the same John Roscoe, the captivating orator who had studied under the legendary senators Webster, Clay, and Calhoun, who with those same senators had crafted the famous Compromise of 1850 that pulled the Union back from the brink of civil war. This could not be the imposing figure who dominated every room and every conversation, who seemed to know the thoughts of any man who spoke to him before he uttered them. This could not be Father, *his* father, the man who professed to love his children while spending as much time away from them as he could.

But all other passengers, able and swift, had already pushed their way past, leaving Father alone and struggling. The conductors stepped off the train with their lunch pails and meandered across the station platform. Black porters and laborers stepped up to load and offload trunks and boxes. Three engineers leaned against the massive iron wheels to smoke their pipes and talk in loud voices. These men became silent and watchful as Father hobbled past them.

Jem squinted against the dust whipped up by the wind, and slowly his eyes widened with recognition. Father had the same bull-mastiff head, shock of white hair, and long white sideburns riding down his cheeks to stop on a razor's edge of a clean-shaven chin and mouth. Father's cheeks were sunken and the skin around his small, piercing eyes was faded and yellow like old parchment. He had more wrinkles than when Jem had seen him last, which to his reckoning was over six months ago. Father came home to Mayfair only once or twice a year, always professing that there was too much work to be done in Washington. Since Father had developed his 'lingering ailment', as he described his case of tuberculosis, he had spent more time away than ever before.

Sarah rushed forward to kiss Father's cheek.

"*Daddy*!"

Father accepted Sarah's touch but briefly before averting his eyes and pulling away with an embarrassed expression. Jem watched Sarah's smile fade at the rejection. Father said something about the cut of Sarah's dress in a disapproving tone. Sarah laughed and smiled again, but this time Jem knew she was forcing it.

"It's the latest style from Europe, Daddy. The Garibaldi dress, folded and pinched at the waist to accentuate the flowering of the hips."

Father gawked at her a moment. "Accentuate the flowering of the...?" He turned away and shook his head with a sigh.

Jem stood back as Father spoke with Sarah, hearing nothing they said, only watching them. At times Father would turn and stare at Jem even as he continued speaking to Sarah. Jem resisted the urge to squirm like a specimen, which is exactly what he felt like under Father's microscopic gaze. Father had a talent for hypnotizing his subjects with an opaque, unblinking gaze that compelled them to reveal their true thoughts, even their darkest secrets. Jem's only defense, which he admitted wasn't a very good one, was to look at the bridge of Father's nose rather than into his eyes directly. This he did even now, with nothing to hide. But that was Father's true talent, after all: whenever anyone spoke to John Roscoe, they always came away feeling confused, exhausted, and something like a criminal whose guilt is finally exposed.

Father's eyes were ever probing and studying the expressions of others, but his own eyes and the mind behind them were opaque and unknowable. Even their color evaded description, constantly shifting between blue, gray, and green. The colors swirled, cloud-like, like the smoking steam of the train resting nearby.

"And of course they won't be dressing like this in Washington until next summer," Sarah concluded proudly. "Everyone knows Richmond sets the trend for every season, right after New Orleans of course."

"Oh, of course," Father said.

Jem realized he was still staring at Sarah's hips and looked away red-faced and blinking, and he decided he would wait to study such fashion until it was worn by anyone other than his sister.

Father, meanwhile, was unimpressed. "There's little wonder why I must introduce you to society yet again," he said to Sarah. His voice, despite his sickly appearance, remained sharp and strong. It was clean, crisp, like the first bite of a cold ripe apple. No one had ever been able to guess the origin of his accent. One moment Father might be a Manhattan aristocrat, the next a Georgian planter. Certainly he didn't have the dry, drawling vocal flavor peculiar to the Mayfair Valley. "In my time," Father continued with his chin held high, "young ladies were creatures of Christian humility. Remember, Sarah, that a man won't buy the cow if he gets the milk for free."

Sarah looked uncertain whether to submit in silence to Father's remark or lash out in protest. Jem gave her an eager nod of encouragement, goading her to fight if only so he could see what happened next. She smiled, hurt, and turned away to glower in gloomy silence.

Jem's grin quickly faded. She wanted to be alone with Father's insult, and Jem supposed he could well understand that. After all, Jem had suffered his fair share of blows from Father; the old man had a talent for cutting to the bone.

Father turned now to Ben Freeman. He embraced Ben like a son, and they spoke together as if they were the only two people in the world. They were kindred spirits, if nothing else. Ben was a keen student of the law and politics despite there being no prospects for him anywhere. Whenever Father came home, they spent a good deal of time in the library debating and discussing the political world in Washington.

Jem reminded himself to be patient. He would be lying to himself if he didn't admit he was rather jealous of Ben's close relationship with Father. But then again,

Jem was often invited to join their 'policy sessions' and instead chose to ride across the Valley and jump fences. Just now, Jem decided he would take Father up on his offer the next time the old man asked to share cigars and brandy.

Father went stiff as a violent cough tore through him. He shuddered and put a hand up in the air, and there was sudden concern on his face. A heavy wetness rattled in his chest as he coughed again, again, harsh and raw, not able to stop despite the tears welling in his eyes.

Jem went pale. "...Father? Father, are you—?"

He reached out and put his hands on Father to soothe him somehow. Mercifully, the coughing fit ended as abruptly as it had begun. But even after the episode ended, Father remained hunched over, a hand clasped over his chest.

"Father?" Jem repeated. "Can you look at me, sir?"

When Father looked up again, when his gaze fixed upon Jem, the old man's whole manner slowly changed. His hard scowl vanished, replaced by a plain face, a docile — almost *stupid*, as much as Jem hated the word — manner that was wholly alien for Father. It was as if Father had been hypnotized, but of course that idea was ridiculous...

Looking at Jem, Father's lips stretched into a wide smile, and they began to tremble. His eyes, filling with dawning adoration, drank in Jem's beautiful homemade militia uniform. There was nothing senile in Father's manner — quite the opposite. He wore the look of a man who had finally woken up from a terrible dream in which all others were still trapped.

Father breathed one word, a question hissed to a ghost on the air:

"Jonathan?"

Father's smile broadened. There were tears in his eyes. Quiet joy, pride.

"Jonathan, my boy!"

Jem stared back, stunned. Slowly, a cold realization washed over him. Part of Jem wanted to say '*Yes, it's me,*' but he didn't. Swallowing, Jem took Father's hand into his own and squeezed it gently.

"It's Jeremiah. It's *Jeremiah*, Father. Are you feeling all right?"

Father blinked, and suddenly his shifting gray eyes darkened. The light of loving pride glinted once and went out, and then the old man's eyes shrank to pinholes of crestfallen recognition.

"Of course," Father said, and Jem felt the old man's gaze bore through him. "Jonathan's eyes were green, not blue."

Father looked away abruptly and let out a nervous laugh, as if he'd just made a clever joke. Suddenly, his body was wracked by another series of vicious, painful coughs. He doubled over and was caught by Sarah and Ben together. Ben offered a handkerchief, and the old man took it and proceeded to hack into its folds. Finally, this second fit passed as well. Father straightened up, at least as much as his crooked back would allow. He looked weaker now, even worse than a few minutes ago.

Ben started to help the old man across the platform to the waiting coach. Jem lingered, dumbstruck. He opened his mouth to say something after Father, but no words came. Instead, he could only think of the pitiful, searching light in the old man's gaze…the smile of mistaken recognition, and then the desolate look of realization…

Sarah touched Jem's arm and whispered, "Jonathan's eyes *are* green."

Jem shook his head. "What?"

Sarah nodded toward Father. "He said JJ's eyes *were* green. But…they *are* green."

They shared a long look of confusion, concern. Watching a wheezing, trembling Father struggle aboard the six-seat coach only after a great effort, Jem's face became hard-set.

"It's nothing," he said. "A touch of the sun is all. Father is understandably tired from his long journey."

❧

Long ago, the Mayfair Valley had been regarded as a sacred place by the Shawnee, and by the unnamed peoples who came before them. Cut into the foothills of the Blue Ridge, and with the grand Alleghenies standing to the west, the 'Little Valley' was an offshoot of what Mayfair folks called the 'Great Valley' of the Shenandoah.

Looking down from on high, one might mistake the Mayfair Valley for a whole world in miniature. Shaped like a long canoe, the Valley was anchored by the twin mountains called the North and South Branch respectively. Bordering the eastern and western sides of the canoe were the Cuts: high forested ridges that protected the lush woodlands below. Tucked between the Branches and the Cuts lay several miles of lush Appalachian forests, dense thickets, a handsome burg clustered around a collection of churches, and rolling green pastures dotted with tiny farms and sprawling plantations. Along the snaking tract of a river called Sleepy Creek lay boggy lowlands where a great battle of the Revolution had once been fought. The Sleepy's steady trickle eventually became a roaring chute of water where it joined the Shenandoah and then on to the mighty Potomac.

It was over the aptly named Stony Bridge, one of the bridges that spanned the Sleepy, that the Roscoe coach now passed, with Jem taking up the rear upon his young colt Greenbrier.

"I don't know how you manage him," Ben called back from the coach cab. "That horse is wood-wild. He nips at me any time I try to muck his stall, and I swear he laughs at me."

"He'll straighten out in time," Jem said.

"Not with you riding him," Sarah called from the coach.

Jem laughed and stroked Greenbrier's neck. The Saddlebred colt was plucky and headstrong, and already as big as his mother Mabel (Jem expected him to grow to an impressive 16 hands before long). Greenbrier was a beautiful gray with black point coloration, and in the morning light he appeared almost ivory white.

Jem reached into one of the pockets of his militia uniform and pulled a handful of crabapples he'd picked up on the South Branch. He leaned down in the saddle and offered them to Greenbrier. The colt turned his head and mashed the apples against Jem's palm and gulped them down with a slathering tongue. He nipped Jem's fingers and Jem laughed and clenched a fist. The colt gnawed timidly on Jem's knuckles but a moment before losing interest, and now Jem reached out and ran his hand up and down the colt's velvety snout.

With Greenbrier somewhat appeased, Jem sat upright in the saddle and urged him on at a faster pace. It was getting hot and humid, and there was talk in the Valley of a big storm coming up from the south. Then again, there was *always* talk of a big storm from the south.

Sarah's excitable chatter soon dominated the conversation. She was overjoyed with the shape and color of the dress she would wear to Mr. Claiborne's barbecue later that night, and she was very much looking forward to walking the famed gardens at Wyolah Hall, and she was beyond thankful to her father for handling the 'Sam Hanley situation' so delicately.

"And I'm happy to be back in Mayfair," she said, "although I do miss Richmond and my school friends dearly. I realized today it's been six months since I brought my books home. Once the party season is over, I'm ever so excited to return to school. I have my final examinations next spring, you know. Oh, won't it be great to have your daughter *educated* before she is married, Daddy? I should think it will be a considerable boon to my prospects. And in the meantime, Madam Worth — you remember my teacher, don't you? Madam Worth offered me a teaching post with the city's underprivileged children, to accept upon graduation! Wouldn't it be wonderful, Daddy? I could live and teach in Richmond for a time. Oh, I detest talking about dirty things like money, but Madam Worth promised a salary that is most agreeable. I would be able to afford a place of my own, furnishings and all, in which to stay until I find a suitable husband."

Pulling up to ride alongside the coach, Jem laughed. "I pity the poor fellow, if he even exists."

Sarah sniffed. "You are a pig, Jeremiah. Truly."

"Congratulations, Miss Sarah," Ben called back from the cab. "You would make a great teacher."

Sarah beamed. "Thank you, Ben."

Jem recognized the glint in Ben's eye, and the blush color in Sarah's cheeks too. He directed a knowing grin at Ben. Ben's wistful smile vanished and his head snapped forward to focus on the road ahead.

Father, who had been watching the bright and beautiful world go by with a gloomy grimace set on his face, finally turned to Sarah.

"Your brother and I work so that you don't have to, my dear. And besides, none of us can avoid the responsibilities of life forever. Your time would be better spent learning to mind hearth and home. Speak to Mae Jane; she ought to offer sound instruction on the matter. If all goes well at Wyolah Hall tonight, as I hope and expect it will, you won't have to worry about anything except raising a Christian family. Whatever you do, do not dangle your education over the heads of your suitors."

Jem watched Sarah's face shift from one outraged expression to another, settling at last on dutiful compliance. Taking a long breath, Sarah said, "Yes, Daddy."

Father said, "I will write to Madam Worth and tell her that you won't be returning to school this fall. You may have your books as keepsakes, but the time for such distractions has passed."

Despite the smile she forced across her lips, tears welled in Sarah's eyes. She swallowed hard and said, "You know these things best, Daddy."

Jem watched the red road pass under the coach's rumbling wheels and Mabel's stepping hooves, its surface beaten down by endless comings and goings.

"There seemed to be quite the commotion in town when we passed through," Father said. "They held court today, correct?"

"Yes, sir," Ben said from the cab. "A busy auction as well, I've never seen such a crowded harvest market."

Jem said dryly, "Don't forget the good old-fashioned slave beating too."

Sarah turned on Jem and snapped, "That's an awful thing to say, Jeremiah."

Jem shrugged. "Why lambast me? It wasn't me who broke that child's arm. Some fellow yanked it right out of the socket, Father."

Father shook his head with disgust. "I don't want to hear about it."

Stirred at the prospect of gossip, Sarah sat upright and returned her attention to the coach. She offered her estimation of the 'singsong situation' that occurred in the town square. She concluded her report with a suggestion: "I should think the slaves deserve some kind of punishment."

Jem laughed aloud at the absurdity of the idea. "Punishment? For singing a song?"

"It's not the singing," Sarah explained. "It's the acting out that was so, well, *embarrassing*. It's disrespectful to their owners, and it upset the entire community. You saw how disturbed the people were, didn't you, Ben? Oh, I'm sure you'll hear all about it from Mr. Claiborne tonight, Daddy. The entire ordeal was *most* unpleasant."

Jem noted the somber grimace on Ben's face. He watched Ben's jaw tighten as Sarah spoke, watched his Adam's apple buck up and down as he swallowed down the bile that must have been coursing up his throat.

Jem turned to Sarah. "The day we punish someone, white or black, for *singing*," he said, "will be the day pigs fly. In Virginia — in Mayfair of all places — no one should be restricted in what they say. They shouldn't be restricted in their singing either." He grinned. "Unless they can't carry a tune, of course."

He'd hoped his little joke would make Ben laugh, but Ben just stared ahead with a mask of stone.

"In any case," Sarah said, "it's an owner's right to put a stop to troublemakers."

Here, Ben cleared his throat. "On quiet mornings on the veranda, you can hear voices on the wind, coming clear across the Valley. Voices singing from the plantation fields on the South Branch. The voices are sorrowful, full of pain, very much like they were today. But in their songs is a sense of hope too, maybe." Still looking at the road, Ben said, "Sometimes I like to wake up early and just listen to the people sing."

Sarah looked down and picked at her gloved fingertips while Father cleared his throat with a low rumble. After a time, Sarah continued with her earlier point. "However regretful *the institution* may be at times, it is important that all of us respect its integral importance to maintaining balance and harmony in our society. We could all do with a little more humility and fortitude. Servants especially."

Again Jem saw the forlorn, exasperated expression on Ben's face. Jem tried to dispel the clouds that had fallen over their little party with a great laugh. "Perhaps you should open a school for *servants*, dear sister."

Evidently taking the remark seriously, Sarah perked up. "Actually," she said, "I have given that idea a good deal of thought, dear brother."

"Better give it a good deal more," Jem replied. "There's human nature to consider. No master wants a civilized slave."

"You mean no massa wants a nigger who can think," Ben said hotly.

Jem cracked a smile at Ben's outburst, but then he saw how Ben's eyes reflected a bitterness at the world around them.

"You must watch your language, Benjamin," Sarah said, her voice patronizing and disapproving. "You know Daddy doesn't like *that word*."

Jem looked at Father, who was presently directing a glare of cold disapproval at the back of Ben's head.

Ben straightened his back and assumed a stiff decorum. "Of course, Miss Sarah," he said. "I do sincerely apologize, Senator."

As he rode beside the coach, Jem watched Ben for a while. Ben's shoulders slackened once more, and his head turned low, and he bent down to the task of driving the coach as if they were plowing through a heavy blizzard.

"You seem rather on edge today, Ben," Jem said.

Ben looked up with some surprise before he shook his head. "I don't know what you mean."

"It just seems something is on your mind, is all."

"Something is *always* on his mind," Sarah said. "You know, just this morning, he was writing about…oh, what was it you were writing, Ben? A letter to the Supreme Court? Something very high and mighty, is what it sounded like. Something about negro citizenship. Oh won't you tell Daddy about it, Ben?"

Before Jem's eyes, Ben shriveled with embarrassment. "Miss Sarah, *please*. I—"

"A letter to the Supreme Court?" Father said. "That certainly does sound high and mighty. What could have possibly inspired you to draft something like that?" His query was doubtful, a challenge intended to send its recipient back on his heels. Such a tactic was Father's specialty, even in normal discourse. For John Roscoe, every conversation was a means of exercising power over others.

Ben shook his head urgently. "Just fooling around is all," he mumbled. "It was an exercise in logic and argument, sir. That's all there is to it, really. Certainly it's not the kind of letter one would actually mail."

"I should hope not," Father replied. "A Court clerk need only inquire about the return address on the envelope to trace its origins back to Clarendon, and thus to me. You can understand, Ben, the sore spot in which I'd find myself if the Senate majority whip became associated with any sentimental radicalism — *especially* radicalism of a distinctly Republican flavor."

"Yes, sir," Ben said huskily.

"You know Chief Justice Taney is a good friend of mine," Father said, continuing to drive down on the same nail, as was his way. "Were the public to hear grumblings that any Democrats disapproved of, say, the decision on the Dred Scott case — a *closed* case, I might remind you — our plans for next year's election would be thrown into disarray. Stephen Douglas is counting on me to help him secure the Democratic nomination next year."

Ben gave an eager nod, but his tone was muted. "Yes, sir. You need not concern yourself with any of it, sir. I'll put the letter away, sir. Better yet, I'll burn it."

This seemed to satisfy Father, for he nodded with a smile of approval.

Jem grimaced. There was, and always had been, a keen irony to Father's indulgence of Ben Freeman. The two often held long conversations about politics and philosophy, about truth and morality and the nature of American democracy. And yet, as far as Jem could tell, Father was never interested in what Ben himself had to say. After all, Father was a conservative Democrat who came of age in the time of Andrew Jackson, while Ben used clippings of Republican Party speeches to bookmark passages of anti-slavery literature like *Uncle Tom's Cabin* and the autobiography of Frederick Douglass. There burned in Ben's heart a kerosene flame which Father perhaps marveled at for its beauty, but only if it could be contained within panes of glass. And Ben, sharp as he was, was still only beginning to grasp that Father considered him little more than a sounding board, and a flimsy one at that.

But now there seemed to be within Ben an awakening of sorts. Even since Jem left home with the militia three days ago, Ben's candor was different. He was testy and defiant, as if he was mourning the failure of John Brown's rebellion. But there was more to it than that. Ben was starting to test the borders of the box in which Father had placed him, itself just one of the boxes in which Father placed everyone.

Jem turned and looked out at the dry brush, where withering leaves danced themselves to death in the autumn wind. Despite the happy chirruping of birds, Jem could not help but feel a peculiar sense of loneliness.

"...Jeremiah?"

Jem turned his head to Sarah. "Pardon?"

"Father just asked you a question," Sarah said.

"Oh. Apologies, Father. You were saying?"

Father cleared his throat. "I said, I want you to send three deposits to Washington next month. And for God's sake, boy, don't send them to my office. Tenth Street is the destination, as always. Send them individually, but double the amount on each from last month. By the time I return to Washington, the funds ought to be ready for me to put them to good use."

Sarah stared into her lap with a look of embarrassment. Grimacing, Ben kept his eyes fixed on the road ahead. Meanwhile, Jem shifted uncomfortably in his saddle. Father had a rough, rather direct way of talking about money that always made his children cringe. It was impolite in Mayfair, even in a family setting, to discuss dollars and cents so openly. The old man's attitude was more akin to that of a Yankee, not a Southern gentleman.

"*Three* deposits, Father?"

"One won't be enough. I'll also be requesting some personal donations from Clay Claiborne and others tonight at the barbecue. There are some important bills that must be passed before Congress adjourns in December. Time is running short to inspire some charitable feeling among some of my colleagues."

That meant Father wanted to buy other senators' votes, of course, and to buy a lot of them.

Jem knew that his father was an idealist (at least that's what Father claimed to be), but if there was anyone who understood the pragmatic aspects of Senate politics it was Big John Roscoe. Father considered the buying of votes a natural and time-honored process, nothing to keep concealed in the shadows but to be discussed openly. Indeed, it was Father's ability to 'get out the vote' that had made him such an influential figure in the Senate. Father prided himself on knowing the strengths and weaknesses of each of his colleagues, and how to inspire them to join causes in which he had a personal stake. In short, Father knew every man's price.

"...Well?" Father said, waiting for an answer.

Jem swallowed hard. First Father had cut into Sarah, then Ben. Now the thrashing was about to begin again, and this time Jem was on the whipping post. He cleared his throat and began the speech he had been preparing for several days now.

"There's only one problem with that idea, Father..."

"It's not an idea, it's an order. You may be acting President of the RRC, but don't forget you derive your authority from M-E me."

Jem tried to keep calm, composed. "I understand that, sir. It's just that—"

"What's the matter? Did you drink away all our profits? Lose it at the dominoes table?"

"*No*, sir. Nothing like that. It's just that—"

"The North Branch Mine has served us well these past many years," Father interrupted, "but I don't intend to restrict my legacy to that of a lowly prospector. You must dig deeper, Jeremiah, so that we may invest the mine's revenue into other, more productive ventures is necessary, rather *imperative*, to our plans — *my plans* — for this family's future."

Jem nodded. "I understand that, sir. It's just—"

"Spit it out already, boy!"

Jem bit his tongue and took a deep breath. "It's not as simple as 'digging deeper', Father. There are the Northern tariffs to consider. Nearly all our coal ships to Northern customers, but we earn only a pittance once the vultures wet their beaks. Meanwhile there are coal mines springing up all over the Northeast. The Yankees have no tariffs to worry about, and so can afford to expand even while driving the price down for the rest of us. What I'm saying, Father is that...well, the North Branch doesn't have the means to...there's nothing in our accounts to *draw from*, Father. There's nothing to take out. It's all gone — not from mismanagement, Father, I never touched a cent except to make payroll. Mr. Trask and I secured a few more months' credit, but it won't be enough unless there's a change of some kind. If you want to inspire any *charitable feeling* among your colleagues, then the Senate must pass a bill that protects Southern producers from Federal greed."

Jem finished at last, breathless.

Father looked out at the beautiful world around him and scowled at all of it. "When I need political advice from you, Jeremiah, I will ask for it."

"Yes, sir. But you must understand that—"

"I understand perfectly well," Father growled. "Easy enough to blame our woes on the government or other business interests. But the issue remains. We *must* have the means to finance the great projects to come. The *railroad*, Jeremiah..."

Jem sighed. "Yes, Father, the railroad."

"Don't be smug! Who do you think lobbied to extend the Baltimore & Ohio Railroad south to the Valley? What do you think would happen to this bright little town in another ten years, were it to remain cut off from the rest of the Union? I needn't remind you that rail is the way of the future, Jeremiah. Well, it is one thing to build a small station in a small country town. It's another matter entirely to lay thousands of miles of track from here to the Pacific, over mountains and across deserts, and to give birth to villages that will become enormous cities in a hundred years' time. Yes, all in *good time*. But first, the groundwork must be laid. At long last, the Senate will soon enact the law calling for the construction of the transcontinental railroad. When the RRC is awarded the contract, we will—"

"And you're certain that will happen?" Jem said doubtfully.

"Beyond certain," Father replied. "Stephen Douglas is Chairman of the Committee on Territories, the committee that oversees the railway project. The contract cannot be given to a sitting senator of course, but come next fall that won't be an issue. Stephen will be elected president in November, and my last term in Congress will end. I will officially retire into private life the day President Douglas enters the White House. Once in office, he has graciously agreed to apply appropriate pressure in the appropriate places. In two years' time, the Roscoes will be blasting rock through the Alleghenies. In another five, we will have reached the blue Pacific. But before all that can happen, we *must* secure the financial means to help Stephen win the election."

Jem turned away and rode on. He had heard all this before.

"Come now, Jeremiah," Father said. No doubt the old man had detected his Jem's gloomy temper. "I know babysitting a coal mine was never your idea of greatness either. You aspire to go out and make something of yourself, and I can well appreciate that sentiment. Imagine yourself overseeing a massive public works project such as this. You don't have to worry about the particulars; there are plenty of engineers to do the thinking for us. What matters to history are not the efforts of a monument's laborers, but the names of its *architects*. One day, children might read your name in their schoolbooks."

"But I don't care about such things, Father. What you speak of is JJ's dream, not mine."

Father tensed at the mention of JJ's name.

"In fact, it's about time we talked about JJ," Jem said. "He'll be back from the Academy next year. I'll be twenty-one in July, Father, which means he'll turn the same age the same day, only three minutes earlier than me. At twenty-one, JJ takes over the RRC, just like he was supposed to before everything happened. That was our deal."

"Insolent brat," Father barked. "There is no *deal*. A man does not make deals with his own children."

In his periphery, Jem saw the shocked faces of Sarah and Ben, who looked upon the scene with dismay and helplessness. He knew that neither of them could step in to aid him, and certainly he could not blame them for keeping back. One did not lightly tempt John Roscoe's rage. Jem would have to face the rest of Father's vitriol alone.

Still, Jem was adamant in his position. "The only reason I gave up my place at West Point was to—"

"It was your choice to fall on your own sword to save your brother," Father growled, his eyes gleaming with cold derision. "It was no fault of mine that Jonathan nearly destroyed this family's reputation, and during an election year no less. It was *you* who willingly offered your place at the Academy so that he could save face. So do not speak to me about *deals*. Look at me, Jeremiah."

Jem tore his eyes away and resolved to not look at Father again. He could not stare into those penetrating eyes. No, he *would* not—

"*Look at me*, boy."

Heaving a sigh, Jem finally relented and turned back.

"It is a real man who understands there is no thread of fate spun and woven for him," Father said. "There is no terminal destiny that predetermines the course of his life. The self-aware man knows he will never possess anything which he doesn't have the courage to seize for himself." Father pointed his cane at Jem as if it were a long, accusing finger. "A man's fate is nothing but the sum of his choices. Your brother made his choice a long time ago, and you made yours. Now I am giving you — and *only* you, Jeremiah — the opportunity to make another choice, and one of great consequence."

"You give only the illusion of choice," Jem said. With that, he dug his heels into Greenbrier's sides and urged the young colt forward.

Father's mocking voice trailed behind him. "Oh, yes. Ride on, my brave soldier-boy! You think yourself some kind of conquering hero in that getup?"

Jem rode on, making a good distance between himself and the coach. All the while he could still hear the venomous lashings from Father's tongue, but he was no longer listening.

As the North Branch loomed ahead, Jem looked up at the mountain. He saw the pillars of smoke rising from the coal mine and studied the squat cabins tucked against the rock cliffs. As he looked, he saw himself in tiny miniature up there on the mountain, marching up and down like a weary Sisyphus. He imagined himself as a mote of dust, moving not by his own agency but by the wind and other forces which swept him one way or another. He was still only *acting* president of the RRC, but soon enough Father would name his successor.

And, judging from the syrupy coughs that wracked the old man's lungs, that time would come sooner rather than later.

There was a chance (and seemingly an increasing likelihood), that Father would choose Jem to lead the RRC in an official capacity. But the real company man, Jem well knew, was always supposed to be JJ. It was JJ who had spent his childhood talking with Father about 'the Roscoe family legacy' (whatever the hell that meant), while Jem struck off into the woods to play War with his friends. If there was such a thing as destiny, it was JJ who was destined to sit at Father's right hand. For Jem, the idea of living his life according to the whims of another, even (and especially) someone like Father, was anathema.

And so, what was the alternative? What was stopping him from turning and digging his heels into Greenbrier's sides and galloping up the Capon Bridge Road that would lead him out of the Valley forever? Where would he go, what would he do? He would live the life that *inspired* him, of course. But what the hell did that even mean?

And what about Audrey?

Audrey. Now *there* was a reason to favor remaining in Mayfair.

Jem had first seen her a few weeks ago, on a mild September evening on his way home from the North Branch Mine. The craggy mountainside was dotted with tiny farms that never grew much of anything. The Blake farm, with its rotting barn and field full of rocks, was the most hardscrabble plot of land in the Valley. Old Everett Blake was a poor goat farmer and widower with three sons, each uglier than the last. The line ended with Ezra, the ugliest of all. But this was not the case with Everett's only daughter.

As Jem passed by the broken rail-fence, same as he'd done a thousand times before, he chanced to look across the Blake farmyard.

And there she was, hanging laundry from a clothesline made of chickenwire. Her white-blonde hair was pulled back to reveal high cheekbones and a long, elegant neck that disappeared under a simple homespun dress. She was barefoot, with chickens pecking the mud all around her. As Jem watched she rose up on her tiptoes with all the strength and grace of a dancer, and in this manner she moved down the chickenwire hanging linens as she went. When a hen pecked her foot, she did not yelp but instead laughed and gently scolded the thing. Jem might have stood there watching her forever if she hadn't looked over and spotted him gawking. It was only when she gave him a slightly bemused wave that he snapped back into reality.

"Evening!" he said, waving back with great enthusiasm.

The warmth of her smile rooted him to the spot. She had turned back to continue her work, but with another glance toward the road she saw that Jem had not moved on. Leaving the line for now, she crossed the farmyard until she stood on the other side of the rail fence. Jem tried his best not to stare, but it was a poor effort. The girl was small and thin, but not frail. She had green eyes that danced in the morning light. And her smile — *Lord Almighty.*

"Can I help you with anything, sir?"

Jem tore his eyes away and forced himself to look down at his feet. "Er...well... no, no, you're fine. *I'm* fine, I mean. You are fine too, I trust."

She laughed and said, "You're Jem Roscoe."

"Only to some," he said, thinking this would lead into a clever joke. Nothing came next, and so he added lamely, "To everyone, rather. I'm Jem Roscoe to everyone." He silently cursed himself for being an idiot.

"Do you remember me?"

Jem smiled, and all pretensions were gone. "Of course I do," he said. "You're Audrey Blake. We used to run together as children, in those footraces at church picnics."

Audrey laughed. "Yes. And I used to beat you and your brother JJ to the finish line." There was a teasing glint in her eyes. "I beat you every year, as I recall."

Jem laughed and shook his head. "I seem to have forgotten that aspect. Maybe intentionally."

He glanced at her again, careful not to linger but not wanting to look away. She smiled, and the effect was contagious.

"You've been away?" Jem said. "I feel like I haven't seen you in the Valley in years."

"Almost ten," she said, nodding toward the plume of smoke rising from the mountain. "My brothers work at your father's mine, you probably know. Daddy sent me down to a girls' school in Staunton after Mama died. I enjoyed it, most of the time." The brightness of her face dimmed a little. "The other girls didn't care for me so much."

Jem understood without her having to say anything else. The world of a girl like Audrey Blake was not a world of fancy balls and barbecues like the one Sarah inhabited. Still, Audrey was as beautiful — no, *more* beautiful — than any debutante Jem had ever seen. The Valley's rich mocked slaveless commoners as 'mud-eaters', and the Blakes were considered the lowest of the low. Wherever Audrey went, no matter how practiced she became in fine manners and elocution, she would never be anything more than a mud-eater's daughter.

"Well," Jem said, "all those painted princesses were probably just jealous."

Audrey laughed and shook her head. "I can't imagine why."

Jem marveled at her green eyes and said, "I don't have to imagine."

The words had just slipped out of him like a wayward breath. For an instant he panicked, thinking she might sneer at the sentiment as a bold *line*. Other girls surely would have. But laws, he'd really meant it, and he offered a shy smile to prove it.

Blushing, Audrey looked down at her feet. "I appreciate that, Mr. Roscoe."

"Please," he said. "You can call me—"

The screen door of the farmhouse slammed shut. Looking over Audrey's shoulder, Jem saw Ezra Blake glaring at them from the rickety front porch.

Ezra Blake had the same green eyes as his sister, but his were filled with contempt. Swarthy and built like a bull, he carried a massive head on a neck thick with wild blonde whiskers that saw no grooming save the idle picking out of food scraps. Two massive hounds curled around his legs, each with gobs of saliva dripping from quivering jaws. When the dogs saw Jem at the edge of the property standing so close to Audrey, they began to growl and foam. The dogs, like all their Blake masters and especially Ezra, harbored an instant hatred for any outsider who dared approach their darling sister.

"Who's that yackin at you, Audie?"

She turned and called back, "Mr. Roscoe, Ez. Your employer."

Ezra Blake turned and spat.

Audrey turned back to Jem and gave an embarrassed smile that made him adore her all the more. "I should get back to my chores," she said. "It was very nice speaking with you, Mr. Roscoe."

"And you," he said. He wanted to say more, but no other words came to him.

She'd turned and crossed the farmyard again. For a moment he studied her walk, how her hair bounced on her shoulders, the slight sway of her hips — but then Jem realized Ezra Blake was glaring at him and his snarling dogs had crept halfway to the rail fence. Jem waved to Ezra and bid him good evening, and then he'd turned and carried on home.

Since that day, Jem began to look forward to his journeys up and down the North Branch. He made a point to pass by the Blake farm, and every time he searched the farmyard for a sign of Audrey. Whenever he found the yard empty, he would carry on to the mine with a heavy heart and a hope that she'd be there when the day was over. But the few times when she was out doing chores, she would see him and cross over to the fence so they could speak together a little while. Always their conversations were cut short by Audrey's father or brothers, or the dogs that barked like mad whenever they caught a whiff of Jem's scent. But the anticipation of a few moments alone with Audrey was what spurred Jem out of bed every morning, and the memory of her smile kept him awake late at night.

❧

Jem was still riding on, still studying the slope of the North Branch, when he heard Sarah scream.

"Daddy?" Sarah cried, her voice sharp with alarm. "*Daddy?!*"

With his heart in his throat, Jem turned Greenbrier around and pointed back toward the coach. Father was keeled over in his seat, coughing and retching, one hand clutching the side of the coach and the other clawing the air. A spasm flung him back onto the coach seat as if an invisible set of hands had shoved him.

Jem galloped back toward the coach and swung down from the saddle. He leaped upon the coach as Ben struggled to hold a frightened Mabel in place.

Jem put his hand on Father's shoulder while Sarah clutched the old man's hands. Father was doubled over, still coughing, his breath no more than a pitiful wet rattle.

Brother and sister shared a silent look of fear and helplessness.

"Mind his head!" Ben cried, whipping Mabel into action. "We'll drive to Dr. Harper's house immediately."

With tears in her eyes, Sarah embraced Father. The old man had strength enough to push her away. He turned his head high to the sky, his fleshy gullet wagging, his eyes blinking furiously. He managed a single shallow breath before another spasm of coughing wracked his body.

But then, just as the thought dawned on Jem that they might all be witnessing Father's last breaths, the coughing fit subsided. Father's shoulders sagged and his head drooped low. He slumped weakly against Sarah, able to breathe only by taking in ragged sips of air.

Slowly, Jem and Sarah guided Father to an upright sitting position. The old man gawked around him, as if he was an infant seeing the wide, terrifying world for the first time. Slowly, Ben pulled Mabel to a halt once more.

Trembling, Sarah said, "How are you feeling, Daddy?"

Grimacing, Father mumbled, "Peculiar, in fact." He coughed sharply again, and this caused the three watching him to anticipate another fit. But instead, the old man shook his head and cleared his throat. Reassuming a dignified air despite the red embarrassment that colored his cheeks, he gruffly shrugged off the grasp of both Jem and Sarah.

"What are we waiting for?" Father said, the strength returned to his voice. "Your horse is blocking the damn road, Jeremiah." He rapped his knuckles against the side of the coach. "Get this thing moving, Ben! I'd like to get home before Thanksgiving, if you please. And where's my cane?"

No one moved to comply. Instead Sarah took Father's hand again and looked into his eyes. "Daddy, you're unwell. Perhaps we'll take you to see Dr. Harper, as Ben said. Or perhaps we'll call for him to visit you at home, if you'd prefer."

"I want nothing to do with the damn *Harpers*," Father snarled. "Why they haven't been driven out of the Valley for what they did to us, I'll never understand."

Father coughed again and cleared his throat with a low rumble.

"Besides," he said, "I already have a doctor in Washington. We all arrive at death's door eventually, but I am far from the threshold yet. I refuse to let any infirmities command my life when there is so much to be done."

Father smashed his hand against the coach again.

"Onward, Ben! And push that beast faster than a plod, for God's sake. Whip it if you have to."

Still grumbling, Father collected phlegm in his throat and spat off the side of the coach. Looking up at Jem now, the old man scowled.

"*Away*, boy, and clear my road. Who do you think pays for its upkeep? Certainly not the planters, I can assure you of that. Were the Branches not carved out of the earth by glaciers, they might say the Mayfair Valley was made by John Roscoe. But do even my own children care? *Away*!"

Jem staggered down from the coach. Moving as if in a daze, he returned to Greenbrier and mounted up. Jem exchanged a silent, disbelieving look with Ben. Then Ben clicked his tongue at Mabel and the coach started off, once more rolling up the long climb toward Clarendon perched upon the North Branch.

Lingering in a cloud of road dust, Jem watched the coach roll on. Turning, he looked down at the road beneath him. There, speckled red along the stones near where the coach had rested, were drops of Father's blood.

Chapter 6
TOM

Slowly, he cocked his pistol and waited.

Hidden behind the thick base of a tree, he caught his breath and stared out at the surrounding forest. The sun was fading fast through the trees. In the waning light the forest was serene, pleasant, but too quiet.

Curse it, he'd hunted too long into the afternoon. Night came quickly in these mountain valleys, and he'd had no time to build a fire. Tonight, that mistake might mean his death.

There — what was that? A voice called out from somewhere hidden. Bristling, Tom heard leaves rustling and twigs snapping in the undergrowth to his right. A raven shrieked and flew off from a nearby tree branch, startled by something unseen in the brush.

The savages were approaching, maybe from every direction. He might already be surrounded…

He took a deep breath and peered over the side of the trunk. He heard it before he saw it: a small savage barreling through the foliage, thwacking branches aside with a savage war club. The savage wore face paint and white man's clothes, no doubt stolen from the body of a poor settler freshly killed. So far, the savage did not see Tom. But when there was an opportunity for an ambush, it was an opportunity worth taking.

Tom raised his pistol and inched forward. As he did, he stepped on a dry branch.

Crrrraack!

The savage looked up and bared white teeth. It cried out in some strangled, heathen tongue and raced toward him.

Tom leveled his weapon.

"*Blam*!"

The savage fell dead in the leaves.

Tom leaped into the air. "Take *that*, pagan!"

From behind came a fierce battle cry. Tom whirled just in time to see the Black Knight charging at him astride a massive warhorse. Tom's single-shot pistol was spent, but he drew his greatsword from the sheath strapped to his back and parried the Knight's powerful first strike. The Knight wheeled his horse, dismounted, and brought up a great shield.

"Surrender or die, Roscoe."

Tom stood defiant. "Never surrender!"

The Knight laughed. "Then prepare to meet your maker."

Now it was Tom's turn to laugh. "Prepare to meet yours, you son of a—"

Stars. Tom's vision suddenly blurred. The savage's war club had struck him across the face, knocking him flat on his back. He put a hand to his stinging nose and felt warm blood stream from his nostrils. He glared up at the revived savage leering down at him with a victorious grin.

Tom was on his feet the next instant. He shoved Bayard to the ground.

"Stupid! You were supposed to stay dead for twenty seconds. *Twenty seconds*! Can't you count?!"

Confused tears welled in Bayard's eyes. He shook his head. He counted fingers on his hands, counted them again.

Tom picked up Bayard's warclub, a gnarled stick.

Bayard's eyes widened: *No, don't—*

Tom hurled the stick into the trees. Bayard hung his head and sobbed, with gobs of snot running from his nose and his tears leaving tracks in the crude warpaint on his cheeks.

The Black Knight lowered his sword. "Ease up, Tommy..."

Tom stomped away from them. "To hell with you both."

Billy Clements sighed and followed. "Bay didn't mean it."

Tom threw his head back and squeezed his nose to stem the blood. "Bull."

Bayard sat crying on the ground, his sobs quickly devolving to strange grunts and shrieks of rage.

"Oh, shut up!" Tom snarled. "Cut it out just *once*, will you?" He reached down and hauled his little brother up by the shirt collar. Bayard fought back scratching. Standing Bayard up straight, Tom balled a fist and hurled it. His knuckles slammed into Bayard's right cheek, sending the boy down in a spray of spit, tears, and blood.

Tom cursed and clutched his ballooning knuckles, already blue with bruises.

"I think I broke it," he wheezed to Billy. "*I think I broke my hand.*"

Billy could only watch, his mouth hanging on a hinge.

Nearby, Bayard whimpered. He picked himself up slowly, bewildered. He reached into the bed of leaves and produced a white tooth, with thin nerves still clinging to it. Blood and saliva dripped from his mouth in a constant stream. He looked up at the older boys, who stared at him with horrified fascination.

Faced with the results of his rage, Tom's face paled. He stepped forward.

"Bayard, I'm sorry—"

Then Bayard was up and running away back to the house beyond the woods.

Tom and Billy watched him go.

Stung by the rebuke, Tom shouted, "I hope you get lost! I hope you get lost in the dark and a witch finds you! *I hope she finds you and eats you!*"

Still sobbing, Bayard ran on until he was out of sight.

Billy sighed and reached for his warhorse, an old broomstick, and set it on his shoulder. "You're really gonna get it now," he said.

Tom sniffed. The blood had finally stopped. "He's the one who should get it. He could have broken my nose with that damn stick." He shook his head. The pain was still there, but abating.

"Might've broke his nose back," Billy said. Absentmindedly, he set to hacking at a bush with his wooden sword. "You know he's simple. He don't know any better."

"Well he should," Tom snapped. "He ruins War every time."

They walked on for a time, neither enjoying the pervading silence.

Then, Billy's eyes brightened. He turned on Tom and assumed his evil Black Knight voice.

"*I shall avenge his honor!*"

Tom brightened at the prospect of resuming the battle. He brandished his sword again and dropped into a low stance. "Do your worst, you black-hearted bastard."

Billy rattled his sword against his shield. "Time to die!"

They fought like titans. Tom charged first, swiping at Billy with his greatsword. Billy deflected the blow with his shield and struck out at Tom's exposed hand. Tom yowled and retreated a few paces to whirl about and face his opponent again. This time he let Billy lunge first, parrying the Knight's thrust and using his body weight to slam against the shield and knock Billy on his back. Breathless, Tom dropped his sword to Billy's pulsing throat.

"Do you submit?"

Billy glared up at him. "Not for all the gold in Camelot."

Tom spoke through his teeth. "*Submit.*"

Billy drew an invisible knife from underneath his armor and stabbed himself in the heart. "You said it yourself: never surrender." Then he shuddered and died, his tongue lolling out of his mouth. So ended the terrible reign of the Black Knight.

Tom stepped back from his fallen foe and sheathed his sword. Standing in silhouette against the fading sun, he was the vision of King Arthur returned.

The crickets chirped merrily as Tom and Billy walked side by side, soaked with sweat and laughing softly together.

"Your mammy's gonna be mad," Billy said. "Think she'll whip you?"

"Not if I whip her first," Tom replied. He snatched Billy's wooden sword and swung it through the air. "Or maybe I'll just cut her down where she stands, *like this*!"

"Would you kill her?"

"Likely!"

"Liar," Billy laughed.

"Sodomite," Tom countered, watching and waiting for a response.

Confused, Billy furrowed his brow. "What the hell is that?"

Tom grinned. "Your brother's one!"

"No he ain't. I don't even know what you called him, but he ain't what you called him."

"Well then, your mother's one."

"One a what?"

"A sodomite. Like from the Bible or whatever."

"She's dead," Billy said. "My mother's dead."

"Oh." Tom felt a sudden hollowing sensation in the pit of his stomach. "I knew that," he said. He sighed and shook his head. "Laws, Billy, I'm...I didn't mean—"

"My birthday's next month," Billy said abruptly, his best attempt at changing the subject. "You remember the date, Tommy? I turn thirteen. Pa says I'll be a man, he says. Course, he said *he* became a man when he was nine. Says this generation is a bunch of babies."

"Sodomites," Tom clarified.

"Right. Anyway, he says I could leave school after the harvest if I wanted, long as I stayed on the farm."

Tom's jaw fell open. "You're going to leave school?"

Billy shrugged. "Pa says readin books, and countin numbers, it all adds up to nothin. I'd ruther work, save my pennies, then buy myself a darkie." He nudged Tom's shoulder. "You should quit too, Tommy, soon as you get the chance. Then we can ship off like we always talked about. Visit them fancy gals in Nawlins."

Tom grinned. He put his hands on his hips and drawled, "*Naw*lins."

Billy laughed and tried his best Creole: "Nuh-*Aw*lins."

Tom jerked his body about and strutted like a peacock. "Nuh-*Aww*-lins!"

They fell together laughing.

They were still catching their breath when they burst through the thickets and entered the wide lawn leading to Clarendon. The big white house loomed before them. Through the corner of his eye Tom registered Billy's awe at the size and grandeur of the place, and just now he tried to see Clarendon through his friend's eyes.

The house was a full-three storeys, glittering with windows that reflected the day's last sunlight. Tall Corinthian columns stretched up from the veranda to the highest balcony. From east to west wing there were some forty rooms in the place. Father liked to say that no Roman had ever built a more impressive structure.

But Clarendon was not without its ugliness, and its defects were what always caught Tom's eye first. The lawn was sickly and overgrown, and over yonder behind a copse of trees squatted a row of old slave houses left over from what the family called 'the Colonel's time.' Tom and Billy used to play in the rotting slave houses until one day Tom pierced his foot on a rusty nail and nearly died from the resulting infection. The scattered wrecks and ruins of the old plantation days had once upon a time stimulated Tom's imagination, but the older he grew the more he considered them terrible eyesores in need of destruction and removal.

Clarendon, being built on the craggy, forested North Branch, was surrounded on all sides by trees. But these trees had not been cleared or cared for, and over many years the handsome tree line devolved into snarling, impenetrable thickets that seemed to creep in closer with each passing year. Tom did not like to venture through the thickets alone, for often he would stumble upon worn headstones that indicated the graves of unknown persons. Tom's best guess was that they were the shallow graves of the Colonel's slaves. Once, he discovered a giant pit that had been dug out of the earth and never filled in, its base occupied now by standing water and sparse grass. Tom was convinced that the pit had been dug to serve as a mass grave. But where were the bodies?

It was these deformities and more that gave the towering house of Clarendon a singularly lonely character, like that of an abandoned castle hidden deep in a forest in which there lurked witches and monsters. Little wonder then why Tom sometimes referred to the place as 'the dead house'.

Suddenly, Tom spotted the old housemaid Mae Jane. She was clutching a shawl to her chest and peering out into the twilight forest from the back portico. Even in the gathering dark, Tom could see the deep creases of anger set in her face. Bayard sat on a chair nearby holding a raw slab of beef to his injured mouth. Tipper the dog sniffed about the lawn.

"Quick!" Tom said to Billy. They darted back into the trees and skirted the side of the house, aiming to circle to the front.

They had not gone ten yards when Billy snapped a dry branch underfoot. Tipper was old but his ears were sharp, and he bounded over to them and announced their arrival with incessant barking.

Mae Jane's head snapped to them like a hawk spotting prey.

"Thomas Nathaniel Roscoe!"

Tom groaned. There was no point in running now. Tipper found them in the bushes, and the dog was happy to see his boy and his boy's friend safely returned. Billy relented and stooped to pet Tipper, but Tom looked away from the wagging tail with disgust.

"Stupid dog."

Mae Jane tramped across the grounds with murder in her eyes. She was a short, wiry woman with a large nose. Tom had never seen her hair down, for she always kept it wrapped in a tight kerchief. Seeing the wrath in the old mammy's eyes, Tom looked down and stared at his dirty feet when suddenly she slapped him across the face with the back of her hand.

Tom dropped his toy weapons and clutched his nose, where fresh blood flowed.

"I oughta tan you," Mae Jane growled. She was beside herself with anger, her words tumbling over each other. She gestured at the tiny figure of Bayard, who watched wide-eyed from the portico. "I oughta tan you right here and now for what you done to your brother."

"I didn't hit him," Tom protested. "I only pushed—"

The words were barely out of his mouth before Mae Jane slapped him again.

Tom screamed, "*He hit me first*!"

Out of nowhere Billy Clements burst out laughing, a bizarre reaction inspired by shaking fear of the old maid.

Mae Jane turned on him with blazing fury. "You got somethin to say, boy?"

Billy staggered backward and shook his head dumbly.

"Best you run off home," Mae Jane said. "G'won, get!"

Billy muttered, "Goodbye, Tommy," and turned and ran.

Tom watched Billy go with a quiet yearning.

Mae Jane shook him again. "I *won't* have violence like that in my house, Thomas Roscoe. Not in it, and not in the woods round it. For God's sake, *look at me*, Thomas."

Tom squeezed his eyes shut. When he opened them again, they burned hotter than the red blotch on his cheek.

"This isn't *your house*!" he snarled. "You're just a dumb *nigger* and you own *nothing*. If I wanted to, I could get Father to throw you out to starve and die." Tom puffed out his chest. "So go on and hit me again, *nigger*."

Something in his threat stung, for Mae Jane's wrath suddenly vanished. Tom searched eagerly for fear and defeat in her eyes, but instead he saw the old lady's expression cloud with a heavy sadness.

"Who taught you to say that?" she said. She let go of him suddenly and took a step back, as if his words had injured her somehow. Her voice was raspy, like an old broom sweeping dead leaves. "*Who taught you to say that?*"

Tom glared at her and refused to answer.

Mae Jane opened her mouth to say something more, maybe with a mind to scold Tom further. But instead she wrung her hands together and turned away with tears welling in her eyes. "You shouldn't say such things," she murmured. "Shouldn't say such things...God, keep him...Lord, keep him..."

Stunned, Tom called out, "Mae Jane?"

But she didn't answer. She just took the hand of an awestruck Bayard and went inside the house. Tipper the dog watched them go, offering a low, sad whine. The dog looked at Tom with a cocked head, as if trying to make sense of him. Then the dog turned away and padded quietly after Mae Jane.

Alone now, Tom stood on the veranda in shocked silence. At last, the crickets resumed their night song.

Tom could hardly believe his luck. He had finally stood up to Mae Jane, and there she went, fleeing with her tail between her legs. But whatever sense of victory he felt quickly faded. Now he just felt nauseous.

❧

Supper that evening was quiet, at least to start. Tom lingered at the entrance of the dining room with some reservation, wondering whether Mae Jane had tattle-taled about his outburst to Father. Tom peered around the corner and saw that Father was casually reading a copy of the *Mayfair First Witness*. If Mae Jane *had* said anything, Father did not seem all that concerned. Whistling, Tom strolled into the dining room with swagger.

"Hello, Father! Welcome home."

Father had the peculiar habit of reading newspapers from back to front, for he believed that obituaries were the most important element contained within them. Father looked up only briefly at Tom, long enough to smile and murmur a distracted hello before he turned his attention back to the paper.

Tom was still smiling at Father, maybe waiting for him to say something more. But evidently that was all the attention Father would give him, at least for now. Tom found his chair next to Sarah and sat down. He resumed whistling until Sarah rapped him on the wrist and warned him to cut it out. Tom stuck out his tongue and she kicked at him under the table. Crying out, Tom snatched up his fork and made ready to stab.

"*Enough*," Father said sharply, not even bothering to look up from his newspaper.

Jem soon entered, and floating in with him came the musky, pine-needle aroma of gin. Jem was all dandied up for the dance, and he turned red when Sarah teased him for finally combing his hair. Jem sat down heavily in his chair and promptly uncorked a bottle of merlot on the table and filled his glass.

"Not yet," Father said, folding his newspaper. He indicated a stack of documents beside him and held up a pen. "These withdrawal requests won't sign themselves."

"Can't it wait?" Jem said. He nodded at the darkness beyond the windows. "It's well past candle-lighting, and the barbecue's soon. Now's a time for celebration and—"

"There will be time yet for celebrating later," Father replied gruffly. "You are President of the Roscoe Railroad Company, which means I can't transfer funds from the company without both our signatures." Father gave a curt nod to Ben Freeman, and Ben dutifully stood up to help pass page after page to Jem in a sort of assembly line.

Taking Father's pen, Jem scrawled his signature on page after page. "You do know, Father, there is such a thing as a telegraph. If you want to pilfer your own pockets, you can just use the wire."

Father's upper lip curled up in preparation for a retort, but just then Mae Jane entered the room with an array of steaming dishes.

"Somethin good from the kitchens tonight!" Mae Jane called. She served Father first, and then the empty space where Mother would soon sit. Mae Jane snapped her fingers at Ben, who abandoned the assembly line to fetch more dishes from the kitchen (which the Freemans called 'the kitchens').

Mother joined very late. Father stood up and addressed her with a sense of humility that only Mother could conjure in him. Tom recalled Jem's theory, which he himself had never been able to fully understand: that Mother had married Father not out of enthusiasm, but because her own father had told her so.

Father leaned in to kiss Mother on the lips; she grimaced and gave him her cheek. It had been several weeks since Tom had seen Mother outside her self-imposed exile within the east wing study. He wanted to embrace her, to speak with her awhile, but Mother had eyes only for Bayard. At first, Tom felt a knot of jealousy and hated Bayard for all the attention he was receiving. But then, watching Mother stroke and pet Bayard as if he was a housecat or a favorite doll, Tom decided he didn't want attention of *that* kind.

As everyone tucked into their meal, Tom's anxiousness returned. He wondered whether Mae Jane had been waiting until just now to tell Father that his son had called her a terrible word. Tom's mind raced to develop arguments in defense of his actions. Was the word really so terrible? Mother used it all the time, and so did plenty of other people, and nobody ever seemed too bothered by it. Why, even the Freemans used the word themselves, and often rather casually. Maybe it was just like Jem sometimes said, that society was becoming too sensitive to the words people used. Free speech is free speech is free speech. Sticks and stones and all that, right? In any case, Tom's stomach soon overpowered his mind and he dug into his meal with ferocious energy. Killing Indians and wayward knights, as it turned out, worked up an appetite.

After some time had passed, with the only sounds the scraping of cutlery and quiet chewing of food, Tom looked down the table toward Father.

"I want to go to the barbecue tonight. May I please, Father? Tell me I can go."

Sarah shook her head. "You're too young."

Tom turned on her with a scowl. "I'm almost thirteen. Some boys become men at nine."

Jem laughed. "At nine, you still needed Mae Jane's help to wipe your own ass."

"*Hush,*" Mae Jane chided. "You ought to watch your language at your father's table, Jeremiah." She turned to Ben, who was using a napkin to stifle a laugh of his own, and she glared at him until he fell silent.

"Thirteen is still too young," Sarah insisted. "*I'm* certainly not spending all my time babysitting you. Maybe Jem will let you tag along with him and his riff-raff friends."

Jem laughed. "Not a chance."

"I'd be your chaperone, Tom," Ben said, "but I'll be waiting on your father tonight."

Tom looked to Father for aid, but Father was still engaged with the newspaper. With a heavy sigh, Tom dropped the conversation altogether.

Supper dragged on. By and by, Father asked Tom how school was going. The old man's cloudy gaze was still fixed on the newspaper clutched in his hands, so Tom could not be sure whether Father was even listening to him. All the same, he gave a brief and banal account of prison life under the ancient schoolmaster Mr. Braxton. Father did not respond except to grunt or sigh once or twice. Eager to wrap up his story, Tom finished with a noncommittal stance on the news of Mr. Braxton's long-awaited retirement, with the arrival of an unknown schoolmistress starting Monday.

"Who is she?" Sarah asked with intense interest. "Is she from beyond the Branches?"

Tom shrugged. "How should I know?"

Jem cleared his throat with a loud cough and sipped at his wine.

"You will report to me on her efficacy, won't you?" Father said. "I'm all for country education. Don't forget, you're only at Mayfair School to establish a history of relations with the common people. The experience will toughen you up, and give you greater respect for the boarding schools and colleges to come. But I must know whether or not you are receiving sufficient instruction. I will expect a thorough analysis from you by Christmastime."

Tom nodded. "Yes, sir."

Here, Father finally looked at Tom directly. Though up to now Tom had wished for Father's attention, he quickly decided he didn't want it anymore. Father repeated his usual lecture about Tom's responsibility to uphold the Roscoe legacy, and how Father and Mother had great expectations that Tom would attend the College of William and Mary when he was older. "After that, you will study a useful trade," Father said. "The law would be most suitable for you, I think. After establishing a practice for a yet-to-be-determined period of time, you will run for public office." Father added, almost as an afterthought, "Only if you so desire, of course."

Across the table, Jem snorted with laughter.

Father glared at Jem and was quiet. Then he looked down at his plate and attacked it with fork and knife. As he chewed, he said: "By the time you are ready for politics, Thomas, Jeremiah ought to be driving the last spikes in my railroad. *If* he has not drunk himself to death by then." Father looked sidelong at Jem with a watchful eye, but when he looked at Tom again he pushed a smile over his thin lips. Most smiles made Tom smile back almost by instinct, but Father's smile only made him feel sick.

"In the meantime," Father said, "our enterprises will be enough to finance all of your ambitions, Thomas. Of that you can be sure."

Here, Mother spoke up for the first time: "We must all do our duty for the family."

By now Tom's food had turned to mush in his mouth. With a gulping swallow, Tom offered a meek nod of understanding to his parents. "I'd like all that very much. But…But why me? I don't…" Tom searched for the right words. He could only shake his head. "I don't even know what it is I gotta do."

Something in Father's eyes quivered. Mother's head jerked but an inch.

"*Must do*," Father said, his voice tight.

Tom blinked. "What?"

"*Pardon*," Mae Jane corrected, her voice hushed.

"Pardon, Father," Tom said. He looked across the table, wanting to thank Mae Jane, but she had turned to help Bayard.

"It's not something you *gotta* do," Father said, his voice filled with disgust, "it's something you *must* do. Do you understand?"

Tom bowed his head. "Yes, Father."

Father ripped his napkin from his throat and pushed his plate aside. "Clearly you don't. Who is teaching you to speak like that? You sound like a goddamn mud-eater."

Across the table, Jem clenched a fist but stayed silent.

"*Please*, Daddy," Sarah said. "Like Mae Jane said, it's improper to swear at the—

"Who is your teacher?" Father demanded. "Some old bumpkin?" His voice was tinged with mockery, and somewhere in there was resentment also. "Does he teach my son grammar after mucking out the pig stalls? Oh, he's just some country coot in a one-room schoolhouse. What would he know of your abilities? What would he know of your potential? You're a *Roscoe*, goddammit, and shouldn't that *mean* something to him? To anyone?"

Somehow, Tom could see behind Father's eyes a furious cranking of clockwork, a deadly whir of machinery moving so fast that it couldn't possibly keep going, or go faster.

"No more," Father breathed to himself, so quiet that maybe only Tom caught it. "No more dirt floors for the Roscoes."

When Father looked up again, his face had swollen to twice its normal size. A vein in his left temple throbbed, as if a purple worm were squirming across his brow.

"I don't need to wait until Christmastime after all," Father said. "I was wrong to think country schooling would be good for us." He spoke building energy, his voice sharp and exact, as if he was dictating his thoughts to an invisible stenographer. "Your Mother will find a better school than that *shack* down the Valley. We'll get us into a bonafide institution this year, instead of waiting until next. Still, we'll put you in the *advanced* classes, with the older pupils. You'll shine as bright as they, I haven't a doubt about it. Your new teachers — your *professors* — shall wipe that country-talk off your tongue, even if they have to scrub it out. They'll clean you up, Thomas. Because Roscoes are *clean* people, you understand? We are clean, which means *you* must be clean."

Exhausted of bearing the brunt of Father's heavy gaze, Tom looked down into his lap. He decided another question he had in mind just wasn't worth the asking. All he could say was:

"I'd like it all very much, Father."

For a long while, the Roscoes and Freemans ate in silence.

By and by, conversations were reborn. Tom slumped down in his chair and picked at his food while talk buzzed overhead. As dessert time neared, the conversation eventually landed on the 'goings-on' at Harper's Ferry.

"Just a terrible thing what happened," Mae Jane murmured, shaking her head. "All those people killed, Lord bless them. And all for what? *Nothing*."

Tom watched a grimace pass over Ben's face, as if the food in his mouth had turned to ash. Just then, a question popped into Tom's mind.

"Why didn't they go to him?"

At first, the others ignored the question. This was a common tactic used against Tom's dinner table queries. Only Ben looked up at Tom, but he didn't say anything.

And so, Tom tried again.

"Why didn't the nig — the *negroes* — why didn't they go to John Brown?"

Finally, Ben set his cutlery down and looked at him. "It's a good question, Tom."

For a while, it seemed that was all Ben was going to say. Then he coughed and cleared his throat.

"If you throw a man down a hole, he'll try to scramble out. But as his strength weakens, you might in time convince him that his dark little hole is his home. That it's the nicest, safest hole he could ever want, and that everything outside the man's hole is hostile and dangerous, including strangers who try to help the man out. Well, after enough time passes the man in the hole might start to believe it's all true. And when his children are born in that hole, and his children's children too, soon enough you'll have an entire people who believe they'll never climb out, and were never meant to. It will take a fundamental shift of thinking — in short, a revolution

— to change attitudes, both of the people in the hole, and those who feel it their duty to keep them there."

Tom heard all this and nodded slowly. He imagined himself literally down a wet hole, looking up at the world as a circle within darkness, able to see the sun pass by for just a few hours a day.

From the head of the table, Father said, "Slavery will end not through revolution, but through *evolution*. Peace and compromise must be maintained while solutions to problems are worked out in their own time. Evolution is slow, but it is steady. What's more, it is right. Revolution does nothing but get people killed, and there is always a regression to follow."

Ben's jaw clenched up. "I don't suggest what John Brown's done is *right* on its own terms," he said. "One might ask another, 'Do the ends justify the means?' Well, let the answer be, 'Give me the means and the ends, and I will reason whether it's justified.' There is a broader context to this whole affair that can't be ignored. What if, finally, after years of suffering harassment and injury and oftentimes murder, the proponents of slavery's abolition — not to mention the *four million* negro slaves who live in the South — have decided that revolution is the last remaining option to effect some kind of meaningful change?"

"The sum total of killing one man to free another is zero," Jem replied. "Do I understand the moral nature of the abolitionist cause? Of course I do. If it were up to me there would be no slavery at all. If it were up to the Roscoe family, we'd have many more dining tables across the Union look like ours here, black and white living together in peace. But should such a cause as abolition ever necessitate violence to achieve its aims? If men like John Brown were truly righteous, if they were truly committed to the spirit of their cause, they would work toward peaceful solutions by peaceful means."

Ben's eyes bulged out of his head. "*Peaceful solutions*? Easier said than done when lynch mobs stand ready to intimidate or kill anyone who speaks out against the slave powers. Easier said than done when four million human beings suffer legalized torture, rape, and humiliation, to be cast out to a refuse pile the moment they've outlived they're usefulness."

"*Mae Jane*," Mother said sharply, "won't you tell your boy to keep quiet? When the Colonel sat at this table, negroes spoke only when they were spoken to."

"Yes, ma'am," Mae Jane said, nodding dutifully. Now she turned on Ben with a scowl and hissed, "*Hush*!"

A moment of strangled silence came and went.

Jem polished off the last of his wine and reached for more. He looked to be itching for a good old-fashioned sparring.

"I say too little attention is paid to the Valley's yeomen. By that I mean the poor farmers who own no slaves, and by *that* I mean eight out of ten men here in Mayfair.

Do the Northern newspapers ever talk about that? *Eight out of ten* Southerners own no slaves at all. 'Poor white trash' some people call them. Why, I've even overheard some slaves ridicule the 'mud-eaters' for not living up to the abilities of white men."

Ben shook his head. "If the Valley's farmers realized the power they actually hold over the First Families, Mayfair would be a much different place. Legitimacy — of a government or an institution or anything else — is conferred by consent. As it is, men like Clay Claiborne feed lies to the population. They convince even the poorest farmer that he can still hold his head up high because, 'Well, at least I'm not a nigger.' But what does such an empty consolation really mean? What does—?"

Tom cleared his throat. "You shouldn't say *that word*, Ben." Tom's eyes flickered to Mae Jane, then back to Ben. "It's a dirty word."

Ben was quiet for a long moment. "Thank you, Tom," he said at last. "I'll try to keep that in mind."

Ignoring the distraction, Jem pressed his case. "Maybe the way out of slavery is not through violent revolution, but through opportunity. For instance: that same poor farmer can come work up at the North Branch Mine. With his wages he can buy better food for his family and keep his children in school year-round. Maybe his sons won't have to mine coal when they grow older. Our workers can hold their heads up high and feel great pride — not in the apparent supremacy of their skin color, as the Families would have them believe — but in their status as able-bodied men of responsibility. Maybe, over time, these men will realize that the slave-masters in fact do very little *good* for the Valley, preferring instead to whip up racial fear and resentment. Maybe, over time, attitudes about our peculiar institution will change. Maybe one day the people of Mayfair will do away with it completely. They'll withdraw their consent, as you say."

Ben sighed. "Do you really believe all that, Jem? Your workers save their wages not for some noble purpose, but only so they can buy themselves a slave to cook their meals and clean their house."

Jem shrugged. "They are only trying to get ahead using the means available to them."

"Sure, and they're doing it on the backs of negroes," Ben said. "Don't you see the insanity of it all? For every one white person in the Valley, there are four slaves. There's some two thousand whites in Mayfair, which makes eight thousand blacks. Must eight thousand souls suffer on a daily basis in order to help a handful of white men fulfill their ambitions?"

Here, Father heaved a great sigh. "This is all terribly interesting," he said with a thick note of sarcasm, "but it seems to me that you're missing a key point, Ben."

"Then please enlighten me, Senator," Ben said haughtily. There was a smoldering fire in his voice and eyes, and for a moment Tom thought Mae Jane would reach out and slap her son across the face for speaking such a way.

Father made nothing of Ben's animosity. Instead, he folded his hands together and stared down the table, deep in thought.

"Picture yourself walking with another man down a road, both trying to get to the same place. Together, you might come to a fork with two available paths. In your heart of hearts, you know the rightward path leads to your shared destination. Meanwhile, the other man insists on going left, for his own perfectly valid reasons. You might consider the act of going right a moral imperative, but of course the other man tells you the very same thing about his going left.

"In making any choice of consequence, a man must feel that the choice is *his* to make. If the choice is made for him, or pushed upon him as a *fait accompli*, he will deny its good sense and credibility. Try to drag the other man your way, and he will dig in his heels — even if by doing so he works against his own self-interests. And always, those who profit on fear and resentment will be there to cheer such men on."

"Try to force an idea down my throat, however morally right the idea may be, and you've lost," Jem said.

Ben shook his head. "But, sir, there are some roads that should not be traveled," he said. "There are some ideas that are objectively *right*, and to refuse them is insanity. I'm all for free choice, Senator, but there are limits. Outlawing slavery might restrict certain rights, but in such a case the good far outweighs the bad. Before Moses, I might have thought I had the right to murder. Now we all agree murder is a crime against God and Man."

"You're right," Father said. "My point, and I believe Jeremiah's as well, is that most men do not believe slavery is a crime. Rather, they consider slavery an inherent good. They believe it is a peaceful solution when there is so much fear and distrust between the races."

"There need not be *fear*," Ben said. "There need not be *distrust*. If there were no crutch of slavery, then maybe—"

"Again you are right," Father said. "But whatever need or need not be is not, unfortunately, what *is*. Whatever example this family might set, we must remember it is an anomaly. Whether rightly or wrongly, the people of Mayfair fear the consequences of racial equality. Hearts and minds may change in time. But such persons must be coaxed down the right path, not forced there by the point of a knife."

"Again I call it insanity," Ben said. "These are grown men we're talking about, not babies. We ought not to coddle them with promises that negroes will be kept in their place. If you want opportunity, as Jem says, then let there be free opportunity *for all people*. Then and only then, the cream will rise to the top. Then and only then, we will have a true democracy. Then and only then, we will have peace."

Mae Jane turned and directed an overlarge grin at her son, but her eyes were deadly serious. "Then I suppose we'll all just have to agree to disagree bout this," she said through her teeth, feigning cheer and promising a final warning before retribution. "*Ain't that the case,* Mr. Freeman?"

Ben opened his mouth to say something more, but he could not withstand his mother's power. Relenting, Ben gave a quiet sigh and nodded.

"Now," Mae Jane said, a genuine smile returning to her lips. "What do you-all think of my collards?"

They ate in stilted silence. Tom looked around, taking in everything. Ben glared down at his plate, having apparently lost his appetite. Mae Jane watched her son with tired eyes. Jem polished his glass and filled it up again, spilling some wine on the tablecloth in the process. Bayard was gawking at Father, who coughed and spat into his handkerchief. Mother's eyes were fixed on a portrait of the Colonel on the far wall. Clutching her white party gloves, Sarah's impatient eyes looked toward the grandfather clock in the opposite corner.

Tom's ears twitched at the sound of the front door opening. Tipper the dog, who had been dozing by the fire, suddenly sprang into action. The dog quit the room in a frenzy, barking at the top of his lungs.

"That *dog,*" Jem groaned, clutching his head. "Shut him up, Tom, will you?"

"I didn't know we were expecting company," Mother said stiffly.

Mae Jane stood up and wrung her hands. "We ain't expectin nobody, so far as I know."

At the head of the table, Father continued to eat in silence.

"Oh!" Sarah gasped. "I can't be seen by guests in *these* rags. Keep them busy while I change—"

Tom pushed his chair back and hurried after Tipper. "Here, Tip! What's the matter, boy?"

Exiting the dining room, following the sound of Tipper's barking, Tom rounded the corner and looked down the long hallway toward the grand foyer. A tall figure in mud-caked clothes stood there in the expanse, admiring the glittering chandelier suspended from the ceiling.

Tipper, barking and baying, rushed the figure and leaped up with his paws outstretched. Man and dog locked together in a strange sort of dance before the man brought up his knee—"*Down,* damn dog!"—and knocked Tipper bodily across the floor. Splayed out, Tipper whined and went still.

"Hey!" Tom cried, his blood running hot. He hurried down the hall, meaning to thrash the stranger — whoever he was. "You can't just waltz in here and kick at my..."

Tom stopped. His eyes bulged.

"*JJ?!*"

And there JJ was, his green-gray eyes smiling at Tom. He was a perfect double of Jem (or rather Jem was a perfect double of *him*), except while Jem had a habit of slouching JJ held his chin up and shoulders back, proud and dignified. Slowly,

Tom inched forward, trying to see if the figure of JJ was real or just some kind of apparition.

"Hello, Tom," JJ said, still smiling. "Well, I'm back."

Chapter 7

THE HERO OF HARPER'S FERRY

"*Wait*, Tom! Not just yet—"

With a laugh, Tom threw the door of the dining room open and stepped inside. He gestured toward the open space with dramatic flourish, as if he was a ringmaster introducing a star circus animal.

"Look who I found!"

All at once, the eyes of the Roscoes and Freemans fell upon the looming figure in the doorway. Arms suspended in mid-motion, with forkfuls of food hovering in gaping mouths, as JJ stepped into the light of the room. For a long, excruciating moment, there was nothing but stunned silence broken only by the slight ticking of the grandfather clock.

At last, the silence was broken by JJ, who finally found his voice:

"Hello, everyone."

Looks of confusion and disbelief now gave way to delayed expressions of joy and delight. Bursting with excitement, Sarah abandoned all formalities; she stood up and hurled herself against JJ's chest with a girlish shriek.

"JJ! My word, what a surprise. *Look at you,* all grown up..."

Mae Jane stood up next, beaming. "Handsome as ever," she agreed. She went to JJ and gave him a warm, tender embrace. "Jon Jacob," she said. "Oh, it does this old heart good to see you, child."

Ben approached next, first offering JJ a formal handshake before thinking better of it. Laughing, the two hugged as old friends — as brothers.

Watching all these greetings, Tom's heart swelled with quiet joy. He could barely remember life when JJ had been home. Tom himself had only been eight years old when JJ left for New York in a terrible hurry. He vaguely remembered hearing voices crying down hallways and behind shut doors, and he remembered a dark cloud that hung over Clarendon in the days that followed.

Up to now, the name 'JJ' had been uttered only rarely, and always in a hushed tone. The last three Christmases, Jem had whispered of JJ's looked-for homecoming like he was predicting the Second Coming. The rest of the family talked about its eldest son as one might talk about a ghost. Every time someone brought up JJ's name, Father and Mother would insist the family pray to God for 'the souls of the misbegotten', as if doing so might have some cleansing effect.

But now, at least as far as Tom could tell, all those dark and confusing sentiments were gone.

Ben drew back from his embrace with JJ. "We had no idea you were coming home. *I* had no idea — I didn't think you'd be finished at the Point until next summer."

JJ laughed. "Of course you had to know, Ben. You know everything Father says and does, sometimes before *he* knows it." JJ beamed his smile at the others around the table. "The letter said you'd be waiting for my arrival. I'm just glad you-all weren't waiting with torches and pitchforks."

Ben laughed at the joke, but Tom could see confusion behind his eyes. In truth, Tom felt some measure of confusion himself. What letter? He didn't know about any letter. Then again, nobody around here ever told Tom anything. He knew his family still treated him like he was nothing but a damn stupid kid. Meanwhile, down the Branch was Billy Clements, whose pa said he could quit school anytime he wanted! The irony was, some classmates actually *envied* Tom for growing up a Roscoe...

Tom followed Ben's uncertain gaze to Father, who sat at the head of the table and kept his eyes fixed on a line of tallow candles.

JJ gave a nonchalant shrug. "Well, it seems I nevertheless surprised you-all. And at suppertime, no less. But I assure you, there's a good reason for my tardiness. We'll get to that in good time. But first..."

JJ turned and rounded the table. He paused to ruffle Bayard's hair and pinch his cheeks.

"My word, look how you've grown, Bayard. You'll be bigger than all of us one day. Understand, Bayard? I said, *you'll-be-bigger-than-all-of-us-one-day*."

"He can hear you," Mae Jane said quietly.

JJ turned to her with a questioning look.

"He can hear you," she repeated. "You know Bay can't much talk but he...he understands. He understands most things better than do most folks, I reckon."

Though he rarely said anything beyond the odd boyish grunt of yes or no, Bayard was indeed lucid and watchful. He smiled politely at JJ, but there was a hint of fear in his eyes, as if he had no idea who JJ was. And thinking about it, Tom realized such a reaction only made sense; Bayard had only been four years old when JJ left home. Even then, JJ had never paid much attention to his younger siblings. To Tom's memory, JJ had usually been off somewhere with Father.

Looking at Bayard now, JJ's smile faltered. "Right. Of course. Well, I suppose it's just that I've been away so long." Keeping his distance, he studied Bayard with the air of a naturalist. "Couldn't be helped, Bayard. But we'll get to know each other again, I'm sure of it."

There was movement beside Tom that caught his attention. Jem pushed back from the table and now stood opposite JJ. The twins were identical except for the slight difference in eye color; both were a shade of Father's gray, but JJ's were shaded green and Jem's were misted blue. Together, the twins appeared as both window and mirror.

To Tom's eyes, each twin seemed to be trying to read the mind of the other. JJ watched Jem with an almost cautious air, while Jem was distracted by his brother's blue uniform. Slowly, moving like two strange dogs investigating each other, the twins came together. They reached out and touched each other. They stared long into each other's eyes, each feeling the weight of the moment.

"Four years," Jem said stonily, his lips pursed. "In all that time, precious few letters home."

JJ remained still, watchful. "Well, I've been busy."

Jem cocked an eyebrow. "Hm. Too busy for your own family?"

Somehow, Tom felt the candlelight in the dining room begin to dim. He felt his shoulders tense up with anticipation. Maybe he'd been too quick in thinking all the dark clouds had cleared…

JJ made a show of looking all around the room, and then his eyes landed on Jem once more. Slowly, he strode forward until the twins stood nose to nose. "I don't see any family around here," he muttered. "All I see is an ugly bastard wearing my old riding boots."

Jem flinched. "These are *my* riding boots."

Suddenly, the mood in the room changed, as if a spell had been broken. JJ cracked a smile and waved an admonishing finger in Jem's face. Growling, Jem leaped forward and wrapped JJ in a laughing bear hug.

"*Bastard!*"

Hollering in answer to Jem's hooting, JJ tried to wrestle free. The two huffed and stamped as if engaged in some absurd interpretive dance, and neither could stop laughing. All at once, the stale air in the room freshened, and the candles seemed to burn brighter.

"Thank the Lord," Sarah laughed, fanning her flushed cheeks. "I was beginning to think this had all taken a *turn*."

Tom shook his head, incredulous. "I have no idea what's happening."

Ben laughed and shook his head. "They're still rabid dogs, after all this time. That's the idea."

Watching the twins play-wrestle, Tom laughed when they laughed. He yearned to share in the joy of the moment, but somehow he felt strange watching the reunion. Nobody had seen JJ in years, but that long separation had to have hit the twins hardest of all.

Tom had no idea what it was like to have a twin sibling. He'd never had to share anything with anyone — not a toy, not a bedroom (Clarendon was just so damn *big*), and certainly not a womb. But seeing JJ and Jem together, he could begin to appreciate just how intimate their connection was. They were so different, and yet they moved as one body, right down to how they clenched their jaws when thinking about something.

The twins' battle ended in a draw, as always, with each claiming victory, as always. Catching his breath, Jem eagerly led the way to JJ's seat across the table. Jem passed around Mother without a second thought, but JJ made a point of stopping before her chair. Bowing, he leaned down and kissed Mother on the cheek.

"Lady Spencer, you look as beautiful as ever."

Mother offered a thin smile with pressed lips. She gently tapped JJ's hand once or twice and murmured something inaudible, as if talking while asleep. This was the extent of Mother's welcoming affection. For Tom, the mild reaction wasn't altogether surprising. His own experience with Mother, made common enough in their interactions (which were always few and far between), was the experience of being *looked through* — as if Mother could not see him or else chose not to. Tom was used to this and many other peculiar things relating to Mother and Father and life at Clarendon itself. Most of the time, he chalked it all up to the philosophy Mae Jane called 'the way it go.'

But the difference, Tom supposed, was that JJ had been away for a very long time. Was it too much to expect a warmer welcome from one's own mother? If the same thought crossed JJ's mind, he did not express it. Still, Tom thought he saw a wounded look in JJ's eyes, but JJ quickly blinked it away.

At the head of the table, Father pushed back from his chair and pressed his trembling cane upon the floor. Grunting, he began to stand upright to formally recognize JJ's arrival. But as Father rose, his body shook and wavered — the cane that held his weight bowed and bulged, threatening to give out.

Sucking in his breath, JJ lunged forward and caught one of Father's arms.

"Here, Father, let me help—"

"*I can stand on my own damn feet,*" Father snapped.

Unnerved, JJ stepped back. His cheeks blushed red.

Father stood upright and tilted his chin skyward. After a moment, Father's frustration gave way to a begrudging sort of regret. "I thank you for wanting to help," he murmured. It wasn't exactly an apology (for Father never apologized), but it was clear enough that Father meant what he said. "It hasn't been easy, learning to live with another limb."

JJ smiled as a fond memory glinted in his eyes. "What walks on three legs in the evening-time?"

Father returned a smile, though it was bloodless and unconvincing. Turning, Father gestured toward a vacant dining chair at his right side.

"As you can see, Jonathan, there is still a place for you at the table. You—"

Father's voice cut out as JJ threw himself into the old man's arms in a tight embrace. Tom's first instinct was to burst out laughing, especially because Father's face was stamped with a comical sort of embarrassment.

The longer he watched, however, the more Tom felt a hot tightening in his throat. JJ, his trembling fingers searching and clutching, his face buried against Father's crooked shoulder, looked so much like a lost child finally reclaimed. Tom suddenly remembered a story Reverend Cutler had told in his sermon the other week, something about the prodigal son returned.

Meanwhile, Father stood rigid, his arms drooping at his sides, having no idea what to do about the creature that had latched itself to him. The longer Tom looked at Father, the more he detected a conflict raging behind those elusive gray eyes. Somewhere in Father was the instinct to reach up and hug JJ closer, and maybe there was also the impulse to push JJ away.

"There, there," Father said, finally compelled to reach up and pat JJ's forearm in an awkward show of assurance. "There, there. That's enough now."

JJ drew back from his embrace and, hiding his face from the others, went to his seat. Clearing his throat with a low rumble, Father sat down again.

Mae Jane went to the kitchens and soon returned with a heaping plate of hot food. Grinning with delight, she set the plate before JJ and urged him to eat.

And eat the Roscoe family did, together with the Freemans. By and by, and rather to Tom's surprise, the routine dreariness of Clarendon's supper hour became something different. Soon enough the dining room hummed with bubbling conversations, until the Roscoes really did resemble something of a happy clan. JJ politely dismissed questions about his journey home from New York, suggesting he would get to such matters in good time.

As Tom listened to his family talk together, as he saw the smiles on their faces — even Father and Mother seemed relaxed and light-hearted — Tom felt a simple contentment he had never known before.

But no, he realized he *had* known it before, or else imagined he had, a long time ago. Before JJ had left for New York. That was the time — meaning before whatever happened, had happened. And in that distant time, which somehow felt not so long ago, there had been more smiles, more laughter. Somewhere along the way, those joyful sounds went silent.

But now the smiles and laughter had returned. The family was whole again. The dining room, and Clarendon itself, seemed to feel more expansive, and somehow the candlelight became still brighter. If houses contained spirits, then maybe there was a long-slumbering sentiment in the creaking old house that was just now reawakening: a quiet joy that stirred within Tom a feeling of hope and optimism.

"It does my heart good to see everyone again," JJ said, indulging a smile of sincere joy. "I've been looking forward to this for…well, for a very long time."

Tom looked up from his plate. "You mean you don't like being a soldier?"

"Oh, I like it well enough," JJ said. "I'm good at it, and that helps." Here, JJ cast a meaningful look toward Father. "But I like to think I'm destined for a different path through life."

The meaning of the look was not lost on the others, and there were some smiles shared around the table. But Father, at the table's head, only shrugged and stabbed at the chicken on his plate with his fork.

"I've always been of the opinion," Father said, "that no one is *destined* for anything at all. It's an anarchic world we inhabit. Nothing is guaranteed but what we secure for ourselves."

JJ offered a humble bow, as if he was addressing a king or emperor. "How true, Father. I suppose it was only a manner of speaking."

Saying nothing, Father gulped a morsel and continued eating.

Maintaining a polite smile, JJ asked Father a number of polite questions, to which he received a number of polite, but short, answers. JJ asked about Father's health, and about the latest news from Washington. He also inquired about 'the Company', meaning Father's company, the one Jem managed day to day and which Tom was supposedly destined to join when he was older.

"I've developed some ideas," JJ explained. "No doubt you've considered that the coal deposits below the North Branch won't last forever, Father. We ought to have a chain of camps all down the Blue Ridge before someone else secures the rights. What's more, we ought to diversify our holdings. For instance, there was a discovery in Pennsylvania a few months ago — black oil, like whale oil, only from underground. There could be practical applications related to the railroad, and maybe well beyond it too. I'm only back for a few weeks, Father, so perhaps you and I could go up the Branch together tomorrow. We can discuss how to make 1860 a banner year for us."

With a gloomy expression, Father shifted in his chair.

Seeing this reaction, JJ's smile faded. "Or perhaps you'd rather not discuss business at the table?"

Father pointed at Jem with his fork. "You may discuss Company matters with your brother. Jeremiah is acting president."

JJ's smile returned, though it was strained, deliberate. "I'd rather hoped I might speak with *you* about Company matters personally, sir. Your letter led me to believe—"

"What's this letter you keep talking about?" Jem asked. He sat up tall in his chair, as if trying to make his presence at the table known and felt.

JJ seemed to note Jem's discomfort and gave a dismissive shrug. "Private correspondence between a father and his son. Nothing that concerns you, baby brother."

Veins bulged from Jem's neck. "Don't call me that," he muttered.

"Don't call you what?"

"*Baby brother.*"

Tom snorted, "Ha!" This had to be another game between the twins, one he might finally join. He made crybaby noises and pointed mockingly at Jem. "Baby brother! *Baby* Jem!"

Jem turned and shot a deadly glare at Tom, and the sight of it made Tom clamp his mouth shut. So, it wasn't a game after all. Tom put his head down and kept it there.

Jem directed a sour look at JJ. "If any matter concerns the North Branch, or the Roscoe Railroad Company itself," he said, "then it concerns me also. You might recall, I've been in charge there for several years now."

JJ laughed. "You mean the foreman has been in charge. Without Joe Trask running that place, you would have run it into the ground a long time ago."

Jem bristled. "What, you really think you can do better?"

Grinning, JJ shrugged. "I rather think that's for Father to decide, don't you? You know, I stopped into the Branch on my way into the Valley. There was talk of expanding the shafts years ago before I left, except it seems nothing close to that has happened. I wonder why?"

Seething, Jem reached for his wine glass and found it empty. As he reached for the decanter, he muttered, "We've encountered some...financial setbacks."

"Setbacks?" JJ echoed with a laugh. "What are you going to do, Jem, when the Roscoe Railroad Company actually *becomes* a railroad company? Delays and setbacks must be worked into the firm's operational strategy. You must think like a soldier about these things, Jem, like a general. At the Point, they tell us to consider—"

"Yes, well, what a bunch of powdered wigs tell you at the Point doesn't exactly apply to the real world," Jem muttered. He dried his freshly-filled glass in almost a single gulp.

JJ showed a grin to Tom. "My, my," he said. "Struck a nerve, have I? You've become testier these last few years, dear brother."

Sarah looked up from her end of the table. "Oh, Jeremiah's always had a boulder for a brain, didn't you know?"

There was some quiet laughter among the siblings, but of course Jem stewed in silence. Seeking a more conciliatory tone, JJ looked at Jem once more.

"It's all in good fun, Jem. But the fact remains that Father will soon need someone he can depend on, someone who can *commit* to seeing the entire job through. Once Congress awards Father the transcontinental railroad contract..."

Suddenly, Mother burst out laughing across the table.

Father's head snapped to her. "What's so funny?" he demanded, his voice hoarse.

Mother snorted. "Oh, nothing, my dear. It's just that you've been waiting fifteen years for that silly little prize. And they're *still* dangling it in front of your nose? Even a dog knows when it's being teased."

A flush of red colored Father's pallid cheeks. "I am very close to gaining the railroad contract, as a matter of fact. So close, as it happens, that I am considering moving the Roscoe family away from Mayfair to somewhere more appropriate for managing railroad construction..."

Suddenly alert, everyone looked to Father.

"Where?" Jem asked urgently.

"Washington City," JJ guessed, his eyes dancing.

"California!" Tom shouted.

"New York," Ben breathed.

"Atlanta?" Sarah wondered, already lost in a wistful dream of her new life.

Father echoed none of these names.

"Missouri," he said, beaming a broad smile.

A long, uncomfortable silence hung in the air.

"*Missouri*?!" Sarah said, spitting the word out as if it were a bug. "Why would you *ever* want to drag us to that horrid place? They have no *culture* there!"

"It's a Southern culture, and fine enough for our tastes," Father said. "I tell you, what we now call the West, we'll call the *Mid*west in less than a quarter century. No longer is Mississippi the frontier. The state of Missouri is connected to the East by the Mississippi, and to the North and South by that same artery. West from Kansas City are the open plains of the Territories, all of it virgin land. From its prospective headquarters in St. Louis, the RRC can lay track in two directions at the same time: one east to the planned terminus at Richmond, the other west to San Francisco."

Mother set her cutlery down, having lost all interest in her food. "You-all may go off and become cattle drivers and live among the redskins if you wish. *I*, for one, will be staying here at Clarendon, where at least there is some semblance of human civilization. I was born a Virginian, and I shall die a Virginian."

"I agree with Cousin Isabella," Sarah said, looking astounded with herself for uttering such words. "I wish to stay as well. Can you imagine *me* at a ball in St. Louis?"

"I's stayin too," Mae Jane said. "This un's too old to be rollin round in a covered wagon."

Tom nearly leapt onto the table, such was his excitement. "I'll go!" he shouted, "I'll go!" Already he was trying to imagine what it would be like to meet a real-life Indian, and to see the wide open plains of the West.

"I'll go too," JJ said, smiling at Father. "I'd be proud to serve in the RRC's St. Louis office."

Father returned the smile, though it maybe looked more like a grimace.

"But who's going to look after the North Branch?" Jem said. "There's more than a hundred of our neighbors who are—"

"A means to an end," JJ finished. "Jem, this has been Father's plan since the beginning. We are talking about our family building the longest railroad in the Union's history — in *world* history — and you're worried about a few mud-eating yeomen choking on coal dust?"

Jem scowled at JJ. "With an attitude like that, it's no wonder everyone in Mayfair hates us."

"They admire us," JJ corrected, "and rightfully so. Right, Father?"

Father shrugged and gave a mumbled reply.

While the family continued to debate, Tom became lost in his own thoughts. He imagined himself striking West like he was the intrepid Merriweather Lewis. Maybe he'd become an Indian fighter like those he read about in dime novels. Out there in the wild, there were no halfwit baby brothers whining or old mammies telling you what to do. Out there, a boy — a *man*, rather — had only himself to answer to, and to hell with everyone else. Out there lay danger, fortune, adventure, and one fantastic story to tell when he returned — *if* he decided to return. If he came back, he would be rich (richer than now, at least) — oh, and handsome too (more handsome than now). And little Penelope Cutler, who had rejected his marriage proposal at Sunday school two weeks ago? She would beg to have his attention again, and when he refused *her*, he'd watch her jump into the Sleepy Creek and drown herself. Oh, happy times! The more he considered all these possibilities, the more they felt like certainties.

"While we're on the topic of good news," JJ said, "I suspect you all have your thoughts about the events at Harper's Ferry?"

Hearing this, Jem and Ben turned to face each other.

"Oh no," Sarah groaned. "Here we go again..."

Jem pointed his thumb over at Ben. "This one thinks we locked up the wrong criminals."

Ben shook his head. "I never said that."

"But you mean it, don't you?"

"I'm interested in what JJ thinks," Ben replied.

JJ shrugged. "If you're suggesting the slave-owners John Brown tried to round up and kill are themselves criminals, well, you'd have a tough time convincing most folks of that."

"Only folks down here," Ben said. "I'd wager over half the country thinks exactly that."

Father heaved a sigh. "Be careful you don't inflate a few Republican news editorials with majority opinion."

"Slavery is not altogether moral in my estimation," JJ said, "but it *is* the law of the land. And since I swore to defend the flag of the United States, including all the laws it represents, then it doesn't matter to me if a rebel owns slaves or not. A traitor is a traitor."

"Amen," Jem agreed. "And a patriot is a patriot, so long as he defends the principles of American democracy."

Now it was Ben's turn to shrug. "Except it seems no one can agree on what those principles are, or what they ought to mean in practice. We couldn't agree before the Revolution, nor after it, and we still can't agree now."

"There is always the opportunity for compromise," Father noted. "After all, democracy *is* compromise. What is the alternative? Admit we exist in a state of anarchy, and go at each other's throats like animals?"

"It seems to me we're doing just that," Ben said. "We should stop pretending. We should set self-interest aside and acknowledge that there is an objective *right way* of thinking about this issue."

"Hoe your own row," Jem said. "That's the only right way. It's not for one mind, or even one small collection of minds, to decide what is best for everyone, everywhere, at all times."

Ben shook his head. "You wouldn't say that if you were born in one of those shacks on the back lawn."

"Of course I would," Jem said. "King or slave, it doesn't matter. We don't choose the hand we're dealt. But a poor hand can still win the pot."

Ben sighed. "Sure, and a broken clock is still right twice a day."

JJ said, "You're both missing the point about John Brown."

Ben and Jem looked at him. "Which is what?" Ben asked.

Watching from his chair, Tom saw that JJ's answer was directed as much toward Father as it was to the others.

"It seems there will always be an impulse to condemn higher authority," JJ said. "But the fact remains that every society, in order to function peacefully, needs a nightwatchman to keep guard. Sometimes the nightwatchman is a tyrant, but we in America would rather prefer he serve *us*, not himself. Still, we must surrender some of our own liberties so that he may exert protective power."

"And what's your point?" Jem said. "Is this more philosophy from Yankeeland?"

JJ sighed. "My point, is that those who would try to delegitimize a freely-elected authority, or else try to usurp that authority, are enemies of the American people. That's not opinion — that's fact. Was John Brown's cause righteous, as you suggest, Ben? Perhaps. But as soon as he committed violence against his citizens who had committed no violence against *him*, he lost all claim to any moral high ground. As far as I'm concerned he's scum, no better than Benedict Arnold. Still, I don't doubt that, while he was busy murdering and terrorizing his own countrymen, John Brown believed he was a true American patriot. In my estimation, that is the most dangerous traitor of all."

With a shrug, Jem held out his wine glass with a grin. "It seems we don't agree on much anymore, but I'll drink to that."

From down the table, Sarah smiled and said, "You'd make a fine politician someday, JJ."

Hearing this, JJ turned to Father and smiled. "That reminds me of something, in fact." Turning to Ben now, he said, "Mr. Freeman. Are you still reading every scrap of paper you can get your hands on?"

Ben laughed. "Most of them, yes."

Reaching into the inside pocket of his uniform, JJ produced a newspaper cutout. "Read that aloud for everyone, would you, Ben? Since we're still on the topic of good news."

"My, of course." Ben accepted the clipping, which showed the front page of yesterday's copy of the *Winchester Advertiser*.

"I picked it up on my way home," JJ said proudly. "I know we're more of a *Mayfair First Witness* family, but I thought the leading story would be of keen interest."

Tom looked up from his plate and caught a glimpse of the front-page headline, printed in bold letters:

THE HERO OF HARPER'S FERRY

"Is this the one?" Ben asked, pointing at the lead article.

JJ caught Tom's eye and winked at him from across the table. "That's the one."

Clearing his throat, Ben began to read. The article was a summary of the bloody events up at Harper's Ferry. Tom listened, registering only every other word. He had only a vague understanding of *why* what had happened there *had* happened, that somehow renegade slaves and Yankees had been involved. Some folks thought that some other folks called Republicans had organized the whole thing. Earlier that day, Billy Clements had told Tom that the rebel leader, a Satan-worshiper named John Brown, had cut out the heart of a man and fed it raw to the negroes under his command. Of course Tom didn't believe such nonsense, but he had to admit that such a grisly act was at least *possible*.

Ben's recitation continued. Suddenly he stopped, reread the next section in silence, and turned to JJ with a look of disbelief.

JJ nodded. "Go ahead."

After clearing his throat a second time, Ben read aloud:

"This editor has the duty to report that one of Virginia's own, Jonathan Roscoe of Mayfair, led the charge that ended John Brown's reign of terror."

Everyone at the table now went very still. Their shoulders hunched, and they hung on every word that followed.

"According to Colonel Robert Lee, the operation's commanding officer, the attack on

Brown's stronghold was executed and concluded with utmost expediency, and with relatively few casualties. 'At the threshold one soldier fell mortally wounded,' Lee said. 'The rest, led by one Lieutenant Roscoe, quickly ended the contest. The insurgents who resisted were bayoneted. Their leader, John Brown, was cut down by the sword of Lieutenant Roscoe, and all hostages were rescued by officers and enlisted men. The whole was over in but a few minutes.'"

Mother let out a quiet gasp. Even Father was shaken by the revelation. And for Tom, he was grinning from ear to ear. JJ had captured John Brown! And that meant...well, that had to mean—

"You're *famous?*" Tom said.

JJ laughed, but it was clear he liked the idea. "Maybe so. Not as famous as Mr. Brown, that's for sure."

But not everyone wore a dazed smile of wonderment. Jem shook his head slowly, his face registering disbelief and the first shadows of frustration. "*Lieutenant* Roscoe? But that doesn't make any...how can that—?"

"Laws!" Tom shouted. "Tell us how many Yankees you killed, JJ!" He brought up an imaginary musket and shot out one of the candles on the table, imagining it to be John Brown himself.

"*You hush,*" Sarah hissed. "That's no talk for the table, Tom."

When Tom stuck his tongue out, Sarah leaned over and rapped his wrist to censure him. They squabbled and picked at each other for several furious moments before Mae Jane demanded an immediate ceasefire. Order was grudgingly resorted, for now.

JJ now turned to Father with a broad smile. "This is my gift to you, Father."

Father's face registered genuine surprise, a rare look for him. "Gift?"

JJ nodded. "Go on, Ben."

Ben kept reading: "*While the elusive Lieutenant Roscoe was not available for comment, rumors abound as to the identity of this unswerving hero. One possibility is that Roscoe, being from Mayfair, is more than likely a close relative of Virginia's eminent Senator John Roscoe (D), a man who has long sought to keep the forces of abolitionism in check. Our editor has dispatched a correspondent to the Valley to confirm the truth of this information. What we know is true already is that Senator Roscoe stands as one of the few stalwart men in Congress who stands against violent radicalism in the name of peace, prosperity, and Union. Might this conquering hero be the noble senator's son? While we verify the extent of the relation between the two men, let it be said by at least one publication that, truly, the high-blooded spirit of patriotism runs hot in Roscoe veins.*"

Finished, Ben set the newspaper clipping down on the table. A brief silence passed, and then JJ stood up. Using his chair as a sort of pulpit, he addressed the whole family together.

"If properly endorsed," JJ said, "that article could be printed and reprinted in dailies all across the Union. All we need do is meet with that correspondent and confirm that, indeed, it was Senator John Roscoe's son who defeated the anti-government rebels."

From his seat down the table, Tom studied Father's reaction. The old man began to blink a great deal (and so far as Tom could tell, Father never paused to *blink*). Father's sunken cheeks turned a dark purple, and suddenly Tom realized this was Father's manner of blushing from pride.

"From Mayfair to the Dakotas," JJ went on, "and at all points of the compass in between, millions of people will read the name 'Roscoe' and regard it with pride and honor." Turning to Father once more, JJ said, "They will regard our *family* with pride and honor here at home, and perhaps even at our Missouri home too. Certainly, Washington will look most favorably upon this news."

Here, JJ was compelled to hang his head for a long moment of silence.

"I know how I hurt this family, years ago," JJ said, his voice quieter now. "I know I will need to do much to repair the damage I wrought as a child. But let this"—and he lifted the clipping from the table, and to Tom it looked like a flag of truce—"let this be the first of a *man's* reparations for a boy's failures."

JJ seemed to speak only to Father now, as if Tom and the others were not even there. Indeed, JJ began to step closer to Father. He set the clipping down before Father as if it were a kingly gift.

"Everything I have to give, I give to my family. Whatever may be asked of me, I will see it done. Whatever object is required, I will procure it. Whatever ambition, I will realize it."

When JJ was finished, a thick silence hung over the table. If JJ had been expecting some kind of response from Father, Father was very slow in giving one. And the longer the silence persisted, the less it seemed that Father was going to say anything at all. The proud smile on JJ's face became plastered there, even while his eyes glazed over from the strain of waiting, waiting, waiting...

Suddenly, Tom laughed. He had no idea why — maybe in reaction to the strangling awkwardness of the moment — but laugh he did. Though it was only a quiet titter, it was enough to invite a wrathful glare from JJ that nailed Tom to the back of his chair.

"What's so *funny* about it?" JJ seethed. His whole manner had changed in an instant, from warm-hearted charm to cold, ugly spite.

Tom's stillborn laughter churned in his guts. He shook his head and mumbled a sorry sort of answer.

Finally breaking the silence was Jem, who shook his head in disbelief. "I still don't understand it," he said. "You're not a lieutenant. You're not an officer of any kind."

Exasperated, JJ turned to Jem. Before JJ could provide an answer, Mae Jane clapped her hands together with a laugh.

"Wonderful, Jon Jacob, just wonderful! We's all *very* proud!"

Sarah nodded in agreement. "You'll be the toast of tonight's ball!" she said.

"Ball?" JJ whitened and turned to her, with something like panic in his eyes. "*Here?!*"

"Of course not *here*," Sarah said, as if it were obvious. "Wyolah Hall, same as it's been for years. A ball for the civilized, and a harvest dance for the commons. *Everyone's* going to be there, JJ. Even the colored folk will be dressed up." She beamed at JJ. "And no doubt our brave lieutenant will be the guest of honor!"

JJ seemed to be barely listening to her, the color only just beginning to return to his face. It wasn't until Ben leaned over and touched JJ's shoulder that JJ came back to life.

"Whatever one may think of events at Harper's Ferry," Ben said, "whatever the consequences may be, right now it doesn't matter." He offered his hand to JJ. "I'm just glad you made it through safe and sound, brother."

There was some muted agreement around the table, but then Father cleared his throat and announced, with a touch of pride in his voice:

"Hear-hear. We're all very glad for you, Jonathan."

No one said anything for a long moment, while in his chair JJ began to tremble. Meanwhile, Father wore a shaky, uneven smile, as if he had just landed on a decision about which he was still uncertain.

Father fumbled for a glass of wine. He had barely touched the wine all evening, for Father never drank unless it was, as he said, "on purpose." He held the glass out to JJ in a sort of toast, and Father's smile broadened. Secretly, Tom wished the smile was for him.

"You did well, Jonathan. You've done very well by our family." Father held his glass aloft. "To the Roscoe family."

"To the Roscoes!" the Freemans said together.

"The Roscoes," JJ said, his voice choked with emotion.

For her part, Mother murmured, "Spencers..."

"*The Roscoes*!" Tom shouted with Sarah, and grinning they cheersed each other with glasses of water. A laughing Bayard joined in too, offering his glass in approval.

Jem pounded the table. "Now just *hold on*!" he shouted over the rattle of dishes. "I can't damn well think straight. You're still a *cadet*, aren't you, JJ? How is it a cadet — a *boy* — came to command all those soldiers?"

Puffed up by so many compliments, JJ's reply to Jem was dismissive.

"What of it? My country was in need. I found myself on the same train as the soldiers assigned to stop John Brown's rebels. They had no leader, and so I answered the call of duty. Besides, I'll be commissioned as a lieutenant when I graduate next year anyway. What's a few months in the difference?"

Jem frowned. "Impersonating an officer of the United States Army is the difference. You could be charged with treason, and your being a 'hero' might not be enough to prevent a conviction."

Sarah laughed. "It sounds like someone is just jealous."

"I resent that," Jem growled.

"I impersonated nothing and no one," JJ said. "This was an emergency. Through Colonel Lee, I was following orders from President Buchanan himself. The real traitors are John Brown and his men, and they've been charged as such. There's a criminal trial starting next week over in Charles Town, and I plan to be there. I plan to be there when they hang Brown too, as a matter of fact."

From the head of the table, Father looked up again. "You mean you don't plan on returning to New York?"

JJ turned to address Father directly. "Oh, certainly, sir. I fully intend on finishing my studies." Here, JJ tested a hopeful smile. "Unless, perhaps, you've made other arrangements in the meantime? Perhaps you need someone to establish the Company's presence in St. Louis?"

Father's face became stonelike once again. The loving emotion that had overtaken him a moment ago cooled and faded.

"I see," Father said. "Well, of course, I've made no official decisions just yet. Nothing good may happen before its proper time, of course."

JJ's smile weakened. "Of course, Father."

"We will talk about it tomorrow," Father said. His featureless expression hinted at some meager assurance, though assurance it was. Father thought about it some more, and then he nodded. "Yes, tomorrow will do. You and I will go for a walk through the grove.

JJ's smile returned; he was positively beaming. "The grove? That sounds fine, Father. Oh, that sounds very fine."

Mae Jane stood up and clapped her hands. "Seems everybody enjoyed they sup," she said. "Now, how bout some dessert?"

"Oh, no," Sarah said, pushing back from the table. "We're terribly late for the Claibornes' party as it is. Are you ready to go, Daddy?"

Tom flinched as Father was stricken by a series of violent coughs. After clearing his throat, Father reached for his cane and stood up shakily.

"I'm not ready to leave just yet. I've some business to attend to first. Ben? Fetch something to write with and meet me in my study. *No visitors*. We're not to be disturbed."

"But *Daddy*!" Sarah cried. "What about the ball and barbecue?!"

Father shook his head and departed without giving an answer.

After Father had gone, Tom turned to Sarah and pretended to faint. "*But Daddy*!"

Sarah bunched up her napkin and hurled it at him. "Shut up, you little monster." She glared at the twins now, and Ben too. "Oh, you boys and your stupid politics.

You've gone and upset Daddy somehow. Now we won't get to the barbecue for, what, another hour? I don't even want to go anymore. I'd rather stay home than show up so horribly *late*."

Dishes rattled as Sarah pushed away from the table and stormed out of the dining room.

After Sarah had gone, JJ whistled. "Seems some things haven't changed."

Jem shrugged and drained the last of his wine. Ben soon excused himself and departed so he could join Father in his study down the hall. After a few moments, Mother stood up to leave. The Roscoe boys — Tom included — were obliged to stand up in recognition. Mother went to Bayard and took the boy's hand, and they left together.

"Mother certainly loves Bayard," JJ observed in a quiet voice.

"Only because he won't talk back," Tom said.

The twins each gave a dry laugh, and Tom laughed with them, but then he felt Mae Jane's watchful eyes on him. The old mammy had begun to clear the table, stacking dirty dishes atop one another. The twins took this as their cue to depart together, each complimenting Mae Jane on a fine meal. They both reached the door at the same time, and neither looked willing to make way for the other. Grimacing, they managed to slip through the door side by side.

Now there remained only Tom together with Mae Jane. Sensing the formation of an awkward silence, Tom pushed back from the table.

"May I be excused?"

But it wasn't a question; he made haste to quit the dining room altogether and catch up with the twins. He pushed his chair in, thinking this little show of good manners might provide sufficient cover for him to—

"Thomas?"

He froze, his hands still on the chair, poised to push. "Yes, Mae Jane?"

A brief silence. Then: "About what you said earlier. That *word*."

Tom stared down at his feet. He believed he knew what she wanted to hear. "I'm sorry, Mae Jane. I won't say it again, not ever, I promise."

Mae Jane sighed. "I don't want you *promises*, Thomas. If you gonna promise anythin, promise you ain't gonna push you brother round no more."

"But he started—"

"I ain't barterin with you, Thomas. He don't know no better."

"*Fine*. I promise, I won't push Bayard around anymore."

"Thank you." Mae Jane held her arms out wide. "Will you give me a hug, Tommy?"

Tom grimaced. "Do I *have* to?"

Mae Jane smiled. "I know I'd appreciate it." She beckoned him again.

Slowly, Tom trudged around the table and allowed himself to be pulled into Mae

Jane's wiry grasp. She smelled of lye soap and her clothes were rough to the touch. Pressed against her, Tom felt a stiffness in the old lady's bones begin to melt away. It was like touching a statue and feeling it come to life, hearing its stone heart begin to swell and beat the rhythm of living. All the while, Tom's arms remained at his sides like the stitched limbs of a doll. Mae Jane sighed and squeezed Tom tighter for just a moment longer, as if she might hold him there forever. But then she finally let go. When Tom pulled back, he thought he saw tears in his old mammy's eyes.

"What's wrong?"

"Oh!" she said, wiping at her eyes and laughing a little. "Nothin's wrong, Tommy — Mr. Thomas, I mean. Well now. Ain't you gettin so tall? And so strong? You older now, just like you brothers. I s'pect that means I should start addressin you as a man, hm? It'll be 'Mr. Thomas' from now on."

Tom shook his head. "I don't like that name."

"It's a fine name, Tomm—Mr. Thomas. You learn to like it, you see."

"Yeah."

Mae Jane drew a sharp breath and returned to her work. "Well, lots to be done. Lots to be done..."

"Mae Jane?"

She turned and looked at him. "Yes, Mr. Thomas?"

Tom's voice failed him for a moment. Damn, was *he* getting choked up too? He fought through it, stamping the raw feeling down, and finally he managed: "I'm sorry again. For what I said. For what I called you. I swear to you, I ain't a bad kind of person."

Mae Jane reached out and touched his cheek, and with her thumb she caressed his skin, still soft and babylike. "No you ain't," she said, her voice barely above a whisper. "You ain't a bad person. There ain't nobody in the world who's all one kind, Tommy."

"Mr. Thomas," he corrected, with a small smile.

Mae Jane laughed. "Get on with you."

"Yes, ma'am."

Tom went out to the hallway. For whatever reason, his instincts gave him pause. Turning back, he crept toward the dining room and looked in. There, sitting alone amidst the empty chairs strewn about and heaps of abandoned dishes on the table, Mae Jane was bent over her head in her hands. Maybe she was praying, or maybe crying (except Mae Jane always proclaimed that she didn't know how to cry).

Tom felt an urge to go back into the dining room, just to check. He wouldn't ask Mae Jane what she was thinking about. She wouldn't have to say anything to him at all. Just as long she knew he was there, that she wasn't alone.

In any case, Tom didn't go back. Instead he crept away, moving slowly at first and then faster. By the time he reached his bedroom, he forgot about Mae Jane and thought only of his toy soldiers scattered on the floor. Tonight, he decided that he, Colonel Thomas Roscoe, was going to win the American Revolution single-handedly.

Chapter 8

OF DANCES AND DEBUTANTES

Lord help her, Sarah Roscoe prayed that tonight would not be a complete and utter disaster.

It wasn't embarrassing enough that the Roscoes had arrived so horribly late to Wyolah Hall, all tumbling out of their rickety coach like a company of serfs. And it wasn't embarrassing enough that Jem was already drunk by the time they got there, or that Daddy had sunken into such a morose mood when the night was supposed to be gay and carefree. And it wasn't embarrassing enough that JJ had eschewed a tailored suit in favor of his mud-caked, ill-fitting uniform, ostensibly because he was the 'hero of Harper's Wherever' and wanted everyone to know about it. Sarah had done her best to clean JJ up on the drive over, but only so much could be done to turn a pig into a prince.

"I thought *I* was the pig," Jem said to Sarah. "That's what you always call me."

"I do, and you are," Sarah replied, still furiously trying to polish JJ's brass buttons. "JJ might look worse for wear, but at least he doesn't look like a down-and-out tramp."

Jem grinned. "I'll take that as a compliment."

A small army of Wyolah Hall servants in Claiborne livery greeted the Roscoes when they arrived. The servants kept their eyes fixed on distant points as the Roscoe men passed, but Sarah noticed that their eyes flickered to Ben Freeman as soon as they deemed it safe to stare. Several of the servants scowled openly at Ben, though their faces turned to stone when they became aware of Sarah's eyes on them. It was strange, this behavior between blacks, and Sarah couldn't make heads nor tails of it.

Feeling the weight of all those staring eyes, Ben tucked his head low between his shoulders. But when Sarah touched his arm, he perked up again.

Sarah asked, "Are you all right, Ben?"

"Me? Oh, I'm fine. All's well. It's nice to have everyone home again."

Sarah spied a small leather bag tucked under Ben's arm. "What's that for?" she asked. "You fancy yourself a burglar or something?"

Ben laughed. "It's for your father." His smile faded a little, and he wouldn't elaborate further.

"I see," Sarah said, and then she did her best impression of a South Branch planter. "It's a *gentleman's business*, hm? Don't ask, old sport, and don't you dare tell."

Ben laughed again. "Something like that."

They all paused before the great doors of the Hall, which was an ornate structure built of fine red brick. From within came the sounds of chamber music, laughter, and a thousand cordial conversations.

Daddy turned to the boys. "Consult your pocket watches."

Dutifully, JJ and Ben each produced a watch; Jem gawked at Daddy a moment before he patted his pockets and turned around in circles, as if he'd dropped his own watch somewhere between here and the several miles back to Clarendon.

"For God's sake, never mind," Daddy said. "Ben will take Sarah and myself home at one o'clock. If you two boys are not waiting near the coach at that time, you will have to find your own way home. I shan't wait for you."

JJ agreed and gave an obedient nod, while Jem said nothing. Just now, Jem perked up at the soaring cry of a fiddle somewhere behind Wyolah Hall. From that direction, Sarah could hear laughter and drunken shouts punctuating the wild music. With a gleeful grin, Jem turned and made a beeline for the back lawn.

"Wait!" Sarah protested. "Jeremiah, can't you commit even *five minutes* to civilized society? We must pay our respects to the Clairbornes and—"

"I'll be along in a few minutes!" Jem called, not breaking his stride. "You-all run along and I'll be with you shortly." With that, he disappeared around the corner of the house.

Ben gave a quiet laugh and shook his head. "He won't be back."

JJ, who was still watching the empty space where Jem had disappeared around the corner, didn't say anything.

"Well," Daddy muttered. "At least I won't have to suffer the stench of his gin-breath." Brightening a little, he offered his arm to Sarah and she took it. "Sarah, my rose. Come along, and let us inside."

❧

The Roscoes entered a grand hallway that was all but deserted. Two servants slouching before the door flinched and shot upright, as if they had not been expecting any more guests, and certainly not so late into the festivities. Sarah's stomach, which had been churning from worry all the way to the Hall, went numb at the realization that her family's lateness was now well beyond fashionable.

"They've already *begun*," Sarah moaned, wanting to wail her lament to the vaunted ceilings.

"Hush," Daddy said, and he guided them forward, his cane *thump-thumping* on the Persian runner that stretched down the hallway.

They neared a wide archway that led into Wyolah Hall's main ballroom. There were shadowy figures milling about the arch whose heads now turned to the sound of newcomers. At first, Sarah thought the eyes of the other guests were admiring her. (And if she was being honest, she believed they *ought* to be.) But instead, their eyes were staring at Daddy. And just now, some of those eyes narrowed.

Sarah felt Daddy tense up under the weight of stares, watched him flash his usually charming smile at so many blank faces. Why should so many guests look upon Daddy with, well, with such *distaste*? Daddy was their senator after all (a title she knew precious little about except to know it was IMPORTANT), and therefore Daddy was deserving of respect and deference. Never before had Sarah seen any of Daddy's constituents look upon him with anything less than gratitude and wonderment. Looking closer at the guests, Sarah realized their eyes flickered from Daddy to JJ and back again.

Could *that* be it?

Thankfully, all those staring eyes and heads turned away again, for within the ballroom floated the voice of a single speaker. A speech of some kind was being delivered.

As she stepped into the light and looked into the ballroom, Sarah saw a great host of ladies and gentlemen dressed in colorful finery. Here and there stood handsome black servants in tailored broadcloth. Hundreds of candles glittered from chandeliers high overhead, casting everyone in a warm, angelic glow.

Standing upon the third step of a great staircase was the evening's resplendent host, Mr. Clay Claiborne, basking in the rosy attention of all present.

"Ladies and gentlemen," Mr. Claiborne said, beaming. "I want to take this opportunity to welcome you-all to Wyolah Hall for this evening's festivities. It's my sincere pleasure to have each and every one of you here with us tonight."

Sighs of pleasure and gratitude rose up from the crowd, and Mr. Claiborne's smile broadened.

"There's a special someone in the audience here tonight who deserves recognition..."

As he spoke, Mr. Claiborne looked several of his guests in the eye. Presently, his gaze seemed to linger over the place where Sarah and Daddy stood. Sarah felt Daddy twitch with anticipation.

"There's a gentleman here tonight who has been ever loyal, ever committed, to our beautiful Valley home and especially to our traditions. What's more, he's been a very good friend to me, and to many others, for as long as I can remember. I'd humbly ask you-all to thank this man tonight."

Smiling, Daddy let go of Sarah's arm and started forward to be recognized.

But Mr. Claiborne now gestured in the opposite direction, toward a gray-haired black man standing below the staircase.

"My Uncle Jupiter has organized such a *fine* evening for us tonight. Won't you thank him with me? Go on now, do be kind."

All at once, the ladies and gentlemen of the ball applauded the bashful black man, who was the butler of Wyolah Hall.

Sarah felt Daddy freeze up beside her, as if he'd forgotten how to breathe. His eyes darted all around in search of disapproving glances. Then, his movements sharp and jerking, Daddy bashed his palms together and insisted on clapping louder than all the others around him.

The butler named Jupiter wore a red ribbon on his lapel that indicated he was 'prominent among negroes.' The guests' applause was endearing, as if the people were cheering a prize-winning dog.

"And truly," Mr. Claiborne went on, "what is a negro without his mistress? Who has a better mind in the Valley for hosting such fine soirées? Take a bow, if you please, Mrs. Claiborne."

The pomp and circumstance went on, but Daddy had evidently had enough. Turning to Sarah, he whispered, "I trust you'll be fine from here, my dear. There's important work that needs tending."

Sarah smiled and squeezed his hand. "Of course, Daddy." In fact, she'd been waiting for this very chance to break off and strike out on her own. All her friends were out there in the crowd, and all those handsome bachelors too.

"You don't need Ben to escort you?"

Somehow she felt Ben's eyes watching her meaningfully, but she shook her head. What good would it do, trying to find a dance partner with a shadow following her around?

"Mary Beth Merrick is here somewhere, Daddy. She'll be my escort."

A final applause sounded; Mr. Claiborne's speech had finally drawn to a close. While he clapped his hands, his expression soured by embarrassment and impatience, Daddy nodded his curt assent.

"Very well. Off you go then."

Beaming, Sarah turned away, remembering to avoid Ben's gaze just in case he was still looking at her. (He was.)

Sarah wove her way into the crowd just as the assembly of guests began to fracture and break up. She wound through the crush of bodies, pausing here and there to indulge the fawning greetings of certain boys who, while they were nice enough, she'd nevertheless dismissed as improper matches long ago.

Presently, a string ensemble took up their bows and instruments and began to play. Almost at the same time, the dance began. Prim ladies and gentlemen of Mayfair's First Families joined together and danced in sweeping circles. There were guests from 'beyond the Branches' as well, including young ladies and bachelors from as far away as Richmond and Fredericksburg, and even from distant Baltimore. A long table filled with delectables had been ransacked and refilled and then ransacked again.

According to Mr. Claiborne, he had instructed Wyolah Hall's chief architect to build the 'Tuileries of America.' A grand staircase, polished and shining, ascended into the domed heavens above. The entryways were adorned with Greek pillars and Roman arches. The works of German romanticists and English realists enriched the walls, while the floors were furnished with Bourbon French furniture and Oriental rugs. A massive agrarian scene inked on wallpaper stretched across the entire hall in a style to rival the tapestry at Bayeux.

"All rather grand," Sarah heard some of the guests say, "though a bit lacking in cohesive good taste."

As she swept from room to room, a voice in Sarah's head made a flurry of demands and instructions. Keep the head up, chin out — *not that much*. Shoulders back and down; gentlemen don't want a hunchbacked troll. Arms out and hands clasped together — *must cover that hideous paunch*. Suck in, don't let it out. And remember to SMILE.

Percy Claiborne had committed three dances to Sarah, and she was very much looking forward to them. Percy was as fine a catch as the Valley could produce. But looking around, she saw no sign of Percy anywhere. As she spotted some new guests arriving, she reassured herself that some handsome bachelor would soon approach and ask for her attention.

At one point Sarah's eyes met those of Sam Hanley, a boyish young man who was heir to another South Branch plantation. Sam beamed at her, but she quickly averted her gaze and hurried on. She wanted no attention from *him*, that was for certain. Poor Sam had professed his undying love to Sarah a few weeks ago, with an earnestness that would have been gut-bustingly funny were it not so, well, so *sad*. When she explained to him that, "It would never work between us," or some such excuse, the boy had broken down weeping. Weeping! Well, Sarah was sure she'd dodged a bullet all right. It wasn't like she was a heartless person. A fellow like Sam Hanley was handsome of course, but handsome in the way a *horse* is handsome. Poor Sam just couldn't seem to understand that.

Still, the longer Sarah searched for a beau, the more she despaired. She was older than almost every other debutante at the ball, and instead of drawing the attention of the young bachelors prowling the ballroom she instead had the undivided (and unwanted) attention of leering widowers, some of them even older than Daddy. She started to wonder just what was *wrong* with her.

Did she still carry the stain of Richard Harper, perhaps?

Sarah had been infatuated with a boy named Richard Harper several years ago, but — oh, forget it, she didn't want to think about any of *that* right now. She needed to find herself a dance partner!

Sarah reminded herself not to look so desperate. People could smell desperation on a girl, especially as she grew older. Then again, Sarah reminded herself she wasn't *old* at all. She was only twenty-three...

Ah, but soon to be twenty-four! This was the voice of Cousin Isabella mocking Sarah in the space between her ears. *Meanwhile those girls across the floor are no older than seventeen, perky everywhere, and with five salivating bachelors apiece.*

Upon returning to Clarendon from Richmond, Sarah had promised herself that she would cease to be a Roscoe (such a rough, uncivilized name) come next autumn. By that time she wished — no, she *demanded* — that fate would take her away from Clarendon and into the home of a new family, a dynasty with bonafide roots, as close to perfect as any family could be. And then she would finally be happy and content, and held in the loving arms of a great man.

But just who *was* that man? And why hadn't he arrived yet?

Across the vast room, from behind a parlor door, ashen-faced women in black peered out at the fun and festivities. These were the patrician widows of Mayfair who mourned dead husbands. Though a gentleman who lost his wife was welcome (and indeed encouraged) to soothe his fractured soul by pursuing a young debutante, it was custom in the Valley — or strange torture, in Sarah's estimation — to cordon widowed women off from larger celebrations as if they were a community of lepers.

Widows young and old could share only in the company of other widows, and always tucked away in some obscure corner. Some of the widows were no older than eighteen. Some had been brides not six months earlier, until their husbands died from typhus or measles or just plain bad luck. For these women, these *girls*, there would be no more parties, no more dancing, no more chances to be young again. The only world they knew had shut itself against them, maybe forever.

As Sarah studied those poor girls who looked so much like quarantined shut-ins, she felt the grip of anxiety around her heart. What if she should *never* find a match? What if she remained *Spinster Sarah* forever? What if her case became so desperate that she was locked up with the widows, never again to dance or flirt or be wooed? Just as she considered this desolate future, an older widow stepped forward and put her hand on the parlor's sliding door. She looked at the teenage widows and shook her head with a knowing sorrow, and then she slid the door shut.

While Sarah was still searching desperately for a means of distraction from a hundred worst-case scenarios, she felt JJ step up beside her.

"Do you mind if I join you?" JJ said. He had a nervous, fish-out-of-water look in his eyes that was most unusual for him. "I haven't been to a ball like this in, well, since the last time I was home, I should think. Everyone looks much older than before."

"Mhm." Sarah was trying to distract herself by critiquing the styles and cuts of the other debutantes' dresses.

JJ was also scanning the room, as if looking for someone in particular. "Do the… um, does the Harper family still frequent these events?"

Sarah gave a start, as if she had just realized JJ was there beside her. "Pardon? Oh, wait — oh, *look*!" With a gleeful laugh, she rushed across the ballroom. "Mary Beth! Mary Beth, my darling, hello!"

Across the dance floor, a rosy-cheeked girl waved and shrieked with delight as Sarah approached. Mary Beth Merrick was Sarah's dearest friend. She was a planter's daughter who had never wanted for anything in her entire life and was rather used to having men, including her father, wrapped around her finger. Mary Beth was plump, though no less beautiful. This was the first time Sarah had seen her friend in several months.

After embracing, the girls talked excitedly together. They showered compliments upon each other, remarking upon the beauty of their respective gowns and hairstyles and makeup and jewelry and on and on and on. Sarah grimaced a little when she felt JJ step up beside her once more, fearing that his presence might drive Mary Beth off.

Instead, Mary used JJ's arrival as an excuse to introduce the beau on her arm, a handsome lawyer from Richmond named Chandler Wise.

"He's the governor's nephew," Mary added with a knowing smile.

"The governor is *my* uncle," Chandler corrected.

Chandler kissed Sarah's hand, and she smiled and offered a polite curtsy in return. The boy was really rather ugly in her estimation, with beady eyes and a grotesque head shaped like a tombstone. Still, being related to such an esteemed gentleman as the Governor of Virginia was evidently enough to make most girls (Mary, at least) overlook such an unfortunate feature.

Sarah nodded to JJ. "Mr. Wise, allow me to introduce my brother."

Chandler turned to shake JJ's hand. "Ah, yes. Jeremiah, is it? Roscoe Railroad Company? My uncle — that's *Governor* Wise — is very supportive of your family's efforts to—"

"JJ."

Chandler paused. "Pardon me?"

"My name is JJ Roscoe. *Lieutenant* Roscoe, as a matter of fact."

Chandler nodded. "Oh, I see. You must be Jeremiah's brother then."

"Certainly not." JJ flashed a grin. "Jem is *my* brother."

Chandler offered the weakest of obliging laughs, but the joke, bad as it was, had gone over his head.

JJ turned to Sarah. He wore a look that suggested he'd outstayed his welcome within the conversation. "Well now, I think I'll be off. People to see and…well, you know."

"Very well," Sarah said with a polite smile. "I'll be here."

JJ bid the others adieu and left their circle. No sooner had JJ gone than Mary Beth lunged forward and grabbed Sarah's hands.

"Since when did *he* get back?"

"Just this evening," Sarah said. "Isn't it wonderful? He's perhaps a bit out of touch socially, but..."

Mary Beth cast a watchful grimace after JJ. "He isn't...*diseased*, is he?"

Chandler looked down at his hand. "Diseased? What do you mean?"

"He's nothing of the sort," Sarah said, forcing a laugh. She turned and watched JJ work his way through the crowd. "He's just...well, I should think being in New York has been rather good for JJ. He has a good head on his shoulders now. I think he's truly sorry for what he did, for all the trouble he caused. In fact, I believe Daddy is even thinking of..."

Sarah's voice drifted when she turned back and saw Mary Beth whispering into Chandler's ear. Chandler's face turned gray and twisted with revulsion.

"And you let me *shake his hand*?"

Sarah pushed a pleasant smile across her lips and waited patiently for someone to change the subject.

❧

As the ball progressed, Sarah became hopelessly convinced that the whole affair really was a disaster.

It wasn't frustrating enough that perfect Pippa Claiborne, with her perfect teeth and perfect figure and perfect diction, had the undivided attention of every young man at Wyolah Hall. And it wasn't frustrating enough that Pippa's brother Percy was apparently down in the plantation yard lusting after some 'poor white trash' girls with loose morals. As more girls paired up with young bachelors, despair threatened to consume Sarah's mind. At this point she'd take anyone for a partner — even Sam Hanley.

Later on came the most crushing blow of the evening. Dora McGinley, that giggling little Irish monster from Mountain Falls, had arrived at the ball in the *exact same dress as Sarah now wore*. Not a similar dress. *The same dress*. Sarah had been more than certain that her ball gown — a shapely blue satin gown with cream-colored trim, cut low to show off her slender, milk-white shoulders, and with puffed sleeves that exposed her long, graceful arms — was one of a kind. *Unique*. Well, she supposed that such a word no longer qualified.

"I don't see the reason why we can't speak *alone*, Mary." That was Chandler Wise, still the governor's nephew and starting to become a real pain in the you-know-what. He was practically salivating over Mary Beth Merrick's massive bosom, which she'd taken great pains to showcase to perfection in a custom-fit basque shipped all the way from Baton Rouge.

Mary Beth pushed Chandler's leering face away from her. "Sarah is my closest and dearest friend, Chandler. I can't simply abandon her to the wolves." She wrinkled her cute button nose, the feature rated by most gentlemen her second best, or third if each breast was counted separately.

Sarah sighed. "I'd like to go home."

Chandler appeared positively relieved at the prospect of being alone with Mary. He extended his hand eagerly. "Well, it was nice meeting you and all, Miss Roscoe. Too bad our time was so short. Bonsoir!"

Mary glared at Chandler until he stepped back. She squeezed Sarah's hands. "Dear sister, you've only just arrived! What's wrong?"

Near tears, Sarah hung her head. "*Everything* is wrong."

Mary knew what to do. She turned to Chandler. "Help me find her a beau."

Sarah looked up suddenly, her glistening eyes hot with rage. "I don't need *another beau*," she snapped. "I have plenty already."

Chandler Wise laughed in the manner Sarah could only describe as a guffaw. "Plenty of bachelors waiting on your hand and foot, have you?" He made a show of searching the room like a sailor scanning an empty horizon. "Hmm, plenty indeed."

"There," Sarah said, pointing. "Sam Hanley asked me for a dance tonight."

They all looked across the room at Sam Hanley, who stood with nine or ten other infatuated suitors all staring puppy-eyed at a breathtaking Pippa Claiborne.

Chandler's eyebrows danced like waltzing caterpillars. "He seems a bit predisposed, don't you think?" He guffawed again, and Sarah suppressed the urge to strike him. Apparently everyone from Richmond guffawed when they laughed.

Chandler again insisted on going for a long walk in the garden, which could only mean one thing.

"I told you, I *can't*," Mary said. She had already adopted the faux-English accent of high Richmond society. She pronounced her *can't* as *caun't*.

For her part, Sarah considered it rather unbecoming for a young lady to take so quickly to a new man, and to change her personality so dramatically to try and impress him. But then, she'd learned in school that womanly love depended on adaptation and resilience. Still, however Sarah tried to rationalize, she couldn't help wanting to take Mary's hand and run away from Chandler, from everything, run upstairs somewhere and lock themselves in a room where she and Mary could forget everything *proper* and just be themselves, like they were little girls again.

But Mary Beth was simply adapting, and maybe she was right to do it. Maybe Chandler Wise was really worth it.

"Oh, please," Chandler drawled. "Let's find the girl a little boy to pull her hair and be done with it."

No. Sarah decided it. All the money in the world wouldn't make Chandler Wise any less of an ape. She wheeled on Chandler and scowled up at him.

"Pull the hair yourself, Mr. Wise. You'll find this girl has talons for fingernails."

Mary gasped, her face registering shock and delight.

Chandler retreated as if he'd been struck. "I've not heard a woman speak to me like *that,* ever in all my life." He tugged fitfully at his collar and bowed formally to Mary. "Miss Mary, I'm away to fetch a drink. When I return, I do hope you'll allow me to escort you through the garden"—and here he glowered at Sarah—*"alone, and undisturbed."*

Having made his point, Chandler Wise turned on his heels and stalked through the crowd.

Sarah watched him go and laughed. "Look at him walk." She performed a cruel pantomime. "Looks rather like a penguin, doesn't he?"

Mary giggled. "You are *bold,* Sarah Roscoe."

"Any of the weight on his bones is certainly not spared on brains," Sarah said.

"Likely it's kept somewhere far more tantalizing," Mary said.

Sarah rolled her eyes. "I should at least hope so, for your sake."

Mary traced a finger along her neckline down to her bosom. "Do you think he likes me?"

"Likes you? He positively drools over you. He's ready to propose. As long as you can keep him away from that garden, of course."

Mary smiled, her eyes cast inward. "I might let him take me."

Sarah's eyes went wide with shock. She grabbed Mary's hand. "You *wouldn't."*

"Oh, why not? He seems very fine, Sarah. *Very* fine indeed."

"I'm not concerned with *him,* Mary. Think clearly. There are *consequences."*

Mary laughed; it was very close to a guffaw. "Like what? I've far more to gain from a leisurely stroll through the rose-bushes with Mr. Wise than not going at all." She counted on her fingers. "A wealthy husband and pretty children, that's one and two. A beautiful house in Richmond, there's three. Four, the finest dressmakers in Virginia with shops all within a carriage ride away. And let's not forget the *real* reason for marrying a man in the first place." Now her face darkened with a mischievous grin. "Did you notice how tall Chandler is? A full head taller than most of these little Mayfair boys. It makes a girl wonder…"

Sarah shook her head. "Don't you dare go into that garden with him, Mary. People will find out. They will *talk.* You'll be disgraced, and no young gentleman will marry a girl who has blackened her father's name." She lowered her voice to a hoarse whisper. "And what if you *did* have a child? Chandler would abandon you, and you'd be left with"—she cast her eyes around for eavesdroppers—"a *bastard."*

"Oh, *pshaw!"* Mary cried. "You're only sour because no man has walked you through the garden."

"Exactly!" Sarah was nearly in hysterics. "Because I'd never let them!"

Mary gripped both of Sarah's hands. "Well then, dear sister, that's simply the difference between a girl like you and a woman like me. The truth is, I've been on a number of walks with a number of men."

Sarah snorted with laughter. She was not proud of her snort, but at least it was not a guffaw. "Indeed? A real lady of the night, are you, Mary? Who are these men, and tell me how many." Her mocking challenge suddenly evaporated. "Never with my brothers...?"

Mary squeezed Sarah's hands tighter. "Hush now, dear sister. Here comes the potato-eater."

They watched Dora McGinley float toward them flashing a dazzling white smile.

Sarah's voice dropped to a conspiratorial whisper. "Sadie Mae Armitage says she saw Dora and her mother enter the seamstress' shop right after I left. Sadie Mae says Dora asked for the *very same* gown."

Mary grimaced. "Oh, that rag is absolutely *hideous*." Instantly, Mary changed course and turned the grimace into an encouraging smile. "Oh, but not on you of course, Sarah-darling. On you the dress looks wonderful. It's only on the potato-eater that it looks like a smock."

Dora passed by the girls and smiled at them. "Hello, Sarah. Hello, Mary." Her voice had a pretty Irish lilt that the Mayfair girls considered sincerely distasteful.

Sarah and Mary said together, in smiling unison: "*Hello, Dora.*"

The three girls glowed, beaming at each other with fluttering eyes, and to the casual observer they appeared to be lifelong friends. They exchanged brief cordial pleasantries before Dora moved on. Sarah and Mary's cheerful smiles disappeared as soon as Dora turned her head.

"She didn't even mention the similarities of her dress," Sarah said with disbelief. "She thinks she can put a white bow in her hair and consider it *couture*."

"Those dirty, *dirty* Papists," Mary said. "Why we let them into our country at all is beyond me. No worse than darkies, says Daddy. Daddy thinks we should send the lot of them back to Dublin and make the Pope pay for all the tickets."

Sarah remembered their earlier conversation. "My brothers, Mary. Have you—?"

Mary winked at her. "Well, I once fancied JJ..."

Sarah groaned.

"...but he showed no interest at all," Mary went on. "Was rather odd, I should think. But I suppose it makes sense now, given what happened."

Sarah laughed nervously but said nothing. She only had a vague idea of THE INCIDENT that happened all those years ago, for Daddy refused any talk about it. Among Mayfair society there had been nasty whispers, but it was easier to close one's ears to such gossip. All Sarah knew was that JJ and her dear friend Richard Harper had committed what some called a 'sin against nature', and that the mere mention of the act inspired rank disgust among even the most open-minded members of the First Families. Sarah tried her best, then and now, not to ask questions, nor to even think about it. Richard had humiliated her after all, what with his sudden running away from the Valley like he was some sort of criminal. The Harpers were made into social outcasts, but what good had any of it done for *her?*

Looking around the ballroom, Sarah's eyes found JJ again. He was standing alone in the far corner watching the string ensemble and pretending to be intensely interested. Earlier that evening, Sarah's heart had leapt at seeing her brother again. But now that she stood with Mary, and now that she became aware of how the party guests looked at JJ and whispered, Sarah's cheeks reddened with shame.

But oh, what was she thinking? JJ was her *brother*. How could she feel ashamed? She loved him and accepted him for who he was, no matter what.

...But did she really believe all that?

A curious silence filled the air, and then Sarah realized that the musicians had ceased playing. Taking a silver fork to a crystal glass, Mr. Claiborne chimed for his guests' attention. Slowly, conversations faded and heads turned to look once more upon the party's host.

"Forgive my intrusion, ladies and gentlemen. Before we carry on, I have just a few words to impart. I know many of you have on your minds the troubling episode over in Harper's Ferry..."

Here, the guests turned their heads together. There was great activity of shaking heads and clicking tongues. Mr. Claiborne held a hand up in the air to redirect attention back to himself.

"But of course we have nothing to fear here in our beautiful Mayfair Valley. What's more, our proud Commonwealth of Virginia has nothing to fear. By extension, our noble Southland and the whole Union have been delivered. And for all this, I consider myself proud to say, we must thank one of the Valley's own."

The crowd gasped with delight. Evidently the latest news from Harper's Ferry had not yet reached every ear, but just now Mr. Claiborne gestured broadly in JJ's direction. As one body the whole crowd looked upon JJ standing alone in the corner.

"Here tonight," Mr. Claiborne said, "we are graced by the presence of a *hero*. Jonathan Roscoe, son of our honorable Senator John, led the final charge that broke the defenses of the rebel horde which had besieged Harper's Ferry. It was our own JJ who rescued several hostages, including one Mr. Lewis Washington, great grand-nephew of General Washington himself. Give us a wave, JJ, go on!"

With a weak smile, JJ held his hand out to the crowd. Under the weight of so many stares, JJ seemed to tremble under his uniform. Sarah wanted to rush over and take her brother's hand and lead him outside, to take him away from everyone. Mr. Claiborne meant well, surely, but she detected a mocking gleam in more than a few eyes among the party guests. Even while they indulged their host, their sneering derision was still visible below the surface.

Even now a curious smile flashed across Mr. Claiborne's lips, and Sarah had only begun to wonder what the smile meant before it vanished. Mr. Claiborne held his glass up high for all to see.

"I wish to make a toast. To our hero of Harper's Ferry, our hero of the Mayfair Valley. To JJ Roscoe: our *man* of the hour!"

Together, the crowd answered: *JJ Roscoe, man of the hour!*

Grinning lips pressed against glasses, and their contents washed down giddy laughter. Having finished his own drink, Mr. Claiborne beamed at JJ. For his part, JJ offered a weak nod of thanks.

"And now, my friends," Mr. Claiborne said, holding his hands out wide, "no more interruptions. Let us dance and make merry!"

The crowd applauded, showering praise and cheers upon their benevolent host. Meanwhile, JJ remained alone in the corner. No one approached him to extend their personal congratulations. As the musicians took up their instruments and began to play again, JJ began to search for an exit.

Feeling a clenching sensation around her heart, Sarah started toward JJ.

"Oh, maybe I should ask him to dance."

Mary was aghast. "No you will not!" She grabbed Sarah by the hand and held her back. "You will put that idea out of your mind, Sarah Roscoe. A girl waltzing with her brother is one thing. But if any of these bachelors see you giving the time of day to a filthy *sodo*..."

Catching herself, Mary blushed and trailed off.

"Well," Mary went on, "Mr. Claiborne made a nice speech and all. Perhaps JJ's recovered some face among the community...perhaps. But for *you*, dear sister, we must find you a real man to dance with."

Mary dragged Sarah toward the dance floor. Sarah planted her feet and tried to protest, but the tug-of-war was lost before it began.

In the midst of dancing couples who swept about the room in great circles, Mary's head swiveled back and forth. At last, her gaze fixed on a pair of glittering blue eyes watching them from across the room.

"There," Mary said, nodding. "Henry Cutler."

Sarah gasped, "*Henry Cutler?*" Her eyes searched the room with sudden desperation.

Mary blushed and looked down at the floor. "Oh, he's staring at me!"

At last, Sarah found the pair of blue eyes she sought. They glowed cold like ice, and at once they fixed upon her gaze so that she could not look away. She realized immediately that Henry Cutler was not looking at Mary Beth at all.

He was looking at *her*.

Sarah tore her eyes away and looked into her white-gloved hands.

"Oh!" Mary pouted. She pretended to ignore Henry's staring. "Can you believe the *nerve*? Doesn't he see I've been with Chandler all evening? When a man looks at you like that, you can tell right away what he's thinking about."

Sarah looked up again, attempting with great effort to appear aloof. She had lost Henry in the crowd. Scanning the faces moving through the hall, she at last saw those clear blue eyes again. Henry was speaking with a group of young men. When he laughed, his white teeth glittered.

Sarah sighed, "Henry Cutler."

How could she have forgotten about Henry Cutler? She'd even seen him earlier today in the town square. But of course, she never once thought he would ever be interested in *her*...

Suddenly, Sarah's chest tightened with jealousy. She squared on Mary and tried to steel herself for the worst. "Please, Mary, you must tell me. Of all the boys who you've...*walked* with..." Sarah looked back at Henry for a moment. "Was he one of them?"

"Of course," Mary said cheerily. "He's such a prize, isn't he? I simply had to. But oh, that was *years* ago, Sarah-darling." Mary turned away and groaned. "Is he still staring?" Now her face lit up with another of her mischievous grins. "I'll bet he has some rather fond memories of me."

Sarah's heart tightened with inexplicable rage. She wanted to slap Mary across the face and spit in her eye, and for a frightening moment she thought she just might do it. But in another moment the rage was gone, though her cheeks were still flaming hot. She tried to refocus by staring at Henry again. As she drank in the sight of him, she felt a wave of something — suddenly she realized the feeling was *desire* — wash over her.

He's such a prize, isn't he?

Well, yes, he certainly was.

Then Sarah realized her eyes had lingered too long. From across the room, Henry's gaze caught hers once again. He smiled and nodded.

She turned away again, blushing. She pulled at her gloved fingers to distract herself, but the two glowing blue eyes were seared in her vision. Sarah forgot about Mary, the guffawing Chandler Wise, the ball — everything. She only thought of Henry Cutler's eyes.

She had known Henry all her life, or at least had known *of* him. He was several years older than she. Oh, Henry had looked her way once or twice maybe, and even back then she noticed the cool glowing in his eyes. He had perhaps even spoken a word or two to her here and there, but she was too afraid, and in any case too young to speak to any young gentleman of consequence. She'd only been a silly girl in those times. Besides, Henry had always been more interested in the plump girls with the pretty smiles and something to touch. Raw pangs of jealousy stabbed at Sarah again as she considered that Mary might actually be telling the truth about her and Henry. She was his type, after all. Mary Beth Merrick was *every* man's type.

Years ago, and as Sarah thought about it she decided it must have been four, Henry left Mayfair. Yes, it was around the same time of JJ's INCIDENT. Henry went South to learn the delicate craft of negro-breaking on his uncle's okra plantation outside Corinth, Mississippi. Seasons passed, time stretched on. Once Sarah began school in Richmond, she had forgotten all about Henry Cutler.

But when he reappeared to her on the courthouse steps earlier today, he had been like a dark, handsome stranger emerging from those romance tales she adored as a little girl. The Mississippi sun had browned his skin to rich caramel. A muscled chest and broad shoulders stretching his jacket. And his eyes sparkled with the same blue fire as she remembered.

Sarah flinched at a nudge from Mary and heard the girl's whining voice ask if she was all right. Flustered, Sarah dismissed her curtly. Yes, of course she was all right. She saw the hurt in Mary's eyes, but she remained cold. No, not cold. Simply indifferent, and could Mary really blame her for that? Mary had the guffawing Chandler Wise to shower attention on her. And she had *had* most of Mayfair's young men by now anyway. That should be more than enough for her.

Turning her attention to Henry again, Sarah's hardness melted.

"Where are you going?" Mary said.

Sarah called back, "To see if all the stories are true."

He was standing there, shoulders square and chin high, both mesmerizing and menacing in the way he looked out at the party with a quiet scowl set on his face. But when he saw her approaching, his smile returned. Sarah's instincts were about to send her veering off to flee upstairs. She stood before him now, and she shivered watching his eyes take her in, from head to toe and back up again.

Henry Cutler smiled. "Good evening, *mademoiselle*."

She laughed. "Good evening, *monsieur*."

She felt his touch, and then he lifted up one of her hands and kissed it gently. She wished to God she wasn't wearing gloves. Turning away to blush, she looked up toward the ceiling and saw a shadowy figure watching her from the third floor landing. She blinked and looked again, but the figure was gone.

"*Voulez vous danser?*"

Snapping back to Henry, she blushed. "I'm sorry, I don't—"

"Don't worry," he said with a grin. "Those are all the words I know. Learned them down in Baton Rouge. But I've always considered French a dirty language, much less preferable to American. Wouldn't you agree?"

"Well, I suppose—"

"Would you like to dance with me?"

Dazed, she nodded. With a smile, Henry led her toward the center of the dance floor. His hand was large and warm and cupped her own hand perfectly, as if the two had been made for each other.

Henry stopped suddenly in the middle of the floor, and his expression became grim. "I should warn you..."

Feeling hairs pricking on the back of her neck, Sarah tried desperately to read him.

"...Yes?"

"I take dancing very, *very* seriously." Henry cracked a grin and winked at her.

Sarah laughed. As the violins sang, Sarah felt Henry gently pull her closer. Her hands felt small in his. Her body felt small against his. Timidly, she looked up into his face. He was smiling at her, his gaze soft yet constant. Outwardly he presented the picture of confidence, but she could see in his eyes a timidity of his own, a sense of wonder reflecting back at her. Blushing, she looked away. After a time, she rested her cheek on his shoulder.

A small hand — not Henry's — now fell on Sarah's shoulder.

"Purity for your Lord."

Sarah turned and looked into a pair of tiny, flickering eyes. They were the same blue as Henry's, but without the same beauty and charm. A thought flashed through Sarah's mind upon seeing those eyes up close — a persistent, regretful thought she would subsequently try to suppress many times without success. She saw Reverend Lucas Cutler's shifting eyes as those of a reptile.

Sarah pulled away from Henry and looked down shamefaced. She felt Henry's body tense, and with a broad arm he squeezed her against him and turned his shoulder to his brother. It was a subtle show, but it was a show nonetheless.

"Must you barge in like this, baby brother?"

Lucas was not intimidated. "I promised the Judge a clean dance."

"The Judge? Father's expectations don't apply to all four corners of the Valley."

"Exactly the Judge's concern. Wyolah Hall is rife with depravity. Not all families are as pure-minded as the Cutlers."

Somehow, Sarah guessed that Lucas Cutler was talking about the Roscoes. *Her* family. And as she thought this, she noted the boy-reverend's eyes flashing toward JJ in the corner.

Henry was having none of it. "*Depravity*, eh? Honestly, do you see any girls here flashing their shifts?"

Sarah blushed and couldn't help but laugh. Immediately, Lucas' gaze fell upon her.

"I see your brother Jonathan's returned home, Miss Roscoe. I trust he won't cause any trouble here tonight?"

With a grunt, Henry broke away from Sarah and turned upon Lucas. Henry, tall and muscled, loomed over the smaller brother, but Lucas' eyes gleamed brighter, as if goading Henry on. A painful silence lingered between the brothers such that Sarah could no longer hear the music or conversations bubbling around them.

At last, Lucas smiled and offered a small bow. "But then again, how can there be trouble with my dear brother around? I know he will protect even the least of my Father's sheep." Glancing at Sarah again, he said, "I bid you good evening, Miss Roscoe."

With that, the boy-reverend moved on to inspect and correct the closeness of other dancing couples.

"Purity for your Lord…Purity for your Lord…"

Henry took Sarah's hand again. "I apologize for St. Luke," he said. "He considers himself the Second Coming."

Sarah frowned and pinched his arm. "Such blasphemy, Henry Cutler," she chided. But after a short moment she giggled. "He is, perhaps, rather fervent."

He grinned. "Don't you mean *holier than thou?*"

A piggish snort of laughter escaped before she could stop it. Sarah slapped a hand to her mouth and froze with shock. *There. Take me now, Lord.* Sarah Roscoe was ready to die of embarrassment.

"That's the most beautiful laugh I've ever heard," Henry said.

She couldn't believe it, *wouldn't* believe it, and she said as much.

"Of course I mean it. Most girls I've known never allow themselves more than a bland titter."

Sarah shrugged. "Most men I've known don't laugh at all. They guffaw."

"Guffaw?" He grinned. "That's rather descriptive."

"Certainly," she said. "I've met enough drunken boors in my time to know how they sound."

"I see. And am I a drunken boor?"

"Of course not!"

"I warn you, I can be."

"Well, I don't believe it."

He smiled. "I *am* drunk." He pulled her closer. "And I can be bold."

She looked away from his gleaming eyes and searched the crowd for Lucas, who might be watching them…

"He won't bother us again," Henry said. "Come."

He touched her chin and guided it back to face him. Each stared into the eyes of the other for a long, unblinking moment. At last she tore her eyes away. Her pulse rattled like a snare drum in her throat.

Henry asked, "Does my boldness offend you?"

Her mouth was dry, but she managed: "No."

His face was now very close to hers. She could smell his unique bodily perfume of leather and brandy and musk, could see her watery reflection in his azure blue eyes, could trace the outline of his jaw and his lips and singular grains of stubble threatening his angled, clean-shaven chin. As Henry spoke, his voice warm, soothing and yet dark, secretive, she felt a comforting haze swallow her senses.

"Does the way I'm looking at you now offend you?"

She could only breathe, "No..."

"Does my closeness offend you?"

"No..."

He said nothing for a time. Then: "Does the way I touch you offend you?"

She closed her eyes and trembled. "No..."

There was another long pause. She waited, eyes closed.

"May I call on you next Sunday?"

"No—"

Her eyes opened. The realization of what she'd said struck her and—

"Yes!" she cried, almost shouting in his ear. She looked up at him and smiled with wide, marveling eyes. "Yes, yes, Henry, of course you can, yes!"

Laughing, Henry flashed a knowing grin. "Well then. For all your apparent loathing of drunken boors, Sarah Roscoe, you seem rather open to letting this one hang around you."

Sarah laughed again, another snort, but she no longer cared. As she folded once more into Henry's arms, she realized this night was not so terrible after all. In fact, she was very glad she'd stayed at the Claiborne ball.

Very glad indeed.

Chapter 9

A MAN OF COMPROMISE

Lurking in the shadows of Wyolah Hall's third floor landing, Ben Freeman gazed down at the great ballroom lit up far below.

Wide-eyed debutantes, young and beautiful, fluttered about in close pairs or groups of three, most of them terrified and none of them particularly loyal to each other. Meanwhile, scores of men both young and old hounded them like wolves, though no sooner did the boys form packs to encircle the debutantes did they disband at the slightest prospect of sneaking off alone with their intended.

As Ben watched the peculiar rituals of Mayfair's 'high society', he noted that it was rather like observing animals in a zoo. Except instead of feeling awestruck at the wonders of nature, he instead felt a damp blanket of melancholy weigh down.

Ben's eyes caught sight of JJ alone in the crowd.

JJ had cleaned and polished his uniform before the party. He had insisted not just on wearing his saber but a holstered revolver too. He sometimes paused to exchange brief words with various guests, JJ looked distinctly out of place amid the suits and flowing gowns of the other guests. He walked with his chin high and chest puffed out, hand on the hilt of his sword, as if he dared anyone to challenge his standing as a man or to bring up the sorry events of *that night*. At the same time, JJ seemed to be searching for someone.

Many guests regarded JJ's presence with thinly disguised distaste. Heads turned together to whisper, and the old rumors of four years ago began to circulate anew. Though he knew negroes were not welcome down on the ballroom floor, Ben considered going down to try and keep JJ company, or else to invite him up here to—

And there she was.

Sarah Roscoe was laughing, her eyes shining. He could see her green eyes even from this far away. She was intensely engaged in an intimate conversation with Henry Cutler. Ben sank down, but he didn't let himself turn away just yet. Whatever Henry was saying to her, she was clearly enthralled. Ben studied how the gleaming candles of the ballroom chandelier glittered in the quivering wet darks of her eyes. He willed himself to look longer, thinking vainly it might make him stronger somehow, but all it really made him was dog-sick.

Sarah looked up; their eyes met and held, but only for a moment. The lights in her eyes dimmed a little and then went out completely. It was as if she chose not to see Ben standing there.

Henry Cutler turned his head and followed Sarah's eyes, but Ben had already stepped back from the railing and stood hidden in the shadows, breathless.

"'Scuse me?"

Ben turned to the voice and saw Moses, the slave he'd met earlier that day, standing across the landing. The man was no longer dressed in rags, but wore a plain black suit pressed for the occasion.

Moses was quiet, but not timid. "Your massa..."

Ben understood. Turning to a small table nearby, he reached for the leather bag that he'd brought to Wyolah Hall. The bag had been empty when he first arrived, but since then a procession of dull-eyed slaves had slunk over to him, each of them pushing a wrapped bundle into his hands. Ben had placed each of these bundles into the bag and noted the names of the gift-givers: Hanley, Merrick, Warren, and the other planters too. There were many bundles, and many givers, but only one recipient.

'Holding the bag' had been one of Ben's responsibilities to Senator Roscoe for as long as he could remember. Whenever the old man came home to Mayfair, he would always collect political donations from his most ardent supporters, meaning the patriarchs of the First Families. But John Roscoe never accepted donations personally. He was aligned with most planters in the Valley in the firm belief that handling money was *dirty*. In fact, the old man often mused about the story of Jesus casting the moneychangers out of the Temple. Of course, he was nevertheless always happy to see Ben approach at the end of the night with his leather bag stuffed to the brim with 'notes of support'.

Ben normally didn't think much about gathering donations, which was really a rather banal part of his duties. Though he found the act of money-gathering itself distasteful, for reasons he couldn't quite put his finger on, he reminded himself of the bright side. While the planters believed their donations ensured John Roscoe's support for pro-slavery measures in the Senate, Ben knew that the cold hard cash from all those slave-owning bastards was actually helping John Roscoe build a large enough power base to eventually *undermine* the institution of slavery. The Senator had explained to Ben that it was a long game, and one in which, as he so often said, "Nothing good may happen before its proper time."

Ben held the bag open to Moses in anticipation of a new donation, but Moses only expressed alarm and confusion.

"No, no," Moses said, shaking his head. "Your massa, he *asked* for you."

Now Ben truly understood. "Senator Roscoe wants to see me?"

Moses nodded. "Yessuh, that's right. He's outside on the balcony."

Feeling a pang of embarrassment, Ben closed the bag. He felt like throwing it away.

Moses turned to go, and Ben followed him across the landing. As they neared a set of French doors, Ben asked if Moses was keeping well.

There was numb shock in Moses' voice. "I...I beg you pardon?"

"I asked, are you keeping well? You know, how you're doing."

Moses had no answer, or else wouldn't give one, and Ben did not insist.

They passed through the doors and came out to a broad balcony. Here, looking out at Wyolah Hall's south lawn, one could see the gardens of Versailles in miniature. Except these gardens were rotting, with disease leaching through the roots. Two shallow green pools ran parallel, and though Clay Claiborne had long abandoned the expensive chore of keeping the pools clean, the night's pale moon still shone on the slivers of water not choked by brown algae.

Beyond the pools much cleaner water chuckled forth from a handsome marble fountain. Here and there among groomed shrubbery stood a collection of statues. Each statue wore the same blank, featureless face created by a single mold. Claiborne proudly announced to all who would listen that his prized statues were in fact pieces of excess stock from the Uffizi in Florence. He had purchased the collection in New Orleans from an Italian art dealer who was, to Claiborne's great pleasure and amazement, willing to part with such rare antiquities for a truly astonishing price. Evidently none of Claiborne's many friends and admirers were willing to question aloud whether the statues were fakes.

But there was a feature of Wyolah's yawning gardens that was not known in Versailles, nor anywhere else for that matter. Near the extreme edge of the Claiborne plantation was a huge jacaranda tree, transplanted there from South America, somewhere with an older and wilder backcountry than anyone in the Valley knew.

Strewn before the purple jacaranda were lanterns and clusters of tables and a crowd of several hundred people gathered together. There were tents and pavilions set up on the lawn for overnight stays. If Wyolah Hall was Clay Claiborne's idea of a castle, then here were the grounds of some grand tournament all laid out. Before the string band danced many couples, and apart from the dancers stood a throng of onlookers, and beyond the onlookers stirred countless minglings, merry conversations, and various comings and goings so that the gathering resembled a human hive. Music and laughter filled the night air as much as the sweet, pungent smell of barbecued meats roasting in deep rose-embered pits cut into the earth.

Ben spotted Senator Roscoe seated apart from the others at the far end of the balcony. Moses led Ben past two slaves dressed in sharp-looking waiter's uniforms.

"Hey, boy."

Ben halted and looked up. The two men ogled Ben with laughing eyes.

"We was just wonderin," the first man said. "You dress youself tonight, or you let you white folks do it for you?"

The muscles in Ben's neck corded, and he curled a hand into a fist. The slaves, bigger and stronger than he, towered over him. The joker's mocking eyes goaded him to just try it, and see what happened next.

A sharp voice called, "Israel!"

The joker's grin vanished and he shot to servile attention. "Yessuh, Marse Clay."

"Take Boz and fetch these gents some fresh drinks, would you?"

"Yessuh."

Sour and subdued, the two slaves glared at Ben a moment longer before they turned inside. Ben's ears burned with the sound of mocking laughter from within. Slowly, Ben loosened his fist. What was he thinking? This was no place for a confrontation.

"Get a hold of yourself," Ben muttered to himself. "Where's your head?"

❧

Ben approached the Senator. Ever since he was a child, Ben referred to John Roscoe as *the* Senator, capital *S* and all, as if the old man's name and title were one and the same. The man's stature loomed so large in Ben's mind that he could not bear to call him an affectionate name like 'Mr. John' as Mama did. After all, this was the Great Liberator: the man who had, after inheriting Clarendon from Colonel Spencer, freed almost five hundred slaves, including Ben and Mama, with a single stroke of his pen.

The Senator sat in a chair and nursed a glass of brandy while he listened to the man seated beside him. The Senator looked tired, and Ben could plainly see that the pale red in his cheeks was not his own healthy color but rouge makeup applied by Sarah's hand. There were deep wrinkles furrowed on the Senator's brow, and the heavy bags under his eyes were a jaundiced yellow. Seeing Ben and Moses approach, the old man nodded to them.

"Good evening, gentlemen. Ben, you remember Judge Cutler, don't you?"

Feeling his blood run cold, Ben turned and looked at the man seated beside the Senator.

Oh, he remembered the man all right.

Judge Tobias Cutler was not altogether ugly, though the many long years of his life had not been kind to him. A bulbous head spilled out from a bulging neck like raw sausage from its casing. His nose and cheeks were vein-broken, maybe from too many glasses of brandy like the one now clasped in his long fingers. His eyes, like those of his son Henry, were a cold and shining blue. But Tobias Cutler's eyes were translucent, and within them was detached restraint that belied a deeper, more cunning intelligence.

Suddenly, dreams of terror flooded Ben's vision. He was back in the grove at Clarendon watching Daddy bleeding in the dirt while a young man with rusty shears stood over him. From some dark crevice of Ben's subconscious, Colonel Spencer's drawling voice floated up:

Go ahead, Tobias.

Ben blinked and it was all gone. Once again he stood on the balcony of Wyolah Hall on a late October night, except now he stood shivering from the cold sweat that had soaked through his clothes.

Cutler was still watching Ben with creeping distrust, and not a little contempt. "JR," he said cautiously, "I do believe your boy is *staring* at me."

The Senator looked at Ben with a tight-lipped smile. "Ben, please don't make the Judge uncomfortable."

"Apologies, Congressman," Ben said. "I meant no offence."

Cutler turned to the Senator. "JR, tell your boy to call me 'Judge' when he speaks to me. I've been in Congress for but three years, but I sat behind the bench for over twenty. Few men respect a congressman, but everyone respects the robes and gavel."

"Ben already knows that, or at least he should," the Senator said. He took out his handkerchief and held it across his mouth as several wet coughs racked his body. At length he sat upright again.

Cutler grunted as a means of dismissing Moses. Bowing low, Moses turned and departed. Ben was sorry to see Moses leave, for now he stood alone before the two old men.

The Senator said, "I wanted to ask you something, Ben. Where are the twins?"

As if in answer, they heard a sort of battle cry from across the south lawn as a string band struck up the jangling tune of *Dixie*.

Ben gestured toward the milling crowd in the field. "Mr. Jem's down on the lawn, sir." He couldn't help but smile. "I think I saw him...dancing, sir."

The Senator resisted a scowl. "And Jonathan?"

"I'm not sure, sir. He might be here in the Hall somewhere—"

"Find them," the Senator said. It didn't sound as though he cared much where his sons were, so long as they came to him, immediately. "The Judge and I are discussing matters relevant to our family, and they should be here to heed our counsel."

With a smile, Cutler pulled a silver cigar case from his pocket and opened it. "Not to worry, JR," he said. "Let the boys have their fun. It's for us old fogies to worry about the world, not them." Cutler ran his fingers, each adorned with a gaudy ring, through a selection of hand-rolled cigars. "Jonathan in particular. If he's as loyal as you say, he'll obey whatever your instructions may be."

Ben looked out at the field again, toward the barbecue pits and the white minstrels in blackface and the people dancing in wide circles. He spotted, there under the purple-blossomed jacaranda tree, Jem Roscoe square-dancing with a blonde girl. (And Jem really wasn't half bad, Ben noted with a grin.) And just over there stood JJ watching his brother. Even from this distance, Ben thought he saw a proud smile on JJ's lips. Ben made no announcement to the Senator, for the twins were far out of earshot. Maybe that was just as well.

"Will that be all, Senator?" Ben asked. "Perhaps I should leave you two gentlemen to your business and—"

"Stay," the Senator said.

Cutler offered a tight-lipped smile of discomfort. "No need for an extra body, JR. The Hall's help is perfectly capable of serving us. And if you desire anything in particular, my Moses is most able."

"Ben is my eyes and ears when I'm home in the Valley," the Senator replied. "If it's not too much trouble, I'd like him here with me."

Cutler's smile broadened, though his eyes dimmed. "As is your right, of course." He offered a cigar. "Will you smoke, JR?"

"Thank you kindly."

Ben watched as the Senator accepted Cutler's cigar.

"Excuse me," Ben said. "Senator, sir? Perhaps it's not a good idea to..."

"...Yes?" The Senator raised his eyebrows at Ben, looking surprised and annoyed.

"Smoking, sir," Ben said. "Your doctor's orders, sir — *advice*, rather. It's just, well, perhaps it's not...Perhaps it's not advisable to, given your diagnosis..."

Ben's voice failed him at last. Under the weight of the Senator's unblinking stare, his mind went blank.

Silence persisted, and the message was made clear. If the old man wanted to smoke, he would smoke.

Cutler grinned. "Your eyes and ears, is he?" Cutler looked Ben up and down. "He seems to fancy himself your mouthpiece as well."

The Senator said, "He'll hold his tongue, I assure you."

Ben hung his head and looked away.

"And tell him to keep away from the balcony," Cutler said. "We don't want to embarrass Claiborne by having any of his guests look up and see a darkie staring down at them."

While Cutler and the Senator exchanged small talk, the pungent smell of their tobacco smoke wafted in Ben's nostrils. He craved a cigar too, but he had none of his own.

Cutler exhaled a screen of smoke. He murmured, "Did you notice the others before we sat down?"

The Senator, meanwhile, puffed on his cigar and stared ahead, as if he hadn't heard the question. But after a moment, he stretched out and peered down the balcony. A group of esteemed Valley gentlemen held court there. They were the patriarchs of the old First Families: Merrick, Hanley, Warren, Claiborne, and a smattering of others, all of whom could trace their ancestors back nine generations. As an outsider coming from 'beyond the Branches,' even despite his incredible wealth, John Roscoe could be like such men but could never be one of them. Ben knew as well as anyone that it was this one brute fact that John Roscoe lamented the most, and tried his hardest to disprove. Maybe, in a roundabout way, this was why the Senator spent so much time in Washington working on behalf of his most important constituents.

Claiborne and the others were laughing about something, their heads turned together. A sensible cheer sounded, and the men put their glasses together and drank.

Having seen enough, the Senator sat back in his chair and turned to Cutler once more.

"When I arrived here this evening, the reception I met was…peculiar, to say the least."

Cutler puffed rings of smoke. "Cold, would you say?"

"You too?" Here, the Senator looked over at Ben. The old man's eyes went next to the leather bag resting on the balcony floor. The Senator's hard gaze now communicated a single question.

Ben understand the question, and his answer was a shake of his head. Tonight, only a handful of slaves had approached him with donations. The bag was only half-full, which to the Senator meant it was half-empty.

Chewing distractedly on his cigar, the Senator glared out at the party lights below.

"There is only so much that a man can do in Congress, without necessary support. My enterprises serve me well, but no man's coffers are boundless. Don't I give enough in public service? When there is a floor vote, I *always* know the count. I champion the bills my constituents support, and I kill in committee the bills they don't. But now they expect their champion to pay out of pocket so that their voices may be heard?"

Cutler shook his head ruefully. "You don't have to tell me about any of it, JR. It's been like pulling teeth to get Hanley's donation to my campaign for next year."

The Senator heaved a sigh and shook his head. He chomped on his cigar as if it had offended him. "It's Claiborne who concerns me. All the rest of them defer to good ol Clay."

Cutler shrugged. "I like Claiborne, when he's drunk. He's easier to deal with."

The two men laughed together. Ben could see that, even as he watched the two men laugh, Cutler was watching the Senator closely. Cutler stopped laughing only when the Senator went quiet. After a time, Cutler pulled his chair a little closer to the Senator's. He leaned over, and he dropped his voice low.

"Now I must be honest with you, JR. The Valley is full of rumors."

The Senator was not interested in any conspiratorial gestures. "Oh?" he said loudly, as if he wanted the others down the balcony to hear him. "What are they saying that I haven't already heard before?"

Cutler's expression turned gray. "Nothing good, my friend."

The haughty light in the Senator's eyes went out. He concentrated on puffing a brooding cloud of smoke.

"Nothing good," Cutler echoed. "It's never open, never raw. There are no ill words spoken. But the sentiments, JR, are impossible to ignore. The sentiment that you might betray your people when the time comes. The sentiment that you might choose your own interests over those of your neighbors, over your section...over your *country*."

The Senator gave an amused scoff. "Country? Exactly what country are you and the others referring to? It's the United States, I hope, and not some antiquated idea that Virginia, like all other states, is independent and sovereign, and that the Union that binds them is made of nothing but lace ribbons."

Cutler placed a hand over his heart. "JR, please, you mistake me. These aren't *my* words. But that's what the others think."

The Senator registered nothing of the joyous voices in the air, nor the rich scents from makeshift smokehouses, nor the kissing touch of the night's humid breeze.

"Well," the old man said at last, "I don't care what *they* think."

But of course he was lying; Ben knew it, and so did Cutler. John Roscoe cared a great deal about what others thought of him. In fact, it was the only thing that seemed to frighten him.

"Of course you don't care," Cutler said. "You'll soon be twenty years in Congress. You helped craft the Compromise of 1850 that spared the South — and the Union — from certain destruction. You came from nowhere, up from nothing, and look where you are now. And so what if you're not part of the old Jamestown stock? Take it from me, JR, being one of the First Families of Virginia is nothing to envy. If you don't think and do *exactly* like everyone else, they will crucify you for it."

"My father-in-law seemed to appreciate me for a breath of fresh air," the Senator said. "The Colonel supported my taking over Clarendon, every step of the way. The Spencer fortune didn't just fall into my lap, after all. I saw what I wanted and I *took* it, as any man should."

"Of course, JR. Of course."

All this time, Ben stood with his back to the balcony railing. As Cutler and the Senator went on talking, Ben sank against the railing to rest his lower back. Seeing this, Tobias Cutler flashed with anger.

"Nigger, you better *stand up* in my line of sight."

Instinctively, Ben obeyed and stood up straight. He hated himself for it, but there was nothing else to do. His body twitched, urging him to slouch back down out of spite, but Ben remained upright and murmured some apology to Cutler. A voice in his head told him to spit in the bastards' face, but he didn't. After all, the Senator was watching him.

The two old men continued to smoke together in silence.

"If you'll permit my saying," Cutler said after some time, "I think I can understand where Claiborne and the others are coming from. It's one thing to balk at a few traditions, but you've proven yourself to be a bonafide iconoclast. It's not just that you drag around your pet nigger everywhere you go. It's difficult for our friends to forget that, not a moment after you inherited all those slaves from Colonel Spencer, may he rest in peace, you freed the brutes and sent them God knows where..."

"As freedmen, their destination was their first free choice to make," the Senator said.

"Indeed," Cutler said dryly. "But in the meantime, you scared the entire Valley half to death. Even *I* was convinced a mob of darkies would set upon my family in their beds. You know how we fear a repeat of Nat Turner, JR."

Ben knew well enough that the name *Nat Turner* was hated in the minds of every white person in the Valley. Some thirty years ago, there had been a slave uprising downstate in Southampton County. Led by a black preacher named Nat Turner, a small band of slaves had attacked their masters and killed some fifty white folks while making a bid for escape. The rebellion was put down within a few short days, and afterward the vengeful authorities had murdered countless men, women, and children, whether they'd been part of the rebellion or not. Nat Turner's body was never found.

The Senator nodded slowly. "I suppose I can understand the concern. In my younger days I was given to throes of sentimentality. But I saw an opportunity to do good and I acted upon it. Maybe foolishly, but I acted."

"You were mourning your first wife," Cutler said. "Grief affects men in different ways."

More than ever before, Ben wanted to speak up. For God's sake, John Roscoe's decision to free Clarendon's slaves had been no foolish act of grief! It had been an act of honor and nobility — of the true *goodness* that rested deep within every human heart, if only it could be kindled. Instead of assuming the easy riches of being a slave-owner, John Roscoe had chosen to do the right thing.

Maybe the Senator had become somewhat jaded about the cause of abolitionism during his time in Washington. After all, some abolitionist writers and politicians had called for the complete dissolution of the Union on the basis that its slave-owning founders were irredeemable in the eyes of God. These radical ideas were anathema to the Senator, especially when they inspired violence like that perpetrated by men such as John Brown.

Still, the Senator's pure and noble act of liberating Clarendon's enslaved people could never be tarnished. Twenty years later, those five hundred freedmen might now be a thousand, maybe even *two* thousand. Soon enough those people would stop thinking of themselves as ex-slaves, or even freedmen. Certainly their children wouldn't think of themselves in such a way. Instead they would think of themselves as Americans — as American *citizens* — who were as motivated to serve their country as anyone else, as deserving of every constitutional right as anyone else.

Five hundred people. And all thanks to John Roscoe.

"Another cigar for you, JR?"

"Thank you very much."

While the two old men continued to smoke and talk together, Ben's attention drifted away. He stared out at the sloping lawn of Wyolah Hall. Squinting, he saw the plantation's cramped and weathered slave cabins standing far past the merriment. There were some dark shapes standing under the willow trees and gazing upon the white man's party from afar. In fact, there appeared to be some kind of party in the works at the cabins themselves: the shadowed forms of people were gathered around campfires where voices sang, and hands and dancing feet held rhythm together.

Ben tugged at his stiff collar, which was chafing his neck. Damn these starched clothes. He wanted to take everything off and slip on simple homespun threads and join the people over at the cabins. He wanted to sit and listen to their songs, to feel all those deep voices resonate in his chest.

"She's a lovely girl," Cutler was saying, "and of the right age."

Ben perked up and listened intently. Who was lovely?

When the Senator said nothing, Cutler continued. "It's unfortunate she could not attract a suitable gentleman in Richmond."

The Senator rolled his eyes. "She says she went to Richmond to study, not to find a husband."

"Well," Cutler said with a laugh, "it's good that you called the girl home. Perhaps she will have an easier time finding a husband here in Mayfair."

Ben's heart clenched up. *Sarah*. They were talking about Sarah.

Cutler breathed a cloud of smoke. "You know, JR, my Henry has taken quite a cotton to her."

"Is that so?" The Senator did not seem exactly surprised.

"It is," Cutler said with a smile. "And I must admit, when he told me I couldn't help but consider the idea with considerable favor. We could meld our two families together and make something stronger. A new American dynasty, with a commitment to tradition and a, well, an *openness* to the future." Cutler's smile broadened. "We could be like the Lees and the Washingtons."

The Senator cracked a rare grin. "Maybe. Or perhaps we'll turn out like the Yorks and Lancasters. Hm?"

Cutler's own smile faded. "I...I don't know those people. Are they Republicans?"

The Senator shook his head and let the matter go.

It did not take long for Cutler to press his case further. How Henry was a skilled planter, a hard but not cruel driver of field hands, and that he would one day soon take over the Cutler plantation of Arcadia, which lay just over the hill from Wyolah Hall. Henry was, in his father's estimation, a great man. But behind every great man, there was of course a great woman.

Ben listened, barely breathing. So this was how it happened, how it had always happened in old families for millennia. Here was the song and dance of two patriarchs deciding the fate of their children. But how in God's name, in this modern age, could two men talk of love and marriage as a mere matter of transaction?

Ben was certain that Sarah, despite entertaining a dance with the man, wouldn't see anything of value in Henry Cutler. How could she? The man was goddamn vile, and that was plain enough for anyone to see. Sarah, well, she was too *good* for a man like that. She'd be better suited with someone who didn't make a living by whipping people, someone with whom she could really speak her mind, someone who made her laugh. Someone like—

Someone like who? Him? '*A nigger in white man's clothes*', as Henry Cutler had called him?

Of course, what Sarah really deserved was the opportunity to make her own choice of partner. And had Ben ever considered that maybe she'd want no partner at all? Some women balked at the strictures of married life in the same ways men did. And if she did fall in love and wish to marry, then her choice of husband was *hers* and hers alone. There should be no undue influence from anybody.

Not even, he realized, from himself.

Looking up, Ben saw the Senator was watching him. The Senator had a talent for reading minds, or at least giving the impression that he could.

Ben turned away and put his head in his hand. He felt a headache coming on. Surely if he could somehow explain to the Senator that Henry Cutler was a fine gentleman, sure, but not *the one* for his daughter. The Senator would surely understand. John Roscoe always understood.

"I appreciate this offer very much," the Senator said. "It humbles me. But I cannot help but wonder, why? Is it really that Henry is so infatuated with my daughter, or is there another reason for your proposal?"

Ben smiled. And there it was. The Senator's polite refusal was sure to come next.

The ashes hanging from the tip of Judge Cutler's cigar defied gravity. Finally, Cutler tapped his cigar and the ashes dropped.

"There's a great storm gathering, JR, and I know you feel it too. John Brown was just the beginning. If we Virginians are to survive the coming tempest, and still hold on to what matters most to us, then we ought to work together. Why shouldn't

Noah's neighbor have helped him build the Ark? And besides, haven't I always been a friend to you?"

The Senator nodded slowly. "A great friend," he said. With a somber sigh, the Senator looked out at the party lights below. "You must have seen him here tonight."

"Him?" Cutler echoed. "You mean..."

"That's right," the Senator said. "I haven't forgotten what you did for Jonathan that night, Tobias. What you did for *me*, for the Roscoe family. You delivered me safely from that...unfortunate episode. My career, all my future prospects, they might have turned to dust if you hadn't—"

"Say no more," Cutler said. "My own family has seen its fair share of shameful happenings in the past. Too often, in the wake of a scandal, people are so busy wondering about dramatic details and gossip that they completely forget about the well-being of the aggrieved family. Some families never recover from such affairs. What it takes is for a man of authority to stand up and defend the honor of his neighbors." Cutler exhaled a cloud of smoke and shrugged. "It's unfortunate that the Harpers had to fall on the sword, but a tough choice had to be made."

The Senator gave a stiff nod and continued smoking.

"And how is your JJ doing at the Point?" Cutler asked. "I trust the trials of military life have done much to straighten him out."

The Senator shrugged. "He's getting on fine enough," he said. Maybe sensing something in Cutler's line of questioning, he added, "It seems he got himself roped up in that John Brown debacle over at Harper's Ferry earlier this week."

"I heard Claiborne's speech," Cutler said. "And serving under R.E. Lee, no less."

The Senator nodded. "He might prove to be a valuable asset after all. He was certain to be one, a long time ago." With a sigh, the old man shrugged. "In truth, I've missed my boy a great deal. Seeing him again, I...well, of course I couldn't let my feelings be known to him. That would not be proper. But still I...I felt as though..."

Looking up and seeing Ben, the Senator suddenly reddened and shifted in his seat.

"Anyway," the Senator said hastily, "I haven't yet decided what I shall do with him."

Cutler pulled at the many clacking rings he wore on his fingers. "Of course he's your son. But be wary of your emotions in this matter, JR. Better to think with the head than the heart. If his reputation is a danger to *your* reputation..."

"I know, Tobias. I understand the risks to my work. But maybe the fame from Harper's Ferry will give him a clean slate."

"He'll never get out from under that cloud," Cutler replied. "It will follow JJ everywhere, for the rest of his life." With smoke curling from his nostrils, Cutler nodded slowly. "But if gangrene infects an extremity, one must cut off a limb to save the body."

Listening to Cutler, Ben resisted a hateful scowl. Just what was Cutler trying to suggest? With such a father as Tobias Cutler, it was no wonder that his son Henry had grown up to be such a bastard.

"Changing the subject," Cutler said. "I heard a rumor that you're going to support Stephen Douglas's bid for the nomination next spring."

The Senator sighed. "Rumors, rumors."

"Yet you don't deny it," Cutler said. "Really, JR, I wish you'd reconsider your endorsement of that lying pig."

The Senator laughed. "That lying pig is one of my oldest friends in Congress."

"He's the king cobra of a snake pit," Cutler said.

"Is he a pig or a snake? Come now, Tobias. Stephen Douglas will make a good president. He's a Northerner who understands and respects the Southern way of life."

"Maybe he understands it," Cutler muttered. "I wouldn't say he respects it."

The Senator shrugged. "In any case, I've committed myself to his cause. Another railroad bill will soon make its way through Congress. By supporting Stephen's bid for the White House—"

"He's pledged the railroad contract to you, yes, I've heard," Cutler said. "Still, I wouldn't trust any of that man's pledges. Don't forget the promises he made to the South six years ago. He promised the Kansas and Nebraska territories would remain open to Southern institutions after their statehood was ratified."

Ben grimaced. *Southern institutions*. Of course Cutler meant slavery.

"Instead, the Western Territories have been in flames for half a decade now," Cutler went on. "Abolitionist settlers and Southern planters squabbling over the same tracts of land. Now what do we have? Anarchy, that's what. And all that blood is on the hands of Stephen Douglas."

"Stephen had good intentions," the Senator said.

"His only intention was to line his own pockets," Cutler said. "I don't have to remind you, JR, that my own nephew packed up his farm and took his family to Kansas. He was lured by the hopes that Stephen Douglas wrought. And it *was* Douglas who gave hope to so many. His promises are in the Congressional record."

For a moment, Cutler choked up. He pressed on only with great difficulty, his eyes misty.

"They found my nephew's farm destroyed, himself just a pile of burnt ash, his wife and girls raped and massacred in the barn. Wherever the abolitionists took his slaves, I don't know." Cutler closed his eyes and shook his head slowly. "That was five years ago now."

The Senator withdrew his cigar and let the ashen tip grow longer. "I'm sorry, Tobias."

Cutler's eyes shot open again. "Yankees lambast Southerners for their apparently boundless greed, yet in the North there is no shortage of thieves who call themselves public servants. Stephen Douglas is one of them. You know he bought thousands of acres of land out in Missouri and Kansas, intending to sell it back to the government when the railroad came through? Oh, but of course you know about it, JR. You bought several hundred acres yourself."

The Senator did not answer right away. Evidently he was employing a strategy that Ben had learned from him a long time ago. Sometimes it was better to answer a thorny question right away, lest one's sincerity be doubted. But if the question seemed like bait on a beckoning hook, it was better to keep quiet rather than spill a rushed, unthinking answer.

"I do own land out there," the Senator replied. "Stephen and I own some land together, in fact. We went into it together, some ten years ago, piece by piece. It's no secret, really. The tracts have been surveyed thoroughly and determined to be quite amenable to railroad construction."

"So what went wrong?" Cutler asked. "Did your Yankee investors turn green at the idea of looking out the south window and seeing negroes in the fields?"

"The goal was *compromise*, as ever," the Senator said. "Nebraska was supposed to become a free-soil state, and meanwhile Kansas was supposed to legalize slavery and join the South. In this way, the Missouri Compromise would remain more or less intact. In this way, the balance of power between North and South would hold."

"But the balance *didn't* hold," Cutler said. "It collapsed. Neither territory became a state; instead they both became charnel houses. And now all that land you own is littered with the bones of children. My nephew's girls are buried out there somewhere, in some shallow prairie grave. Civil war, JR. That's the legacy of all this."

Here, Cutler leaned in close to the Senator.

"But I don't blame *you* for what happened, JR. Please believe me when I say that. It's Douglas who ought to be crushed under the wheel."

The Senator shook his head. "Public opinion holds Stephen Douglas in high regard."

"Not anywhere south of Baltimore," Cutler noted.

"But certainly in the North," the Senator said. "And you well know by now, Tobias, that the North's voting population exceeds ours by some three to one. You might be surprised to know, Northerners have as little affection for the abolitionist movement as any Southern man. They abhor the idea of racial equality."

Cutler harrumphed. "And congratulations to them, for finally listening to some common sense."

"But neither do they approve of slavery's expansion," the Senator said. "Next fall, there will be a battle for the White House unlike anything we've ever seen. The Republicans are sure to put forward a moderate candidate, which means we must act in kind. Stephen Douglas is the Democratic Party's best hope of winning the presidency and healing the Union's divisions."

"Our best hope?" Cutler wondered aloud. "There are some Democrats — a growing number of us, in fact — who believe we can win the White House *without* Stephen Douglas."

"You mean your little club of radicals," the Senator said with a laugh. "What is it they call your friend William Yancey? The 'Prince of Fire-Breathers' or some such nonsense?"

"Fire *Eaters*," Cutler corrected, not without a little sourness. "And we aren't *radicals*, JR. We are conservatives, and Mr. Yancey is a patriot. While abolitionists and European aliens burn the national flag in Northern cities, we in the South are marshalling a resistance. We're readying to take our country back, to snatch it out of the maw of Black Republicanism. Because if the nigger-lovers win, they'll make it so that our daughters are forced to marry brutes like your black boy there. I do apologize for such a disgusting example, JR, but now you know how serious I am about this."

Ben maintained a stony silence.

"I don't doubt your passion," the Senator said. "But assuming the South's support of the Democratic Party is assured—"

"But that's just the trouble," Cutler said. "For too long, Democrats have *assumed* the South's unwavering support. Meanwhile, our colleagues have conceded to the Yankees on almost every anti-slavery proviso, on almost every pro-Northern bill. But what if we suddenly refused to give our consent? After all, what have the Northerners ever done to protect their Southern allies in the Party? This isn't just about an election, JR; it's a fight for survival. If we don't put a Southern man in the White House next fall, the South as we know it will cease to exist."

The Senator asked pointedly, "And just who do you think that Southern man should be?"

Cutler huffed. "Not me, surely. There was talk of Jefferson Davis from Mississippi, but he's told us time and again he does not wish to be president. But maybe there is another..."

The Senator groaned. "Don't tell me you want William Yancey."

Cutler shook his head. "Yancey doesn't want the White House either."

"No," the Senator said with a wry smile. "He'd rather watch it burn."

Cutler sighed. "I don't know who the candidate will be in the end," he said. "All I know is, the candidate must be a man of vision. He must be a man of moderation. In short, a man of compromise." Cutler sat back in his chair. "And I say he ought to be a Virginian."

Hearing that last remark, the Senator exhaled a billowing cloud of cigar smoke.

Ben watched a shift in John Roscoe's eyes. They had widened to become like saucers, bulging with expectation and dancing with the light of new possibility. But in an instant it was all gone, buried, and when the Senator looked at Cutler again his expression was flat and his eyes dull.

"It's a good thing *I'm* not a Virginian," the Senator said.

The two old men stared at each other a long while, each trying to read the other. Cutler had not so much as blinked, but presently a smile stretched across his lips. It reminded Ben of a sketch in one of Tom's nature books that depicted a laughing hyena.

"Oh, JR, you are clever," Cutler said, laughing and wagging a finger. "Very, very clever." He puffed rings of smoke, trying very hard to appear nonchalant. "I expected you to turn the idea down without a second thought. But at the very least, for my sake, you ought to at least consider the idea. Seven of our fifteen presidents have been Virginians, from Washington to Jefferson to Madison and beyond."

"According to Claiborne and the others, I'll never be a Virginian," the Senator replied. "In their eyes, I'm nothing but a Yankee wearing a Georgian necktie."

"You are a *Virginian*," Cutler said assuredly. "What's more, you are a conservative with certain progressive ideals. You understand the South because you were raised up within it. I'd like the Party's leaders to name a better candidate who represents the middle path." Cutler's smile stretched wider. "And besides, I imagine the Executive Mansion is far more comfortable than even the most luxurious railcar."

The Senator smiled and sat back to consider the idea deeply. With his cigar clamped between his teeth, the old man rested one hand on his lap and turned it palm upward. With the index finger of the other hand he slowly traced lines and ciphers across his palm. As if he was recording the secrets of his mind with invisible ink. Whatever message was there was lost when the Senator closed his hand and reached up to pull his cigar from his lips.

"If you are suggesting what I think you're suggesting," the Senator said quietly, "then this conversation has taken a very serious turn."

"I prefer the term 'consequential,'" Cutler said, winking.

A knot tightened in Ben's chest. Cutler was dangling a jeweled pendant before the Senator's eyes. Ben knew it had to be bait of some kind.

"Any man on Capitol Hill who says he's never entertained the idea of being president is a liar," the Senator said. "But all the same, a 'man of compromise', as you put it, must necessarily be a man of his word. I gave my word to my friend, Stephen Douglas, that I would help *him* secure the nomination. This will be his third try at the White House, after all. It will probably be his last. And speaking of *lasts*, I myself am not much longer for this earth. As easy as it is for me to forget that, my doctor insists on reminding me. Maybe I have a year, maybe two, maybe less. Beyond safeguarding the position of my family — which to me, has always meant the Company — beyond that, it would be irresponsible to indulge any vain ambitions."

Ben's chest tightened with quiet pride. Whatever thorns the Senator had sprouted as he aged, whatever mistakes the man had made regarding his family (and there were many), this here was the man whom Ben admired. This here was the father figure who gave him a reason to believe in better days coming. *This* was John Roscoe.

Cutler, meanwhile, had slumped down in his chair. He barely tried to conceal the scowl on his face. Evidently the man was not gracious in defeat.

"I only hope that Douglas keeps *his* word to you, JR," he said. "Time and again he's demonstrated his penchant for weaseling his way out of commitments — even those to whom he calls friends."

The Senator nodded. "I understand your concern, Tobias. Perhaps I prefer to take a larger view of things. One day, people will cease saying 'the United States *are*' and instead say 'the United States *is*.' In this election, now more than ever, Democrats ought to set the ideas of 'North' and 'South' aside. We ought to think not of sectional interests, but *national* interests. If the Democrats fracture, the Republicans are guaranteed to win the White House, and maybe the whole of Congress with it."

Cutler puffed on his cigar. It wasn't clear whether he was listening anymore.

"Tobias," the Senator said. "I want you to meet Stephen Douglas."

The other man scoffed at the suggestion. "I've already met him," Cutler said. "I've met him, and I don't like him."

"Meet with him," the Senator said. "Charleston. Next spring, before the Convention. I will moderate the discussion, as much as I can. I'm certain we can all reach an understanding of some kind."

Cutler took in a long breath. "And if we cannot? Would you reconsider my proposal?"

The Senator watched tendrils of smoke curl in the air. "I can only say that perhaps we'll discuss these matters again. Down the line, so to speak."

Cutler chewed on all this for a moment. At length, a smile returned to his lips and he extended his hand. "*Perhaps* is all I can ask for, JR."

Ben watched as the Senator reached out and took Cutler's hand.

"Your boy Henry may call on Sarah," the Senator said, as if their conversation had never diverted from that subject. "Their courtship has my blessing."

Invigorated at this news, Cutler laughed. "I'll drink to that!" he said, and he slapped the Senator on the back. "This calls for a celebration. Servant, waiter, whatever! *Moses!*"

The slave Moses soon appeared at Cutler's side. "Yessuh?"

"Fresh drinks, and be quick about it."

"Yessuh."

Cutler tossed his half-smoked cigar on the whitewashed floor and ground it under his heel, all as he took out his cigar case and picked out yet another fresh cigar.

"Where are my damn matches?"

Looking up at Ben, Cutler snapped his fingers.

"You, nigger. Oh, what's your boy's name again, JR?"

Ben had already struck a match of his own. "My name is Ben Freeman." After a pause, he added, "*Judge*."

Again Cutler studied him, trying to place him.

Ben held the burning match in his fingers. His voice was taut, the words grinding between his teeth. "My father, Joby. I think you knew each other, sir. During your time working at Clarendon."

Cutler chuckled and nudged the Senator with his elbow. "I've certainly seen a lot of their kind in my time, JR. Never would I go so far as to say I *know* any of them. I know darkies like the redskins know buffalo."

The Senator's eyes flickered to Ben for a moment. Turning to Cutler, the Senator offered the man an obliging laugh. The sound of it cut into Ben, and though he knew the Senator was only playing a part, the sting was no less painful. Still, he knew he would never say anything to the Senator. The old man would only huff and say that Ben was too sensitive, that it was 'only politics' and nothing more.

Pushing a fake smile across his lips, Ben leaned forward and lit Cutler's cigar. Standing so close to the man, Ben felt the flesh of his scarred ear begin to twitch. He was close enough now to spit in the man's eye. It was a simple opportunity, maybe a perfect moment unfolding right before him, and perhaps one he would not soon have again, if ever. But at what cost? He would be dead within the hour, strung up and mutilated for assaulting a white man. And what would be gained? What would be accomplished? A moment's dark glee, and nothing more.

Nothing good may happen before its proper time.

When Moses returned with fresh brandies, the two old gentlemen held their glasses aloft.

"To you, JR," Cutler said, grinning.

"To the Union," the Senator said. "And to the union of man and wife under God."

The old men drank.

Cutler licked his lips. "My, that's damn good brandy." Turning in his chair, he looked toward Moses and murmured, "I trust the party is going well down there?"

The Senator, staring out at the jacaranda tree, seemed not to hear or register such an idle question. But as Ben watched, Moses gave a curious sort of nod to Cutler, as if he was responding to a more meaningful inquiry. Moses' eyes darted toward Ben and flickered away.

Ben winced and looked down at the still-lit match, which had burned down to a blackened stem between his fingertips. The skin there had bubbled and turned pink. He had not felt any pain until this very moment, and now it was coming to him all at once. And yet, he did not move. He watched with morbid fascination as tiny tendrils of smoke curled out from the burnt edges of his fingertips.

"Well, well!" Cutler said with a satisfied smile. He turned to the Senator now and offered a knowing grin. "You know something, JR? I feel that love is in the air tonight. It may be, with respect to 'man and wife', that God is working His mysteries upon us as we speak."

The Senator smiled and shrugged. "Maybe so."

Chapter 10

UNDER THE JACARANDA

Outside on the south lawn of Wyolah Hall, the string band thrashed like madmen. This was no group of refined gentlemen performing gentle nocturnes like the string ensemble up at Wyolah Hall. Dueling singers, one a bearded man in drag and the other a dwarf in blackface, traded verses back and forth and hurled jokes and insults at the crowd between choruses. The red fires of the barbecue pits cast long black shadows that danced in the hellish light.

Looming above the firelights was the mighty jacaranda tree with its violet-colored blossoms. To look upon the jacaranda with the whole of the eye was quite the sight indeed. At twenty-two feet around and forty feet tall, it stretched higher than any of Mayfair's manmade structures, not counting the steeple of the First Church.

Hunched over a makeshift bar, Jem tossed a thumb of gin down his throat and coughed for another.

Baby-faced Sugar Dave Dixon shook his head. "I don't know, Jem. You've had half the bottle already..."

"Give me the other half," Jem said. "I need to take my mind off things."

"Of course you do!" a voice boomed. George Hunt, slick and fox-eyed, appeared at Jem's side. "Remind us once again of the great tragedy of your life, Mr. Roscoe. How does the story go again? Rich boy wants to come down from his mountain to play in the muck with us yokels, but he's afraid of making his daddy angry."

With that, Hunt snatched the bottle from Sugar Dave's hand and held it just out of Jem's reach while he poured himself a stiff drink. Jem growled and lunged for the bottle again, but Hunt gave him nothing but a playful grin.

"Although I have to say," Hunt said, nodding toward a group of girls dancing upon the grass dance floor yards away, "*our* gals have a hell of a lot more fun than those painted belles up at the big-house."

Sugar Dave looked toward Wyolah Hall and sighed adoringly. "Oh, but did you see Pippa Claiborne tonight? I caught a glimpse of her through those big windows. She looked positively di-vine."

"She's got a mustache," Hunt said flatly. "That's right, I said it. The sister's got hair in all the places her brother Percy ain't manly enough to sustain."

Ignoring him, Sugar Dave turned back to Jem. "What's the trouble, Jem, really? You were saying earlier that JJ's come home. But where is he?"

Jem shrugged. He wasn't much interested in talking right now, only in drinking. "Up at the ball, I think. Strutting around in his uniform, no doubt."

Hunt winked at Sugar Dave. "Watch out, Davey. We've made friends with a real Cain over here."

"*Laws*," Dave said, "we-all should have worn our militia uniforms tonight! Then we'd have to beat the girls back with a stick."

Hunt said, "Careful the girls don't take the stick to you instead, Davey."

Jem turned on Hunt. "I'm *not* a jealous Cain, thank you very much. But maybe you can appreciate my head's a little spun. It's been years since JJ's been home, meanwhile I've been stuck here. Suddenly he's back and everyone's praising his name and calling him a hero. Next thing you know, my father will probably name him President of the RRC and—"

"But that's what you want, isn't it?" Hunt said. "You hate being stuck in that damn matchbox up on the Branch. You're always talking about how you can't wait until your brother gets back so that you can finally leave it all behind. Well, your wish finally came true."

Jem shrugged. "I suppose so. But now the question is, what the hell am I supposed to do with myself now?"

Hunt laughed. "Get the hell out of the Valley, like you've always talked about. Oh yes, best say your goodbyes now, Davey. Our Jemmo here will soon be a man of the world, bound for Richmond or Calcutta or some damn place."

Sugar Dave smiled. "Oh, I think Jem will stay right where he is."

Hunt furrowed his brow. "State your reasons."

Still smiling, Sugar Dave nodded toward the dance floor. "There's one."

Together, the three of them turned their heads. And there, within the circle of dancers, was Audrey Blake.

Jem's cheeks flushed as he watched her move. Her ashen blonde hair, held up with simple flair, rose and fell on slender pale shoulders covered by a homemade green dress that swayed and curled as she circled. She whirled in the wet grass without shoes, her bare feet white like porcelain.

"See?" Sugar Dave said, with a knowing look at Jem's puppy-eyed expression. "Jem's been crazy about her since, well, since forever. Certainly since Audrey got back from teacher's school down in Staunton."

"Gets me, why she came back," Hunt said. "The Blake farm ain't no place for a woman. Or a goat, for that matter." He analyzed the dancing circle while tugging fitfully at the black sideburns he was attempting to grow. "It's almost November. What the hell is she doing dancing without shoes? She's loon-crazy. Maybe she's the one for you after all, Jemmo."

Jem laughed. "I'll drink to the hope, at least."

Hunt grinned and offered the bottle. "Hold out your cup. That's it. Up and back, boys!"

They drank. Jem and Hunt downed gin while Sugar Dave nursed a glass of buttermilk.

"You better acknowledge the corn now," Hunt said to Jem after a while. "I see a few eyes roving about these gardens, and most in the direction of Miss Blake's pretty figure. And that's of course not mentioning one Percy Claiborne, *esquire*." Hunt winked at Sugar Dave. "He might make you think twice about any courting plans."

Jem's eyes focused on a prissy-looking boy in a dazzling cream-colored suit speaking to Audrey Blake on the grass dance floor. It was Percy Claiborne, who referred to himself as a 'well-bred highborn' and actually meant it. The pit in Jem's stomach hardened to a rock.

"Percy Claiborne can't wipe his own ass without ordering one of his slaves to check if he missed a spot," Jem said. "I think I can at least handle *that* competition."

"Oh yes?" Hunt laughed. "Tell us then, what about her brothers?"

Jem looked across the way. The three Blake brothers were each hearty and fibrous as beanstalks. They were dressed in ragged overalls and wore long, unkempt beards, and they scowled at the world behind squinting blue eyes. Their brute strength was fabled throughout the Valley. Jem knew the North Branch Mine was lucky to have the Blakes on its payroll, for together the three giants could do the work of ten men.

Ezra Blake, the youngest brother and the trio's leader, looked over and his eyes met Jem's. Instantly Ezra's eyes narrowed and he muttered some hideous invective in Jem's direction. Maybe it was because Ezra had heard the rumors that Jem was infatuated with his younger sister. Or maybe it was because Jem was the 'boss-man', and therefore a natural target of derision. But even as boys, the Blake brothers and the Roscoe twins had never seen eye to eye — no doubt because Jem and JJ had a black playmate, and a *freedman* no less.

Jem promptly turned away and set to refilling his cup. "Well, perhaps tonight isn't the right time..."

Hunt laughed and shook his head. "I see our loverboy's turned yellow, Davey. Of course, you don't stand a chance with Audrey Blake no-how. Her family sharecrops Claiborne land, which means the Claibornes all but own them. Doesn't matter if they hate Percy's guts as much as they hate yours, they'll serve Percy because his money talks loudest. Still, that doesn't mean you should just give up like some cussed lickfinger. What the hell's wrong with you, boy?"

Jem shot an impetuous glare at the three George Hunts standing before him. "Pile on the agony, George," he said, slurring his words a little. The gin was really starting to hit him. "You really ought to try motivational speaking. You'd make a great preacher, or a general for that matter. Soldiers like Dave and I would follow you anywhere with your sunny optimism."

Hunt laughed and waved him off. "Show me a money-grubbing Yankee and I'll shoot him, but I wouldn't waste my talents taking charge of you sorry bastards." He stepped away from the bar and started toward the dance circle. He gestured toward the dance circle. "Anyhow, I'm off. Going to try and find some poor girl severely lacking in self-respect."

"Try the stables!" Jem cried.

Hunt laughed and strode off into the crowd.

Jem took another drink and felt a pit in his stomach. Damn the gin — he was starting to feel sick. But the imp in his head urged him on, and he downed another gulp.

Many times, after waking up to yet another aching hangover, Jem would descend into a fit of self-loathing and hurl his trusty bottle of gin out the window or into the woods. *No more drinking,* he would tell himself, or at least not in private. But by and by, a bottle would find its way back to the cozy little drawer in his desk. He would have the same epiphany many times more, and always when he was drunk.

Returning to the barbecue, Jem saw that Percy was still talking to Audrey. He was telling a joke with casual, perfectly-timed delivery. And Audrey flashed a smile, a laugh. One foot, bare and beautiful, she placed atop the other, her toes bending and curling with dazzled anticipation. She took a small step closer to Percy. The Blake brothers, looking on with vague disinterest, appeared content to stand back.

Jem's heart sank. He broke away and watched without interest as several men raked hot coals in the long barbecue beds where the sweet meats were roasting. He pulled at his sweat-soaked collar. The pit in his stomach was now a boulder churning his guts. The world was murky, his senses cloudy. Sugar Dave was talking to him. Was he all right? Jem nodded, wagged his head to shake off the fog. Sure he was all right. He held his cup of gin up high.

"What shall we drink to, Davey?"

A voice answered: "How about a toast to all the untamed hearts?"

Jem turned. The voice didn't belong to Sugar Dave, but—

"JJ?"

For a moment, Jem was lost for words. "I…I'm surprised to see you down here. I didn't think this would be your kind of party."

JJ shrugged. "I forgot how boring all those stuffy balls used to be. Besides, I wanted to come spend some quality time with baby brother."

Jem frowned. "When are you going to stop calling me that?"

JJ smiled. "Whenever it is you age three minutes faster than I do."

With great excitement, Sugar Dave stuck his hand under JJ's nose. "Hiya, JJ! Been a long time, very long time. You remember me, don't you? We never talked much — not at all, really. Dave Dixon?"

Jem noticed that JJ's smile faded. JJ had never been one to mingle with the Valley's yeomen, and that was one of the chief differences between the twins. Jem tried to see and appreciate people for who they were. JJ was too much like Father in that he saw people as a means to an end, the end so often being an increase in social standing among the rich and powerful, or rather the 'well-bred highborn.' And since a poor boy like Sugar Dave had little to offer in such a respect…

"Dixon, right. The miller's boy."

Sugar Dave beamed. "That's right! He's remembered! Laws, it's been such a long time. I heard you been busy killing Yankees." Grinning, Dave looked down expectantly at his outstretched hand.

JJ finally shook Dave's hand, but a slight grimace replaced his smile. "Something like that, yes."

Dave nodded, still grinning, and an awkward silence persisted. Seeking to fill it, Jem cleared his throat with a loud rumble. He reached for an empty pewter cup and the bottle of gin.

"A drink for you, JJ?"

"No, thank you."

Jem cocked an eyebrow. "What, are you a teetotaler or something? Spent too much time with all those Quakers up in Yankeeland, have you?"

JJ nodded toward Sugar Dave's glass of buttermilk. "I'll have what he's having."

Jem laughed, and then he realized JJ was serious. He felt suddenly self-conscious, as if he wanted to turn and pitch the bottle of gin into the trees and sober up on the spot. But of course that was ridiculous — *JJ* was ridiculous. Even Sugar Dave had a drop of the satanic syrup now and then. What kind of man refused to drink outright?

Jem looked at Sugar Dave and shrugged. "Well, Davey, would you mind finding my brother some of that milk?"

"Sure thing," Dave said. He offered an encouraging smile. "I'm sure you two have a lot to catch up about."

Together, the twins watched as Sugar Dave melted into the crowd. For a long while, neither brother said anything. A lot to catch up about? That was one way to put it. The weight of four years of questions pressed on Jem's mind. So many questions, many profound and many others mundane, some of them utterly unspeakable. But where to begin?

"You're looking well," Jem said at last.

"Pardon?"

"I said, you're looking well." Jem nodded at JJ's uniform, but his eyes were on the saber and revolver on JJ's belt. "You look like a real soldier."

JJ nodded. "I suppose that's what I am."

"That a six-shooter?"

"Yes."

"It's nice."

JJ's response was to smile. He looked out at the party around them.

Jem looked around too, but his vision was starting to blur again. Still slumped against the bar, he turned to JJ and saw that his brother stood erect, chin up, back straight, the buttons on his uniform gleaming. Slowly, Jem pulled himself upright so that they stood shoulder to shoulder. He tried to gauge whether JJ had grown taller than he had in the last four years. When JJ turned back to him, Jem offered a disarming smile.

"So..."

JJ turned away again. "So."

"Do you like New York?"

"I like the Point."

"Mhm. Many Southerners there? Virginians?"

"A few Virginians. Over half my class are Southerners, in fact."

"I imagine the Yankees don't make great soldiers."

JJ scoffed. "Why, what makes you think so?"

Jem shrugged. "It's just common knowledge, isn't it? They say if there was ever a war between the states that the South would win in a single battle. They say one Southern man would have the courage and grit of ten Yankees."

"Oh yes?" JJ said. "And who is *they* exactly?"

"Stands to reason, doesn't it?" Jem said. "Northerners aren't raised like us. They're all merchants and mechanics — city-folk. They think first of dollars and cents. They don't know their history, they don't know tradition. Most of them are immigrants who don't even know English, or else they're the money-grubbing industrialists who make money off wage-slaves. Meanwhile, Southerners consider honor, merit, and noble living. Yankees grew up in dog-eat-dog city slums, while we were lucky to be raised within a quiet society of tradition and values."

JJ laughed and pointed all around. "Is that what you call all this?" His gesture landed at last on Wyolah Hall's slave shacks tucked back against the woods.

Jem bristled. "At least we're trying to right the wrongs within our society. It will take time, but we're better off fixing things ourselves than asking the Yankees to come down and turn everything on its head. I can tell you this much, Mayfair is a damn sight better than the New York waterfront. I've read about that place; it sounds plain awful."

"To read about a place doesn't mean you know it," JJ said. "And knowing it doesn't mean you understand it."

"Well, I stick to what I said."

"Of course you will, because you're stubborn. That's the Spencer blood in you.

But before you go condemning Yankees, you might first look after your own self. For instance, you could start by cutting that mane of yours."

Jem balked. "I like my hair. Makes me look, I don't know, like a rapscallion or something."

"You look like a mud-eater," JJ said, unimpressed. "It's undignified."

Frowning, Jem ran his fingers through his hair and said nothing.

"Yankees aren't nearly so shaggy as you are," JJ went on. "They take pride in appearances. They are a hard-working people. Ambitious, industrious. If they own a piece of land, they care for it. They don't let rot or decay take hold. As a population they're really quite remarkable, I must say."

"*Pshaw*," Jem groaned. "They sweep their dirt under the rug, same as anyone else. Certainly they're no better than we are."

"Certainly not," JJ said. "But you might be surprised to know the North isn't some big industrial wasteland full of diseased immigrants. I thought the same way before I went there. But in fact, they have as much gentle, rolling farm country as we do. *More* of it, probably. And their farms and villages, they were *pristine*. As pristine as country towns can be, anyway. Don't misunderstand me, some places are still crawling with dirty Irish peasants. But there's more than enough room for everyone up there. More than enough room down here too, for that matter."

Here, JJ looked toward the lighted windows of Wyolah Hall. Jem followed his brother's gaze until he looked upon the third floor balcony. There sat the Valley's patriarchs, smoking and drinking together. Father would be up there somewhere, mingling with his most important constituents.

JJ said, "The North feels like the sort of place where anyone can make a fresh start; where people can create new, better versions of themselves. And if you desire riches, you must *earn* them. There are no fat-cat planters up there taking all the spoils for themselves. Up there, there is a sense of industriousness that we seem to lack here in the Valley, and maybe across the whole South. There is a sense that things are moving steadily *onward, upward*. I don't think it has anything to do with them being Northerners and we Southerners. It's nothing to do with there being anything like separate nations within the Union. Maybe it's something else. In any case, everyone up there seems to share in a belief in something better coming. A dream of the future."

Jem considered these ideas for a moment, but then he shrugged them off. "Well, I can't believe it."

"You can't," JJ said, "or you won't? Maybe if we did things differently down here, Mayfair could change for the better. We could right our own wrongs, like you said. Because the Union — the whole *world* — is entering a new age. An age of machines and industry, of greater prosperity than mankind has ever known. America is at the forefront of the change; we're *driving* it, especially in the North." Once again JJ looked toward the slave shacks across the darkened lawn. "The South could be part of it too, if only we could rid ourselves of *all this*."

Jem watched as the red firelight danced upon JJ's face. His brother's eyes shone with hope and expectation.

"Finally, I understand what Father means when he says Mayfair can be more than what it is today. I understand what he means when he says the *Roscoes* can be more than what we are today. Everything in this new world is up for the taking, Jem, but only those with the courage to take charge of their destiny will be the ones to rise up. Only those with great ambition will be the ones to establish a legacy."

Jem sighed and shook his head. "You sound just like him."

"Who?"

Jem nodded toward Wyolah Hall. "Who do you think?"

"And since when did that become a bad thing?" JJ said.

Jem downed the last of his gin and refilled his cup. "You'll never stop defending the man, even after what he did to you."

"He's still my father," JJ said. "I'm still his son. None of that has changed."

Jem thought back to the rail station, and how Father had, maybe in a fit of delirium, mistaken him for JJ. There had been such a look of longing on Father's face in that moment, as if, for a precious few seconds, the truth of Father's mind had been laid bare.

"He doesn't talk about you," Jem said. "Not that he waxes poetic about the rest of us anyway. But in all the time you've been gone, he's sent no letters, offered no invitations calling you home — not even for Christmas for Christ's sake. And suddenly, out of the blue, he calls you home?"

JJ nodded. "It is curious, I'll give you that. But when I left, Father was in good health. Maybe, now that he can glimpse the end, he's trying to make things right again. Maybe he'll apologize."

Jem shook his head. "When have you ever seen the old man apologize for anything?"

"This is different," JJ said, with confidence in his voice. "This is the family legacy."

Jem took another drink and looked out at the party. For a long while, the twins stood side by side in silence.

"I feel *I* should apologize," Jem said at length. "About earlier tonight, back home. I *am* proud of you, JJ. I'm proud of what you did at Harper's Ferry. It was a noble thing."

JJ gave a nod and said a curt, "Thank you," as if the whole thing didn't mean very much to him, but of course Jem knew it did. JJ being JJ, he didn't make anything easy, including apologies.

"Were you scared?" Jem asked. "During the fighting, I mean. Were you frightened?"

"I was," JJ said, and it seemed that was all he'd say about it. After a moment, however, he turned to Jem. "But I remembered what Father always told tell us as children. 'Acknowledge your fear, let yourself feel it. Then set it aside and do whatever needs doing.'"

Jem laughed. "I must have missed that lecture," he said. "Oh, his musings were really awful, weren't they?"

JJ shrugged. "I happened to like them very much."

"Of course you did." Jem put his cup to his lips. "I prefer a different strain of advice. 'Never fold on a three-pair,' for instance."

Before Jem could drink again, JJ reached over and took the cup from Jem's hand and set it down on the bar.

"Hey, what's the idea?" Jem protested.

JJ turned squarely to Jem. "I've been away from home a long time," he said. "And in that time, we've both learned to live alone — without each other. But I'll be coming back to Mayfair again very soon, and for *good*." Here, JJ placed a hand on Jem's shoulder. "I know what you did for me, Jem. I know it was you who offered your seat at the Point. When I'm back with you, and Father, and the Company, I want to return the favor somehow. I don't know exactly how I'll do it. But we needn't act like squabbling strangers to each other. We'll need to learn how to be brothers again — for the good of the family, and for ourselves."

Jem laughed. "We've squabbled since the day we were born. That's never going to change."

Side by side, the twins looked out at the party. Jem's eyes settled once more on Audrey Blake. She was alone again, swirling about the trampled grass with her blonde hair rising and falling on her shoulders.

Jem blinked and tried to focus his attention elsewhere. "So then," he said. "Since we're going back to the beginning, what shall we talk about?"

JJ shrugged. "I don't know." His eyes shot toward the dance floor. "Maybe you could start by telling me about that blonde girl out there, the one you can't stop gawking at."

Jem's smile froze on his lips. "Audrey? You mean—"

"*Audrey*," JJ echoed, remembering the name. "Now it makes sense. Audrey Blake, right? Quite a family, hers."

Jem nodded, a small smile on his lips. "Quite a woman."

JJ rolled his eyes. "And she's captured your poor, sappy heart."

Jem shook his head. "What? *No*. Not a chance."

"No?" JJ gave a little shrug, but he didn't look convinced. "My mistake then."

Jem worked his jaw. "Well...it's just...it isn't that *simple*—"

"It's for the best, you mean," JJ said. "After all, pretty as she is, the poor girl's nothing but a white trash mud-eater."

Jem's throat tightened. "Don't call her that."

"What, a mud—?"

"*Don't*. Her name is Audrey. Miss Blake, to you."

"Fine, fine," JJ said. "But still, I'd say it's for the best you move on."

"Move on? What do you mean?"

"What I mean is, you deserve better."

Jem's jaw dropped open. "Better than Audrey Blake? My apologies, dear brother, but are you goddamn blind?"

"You know what I mean," JJ said. "The prince and the pauper. The Blake family doesn't have a pot to piss in. Never have and never will. Bad enough you run around with the likes of that Dixon fellow. Father would never approve a match with a girl like that."

With a sigh, Jem turned away. He considered a green-bellied fly that had landed in his gin. Jem took up the cup and angrily pitched its contents. Looking at the empty cup, he saw the fly was gone. He reached for the bottle and poured himself a fresh drink. As he measured up, his head began to swim again from drunkenness.

"To hell with Father's *approval*," he growled. "The day we let other people decide the course of our own lives is the day we stop living."

"I agree in theory," JJ said. "But he's our father, after all."

"Maybe that matters to you," Jem said, "but it doesn't make a difference to me. He's just a man, like any of us."

JJ laughed. "And you're the one who always wanted to be a soldier? Taking orders with no questions asked is one of the fundamental requirements. But anytime someone tells Jem Roscoe to do something — *anything* — you get it in your mind to do the exact opposite."

Hearing that, Jem had to laugh. "Maybe you're right."

"I usually am," JJ said. "But just tell me one thing. What are you so scared of?"

"*Scared*? I'm not scared, not by anything."

"You whine about Father's heavy hand over your life. You moan about never leaving the Valley. But whose fault is any of that, truly? You're a man, Jem, not a boy; whatever you do or don't do is up to *you*, and no one else. Meanwhile, the idea of asking a poor village girl to dance makes you shake in your boots. That's plain enough to see."

"*Bastard*. That's just not true—"

"Then prove it."

Jem blinked. "What?"

"I said, then prove it. Go ask her."

Just then, the string band held the final screeching note of *Dixie*. The dancers stopped to applaud and cheer wildly. The fiddlers nodded to each other and began to play a slow, sentimental ballad.

Feeling JJ's laughing eyes on him, Jem swallowed hard and stared at Audrey

Blake. He waited in expectant agony for another man to take her by the hand for the next song.

"Come on now, baby brother," JJ whispered. "She must know you're sweet on her. Maybe she's sweet on you too. Or else, maybe she'll take pity on you. There's nothing wrong with a dance. Just don't bring her home to Mother and Father, hm?"

Still rooted to his spot, Jem had a vision of himself crossing the floor, nearly reaching Audrey, only to be intercepted by Percy Claiborne or Sam Hanley or some other handsome bachelor. And Audrey would go with the other boy and then Jem would turn around and slink quietly back to his gin and maybe he really was better off and—

"Up and at em!" JJ cried, pushing Jem away from the bar. "Time to prove your courage and grit to me, O noble Southern knight."

Jem staggered forward and nearly toppled from drunkenness. Standing upright again, he slapped his cheeks to liven his senses. He took another step forward, then promptly turned back and held his empty cup to JJ with a sheepish grin.

"One more drink, JJ? For good luck?"

JJ took the cup from Jem's hand. With a wolfish grin, he tossed it over his shoulder and smiled wider when it crashed through the bushes.

"Go. 'Do what needs doing,' baby brother."

Jem flashed a grin. "And never fold on a three-pair."

JJ laughed, his face shining in the firelight. Jem turned toward the dance floor. Mustering his courage, he took a breath and plunged into the crowd.

As he wove through the throng of people, Jem rehearsed under his breath.

"Audrey... Hello, Audrey... Good evening, Audrey... Good evening, Miss, don't I know you from somewhere? No — stupid. Good evening, Miss Blake. May I have this dance?"

She stood there speaking with two friends. The friends were both pretty enough, but in Jem's eyes Audrey glowed brighter than either of them. When the other girls saw him approaching, they whispered hastily to Audrey and melted into the crowd, laughing and covering their mouths with their hands.

Jem hesitated. What had the girls said? He looked down at his clothes, smoothed his jacket, ran his tongue over his teeth. Looking up again, he saw Audrey alone, watching him. A voice in Jem's head urged him to run and never look back. But somehow his feet carried him forward until at last he stood before her.

Too close, he realized too late. A heavy man passing behind him turned suddenly and bumped Jem forward, and Jem's last step brought him careening forward until he stood nose to nose with Audrey. She instinctively leaned back, alarmed and maybe amused. Flushing red, Jem retreated a step back.

"Er, sorry..."

Audrey offered a wry smile. "You come on rather strong, Mr. Roscoe."

Jem was suddenly aware they were being watched. He felt a dozen pairs of eyes trained on him, boring into his head like hard screws into soft lumber. A suitor was never alone with his sweetheart. Not until their wedding night, whenever that might be. Anyway, he was getting ahead of himself. *Say something.*

"Goodnight."

She laughed. "Goodnight?"

He wagged his head. "Good *evening*," he said. "It is a *good* night. Beautiful, one might say, like you."

She looked at him, baffled. "You're really terrible at this, aren't you?"

Jem's mouth worked, but no sound came. Then he felt a soft touch on his hand. Audrey was now leading him to the dance floor.

"Come on," she said. "And mind my feet."

He blinked. "Sorry?"

"You were about to ask for a dance, weren't you? The song's half finished, so we'd best get to work."

Jem looked to the spectators watching from the crowd. He caught Percy Claiborne's jealous red face glaring at him. But feeling the soft touch of Audrey's hand in his own, Jem felt invincible.

Now Jem and Audrey stood together in the trampled grass. The current song finished and the next was set to begin. A caller stepped up and shouted for ladies and gentlemen to take their places.

The fiddlers struck up *Wait for the Wagon* and the caller called for ready. Jem bowed and Audrey curtsied. He took his position beside her for the promenade. He took her left hand in his and stretched his right hand over her shoulders to grasp hers. She leaned into him and he felt her hips push against his. He wished he had another damn drink — just to keep himself alert and focused. Looking across the way, he saw JJ nodding at him with a proud smile plastered on his face. A grinning Sugar Dave stood with JJ now, two glasses of buttermilk in hand.

The caller counted off and the promenade began.

Audrey turned her body into his. "I must say, you're a better dancer than a talker."

Jem murmured into her ear: "You can't learn everything from books."

"Had many lessons, then?"

"Enough to be dangerous."

Cheek to cheek, Jem breathed in her fragrance. The eyes watching from the crowd had not lost their vigilance. The promenade soon finished, and the dancers moved to change partners. While they were separated, Jem searched for Audrey in the circle. The other girls had no faces. When he at last made the full circle and was reunited with Audrey, perhaps a mere minute had passed, but it was more like an eternity. Jem smiled from ear to ear.

She laughed at him. "Happy to see me?"

"You have no idea."

The do-si-do was next. She turned her back to him and they circled each other. He watched her hips sway. The gin suddenly overcame him for a moment and he staggered back, blinking. Laws, he'd nearly passed out just now.

Audrey laughed and, taking his hand, pulled him back into position again. "Maybe I spoke too soon," she said with a wink. "You're growing two left feet."

He forced a smile and swallowed hard. The pit in his stomach had returned with a vengeance. Cold sweat dripped down his face.

"Nothing to it," he croaked.

Mercifully, the song finished. The dancers slowed and clapped for the band. Jem and Audrey turned to each other. She curtsied, he bowed. As Jem straightened again, the bile bubbling in his stomach suddenly shot up his throat. He slapped a hand over his mouth.

Audrey took his other hand and squeezed it. "Jem? Jem, are you all right?"

Red with shame, Jem turned sharply and staggered away. He'd go off somewhere and be sick, because that was going to happen whether he liked it or not. But when he felt better, he'd come back to Audrey and apologize, and maybe he'd ask her for another—

Jem froze as he saw Percy Claiborne moving in to cut him off.

Reduced to animal instinct, Jem's mind searched frantically for an exit. Finding his path blocked by a line of dancers, Jem pivoted and turned abruptly into Percy's path. He pushed a stunned Percy aside and made a beeline for the huge jacaranda tree several yards away.

Jem had nearly made it when his path was again blocked, this time by three barrel-chested figures. There was no pushing by or through them. Jem craned his neck and stared up into the brutish scowls of the Blake brothers.

Snorting and grunting like a bull, Ezra Blake pushed at Jem with a meaty arm.

"Keep away from my sister, nigger-lover."

Jem blinked. There were six Blakes in front of him, now nine. The whole world was spinning, faster and faster. There was no time for this.

"Please, fellas. I meant no disrespect—"

"Beg all you want," Blake growled. "If I see you talk to her again, so much as look at her again..."

"There's no need for threats, Ezra. I'm your employer, aren't I? You wouldn't really—"

"I don't care if you're the goddamn Pope of Rome," Ezra Blake hissed. "If I see you with Audrey again, I'll fuckin kill you. Got it?"

Jem's eyes shot wide open. It was coming. He needed to get away. Now.

Ezra Blake grabbed his arm and squeezed. "*Got it?*"

Jem shook his head. No *time*! He was going to be—*Oh, God.*

Jem turned away from Blake just as vomit shot up his throat like a hot, stinking geyser. In the meantime, Percy Claiborne had stepped up right behind Jem, finger outstretched, ready to tap his insolent foe on the shoulder before knocking the knave senseless. Instead, Percy was met with a spray of tarlike bile from Jem's volcanic stomach. The militia captain's dazzling cream suit turned a horrifying yellow.

"*Sonofabitch!*" Ezra Blake shouted.

The crowd groaned and then roared with laughter. Meanwhile, Jem tried to catch his breath. He thought he was finished, but just then another wave of vomit surged out from his guts. This time Percy had the sense to step back, but his fine boots were drenched in a putrid mess that made several ladies in the crowd faint from shock. The men standing around bellowed with fresh laughter. Jem stood there, stunned, his hands outstretched as if pleading his innocence.

The next instant, meaty hands were all over Jem. Ezra Blake yanked Jem around with a snarl and hurled a punch. Before the connection was made, a sudden wave of exhaustion flattened Jem and he fell back out of harm's way. Blake's fist rushed over Jem's head and instead connected with Percy Claiborne's dumbfounded mug. The crowd bellowed harder as Percy found himself flat on the ground in a stinking wet mess, massaging his cracked jaw.

Seeing his window of escape, Jem shot to his feet. He dodged grabbing hands and broke through the crowd to the woods beyond.

The Blakes helped a dazed Percy Claiborne to his feet.

"Find him!" Percy shouted. "Spread out and find the bastard!"

Chapter II

FREE-MAN

The nightmare drove Mae Jane out of bed for the third time that week.

She awoke with a start, breathing hard, not knowing if she was alive or dead. She put a hand to her mouth and it came away smeared with blood from where she'd bitten into her lip. She fumbled in the darkness and finally managed to light a small candle at her bedside. The tiny light it produced shone bravely, but an all-swallowing darkness loomed everywhere.

Ben's cot across the small pantry apartment was empty, the corners neatly tucked in. He had to be still across the Valley with the Roscoes. Mae Jane had no idea of the time, but she guessed it was well past midnight. And since she knew getting back to sleep was out of the question, she swung her legs out from under the covers. She braced for the cold of the floor as she pressed her feet down. As she stood, her hip gave an audible *pop*.

"Damn old bones," she murmured to the darkness.

She dressed quickly, simply. She had not decided what she would exactly do with the night that remained, but she was confident she'd think of something. There was always a wall to wash, a hall to sweep, a closet to organize. There had once been a time when Clarendon bustled day and night, its slaves constantly working to keep the place tidy. In the years since the Spencer place became the Roscoe place, and without fifty or more other servants to aid in even the most modest of cleaning efforts, the glittering white palace of Clarendon had slowly but surely yellowed over time.

Mae Jane lit a kerosene lantern, which afforded better light. She blew out the candle by her bedside and watched as a curious air current sucked the smoke through the crack of a nearby door. The door looked to lead into a closet, but it was of course the entrance to the cellar, and the underground tunnel that led to the slave cabins far across the lawn.

In the old days, during harsh winter months when blizzards made the lawn nigh impassable, the most trusted of the help would rise early and gather in slave cabin three to make the dark trek underground toward Clarendon's pantry. Eventually the tunnel became a common passageway, for Colonel Spencer had claimed he didn't like the idea of his slaves roaming the grounds of his estate after dark.

After Mr. John freed all of Clarendon's slaves, and after Mae Jane elected to stay on the estate to help the Roscoe family, Mr. John had invited her to live *in* Clarendon. Of course Mae Jane refused to move out of the cabin she and Ben had shared with two other families. "It ain't right for whites and coloreds to live together under the same roof," she had professed to Mr. John at the time.

Lady Isabella was of a similar opinion. She had balked at her husband's suggestion that the Freemans should sleep in bedrooms that had been constructed for the Spencer family and their guests. It didn't matter to Isabella that over twenty guest rooms, each of them furnished with fine beds and linens, went unoccupied for months and, lately, years at a time.

"We can't have visitors think we live in a *commune* or something," the Lady of Clarendon complained. "We must maintain some kind of order, some kind of hierarchy." Evidently, Isabella had no issue with the family dog Tipper sleeping in an upstairs bedroom.

But in those early years of the Roscoe family, after it became apparent that Mae Jane needed to be within earshot of the infant Sarah, and later to dote on the newborn twins, the Freemans were asked to make their own private apartment out of the pantry. Clarendon's massive and now mostly unused kitchen complex ('the kitchens') was large enough to render the pantry superfluous anyway, especially since it was no longer necessary to keep dry stores for several hundred slaves. The Roscoes gave the Freemans two feather cots, the first bed above the floor that Mae Jane had ever slept on. Sometimes, when her spine or joints gave her grief, she still preferred to sleep on the hard floor.

As she passed through the darkened pantry door, Mae Jane paused and touched the jamb. There, notched into the worn oak, were the faded markers of Ben's age and growing height: *Ben 7*; *Ben 8*; a great spurt at *Ben 9*. The handwriting was Ben's, etched in an uncertain childish scrawl, for Mae Jane couldn't read or write. Another height marker was noted *Mama*. There was no indication of Mae Jane's age, because she didn't know when she was born or how old she really was.

"And I prefer to keep it that way," she liked to tell Ben.

With the lantern in hand, Mae Jane padded through the silent hallways of the towering mansion. Gone were the days of magnificent balls and barbecues of the kind the Roscoes were attending tonight across the Valley. Instead, the parlors and drawing rooms hosted only abandoned furniture, each piece shrouded in ghostly white linen. Whenever she walked alone through the halls at night, Mae Jane could not help but feel the haunting presence of people she'd once known. She saw shadows slipping around corners, imagined figures occupying covered chairs as if engaged in conversation together.

Never did she feel hostility from such ghosts, but rather a creeping sadness, a sense that such sentinels missed their former lives. Mae Jane certainly missed the people whose shadows she recognized. She missed old Aunt Bess (Not Aunt *Bessie* — call her that and you were liable to get your ears boxed), the head maid who had run Clarendon like a hard-nosed Yankee skipper might run a whaling ship at sea. Mae Jane also missed Cici and Phibe, who had been like sisters to her. She missed Carlotta-George, the kindly, plump lady who had raised her after Mama died and who had taught her how to become good help. And she missed Mack and Jem, who had been good friends of Joby's and later looked after her and Ben until they themselves were sold away somewhere. (Lady Isabella had never guessed there was a namesake when Mae Jane had suggested the name 'Jeremiah' for her second twin son.)

Most of all, Mae Jane missed Evie.

Evie had been Mae Jane's younger sister. *Was* her younger sister. Evie had been born with a clubbed hand, but that didn't make her any less beautiful. She was gregarious and bursting with energy, and she enchanted all who looked upon her. She especially liked to dance, and always had an audience to watch her move. She wore bracelets and anklets which she carved herself out of wood and animal bone and some small glittering stones, and these pieces clacked and rattled as she danced in the dirt. Mae Jane knew she'd be lying if she said she'd never been jealous of Evie's talents, or simply of her sister's joyous spirit. Some people choose to see the goodness in the world, but Evie *felt* it. To Evie, there was nothing to the world *but* goodness.

"You too rambunctious," their adopted mother Carlotta-George would scold. "You keep you head too high, child. You wanna know why all the old timers got our heads crooked and our backs stooped? It ain't 'cause we enjoy the view from down here. It's because smart niggers keep they heads low, and the low-headed uns live long enough to win a little rest before the Lord take em. You ever see any uppity niggers with gray hair? They all buried in the same hole where the Colonel puts em, maid and bull alike. Mind you don't join em, Evie. Mind you keep you head down!"

Evie had been so beautiful, in fact, that Colonel Spencer's wife — Lord, it had been *years* since Mae Jane had thought of Lady Anna — begged her husband to sell Evie lest she corrupt the young white gentlemen coming to call on their daughters (including Isabella). Lady Anna believed Evie was a witch who could cast voodoo spells upon white men. It didn't matter to Lady Anna that Evie was only twelve years old.

In any case, it wasn't a gentleman caller who was 'corrupted' by Evie's charm, but a young drifter hired on as an extra whip for the cotton harvest. The drifter took a liking to Evie and interrupted her work to make her to dance for him. The head overseer had words with the drifter over this infatuation, and in anger the drifter struck the man down. The drifter then grabbed Evie and fled with her.

For many years afterward, Mae Jane wondered to herself *why* Evie had gone with the man so easily. Being ushered off in full view of an entire field of hands, Evie need only have cried out or tried to fight the man off. The other hands would have stepped in, and surely the Colonel would have forgiven their beating of the drifter as small justice for his killing of the head overseer.

But Evie didn't cry out. She didn't even look afraid. Rather, she looked *thrilled*, as if she was embarking on a great adventure. Mae Jane could still see the expression on her sister's face as she turned in her direction. Evie was smiling, and she *waved goodbye to her*. That was what stayed with Mae Jane the most: that carefree wave and happy grin, as if the trip was a roundabout stroll through the garden, back in a jiffy.

Evie never came back. The Colonel's men found her body sprawled out on the bank of the Sleepy Creek some three miles away from Clarendon. The drifter had evidently had his way with Evie and then cut her throat, all of it done quickly and without fanfare. The Colonel determined the drifter was not an insane killer, only an opportunistic one. They decided not to pursue him, and rumors went around that the man traveled farther south.

None of this did anything for Evie, of course. The Colonel's men opened up one of the mass graves at the edge of the estate and buried Evie there among all the generations that had gone before her, with space remaining for those of generations to come. They hadn't even wrapped her up, but gave her naked to the soil. For whatever reason, they had left Evie's jewelry clasped to her hands and feet.

"Just the way it go," Carlotta-George had told Mae Jane when the terrible news broke. The old lady refused to tell Mae Jane that her sister was *dead*. She repeated her best version of a euphemism over and over for many days, her voice barely a whisper: "Just the way it go…Just the way it go…"

For some years after Evie's death, Mae Jane considered digging up her body to remove those pieces of jewelry; not for any sentimental value, but because Mae Jane could not bear the thought of her sister wearing anything resembling chains on her way to the afterlife. But Mae Jane never had the courage to confront the mass grave, and Joby was always quick to talk her out of it. By the time Ben was born, Mae Jane had given up hope of trying. Evie would remain where she was, jeweled shackles and all.

Just the way it go.

Back in the present, Mae Jane turned her head to the sound of the front door opening. She heard the voices echo across the quiet house. Cupping her candle with a hand, Mae Jane turned away from the empty parlors and drawing rooms and padded toward the grand foyer.

She greeted Sarah and Mr. John in the puppy ballroom. Sarah was flushed and giddy with happiness. Sarah kissed Mae Jane on the cheek and professed she might fall asleep halfway up the stairs.

"And you, Mr. John?" Mae Jane asked the old man. "You had a long day, what with you travels and the party and all. I got a bed in the sunroom all made up for you, right this way."

Mr. John hesitated a moment and waited for Sarah to ascend the stairs. In a low voice he asked Mae Jane, "Has the Lady of Clarendon left her door unlocked tonight?"

Mae Jane shook her head. "I don't rightly know, sir. I…I could check for you, if you—"

"No, no. No, that's fine, Mae Jane, thank you."

"It's really no trouble, Mr. John—"

"Indeed it isn't," he said, pushing a smile across his lips. "Thank you, Mae Jane. Down here will be just fine for tonight."

She led Mr. John to a guest bedroom just down the hall that she called the 'sunroom,' for it featured large windows that enjoyed sunshine through most of the day. Looking through the panes of glass, one could just barely make out the decrepit slave cabins tucked around the corner of the willow grove.

"That will be all, Mae Jane, thank you."

"Is you sure you don't need me to—?"

"I've got everything I need for tonight, thank you."

She nodded and went to the door. There, she paused.

"Mr. John?"

The old man eased himself down onto the bed. He leaned on his cane and looked at her with an inquiring expression. "Yes?"

"Was my Ben all right for you tonight, Mr. John?"

"Was he all right?"

"I mean, was he behavin himself. It's his business with Mr. Jem at the table tonight that got me thinkin. I warn Benny all the time about his speakin-up and speakin-out, and how it does no good for nobody. But, Mr. John, you know how it is when you young. They think they know everthin there is to know about anythin."

Mr. John laughed in the darkness. "Yes, I know what you mean. But sometimes I doubt if age really does bring any greater measure of wisdom."

Mae Jane nodded eagerly, as if the answer was self-evidently *of course it does*. "I know a lot thanks to these gray hairs, Mr. John. Mostly, I know that I don't know much at all."

The old man laughed again and bid Mae Jane goodnight.

"Goodnight, Mr. John."

She left the candle in the room and shut the door behind her. Plunged in darkness, she waited a moment for her eyes to adjust. Slowly, she waded through the blackness toward the ethereal night light that frosted the windows.

Yawning, Mae Jane determined it was time to turn in once more. Ben was likely outside seeing to Mabel and the coach, and would be inside soon.

She passed back into the pantry apartment and lit a new candle. She looked over at the small cot where Ben slept. Stacked on the windowsill above was a collection of books. She couldn't read the titles, but Ben had told her about all of them. He was particularly proud of one, which he claimed was written by an escaped slave named...what was it, Douglass? Frederick Douglass. A man who was born into slavery in Maryland and who escaped to New England, taught himself to read and write, and was now an outspoken advocate against slavery. Douglass was Ben's hero, and he'd read the man's autobiography countless times. He'd even tried to read passages aloud to her, but she would not permit it. She didn't have time, she claimed, to listen to other people's problems. She had enough of her own as it was.

Turning to her own cot, Mae Jane kneeled down. She winced a little as her knees *popped*. She put her hands together and bowed her head to pray.

A few minutes later, Ben burst inside the apartment. He was flustered, distracted, evidently with great matters on his mind. His entrance sent a gust across the tiny room that snuffed out Mae Jane's prayer candle.

Calmly and quietly, Mae Jane struck a fresh match and relit the candle. Its flame glowed white.

"You wake the devil comin in like that," she said to Ben.

"Sorry, Mama."

Standing there, Ben looked so much like Evie.

Mae Jane turned and shut the world out by putting her head in her hands. She was thankful for the cover of darkness.

Ben went to the small dresser beside his bed and began to undress. His shirt collar was wilted with sweat from a long day, and he removed it with a sigh of relief. He dropped his suit clothes to the floor to be dealt with tomorrow. He pulled a long nightshirt over his shoulders and spread the cotton fabric down to his knees.

"You gonna clean up your mess?"

"I'm tired, Mama. It will only take a minute tomorrow."

"God gave you a minute right now. Ain't no guarantee He'll do the same come morn."

Ben sighed. "Yes, Mama."

After putting his clothes away, Ben sat down heavily on his bed. Mae Jane did not hear the rustle of sheets. Instead she felt that Ben was suffering a quiet torment.

"What's on you mind, child?"

She felt Ben's eyes on her. Her own gaze was still fixed in darkness, and she rubbed her dry hands together slowly, vigorously. She murmured something to God and now she looked up, her prayers finished at last.

"It's past midnight," was Ben's answer. "You should be long asleep."

"I don't sleep much these days. Never really did. Bad dreams."

"About the old days?"

Old days. That was their euphemism for the days of terror: of whipping and raping and killing and stamping out the humanity of human beings. Other folks in Mayfair called them the *good* old days. Strangely enough, Mae Jane sometimes thought of them as such too, but she never let on about that to Ben. Mostly they had been days of horror and humiliation, but there had been moments of *goodness* too. Carlotta-George teaching her to make hot cakes on Sunday afternoons. The harsh beauty of a blood red sun setting over the fields at harvest time, and the sound of those old soulful songs ringing in her ears. Maybe time didn't heal all wounds, but everything that could bleed eventually dripped dry.

Mae Jane shook her head. "Not the old days. About the Roscoes."

"The Roscoes?"

She looked at Ben sitting there on the bed, watching her intently. The white candle reflected in just one of his eyes, wide and glassy. The other half of his face was darkened by shadows.

Mae Jane shook her head a second time. "You wouldn't want to hear none of it," she said. "It's all nonsense."

Ben said, "I want to hear it, Mama, I do. But only if you want to tell me about it."

She looked at him and offered the best smile she could manage. Her deep voice was hesitant, shaky, as if saying anything at all might bring a curse down upon the entire house.

"I dream I'm in the kitchens," she said. "It's boiling hot, as usual. Can't see for the sweat in my eyes. I bring the sup dishes out one by one, set em on the dining table. But all the chairs is empty. The wine glasses is full to the brim. I sit there alone, all this big sup laid out, and I get to wonderin where everybody's gone. Then I get to thinkin — why, Mae Jane, you ought to have youself a drink. Never had a drop in my life, but…but that wine, it *smells good*. Smells like the feelin you get, sittin warm by the fire in winter. Somehow it smells like that. So I pick up the glass and I put it to my lips, and before I drink I smile and take another whiff, to really relish it. Suddenly my stomach turns. It don't smell right no more. It smells rank and rotten, like a slab of meat left out in high August. And there's…there's that iron smell too, and it runs down my throat. I hold the glass up in the light. Then I see. The glass is filled with blood. All them glasses on the table, they's all filled with blood. The Devil's invisible hand keeps pourin, keeps fillin em up, until finally they run over and blood spills over the table, over all the sup I made for nobody. I feel sick and I push myself away from the table, but I knock my glass over and it shatters on the floor and blood runs along the boards. I feel very afraid — cold. The fire's gone out, and I'm there all alone. Except no, not alone. I feel somebody beside me and I look. There's Evie, my baby sister, and she's laughin at me. I don't know why she's laughin, but she is. *Was*. And then I hear screamin upstairs. A scream I ain't never heard before. Maybe a baby, but no baby I ever heard of. Maybe a mama…but not even a new mama who delivers a dead baby could scream like that. I figure whatever's up there, it ain't livin. But it's gettin louder, closer. It smells like hot iron, like blood turned bad. And Evie's laughin, it's mixin with the screaming, until it's so I can't tell the difference. And then I…well, then I wake up."

Ben said nothing. He stood up and walked over to Mae Jane's bed, and he knelt down beside her and put his arms around her.

"Oh, stop it, child."

"No, Mama."

"I said stop—"

"Please, Mama…"

They held each other like that for a long while. Mae Jane wanted to cry and almost felt like she should, but she couldn't. No matter how many times in her life she'd wanted to cry, the tears would never come. When they pulled back from their embrace, however, she saw that Ben's eyes were wet with tears.

"Mama," Ben said, his voice croaking. He swallowed down a frog in his throat. "Mama, I think we ought to leave Clarendon. We ought to leave the Valley and head north."

Mae Jane shook her head. "Benny, child, what nonsense you got in your head now?"

Gently, Ben turned her shoulders toward him so that she could look in his eyes.

"I saw him again, Mama. I saw Cutler."

Mae Jane felt a chill run through her; there was nothing she could do against it. But in an instant she snatched Ben's wrist and glared at him. "*Enough with that,*" she said in a warning tone. "I don't want to hear *none* of it, child."

Ben shook his head. "He's got Senator Roscoe's ear, Mama. I don't know what he's aiming for, but no doubt Clarendon factors into his plans somehow—"

"*None of it,* Benjamin. I told you. Not another word."

Ben pulled his arm free from her grasp. "What's the matter? You just want to pretend none of those horrible things happened?"

"Of course they happened," Mae Jane said. "But that don't mean we gotta dwell on em. You and me, child, we freedmen now. We ain't got no concern with Mr. Cutler no more, 'cause he ain't got no concern with us."

Ben turned and glared at the white light of the candle. "Freedom," he muttered. "What's freedom really mean down here in the Valley? What's the life of a free negro worth in Virginia? It's an illusion. We aren't *free* down here, Mama, not really."

"Of course we is," she said with a huff. Her sadness and fright were gone, and her typical dry candor had returned. "Mr. John pays the both of us by the week and we keep every penny. Ain't that bein free, child? We's lucky, bless the Lord, we's luckier than most other folks I've ever known."

Deflated, but still stubborn, Ben shook his head. "No, Mama. Down here we can't go where we want, we can't say what we want. They gave us the name '*Freeman*', but it doesn't mean a damn thing. Whatever our real names were, they took them away a long time ago. Around here we'll never be anything more than *niggers*, and here in the big-house we'll never be anything more than the servants of rich white folks. For God's sake, Mama, we sleep in a pantry."

Mae Jane stiffened with indignation. "And maybe that's good enough for me. Ever think of that, Benny? Maybe *this*, right here, is more than good enough for you mama. You forget, child, the dirt floor you was born on, and *in the dark*. This is paradise compared to them old times. And you know, child, maybe all them books you like to read done nothin but make you ungrateful. They just fill you head with hot air, make you insufferable."

Ben took her hand. There was a pleading look in his eyes. "We could have a life of our own, Mama. A *real* life, someplace else. I could build you a house—"

Mae Jane laughed. "You, build me a house? Oh, child..."

"I'm serious, Mama."

Her laughter disappeared, and all that remained was a stern glare. "I am too," she said in an urgent whisper. She had never quite gotten over the idea that a master and his family had the right to eavesdrop on their slaves' conversations. Growing up at Clarendon, a slave had no concept of privacy. Even today, Mae Jane always looked over her shoulder before engaging in any discussion of THE FAMILY.

"Mr. John?" she whispered. "The Roscoes? They's *family*, Benny."

"*We* are family, Mama. *They* are—"

"Don't you finish, child." She shook her head furiously. "Don't you dare finish. You gonna look you mama in the eye and tell me them Roscoe boys ain't you brothers? You gonna tell me Miss Sarah ain't you sister?"

At that, Ben tore his eyes away. Hot sweat beaded on his pulsing brow.

Mae Jane groaned, realizing that she'd hit some kind of nerve in her son.

"I see. So maybe that's part of it too. But even so. You gonna tell you mama that Mr. John ain't been like a daddy—"

"I *have* a father," Ben muttered. "Or at least I *had* one. And John Roscoe just stood there watching while he was maimed and sold away like a goddamn animal."

Mae Jane struck Ben across the face. After a long moment of shock, Ben scowled at her before he glared at the far wall.

"Look at me, child."

He wouldn't.

"*Look at me*, child."

Still, Ben kept his gaze on the far wall.

Mae Jane reached out and took Ben's fingertips, and she kissed them and touched them to his own stinging cheek.

"Benny. Child. It don't gotta be like this."

Ben shivered at her touch. He turned back to her with fresh tears in his eyes, and gently, Mae Jane wiped them away.

"It ain't blood that makes a family," she said. "We don't get to choose how or where we's born. We don't get to choose our family. God don't let us choose anythin — He just give it to us, be it good or bad. But what we *can* choose is to love what we got, who we got, and remind ourselves that none of it lasts long. That's what family is, Benny. It's folks who choose to love each other, no matter who they is or how they all different, because they believe the sameness outweighs the different. Family chooses to love each other, even when they don't feel like it. 'Specially when they don't feel like it."

The low-burning bedside candle went out at last, and suddenly all was darkness.

"Now," Mae Jane said. "You should get youself to bed and get some sleep. I don't wanna hear no more about this runnin-off business. This is home, and home this is." After a quiet moment, she added, "It's just the way it go."

Ben stood up and Mae Jane held out her hands, and he helped her to her feet. Mae Jane settled into bed again while Ben crossed the room to his own mattress. He slipped under the covers and stared up at the darkened ceiling.

"Mama?"

Mae Jane spread the covers about her. "Yes, Benny."

"Do you...do you think Daddy's still alive? Do you think he's still alive somewhere?"

It was very quiet. Whatever thoughts had been coursing through Mae Jane's mind in that instant, Ben's question scattered every one of them. All she could do was lay back and pull the covers up over her head.

"...Mama?"

The only response to Ben's question was the creaking springs of Mae Jane's cot as she rolled over on her side. If she was going to cry — and she knew she wouldn't, no matter how much she might want to — she didn't want Ben to see.

Just the way it go.

"Goodnight, child," she said. "Sweet dreams."

Silence filled the small pantry. In her mind's eye, Mae Jane saw Ben looking at her from across the room, peering toward his mother but seeing little in the inky blackness. Ben waited a moment longer, but there was no point in it. He lay his head down on the pillow once more.

"Goodnight, Mama."

Chapter 12

THE DUELISTS

In the early hours of the morning, moving like a shadow across a starry sky, a barefoot boy stole through the tobacco fields of Wyolah Hall.

Tom stalked in like a painted Comanche brave on a suicide mission. Twice on the way there he fled the familiar dirt roads of the Valley to avoid buggies and wagons going to and fro. Once, he glimpsed Ben driving Father and Sarah back home to Clarendon and was glad he'd been out of sight when the coach passed by.

Tom had made the decision earlier that night, permissions be damned, to attend the Clairbornes' ball and barbecue. After bidding goodnight to Mother (she was in the parlor calmly listening to Bayard on the piano) and to Mae Jane too, Tom closed the door of his bedroom and immediately set to work on his breakout plan. He stuffed his bed to make it look like he was sleeping there. His bedroom window opened to the second story veranda, so it was an easy task to get down. From there, Tom raced up Clarendon's tree-lined path and turned south across the Valley.

Hours later, walking on sore feet but still with a pep in his step, Tom reached Wyolah Hall. He was certain he would have enough time to poke around, maybe pinch a forgotten tankard of ale or a half-smoked cigar, and get back to Clarendon before sunrise.

At Wyolah Hall, the festivities were in full swing. From the cover of a tobacco field, Tom knelt down and observed. There were hundreds of faces laughing together in the searing light of the smoke pits. Blacks and whites stood mostly apart, but some had gathered together. It was a real *amalgamation*, which is how Tom had always heard the older folks put it. Seeing those red faces in the firelight, Tom's first thought was of a fairly agreeable vision of Hell filled with demons eating racks of pork ribs. Off in the distance, Tom heard thunder but thought nothing of it.

"Kid."

Looking down, Tom leaped back and resisted the urge to scream. Instead a high, strangled mumble left his lips that made him bring up his hands to cover his mouth. On the ground before him was a talking corpse, a drunk draped over a thick pile of shredded grass. The drunk had his hand outstretched. He was shamelessly matter of fact in saying: "Kid, you really gotta get me another drink."

Without a word Tom steadied himself, set his eyes forward, and walked steadily ahead without looking back. He heard the drunk say something but didn't stop to listen. After finally shaking the last of his jangled nerves, he dropped back into Comanche character, and though he certainly didn't want to stumble over another drunk in the dark he clung to the safety of the forest while rounding the Hall's perimeter. He looked over his shoulder to ensure the drunk corpse was not coming after him in a death-shuffle, and then he pressed on.

From a thick cover of trees, Tom looked up at the big mansion atop the hill. It was a magnificent palace of the kind written about in every fairy tale Tom had ever read. Orange lights shone out from every window to ward off the deepening night.

Suddenly, a dark shape crashed through the undergrowth — terribly close. Tom froze and watched. The shape turned around and Tom recognized the face in a sliver of moonlight.

Jem!

Except Jem didn't see him, thank the Lord. Instead Jem staggered a few yards more, keeled over, and vomited in the bushes. Tom resisted the urge to puke in turn.

"Christ," Jem was muttering between spasms, his voice weak and pitiful. "Why, why, why..."

And then, from somewhere, a woman's voice said, "Well, that's one way to say goodnight."

Tom's heart leapt into his throat. Jem likewise whirled around, startled. Tom was certain that Jem would see him now. It was dark, but not *so* dark that he could not be seen. Instead, Jem looked off toward the sound of the voice.

A blonde girl was standing there in the moonlight. Her dress rippled against her body in the soft breeze. Tom thought her beautiful, but somehow unreal. He suspected she was the kind of girl he would fall in love with when he was older. If only he was older already.

"It's late," the girl said to Jem. "And cold. My brothers are set to take me home."

Jem nodded and was about to say something, but then he clutched his stomach and groaned.

"Are you all right?" the girl asked.

Jem turned away from her to spit. He shuddered. "I will be."

Tom grinned. Poor Jem, he had to be in love with this girl! Tom couldn't wait to torture Jem with cries of *loverboy* later, but then he realized he couldn't tease his brother without also asking for a whupping.

Tom heard dozens of voices and rushing feet, and beyond the trees he saw many bodies stalking about the firelights, searching for something — or someone.

"I have to go now," the girl said to Jem. "I'm sorry."

"Audrey." Jem stepped toward the girl. "I'm sorry. I've acted like a real fool. Worst of all, I embarrassed you. Did...did I embarrass you?"

The girl named Audrey nodded. "A little," she said. But now she smiled. "Luckily, I'm terribly forgetful of bad memories and rather fond of good ones. How about you, Mr. Roscoe?"

Jem laughed. "I don't know if anyone will let me forget this one." He gestured back toward the party. "I suppose you shouldn't keep your bodyguards waiting."

"Let me worry about them," she said. "You take care of yourself, Mr. Roscoe. And make sure your own brothers come to school on Monday. Mr. Braxton has told me all I need to know about your Tom."

Tom's mouth fell open. The new schoolmistress!

So Jem was in love with Mayfair's newest prison warden. Tom shivered, maybe from a cool wind, but more likely from the sinking reality that his plans for skipping school and going quarry-diving with Billy Clements were now squandered without question. In that moment, Tom decided it was his solemn duty to make Jem and the girl somehow fall *out* of love and never speak to each other again. Then he would have free reign over the school, which of course meant never darkening the door ever again. Perhaps he could solicit help from Billy for the dirtiest deeds that would need doing, and maybe even ask some of the girls at school about their knowledge of *anti*-love potions.

"Audrey?"

The girl paused and turned back. "Yes?"

Jem gazed at her for a long, quiet moment. "You were breathtaking tonight."

The girl named Audrey looked down and her cheeks blushed deep red in the darkness. When she looked up at Jem again, she beamed.

"You have vomit on your chin."

Tom chewed on his tongue to keep himself from laughing. He watched as Audrey Blake turned and departed from the woods. She walked across a field toward the big jacaranda tree and the party, and there a circle of men — her brothers, Tom guessed — whisked her away. But even as this group departed, an even larger group stalked toward the treeline.

Suddenly, Jem pitched forward again and retched the last of the mess churning in his stomach. Tom heard him groan between spasms of pathetic dry-heaving: "Lord in Heaven, I love her. Lord in Heaven..."

"*Jem?* Jem!"

Tom peered through the brooding black of night. Three men approached ahead of the massed crowd, and Tom knew one of them instantly.

"You beautiful bastard," JJ said with a laugh. "You should have seen the look on Percy Claiborne's face when you soaked him."

"It ain't good, Jemmo," one of the others said. Tom thought his name was George Something-or-other. "It ain't good at all."

Tom listened to the voices in the distant crowd. The music had not stopped. But now came a shrill, bloodcurdling wail: a hunter's call. And just then, tree branches snapped as the crowd pushed into the forest.

"There's all wrath about to come looking for you," said the third man. "I reckon you've inspired a lynching. You think he needs a gun, George?"

"Son of a bitch," George said. *Hunt*, that was his other name: George Hunt. "You really need to ask the question, Davey?"

Without a word, JJ put a hand on the holstered revolver at his side. "If Jem needs a weapon, I've got one for him."

Jem swayed on his feet. His voice sounded stronger than he looked. "No, JJ. With a gun in my hand I know there'll be a man shot dead here tonight, and maybe two."

The others looked at each other, and then they burst into laughter.

"Never mind the chivalry," the man named Dave said. "You need a gun."

"Why?"

Hunt nodded toward the approaching crowd. "Because *they* have guns. A lot of them."

JJ drew his revolver, a gesture that was met with stunned silence. JJ flipped the revolver round and offered the handle to Jem.

"Here," JJ said. "You're the better shot. For God's sake, don't use it if you don't have to. But if you have to..."

Shouts and whistles reached Tom's ears. Looking out, he saw a mass of approaching men, heard them snarling like wolves. And at the head of the gang was a tall man in a white suit that had been turned a yellowish-gray by a spill of some kind. Feeling bodies press in from all sides, Tom knelt down and hid himself within the broad leaves of a fern, and prayed that no one noticed him there.

The gang of men swelled out to form a wide semicircle around the twins and their two friends. Some in the crowd were armed with crude weapons and others curled bare fists. The man in white, Percy Claiborne, stepped forward with murder in his eyes.

"Jeremiah Roscoe..."

There was a long pause. No one breathed a word.

Jem cocked an eyebrow. "...Yes?"

Percy struck out with an open hand, and one of his fine sterling rings split Jem's lip open. When Jem looked up bleeding, Percy grinned and turned back to the crowd. They whooped and whistled as if a boxing match had just begun.

"I demand satisfaction!" Percy cried, and he smiled when the crowd cheered louder.

Over the cheers, George Hunt leaned forward with his arms crossed. "How about a hot poker up your ass, Percival? Would that *satisfy* you?"

Percy sneered, "I'll deal with you after I've put a bullet through Roscoe's heart." Here, the crowd renewed its fervent support. By now the crowd had swelled even larger. The dance, the barbecue, everything else had been forgotten.

"There's no need for this nonsense," Jem said.

"Says the man holding a gun," Percy snapped. "You've stained my honor!"

Here, JJ stepped between the two opponents. His looming presence created a ripple effect of doubt among the crowd.

"My brother's stained your shirt," JJ said, "and for that I suppose he's sorry. But the only one doing any damage to your honor, Percy, is yourself." JJ now offered a conciliatory handshake. "There's still a way out of this that saves both of you any further embarrassment. So please, Percy, for old time's sake, for an old friend, let all this go. It's beneath you."

The crowd was quiet. Whispers and murmurs were exchanged. Percy seemed to sincerely consider JJ's words. But then, after the moment passed, and maybe feeling the energy of the crowd seeping away, Percy slapped away JJ's outstretched hand.

"Don't you dare touch me, *cocksucker*."

The crowd gasped. Gleeful grins lit up dark faces.

Percy made his voice ring louder. "I have no grievance with you, JJ Roscoe. Unless, of course, you put your filthy, sodomizing hands on me again."

The crowd snickered and waited for a reaction. JJ's fists were clenched, his jaw pulsing, but he stood very still. His eyes studied every laughing face — old friends and neighbors — and he seemed to make a silent oath against each of them.

"Well?" Percy said, stepping nose-to-nose with JJ. "Are you going to get out of my way, cocksucker?"

The hammer of the revolver *clicked* as Jem cocked it. Next instant, the barrel was pointed at Percy Claiborne's temple. The crowd stepped back in mute shock.

Jem's eyes had become slits. "Insult my brother one more time, Claiborne, and see what happens to you."

Terror filled Percy Claiborne's eyes, but he managed a haughty laugh. "You'd shoot a defenseless man like a dog? And for what? All this show of so-called bravery just so you can bed the little Blake whore?"

A thick silence spread over the whole scene. No one breathed, but Jem's eyes widened with white hot rage.

George Hunt clicked his tongue and his impish grin widened. "You're one dumb son of a bitch, Percival."

The next instant, Jem turned the revolver in his hand and brought the butt of the weapon down on Percy Claiborne's skull. With a savage cry, Jem threw himself upon Percy and rode him to the ground and wrapped his knuckles around his windpipe.

The crowd whooped and hollered. JJ and several others swarmed in trying to pry Jem's vice grip loose, and at last they tore him away and hurled him to the dew-soaked grass. Cool shadows grappled in the chilly wet, and Jem reeled at a blow to his mouth and went still.

Gasping and hacking, Percy Claiborne staggered upright with the help of his supporters.

JJ hauled Jem to his feet. Lone voices in the crowd cheered for the twins like two heroes vindicated, but the greater hive mind howled with displeasure and urged Percy to teach the Roscoe bastards a lesson they wouldn't soon forget.

Percy Claiborne staggered upright. "You two make a lovely pair!" he shouted. "A sodomite and a whoremonger."

Jem spat blood. "You're lucky the Blakes aren't here, Claiborne. What would they say about your insulting their sister like that?"

Percy leveled a long, accusing finger. "The Blakes know their place. You, on the other hand, need to be *put* where you belong: in the ground."

A great flash and crash of thunder split the charged air. The crowd threatened to scatter, and some did. The heat of the night was thick, and in the sucking wind a great hush seemed to fall over the entire world.

One of Percy's cronies spotted something on the wet ground and reached for it. In a flash, JJ drew his saber and set the blade on the man's shoulder, inches from the man's white throat.

"I see you've found my revolver," JJ said. "Kindly hand that back to me, would you?"

Scowling, the man handed the revolver over to JJ.

Staggering drunk from both liquor and punches, Jem reached out to a bottle of gin offered by a gleeful George Hunt. He took several gulps from the bottle before passing it back. Sugar Dave looked on, shocked.

"Oh, Jemmo, I don't think that's such a good—"

"You said you want *satisfaction*?" Jem drawled. He stepped up beside JJ and took the revolver into his hands once more. "If we're to settle this matter with a fight, Percy Claiborne, you're looking at an armed man."

JJ wheeled and grabbed Jem's arm. "*Stop it*, Jem," he hissed. "Don't make a challenge you can't meet. You don't know what you're—"

"*Challenge*!" Jem shouted.

Percy scowled at him. "I *already* challenged you, idiot."

"*Considered*!" Jem said.

JJ squeezed Jem's arm. "For God's sake, *no*—"

"*Terms*!" Percy cried.

Here, a hush quieted the crowd. Now that the ritual had begun, no one could stop it.

Jem winked at JJ and turned his attention back to Percy. With a shrug, he said, "This is your neck of the woods. You state the terms."

"Very well," Percy said, suppressing a smile. "The stone wall along the western property line. Each man may choose his own weapon, but he may fire only once.

Seconds may be present, but they shall not fight. Failure to stand when called is immediate forfeit." Here, Percy allowed himself a haughty grin. "And if a man forfeits, the whole Valley will know he is a white-feather coward. Then, not even a mud-eating whore will give him a second look."

Jem's eyes turned black at the insult.

"*Accepted?*" Percy challenged.

"*Accepted*," Jem said.

The crowd sighed and began to babble excitedly. Percy turned away and was immediately flocked by friends as if he was already victorious. Jem was likewise jubilant; he turned to George and Dave, who clapped him on the back. Hunt offered Jem more gin and Jem drank it greedily.

Meanwhile, JJ shut his eyes tight and shook his head.

"You stupid goddamn bastard."

❧

In the gathering dawn, Tom's thin legs carried him to a copse of slender trees that stood across from a green pasture. Yonder, a long stone wall rolled up the hill and out of sight.

Breathless, Tom searched for a hiding place with a good vantage point. His arms were as thin as his legs, but they were strong and he lifted himself up into the highest limbs of the nearest tree he could find. He planted one foot against the *y* of a strong bough, and the other against a higher branch that he could press his weight into to bounce himself up for a clearer view of the pasture. As long as he didn't look down, he'd be fine.

Just don't look down.

Below, the gathering crowd lined the stone wall where Percy Claiborne and his supporters prepared themselves.

By luck, the twins approached the copse of trees where Tom had hidden himself. Peering through the auburn leaves, Tom quieted his breath and listened.

"Maybe we ought to hold on all this until tomorrow," Sugar Dave said, trying his best to sound casual. His neck was craned up at the thunderheads moving in. "It's getting into Sunday is all. Ain't there some kind of rule against dueling on Sundays?"

JJ inspected the hammer of his revolver and handed it to Jem. "I want that back when you're done with it."

Tom watched as Jem took the weapon and measured it in his hand.

"You look sick," George Hunt said.

Jem grimaced. "Don't remind me." He leveled the revolver as if to fire.

JJ corrected Jem's form. "You wanna *kill* him, don't you?"

Jem didn't answer the question. He closed an eye and aimed down the sight. As he did, he lost his footing and staggered.

"I don't...I don't feel so good..."

"Maybe it's that extra half bottle you just drank," Sugar Dave said, eyeing George Hunt.

"What are you looking at me for?" Hunt said. "The man wanted another drink."

"Listen to me," JJ said to Jem. He grabbed the revolver and emptied all the rounds except for one, which he ensured was ready for firing. "*Look at me*, Jem. You got yourself into this fix, but if you listen up you may just get yourself out of it. Claiborne will choose a smaller caliber. He'll choose a real bastard, something fast. He'll try to shoot first. Dammit, Jem, *look at me*. You have to let him do it. All right? You have to take that chance. Draw fast with this piece and you won't hit a barn. Aim, correct, exhale, squeeze." JJ handed the revolver back to Jem. "You have all the power you need right there. Let it do the killing for you."

A nervous laugh escaped Jem. "Killing. Huh." Then he huffed for breath and wiped cold sweat from his brow. He peeled away and began to retch.

"Oh, what's Audrey Blake gonna say about all this?" Sugar Dave said. "What's she gonna think of you, being a killer and all?"

"This is bigger than that," Hunt replied. "This is about honor."

"*Honor?* This ain't nothing but two bucks sparring over a doe."

Tom watched all this, breathless. For himself, he had always wanted to see a duel. They were outlawed of course, which didn't exactly mean they were rare, but in Mayfair's public memory there had only been two duels before in the Valley, one of them fatal. Tom had expected to feel more excitement, but instead he was preoccupied with cold, hunger, and a pulse-throbbing anxiety.

JJ squared up to Jem again. "Jeremiah Roscoe: As your designated second, it's my duty to load and ready your weapon. I have done so. Terms restrict me from finishing the duel in your place, should the hand of God strike you down. Do you understand?"

While JJ spoke, Jem went on retching. It was a horrible sound. From high in the tree, Tom watched the pitiful sight with creeping embarrassment. Here was big brother Jem, for so long an invincible hero in Tom's eyes, now pale and shaking.

"Do you understand?" JJ repeated.

Still bent over, Jem croaked: "Yes, yes!" He spat himself dry and shuddered. Finally, Jem stood upright again. His face was gray, his lips blue. "Well, at least I'm feeling better."

The others watched him with skeptical looks.

"Really?" Sugar Dave asked.

"No," Jem said, his eyelids fluttering. "In fact, I feel...I feel really sort of...sort of..."

Suddenly—"*Watch it!*"—Jem's eyes rolled back and his knees buckled. He dropped to the ground like a stone, his fall broken at the last moment by Hunt and Sugar Dave's catching hands. They eased Jem to the ground.

JJ turned and watched for witnesses of Jem's collapse. "Fuck. I hope no one saw that."

But luckily it seemed no one had. With a bottle in hand, Percy Claiborne was presently delivering a haughty speech to a fired-up audience at the stone wall.

"Jem?" Sugar Dave said, tapping Jem's cheeks. "Jem? Oh, Jem, can you hear me?"

"Move aside," Hunt growled. He took firm hold of Jem's collar and slapped his friend across the face, as hard as he could. "Wake up, you ugly bastard. Wake up!"

"Quit it," JJ said. "He's out cold."

Now came the drunken trill of handsome Sam Hanley, who was officiating the duel: "*Two minutes*, gentlemen! Two minutes until destiny calls!"

Cursing, JJ pulled at his hair. Suddenly, an idea flashed in his eyes. Immediately he started to tear at the buttons of his uniform. He undid his belt next and prepared to drop his trousers.

"This ain't no time for funny stuff," George Hunt said.

JJ snapped his fingers. "Take him around those trees and take off his clothes."

The others stared at him, dumbstruck.

"*What?*"

"*Move!*" JJ ordered. "Take him there, strip him down." JJ led the way as he continued to undress. He pushed his clothes into Sugar Dave's hands. "Put these on him."

Sugar Dave balked. "You're…you're gonna fight in his place?"

"It's forfeit," Hunt said. "Nobody can fight for Jem. It's against the terms."

"Fuck all that," JJ muttered. "If Jem forfeits this duel, you know as well as I do what it will mean for his reputation — and mine. It's a point of honor."

Looking from Jem to JJ, George Hunt shook his head. "You might be twins, but you don't look a thing like Jemmo, even with his clothes on."

"You think anyone up there is going to know the difference?" JJ said. "It's still half dark and they're all piss-drunk."

The cry echoed down: "*One minute*, gentlemen!"

Sugar Dave shook his head with dismay. "This is insane. This whole thing is loon crazy!"

"No," George Hunt said in a whisper. The cold realization had finally struck him. "JJ's right, Davey. If 'Jem Roscoe' don't show himself, he ain't gonna be able to hold his head high in town ever again."

Sugar Dave protested: "For a while, maybe, but not forever. Besides, there will be other girls—"

"It ain't *like that*, Davey," Hunt said. "If Jem don't show, he'll be a laughingstock."

"And that'll make two of us," JJ said. "And our family's name will be ruined for a whole generation."

Tom understood JJ's point, if only in part. But the part he knew he knew *deep*, as instinctual as knowing not to touch your hand to fire. In the Valley, when a man's honor was disputed (any man, no matter if he was rich or poor), that man had a responsibility to answer the challenge. To let any accusation or insult go unanswered, to shirk the necessity of proving one's character in a public display of courage, was to admit a crushing defeat. Worse, in a way it meant the other man owned a piece of you forever. Men who forfeited duels spent the rest of their lives in shame, and some chose suicide rather than suffer further humiliation.

JJ stole a look over his shoulder to confirm no one was watching. Then he stooped low and undressed and passed his uniform to Hunt, who stripped Jem and passed his clothes back to JJ. When JJ stood up again, he was the spitting image of his twin brother.

"Except for the hair," Hunt noted. "Yours is much shorter. That's a dead giveaway."

JJ snapped his fingers at Sugar Dave, who wore a straw hat. "Give me that. Come on, quick!"

"*Gentlemen*!" Sam Hanley called. "It is time."

The hat looked ridiculous on JJ, but it helped with the disguise. JJ checked the revolver and held it at his side. Looking up, his eyes drank in the world with unquenching focus. In an instant, he accepted the stakes laid before him.

"Keep Jem out of sight," JJ said to the others. "Better yet, get him home, and for God's sake tell nobody about this. I'll be along shortly."

With that, JJ turned and walked toward the pasture. He became like a greasy figure upon an oil canvas. High on the hill, Percy Claiborne and his entourage of silhouettes had gathered together. They were a curious amalgamation: sons of Mayfair's richest planters stood with the ragged sons of slaveless sharecroppers as their bodyguards.

The clouds overhead threatened to open up any minute. The gathering storm looked like it was going to be a real thrasher. The audience at the wall looked upon the proceedings with morbid expectation. After the building ecstasy of the carryings-on at Wyolah Hall, they were anxious and hungry for a show-stopping thrill. But they were watchful of the storm too, and they looked up at the dark clouds with growing dread.

Suddenly, an urgent idea slashed through Tom's mind. Someone ought to call the whole thing off. Then, no one would be hurt. All these people would go home, and on the way home maybe laugh about it all. A real lark, that near-duel, wasn't it? An absurd relief.

Tom waited, but no one moved — no one said anything. With a chill shiver, Tom realized that no one — not even himself — was about to stop anything. That opportunity had long since passed, and now JJ's silhouette stood prominently right of center in the oil pastoral of Tom's vision.

Sam Hanley's slurring voice floated across the field.

"Gentlemen, you may shake hands."

The wind lessened. The next moment the wind died, and as Tom looked around the rippling autumn leaves and dancing boughs of the trees sagged and went miraculously still. The first signs of a steely gray dawn crept up in the east. Thunder rumbled directly overhead.

With his straw-hatted head bent low, JJ stretched out his hand.

Percy Claiborne's hands stayed where they were, but his figure seemed to twitch with mild convulsions. He turned and faced away, and slowly JJ rounded about too. They trudged in opposite directions, marking twenty-four paces' distance.

"Find your marks!"

Tom looked around for signs of a party of grownups on horseback, driving their mounts like mad to stop this infernal charade before it commenced. But none were coming.

JJ found his mark. He turned around and faced his opponent.

The caller's arm rose slowly into the air.

"Ready..."

Two weapons were raised. Hammers cocked. The crowd flinched together and now went stock still, silent. Fingers brushed triggers.

Tom's breath caught in his throat, and he held it.

"*FIRE*!"

Percy Claiborne's pistol sparked, but no giant orange flame erupted as Tom expected. There was, however, a great deal of smoke that obscured part of the field. Icy fear clutched at Tom's chest as a gust of smoke swallowed JJ whole.

Sugar Dave whimpered, "I can't look..."

But there, through the slow clearing of the smoke, was JJ. He was still standing, and still holding a loaded weapon.

Percy had fired too high!

Tom grinned as the crowd sighed and cheered, while some moaned with despair and others hurled insults. Tom could see clearly, even from this distance, Percy Claiborne's face drain of color.

The next instant, JJ's weapon roared in answer. Percy reeled and crumpled to the ground as a spray of blood spattered the faces of his supporters.

Tom's jaw dropped open as the crowd gasped and went silent. Percy's entourage rushed forward, and a few spectators leaped over the stone wall to get a closer look.

Upon the field, 'Jem Roscoe' stood very still. Finally he lowered his arm and turned, and he began a slow, solemn march back to the copse of trees. Just then, the sky opened up and rain began to pelt down.

At last, JJ returned.

"I thought I told you to get him out of here! Quick, let's go."

Tom had to bite his knuckles to keep himself from crying out with joy. Fascinated, he watched as they tried to get a comatose Jem onto his feet. Tom moved slowly across a stout limb until he could hang down to read their faces. Jem was deathly pale, looking much worse than before.

Tom looked back up the hill at the fallen Percy, who lay convulsing in the wet grass. The boy's friends and supporters surrounded him and closed in.

"Give him air, for God's sake—"

They all stepped back, only to creep in again.

Sugar Dave looked upon the scene with awed fascination. "Can you see anything?"

"I think you got him in the head," George Hunt said. "It was a damn smart shot."

Tom thought of what Percy's head must look like — split open, oozing, with a welcoming hole for the worms to enter — and shuddered at a cold screwing in his own head.

"Wait a minute," Sugar Dave said, freezing. "Look — Percy's *moving*..."

"Come on," JJ urged. "We need to get the hell out of here."

George Hunt had stopped too. "Lord Almighty, he's getting up! The bastard survived!"

Then, before the stunned eyes of all present, Sam Hanley and a few others helped Percy Claiborne sit up straight. A great cheer went up from his entourage. Roscoe might have won the duel, some later said, but the true victory was Percy's. One man bundled a handkerchief and pressed it against Percy's right ear, or rather what remained of it — more than half a lobe had been shot off.

Sugar Dave gawked at JJ. "You missed. You *tried* to miss, and you spared Percy's life!"

JJ tore the straw hat from his head and pushed it into Sugar Dave's arms. "I did no such thing. I aimed for the space between his eyes. Now come on and help me with this lug."

Grunting under Jem's dead weight, JJ's gaze went to the sky and passed over Tom hidden high in the tree. Startled, JJ squinted and did a double-take.

"What the—?"

His heart in his mouth, Tom tried to climb higher, out of sight. The rain was picking up, and the bark was slick. He felt a round branch and tested it briefly before he began to pull himself up and—

CRACK!

He was falling through the air with the splintered branch still in hand. He let it go and pushed out with his palms as the dark ground came rushing up.

Tom landed face first, but his right arm had broken some of the fall. Still conscious, he rolled quickly on his back and stretched out as if going to sleep and — *Oh God, he couldn't breathe!*

Tom's lungs had been emptied by the impact. He flopped around, gasping for air like a landed fish.

And then, the pain in his arm found him.

"*Yeesh*," Sugar Dave said.

George Hunt clicked his tongue. "That doesn't look good."

JJ cursed violently and shook his head. "Just our goddamn fucking luck..."

Tom inhaled sharply as bolts of pain ran up and down his right arm. His arm was popped from its socket, bent at a grotesque angle. Through the angry waves of pain, he was dimly aware of the others standing around him.

Tom felt JJ's glare — a hateful glare that made Tom almost forget the pain and feel sick to his stomach. No one had ever looked at him such a way before, but now he knew what complete abhorrence looked like. The words '*I'm sorry*' began to form on Tom's trembling lips, but his voice was lodged under a burning lump forming in his throat. Despite his best efforts to hold it in, Tom began to cry.

From across the pasture staggered Sam Hanley, the duel-caller. Drunk as he was, he kept his hands out in front of him as if he might trip over.

"Christ," JJ said. He pointed at Sugar Dave. "Get Tom and *let's go*."

Sugar Dave stepped up to Tom. "C'mon, Tommy. We gotta go." He reached out and touched Tom's arm to help him up and—

"*DON'T TOUCH IT*!"

Blinking away tears, Tom squeezed his eyes shut and wished it all away — the duel, all these people, the mind-numbing pain, everything. Just let him be back home in bed, and let his arm not hurt so goddamn much.

It was too late. Sam Hanley reached them and stepped behind JJ, whose back was turned to him. Wearing an expression of apathetic disgust, Hanley lobbed his announcement without care.

"Roscoe, you're the winner."

George Hunt turned and sneered, "Mighty fine eyes you have, Sam."

Hanley waved him off. The planter's son was turning around to trudge back toward Percy, who he'd of course been rooting for. But just as he was departing, he turned and looked down at Tom.

"What the hell happened to him?"

Hanley looked back at the others, and then his jaw dropped open when he realized there were not one but *two* Roscoe brothers lying prostrate on the ground. And focusing on the larger of the two, the one in the blue uniform...

"*Cheat*!" Sam Hanley shouted, his arms flailing. "*Cheat*! *Cheat*!"

JJ brought up his revolver as if to threaten Hanley into silence, but it was no use. The accusation echoed over the hills and back toward Wyolah Hall.

Tom screamed at another attempt by Sugar Dave to help him upright.

"*Leave*...leave me alone—"

Furious, JJ knelt down and shoved Dave aside. Without a word or second thought he grabbed Tom's arm with both hands and before Tom knew what was happening JJ was PULLING AND TWISTING AND TOM SCREAMED LOUDER THAN HE EVER KNEW POSSIBLE AND—

And then Tom passed out.

A mute scowl on his face, JJ pushed Tom's hand and arm into its crook. He took Tom's other hand and placed it atop the dislocated shoulder to hold the injured arm there. Pushing back on his knees, JJ tore off one of the sleeves of Jem's shirt. He fashioned a makeshift sling and wrapped it around Tom's shoulder.

Tom woke up again in a half-daze, whimpering, he didn't dare cry out again lest JJ wrench his arm around a second time. Once his arm was balanced in the sling, he felt some relief. His shoulder muscles, aching with tension, finally relaxed.

With his other hand, Tom reached out for JJ's help up.

Instead of helping, JJ turned away. Tom didn't know whether he'd glimpsed tears of rage or shame stinging JJ's eyes. The driving rain made it all the same anyway.

Tom sat in the sopping wet, feeling utterly sorry for himself. Sugar Dave came forward again and draped his coat over Tom's shoulders. The gesture was appreciated, but it did little; Tom and the coat were already soaked.

Nearby, a groggy voice murmured, "…happened?"

Slowly, Jem came to. He opened his eyes, and they didn't blink even when raindrops landed in them. Thrusting his hands in the air, seeming to swim through the falling rain, Jem brought himself up into a sitting position and looked around. He looked stupidly at the woolen blue coat someone had put on him. He turned and saw a sniffling Tom beside him wearing a makeshift sling, and his eyes bulged wide. Now he looked up at his friends.

George Hunt spat — another raindrop among millions — and shook his head. "Don't you dare ask what happened."

Sugar Dave sighed. "Come on," he said, helping Tom to his feet. "Let's get you two on home."

Jem let Hunt pull him to his feet. He looked around, dazed, a touch of panic in his eyes, but he couldn't decide which question to ask first.

The rain kept pouring, and thunder rumbled again. Trudging slowly, his chest still heaving with sobs, Tom followed the older boys while Jem's companions tried to explain what had just happened. JJ was far ahead, wearing only Jem's torn undershirt, prowling through the mists like a man wanting to kill someone (and not just to nick them in the ear this time). Tom turned and looked back at the tree, and a shiver ran down his back when he realized the height from which he'd fallen.

Up ahead, still listening to his friends' recounting, Jem suddenly became a wild animal. He threw off their beseeching arms and started at a run for JJ, who had disappeared into the treeline far ahead. Tom was vaguely aware they were heading north; he could just make out the peak of the North Branch despite the wall of fog and rain.

Dejected, Sugar Dave turned back and beckoned Tom forward. George Hunt had no choice but to hang back with them.

"We're with you, Tommy," Dave said in a reassuring voice.

"You'll be all right soon, kid," George Hunt said.

Tom refused to believe such a thing could ever be true ever again, but he did his best to blink away his tears despite the rain.

The miller's boy attempted to cheer Tom up a little. "It could have been worse, you know. A lot worse."

George Hunt nodded toward the tiny figures of the twin Roscoe brothers, who could be seen circling each other like wolves even as they stalked up to the next line of trees. Hunt gave a humorless laugh and said, "No, Davey. I really don't think it could be any worse."

Far in the distance, beyond the haze of locally falling rain, the far eastern sky bore a blood red sun that was palest white in the center. As it crested the eastern horizon, the freakish sun cut ribbons of red light into the blackness of the storm clouds. And then the clouds overtook the sun and swallowed it whole, and the Mayfair Valley was covered in fog and darkness.

Watchful of forked lightning fast approaching, three men scoured the place where Percy Claiborne had fallen. Then one cried out and picked at something on the ground. He whipped out a handkerchief, bent down, and swaddled a singed chunk of Percy's ear in the fabric. He thrust the ear into the air with a victorious shout.

An earsplitting crash of thunder turned the man's shout into a terrified shriek. The treasure hunter and his companions raced off to rejoin the procession that carried Percy, the proud hero of Wyolah Hall, back to his palatial home.

Chapter 13

PRODIGAL SONS

It was Sunday, and so the North Branch Mine was deserted. Seeing no other living thing in sight, JJ dismounted his horse (the same nag he'd taken home from Harper's Ferry) and led her forward.

When JJ had been just a boy, this place on the mountainside had been a teeming forest. In the years since, it had been cut clear to the cliffside, with ugly stumps marking the graves of dead trees. The rest of the ridge had been churned up by the mine and the men who worked it, with great mounds of earth standing beside deep pits. A gravel path led up to a yawning black pit that plunged down into the earth's heart. Small chimneys protruded from mounded clay and soil. By tomorrow at dawn, not far off now, those chimneys would start to belch black smoke as the miners' work week began anew.

Leading the old nag, JJ wandered among squat, tin-roofed buildings and gazed upon the mine's gaping mouth. He could almost hear the sounds of industry: the heavy rattle of coal cars on tracks, the clanging of a blacksmith's hammer on an anvil, the baying of mules and whinnies of workhorses, the gnashing and scraping of picks and shovels.

Set apart from the pit and outbuildings was a lonely log cabin with a porch and a commanding view of the Mayfair Valley. The hand-painted sign above the door read, in white letters: OFFICE.

JJ tied the nag to a nearby post and climbed up the porch. He was thankful to be out of the rain, which despite no longer being an icy downpour was still a foggy, bone-chilling drizzle. He tried the door, expecting it to be locked, but the latch *clicked* and the door yawned open.

It was dark inside the cabin. Rain pelted the tin roof overhead. JJ had no matches, and even if he did they would be no use to him wet. He groped in the dry darkness and nearly knocked over a kerosene lantern. He found a packet of matches, lit one, and fed the lantern until it glowed. Taking up the lantern, JJ began to explore the cabin.

There was a single room, with slivers of pale light filtering in from three misshapen windows. There was a small wood stove, and two work desks were tucked into opposite corners. A large table dominated the middle of the floor, ostensibly for company meetings, but there were no chairs around it. The table and desks were strewn with maps, blueprints, old newspapers, and coffee-stained documents of all kinds. JJ counted six overflowing ashtrays which hadn't done much to keep ash and cigar butts off the sooty, mud-caked floor.

At the table, JJ sifted through the documents. A few newspaper headlines caught his eye, particularly a story about how the Sioux civilization out in the Dakotas was growing 'restless', with braves taking to the warpath against whites. Another story told of more violence out west, this time between pro- and anti-slavery forces in Kansas. A slave-owner and his family had been butchered, apparently, by abolitionist militiamen inspired by John Brown's raid.

Next, JJ read about the death of a family of free blacks in Staunton down the Shenandoah. The entire family had been lynched because the father, according to the authorities, was an illegitimate preacher stirring up resentment among the local slave population. The youngest person killed was just ten years old. Photographs of militiamen posing with the dead family were being sold for a penny, with proceeds going to support Staunton's local militia.

Most of the articles were about the upcoming presidential election set for next fall. The Republicans had a slew of candidates running to be their nominee. William Seward, who had publicly criticized slavery as defying a 'higher law' of morality, was the front-runner, though he had a gang of unknowns nipping at his heels: Salmon Chase, Abraham Lincoln, Edward Bates, Benjamin Wade, and the list went on. The Republican Party had been founded just three years earlier, around the same time the old Whig Party had collapsed. The Republicans had made strong gains in the House and Senate in the '56 elections, and were widely expected to give Democrats a significant challenge in the year to come.

Way up in Chicago, Senator Stephen Douglas had officially announced his intention to become the Democratic Party's candidate. Douglas was considered by most to be the logical successor to the presidency, having outlived all of his rivals. And Douglas was a good friend of Father's, so his likely nomination promised very good things for the Roscoe family.

JJ's thoughts drifted away from the news stories. His eyes scanned more headlines and articles, but he registered little of what he read. He came to think only of the envelope in his pocket.

...come home to receive news of the Roscoe family legacy, and your rightful place.

JJ started to wonder what *home* even meant anymore. Now that he had come back to Mayfair — now that he had seen, as if for the first time, the gaudy decadence of places like Wyolah Hall, with its gaunt black shadows creeping in the background — JJ realized just how much he had changed in four years, and how little had changed in the Valley. In any case, it wasn't Mayfair that mattered at all, but his rightful place at Father's side. Wherever Father went, *that* was where JJ was meant to be.

But what would Father say about what happened last night — in reality just a few hours ago — at Wyolah Hall? By now, news of the duel would have spread clear across the Valley, and perhaps beyond the Branches too. No doubt rumors were spreading too: that Jem Roscoe had been too chickenshit to fight, and that JJ had disguised himself as his brother in order to murder Percy Claiborne for any number of make-believe reasons. Leave it to those Roscoe twins, a sodomite and a fall-down drunk, neither of them good for anything.

But the plain fact of the matter was that Percy now lay mutilated, and possibly dying. The son of one of the Valley's most powerful men, might die of shock or blood loss — and all because of JJ.

Of course, JJ could claim it was all to protect Jem, to uphold the Roscoe family's honor when its honor was questioned. And truthfully, that was most of it. Jem, that dumb romantic bastard, had gotten himself into a real fix over some pretty face. It was a good thing JJ had been there to help get him out!

But there was something else too, some other idea rattling in JJ's mind that he would not dare try to explain to Father.

During the attack on Harper's Ferry, JJ had killed a man. Even putting those words together in the same sentence was surreal, but he had really done it. He had run his sword through a human body — with everything happening so fast he'd barely realized he'd done it. But later, after the smoke had cleared, JJ went back and examined the body, which not an hour before had been a living, breathing person. Checking to make sure no one else was watching, he went down on his knees and leaned down. He let the iron odor of the man's blood waft in his nostrils. It struck JJ then, the realization of the great and terrible power in his possession. In one stroke, he had seized another's past, present, and future for himself.

And he had never felt so alive in all his life.

Last night, he might have simply pulled Jem away from the confrontation with Percy and the others. He might have simply taken Jem home and withstood the stinging insults hurled at their backs. But looking at Percy — Percy, one of his childhood friends, who had later been one of the first to fling the sodomite rumors against him, and who had become the personification of everything that was *wrong* about Mayfair — JJ felt the inexplicable urge to reclaim that vibrating sense of power. And so, when it seemed certain that Jem would forfeit the duel, JJ's decision to take his place hadn't been a decision at all, but base instinct.

Well, he'd had a taste of that power again, so to speak. But at what cost? Of course he didn't give a damn about Percy Claiborne…

But what was Father going to say?

After the duel, Jem's mud-eating friends George Hunt and Dave Dixon had driven the Roscoe brothers back to Clarendon in a rickety one-horse wagon. The closer the wagon rolled to home, the more JJ felt a numbing anxiety grip his chest. Driving up the clay path toward the white mansion, JJ decided he could not face the old man — not yet. He needed time. Time to think, time to make sense of the nonsensical.

And so, here he was, alone on the North Branch.

JJ went to the cabin's stove and piled several logs inside. He lit another match and set a scrap of newspaper alight to get the fire going. After nurturing the tiny fire, JJ stood back and lost himself in the hot glow and crackle of the flames.

In his mind's eye, he was transported back in time — not to Wyolah Hall a few hours ago, but back to Clarendon, four years ago. JJ was sixteen, and he could almost hear the sounds of the party, the fundraising dance that Father had hosted for his friend Stephen Douglas. He remembered circling about Clarendon's grand ballroom with the most prized debutantes of the day. JJ was about to travel the Union on campaign with Father and Senator Douglas, and Jem was all set to attend West Point. Jem was set to leave the very next day in fact, and he wore his new cadet's uniform as proudly as a peacock.

Most clearly of all, JJ remembered the proud, reverent, almost wistful look on Father's face as he watched his boys work the crowd. At that time Father had been healthy and vibrant, his lungs yet untouched by the thick, soupy consumption that would soon take hold. JJ felt Father's gaze shine brightest on him, and though he always denied Jem and Sarah's jokes that he was Father's favorite, JJ happened to know it was true.

Father's voice, ringing in his ears: "My boy..."

But there was another gaze that caught JJ's attention that night, and indeed had for some time. Sarah, then a shining nineteen, and her beau Richard Harper, son of the prominent family of physicians, made the most handsome couple at the ball. Still, JJ could tell that Sarah was not the focus of Richard's attention, but JJ himself.

JJ couldn't remember feeling any strange sort of way as a child. It was only when he and Jem began to attend society debuts and dances as 'eligibles', only when Father started murmuring to them about 'proper matches with proper ladies', that the pieces of the puzzle started to fall together. Except JJ's puzzle wasn't like the others. Nothing fit together as it was supposed to, and eventually JJ gave up trying.

Until Richard Harper. Until *that look* across Clarendon's ballroom floor, while Richard danced hand in hand with Sarah. A silent, unspoken message that had made JJ's hair stand on end. An *unspeakable* message. Unwarranted, unclean...

But not unwanted.

JJ had followed Richard upstairs. He had to know, had to be sure. But though he hadn't known it at the time, someone's watchful eyes had followed *JJ* upstairs, had read the hopeful hesitation on his face before he reached out and took Richard's beckoning hand.

Despite having to grope in the dark, JJ remembered the electric sensation of Richard's touch, and the realization that he had never felt so happy in all his life. But then the door rattled and was flung open, and in the blinding light JJ saw a monstrous shadow appear on the far wall. Turning, he went cold when he saw the figure of Father standing like some crazed Prometheus holding the god-fire that shone light upon everything. In an instant, all secrets were exposed and laid bare, and not a lifetime's worth of explanations could have erased the desolate, heartbroken expression on Father's face that turned JJ's newfound joy to ashes in his mouth.

Rumors spread quickly among the guests. The official word, as relayed by Judge Cutler, was that Richard Harper, the doctor's son, had been discovered in a state of undress with a black manservant who had attended the party with Clay Claiborne. The shock of the news forced the Harper family to flee the party in horror. Meanwhile, Mr. Claiborne exploded in a fit of fury and threatened a mortal challenge to any man who dared utter another word about his connection to the scandal. Claiborne soon abandoned the party to deal with his wayward unit of property in private. The party soon disintegrated and the guests departed, with not a few noticing that John Roscoe and his son JJ had been conspicuously absent during all the goings-on. Though no one realized it at the time, Clarendon had hosted its last soirée.

To this day, JJ did not know who could have uttered the first whisper. He learned later that Judge Cutler had told Father, and Lucas Cutler (not yet a reverend) had told the Judge. But who had told Lucas?

In the end, it didn't matter. Whoever had talked first had committed no sin, and no fault could be laid at their feet. The fault belonged only to the two wrapped together in the darkness, for the weakness — the disease — had been theirs and theirs alone.

The Harpers, being of relatively lowborn status, were relegated to pariahs; none of the Valley's gentry ever invited that family to another prominent social function again. Richard Harper himself disappeared without a trace, and so far as JJ knew, he had moved to some obscure burg under an assumed name.

The morning after THE INCIDENT, JJ rose from bed (he hadn't been able to sleep) and went downstairs. He found Father in the library. Jem was there too, and Ben, and even Mother. The younger boys had no concept of what had happened, and Sarah had locked herself in her room to weep over the confusing, humiliating loss of Richard, not realizing her beau's connection with JJ.

Father's head was down, and his eyes were red and puffy. Ben was sorrowful, and Jem could do nothing but glare out the far window. While JJ stood like a convicted felon, it was Mother, not Father, who explained his future to him.

He would go to West Point, in Jem's place. He was to leave that very day, to pack presently, to be ready to leave by noon. Four years of education, moral training, spiritual rehabilitation awaited him. Personal correspondence home would be restricted, and there would be no visits back to the Valley, at least until the storm clouds hanging around Clarendon had dissipated. It was an election year, after all.

The news sank in, and JJ felt heavy. Four years. It really was something like a prison sentence.

But what happened after four years? What happened after graduation?

Mother pursed her lips and shrugged. "It remains to be seen where your rightful place shall be, Jonathan."

JJ remembered looking at Father again, who clutched his head in his hands. JJ tried half a dozen strangled versions of an apology but could finish none of them. It all sounded *wrong*, unreal. And still Father refused to speak, and Mother only expressed her tearful regret that her firstborn had inherited nothing of the Colonel's purity of character.

It was a half-day's journey to the rail station in Winchester (for no rail track had yet been laid to Mayfair). Jem rode with JJ, but only to the edges of the Valley. Jem had never been beyond the Branches, and his journey to New York had been intended as his first adventure. Instead, it was JJ who wore the shining new cadet uniform (a perfect fit).

The twins didn't say much during the slow ride up the Capon Bridge Road. At the crest of a high hill where stood a weathered white birch, JJ implored Jem to keep him company a little farther. He didn't remember what he or Jem said to each other, but he did remember pushing on, fighting back tears as he went. He remembered turning around, thinking he'd look back and see the hill barren, Jem gone. But Jem was still there, he and the birch in silhouette, and Jem watched JJ go. When JJ raised a hand in farewell, the silhouette of Jem returned the gesture.

Somehow, JJ took comfort in that.

❧

JJ shivered. Blinking, he realized he was still high up on the North Branch, standing in a dank cabin before its tiny stove, his mind lost somewhere while he stared at glowing chunks of coal. After adding three more pieces of coal, JJ shut the stove lid.

Suddenly aware of just how quiet it was, JJ looked up. The tin roof was no longer making noise, for the rain had stopped. Just then, JJ heard a new sound from somewhere distant.

Hoofsteps?

He crossed to a rain-slicked window that looked out at the mineyard. Jem was outside, riding a young colt that JJ had never seen before. Jem rode up beside the old nag and dismounted, and he hitched the colt to the same post. Jem looked toward the window, but JJ drew back into the shadows, not knowing exactly why.

JJ tried to busy himself with making coffee, but he had no idea where to start. He heard the porch boards squeak and groan and then the door of the cabin opened up and a chill breeze blew inside. Looking toward the door, JJ saw Jem standing there against the fading daylight.

"So here you are," Jem said.

JJ turned back to his business. He found the kettle and set it on the stovetop. There was a ladle and a galvanized bucket of water next to the stove; JJ dipped the ladle into the water and filled the kettle.

"How did you find me?"

"Chimney smoke," Jem said, pointing vaguely skyward.

JJ nodded and turned back to the stove. "I'm making coffee."

Jem joined him at the stove and planted his feet. "I'll take care of it."

When JJ continued to rummage, Jem pushed him aside.

"I'll take care of it."

Sighing, JJ straightened and stepped back. While his brother thrashed about making coffee as if pursued by a hornet, JJ traced a meandering path through the cabin.

"This place is a damn pigsty," he observed.

Jem worked in stony silence.

"How's Tom?" JJ asked. "Is he doing all right?"

"He'll live," Jem murmured. "Doc Harper says you set his shoulder wrong. He had to pop it out again."

JJ stopped at the mention of *Harper*. "Doc…?"

"Ira," Jem said.

JJ nodded, trying to appear nonchalant.

"Have you seen much of him?" JJ asked. "Richard, I mean. You know, ever since…"

Jem stared down at the kettle as steam began to rise. "Pardon?" he said, distracted. "Oh, well…Richard, right."

JJ sighed and shook his head. "If it bothers you to say, you—"

"It doesn't bother me," Jem said, and it was clear that he meant it. "The truth is, I haven't seen him in years. Last I heard, he moved down to Lost River."

JJ nodded. "I see. Nice country down there, I hear."

Jem shrugged. "I've never been."

JJ turned to look out the window. A weak sun was peeking out from behind a thick cloud cover. The storm was moving off to the west, and through the warped glass JJ saw bulbous clouds hurrying across a desolate sky.

JJ turned back to Jem. "So he's never written? Reached out?"

Jem shook his head, no.

And there it was, question and answer. The answer was something like what JJ had expected, but he hadn't expected to feel this rotten upon hearing it. In truth, he had been hoping for a different sort of answer.

JJ pushed against the screen door and stepped out to the porch. The rickety boards wrapped around the cabin and offered a commanding view of the Valley. The wind bit at his bones, but he gritted his teeth and went to the side overlooking the slope of the North Branch, with the Cuts on either side, pointing like a finger toward the South Branch and the rolling hill country beyond. To the west lay the Alleghenies under a setting sun, while to the east the spine of the Blue Ridge darkened as night rolled over the world.

Down below, the Valley was still obscured in a thick mist from where the rains had rolled through. Quaint chimneys and squat houses broke the mist here and there, and barely visible there on the far hillsides of the South Branch were the marble white homes of the planter gentry, with their barracks-like slave shacks nailed up next to huge liver-colored cotton fields. The sight of the slave shacks disturbed JJ, though he could not decide exactly why. Maybe it was because the sprawling mansions looked as ready to collapse as the huts of the oppressed.

The cabin door opened and Jem joined him at the railing. He had two cups of steaming coffee in hand and a bottle tucked under one arm.

"It's warmer inside," Jem said, handing over a cup of coffee.

JJ accepted the coffee gratefully. "I could use the fresh air."

Jem shrugged. "Suit yourself. But as soon as my teeth chatter, I'm going back in. Irish?"

JJ stared at him. "What?"

Jem held up a bottle of whiskey.

"Oh," JJ said. "No."

"I'm afraid I'm all out of buttermilk," Jem said.

Jem balanced his half-filled coffee cup on the railing and filled the other half with whiskey. He stuck a finger in the steaming mixture to stir it, then—"*Ow!*"—retracted his finger and sucked on it. Satisfied, he lifted the cup with his other hand and offered it for a cheers.

"Here's to you," Jem said groggily.

JJ watched his brother gulp half the mixture down and shook his head with disgust.

"What?" Jem said, wiping his lips. "Don't give me that look."

JJ looked toward the horizon. "You're bitching about something."

"Am I?" Jem asked.

"It's not exactly hard to tell."

"I might say the same about yourself." Jem joined JJ at the railing. "Aren't you going to ask me?"

JJ shook his head. "Ask you what?"

"What it was like, getting flogged by Father and all."

"I can't imagine it was pretty."

"It wasn't."

"Well, I suppose I don't need to ask then, do I?"

"It was good timing, your running away."

"I didn't run away."

"Sure looked like it to me. If you can believe it, Mae Jane gave me a worse whipping than the old man did. Hell of a lot worse."

JJ nodded. "I believe it."

"Old woman blew her top in a way I haven't seen since we were kids. She was as fired up as the day she found our chicken coop in the yellow parlor."

Jem laughed at the memory, and he looked for JJ to laugh too, but JJ was still staring out at the Valley.

"My, my," Jem muttered. "You're cheery. Maybe you ought to bitch about something too. It won't make you feel any better, but it'll give you something to do."

JJ gave an exasperated sigh. "Forgive me, dear brother. I've got a lot on my mind. For all I know, I've just plunged our family into a blood feud. There will be hell to pay if Claiborne dies."

Jem shook his head. "Not if the old man has anything to say about it."

JJ became very still. "What does Father say about it?"

"All I know is, Judge Cutler came to Clarendon this morning, and they've been shut up together for hours. Besides Father calling me in to sign a few RRC papers, I've barely seen him. He's only decided to speak with you now — both of us, for that matter. I told Father you were probably halfway to New York by now, but I had a hunch this is where you'd be."

RRC papers? JJ thought to ask about exactly what Jem meant, but he knew Jem didn't have a clue. JJ watched his brother try to slurp his 'coffee', filled to the brim with whiskey, but only managing to scald his hands.

Jem winced. "God*dammit*..."

JJ sighed. "You're better than this, Jem. You *could* be better."

"You're one to talk," Jem muttered, wiping his hands. "You realize I won't be able to show my face in Mayfair again? Everywhere I go, folks will say, 'There goes Jem Roscoe, too chickenshit to fight his own battles. Jem Roscoe, who cowers behind his brother's skirts.'"

"You did that to yourself," JJ said. "You passed out with a fucking brick in your hat. Besides, you should be thanking me for what I did."

Jem scoffed and shook his head.

"What?" JJ said. "You don't think so? I've been away a long while, but I still remember who Percy Claiborne is. He could have killed you. He *would* have killed you, the state you were in. Meanwhile, you know what I smelled on *his* breath? Nothing. He was sober as a judge, and he would have put you in your grave last night, Jem. If you think anything different, you're only deluding yourself."

To all this, Jem said nothing. Sensing he was getting through to his brother, JJ pressed his case.

"So they drag your name in the mud. They're all country simpletons, even the sons of the Families."

Jem said, "We *are* part of the Families, you know."

"Only the Spencer half, and there's not much of that blood left," JJ said. "We're a new sort of family, for a new sort of America. That's what Father's been trying to say for years — you'd know it, if only you opened your ears. Nothing those yokels think about us will matter when we're standing there, on the furthest, highest peak."

"There's no way to go from a peak but down," Jem said. "And sometimes it's a sheer fall." A slow, painful realization shone in his eyes, and he let out a low groan. "Audrey..."

"I wouldn't worry," JJ said. "You think a girl like that gives a damn about your 'honor and prestige'? Where'd you find yourself a piece of ass like that anyway? Just some barefoot mud-eater who probably—"

"*Shut up*," Jem snapped. "You call her that again, JJ, and I'll break your teeth, I swear on it."

At first JJ stood stunned, but then he burst out laughing. "*Laws*, Jem. Again with your self-righteous pissings. For Christ's sake, when did your sense of humor completely abandon you?"

"It's right here," Jem muttered. "You just keep missing it."

The twins glared out at separate landscapes. Across the western expanse, beyond the reach of the storm clouds, the sun began to set in a sliver of clear, blazing sky. The rumbling storm was carrying on, and the distant collision of black clouds and vibrant red light gave the impression that a great smoking battle had just been fought in the heavens. Over it all rose a pale moon tinged yellow.

After a long while, JJ cleared his throat.

"I think it's time we speak plainly."

Jem wore a wry smile. "Haven't we been doing that already?"

JJ kept his eyes on the moon. It was somehow easier to speak with Jem this way. "Ben told me how much time Father has left — how much time *really*."

Jem didn't answer right way. "There's still lots of time," he said at length. Jem nodded slowly, and kept nodding, as if the more he did he more he would convince himself this was the case.

But of course JJ knew there wasn't much time at all. Not for all that Father wanted to do, all that JJ wanted to do alongside him. So much time had been lost between them, and now it was a matter of racing the clock. Six months to a year, Ben had said. Some patients with cases of his nature went another eighteen months, but never twenty-four.

JJ turned to Jem. It was past time for beating around the bush. "I ought to just come out and say what it is I've been meaning to say."

Jem shrugged. "By all means."

Looking at him squarely, JJ said, "It's going to be me, Jem."

Jem held an expectant look, as if he was still waiting for JJ to come to the point.

"Father's estate," JJ clarified. When Jem still offered little more than a blank look, JJ shook his head with frustration. "For God's sake, you know what I mean by it, Jem. Clarendon, the Roscoe Company. The *contract...*"

Jem shook his head and looked away. "You really think I want any of that? Laws, if it means so much to you, JJ, you can have it. All of it."

"You're going to receive a portion," JJ said, as if he'd had to push this same point in a thousand previous conversations. "Father's giving something of Clarendon to everyone, even the Freemans. But the *Company*, JJ. The contract to build the railroad, that will go to just one person."

"Exactly," Jem said. "The contract will have no name on it but John Roscoe. Don't you get it? Meeting the terms of the contract will fall to his heirs and assigns, when the time comes, of course. It could take ten years to lay all that track, or it could take twenty, or it might never happen. But if it does, it won't be my name in the newspapers, and it won't be yours either. It will be his, because it was always meant to be his, and his alone. But if you want to lead the Light Brigade for the King's glory, be my guest."

JJ shook his head. "It's not only about him. The *Roscoe* Railroad Company, Jem. It's bigger than any one man. It's a dynasty, a *legacy*—"

"Vanity," Jem grumbled.

JJ heaved a great sigh. For God's sake, where was he to go from here?

"Jem, I know you're capable. I know you're capable of understanding the broader scope. This, the mine, the Valley, it's all the first step on a long journey. What else are you going to do? Stay here and continue your feuds with pompous fools, dress up and playing soldier, drink and whore yourself to death with squirrel-shooting slackjaws?"

Jem scoffed. "Brother. How I've missed you, JJ..."

"You *are* better than all this," JJ insisted. "You could be out there somewhere, far beyond the Branches, really doing something. *We* could be out there, together."

"To what end?" Jem countered. "Tell me, is there anything I might find out there that cannot be discovered right here? Is there anything to know out there that I cannot learn for myself here?" His eyes looked off somewhere. "Maybe I prefer to spend my time shooting squirrels. Maybe I don't want to be out there on the edge of nowhere, watching men break their backs from the comfort of my padded railcar."

JJ studied Jem closely. "You're afraid of command?"

Jem scowled. "Fear has nothing to do with it."

"Oh no," JJ said. "No, of course not. My mistake."

Jem ignored the slight. His eyes turned inward. "If you want to know the truth, every day I come up here, I get sick. I feel my stomach twist a little tighter the closer I get to the top. Men go down that pit there, and when they come back up they're... different. You know the air you breathe down there? It's not air at all; it's just dust, the breath of a million little rocks, and something in the dust makes men *wrong*. I'm down there only as often as I need to be — I'm goddamn terrified of turning down the wrong shaft. But the others, they go down *every day*. I watch them arrive laughing and singing and joking in their lamp-hats, and at sundown I watch them come up from below with their flames extinguished. No one makes a sound but to hack and cough. I hand them their pay on their way out the door. Eventually, every man hits their limit."

JJ heard all these things, but he'd stopped listening.

"You don't have the stomach for it," he said. "For any of it. Which is all the more reason why Father will choose me to lead the Company. This family, the world, they need men of action, Jem, not whinging self-doubters."

Jem glared out at the darkening sky and refused to say anything.

JJ studied his brother there, exuding a spirit of defiance that, however maddening, was perhaps admirable in its purity of feeling. Jem would adhere to no authority he deemed arbitrary. He would drink a deadly cup of hemlock to spite the powers-that-be. JJ knew that Jem, if compelled, would spit in the face of anything approximating tyranny and strut down the same shortcut to Oblivion trodden by so many deviants before him, and he wouldn't think twice about it. Still, JJ suspected that Jem's steadfastness, if it was anything like his own, had some vulnerability to the cancer of self-doubt.

"Father called me home for a reason," JJ said, feeling that now was finally the right time to lay cards upon the table. "His letter spoke of my 'rightful place.' I'll give you three guesses what a dying man might mean by that. But now, after all this business with Claiborne...I don't know what to think. I yet believe it will be me he chooses to head the Company going forward. But still, Jem, I need you. I need you to stand with me when I speak with Father."

Jem pursed his lips. "Why would you need a, what am I again? A whinging self-doubter?"

JJ sighed. "I need my brother. That's all."

Jem stared out at the Valley. "That's all."

"That's all," JJ echoed.

The twins stood together in silence for a long while.

At length, Jem said, "Shouldn't I be asking what I stand to gain?"

"You'll get what I told you last night at the Hall," JJ said.

Jem tried a weary grin. "I don't remember much from last night, to tell you the truth."

"Well," JJ said with a shrug, "like I said, you had a brick in your hat. Everybody knew it."

Jem stared out at the view and nodded slowly, chagrined. "Right..."

"But you know," JJ said. "Audrey Blake, she—"

"If you're going to say what I think you're going to say..."

"It's not that," JJ said, shaking his head. "It was...well, it was nice seeing you like that. Not that I was watching or anything, but...you know, it was a nice thing."

Jem blushed with embarrassment and turned away. "Laws...Well, I suppose she's factored into some of my ideas for the future."

JJ cocked an eyebrow. "Only some of them?"

The twins laughed together, and finally the knot of tension between them began to loosen. They laughed a long time, their cares forgotten. It felt good to laugh together, almost as if time had run backwards to BEFORE, when there had been more to laugh about. After a while, though, both twins fell silent again. Once more JJ felt the cold, searching fingers of the wind, and he remembered where he was. He remembered who was waiting down the mountain.

"I know I ran away this morning," JJ said. "I know I left you alone to answer to him. And maybe...maybe I haven't ever dug in my heels quite the way I like to remember. I'm not like you in that respect, Jem. But still, I'm asking you..."

"All right," Jem said.

"What?"

"I said, all right."

Jem looked up at the sky then, and JJ followed his gaze. Stars were coming out in the darkening sky overhead.

"Meteor," Jem said, pointing.

JJ shook his head. "I didn't see it."

Jem craned his neck, marveling at the patterns in the heavens. "I know what you're really asking for, JJ."

JJ kept his eyes on the sky, but he could discern no pattern in the winking lights overhead. "And what am I asking for?"

When there was no answer, JJ looked at his brother. Jem offered him a small, encouraging smile.

"I'll go along with whatever Father decides," Jem said.

JJ considered this for a time. He nodded, smiled, and stretched out his hand.

"That's all I can ask, brother."

Jem accepted the gesture, and the twins shook hands. From afar, an onlooker might have seen the miraculous image of a man shaking hands with himself.

"Now," Jem said, looking decidedly more relaxed than before. "What do you say we get the hell out of here?"

"I couldn't agree more," JJ said. He looked toward the horses tied up across the yard, and a thought popped into his head. "What do you say to a good old-fashioned race?"

Jem blinked. "Race?"

"Down the Branch," JJ said. "You know, for old times' sake."

The clouds of Jem's hangover cleared as the spark of competition glowed in his eyes. "You still slump in the saddle?"

"Far from it," JJ laughed. "I'm the best rider at the Point."

"That can't be saying much," Jem replied. "All the other cadets are Yankees."

JJ shrugged. "Why don't you find out?"

Jem flashed a grin. "Dear brother, you don't know what you're in for." He knocked his riding boots together, heel to heel. "These are Hermes' wingtips, you know, and my steed over there is called Pegasus. You haven't seen that Greenbrier fly!"

Laughing, JJ went back inside the cabin to fetch his still-wet uniform coat. Pulling it on, JJ hurried outside and leaped from the porch. "Then quit jabbering and show me!" he called, hurrying across the mineyard. "That is, *if* your runty little colt can keep up!"

"Wait," Jem said, still standing on the porch. "We're starting *now?*"

JJ unhitched his old nag and mounted her. With a cry, he wheeled her in circles, her stomping hooves spraying mud in every direction.

"It's now or never!" JJ cried. "Come on, Hermes. Last one to Clarendon stables the horses. Ready? And…"

Jem jumped down from the cabin's porch. "*Hold it*! Just let me get up and—"

"*Go*!" JJ shouted, and he was off, becoming a blur in the black night.

JJ spurred the nag's sides and she shot forward like a bolt. Laughing as he tore past the gate of the North Branch Mine, JJ turned in his saddle and saw Jem still trying to mount his colt.

Facing forward again, JJ urged the nag faster. She whinnied and wheezed and pushed, and for a brief moment JJ closed his eyes and felt the wind rush against his cheeks and—

"*Fly*, Pegasus! *Fly*, Greenbrier!"

Cursing, JJ's eyes snapped open just in time to see a laughing Jem and his gray-maned colt overtake him. Before JJ knew what was happening, Jem had already rounded the next bend and disappeared.

With a cry, JJ dug his spurs into the sides of the little nag. Off she went with another frantic burst of energy. JJ spurred her again, and again. She foamed and grunted. He took corners sharper than he knew was safe, risking the nag snapping a leg or his being thrown from the saddle to plummet down the cliffside. But the old beast was steady and sure-footed, and she took each turn with the instincts of a mountain mule.

Rounding another bend near the base of the mountain, JJ finally caught sight of Jem and Greenbrier a quarter mile ahead. Here was the last of it, a flat stretch leading home to Clarendon. With sinking hope, JJ realized he would never catch up.

But up ahead, Greenbrier began to lag and shuffle. The colt was young and strong but his flame, hot as it was, burned out too soon. Despite Jem's urging, the colt began to slow and would fly no faster.

The plucky nag gained ground in her steady, plodding canter, and JJ whooped as he overtook Jem. He even managed to put a few lengths' distance between them, until finally he could see the gates of Clarendon up ahead.

After bursting victorious through the gate, JJ let out a halloo and slowed the frothing nag to a trot. Jem caught up drenched in sweat and breathing as hard as the colt.

"Just wait until next season," Jem gasped. "Greenbrier will be ready. He'll be a winner."

"Next season this one will be dead," JJ said, meaning the nag.

"She doesn't have a name?"

Winded, JJ dismounted. "It doesn't need a name," he said after catching his breath. "It's just a horse, or maybe something more mulish."

Jem laughed and shook his head. "Cold bastard. Every animal needs a name." He dismounted and they walked their horses down the path. Jem studied the nag with a lover's eye. "How about Nelly?"

"*You* can call it Nelly," JJ replied. "I'll keep calling it *Hey-You*! See? It responds well enough to that."

The great house of Clarendon loomed like a silent fortress. A hazy mist clung to the ground, and the lights in the windows glowed like the gatelamps to a dark netherworld.

The twins went first to the stables. Though he'd won the race home, JJ helped Jem stable the horses. They worked well together, Jem unsaddling and currying the horses (he was better with animals, and always had been) while JJ prepared the stalls with fresh hay and water.

With the horses seen to, the twins emerged from the stables. JJ was hungry, and he almost wanted to have a drink of some kind. But first, he knew that more important business waited for him, and for Jem too. Looking toward the darkened house, JJ saw a single light shining from within the huge windows of the library.

"He's in there," JJ said.

"It could just be Ben, bookworm that he is," Jem said, a rare note of nervousness in his voice.

"It's Father," JJ said. "I'm sure of it."

As they approached the front entrance, JJ could not help but feel that he stood upon a great threshold of some kind, not of wood or stone but of being. Four years ago, he had fled home and family in utter shame for a horrible, confusing sin. But now, with Father's letter in his pocket, he felt certain that the time for forgiveness and reconciliation had finally arrived. Still, he felt within himself a creeping sensation, a warning that it would be better to leave the future beyond this door unopened, unknown.

"You know," Jem said, maybe feeling a similar way. "We could always keep him waiting a little while longer."

For a moment, JJ considered the suggestion. More than that, he considered the possibility, bleak as it was, that he'd spent the last four years dreaming of a home that no longer existed, and maybe never had.

Your rightful place.

But Father could not have called JJ home for any idle purpose! Truth be told, JJ could already feel the warmth of Father's embrace. He could already feel the strain of years lifting from his shoulders as if he had just sunk into a steaming bath. He could already see himself sitting before the fire with Father, the old man's requisite reprimand finished, as father and firstborn son shared all the stories, ideas, and philosophies that could be bottled up in so many years of separation. In time, the lingering sorrow and rejection of the past would become nothing more than a bad dream, and JJ knew that all dreams faded away eventually.

"No," JJ said at last. He squared his shoulders. "I've waited — *we've* waited — long enough for this."

And then, taking a deep breath, JJ opened the door and crossed the threshold.

Chapter 14
THE CODICIL

Clarendon's great library was lit by a single candle. Its plucky yet meager glow cast huge shadows upon the walls and vaulted ceiling, and maybe upon the entire world. Here in the dark Jem Roscoe was reminded of a cathedral, even though he'd never been in one.

But the sad beauty of the usually bright and welcoming library was less impressionable than the frigid cold that bit at his bones. Jem gazed upon the bear-sized hearth and saw the smoldering dust of a long-dying fire now finally dead. His fingers were numb, the little bones in them screaming. Jem heard a strange sound from outside — the ghoulish shriek of a barn owl — and turning his head he finally realized the windows were all open.

Father sat exactly where Jem had left him earlier in the day, presiding over his desk like a condemning judge. Beside Father stood Ben Freeman, who looked like he craved to be anywhere else. Well, at least Ben wasn't alone in that feeling.

Jem looked at Father again and noticed the old man's teeth were chattering. Looking closer, he saw the old man was drenched with sweat, and there was steam rising from Father's pulsating brow.

Father's desk was strewn with books and papers. Among them Jem spied the clipping of the Winchester newspaper that contained JJ's 'Hero of Harper's Ferry' story. When he and JJ had first entered the library, Jem had seen Father leafing through a series of documents that Father now set down next to the candle. If there was anything Jem admired about his father, it was his capacity for long hours of work.

Jem listened and said nothing as mild pleasantries, stiff and formal, passed between JJ and Father. JJ stood ramrod straight at attention, the dutiful boy-soldier. He was still wearing his blue uniform, mud-caked and unwashed for many days, and on his belt hung his sheathed saber and holstered revolver.

Jem held a measure of pity for JJ. His brother still looked upon Father with the wide-eyed reverence of an acolyte, who would gladly throw himself from a cliff if given the command. Not even Tom still looked at Father in such a way, and Bayard — well, who knew what Bayard thought about it? The point was, even after everything Father had done to JJ, JJ still loved him. More than that, JJ craved Father's approval without really stopping to consider who the man was.

But Jem, he knew who John Roscoe was — who he *really* was. Some men earned the admiration of their children for simply doing the right thing, in all cases, without expectation of reward. Other men only cared to be known for doing the right thing, and in this pursuit the feelings of a child matter not at all. JJ's mind was sharp — sharper than any of the siblings, Jem included — but still JJ seemed unable or unwilling to detect the snake coiled at his feet.

Jem looked at Ben, who was staring vacantly at some distant space on the floor. Jem caught Ben's gaze and asked a series of silent questions, but Ben would not (or could not) give any answers. Instead, Ben only shook his head slowly, back and forth.

Perched behind his great desk, Father closed his eyes under the weight of some quiet torment. When they opened again and reflected the sickly candlelight, the old man's pupils shrank to black orbs suspended in pools of blood-stained milk. Father looked at both of his sons, but his eyes lingered especially on JJ.

Watching Father, Jem thought he detected within him a great and violent upheaval. It was as if some raw element within Father compelled him to leap up and grab JJ in a tearful, all-forgiving embrace, while at the same time some inner voice demanded stoic dispassion. Evidently the inner voice won out, for Father remained seated. Finally, he opened his mouth to speak.

"I haven't the time to be pedantic," Father said. "What I have to say I will simply *say*, and there will be no more said about it."

Jem didn't look at JJ, but they exchanged a wordless, telepathic debate. Who would speak for both of them? Who would stand before Father, and possibly stand *against* him? Who would take the lion's share of the lashings?

Jem opened his mouth to answer, but JJ was faster.

"Of course, sir," JJ said. "We adhere to your wishes in all things, Father."

Jem chewed his tongue and remained quiet.

For a time, there was only silence. The library was cold and cryptlike. Jem imagined how many steps it would take to reach the hallway and freedom beyond. Whatever was about to unfold, he would sooner not experience it firsthand. Still, Jem nevertheless felt the compulsion to stand with JJ and *take it*, whatever it was going to be. After all, it was Jem who had gotten them into the whole mess with Percy Claiborne. It was Jem who had—

"I'll see to the fire," Ben blurted. He turned and made a beeline for the hearth. He knelt near the bed of cold ash and began to stack cords of wood together. The arms of Colonel Spencer — his rusted saber, long rifle, and twin dueling pistols — hung over the mantle, and it looked now as if the kneeling Ben was worshiping these weapons of war.

Jem tried a strained laugh. "Yes to a fire, Ben. Laws, my teeth are chattering. Let's all get *comfortable*, shall we?" Looking at the somber faces of Father and JJ together, Jem's grin weakened. Still, he nodded to JJ. "What do you say about a drink to warm us up?"

JJ, who had eyes only for Father in that moment, shook his head no.

"There will be no libations tonight," Father muttered. "You had your fill last night, at the expense of your reputation. *And* mine."

Again Jem laughed, maybe trying to cut through the thick, sludge-like silence.

"Well, I'll take personal integrity over reputation any day, Father. Besides, a little hair of the dog never hurts..."

Dull-eyed, the old man set his teeth forward and folded his hands together.

"Jeremiah..."

"Yes, sir."

"Mind you don't open your mouth again unless I permit you to do so. Understood?"

Jem clenched his jaw and said nothing. He knew how this sort of test worked.

Father gave a thin, pleasureless smile. "Good. Now..."

At the hearth Ben lit a match, and it had the effect of a thunderclap. Kindling began to catch. Jem felt a little better knowing that the empty, gnawing silence in the library would soon be filled by the crackling of the fire.

Father said, "I spoke with Judge Cutler earlier this evening. About the Claiborne boy."

JJ nodded. "Yes, sir." There was a sickly hope in his eyes, the kind that flushes the veins of a condemned man awaiting an eleventh-hour pardon that might never manifest.

Father sat back in his chair and stretched. "Well, good news first. Percy Claiborne will live, though he will be permanently disfigured."

Jem felt JJ shudder a sigh of relief beside him. Jem felt relief too — he didn't have murder in his heart, nor wished death on anyone — but in a twisted way he wished he'd been conscious so he could have seen Percy get blasted.

"Tobias assured me that Clay Claiborne has declined to press charges for Percy's maiming."

JJ gave a smile of relief. "Oh, that's very good news, Father. Very good news indeed. I'm so relieved to know that—"

"*The bad news*," Father went on, "is that Claiborne has decided to cancel his financial contributions to my campaign."

Silence hung like a shroud. The relieved smile on JJ's lips began to curdle.

"And that is not all," Father said. "Claiborne is already encouraging the other First Families to cancel their donations in turn, suggesting that I can no longer be trusted to represent their concerns and interests. Of course you're aware that the Families are a powerful political force with influence far beyond the Branches, beyond even Virginia's borders. They can buy any number of votes in Richmond, and they can buy them in Washington too. But now, after the events of last night, they will no longer buy them through *me*."

Jem waited for Father's wrathful glare to fix upon him, but for now Father seemed to have eyes only for JJ.

"Without the financial support of my own constituents," Father said, "you can imagine what will happen to my alliances in Washington. My means of influence gone in an instant. If the well dries up — and it soon will, if something is not done — I'll have no ability to support Senator Douglas' bid for president. In turn, he'll have no reason to support my own ambitions. And if it comes to *that*, it will only be a matter of time until this session of Congress ends, until the railroad bill dies in committee. When that happens, I'll have the choice of running for yet another term in the Senate to resurrect the bill, but this time with no base of support, and here after I've already announced my intention to retire from public life next year..."

Jem heard the growing anxiety in Father's voice, noted the violent seesawing between spiked panic and flaccid reassurance that, of course, the worst could never happen, *would* never happen — not to John Roscoe, of all people.

After a long silence, it was JJ who spoke up first.

"If I may, Father," he said, trying his words out carefully. "I can give no excuse for the events of last night. Tempers ran hot, and perhaps for Mr. Claiborne they run hot still. But I believe this cloud will blow over, sir. I believe Claiborne's threats to be empty. And even if they're not empty, I believe the Families' withdrawal of support is not a catastrophe so much as a...well, a bump in the road, so to speak."

Father raised an eyebrow. "*A bump in the road?*"

JJ nodded. "Yes, sir."

Father pressed his lips together until they were white. "You're certain of that? You'd stake your reputation on it?"

JJ nodded again. "I would, sir."

Father barely moved, seemed not even to breathe. "And what about the family's reputation? Would you stake *my* reputation on your belief that all this is but a minor concern?"

JJ was quiet for a long while. Finally, he took a deep breath.

"'The world gives nothing to a man of action. Whatever he wants, he must take.' Those are your words, Father, and I've lived true to them for a long time. I live them to this day — and I say, we ought to keep living them still. So what if the First Families turn against us? We do not need them, and maybe we never did. We are *Roscoes*: independent and enterprising. You talked about taking our family elsewhere. Well, perhaps it's time we go. We've outgrown Mayfair, and perhaps we've outgrown Virginia too. Let us move on from here, and take whatever we intend for ourselves. You may talk of the Roscoe family's legacy, but I think we ought to speak of its destiny."

While JJ spoke, Jem watched a dark light grow in each of his brother's eyes. JJ's unblinking gaze brimmed with conviction and self-certainty, and suddenly the son appeared more than ever the spitting image of his father.

Pointing at the newspaper clipping, JJ indicated the front-page headline.

"When my story goes Union-wide, Father — when *our* story goes national — the Roscoe family will be untouchable." Here, JJ offered a hopeful smile. "I gave you John Brown. Now, *you* can give him to the people, to the Union. The question is, what will the people give to you in return? What will the Union give to our family? Whatever the Roscoes can claim, we can gain it — *together*. I'm certain of it, Father."

No one said anything. Jem saw JJ stand tall, his hands placed powerfully on the belt where his saber and revolver were holstered, but JJ was nevertheless trembling with nervous anticipation.

Meanwhile, a glimmer of consideration flared in Father's eyes, and it lingered there a long while. Again Jem saw an inward battle roiling within those clouds of gray. Father looked like a paranoid king clutching at the sides of his throne.

Still, Jem waited for the clouds to pass, for the king to come to his senses. Maybe JJ was right when he talked about reconciliation. Somewhere behind the mask that Father wore so well, Jem could detect that same vulnerable, loving spirit that Father had let slip to him on the train station platform. He waited for that spirit to return, for Father to cast off the veil once and for all.

...Jonathan?

But instead, the hinted spirit of forgiveness vanished. The old man's expression darkened, and he assumed a hard-set look of grim determination. He pressed the tips of his fingers together, five to five, as if testing their will for shaping what was to come.

And then, with a quiet sigh of resignation, Father reached out and picked up the newspaper clipping and set it atop an idle stack of papers.

"Ben, set these scraps in the fire."

Ben gawked at the old man and didn't move. When Father turned and leveled a stare at him, Ben dragged his feet forward and took the papers into his hands.

With an uncertain look toward Jem and JJ, Ben turned and stood before the glowing hearth. Jem could almost hear JJ shout for Ben not to move another muscle. After some hesitation, Ben finally reached out and fed the papers to the hungry flames. Jem watched, fascinated, as the blackening pages of the clipping writhed and curled.

Father said, "A correspondent from the *Winchester Advertiser* arrived here about two hours ago, while you were both out. The man wanted to know about the nature of my relationship with the 'hero of Harper's Ferry'..."

JJ started forward with searching eyes, as if he might find the correspondent hiding behind the old man's desk.

"And is he still here, Father? I should like to speak with the man so I may answer his—"

"I sent him away," the old man replied flatly. "I explained to the correspondent, who was pleasant enough to deal with, that in fact I had no idea what he was talking about, nor why he'd come such a long way to speak with me. I told him I was not aware of any relation to a 'Lieutenant Jonathan Roscoe.' I did, however, note I was father to a 'Jonathan Roscoe', presently a cadet enrolled at the Military Academy at West Point, though I clarified that fact with the insistence that *my* Jonathan was studying in New York during the attack on Harper's Ferry, and therefore couldn't possibly have participated in John Brown's capture."

Here, Father gave a dismissive shrug.

"You can imagine the young man's surprise at hearing all this, but I suggested to him that either his sources were mistaken, or else there was some kind of misprint—"

"*Father*," JJ gasped, his voice shaking. "There was no misprint. The sources were not mistaken. I was *there*, Father, and it was me who—"

"John Brown will answer for his crimes," Father went on blandly, "and that is all that matters. As the commanding officer of the soldiers present, Robert E. Lee naturally deserves the praise for Brown's capture. Oh, and who else did the correspondent identify? Someone named Stuart, I believe, will share some part of the praise."

JJ stared back at him in stunned disbelief.

"It is all just as well," Father said, "for if I allowed you to traipse about on the national stage in a fit of self-congratulation, this would only invite Claiborne and the others to plant a follow-up story. A story that reveals the erstwhile 'hero of Harper's Ferry' is in fact a carnal degenerate from a family of degenerates. No sooner would *Roscoe* become a household name than it would become a laughingstock — not just here in the Valley, which it already is, but across the entire continent. Exactly what do you think will happen to a sitting senator who is revealed to indulge the unholy predations of his sodomite son?"

At the word *sodomite*, JJ hung his head and looked down at the floor.

"But of course," Father went on, "I couldn't let the young man go back to Winchester empty-handed after traveling all this way. I gave him what change I could spare and sent him on his way with the understanding that, in fact, there was no one named 'Roscoe' at Harper's Ferry."

Unable to comprehend what the old man was saying, JJ could only shake his head. "But that…that isn't the *truth*, Father…"

"It's enough of the truth," Father replied, "and that's good enough for me."

Watching and listening to all this, Jem pulsed with the need to *do something*. But still, he stood there in silence with his head bowed.

After breathing a heavy sigh, Father looked determined to press on with the business of the moment. He reached across the desk and indicated a nearby leather-bound case.

"I don't think I need to tell either of you what is written in here," Father said. "It's only natural that a dying man should write one, and better to write one while he possesses a sound mind. Indeed, that is the whole purpose of my visit home. Tomorrow, I will share the full details with the rest of the family."

Slowly, Father opened the case and drew out the pages within.

"As far as these things go, it is rather ordinary and predictable. However, there is one clause, regarding my successor, that deserves special consideration. I heard Judge Cutler's advice on the matter, and with that advice in mind I appended a codicil, a sort of modification, that supersedes the original document. And since the Lord may take me at any moment, I want to clarify that clause for the two of you now, so that there will be no confusion during the document's official reading."

In the thick silence that followed, Jem looked upon the leather case and tried to think back to earlier in the day. Had any of the RRC documents he'd signed ended up in that case? He didn't think so — he was certain of it. Still, Jem nevertheless felt his heart drop into his stomach.

Father looked at JJ and pushed the leather case to the edge of the desk.

"I think you ought to read what is written here, Jonathan. You may ask clarifying questions if you wish, but afterward I would like you to witness the document personally."

Jem turned and watched JJ's face drain of color. The fingers of a cold realization had seized him, and the last traces of a hopeful expectation were stripped from his face. Then, Jem heard a rather strange sound.

JJ was laughing.

"Come, Father," he said. "Surely you don't intend to cast your firstborn son into the cold over a foolish matter like a duel."

Father's face was blank, stonelike. "In fact, that is precisely what I intend."

JJ went on laughing, but his laugh became choked, forced. At last, he managed to gasp, "*Why?*"

Father shook his head. He spoke now in a tired, explanatory manner, as if he'd pressed upon this same point a thousand times before.

"The plain fact of the matter is that I haven't much longer for this world. And you of all people must understand, Jonathan, how imperative it is that I secure a position of strength for this family that will last long after I am gone. The national railroad, the vanguard of an American empire, the opening of the West — it is all within our grasp. But a great idea is never the domain of a single mind. Others are scrambling to seize upon our plans, *my* plans. It will be up to the rest of this family to carry on the legacy which I impart. The die has been cast, and this family can afford no missteps, no scandals, no clouds of dishonor or distrust. Twice now, Jonathan, once before and once again last night, your actions have brought my life's work to the brink of disaster. Now that I am finally so close to achieving my ambitions — now that I am so close to the *end* — do you really think I'm going to risk a third chance at catastrophe? Would *you* risk it, were you in my position?"

JJ shook his head furiously. "But this...it doesn't make any sense. Father, of course I recognize the shame I once brought on this family. I will spend the rest of my life correcting myself, stamping out all effeminate feeling. I am committed to that practice, Father. But this spat with the Claibornes is all *Jem's* fault, not mine."

Stunned, Jem turned and stared at his brother with disbelief. "I beg your goddamn pardon?"

"*He's* the one who deserves to be punished," JJ said, ignoring Jem and appealing to Father directly. "He's the one who's been feuding for months with Percy Claiborne over some village whore. I was only defending our family's honor. I was only trying to preserve the legacy that *you* created."

"So much for standing together," Jem muttered. Looking up at Father now, he said, "I don't care what you give or don't give to me in that piece of paper, Father. I'd sooner receive nothing and be free to do as I please." He cast a meaningful look toward JJ. "All this rambling about *legacy* and what one *deserves* is enough to give me a headache."

"You're sure that's not the gin?" JJ said. There was a wild, cagey look in his eyes. "Father, please. The Roscoe Company will need leadership after you're gone — *true* leadership, not uncaring incompetence. You know it's me, Father. Despite my missteps, you know it's always been me."

Father sat back and began to wring his hands together, as if shaping something between his palms. In a soft voice, he admitted, "It was always supposed to be you, Jonathan..."

JJ nodded and smiled, and he waited for Father to say something more.

Father set his mouth against his hands, as if whispering a prayer into them. Presently his gaze shifted to the single candle on his desk. Within the old man's eyes, it was now plain enough to see: the hopeful light of mercy and forgiveness was dimming, fading, and finally gone.

"But it won't be who you takes over," Father said. "It will be Jeremiah. He has proven himself to be capable enough, despite your claims to the contrary."

JJ spat the words back. "*Capable enough?*"

"What's more," Father went on. "He harbors no delusions of grandeur. Of course Jeremiah has his own failings; we all do. But the very fact that he does not crave the responsibility of shouldering the Roscoe family legacy is what assures me that he is the one who can best meet the challenges that lay ahead."

JJ threw a bitter laugh on the floor. "Bullshit."

There followed a great silence. Looming overhead, the library's great bookshelves looked like rows of box seats in some sort of mad peanut gallery, with imagined whispers of ghoulish laughter settling upon everything like cold sleet.

Father's eyes were hard, narrow. Again he put his hands upon the document before him. "It would be best if you simply wrote your signature and we said no more about any of this. What's done is done."

JJ trembled, his whole body tensed as if ready to do physical battle. He reached into the breast pocket of his coat and withdrew a battered envelope.

"What about this? Your letter, Father. 'Your rightful place.' Was all of it a lie, nothing but a goddamn ruse?" With a snarl, JJ now turned on Jem. "And you, baby brother. You'll 'go along with whatever Father decides,' will you? All this time, you *knew* what this really was."

Jem shook his head. He tried to protest, but the accusation had been so sudden, so appalling *false*, that he could not—

"This was your intention from the beginning," JJ said. "All of you, the whole fucking family, you led me here like a rabbit to the snare, just so you could have a laugh at my expense. You wanted me here so you could humiliate me and—"

"Your talents are undeniable," Father said, his voice sharpening, "but your skin is much too thin. You believe the world is yours to inhabit, and yours alone. You think reality ought to unfold in the manner of your desires, adhering always to your own notions of 'destiny.' Meanwhile, you see a threat in every man's intentions. You read every action as a personal attack. You are incapable of trusting anyone, even yourself."

JJ flashed an acidic smile. "Well then, am I not John Roscoe's son?" The smile twisted and became a grotesque sneer. "I know my failures, but I know my triumphs too. You cannot erase them like you can burn a few scraps of paper. I earned glory for our family, and for our country, at Harper's Ferry. I know my rightful place is here with you, Father, and one day, at the head of this family. If you cannot see that, then perhaps the corruption in your lungs has taken hold of your mind."

The old man's eyes and nostrils flared, his hair seeming to stand on end. The effect reminded Jem of predators puffing up before rivals to claim a fresh kill for their own.

"You accuse *me* of corruption?" Father hissed. "You, the golden child, fallen from grace when the impulse of degeneracy seized you…*you* would accuse me of corruption? Oh, Jonathan, my boy, how I do pity you. I pity you, and I will pray for you. I will pray for you, and for the departed soul of that poor Harper boy."

JJ opened his mouth to retort, but no sound came. Slowly, his face registered confusion. In time, the raw meaning of Father's words began to sink in.

"Or do you not know?" Father said, a hint of vindication gleaming in his eyes.

"Did Jeremiah not tell you? Did not Ben tell you, or Sarah? *Richard Harper is dead.*"

JJ said nothing. He could only look away, his eyes darting all around the darkened room, unable or unwilling to rest anywhere lest tears take control.

"I understand the poor boy hanged himself," Father went on. "Such was the shame that followed him, even to a place where he was a stranger to all. Such was the torment that gnawed at him from within. Perhaps it was better that he chose to end his life in such a way. Who could ever wish for their own son to suffer endlessly, needlessly?"

All this time, Jem had stood helpless beside JJ. He wanted nothing more than to turn away and flee.

Meanwhile, JJ's mouth moved, but no sound came. When JJ finally found his voice again, it was a dry croak, the sound of a person fighting off nausea.

"When?"

Father shrugged. "Oh, some months ago now, I'm not entirely sure. Do you know, Jeremiah? You were the one to tell me the news, after all."

Jem's stomach reeled. Instantly, he felt JJ's wrathful eyes on him. Deciding there was nothing he could say, Jem only shook his head and looked down at the floor.

JJ heaved a shuddering breath. He lifted his chin high and glared his hatreds at the far wall, as might a man resisting torture.

"Well," JJ said. "What do I care about any of that? Richard Harper means nothing to me. He *meant* nothing to me."

"Don't lie to me, boy," Father growled. "It insults my intelligence. You still retain some twisted notion of love for the Harper boy, a 'love' that is nothing more than a tumor in your brain. You think it gives me any pleasure to watch this sickness take hold of you, and *keep* hold of you, despite your intentions to 'correct' yourself? There is no correcting nature, Jonathan, and *your* nature is one of corruption — corruption which, like a gangrenous limb, must be cut off in order to save the body."

In his periphery, Jem watched JJ hang his head in shame and defeat. And finally, the tears came. They cut tracks down JJ's cheeks, and despite his best efforts he could not stop them.

Jem turned now to Ben Freeman, who all this time had seemed to shrink smaller and smaller. Ben wore a look of misery; he too appeared defeated, unable to do or say anything. And Father, he remained powerful in his chair, unsmiling but clearly satisfied with the evening's progress.

"All this need not be so dramatic," Father said. "There need be no tears shed over a few dollars and cents. You can take comfort, Jonathan, that I will not leave you adrift, so to speak. Within the terms of my will, you are to receive a fair and suitable portion of—"

"I don't want a fucking *portion*," JJ growled. "I want what I deserve. I want what was promised. I demand what's *owed* to me."

Father stared back at him, stone-faced.

"Very well," the old man said. "Then it shall be nothing." Looking down at the papers before him, Father reached for a nearby fountain pen. "All the same, in order to conclude our business here this evening, I need at least *one* signature." Father looked up now, pen in hand. "Jeremiah?"

Stunned, Jem stood frozen. He felt his pulse pumping in his throat. He felt JJ's hateful gaze in his periphery, while before him Father extended his arm and offered the pen as if it was some kind of scepter.

"Will you do the honors, Jeremiah?" Still holding out the pen, Father offered a smile that might have been loving. "Will you do this, my boy, for me?"

Jem's answer was to turn and look at JJ for a long while. In one sense, he wanted nothing more than to put his arm around JJ and flee the library together, and with Ben too. Everyone, the whole family, would abandon Clarendon and leave the wretched old patriarch to gnaw on bones in the dark. But in the same breath, Jem resisted the impulse to spit in JJ's face. He'd injured his brother in no conceivable way, yet JJ glared at him as if he was an utter traitor. Perhaps JJ really did inhabit the self-absorbed spirit of John Roscoe, in that he showed affection for others only when he stood to gain something from them.

Well, to hell with all that.

"I *may* sign it," Jem said, not taking his eyes off JJ. "First, I'd like to read what you've written, Father, and thoroughly, before I make a decision."

Father nodded slowly and set the pen down on the desk. "The boy is learning. Well, come over here to the light so you may see properly..."

Taking a breath, Jem turned away from JJ and started toward the desk. Already he felt a sense of shame welling up, heard a quiet voice compelling him to assume the role of mediator, to set all personal grievances aside and try to be the voice of reason, and he was so consumed by these thoughts that he was not aware of the sudden movement behind him — not until, through the corner of his eye, he saw Ben raise his hands with a look of horror stamped on his face.

"JJ," Ben breathed, "JJ, no, *don't*!"

Jem turned just in time to see JJ draw his Colt revolver from its holster and point the barrel at Father's heart.

Without thinking, Jem lunged. He clasped the killing arm with both hands and tried to wrench the revolver free, tried to point it away. He succeeded only in knocking JJ off balance just as JJ squeezed the trigger.

The gunshot split Jem's ears open. Somehow there was barely any smoke from the revolver, but in the same instant he heard a violent *shunk*! from above, where the bullet had punched a black hole. Dust and debris fell from on high and doused them in a fine yellow powder. It was as if the old house was weeping, or bleeding, or both.

Roaring, the twins grappled together. The revolver dropped to the floor and was kicked away in the scuffle. The candle on Father's desk was knocked over and snuffed out, and suddenly Jem and JJ fought as shadows in a firelit deathmatch. JJ suckered Jem once, twice, and then dealt a gut-wrenching blow to Jem's kidneys.

Jem grabbed fistfuls of JJ's uniform and pulled his brother close as if to kiss him; instead he cracked his forehead against JJ's skull and sent JJ staggering back.

JJ wavered, punch drunk, and fought to remain standing. Wheezing, Jem advanced sluggishly and turned his brother around, aiming to lock an arm around his neck.

Suddenly JJ came back to life; he drove his elbow at his brother's ribcage, forcing *in* and *up*. Jem croaked and staggered backward, the breath blown from his lungs. Groping his way forward, JJ made a fist and hurled it at Jem with all his might. The blow picked Jem up off the ground and threw him down upon Father's great desk. A dull *crunch* sounded as the top of the desk split in two.

Stunned, blood streaming from his nose, Jem collapsed to the ground. He groaned and groped at the air as if he was blind. He felt his lungs shrink inside him like neglected bellows. But so strong was the primeval instinct to *breathe* that something deeper in him took control of his body. An unearthly wheeze escaped him. His eyes rolled around in his skull, as if they'd been knocked loose somehow. Slowly, excruciatingly, his lungs began to fill with air again.

JJ, startled by his own strength, staggered back and looked on at what he'd done, his cheeks flushed red, his eyes gleaming with conviction and pride.

Ben started forward to intercede, but he stopped when he caught a staying look from JJ.

Slowly, white shock bled the red from JJ's cheeks. He blinked, and blinked again, such a simple act that in the moment seemed to require gargantuan strength. A realization lit up in JJ's eyes, and he went searching. Seeing the revolver across the floor where it had landed during the struggle, JJ went over and picked it up again. He marveled at the weapon as if he'd never seen such a thing before.

Unable to move from his heap of limbs, still covetous of every ragged breath he could take in, Jem could do nothing but watch as JJ stepped forward again with his revolver in hand. Jem imagined the ticking clockwork of JJ's mind, and then imagined it running faster. He could almost see the cogs begin to fracture and the gears break asunder, and from the collapsed wreckage of reason and rationality spewed an unthinking malcontent that filled JJ's eyes like black smoke.

And then Jem saw that his brother was smiling.

Maybe JJ smiled because Father, whose face Jem could not see, had become a rictus of terror. Indeed, Jem could hear a low whimpering from behind the desk. He imagined tears and snot running the length of the old man's face. Maybe JJ was smiling at the sight of his father's wrinkled, beseeching hands thrust out before him, as if they would be enough to stop another bullet.

Slowly, JJ lowered his hand until the barrel of the revolver was level with the bridge of Jem's nose.

Jem fought to sit up as straight as he could. He glared past the barrel and looked into his brother's eyes, which gleamed with bloodlust. But Jem did not cower; he did not hold up his hands nor shut his eyes tight to await the inevitable. Instead he glared back at JJ, his eyes meeting hate with hate, and though Jem said nothing his goading challenge was made clear.

Go ahead.

At any moment, any split second now, Jem was certain that JJ would in fact *go ahead*, that Jem would soon greet a bullet. But suddenly, he could see JJ's hardened determination begin to tremble and crack, as if his resolve was a stone pillar finally about to give way under the bite of ropes and chains.

Still no bullet came. And just as Jem felt he must scream or lose his mind from the insanity of the moment, JJ's bloodlust vanished. JJ now looked up to Father again, now to Ben, and finally to Jem once more, but he could look no one in the eye for very long. A hundred expressions chased themselves across his face, all of them versions of shame and horror and loathing regret. JJ opened his mouth to say something, maybe to explain himself, but nothing came out of him except for a guttural croak. There were no more proud opinions or self-righteous declarations. Instead, JJ turned and fled the library.

Jem watched JJ go, watched him turn the corner and heard his hurried bootsteps decay down the hall, like a shackled ghost fleeing through catacombs. Far away — across the world, maybe — Clarendon's front door creaked open and clanged shut.

Jem finally snapped back to reality when he heard Father coughing. The old man doubled over and snatched up a nearby handkerchief. Between coughs the old man tried in vain to gasp for breath. A gout of blood splattered the fabric, and Father made no show of trying to hide it. There was no point now, for more blood was coming up.

"Christ Almighty," Ben whispered. He went at once to the old man's side and put a hand on him, gingerly, as if his touch might only make things worse. "I'm here, sir. Can you breathe for me, sir? *God's sake*...You're all right now, sir. You're all right now..."

Moving sluggishly, the world around him awash, Jem staggered to his feet.

"Jem?" Ben said. There was unthinking panic in Ben's normally calm, measured voice. "Jem, you should stay down. *Jem*, where the hell are you going?"

Jem only grunted and staggered toward the space over the blazing hearth, where Colonel Spencer's weapons were displayed. Ignoring the blast of heat on his legs, Jem reached up for one of the dueling pistols. Holding the aged flintlock in one hand, he hurried away from the fire to a cabinet in the far corner.

While Ben hurled urgent protests at him, Jem hauled a drawer open and dug about, snatching up a fistful of flint and lead balls and several packets of gunpowder. He pushed the balls and packets into his pocket, saving one of each for loading. He tore a packet open with his teeth as he made for the hallway — this he could do without thinking, punch-drunk or not — and he drove a ball in and packed everything with the flintlock's small ramrod.

"Jem!" Ben called. "Jem, whatever you're about to do with that, I beg you, *don't*—"

But Jem had already quit the library. He was already plunging down the darkened hallway before he realized that, yes, he was committing to this course of action. JJ had forced his hand — traitor! A would-be murderer, foiled only by the realization of the ruin he would bring down on himself. And all for what, a few pieces of paper? A goddamn hole in the ground, a few miles of goddamn steel track?

Clutching the flintlock, Jem turned out the main door and saw JJ nowhere in sight, but of course he knew where he'd gone. Picking up his feet, he ran around the house toward the stables.

He found JJ there in the barnyard, having just secured the saddle on his nag. As JJ prepared to mount up, Jem cried out and drew the pistol to full cock and leveled it at his brother.

Standing beside his horse, JJ became very still, watchful. His own weapon was holstered — he was defenseless — but he kept his hands at his sides. His face was hard-set, his eyes cold and unblinking. It was as if he was appealing Jem to shoot him, just as Jem had done within the library. Shoot him, and quick; he'd be doing him a goddamn favor.

And Jem wanted to shoot — God, he wanted to. But just as his finger graced the trigger, the full insanity of the situation struck him. Out of nowhere, the term for what he was about to do sliced through his thoughts like a sharp blade.

Fratricide.

Though Jem's trembling arm fought against it, he felt an overwhelming pressure on his killing arm, as if some invisible hand were pushing it down.

JJ shook his head slowly. "You don't have it in your heart, Jem."

Grimacing, Jem held the pistol steady. "You do," he muttered. "You pulled the trigger, and were about to do it again. There's a darkness in your heart, JJ. And aren't you and I one and the same?"

JJ didn't answer. While they stood watching each other, their haggard breaths gusting in the cold night air, freezing raindrops began to fall. Soon enough the only movement in the barnyard was the plunging rain, a million myriad drops falling in an endless, indiscernible pattern.

JJ placed his army forage cap, sopping wet, upon his head.

"Goodbye, baby brother."

There might have been a smile on his lips — not mocking, but almost wistful — and then JJ turned and mounted his horse.

While Jem stood there, uncertain what to do or how even to think, he watched JJ ride down the clay path.

Thinking about it later, Jem couldn't be sure whether he'd actually pulled the trigger or whether the pistol itself had malfunctioned. But with the weapon still pointed at his brother's back, the consideration of a hateful opportunity *did* flare in Jem's mind. If only JJ were gone, then maybe...

And in the same instant that thought gripped Jem's mind, he flinched as a thunderclap struck — the pistol flashed and bucked in his hand, and gunsmoke gusted into the rain-filled air.

Shocked, Jem peered through the smoke. He thought he saw JJ reel in the saddle. But then again, maybe not. JJ kept on riding, tall and erect, and the beech trees stood weeping raindrops for him, their huge frames seeming to stand at attention for him.

Jem watched as the mounted figure of his brother became smaller and smaller, and finally it turned northward and vanished. The drumming rain was already filling in the receding hoofprints, already washing them out, and after a while it was as if JJ had never been there at all.

Alone, Jem stood there in the icy rain. It took everything for him not to collapse to his knees. Turning his head to the sky, feeling the pelting raindrops course down his bleeding, battered face, Jem closed his swollen eyes and welcomed the deluge.

Chapter 15
RUNAWAY

The next morning, November arrived gray and cold.

Clarendon remained quiet for much of the day. Outside, the gnarled trees and shrubbery wept the last of their leaves. The grass turned to slate. The grounds became the domain of mean-eyed crows who scared away the last of summertime's plump songbirds. The front door of the stables was not quite closed; it yawned open and swung shut according to the whims of a biting north wind. The Mayfair Valley's long summer was indeed over.

Ben awoke from a fitful sleep (he'd only caught a few hours' rest) to the sounds and smells of Mama frying up breakfast. He shuffled into the kitchens to help her. Mama asked no questions — she'd heard the gunshot in the night, and the screaming and scuffling, the ragged coughing, and finally the low weeping. No doubt she'd heard the second gunshot too, and the hooves galloping away until they faded.

In the dining room, Ben and Mama served breakfast to a table of no one. After waiting a little while, they carried trays up to bedroom doors that would not open.

Ben spent much of the day wandering around Clarendon in a cloud of his own thoughts. He was comforted when the dog Tipper padded up to him and pushed his snout against him, his way of asking for attention. With the dog at his side, Ben continued to wander. He could walk Clarendon in his sleep, but today the parlors were alien and foreboding, the corridors empty except for the gnawing feeling of something watching from the shadows.

By and by, Ben found himself in the library to take on the chore he had been putting off for most of the day. Approaching the large desk before the hearth, Ben studied the small pile of dust and debris that had appeared on the carpeted floor, as if some gopher or field mouse had dug a burrow there. There were spots of dried blood staining the carpet, but as to which twins' blood it was, Ben had no idea. Tipper bent down to investigate but Ben whispered the dog away. Craning his neck, he looked up at the hole in the ceiling where JJ's bullet had struck and disappeared.

From nowhere, a voice said: "I'm thinking I might just leave it like that. Good craftsmen are expensive these days. And what's more, it gives the place character."

Ben looked all around, but of course he knew who had spoken. He saw Senator

Roscoe standing at the entrance to the library, cane in hand. He looked a little better this morning after some rest.

As the old man picked his way across the carpeted floor, Tipper assumed a stance of tense readiness, his dark eyes watchful. As he stepped up beside Ben, the Senator noticed Tipper and reached out to him with a smile, but the dog evaded his touch with a low growl, and soon quit the room.

A flash of anger passed over the Senator's face as he watched the dog go. "And I sometimes wonder why I don't like animals," he murmured. Turning to Ben now, the Senator nodded skyward at the bullet hole. "Do you think he really meant to kill me last night?"

Ben wished he knew the answer, but he could only shake his head. "I don't know, sir. The hole in the ceiling suggests one answer. But if the case were as clear as that, maybe you wouldn't feel the need to ask the question."

A curious smile passed over the Senator's white lips. "No. I suppose not." With a tired sigh, the old man went up to his desk and placed his ringed knuckles upon the lacquered wood surface. He ran his palm over the hairline fracture where the wood had split under Jem's weight. "Let me ask you another question then, Ben. Do you think I'm a monster?"

Ben blinked. "Sir?"

"I said, do you think I'm a monster? For the decision I made?"

Ben felt the ensuing silence threaten to swallow him whole. He didn't know how to answer this question either, and he said as much. But he also explained that he had seen plenty of monsters in his short time, and he did not believe John Roscoe was one of them.

The Senator nodded and smiled, satisfied.

"...but that doesn't mean," Ben went on, "that the decision you made regarding JJ was wise, or just."

The old man's smile soured. "You don't think so?"

Ben searched for the right words. "I wonder, sir. Was last night really about the twins playing with guns? They were wrong to fight Claiborne, surely, but they kept their honor. And the Families were preparing to turn against you even if the duel had never happened. After all, the bag I brought to you at Wyolah Hall was half empty."

"The remaining contributions will arrive in good time," the Senator said. "Tobias assures me, it will only be a matter of time until Claiborne and the others come to their senses. They know what's at stake here, and in Washington too."

Ben's eyes narrowed at the mention of Tobias Cutler. He had been hearing that name a lot lately, and rather too much for his liking.

"I wonder, sir..."

Ben hesitated, unsure whether to proceed with what he really wanted to say next. But now he swallowed, found his voice again, and pressed on.

"I wonder if last night was really about something else entirely. An old wound you thought had closed over a long time ago. When you realized it was still open, still raw, you decided to cauterize it."

The Senator laughed and shook his head. "You're not making much sense, Ben. *I* wonder if all the commotion last night might have rattled your brain."

Ben tried to catch the old man's gaze and hold it, but the old man would not look at him. "I'm only saying, sir, that perhaps you were looking for an excuse to send JJ away. You were punishing him for a sin you believed he has yet to atone for."

"*Punish?*" the old man echoed with disdain. "Did you and I not witness the same events last night? If I'm guilty of anything in all this, it's that I've been too soft."

"Forgive me, sir," Ben said. "I'm not trying to point fingers. But since you asked my opinion, I wonder if there might have been a better way to right whatever wrongs exist between you and JJ, both real and imagined—"

"There was no other way," the old man said flatly. "I assure you, Mr. Freeman, his *wrongs* were very *real*. What I did, I did for the good of the entire family."

Ben opened his mouth to clarify, or maybe in fact to argue, but then he hung his head and nodded.

"Yes, sir."

"What, you don't believe me?"

"It's not that, sir."

The Senator sat down behind the desk. "Then what is it?"

Ben realized he was standing in the same place where JJ had stood last night, the focus of the old man's withering stare. At length, Ben shrugged. "Perhaps I've said too much already. Perhaps it's not my place to say anything more than—"

"I wish you just would say it, whatever it is."

"Yes, sir. Well, it's just that…I don't understand how any of it is *good*."

The old man blinked and looked away. He stared off somewhere unknowable, and despite the hardness in his eyes and the firmness of his jaw, the Senator appeared as a man clutching a cliff face who was losing his grip.

"No," the Senator murmured quietly. "No, it is not *good*, you're right. I wrestled with that decision for years. Somehow, last night, what I had to do was made clear to me. But now that the deed is done, I still don't know if I was right. If a man could choose his fate, I would not have chosen this one."

Ben shook his head. "But, sir, you *did* choose to—"

"*Nevertheless*," the Senator continued sharply, "it is what it is." As he looked off, keeping his eyes fixed on some distant point, the old man seemed to speak only to himself. "Sometimes there are no right answers in a situation that is entirely wrong and hopeless. But what can a man do? He cannot slink away — he must *act*. I *acted*. I explained to him, in no uncertain terms, that for him to remain my successor was a categorical impossibility. And yet, I assured him that, despite the dishonor he brought upon this family, this family would not abandon him. And what did he do? He spurned me. Like a mongrel dog, he bit the hand of charity."

Ben drew a deep breath. "If I may, sir. Perhaps JJ didn't come home wishing for charity, but to reconcile with his father."

The Senator wore a grimace of pain and was silent for a long moment. Ben wondered if, somehow, he had broken through a wall of some kind.

"Jonathan is young," the Senator said at last. "He has a whole life ahead of him. Perhaps this is only a period of confusion, and someday soon he will realize the hideous errors in his ways. But *I* do not have the luxury of time to wait until he comes to his senses. I must proceed. We, the family, must carry on. We must imagine Jonathan is dead and buried, for in a sense that is exactly what has happened. If my hopes are realized, Jeremiah and Thomas shall become some of this century's great men. I regret that Jonathan will not be ranked with them, but *it is what it is*."

Ben offered a relenting nod. "Yes, sir."

The Senator put his head in his hands, and it was into his palms that he now spoke.

"My legacy is all I have to give to the world, Ben. It is all I may consign to history. My own father gave me nothing but the stench of failure, the gnawing hunger of poverty. In my time, I bore witness to the exponential growth of these United States, and indeed I have played a part in its shaping. Indeed, its riches became *my* riches, and I sleep well knowing that I *earned* everything I own. Nothing was given to me which I did not have the courage and creativity to take for myself. I have no doubt that one day the industrious, entrepreneurial Union shall eclipse the empires of Europe and stand paramount among all the nations of the earth. Indeed, I believe this is already happening. When my time is over, a bold future will be placed in the hands of my children, and their children after them. I have lived with the singular aim of dragging the Roscoe family out of the gutter, and that aim has been achieved. I must die knowing that those who come after me will not plunge this family back into the muck."

The Senator went on talking, but after a while Ben stopped listening. Eventually he excused himself and turned to go. Leaving the library, he chanced a look back and saw the old man staring up at the bullet hole in the ceiling.

Walking up the long, darkened hallway, Ben forgot briefly who he was and where he was going. Some force drew him to the nearest door. Stepping out on the veranda, he felt the cold late afternoon air and found he could finally breathe again.

Feeling the impulse to write, Ben fetched his notebook and returned to a chair upon the veranda, and he sat there until the sun began to set. As darkness crept in, Ben rolled a cigar and began to smoke. Within his notebook, he had managed to write only a few words:

Only a true monster could deny the authentic spirit of someone they purport to love. To demand a loved one deny the essence of their own being is to command suicide, if not of body, then of the soul.

Still smoking now, his notebook splayed upon his lap, Ben watched as the darkening clouds in the west broke to reveal a last sliver of blazing orange light. The dying sun cast along the underside of the heavy gray clouds so that it seemed the sky was a frothing sea turned upside down.

Ben turned his head and stared down the long clay driveway, past the ancient beech trees lining either side, and studied the rays of light filtering down to the cold, hard-packed earth. It was very cold, but he had no wish to go back inside.

Suddenly, Ben hunched forward and hacked a series of ragged coughs until he retched. He spat, and he heard a nasty gurgling in his lungs as he took in a rattling breath. Perhaps he had been smoking too much lately. Or perhaps he had caught consumption like Senator Roscoe. Ben laughed darkly at that thought, until another fit of coughing forced him to focus just on catching his breath. When the coughing had finally passed, he turned his head skyward once more and realized the sun was gone. The land all around Clarendon was dark and, despite the blowing wind, suffocating.

Just then, something caught Ben's eye in the distance. He looked across the fields.

There was an animal moving through the thickets.

A fox, or maybe something bigger. No, definitely bigger. Ben sat up and watched. The animal was moving closer, now tracking slowly across the fields. The thing seemed to limp, to stumble along as if injured. Ben sat back again. Some predator would likely get it in the night, whatever it was. Maybe one of its own kind.

But the animal kept coming. And as Ben watched, his eyes at last focused in the darkness. This was no fox. It was much, much bigger. And faster.

And moving right toward him.

Ben stood up straight. His mind raced with explanations. A bear? In these mountains? Whatever the hell it was, he had no weapon to use against it. Ben tossed his cigar and stood bristling on the veranda. Squinting against the dark, he heard heavy breathing, and feet running. Two feet, not four.

A man.

Ben called in a deep voice: "Who goes there?"

The feet stopped. The wind picked up. Ben could see little in the gathering dark, but he caught the shape of a man standing in the field beyond the grounds. A dark head appeared, the body concealed by the heavy brush. A low voice carried over the dying grass and into Ben's ears:

"I ain't goin back. Don't let them take me back."

Ben knew the voice. It carried a faint memory that became clearer with each passing moment. He walked to the steps of the veranda and went down to stand on the lawn. Somewhere far off, maybe a mile away, a dog barked idly. The man in the field jumped at the sound, and despite the darkness Ben saw icy white fear gleaming in his large eyes. It was not the first time Ben Freeman had seen fear reduce a man to something less than human. This man had become a thing hunted. And the thing hunted wore a silver cross with the visage of Saint Anthony.

Ben's eyes widened. "Moses?"

Upon hearing its name, the thing hunted became a man once more. He looked at Ben and pushed through the brush, and now he stood upon Clarendon's front lawn. He was a large man and towered over Ben even from a distance, but something had made him appear very small. Perhaps it was the shroud of fear that covered him. Perhaps it was the fresh and still bleeding wounds on his back, where a rag of a shirt had fallen away.

"Gotta get north," Moses said. "Gotta get away. Lord knows, I ain't goin back."

Sucking a breath, Ben looked back at the house. Light shone from within, but nothing stirred at the windows. Jem was still off riding, but he might return at any moment to find a runaway slave standing on the grounds. Without a second thought, Ben turned back to Moses.

"We will hide you."

"I ain't goin in there," Moses said. He took a step back toward the field. "I ain't stayin anywheres near here. Shouldn't even be talkin to you."

Ben held out a hand. "It's all right. I will hide you."

Moses shivered in the wind. "Can't trust no one. Our folk give each other up just like whites. Our folk whip each other just like the whites do, if you let em. I seen niggers what own other niggers just like the whites. You and me may look the same, but we ain't the same." Moses eyed Ben's fine gray suit. "Not when you look like that. Not when you talk the way you talk. Not when things is the way they is." Moses took another step back, his nostrils twitching, like a rabbit ready to bolt. "I never shoulda come here. I shoulda kept running."

"You're hurt," Ben said. "You won't get far. Not tonight."

Moses flinched. He made ready to run.

"*Think*," Ben said. "Look at you, dripping blood. You think their hounds won't catch your scent? When they catch you, they'll tear you to pieces. We need to clean you, bandage you."

Moses looked skyward, helpless and miserable. He closed his eyes and murmured a low prayer. When he opened his eyes again, he looked at Ben. "I gotta know you ain't gonna give me up."

Ben stretched his hand out again. "You have my word."

Moses looked at Ben's hand, then looked up at Ben's face. He turned and looked out at the wild country around them, then back at Ben one more time. Slowly, Moses took Ben's hand.

"Follow me," Ben said. "I know a place you can hide."

❧

The next day, the Roscoe family gathered on the front veranda to see their patriarch off. The Senator explained the abruptness of his departure by claiming that there was too much work to be done in the capital, and that his short trip home had indeed been sufficient to rest and re-energize. The old man's last will and testament was given to Ben to keep safe.

The old man went down the line as if bidding farewell to court magistrates. He tousled young Bayard's hair but could think of nothing to say to his youngest boy. He shook Tom's uninjured hand and assured him he would find a "better, more proper educational institution" for him in the New Year. Sarah kissed her father on both cheeks and looked ready to break down into tears at any moment.

JJ's absence had a dark presence of its own. To Ben it seemed almost a dream that JJ had come home at all. All that confirmed the event was the black bruise around one of Jem's eyes, and of course the bullet hole in the library's ceiling, and the bitter tang of gunpowder that still hung in the air.

Stiff and formal, Jem shook hands with the Senator. Father and son spoke together in low voices that Ben could not hear. But he could see part of Jem's face over the old man's bony shoulder: it was a face of stone, and the debonair glint in his eyes had faded to a dull and glassy stare. Jem seemed to accept whatever the old man had to say without emotion, without resistance. When the Senator at last moved on, Ben exchanged a long look with Jem. Ben offered him the most reassuring smile he could manage, but Jem only turned his head and looked away.

Finally, the Senator bid farewell to Lady Isabella. Husband and wife exchanged a stilted farewell with requisite murmurings and mutterings, and in parting they pecked each other on the cheek with pursed lips. Isabella did not linger to see her husband climb into the coach and drive off. Instead, she turned immediately and disappeared into the house, her long black dress following her like a storm cloud.

Ben helped the Senator aboard the coach, and then they started up the long clay path. The Senator turned and held up a hand to his family, who waved goodbye with limp and joyless gestures. Ben was relieved to pass through the gate and turn down the road toward Mayfair and the train station beyond.

The journey to the station was cold and quiet. No birds sang in the trees, but the November wind sighed and whistled. Ben pulled his collar close and silently cursed himself for forgetting to wear gloves or a scarf.

As the world passed by, Ben's thoughts drifted to Moses. Very soon something would need to be done. If they were not combing the Valley for him already, Mayfair's planters would soon form a search party. If Ben was going to get Moses across the Potomac into Maryland, and then across Maryland to the Pennsylvania border, then they would have to go immediately. That meant they would have to leave tonight.

Behind him, the Senator cleared his throat. "Are you happy to see me go, Ben?"

Ben sat up straight. Had he heard that question correctly? He turned in his seat and looked back at the Senator. "I don't know what you mean, sir."

The Senator smiled and shrugged. "What I mean is, I'm leaving Mayfair once again. I may not come back for a long while. That ought to be cause for celebration, isn't it? Now you can finally get back to your important work."

Alarmed, Ben thought of Moses hiding under the bunk in Cabin Three.

"My work, sir?"

The Senator looked out at the ashen autumn world passing by. "Maybe you are writing more of those letters and speeches of yours in the hopes that I will deliver them in the Senate one day. Or maybe you hope I will give them to some newspaper to publish. And perhaps the fault is mine for inspiring you to hold such hopes. I've told you your whole life that I am committed to the cause of gradual emancipation — the key word being *gradual*. And I am honest when I say that I am indeed committed to the idea, or at least its consideration. But no matter what I've ever done, it's never been fast enough for your liking. You seek immediate, radical solutions — the John Brown kinds of solutions — which in fact are not solutions at all. They are distractions at best. At worst, they are anathema to the very principles of American democracy."

Ben swallowed hard. If it was true the Senator could read minds, maybe here was a good example of such. He stamped down any thoughts of his escape plan with Moses, lest he betray anything to the old man. But surely the Senator, if he knew of Ben's plans, wouldn't stop him? Maybe the Senator would even offer to help?

After all, it was John Roscoe who had set *five hundred people* free once upon a time, including Ben and Mama. Perhaps the Senator could help Ben smuggle Moses aboard the departing train. Once in Washington, Moses would have a far better chance of escape than being dropped near some country town along the Potomac. But somehow, Ben knew he couldn't take that chance. It wasn't that he didn't trust John Roscoe with the Moses situation, but rather that he didn't know if he could trust anyone. Moses might become too cagey with a third party involved.

Ben said, "I sometimes wonder, sir, whether by allying yourself with men like Tobias Cutler, you will end up on the wrong side of history. They don't share your vision of society's slow, tempered progression. They would rather see us go back to some imagined golden age, and go back immediately. In reversing whatever social progress we've made, they'd plunge us back into the dark ages."

The Senator laughed. "My God, Ben. What, you think the existence of slavery is some criminal conspiracy? The institution is all around us. It is *within* us as a people. Whatever slavery's evils, there is not a single American that it has not touched in some positive way. The food we eat, the clothes on our backs, the very paper upon which you write your treatises and memorandums — one way or another, slavery is the source and foundation of America's economic might. Must it always be this way? Of course not. As we speak, the minds that will solve the slavery question are being nourished by the excess bounty that slavery produces. For thousands of years, slavery has been a driver of human flourishing. We are only just now beginning to emerge into a new realm of consciousness. But old habits, as they say, die hard. To unravel such an institution is no simple matter. We cannot simply cut a thread and say the thing is finished. We must listen, understand other points of view, question our own assumptions, and find a means of compromise."

Ben shook his head. "But we are not engaged in a debate over cold abstractions, sir. Human lives hang in the balance. When faced against men who spit on science and progress, who instead cling to an archaic belief that God created some lesser men to serve superior mortals, I find *compromise* a poor substitution for justice. I have no interest in hearing the point of view of a man who chains and rapes women in order to produce more workers to till his fields."

The Senator took a long, deep breath. "Ben…Ben, sometimes I wonder about you. You and I are on the same side of this debate."

Now it was Ben's turn to laugh, though it held no humor. "Then why do you and Judge Cutler seem to agree on so much? I cannot fathom why you attach yourself to the man whose values are the antithesis of yours, or so I've always thought."

The Senator's voice sharpened. "Because if the banker decides to go to war with the baker, he'll soon find himself without bread to feed his family. Why do you think I kept the Roscoe family here in Mayfair? I could have taken all our inherited wealth and moved elsewhere. I could be enjoying champagne and oysters with men who think exactly like I do. Instead I remain here because there is work to be done here. *Good* work, the work of *politics*. And politics begins and ends with speaking to people in terms they can understand. The work is in choosing the right words."

"I admire the right words," Ben said. "But what are the right words without right action? Thomas Jefferson declared all men equal when he himself owned human beings. He wrote the right words when a fifth of all Americans were owned by their neighbors."

"And what of Jefferson?" the Senator countered. "His administration coexisted with kings and queens and covens of democracy-hating aristocrats. Many times during his presidency, Jefferson sought to pass legislation intended to restrict and even doom slavery. And every time, overwhelming negative opinion crashed down upon him. Congress was compelled to block him at every turn. He could not solve the problem of slavery *because it was not the right time*."

Ben scowled. "If he really believed in his own words, he should have freed his slaves like you did."

The Senator shrugged. "Maybe you're right. But at a certain point, a man comes to understand that though there are many great and noble hills to die upon, he may only die upon *one*. What's more, he must have confidence that his death will come with the promise of meaningful impact. If a river is shown to be impassable, it is not a selfless martyr but a deranged fool who drowns himself in the crossing. Jefferson gave our country an ideal to strive for. Poetic, I think, that he didn't live up to his own dream."

Ben sighed and went silent for a long while. He felt the Senator's incisive gaze on him.

"You know something, Ben? When I was a young boy, only wealthy landowners could vote in elections. The poorest among us, which indeed was most of the country, were barred from participating in our own democracy. When I came of age, finally, such limits began to be lifted. Now it's almost 1860, and nearly every white man in the Union has earned the right to take part in democracy.

"Who is the poorest family in the Valley? The Blakes, perhaps? Poor Everett Blake cannot get a loan from a bank, but he can still cast a ballot that might determine who becomes the next president. Say what you will about inequality and justice, but I must say I think we're on the right track. American democracy could not progress in such a way were the Union not *rich*, and the Union became rich because of its system of labor. I am not saying this was the best way history could have unfolded, but unfold it did. Someday, through the natural progress of all things, perhaps African men in this country will earn their freedom."

Ben bit his tongue. *Earn* their freedom?! Was it only for some people to be born with their freedom, together with all the inalienable, God-given rights that they took for granted, while for so many others freedom was merely a carrot on a stick?

"And perhaps," the Senator said, "after African men become sufficiently enlightened in a few hundred years, we may find that white women have earned the right to vote. And a few hundred years after that, perhaps African women too. The progress of Man is slow and fickle, but it never ceases. I counsel patience. *Patience*, Ben. Nothing good may happen—"

"Before its proper time — yes, I *know*. Except it seems that the 'proper time' will never come. Or maybe that's the whole damn point of it?"

Almost immediately, Ben cursed himself for his show of disrespect. By lashing out, any argument was already lost. Ben felt the Senator's wrathful glare hot on his back, and he knew that in some corners of the Valley a man like him could expect to have his tongue pulled out for talking back like that.

For a long while afterward, there was only the sound of the wind and the coach's wheels turning and grinding against the hardpacked road. Nothing more was said between the two men until the coach neared the train station.

Upon reaching the station, Ben slowed the coach to a stop and climbed down. Without a word, he guided the Senator down to the ground and collected the old man's bags. They walked slowly toward the platform, the Senator's cane bending and bowing with each heavy step. When at last the Senator's bags were loaded upon the train and the old man stood ready to depart at last, he turned and looked upon Ben.

"I want you to come with me to Charleston in the springtime," the Senator said. "I want you at the Democratic Convention when we nominate Stephen Douglas for president. I'm to deliver remarks at the Convention, and I would be honored if you'd help me write them."

At first, Ben thought the Senator was only joking. But then he remembered the Senator had a boulder's sense of humor.

"You're serious?" Ben said, his voice barely above a whisper.

"Of course I am. I take speechcraft very seriously, as you know. After all, my seat in the Senate Chamber is the same seat which Henry Clay used to occupy. Those are mighty big shoes to fill, but I do intend on filling them."

"Senator, sir, I don't know if I..."

"If you're about to say you can't, I assure you that you *can*," the Senator said. "If you only knew the incoherent drivel that most congressmen spew from their mouths, you'd be ashamed of the whole business of lawmaking."

People were hurriedly boarding the train. Still standing upon the platform, the old man turned and looked toward the mounded summit of the South Branch, and the craggy North Branch several miles distant.

Ben shook his head. "I don't know, sir. Perhaps it's best I remain at Clarendon in the springtime..."

"Why?"

Ben thought of a dozen different answers, but none of them were the truth. "Well," he said, "I suppose I've never been much of a flag-waving Democrat. Not with men like Tobias Cutler involved."

The Senator smiled at him then, and the smile was kind. The old man reached out and took Ben's hand. It was a warm, fatherly gesture, a touch that Ben only now realized he had been yearning for ever since the old man had come home. And yet, Ben felt a shiver streak down his spine. Was this the same John Roscoe who had, just last night, humiliated and all but disowned his firstborn son with vindictive spirit? Was this the same John Roscoe who had all but sold his daughter to a slave-owning bastard in exchange for political goodwill? How could the old man look at Ben with such promise, touch him with such fatherly love, and yet for his own children seem to feel nothing at all? Might there come a day when he abandoned Ben too?

All these questions were soon forgotten, however, for the Senator's gray eyes had fixed themselves upon Ben and held him there.

"In Charleston, we'll have a chance to change things, Ben — change them for the better. I want you to witness for yourself the slow progress of which our country is capable. For the last thirty years, the Union has been hamstrung by the so-called slavery question. For over a generation, no one has discussed the possibilities of the future, only debated the travesties of the past and present. But now, I feel we are nearing a tipping point.

"The United States are strong, Ben, but they are not invincible — certainly not when they are divided. Right now, our country is under threat from radicals who hold sway over the will of the people. Our democracy must be protected, and I tell you that despite our collective sins, the Union is altogether worthy of protection. Only when the Union is secure can we move toward making it the Union that *you* wish it to be. And all that can begin next year, starting with the man we make our next president."

Ben wanted to nod his head. He wanted to say yes. But still, he remained silent and unmoved.

"Ben, I am not asking you to become a fire-breathing partisan. I am not asking you to stand shoulder to shoulder with Tobias Cutler. But I *am* offering you the opportunity to help shape a new era of American politics — one that will yet include men like Cutler, and men like yourself too. It's up to you to decide if you'll seize this opportunity, or let it pass."

The train whistle shrieked. Both Ben and the Senator looked toward the sound, then returned to look at each other.

"I don't pretend to consider myself a good father," the Senator said, his eyes turning inward. "You saw that for yourself last night. But at least let me show you I am a good American, that I believe in something *good*. Something greater than any one man. Something greater than any one family."

The train whistle shrieked again, and now it was time for the Senator to go. Ben embraced the old man. He felt his weak, gelatinous flesh moving under brittle bones, and with a lump forming in his throat Ben realized that he could not remember the last time he hugged John Roscoe, the man whom he knew better than his own father. Ben wondered whether this might be the last time he ever embraced the Senator. Thinking of that, he squeezed a little harder.

As they pulled back, the Senator offered a small smile and took up his cane. He turned and struggled up the small steps until he stood upon the railcar. "Onward and upward," he said. His lips were trembling, whether from emotion or physical strain Ben could not be sure.

Ben stepped away from the train. The steam engine hissed, and its lumbering bulk began to roll out of the station. Over the grinding and screeching of iron wheels, Ben smiled and said, "You are a good man, sir."

The Senator held a hand over his ear. He had not heard Ben, and when he called out to say as much Ben could not hear him either.

"*You're a good man*!" Ben called again, louder this time, but still with no effect.

Instead the Senator smiled and waved, still uncomprehending. Ben lifted a hand to wave back, but by then the old man had turned into the car and disappeared as the long train shuddered out of the station, rolling and rolling until it was out of sight, until all that was left was the fading sound of its lonely whistle carrying over the Valley with the wind.

❧

After supper, each of the Roscoes skulked to isolated corners of Clarendon while the Freemans worked together to clear the table. They were washing dishes in the kitchens when Mama informed Ben he was to chaperone Sarah's rendezvous with Henry Cutler, happening tomorrow.

Ben winced. "Chaperone? When? *Why?*"

"*Tomorrow*, like I said, and because you mama said so." Now Mama released a sighing smile that made Ben grimace. "Oh, a nice Valley drive for the two young lovers. Wonderful! That Henry Cutler is ever so handsome. Mr. John finally caught Miss Sarah a good one." She looked at Ben sidelong. "You 'member to drive slow for em, child, and mind them potholes."

Ben abandoned the dishes in the washbasin and went to the nearest window. "Why can't Jem be their chaperone? He's her brother, after all. Why must I be part of it?"

"Mind you manners, child," Mama said. "When a young man calls on a young lady, they gotta have a chap'rone."

"I understand that," Ben said. "But why must it be *me*?"

"Oh, fine," Mama said. "Maybe you just wanna put you feet up and take a load off. Never work for you dinner, never earn you keep. Maybe I raised a loaf of a son who don't care to serve his betters."

Ben groaned and rubbed at his temples.

"Just what's got into you?" Mama questioned. "I thought I told you a long time ago to give up that nonsense with Miss Sarah. It's one thing for two children to play games. But she's a grown woman now, Benny. And *you* a grown man. A grown *colored* man, no less. I don't gotta tell you anythin more about it."

"It's not that," Ben said urgently. "Mama, it has *nothing to do* with—"

"Then what is it? Hm? You tell me what it is then."

Ben tried, and tried again. But all he could do in the end was shake his head violently. "It's nothing." He turned away and fished for dishes underneath the soapy surface of the water.

Mama returned to her own business of collecting food scraps. Most of the left-overs would be saved, and some would be set aside for Tipper the dog. The rest would be composted and used for fertilizer. From the washbasin, Ben watched as Mama tipped a plate of chicken and string beans and added its contents to a growing pile of mush.

Ben turned back to Mama and offered her the sincere smile of a doting son. "You look tired, Mama. Why don't you go into the apartment and get some rest? I'll finish up here."

Mama gave him a curious side-eyed glance. "You got a fever or somethin?"

"I'm fine, Mama," Ben said, and he swept his hands vigorously through the wash basin to demonstrate as such. He set several clean dishes out to dry. "There's just things on my mind, is all."

"Mr. John's right, Benny. You think too much. Too much for you own good."

"Yes, Mama."

Mama yawned. She seemed to be in a trance, her eyes half-glazed and her body wavering on her feet. She had not been sleeping well, and certainly not since JJ's visit days before.

"Well," she said, "maybe you right. Maybe I ought to lay down." She looked around the kitchens, where there were still plenty of pots and pans to be scoured. "But there's plenty work to be done yet."

Ben touched her shoulder gently. "But God didn't make all Creation in a day. Go on, Mama. I'll clean up."

Mama heaved a sigh and wiped her hands on her apron, her signature sign that she was 'done.'

"Bless you, child," she said, and she put a hand to her forehead. "I feel I could sleep for a week."

"Maybe you ought to," Ben said. "The rest would do you good."

She kissed him on the cheek. "Goodnight, child."

"Goodnight, Mama."

Ben watched her shuffle away. She entered the small apartment across the kitchens and closed the thin door behind her.

With the kitchens to himself now, Ben promptly abandoned his task of washing dishes and went to the counter. He unfolded a large hand towel and draped it on the countertop, and then he placed another towel on top. He collected a selection of uncooked ingredients that had gone into the evening's supper: raw string beans, carrots, and sliced yams. He went to the pantry and collected a handful of apples and okra, and these he placed with the other items. Ben thought to add potatoes and even a slab of raw meat wrapped in paper, but he thought better of it. The name of the game was speed, and there would be no time to make a fire for cooking. What's more, making a fire would be too conspicuous. The food he packed now would have to be consumed raw, and on the move. Ben bundled the towels up and tied them together.

Now he assembled a collection of unwashed cooking pots, which still had various scraps left over from the evening's supper. Luckily, he found some significant morsels stuck to the bottom rims. He scraped these onto his own plate, the contents of which he'd purposefully only half-consumed. Quickly, he assembled a meal intended to sustain a grown man for a full day or more. There was some chicken and potatoes and cooked string beans. Ben found some cold, gelatinous gravy stuck to a ladle and drizzled the last drops upon the plate. He took up a freshly washed fork and set it upon the plate, and then he carried the plate and the toweled bundle out of the kitchens.

Moving noiselessly down the hallway, he passed a drawing room in which Jem lay slumped over in a chair, comatose, a near-empty gin bottle perched on the table beside him. Ben went inside and picked up the bottle and tucked it under his arm.

Ben moved on and slipped out the east door to the veranda. Confirming that all was clear, he descended the veranda steps and started across the lawn. Darkness was descending quickly.

That goddamn Henry Cutler. How the hell was Ben supposed to drive all night for the Potomac, drop Moses off somewhere near the Maryland border, and return to Mayfair in time to serve as Sarah's chaperone by noon? Was there anyone else he could trust with this?

Ben hurried through the twilight.

What about Jem? No doubt Moses' plight would appeal to Jem's notions of personal liberty, but Jem himself was no abolitionist. He was a man of murky morals; on the one hand he would claim that for Moses to fly from oppression was a commendable act of bravery, but in the same instant he would try to convince Ben that helping Moses wasn't worth the risk, that it was better to send the runaway off and wash one's hands of the situation.

Mama, then? But no, that would never do. Mama would throw a fit. She would alert all the Roscoes, and soon enough the whole Valley would show up to collect Moses. All her life, Mama had always detested runaways. "Everythin'll be gettin on fine, the whites finally give us our space, and then somebody gets it in they head to split. But they's always captured. Then the hammer comes down on everybody."

It was not long before Ben passed the grove and came upon the old slave cabins standing in the quiet shadows at the far edge of the estate.

Ben resolved to leave now. Not at midnight, when the night was darkest. They would leave now and cross the Potomac by the early hours, and Moses could clamber down from the coach outside Hancock, Maryland, which was just across the river. From there Moses would press northward on foot, and Ben would turn around and head back for home. He'd return to the Valley by mid-morning, and no one would think to ask any questions.

And then he'd take Henry Cutler riding in the coach. The same coach with which he'd whisked away one of the Cutlers' precious slaves!

At the third cabin, Ben tried the door. It opened with a low groan. Stale, musty air met his nostrils.

"It's me," Ben said.

A figure moved in the dark, and Moses emerged to accept the plate of food. He was dressed in a fine white shirt and waistcoat, with clean trousers and a pair of JJ's old shoes. It was all too small for the big man, but at least he was out of his bloody rags. Moses sat down on one of the bunks and wolfed everything down.

"Easy does it," Ben said. "You'll make yourself sick." The words sounded ridiculous as soon as he said them. The man was starving.

Ben reached into his jacket pocket and pulled out a piece of paper. He unfolded it and held it out for Moses to see. There was still enough twilight to read by, but only barely. "Here's a map I made up yesterday," Ben said. "There's been a slight change of plans. We'll head out now, as soon as you're done eating. Once beyond the North Branch, we'll take these side roads up to the Maryland border. See? We'll lose time, but that way we'll avoid other travelers who might ask questions. Once we get to Hancock, you'll be on your own. Take this compass. You know how to use it? A few miles north of Hancock is the Pennsylvania border at Warfordsburg. See? But you can't stop there. You keep pushing north, as long as you can, until you find someone who can help you."

Moses nodded quietly. "Just came to me," he murmured. "What if nobody wants to help?"

"Someone, somewhere, will help," Ben said. "But the masters, they'll send slave-catchers looking for you all over. They might follow you into the North. With this being Judge Cutler, his following you is beyond certainty."

"How will I know who's a catcher?"

Ben thought about it. "They'll be friendly," he said. "Too friendly. They'll offer to help you before you even think to ask. If that happens, run the other way." Ben folded the map and offered it together with the compass to Moses, and then he pulled out a coin purse and offered that too. "That should be enough to buy food for a few weeks, and some train tickets. But only venture out in public if you absolutely need to, and only once you're in Pennsylvania. And don't tell anyone you're heading straight north, or they'll start asking questions."

"I ain't stupid," Moses said.

Ben nodded. "Right. Of course."

Moses held the items solemnly in his hands, weighing first one and then the other. He sat back and looked around the tiny slave cabin. "Being in here. Like I never left."

Ben looked at the four walls. "I know what you mean."

Moses turned on him. "No, *you don't*."

Ben stepped back in surprise. Moses had forgotten his hunger and was now shaking with anger. He pointed an accusing finger at Ben. "You keep sayin you know who I is, what it's like to be me. To be any of us. You don't know it." Tears welled in the man's eyes. "*You don't know it.* You ever take a whip to the back for breakin eggs? For breakin a dozen goddamn eggs? My daughter did. Eleven years old, and them boys strung her up screamin. I begged em to punish me instead — they said they'd take care of me later." Moses hung his head. "They gave her ten lashes. Reckon would've been more if Marse Tobe hadn't stopped em. Wasn't out of no pity neither. He said he had guests and they was tired of all the hollerin." Moses' voice was barely above a whisper now. "You don't know *any* of it."

Ben said nothing for a long time.

"You're right, Moses," Ben said at last. "I don't know what it's like to be you. I was lucky, damn lucky, for that. But you're wrong to say I don't know *any* of it. I was born on this clay floor. The brand you have is the same one they burned into my skin. And as for the whipping. Maybe I don't have scars on my back, but I've got more than a few in my head."

Moses continued eating. "It's not that I don't appreciate what you doin. Lord knows I do. But it ain't easy. Ain't easy to, what's the word. Ain't easy to trust a—"

"—a nigger in white man's clothes," Ben finished. Now he felt a rising anger of his own, though he maintained a low whisper. "I've heard that a hundred times before. And it still doesn't make any sense. I dress white, I talk white, I *walk* white? What the hell does any of that even mean? I'm my own self, and nobody but. It might occur to you that there are plenty parts of a man that have nothing to do with the color of his damn skin." He tried to say more, but no words came. All he could do was shake his head and laugh at it all.

Moses finished eating and licked his fingers, then the plate. "It ain't the clothes," he said. "I ran all the way here. Straight across the Sleepy, straight across the Valley. It's only a few miles."

"What are you getting at?"

"I think what I'm gettin at is, when we see you walkin all around town takin care of business for that old white fella—"

"His name is John Roscoe."

"—takin care of business for that fella, we get to thinkin. Here's this free boy here, livin among good food and riches. He don't gotta stay. He *chooses* to stay. He chooses to drink whiskey with the white men. But for the rest of us..." and then Moses trailed off for a moment. He picked at something in his teeth. "Maybe we look at you, we don't get no hope in our hearts. Because even if we get free, maybe we'll never stop servin the whites. You name's Ben, right?"

"Right."

Moses leaned in close. "Ben, our folks is dyin. They being beaten, whipped, raped, starved, killed. And it's all happenin just a couple miles down the road." He folded his arms and leaned back. "Maybe it's been so long that it all feels more like a dream to you than anythin real. But I bet you hear us singin in the fields."

Ben nodded. "Yes, I do. But I don't know if it's the Claiborne farm, or the Cutlers', or the Hanleys', or any of the others."

"It's all-us," said Moses. "Every out-farm, all-us all over the place. We don't sing to make the work day pass. Sing to stay alive. Keep each other alive. Give us a reason to believe."

Ben took the empty plate from Moses. "Do you believe all of it will end one day?"

Moses scowled. "Bible says it will, but don't say when. Marse Lucas — that's Marse Tobe's boy — he says the Bible says we'll be slaves to Jesus when we meet him, and he'll be so happy to have us."

Ben offered a sour smile to the floorboards. "'Nothing good may happen before its proper time.'"

"*I* say it ain't gonna happen unless we make it," Moses said. "That's one thing them other niggers don't get. There's believin somethin's gonna happen, and there's *makin it happen*. I'm makin it happen."

The heavy weight of silence pressed upon the dark cabin.

"What can I do?" Ben said, with quiet desperation in his voice. "How can I—?"

He fell silent and hung his head.

Moses stared at Ben for a long time. He reached out and offered his hand.

"You doin it right now," he said. "You ain't standin by. You ain't just livin life tryin to pretend what's goin on five miles down the road ain't goin on. You helpin me, and if I get outta here I'll owe you my life."

Ben took Moses' hand. They shook, and Moses didn't let go.

"But you can't stop at this," he said. "You can't think this is it. We ain't won until everybody can walk away free. And even then we ain't won, cause they'll be powers tryin to chain us up again in a different way. I don't know when the fight will be over. All I know is the fight ain't even started yet."

Ben smiled, blinking back tears in his eyes. At last, he let go of Moses' hand. "We should get going," he said. "I'll take you to the other side of the North Branch. Remember, from there, you'll follow the compass heading—"

"*Shh!*" Suddenly, Moses sat up straight. His eyes were wide, fearful.

Ben turned. "What is it?"

Moses was on his feet. Together they listened, ears straining, and finally Ben heard it.

Horses. Lots of them. Coming this way.

Moses' hand, which just a moment ago clasped Ben's hand in a warm gesture, now clutched at Ben's throat. "You tell em I was here?" Moses snarled. "*You tell em I was here?!*"

Unable to speak, unable to *breathe*, Ben gargled and shook his head furiously — *NO!*

Slowly, Moses loosened his grip and let Ben go. Ben coughed and clutched at his throat. The horses were closer now. Together, Ben and Moses inched over to the tiny window near the door. Moses swept a hand through cobwebs and they peered out. They saw nothing.

"I can't stay here," said Moses. He reached for the door.

Ben blocked his way. "No. If you leave now, you won't make it another mile before they pick up your trail and run you down."

Moses pointed out the dirty window. "The only way I'm gonna make it is to be where they ain't. And right now, they comin here."

"I'll find out what's happening," Ben said. "I'll tell them you were never here." He opened the door and stepped out. He turned his head to say, "*Stay here*," but was nearly bowled over when Moses, wild-eyed, rushed him again. Ben stood his ground and forced Moses back with all his strength.

"I ain't gonna stay caged up!"

Ben pushed against him. "If you leave right now, you'll die."

"And if I stay? You can't promise it won't end no different."

Ben looked at the lights of Clarendon, and at the driveway beyond. There were no horses to be seen, but they were surely getting closer. He looked back at Moses. "No," he said, "I can't. But I'm going to try. Do you trust me?"

Moses said nothing. He tried to push again, and Ben held him back.

"Do you trust me, Moses?"

The man heaved a deep sigh. Finally, he dropped his arms. "I trust you, Ben."

"All right." Ben nodded and went to the door. "I'll be back," he said, and he smiled at Moses. Moses looked back at him grimly, still looking like he would bolt at any moment. And with that, Ben closed the door and shut Moses inside the cabin.

The anxiety of the moment hit Ben all at once, and with each shallow breath he felt as though his lungs were filling with sand. "All right," he gasped to himself. "All right. Now let's just—"

Turning, Ben finally saw them. The riders came down the driveway by torchlight. He counted six torches, now eight, a lantern or two bouncing in the dark, pale hard lights splashing on sinewy horse bodies and men's hard scowls. As the riders spurred their horses forward, Ben felt an icy fear crawl down his neck like a giant millipede, a thousand spiny legs pricking his skin.

Keeping to the shadows, Ben ran for the house.

Chapter 16

BOUND FOR CANAAN

Sarah heard Jem's hurried steps echo across the floor of the grand foyer. The front door groaned and she saw Jem pass outside just as she entered the hall. Through the thick glass of the windows, she could see several men on horses.

It was strange to have visitors calling so late into the evening. More than strange, it was embarrassing. In the name of good taste she thought to climb the stairs to her room and change into a different dress, just in case, but she found herself drawn closer to the nearest window by something she could only call an intense curiosity.

But of course, just peering out the window in full sight of the newcomers would be too conspicuous. Instead Sarah slipped into the darkened front parlor, which had windows that looked toward the front veranda from a side angle. She peeled one of the curtains back and saw a company of riders sitting their horses on the clay path before the house. Jem stood in silhouette on the veranda steps, and she could just make out the conversation passing back and forth.

"...fine evening, indeed," Jem was saying. He had been drunk since his fight with JJ, and just now he moved sluggishly and slurred his words. Sarah silently cursed her brother for shaming himself and the whole family.

"To what do I owe the pleasure, gentlemen?"

A rider came forward with a kerosene lamp in hand, and Sarah saw that it was Henry's father, Judge Cutler. The Judge's face was grim and earnest. "Is your daddy home, Jem?"

"He's not, Judge. He took the train back to Washington this afternoon."

The Judge nodded. "And your brother Jon, is he still home? He in charge around here?"

Jem flared up at the suggestion. "Absolutely not. He's gone." As if to underline the idea, Jem added, "For good."

The Judge nodded again, much slower this time. "I see." He reached up and touched the skin under his eye with a long forefinger. "That's quite a shiner you got there, son."

As Jem fumbled through some explanation, something that had absolutely nothing to do with JJ's leaving *for good*, Sarah studied the other riders through the window.

She recognized Lucas Cutler, the Judge's son and Henry's younger brother, who wore a stiff preacher's collar and sat erect in the saddle. There was broad-faced Clay Claiborne, whose usual jollity was gone, replaced by a stern frown that was either an indication of his lower-than-dirt opinion of Jem, or the anticipation of ugly business that needed doing, or maybe both. Over yonder was Mr. Hanley, Sam's father, a mouse of a man who was in a state of supreme agitation. Beside him was Sam Hanley himself, and over there was Percy Claiborne, his injured head still wrapped in thick bandages. Percy's eyes stabbed in Jem's direction like a pair of cold daggers.

Upon recognizing the next rider, Sarah gasped and retreated from the window. Cautiously stepping forward again, she peered out and saw Henry under the blazing light of a torch held in a black-gloved hand. He was listening patiently to the exchange between his father and Jem, but his eyes were turned up at the windows of the second and third storeys of the house. As if he was looking for something.

Or some*one*.

Oh, now it was absolutely critical that Sarah get herself upstairs to change. It would not do for a young lady to be seen by her beau in such a slovenly dress as she was wearing now. She picked up her skirts and turned away from the window, and that was when she crashed into Ben Freeman.

Sarah's first instinct was to cry out in fear, but then she felt Ben's hand over her mouth and his other hand hauling her back from the window. He held her close against the door, their cheeks pressed against each other. She squirmed against him and pulled herself free, and then she turned an indignant glare upon him.

"It's not right of you to touch me like that," she said. "It's not at all proper to—"

"*Shh!*"

Ben crept toward the window and peered beyond the curtains with fearful eyes.

Sarah furrowed her brow. "You can't *shh* me, Ben. I'm your…well, I don't know exactly what I am to you. But you are nevertheless a servant of this house."

Ben hissed at her, "Miss Sarah, please!"

She crossed her arms. "Just what's the matter with you anyway?"

Ben stared out the window, studying the faces suspended in the darkness. "Just coming to see who's calling," he said, his voice like gravel.

Sarah studied Ben and decided she didn't like what she saw. "You look ill, Ben. You look like you've seen a ghost."

Ben did not look at her; in fact he seemed not to hear her at all. But then he asked in a murmur, "Is Jem inviting those gentlemen into the house?"

"I don't know," she said, paling at the thought. "I hope not! Of course I'd adore spending time with Henry, but I'd rather not put on a fresh face at this hour."

Ben said nothing and remained watchful. Slowly, Sarah crept forward until they stood side by side at the window. Together, they listened to the conversation outside.

"Judge," Jem was saying, "if this is about me and Percy..."

"I'm afraid this is far more serious than a scrap over a girl, son," Judge Cutler said.

Percy Claiborne shot the Judge an indignant glare. "*Scrap*?! That nigger-loving, whoremongering bastard nearly killed me!"

"It wasn't him at all," Sam Hanley drawled. "It was his brother, little Jonny the cocksuck—"

"That's enough!" Mr. Hanley growled.

In the flaring light of the torches, Clay Claiborne rode forward and his horse stamped its hooves in the dirt. "Enough of this," the big man growled. The reins in his massive hands looked like strings of brown licorice. "You tell us where your black boy's at, Mr. Roscoe. I thought I seen him there on your back veranda but a moment ago. We'd like to speak with him."

Ben shrank back from the window. Sarah noted the raw fear in his eyes. His face swelled and contorted, as if he was trying to decide upon a course of action amid myriad choices, none of them appealing nor likely of success.

"What do you want with Ben?" Jem said cautiously.

"One of my father's hands ran out on us," Lucas Cutler replied in his soft, serene voice. "Our men didn't report the bull missing until a short while ago, fearing for their jobs. Since then we've been searching all over the Valley."

"Seems like an awful quick search," Jem said doubtfully. "There's a lot of ground to cover from the South Branch to here, but it seems you made a beeline for Clarendon. Why is that?"

Judge Cutler sniffed. "I know your nigger has...*ideals*." Bitterness dripped from his tongue. "If there's anyone who would make uppity designs toward stealing the Valley's colored folk, it's *your* boy."

Jem shook his head. "With respect, Judge, that's just not right."

Percy Claiborne spat. "*With respect*," he growled, "a gentlemen has the constitutional *right* to collect his niggers if they run away. And his neighbors have the *obligation* to help him. Anyone who harbors a slave is a criminal under federal law. Your daddy of all people ought to know that."

Jem remained stone-faced. "I already told you, my father's gone back to Washington. Ben drove him there this afternoon, and he returned without making a detour."

"You'll vouch for the boy?" Judge Cutler said.

"Of course he will," Percy muttered.

Lucas Cutler cleared his throat. "My dear Jeremiah, this is a matter of community security. Our bull, Moses, he's a good negro. But he's not well in the head."

"Why don't I join you gentlemen in your search?" Jem said. "If you'll just give me a few minutes..."

"We wonder," Lucas went on, "whether Moses might have gained the confidence of your butler-boy by some trickery. Moses is supremely capable of moral manipulation."

Jem turned his head and looked back at the house. His eyes flashed over the spot where Sarah and Ben stood and lingered there for a long moment, and Sarah could not tell whether Jem had seen them or not.

Turning back to the riders now, Jem shrugged and said, "I beg your pardon, gentlemen. But you do realize there's a big world out there? The Valley is only so many miles by so many miles. It's entirely possible that your man…what was his name again, Reverend?"

"Moses."

"It's entirely possible that your chicken has not just flown the coop, but has made for the next county. He could be away in Mountain Falls by now, or Capon Bridge, or even up in Romney—"

"It's possible," Judge Cutler said, offering a tight-lipped smile. "But you do understand, Jem, we must leave no stone unturned."

Jem was quiet for a long moment, as if considering his options. Finally he said, "You've a right by law to try and secure your property, Judge. You-all are free to search the woods and fields around Clarendon. But I won't allow a search of the house or its grounds, and I won't allow you to question Ben. I can assure you he had nothing to do with, well, with anything. This is my property — my Father's property — and I trust you gentlemen will abide by my decision."

"Come now, son," Judge Cutler said. "As the reverend here said, this is a matter of community security. If there's a rogue darkie about, you best believe we're here to protect you and yours."

"I understand that, but—"

"Might we say," Judge Cutler said, "that the missing nigger has a certain predilection toward white women. White *girls*, I should clarify. And if this boy's prowling about the North Branch, there's quite a few farms he might target. If anything horrible were to happen, and we didn't use the opportunity to stop it beforehand…"

After taking all this in, Jem nodded with understanding. "Of course, Judge. We all want to protect the vulnerable."

Judge Cutler smiled. "I'm glad you see it that way, Jem. We'll just take a quick look around. In the meantime, you bring out your Mr. Free-Man and we'll have ourselves a little discussion." With the matter settled, the Judge looked at the other riders and nodded.

Claiborne swung into action. "Percy, Sam, Reverend, take the left. Hanley and I will take the right. Henry, Glanton, circle round back and follow the property line." Claiborne clicked his tongue and the riders turned their horses.

Judge Cutler nodded at Jem with a thin smile. "We appreciate your cooperation here, Jem. It's mighty fine neighbor-work, this is. Now, I won't be back in Washington for some weeks. I wonder if you might be able to pass a message to your daddy for me in the meantime..."

As the riders scattered in every direction, Sarah became aware that Ben was creeping back, inching away from the window. She turned to him. "Are you all right, Ben? You're acting very strange."

Ben wore a smile that was a plain put-on. "Oh, I'm fine, Miss Sarah. Perfectly fine. I just forgot I have some things to see about in the kitchens."

"Now?" she said, but Ben had already quit the parlor and she could hear him going up the hall in a sort of run-walk shuffle. With her curiosity quickly turning to suspicion, she left the parlor and followed after him.

"Ben," she said carefully, "are you in some sort of trouble?"

Ben halted. He turned around to face her, and she could almost see the machinery of his mind spinning and turning with frantic energy behind his eyes. "Me?" he said, nearly breathless. "Of course not. What would make you think that?"

Ben left, and Sarah stood there looking after him as his shape receded. As she watched him turn a hasty corner, seeming to break into a silent run just before he disappeared, a cold shiver ran down her spine.

Something wasn't right.

Picking up her skirts, Sarah hurried up the dark hallway. Turning down another long corridor, she caught a glimpse of Ben turning into the kitchens like a shadowy thief. Moving as quietly as her bustling dress would allow, she advanced in pursuit. From within the kitchens she heard the creaking sound of a thin door opening and closing, and she stopped to listen a moment before starting again.

Entering the kitchens, she found them empty. But there in the far corner, next to the pantry door, was a smaller door that one might assume led to a crawlspace. The door was slightly ajar, and the doorlatch was still quivering. Approaching the door, Sarah studied the sliver of pitch-black darkness beyond the threshold and knew that Ben had gone through it. She also knew where the passage led.

It was a tunnel to the slave cabins.

For herself, Sarah remembered the door as something more than the mere entrance to a tunnel. When they were young — meaning herself, Ben, and the twins, (the other boys were only babies then) — Sarah once saw Ben use this tunnel as a hiding place in a game of hide-and-seek. Thereafter, the tunnel became Ben and Sarah's secret place to hide away whenever they wanted to play by themselves.

Sarah had always feared the tunnel because she imagined dark, monstrous things crawling along the hard-packed walls. But even still, there was a sense of comfort from being shut up inside, where you were deaf and blind to the outside world and it couldn't see or hear you either. During those times, it was only Sarah and Ben.

Even as they grew too old for hide-and-seek, they continued to retreat to the tunnel together. Ben was getting bigger and stronger, sprouting pimples all over his face, and Sarah was blossoming into a young woman. During such embarrassing and confusing times, they needed each other's counsel more than ever. She remembered a few times, after fleeing from Cousin Isabella's frequent tongue-lashings, she grabbed Ben's hand and pulled him into the tunnel so she could talk and cry and he could listen and give advice. Mostly, Ben just listened, and that was what she appreciated the most. Thinking back, she could not remember the details of anything they talked about, recalling only that when they emerged hours later, dirty and squinting from the light, she felt somehow better, surer of herself, and not so alone. Of course, there were far better places to hide away. Still, they kept going down. Maybe it was because the tunnel was a secret that only she and Ben shared.

But somehow, at some point, they stopped going down. Maybe it was because of how Ben started to look at her. In any case, Sarah developed a renewed fear of things crawling along the walls and decided she was too fearful to crawl inside again, and after enough time passed she had forgotten the tunnels completely.

Until now.

Standing before the open door of the tunnel, Sarah stared down into the pitch blackness. She went to the nearest table and found a single candle and a box of matches there, and after lighting the candle she returned and held it out. The light was pitiful, but now she could see steps leading down into the darkness. Then, hiking up her skirts high as she could so that they did not become hopelessly filthy, she descended the creaking steps one by one.

The air in the tunnel was still, stale, and had been undisturbed for many years. Even with the light of the candle, impenetrable darkness threatened all around her.

The tunnel felt longer than it really was, though she remembered Ben saying that it stretched five hundred yards under the estate. That said, she didn't exactly know the length of a single yard, let alone five hundred. All she knew was that the tunnel passed under the grove of trees that concealed the slave cabins from view of the house, and she knew she was there when her shoulder brushed against an exposed tree root and she nearly fainted with fright. Taking a breath, she whispered assurances to herself that it was not much further to the end.

And now, barely visible by the light of the candle, Sarah saw plank boards leading upward — a staircase. She looked up and saw thin slivers of moonlight slashing through crooked slats. Holding the candle in one hand, she pushed against the trapdoor with the other.

It wouldn't budge.

Grimacing at the filth she knew would stain her dress, Sarah set the candle down on the ground and stepped up. She pushed both hands, together with her shoulder, against the door. She was naturally strong, and she opened the door with ease. A square of blue cut into the black, and taking up the candle once more, Sarah ascended the worn steps.

Standing up in the open space, Sarah raised the quivering candle and held it out, and its tiny fingers of light stretched to reveal an empty cabin. A dining plate lay in broken shards on the floor, and turning her head she saw that the cabin's front door had been flung open and was yawning in the night breeze.

Sarah pulled herself up and out of the trapdoor, and carefully she closed it again. She studied her dress and found it hopelessly dirty, but she no longer cared. Wherever Ben was, he wasn't here. And there, just outside the cabin windows, she saw torchlights moving about in the darkness.

If Mr. Claiborne or the others found Ben, they might hurt him before he had a chance to explain himself. But if Sarah found him, she might be able to help him somehow. At the very least, she could speak with Henry. Surely Henry would understand that whatever mistake Ben had made, he had made it out of ignorance. Ben would never do anything to harm anyone, and certainly he would not intentionally insult Judge Cutler or any other member of the Valley gentry. Ben had been raised under the Roscoe roof, after all. He knew better.

Sarah crept out of the cabin and looked around. The torches and lanterns had not yet reached the cabins, but they were moving this way. Turning, she froze when she saw two figures standing at the far edge of the lawn, obscured by a clump of thickets.

Sarah squinted and determined the figures were not slavecatchers — which meant Ben had to be one of them. Beyond the lawn lay a vast field of tall, overgrown grass and clusters of thickets leading down the slope of the North Branch, toward a sea of trees. Hanging over it all was a pale moon suspended on a night sky of dark velvet.

Sarah moved toward the figures. She recognized Ben as she drew closer, but the other man she could not place. They were speaking in hushed voices, but as she neared them she could begin to make out what they were saying.

"There," Ben said, pointing west toward the thickets. "Head for that tree line down the slope. Stay off the roads and—"

"No," the other man said. He pointed northeast, indicating a destination across the exposed open field. "Gotta follow the light."

Ben was exasperated. "Follow this compass," he hissed. "Strike west into the thickets where their horses can't follow, then north. They'll finish searching around the house soon. They'll soon be *here*. You have to get under cover, Moses, and quickly."

The man named Moses looked at Ben with a puzzled expression. Shaking his head, he pointed up at the sky. Sarah looked up and saw a bright white dot high above. The North Star.

"Gotta follow the light to Canaan," Moses said.

"Will you listen to me?" Ben growled. "You go that way directly, they'll see you. They'll..."

Moses extended his hand. The gesture was a sign of thanks, maybe friendship. At least, an understanding. For a time Ben stood frozen. Then he reached out and accepted the other man's handshake. Ben pointed at the cross around the man's neck.

"Saint Anthony," Ben said. "Patron saint of the lost and stolen."

Moses nodded. "When I get where I'm goin, I'm gonna take it off and bury it."

They smiled at each other. Then Moses turned and ran silently across the pasture, crouching low and dropping to the ground every few yards. Ben watched Moses run, and Sarah watched Ben.

Suddenly, a horse whinnied nearby and Ben's head turned to the sound. His gaze finally met Sarah's, and she watched his eyes widen with surprise and fear.

"Sarah? What...what are you...?"

Shivering, Sarah looked from Ben to the running man, from the running man to Ben.

Ben's body sagged under his suit. His expression of guilt was naked to her. She saw the formation of one proposed lie after another in the clear glittering of his eyes. He opened his mouth, and she watched each falsehood fall to ashes on his tongue. Before he could offer his last and strongest attempt at an explanation, she silenced him with a hard glare.

"Who is that man?" she demanded. Sarah turned her gaze upon the silhouetted figure running across a blue-stained night sky, a man desperately lunging for the horizon line. "Where is he going? Do you know him? Well, of course you know him. You were just *conspiring* with him."

Ben's eyes dropped to his shoes. When he looked up at her again, she knew he was about to tell the truth, or at least the better part of it.

"His name is Moses," Ben said. "He's going north, far away from here."

Sarah stared at Ben and said nothing. There he stood: tall, stern, earnest. She admired him whenever he looked that way, and maybe once she had adored him for it. But then she heard the sound of horses and men's voices all around them, and she knew that Henry would be among them.

And Henry, he was someone she understood. Ben had always been a mosaic with missing tiles. And whatever Ben was doing now, whatever he had done to help that ragged figure in the distance, she knew it was not right. It *couldn't* be right. Nothing right ever happened in the dark, in secret.

"I'll explain everything later," Ben said.

Sarah found the words she needed. "*No*," she said. "You'll explain it to me now, Ben."

"There's no time to—"

"Now."

Ben turned his head. They both watched in silence as the running man slipped over the crest of a tree-topped hill and out of sight.

"He came to me for help," Ben explained. "And I was glad to do what I could. I wish I could have done more."

Sarah balked at the very notion. "*More?*"

She heard the riders drawing very near. Any moment now, someone would see their silhouettes from a distance just as she had seen Ben and Moses. She wanted to call out to the riders, to invite Henry and his companions over to settle what clearly had to be a gross misunderstanding.

Instead, she looked squarely at Ben and glared at him. "A servant belongs with his master, Ben. Alone they are vulnerable, confused, and dangerous. Oh, just look at the poor thing! He'll be lost, he might die." She shook her head fiercely. "What you've done is not noble, Ben. It's un-Christian, it's immoral, and what's more, you cannot steal what does not belong to you."

Those last words were barely out of her mouth before Ben snarled, with sudden fury: "Goddammit, Sarah, you cannot steal a man because you cannot *own* him."

Sarah stared at him, shocked and wide-eyed. Ben seemed to transform before her very eyes, and she realized she had forgotten what he used to look like, if she ever remembered at all. She focused, trying very hard to tame this warped vision and recall the happy face of quiet, faithful Ben — happy Ben, obliging Ben, who never spoke in anger or out of turn. But again her vision of him blurred.

This was not the Ben she knew. This wasn't the Ben she *wanted* to know.

"It's not right," Sarah said. "Henry's family—"

"To hell with Henry and his family," Ben cursed. He advanced toward her, his entire body shaking. "It is evil, Sarah — *all of it* — and no matter how tightly you close your eyes and pretend none of it is happening, that is the truth of the thing."

Some instinct within Sarah made her put her hands up, and she stepped back. "*Don't come any closer.*"

In an instant, Ben's anger was gone. "Sarah, I…I'm sorry." He approached again, slower this time. "I'd never try to hurt—"

"*Don't,*" she warned. "Don't, or I'll scream. I'll—"

"Who's there?" a voice called from beyond the trees. "That you, Moses?"

Frozen, Sarah and Ben looked at each other. There was fear in Ben's eyes; indeed he looked ready to bolt after Moses. Sarah felt the night's chill more than ever now, and though her cheeks flamed hot she felt a raw wind pass through her bones. She wanted to go back inside, to be warm and safe and *clean* and done with all this.

"Come out!" the voice cried again. "Show yourself, boy!"

Sarah's heart clenched in her chest. She knew who that voice belonged to! Turning back to Ben, she saw in his eyes a cold panic. He pressed his finger to his lips, pleading with her to remain silent.

But Sarah turned her head and called:

"Hen—!"

Ben's hands were on her before she knew what had happened. One hand muffled her mouth while the other went to her waist, as if Ben meant to guide her to some darker corner of the estate. Terror flooded her thoughts, and she fought against Ben's grasp to no avail.

An idea sparked in Sarah's mind, and she bit down as hard as she could on Ben's hand. With a yowl, Ben yanked his hand away and Sarah was free. Throwing her head back, Sarah screamed to the high heavens:

"I'm here, Henry! Help, please!"

And everything that happened next, happened very quickly.

Henry burst out of a nearby thicket astride his horse. She imagined the scene through his ice-blue eyes: a virgin in a thin dress standing opposite a hulking black man in the moonlight. Before she had even the chance to smile at him and offer the beginnings of an explanation, Henry threw himself off his horse with a savage cry and advanced toward them. Drunk with relief, Sarah went to Henry. He pushed past her and leapt upon Ben with a raised fist, and clenched in that fist was his riding crop.

"*Stop*!" Sarah cried. "No, Henry, wait!"

Ben lifted his chin and waited bravely for the first blow. Henry struck, and Ben went down. Henry flailed Ben in the head again and again. He quickly discovered the crop was an insufficient bludgeon, and so he pounded Ben with his fists until they were bruised and slicked with blood.

Sarah's screams echoed across the estate grounds, and suddenly there was a great deal of shouting and pounding of hooves.

Riders thundered over, all of them shouting. One of the men raised himself up in the saddle and peered over the sliver of horizon beyond Sarah's vision. Whistling, the rider spurred his horse forward and with a fox hunter's yelp he went charging over the pasture. Ben groaned, maybe an attempt to yell out a warning to Moses, but then Henry cracked his elbow across Ben's forehead and Ben fell limp.

The others made a circle around Henry, who finally staggered upright and spat on Ben's unconscious form. Looking to Sarah at last, Henry approached her with great and loving concern. His coat was already off and he wrapped it around her like a blanket. Next came his cravat, which he tugged from his throat and draped around her neck like a scarf. She was sobbing, her body aching from the cold, and he hushed her and stroked her hair. He clicked for his horse and he held the animal still while at the same time he helped Sarah into the saddle.

"Drag that beast round the front," Henry said, pointing at Ben's limp form. "I'll fetch Miss Roscoe home to get warm, and then we'll deal with the runaway."

Standing on the veranda wrapped in a shawl, Sarah watched as the riders returned to the front of the house. Ben, his hands bound and lashed to Percy Claiborne's saddle, had to sprint to keep up. Sarah turned cold when she saw his face broken and bleeding, with both eyes closed shut from heavy swelling. She gasped when Ben tripped and staggered, for then the rope went taut and for the last hundred yards Percy dragged Ben along the ground.

From out of the darkness came Horace Glanton cackling with glee as he dragged yet another crumped form — Moses — behind him.

Seeing all this, Jem stepped down from the veranda. "Stop that!" he shouted. "I won't have men killed on my family's doorstep."

Sarah felt Henry's bruised, red-knuckled hand on her shoulder, felt it give a gentle squeeze. She had seen that same hand bludgeoning Ben's head just a few minutes ago. But when she looked up to see Henry's reassuring smile, she suddenly felt much better.

"Stay here, honey," Henry said. "You'll be all right now."

She nodded and nestled under Henry's coat. She watched him step down to the lawn.

"Easy does it, Horace," Henry called. "Watch you don't tear up the front lawn."

Jem hurried over to Ben, who was on his knees trying to catch his breath. Kneeling down beside him, Jem looked up at the riders and snarled, "Just what the hell have you done to him?"

It was Judge Cutler who answered. "Your black boy," he said, "was aiding and abetting a fugitive slave. He stole my Moses."

"And he must be punished," Mr. Claiborne said.

Jem pointed at Moses, who lay unconscious in the mud. "What about *him?* It seems to me your Moses stole himself, Judge." With that, he set to untying the knots that bound Ben's hands.

"I'm sorry to be the one to say, Jem," Henry said in a low voice. "I found that brute you call Ben in the act of violating your sister."

Ben spat blood on the ground. "*Liar!*" he shouted, despite a swollen tongue.

Jem scowled at Henry. "I don't believe it. He'd never do such a thing. He's not capable—"

"We are all capable of mortal sin," Lucas Cutler said from atop his horse. "It is a fact, Mr. Roscoe, that the dark hearts of Africans are most susceptible to the sin of lust."

"And don't forget about sodomites," Percy Claiborne said with a callous grin.

Jem turned on Percy with wrathful eyes, and Percy's face went pale.

Henry stayed Jem by throwing a friendly arm over his shoulder. "What matters is that I *feared* for Sarah. For her sanctity, for her life. If I hadn't stepped in, I hate to think what might have happened to her."

"It's not true!" Ben shouted.

Jem shook his head. "I *can't* believe it. Ben's like a brother — he *is* a brother—"

Percy sneered, "Could be the whole Roscoe clan was in on the deed, Judge. Maybe we clasp them all in chains."

"Shut up," Henry muttered. He turned once more to Jem. "Listen to me, Roscoe. All I know is I found your sister out in the cold, in a dirty dress, and *that* creature had his paws on her." Dropping his voice lower, Henry said, "I bet you've seen how he looks at her. You're not blind, Jem. You've seen what's behind his eyes. You've felt it yourself, about other women of course. But knowing that *he* thinks that way, and about your own *sister*? How long has he been waiting for his chance?"

Jem's body tensed. Turning, he looked at Ben with a blank expression. He ceased untying Ben's bonds and walked slowly backward.

Ben shook his head furiously. "Jem, *no*! You can't believe it. *I* don't believe you would ever think it, that you *could* ever think—"

"It's not a matter of belief," Henry said. "It's a matter of what I saw."

Ben shot a hateful glare at Henry. "Goddammit, I would never—"

"Blasphemy," Lucas Cutler hissed. The boy-reverend reached out and took the rope from Percy Claiborne's hands and yanked on it, and this sent Ben careening forward into the mud.

Sarah heard the door behind her yawn open, and turning she saw Mae Jane clutching a shawl over her nightgown. Looking upon the scene, the old maid's face was a rictus of horror.

"Ben!" she cried, her usually deep and calming voice now a frantic shriek. "My child, *Ben*!"

Ben moaned, "Mama..." but Lucas Cutler tugged on the rope again and choked off Ben's breath.

With a cry of dismay, Mae Jane hurried forward. Sarah blocked her path, catching the old maid in her arms and holding her. Mae Jane began to sob against Sarah's shoulder.

"Not my boy...not my boy..."

Down on the lawn, Jem turned away from Ben and looked at Henry. Whatever exchange their eyes made, it was enough for Jem to abandon Ben where he lay. Jem climbed the creaking steps of the veranda until he stood in stunned silence beside Sarah and Mae Jane. Looking at Sarah, Jem said through tight lips, "Tell us what happened."

Sarah broke from her daze and looked up at Jem. His eyes, and the eyes of all the others, were fixed on her. Even Mae Jane, shaking in her arms, was watching and waiting for an answer.

Jem's voice hardened. "*Speak up*, sister. What did Ben do?"

"He ain't done a thing!" Mae Jane cried. "Mr. Jem, we's all *family*—"

"And we all know what this *family* is capable of doing to each other," Jem snarled in reply. He pointed across the lawn. "Tell me, Sarah. Did Ben put his hands on you?"

Mae Jane began to sob again. She gasped, "No, no, no..."

Sarah looked past the firelights toward the darkness beyond, and she wished more than anything she could close her eyes and open them again and it would be a bright morning, with all these terrible shadows fading away as nightmares always did upon waking. Instead she remained on the veranda, cold and shivering. Hard, distrustful eyes bored into her, waiting for her to say something, anything, before they could dismiss all of it and believe whatever they wanted to be true.

She looked at Henry. He offered a reassuring smile, an encouraging nod.

Finally, Sarah pointed at the man called Moses. "That man came here for refuge."

There were tears in Ben's eyes. "Sarah, no—"

"*Shut up*," Judge Cutler hissed. He pointed at Lucas. "He squawks again, you hang him by that tree yonder."

Sarah could not bear to look at Ben any longer. Looking away, she began her explanation. Her voice was shaky, the forming of each word a titanic struggle. "Moses was trying to escape north, out of Virginia and maybe farther. Mr. Freeman tried to help him." When she finished at last, she hung her head, exhausted.

Judge Cutler stepped forward. He wore the concerned, understanding face of a doting father. "And did either of them lay a hand on you, honey? Did either of those beasts touch you in any way? Be honest with us, honey. Be honest with us, and with God." He pointed at Ben. "Was it this boy?" Now he pointed at Moses. "Or was it him?"

Henry gestured at Ben and growled, "It was that one. Why else do you think I beat him?"

"Silence," the Judge snapped. "Let the girl speak."

"But it was neither of them," Sarah cried. "Neither man—"

The Judge cut in suddenly, his voice tender but assertive. "These boys ain't men, honey. They're niggers, and even when domesticated they've got minds like wolves. Now we know it was either one, or the other. So which boy touched you? You don't have to be afraid, honey. Tell us, which boy *tried*?"

Sarah saw that the other riders were tense, ready for action, and overly eager to get started on the bloody business they had come here to do. She felt Mae Jane against her, her old body quivering, but though tears welled in Mae Jane's eyes her leather face had become like stone. Jem's face was haggard and drawn, as if he had aged a hundred years in the course of a few minutes. The man called Moses, who lay in the dirt nearby, was murmuring a string of quiet prayers.

"Come, Sarah, honey," the Judge said, cooing. "All you gotta do is point."

At last, Sarah saw Ben Freeman looking at her from his place on the ground.

His eyes were wide and pleading, though not for mercy. Not mercy for himself, at least. Ben's was the same expression of the crucified Christ in all the paintings and in all the stained-glass reliefs she had ever seen, that same look of abject sorrow and weariness and a fading will to live that made even the cruelest blade appear a tender means of mercy.

Shaking, Sarah raised an accusing finger and pointed.

Judge Cutler closed his eyes wearily. When he opened them again, with some faint satisfaction hidden deep within himself, he nodded with a small smile.

"Boys?"

With jolly whoops and hollers, the riders dismounted and leapt upon Moses as wolves upon a screaming calf, and they kicked and thrashed while Lucas Cutler watched from his horse.

"I loved that man!" the boy-reverend shouted, to the Judge and to Jem and to anyone who would listen. "I loved my Moses!" Over the sounds of the kicking and yelping Lucas cried, "Moses, my boy, fear not the pain! You will be with God soon, my son! If not for your sinful ways, you might have yet achieved redemption."

"Stop!" Jem cried. He stepped down from the veranda to appeal to Judge Cutler directly. "Stop this, Judge. I don't care who owns this man or what he did or didn't do. You won't lynch him on my property."

Judge Cutler sighed and nodded. "I'll surely adhere to that, Jem. After all, such business shouldn't be conducted within earshot of our womenfolk. Don't you worry; we'll take Moses away from here, someplace safe. We'll take your boy with us too."

"No," Jem said, standing tall. "Spare my man, Judge. Spare Ben Freeman, and let there be but one death tonight."

The Judge shook his head. "You know the law, young sir. This boy here aided and abetted a fugitive slave. And if it's true he has a mind for Miss Sarah there..."

"I'll take care of Ben," Jem said stiffly. "He's a servant of Clarendon, in the employ of the Roscoe family. Therefore, he's my responsibility."

Sarah watched, awestruck, as Mr. Claiborne pushed a crude noose over Moses' neck while the other men mounted their horses again. Percy, together with Sam Hanley and Horace Glanton, laughed together like they were little boys playing a game. Turning their horses, they led Moses up the clay path.

Fighting the rope around his neck, Moses managed to turn his head and look back. Sarah could not be sure who Moses looked at exactly. Maybe he looked at Ben, who was crouched on his knees, moaning as if he'd been mortally wounded. Maybe Moses looked at Jem, quietly judging him for standing back and standing by. Or maybe Moses looked at Sarah herself, knowing that it was she who had been the chief betrayer. Moses' eyes flashed up at Clarendon itself, as if cursing the great white mansion and all who lived under its roof, and all that it represented.

Or maybe Moses thought none of these things. In any case, someone jerked on the rope around his neck and he turned away for the last time.

Henry still stood beside his father. Gritting his teeth, Henry went over to Ben and hauled him to his feet. As he did this, Mae Jane cried out as if in physical pain. Sarah reeled as Mae Jane threw her off, and then the old maid was running down the steps.

"No…no…Ben…*Joby*—"

Jem caught Mae Jane in her arms and hushed her. She fought against him, but he only held her tighter.

As he watched all this, Judge Cutler's upper lip twitched. "These have been dark times for all of us. I ain't a hateful man, Jem Roscoe, you understand that. All I want is peace and good order. Now, I've got a right to demand compensation for Moses. He's no good to me now, and you know what I mean by that. I've got that right, same as I've got the right to take your boy here away with me." Here, the Judge looked down at the rope in his hands, the one that was fixed around Ben's neck. "But maybe it's like you said. Maybe there need only be one death tonight. If you're sure you can put the fear of God into him…"

Henry looked at his father with dismay. But the Judge's decision had been made, and presently he pushed the knotted rope into Jem's hands.

Mae Jane broke free from Jem and collapsed in the dirt beside Ben. She threw her arms around her son, and they sobbed against each other. Henry stepped back from them, wearing a look of rank disgust.

"Daddy," Henry protested. "Daddy, this ain't right."

"It's done, Henry. We're going." Here, Judge Cutler extended his hand to Jem, and the two men shook. "I apologize for the dramatics this evening."

Somberly, Jem said, "Think nothing of it, Judge."

The Judge brightened a little. "All this aside, I suppose congratulations are in order."

Jem became very still. "Congratulations?"

"On your promotion," the Judge said with a broad smile. "I hear you'll no longer be just *acting* President of the Roscoe Railroad Company. It's a good thing your brother Jon decided to step back after all. I don't believe he has the right mind for the kind of work you boys do."

A shadow darkened Jem's face. After a long silence, he murmured, "Word travels fast, it seems."

"And here in the Valley, it travels fastest," the Judge said. With that, he turned and mounted his horse. "Come on, Henry. Let's catch up with the others."

Sarah watched as Henry strode toward her. Climbing the steps of the veranda, he reached out and took Sarah's hand in his own.

"You'll be all right, darling?"

Sarah tried to speak, but couldn't. She wished she could go with Henry. She wished they could go somewhere, just the two of them. She needed time to make sense of all that had happened, but she didn't want to be alone to do it. She needed someone to listen, to reassure.

Sarah nodded. "I'll be fine, Henry. *Thank you.*"

He squeezed her hand. "I'll write to you."

"No," she said. She pulled his coat from her shoulders and offered it back to him. "Visit me, Henry. Call on me here, and soon. Won't you?"

Smiling, Henry kissed her hand. "Of course I will."

From the path, the Judge called, "Let's be off, Henry."

Henry kissed Sarah's hand again, and then he turned away and pulled on his coat. He paused to shake hands with Jem. As he passed by Ben and Mae Jane, Henry stopped. He murmured something to Ben that Sarah could not hear.

Suddenly, Ben lifted his head and spat in Henry's face.

Shocked, the two Cutlers looked ready to draw their pistols. They might have done just that, and shot Ben on the spot, but Jem stepped forward with a clenched fist and cold fury in his eyes. With a bitter cry, Jem swung down and struck Ben across the face. This last and heaviest of a long succession of blows was too much for Ben, and he collapsed unconscious in the dirt. With a wail, Mae Jane threw herself over Ben's prostrate form.

Terrified, and sickened by everything she saw, Sarah put a hand around her throat and felt her pulse pound against her fingers.

Jem turned to the Cutlers. He attempted an apology, an explanation, but Henry only turned away and mounted his horse. Judge Cutler stared down at Ben with a look of stony detachment.

"Your boy's more trouble than he's worth," the Judge said. "And since he ain't worth a dime..."

Henry and the Judge turned their horses and started up the path. They struck out with their crops and broke into a gallop, the thundering of their horses' hooves drowning out all other sounds in the night.

Jem stood watching the Cutlers go. Slowly, he turned around to face the Freemans. To the unhearing, unconscious Ben, Jem muttered, "You just don't ever fucking learn, do you?"

Through stinging tears, Mae Jane glared up at Jem. "How dare you, Mr. Jem. How dare you..."

"How dare *I?*" Jem said. Shaking, he pointed at the receding shapes of the Cutlers on their horses. "What kind of world do you think we live in?"

Having said this, Jem turned and made for the house. He thundered up the steps past Sarah, and she saw in his eyes a tortured mix of anger and shame. Indeed Jem looked ready to burst into tears. Staring out at the dark night, Sarah heard Jem throw the front door open and stomp inside, and she heard his boots echo down the hallway. She knew where he was heading without having to guess: the library, straight to Father's liquor cabinet.

Down the long clay path, the riders and their torches and their recaptured runaway disappeared around the bend. She wondered about Moses, and what might happen to him. Surely the Judge and the others weren't serious when they talked about there being a 'death' tonight. Surely it was all a ruse, just a show intended to scare Moses and other slaves against running away again.

Sarah felt numb from the cold. Looking down at the Freemans — Ben splayed out unconscious, and Mae Jane cradling him in her lap as if he was a baby — Sarah felt the sting of her own shame. No sooner did she sense it, however, did she try to dismiss it. She'd done the right thing after all. She'd helped Henry and his father reclaim their property — their God-given, constitutionally-protected property. Jem was correct; the world was one way, and there was no sense fighting against it.

Sarah decided it was time to go inside, and she began to turn away. Out of nowhere, the Bible story of Lot's wife popped into her mind. When God's angels destroyed the wicked cities of Sodom and Gomorrah, and the good Lot and his family were commanded to flee. Curious to witness God's power, Lot's wife turned back to look upon the horror, and in doing so she was destroyed.

As she stood on the veranda, one foot facing the Freemans and the other pointing away toward Clarendon, Sarah wondered whether it was possible to be punished for looking *away* from some horrors. Perhaps some horrible things deserved to be seen and recognized, provided the observer could keep her sanity.

Floating up from somewhere came the song sung in Mayfair a few days earlier, which now felt like a lifetime ago.

Look away! Look away! Look away, Dixieland!

Exhausted, Sarah did indeed look away. What else could she possibly do? She turned her back on the Freemans, intent on going inside — inside, and straight to bed. For whatever reason, she looked up at the shadowed house. There, peering down from one of the high windows, was a dark shape set against a candlelit ceiling. She knew it must be Tom watching from above.

Sarah pulled the front door open and hurried inside, and the slow-swinging door remained ajar. Standing upon the threshold, one could look out from the darkness of Clarendon into a still deeper darkness beyond, and perched there in the dim, fading moonlight was a mother cradling her son and praying, praying for deliverance and the light of a new day.

Chapter 17

THIS GUILTY LAND

December 2, 1859. A bitter wind whipped up from the Blue Ridge Mountains. An icy rain had fallen for two days prior, and the wayside burg of Charles Town, Virginia was all but consumed by thick, freezing mud.

A set of mud-caked boots moved through the center of town and stopped before the gallows just outside the county courthouse. JJ Roscoe, stiff against the biting cold, watched as the hangman prepared a noose.

JJ had yet to return to West Point, as he still had another few days of his official furlough to enjoy. The superintendent Colonel Beauregard had granted him a full month of leave to visit Mayfair, though JJ had spent little more than twenty-four hours actually there. In any case, the other cadets would soon be released on Christmas break. For himself, JJ knew he was destined to spend yet another Christmas holiday alone in the barracks.

Besides the one story in the *Winchester Advertiser* that attached him to the quelling of John Brown's uprising, JJ had read no other mention in any other publications. As far as the American public knew, Robert E. Lee had been the hero of Harper's Ferry (together with his flamboyant second in command, Jeb Stuart).

This likely meant no one at West Point, including Colonel Beauregard, knew of JJ's recent escapades. Even if JJ wanted to claim that he had served under Robert Lee at Harper's Ferry, that he had led the charge against the fire engine house, that he personally had laid John Brown low, and that he had *killed a man* with his own hands, none of his classmates would believe him. The history of the Harper's Ferry raid had been written, and the name JJ Roscoe would remain unmentioned.

But maybe that was all just as well. To share his story would be to invite any number of thorny questions about how a cadet had come to command United States troops. Nevertheless, JJ was still trying to come up with a good answer to a particular question that had been posed to him more than once while he was in Charles Town.

"*Roscoe*? You ain't Senator *John* Roscoe's son, is you?"

Answering that question was much more difficult than it used to be.

Oh, what a waste. What a goddamn, sorry waste.

As he felt the cold wind on his face, JJ winced at a searing pain running the length of his right cheekbone. The painkilling whiskey he forced himself to drink earlier this morning was wearing off, and his wound began to gnaw at him again.

JJ remembered that fateful night back home, when Jem had fired a shot at him. JJ rode on through the gusts of gunsmoke as if his brother had missed, but in fact the ball had split JJ's right cheek wide open and chipped away part of his cheekbone.

Fighting through agonizing, head-splitting pain, JJ had ridden north several miles before he finally collapsed somewhere beyond the Branches. He was discovered and taken in by an elderly couple who nursed him for a night and day, and the woman did what she could to dress the wound. Eager to be on his way, JJ quit the small farm in the dead of night, leaving behind a terse note of thanks.

Eventually JJ made his way here to Charles Town, just a few miles southwest of Harper's Ferry. Here, the trial of John Brown and his co-conspirators was already underway. After securing himself room and board and hiring the services of a doctor (who explained the hole in his cheek would eventually cover over with scar tissue), JJ decided to linger in Virginia a few extra weeks. He felt he needed some element of closure to complete the chapter of his terrible, twisted homecoming. To JJ, the impending execution of John Brown seemed to be the proper symbol. He deemed it a sacrificial bloodletting, a catharsis of a kind.

After he had settled in Charles Town, JJ took off the uniform he'd been wearing for God knew how long and donned civilian clothes. After dressing, JJ went to the courthouse and joined the crush of spectators packed into a tiny room. Within, what the newspapers called the 'trial of the century' was in full swing. John Brown, wounded during the last moments of his insurrection, lay on a cot during the proceedings. Though he was compelled to testify many times, Brown refused to speak. After the prosecution rested on a case with overwhelming evidence, including a small army of eyewitnesses who before all present fingered Brown for the murderous rebel leader, the jury deliberated a mere ten minutes. There was never any doubting their ultimate verdict: guilty, with a recommended sentence of death by hanging.

And today was the day.

As he wandered the muddy yard before the scaffolding, clenching his jaw to ward off the pain in his cheek, JJ looked upon the young cadets from the Virginia Military Institute, who were standing guard against abolitionist agitators. The cadets looked fine enough, but to JJ's eye they were nothing compared to the cadets of West Point.

JJ did, however, admire their leader, one Major Thomas Jackson. In his late thirties, Jackson was a Virginian and a West Point graduate. That was all JJ knew about the man, except that presently he also learned that Jackson was rather an odd duck. While riding about the yard inspecting his cadets, Jackson thrust his left hand into the air and held it erect — for what purpose, JJ didn't have the slightest idea. With his other hand, Jackson reached down to an icebox strapped to his saddle and produced a plump lemon, and he proceeded to eat the lemon whole.

As JJ moved through the crowd, he saw that the entire countryside had come out for the hanging. The air was alive with the buzzing conversations of thousands of spectators waiting before the gallows. Congressmen had also come from far-flung places North and South, and everywhere news correspondents scurried about waving scraps of paper and thrusting pencils in the air like tiny pikes.

JJ passed one reporter interviewing a handsome young militiaman. "...Wilkes Booth, no *e* in Booth," the militiaman said in a smooth baritone. When asked his opinion of the hanging, the man gestured at the hanging platform. "Oh, I don't doubt Yankee conspirators put the old traitor up to all this. And there's little doubt they will continue to work against their Southern neighbors. 'Tis time to fear when tyrants seem to kiss,' hm? But I say the South will prevail."

JJ made his way over to the courthouse. Any moment now, John Brown would be brought outside to begin the long march up to the gallows. JJ wished he could find a way to get inside and speak to Brown privately. He wanted to ask the old man the same question that so many others had asked.

Why?

JJ had been asking that same question regarding a great many matters lately, most of them having nothing to do with John Brown. Most of the time, the answers to *what* and *how* were usually easy to identify. *Why* was ever elusive, and in most cases went unanswered.

JJ's mind wandered to the envelope he still kept in his breast pocket. Again, the thorny question of *why* pricked at him. Why had Father invited him home, ostensibly for a reconciliation, only to ultimately reject him? Why had JJ been so naïve, so eager to dismiss four years of silence from Father, and believe that suddenly all would be made right? Why had JJ thought he could trust Jem? For God's sake, his own brother had nearly killed him!

And why, *why* did JJ still carry Father's goddamn letter in his pocket?

"*Hark*!" a voice cried. "He's coming out!"

All at once, the crowd began to mumble and murmur. The side door of the courthouse opened inward, revealing a tunnel of impenetrable black that suggested a chill, tomblike cold within. From the gloom emerged soldiers and police constables, and now a stone-faced reverend clasping a Bible against his breast. When at last the man of hour stepped into the cold, flat daylight, any and all whispers died on the wind.

John Brown was filthy and bruised, his shock of white hair astray and his long beard mangy. He stared blankly out at the crowd gathered to see him before he started slowly down the wooden steps, taking them one at a time, as if the slightest movement caused him considerable pain.

Soldiers and constables created a path through the crowd, warning onlookers away with hard glares and batons. A mother stepped forward and begged Brown to kiss the young baby in her hands, but the soldiers pushed the woman away. Brown walked on, his eyes focused on the steel gray sky overhead.

JJ found himself at the front of the assembly, standing where he had a clear view of Brown's solemn march. He remained there until a broad-chested constable stepped up and ordered him back with the others. With his eyes fixed on Brown, JJ refused to budge.

The constable pushed him. "I said, *get back*."

Raising his chin in a show of defiance, JJ muttered, "Touch me again and see what happens."

The constable laughed and pushed at him again. Just then, John Brown turned his head and saw JJ. Though JJ was wearing civilian clothes and was otherwise indistinguishable from the rest of the crowd, Brown's eyes widened with recognition.

Lunging forward, Brown snatched JJ's arm with one huge, claw-like hand. With the other, Brown pushed something — a folded scrap of paper — into JJ's grasp. All the while, JJ's vision was filled with Brown's blue, rapier-like eyes. The old man's gaze was something like Father's: incisive, somehow *knowing*. In a raspy voice, John Brown said: "Are you in very much pain, my boy?"

Before JJ could answer, or even comprehend the real meaning of the question, a group of soldiers and constables advanced. Several sets of burly arms hurled JJ back against the crowd. All at once, the fragile peace in the yard threatened to descend into chaos. Cries of '*TRAITOR!*' were flung at Brown, while other voices praised Brown: '*Loving patriot! God's man!*'

The cadets of the VMI plunged into the fray. After a brief jostling between the crowd and the authorities, order was restored and the path to the gallows remained open.

JJ had been swallowed up by the swarming crowd. He soon found himself pushed all the way back to rear, still stunned by his encounter with John Brown. Feeling the scrap of paper clutched in his palm, he opened his hand with a mind to read whatever was written there.

Are you in very much pain, my boy?

Before JJ could read the message, drums shattered the air like a musket volley. Looking up, JJ watched the distant figure of John Brown ascend the final steps of the hanging platform. Deciding to read Brown's message later, JJ tucked the scrap of paper into the breast pocket of his jacket.

Faces in the crowd were hard, solemn, merciless. Some onlookers wept, maybe for the soul of John Brown or maybe for some other reason.

Before all present, Brown declined a final religious service or blessing of any kind because the local reverend owned three female slaves. The reverend could do nothing but bow his head and step back with as much grace as he could muster.

JJ scanned the crowd. There across the square sat Major Jackson atop his great warhorse. Some of Jackson's cadets stood around the platform with their muskets shouldered. The rest of the company stood at rapt attention as the pattering drums shifted to a steady, endless roll.

And at last, the drumming ceased.

Charles Town's sheriff examined the hangman's noose. A deputy placed it over John Brown's neck. Brown coughed and then winced, and JJ imagined a thousand tiny splinters from the rough noose pricking his flesh.

The sheriff read out the sentence to all:

"John Brown, you stand charged, tried, and convicted of treason against the Commonwealth of Virginia. You have been sentenced to hang until you are dead. Do you have any final words?"

Brown shook his head slowly, left to right. His eyes burned with vindictive hatred at every man, woman, and child they fell upon. But then the old man closed his eyes. When he opened them again, the hate was gone. He seemed to be at peace with his fate.

The sheriff called for a black hood. A deputy stepped forward and slipped the hood over Brown's head. JJ imagined the world through John Brown's eyes, the sudden shift from a bright world to inky darkness, a mere glimpse of what awaited him in Oblivion.

A clear voice called out: "*Stop*!"

Eyes turned. Major Jackson rode forward, his eyes shining a brilliant, ghoulish blue. In a low drawl, he said, "Let the traitor see with open eyes God's country and people, which he has forsaken."

While the crowd murmured, the sheriff paused and considered Jackson's request. The hanging was, after all, the law's affair. But under Jackson's stern glare and the cheers that now burst from the crowd, the sheriff looked to his deputies and the reverend and finally to the condemned man himself for guidance.

The sheriff pulled the hood from John Brown's head. Major Jackson smiled, and the crowd cheered with frantic energy.

Brown blinked furiously, blinded by the sudden light. But just as Brown's eyes finally focused, the sheriff reached for the lever that would drop the gallows' platform. A passing crow splattered white feces over several VMI cadets. There was no time to ponder this strange omen before the platform fell open with a creaking groan.

Brown's dead weight dropped, and the slack rope resting on his shoulders snapped taut with a sickening crunch. But death did not come instantly, even as the crowd sighed and cheered and a marching band trumpeted joyful songs.

Instead Brown swung there from the killing rope, his body erect and trembling. His face turned blue, now black. His eyes bulged from their sockets, his head twisted by the noose where it held together the jagged fragments of his spinal cord.

"His neck ain't broke!" a voice cried.

Brown's neck was in fact broken, though somehow he was still alive and conscious. While thousands watched, he swung there in the open air for nearly half an hour. Shards of his spine had punctured his neck, but by some miracle a pin-sized tube of air remained for him to breathe through. Soon enough, however, Brown's chest cavity filled with blood and the man began to drown.

Long before Brown himself expired, many of the onlookers left and went about their daily business. Many noted that Brown's was perhaps the least interesting hanging they'd ever seen, notable only because the man himself was so controversial. A quick death, they determined, was fun and exciting. A slow, drawn-out dying was much too disconcerting to be enjoyed.

JJ stood like a rock against the departing tide of onlookers. He could not take his eyes off Brown, who seemed to be looking directly at him, his eyes asking any number of unspoken questions.

Are you in very much pain, my boy?

It was not just John Brown that JJ looked upon. He saw Father hanging there, and it felt *good* to bear witness. He saw Jem hanging there, and he felt a cheer rising in his throat. He saw hanging there every person who had ever sneered at him, every person who had ever laughed at him or mocked him, every person who had wronged him or wished ill upon him or had pretended to care for him. Indeed JJ saw a great many faces — even Mother, who treated him like a ghost, and even Ben Freeman, who could have spoken in his defense that night in the library but didn't. He even saw Richard Harper swaying back and forth — Richard, who had led him down a path from which there seemed no hope of returning. Indeed JJ saw many faces, too many to count, all of them contorted with the pain of suffering. He saw Father there again — all the faces eventually became Father, upon whose face was stamped the despairing regret of the eternally damned — and seeing all this, JJ smiled.

...very much pain?

JJ reached into his breast pocket and pulled out the dirty scrap of paper that Brown had given to him. In doing so, his hand also carried up Father's letter. The battered envelope slipped from his grasp and landed in the muddy slush between JJ's feet, and as JJ watched in unmoved silence the envelope became wet and dark and the ink on the front leached away until it was unreadable. He thought of those words — *your rightful place* — melting and disappearing.

JJ turned away from that spot and left Father's disintegrating letter where it lay. He moved against the parting crowd until he stood closer to the platform. Here, he looked up at watched John Brown as the life began to fade from those piercing eyes.

Brown's mouth opened and closed in some grotesque effort to speak. His swollen tongue wagged about and pushed gobs of blood and saliva over the bulkheads of his lips. And maybe, as JJ presently wondered, John Brown was speaking to him, or maybe he was gurgling some final condemnation to the whole world. Brown's final words went unheard in any case, for they died in his throat.

JJ stood watching the expired John Brown for a long time. Finally he remembered the scrap of paper between his fingers. Slowly, he unfolded it flap by flap and looked upon the words the dead man had scrawled on it a short time before. And while the memory of his father's fateful letter was already fading, JJ shuddered as he read a new prophecy.

I, John Brown, am now quite certain that the crimes of this guilty land will never be purged away but with blood.

❧

In the Mayfair Valley, as in the wider Shenandoah, the summers are joyous but the winters are dark and trying. Much of the Sleepy Creek freezes over in December, and many animals come down from the Alleghenies to cross the icy highway and feed in the low country. Among the migrants are white-tailed deer, and with them come the coyotes.

Except in truly desperate times, Valley coyotes rarely bother humans. In fact, some wanderers in the woods may even stumble upon the rare sight of a pack of wild dogs consuming a fresh kill. The wanderer can watch in peace and safety from a distance as the dogs tear at frozen flesh with bloody jowls. The dogs may even pause to look up at the stranger before continuing to feed. And the wanderer can then push on uninhibited, sighing at the wonders of nature and his good fortune for seeing the ways of God and life unfold before his very eyes.

On a winter's day near Christmas 1859, such a nameless wanderer paused atop a bluff to look down at a pack of coyotes in a feeding frenzy. The kill lay in a depression near the base of the North Branch, next to the banks of the frozen Sleepy Creek. The carcass was frozen, as if it had been there a long time. Why, even under several inches of snow it almost seemed as if the carcass had been buried in a shallow grave. Indeed, the coyotes paused now and then to dig at the hard-packed earth, scratching and clawing at the frozen ground and throwing up clods of dark dirt to reveal more of the carcass underneath. The coyotes snapped at each other as each maneuvered for access to the best strips of meat. Black crows landed nearby and tucked their wings and watched with heads flitting back and forth, patiently waiting their turn.

The wanderer was in a state of bliss. Well, just look at that. There it was again, the ways of God and life unfolding before the wanderer's very eyes. Bless his good fortune!

Seeking relief from the cold, the wanderer moved on and never saw that part of the world again. The coyotes in the depression wailed and dug at the earth and found nothing more. The carcass was very old after all, and the best parts had already been picked over or taken by worms. They sniffed at the shreds of bloody cloth nearby and left them alone. They sniffed at the small skull and pushed their tongues through the eye sockets. They had polished off what little flesh the old carcass had to give, and they left the shattered bones to the beady-eyed crows who hopped through the snow in frantic excitement.

Perched nearby, a lone owl watched all these things with detachment until she saw something shining in the snow. She flew down and drove off the crows long enough to stab down into the ice and extract a silver chain. On the chain was a silver cross bearing the visage of St. Anthony, though of course the owl saw only how the thing glinted and gleamed.

The chain was heavy, but the owl lifted it up into the sky and carried it to her nest within the hollow of a tree. It was dark in the hollow, but when the sun was at the right angle the glittering ornament cast specks of light on the walls of her quiet sanctuary, much to the delight of her chirping young. If owls can feel contentment, this one looked at the silver light reflecting all around her and was pleased.

II

SECESSIONITIS

April – December 1860

When the government gets into the hands of the Republican Party, the arm of the government, we are told, will not be raised for the protection of our slave property. Then John Brown, and a thousand John Browns, can invade us and yet the government will not protect us...

Have we then no right to announce upon this floor that if we are not to be protected in our property and sovereignty, we are therefore released from our allegiance, and will protect ourselves out of the Union, if we cannot within the Union? Have we no right to allege that to secure our rights and protect our honor we will dissever the ties that bind us together, even if it rushes us into a sea of blood?

A Representative from Mississippi,
speaking on the floor of the House

April 22nd, 1860

Charleston, South Carolina

We are finally pulling into the terminus at Charleston after two endless weeks of train travel. We've changed trains more than a dozen times, for as we passed from state to state, and even from county to county, the gauge of the tracks changed. The places we are passing through — southern Virginia, into North and South Carolina — are so skeptical of anything resembling central, federalized authority that they prefer to build their own railroads according to their own 'native' specifications. It's a policy that Jem would surely applaud.

I'm keeping this journal and intend to fill its pages with notes and observations throughout my trip. I don't fool myself with thinking that anyone will ever read this. But as it is, I've felt a growing need to step outside the flesh and bone of this life, so to speak. I'm tired of wandering about the grounds of Clarendon and the Mayfair Valley without the ability to speak and be heard.

And since November, since Moses, I've felt invisible too.

I've heard no word about Moses' well-being, not that I expected any. Around Christmastime I did ask Jem, who was due to attend a ball at the Cutler family's plantation, to inquire in a subtle way with Henry Cutler. Jem said of course he would, but when he came back from the party he explained he couldn't find the right moment to broach the subject. It was during that same ball, I learned, that Sarah said yes to Henry Cutler's marriage proposal.

Sarah and I have barely spoken since last November. Whenever we are together (a very rare phenomenon these days), there is an undeniable chill in the air. Sarah's wedding, to be held at Clarendon later in May, is all anyone seems to want to talk about — including Mama. I for one am glad to be away from it all, if only for a little while. And I suspect Sarah was happy to see the back of my head too. I could almost hear her calling:

"Goodbye, Mr. Freeman, and good riddance."

Sleeping aboard these shuddering, jerking hunks of rolling iron is a rather fitful business. I feel I've aged twenty years in two weeks, so far as my lower back is concerned. I remember a few days ago, I was finally able to catch a few winks when a great rumbling jolted me from a fitful sleep. The train had stopped in the middle of the track for reasons of maintenance, an occurrence that I no longer considered rare or peculiar.

Turning my head, I looked out the window to the world beyond. Of course, this being God's country, what did I see in the early morning light?

Negroes bent to work in a cotton field.

Hands picked bolls and pushed them into canvas sacks. The people worked quietly, trancelike, for it was that early hour of the workday when the drudgery seemed somehow and only briefly novel. I saw the silhouettes of riders against the newborn sun. It seemed to me the kind of image an artist might wish to immortalize with oil and canvas. Here were proud riders passing under the sun — the artist would surely render the sun as setting rather than rising, to hint at some unspoken notion of time and tradition passing away — and the sun's glow shone down on humble people bent to humble service. Perhaps such a painting would be beautiful, as indeed the image seared in my memory was, in its own way.

But would the artist also choose to detail the arcing whips in the hands of the riders, or the bulging shape of pistols on their belts, or the drawn expressions of sorrow and torment etched into the faces of those ostensibly humble field hands?

No, I suspect no museum or gallery would ever hang an image that humanized such abject sorrow — not unless the artist attempted the favored depiction of the noble death of pale, perfect Jesus Christ, with the sin of mankind running red along the sunken contours of his white flesh. Only through the example of a blue-eyed Prince of Peace are people willing to face the hideous aspects of human nature. But when ordinary men and women personify a collective suffering felt daily, all over the world, these figures are relegated to the shadowy background. It seems that immortality belongs only to the noble white knights keeping watch over a time of order and tradition.

As I looked at the slaves, I asked myself: why don't they fight back? Why do they bend to work while the whips crack over their heads? Why do they toil, owning none of the fruits of their labor while stoically shouldering its tragedies and travesties? I think of what I said to Tom when he asked, a long time ago it seems now, why the slaves around Harper's Ferry did not flock to John Brown's revolutionary banner. A human life, like water, takes the shape of its confines. Whether he presses against the walls of a deep hole or traces the borders of a cotton field, few will ever have the courage to explore the unknown, the undefined. The suffering which one knows is just that: known, familiar, its borders clearly marked. Who can say whether the claim of a 'better world' beyond is not an empty promise that leads to ruin? Besides, the overseers had more than whips to smother ideas of escape and freedom.

Placed in the same situation, I cannot say I would not be there among those field hands, wallowing in resentful docility. I am reminded of what Moses told me many months ago, on the night he died. Who am I to question the will of these people when I myself do not face the lash of the whip, day in and day out? I've known freedom, or at least a version of it, since I was but a small child.

Still, I cannot help but yearn for one of those crooked heads to look up, to see a man or woman stand up in erect defiance to the riders and disrupt the pretty picture. I counted three or four dozen field hands, but only three overseers to watch them. The overseers had weapons, to be sure, but it would not take much for ten men and women to surround a single horseman and pull him down and wrestle his weapons away from him. Of course there would be the immediate consequences to contend with: namely, the fact that every white man within a hundred miles would come running with a loaded weapon and a vision of holy retribution to manifest. But if it is true, as I've heard it said, that some eight in ten people in the Carolinas are negro slaves, then the hands out in the field — and maybe all the slaves in the South, if they could only gather together — have an advantage of numbers that cannot be ignored. They don't need a John Brown; they only need themselves.

Even as I pondered these things, the train rumbled back to life and resumed its slow rolling down the track. And before long the field and the hands in it were gone, and in my mind's eye there remains only the vague image that deserves to be recorded for posterity in all its rawness, but which is destined only to fade away in time.

Chapter 18

THE LITTLE GIANT

The sun slipped over the hills to the west. Seagulls and pelicans announced the day's ending like a cult of town criers gone mad. And all the while a great darkness crept ashore from the Atlantic. It was as if the darkness came out of the sea itself, swept to this particular shoreline from a rolling, featureless expanse far beyond human sight and comprehension.

There was a strangeness to Charleston that Ben Freeman could not quite put a finger on. Maybe it was the salt tang that was foreign to his Valley nose. He knew manure well enough back home, but the first whiff of a low tide baking under the Carolina sun nearly set him back on his feet.

Maybe it was the alien aspect of the sea that bothered him. Ben still dreamed to look upon the full brunt of the Atlantic up close, to feel its elemental power. From Charleston Battery he could glimpse the swell of the ocean as it vibrated along the horizon line. The city was tucked away inside the relative comforts of Charleston Harbor, which just now as Ben watched started to come alive with its own frothing whitecaps. The retreating light in the west seemed to make way for a tempest, one that always brought night with it.

And it was hot. Damn hot.

A taxi-coach pulled up to the steps of the Rutledge Hotel. Ben reached for the taxi door and felt Judge Tobias Cutler push by him. Ben swallowed the pit of anger in his throat and helped Senator Roscoe into the coach next, then waited for Cutler's ancient manservant Solomon to climb up. Ben went in last, and soon the Mayfair men were off.

As the coach passed the docks, Ben saw crowds of slaves loading and unloading scores of merchant ships. Hundreds of slaves, nearly all of them strong young men like himself, lugged bales of fresh cotton aboard the ships. Ferocious policemen carrying large clubs watched over them, barking orders and routinely striking out with their clubs. But mostly the loading and unloading went on like clockwork, and from this distance the bustling slaves looked like so many busy ants.

"Look at those boys *work*," Cutler marveled, his gaze falling on the docks. "Lord, they've got a real society down here, don't they?"

The 'society' Cutler admired had existed since Spanish settlers first landed in the Carolinas. The next three hundred years had seen the tiny port village that would become Charleston flourish, it success driven mainly by the port's use as a slave market. Here was the terminus of despair, where untold hundreds of thousands of people, kidnapped from another continent, were lined up to be poked, prodded, and sold to the highest bidder. Entire nations and tribes, each with distinct identities and cultures, became one mass of beings — 'niggers' — and native tongues were lost as all learned the universal language of fear. Though the overseas slave trade was no more, Ben knew the city's Old Slave Mart was still one of the busiest marketplaces in the Union.

The coach rolled past walled mansions that looked like fortresses, and indeed some of them were, sporting cannons and the like. The city's cobbled streets were lined with palmetto trees, the facades of its buildings painted in bright pastels, its gates grinning with ornate iron spikes. Even in the fading light of day, the city seemed to Ben like an island lost in time, a drowsy paradise baking in the heat of an eternal tropical summer.

Gazing beyond the glassy waters of the harbor, Ben spied a cluster of distant lights illuminating walls and battlements on a distant island.

"Driver," Ben called, "what is that island there?"

There was no answer. After a moment, the Senator turned and repeated the question to the driver.

"Fort Sumter," the driver replied, having apparently only registered the Senator's voice. "Damn rock ready to fall into the sea. They been buildin it and buildin it for Lord knows how long."

The Senator looked at Ben again, offering a small shrug. "There's the answer."

Ben nodded and looked out the window.

The coach turned away from the Battery and wound through a series of streets that led into the knot of Charleston's downtown core. Lamplighters moved from streetlamp to streetlamp, illuminating the city against encroaching darkness.

"Ben?"

Ben turned to Senator Roscoe. "Yes, sir?"

The old man held a collection of papers in his hands. They were the contents of the latest draft of his Convention speech.

"There are a few passages in this speech that I find…rather disconcerting. They are the rantings of a radical."

"Oh, *come now,*" Cutler said, turning to the Senator. "You're not seriously having the boy write your *speeches* for you now, are you, JR? That is a sick joke, really."

"Ben is a fine writer," the Senator replied. He reached into his coat pocket and withdrew a fountain pen. "Unfortunately, he seems to have forgotten that this is a speech to be delivered before some two-thousand Democrats, not a raving mob of subscribers to *The Liberator*."

The Senator proceeded to cross out several lines and passages. Each time the pen stabbed paper, Ben felt an ache in his chest.

"That rag ought to be banned," Cutler growled. "It was that paper's editor who inspired John Brown, no doubt about it. Those Yankee sons of bitches call for national insurrection at least once a week."

Ben leaned toward the Senator. "What is so radical about what I've written?"

The Senator looked at him as if the answer was self-evident. "We should say nothing of moral law or the rights of man," he replied. "This is not a treatise of political philosophy. All we need do is declare that Stephen Douglas is a moderate, Unionist candidate. There should be no mention of abolishing slavery, nor should we take the opposite position. A little flourish is fine, but to wax poetic about aspirational ideals will only confuse the delegates."

Ben nodded, but he wasn't convinced. "Shouldn't a candidate for president be an idealist?"

The Senator offered a dry laugh. "The delegates don't quote Locke and Rousseau at the dinner table, if that's what you mean." Again, the Senator's censuring pen painted the speech black. "And certainly they don't quote such thinkers out of context."

The taxi coach turned down Broad Street, a handsome thoroughfare lined with stout palmetto trees. City constables roamed about on horses while small groups of citizens meandered (with handservant slaves in tow) between the windows of shops and sundry stores that were near to closing. As the coach drove deeper into the city, Ben detected the sounds of drunken revelry from the tavern district.

"Just where are we meeting Douglas anyway?" Cutler asked the Senator. "I was thinking we could stop at the Charleston Hotel on the way. There are some men there I'd like to speak with."

The Senator nodded. "Perhaps later, Tobias. For the present, we owe Stephen Douglas some of our time."

"I owe him nothing," Cutler grunted. "A parley with Douglas is a waste of time, if you ask me. I for one did not come to Charleston to fraternize with Northerners, let alone North*westerners*. I came here to meet with our Southern brothers and plan a strategy to protect our rights from the Federal government."

The Senator laughed. "Don't forget you're a Representative, Tobias. You *are* the Federal government."

The coach stopped before a handsome tavern called The Blind Tiger. Ben stepped out of the coach and helped both Cutler and the Senator down to the street.

"I just ask you to remember what we agreed before coming down here, JR," Cutler said to the Senator. "I represent a passionate section of our party, and they trust me to protect their interests. If Stephen Douglas does not impress me, he will not impress *them*. That will not bode well for his nomination. And then you will have to make a difficult choice, JR. A necessary choice."

Just then, a lamplighter lit a nearby streetlight. In the gathering dark, the lamp's harsh glow cut deep shadows into the Senator's face and obscured his eyes. The old man took up his handkerchief and hacked several wet coughs.

"I have not forgotten, Tobias."

❧

The Blind Tiger was packed wall to wall with men crunched over tables and slumped over at the long bar. The smoky room baked in the tallow light of candles and oil lamps. Feeling the hot, condescending gaze of many red-rimmed eyes, Ben snaked his way past tables of sneering faces.

"There he is," the Senator said, pointing with his cane.

They approached a table in the middle of the tavern. It was occupied by several men in neat suits with flowers of yellow-colored paper pinned to their lapels. Upon seeing the newcomers, the men stood up in unison. A plump, balding man in their midst remained seated.

"Now go and do your jobs," the plump man said. His voice was powerful and deep, like the sliding drone of a trombone. "You think I'm paying you to keep me company?"

The departing men nodded to the Senator and Judge Cutler both, and they ignored Ben altogether. Then they split up and scattered across the tavern, sidling up beside loners and small groups alike.

As Ben turned back to the table, he found himself nose to nose with a scowling waiter who wore a trim waistcoat with a tiger crest embroidered over its front pocket.

"Shoo, damn nigger," the waiter said. "G'won, get with you. Out."

"That's fine, sir," the Senator called. "That man is with us."

The waiter turned to the Senator and bowed. "I'm sorry, sir. We don't serve negroes in this establishment."

The Senator smiled. "That's fine. You won't have to serve them. They'll merely sit with us and—"

"It's fine, JR," Cutler said quietly. He smiled at the waiter. "Not a problem, my good man. The negroes will eat in the back room."

"*Down the street,*" the waiter corrected. "There's a place for their kind around the corner."

Ben desperately wanted to protest, and words began to form on his tongue. But he remained silent, especially when he saw Senator Roscoe wavering. The old man looked toward Ben helplessly and shrugged. *What can be done?* his expression said.

What can be done? Ben knew the Senator could do a great deal, in fact. Like standing his ground, to start with.

Just then, the plump man at the table reached for a chair beside him and dragged it toward him, causing a great deal of noise. "Just seat the boys there and be done with it," he boomed. "This posturing is all laughable nonsense."

Heads turned, and a hush fell over the surrounding tables. Ben felt eyes crawling all over him, none of them friendly. He looked once more upon the strange man at the table. Short and squat, with a shock of dark hair curling around a pallid, flabby face, the man stared up at the waiter with a patronizing grin. "God won't bring his wrath down upon this cramped piss-pot just because you let a brace of negroes warm some chairs."

The waiter gritted his teeth. "I'd sooner die than stain my honor by serving a nigger."

"Then get on with serving the rest of us," the squat man said. "Problem solved." He reached into his pocket, pulled out a thick clip of rolled bills, and slapped it on the table. "A hundred glasses of brandy, if you please. That should be enough for every man here, I trust? Hell, just open the taps and keep em flowing. Beer, whiskey, what have you. And if one of us happens to slip a dram to the negroes, so be it." The man grinned. "Your honor, noble tavern knight, will remain untarnished."

The watching crowd cheered and broke into laughter, but not out of any sense of witnessing justice served. Rather, they brashly demanded their promised drinks. Finally, the waiter was compelled to take the money and hurry off.

"There's a good lad!" the squat man shouted, and the crowd laughed and whooped.

From the back, a man cried, "Three cheers for Steve Douglas!"

Stephen Douglas shrugged off the applause and downed a glass of brandy, much to the thrill of his supporters. Ben realized just how fitting the popular nickname 'the Little Giant' was for Douglas. The man was flabby and diminutive, but in spite of his small size he puffed out his cheeks and body in the manner of Napoleon.

"If there's one thing I know," Douglas called to the assembly, "it's to never get between a good liquor and his Democrat! Or wait, was it the other way around? Let me see..."

The crowd laughed again. Douglas beckoned the Senator and Cutler to sit with him, and this they did. Two chairs were set apart from the table for Ben and Solomon.

As Douglas' supporters turned back to their drinks and a dull roar filled the air again, Ben leaned forward. "Thank you, Senator Douglas. That was very kind of you."

Douglas squinted at Ben and waved him off. "Oh, don't thank me, er, Mister..."

"Freeman."

"Mr. Freeman." Douglas seemed amused by the name. "I don't have a particularly charitable heart, I'm afraid, Mr. Freeman. But if a glorified bootblack is going to tell my friend John what he can and cannot do, then I make it my business to tell him otherwise."

"You have no *business* upending Southern traditions," Cutler said sharply.

In response, Douglas extended his hand. "Congressman Tobias Cutler, is it? Your reputation precedes you, sir."

Cutler's scowl melted away as his cheeks flushed red. He took Douglas' hand and the two men shook firmly. "A noble reputation, surely?"

Douglas grinned. "You are the *noble* negro-hanging judge of Virginia's Mayfair Valley, yes? And you associate with men who are openly seditious in their plot to form a Southern Confederacy, are you not? O-ho, yes. In that case, Mr. Cutler, *surely* indeed."

Cutler's smile vanished and his arm went limp. "The pleasure is all mine."

"I'm certain of it," Douglas replied. He nodded at Solomon. "And who is this chap, Mr. Cutler? Is this your brother-in-law?"

Fuming, Cutler replied stiffly, "Solomon here has served three generations of the Cutler family."

"Is that so?" Douglas said, pleasantly intrigued. "He must enjoy his job then, if he's been doing it for so long. Oh, but can't he speak for himself? You there, King Solomon. Do you enjoy the life of a beast, or do you find it rather burdensome?"

Solomon did not answer; instead he looked at Cutler with a questioning, almost fearful expression.

"Solomon ain't very talkative," Cutler muttered.

"No," Douglas said, "I shouldn't think he is." Now he turned to the Senator. "And you, John. You're much too thin. A light breeze would carry you off."

The Senator shrugged. "I gnaw on my cane every supper."

Douglas laughed. "Then I'm afraid we shan't be friends much longer. It was a long journey from Chicago, and I'm absolutely starved." The Little Giant patted his bulging stomach. "I could eat for a week and still consider myself famished. Waiter! Be kind to some poor, hungry travelers and fetch us some sandwiches. And where the hell are our drinks?"

The conversation between Douglas, Cutler, and Senator Roscoe was broad and far-reaching. First they spoke of the hanging of John Brown, and all three were in agreement that Brown deserved his gruesome fate. Next they spoke about the myriad frustrations of the current lame-duck Congress, which was hamstrung by a Republican-controlled House and a Democratic Senate. Douglas was quick to blame the ineffectual Congress on President James Buchanan, whom he deemed a corrupt, double-crossing fool.

"I've heard the president's feeling about you is mutual," Cutler said with a veiled smile.

There were personal matters to speak of as well. Stephen Douglas received the news of Henry Cutler's engagement to Sarah Roscoe with tepid approval. "It's a fine match," was all he seemed willing to say.

The tavern waiters served trays of brandy glasses. Nothing was given to Ben or Solomon.

Ben found the eyes of a young waiter who appeared to have a kindly disposition. "Excuse me, sir," Ben said. "May I please have a glass of milk?"

The waiter looked at Ben, and for a brief moment there was a hint of recognition in his eyes. But then those same eyes glazed over, and the waiter saw nothing except an empty chair.

"A glass of milk," the Senator said to the waiter. "If you please."

The waiter nodded to the Senator. Evidently he could still see the old man. "Right away, sir."

Dispirited but not surprised, Ben watched the waiter disappear into the smoky haze before he turned back to gauge the Senator's reaction. The old man merely shrugged at him and turned his attention back to the wider conversation.

"And that damn Lincoln is on the warpath again," Douglas was saying. "All the papers are printing excerpts of the speech he gave in New York back in February. In one night he went from regional hayseed to national figure. Now there's talk of him being a contender at the Republican Convention."

Cutler shook his head. "The Republicans will nominate William Seward. He's the wiliest of the bunch."

"Salmon Chase is my guess," the Senator said. "No man is more ambitious."

"I underestimated Lincoln once when he tried to take my seat from me," Douglas said. "I won't make the same mistake twice."

Cutler offered Douglas a beguiling smile. "Perhaps it wasn't your opponent who nearly toppled you, Mr. Douglas, but your own policies. You did, after all, throw President Buchanan under the train with your anti-Southern sentiments."

Hearing this, Douglas rolled his eyes with dramatic flair. "Anti-Southern? My wife is a Southerner, and her family's plantation has enriched me as much as John's wife has enriched him. I can appreciate the fortunate aspects of slavery, as well as its evils. I simply believe that if the people of a United States territory are in the process of lobbying for statehood, they ought to have the opportunity to vote on the *kind* of society in which they will live. It's a question as old as Socrates. In the American context, will the people have a free-soil state, or a slave state? I say the choice ought to be left to the local people to decide, not the power-brokers of Washington."

Ben looked toward Douglas. "Popular sovereignty," he offered.

Douglas smiled at him. "That's exactly right, Mr. Freeman. Smart fellow you have here, John."

Cutler shot Ben a quiet glare. "JR," he said to the Senator, "I ask you to ask your boy there not to interrupt our conversation."

The Senator merely gave a warning look to Ben, and Ben was silent again.

Cutler cleared his throat and continued. "The issue ain't whether the American people can vote. The issue is that the American people are being *misled*: by anti-Southern newspapers, by abolitionist politicians, by neighbors who claim to be philosophers. Why must we differentiate 'free-soil' and 'slave' states? Such terminology is needlessly confusing and divisive."

Douglas laughed. "Don't lecture me about divisive politics, Mr. Cutler. I know who waits for you at the Charleston Hotel tonight. They are the same men who were the first to claim that I betrayed Buchanan by straying from the party line."

Cutler flushed with embarrassment. "In any case, the Supreme Court—"

"We could go on and on about the particulars," Douglas said, "but it's really very simple. If you are a states' rights man, as I am, then you *must* be for my notion of popular sovereignty. The people of a locality have the right to determine the kind of local society in which they shall live. Whether the Federal government abolishes slavery or enshrines it as a citizen's right in the Constitution — in *either case*, the Federal government would be overstepping the bounds of its power."

Cutler withdrew from the conversation with a heavy sigh.

Seeming to sense a window of opportunity, Senator Roscoe inched closer to Douglas. "I've been thinking, Stephen, about a possible strategy for your campaign this fall. I think we need to change the national conversation away from slavery. As Tobias says, it's divisive. After all, as many Northerners hate negroes as do Southerners..."

Douglas glanced over at Ben and held up his glass. "Cheers to you," he said with a wink.

The Senator smiled at the joke, but his good humor was short-lived. "We need to give the people something to look *forward to*," he said. "We must give them an aspiration. A national dream, if you will. We must give them a public works project where America can flex the muscles of manifest destiny."

Douglas turned away from the Senator and looked squarely at Ben.

"So, Mr. Freeman. How long have you known my friend John here?"

Ben sat frozen, still in the midst of comprehending that the Little Giant was indeed asking him a question.

"Come now — Ben, was it? It isn't a difficult question."

Ben searched for the answer. "Well," he said, "I think...I think it's about twenty years. Most of my life, at least."

"I see," Douglas said, smiling. "I always found it fascinating that our friend John here, a young nobody from nowhere, could have possibly wooed not one but *two* daughters of the First Families of Virginia. People can say what they will of our friend

John, but they cannot say he is not ambitious. He never seems to rest, our John. He's always in the midst of some project or other."

Here, Douglas leveled a wry sort of smile in the Senator's direction. For the very first time, Ben saw John Roscoe deflate in the presence of another.

"JR has always been a friend of the Valley," Cutler said, rejoining the conversation. "What's more, he's become *part* of the Valley."

"Indeed?" Douglas said.

Ben felt the need to support the Senator somehow. "I've known John Roscoe most of my life, as I said. And I've known him to be an honest, forthright man. In all things, he does the right thing. Perhaps that is why the Spencer family embraced him, Senator Douglas. Like attracts like. In this case, good attracted good."

Douglas grinned at Ben, as if he knew well enough that Ben hadn't meant what he said. But Ben *did* mean what he said. Didn't he?

Meanwhile, the Senator's eyes continued to sparkle with genuine hope. "No more jokes, Stephen," he said. "No more distractions. Tell me the news from the Committee on Territories. Tell me when I can expect my railroad bill to be brought up for the vote."

Here, Douglas' grin soured. "Need I remind you, John, that this is not *your* bill — not yet. To speak of it as such puts both of us in a difficult position."

The Senator laughed. "Need I remind *you*, Stephen, to leave the cloak and dagger back in the Senate lobby. We can speak frankly here, can we not? So speak up, I beg you. When can we expect shovels in the ground for my railroad?"

Douglas leaned across the table and spoke slowly, as if he was addressing a child. "I've told you time and again, John, you've no need to worry. The contract to build the national railroad will be yours, but only *after* I win the election."

That seemed to be the end of it. Senator Roscoe, though quiet, still seemed pleased with Douglas' remarks.

But after a brief pause, Douglas added in a low murmur: "And if the bill survives the filibuster."

The Senator choked on his drink. "*If?*" he echoed, his eyes bulging with disbelief. "What do you mean *if?*"

Across the table, Tobias Cutler's eyes narrowed with intense interest.

"I mean *if*," Douglas said. "You know better than anyone the Republicans are expected to win most of the Northern seats next year, in the House and in the Senate. Even if I gain the White House, no vote will be a sure thing. The Republicans would have the ability, perhaps even the power, to rally enough Democrats to kill a vote they don't like — *especially* one that is not Republican versus Democrat, but North versus South."

The Senator became exasperated. "What man calling himself a patriotic American doesn't like territorial expansion? America will finally sweep the reds aside, finally settle those lands and claim our right as a continental power. *Finally*, West and East will be united as one."

Douglas shook his head. "But your proposal to link them via the *South*, with your railroad beginning in Richmond, is not exactly a popular idea in the North."

Cutler harrumphed. "Of course not. Yankees and their Quaker jealousy..."

"Stephen," the Senator said, "I think you've been reading too many Northern newspapers. The Democrats will maintain their majorities in both houses. And with a Democrat in the White House—"

"There is still only so much I can do," Douglas said. "It's no secret to anyone that President Buchanan — the Democrat currently *in* the White House — loathes me more than Lucifer. He's going to award me no favors in the meantime, certainly none to my allies."

The Senator put his head in his hands. "This cannot be," he murmured. "This cannot *be*."

"Fear not," Douglas said with a reassuring smile. "Buchanan made a fine move, but it's no check-mate. When *I'm* president, it will be nothing for me to arrange the pieces how I like. You might even decide to forgo your toy trains, JR, and consider a project of a different sort." Douglas' voice went low. "The vice presidency, for instance. How would you like it, John, to take your seat behind the Senate rostrum?"

The Senator's eyes misted with rageful tears, a rare sight for the old man. "I'm sick of the goddamn Senate," he growled, his whole body shaking. "I want the *railroad*."

A thick, smoky silence hung over the table, and the rollicking sounds of the tavern became louder. The attention of several men surrounding them, alerted by the Senator's outburst, looked upon the strained scene with watchful eyes.

Through gritted teeth, Douglas murmured, "And you'll get it, John, *in good time*. Until then, be prepared for coming amendments. With all due respect, I would rather pass *a* railroad bill than *your* railroad bill. We must consider the possibility that, in order to build a railroad at all, it may need to have a Northern terminus, such as Chicago. Why, the infrastructure is already there under the Illinois Central Railroad. No doubt you will have a say in the project's operations, John. But I'm sure you can understand that Chicago has the necessary talent and experience to really get the railroad up and running. You should meet their president, he's a bright young lad named George McClellan. Reminds me of your JJ a little, in fact. Very serious, very capable. Next time he's in Washington, I'll set up a luncheon. Maybe you could invite JJ, and we could all—"

"This isn't *right*," the Senator growled. "I had your assurances that the bill would pass, and easily. I had your assurances I could run the railroad at my pleasure, together with the choice of its eastern terminus. And now you speak about Chicago? You say there's some *other* party that's inserted itself into the affair? Stephen, this isn't what we *agreed*."

Douglas' reply was stiff. The Little Giant appeared to be losing patience, and quickly. "What we agreed upon may soon be an impossibility, John. If, as president, I'm faced with treasonous radicals on both sides of the Mason-Dixon, then charging blindly westward with a multi-million-dollar railroad will do nothing more than bog my administration down in a quagmire of territorial pissings. You'll just have to trust me on this."

The Senator's patience, meanwhile, had long since vanished. "You can't mean this," he said, his voice shrill with desperation. "You gave me your assurances, Stephen. Your *assurances* that the national railroad would go to Virginia, that it would pass through the American heartland like a life-giving artery. I've *promised* my constituents—"

"I gave you no assurances of any kind," Douglas growled. His candid conduct had eroded at last. "If you've made promises you can't keep, that is your own misstep. I won't be pegged for a mess I had no part in making, and Lord knows I've made my share of messes in the past. We only ever spoke of possibilities, John, never certainties. And obviously I can do nothing to explore *any* possibilities regarding the railroad until I am president. Until then, my word ought to be enough. It *will* be enough."

A strained silence persisted. Ben watched as the Senator withdrew into himself, his gray eyes gloomy and portentous. Douglas gave a dismissive shrug and wet his lips with brandy, remarking loudly about its fine quality. Cutler watched both men keenly, his trenchant gaze flitting from one to the other in turn.

Suddenly, a drunk man approached Douglas from behind and clapped him on the shoulders. "Congratulations, *Mr. President*!"

The dreary mood at the table became one of forced jollity. Senator Roscoe and Douglas laughed together as a number of drunken men burst into applause and singing. One of the men began to sing *For He's a Jolly Good Fellow* until nearly the entire tavern was in an uproar. The Senator sang as loudly as anyone, but his song was one of bellowing rage, the words devoid of their happy meaning. Cutler, meanwhile, downed a second and then a third glass of brandy and waited for the whole charade to be over.

After the song ended, Ben looked around and noticed even more men with flowered lapels scattered across the room. These men bought drinks by the score for others, and that didn't count the hundred glasses of brandy Douglas had just ordered. Everywhere, Ben heard exuberant voices extolling the virtues of a Democratic Party led by one Stephen Douglas.

"Why do they congratulate you now?" Cutler said. "The Convention only starts tomorrow, and you may very well lose. Then all your 'once I'm president' stratagems against your enemies will be for naught."

Douglas indicated the drunken chaos around them. "I don't know with any certainty how the Party's delegates will vote tomorrow, Mr. Cutler." He winked. "All I know is that my staff is working very hard to ensure the delegates vote the way I'd prefer."

Cutler took a glass and finished most of it in one gulp. "I know many men who won't vote for you tomorrow, Mr. Douglas. I hate to say it, but it's true. Our Christian civilization is under threat from all sides: from abolitionists, Papists, Jews, and all those so-called Northern Democrats who claim to be friends of the South, yet work toward our destruction."

Douglas shrugged. "You describe quite the conspiracy, to be sure. But we put your friend Buchanan in the White House for you, didn't we? Where else could you find a Northern president with explicitly pro-Southern, pro-slavery sympathies? Of course, it wasn't much help that Buchanan was an asinine fool, but he'll soon be gone. I fully intend on breathing new life into the Executive Mansion come inauguration day."

"It's all the fault of the Republicans," Cutler said. "They are openly hostile to the Southern way of life. William Seward of New York has all but predicted civil war, suggesting the elimination of slavery is part of some 'irrepressible conflict' that must be fought out, sooner or later. And as you know, Seward is going to be the Republican candidate. So what exactly do you plan on doing about him?"

Douglas grinned. "Defeat him, of course. Why, what is your suggestion?"

"*I* say the South must act preemptively to avoid such a terrible fate as a Seward presidency," Cutler declared. "I'm among the men who understand that the best way to prevent tyranny from infecting Washington is to start over; rebuild America such that it can withstand dangerous and oppressive ideas that are seeping into the Federal system. We envision a republic within the Republic, a ready-made nation that can abandon the Union if and when it succumbs to Black Republican dogma. If we are faced with the likes of a President Seward, wouldn't you agree secession is a justifiable course of action?"

Douglas did not flinch. "Secession! Of course not. You speak of a fantasy world at best, Mr. Cutler, and sedition at worst. The election of a president by the American people, in conformity with the Constitution, would not justify any attempt to dissolve the Union itself. Sometimes the player you don't like wins the game, Mr. Cutler, and that is that. And your solution is to abandon democracy altogether?"

"Unless the next president is a Southerner," Cutler replied.

Douglas balked. "So his being a Democrat is no longer enough for you?"

Cutler shrugged. "Even with a friendly administration, it is still the case that our democracy is under attack from within. There are extremists who—"

"You speak of destroying democratic institutions because you feel they have wronged you in some way," Douglas interjected. "In that sense, you are no different from John Brown or any other radical."

"I resent that!" Cutler barked. Red-faced, he downed the last of his brandy. "The Constitution was ratified by state conventions, not a binding referendum. The states delegated certain aspects of governance to a federal entity, but they did not surrender their inherent sovereignty. Therefore, if a state entered the Union willingly, it ought to be able to leave the Union at will."

Douglas shrugged. "I know a constitutional lawyer who would think otherwise."

"And I know another who would agree with me," Cutler snarled. The Judge took a deep breath to collect himself, but it was all in vain. The blotchy veins in his face looked about to burst. "Suppose Seward was to send troops down here to Charleston the day after his election. The invasion of a state by the Federal government or any other state is blatantly criminal, that much is true. Tell me then, Mr. Douglas. Would you support the South's secession after the Yankees turn their guns on their neighbors?"

"No," Douglas said.

"*No?!*"

"First of all, the idea of an unprovoked Northern invasion of the South is ridiculous."

"Provocations are fickle things," Cutler said. "Countless wars have been sparked by causes less profound than personal trifles."

Douglas added with an impatient growl of warning, "And there are always fools ready to fight them, or else convince poor saps to fight it for him. But if there is to be any conflict, the first shot would have to be from the gun of a revolutionary, a bullet fired in anger upon the Union flag or someone in its service. Any man who makes war upon the United States has already lost, no matter the apparent virtue of his cause." Finally, Douglas' sour pout brightened and he laughed. "But all of this doesn't matter anyway, Mr. Cutler."

Cutler's eyes flashed with indignation. "What do you mean it *doesn't matter?!*"

Douglas flashed a haughty grin. "There won't *be* a war, Mr. Cutler, and there won't *be* a President Seward in the Executive Mansion next year. There will only be me."

Cutler cleared his throat. "Allow me to be abundantly clear, Mr. Douglas. If you want to win the presidency in November, you will first need the support of Southern Democrats. While the North has turned staunchly Republican in the last few years, the Democratic Party has become the champion of patriotic, native-born Americans. Nowhere can you find more true-blooded Americans than in the Southland. And this year's election will be the South's last chance to make its voice heard. By 1864, the North's population — meaning the ranks of the Republicans — will be too numerous to overcome. *This* election, 1860, the South *must* be victorious. And the new president *must* make sweeping electoral changes to ensure the South's survival in the hard years to come. Therefore, the Democratic nominee for president must be a man who is prepared to defend the South against the Yankee mob at all costs."

Here, Cutler leaned in over the table and spoke in a conspiratorial whisper.

"Commit yourself to the South, Mr. Douglas, and we will give the White House to you, just as you once gave it Buchanan. But if you will not commit yourself..."

Douglas sniffed with indignation. "So there are terms to your patriotism? Your love of Union is conditional?"

"Democracy is a social contract," Cutler replied. "The Republicans and their abolitionist base want to tear the contract to pieces. I, and the men I represent, simply want the contract we signed to be enforced. Even better, we want it amended."

Douglas had been sipping his brandy while Cutler spoke. Suddenly the Little Giant choked and spat. His eyes bulged wide with disbelief.

"*Amend* the Constitution?"

Cutler shrugged. "Nothing new about that, is there? It's a living document, after all."

Douglas shook his head furiously. "Not *that*, you idiot. There hasn't been an amendment in sixty years, and for good reason. You are actually suggesting I campaign on the promise that every damn citizen of the Union ought to own an African washerwoman? You want me to sign a decree that every American has a right to life, liberty, and a whip to keep his negroes in line?"

"It need be nothing quite so extreme," Cutler said.

"*Bah*!" Douglas cried. "Here we have a *moderate* secessionist." Douglas turned angrily to the Senator. "Are you *listening* to this, John? This is the company you keep?"

The Senator blushed a deep red. He opened his mouth to reply, but—

"JR supports the idea," Cutler said. "He assured me that you would be open to a possible amendment. At least in terms of political expediency, you'd give it consideration."

Douglas spat the word back. "Consideration?! It's political suicide."

By now, the duel between Douglas and Cutler had attracted the attention of not a few curious onlookers. As the two men sparred, their audience grew larger.

Cutler reached into his jacket pocket and produced a small letter. "It's really rather simple," he said. "Alexander Stephens of Georgia, together with myself, drafted a fine version of the proposed 13th Amendment. Allow me, Mr. Douglas:

"'Section One: The cornerstone of the United States' government rests upon the great truth that the negro is not equal to the white man; that slavery subordination to the superior race is his natural and normal condition. Section Two: Congress shall have no power to repeal this article, but shall have power to enforce it by appropriate legislation.'"

Douglas bellowed with laughter, but there was no joy in his voice. Rather, he seemed to be trying to draw attention to the table so that he would have witnesses to his ensuing lambasting of Tobias Cutler.

"This has to be some kind of joke."

Cutler was keenly aware of the attention now fixed on their debate. "I assure you, sir, this is no joke. The Convention opens tomorrow morning. You will need the support of all Southern delegates in order to clinch the nomination. William Yancey, Jefferson Davis, Robert Toombs — these are all fine and respectable patriots. What if one of those men should be nominated to the ticket in your place? Do you think you could muster the necessary votes to defeat a man like Davis, for example?"

"Davis and all the others are Southern nationalists," Douglas replied. "They would rather see my head on a spike before—"

"They know you would be more than capable in the White House," Cutler affirmed. "But before they would even consider supporting you, they need to know that you have their interests at heart. This goes beyond a man's word. This requires a demonstration of your commitment." Cutler held his letter aloft. "And this here is a good start."

Douglas had turned purple with rage. "If we take a pro-slavery platform into the national contest, the Republicans will eat us alive! Don't you see? They already *have* the numbers they need to wrest the presidency from us. The only faction Northerners detest more than the damned abolitionists are the bloody Southern nationalists. Why? Because abolitionists and Fire Eaters alike would rather see the Union destroyed than give an inch to their mortal enemies — which is to say, *anyone* who does not agree with them. If we appeal only to the most radical sections of our base, every moderate voter in America will be forced to vote Republican."

The Senator leaned into the conversation. "If I may, Stephen. Without a united South behind you, your bid for the White House will never succeed. A select few calculated concessions to Mr. Cutler and his allies is a small price to pay for—"

"I refuse to concede anything to disunionists," Douglas snapped. "I'm disappointed in you, JR. If we give *anything* to those fire-eating bastards, they will be back again demanding more, more, more. Charm a snake and he'll bite you all the same."

Cutler grinned. "I see only one snake at this table, Mr. Douglas. It's clear you despise anyone who disagrees with you. You despise a proud society founded on Christian ideals and which command the most powerful economy the world has ever seen. You despise Southerners and the Southern states alike, maybe because you are jealous and resentful. And yet you think you are fit to be president of the *United* States? You live in a world of delusions."

Charged for a fight, Douglas downed his brandy and puffed his cheeks. "I *despise* no man and no section, sir, unless that man or section defies the Union."

"*Here-here*!" a voice called from the crowd.

Cutler turned to confront the stranger, but Douglas was already pushing on. "Your personal, childish effrontery to the simple statement of facts and honorable pledges is the only thing at this table that I could say I despise," Douglas said.

Red-faced, Cutler slammed his fist down on the table. "*Traitor*!"

This accusation shattered the hubbub of the tavern. For a long moment, all was silence.

Gazes fixed on Tobias Cutler, who brought up a bleeding hand glittering with shards of broken glass. Undeterred, Cutler swept his arm across the table, knocking several glasses and dishes to the floor, and now he rocketed to his feet and towered over Douglas. His eyes, blazing with contempt, were fixed on the little man sitting across the table.

"Insult me all you like," Cutler snarled. "Just know, Mr. Douglas, that should you spurn the South tomorrow at the Convention, the South *will* respond. Should you try to deliver the Democratic Party into the hands of men who pander to foreigners and abolitionists in order to keep a grip on power, the South *will* sabotage you. We will sink your hopes for the presidency. Not only that, but we will also consider it our moral duty to watch you flounder in the storm you yourself have conjured. Adieu, Mr. Douglas."

With that, Cutler turned his back on Douglas. Before abandoning the table completely, Cutler lingered to deliver a meaningful look toward Senator Roscoe. A silent message was exchanged between them, but the Senator's back was turned and Ben could not read his reaction. Cutler ignored a shower of jeers and vitriol.

"Bastard!"

"Massa needs some shut-eye, boys."

"Traitorous cur!"

Cutler slammed the tavern door shut behind him, and this inspired a great cheer from the tavern's crowd of drunks. But slowly, men turned back into their circles and began to talk excitedly amongst themselves. Drinks began to flow and the music started up again. Soon enough, the whole episode was forgotten.

Ben surveyed the destruction on the table: shards of broken glass, rivers of running liquor, abandoned plates of half-eaten, brandy-soaked sandwiches. Looking up at the Senator, Ben tried to draw some meaning from the old man's cloudy gaze but found it impenetrable. Stephen Douglas, meanwhile, sat back and heaved a weary sigh.

"Well," he said, finishing the last of his drink. "I suppose that could have gone better."

Putting his head in his hands, the Senator groaned, "My God, Stephen...What have you done?"

"What have *I* done?" Douglas exclaimed. "The better question is what *we* shall do together, John. Tomorrow, democracy will have its day."

At the next table, a man stood up. "Three cheers for Steve Douglas!"

And all around the tavern, drunken voices shouted together:

HIP-HIP HOORAY, HIP-HIP-HOORAY, HIP-HIP-HOORAY!

Chapter 19

THE LONG RIFLE

The April earth was cold, parts of it still frozen and snow-covered, but the sky over the Valley was a clear blue and the sun felt warm for the first time in months.

As Tom and Jem walked along the mountain path, Tom rolled his shoulder in its socket and listened for curious pops and clicks. His shoulder had healed fairly well, but there was a lingering stiffness. Sometimes the nerves running up and down his arm got themselves twisted into pinching bundles of pain. The only solution was to shake his arm and try to 'work out the kinks,' as Mae Jane put it.

Jem, meanwhile, strode ahead with vibrant energy. Though there had been no fanfare to it, Jem had given up drinking months ago, after a particularly nightmarish bender following the incidents of both JJ's leaving and the runaway Cutler slave.

Jem was looking brighter and stronger, and he claimed to feel the effects of good health even as he exuded them. All this, Jem had been spending precious little time at home. He went to work each morning as usual, but he was rarely home otherwise. Just what was Jem doing with all his time if he wasn't spending it drinking with George Hunt and Sugar Dave Dixon?

Of course, Tom had considered that perhaps Miss Blake was involved somehow.

There had been many clues supporting that theory, but it was all but confirmed when Jem burst into Tom's bedroom earlier that day at dawn. Hurrying about the place, Jem announced that he was taking Tom hunting on the northeast slope of the North Branch that very day.

"But I still have school tomorrow," Tom had groaned, one eye still shut with sleep. "I have school *today*."

"I already told Miss Blake that you're sick," Jem said breezily. He went to the window shutters and opened them, letting in more bluish predawn light. "Besides, you'll be heading downstate next week. Off to your new school, hm? No more dirt floors and all that. Off to your little *institution*. Oh yes, to your asylum, Tom, where you'll finally fit in with all the other drooling crazies."

Tom threw his pillow at Jem, who caught it with a laugh. Tom fell back on his mattress and groaned.

"Come on," Jem said. "We'll go hunting, go check my traps at least. For old time's sake. When was the last time it was just me and you?"

Tom really thought about that. In fact, he couldn't remember the last time he and Jem had spent much time together. Come to think of it he couldn't remember the last time all the Roscoe brothers, and Ben too, had been together. Just that one dinner back in November, but that hadn't really counted because the rest of the family was there too. It had been years since the boys had gone traipsing through the woods together, just themselves.

With the Roscoes, the hunt was really all about *the hunt*. No time was spent on carousing or idling the day away. Instead, the brothers became like a tiny war party embarking on a mission of utmost importance. JJ was an expert tracker, Jem the best shot Tom had ever seen, and Ben could carry two dozen traps on his shoulders the distance of ten miles and not show signs of tiring. Still lodged in Tom's mind were fragmented memories of *other* times, older times, when Tom had tagged along but was still too young to appreciate much. He remembered complaining and looking after Bayard, who really shouldn't have been part of the expedition at all.

Here on the northeast slope of the North Branch, Tom could see the sun rising fast. He and Jem picked their way on foot along an overgrown path. The horses Mabel and Greenbrier, laden with traps and other hunting gear, trudged along with them.

As they hiked, Tom looked up at a few patches of thin gray clouds smeared over the brilliant blue. The clouds rushed across the sky at a feverish pace, and Tom realized the wind must be stronger way up there than it was down near the ground. Here on the mountain path there was barely a whisper of wind; but way up in the sky, where the faded moon still lay nestled in the blue, the winds had to be gale-force.

"Breath of a Yankee witch," Tom murmured.

"What's that?"

Tom shook his head. "Nothing. Just something Mae Jane says sometimes."

They pushed on.

After a time, Jem asked, "Are you getting along with her?"

"With who?"

"What, cobwebs in your ears? Mae Jane, of course."

"Oh." Tom shrugged. "Fine, I guess."

"She deserves more respect than you give her, Tom."

"Why? She ain't our mother."

"*Isn't*."

"*Isn't* our mother. There. Happy?"

Jem shook his head. "Doesn't matter. She's been more a mother to you, to all of us, than—"

"That's not true," Tom said. "Mother is mother. Father is father."

"If that's the way you feel about it."

On the left, something crashed through the bushes. Tom tensed, fearing the approach of some monstrous bear or mountain lion. But now he saw Tipper the dog burst from the thickets with a happy smile, his tongue lolling, his fur covered in leaves and mud. Almost immediately Tipper discovered a new scent and set to tracking it. Greenbrier saw the dog approaching and stamped his hooves in protest, so Tipper kept his distance and loped ahead.

"That damn dog's going to scare off the whole country," Jem said.

"He's a good dog," Tom said.

"Sure he is. But he's not fit for hunting."

"Get yourself a hound then."

"I might. One of these days."

Tom gave a mocking laugh. "You never do any of the things you say you'll do."

Jem opened his mouth in a snarl as if to tell Tom to shut up, but after a moment he only turned away and trudged on in silence.

They pushed on for a time, with Jem leading the way. After they advanced another quarter mile, Jem looked back and said, "What do you mean by it?"

"By what?" Tom said.

"By what you just said, idiot. That I don't do the things I say."

Tom shrugged. "I dunno. You got no shortage of ideas. You just don't see em through."

"Listen to yourself," Jem said. "Hanging around those school-pals of yours has shrunken your brain. 'I *don't* know. You *have* no shortage. Don't see *them* through.'"

"It ain't — *isn't* — courteous to correct a man's grammar."

"Oh yeah? Who said that?"

"Miss Blake said so."

There was a long pause as Jem considered this new information. Finally he shook his head and grumbled, "Up this way, and hurry up. We're burning daylight."

The morning stretched on. They left the path and picked their way along the eastern slope of the North Branch. They paused along a ridge and Jem poured each of them a cup of coffee, cold now after two hours of walking, and they stared out at the vast Shenandoah Valley.

Jem pointed to a distant cluster of smoke tendrils rising from puffing chimneys. "That's Winchester there."

"How far away?"

"A day's ride at least, through this country," Jem said. He finished his coffee. "But I don't know for sure. I've never gone that far." He pitched the coffee grinds from his cup over the side of the ridge. "Always said I would. I suppose it's just like you said, isn't it?"

They stood there for a long time gazing out at the wider Shenandoah, what in Mayfair everyone called the *Great* Valley. Somewhere over there, obscured by the knotted trees and green hills, the Shenandoah River flowed northeast to meet the mighty Potomac at Harper's Ferry. Tom pointed out a column of smoke that was presently carving a path through the sea of trees and rightly guessed it was a train. They stood in silence, and finally their ears perked at the distant sound of the chugging locomotive.

"Wonder where it's off to," Tom said. He turned to Jem. "How far do the trains go west?"

"St. Louis, I think," Jem said. "Somewhere in Missouri, anyway."

"*Missouri.*" The word tasted exotic on Tom's tongue, as rich-sounding to his ears as Peking or Timbuktu. "You think Father still means to take us there?"

Jem shrugged. He pointed northward, vaguely in the direction of Harper's Ferry. "If you can get on a B&O train, you could ride an engine all the way out to St. Louis. That's right on the Mississippi River. Cross the river and you've gone as far west as most people ever get."

"We'll get farther," Tom assured him.

Tom was still looking out at the vista when Jem turned and gathered up the steel traps lashed to Greenbrier.

"We'll leave the horses here," Jem said. "I've got some old traps nearby, just down this slope."

Tom was very aware of Greenbrier's watchful eyes. The stringy colt, who usually wasted no opportunity to chomp at Tom when he wasn't paying attention, now seemed to appeal to Tom's sense of empathy. The brute seemed awfully concerned about Jem's plan to leave him behind. Nearby, Mabel sniffed the sparse grass without care.

"What about the horses?" Tom asked. "There could be wolves."

"There aren't any wolves in the Shenandoah," Jem said. "Not anymore." He patted Greenbrier's fibrous neck. "And coyotes won't come anywhere near these two."

Tom looked at Greenbrier again. The horse clearly wasn't convinced, and neither was Tom. "What about cougars? Or bears?"

"Horses are smart," Jem said. "Nothing can sneak up on these two. If anything tries, they can outrun them."

"Horses ain't—"

"Aren't."

"Horses aren't built for running up and down mountains."

Jem sighed. "Just hurry up and get your things, Tom. You carry the traps, hm?"

They followed the ridge until it eased to a gentle slope. Tom lumbered under the weight of the traps and tilted his head up so that the rank bait would not overpower his nostrils. Jem trudged ahead with the Colonel's long rifle slung over his shoulder. To keep his mind busy, Tom silently rhymed off everything he knew about the long rifle.

It was an old Model 1814 designed by somebody named Wickham, the fifty-ninth of the famed 'First 1000' produced by somebody else named Deringer. The barrel was 33 inches long and loaded a .54 caliber bullet. The Colonel had never used the rifle in combat, but it had accompanied him on many hunting trips during lulls in the New Orleans campaign during the Second War of Independence (what the British called the War of 1812). The Colonel's long rifle was the weapon responsible for all the stuffed trophies in Clarendon's library. The rifle's stock was flame maple, with a silver inlay that depicted twin eagles clashing in mid-air.

Over time, the dueling eagles had become something of a family sigil. The same image was etched into the stock of the Colonel's long rifle, on the grips of a pair of old pistols, and even into the hilt of the Colonel's cavalry saber.

The story went that, on the night before the Battle of New Orleans, the Colonel had seen two eagles, one white and one red, slashing at each other in the fading light of dusk. The Colonel had fired a shot that passed between them, but the eagles kept fighting until they plummeted to their deaths.

"That's true?" Tom asked, trying to picture the eagles falling like meteors, their talons tangled together.

"Of course it's true," Jem said. "The Colonel never told a lie, you know. He was a good man. A *great* man. It's a pity he didn't live longer. You would have liked him."

Tom nodded and said nothing. It felt strange to hear so many stories about his grandfather, to be named after him even, and to have never met him. Tom didn't even know what the Colonel really looked like, because none of his portraits looked the same.

"Mother's told me all the stories," Jem said. "Stories she's long since forgotten about. You know the Colonel met General Washington during the Revolution? He was a drummer in the Continental Army, no older than Bayard at the time. Can you imagine? Redcoats firing at you, men dying all around you, and you've just barely grown beyond the age where you still shit your pants."

Tom wailed with laughter.

"To be fair," Jem said, laughing with Tom, "I'd expect it would be easy to forget all that wisdom when the bullets start flying."

The brothers laughed together. They pushed on, their hearts and feet lightened by good humor. Tom imagined they were on a fur-trapping expedition somewhere way far north, where the breath of Yankee witches blew without ceasing. But the more Tom imagined, the larger he wished their company was. Two trappers were not nearly enough.

"Bayard would have liked this," Tom said. "And Ben too."

"Ben's gone down south with Father," Jem said. "And Bayard, well...Mother's become more protective of him of late. You know how it is."

Tom didn't really know how it was, but he nodded anyway. As they walked along, another thought popped into Tom's head.

"You and Ben don't talk much anymore."

Jem didn't stop outright, but his steady pace slowed noticeably. Jem kept his gaze fixed on some far-off point.

"We do talk," Jem said. "It's just that, well, maybe we have different ideas. Different ideas about how the world works."

Tom was quiet for a time. After a long silence, he said, "I seen you hit him. Ben, I mean. I was watching from the window."

Jem said nothing and kept walking. Tom was starting to wonder whether he should repeat himself when—

"Saw."

"What?"

"I *saw* you hit him," Jem said, his voice raspy. "*Saw*, not *seen*."

Tom shrugged. "All right."

They pushed on in silence. After they crested the next hill, Tom felt it a good time to speak up again.

"I saw the slave they took away too. The one Ben tried to hide. Ben said he was innocent."

"Innocent has nothing to do with it," Jem snapped, his voice raw and irritated. "For all Ben's talk about the law, he likes to ignore the ones he doesn't agree with. The Fugitive Slave Law says it's illegal to harbor or help runaways. That law extends all across the Union. And until such time as Congress decides to do away with that law, it is *the law*. So if you can't adhere to that one law, then what good are all the others? Besides, the Cutlers knew that runaway better than the rest of us did, and *they* said he was dangerous. What reason would they have for lying about such a thing?"

Jem pushed on, moving faster. Adjusting the weight of the traps, Tom trudged after his brother. He was sweating from the effort of carrying the traps uphill and downhill, seemingly with no end in sight. He felt himself start to lag behind, to lose interest in their surroundings. It was all just *trees*, in every direction, as far as the eye could see.

Up ahead, Tipper barked and crashed through the undergrowth.

"Here, Tipper!" Jem cried.

Tom looked up. Tipper was frolicking in the bushes ahead, perhaps triggered by the sight of some tiny animal. Tipper thrust his rump in the air and barked at a small burrow next to a fallen tree.

"Call your damn dog, Tom."

"Tipper! Tipper! C'mere, boy."

The dog barked and came trotting back, his tail wagging.

His face grave, Jem pointed at the thick cover of dead leaves spread out before them. "Keep him close by your side, Tom. He might walk right into somebody's old forgotten trap-jaws and it would be all over for him."

They found the first trap near a marked tree. The mechanism of the jaws had been triggered, but whatever animal had snatched the bait had made off seemingly without a scratch. The tracks were two weeks old, and maybe older.

"We'd need to be Chickahominy to make any more sense of it," Jem said.

Tom helped bait and reset the trap, and they pushed on.

Farther along they found a hare, or rather what remained of a hare, snagged in the next trap. Disturbed leaves were crusty with dried blood, and something had torn most of the hare's body loose from the trap-jaws. All that remained was part of the dead animal's foot. Covered with maggots, the foot squirmed as if it was alive.

Jem wrapped his hand in a handkerchief, pulled the foot free, and held it up for Tom to see.

"Rabbit's foot. It's your lucky day, Tom."

They laughed, and then Jem pitched the foot into the trees. Tipper gave a pitiful whine. He was eager to run after such a fine trophy, but he stayed put at Tom's command.

"It's too bad," Tom said as he watched Jem lay down a fresh trap. "Rabbit's my favorite."

"You've got that squirrel gun," Jem said. "You might get lucky and spy one."

"Can I use the rifle?"

"No. Not until you're older."

"I *am* older. I'm thirteen now, and a full month into it."

"Father didn't let me touch the rifle until I was fifteen."

"But you're not Father," Tom noted. "You can break the rules if you want. Make up your own. Whatever they are, I'll follow them."

Jem laughed. "Sneaky knave. You're just trying to butter me up. All right, new rule. Walk on your hands and eat with your feet 'til sundown. Hey, get to it!"

They pressed on through the woods. Jem said he was hopeful to find foxes in the late afternoon, once they ventured up the slope to find shade in the Branch's shadow.

"Foxes wait until the sun shines right into a burrow hole," Jem explained. "Their prey is blind when it comes out, and the fox can pick them right up. And if we're lucky, maybe we'll spot some deer. There are usually whitetails yonder, where the thickets thin out."

While Jem talked, Tom's mind was busy thinking about other things. An idea took hold of him, and he spoke up before he had a chance to really think about it.

"JJ's a sodomite," Tom said suddenly. "He's a nancy-boy. That's why Father sent him away, wasn't it?"

At first, Jem did not seem to hear him, but now Jem looked back over his shoulder.

"JJ is your brother, Tom. There's no reason to call him anything other than that.

Besides, there was more to it than just that."

Tom shrugged. "I heard the big argument that night, back last autumn. Most of it, anyway. I sat on the stairs and listened. I heard the shouting and the gunshot... and the crying."

Jem said nothing and quickened his pace.

Tom followed behind. "The Bible says sodomites are sinners. I looked it up. Says they should be outcast and punished and killed with stones. Says God burned down a whole city full of them, and turned to stone a lady who looked back. But what is it that's wrong with them exactly?"

"Tom, you're too young to talk about these things."

"I told you, I'm thirteen. In the Revolution days I'd have killed my first redcoat already."

Jem laughed. "I'd bet on it."

Tom halted and refused to go farther until Jem provided an answer.

Sighing, Jem turned around and faced him. "Do I really need to explain it all?"

Tom nodded. "I tried to ask Mae Jane about it. She said there's no such thing. There's only those who sin, and those who don't."

Jem unslung the long rifle. He made room so they could walk side-by-side through the underbrush. "I'll make this as simple as I can," he said. "Sleeping with a woman is sinful, unless she's your wife. That's what the Bible says, anyway. It's what Mother and Father say too. And it's what *I* say, so at the very least you should listen to me."

Tom furrowed his brow. "What's wrong with just sleeping—?"

"Come on, Tom. You know what I mean."

Tom thought he knew, but...he didn't *know* he knew. Thirteen was old enough to know lots about the world, but not everything. Still, he wasn't going to ask Jem to spell it all out for him, or at least not right now.

"Well," Tom said. "Have you ever...you know...*slept?*"

Jem blinked, looking as if he'd just been stung on the nose. His eyes narrowed and he glared at Tom. "That's irrelevant. Besides, it's none of your damn business."

Tom suppressed a grin. So the answer was yes!

"Was it Miss Blake? Oh, tell me it was! Tell me it *is*! I can't wait to tell Billy about this and—"

Jem suddenly grabbed Tom by the shirt collar and shook him, and his scowl filled the whole of Tom's vision. "Let's just keep to the one subject. And you're not going to breathe a word of any of this to *anyone*. All right?"

When Tom said nothing, Jem shook him again, harder.

"All right?"

"All right, all right!" Tom cried. "*Laws*, some temper..."

Grudgingly, Jem let Tom go and turned down the trail again.

Tom hurried to keep up. Far from feeling cowed, an impish grin flashed across Tom's face. So it really *was* true: Jem and Miss Blake were lovers! And based on Jem's reaction, they were *secret* lovers too. The whole thing reminded Tom of those sappy romance novels that Sarah liked to read. In order for such a story to be even half interesting, Tom knew there needed to be guns and Indians and a kidnapping, and stolen treasure of some kind, and—

"Are you in love with Miss Blake or something?"

Jem stopped again and Tom flinched, waiting for the delivery of some nasty retort. But instead Jem looked at him with a shy smile.

"Or something," Jem said.

They walked on again, slower now. Tom's impish grin returned. "I knew it! You gonna marry her?"

Jem shrugged and smiled. "I'm going to ask her, at least. One day. But that doesn't mean she'll say yes."

"She'll say yes," Tom said.

Jem laughed. "Well, I certainly hope you're right."

"Father doesn't want you to ask her, does he?" Tom said. "He says you should marry somebody else. Cousin Talia, maybe, or Cousin India from Fredericksburg. Or maybe that Claiborne girl."

Jem's gaze was fixed straight ahead. "Father says a lot of things," he said grimly.

"Sure, but you always do them."

"What?"

"I mean, you do what he says. Whatever Father tells you, you always see it through."

Jem's shoulders tensed up. "Father may suggest a course of action, but it's *me* who chooses which course to take."

Tom nodded his understanding, but he didn't exactly believe what Jem had said.

"You're still young," Jem said. "But soon enough, Tom, you'll discover that the world is full of folks itching to tell you what you can and can't do, and most folks have opinions aplenty on the latter point. At some stage, folks made a rule that men can only love women. That rule came naturally enough I'd say, but some folks took it to heart that to deviate from that rule meant some sickness had taken hold of you. Later on somebody made a rule that you can only love someone with the same color skin that you have. Again, it makes sense where the rule came from, though I can't say whether it's *right* or not. And in time, somebody like Father made *another* rule, one that you can only love someone who looks like you, meaning who dresses and acts like you. Probably some lonely, snot-nosed bastard who was tired of rejection suddenly found himself in a position of influence and decreed that a 'gentleman' can't marry a 'mud-eater.' And on and on and on, with a thousand contradictions in between."

Tom said, "I take it you don't like all those rules then."

Jem laughed. "Not particularly. But what use is it shouting down the wind? The point is, so far as I can tell, Father was a mud-eater himself once upon a time. He came up from nowhere selling cotton gins, and that's how he came to meet the Colonel. That's how he came to meet Mother. I don't exactly know how he made that leap from trash to gentry, but he did it. It's men like Father, the ones who pass through that door, who try hardest to shut the door behind them."

Tom nodded. "I reckon at some point, somebody made a rule that some folks had to be slaves, and others had to be masters. What do you make of that?"

Jem shrugged. "That's for every man to decide for himself. All I know is, wherever you choose to stand on an issue, you'd best be sure of your ground, because sooner or later you'll have to defend it."

Tom only half understood what Jem was talking about. He had no opportunity ask more questions, for suddenly Jem stopped in his tracks.

"What is it?" Tom asked.

Jem crouched down and gestured for Tom to do the same. Pointing down at the ground, Jem indicated a pile of droppings. Looking up at Tom again, Jem smiled.

Tom whispered, "Is it...?"

"Yes," Jem said. "Deer, and only a day or two old. They must take water nearby."

They crept forward on their haunches. Tipper sensed the situation and quietly edged forward beside them, his snout twitching as it followed the scent from the droppings.

At length they reached the edge of a clearing through which a bubbling stream had cut a shallow trough, its banks still covered with snow and ice. Jem tested the wind and they repositioned themselves across the clearing, careful not to break any branches dried out by the winter cold.

They sat down in the cover of withered thickets. Tipper lay down and slept for a time. Tom and Jem watched the stream in silence. Eventually, a deer or some other creature might make its way to the water for a drink, but Tom knew it might take hours for that to happen.

"I wonder about JJ," Tom whispered.

Jem's eyes dulled, as if he was not particularly pleased to be returning to the subject. "What about him?"

Tom picked at the dead grass next to him. "JJ tried to kill Father. Would he have killed the rest of us too?"

Jem remained silent for a long time, and Tom wondered whether his brother was ignoring him intentionally. At length, Jem shook his head. "No, Tom. Of course not. JJ may be lots of things, but he's not a monster. His fight was against Father, and maybe against me. But that's all over now. It's finished."

Tom looked up at the pine branches swaying in the soft wind. He listened to the trickling of the stream.

"I'm glad he's gone," Tom said. "JJ, I mean. I'm glad you chased him off. Whatever Father did or didn't do to him, there's no call for murder. Not ever."

Jem's gaze was turned inward. "You're right."

"Unless you're defending yourself," Tom went on. "Like if JJ came back to the Valley. Like if he came back and was real angry about something, real vicious about it. You could kill him and it would be just fine, because who's to say he wouldn't try to kill you first? He's still your brother, you still love him, but something needs to be *done*." Tom nodded as the pieces of his own logic fell into place. "*I'd* kill JJ. For what he did, what he might still try to do. I wouldn't think twice about it."

Jem shook his head and sighed. "I'd rather...I'd rather not talk about this anymore, Tom."

Tom shrugged and let it go. Reaching down, Tom dipped his hand in the stream and let the ice cold water flow against his palm, around his fingers. Slowly, Tom withdrew his dripping hand from the stream. Already his fingers had gone numb. He rubbed his hands together to stay warm.

Just then, there came the sound of a snapping branch.

Tom sat bolt upright. "What was—?"

Jem put a hand against Tom's chest and mouthed at him to keep quiet. Beside them Tipper lay on his belly, his unblinking eyes fixed upstream. He wasn't barking, nor barely even breathing, only watching and waiting.

When Tom and Jem looked across the stream, they saw a young doe drinking at the water's edge.

Jem brought up the Colonel's long rifle and shouldered it. Tom watched expectantly as Jem carefully aimed (he'd already loaded and primed the rifle well before). He saw Jem's finger grace the trigger and prepare to squeeze. But then Jem looked up, turned to Tom, and held his arms out.

Jem was offering the long rifle to him.

Stunned, Tom looked from the rifle to Jem and back to the rifle. Jem offered the rifle again, his eyes urgent. *Not much time.*

Tom gingerly took the ancient weapon into his arms. Moving as slowly as possible, Tom pushed the butt against his left shoulder and raised the barrel. Jem corrected his form. Tom squinted down the sight until his eye found the fleshy ripple running down the doe's neck that Jem called 'the killing vein.' Jem corrected his form again, and then sat back to watch.

Tom put his finger on the trigger and prepared to fire, but then he remembered to pull the hammer back first. The lock *clicked* and the doe's ears perked up, and for an anxious moment Tom was certain she would turn and bolt. But she remained there drinking, and even from this distance Tom saw the flowing water of the stream reflecting in her large, dark eyes.

Tom felt Jem's hand squeeze his shoulder softly. In his periphery, he saw Jem nod.

Tom took a deep breath. He knew what happened next. He'd watched Jem and JJ and even Ben do it a hundred times before. A long exhale, the opening of both eyes, a final correction, and a gentle squeeze when his lungs were finally empty. His next breath would come after the shot was fired, after the animal had drawn its last.

But looking once more at the young doe's dark eyes, Tom's vision wavered. His breath became short and ragged, and the barrel of the long rifle dipped in his trembling hands.

Tom shook his head and pushed the rifle back into Jem's hands. Jem said nothing, but he looked at Tom for a long moment. Was he sure?

Tom nodded, thankful to be free of the rifle's dead weight. Yes, he was sure.

Tipper still lay ready to spring, his eyes fixed on the doe. Tom looked at his dog, who glanced sidelong at Tom but a moment before focusing on the doe again. Tom thought about the slumbering wolf instinct that was awake within Tipper's usually docile eyes.

Tom sat back and shut his eyes and put his hands over his ears and waited for—

CRACK!

The crash of the rifle was deafening, the heat from the flash hot enough to rip the breath from Tom's lungs. When Tom took in an eager breath, his lungs instead filled with gunsmoke. Squinting through his bleary, watering eyes, he watched the smoke dissipate in the cool spring air. He looked at Jem's face, which was grim but content. Then, looking across the stream, Tom's heart tightened in his chest.

The doe lay at the water's edge, still alive but only barely so, her legs sprawled out beside her and a heavy redness flowing from the base of her throat. Tom stood up then, and for Tipper this was the signal ending an excruciating wait. The dog went bounding through the stream barking like mad.

Upon reaching the deer, Tipper sniffed its sides and rear. He flinched as she raised up a powerful, skull-crushing leg to kick at him. A guttural warning shot up Tom's throat but became lodged there. Instead of kicking, the leg only dropped down again, lifeless, and the doe died.

Tom and Jem crossed the chilly stream. Jem was ecstatic, speaking at a run. It wasn't a buck to be sure, but the girl was *big* and she'd make good meat. He'd salt most of it and bring it to the North Branch Mine to distribute chunks of venison to the miners. He talked of sending a parcel of meat to the Blake homestead as well.

And Tom, hearing all this, found that he understood nothing of what Jem was saying. He could only study the chuckling stream as a hot lump formed in his throat and tears welled in his eyes. He could only watch as the warm blood of living spilled into the cool water in curling tendrils, with nothing else to do but be swept away.

"Tom."

Tom looked at Jem, whose smile had faded.

"Are you all right, Tom?"

Angry with himself, Tom wiped at his tears. "Of course I am. Just the wind..."

He knew Jem didn't believe him. Kneeling beside his quarry, Jem motioned for Tom to join him. Slowly, feeling nauseous, Tom inched his way over and knelt down beside his brother.

Tom forced himself to look upon the dead doe. He realized he'd never really *looked* at a dead thing before. All those times he tagged along with the older boys on their summer hunting excursions, he always shut his eyes tight when the killing began. Ben often played War with Tom and Bayard while the twins cut up the meat, and only now did Tom realize Ben had been trying to distract him. Sure, maybe Tom had seen a robin's egg broken on the ground, or had glimpsed an eagle with something clutched in its talons, and somehow the half-eaten rabbit's foot from earlier was such an abstract thing that Tom didn't think twice about it. But he'd never confronted the stillness of death like this before. He'd never had to.

"I know," Jem said softly, and somehow this seemed to say everything.

Tom felt his tongue retreating down his throat. He tasted salt.

"I know," Jem said again, and he rubbed Tom's back while Tom vomited.

When he was finished, Tom wiped his mouth and sat back. He felt better — a *little bit*, anyway. He bent down and drank from the stream, minding that he drank upstream from where the doe had fallen. He gulped several mouthfuls of water, and then he plunged his entire face into the stream and felt the icy thrill of the current. When he drew himself up again dripping, he saw that Jem was studying the long rifle in his lap.

"One day you'll pull the trigger," Jem said. "It isn't today, and that's fine. But one day, Tom, you will. Maybe to hunt so you can eat. Or maybe you'll *need* to pull the trigger: to defend yourself, or someone you love. For one reason or another, you'll need to do it. You may not have a second chance, Tom. You'll have only one shot, so you must make it count. You will need to do what needs doing, and you can't allow yourself another thought about it."

Tom looked at the doe. Feeling the stream water trickle down his neck, he shivered.

"Do you understand what I mean, Tom?"

Tipper began to whine, and plopping down before Tom the dog offered his belly to his boy. Absentmindedly, Tom reached out and rubbed Tipper's soft fur. He tried to make sense of what Jem had just said. Just then, Tom noticed that Tipper's muzzle was red, that his happy, friendly dog was covered in the doe's blood. Like a wolf.

Nodding, Tom whispered, "I understand."

Jem nodded with him, smiled. "Good," he said, and then Jem drew a large knife from his belt. He offered the knife to Tom. "And now, will you help me clean her?"

Slowly, without a word, Tom reached out and took the knife into his hand.

Chapter 20

FIRE EATERS

Charleston's Institute Hall was an imposing structure of stark gray stone, a Bastille that had never been torn down. In the soft light of the gray, humid morning, the throngs of men entering its doors looked like mourners in an endless funeral procession. Tucked under the cover of an umbrella, Ben joined the shuffling crowd on its excruciatingly slow procession through the main doors.

Inside, a wall of thick, grimy heat hit Ben as he entered Institute Hall's wide foyer. Gray light shone upon the grim, colorless walls. Deafening footsteps echoed along the marble floor.

From far across the corridor, Ben recognized Tobias Cutler hurrying into the Hall's main chamber flanked by a gang of prim men in fine suits. Ben stepped away from the shuffling mass of people to linger by the wall and study faces in the crowd.

Finally, Ben saw him.

"Senator!" Ben called. He reached into his jacket pocket and pulled out the creased pages of the old man's speech, which Ben had finished just the night before. "Senator Roscoe, sir!"

The Senator turned away from a circle of dour-faced men. There were purple bags under the old man's sunken eyes, as if he had not slept all night. Seeing this, Ben couldn't help but laugh.

"Late night for you, sir?"

The Senator squinted at him. "What?" he muttered. "Oh..."

"You must have gone out again after we returned to the Rutledge last night," Ben said, trying to clarify.

The old man scowled at him. "Yes? And what business is that of yours?"

Taken aback, Ben's words wouldn't come just right. Instead, he managed to say, "Just a bad joke, sir."

The old man huffed with impatience. "Indeed. Now, what do you want?"

Ben held out the pages of the speech. "This is the final draft, sir."

With a greedy glare, the Senator snatched the speech and tore through it page by page. "About damn time. What have you changed? Any more abolitionist nonsense?"

Ben felt the glowering stares of several onlookers. "There's nothing in there which we haven't discussed at length, sir. The statements and positions are your own, sir, corrections and all."

With a heavy sigh, the Senator folded the pages together and stuffed them in his breast pocket. Without a word, the old man turned away and quickened his limping step. Confused, and not a little angry either, Ben watched the Senator's reflection on the shimmering marble floor. The twin images of the old man, hunched over in pain, fled toward the deafening sounds and activity within Institute Hall's main chamber.

Inside, the Convention was about to begin.

After weaving against the steady flow of spectators heading upstairs to the galleries, Ben found Solomon alone in the crowd. The Cutler manservant was plastered against the wall, trying to make himself as small as possible.

"Are you all right, Solomon?"

"Leave me be," Solomon muttered angrily, scowling at him as if Ben had given away his hiding place.

With a sigh, Ben looked around the broad corridor. It was alive with eager spectators, lobbyists, hucksters, journalists, and a gang of bewildered workmen who were only there to fulfill a day's labor painting signs on office doors.

A passing man carelessly spat tobacco juice on Ben's shoes and hurried by.

"They so many," Solomon said, his eyes watchful of every passing face. "Where they all come from?"

Ben drew a handkerchief, leaned down, and wiped his shoes clean. When he stood up again, he folded the kerchief and tucked it in his pocket. "Out of the woodwork," he said. He gestured toward the stairwell. "Come on, up this way. There's got to be a colored section up here somewhere."

❧

The main chamber of Institute Hall appeared as a massive cathedral, a giant open space thronged by several hundred delegates of the Democratic Party and thousands of watchful spectators in the galleries. Down below on the chamber floor, several chairs like wooden thrones were set upon risers for the Convention's chairman and other Party officials. Twin pulpits stood opposite each other, with a clear line of demarcation separating the Northern delegates from those of the South. The battle lines had already been drawn, and upon this very border sat John Roscoe and the Virginia delegation. Missing from this delegation, of course, was Tobias Cutler; he was seated at the furthest extreme of the Southern wing, flanked by dour Georgians and crusading Texans and vengeful Carolinians.

By now, thousands of spectators had packed themselves in the galleries. Twice, constables approached the slave section and ordered the slaves to push over and make room for more whites. Ben soon found himself squashed in a stinking crush of seated bodies.

Looking across the vast Hall, Ben studied other faces in the galleries. Suddenly he did a double-take and his heart leapt into his throat. In the far gallery, he locked eyes with a beautiful young woman: pale, freckled, raven-haired. She bore a stunning resemblance to Sarah Roscoe, and yet at the same time she was—

"Not even close..."

Grunting, old Solomon leaned over and cupped his ears. "Whatsay?"

"Nothing," Ben said.

Down below, the Convention chairman rapped a gavel. Amid cheers and applause, the chairman stood up to address the congregation with a booming voice.

"*Gentlemen of the Convention*: We are assembled here on this occasion as the National Democratic Convention, called by the National Democratic Committee, to nominate candidates for President and Vice President of the United States, and to transact such other business as the interests of the Party may dictate. What is your pleasure?"

The room erupted with frantic applause, cheering, and whistling.

Amid the din, a delegate from Ohio stood up.

"Let's be quick and unified about this!" the Ohioan cried out. "A motion for *cloture*, Mr. Chairman. I move for the Party to bypass the platform discussion altogether and nominate Stephen A. Douglas our candidate for president. Our leader ought to dictate his own policies. So let us vote at once then, without debate!"

The motion floundered under a tidal wave of wails and lewd insults from a block of Southern delegates. In the face of the onslaught, another Northerner stood up to second the motion. Before the man could open his mouth, two dozen Southerners shot to their feet and screamed at the chairman:

"POINT OF ORDER! POINT OF ORDER!"

The chairman rapped his gavel. "Gentlemen, please. One at a time."

Over the commotion, the Ohio delegate shouted, "Let's be civil about this!"

To that, a Southern delegate groaned loudly, "*Civil?* Don't you mean 'quick and unified'?"

Great laughter rolled through the Convention, after which the same Southerner requested the floor. The chairman granted the floor to "the gentleman from Alabama, Mr. William Yancey."

Over the wild cheers that followed, Ben heard a slave in front of him mutter to the man next to him: "They like a darn bunch of children."

"Hush," the other man replied. "They runnin our country."

"*They* country," the first man said.

Spurred by the attention and with the floor at his command, a man with coiffed hair and beady, sunken eyes shot from his seat and leaped to the center of the chamber. With the attention of the entire Convention upon him, William Yancey bowed to his fellow Southern delegates and the Charleston ladies in the gallery. Smiling, he seemed to revel at the sound of Northern boos and catcalls as much as the deafening praise showered upon him by Southerners.

Ben had only read of William Yancey in newspapers, but his reputation as a fiercely pro-slavery Southern nationalist had made him famous across the South and infamous across the North as the 'Prince of Fire Eaters.'

Standing tall now, Yancey made a show of straightening his tie. He folded his hands behind his back and paced the floor like a reflective scholar.

"A point of order has been made, gentlemen. We cannot *vote* without a *debate*. What, pray tell, would be the point of gathering all our brains in one room if not to pick at them? Of course you may find, as in the case of the gentleman from Ohio, that some of the brains in this room are rather more overripe than others. Their contents are of a softer, soupier texture."

More laughter rolled through the hall. Smiling, Yancey continued.

"We like to call our Party the 'One and Indivisible Democracy.' I happen to be very fond of that name, gentlemen. I'm fond of the name because our Party is supposed to be unified on *every* issue we face in these dark and trying times. As we prepare to face the 'Black' Republican Party, who is at this very moment conspiring to nominate his holiness Pope Seward of New York—"

Yancey was immediately interrupted by a chorus of boos and wails, and this time both Northern and Southern delegates were united in their vocal loathing of William Seward, the de-facto Republican leader. This made Yancey's smile stretch wider, and to Ben the man appeared as a grinning clown commanding a mad circus.

"—Mr. Seward, a man who speaks so *darkly* of a so-called irrepressible conflict, and whose election might fulfill his own *dark* prophecy of racial violence. As we prepare to face the trials of a generation, gentlemen, the One and Indivisible Democratic Party must be just so: *one*, and indivisible."

As the cheering crashed down from the galleries, Yancey placed his hands over his heart and hung his head in a show of mock humility.

"And yet I am only one man. Even the One and Indivisible Democracy may, yea, indeed *should*, have healthy dissent within. Yes, my friends, a good debate will only make us stronger. Therefore, with the floor offered to me thus by our esteemed Chair, I shall open our debate."

Scanning the room, Ben's eyes landed on Senator Roscoe. The Senator, rather than listening to Yancey's rhetoric, was instead bent over at his desk with a pen in hand and the pages of his own speech spread out before him. Ben's heart sank as the Senator dragged his pen across the pages again and again, eliminating whole paragraphs and entire sections with vicious zeal.

"Our Northern colleagues wish us to ordain Stephen Douglas as our heroic leader. But does Mr. Douglas have what it takes to stand up against the Black Republicans? Is Mr. Douglas a leader in whom Southerners can place our trust? Or is he a man who would set fire to our democratic institutions if it gave him the chance to line his own pockets with loot? Is Stephen Douglas merely a foil for the hordes of diseased, negro-loving, America-hating immigrants who want to usurp and destroy our native culture and heritage?"

Yancey paused as cheers and cries of *Hear-hear*! thundered across the floor. Tobias Cutler howled and applauded his ringmaster.

The Prince of Fire Eaters continued:

"Allow me to share but a brief history lesson. It's been six months since John Brown assaulted proud Virginia, the crown jewel of the Union, and yet some of our Northern colleagues are too eager to forget that John Brown's crimes were the result of their unwillingness to quash radical Yankee abolitionism in its infancy. Now that the disease has infected the entire North, there may be no stopping it."

A number of colorful outcries followed. Yancey swept up and down the lines of delegates at a hurried pace.

"Six years ago," Yancey continued, "President Franklin Pierce declared the future of the Union lay in the unconquered west — *the West*, as we've come to call it. The president looked to Stephen A. Douglas, who was Chairman of the Congressional Committee on the Western Territories, to propose a strategy of expansion. Douglas offered the idea of a great national railroad.

"The railroad, beginning somewhere in the civilized East, would traverse the continent following the rough line of the Missouri Compromise. Together with his allies, Mr. Douglas began his humble work 'for the people.' But even as they laid their plans, Mr. Douglas and his friends were also busy buying up great swathes of land in the unorganized territories of Kansas and Nebraska. Their plot, of course, was to generate exorbitant profits once the coming railroad turned these otherwise worthless tracts into priceless real estate."

A low rumble of whispers and murmurings sounded throughout the chamber.

"*Lies*!" a lone voice shouted from the Douglas wing, but the chairman's rapping gavel warned against further outbursts.

"Of course," Yancey said, "even in 1854 the Northern states were hemorrhaging American patriots due to pro-abolitionist policies, together with crooked schemes to bring more diseased immigrants to our shores. The resulting political pressure came down hard on President Pierce, and thence upon the head of poor Mr. Douglas. Weak-willed Northern elitists in the administration threatened Mr. Douglas with the railroad's cancellation, citing an unwillingness to see the Union's proud railroad pass through even a single acre of 'slave soil.' The North wanted the West for its own. No doubt they were far more concerned with impressing European diplomats by showing just how 'enlightened' American society had become, rather than protect the interests of our own citizens."

Wild cheers clashed with howls of protest in the chamber's thick, smoky air.

"And so, Mr. Douglas conjured another idea. He championed a bill that effectively nullified the Missouri Compromise line — *quashed,* in other words, that neat North-South divide that had kept our Union together for the better part of forty years. Douglas claimed that whomsoever settled the territories of Kansas and Nebraska could choose for themselves, vis-a-vis the doctrine of *popular sovereignty,* whether they would live in a 'free' state or a 'slave' state. Mr. Douglas had little doubt that, after applying the right pressure in the right places, Kansas and Nebraska would join the free-soil North. This strategy, he determined, would satisfy both the Northern lobbyists and grant him his railroad, land, and all the power a would-be despot could want."

"*LIES!*" came the cry again. Immediately this dissenting voice was drowned out by hisses and boos from Southern delegates and the gallery audience. Not even the chairman's gavel could silence the crowd.

Yancey, on the other hand, had the crowd in his palm. Flashing a grin to the galleries, he yelled, "Am I getting warmer?" to great laughter and applause.

Presently, Yancey's grin curdled. He turned a look of cold derision upon Stephen Douglas and the delegates who surrounded him.

"Douglas told the Southern people to go west. 'Go with your American vigor, go with your families, go with your *property.*' And the Southern people went, assured of America's manifest destiny. None of these settlers were the cruel, abusive slave-masters that Northern newspapers make them out to be. They were humble, hardworking farmers who tilled their modest plots *alongside* their negro hands. Southern planters found themselves neighbored with Northern free-soilers, and never was there animosity or violence between them. Indeed, ladies and gentlemen, for a brief time the open country of the West was the American idyll. Even when the territories began to lobby for statehood, and when the question of 'slave' or 'free-soil' was foremost in the minds of all, these unlikely neighbors agreed to hold peaceful debates and discussions, and to let democracy take its natural course.

"But encroaching upon this tranquil landscape were sinister forces bent upon division, terror, and violence. For the same anti-slavery Northern capitalists who threatened to destroy Mr. Douglas' railroad now sent private companies of brigands into Kansas and Nebraska. Many of these abolitionist criminals were paid handsome salaries, with their only instructions being to stamp out the seeds of slavery by any means necessary — even if it meant soaking the soil with innocent blood. These criminals pitted neighbor against neighbor, until suddenly violence exploded all across the prairies. 'Bleeding Kansas,' we've come to call it, our Union's first and, I hope, *only* instance of civil war. But when the smoke cleared and the bodies were buried, it was all too horribly obvious that the Northerners had won their slimy victory. After all, there is no surer way to win a popular referendum on such a divisive issue than if the other side never makes it to the ballot box alive."

This charge inspired a great many shocked gasps and low murmurings.

Yancey gave a dramatic shrug. "Of course, none of this mattered to Mr. Douglas. By this time, there was a new administration in the White House. And *finally*, the issue was on the verge of being settled. The people of Kansas submitted to President James Buchanan a state constitution that, shockingly, *upheld* the American right to uphold property of any kind — including property in negro slaves. Well, of course the Northern captains of industry were outraged. And being their lowly minion, Stephen Douglas danced for them. He *denounced* our president and claimed that Kansas had been stolen by the so-called slave powers. Mr. Douglas is happy to play the game of power, it seems, but only if he is assured to win."

Before the earnest cheering began again, several voices from the Douglas wing shouted out:

"*What of the free-soil ballots stolen by Southerners?*"

"*What of the free-soil families murdered in the night?*"

"*The Dred Scott decision killed the Compromise!*"

"*Slavers fired the first shots of the border war!*"

"*Lies!*" the first dissenter cried again. "*All of it, damn secessionist lies!*"

Outraged, Tobias Cutler shot to his feet in defense of Yancey. "*These are not lies,*" he screamed, "but facts of public record!" With heaving breath, he shouted down the snarling calls of '*Point of order!*' and stepped up to Yancey's side. "My own nephew was among the murdered! My own nephew was among the proud Southerners who went west. He and his family were murdered before the vote!"

"Which begs the question!" Yancey said, shouting louder than all the rest. "All of this invites the most obvious question, ladies and gentlemen, and perhaps we fear the answer for being so damning. But all the same, the question must be asked:

"*Why* is it that our Northern colleagues, and especially Stephen Douglas, would betray their Southern allies in order to serve hordes of unwashed, pagan foreigners and the self-hating, self-flagellating radicals who whip them into negro-loving frenzies? Why do our Northern friends do this, and thus endanger the lives and livelihoods of their Southern brethren? I ask you, ladies and gentlemen, where is their pride? Where is their love of country? Where is their love of the true God? I needn't tell you that ours is a white, Christian nation. Since when did that *ever* become something to be ashamed of?"

Amid a passionate roar of applause, Yancey turned and thrust his hands out into the entire crowd like a mad preacher commanding a church of thousands.

"*Ours* are the institutions which are at stake. *Ours* is the racial peace that teeters near disaster. *Ours* is the property that is to be stolen from us on the false pretext of *freedom*. Ours is the honor at stake — the honor of standing up for our children, for the honor of our family names."

Just then, a young Douglas supporter stood up. "I demand the gentleman from Alabama yield the floor so I may respond—"

Yancey turned on the man with hot rage in his eyes.

"I demand *you* to yield, sir! You and all your ilk. What right of yours, gentlemen of the North, have we of the South ever invaded? What institution of *yours* have we ever assailed, directly or indirectly? Have we ever commanded you to turn your horses loose, because we do not like how you ride them? Have we ever questioned the moral standing of your factory owners — your captains of *white slavery* — who pluck Irish orphans off the streets to run Southern textiles through your godforsaken machines? What laws have we ever passed that have invaded, or induced others to invade, the sanctity of your homes, or to put your lives in jeopardy, or that were likely to destroy the foundations of your society? Bear with us then, you Northerners, while we say that we can yield no position until we are convinced that you are right and we are wrong. That is to say, we will never yield an inch."

Weakened by this onslaught, the Douglas supporter sat down heavily, his spirit pierced with boos and catcalls from the galleries.

Yancey flashed a broad grin. "'I demand.' Is that what our democracy has come to? No more discussion, no more debate. Only ultimatums from a first-term Yankee congressman who doesn't have the sense to know he'll soon be a *one-term* congressman." Yancey shrugged, feigning nonchalance. "But whether this pipsqueak's career is cut short by negroes in the ballot box or by the bullet of a patriotic Charlestonian, I cannot rightly say."

Mocking laughter rolled through Institute Hall, booming like the thunder that crashed outside. Up in the galleries, Ben watched the dark glee on the faces of so many thousands of people. But within their sparkling eyes was not mere vindictive loathing, but cathartic relief. It was as if the people of Charleston had for years been suffering under some unnamable, unspeakable cloud of misery and forlorn hope, and finally, in the form of William Yancey, they had found a shining lamppost guiding their way through the dark. It was then that Ben first grasped the idea, still nebulous in his mind, that just as the first-hand accounts of Frederick Douglass' escape from slavery stirred his own heart with hope, the lambasting wit of William Yancey sparked a different kind of hope entirely within the hearts of so many others.

Yancey went to his desk and picked up a piece of paper. This he held up for all to see as a document of salvation. He was Moses clutching the Commandments, and upon Yancey's face was an expression of fervent righteousness.

"Though I am loath to yield the floor, Mr. Chairman, I know that proper manners insist upon my allowing a rebuttal from our Northern colleagues. But let me finish with this. We have but one request of our Northern colleagues. Surely you, with your infinite power and wisdom, may grant us just *one* humble request? We ask for the Democratic Party to accept the following as its national platform for the coming presidential contest:

"Resolved: That the Democratic Party of the United States hold these cardinal policies on the subject of negro slavery:

"*First*, that Congress has *no power* to abolish slavery in any state;

"*Second*, that Congress has *no power* to abolish slavery in the Western Territories, nor in any states that may be created from those territories;

"*Third*, that territorial legislatures themselves have no power to abolish slavery in any new territory, nor to prohibit the introduction of slaves, nor any power to destroy or impair the rights of slave owners by *any* legislation whatsoever.

"These, ladies and gentlemen, are our humble terms. Rather, it is our vision for a new and more just America."

Wild cheers clashed with howls of protest in the chamber's thick, smoky air.

Yancey gently placed the paper back on the table as if it were as revered a document as the Declaration of Independence. Turning once more to the rapt crowd, he said:

"We ask that the Democratic Party, our One and Indivisible Democracy, stands united on an issue that threatens to divide North and South forever. Stand *with* the South, Northerners, and we will forever be your friends and brothers. But should you deny us this one request — and should you think that by some trickery you might yet quietly nominate Stephen Douglas while we stand in shock at your betrayal — then I must tell you what the South will do. Should you extend no saving lifeline to us, the South will as one body *abandon this Convention*. I warn you now, Southern Democrats will convene elsewhere to nominate our own man for president. I counsel you to consider deeply the grave consequences which will inevitably result from your refusal to compromise. Thank you, Mr. Chairman."

With that, Yancey strolled back to his seat while the Fire Eaters rose to their feet. The Cheering and jeering continued long after Yancey was seated once more, until finally the wheezing chairman managed to quiet the crowd with repeated cracks of his gavel.

A stuffy silence filled Institute Hall that belied the roiling tempers just beneath the surface of calm. Minutes stretched on in silence, interrupted at times by lone coughs, sneezes, and the sterile shuffling of papers. No man on the floor moved to uphold Yancey's theatrics, and none dared criticize them. To do either would be an open declaration of war between the Northern faction and the Southern bloc, and all the delegates in the middle would be forced to choose sides.

But frantic looks and glances exchanged urgent questions. Surely Yancey had been misheard — surely he hadn't actually said the South would *abandon* the Convention? Why, without Southern delegates the Convention would cease to be much of a body at all. No sane Democrat would seek to divide the Party in two. And all over the question of *slavery?* It was an almost laughable absurdity. Shouldn't someone now stand up to call the man's bluff, the existence of which was beyond certainty? Clearly Yancey's threats were puffy exaggerations, harmless hyperbolics merely intended to rile up his supporters.

Or could it be that the man truly meant what he said?

In the thick silence, Ben looked up. The chamber, so cavernous and so dark, was alive with the musty energy of hot tempers. The ceiling, ashed black over decades by rising cigar smoke, seemed to be made of the same dark storm clouds that thrashed outside the shelter of the roof and grim walls.

Just now a chair creaked, and a desk groaned under a heavy weight.

"Mr. Chairman," a voice said, floating up like candle smoke. "Mr. Chairman, I would like to respond to that resolution just now proposed by the gentleman from Alabama."

The chamber filled with low murmurings until they were silenced by the chairman's gavel.

"The Chair recognizes Senator John Roscoe of Virginia."

❧

A deep hush lingered over the chamber.

Ben leaned forward. Spread out before him was a canvas of gray light and black shadow: a lone man stood tall above thousands of seated delegates, his head bowed slightly, his eyes glancing up at the thousands of spectators lining the packed galleries. Murky light seeped into the dark room through large, church-like windows cut into the east wall, so that the lone man stood bathed in a ghostly aura while living color rippled out in all directions.

John Roscoe took a deep breath and began.

"I will answer to the national platform which Mr. Yancey has proposed, Mr. Chairman. In so doing, I wish also to comment on the peculiar nature of our gathering here, today." The Senator turned his head up so that his voice might reach the furthest corner of the highest gallery. "For millennia—"

Suddenly the Senator bowed over, and Ben's heart leapt into his throat as he heard the old man's hacking, rib-busting cough.

Several delegates turned to look upon the Senator with alarm, and one stepped forward with a handkerchief. The Senator gave this man an amiable wave and cleared his throat with a low rumble, the coughing fit finally subsided. Ben heaved a sigh of relief and watched anxiously as the Senator stood upright again.

"For millennia," the Senator said, "the greatest philosophers of every age argued that democracy was a form of government that was impossible to sustain. Democracy was considered to be too impulsive, too revolutionary, anarchic in its character, and ultimately doomed to devolve into chaos. After so many generations of freely elected leaders, so the theorists surmised, there would come one leader who would seize upon the resentments of an alienated group and leverage their support to inaugurate an autocratic regime of the very kind which democracy sought to eliminate in the first place. If the examples of Rome and France and countless others are any indication, a free and democratic society is nothing to be taken for granted. There are always would-be despots lurking in our midst. Even if the comforts of democracy lull most of us into complacency, the myriad threats facing democracy do not sleep."

Some in the galleries shouted: "*The traitor Steve Douglas! Down with the Chicago tyrant!*"

Across the aisle, William Yancey folded his arms and tilted his chin, smiling.

The Senator slowly scanned the galleries above until his heavy, measured gaze silenced the brash and outspoken. Then he began anew.

"There is little doubt the separate sections of our Union have separate ideas about which course this ark ought to take; that is, how the country ought to be governed. What we have come to call the Northern section wishes, broadly, for us to fulfill the promises of a people's government laid out in the Declaration of Independence and the Constitution. What we call the Southern section wishes, broadly, for the very same thing.

"We may tread different paths, gentlemen, we may chart different courses, but I believe we are all heading in the same direction. And since the days of 1776, we, as elected representatives, have always come together on behalf of the *demos* — the common people — to transcend our differences and share a common voice inspired by the millions. We come together, in short, to *compromise*. We, the people's representatives, owe this much to our fellow citizens, and to our millions of unborn countrymen."

Up in the gallery, a smile brightened Ben's face. As John Roscoe's speech continued, Ben's anxiety melted away.

Solomon leaned over and whispered, "The hell you grinnin about?"

Ben shook his head and said nothing, but he couldn't stop smiling. The Senator was reading, verbatim, the final draft of the speech Ben had prepared the night before!

"When Washington was president," the Senator continued, "the different sections of the Union basked together in the warm afterglow of a new nation's birth. Only when it came time to choose our good general's successor did the infighting begin. Only after we split into factions did we truly conceive of a North distinct from the South, East separate from West. And though our sectional disagreements have increased in number and intensified in ferocity, it is *compromise* that has tempered passions and held our ark together. For compromise is the very thing the selfish tyrants of old Europe would never suffer — not until it was forced upon them with knives at their throats and guillotines overhead. Compromise is the beating heart of democracy."

Here the Senator paused for a long moment while the chamber went completely silent.

Ben held his breath. He knew that next, the Senator would conclude by declaring his support for Stephen Douglas, finishing with a motion to nominate Douglas as a candidate. Watching the old man, Ben could not help but feel the quiet stirrings of a son's pride.

"Therefore, I urge our Party to nominate a man of compromise. We must nominate a man whose pursuit of compromise is uncompromising. We must nominate a man who is committed not to just one section, but to the *whole* of the Union. Then and only then will we be able to defeat the rebels of the Republican Party.

"It is my estimation that the great majority of Americans, in both the North and the South, will put their faith in a man who has shown many times before that he has a steady hand when navigating dangerous waters. Who shall this helmsman be? I say, let it be Stephen A. Douglas of Illinois."

The Douglas faction began to cheer wildly. Slowly, all eyes turned to look upon the Little Giant, who wore the contented look of a man who was patiently biding his time; a general who was confident in the calculations of his battle-plan. Looking around, Ben noticed for the first time just how many yellow-colored paper flowers could be counted in the crowd, the same ornaments that he had seen decorating so many jacket collars at The Blind Tiger the night before.

"—and let us, together," John Roscoe said, "do everything we can to help our undaunted pilot guide our ship of democracy to safer waters."

And this, Ben knew, was the end of John Roscoe's written speech. But instead of taking a humble bow and returning to his seat, the Senator remained at the pulpit.

Presently, John Roscoe looked across the mass of faces. From up high, Ben followed the old man's gaze and realized that the Senator was looking squarely at Tobias Cutler.

Slowly, Cutler gave a small nod.

Ben's breath caught in his throat. But before he had time to comprehend the meaning of the look between the two men, John Roscoe produced a new paper from underneath the first and set it out before him. Now he opened up to face the whole of Institute Hall once more.

"While Stephen Douglas ought to be our man in the White House," the Senator said, "we must remember that it is not for the president alone to shape the Union according to his will. Instead he must heed the will of the American people, including the will of their elected representatives. After all, the president is not a king."

Ben's gaze went to Stephen Douglas. When the Senator's 'king' line, delivered with such pointed meaning, echoed in the air, Douglas' face drained of color and the little man leaned forward with an expression of deep consternation.

The Senator, it seemed, was fully aware of the nervous energy building among the Northerners. Still he pushed on.

"It is no surprise, therefore, that the success or failure of an American president depends greatly on his relationship with the two branches of government that both provide and check his power. If the president has no rapport with Congress, and should he bicker with Supreme Court justices, his administration will be hamstrung. If there can be no compromise between the president and the institutions that support him, our democracy will flounder.

"Let us not be like those Romans who plunged their republic into civil strife when their fraternal bonds showed signs of fraying. If we are to shed ourselves of this idea of 'North versus South,' we must rekindle the fires of patriotism in every American heart. Therefore, we must embrace *compromise* not as a means to an end, but as an end in itself."

The Senator thrust his hands out on either side: one appealing to the Southern wing of the chamber, the other to the North.

"Mr. Yancey, it is plain to see that the South is firmly behind you. I wish to tell you that the Democratic Party, including its Northern delegation, hears you. We see you. Indeed, the *Union* sees and hears you. We wish for no fractured Party, lest that deliver victory into Republican hands. We can well appreciate your conservative calls for the protection of your social and economic institutions."

Ben cocked his head. Was he hearing this right? Had he missed something? Was the Senator actually *agreeing* with Yancey? Surely he was—

No, Ben realized. No, he wasn't imagining things. All across the Northern section of the chamber, heads turned together. Murmurings and frantic mutterings swept across Institute Hall like an encroaching rainstorm.

"And I say, our Party *must* adopt Mr. Yancey's proposed platform," the Senator declared.

Hearing this, Ben's jaw dropped open. All around, audible gasps and grunts of surprise echoed in the air. From the galleries, some Charlestonians shouted their frenzied approval and adoration.

Amid the growing frenzy, the Senator struggled to maintain his voice. He cried out:

"For what, ladies and gentlemen, could present a more attractive alternative to Black Republicanism? On the one hand we have the Northern Democrat who defeated the upstart Lincoln deep in Republican country, the same man who *will* defeat Seward on the national stage. And on the other hand we have the ardent conviction of the South, an army of patriots that is millions-strong, an army ready to preserve the rights bestowed on them by God and our Constitution. So let us nominate Stephen Douglas together with Mr. Yancey's pro-Southern platform, and we will have both the man and the policy which will earn us national victory in November. But if instead we continue to play games of principles, this proud ship we call the Union will be wrecked on the rocks. It is our responsibility, gentlemen — our *duty* — to deliver this ark of democracy to safe harbors."

Ben winced as a knot tightened in his chest. He could barely breathe. He could barely *think*. It was as if someone had pushed his head underwater. He was no longer listening to John Roscoe's speech, even as the Senator lifted his head and delivered his concluding statements.

"Will we pursue the death of slavery and thus plunge our beloved Union into civil war?" the Senator cried out, to be answered by howls from the Southern wing. "Or will we, by swallowing this bitter pill, safeguard this land of the free for those future generations who will solve the challenges which we cannot?" Here the Southerners cheered. "I tell you: *now* is not the time for sweeping reforms. Now is the time to be the *One and Indivisible* Democratic Party!"

John Roscoe held one hand out to Douglas, and the other toward Yancey.

"With this leader, and with this platform, victory will be ours. Thank you, Mr. Chairman."

As the Senator finally turned to take his seat, Institute Hall erupted. Northerners and Southerners shot to their feet in the same instant, the one section howling with rage and the other cheering wildly and embracing each other with tears in their eyes. Up in the galleries, the slave section was eager to appear excited and supportive of anything their masters approved. Old Solomon stuck a hand between his gums and whistled, but he did not seem to know exactly what he was whistling about.

Feeling cold despite the clammy heat in the galleries, Ben now turned to look upon the Little Giant. Stephen Douglas sat stoically while all around men flew about in a frenzy. Several supporters stepped up to conspire in whispers, but Douglas swatted them angrily away. He remained a lone, desolate figure amidst the throng, his face pale and his body convulsing with heavy breathing, his hands clasped across his chest as if someone had just delivered a mortal wound.

Over the chaos, the chairman's furious gaveling went unheard and unheeded. "*Order!*" the chairman cried, his voice failing him. "*Order*, gentlemen! May we have order? *Please*, gentlemen, we must have order!"

From the stunned shock of the Douglas men to the dejected air of depression hanging over John Roscoe's seat, Ben looked at last upon the Fire Eaters, who in the wake of the Senator's explosive speech had turned and clasped each other in tearful embraces. And amid the throng of cheering, exuberant faces, a giddy Tobias Cutler turned and shook hands with William Yancey.

Now, Yancey turned his face up to marvel at the wild energy in the galleries high above. Doubtful that Yancey's eyes met Ben's directly; very likely it was just a trick of light that suggested their gazes met with intimate focus, however brief. But in that moment, seeing the lurid look of glee on Yancey's face, Ben could not help but tremble with despair as the last hope within him crumbled.

The Prince of the Fire Eaters was laughing.

Chapter 21

STAR AFTER STAR

During the Convention's recess, delegates wandered about in pale shock. Under the high arches of the Institute's hallways, away from the roaring in the public gallery, the quiet, earnest discussions began.

Stephen Douglas was a strong candidate, but was his nomination worth breaking the Democratic Party in two? Some asked, how could the Party's old conservatives help the radical Fire Eaters understand reason? As far as the old timers were concerned, this latest sectional crisis would pass just like the last North-South spat in the early '50s, and the Congressional battles in the '20s and '30s. There had been presidents hostile to slavery before; there would be again. And Douglas was not necessarily hostile to the peculiar institution, but rather indifferent to it. What more, then, could Yancey and his good old boys hope for? Whatever Douglas' intentions, the Party's elders were certain that no Democratic president would ever defy their counsel. After all, these were the men who had been running the clockwork of Congress for fifty years. They knew better than anyone that what mattered above all was *unity* (with the elders being first among equals, of course). If John Roscoe counseled a Douglas candidacy with a pro-slavery platform, then wasn't that the greatest of all compromises? Couldn't it be at least the lesser of two evils?

But the radicals at both ends of the spectrum were beyond discussion. They met in closed sessions to conduct urgent business. The Douglas supporters hotly debated how to bypass the so-called 'Yancey platform.' Meanwhile, the Fire Eaters calmly discussed what they would do should the Northern delegates attempt to fast-track Douglas' nomination while blocking any vote on the national platform.

The men who stood outside these radical clubs drifted through the hallways like lepers. But in their exile the lepers found community. They were Northerners, a few conflicted Southerners whose constituents in Kentucky and eastern Tennessee were moderates, most of them more than willing to swing to whichever side sounded the least insane. These men, if not abolitionists per se, at least found the institution of slavery 'disagreeable.' Whatever degree of opposition they had to the Fire Eaters and to the Douglas conservatives both, the lepers eagerly formed a block. But no man had the backbone to go back into the Hall to stand and be heard lest the roaring tide of popular opinion crush them against their desks. Many of them fled the Convention and returned to their hotels to pack for home.

For his part, Ben wanted to ask Senator Roscoe exactly where he had gone the night before, after the testy meeting with Douglas. Further to the point, why had he, seemingly out of nowhere, decided to endorse a pro-slavery platform? Wasn't this the man who had freed the slaves he inherited?

Ben imagined John Roscoe walking about the streets of Charleston the night before, his cane tap-tapping along the cobblestones. He imagined the Senator entering the smoky lobby of the Charleston Hotel, the makeshift headquarters of William Yancey and his Fire Eaters. Ben saw Tobias Cutler welcoming the Senator in, sitting him down beside eminent Southern gentlemen like Jefferson Davis of Mississippi and Thomas Hindman of Arkansas. Of course John Roscoe would already be familiar with Vice President John Breckinridge, who some claimed was the real power in the Buchanan White House. And there in the middle, chairman of their own miniature Convention, was the master puppeteer William Yancey. Ben imagined hands filled John Roscoe's drink and pushing a cigar between his fingers. Then came the debates and deliberations, the extolling of the virtues of a solid Southern alliance against Yankee corruption. Ben could almost hear William Yancey's whispered promises of everything under the sun — the national railroad, to be sure, and maybe something else too. Maybe something bigger. After all, the Fire Eaters, for all their railing against Stephen Douglas, had not yet named a rival candidate of their own...

Ben searched the crowded foyer for some sign of Senator Roscoe. Standing apart from the crowd were two men silhouetted by a large stained-glass window. Ben recognized the Senator instantly. The diminutive man beside him took Ben a moment longer to recognize, but as he approached he saw that it was none other than Stephen Douglas who now had the Senator's ear.

Ben kept back, and from his vantage point he could just barely make out pieces of the hushed conversation over the crowd's dull roar.

"Stephen, please—"

"Did you really think that after thirty years of friendship that I would simply leave you to the wolves?" Douglas growled. "For God's sake, John, what kind of man do you think I am?"

The Senator said quietly, "It must be this way, Stephen."

"No it mustn't," Douglas said. "And it won't be. You realize you've forced me into a corner? For God's sake, the only reason I kept my Senate seat when that upstart Lincoln tried to take it from me was because I expressly said *I would not touch the issue of slavery*. I won't condemn it, but neither will I support it. And there you were, waxing about Yancey's platform as if it was the goddamn heir to the Declaration of Independence."

"It is the middle path that could—"

"To hell with the middle path," Douglas growled. "In any case, it doesn't matter. My men have been busy whipping votes while your Fire Eater overlords sit there gloating. And after the recess, they're going to present an alternative platform. One that *doesn't* play right into the hands of those pock-faced secessionists. For God's sake, John, what was it those bastards said to you? What did Yancey and his minion Cutler promise you?"

"It's not a matter of promises," the Senator said. "It's a matter of principles. The South must protect its institutions, however dilapidated they may be. The South must—"

"Oh for God's sake, *listen to yourself*," Douglas snarled. "You're no more a Southern man than I am. You're a stranger in a strange land. You know it, they know it. You will never be *one of them*, John. No matter how many goddamn trains you build or how much wealth you acquire, to them you're nothing more than 'new money.' They look at you, the foreigner who inherited a cotton kingdom and sold all his slaves to the Deep South, and they laugh at you."

Ben turned his head and strained to listen over the din of the crowd. He must have misheard Douglas, or else the Little Giant had misspoken about the selling of slaves. But before he could think any more about it, Douglas had already pushed on.

"You do realize how much they laugh at you — don't you, John? To them you are the money-grubbing fool who sought easy wealth instead of power, *real* power that can only be felt by gripping a nine-tailed whip. And so while one of them butters you up with promises of power — goddammit, maybe even the *presidency* — the others point and snicker behind your back. Whatever they've promised you, you won't get it. They'll offer you a concession prize and they know you'll take it anyway, whatever it is. You're not their friend, John, and you're not their ally. To them, you're a practical joke."

The Senator gave an exasperated sigh. "Please, Stephen. I am *your* friend—"

"*No*. You are a worm, John Roscoe. I'd rather play blackjack with Brutus himself than suffer a friend like you."

Douglas looked away, and suddenly his eyes landed on Ben.

Standing frozen, Ben tore his eyes away and tried to pretend he had not been staring or eavesdropping. But just as he thought to turn and flee, Douglas called out:

"Hello, Mr. Freeman! Come and join us, won't you?"

Ben felt the Senator's eyes on him now, and he felt he might be sick.

"Come now!" Douglas bellowed. "Join in the fun."

Moving stiffly, Ben shuffled forward. He was keenly aware of the Senator's wrathful glower, but just now he decided he didn't care what the old man thought.

"You're enjoying the Convention?" Douglas asked, directing a knowing look at the Senator.

Ben shrugged. "I suppose I have nothing to compare it to. But no, not really."

"Shame," Douglas said. "But not to worry, dear boy. This circus will liven up soon. I hear that next up, they're going to let a bull elephant rampage on the Convention floor."

"*Please*, Stephen," the Senator hissed, "can we not speak rationally about all this?"

"What was it you said to me the other night about our friend John here?" Douglas said to Ben. "Come now, help me out, Mr. Freeman. *In all things, he does the right thing*. Isn't that what you said to me?"

Ben looked to the Senator before answering. "That's what I said, sir."

Douglas cracked a grin. While he spoke, his eyes never left the Senator. "You've known John Roscoe a long time, Mr. Freeman, but you haven't known him as long as I have. The day I met him, he showed up on my doorstep one day in Springfield — this is thirty years ago now — attempting to hoodwink my wife into buying a new cotton gin for her family's plantation down in Mississippi. He said the contraption, which *he'd* invented, was the latest revolution of Eli Whitney's cotton gin. Indeed, John here claimed his invention was going to change cotton production forever, and that he was going down to Virginia the next month to install units on several large plantations there. Rather than throw the knave out as a snake oil salesman, I allowed him to talk me into buying *two* of his damned machines. Later on, I discovered I'd purchased two of what they call 'McCarthy gins', except I'd bought mine before Mr. McCarthy ever filed his patent. That was certainly curious, but still I liked John Roscoe all the same. He had a *drive* in him that I found inspiring. Even then, he dreamed of becoming a *someone*, by any means necessary. Still, however hard I tried, I couldn't figure out where he came from. His strange accent, and that starved sort of look in his eyes? He wasn't from Illinois, that was for sure. It was as if he'd floated down from the Moon. I was certainly sorry when my friend John left for some backwater in Virginia, and sorrier still when he decided to stay there. But I knew that, somehow, the next time I saw him, he would indeed be *someone*."

While Douglas talked, Ben's gaze drifted to the Senator. The old man was staring down at his shoes, his cheeks flushed purple, looking like a scolded child.

"Did you ever tell anyone *exactly* how you financed that coal mine of yours, John? Of course I know your father-in-law wasn't of much help, may he rest in peace. What was it again, gambling debts? Poor man. No doubt your fledgling Roscoe Company required substantial upfront investment — and there you were, running for a seat in the Senate at the same time!"

Douglas clicked his tongue and placed a hand on the Senator's shoulder as a friend might. Ben could not be sure how hard Douglas squeezed, but he did see the Senator grimace.

"You always liked long odds," Douglas said, "but you always knew what hand to play. You always knew how to win, John. By any means necessary."

Having said this, Stephen Douglas spat at the Senator's feet. He offered his hand to Ben, and Ben took it, dazed.

"Enjoy the rest of the show, Mr. Freeman."

The Little Giant turned away and prowled across the marble floor. Upon recognizing him, the shuffling crowd erupted with equal measure of applause and jeering. Scowling, Douglas pushed his way into the main chamber beyond.

At last, the Senator looked up at Ben. They stood there staring at each other, and for a long while neither of them spoke.

Ben studied the Senator's expressions as they moved in a shifting mosaic: aloof, defiant, abashed, and now mournful. Maybe the old man saw something in Ben's face too — something that frightened him, or shamed him. Whatever he saw, the Senator now turned away from Ben and hobbled with his cane across the marble floor.

"Senator!" Ben called. "Senator Roscoe, sir—?"

But the old man did not look back.

Inside Institute Hall's main chamber, a great cheer went up and the chairman rapped his gavel. The Convention was about to resume.

❧

Up in the galleries, Ben felt a charge in the air. The *something* that had filled him with so much dread when he awoke that morning was finally set to unfold.

To answer Yancey's platform proposal, several Douglas supporters set up a series of maps and charts to visualize their dry assessment of the Democratic Party's prospects for the upcoming presidential election.

"There are 303 votes in the Electoral College," one of the Douglas men explained. "On election day in November, the candidate who secures 152 of those votes will be our next president. We can be sure that the Republican candidate, whoever he may be, will not take a single vote from any Southern state. That means we Democrats can expect our man to gain 120 votes in the South and along the border. Thirty-two votes remain, and we feel our best chances lie in the Northwest: Wisconsin, Illinois, Indiana, Ohio, et cetera. This region is hostile to abolitionism, yet unfriendly to the prospect that slavery might become protected by federal law. Gentlemen, this region is Stephen A. Douglas' back yard. There is no other candidate we may put forward in the national race with half as strong a chance at victory as our Little Giant. But if Mr. Douglas must run with a pro-slavery platform of the kind put forth by our colleague from Alabama, no Democrat — and I mean *no* Democrat, not even Mr. Douglas — has a hope of winning the presidency. These are the facts; ignore them at your peril!"

The Douglas men then laid down a new platform, henceforth called the 'Douglas platform' as opposed to the 'Yancey platform.' The new platform was remarkably straightforward, stating that the Democratic Party would abide by the decisions of the Supreme Court on any question regarding constitutional law. The platform also suggested that Cuba ought to be 'acquired' (for reasons unknown, but no doubt as a concession to slaveholders). And finally, the platform called for a national railroad to commence construction at the earliest opportunity.

Hearing this last point, Ben looked down at Senator Roscoe. Pale and shivering, the old man looked as though he might at any moment become violently sick.

As expected, Southerners decried the new platform as a crude trick. Urged on by the Fire Eaters who sat around him, Tobias Cutler stood up.

"What is there to differentiate Mr. Douglas' platform from that of the Republicans?" Cutler questioned. "All across the North, dark forces are marshaling to overwhelm Southern civilization. The Democratic Party must make a firm stand against the stupid and half-insane spirit of faction and fanaticism which would hurry our land on to revolution and civil war. What does it mean when our very own President Buchanan himself detests Mr. Douglas as a man without principles, as nothing more than a scheming politico?

"You gentlemen of the North insist that our Party cannot win the presidency without Mr. Douglas or his weak-boned platform. I tell you, as Mr. Yancey and others have already done, that *this is exactly the point*! We do not *want* that man, nor his criminal, unfaithful promises. And let this resounding rejection be his last and ultimate defeat, for Stephen A. Douglas has never stood for anything except his own self-interests. I will remind Mr. Douglas that not since Andrew Jackson has a Democrat ever stood against his own party and survived!"

Amid the roar of applause that followed Cutler's remarks, Stephen Douglas stood up red-faced and spoiling for a fight. So rare was it for a nominee to speak for himself that a great hush immediately descended over the whole of Institute Hall.

"And I remind *you*, sir," Douglas boomed, "that Andrew Jackson is dead!"

Whoops of Northern laughter clashed with bellows of Southern vitriol. When the chairman finally regained calm control of the proceedings, the two competing platform proposals were locked in.

Finally, the voting began.

Ben anxiously tallied the votes as they were roared out by state delegations. All told there were some 300 delegates, nearly half of them Southerners, which meant the margin of victory would be razor-thin. Institute Hall's chamber, so cavernous and so dark, was alive with the musty energy of hot tempers. The ceiling, ashed black over decades by rising cigar smoke, seemed to be made of the same dark storm clouds that thrashed outside the shelter of the roof and grim walls.

Ben felt Solomon tug at his sleeve. "Did Marse Cutler win?"

Ben turned to answer, but suddenly the chairman rapped his gavel.

One of the Convention's secretaries stood up and cleared his throat.

"The vote. Delegates in favor of Mr. Yancey's platform, one hundred thirty-eight. Delegates in favor of the Douglas platform...one hundred *sixty-five*."

Institute Hall exploded with shouts of anger and protest from Southern delegates and spectators alike.

Upon hearing the results, Ben had breathed a heavy sigh of relief. Yancey's pro-slavery platform had been rejected! Now there was reason for hope. Even if Douglas himself lost the nomination, the Democrats had refused to become the party of slavery.

But then, as quickly as the protests began, they lessened to groans and whimpers. Eventually they died completely. The astonished chairman still had his arm stretched in the air, ready to bring the gavel crashing down. Slowly, meekly, he lowered his arm once more. Incredibly, Institute Hall was now completely silent, with not even the shuffling of papers or low whispers between gallery onlookers.

But down below, among the Alabama delegation, there was movement. A hand shot into the air, and presently the fingers curled in one by one to form a defiant white fist.

The fist belonged to William Yancey, who stretched his arm up and out, reaching for the ceiling and the heavens beyond.

It was a signal.

Up and down the Southern wing heads turned, eyes met, and delegates exchanged curt, knowing nods. There was no pleasure in their expressions, no put-on of chummy bravery. Presently the movements hastened, intensified. Several dozen Southern delegates gathered their papers and capped their pens and closed their ink bottles with dramatic flourish.

Twenty Southerners stood up at once, like a small army ready for battle. A days-old baby in the galleries, maybe sensing a dark energy in the air, began to cry. Its lone, helpless wail triggered a thousand hushed conversations.

The head-splitting clatter of the chairman's gavel came almost as a relief. Men and women in the galleries eagerly hushed each other and looked upon the proceedings with deep and silent anxiety. Ben felt a sickness growing in his heart, and looking around he saw that the same sickness must have infected every single person in the room.

The chairman's voice was quiet, careful. "The Chair cannot recognize all of you at once, gentlemen. I ask that you sit down and address the Chair one by one."

The twenty men did not sit down. Instead, they made way as one of their own stepped forward. This time it was not Yancey, but a handsome man in a dark suit and an aura of grim contemplation, as if he was a soothsayer who had seen a dark and inevitable future.

"We will not sit down, Mr. Chairman."

Shock hit, and then the whispers began again until the gavel silenced them.

"The Chair recognizes Senator Jefferson Davis of Mississippi."

Ben focused his attention on this man, for Jefferson Davis was a hero of the Mexican War, former Secretary of the War Department, and a popular figure in national politics. He was thin, dressed all in black, and his eyes were half-hidden in the leathery seams of his face. He was blind in one of his eyes, in fact; while one was steel blue, the other was colored milky white.

"Mr. Chairman," Davis said, "we have worked long and tirelessly to promote a truly national platform that both protects Southern institutions and satisfies Northern ambitions. It seems that said Northern ambition is in fact insatiable. Well, the people of the South will not stand idly by until we are overrun by Yankee civilization. Here, in the proud city that has always fought for its rights against Federal tyranny, we must defend ourselves. Therefore, my compatriots and I shall now retire from the Convention. Good day, gentlemen, and God bless the united Southlands."

With that, Davis stepped out from his desk and walked silently up the aisle. Nearly twenty Southern delegates joined him in the slow, solemn march out of Institute Hall.

Chaos erupted among the bureaucrats seated around the chairman's desk. The chairman looked to his secretaries and Party officials. Was this permitted? Was this legal? *Possible?* The secretaries shrugged lamely — they had no idea. The chairman raised his gavel to strike, but just then another block of delegates stood up.

"I wish to be recognized, Mr. Chairman."

Even from a great distance, Ben thought he saw the chairman's Adam's apple buck as the old man swallowed hard. After a stern throat-clearing, he said, "The Chair recognizes Robert Rhett of South Carolina."

"Our Northern brothers have determined to call the South's bluff," the Carolinian said. "Well, gentlemen, I am both sorry and proud to say, that was a grievous mistake. You are our brothers no longer. Farewell, gentlemen."

Then, almost as if reading a list of obituaries, the chairman hailed: "Robert Toombs of Georgia...David Yulee of Florida...James De Bow of Louisiana..."

One by one, the delegations of the Deep South departed the Convention. First went Mississippi and South Carolina. Next went Georgia, Florida, Louisiana, Texas. Then the delegates of Arkansas stood and locked arms to leave the Convention floor as one mass, and after their departure the Convention floor looked like a broken puzzle. Empty blocks of abandoned desks and chairs bordered clusters of confused Northern delegates. To Ben's count, over a hundred men had left the Convention.

Nearby, one slave said to another, "Is this normal-like?"

His companion's answer came with a shrug: "Lord knows. Sure don't seem it."

Solomon whispered in Ben's ear, "We won. Looks like we won, don't it?"

In answer to the sudden departures, a Northern delegate stood to address the chairman.

"Here we find star after star madly shooting from the great Democratic galaxy," the delegate said. "Why is it, and what is to come of it? Does it presage that, hereafter, stars will shoot from the galaxy of the Republic, and the Union will become nothing but a parcel of sectional republics?"

The man's questions went unanswered. By now, half the Southern states had departed Institute Hall's main chamber. With Alabama the last of the Deep South states remaining, and with no one doubting that the state would eventually abandon the Convention, all anxious eyes now fell on the remaining Southern state delegations. These were the so-called Border States: Tennessee, Kentucky, North Carolina, Maryland, and Missouri also. Their societies knew slavery well, but their people were fiercely loyal to the Union. What would these states do? Would they too abandon the Convention in mass protest?

Ben believed he knew the answer.

The Border States would go with Virginia, whichever way she went. And just now, a man stood up to confirm that this was to be exactly the case.

"The Chair recognizes John Roscoe of Virginia."

Ben swallowed hard and found a lump had formed in his throat.

As the Senator rose shakily to his feet, he looked across the chamber toward Stephen Douglas. Boos and hideous insults fell at the Senator's feet, but the Senator lifted his head as if to speak to the heavens themselves. Ben wondered if he did this because he could not look any of the men around him in the eye.

"If there is a break-up of the Democratic Party indeed at hand," John Roscoe announced to the Convention, "then Virginia will march out with her Southern sisters."

A hush fell over the entire chamber.

The Senator's voice quavered. Indeed, the old man seemed to be on the verge of tears. He strained to speak, as if the delivery of each word cut a new wound in his own flesh.

"I've always considered myself a Union man. But today I must stand before you as a Virginian. It was the people of Virginia, and nowhere else, who selected me as their representative. Therefore, I must think first of my neighbors, my *community*. For now, everything else is an abstraction.

"Six months ago, Virginia survived a near-massacre in a peaceful railroad town; a massacre that could have been larger and more widespread. When I first called for compromise at this Convention, perhaps I did not appreciate the simple fact that for two opponents to compromise, they must each make *concessions*. They must *agree* to *give up* certain demands they hold dear, in the interest of a common utility. But our Northern delegates refuse to concede any of their policies to support the

South's fight for its own survival. They are stubborn in their ardent belief that since they are right, all others must be wrong. As a Southern man, as a Virginian, I cannot swallow such an insult."

A great cheer soared among the Charlestonians who dominated the galleries.

The Northern faction stared open-mouthed at John Roscoe, formerly one of the closest Southern allies, in a state of shock. Just then, a burly delegate seated beside Stephen Douglas stood up and shouted in a booming voice:

"*TRAITOR*!"

A stunned silence hung over the Hall.

Now, delayed, came the howling. William Yancey now leaped into the aisles, ostensibly to defend John Roscoe's honor. Meanwhile, Northern delegates stood and hurled insults at the Senator, and in response the remaining Southerners climbed upon their chairs and lobbed curses and invective across the Convention floor. The chairman's pounding gavel did nothing but keep a beat to the catastrophe. When at last the delegates had shouted themselves hoarse they fell quiet but remained standing, some poised to give and receive blows.

The Senator stood pale and shaking, like an aged buck surrounded by wolves and a host of carrion.

For himself, Ben's blood boiled. He might have shouted the cry of *Traitor* himself; he wanted to jump up and cry out, to hurl himself down upon the old man — anything to stop him from delivering the words he would say next. What the hell was he doing? Here, in front of thousands, John Roscoe was bowing down to the slave powers. He was bowing down to *Cutler* and Yancey and all their ilk. But though Ben's body twitched and the voice in his head screamed with primal fury, he found himself frozen to the bench on which he sat.

Meanwhile, John Roscoe's voice was grim, heartfelt. The old man seemed fully aware of his status as a foil of the Fire Eaters and a traitor to Douglas' Northerners. But for whatever reason, the old man pushed on. "And yet," the Senator said, "not even when her own children fell on a black night last October was Virginia's heart pierced with so profound a grief as the sorrow she will feel at having to choose between a separate destiny with the South and a common destiny with the whole Republic."

This sobering statement rang out louder than any curse or threat. For a long moment, the delegates and the people in the galleries took a good look around them. The number of empty chairs rivaled the number of delegates who remained.

"For so long, I have refused to believe we are witnessing the slow death of the Union," the Senator said. "I have refused to believe that such a travesty could ever come to pass as the collapse of compromise. But maybe I, and we together, ought to truly consider such a possibility with the deadly seriousness it deserves. What do all the great civilizations of humanity have in common? They all collapsed, sooner or later. Will America share in the fate of empires, or shall we transcend our divisions, together?

"For now, we must find a better way forward, even if we must push on separately for a time. And if we must choose a separate destiny — if radicals on both sides of the great slavery question insist, as a culmination of all their hideous rhetoric, that there must be a final, apocalyptic showdown — then the Commonwealth of Virginia will carve its own legacy separate from those debilitating spirits of division and resentment. We Virginians do not reject the Union, and we do not embrace Southern nationalism. But we do reject all those who would try to drag us down the path toward a destiny we do not want. To reflect on words I said earlier, we will place ourselves at the helm of our own legacy. We will navigate these waters ourselves. We are Americans, after all. Independent spirit is in our blood."

Bursting from the galleries came heartfelt cries of support and adoration. As the applause continued, the Senator collected his things. Standing now, he moved for the exit. His face was grim, contorted, as if the old man might burst into tears of despair at any moment. He was promptly joined by a smiling, vindicated Tobias Cutler and several other Virginia delegates. Behind them trailed men from Tennessee, Maryland, and Missouri, who had been inspired to action by the Senator's words.

As the chamber floor emptied of yet more Southerners, the Alabama delegation finally stood up. William Yancey delivered a graceful bow to the Convention chairman while the adoring crowd chanted the man's name. Smiling, satisfied, Yancey led the Alabamans up the long aisle and out of the chamber.

The crowd in the galleries began to depart too. Amid the sudden jockeying and jostling, Ben stood up and looked down at the chamber. So many seats were empty, such that the Convention floor resembled a tiled floor cracked and fractured by an earthquake. Down below, Stephen Douglas sat disconsolate. The Northern section devolved into anarchy, with delegates turning upon each other with wild accusations. The chairman banged the gavel until he had order once more; this was far easier to achieve without the clamor of the Southern bloc.

"The Convention secretariat assures me we still have a quorum, gentlemen. We may move on to select nominees for president with those delegates still remaining. Do I have a motion to proceed?"

❧

The evening train pulled slowly out of Charleston, now picking up speed, and with a steaming shriek went rolling up a northbound track. But for Ben, the train could not move fast enough. He turned away from the sights of Charleston falling away and instead tried to focus on the newspaper clutched in his hands. He read the same paragraph three, four times before he finally gave up and set upon rolling a cigar for himself.

"I'll miss this place," Cutler said from his seat across the private cabin. He sipped a cup of coffee and smiled out the window. "The city by the sea. What we've done here might go down in history. It *will* go down in history."

"Too bad the sun started shinin only now we leavin," old Solomon mused, watching the rainclouds finally moving off.

Beside Ben, the Senator coughed into his handkerchief. The old man was weak today, and very congested.

"There's much work to be done before we convene the new Convention in Baltimore," the Senator said. "Before Democrats can meet again, the Republicans will have already chosen their nominee."

Baltimore. The madness of the whole situation was too much for Ben to grasp. After the Southern walkout, the remnants of the Democratic Party proceeded to nominate Stephen Douglas as the candidate for the presidential race. But already, Southern Democrats (a group that now included John Roscoe, apparently) were busy planning a different National Convention to be held next month in Baltimore. At this 'official' Convention, the 'real' Democratic Party would nominate a 'legitimate' candidate, which meant a pro-slavery Southerner.

Cutler shrugged. "Whoever takes the Republican nomination, we'll still have the numbers to block their ballots in every constituency south of the Susquehanna."

"But that will depend greatly on who *our* nominee will be," the Senator said. "The Republicans are one obstacle, but campaigning against Stephen Douglas will be another feat entirely. What did Mr. Yancey say about me? When will he make his endorsement public?"

Cutler shifted in his seat. He turned to Solomon seated beside him and held out his cup and saucer. With an obedient bow, Solomon lifted a coffee pot off the small dining trolley tucked in the corner and poured a fresh cup of steaming coffee for his master.

"We didn't have the chance to speak of such matters," Cutler said, his eyes following the rising steam of his filling cup.

"But you were together all night!" the Senator protested. "You and Yancey, and Jeff Davis and Robert Toombs, all the others." The old man shook his head with dismay. "I should have gone to the Charleston Hotel with you last night. I wish you hadn't convinced me to attend that meeting at the governor's house. I might have been of some help at the meeting."

"No doubt," Cutler replied. "But it was important that we keep good relations with Governor Pickens and his men. Besides, I thought perhaps you'd appreciate a more restful social outing. I know how difficult these last few days have been for you."

The Senator huffed and looked out the window. "I can already imagine what all the newspaper editors will say come tomorrow's first edition."

"Yancey has agreed to take care of that," Cutler said. "No unfounded criticism of you shall be read in any Southern paper. If anything, your patriotism will be the subject of considerable praise. And you have my personal guarantee for that, so far as the *Mayfair First Witness* is concerned."

"I appreciate that," the Senator said, "but I really do think we ought to talk seriously about Baltimore. No doubt there are others who sense opportunity. I do not expect to be the only nominee, but I do expect that Yancey, Davis, and the others will provide their endorsement sooner rather than later. If we can establish me as the front-runner right out of the gate, then we may very well trot to the finish."

Once again, Cutler grimaced and shifted about. "This all reminds me of something I've been meaning to mention." He turned on Solomon and hissed at him to refill the Senator's cup, and be quick about it. As the Senator leaned forward to receive fresh coffee, Cutler smiled and said, rather abruptly and matter of fact, "You won't have any endorsements, I'm afraid."

The Senator flinched and a stream of hot coffee spilled over his quivering hand. The old man yowled and dropped the cup and saucer to the carpeted floor. The pieces did not shatter, but coffee splashed in every direction.

Red-faced, Cutler shouted, "Goddammit, Solomon, look what you've done!"

"I'm sorry, sir, Massa Tobe, sir. I'm sorry, Senator Ros—"

"Get out!" Cutler snarled. "Why I invited you up here in the first place is beyond me. Back to the nigger-car. Out, get out!"

Shaking, Solomon struggled upright and fled as quickly as his feeble form could manage.

Cutler clicked his tongue while wiping at the stains on the floor with a handkerchief. "What a mess..."

The Senator, meanwhile, paid no attention to the spilled coffee or his scalded hand. "What the hell do you mean I'll have no endorsements?"

Cutler shrugged and offered a weak smile. "Mr. Yancey, together with others in our circle, believe that our candidate ought to be a man who has...an *existing* reputation as a states' rights man."

The Senator scowled. "Come off it, Tobias. What about all that talk about nominating a man of compromise? Tell me exactly what Yancey said."

With a sigh, Cutler sat back. "Yancey wants Breckinridge."

Hearing that name, Ben looked up with surprise. John Breckinridge was Vice President of the United States. The son of a prominent Kentucky planter family, Breckinridge was said to be an advocate of Southern secession even while occupying the Union's second greatest seat of power.

"*Breckinridge?*" the Senator echoed, his voice dripping with venomous disgust.

"The vice president was at the governor's dinner last night. Are you really telling me that while I shared a table with Breckinridge, you and Yancey were discussing *his* nomination instead of mine?"

Cutler shook his head. "That's a mere coincidence, JR, and nothing more."

The Senator shook his head with disbelief. "James Buchanan will go down in American history as being one of the most ineffectual presidents to sit in the White House, and Yancey wants to endorse his number two? No, no, this can't be true, Tobias. What did Jeff Davis say about this? Jeff and I have been friends for years, and I know he's no fool. Surely he sees the folly in ticketing what would be little more than the continuation of a failed administration?"

In body and spirit, Cutler distanced himself from the conversation. "I'm afraid Jeff Davis concurs with Yancey, JR, as do the other gentlemen. They believe your relationship with Stephen Douglas, though severed, raises some doubt about your loyalty to the Southern cause."

With a loud grunt, the Senator drove his cane down. The cup, which still lay on the floor, cracked under the weight of the blow.

Seething, the Senator said, "I did all but plunge a knife into Stephen Douglas' spine. Thirty years of friendship, and I threw it away so that I — so that *we*, Tobias — might build a new, modern administration that finally settles the North-South crisis for once and for all. Machiavelli himself would not have attempted such a coup were he not certain that the ends would justify the means."

"You know as well as I do," Cutler said, "that politics offers no certainties."

"But men of good faith *do* offer their word," the Senator growled, "and men of honor *keep* it."

Ben wanted to laugh at that, but he kept quiet.

Here, Cutler bristled. "I don't know why you're angry with me, JR. It was not *my* decision to endorse Breckinridge. I'm blameless in all this. I even lobbied to Yancey on your behalf. I explained to him that, of course, you were just as worthy a candidate as anyone else."

The Senator offered a curdled smile. "But my dear Tobias, I thought you and Yancey did not have a chance to speak of such matters? Isn't that what you just told me?"

Cutler finished the rest of his coffee with one gulp. With a sigh, he set his cup and saucer down on the small table beside him and stood up. Smoothing down his suit, Cutler sniffed and said, "I understand you're upset, JR. I share much of your disappointment, but a friend can only offer so much by way of condolences. I'll leave you now to think on these developments. I'm going to the observation car for a smoke."

The Senator grunted and waved him off.

Cutler paused at the door leading to the aisle. He looked down at Ben.

"I do hope," Cutler said to the Senator, "that your boy here will be gone when I get back. I don't relish the thought of sharing my air with him the entire journey home. Besides, he ought to keep Solomon company in the nigger-car."

With that, Cutler left the private cabin.

For a long moment, Ben and the Senator sat side by side in silence. Finally, Ben turned and looked upon the old man. With a cold stare, Ben studied the multitude of facial contortions that John Roscoe exhibited like so many masks from Greek theatre. The old man pulled on one frozen visage of emotion only to find it ineffective before hastily discarding it for another. In this display, which Ben could see as nothing more than mere performance, Ben saw the Senator offer looks of dismay, remorse, shame, anger, regret, and countless variations in between. All during this time, Ben strained to keep his own hateful emotions from bursting out.

Ben wanted to hit the old man, but he didn't. He wanted to scream at the old man, but he didn't. On instinct, as one might reel from a snake, Ben rose to his feet and backed toward the door. A tempest of rageful tirades rose up from within him. He wanted nothing more than to pummel the stupid old sellout with abuses and condemnations.

"Ben," the Senator said pitifully, "Ben, I need to…Ben, I want to explain…"

Ben did not linger to hear the rest. He pushed the cabin door open and slammed it shut behind him. He stood in the aisle of the railcar, breathing hard. He looked up and down to ensure there were no watchful eyes staring. Sensing no one was looking, Ben stuffed his hand in his mouth and bit down on his fingers as hot tears streamed down his cheeks. Shaking his head, he hastily wiped the tears from his face with his hand and sleeve.

Ben turned to walk down toward the 'negro car' at the train's rear. He wasn't going there because goddamn Cutler wanted him to. It was because he had no interest in spending another stifling minute with neither Cutler nor John Roscoe. The two men were more alike than different, and to hell with them both.

Just as he was about to start off, Ben caught sight of the Senator through a thick pane of glass looking into the private cabin. The warped image of the old man was grotesque in shape and color, but the essence of the man was clear. John Roscoe was stooped over in his seat, his head buried in his hands. Ben could hear no sounds from within the cabin, but he saw the old man quake and shudder as if suffering excruciating, bone-rending pain.

For how long Ben stood there staring, he didn't know. Eventually his wits returned and he hurried down the aisle toward the next car. He passed Cutler on the way and was obliged to stand back and bow his head to the man, resisting every urge to leap upon him and somehow tear out his throat. When Ben finally reached the cramped negro car and was met with countless cold, dismissive stares, he realized he had found no refuge. He barreled forward, moving like a man through blinding smoke, until at last he burst out into the fresh air of the caboose's observation deck.

Ben clutched the rail and stared down at the ground running up from underneath, as if the whole world were spilling from the train's metal maw in some bizarre act of cosmic regurgitation. The track lengthened through miles of sloping green country, stretching back across lifetimes and eons, the landscape ever fading into the distance. This train was bearing him back to Mayfair, back to what he knew, and yet somehow he felt the sensation of moving forward into the unknown. The whole history of the world seemed laid out upon the country he was so swiftly departing, visible but unreachable. He wanted to turn and look toward what was coming, but the courage to do so was sapped from his bones. Instead, he kept his back turned against whatever he might call the future, with the uncertain present ever forming underfoot.

CHAPTER 22

THE DUCHESS OF ARCADIA

THAT CLOUDLESS SATURDAY, forever etched into the happy couple's gilded wedding china as May 19th, 1860, was a day which many within Mayfair's high society would long remember as one of the finest and final days of the Antebellum.

It was a day when the Virginia sun shone proud and bright, but no collars were wilted. It was a day when husbands and wives linked arms with tenderness, showered kisses on their children, and marveled at the beauty of their humble little world while pondering the gifts of God. For all the troubles brewing across the Union, for all the troubles across the entire world, here and now there was only a pleasant hum in the air from droning insects, the pungent smell of dogwood and magnolia and cherry, the enchanting sound of the wind through the branches of Clarendon's tall beeches and drooping willows trees.

In the grove behind Clarendon's back portico, two wide columns of whitewashed chairs sat in the shade of willow trees. The boughs of the trees were entwined, like the great roof of a massive green cathedral. Before the chairs was a new altar made of fresh-cut pine, constructed and sanded and whitewashed just days before. The bridegroom Henry Cutler stood upon the altar with his reverend brother beside him, and off to the side stood Horace Glanton and several other men dressed in Cutler livery.

In the chairs sat over three hundred guests. They were old friends, cousins, and neighbors: the Merricks, Hanleys, Claibornes, and other First Families of Mayfair; the Blairs from Rich Neck; the Archers from Williamsburg and College Creek; the Rolfes, descended from the first master of Jamestown himself, John Rolfe. Also present was the family of Isabella's younger sister Anna: the exotic Taliaferros from Fredericksburg. Of the younger generation, the breathtaking India Taliaferro, with caramel skin and piercing amber eyes, was expected to gain a fiancé during the course of the wedding. (Rumors circulated that a match had already been arranged for India and Jem Roscoe.) A star guest was India's brother Fitzhugh, heir to the family fortune at Hagley Plantation and a dashing cavalry officer on furlough from Indian fighting in the far west. There were many dignitaries present also: congressmen, governors, military officers, all with their stately wives in gorgeous designer gowns. The pomp and pageantry exceeded even the highest expectations.

Looking out at the scene from the safety of the big house, Sarah Roscoe felt a sudden wave of nausea. There were so many people. Too many people. And all here for her? She knew less than half of them, and half *that* amount were mere acquaintances. The sentiment was exhilarating and terrifying at the same time.

Sarah realized just then that she was living the last minutes of her life as Sarah 'Roscoe'; in a few minutes more, she would become someone new. She would become a Cutler.

A new life awaited her just outside Clarendon's doors, the doors that she once felt had kept her trapped inside. For so long she counted herself among the miserable heroines of all those fairy tales, the ones shut up in castles by evil witches who had cast spells of negligence upon bumbling fathers. But tonight, Sarah would be free. She would be *the orphan* no more, and instead be a wife, and someday soon, a mother. Tonight she would go with Henry to his plantation home at Arcadia, and there they would build a new life together. A happy life.

The last few months had been a whirlwind. Sarah remembered vividly the first time Henry came to call on her. She could still see him pounding up Clarendon's gravel driveway atop his horse. Henry clicked his tongue and made his horse dance in circles, and Sarah had laughed with delight. She could still remember how handsome Henry looked in the Valley twilight, with his hair tumbling down and with the frills of his shirt protruding from a chest-fitting broadcloth.

Sarah recalled a courtship that was beautiful and sweet. They walked together around Clarendon's gardens and sat together in the grove where twin willows wept together. Sometimes Henry took Sarah out on carriage rides around the Valley.

Of course, that nasty business with Ben Freeman and the Cutlers' runaway slave had threatened to ruin everything. But Henry was most gracious about everything, assuring her that justice had been served and that there was no ill will between their families. After all, the Roscoes had done what any Valley family would have been expected to do in such a situation: they complied with the proper authorities. "And you, more than anyone, did the right thing," Henry had told her. "You helped bring a criminal to justice, Sarah. You made the world a better place that night."

In truth, Sarah didn't know if what she'd done had been right. But *Henry* believed it was right, and that made her *want* to believe it, and after some time passed she decided that she'd changed her mind about everything. She decided that what she'd done *had* been right, and that she would do it again.

A few months later, just before Christmas, Henry and Sarah were riding through the Valley when he took her hands into her own. Touching the ring — Mother's ring — on her right hand, Henry gently pulled the ring free. While he started into an incoherent but nevertheless adorable discussion of Christian marriage, Sarah felt her pulse quicken. And when Henry looked at her and said those five little words—

"Will you marry me, Sarah?"

—she felt a shudder travel down her spine, the same blissful shiver she'd anticipated for so many years. As Henry took up Mother's ring and gently pushed it onto the ring finger of her left hand, Sarah closed her eyes and basked in the agonizing joy that pulsed through her. In that moment she felt a greater peace than any she had ever known in her life. Opening her eyes again, she gave her beau — her *fiancé* — a playful smile.

"Why don't you kiss me, Mr. Cutler. I'll think on your proposition while you do."

❧

Out on the grounds, a string quartet picked up their instruments and began to play. It was a song she recognized but could not name. Something rather baroque, but nonetheless enchanting. Now Sarah began to feel right again. She was a princess after all, a woman of Southern nobility.

And there, upon the altar, stood her handsome duke. Henry, for once looking shy and uncomfortable with so many eyes on him, stood wringing his hands and looking around nervously. Sarah stared at him, loving him, until she forgot how much time had passed.

Henry's little sister Penelope led the way down the aisle, scattering white flower petals at her feet as she went. The bridesmaids were debutantes, each handpicked by Sarah to shine brighter than the one who came before, but with careful assurances that even the most beautiful among them could not eclipse Sarah's grand entrance.

As the music swelled, Sarah realized it was time to go. Taking a deep breath, she passed through the door and stepped outside to meet her future.

She stood there on the threshold, with just one step separating her from womanhood. Three hundred bodies and heads turned toward her. Taking that final step, she walked to the edge of the shaded veranda and marveled at the sight before her. The people were all looking at *her*, and her alone. Fear froze her to the spot for a long moment, but then she saw Daddy in a fine suit waiting for her on the grass.

Daddy had lost even more weight than the last time he visited home. He had been in Washington for most of the winter and spring, and she knew his work had taken a toll on him. His skin was thinner than she had ever known it to be, his hair whiter and his eyes darker, but he was still a handsome man nonetheless. She was proud to walk alongside him.

Sarah embraced Daddy for a long moment. A thought came to mind that this would be the last time she hugged Daddy as his little girl. As they drew back, she saw that Daddy looked upon her not with his usual barely concealed disappointment, but with a tearful expression of sincere pride. When he offered his arm to her, she clutched to him and rested her head on his shoulder.

They moved slowly up the grassy aisle. The pace was fine enough for Sarah, for it gave her more time to look out and smile at her guests. She beamed at Mary Beth Wise, who stood arm in arm with her husband Chandler (they had married back in December). Old society rivals like Pippa Claiborne looked upon Sarah with adoration and yearning, and not a little jealousy.

With no small satisfaction, Sarah looked upon the faces of failed suitors: Percy Claiborne, Sam Hanley, even her cousin Fitzhugh Taliaferro. All stared at her with forlorn expressions that were rather touching, but they did nothing for her but confirm the realization that Henry Cutler was really and truly *the one*.

Before the altar now, Sarah hugged Daddy one last time. Henry stepped forward and warmly shook Daddy's hand. Daddy shuffled slowly to his seat while Henry took Sarah's hand and led her up the altar.

Facing each other, Sarah marveled at the sensation of holding both of Henry's hands in her own. The long, watchful moment between them was loving, sincere, and perhaps just a little too serious. Henry made a funny face and Sarah giggled. A gentle, adoring *Ahh* rolled through the guests. Someone snorted loudly at the sentimentality of the moment and Sarah was almost certain it was Tom.

Reverend Lucas Cutler cleared his throat.

"Family, friends, and faithful servants of the Lord Jesus Christ. Today we share a very special blessing under God's own perfect sky. Today we stand witness to the holy vows of marriage between man and wife."

Henry flashed his eyebrows at Sarah: *Here we go*.

Sarah took a deep breath and smiled.

"In the Garden," Lucas said, "when the world was young, God determined it was not good for Man to live alone. And so from his rib he crafted a suitable companion to care for Man, to obey Man, and to help Man embrace God's grace. And thus marriage was created, and standing witness to this creation was the whole of the heavenly host. And God smiled upon all this and decided that it was very good indeed."

As the ceremony went on, Sarah looked upon her family in the front row. Daddy beamed at her and nodded. Cousin Isabella sat with her hands folded neatly on her lap with a smile, undoubtedly false, set on pursed lips. Jem was not even paying attention to the ceremony, but instead was gazing up at the trees, his eyes far off somewhere else. Next was Bayard, docile and smiling, and next to him sat Tom, who stared blankly at the proceedings without interest.

Sarah had already made peace with the knowledge that JJ would not be at her wedding, but all the same his absence had a presence of its own. Seeing Mae Jane watching the ceremony with tears of joy streaming down her weathered cheeks, Sarah's own eyes welled as she offered her old mammy a quivering smile.

Her eyes fell on Ben Freeman last. He was busy staring into his hands, but when he looked up he offered a small smile of encouragement, and then he looked down into his hands again. And that was it, nothing more.

Sarah felt Henry squeeze her hands and she turned to face him again. He mouthed the words *I love you*, and she blushed furiously. Knowing she was being watched by hundreds, she mouthed the words back to Henry. Not a few of the guests sighed another great *Ahh* at the blessed sight.

By and by, Henry Cutler and Sarah Roscoe recited their vows. The boy-reverend blessed the couple with a high appeal to God for "His guidance, His wisdom, and His instruction to the daughters of Eve to serve and obey the sons of Adam."

And now, amidst frantic cheering and applause, Henry and Sarah Cutler kissed for the first time as husband and wife.

❧

"Hold on a moment…there we are…and three, two, one…patience, please…"

Click.

Was…was that it?

Sarah was still looking at the child-sized contraption suspended on wooden legs when suddenly Henry abandoned his position at her side to greet a circle of his friends. Sarah watched him go but remained frozen in place wearing a tight-lipped smile — not too wide, she was instructed, for only soft-brained idiots actually smiled for 'photo-graphs.'

At last Sarah broke character and looked over at the photographer, who was fussing with his contraption and muttering to himself.

"Did everything work as expected, sir?"

The photographer flinched and looked at her. "Well, I think so. I mean *yes*, yes, of course it did. I mean, I'll know for sure in a few days' time. But yes, I'm certain of it. I'm a professional after all, miss."

"*Missus*," Henry corrected. He had just now returned with a fresh drink in hand.

Sarah turned to Henry and beamed at him. "Oh, isn't it wonderful, Henry? Our very own *wedding photo*, the very first ever taken in the Valley."

"Splendid indeed," he said. Now he swept her in close and whispered in her ear, "I want you."

She resisted the urge to wrinkle her nose at the stench of his whiskey-soaked breath. Instead she smiled at him and said, "You have me, silly."

Henry kissed her. Such bold public affection between men and women was frowned upon in all circles, but she knew people would forgive them on this one day. He thrust his hips against the folds of her dress and murmured, "I want you, and you know what I mean by it. No more child's play."

Sarah, seeing the photographer gawking at them in her periphery, gently pushed

Henry back and blushed. "You've been drinking, Henry."

He grinned at her. "Of course, honey. It's our wedding after all. Didn't I tell you long ago what a boor I am?" He lowered his voice. "A passionate boor at that."

She squeezed his hand. "Soon," she whispered. "Very soon you shall have me."

Speaking in such a way was like learning a foreign language. She was terribly frightened she would say something wrong, that Henry would return a strangled look of embarrassment that would kill her if she saw it. But still his eyes were fixed on her, and with a dark joy she realized that Henry hung on her every word. After some hesitation she added slyly, "Tonight, you shall have *all* of me."

She watched his eyes shine with anticipation. It was very interesting indeed, this newlywed game of cat and mouse. Perhaps she would enjoy it a little while longer. She let go of his hand with a teasing smile. She twirled in her wedding dress and stepped away as Henry reached out for her.

"Not so fast," she said with a wagging finger. "I'm going to say hello to our guests." She could feel his eyes hot on her back, trailing down, watching her hips and legs move under the rustling dress.

The wedding feast had begun, and Mrs. Sarah Cutler — oh, she would *never* tire of hearing that name — looked up at the patches of blue sky cut from a passing blanket of gray clouds. Thank God the rain was holding off. The air was heavy with humidity, but the guests were seated around all the tables under the open air and the musicians continued to play. So far, Sarah's perfect day was a complete success.

Black servants dressed in fine Cutler livery served drinks and canapes to guests. In a fine gesture of solidarity, the Cutlers had loaned some fifty servants to Clarendon to help prepare the wedding feast and other matters. Mae Jane Freeman had received quite a shock to see fifty servants, most of them women, march into the house and proceed to dust and mop and polish everything in sight. Clarendon had not seen anything like it in over twenty years.

Looking across the lawn now, Sarah saw Mae Jane standing in the doorway that connected the kitchens to the veranda. Servants hurried out of the door carrying platters of drinks and of foodstuffs, and they hustled back inside with trays of empty dishes. Old Solomon, the Cutlers' butler, clasped a pocket watch and urged the servants to move faster, with more liveliness. Meanwhile, the visibly exhausted old maid caught her breath and wiped her brow, but she was likewise observing the bustling scene with a look of pride.

Sarah floated through the gardens of Clarendon as if in a dream. Young women from all over the Valley and places far beyond approached Sarah and spoke adoringly about her dress and her hair and her radiance, and for once Sarah allowed herself to believe every word. All the young bachelors kissed her on the cheek, and though she knew this sight would make Henry terribly jealous she allowed it all the same. Why, she was a married woman now, and would be so forever. Couldn't she have a last bit of childish fun?

Looking around, Sarah surveyed a curious divide between the wedding guests. It was almost like observing two opposing colonies of ants. On one side of the lawn, a large group of gentlemen clustered around Daddy. Most of these guests were from beyond the Branches and had to be political friends from Washington and elsewhere. Meanwhile, on the opposite side of the lawn, her father-in-law Judge Cutler held court with notable guests including Vice President John Breckinridge, whom Sarah understood was a candidate for president.

A man who might become president, at *her* wedding. How splendid! But why was it that Daddy and Judge Cutler were not speaking to each other? Indeed they seemed to have avoided each other during the whole day so far, interacting only when custom required. Henry had told her some of what had happened during Daddy's trip to Charleston earlier in the spring, but she'd been too embarrassed to ask for the full story. Well, maybe it was true that the Roscoes stumbled from one scandal to another. But since she herself was now a Cutler, she didn't have to worry about her family's antics any longer.

Out of the corner of her eye, Sarah spotted Mary Beth Wise across the lawn. Picking up her dress, Sarah turned and crashed right into a servant carrying a tray of drinks.

Guests gasped in shock, and Sarah's heart leaped into her mouth. Horrified, she staggered back and looked down at her white dress. She expected to see horrible, discolored stains, but miraculously her dress was dry and spotless. Looking up again, she saw that the slave girl who had crashed into her was doused in julep and brandy, the entire front of her dress and apron soaked completely through. The girl stared at Sarah with an expression of cold shock, and suddenly her mouth began to move as she stuttered her way through a thousand apologies.

"It's fine," Sarah said, still shaken. "Really, it is. But next time, I ask you to be more—"

"TATTIE!"

Turning, Sarah looked upon old Solomon, the Cutlers' chief servant. The girl named Tattie froze with fear and held the empty tray at her side with her eyes cast down. Solomon approached and grabbed the girl's ear and twisted it until she screamed, and then he hauled her away from the scene and around the corner of the house. Watching from a few tables over, Horace Glanton stood up and adjusted his belt and followed them around the corner.

An old woman touched Sarah's arm. "Are you all right, miss?"

Sarah smiled at the woman and nodded. "Yes, very fine," she said. "A bit shaken of course. But all's well that ends well, isn't it?"

The guests around her smiled and laughed. With a sigh of relief, Sarah turned and carried on enjoying the reception. With a final glance over her shoulder she looked for the girl named Tattie, but she was nowhere to be seen.

"Sarah? Dear Sarah, darling, a word with you?"

Her new mother-in-law, Mrs. Lucretia Cutler, pulled her toward a small circle of finely dressed ladies and gentlemen. Their pungent perfumes invaded Sarah's nostrils and made her eyes water.

Mrs. Cutler made introductions at a blistering pace: "My sister Marion and her husband, Mr. Aldous Hammond…Mr. Roger Pryor, one of Tobias' good friends… and this is James De Bow, a fabulous writer from New Orleans. (You regale your readers with the latest advancements in cotton ginning technology, don't you, James? Oh, among other people-keeping topics, yes of course.) Sarah, you must know Mr. William Yancey of Alabama…"

Sarah nodded and smiled obligingly to each guest in turn until she began to feel dizzy.

"And here," Mrs. Cutler said, "is my first cousin, Mr. Nathan Bedford Forrest."

Sarah smiled and shook hands with a tall, handsome man with wild hair and a dark beard. "A pleasure to meet you, Mr. Forrest. Henry's told me of his admiration for you."

The man named Forrest offered a mellow, disarming smile that was positively enchanting. Still holding Sarah's hand, he held her fingers to his mouth and kissed her wedding ring. "Charmed to the last, ma'am."

Mrs. Cutler let out a giddy, girlish laugh. "Nathan surprised us with a visit this week, so we simply had to invite him to the wedding." Mrs. Cutler was incapable of keeping her hands away from her cousin, and was set on stroking and pawing him without relent. "And he's been *so* kind as to offer a negro-breaking job to my Henry. Henry just might take it, but only if his new bride could be convinced to move to the wilds of Mississippi!"

Forrest grinned. "I just bought two plantations down in Coahoma County. The country there may be wild, but at least the coloreds don't make a fuss." He winked at Mrs. Cutler. "Not like *this* horrid place, Lucretia. You might as well live in Nantucket the way your darkies behave."

Mrs. Cutler gave him a playful push. "Oh, you are a terrible tease, Nathan."

Sarah bowed her head graciously. "Wherever my husband wishes to go, I shall of course follow. On behalf of my husband, I thank you for the opportunity, sir."

Forrest drained his brandy glass and caught sight of a passing servant wearing all black. "You there, boy!"

The servant turned, and Sarah saw it was Ben Freeman.

Forrest tossed his empty glass to Ben without ceremony; Ben nearly dropped it. "Fetch me a fresh drink," Forrest called.

For a long moment, Ben held the glass and stood in silence. Sarah recognized a burning resentment behind his eyes, a blazing anger directed at the entire group of prim ladies and gentlemen. When she caught Ben's gaze she realized that she herself was likewise a target of his naked animosity.

Turning to Mrs. Cutler, Sarah saw her mother-in-law's eyes flash with panicked shame. Just how, those eyes wondered, would this unkempt Roscoe negro embarrass her? Meanwhile, Forrest's eyes dared this uppity bull before him to just try and talk back. Try it, those eyes said, and Ben would learn how they dealt with lippy darkies back in Coahoma County.

Sarah felt fear for Ben. But then she felt the cold sweat of humiliation. She could not let her new mother-in-law be embarrassed by Ben's petulance. Not here, not today, not when she'd only just become a Cutler herself. For pity's sake, shouldn't Ben *know better* by now?

"Well?" Sarah snapped at Ben. "The gentleman has given you an order, Mr. Freeman, so be quick about it."

Ben blinked, his anger instantly replaced by numb shock. He stared at Sarah with a slack jaw and eyes filled with pain. But he did not expose his hurt for long; nodding curtly to Sarah and the assembled ladies and gentlemen, Ben put his head down and rushed off through the crowd.

Watching Ben go, Forrest laughed and shook his head. "Mr. Freeman, is it? His master must have been a cruel man. But now do you see, Lucretia? Our niggers don't have that questioning look in their eyes, like they're almost about to ask you *why* they must submit to your commands. We've bred it out of them."

"Virginia planters are too soft," the man named Mr. Yancey agreed with a shrug. "It's no wonder the abolitionists are stealing away more and more hands every month. The masters practically let the poor things walk out the front door."

Sarah looked around and tried to spot Ben in the milling crowd. She could not understand what had come over her a moment ago. Seeing Ben's anger, his indignation, had simply enraged her beyond comprehension. She could not understand why Ben should look with such raw contempt upon noble men like Mr. Forrest. But neither could she understand how it was so easy for her to speak to her oldest and dearest friend as if he was...well, as if he was a *servant*.

But wasn't that just what he was?

There. There was Ben, tracing a path along the side of the house. He stopped before a set of French doors that led into the library and slipped inside, but not before pitching Bedford Forrest's glass into the bushes nearby.

"If you'll excuse me," Sarah said to Mrs. Cutler and her guests, "I just have to see about something. Something regarding the...um...the wedding cake."

"Bless your heart!" Mrs. Cutler said with a laugh. "This is your *wedding day*. You of all people shouldn't be concerned with matters of hosting, dear girl. Let someone else worry about such particulars."

Bedford Forrest offered a charming smile. "Particulars is why we have niggers, after all."

Sarah smiled and curtsied. "I do apologize. If you'll excuse me, please."

As she wove her way through the crowd, Sarah felt lightheaded and nauseous, and not a little dizzy. She needed a break from it all, if only for a few minutes. Hundreds of beaming faces commanded her attention but she could only offer them the faintest of smiles as she hurried past them and made a beeline for the cool, dark safety of the house.

Sarah felt a hand on her shoulder and stopped. She had barely started to turn around when she was met by Mary Beth Wise's pouting face.

"And just what do you mean by that?" Mary whined.

Sarah furrowed her brow. "By…mean by what?"

Mary pointed across the lawn, as if indicating a moment back in time. "By waving to me as if you were coming over. You know, fixing me to the ground like a fool, and then turning tail to carry on with all your more important guests."

Stunned, Sarah wracked her mind for some sort of reasonable answer, but she could think of nothing to say. Oh, for God's sake, was there nothing she could do right today? Couldn't all these people just leave her alone? Couldn't they just—

"*Joking*!" Mary cried with a giddy laugh. Now she threw herself into Sarah's arms and squeezed. "You should see the look on your face — *serious married woman*. Oh, dear sister, I'm so happy for you!"

Sarah sighed and melted against Mary's touch. "Thank you, dear. Thank you."

Mary took Sarah by the hand and they passed under the shade of a nearby tree, away from most of the party guests. "Tell me, how are you getting along? Are you wanting to open your wrists in a warm bath just yet?"

Sarah heaved a deep breath. "Well, now that you mention it…"

"You look breathtaking," Mary said admiringly. "Chandler was salivating when he saw you, but I won't hold it against him."

Sarah smiled to hide her grimace. The thought of guffawing Chandler Wise leering at her was not exactly a complimentary idea.

"And your Henry, *my* he's a catch today. Every day, I should say."

Sarah beamed. "Thank you, Mary."

Mary looked over her shoulder in a conspiratorial way, and now she leaned forward and whispered into Sarah's ear. "Now, before the day gets too far along, there's a few things you should know…"

Mary proceeded to spill all the secrets of the marital bed, lessons she'd learned over the past however many months. It all sounded rather sticky and painful, and Sarah said as much. To that, Mary only giggled and told her to *just wait*.

"After your wedding night," she said, "you'll never look at a stud horse the same way again."

Sarah scolded Mary for being immodest, but in truth she supposed she was only trying to hide her jealousy. But all that would end tonight, of course. Tonight, she would finally know why some men looked at her the way they did, and why Henry looked at her the same way. At last, she would know what they were *really* thinking behind those lidded gazes, and she would confirm her own suspicions too.

"It will hurt," Mary went on, "but only a little, and only at first. You cannot show fear or make unpleasant noises, or he shan't touch you ever again. If you decline him even once, he shan't ever touch you again and will take up with a mistress. If you give the impression that his performance is unsatisfactory, he shan't ever touch you again and will take up with a mistress."

Sarah nodded and smiled, despite feeling faint. She wished she had a pencil and piece of paper to take a few notes for later reference.

"Give it to him every time he wants it," Mary said. "Do that, and he will be yours. And trust me, you'll want it too." Losing all sense of decency, Mary's smile twisted into a lascivious grin. "You'll want it *all*. And *all* the time!"

Before Sarah could press for more details, she heard loud applause from across the lawn. Stepping out from under the tree, she and Mary looked out to see Daddy standing up amidst a crowd of fawning guests. Daddy called for the nearby string band to cease its playing, and with a loud voice he called for attention. Slowly, conversations dangled and heads turned to look upon Daddy.

"Here comes the bride," Mary murmured with a dark grin. "How does it feel to be the second most important person at your wedding?"

"Oh hush," Sarah said, rapping Mary's wrist gently. Even still, she found it difficult to laugh it off. Just what was Daddy trying to do, interrupting the party to make a speech? She was too busy trying to remember whether all this was part of the wedding schedule, but of course it wasn't.

"On this joyous day," Daddy began, "we take time to—"

He was cut short as a hoarse coughing fit overtook him. He coughed several times into his handkerchief before folding it and stuffing it in his pocket.

"On this joyous day," he began again, sniffling, "we take time to thank God for His many blessings. We thank our friends and neighbors for joining us, and for giving their support to the new Mr. and Mrs. Henry Cutler."

The crowd offered genial applause, with several loud cries of *Hear-hear*!

Daddy continued. "We can also thank our lucky stars for our being born in this, the greatest and most prosperous time in human history. And we can be likewise thankful for *where* we were born: here, in Virginia, under the banner of the Union. What's more, we must recognize *to whom* we were born: our ancestors, close and distant. They have bestowed on us a great republic which not even Plato could have imagined, and which not even the conquering legions of Rome could have forged."

Another smattering of friendly clapping. Sarah sighed and hoped that Daddy would soon get to his point, whatever it was. *Thank the guests, welcome the groom, and sit down, for God's sake.*

"But while we practice gratitude for our American civilization," Daddy said, "let us also remember that it is our responsibility to safeguard that civilization. It is our responsibility as citizens to shore up the foundations of our own democracy. Indeed, it is our responsibility to form, in the words of our Founding Fathers, a more perfect Union."

From her vantage point, Sarah saw that several of Daddy's friends and supporters met these words with earnest applause, as if urging Daddy on. Sarah noted also that Judge Cutler and his circle were themselves quiet and watchful. The many guests scattered between these factions were no doubt only wondering why the music had stopped.

Daddy beamed at his guests. "This is why, today, on the day of my daughter's wedding, I submit to you — my friends, my neighbors, and the American people — that I, John Roscoe, am ready to accept the responsibility of governance. I will accept the challenge of protecting our beloved Union, of upholding the Constitution, of steering the ship of American democracy toward safe harbors."

Low gasps went up from the crowd as the meaning of those words began to sink in.

Beside Sarah, Mary breathed, "He's not about to say what I think he's about to say, is he?"

Sarah stood frozen, breathless. In her periphery, she saw Judge Cutler, together with Mr. Breckinridge and others in their circle, whisper excitedly amongst themselves. Her gaze was meanwhile fixed on Daddy, who smiled broadly all around.

"Today," he said, "I announce to you that I, together with my esteemed colleagues you see with me today, have formed a new political party: that of the Constitutional Unionists."

Here, several guests turned and looked at each other in confusion. The Constitutional What?

Daddy lifted his chin high. "And, with respect to the founding of this new organization, I must also announce my candidacy for President of the United States of America. Sunday edition headlines stating as such will be printed Union-wide tomorrow."

Sarah felt Mary's hand clasp hers. Meanwhile, gasps of shock echoed among the guests. For a long time, no one moved or said anything. A smattering of applause began, with the trickle now becoming a sweeping wave of jubilation. Many now stood up from their seats to cheer and beam smiles all around.

"Thank you," Daddy said. "Thank you, no need for applause."

For her part, Sarah was still trying to determine whether she'd heard Daddy right or not. Did he just say he was running for *president*?

And why in God's name would her own father make such a grandstanding announcement at *her* wedding? What part of him ever thought such a thing could be right?

Judge Cutler stood up from his table and walked off with Breckinridge and a man Sarah vaguely recognized as Mr. Yancey, one of the Judge's good friends. Daddy seemed to notice this movement from where he stood.

"Now I know this announcement may come as a shock to some of you," Daddy said, a smug smile on his face, "but I at least hope it's at least a *pleasant* shock for most of you..."

The guests laughed and applauded, but by now Sarah could take no more. Her head swam from the heat, from the noise of the crowd, from Daddy's speech, from *everything*.

"Sarah?" Mary said. "Sarah, are you all right?"

"...much to do between now and November, but there is nothing that cannot be achieved if there is concerted action. Now is the time to stand up for Virginia, for *America...*"

Fighting tears, Sarah shrugged off Mary's comforting grasp and fled. She made for the safety of Clarendon. Plunging inside, she threw the door shut behind her. But no sooner did she consider herself safe did she realize that the wedding guests had infested not just Clarendon's grounds, but had also occupied its parlors and sitting rooms.

Sarah hurried down the hallway toward the library and was thankful to find it quiet and empty of guests. She retreated to one of the bookcases at the far end and leaned against it to catch her breath. In that moment she wanted nothing more than to tear open the tight basque of her wedding dress so that she could breathe normally again.

Humiliated. Exhausted. Elated. Confused. She couldn't decide how she felt, as if she had any say in the matter.

No say.

Sarah never had a say in anything. Not while she was here at Clarendon. Under this roof, she never felt like part of the family. She was always a guest, and one who had long outstayed her welcome. The Colonel was gone, this was Cousin Isabella's house now, and Daddy had time and again proved himself incapable of standing up for Sarah. He professed to treasure his daughter, but she could not recall the last meaningful conversation they'd ever shared together.

And to usurp the wedding like that. To turn it into a political rally...

What kind of father — what kind of *man* — could do such a thing?

"Miss Sarah?"

She nearly shrieked with fright. Turning, she saw Ben seated in one of the armchairs before the cold, empty fireplace. He had a book in one hand and a glass of whiskey in the other.

"Are you all right?" he asked.

Sarah tried to answer him, but she found herself unable to speak. Suddenly, the day's emotions came flooding out of her. Amidst her streaming tears she attempted a laugh — a last feeble attempt to play it off — before she broke down completely. She finally caught her breath again.

"I suppose I'm a little…very much…overwhelmed."

Ben watched her for a long moment. He looked to be decided something. But finally he stood up. He went to Daddy's liquor cabinet and fetched a second glass, and he poured half a thumb of whiskey into the glass and offered it.

"This will help."

Her eyes were puffy and sore. "I'm not much for spirits," she murmured.

"Neither am I. But there's a first time for everything." He cheersed her glass. "It's just a little liquid courage."

She managed a weak laugh, and together they drank. The liquor burned on the way down, but afterward she felt better. Somehow, her mind felt clearer.

"There," Ben said. "The color is returning to your cheeks."

She blushed and thanked him for the help. He shrugged, refilled his glass, and wandered over to the armchair to sit down once more. After a moment's hesitation, she followed him and stood next to the chair.

"Mae Jane will be wondering where you've gone."

"I thought I'd take some time to myself," he said.

She nodded. "Well. I can certainly appreciate the need for solitude."

"Even on your wedding day?"

"As I said, it's all a bit much. So many conversations, being pulled in every direction. Oh, everyone is very nice and all, but I just can't help but…I have so much to be thankful for, but it's just…Well, I suppose it's that I've barely had a chance to speak with Henry at all and, well…"

Ben watched her for a long moment. "Why aren't you with him now?"

She opened her mouth to offer a hundred different reasons why, but none of them made sense. All she could do was shrug and look at Ben.

"May I sit with you awhile?"

He gestured at the chair next to his. "By all means."

Their conversation began slowly at first, and they spoke mostly of the day's goings-on. Sarah said she'd seen Mae Jane cry more tears in a few hours than she'd ever seen her cry her whole life, and Ben laughingly agreed. Sarah asked Ben to confirm the rumor that Jem had invited social outsiders like George Hunt and David Dixon to the wedding, and that they were all shut up in the stables drinking themselves to death.

At the mention of Jem, Ben's expression darkened. "I couldn't say what Jem's up to," he murmured. "It used to be I thought I knew his mind, but not anymore."

Sarah nodded slowly. "I've noticed you and Jem have not been…well, you've not been very *close* as late, and…"

"No," Ben said. "No, you're right. We haven't been close." He shrugged. "I wish things were different in that regard. But Jem…I think he's heading down a path where I can't follow."

Sarah thought to ask Ben what exactly he meant by that, but decided against it. "And what of Daddy? Have you spoken with him today?"

Another deep shadow passed over Ben's face. "I've seen him," he said, "but I haven't spoken with him, no. He has a circle of old men gathered around him. They're talking about saving the 'righteous old Union', whatever that means, while just across the lawn another circle talks about the forging of a new Southern nation. And this place, which hasn't seen a slave on the grounds in years…Suddenly the cabins are filled with them. It's like time has turned backward."

"They'll all be gone tomorrow," Sarah said. "You can trust in that, Ben. By tomorrow, you won't have to see or hear any of it ever again. I promise you."

A bitter smile crept across Ben's lips. He shook his head and looked away.

"What's the matter, Ben?" she asked. "Was it something I said?"

"It's nothing."

"Obviously it's not nothing. You can tell me."

"I can't."

"And why not?"

He regarded her cautiously. "Because I'm afraid you'll look at me *that way* again."

Sarah became very still. She blinked, swallowed, and found her breath again. "Which way do you mean?"

Ben turned away again. "People have been looking at me a certain way all my life. I can't tell what it is. Fear, mockery, shame, maybe all of those things at once. It's the kind of look that cuts right through you. You want nothing more than to crawl into a hole somewhere. Your father has given me that look, and Lady Isabella without question, and even the boys too. Even little Bayard, now that he's a little older, though I can't rightly blame him. He doesn't understand like the others should. But I never thought *you* would look at me the same way, Sarah. You never did, until today."

By now, Sarah had already decided to stop listening. This day — *her* day, this most joyous day — had been wasted listening to everyone else's problems. Could no one give her just this *one* occasion to be free and happy? To not have to worry about anyone else? Why was it that everyone she cared about had to be so…well, so goddamn selfish?

She sat up straight. "What, do you mean earlier, with Mrs. Cutler and her friends? I've looked at a great many people today, Mr. Freeman. Do you think any of *them* are upset? I cannot understand what you're even trying to say. I haven't been able to understand you for…well, for a rather long time."

Ben shook his head. "You are more intelligent than you know, Sarah, and certainly more than you permit yourself to be among all those 'high-society' halfwits. And more than intelligence, I believe you possess intuition, deep feeling. Above all, empathy." He looked into the cold ashes of the fireplace. "Which is why I don't understand *you*. I wonder if you'll ever wake up at Arcadia and hear the singing voices of your happy slaves. I wonder if you'll actually take a moment to *listen*."

Sarah pulled distractedly at her wedding ring. "I'm afraid you're not making an ounce of sense, Mr. Freeman."

"That's not my name, you know," he said sharply. "Freeman? Your father gave that name to Mama and me. Whatever name we used to have, whatever name my father used to have, was taken from us a long time ago. Erased. Forgotten. Just like everything else we had, or might have had."

Ben nodded toward the shelves of books and the vaulted ceiling, indicating the whole of Clarendon.

"Oh, but at least we get to be *free*. We get to be thankful for our humble life of service to the noble Roscoe family in their little palace, neatly tucked away from the horrors of the world. Away from the horrors of the Mayfair goddamn Valley."

Sarah's eyes narrowed. "I think you've had too much to drink, Mr. Freeman."

He turned on her and snarled, "*Stop calling me that.*"

Shaking with anger, Sarah stood up. She smoothed down the creases of her wedding dress and turned to leave. But she could not depart without turning back and glaring down at him for one final moment.

"Is it really too much to ask for you to be happy for me on this *one day*, Ben? I always considered you the most decent person here at Clarendon. I always thought you were my dear friend. Now I see, you only care to think about yourself. Could you just once forget all the world's woes and miseries? Could you, just once, stop thinking of yourself as some downtrodden savior — as some kind of sorry *victim* — and see the beauty in the world around you?"

Ben was quiet for a long time.

Breathing hard, Sarah wondered whether something she had said had finally got through to him. Maybe he would finally start acting sensible, and speak sensibly.

Slowly, Ben tipped back his whiskey glass and downed the last of its contents. He held the empty glass in his hand and studied its shape. "You know something?" he said quietly. "All during the ceremony, sitting under those beautiful willow trees in the grove, I could only think of one thing."

Sarah heaved a sigh. "And what is that?"

Ben looked up at her, and his glistening eyes hardened to dark stones without light or color. "The exact spot where you recited your wedding vows was the same place where your grandfather tortured my father. And Judge Cutler, he was the man who gelded my father — a human being — like a goddamn animal. Together those bastards bled my father there in the dirt, and all while your mother just stood there watching it happen. Yes, Sarah Carter was there, together with your father. Miss Carter was the only person in the world who I thought actually *cared* about us poor, helpless negroes. But all she could do was fold her pretty hands together and smile through it all, as if what was happening was just some plain, everyday matter. I remember thinking about the *strength* it must take, if that's what it really is, to smile politely while a human being is tortured before your very eyes. It must take a great deal of strength to blind yourself to horror, to deafen yourself to the screams."

Tears stung Sarah's eyes, but she blinked them back. She was barely able to speak for the bulging lump that had formed in her throat. "You know I've felt just as much of an outcast here at Clarendon as you."

Ben filled his whiskey glass to the brim and laughed bitterly. "Just as much? I beg to differ. But then again, this isn't about me."

Sarah shot to her feet. "Then what *is* this all about?" she snapped. "Tell me what it is you're trying to say, Ben, because evidently I'm not smart enough to understand your word games. Do you delight in making me feel guilty over…what? Something my grandfather did before I was even born? Something my mother or father *didn't* do? I can't change anything about the past, and I've done *nothing* to deserve your empty accusations."

As soon as she finished, Sarah bit her tongue. And Ben, who had been staring at the swirling patterns of his drink, looked up at her then with a knowing sadness in his eyes. She remembered suddenly the dark autumn night, the riders and their horses, and the torchlit eyes of a man she had condemned to death.

"You have your mother's strength too," Ben said. "You watch, and oh, you may disapprove. But you will never do anything to stop it. Instead you are content to remain deaf and blind to the plain horrors upon which your perfect little world is built."

In her mind's eye, Sarah saw with more clarity the sight of the slave Moses being led up the path, of the desolate look of fear in his eyes.

With a violent shake of her head, Sarah banished all memory of that horrible night from her mind. All she could see now was Ben sitting in an armchair in the library, and with great relief she stepped closer to the exit.

"Enjoy your whiskey, Mr. Freeman," she muttered.

She abandoned the library without looking back. She passed down the darkened hallway and stepped out to greet the sun-gorged extravagance of her wedding party once more. Refreshed by a second wind, she laughed and talked cheerily. Sarah Cutler took her bridegroom's hand and danced with him, basking in the glowing attention of her guests, and she did not think of Ben Freeman again.

Around midnight, the newlyweds said their goodbyes and prepared to turn in early. They endured with grace and good humor the grins and winks from their friends and family. Judge Cutler slapped Henry's shoulder and wished him well, and Mrs. Cutler squeezed Sarah's hand and gave her a knowing look of encouragement. On the carriage ride to the Cutlers' ancestral home called Arcadia, Henry kept handing Sarah a tall bottle of wine. Even though she didn't want it, she drank it. She was drunk enough with ecstasy, with such insane happiness that she was sure she must be dreaming.

Sarah entered the gates of her new home in darkness. As the carriage slowed to a halt before the front steps of the brick-walled mansion, Henry hurled the door open and staggered outside, laughing. A black face appeared in the darkness and a white-gloved hand extended to help Sarah down. Sarah took the hand carefully, remembering not to look the valet in the eye as her new in-laws had instructed. Standing in the cool darkness, Sarah marvelled at the size and magnificence of Arcadia's pillars and windows. But it was too dark to see much, and she was too tired to study long. There would be time enough for that tomorrow, and all the days to come.

Besides, now she really was drunk. And she wanted to find out for herself just what Mary Beth Wise meant about stud horses.

"Henry? Henry, where are you?"

She searched the darkened bedroom for her husband. She bumped into the bed, with its fresh sheets and plush pillows, just waiting there like a gift to be unwrapped. She looked at the bed and felt suddenly nervous.

Turning away from the bed, Sarah looked toward the balcony and saw Henry standing there. Wrapping her nightdress tight, she went outside and joined him there. From on high, they had a commanding view of the South Branch and the Valley beyond under the light of a setting spring moon.

"It's beautiful," she breathed.

Henry said nothing. When she turned to look at him, she saw that he was in fact hiding his face from her.

"Henry?" She touched his shoulder gently. "Henry, what's the matter?"

At last, he turned to her. He seemed ashamed, and his voice was choked with emotion. "I'm sorry," he said. "It's just…it's a frightening world we live in, Sarah. I've lived here on the South Branch most of my life, and now this is to be your home too. And it will be home to our children, one day."

Sarah felt a flutter in her chest. Reaching out, she squeezed Henry's hand.

"There are people trying to take all this away from us," Henry said. "All that's simple and good in this world, all that's righteous in God's name. They want to destroy our peace so they may profit. You know of whom I speak, don't you? It's the abolitionists, the capitalists, the corrupt newspapers that serve them. If we do nothing, it will not be long before many people lie dead, and needlessly so. And..."

He broke off for a moment, lost for words. When he turned slightly back to her, so that she saw him in profile against the moonlight, she saw that tears quivered in his eyes but refused to fall.

"And when I think about raising a family," Henry said, "and caring for a wife, and all while this looming *thing* threatens us, I can't help but think: 'Why must I suffer the evils of this period of history? Why must my wife and children suffer? Why must we live in this time, with all its uncertainty and anxiety?"

After a moment he sniffed and wiped at his tears, and when he looked up again they were gone, though his lips trembled.

"Well, maybe it's better off that it *is* me. Maybe I'm better off for it, because I know that I have the strength to meet the coming crisis and rise above it. The task must be mine to meet whatever may come, and thus *overcome*. For the sake of the unborn."

Sarah took his hands in her own. "And it's a wife's duty," she said, "to follow her husband faithfully in all his actions. I would be proud of him for standing up — against tyranny, and standing up for what is right. I would be proud of him for fighting for that which he believes in. And I would wait a hundred years or longer for him to return home to me."

Henry took Sarah into his arms and held her. They swayed together, and she felt her heart beat in time with his.

"So," he said at length, "how does it feel to be a Cutler?"

She beamed at him. "Wonderful, as expected." As they moved together, dancing to a noiseless waltz, she said, "You're sure you won't get bored with me, Henry? You're sure that, as years go by, you won't find me bothersome?"

Henry laughed. "Bothersome? That's ridiculous."

She put her head against his chest. "My father...he and that woman — Cousin Isabella, I mean. They have a passionless marriage. Theirs is a relationship intense only in their quiet loathing of each other. I see that whenever they touch, which is rare, there is no sign of bliss." She closed her fingers tighter around Henry's, and she could feel their wedding bands. "There is no...agony...when they touch."

Lifting her head, she looked up into Henry's eyes.

"I never want to end up like them," she said. "I never want to end up like everyone else. I always want my husband to feel agony when he cannot touch me..."

Sarah smiled then, attempting to project something of Mary Beth's enchanting spirit.

"...and I want to tremble whenever he does."

Henry's body corded with anticipation. He reached out and touched his fingers to her cheek.

"My duchess. The Duchess of Arcadia."

She smiled again. "I could get used to that."

Henry became very still, his eyes fixed on hers. "May I kiss you, Sarah?"

In answer, she lifted her chin and moved her lips to meet his, brushing against them but not yet committing. She felt Henry's body pulse with barely restrained energy. With their lips touching, she said, "Only if you promise one thing, Mr. Cutler: that you never ask permission again."

Henry kissed her then, and she pressed against him. She felt one of his hands reach down, and with a laugh she allowed him to sweep her into his arms. Clutching close to Henry, Sarah looked out and bid goodnight to the moon, and then the new duke and duchess of Arcadia passed into the velvet darkness of their bedchamber.

Chapter 23
LOYALTIES

"Class dismissed!"

All at once, forty-one hats flew into the air as the United States Military Academy's Class of '60 erupted in joyous exaltation.

The watching crowd of proud families, military officials, and other dignitaries cheered and applauded the success of the newly graduated first cadets, who were now officers (second lieutenants, to be exact) of the United States Army. The neat and orderly ranks collapsed as friends and comrades turned to shake hands and embrace each other. A nearby marching band exploded in a frenzy of rolling drums, screaming pipes, and baying trumpets.

JJ Roscoe stood conspicuously alone amidst this roiling river of adulation. Finally some of his classmates turned to him at last and extended firm, formal handshakes and stiff head-nods.

"Congratulations, *Lieutenant*," a sweaty cadet named Cready said. Cready was a sniveling bootlicker of the worst kind. He was the closest thing JJ had to a friend at the Point, which wasn't saying much.

A smug-faced cadet named Osborne pushed beside them. "Family didn't make it up for the big show, eh, Roscoe?"

JJ could have broken Osborne's fucking nose that instant, but he maintained his composure behind an acidic smile. He murmured his way through the resulting small-talk, but his gaze continued to flicker toward the white chairs where the cadets' families sat.

He knew he looked in vain, but he searched for a sign of his family anyway. Deep down there was a lingering hope that they might show up after all. If not the whole family, then at least part of it. He believed that Sarah still held some kind of affection for him, so wouldn't she want to be here to watch him walk across the stage? Mother had never been one for affection, but she understood as well as anyone that to have one's son graduate from the Military Academy was a great and prestigious honor. Wouldn't she want to be here today, at the very least to be *seen?* And Ben and Mae Jane Freeman, he knew they still loved him, even if the affections of the others was in doubt. Tom and Bayard were too young to understand family squabbles, so surely they would want to be here to cheer their older brother on?

A savage voice seized control of JJ's thoughts. Just who was he kidding? *Family squabbles?!* That was putting it goddamn fucking mildly, wasn't it? Wasn't he the one who had determined no other course of action but to level a revolver at his own father's heart and pull the trigger? It was only by a miracle that JJ had not become a patricidal murderer that night.

But no, not a miracle. It was Jem who had stopped him.

What would he do if Jem showed up today? Would JJ choose to extend a gracious hand of forgiveness, asking his brother's forgiveness in kind? Or would he run and fetch that same revolver and put a bullet between the conniving bastard's eyes? Unfinished business, finished. And there would be an element of justice to it too — a settling of old scores. Maybe JJ had *tried* to shoot Father, but Jem *had literally shot* his own brother. For God's sake, Jem might have killed him. The slimy, bootlicking traitor might have actually—

"Congratulations, Roscoe."

Flinching, JJ turned and looked into the eyes of a classmate. It was Dodson Ramseur, a tall North Carolinian cadet who was already balding, though he had a luscious dark beard that made his brown eyes pop like chestnuts against a sheen of his pale skin. Ramseur wore a thin, mocking smile on his face that suggested he was ever amused by the lesser beings around him.

JJ shook hands with Ramseur. "Congratulations, Dod," he said, speaking cordially but without much sincerity.

While still gripping JJ's gloved hand, Ramseur nodded toward the stage upon which stood a congregation of West Point's staff and instructors. "The Supe wants to see us."

JJ followed Ramseur's gaze across the parade grounds until his own fixed upon one man in particular: Colonel Beauregard, the superintendent. The dark-eyed Beauregard saw JJ watching him and gave a small nod. JJ nodded back.

"Now?" JJ asked Ramseur.

"We're to rendezvous at his quarters presently," Ramseur replied. He did not sound particularly pleased at the prospect of being paired with JJ.

Just now, JJ saw Beauregard bid a brief adieu to the circle of dignitaries with whom he was speaking. Beauregard now departed the parade ground.

JJ looked around at their other comrades, who presently were being mobbed by adoring mothers and fathers, sisters, brothers, and sweethearts. Witnessing so many reunions and seeing so much intimate joy, JJ felt suddenly sick to his stomach.

"Fine then," he said. "Let's be off."

The air was filled with birdsong and the crunch of boots on gravel. JJ and Dodson

Ramseur shared no words as they marched down Washington Road toward the superintendent's quarters at Jefferson Place. The heat of the beating sun had already wilted the collar of JJ's dress uniform.

The superintendent's quarters was a fine white farmhouse with a handsome veranda. As JJ and Ramseur approached, the door opened and a black servant stepped outside with an inquiring expression.

"We're here to see Colonel Beauregard at his request," Ramseur said. "First Cadets — I mean, *Lieutenants* — Dodson Ramseur and Jonathan Roscoe reporting."

The servant nodded and beckoned them forward.

"Let's make this quick," Ramseur said to JJ. "They popped champagne just as we were leaving."

The cool dark of the house brought welcome relief from the day's oppressive heat. As they passed down a long hallway, JJ surveyed a series of paintings, all of them relating to war and battle in some way. There was a painting of General Wolfe dying on the Plains of Abraham, the thin red line of English longbowmen at Agincourt, Washington crossing the Delaware River, the Siege of Yorktown, Napoleon in marshal dress, and a massive depiction of the Battle of Lepanto between the Turks and the Venetians. There were numerous artifacts as well: muskets, sabers, and standards from the Revolution, together with antique swords, helms, and chain-mail suits collected from centuries-old battlefields. Seemingly the most prized possession, perched above all other items, was a plumed helmet of Rome's Praetorian Guard that had been restored to its gleaming glory.

"The colonel's in here," the servant said, opening a sliding door that led into a yellow-walled study.

Ramseur pushed by the servant with a sneer. JJ nodded and smiled at the man, but the servant regarded him coldly and turned away.

JJ stepped into the study and joined Ramseur in saluting the groomed officer who stood behind an oak table. The officer returned the salute and invited them to sit down.

"Thank you, Clarence. That will be all."

Pierre Gustave Toutant Beauregard was a prim, handsome Louisianian with caramel skin, black curly hair and mustaches, and dark, intelligent eyes. There was little doubt in JJ's mind that Beauregard, being a Creole, had African blood in him from many generations ago. Of course, Beauregard himself would have refuted this, suggesting that calling himself 'Creole' was simply another way of saying he was a native-born Louisianan Frenchman. This was technically true, but it was interesting that a family that might have been slaves during the time of Spanish and French colonization had, through a centuries-long process of intermarriage, risen to become prominent slave-owners themselves. As if to underline this irony, Beauregard opened the conversation by apologizing for the "terrible manners of my Yankee negro. As you know, I'm not permitted to take my own servants up here with me. I think the issue is my *paying* him. Such sentimental Northern customs tend to chip away at the obliging decorum which we've instilled in our coloreds at home. Wouldn't you agree, Lieutenant Ramseur?"

Ramseur, being from a wealthy planter family himself, offered an eager smile. "Yes, sir. Very much so, sir. That's an astute observation, sir."

JJ grimaced. Evidently his friend Cready wasn't the only bootlicker at the Point. Dod Ramseur had almost perfected the practice.

Beauregard now turned his smile upon JJ. "So, Lieutenant Roscoe. It seems that, despite all the instruction you missed last fall, you've passed through the gauntlet in one piece. Congratulations."

"Thank you, sir."

Beauregard's smile stretched wider. "It's fortunate that your instructors allotted extra time so you could complete your assignments."

"Yes, sir."

Beauregard nodded to both of them. "I won't keep you gentlemen long. Even officers must indulge in idle celebrations now and again. But since both of you are among the finest of this year's class, I wanted to offer your postings to you personally."

"It's a great honor, sir," Ramseur said.

Beauregard went to his desk, upon which were three stamped envelopes. Two bore the crest of the Academy. Beauregard handed one of these to Ramseur.

"To you, Ramseur, the 3rd Artillery Regiment, headquartered at Fort Defiance, Texas."

Ramseur accepted the envelope with a stunned, rather dejected expression. JJ knew that Ramseur, like most bootlickers and ladder-climbers, had wanted a posting in Washington.

Beauregard handed the next envelope to JJ.

"And to you, Roscoe, the 4th Artillery Regiment headquartered in Washington. Incidentally, your commanding officer is my former instructor here at the Point, Major Robert Anderson."

JJ resisted a grimace of his own, for he had wanted to join a cavalry detachment out on the western plains. Ramseur, meanwhile, seemed secretly pleased at JJ's disappointment.

Beauregard folded his hands behind his back and began to pace about the study. "No doubt you gentlemen were hoping for alternative posts," he said. "I can well understand your desire to serve in high command, or to get into the action against the redskins. But I am of the opinion that, within my lifetime and possibly within yours, the art of war will undergo a dramatic transformation. I am of the opinion, gentlemen, that within fifty years the cavalry charge will become obsolete."

JJ and Ramseur exchanged puzzled expressions.

"Obsolete, sir?" Ramseur clarified.

"Indeed. And maybe the infantry charge with it." Beauregard directed their attention to a model cannon perched upon his desk. "The blistering speed of this century's technological innovations will not stop with locomotives and cotton gins, gentlemen. The implications for fighting wars will be vast, perhaps devastating. *Artillery*, gentlemen. Artillery is the way of the future.

"Did you know that, with respect to battle wounds, more men were injured in the Mexican War by metal shrapnel than by bullets or bayonets? We are swiftly approaching a time where battle is no longer an intimate affair. No longer will we march up close until we can look the enemy in the eye. Modern battles will be prosecuted from afar, sometimes out of sight of the enemy. And as guns become larger, as their firepower magnifies and their rate of fire grows exponentially, it will be nothing for a single artillery battery to lay waste to armies that insist on employing traditional tactics. The romantic notion of 'Charge!', courageous as it may be, will become little more than a call for men to commit mass suicide."

JJ listened and considered everything Beauregard had said.

The superintendent sat down behind his desk and looked at JJ and Ramseur together.

"Gentlemen, I needn't tell you that the Union is in dire straits. There are radicals on all sides threatening to pull our democracy apart. There are men in positions of power, even within the War Department, who think themselves Napoleons in the making. There are a growing number of officers, myself included, who have discovered reasons aplenty to distrust the old guard. We may soon find ourselves in a position where we must commit our loyalty to one side or another. We may even have to stand against those men who were our former comrades. The choice will not be easy. But being a proud Louisianian, being a proud *Southern man*, I know where my loyalties lie without having to ask any questions."

Here, Beauregard became very still, very watchful. His eyes tracked slowly from Ramseur to JJ and back again.

"How about you boys? Where do your loyalties lie?"

Ramseur sat up straight and said, "With my state, Colonel. Wherever North Carolina goes, I go also."

Without flinching, Beauregard countered, "Even if Carolina went to war against Louisiana? Would you fight me, your superior, if your home and family were threatened? Would you fight your own classmates if they posed the same threat?"

Ramseur's response was automatic. "Yes, sir, I would. But of course, Carolina and Louisiana would never fight each other. We're all Southerners, after all."

Beauregard beamed with pride. Now he looked at JJ.

"And how about you, Roscoe?"

JJ shifted uncomfortably in his chair and said nothing. Just what the hell was this?

"Well you must have an answer," Beauregard said to JJ, his proud smile becoming a smirk. "You were visiting your home in Virginia when John Brown and his rebels attacked Harper's Ferry, weren't you? What if the next invader was me, leading troops from a sister state? Or what if the invader was the Federal government itself?"

JJ considered his answer carefully. As he did, his mind drifted back to the smoke and noise of the battle for Harper's Ferry. JJ thought of John Brown lying bloody on the ground. He thought of his sword running through that rebel boy's body until its hilt crunched against breastbone. JJ had felt no tender affections for the dead and dying. They had been traitors to the Union — would-be usurpers of a people's freely elected government — which meant they deserved no one's sympathy.

But it was not the fact that Brown and his men were abolitionists that made them traitors. It was only right that the legitimate authority of the United States should shelter a diversity of beliefs and creeds. It was only when a man sought to delegitimate and overthrow that authority that he became a traitor. A patriot was someone who would sacrifice his life for the good of his country; a traitor would sacrifice his country for the good of himself.

JJ spoke up at last. "Today, just before you dismissed our class, Colonel, I swore an oath to defend the flag of the United States of America. The abolitionists at Harper's Ferry didn't just attack my home state, but the entire Union. They attacked the flag of every American, North and South together. In the classroom and on the parade ground, I've repeated the Academy's motto — 'Duty, Honor, *Country*' — every day for the last four years. I would not have uttered those words if I did not believe in them, Colonel. So if you're asking me whether I'd stand with my neighbors if *Virginia* herself attacked the Union, then I would have to answer in the negative, sir. If I stood against my country, I would be breaking my solemn oath to defend it."

A stiff silence filled the air. Beauregard's smirk had long since vanished.

Ramseur, meanwhile, flushed with pride. "My state *is* my country."

To this, Beauregard offered a tight nod. "Once upon a time, most Americans believed as you do, Lieutenant Ramseur. After all, we did not fight a revolution against imperial England to worship a new sort of supreme ruler. The states did not form a union to surrender their sovereignty to a monolithic *Union*."

JJ grimaced. He wanted to say that this was *exactly* what the states had done, and with good reason, but instead he decided to change the subject.

"Permission to speak freely, sir."

Beauregard shrugged. "Granted."

"Your allusions to disloyal factions in the War Department is quite disconcerting, sir."

"As it should be," Beauregard said. "There are powerful men with partisan beliefs working to undermine the American confederacy from within. We must be vigilant against those who would deny our people their democratic freedoms, especially in an election year."

JJ nodded slowly. "And is that why you're sending me to Washington, sir? Because you want me to keep an eye on these men?"

Beauregard chuckled. "I'm sending you to Washington to learn the art and science of ballistics, Lieutenant."

JJ shrugged. "And meanwhile you're sending Ramseur to Texas. Is that because there are more men in Texas who you deem to be 'loyal'? Loyal to what, exactly? Loyal to the flag of the United States, I should hope."

Beauregard's eyes narrowed. "That goes without saying," the colonel replied icily.

"Forgive me, Lieutenant Roscoe," Ramseur said, turning to JJ. "But it sounds to me like you're making vague suggestions that our superior officer might harbor ill will against the Federal government."

"I've suggested no such thing, vaguely or otherwise," JJ replied. "I'm merely trying to ascertain exactly what the colonel is asking us to do."

Beauregard stood up from his chair. "I'm *telling* you to follow orders," he said, "and to follow them without question."

JJ and Beauregard glared at each other, neither one blinking.

Finally, JJ nodded. "Then I must say, Colonel, I'm very much looking forward to studying the art and science of ballistics. Furthermore, I look forward to employing the many lessons I'm sure to learn in the service of the Union, my *country*."

Beauregard opened his mouth to retort, but evidently thought better of it. "Very good," he said curtly. "Very good indeed." He turned his back to his guests and stared out the study's large window. "That will be all, Lieutenant Ramseur."

Ramseur gave JJ a glaring side-eye as he stood up and saluted Beauregard. He promptly departed, shutting the door behind him.

JJ sat in silence while Beauregard continued to stare out the window. At length, Beauregard turned his head so that JJ could see his profile.

"You know, Roscoe, I know your father quite well. When he was still a Democrat, of course, and not engaged in this Constitutional Union nonsense."

"Yes, sir."

"And I know that it was not you who was originally supposed to come here to the Academy, but your brother Jeremiah."

JJ was quiet for a brief moment. "Yes, sir."

Beauregard sniffed. "And your brother, is he a patriot? A Virginia patriot, I mean."

JJ considered his answer, but of course there was only one to give.

"He is, sir."

Beauregard nodded. "So what you're telling me is that, if all our nightmares came true and there was civil war between the states, you would take up arms against your own brother?"

In his mind's eye, JJ was back in Clarendon's library, where debris from the ceiling rained down. He saw Father cowering in his chair, his trembling hands covering his face. He saw Jem at his feet, broken and bloody, and he saw the revolver in his hand pointing down to the space between Jem's eyes. JJ remembered the temptation, the *instinct* to pull the trigger, as if his whole life had been leading up to that one point.

As if it had been his destiny.

Back in Beauregard's office, JJ nodded stiffly. "Yes, Colonel. If my brother tried to overthrow the Union, I would put him down."

"But *why?*" Beauregard was truly astonished, even horrified. "You'd kill your own flesh and blood, for what? For a corrupt bureaucracy?"

JJ swallowed hard. "Colonel, sir. This may not make much sense to you…but while that man may be my flesh and blood, I assure you he is not my brother."

Beauregard sighed heavily. He turned around and faced JJ at last. "Well. It seems your mind is fixed."

JJ nodded. "It seems so, sir."

Beauregard stroked his beard thoughtfully. "I hope I'm not stepping beyond my bounds as a mentor to you, but I could not help notice that your family was not present for today's convocation."

JJ's throat tightened. "No, sir."

"As to why, I know that's none of my business," Beauregard said. "Still, with respect to their absence, I feel I should impart whatever words of wisdom I possess. You are about to meet a cruel world, after all."

JJ maintained a polite disposition, but inwardly he could not picture a situation where he would ever need to follow Beauregard's 'wisdom.'

"I have known many bright officers who peaked early and proceeded to fade away into oblivion," Beauregard said. "Some of them played an active role in their own demise. Others were brought down by hubris. Still others failed because their fellow officers felt they could not be trusted."

JJ sat quietly and listened.

"Loyalty is a critical though easily neglected quality in a good soldier," Beauregard said. "Not loyalty to abstract ideas, nor loyalty to oneself — for that is vanity — but loyalty to one's superiors, to his brothers in arms. If I may speak frankly, Roscoe, you seem to have an aversion for trusting anyone but yourself."

JJ considered these things. At length, he shook his head.

"I do consider myself loyal, Colonel. I am loyal, first and foremost, to the Union.

If you call that loyalty to a mere 'idea,' I suppose I cannot convince you otherwise. As for trusting others…well, I suppose I've encountered enough treachery where I believed there was loyalty, enough heartlessness where I thought there was love, to hold much faith in the essential goodness of Man."

Beauregard shook his head. There was a hint of sadness in his eyes, perhaps even sympathy. "Such a perspective seems to suggest a rather lonely existence."

JJ shrugged. "It's not a philosophy developed without sufficient reason. And in thinking more about it, sir, I am reminded of one of my father's many sayings. 'Nothing is guaranteed but what we secure for ourselves.'"

Beauregard offered a relenting nod. "Wise words, I suppose."

"Yes, sir."

Presently, Beauregard sighed and turned away from the window. Crossing to his desk, he reached down and picked up an envelope there, and this he handed to JJ.

"Before you go, Roscoe. Personal correspondence. From your father, I believe."

JJ accepted the letter. Flipping it over, he read the sender's name in the left-hand corner.

John Methuselah Roscoe
514 10th Street
Washington, District of Columbia

JJ's heart began to throb in his chest. He heard his pulse pound in his ears. Swallowing hard, fighting to maintain a stoic disposition, JJ looked up at the watchful Beauregard.

The Creole offered a thin smile. "I wish you well in all your endeavors, Roscoe. I expect our paths to cross again in the future. When that day comes, I do hope to see you marching alongside America's *true* patriots. In the meantime, I do hope you'll rediscover what it means to hold faith in others — in particular, to hold faith in men of virtue."

Without flinching, JJ said, "You mean men like yourself, Colonel?"

Beauregard's smile vanished. He gestured brusquely toward the door.

"Clarence will see you out."

Letter in hand, JJ shot to his feet and delivered a defiant salute. He held the salute and glared unblinking at the far wall. He did not move a muscle until Beauregard sighed and muttered:

"Dismissed."

JJ turned and briskly departed the superintendent's study. He pushed past the servant named Clarence and abandoned the whitewashed quarters without looking back. It was not until JJ was far up Washington Road that he slowed his urgent step and allowed himself to breathe again.

The barracks was all but deserted when darkness fell that night. Most of JJ's classmates had started their journeys back to their homes with their families, or else had already struck off for their various posts across the Union. The younger classes — the Seconds and Thirds — were on brief holiday. They would return in July to welcome the incoming 'plebes' (Fourth Classmen) with a series of cruel rituals intended to teach the green cadets their manners.

In the meantime, JJ had the barracks to himself.

He wandered through the space by candlelight. The barracks was already sparse and spartan even when furnished with footlockers and thin cots and cadets sleeping in them, but without these things it was little more than a skeletal structure of four walls. It was almost as if JJ had wandered into some ghostly netherworld that *looked* like the West Point he had called home for the last four years. But this home, just like Mayfair, was now alien to him.

As he walked among the empty cot frames, noting this was where so-and-so used to sleep, he thought about his posting to Washington. He was to serve under Major Robert Anderson, a supposed artillery expert. JJ was to serve as Anderson's adjutant, a sort of second-in-command.

JJ was excited to see Washington, determining that it was there where he would find the greatest number of opportunities to advance himself and his career. If he could make a name for himself, might Father take notice of his son's new fame? What would Father say when he learned that the son he rejected became an adjutant to Winfield Scott, the Commanding General of the United States Army? What would Father say when JJ became a senior officer himself? Might Father finally reach out to JJ when he heard that his firstborn had become a major or colonel, or perhaps even a *general?*

Father. Suddenly JJ remembered the letter that Beauregard had given to him earlier that day. He had never forgotten it, in fact; he'd felt the envelope burn a hole through his breast pocket all through the graduation supper. He had put on a cordial smile for his fellow cadets and their insufferable families, but all the while his mind was on Father's letter.

He told himself not to think much of the message, whatever it could be. He'd already suffered the mistake of worshiping another letter of Father's, and he didn't need to remember how that turned out.

Still, what if, this time, it was different? What if, finally, the time had come for forgiveness and acceptance?

"But do you really believe that?" JJ asked the darkness.

The answer, he knew, was *no.* Despite this, the tiny flame of hope within him refused to be snuffed out.

JJ reached into his pocket and pulled out the envelope. Father was indeed the sender, but it was not Father's handwriting that inked the page. The cursive was long and slender, its hooped flourishes bulbous and round like spheres.

Could it be that Father had…*died?* Had tuberculosis finally taken him?

A flurry of thoughts flew through JJ's mind just then. Perhaps the letter was Father's last, a final attempt to forgive JJ for all that had happened between them, and to ask for a measure of JJ's own forgiveness.

JJ imagined Father penning the letter on his deathbed, the candle of his life burning low, his quivering hand shaking with the effort to write *just one more word,* to impart *just one more loving idea* to his firstborn son, the son he had so mistakenly rejected. The letter would say nothing of inheritance or status, and JJ didn't care about any of that anyway — at least, that's what he told himself just now. Father's last letter was an expression of love, of all the things the man had never been able to say in person. And JJ knew that whatever was said in the letter, it would somehow make everything better. The stain upon the past would be cleansed and washed away. JJ might even find the courage to return to Clarendon to ask forgiveness of Jem and the others. And maybe, just maybe, they would ask for JJ's forgiveness too. And he would surely give it to them, if he determined they were sincere.

JJ returned to his cot and set the candle nearby. He sat down and tore the envelope open and drew the letter out. He unfolded it crease by crease, remembering the sweaty anxiety — the same anticipation he felt now — with which he had looked upon Father's last will and testament. But maybe this letter would supersede that other horrible document. Maybe *this letter* was a codicil to end all codicils, a last instruction that would make right all those thoughtless wrongs.

Maybe. And so, taking a deep breath, JJ read:

Jonathan J. Roscoe
US Military Academy
West Point, NY

Dear Mr. Roscoe:

Enclosed are instructions to withdraw the last annuity payment paid to you by my client, John M. Roscoe. The payment will be transferred to your account at West Point First Bank via wire telegraph on or before the instance of 1 June 1860.
Should you have any difficulties accessing said funds, please contact directly the Orangetown First Bank or the Western Union Telegraph Company.
Do not contact my client regarding this or any other matter.

Thank you for your cooperation in this regard.

Sincerely,

R. Daniel Bartholomew, JD
Bartholomew & Sons LLP
Washington, District of Columbia

Slowly, JJ let his arms droop until the letter rested in his lap. The letter was a Trojan horse: an envelope sent by Father, concealing a letter from Father's attorney. Had this been another — seemingly the last — of the old man's cheap tricks? Or perhaps it wasn't a trick at all. Perhaps Father, that unthinking and unfeeling man, simply hadn't considered anything akin to *insinuations* or *suggestions*. Father simply did whatever he pleased, and it was left to others to try and make sense of it.

JJ saw the nearby candle waver in its growing pool of melted wax. The light was fading, about to die. He looked at the letter one last time. Slowly, he reached out and held the letter over the flame.

Within an instant, the paper caught fire. In giving its flame to the paper, the dying candle was snuffed out.

JJ held the burning letter for as long as he could, clutching it in his hand like Prometheus holding the fire of the gods. Then, he reached down and pulled a bedpan from underneath the cot and dropped the writhing fireball into it. He watched the hungry flames consume the letter whole, until finally the light winked out and all was consumed by darkness.

Tears welled in JJ's eyes, but he did not permit them to fall. Sitting there, alone in the pitch black, he whispered quiet assurances to himself in the third person. But when finally he felt he *must* weep or else lose himself in despair, JJ found that his eyes were dry.

Chapter 24
SISTERS

Mae Jane walked outside and was met by a wall of heat. Stepping down from the shade of the veranda, she squinted up at the blazing June sun and reckoned it was hot enough to kill today. Rather, she knew it was hot enough to do so; she'd seen it happen time and again, so often she'd lost count. Maybe that was why she preferred cool, gray days. In the old times, living and working had been easier when it was cool. Without the sun beating down, all one had to worry about was the whipping.

Mae Jane looked around. There was no sign of Ben or the coach.

"Oh, that boy..."

Picking up her skirts, Mae Jane hurried inside again. She was thankful for the relative coolness of the house, but sweat was already dripping from the tip of her nose. Her scalp itched, and she craved the relief of undoing the knots of her headkerchief to let the scrunched-up tufts of her hair breathe a little. She went up and down the hallways, peering into parlors and studies and sitting rooms for sign of Ben. But of course, she knew where he had to be.

Turning into the library, Mae Jane was already launching into a scolding tirade that when she asked Ben to do something, she *expected* him to do it, and do it quick. It took her a few moments to realize that she was speaking to an empty room. The cavernous library stood silent, abandoned. Even the ashtray on Mr. John's huge desk was empty, a clear sign that Ben had not been there.

Mae Jane continued her journey through Clarendon, but she could not find Ben anywhere. As she rounded the far western side of the mansion, she turned down a sunlit hallway that glittered with windows. The baking heat of the sun, made all the more extreme by the warped glass in the windows, made her feel like a salmon in a full-stoked oven.

Lord, why couldn't it be October already? But of course, when the chill of autumn really set in she knew she'd be wishing for the warmth of springtime again.

Gasping for breath against the humidity, Mae Jane stopped and lifted her apron to dab the sweat pouring down her face. As she wiped, her ears perked up to a peculiar sound. It was rhythmic, steady, almost like some kind of signal. Lowering her apron (it was completely soaked), Mae Jane started forward again. She made for the nearest door to the veranda and stepped outside.

Standing there, Mae Jane sighed as a light breeze touched her face. Finally, the sweat was doing its job of cooling her down a little. Turning her head, she listened for the sound that had fixed her attention.

It was the dull chopping of axe on wood.

Mae Jane rounded the corner and looked toward the northwest. There at the chopping stump was Ben, axe in hand, with scores of split lumber pieces around him and scores more to be cut. A discarded white shirt, now translucent with sweat, hung from a nearby tree branch. The loose bands of his suspenders flapped about as he worked with the tireless, unceasing energy of an automaton. A few yards away, sunken into the ground and choked with weeds but nevertheless still there, was Clarendon's old whipping post.

For a time, Mae Jane stood watching her son work. There was a dullish look in his eyes, as if he was blind to his immediate surroundings while his mind was somewhere far away. Chopping wood was a matter of letting the axe do the work, but Ben attacked each log with a brutal, vengeful spirit. After clearing all the pieces around him, Ben began to stagger about like a drunkard and grope for more wood.

Mae Jane could watch no longer. Clicking her tongue, she exclaimed, "Just what the Sam Hill you doin, child?"

Ben stopped and looked up at her, his chest heaving.

Mae Jane raised her eyebrows. "Well?"

"I'm chopping firewood, Mama."

"Firewood? Laws, child, is you head fixed straight? You think this is weather for curlin up by the hearth and roastin chestnuts?"

Slowly, Ben shook his head. "No, Mama."

"No is right. Now you get youself cleaned up and take the coach round front like I asked you. Me and Lady Isabella's goin on our picnic today, and I don't want nothin to spoil it."

"Yes, Mama."

"Well, get to it now! The Lady will be waitin for you round front."

She turned away, shaking her head, and went inside. But as she passed through the door, she looked back and watched Ben from the threshold. She saw him there, staring down at his mess of split logs and wood chips. The boy looked lost, and hopelessly so. Ben's desolate detachment reminded her of how Joby had sometimes looked the day after a particularly bad correction from the Colonel's men. Even now, she could hear Joby's low, raspy voice coming back from the old times.

Not today, Mae. I ain't getting up for them today. I'm at the end of my rope, Mae.

But still, Joby always got out of bed. He always went out to the fields, no matter how much his back bled or how hot the sun was. Joby hated the Colonel's men to be sure, but he took pride in his work. He took pride in always showing up, in never being the kind of person who shied away from doing his bit. What would poor Joby think of Ben's forgetfulness, of his tendency to shirk his duties in favor of sitting around with his nose in a book? If Joby were here, the old man would sooner thrash his boy than see him become anything lazy or coddled. Only white folks were allowed to be lazy and that was *just the way it go.*

Mae Jane went into the kitchens to finalize her preparations for the picnic. It was Lady Isabella's birthday today, and though Mae Jane knew better than to mention the Lady's age, she nevertheless wanted to celebrate this particular milestone with her mistress. Yes, a celebration was just what was needed to bring a little excitement back to Clarendon, which had been very quiet since Miss Sarah's wedding. With Mr. John on the campaign trail, Miss Sarah gone to the South Branch, Mr. Jem at work, Tom at school downstate in Lynchburg and Bayard at the Mayfair School down the road—

And don't forget Jon Jacob, exiled to Yankeeland

—it would be a picnic for two. Ben would escort the ladies of course, but he would keep to himself while Mae Jane and Isabella lounged in the shade. It would be refreshing to get the Lady of Clarendon *out* of Clarendon, and particularly out of her self-imposed dungeon in the east wing study. The plan was to drive across the Valley to a high, grassy hill somewhere and soak up the quiet pleasures of summertime.

Of course, the only problem with that plan was that it required leaving Clarendon, which was something Mae Jane had never done in her life.

Oh, it was true that Mae Jane had probably stepped beyond the property line once or twice. Back in the old times, she and Joby sometimes ran into the woods to be alone together, and he would take her to a place at the far western edge of the property where they could look out at the expanse of the Mayfair Valley. The world had seemed so huge, the distances so unattainable, that she guessed it would take a full year to walk from Clarendon to the distant steeple of the Mayfair First Church. She remembered Joby teasing her about that, and promising that one day he'd take Mae Jane into town and show her the wider world was nothing to shy away from.

Of course, things hadn't worked out that way. Mae Jane remained fearful of the world not just beyond the Branches, but beyond the beech trees that lined Clarendon's clay pathway. And even when Mr. John took over Clarendon from Colonel Spencer and liberated all of the Colonel's people — even then Mae Jane could not bring herself to pass under the front gate. Somehow, it felt wrong to leave behind the only home she had ever known. Her parents were buried at Clarendon, and Evie too, together with so many friends, most of whom had become family.

Mae Jane was certainly sorry to see everyone else go. Those folks departing Clarendon were so happy, and they sang songs together as the Colonel's men (now Mr.

John's men) escorted them in one body down the clay path and up the road toward Winchester, where it was said the people would receive their freedom papers. Mae Jane remembered Ben, just a young boy then, laughing and waving goodbye as the people marched to freedom. She wondered sometimes whether she should have sent Ben off with a young mother who claimed she was heading home to her birthplace in Delaware. Mae Jane didn't know the lay of the land very well, but she guessed that Delaware was at least a little farther north than Virginia. Would Benny have been happier living up there than staying here in the Valley?

In any case, choices had been made, and there was no way to go back upriver where the past was concerned. All that could be done was to keep afloat, to follow the flow of time, and to watch out for rocks.

Tipper the dog padded into the kitchens. The old dog looked sleepy (Mae Jane had passed him a few minutes ago, asleep in a pool of sunlight), but presently the pup looked at Mae Jane with a loving stare.

"Oh, you just want some of what I got," Mae Jane laughed. "Don't you, Tip? Don't you?"

Tipper's tail began to wag.

"Well, let's just see. I ain't makin no promises. Let's just see."

Mae Jane began to pack up the fixings she had prepared: okra fingers fried in egg and cornmeal; chicken, spiced and fried; pickled beets and radishes; turnips, boiled and mashed just this morning; a full quart of North Branch blueberries; and slices of smoked terrapin (Lady Isabella's favorite). Mae Jane had hoped to make ice cream too, but even the smallest of Clarendon's ice boxes was too big for her picnic basket. Still, with cups of cold tea to wash everything down, Mae Jane was confident that she and Isabella were about to enjoy a bonafide feast.

Mae Jane picked up the basket and tossed a forgotten blueberry into the air for Tipper to snatch. Laughing, Mae Jane breezed out of the kitchens with Tipper padding alongside her.

It was a good day, despite the oppressive heat. Oh, just what was she doing, thinking back on dark days? It was a *good day*. And what was Ben doing, acting like the world had done him wrong all his life? It was a *good day*, and Lord knew there weren't many of those to go around.

Mae Jane swept through the grand foyer. Opening the door, she waited for Tipper to bound outside before she went out herself. Looking out from the veranda, she saw Ben waiting there with Mabel harnessed to the coach.

But where was Lady Isabella?

As she drew near, Mae Jane posed this same question to Ben. Ben could only shrug and say that he hadn't seen the Lady at all that day, certainly not in the last few minutes.

Mae Jane looked up at the windows of Clarendon. Sighing, she pushed the picnic basket into Ben's arms and turned around. "I'll be right back," she said, and lifting her skirts she hurried back inside.

Upstairs, Mae Jane found the Lady of Clarendon right where she always found her: wallowing in the artificial darkness of the east wing study, her natural habitat. Isabella lay in the bed that had been moved in there to make her more comfortable. The Lady was asleep, no doubt thanks to liberal doses of her 'medicine.' Indeed, a bottle of Mother Bailey's Quieting Syrup lay on the bedside table, with a dripping spoon next to it.

"Bella?"

The Lady's eyes opened slowly. Her eyes were foggy, her black pupils huge.

"Bella," Mae Jane said again. She sat down on the bed. "Bella, it's time to get up."

A smile crept slowly across Isabella's face. It was the first genuine smile that had touched the woman's face in weeks, maybe months. "Hello, Mae Jane," Isabella said in a soft, almost girlish voice. "Oh, how I've missed you. Is it morning already?"

Mae Jane looked toward the closed curtains. There was a tiny sliver of light between them that hinted at daylight beyond. Looking down at Isabella again, Mae Jane smiled and nodded. "Mornin already. We got a big day ahead. You ready to rise and shine, Bella?"

Isabella's cheeks paled. "I…I don't feel very well…"

Mae Jane pushed her smile wider. "Maybe you just overslept," she said. "I heard sleepin too much is sometimes just as bad as sleepin too little. Gotta be like Goldilocks, hm? Somethin just right?"

Isabella nodded weakly. She began to move, but only to reach for the bottle of Mother Bailey's beside her.

"I…I should take my medicine…"

Mae Jane took Isabella's outstretched hand and squeezed it. "Oh, but you already took you medicine, Bella, just a moment ago. It's time to get up now."

A sneering shadow passed over Isabella's face. Now she looked up at Mae Jane with a mixture of confusion and resentment. Her eyelids fluttered, became heavy, and finally closed again. For a moment, Mae Jane thought her mistress had fallen asleep again. When her eyes slowly opened again, Isabella's darkness had faded and she beamed a contented smile.

"Hello, Mae Jane. Is it morning already?"

Mae Jane sat there, holding Isabella's hand and thinking deeply about what to do next. Pressing her lips together, Mae Jane offered the sincerest smile she could manage.

"Yes, Bella, it's mornin-time already, that's right. And we got a big day ahead, big day. Now, you ready to rise and shine? On the count of three, you ready, Bella?"

They picnicked on a shaded hill near the East Cut, which offered a pleasant view of Mayfair proper on the far side of the Sleepy Creek. Beyond the town, beyond the far ridgeline of the West Cut itself, stood the rugged Alleghenies.

"It really is beautiful," Mae Jane said, marveling at the landscape. "Benny told me that way beyond them big mountains is Ohio, and far down there somewhere is Kentucky. Laws, if it took me this long to get halfway down the Valley, I ain't gonna get way over there 'til I's a hundred years old."

"To what end?" came Isabella's irritable reply. The Lady's mind was clearer now, the laudanum having worn off somewhat, but she had barely touched her food and was constantly pushing up her giant sunhat to dab sweat from her brow. "I never saw much reason in leaving the Valley, nor Clarendon for that matter. I never saw the romance in *travel*. Wherever you go, you are still trapped within your own mind, except there's the added rub of not knowing what's around the next corner. Better to remain close to home and let the world come to you, because at least you still have a chance to lock the door."

Mae Jane nodded slowly. "Well…I s'ppose I never quite thought of it that way before."

"Of course you wouldn't," Isabella said. She sighed. "Oh, I don't know why I let you drag me out here…"

The sunny smile on Mae Jane's face dimmed, but she refused to let a bit of snark ruin a pleasant afternoon.

"Isn't this nice now?" Mae Jane said, sitting back on the quilt spread out around them. "We ain't done a thing like this since we was little girls." She laughed. "Now here we is, two *old ladies*, hm? Two old sister-hens. Ain't that right, Bella?"

Isabella closed her eyes and winced, as if the sudden pain of a headache had overtaken her. "I do wish you would stop calling me *Bella*, for God's sake. Am I not your mistress, Mae Jane? Do I not deserve even an inkling of deference and respect?"

"Yes, ma'am. I do 'pologize, ma'am, sincerely."

"Don't trade in redundancies," Isabella said. "Sincerity is what *makes* an apology what it is. Otherwise, it's just a lie."

Mae Jane bowed her head. "Yes, ma'am." She folded her hands together and massaged one of her wrists with the other thumb. Now she began to rub and pick at her skin.

The Lady let out a great sigh, the kind given when the lateness of the hour is top of mind. "Well, this was all very nice, Mae Jane, and I mean that *sincerely*. But I'm tired, and this blistering sun is giving me squaw-skin. You will call your boy and have him take us home?"

The Lady had a manner of asking questions such that it was not easy to answer but one way: *Yes, of course*. Still wringing her hands, Mae Jane looked across the pasture and saw Ben asleep under a tree, with Mabel and the coach standing in the shade nearby. Turning back to Isabella, Mae Jane shrugged.

"I reckoned we could stay awhile, ma'am. Just enjoy each other's company. Talk bout the old times. Celebrate *you*, and the fine occasion of you birthday."

"I can assure you there's no cause for celebration," Isabella grumbled. As she spoke, she dug into a small bag she had brought with her and, *voilà*, there was a bottle of Mother Bailey's in her hands. She uncorked the bottle and, eschewing a spoon, tipped the bottle back in an unbecoming fashion like she was a sailor downing grog. Smacking her lips, Isabella replaced the bottle in her bag. Looking around at the picnic, she sighed again.

"Besides, this is *some kind* of picnic you've organized, Mae Jane. This nigger-food you've brought is awful, and your iced tea tastes like swill. I declare, I haven't had a decent meal at Clarendon for twenty years, not since Daddy sold away that cook of ours. What was her name again? You knew her, surely."

"Carlotta-George," Mae Jane murmured, feeling very small.

"I do beg your pardon? Speak up for these old ears."

"Carlotta-George," Mae Jane repeated. "And yes, ma'am, I knew her. I knew her real good."

All this time, Mae Jane had been wringing her hands. Feeling sharp pain in her left wrist, she looked down and realized that she'd rubbed the skin there raw. Looking up, she told herself to roll her shoulders and ignore the Lady's remarks, to simply focus on the Valley's beauty.

"Mr. Thomas wrote home," Mae Jane offered. "From that school of his, Lynchburg Academy? Benny read the letter for me. Says he's gettin along fine, makin friends. He'll be home end of this month."

Isabella murmured a vague, "Mhm," but said nothing more.

Mae Jane closed her eyes and prayed for God's patience. "Just thought you'd like to know."

"Pardon?"

"Nothing, ma'am."

"Again with your mumbling. Don't expect me to answer when you speak such a way, Mae Jane."

Mae Jane twitched. "Yes, ma'am."

She knew she ought to just clamp her mouth shut and refuse to say anything more. Sometimes when Isabella got in a mood — a *picking* mood — there was no stopping it but to disengage for a while, sometimes hours at a time. But Isabella always came around again eventually. The real Bella, when she came out, was kind and sweet, and she listened. The real Bella made Mae Jane feel not so lonely in the world.

And so, Mae Jane decided to keep talking. Maybe, if she could only talk long enough, she'd somehow wear Isabella's edge away. The day was young after all, and it might turn out to be a great one yet.

"I got more news," Mae Jane said.

Isabella pursed her lips. "Oh, how wonderful."

Holding a tight smile, Mae Jane pressed on. "Miss Sarah — I s'ppose it's *Mrs.* Sarah now — she's gettin along fine with the Cutlers, as I understand. I invited her to join us today, but she said they was too much to do round the new place. It's a big place as I understand, her new place, as big as Clarendon."

Isabella rolled her eyes. "Oh, what a joy it would have been, picnicking with the Carter bitch."

Mae Jane bit her tongue, but she knew if she bit it any longer or any deeper, she'd bite clean through it.

Meanwhile, Isabella turned her face to the sun. "I wonder if her husband's made her a woman by now." Her voice dropped into a conspiratorial whisper. "You think she's with child already, Mae Jane? Certainly didn't take her mother long..."

Mae Jane grimaced and sat up. "I don't know why you needa call her such awful things," she said, her voice very near a growl.

Isabella's eyebrows met the sky, and she gave a halting laugh. "I do beg your pardon?"

It was very quiet now, and suddenly the droning sounds of the Valley summer were very loud in Mae Jane's ears. She heard the soft buzz of a bumblebee, but then it sharpened and she realized there was a hornet in her ear.

"What'd Miss Sarah ever do to you?" Mae Jane challenged. "What'd she ever do, besides be born into a world when she got no say in the matter? You a full-grown woman, Isabella, and the girl's just that: a *girl*. She may need our help someday. You never know."

Isabella scoffed and shook her head, but for now she had no retort.

"Miss Sarah's always been good to me," Mae Jane went on. "Never demandin, always polite. And she was always good to my Benny too."

Isabella snorted. "Oh, I'm sure she was..."

Mae Jane fought the instinct to thrash out. She was momentarily distracted when a dragonfly flew between them and hovered there awhile, before flitting off in a different direction, moving fast. Isabella had not noticed the creature, but Mae Jane was struck momentarily dumb by this idle demonstration of Nature, which had been almost invasive in the way it cut through all the, well, all the *bullshit* (Lord forgive her) that was piling up around her.

Mae Jane tried to find the dragonfly again, wishing it had lingered a moment longer. She was reminded of Ben, and turning, she looked upon her son. She studied the shape of him, crook-backed asleep under a tree, one foot up on the other knee, hat covering his face, a timothy stalk drooping from a slack jaw.

Mae Jane sat up straight. "I'm very proud of my Ben."

Isabella gave her a blank stare, as if to suggest this was the topic sure to hold the least of her interest. "Oh?"

Mae Jane nodded firmly. "Benny says Mr. John invited him to go campaignin with him later on in the summer. Mr. John told him he needs a speechwriter, which you know Ben's so good at."

"Oh, of course."

"Benny wasn't so excited about it, so he says. Says he ain't sure he gonna go. What I can't figure is, he's always wanted to see all them places beyond the Branches. He's always dreamed of strikin off somewhere, same as you Mr. Jem does."

"Mhm."

"So when the child says he ain't sure, that he ain't sure about *Mr. John*, well, I don't know what to make of that."

"I can tell you," Isabella said. Here she finally became interested in the conversation again. "My beloved husband sees your boy as nothing more than a rabbit he can pull out of a hat whenever it suits him. One night he'll be speaking with Yankee donors, and he'll parade your boy around to demonstrate his progressive ways. Next night, when Mr. Roscoe dines with Southerners — *real* Southerners, mind you, not pretenders like him — he'll serve your boy on a silver platter."

While Isabella spoke, Mae Jane became aware of the frightening hornet sound again, but then she realized that the droning was only in her head. Somehow that was worse.

"Well," Mae Jane managed to say. She gasped and stopped to catch her breath, feeling woozy. Maybe the sun was making her sick. "Well, I don't know enough about all them things to reckon you might be wrong, ma'am, but—"

"I'm not wrong, Mae Jane," Isabella corrected. "Not about *him*." As she spoke, her eyes went far away somewhere. "I wasn't wrong when I first saw John Roscoe coming down the path toward Clarendon. Handsome or not, there was something about him I just didn't trust. I tried to warn Daddy about him, to tell Daddy the man was nothing more than a money-grubbing Yankee. But of course, I didn't appreciate then what I do now. Daddy was the sort of man who wanted only sons, and instead got five daughters. So when Mr. John arrived and they got to know each other, oh, Daddy thought the world of him. It was only a short step from there to handing the deed of Clarendon to the man, especially when all the suitors my sisters attracted were such fools. Here I must say, John Roscoe is a great many things, but he is no fool."

Mae Jane nodded as if she was listening, but in fact she'd heard this sort of story hundreds, maybe thousands of times before. It was always a challenge to get Isabella talking, but when she did, her preferred topic was always how the world (usually represented by Mr. John) had done her so terribly, utterly wrong.

And there was some truth to all of it, Mae Jane knew. John and Isabella's marriage had never been what could be considered a stable relationship. 'Transactional' was Isabella's word for it. So far as the Lady of Clarendon was concerned, she'd done her part in providing her husband with four sons for him to use as 'pawns and paper-pushers.' Still, Mae Jane knew that there had been at least *some* affection between the two in the early days. Mae Jane believed that, in a way, husband and wife had needed each other back then, even while Mr. John quietly pined for the lost Sarah Carter, even while Isabella yearned for her father's approval. After all, why else would Isabella have agreed to marry Mr. John, a man she supposedly despised, if not to please her father? But then the Colonel died before his time, and there was Isabella, a mother to children who represented the whitewashed untruth of her life, who reminded her of choices she'd made out of expedience rather than good faith.

"I know he blames me for how the boys turned out," Isabella said, meaning Mr. John again. "Let's see, what do we have? A sexual deviant, a drunk, an idiot. Lord knows what's wrong with Thomas. I'm sure whatever it is, it will rear its ugly head soon enough."

It was only now that Mae Jane saw that there were tiny black ants crawling over the okra fingers, and she set about picking them off and trying to salvage what she could of the food.

Isabella, meanwhile, was looking off somewhere, into the past. "Do you remember, Mae Jane, how my sisters positively tripped over themselves to impress their 'handsome Mr. Roscoe'? The man might have married one of them and spared me a lifetime of association, if only he hadn't gotten poor Cousin Sarah pregnant in the meantime." Isabella began to giggle like a conniving schoolgirl. "Oh, what a laugh I had when I heard *that* scandal. You should be glad I don't call the Carter bitch the Carter *bastard*, because that's what she really is. Though, I do suppose 'orphan' about sums up all that one needs to know about her."

"*You ain't bein fair,*" Mae Jane snapped. "You ain't bein fair to nobody, on no account."

Isabella laughed, but there was a flash of anger in her eyes. "Watch your tone when you speak to me, Mae Jane. And I'll remind you to address me properly when—"

"You only hate Sarah 'cause you cousin made her and not you," Mae Jane said. "You only hate Mr. John 'cause you let others talk you into a life you never wanted, and now all you got left is him. That's the only reason I can figure for all this godawful bile outta you mouth. Frankly, Bella, I's sick of it. The only reason you don't loathe you own boys worse'n you do, is on account of they got some of *you* inside em, and you like that. 'Cause we all know, Bella, how highly you think of youself."

Isabella was not laughing anymore. Scowling, she snarled, "You insolent bitch. You dare talk to your mistress that way?"

Mae Jane threw up her hands and shook her head. "*Pshaw,* some picnic ain't it? Just this once, I didn't think we was gonna be mistress and mammy. I thought we was gonna be friends — sisters. You know, like old times. I thought we was just gonna *be*."

"Well, that just goes to show how stupid you are, Mae Jane. You are a *stupid* woman, Mae Jane. And vain, too."

With her head down, Mae Jane squeezed her eyes shut. She did not want to be here anymore, wanted in fact to get up and leave this terrible woman here under the sun — and good riddance!

But no, Lord be kind, of course she didn't think such a way. Lady Isabella was *good* to Mae Jane, always had been. And the Lady thought well of others, she really did. Growing up with the Colonel for a father could not have been easy for Isabella. The man was cruel not only to his field hands, but to his wife and girls too. There had indeed been many days when, with the muffled sound of the Colonel's carousing in her ears, Mae Jane was glad to go home to her cabin at the end of the day, all while feeling sorry that Isabella had to sleep in the big-house.

And today was just, well, it was just a day. A bad day, perhaps, but Mae Jane was certain it was not beyond salvaging. Bella always lost her edge in time, always came around in time. There might be some *good* yet to find this day...

Isabella sniffed. "I'm waiting for you to *answer me*, Mae Jane."

Mae Jane drew a deep, resigned breath. She had just wanted this day to be *good*. With all that *bad* going around, with all the bad times that folks kept saying was coming...

"I's a stupid woman," Mae Jane whispered.

"Repeat," Isabella said. "Like it's an elocution lesson."

Mae Jane tasted the salt of her own tears as they ran down her cheeks to rest in the corners of her mouth. She could barely speak for the hot lump in her throat.

"I's a stupid woman. I's a stupid woman..."

As Mae Jane spoke, Isabella slowly turned and reached for something in her leather bag. Once again the Lady pulled out the bottle of Mother Bailey's and took a long drink. While Mae Jane watched this out of the corner of her eye, she was seized by the instinct to knock Isabella down and climb on top of her and pour all the contents of that goddamn bottle down her goddamn throat. She pictured herself and the Lady of Clarendon fighting there on the blanket, amidst smashed cornbread pieces and squashed blueberries. Indeed Mae Jane was shocked by her lustful impulse to *do harm* to the other woman, certain that once she began she would not be able to stop herself.

"Maybe I's a stupid woman," Mae Jane went on, "for thinkin this could be a good day, for tryin so hard to make it so. Seems like they ain't much to celebrate these days. With all them troubles beyond the Branches, and Jon Jacob gone, and Mr. John sick and all. And with you, Bella, wastin you life away in that damn room with that damn Mother B's..."

Mae Jane let out a great sigh and shook her head.

"Well...I s'ppose all I wanted was to sit here and at least pretend things was goin right, that things was *good*."

The women sat there, each locking themselves in a separate silence. The sights and sounds of the summer day were forgotten. Now there was nothing but the sickening humidity, the scorching sun—

Hot enough to kill today

—and a mess of spoiled vittles to be packed up, only to be unpacked again on the return to Clarendon. Mae Jane's thoughts began to turn round and round, as if she was strapped to a water-wheel where she was plunged underwater, going deeper, finally emerging half-drowned and spluttering, only to feel herself be carried around again in a ceaseless pattern.

Mae Jane reached up and pulled her sweat-drenched kerchief from her head. She ran shaking fingers through the coarse, close-cropped tufts of her hair and felt that she wanted to tear it all out, to kick and scream. She only wished she was back at Clarendon, back in her private domain of the kitchens where nothing and no one could bother her, where everything had its place, including herself.

Maybe Isabella was right. It was no good walking out the front door. It was better to see the world from the doorway, with a hand ready to throw the door shut.

"When did you do that to your hair?" Isabella asked suddenly.

Instinctively, Mae Jane's hands went to her scalp. "My...?"

Isabella nodded at Mae Jane's exposed head. "Your hair. It's...when did you cut it? I remember it used to be so long, but now..."

Mae Jane thought about snapping back, but for now she remained quiet. Was this the lead-in for some sort of cutting remark? Mae Jane shut her eyes tight and grimaced against the first hints of a headache.

"Laws. After all that, Bella, you askin about my *hair?*"

Isabella shrugged. "It's a simple question. No need to get defensive."

Mae Jane sighed. "Well, *forgive me...*"

It was quiet again. Mae Jane looked around and saw that there were ants crawling over much of the food, which somehow seemed an appropriate thing given that the whole picnic had been an utter disaster.

"You ought to wear your hair like that more often," Isabella said. "Not keep it hidden up underneath that cloth."

Mae Jane was busy stuffing vittles into the picnic basket. She tossed everything in without care. "Oh?" she murmured, only half listening. "You tryna butter me up now, Bella? Tryna sweet-talk me like we's little girls again? Well, I didn't know no better back then. I do now."

She felt the Lady's hand touch her own.

"Mae Jane," Isabella said. "Mae Jane...*sister...*"

Mae Jane stopped and looked at the white hand over her own. Looking up into Isabella's eyes, she saw that the woman's whole manner had changed. The Lady's medusa-like mask was gone, and here before Mae Jane once again was the old Bella, the *real* Bella, the girl Mae Jane knew a long time ago.

Still, Mae Jane curled her lip and turned away. Sister, was it? Well, Mae Jane already had a sister. She'd *had* one, at least. Evie would have never talked to her such a way. Sisters, real sisters, didn't talk to each other such a way...

"I just think it looks very fine," Isabella said. "Your hair, I mean."

Mae Jane might have scoffed at that. She might have dismissed the Lady and every hollow word the woman uttered. Certainly that's what she felt like doing. But looking up again, Mae Jane saw that Isabella wore a look of sincere self-reproach. The Lady of Clarendon's head was down, her eyes cast to the ground.

Apologizing — saying sorry — Lord knew that just wasn't Isabella Spencer's way. But looking at her now, Mae Jane realized that the Lady's tedious and barely coherent compliments made up her best attempt at conciliation. It was a roundabout apology, a child's apology, but...well, this being that sort of day, Mae Jane supposed she would take whatever she could get.

"I do appreciate it," Mae Jane murmured through tight lips. That was all she was willing to say about it, apology or not. Now she focused on packing up the last of the picnic. Lord, was she looking forward to getting home again.

Isabella took off her sunhat and ran a hand along the brittle strands of her hair that were tied into a tight bun. "Do you...do you think my hair would look as fine as that, Mae Jane? If it looked like yours?"

Mae Jane sat there and tried to make sense of the question. It seemed so strange and out of place, but the Lady's inquiry was no doubt earnest. Suddenly, Mae Jane felt a laugh kick up from somewhere inside her. It surprised her, the laughter, but she indulged it anyway.

"What's wrong?" Isabella said, with a quiet note of concern.

Still laughing softly, Mae Jane shook her head. "It's a picture," she said. "Laws, it sure is a picture..."

Slowly, a smile appeared on Isabella's lips. Before long, the two of them were laughing together. For the longest time, neither had seen the other smile nor heard the other lose control in such a way. Their voices rang out, pure as once upon a time when they were giggling little girls — when they were sisters.

Ben's head looked up from the shaded place under the nearby tree, and probably he wore a look of utter confusion. But for Mae Jane, and for Isabella too, it was only their shared laughter that mattered. Their voices, sounding ageless in that endless moment of quiet joy, traveled down the hill and across the pasture, back across the Mayfair Valley toward Clarendon, reaching back through time to some distant memory when, maybe, *things was good.*

Chapter 25

CAVE-IN!

Jem Roscoe yawned and poured himself another cup of coffee. Pushing back in his chair, he closed his eyes and dozed in the warm light of the late June morning. The rhythmic racket of the mine around him slowly faded away.

It had been another long night, and the morning had come too soon. He and Audrey had spent another night in a clearing near Dixon's Mill. They hadn't slept, instead choosing to nestle closer together under the old horse blanket he'd brought. They watched the stars overhead. They made love, then lay back and talked for a small eternity. They made love again, and then they slumbered in each other's arms until the milky light of dawn crept overhead, and it came time to go.

For months now, Jem and Audrey had been meeting almost daily. Sometimes they met in an open fashion, such as when he would carry her books home from the Mayfair School (always careful to bid adieu to her before getting too close to the Blake farm, of course). Other times they rendezvoused at night, in secret, meeting at agreed-upon places at agreed-upon times.

The first time they made love, with Audrey's blonde hair flashing white in the light of a haloed moon, Jem shuddered at the revelation of a new world, a new manner of being. Over those cold winter months of 1860, he could think of nothing but Audrey. He penned bad poetry and rediscovered what it was like to look at the world around him with the wondering eyes of a child.

Each time they burrowed together, basking in love's warm afterglow, they talked of many things: Audrey's brothers, her schooling downstate, and her dreams to make the Mayfair School 'bonafide.' Audrey didn't seem to mind that most of Jem's dreams were vague and nebulous and scatterbrained, each of them as wild as trying to throw a stone and hit Mars. They talked about JJ too, about that horrible night in Clarendon's library, and Jem was struck by Audrey's ability to listen and comprehend the incomprehensible. It was Audrey who suggested that a reconciliation between the brothers was still possible, however far-off it might be.

"But it will happen, if you want it to," she said. "If you *both* want it, that is."

The lovers met wherever they could: after dark in the stove-heated office cabin up at the North Branch; the dry hayloft of Clarendon's stables; and a time or two they met at Dixon's Mill, where Jem had a key to the storehouse thanks to Sugar Dave.

And now that it was June, with the days hot and the nights warm, a lush clearing near Dixon's Mill had become their preferred hideaway. It was a quiet place hidden in the woods where a young ash tree grew in a spotlight of sunshine. There they would make love on an old horse blanket under the tree's shade, and later when they lay together, Jem believed he could see in the ten thousand leaves rustling overhead the answers to all of life's great mysteries. Any time he tried to explain these answers aloud, however, Audrey would snort with laughter and push him away. It wasn't that she didn't understand what he was trying to say, for she did. She knew exactly the truths hidden within the creamy dollops of light that played upon their eyes. Somehow her understanding was deeper than his own, because she didn't feel the need to explain anything at all.

Last night, the clearing had once again been their hideaway, the horse blanket their veil that blocked out the rest of the world. With dawn breaking, Jem helped Audrey climb atop Greenbrier and rode hard for the North Branch, taking the West Cut to save time.

As he looked out at the Valley, Jem imagined it through Audrey's eyes. Instead of his usual dour sense of disappointment at being 'stuck', he gazed in awe at the rough-hewn beauty of the North Branch, the rolling green hills and the way the sunlight glittered upon Sleepy Creek. The humble sprawl of Mayfair, once so easily dismissed as a one-horse nowhere, now appeared to him an enchanting place of possibility.

For so long a time, Jem Roscoe had dreamed of nothing more than leaving Mayfair behind forever, so long and good riddance. But now, with Audrey pressed against him, the rich smell of her hair and skin filling his nostrils, himself acutely aware of the hot blood pumping in his veins and with almost every thought fixed upon the beauty and grace and joy that was Audrey Blake, Jem looked upon his boring old Valley home with a feeling approaching contentment.

Jem had just barely managed to get Audrey back to the Blake farm before her father and brothers woke for the day. From the cover of the forest, he turned and watched Audrey as she set about her morning chores with pep, as if she'd just woken up.

"I love that woman," Jem whispered to the trees, to nobody.

And now, sipping his coffee up at the mine, Jem was already thinking about how soon it would be until he could see Audrey again. How soon he could touch her, caress her, lay her down and—

"The hell you grinnin about, anyhow?"

Jem sat up straight. He looked over at old Joe Trask, the mine's head foreman, who was watching him from the cabin's large worktable.

Jem shook his head. "It's nothing."

"Sure don't seem like nothin." Trask winked at him. "You been up late with that country girl again?"

Jem laughed. "A gentleman never tells, Mr. Trask."

Trask grunted, "You don't gotta tell. The whole damn Valley knows about you two."

The old man rustled the newspaper in his hands and continued reading. Trask was whip-smart, but like most men in the Valley he'd never darkened the door of a schoolhouse. Over many months, Jem had taught Trask the fundamentals of comprehension. Jem suspected Trask's wife made her husband study the Good News by candlelight at home too, for Trask now carried a dog-eared pocket Bible with him everywhere. He often took it out to stare at its leather covers begrudgingly. He seemed to prefer newspapers because the print was larger. Even now he puttered happily along in his reading, underlining each word with a palsied finger and murmuring under his breath as he went.

Jem watched Trask idly scratch his chin, sending tiny specks of sunlit dust and skin flakes drifting down into his coffee cup. The old man was too busy reading to notice.

"What's the election news this week?" Jem asked.

"Don't rush me, kid."

Jem looked into his coffee cup and smiled.

He felt good today. He couldn't remember the last time he'd felt *bad*, to tell the truth. Maybe that night with JJ, or the night with that runaway slave, but all that seemed like so long ago. Jem wasn't drinking anymore. He'd started taking more pride in his work with the RRC. Now that Father was busy campaigning (and no longer financing his ambitions with the mine's revenue, but through Union Party donations), Jem enjoyed an agency that suited him just fine. Soon enough the Roscoe Company really would be his, and instead of lamenting that fact he started to think about how he might improve things, starting here on the North Branch. He'd be damned if he was going to let the mine fall into disrepair.

After all, a man had to ensure he could provide for his family.

Joe Trask had implored Father to expand the North Branch Mine for years now, suggesting the coal yields from existing shafts were thinning. Father, still believing his railroad was just around the bend, had always been hesitant. But when Jem realized that further delay would spell disaster for the mine and the men who worked within it, Jem quietly gave the go-ahead to Trask and his engineers. Today marked the start of a second week of digging for a new shaft that cut directly into the heart of the mountain.

Joe Trask flipped to the next section and rustled the paper to stiffen the spine. Jem watched the old man read. He smiled at the sight of the shabby, bewhiskered

Trask looking like some Tammany Hall huckster reading *The New York Times*. Then Trask leaned over and spat black tobacco into a spittoon, thus somehow perfecting the image while at the same time destroying it.

The old man's finger traced across the printed pages and he murmured to himself. Looking up at Jem, he said, "It ain't lookin good for your daddy and his new Union Party. He might win Virginia and Kentucky come the fall, but not much else."

Jem nodded slowly. He tested the words *Union Party* on his tongue and then shook his head with barely concealed derision.

For his whole life, Father had professed that he sought no higher office than senator, suggesting the Senate was the noblest of the Republic's institutions. What's more, Father's dream of building the Union's transcontinental railroad had seemed to be the singular goal of his life. But now, suddenly and without warning, Father wanted to become *president?*

Any day now, the old man's consumption might take him. And yet, it seemed that Father's every thought was fixed on attaining the White House. Why? To what end?

The old man had moved quickly in the wake of his campaign announcement. As productive as the North Branch was, one coal mine was far too little to power the engine of an entire presidential campaign, however 'modest' its managers considered the campaign to be. Father began to sell the western tracts of land he had purchased about a decade before. The future of the Roscoe family legacy, it seemed, no longer lay in Missouri. Father made some profit, but it was a pittance against what might sell in the decade to come. Father knew it too; he said as much to Jem in a letter home that showed a rare glimpse into the old man's mind:

> *I've stacked every chip upon this venture. If I am successful, my efforts will have bestowed upon our family a legacy for the next two hundred years. If I fail, I will soon be dead and our family will be ruined. And yet, I can see no better course of action. The die is cast; the Rubicon must be crossed.*

It was as if the weaker Father became with consumption, the more fervently he wanted to consume everything around him: power, prestige, anything that might make him immortal. Jem had long ago realized that 'family legacy' meant nothing more than Father's own personal *kudos*.

Well, all the more reason for Jem to shore up the Roscoe Company, not for his own sake or the sake of his family, but because the Company had become larger than any one person. Now that so many families in the Valley depended on wages from the North Branch Mine, keeping everything going had become in Jem's mind a moral obligation. Still, Jem was under no illusions regarding the mine. The work was difficult, dangerous, and even the hardiest of men worked on borrowed time. Still, something could not come from nothing. If the Company was strong, it could grow and adapt, and all those people connected to it would benefit.

That was the idea, at least.

Outside, a bell rang. Jem stood up and looked out the window. It was a shift change. He watched as soot-covered men sauntered down the slag hill with shovels and pickaxes over their shoulders and flashed toothy grins at their replacements. Moving opposite that line, trudging uphill, was a group of fresh-faced miners and teamsters driving mules and carts toward the mine's open mouth. Jem recognized the Blake brothers — Jonah, Charlie, and Ezra — among the newcomers. One by one, the men and mules passed from the bright, sunlit world and melted into the yawning darkness.

Trask folded his paper and set it down on the table. "I'm gonna head down the throat."

The 'throat' was what the North Branchers called the mineshaft. Jem stared out the window as the last stragglers went down below. "Inspection's at noon, yes?"

Trask checked his pocket watch. "That's right. You'll be fine gettin down on your own?"

Jem loathed going down the mine. There was nothing in the world that terrified him more than dark, tight spaces. Oh, the bitter irony.

"Sure," Jem said. "I'll be fine. Nothing to it."

Trask grinned; he seemed to read Jem like a book. "You just mind your feet and you'll be fine," he said. "You wanna know how I've gone twenty years walkin round the pit? It's 'cause I lead with my toes. Fellas who get into trouble, they lead with their heels."

Jem nodded. "I'll keep that in mind."

Trask whistled and snapped his fingers. "C'mon now, my Lady."

In an instant, there was movement under the table. Trask's dog, a German shepherd named Lady, followed her man outside the cabin with her tail wagging. Jem watched them walk toward the mouth of the mine together, same as they'd been doing for years.

Jem poured himself a fresh cup of coffee. For whatever reason, he felt the watchful presence of another person in the cabin with him.

Turning, Jem saw that, no, he was alone. Still, he could not shake off the idea that someone—

JJ?

—had been watching him. Such an eerie feeling had come over Jem many times in recent months, and sometimes his dreams were haunted by warped memories and troubling visions.

Jem took a drink and set his cup on the table. He wandered out to the porch that looked upon the whole of the Mayfair Valley. He remembered standing here with JJ just a few short months ago. He remembered laughing together, and feeling that, at long last, the wrongs of the past had finally been made right.

But that just wasn't the case.

Maybe Audrey was right that a reunification was possible. Maybe there would come a time when Jem and JJ would reconcile, and maybe even JJ and Father too, before it was too late. But the more Jem considered these possibilities, the less certain he was that either hatchet would be easily buried. JJ had always liked to brand Jem as the stubborn one, but it was JJ who in fact wore blinders to everything but his chosen object, whatever that object happened to be. For such a long time, and probably even still, that object had been to stand where Jem now stood. Audrey might hope the brothers would reunite someday, but Audrey didn't know that JJ was the sort of man who didn't give a damn about means, so long as the ends worked out in his favor.

After all, there was still a bullet hole in the ceiling of Clarendon's library.

Jem was almost certain that, somewhere out there, JJ was praying for some disaster to befall Jem and the RRC. Sometimes, Jem half expected to arrive at the North Branch one morning and find JJ sitting in Jem's chair, his feet propped up, and with a pair of dueling pistols primed and ready on the table.

Winner take all.

Jem's thoughts were suddenly cut short by a deafening explosion that shook the cabin.

Jem's coffee cup fell from the table and shattered on the floor. Dust rained down from the roof overhead. Jem froze, trying to guess the source of the sound. Could it have been thunder?

And then, Jem heard a man cry out.

No, he heard *men* crying out. Lots of them, and all screaming with pain.

Jem bolted around the porch and stepped into the mineyard. Looking up—

"God, no..."

The North Branch was obscured by black smoke. Craning his neck skyward, Jem saw a dark cloud and had only half a moment to wonder—

Rain?

—before a torrent of rocks and rock shards poured down from on high. Every man on the mountain crouched and covered his head as rocks the size of fists rained down upon them. At last, the deluge subsided and a cloud of dust filled the air.

Jem finally caught a ragged breath as his debris-battered lungs began to fill with air again. He watched, horrified, as bleary shapes materialized in the smoky gloom of the mine's mouth. They were men, some burned and others blinded and all of them bloody and naked, moaning and wailing like undead ghouls. Jem saw a lean black shape loping through the dust cloud and realized it was Lady, her eyes huge with panic.

Joe Trask emerged from below and hobbled down the hill. Jem rushed over to him and Trask collapsed in his arms. Jem helped Trask down to the ground while other men gathered around.

"Joe?" Jem said. "Joe, can you hear me? What happened, Joe?"

When Jem brought up his hand again, it was smeared with blood and tissue. Trask's skin had come apart in his fingers. Trask opened his quivering mouth to speak, but instead black smoke issued from his lungs, and he turned on his side to retch and quiver.

Shaking, Jem looked up at the mine. What he saw through the dust and smoke made him go numb with horror.

Half the mountain was gone.

God Almighty. *Half the mountain was gone.*

"They must've hit gas down there," gasped one of the men standing nearby. "They must've hit gas down the new mineshaft."

Jem knew the man was probably right, but it didn't matter what had happened — not right now. Just a few minutes earlier, over fifty men had gone down into the heart of the mountain.

The Blake brothers were down there too.

There were more shapes staggering up from the underworld, all of them blinded by facial burns. Those few unscathed men ran to them and guided them downhill toward the camp. Several men from the previous shift reappeared at the gate and ran up to help.

While Jem lay with Joe Trask cradled in his lap, he felt a dozen pairs of eyes on him, now more. Looking around, he saw nothing but panic and confusion. For a moment he thought he himself might drop to the ground and not have the strength to get back up again. He wondered if he could somehow slip away from the terror and confusion, could somehow run home and pretend none of this had happened…

But then a phantom spirit overtook him. Jem blinked once and his gaze hardened. Finding faces in the small crowd around him, he began to bark orders.

"Ballard, fetch Mr. Trask here some water and help him downhill. Rawlins, take the injured to the cabins. Give them water, whiskey, anything they need. I need ten men to help Rawlins — go *now*. Jackson, take a horse and fetch Dr. Harper in town, and rally anyone else who can lend a hand. You other men, follow me."

With that, Jem left Trask in the care of another and stood up. Turning, he ascended the hill toward the mouth of the mine. A group of men fell in behind. As they neared the mouth, which was still gushing smoke, a second deafening explosion erupted. Sparks of flame ushered forth and sent the men scattering.

Jem fell to his knees and slapped his hands over his ears. The concussion split his ears and filled his lungs with a gust of sulfuric wind. With his head spinning, he lurched forward on his hands and knees and vomited an acidic spray of black coffee and sooty smoke. Struggling to his feet again, he wavered once and then steadied himself.

The smoke was impenetrable. Jem pulled a kerchief from his pocket and wrapped it over his mouth and nose. He gestured for the others to do the same. The smoke stung his eyes and soon tears were pouring down his cheeks. The heat of the smoke burned his skin as if he stood in the embers of a giant bonfire.

Coming up from below was the sound of rushing hooves. Jem cried out and the men stepped back as a wide-eyed mule plunged screaming through the smoke, bursting out of the cloud and skidding down the hill with its unhitched harness dragging behind.

Jem stepped into the maw of the black mine and saw nothing. Turning to the nearest man, he passed the order down to bring up lanterns. No man was to wear the standard-issue wick caps, which featured small, long-burning candles to help guide a miner's way in the dark. They would have to take their chances with cumbersome closed lanterns, no open flames, and hope that whatever gases that had ignited deep below had been cleared by the blast.

When their lanterns had been lit, Jem beckoned for the men with him to follow. "Put a hand on my shoulder," he said to the next man. "Link up! Follow me."

Single file, the men followed. Together, they pushed forward through the smoke and descended into perfect darkness.

❧

Down in the underworld, Jem remembered to lead with his toes. He stumbled a man lying unconscious. While the others gathered around, Jem pinched and slapped the man's cheeks to rouse him.

"You'll be all right. We're taking you up. How many others below?"

The man shook his head. "All dead..."

Jem held the man as he went limp. Jem lifted the man and passed him off to two others and sent them back toward the entrance.

As the search party neared the first junction, where the wide tunnel split into two narrow pathways, cold fear gripped Jem's chest.

Which way to go?

Jem turned first one way, then the other. Now he turned and faced the men with him. He saw only half-faces in the dim light, the men's eyes gleaming with tiny pools of fire.

He thought to give a brusque order, to command one of the men to lead the way and be goddamn quick about it. That was something he thought JJ might say. But JJ would never admit ignorance; he would instead clench up and bark an order to the meekest man he could find.

Taking a breath, Jem shook the thought from his head. He looked squarely at the men gathered next to him and shook his head.

"I'll be honest, boys. I don't know the way down."

For a moment, no one said anything. Jem wondered whether his show of vulnerability had been the wisest choice after all.

Just then, someone stepped forward. The lantern light revealed Ed Ripley, a slight, cockeyed boy who had been playmates with Jem when they were children.

"I know the way," Ripley said.

Jem's heart beat faster in his chest. Good old Rip!

Ripley pointed to the left path. "That way to A-Shaft," he said. "It slopes down to the coal beds. Nice, easy climb." He spoke as if the climb was anything but. Now he pointed back to the right. "That way's the way to B-Shaft. Straight down. Don't know if the pulley's workin, but if she's let go she'll drop full chisel. We got some rope to get down there in any case." Ripley pointed between the two directions. "And we got three crosscut tunnels that connect the shafts. But I don't know which might be blocked up."

One of the men nearby rasped: "We shouldn't all head down one way. We should split up into two teams."

Another man wagged his head. "Ain't no sense goin one way if there's no fellas down there. We might get trapped ourselves."

"We ought to listen for sounds of men and follow em down," another said.

"And if we all get caught in another blow-out, who's gonna come for *us*?"

A grave sense of calm touched Jem on the small of the back and worked its way up his spine until it flowed through his entire body. He thought of JJ once again, but this time the memory was positive. He remembered what JJ had once said about fear: that it was fine to accept it, but only for a moment. Once the fear had been felt, there was only one thing to be done.

To do what needs doing.

Slowly, all heads turned to Jem once more.

Jem nodded, indicating he'd made a decision. He pointed at the shaft leading down to B-Shaft. "If that's a mean drop like you say it is, Rip, I don't want to take a chance on it with all of us. Let's have two men stay up here and try the pulley. Samson, Nichols, that's you. Put some weight on the system, give it some stress. If it holds, send one of the coal trays down. As we bring men forward, we'll load them on a tray and raise them up. And if you don't hear from us in twenty minutes, they can send a message back."

Jem turned to the path sloping down to A-Shaft.

"The rest of us — what are we, nine now? The rest of us will head down the slope. We'll make a square search of it, see? We'll split up at the second crosscut. One team will head across to B-Shaft and search as far in as you can. The other team will search the full length of A, turn down the last crosscut, and link up in B. We'll carry any wounded we find to the shaft and haul them up, then we'll come back up the A-Shaft slope by way of the first crosscut. We cover the whole of it inch by inch, no stone unturned. Understood?"

The men nodded in silence. One of them, an older man named Hall, pressed for more. "But what if there's a shake? What if our way gets blocked?"

"Double back," Jem said. "We'll find another way around, somehow."

"Detour," Ripley said with a grin. "Just like a stroll down-country, boys."

A few smiles broke on their grim faces. It wasn't much, but it was needed. Now the men straightened their backs and got ready to move.

"All right," Jem said. "Let's get down there."

"We ought to say a prayer," Ripley said. "Can we say a prayer?"

Jem knew there wasn't much time — there wasn't *any* time — but the men looked terrified.

"All right," Jem said.

The men joined hands and closed their eyes. Ripley led the group in a hasty, half-muttered prayer. Jem quieted the racing thoughts of his mind and focused on listening. When Ripley was finished and Jem opened his eyes again, he saw that each of the men looked a little better than they had just moments before.

"Now we go," Jem said.

They started off single file, groping their way through the darkness like blind shadows. Their flickering lanterns swayed in the darkness.

When the group passed the first fork in A-Shaft, they pushed on all together. At the second fork, Hall broke off with four others in the direction of B-Shaft.

"See you fellas on the other side," Ripley said.

"See you in hell," Hall said. Then he and the others disappeared into a river of darkness.

Jem nodded to Ripley and the three men remaining with them. Together they continued down the A-Shaft slope. As they journeyed deeper into the heart of the mountain, the God-fearing Ripley began to murmur another string of urgent prayers.

They moved slowly, creeping their way over mounds of earth and rock. In several places the overhead support beams had splintered and huge boulders narrowed the tunnel. Halfway to the next crosscut, the tunnel had caved in from both sides so that Jem and the others needed to squeeze through a sliver of open space to continue. Putting a hand on the rock, Jem could still feel a tremor in the earth and realized he was touching the deep heart of the mountain. He heard the haggard breaths of the men ahead and behind him.

"Easy does it," Jem said, trying to reassure himself as much as anyone else. "Breathe in, breathe out. Easy does—"

There was a sound up ahead. Faint, but growing louder as they inched farther down the tunnel. Jem strained to listen, and there it was: a man screaming, hollering, shouting at someone. Shouting *for* someone.

Jem quickened his pace and the others followed at a trot. Their lanterns bounced crazily, their light stabbing up at the rock crevices and splintering down the tunnel like yellow lightning on a black sky. And always the guttural shouting down the tunnel grew louder, the rage and desperation greater, as if a man was fighting a brutal deathmatch with something lurking in the dark.

Turning down the slope, their lanterns revealed a wall of solid rock that should not have been there. A giant shadow of a man flickered on the wall. The shadow was stooping, heaving up rocks and stones, and hurling them away like a deranged Sisyphus trying to tear down the walls of Tartarus itself.

Under the lantern light, Jem's eyes widened with recognition, but it was Ripley who called out first:

"Blake! Ezra Blake!"

Ezra Blake turned his head into the light, his wild eyes bulging with desperation.

"Help me, goddammit!"

Jem and the others sprang to action. Taking position at the wall, they put their ears against the rock face and listened. They could hear muffled voices from behind the broken wall — voices yelling, crying out, praying with exultant fervor.

"Lord," Ripley whimpered. "They're blocked up."

Blake stepped up to haul another rock from the wall of debris. This next one was a boulder as big as Blake himself. Stunned for a moment, Jem stared at the veins bulging in Blake's neck before he snapped out of his stunned trance and moved to help him.

The others scrambled into place, and now all together they lifted the boulder and rolled it back. It lumbered drunkenly two or three feet before it spun on its axis and collapsed and—"Sonofagun!"—nearly crushed Ripley's foot underneath it.

"You all right?" Jem said.

Ripley shook his ankle free and moved his foot around, and Jem imagined him curling his five toes within the big boot.

Ripley nodded meekly. "Maybe lost a toenail, but I'm good."

Blake stepped up again, his large hands already grabbing at the next rock. He bellowed, *"JONAH! CHARLIE!"* over and over. The muffled screaming from behind the wall continued. There was no way to discern what the trapped men were saying, or who they even were. But there was no questioning that two of them were Ezra Blake's older brothers.

Audrey's brothers.

Trying to hide the desperation growing within him, Jem turned to Ripley. "Can we get around them through the B-Shaft?"

Ripley shook his head. "The last crosscut is back up the slope a ways. This here is the newest section, and the deepest too. The only way through is through."

Jem stepped back and took a true look at the fallen wall. Giant boulders were piled together, with rocks the size of horse heads cramming the spaces between. There was no way around the wall, and no way through it but to pick it apart rock by rock. That would mean splitting rocks with chisels, and it would mean an army of men working around the clock. Explosives weren't an option, not with the trapped men so close and with the mountain as unstable as it was. But how much air was locked behind that wall? Did the trapped men know to limit their talking, to breathe in small sips, to conserve their energy and—

"JONAH! CHARLIE! JO—"

Suddenly, Ezra Blake pitched forward like a toppling tree. Jem caught his arms and the others helped him lay Blake down. Jem pulled one of Blake's eyelids open and saw the eye twitch in the light.

"He's gone out cold," Jem said. He tapped and pinched Blake's cheeks. "Ezra. Ezra, wake up. *Ezra, wake up...*"

"They don't got no time," Ripley said. His spirit had accepted defeat.

"We need to give them time," Jem growled. "This isn't done — not yet."

Ripley patted one of the hulking boulders. "You pull these suckers out, you'll bring the whole mountain down on top of us."

"For God's sake, we have to try!" Jem shouted. He shot to his feet and advanced on Ripley until they stood nose to nose. "There could be twenty men in there. What if it was you in there, Rip? Would you want us to give up on you just like that? What would you do, sit down and say a goddamn prayer?!"

Ripley stared back at Jem with a hurt look of defiance. At length, hearing the muffled shouts from behind the rock, he sighed and spat and gave a relenting nod.

"Right," Jem said. He pointed at two men beside him. "You boys, take Blake up top and tell the others what's happened. We need every able-bodied man down here ready to dig. *Go!*"

The others hauled Ezra Blake to his feet, and they trudged up toward the mine's entrance. At last, it was just Jem and Ed Ripley who remained.

"Rip," Jem said. "I'm sorry for what I—"

"Don't," Ripley said. He put his hands upon a rock as big as he was. "Just help me with this, will you?"

❧

Still coughing up smoke in the fading light of dusk, Jem stood at the mine's entrance and looked out upon the scene before him.

Hundreds of Mayfair folks had climbed the North Branch and gathered around the slag heaps. The cabins were all occupied, and the small tent village built down the slope had grown into a tent city. The injured were attended by nurses, who just minutes ago had been wives, sweethearts, fathers, brothers, and sisters. Dr. Harper hurried from man to man like a battlefield surgeon. The people of Mayfair had built up several cooking fires and were busy making a communal stew. The sweet sounds of a violin echoed along the Branch's outcroppings. In the encroaching darkness a mule wagon rolled up driven by an old woman in her eighties. The wagon was stuffed to overflowing with bedding and feather pillows that soon turned black from soot.

The sight of it all choked Jem with tears. To see all these people coming together, to see the community bonding in such a way...well, such unity would have been even more beautiful were it not for the horror that inspired it.

"Coffee for you, Mr. President."

Jem turned and saw George Hunt and Sugar Dave Dixon standing with him.

Jem scowled. "Don't call me that, George, for God's sake."

Hunt was chagrined. "Sorry. Bad joke."

Sugar Dave offered the coffee to Jem, and Jem accepted it gratefully. His throat was raw and his whole body trembled from exhaustion.

Jem checked his pocket watch in the fading light. Soon it would be time for the next shift, and he'd go back down the throat with them. They had been digging out the caved-in section of A-Shaft for over twelve hours. No, not digging. *Mining.* Splitting and chiseling rock into pieces small enough to be hauled up and out. As hot coffee warmed his throat, a chill ran down Jem's spine. Today, the men of the North Branch weren't mining for coal, but for other men.

"Men comin up!"

Jem's head snapped to the voice. Emerging from the pitch blackness came the twinkling lights of lanterns growing larger and brighter. At last, Jem could make out the faces of the men as they approached. They shuffled forward, their clothes ragged and tattered, their faces blackened and worn. They dragged their shovels and pickaxes behind them.

Jem found Ed Ripley among the men. "What happened? I'm about to lead another group down."

Ripley could not look at Jem. He tried to speak, but no words came. Instead, he stood there jawing at the world. Tears rolled down his cheeks, cutting rivers of pale skin through black soot.

Now he looked at the other men who had come up from below. They were mute to the man, all with their heads hung low in despair. They dropped their spades and pickaxes and wandered out into the open night.

While holding back tears, Ripley explained what he had seen. After several hours of backbreaking effort, Ripley and his team had at last broken through the collapsed wall of rock — but too late. They found some twenty men dead in the darkness. Some had been crushed during the initial explosion and cave-in. The rest had died trying to dig their way out, many still clutching their tools. In their strain and effort they had consumed the last of their oxygen. The would-be rescuers had entered a tomb.

Jem listened to all this, not wanting to believe any of it.

"Twenty men?"

Ripley nodded, dejected. "That's the count. Harris boys, Clay Greene...the Blake boys too. Jonah and Charlie, they was almost out. They'd almost dug their way free, but...there just wasn't enough time."

Jem could do little but put his hand on Ripley's shoulder and squeeze. "You did all you could, Rip. Everybody, they did all they could."

Ripley staggered off with the others moving downhill. At the same time, the crowd forming around the mouth of the mine had grown larger. There were now several hundred people murmuring together. Soon enough, the news from below would spread.

Joe Trask hobbled forward with the help of two others. The old foreman's injured right leg had been set against a plank board and tied there.

"A word with you, kid?"

Jem listened as Trask advised that an official announcement be made, here and now. As the news traveled, so would misinformation. It was time for Jem to gather everyone within shouting distance and explain the situation. This horrible situation. But just exactly what would Jem say? What *could* he say?

And then, Jem saw her.

Audrey was down at the camp, kneeling next to her brother Ezra, who was still unconscious. Audrey dipped a rag in a bucket of water and wrung it, and she used it to wipe the soot from Ezra's face.

"Kid," Trask said to Jem. "Folks gotta know. Somethin's gotta be said."

Jem nodded. "In a minute," he said. "Just give me a minute, Joe."

As he trudged down the hill, Jem felt his blood flow sludge-like through his veins. When Audrey looked up and saw him, she stood up and came to him. They met halfway up the hill. Jem kept his distance, thinking it best to maintain some element of decorum in the situation, but Audrey threw herself at him and squeezed. Jem's heart was in his throat, and he felt he might collapse into tears.

"Audrey," he whispered. "Audrey, I need to tell you something..."

He closed his eyes and held her close. He didn't want this moment to end, knowing that in a moment more, everything would change for the worse.

Then again, everything already had.

Audrey wore a mute expression of shock as Jem told her the horrible news. Her two oldest brothers were down below, two brothers now dead. Audrey closed her eyes for a long while, and when she opened them again she looked at Jem with detached confusion, as if she had forgotten who Jem was and maybe who she was herself.

"Audrey," Jem said. "I'm so sorry, Audrey. Are you…Is there anything…?"

"I need to tell Ezra," Audrey said suddenly, her voice a low, urgent whisper. "I need to tell him what happened."

With that, Audrey pulled back from Jem's embrace. He tried to take her hand, wanting to touch her just a little while longer, but she had already turned away and started down the hillside toward the makeshift hospital below.

Jem watched Audrey go. And then, turning, he began the slow uphill trek toward the mouth of the North Branch Mine. There were several hundred eyes watching him now. As Jem passed into the crowd, he looked at the faces of the miners and their families. The miners, both healthy and injured, were all scarred by the day's nightmare, with each man pondering the sobering realization that one of the rumored dead men below could have easily been himself.

As Jem took his place beside Joe Trask, with Ripley standing nearby and Hunt and Sugar Dave looking on, Jem turned to face the murmuring crowd. He saw in their eyes a collective exhaustion, in some eyes a traumatized detachment, and in others the narrow glare of hate and suspicion directed toward Jem himself. Jem waited for their whispers to subside, until he could hear only the crackling of the campfires below. Behind him, the mountain remained as silent as ever.

"I suppose you-all know by now the terrible news from down there," Jem began. "We know there's about twenty of us down there. We're searching for others, and the roll call list is going around presently."

Heads hung low and shoulders drooped, and Jem's voice faltered. The words he'd spoken hung in the air like the heavy smoke that still clung to the earth.

"What can be said at a time like this? All I can say, for what it's worth, is that we won't leave those men down there. We'll bring them up here — all of them. And then we will honor them."

Jem looked at faces all around, and finally he landed on Ripley.

"In the meantime," Jem said, "I ask that we all bow our heads in silent prayer."

Together, the people of Mayfair bowed their heads.

In the long silence that followed, Jem heard only the summer wind blowing. On the breeze, he detected low campfire conversations at the camp down the hill.

"*No!* No, no — *NO!*"

All heads turned to the sound of Ezra Blake hollering in heartbroken fury. Audrey, kneeling at her brother's side, went very still as Blake shot to his feet. Dr. Harper hurried over, maybe to instill calm in his patient, but Blake grabbed the doctor by the throat and shook him like a ragdoll. He hurled Harper back through the open flame of a nearby campfire where the doctor collapsed smoking on the ground, unhurt but nevertheless stunned beyond speech.

Jem's heart leaped into his throat as he watched Blake storm up the hillside. As Blake reached the mass of people, they slowly parted for him. He trudged forward, limping, straining with every step. At last, he stood before Jem and glared down at him with cold and utter contempt.

"Well?" Blake said, turning to the crowd. "Just what the hell are y'all standing around for? What good's your thoughts and fuckin prayers gonna do? I'm goin down there to get my brothers out, and I'm goin *now*."

Blake started forward with a vicious snarl and knocked Jem out of the way. Ed Ripley moved to block Blake's path, but Jem waved Ripley down.

The people of Mayfair looked at each other, each trying to decide what to do. They watched as Ezra Blake plunged into the depths without a candle or lantern to guide him. Finally, several men stepped forward with haggard sighs. Steeling themselves for the grim work ahead, they took up their lanterns and trudged into the darkness, following the haunting sound of Ezra Blake's quiet, stifled sobbing.

Chapter 26
THE LONG JULY

Tom Roscoe liked trains. He liked them a great deal, as a matter of fact. Sure, he often dreamed about conquering the vast unknowns of the West by trekking mountain ranges on foot like Merriweather Lewis, or driving mules before a lumbering Conestoga wagon across prairie brushland, but he knew that whenever he finally decided to go West, he'd go by train.

The train Tom was in now was bearing him, unfortunately, back to familiar old Mayfair. Still, he knew that Mayfair wasn't the worst of all places. The worst of all places, of course, was Lynchburg Academy.

Tom was en route home from the 'Lynch', and had in fact abandoned that horrid place as soon as he finished his last written examination. He had never experienced much by way of examinations back at the Mayfair School, even when cruel Mr. Braxton had been in charge. At the Lynch, Tom raced his way through the test, barely comprehending the strange hieroglyphics on his slate and fighting to think properly with the voice screaming in his head. He was desperate to leave early, because this gave him a better chance of evading the brutish whims of the Lynch's upperclassmen. Tom had earned a few too many bruises over the semester (all aimed carefully under the neckline so as not to arouse suspicion from prefects and professors) to chance meeting with the bastards when he was so agonizingly close to escape.

The ride north through the Shenandoah had been plodding, but pleasant. Tom spent much of it looking out the window, watching the world go by. At one point an old lady occupied the bench opposite Tom, and she amused herself by glaring at him. When she got off at Staunton and a mustachioed man in a suit sat down in her place, Tom amused himself by imitating the man's movements until the man muttered that Tom's mother would be ashamed of him.

Tom had taken off his stuffy school uniform when the train rolled past Harrisonburg, about halfway to the Mayfair Valley. Tom did not want to draw any unnecessary attention, especially with where he was going.

At last, the country sights hurrying past the window became familiar to Tom's eye. The train soon rolled into Mayfair Station and rested on a bed of steam. Looking out the window, Tom recognized the familiar clear-cut hump of the South

Branch, the cotton fields laid out like a quilt, the bald crown of the mountain dotted with mansions and quiet hamlets, with a large new church well under construction. A hot sun swam in a sky of crystal blue, and the whole world brimmed with the promise of summer.

Summer! Some sixty days — a damn eternity — of freedom!

Climbing down from the train, Tom heaved his heavy trunk onto the platform. There were many people waiting on the platform for loved ones, but Tom could see no one he knew among them. Of course he'd had the good sense to write home and tell them the day and time he was coming home. But as he searched for sign of Jem, Ben, anyone, he began to wonder if he would have to somehow lug his trunk all the way across the Valley, and *then* up the North Branch.

Oh, but maybe someone would give him a ride in their coach. Tom looked in the eyes of some of the people around, trying to discern the Good Samaritans among sinners. When the crowd started to thin out, Tom began to panic.

And then, Tom saw him.

Jem was slouched against the ticket booth, absentmindedly sawing a toothpick with his teeth. He looked not to have noticed a train had arrived at all.

Tom heaved his trunk forward, feeling either his arm might snap off or a vein in his neck might burst. The closer Tom got to Jem, the more pungent the nostril-burning whiff of liquor became.

"Don't you ever wash?" Tom called, breathless.

Sluggish, Jem looked up at him and squinted. "What?"

"The prefects make us wash every day," Tom said. "They run us through these stalls like we're a bunch of animals. They douse us and delouse us."

"Sounds delightful," Jem said.

Tom shrugged. "You ought to try it."

Jem smiled, but there was no laughter. He lit a match and puffed on a cigar, and this brought at least some color back to his pallid cheeks.

Taking a deep breath, Tom hauled his trunk forward again. "Where's the coach?"

"Let me get that," Jem said, and he picked up Tom's travel trunk without the slightest effort.

"Thanks," Tom said, following behind. He decided that he needed to build up his muscles, somehow.

They walked to the coach. Tom said hello to old Mabel. She was the only horse he even remotely cared for; all others could go to hell. Suddenly, Tom thought about his dog Tipper.

Oh, Tipper!

Tom had thought about the mutt almost every day he'd been down at the Lynch. Sometimes he even dreamed about his old dog, and when he woke up he missed Tip all the more. He wondered if Tipper was going to pee on the floor again when they were reunited, which is what he did anytime Tom walked through the front door (much to the eternal dismay of Mae Jane).

"What are you laughing about?" Jem said.

Still laughing, Tom shook his head.

"Nothing."

"You laugh at your own jokes," Jem said.

"What's wrong with that?" Tom said. "No one else will."

Jem gave a thin smile. But still, no laughter.

It was a fine day, so Tom sat with Jem atop the cab of the coach. The coach rolled and rumbled along the Valley road leading down the South Branch toward Mayfair and the North Branch beyond. The sun was still high, but starting to wane. By the time they reached Clarendon, most of this precious summer day would be over.

Why no laughter from Jem? Well, of course Tom had an idea why. Even down at school, everyone had heard the stories about the collapse at the North Branch Mine. (Incidentally, Tom was careful not to associate himself too closely with the whole affair.) Speaking for himself, Tom couldn't wait to climb up to the mine and take a good look around.

Tom turned and looked at Jem. The burning, pinewood smell of gin seemed to ooze from his brother's sallow, sweaty skin. Laws, it was *summertime* after all, the time of year when folks ought to be at their healthiest. But Jem, he looked positively done in.

Tom remembered a dirty joke from the Lynch and thought it might cheer Jem up a little.

"Say, what do you call a blind chinaman's mule?"

Jem didn't say anything. He held the bouncing reins loose against his lap and made a lazy clicking noise out one side of his mouth, a call for Mabel to keep to the left.

Tom leaned into his brother. "I said, what do you call a blind chinaman's mule?"

Still no answer. Jem seemed to be lost in thought, his eyes far away somewhere. But of course Jem had still *heard him*. They were sitting right goddamn next to each other.

"Hey, what's the idea?" Tom whined, waving his hand in front of Jem's face. "*What do you call—?*"

"Dammit, Tom, *enough*. Leave it."

Tom turned and folded his arms and glared out the other side of the coach. As they continued to roll through the Valley, Tom looked out at farms and fields. Most farms were tiny, hardscrabble plots of land with squat cabins and barns that looked ready to collapse. There were some fine country homes here and there, and yonder Tom could see small groups of men, black and white, working together in the fields and building fences along property lines. It was only the rich planters of the First

Families who could afford to keep enough slaves to do all the farm work, let alone hire white overseers to manage them. Most folks in the Valley who owned slaves only owned one or two apiece, and master and slave often toiled side by side.

By and by, Tom's gaze fell upon the North Branch. Way up near the top, he could make out the gray cluster of buildings that marked the North Branch Mine.

"There's no smoke," Tom said.

Jem tossed his head as if shaking a horsefly. "Eh, what?"

"The Branch," Tom said, nodding toward the mountain. "There's no smoke from the chimneys. You've been closed a few weeks, by the looks of it. Will you be starting up again soon?"

Jem looked up at the mountain for only a brief moment before he hung his head and stared down at the reins in his hands. "Closed indefinitely."

"What do you mean indefinitely?"

"I mean a long time," Jem said. "Maybe forever. There are three bodies still down there."

Tom winced. "Three *bodies?*" For some reason — afterward he couldn't figure out exactly why — the absurd vision that popped into his head made him snort with laughter. "Ah, what a stink! Why the hell has no one taken them out yet?"

Jem turned on him suddenly, his face red with indignation. "Because they were *crushed*, Tom. They're fucking pancakes, and they're buried in the deepest part of the shaft where we can't get. Why, you want to go up there and take a look? You want to take a fucking *whiff* and laugh about it some more?"

Frightened, Tom looked away from Jem. His eyes darted around until they landed on something, anything, that he could fix his gaze on. He was left staring at Mabel's huge rolling rump, trying to swallow down the sudden tightness in his throat. Even when he heard Jem heave a great sigh (a sign that his anger had passed, at least for now), Tom did not look up for a long while.

They rode in silence. Jem tried to avoid going through Mayfair directly, but the bridge near Dixon's Mill was undergoing repairs. As the coach rolled through Mayfair, Jem pulled up his collar as if trying to hide his face. Indeed, Tom noticed that they had the attention of a good many folks, and none of them looked particularly happy to see them coming. Tom started to wonder just how badly Jem had messed up to draw such unfriendly scrutiny. As a man passed beside the coach, he turned and spat upon the wheels. Jem kept his eyes forward, his face drawn and tight.

For himself, Tom was glad to see the town again. Now that he'd been away, Mayfair felt like his 'old town,' his starting point, his humble place of origin. He felt older, probably wiser, and, he hoped, a little more handsome. Looking around, he couldn't resist a proud grin.

"Please," Jem mumbled, catching the wistful look in Tom's eye. "You've gone a few miles beyond the Branches and now you think you're Kit Carson."

"I've gone further than you," Tom said pointedly.

"Farther."

"What?"

"Farther *physical*; further *figurative*. Didn't they teach you that at that fancy school?"

"Same difference."

"No, it's not. Maybe you've gone farther than me, but you've got a lot left to learn. You're still a little kid."

"I'm no kid!" Tom exclaimed. "I'm—"

"Thirteen, right, which means you're a kid. You should enjoy it, Tom. Enjoy it while it lasts."

Tom was about to protest further (*farther?*), but then the coach was nearing the Mayfair School, a one-room schoolhouse tucked near the base of the North Branch.

"Stop here!" Tom cried. "I'm getting out. They might not be finished yet."

Jem shook his head and flicked the reins, and Mabel kept plodding along. "It's best we get home, and quickly. Things have changed, Tom. I'll explain later, but for now just trust me and — *hey*, where the hell are you going?"

Tom had clambered down the side of the moving coach and was already racing toward the schoolhouse. "Pull over up there and wait for me!"

Laughing, Tom jogged through a patch of shrubs and long grass until he reached the schoolyard. Mayfair School was built on a hill, one of the foothills of the North Branch, and from here one had a fine view of Mayfair proper. But right now, Tom had eyes only for the humble little schoolhouse itself. Any minute now, classes would be finished for the summer.

And there, from inside, came the clang of a hand-rung cowbell.

Summer!

Tom's former classmates began to pour out of the schoolhouse, the excited hubbub of conversation following them like a cloud. Within a moment, Tom was swallowed up by a sea of chattering youths and children. Some looked at him with surprise, a few said hello, but most were too preoccupied with the promise of summer and fled for home as quickly as their legs could carry them.

As he studied the faces of the other pupils, Tom realized that many of them had changed drastically in just the few months he had been away. Some faces had fattened, others had stretched out, and every *body* seemed to have morphed or shifted in one way or another. He barely recognized Penelope Cutler, for instance, who had once been among the smallest of his classmates but was now a full head taller than he.

Penelope exited the schoolhouse clutching her books to her chest. Seeing Tom she stopped, and she looked him up and down with a skeptical eye. "So," she said, "you decided to come crawling back."

"Hello to you too, Penny."

"I do hope you're taking your studies at Lynchburg Academy seriously," Penelope said.

Tom gave a devilish grin. "Half the time, anyway."

Penelope sighed. "If some of us had only *half* the opportunities you do, Thomas Roscoe, this world would be a better place."

Tom stuffed his hands in the pockets of his trousers and shrugged. "Why? What's stopping you from going to school someplace else? Your daddy can afford it, surely. There's a girls-only academy down in Lynchburg too. And another in Roanoke, as I understand."

Penelope's face darkened with anger and frustration, though not necessarily because of Tom. "You know *exactly* why I can't go, Thomas." She fought back tears. "Take a look at yourself, now look at me. See the difference? Of course, I know I'm a better student than you. I could go to university if I wanted. Instead, I'm stuck here at this country shack. Daddy says it's no use paying for an educated woman when there's no proper need for such a creature." She looked down at her dress, despairing. "Such as it is, it's the debutante ball for me."

Tom kicked a rock at his feet. Speaking for himself, he much preferred the idea of spending one's life going to parties rather than sitting in front of a blackboard. He recalled his sister Sarah had some education, and that had made her *less* attractive to most Valley gentlemen. For whatever reason, Penelope's brother Henry had married Sarah anyway. Tom considered telling Penelope there was little point for a woman to learn things like French or mathematics if she was destined for a life at home anyway, but he decided against it.

"Say, I've got an idea, Penny. Why don't you come down to Lynchburg with me? We'll cut your hair or something. I'll pass all my exams and assignments to you, secret-like. You finish them, and I'll get the credit." Tom laughed. "You'll still have the academic life you've always wanted!"

Penelope sniffed and started forward, her chin held high. "Very funny. Enjoy your summer, Thomas Roscoe."

"Will I be seeing you?" Tom asked hopefully.

The girl rolled her eyes. "Maybe across the aisle at church. Beyond that, I can't imagine it."

Tom tried to think of a few quips to toss at the back of Penelope's head, but he blanked when his eyes fell on her hips and followed the rhythmic swish of her dress. Blinking, he took a long breath. Penelope Cutler was already fourteen, and next year she would debut before Mayfair society. That meant that as early as next spring, Penelope might become engaged to an older boy, and very likely an older man. For whatever reason, thinking about that made Tom's pulse pound.

A finger tapped on Tom's shoulder, and turning around Tom looked into the eyes of—

"Bayard!"

He threw his arms around his little brother and squeezed, and then the realization struck him that Bayard was nearly as tall as he was. Why the hell was everyone else growing so tall while Tom stayed the same size? Pulling back, Tom laughed and put an arm around Bayard's shoulders.

"Say, how'd you do in there? Does Miss Blake make you take examinations? Make you cut shapes out of paper? Count rocks? Come on, Bay, tell me all about your genius breakthroughs."

Speaking in his own manner, Bayard started into a happy explanation of his schooling. Tom listened and understood as best he could, and he nodded along with genuine interest. As godawfully annoying as Bayard could be (he was the baby in the family, after all), Tom was one of the few who actually listened to his brother's perspective of the world. And having been away from home for so many months, having met precious few friendly faces at the Lynch, seeing Bayard again made Tom's heart soar.

"Come on, boys," came the call. It was Jem, standing near the edge of the schoolyard. He kept looking nervously toward the schoolhouse and looked like he was ready to bolt for home any moment. "We should be getting along up the…"

Jem's voice trailed off as he saw something across the schoolyard. Following Jem's gaze, Tom turned his head and looked toward the schoolhouse.

Standing there on the front steps, seeing off the last of her pupils, was Miss Audrey Blake. She wore a blue dress with a high collar, her blonde hair tied back with simple flair.

Cheerily, Tom thrust his hand in the air. "*Hello*, Miss Blake!"

Shielding her eyes with a hand, Miss Blake peered across the schoolyard. She saw Tom and recognized him, and she offered a pleasant wave. But then her gaze went farther and fixed upon Jem, and suddenly her smile froze.

Tom looked between Miss Blake and Jem. For a strangled moment, the two seemed to share some silent, important communication across the schoolyard. Jem, who had been slouching just moments before, stood up straight and put his hands at his sides, his eyes never leaving Miss Blake. When a gaggle of schoolgirls hailed Miss Blake, she tore her gaze away from Jem for but a moment to wave a happy goodbye to the girls.

Just then, the huge bulk of a bewhiskered giant emerged from within the schoolhouse. Tom vaguely recognized the giant as Miss Blake's brother Ezra. Exactly why the schoolmistress' brother was here, Tom couldn't be sure.

As Ezra Blake stepped into the daylight, his lower lip turned up in a hoggish sneer, he glared at the spot where Jem stood. Turning to gauge Jem's reaction, Tom instead saw the back of Jem's head as his brother hurried away from the schoolyard.

"Well, come on, Bay," Tom said. "Let's catch up with him."

As he and Bayard trudged after Jem, Tom heard a familiar laugh ring out. Whirling around again, he watched as Billy Clements came tumbling out of the schoolhouse with two other boys in tow. They were laughing about something, but Tom couldn't tell what about.

"Just a minute," Tom said, and he stepped away from Bayard. He ran toward Billy and beamed a wide smile. "*Hiya*, Bill!" he shouted, finding it funny that Billy flinched a little when he heard his name. A moment later Tom stood right beside his oldest friend, still grinning like mad. "How'd it go in there, partner? You whip em or what?"

The other two boys — Tom recognized them as Joe and Ira, the sons of North Branch farmers — lingered behind Billy like mewling cats. The boys mumbled together and then walked right past Tom without serving a second glance. Tom heard one of them mutter a curse or slur of some kind, but he only caught a piece of it.

"...cussed *lickfinger*..."

Tom decided to ignore the boys. He'd never much cared for Joe or Ira anyway, nor most other boys for that matter. He'd only ever had one friend, and that was Billy. Still smiling, Tom threw a playful punch at Billy's shoulder.

"You hear me, Bill? I said, how'd you do?"

Billy ignored the question outright. "We're gonna head down to the quarry," he said.

Tom's eyes lit up. Swimming at the quarry was exactly what he'd been hoping for, had indeed been thinking about all during the train ride home. "Great! Well, let's vamoose then, partner. You gonna leap the Promontory?"

Jumping from the Promontory, a jagged rock looming over a deep swimming hole, had become a rite of passage for Mayfair's youth. Tom did not know a single person over fifteen who had not made the jump.

"Laws," Tom said, "I'm glad I took off my fancy school getup. Why don't you climb up on the coach? We'll stop at my place on the way, and then we'll head down together."

Billy had the eyes of a cornered animal. Maybe he'd caught a look from his new friends, for he started to creep away from Tom.

"Actually, Tommy, I...well, me and the boys, we was thinkin we'd head down there straight away. Leave it too late and all the babies will take the best rocks. You know how it is."

Stunned, Tom could do nothing but nod in agreement. "Oh, sure. Yeah, best to get there straight away, like you said."

Billy shrugged. "Yeah." Then, with his eyes down and head low, Billy sidestepped Tom and pushed on to catch up with the other boys, who were already a quarter mile up the road.

Tom called, "Maybe I'll just meet you at the quarry then."

If Billy heard Tom, he didn't turn around to make it known. He just ran on. When he caught up with the other boys, Tom heard a gale of laughter. He guessed — no, he *knew* — the joke was about him.

As Tom watched Billy and the other boys go, he felt a nauseous feeling overtake his stomach. What had just happened? The bright summer day, with all its sunny promise, now seemed a waste. Tom found himself wishing for a cold rain so that no one could swim down at the quarry.

At the schoolhouse, Miss Blake was quietly locking the door for the final time of the season. Her brother Ezra stood waiting nearby, his squinty eyes scanning, watching for another sign of...

Jem.

And now it made sense: the Blakes, the scowling faces in town, Jem's whole sorry state. Most of the pupils at Mayfair School had brothers and fathers and uncles who worked up at the North Branch Mine, some of whom were among the dead from the cave-in. Probably there wasn't anyone in the Valley who didn't have a connection to the dead. And whatever rotten ideas grownups tended to think and say, their children absorbed it all like sponges.

The schoolyard was all but deserted now. Even with Bayard standing beside him, Tom felt a gnawing sort of loneliness.

"Come on, Bay," Tom said, putting his arm around Bayard again. "Let's get on."

They turned toward the road. Jem was already up on the driver's bench of the coach, reins in hand, looking as if he'd just lost his lunch.

Tom and Bayard clambered aboard the coach.

Jem released the brake lever. "Any other stops you wish to make?" he asked pointedly.

Tom shook his head in a subdued way. "No," he said, his voice quiet. "Just home."

❧

The summer was already fully baked by the first of July, and by the middle of the month it was burning. Rumors came up from Staunton that a forest fire had killed several families and had driven a herd of deer right through the middle of town, all during Sunday services no less. Tom heard others suggest that the last part was just made up, but he couldn't tell who was right about what.

According to all the old-timers, storms were constantly 'a-brewing.' But somehow, it never rained. The sun disappeared for days at a time, and the clouds pressed the heat down until the whole Valley steamed like the inside of a kettle. But still, no refreshing raindrops fell. Bulbous thunderheads loudly threatened to split cracks in the earth, but the wind always succeeded in hurrying the braggarts along before they burst. Humid dusks against gray walls of clouds colored the world yellow like jaundice. Some folks said it was the glow of the wildfires down in Staunton.

Tom adored his summers to be sure, and devoted painstaking hours in the autumn, winter, and spring planning what he would do each and every blessed day offered by the months of July and August. *Sixty days of freedom*, give or take, according to the old almanac calendar in the twins' room. Sixty days might as well be a thousand days, or ten thousand, one long July that stretched past August into eternity. Summer really did feel like a lifetime, and a glorious one at that.

But for all his planning, most of this summer Tom didn't do much at all. He often woke late and lay in bed studying the trees moving outside his window. At some point he padded downstairs to wail for breakfast from Mae Jane. He protested against house chores, citing summer liberty as a constitutional right. The one chore he permitted himself to do was to fill up Tipper's food dish. Maybe it was how the dog looked at Tom with round, innocent eyes. Mae Jane often chided the whole business of spoiling a dog with meals, saying that when she was a child dogs scrounged for scraps. "That dog eats better than most real folk," she grumbled.

Tom said, "Well, he deserves it."

Tom and Tipper spent most mornings meandering around the estate, daydreaming and swatting lazy flies in the shade. He never tired of exploring the slave shacks, though by now he had thoroughly searched all of them for hidden treasure left behind by dirty Spaniards or noble English privateers. All Tipper was interested in doing was chasing after sticks, but Tom happily obliged him. If he threw as hard as he could, he could send a good-sized branch thirty yards.

If Bayard followed Tom, which happened often, they would play together. Usually Tom would award Bayard some subordinate role in their games: a Sir Gawain to his King Arthur, a nameless Sioux brave to his proud war chieftain. Tipper would run amok between the boys, leaping and barking excitedly.

Lately Tom's preferred game was to kill imaginary redcoats as the famous Colonel Thomas Spencer, his namesake. Many hours were spent locked in battle, clenching his fists together and swinging them through the air, as if he wielded the Colonel's flashing saber. When he wasn't cutting redcoats down by the bushel, he would dream up a flintlock pistol that never required a reload and never ran out of ammunition, and with this magical device he would take down hordes of Hessian mercenaries. Tom would frequently step into the role of one of his innumerable foes and collapse in a dramatic death dance before leaping up again to resume his performance as the Colonel.

Mae Jane's dinnertime call was bittersweet. Tom was always ravenous after killing three hundred men single handedly, but the lunch hour meant that another summer's day was already half over.

Today, however, there would be no games of war. Today, on a bright and dusty day with no clouds in sight (the last would-be storm had moved off west two days before), Tom determined he would finally leap the Promontory.

At some point during the Mayfair Valley's geological history, the receding glacier that had carved out the Cuts and the Branches had left behind a deep sinkhole with a swimming hole at its center. In the summertime, the 'quarry' was the favorite gathering place of Mayfair's children, or at least all of Mayfair's children who were not condemned to toil on family farms. The quarry had also become the site of a solemn rite of passage: 'leaping the Promontory.'

The Promontory was a jagged rock atop the quarry that stretched skyward. Every summer, a handful of children would summon the courage to take the leap. They jumped from the outcrop and dove into the water as boys and girls, but they surged back to the surface as full-blooded grownups shaking victorious fists. There was a quiet understanding among uninitiated boys that, after leaping, if one did not linger deep in the cold depths to drink 'eel water' before ascending to the surface, his voice would never drop and he would sound like a baby for the rest of his life.

Tom was terrified of such a horrible fate. He practiced for the Promontory leap by pushing off from the rocks and diving as deep as he could, gulping water all the while. It occurred to him to ask exactly how or why the swimming hole's apparently transformational abilities had no effect on a boy's larynx unless he plunged into the water from sixty feet up. But then again, Tom didn't dare question what every child of Mayfair accepted as sacred teachings from on high (meaning older brothers and sisters). There were, of course, many unconfirmed tales of children who, whether out of fear or an unfortunate slip, leaped too close to the quarry walls and smashed themselves to pieces against the rocks. Others plunged so far into the depths that they were presumed drowned and never seen again. No one had ever *seen* anyone they knew meet such grisly ends, but the children of Mayfair were dead certain that such horribly interesting events had occurred in the past and would surely happen again.

Tom had attempted to leap the Promontory the previous summer, knowing that by the time he turned thirteen he might attract accusations of being a coward or a nancy. Tom bragged to all who would listen that "Today is the day! Today is the day. And I'll dive it too." But once Tom reached the edge of the rock and sensed the immensity of the fall, all courage abandoned him and he fled back down the quarry trail to the water's edge. No one laughed in his face, but their stifling smirks were somehow worse. Tom had stayed away from the quarry for several weeks until he determined he had the courage to go back. Nobody mentioned anything of the event, but Tom was still compelled to keep to the shallow side of the swimming hole, where a shelf of shale allowed one to swim and run in waist-deep water. In many ways the shallows were actually *better* than the deep section, but of course that was irrelevant.

In any case, Tom continued to swim with the 'babies' in the shallows while the older youths occupied the deeper waters far across the lake. No uninitiated boys and girls were permitted to swim the deeper waters until they'd made the leap.

But this summer, today, *really*, was the day. And he wasn't going to tell anybody about it.

As he approached the quarry, Tom heard the other children laughing and screaming before they came upon the full spectacle of the place. It sounded like a real crowd.

Seeing the quarry emerge through a copse of trees at the top of a high hill was always a fine moment that stirred joy and some kind of purpose in him. The quarry was not large but it was deep, an ancient wound in the earth caused by some great catastrophe: an earthquake or lightning bolt or meteorite or, as Tom believed, a fantastic wrestling match between God and Lucifer. And there at the top, protruding like the finger of a stone titan, was the Promontory.

Tom felt Bayard press up against him. Looking at Bayard, Tom saw that his brother was busy staring across the quarry. Presently Bayard's eyes brightened and he pointed across the way. He delivered, in gestures and whispered grunts, his assessment of the situation.

"Do you see someone?" Tom asked. He followed Bayard's hand toward a group of boys Tom's age swimming near the rocks at the far edge of the quarry. As soon as he found the boys, his eyes dimmed.

Billy Clements was down there.

Tom felt the sudden sickening urge to turn around and go home. Turning to Bayard, he slapped the boy's hand down. "Quit pointing like that."

Sour-faced and hurt, Bayard massaged his hand and stared down at the rocks at his feet. Tom surveyed the rest of the quarry. Besides Billy and the boys, there was a group of 'babies' — young children, anywhere from six to twelve years old, who hadn't jumped the Promontory — splashing in the shallows. Between these two groups was a gaggle of girls tucked along the rocks where the shallows met the cooler, deeper waters of the far end. The girls performed handstands and various underwater acrobatics, undoubtedly aware that by flashing their ankles from under their swimsuits they were drawing the overt attention of the boys across the water.

Fear clenched at Tom's heart. He and Bayard stood isolated and unwanted like outcasts. The girls' group was utterly unapproachable. He outright refused to join the babies lest this invite jeers from across the quarry. And speaking of jeers, the third group (Billy's gang, formerly a motley assembly of Tom's own school-friends) would coldly refuse and hurl insults at Tom the moment he tried to join them.

Nearby, Tom heard a low whine. Turning, he saw Tipper down on all fours with his rump in the air, tail swishing with frenetic energy. Tipper's snout had invaded the round entrance of a small animal's burrow.

"*Quiet*, Tip."

Unable to contain himself, Tipper leapt back from the burrow and howled.

Billy Clements and the boys down below looked up and spotted Tom, exposed and isolated atop the quarry. Indeed, *everyone* was looking up at Tom. His instinct was to flee, but he stayed where he was. Bayard hadn't moved either, but certainly he felt the piercing power of all those staring eyes.

Tom groaned and glared at Tipper. "Damn dog..."

Tipper looked back at him happily, tongue out.

The boys gathered together to point up at them and whisper before they broke off into gales of shrieking laughter. One of them hollered some insult that bounced among the rocks, but Tom couldn't make out what had been said.

And really, he didn't care. Well, he *did* care, and painfully so — that was just the problem. But he'd be damned if he was going to stand around and act the dummy for the sport of all those lickfingers down there. To hell with them, and to hell with Billy Clements. Billy was swimming in the deep waters even though he'd never jumped the Promontory. Just what gave that coward the gumption to make fun of anybody?

"Come on, Bayard," Tom said, taking his brother's hand. "Let's get you in the water."

They snaked their way down the path toward the shallows where the babies played. Tom would get Bayard situated, and then he'd deal with stupid Billy goddamn Clements and his stupid goddamn friends. He'd swim over there to the deep waters, and to hell with the rule that only jumpers could swim across. And then once he was across, he'd climb up on the jagged rocks there and demand an explanation of Billy himself. He'd spill beans about Billy's quirks and shortcomings, and when Billy's new lickfinger friends turned on him and laughed at him, Tom would laugh right along with them.

Tom watched Bayard jump in the water. He could swim just fine. Better than all the babies, anyway. But with his condition, it was assumed that Bayard would never leap the Promontory. Even when he came of age, he'd have to keep swimming in this same shallow section of the hole. It didn't matter that a person's hearing made no difference when it came time to jump.

Jump.

Tom looked up at the Promontory.

The noonday sun had swung west enough that much of the rocks below the Promontory were shaded and the fingerlike rock itself speared the blue sky in black silhouette.

With a quiet sigh, Tom stood up. Bayard made to follow, but Tom warned him away with a wave. "Stay here," he said gruffly. "Don't follow."

With Bayard watching, Tom trudged back up the rocky path toward the grassy lip of the quarry. He passed Tipper, who was still sniffing around. At a slow saunter

Tom ascended the brush-covered path toward the naked rock of the Promontory.

He told himself not to pause to take the measure of the jump, to just start running and spring forward. He kicked his feet, but the ground underfoot disappeared much too quickly. The world seemed to shift suddenly on its axis and Tom's stomach pitched. He skidded and nearly toppled over the side, but he managed to hurl himself back where he collapsed on the hard rock with a groan. He lay on his back catching his breath. Up from below came that vile, mocking, cut-to-the-bone laughter that only children can produce.

Dammit. God*dammit*. Why? Why couldn't he do it?

Red-faced and irritable, Tom sauntered back down the path to the water's edge. He did his best to ignore the jeers from the others, especially those from the deep side of the pool. Even Billy had joined in the ribbing.

Tom stepped into the water and swam through the shallows, letting his hand drift along the velvety sand at the bottom. Opening his eyes, he peered into the gaping maw of darkness where the shelf plunged down into an apparently bottomless abyss. Down there was where the bodies of all the 'unfortunate children' lay, their skulls having long become hiding places for eels. Shivering, Tom kicked back toward the surface.

As Tom came up for air, he decided it was time to leave. To hell with the goddamn quarry. To hell with everybody. Tom fought the urge to cry by swallowing some cool quarry water. As he reached the rocks again, he looked around for Bayard. It was time to go.

"Bayard? Come on, Bayard. We're leaving."

There was no sign of his brother. Tom looked all around.

"Bay?"

His brother had disappeared. He'd been right there in the shallows just a moment ago, but now…nowhere.

"*Hey*!" a girl cried.

Most heads, including Tom's, swiveled to look upon the girl herself. But she was pointing up toward the Promontory, and just as most heads turned to look upon it they saw a blurry shape drop from its heights and plunge into the waters below.

Tom blinked. Turning his head, he scanned the group of babies playing in the shallows. Still, Bayard was nowhere to be seen.

"Hey!" the same girl cried again. "He jumped!" Suddenly, she burst out laughing at the absurdity of her announcement.

With a sudden knot of fear twisting in his chest, Tom turned back and swam for the frothing white where the shape — Bayard! — had hit the water.

"Bayard. *Bayard?*"

The mist of the splash cleared and the surface stilled again, and there was no sign of Bayard.

The word 'Bayard' was on Tom's lips but he didn't ask again. Instead he huffed a deep breath, plunged his arms down and kicked his feet up, and swam down into the darkness.

As he swam down, Tom wished he had taken a deeper breath. He searched the murky depths but could see nothing except for specks of algae floating up from below. Tom's lungs urged him to surface, but still he swam down. He swept his arms and legs about, groping in the dark and hoping he might stumble upon Bayard somewhere in the abyss. Finally, with his lungs bursting, Tom kicked his feet and surged upward. Panic took over his every thought. What if he couldn't find Bayard after another dive? What if Bayard had plunged so deep that he'd somehow gotten himself trapped by a rock? What if his brother was lost to the quarry depths forever, destined to become nothing more than a boogeyman legend for young children to fear and older children to snicker about? What if—?

Tom's head exploded with pain. Someone's foot kicked down from above and cracked him in the nose. Instantly a gush of cold water filled his open mouth. Dazed, his lungs screaming, Tom swept his arms forward but could not understand why he was not surfacing. Suddenly he realized he'd somehow turned himself around, and he was swimming *back down*.

No sooner did Tom turn back for the surface did he begin to lose consciousness. He felt himself fading, his senses slowly blackening. But just as he felt himself slipping beyond a point of no return, he burst out of the depths into the open air.

Tom flailed about, spluttering and hacking up quarry water. Blood ran from his nose where he'd been struck. All Tom could think about was catching his breath in order to dive down again. But just now he felt someone splashing beside him, and turning his head he looked into the grinning face of a victorious Bayard.

Bayard shook a tiny fist in a show of triumph. He'd jumped the Promontory!

All around came applause. *Clapping*! Well, a smattering of it anyway. A number of children wore shocked expressions. Some of the younger children, who had screamed all during Tom's frantic search, now wore baffled smiles.

But Tom was in no mood to celebrate. Instead he swept a tidal wave in Bayard's direction and cursed him loudly. "You broke my nose!" he shouted. "You damn stupid idiot, you broke my nose!"

Tom heard the other children laughing. Billy Clements and the other boys laughed loudest of all. Tom clamped his mouth shut and his face went red. Not only had Bayard stolen his moment of glory, but now Tom looked like a damn fool to boot. Turning angrily away from Bayard, he pulled toward the rocky shore.

Dripping, Tom clambered up the quarry's rocky path. He ignored the laughing voices and mocking stares, stopping once to bark a savage rebuke at a boy several years his junior who dared insult him. He caught sight of Billy across the quarry; Billy was not laughing like the others, but looking at Tom with a pale, shaken expression. Tom turned away and continued up the slope.

Once atop the quarry and out of sight of all below, Tom crouched down and allowed himself a quick and urgent cry. Tipper hurried forward and began to lick the water off Tom's skin, and so Tom grabbed Tipper and pushed his face against the dog's side and wept into his golden fur.

Footsteps drew near, and so Tom pulled away from Tipper and hastily wiped his eyes.

Bayard appeared on the path, looking small and sheepish. A flare of fury burned in Tom's chest, but somehow he had the presence of mind to let it go. Just a few moments ago he'd searched frantically for Bayard, fearing for his life, and only to now resent him for a simple mistake? With a quiet sigh, Tom reached out for his brother. Bayard flinched, but then Tom put his arm around his shoulder and the boy relaxed. Bayard wrapped his arms around Tom and hugged him tightly.

"It's all right," Tom said. He fought against the lump forming in his throat. "It's all right. Just watch where you're flailing next time." Looking into Bayard's eyes, Tom managed a smile. "You did it, Bayard. You did it! You made the leap." He thought to add *I'm proud of you,* but for whatever reason he didn't. Why get mushy about it?

Bayard beamed all the same. After a moment, he gave Tom a questioning look.

"You're about right," Tom replied. "That's enough swimming for one day. Let's get on home."

Arm in arm, the boys started back for the North Branch.

❧

The last days of August arrived, and with them came a creeping realization. Though Tom tried to deny it, there was little refuting the simple observation that the long days of summer were not so long anymore. The long July was slipping away and the forgotten promise of winter wind was no longer a far-off fantasy.

And finally, it seemed the Mayfair Valley would get a good rain.

The day began like any other, with birds chirping and insects droning. Though it was still early morning, the sticky heat was oppressive. The Valley had sat under a stifling cloud of humidity for nearly two weeks now, and though there was moisture in the air the grass continued to brown and the leaves on the trees continued to wilt.

As he lay in bed in a blast of sunshine, Tom pondered what to do with his day. Presently the sunshine dimmed and faded. Tom went to the window and gazed up to where a cloud had enshrouded the sun like a heavenly curtain. Respite from the sun's blazing heat was usually welcome, but it wasn't the sun that seemed to bother anyone. It was the sticky humidity that seemed to set people on edge, and the Roscoes were no exception.

Mae Jane was in a nagging mood that day. She picked at Tom all during breakfast, urging him to do something 'worthwhile' with his time. Bayard was spared all of Mae Jane's carping, an immunity which Tom considered supremely unfair.

"Hmm?" Mae Jane said to Tom. "You might help with the horses today."

"Naw," Tom replied. "I might go hunting pheasants."

The old mammy shook her head. "I don't want you out huntin by youself, nosir."

Tom shrugged. "I'll get Jem to take me."

"Nuh-uh," the old mammy said, and she turned back toward the kitchens. "With all them ne'er-do-wells hangin round the front gate? You liable to get hurt. Besides, you too young, Thomas. Much too young."

Tom's hopes for the day clouded. The more he thought about it, the less hopeful he was that Jem would want to take him hunting. Since the collapse at the North Branch Mine, Jem had become so much like Mother. He left his room only rarely, and whenever Tom did see his brother Jem was usually stinking drunk.

Tom didn't know what exactly inspired him to go into the library. Maybe it was the idea that he *wasn't* too young. He was *thirteen* after all, and wise beyond his years. Wiser than most folks, anyway. Somehow he knew that his destiny was attached to the Colonel's long rifle that hung over the fireplace. Making sure no one was watching him, he pulled a chair over and climbed up and lifted the rifle from its perch, careful not to knock it against the wall.

No hunter was complete without a hound, and so before leaving home Tom found Tipper and gave him a belly-rub. The dog licked Tom's hand. With the long rifle slung awkwardly over his shoulder, Tom crept out one of the side doors to the veranda. Tipper followed eagerly, excited as always to get outside.

With Tom leading, boy and dog crashed off through the thickets, making a point to avoid the main road (which was still occupied by a company of angry toughs who blamed Jem for the mine explosion), and made their way up the North Branch.

Tom traced the same path he and Jem often followed, but an hour into the trek he realized he didn't know the mountain as well as he thought he did. Suddenly he remembered the steel traps that hunters set all through the area, and so Tom kept a close eye on the ground at his feet.

"Stick close to me, Tip. That's it, boy. Stick close to me."

The air in the forest was thick with mosquitos and bad omens. Though just past noon, the world was dark: the sun was veiled by heavy clouds that had rolled in from the south. Tom shivered all over, not from cold but from the tickling sensation of sweat dripping down his body and soaking his clothes to his skin. Sometimes what he thought was the slick tingle of sweat became a sudden sharp pain, and then Tom would slap at the spot with his hand and see another squashed mosquito there. The woods on the east slope of the North Branch seemed to hum and vibrate, as if Tom were drawing ever closer to the living pulse of the forest's dark, ancient heart.

As Tom crept through the underbrush, he heard a low growl nearby.

"Easy, Tip," Tom whispered. "Easy, boy. Not just yet."

Tom and Tipper had been out for a good three hours by now, although Tom had no way to tell the time. All Tom knew was that they were somewhere on the east slope, well beyond shouting distance of any farms or homesteads. Back over his shoulder, Tom could just barely make out the craggy summit of the North Branch. Ahead lay the wild expanse of the Shenandoah — that is, that's what Tom knew *should* be out there; all he could see at present was a gnarled wall of trees and thickets.

And somewhere up ahead, Tom could hear a gang of pheasants clucking about.

Tom inched slowly forward. He brought the long rifle up into a ready position. He'd never fired the weapon before, but he had watched Jem closely. Jem always aimed down, and he braced the butt against his shoulder a certain way to guard against a savage recoil. Tom knew he might only have one shot. He needed to somehow catch the pheasants unaware, to sneak up close, to give himself the time he needed to properly—

"No, Tip."

Tipper's hackles were up, his jaws open. Growling, he saw something through the underbrush: something that triggered his deepest instincts and made him deaf to Tom's appeals.

"*No*, Tip — *don't*."

Suddenly Tipper shot forward, barking and baying like a war hound. He crashed through the undergrowth and heard screeching and squawking on the other side. Tom burst forward and found himself in a clearing, and he was just in time to catch sight of some feathered bodies scurrying into the undergrowth. They disappeared underneath dense brambles and were gone from sight. Tom instinctively lifted the rifle to shoot, but it was pointless. Tipper rushed about the clearing, trying to find a way around the brambles. He lunged at one area but retreated with a yelp after pricking himself with thorns.

As Tom considered the implications of Tipper's attack — another hour or more to track the pheasants down again, and all without the promise of success — the stuffy heat and cloud of insects overwhelmed him. Whirling about with a vicious redness in his eyes, Tom rushed forward with his hand out. He lunged at Tipper and cuffed the dog upside the head, and then he cuffed him again for good measure.

"Stupid mutt. Stupid *fucking* mutt—"

He thought hitting Tipper would make him feel better, but it only enraged him more. Suddenly, Tipper's eyes rolled back and he turned his yellow jaws upon his boy.

Tom reeled and screamed. Blood flowed from puncture wounds in his hand. "Laws — you *bit* me!"

Tipper's eyes bulged with fear and shame. With his tail tucked between his legs, Tipper hurried to the far side of the clearing.

Tom inspected his hand and whimpered at the pulsing pain. When he looked up at Tipper again, his eyes narrowed. He pointed at the dog and then at the ground beside him.

"*Here.* Now."

Tipper knew exactly what kind of mood his boy was in, and so he refused outright. With wide, puppy-like eyes, Tipper sat on his haunches and would not budge.

This simple but complete refusal sent Tom off the edge of rationality. Boiling with rage, he advanced on Tipper with hate in his eyes. He'd teach that goddamn dog to listen to him. Wasn't he Tipper's *master*? Wasn't the dog supposed to obey his owner?

"Fucking mutt — *come here*!"

Tipper shot off through the undergrowth, but Tom got there in time to give the dog a solid kick in the rear. Tipper staggered and then went yelping off, and Tom was left alone with his rage. He screamed aloud for all the world to hear, and he kept screaming until his voice cracked and finally gave out. He hated it all: the fucking birds, the bugs, Jem, Billy Clements, Mayfair, the stupid fucking dog, *all of it*.

Well, now here was another irritation: the act of *finding* his stupid fucking dog somewhere out in the woods and convincing him to come home. That alone might take hours, and Tom couldn't be sure he wouldn't try to beat the dog's head into the dirt as soon as he got his hands on him. The dog had to learn *manners*. The dog had to learn how to obey—

What was that? A sudden yelp, weak, far off somewhere. Maybe Tipper had found a bird in the underbrush and—

That sound…Whining…

Tipper?

Holding the long rifle close, Tom followed the dog's path through the foliage. "Tip?" he called. "Tip, you out there? Tip, I'm sorry. I'm sorry, boy. Tipper! Here, Tipper!"

He searched for several moments without finding anything. He swatted at the swirling cloud of gnats and mosquitos, which had somehow grown larger. The sun faded from view, and suddenly the forest floor was very dark. It was as if Tom had stepped into some deep swath of the Amazon. He felt eyes on him, as if creeping things were watching. Watching and waiting.

"Tipper? Here, Tipper!"

And finally, pushing past a thick stand of trees, Tom saw him.

The words "God, no…" formed on Tom's lips, but no breath ushered forth. Instead he staggered back, blinking, trying to comprehend the sight before him in its full detail.

Tipper lay on his side. At first Tom's heart clenched and he thought Tipper might be dead, killed by some woodland beast who had run off just before Tom arrived. But as he approached, he saw that it wasn't an animal that had taken Tipper down, but a beast of a different kind.

One of Tipper's forelegs was caught in the jaws of a steel-trap.

Tipper lay there, whining a little, but otherwise very still and quiet. His whole body quivered, and at intervals his big head reached forward and he licked at the blood that poured from his wounds. His hind legs twitched and flung themselves at the cloud of insects that was swarming around him, now settling closer to the ground.

Tom knelt down at Tipper's side. The dog gave a start, as if he still feared his boy's repercussions. But instead Tom only touched the dog's head, caressed him softly as if he was a newborn puppy.

There was so much blood, and more seeping out of Tipper's wound. More blood than Tom had ever seen before.

"But it's not so bad," Tom said aloud, unaware that he was crying for all the sweat that stung his eyes. "It's not so bad, Tip." He set the long rifle down and slid his hands around the closed jaws of the trap. "Here, let me help you. Let me help you, Tip."

Tipper howled as Tom tried to pry the jaws open. Tom's fingers slipped; he tried again. He pried the jaws open only a half-inch before they slammed shut again, this time cutting deeper into Tipper's flesh and bone. More blood flowed. What had been a trickle a few minutes ago now became a steady stream. If Tom didn't get Tipper free soon, if he didn't get that wound bandaged up soon…

"I'm sorry, boy. I'm sorry…"

Tipper's tongue lolled and his head fell heavily down. The dog was sick with pain and began to froth at the mouth. His eyes rolled about as if he was counting the flies that buzzed overhead. Joining the cloud of gnats and mosquitos was an army of gray-backed blowflies, the ones that laid their eggs on dying animals so that their larvae might feast upon flesh that would soon be dead and rotting and—

"*NO!*" Tom screamed. He directed his fury up at the cloud, at the swirling personification of unthinking hunger. He swatted, thinking and hoping he might kill hundreds — thousands — of the goddamned things. But the cloud swelled only larger.

"Tell me what to do, Tip. Tell me what to do…"

He put his hands on the jaws again. He strained and cried out but his hands were slick with sweat and the jaws would not budge. Tipper growled and bit at Tom's hand before he lay down again, exhausted, his eyes rolling in their sockets.

Again Tom put his hands on Tipper's head. He sobbed a thousand apologies to his puppy, his grand old puppy. Whining, Tipper weakly licked Tom's fingers as if apologizing for biting him. Gnats dove for Tipper's eyes and he blinked to keep them away, all in vain. When Tom looked down he was shocked by the size of the blood pool that surrounded them.

Maybe he could run for help. But was there enough time to get across the Branch and down in the Valley, and come all the way back? He couldn't leave Tipper alone — not like this.

Desperate, Tom looked all around him. Then he saw the long rifle in the grass.

Tipper whined. The old dog was fading, but he was still in immense pain.

Tom closed his eyes and shut them tight. He leaned down and kissed Tipper's head.

"I love you, Tip," Tom croaked. He was barely able to speak. "I'm sorry, Tip. I'm so sorry. I never meant to…I know I was never…I love you so much, Tip, and I…"

From somewhere, maybe within himself or maybe calling out from the trees, Tom heard Jem's voice:

One day you'll need to pull the trigger. And when that moment is at hand, you'll only get one shot. You will need to do what needs doing, and you can't allow yourself another thought about it.

Tom kissed Tipper. He held his lips against his old pup's golden fur, felt for the briefest of moments his heartbeat and the sound of his labored breathing. Withdrawing from this last kiss, Tom snatched up the long rifle and staggered to his feet. When he looked down at Tipper, he saw Tipper looking up at him with calm, sleepy eyes, and how the dog's black lips were curled up, almost as if he was smiling at his boy.

"I love you, Tip," Tom whispered. Then he pushed the barrel against the dog's head and cocked the hammer, shut his eyes tight, and pulled the trigger.

Nothing happened. Just the dull *click* of the action. And then Tom realized. He hadn't loaded the long rifle with a lead ball, nor had he added any gunpowder.

Tipper wheezed once and then Tom heard from him no more. Looking down, Tom saw that his dog had become very still. Flies landed on unblinking eyes.

Tom's knees buckled. He wanted to drop down and cradle Tipper's head in his lap forever. He wanted to stroke the dog all over, to feel the lingering warmth of the furry body before it cooled. He wanted to close those adoring eyes from those damn flies and pick Tipper up and carry him back to Clarendon.

But Tom did none of these things. He regained his balance just before he toppled. Gripping the long rifle in his hands, he bit down hard on his tongue to stave off a fresh onslaught of tears. Unable to look at Tipper again, he turned and fled from the clearing as fast as he could.

After Tom had gone and the air around the dog's body became still again, the cloud of flies descended once more.

Chapter 27

TATTIE

Alone in her bedroom, Sarah Roscoe — *Cutler,* she still had to remind herself — brushed her long black hair before the vanity. This vanity, much larger than any she had ever known at Clarendon, had been specially ordered for her by Henry. It had more drawers than she could possibly fill, and so Henry lavished her with perfumes, powders, creams, as if Henry had himself consulted an issue of Godey's Fashion Magazine and ordered every last item from the catalogue.

The mirror that reflected her image was three sizes larger than the modest one in her childhood bedroom back home. For many months Sarah had marveled at all these wonderful luxuries. Lately, however, she wondered whether the mirror was rather *too* big. Its wide, angular reflection of the room showed towering ceilings and looming windows, with her tiny, insignificant figure compressed by the surrounding grandeur.

Life at Arcadia had a whole new rhythm from Clarendon. The place hummed with activity. The energy of *work* pulsed and vibrated in every room and across every acre. The place was filled with light, with not a mote of dust to be seen anywhere. Out in the fields, Sarah marveled at the spirit of cooperation and competition among work teams. It was as if a city were being built right before her eyes, with everyone knowing their duty and following it out with utmost passion, skill, and care.

Marriage had provided its own novel experiences. On their wedding night, Henry had been tender and reassuring, and so attentive to Sarah that she felt as the beautiful maiden Psyche must have during her first night with Eros, the god of love. There was a sharp pain when he entered her, and she felt pain when he pulled out later. She caught a blurry glimpse of his dripping member — for a split second she heard laughing Mary Beth Merrick's voice, a voice from another lifetime, talking about stud horses — and then Henry took her in his arms and they both drifted off into a contented slumber.

Those first few days and nights were long and thrilling. Making love was easy, the most blissful experience she'd ever known. Henry called her *duchess,* his pet name for her. *The Duchess of Arcadia.* They would talk for hours about their family, about the children they would soon have together. Henry admitted he was hoping for a son.

"A strong boy," he said. "Someone I can take hunting with me, take nigger-breaking with me." He laughed, and she knew she'd never seen a brighter smile on anyone. "A boy born with a cat o' nine tails in his little fist! A young duke to inherit our little domain. A son who will take over someday, when he is ready."

Sarah knew it was expected in Valley society for a newlywed couple to become pregnant within the first three months of marriage, and ideally much sooner. It did not necessarily matter if the child survived to adulthood, so long as one was born within the first marriage year as a symbol of the couple's virility. But as three months stretched to almost six (it was by now the middle of September), and still with no sign of a little one on the way, Sarah began to feel as though Henry blamed her for the delay. He never said as much, but she knew. Somehow, she knew.

As time stretched on, Henry's attitude toward her began to change. She felt a hesitation in him. As the seasons changed, his lovemaking lost its earnestness. He finished faster, long before she was ready, and afterward instead of talking sweetly of silly things together they would lay apart in silence. She would watch him, guessing, as he stared out the window with a troubling blankness in his eyes.

At parties, Henry's eyes began to roam more than ever before. Of course, a man's gaze was always given to wandering, but lately Sarah had seen Henry *linger* on more than one woman, and on more than one occasion. She sat silently while he whispered into the ear of a laughing Pippa Claiborne, and all while Pippa's beau Sam Hanley sat beside them with a wan smile on his face. Sarah could say nothing about this to Henry, of course. It was a man's right to speak with whomever he wished, whenever he wished. A wife did not have such a privilege in Valley society, and that was just the way it was.

Many nights, Henry did not come to bed at all. He had his own bedroom down the hall which he slept in when field work kept him up late, or if he simply wanted time to himself. During those nights when she was alone, Sarah would lay awake and try to reason just how and why Henry had lost interest in her. God knew she hadn't lost interest in him, but what exactly was she supposed to do? She could always feel when his eyes fell on her not in a loving way, but with a look of austere judgment. It was as if he was inspecting her for imperfections, and there were always imperfections to be found.

There came a soft knocking at the door, and then it opened. Sarah watched a dark face appear in a sliver of yellow light.

"Ma'am? It's candle-lighting now. And I just heard the bell for sup. Would you be needin help with you gown?"

Through the mirror, Sarah looked toward the girl standing at the door against a sliver of darkness.

"Thank you, Tattie. You may enter. Candles first."

Tattie came inside the room and went about lighting candles, including the covered lamp that Sarah used for reading. Still through the mirror's reflection, Sarah watched her closely.

"Come here a moment, Tattie."

"Yes, ma'am."

Tattie did as she was bid. Her head was down and her shoulders were slumped forward, her hands folded together.

Sarah stood up and squared up with the girl. Tattie was pretty — very pretty, for being a darkie, at least. She was small and slender with close-cropped hair held back with a blue kerchief of the kind Mae Jane liked to wear. And she had the most tremendous eyes. Sarah had a penchant for people's eyes, and Tattie's were among the most striking she'd ever seen. They were large, round, deep and dark. Sarah imagined that, with a little blush and a fine costume, Tattie would look as beautiful as any Valley debutante — perhaps even more so. Sarah felt a twinge of jealousy that set a scowl on her face.

"You have terrible posture," Sarah said, and she placed her hands on each of Tattie's shoulders and pushed them back to their proper place. "*There*. You should feel a slight strain in your back. It will pass after a few days of practice. But you must remember. One must always be in a state of self-correction."

"Yes, ma'am."

Sarah touched Tattie's chin and gently raised it up, and all the while she examined the slave girl with a calculating eye, as if she'd been studying negroes for years.

"Pretend you have a string on the top of your head," she said, plucking said imaginary string out of the air and pulling it taut. "Imagine that a puppeteer is pulling on it like this. That should help you stand straight."

Tattie looked at her cautiously. "A puppeteer, ma'am?"

Sarah was taken aback. "What, you've never seen a marionette show?"

Tattie shook her head. "No, ma'am. I'm sorry, ma'am."

"I'm sorry *for* you," Sarah replied with a laugh.

Tattie smiled back, and Sarah liked it.

"You know," Sarah said, softening a little. "You remind me of someone. Someone I love and admire very much."

Tattie shifted uneasily on her feet. Probably no white person had ever said much to the girl that wasn't in the manner of an order.

"Yes, ma'am. Thank you, ma'am."

Sarah smiled. "Do you want to know who it is?"

Tattie smiled back, but there was urgent activity in her eyes, as if she was trying to figure out whether Sarah was tricking her, or setting up some cruel joke. "Only if you fancy tellin me, ma'am. You don't got to if you don't—"

"I don't *have* to."

"Ma'am? Erm, *yes*, ma'am."

"Your diction."

"Ma'am?"

"Your *diction*. Girl, you must clean your ears. I was only pointing out your poor *diction*."

"Ah. Yes, ma'am. Thank you, ma'am. It's just I got bad — I mean, I *have* bad dic… dic…I have a bad one, ma'am."

"How about lessons?" Sarah said. "I will teach you. I was going to be a teacher before I was married, you know. I still might be one, if Mr. Cutler permits."

Tattie looked supremely confused. "Teach me, ma'am? About what?"

"About how to be proper in your speech," Sarah said, as if it were that obvious. "Your diction must be thoroughly examined, to start with."

Tattie smiled, but it was strained. "I see. That sounds very lovely, ma'am. But please, ma'am, you don't gotta waste none of you time on a dumb nigger like me. Uncle Sol says I ain't worth any kind of trouble and he's right most of the time."

Sarah shook her head. "Don't be silly. You're too hard on yourself. It will be *fun*. A chance for two girls to talk. You know, talk?"

Tattie gave another weak smile. "Anything you say, ma'am."

Sarah nodded. There, that was that. Now, to give marching orders. She pointed at the clutter atop the vanity.

"After you help me dress," she said, "I'd like you to clean this up. And the rest of the bedroom, for that matter." She resisted the instinct to add *please* to her request. Here at Arcadia, slaves followed orders, not requests. After all, this wasn't Clarendon.

Tattie looked doubtful. "I'll do that, ma'am. Just as soon as I finish my candle-lighting in the other rooms—"

"You'll do what I tell you," Sarah said, her voice sharpening. "And you'll do it without protest. First, help me dress."

"Yes, ma'am. Right away, ma'am."

See? Pig-headed, the lot of them, just as Henry always told her. She reminded herself to be more forceful with future orders, especially with Tattie. The girl's head seemed thicker than most. Say *please* and Sarah knew she risked losing the slaves' humble deference in all things.

Tattie helped Sarah climb into her dinner gown. While Tattie secured the basque, her nimble hands tying the many strings into knots with expert precision, Sarah felt a quiet satisfaction at the power she held over someone else. It was like Sarah was a princess from those old fairy tales, where her every wish was another's command.

But despite herself, a feeling of shame seeped into Sarah's thoughts. She had never spoken to Mae Jane like she had just now spoken to Tattie, and it was Mae Jane who she thought of when she looked at Tattie. It was important to note, however, that Mae Jane was a free negro and this Tattie was nothing more but a darkie servant. There *was* a difference. Staring longer, Sarah studied the girl's simple housemaid's dress, and she noted with displeasure how it accentuated the curves of her little body. Sarah felt overdressed but outclassed by comparison.

Once again, jealousy gripped Sarah's heart. She wondered whether Henry's wandering eye sometimes lingered on the colored girls in the Cutler family employ. Surely that was a ridiculous notion, for Sarah knew that Henry considered negroes to be no different than barn animals. For Henry to stare at Pippa Claiborne's bosom was one thing; the idea of any self-respecting white person being attracted to a negro was positively absurd.

But what about Ben Freeman?

No — enough of that. Deciding Tattie's job was finished, Sarah slapped the girl's hands away.

"Enough," she said. "Now to the candle-lighting and cleaning. And when you're done in here, you may go to bed. Take the back stairs when you go down. You look slovenly today, Tattie, and I don't want anyone in the house seeing you in such a state. Mind you fix yourself finer for tomorrow, hm?"

Tattie bowed dutifully. "Yes, ma'am. Thank you, ma'am. I appreciate you feedback, ma'am."

❧

Later, dressed in one of her finest gowns, Sarah passed the old grandfather clock on the top landing of the stairs and descended to the main floor. The setting sun still blasted its light through huge, church-like windows.

Arcadia was the most luxurious mansion in the Mayfair Valley. Its decor was tasteful compared to the gaudiness of Wyolah Hall, and though Clarendon was larger Arcadia had none of that old plantation's rough-hewn shabbiness. Arcadia was the most magnificent palace of them all, constructed entirely of brick and marble.

The big-house's grand halls had hosted a storied roster of governors, presidents, and foreign dignitaries. Walking from room to room was like touring a modern American castle of great, looming ceilings and huge windows that opened wide to the beauty of the Valley. The parlors were filled with the finest European sofa sets, ottomans in every color, paintings of stately gentlemen and regal ladies upon the molded walls, and every hallway was lengthened by grand mirrors that reflected perfection from every angle. And it was *bright*. Where Clarendon had been a gloomy, dilapidated manor lost within a sea of gnarled trees, Arcadia was a hilltop mansion, ever basking in the full shine of daylight and moonlight.

Most of the Cutler family were by now gathered in the vast dining room. As Sarah entered, she saw that Henry's chair was empty. Judge Cutler, who had just returned from Washington, stood at attention as Sarah entered the dining room.

"Sarah, my beautiful Virginia rose," the Judge said. Her father-in-law's voice was warm and raspy like hot cider. He extended a hand to an open chair. Sarah joined the family at the table and sat down. Uncle Solomon pushed the chair in for her and stepped back while other servants presented Sarah's meal, which had been kept under cover until her arrival.

The Judge said, "We were just about to say grace, honey."

The Cutlers joined hands and bowed their heads. The boy-reverend Lucas began:

"Oh Lord, we thank thee for this bountiful harvest laid out before us. We thank thee for the good, docile, and compliant hands that prepared it. And we thank thee—"

Somewhere down the hall, a door flew open with a great crash.

"*We're late!*" Henry cried from the parlor.

Moments later he breezed into the dining room in hunting clothes.

"I've brought Glanton with me. He helped me skin our supper. I figured he was worthy of eating some of it."

Sarah waited for Henry to smile at her and say hello, and maybe to approach and kiss her on the cheek. But Henry only crossed the table and plopped down in his chair on the other side.

Just then, a horrid smell invaded Sarah's nostrils. Horace Glanton, the plantation foreman, stomped inside with manure-caked boots.

"Horace!" Mrs. Cutler groaned. "You're tramping mud and sick through the house."

Judge Cutler snapped his fingers at Solomon.

Solomon nodded; he already had a team of maids and footmen at work.

Glanton smiled as he watched three servants get down on their hands and knees to fuss over the cleanliness of his boots. "You missed a spot there," Glanton said. "And hurry up. We're damn near starved."

Horace Glanton was an ill fit for Arcadia's regal dining room. He wore clothes stained with sweat and dirt, his shirt collar was wilted irrevocably out of shape, his patchy beard barely covered a splotch of red acne scars, and his teeth were rotting from their roots. His entire demeanor, meanwhile, was that of what the servants whisperingly called 'white trash.' Apparently no one in Horace Glanton's life had bothered to tell him that the tablecloth was not designed for wiping dirty hands clean. Sarah did her best to ignore him, never understanding why Henry called the man his best friend.

Henry poured himself a tall glass of wine. "You should have seen it. Fifty yards away she was, and picking her away across a fallen log spanning the Sleepy. I shot her and she fell — *splash!* — right into the water. Even then she put up a fight, trying to kick at us, so we held her down and drowned her in the river."

Sarah put a hand to her mouth. "That's horrible..."

"That's my boy," the Judge said, beaming.

"I wish you'd returned earlier," Mrs. Cutler groaned. "Supper is already prepared and piping hot to boot!"

Henry downed the whole of his wine as if it were a mere drop in the glass. "Patience, Mother. Patience! We dropped our quarry off to the kitchens before we stabled. Sol! Sol, get me something stronger than this watery swill. I need a man's drink, goddammit."

"Please, Henry," Sarah said. "Please don't swear at the—"

"I'll have a drink too, Sol," the Judge said, smiling.

As the Cutlers resolved to fill their glasses, Sarah sat alone with her thoughts.

"Lucas, dear," Mrs. Cutler said. "Would you finish grace?"

Lucas Cutler cleared his throat. "Please join hands."

Henry took Sarah's right hand, and tiny Penelope took her left. The Judge and Mrs. Cutler held hands and smiled at each other. Lucas turned his eyes to the heavens and the house servants turned their heads down to the floor. The family all looked very saintly. That is, all except for Glanton. He hung his head with respect but was busy picking at his teeth.

"Oh Lord, we thank thee for this bountiful harvest laid out before us. We thank thee for the good hands that prepared it. And we thank thee for gathering all of us here today with thy eternal love and blessing. In Jesus' name, we thank thee. Amen."

The Judge cleared his throat. "And I just wanted to add." With a pause, he looked each of them in the eye. "I'm a proud and grateful man tonight. I'm thankful to have such a wonderful wife, and children, and someday soon"—he smiled at Sarah—"grandchildren. I've lived a blessed life. We all have." He seemed to want to say something more, but he was overcome with emotion. Finally, he concluded by saying: "Let's eat!"

They all watched in wonder as the Judge sliced into a large goose. Mrs. Cutler passed around the bread. Lucas was quietly praying by himself, for now ignoring the food. Henry made a face at Penelope and made her giggle.

Sarah, for her part, was still dazed by the Judge's remark about grandchildren. That had been, well, rather *forward*, hadn't it? Rather blunt? Then again, no one else seemed to care.

Slowly, as she looked around at the happy scene, she felt the cold stiffness of her mind begin to ease and ebb. The Judge had only been joking after all, or else merely making a light-hearted remark. And everyone around her was smiling and talking together as all close families do. Sarah felt flush with a tender admiration of the peaceful, almost perfect portrait of the Cutler family. Once upon a time she had thought the Roscoes were peaceful and perfect like this, though such a notion had really been more of a desperate hope than acknowledged fact.

Sarah began to count the many blessings of life at Arcadia. For all the growing pains she was suffering, feeling so much like a stranger in another person's home, Arcadia had been good to her. Being a part of a *normal* family — that had been good for her too. And looking at Henry again, studying the light in his eyes, Sarah decided that Arcadia was the place in which she belonged. The place in which she had *always* belonged.

Henry and the Judge discussed the plantation's finances, and Mrs. Cutler scolded her old man for setting his whiskey glass on the tablecloth and not upon one of the provided doilies. Little Penelope asked Sarah endless questions about her schooling in Richmond.

The Cutlers piled sweet potatoes on their plates and soaked them with melted butter. Sarah's stomach growled, and she hoped no one heard it. Minding her manners, she took only the smallest portions and ate nimbly, remembering to leave most of her plate untouched. Such were the manners expected of a young wife.

"You'll need to eat more when you're with child," Mrs. Cutler remarked knowingly.

Sarah smiled. "I only need a little to be satisfied. It's very delicious."

Horace Glanton was wolfing down his food. He snorted air as he chewed, his eyes constantly searching out the next morsel. "My daddy used to say, 'I eat to live, I don't live to eat.'" Glanton swallowed, coughed, and downed his wine greedily. "He died an old skeleton. I got no intention of goin out the same way."

Henry laughed and offered more bread to Glanton.

Mrs. Cutler asked, "And how is your father feeling these days, Sarah?" She sounded rather ambivalent regarding the answer. "I trust the campaign lifestyle would be hard on a man with his condition."

The mood at the table suddenly dimmed. Feeling all eyes on her, Sarah shifted in her seat. "Daddy's doing very well," she said, hoping that wasn't a lie. "He hasn't been home since May, since the wedding. My brother Jem is set to join him soon, I believe. What with the mine still under repair, there isn't much for him to do here at home."

"Is *that* his excuse?" Henry said, grinning.

"I reckon it's the lynch mob that's scared him off," Horace Glanton added.

Henry laughed. "Oh, no. Ezra Blake's all the motivation he needs to quit the Valley for good." With a wink, he tipped an imaginary bottle to his lips. "But I'm sure Jem Roscoe's many talents will be useful on the campaign trail."

Glanton roared with laughter, and the Judge couldn't help but grin in kind.

Sarah maintained a polite smile herself, but behind it she gritted her teeth. She loathed it when Henry mocked her family. Maybe the Roscoes weren't upright like the Cutlers, but that didn't mean her own husband had to talk down about her family. Swallowing her pride, Sarah turned to the Judge.

"And how is Mr. Breckinridge's campaign progressing?"

Her father-in-law chewed and nodded. "As well as can be expected," he said. "What it's looking like now is a two-way race in both the North and the South. In the North, it's Douglas versus the Kentucky ape. From Maryland down, it's the two Johns."

Mrs. Cutler reddened. "*Please*, Tobias. You know the better half of my relations hail from Bowling Green. If you must call Mr. Lincoln an ape, at least say he's from Illinois and not Kentucky."

The Judge grimaced at the naming of Lincoln. "And if you must refer to *that man* at all, Lucretia, I will remind you we don't speak his name in this house."

Mrs. Cutler nodded meekly. "Oh yes, Mr. Cutler. Forgive me, I'd forgotten." Without missing another beat, Mrs. Cutler looked up at Sarah and smiled. "Perhaps your mother could come to tea next week, Sarah. Perhaps your daddy doesn't have the time, but I would surely *love* to see Isabella. We used to be very good friends, you know."

Sarah offered the sweetest smile she could manage. She resisted the urge to correct Mrs. Cutler, for the *n*th time, that Cousin Isabella was not her mother. Besides, how on earth was she going to convince the woman who barely left her room to trek all the way across the Valley?

"I'm sure she would love that, Mrs. Cutler."

"Oh please, dear," the old woman said. "I've told you once, I've told you a hundred times. From now on, you call me 'Mother.'"

Sarah smiled again, but this time it was a strain to hold it. "Yes, *Mother*."

"Splendid," Mrs. Cutler said. "I'll look to you to extend the invitation. Do be prompt."

Sarah nodded and looked down at her plate. She felt a headache coming on. Hope that it had something to do with pregnancy flitted by and left her, and then she was alone with only the pain throbbing in her temple as company.

Lucas Cutler cleared his throat. "Is there much stock in the rumors, Father?"

The Judge was busy heaping pork gravy upon his plate. "About?"

"About South Carolina seceding," Lucas said. "Governor Pickens says that if *that man* is elected president, their state legislature will enact an ordinance of secession and declare themselves a sovereign nation."

The Judge shook his head. "Not to worry. The Republicans won't take the White House without Southern votes, and *that man*'s name won't appear on any ballot south of Baltimore. My colleagues and I have made certain of that."

Sarah thought to ask about the legality of withholding a candidate's name from voting ballots, but she decided against it.

"Yes, Father," Lucas said. "But what if the worst should happen?"

The Judge's eyes darkened, but there was still a gleam shining within them that Sarah could only describe as *cold*. "If the Yankees steal the presidency," he said, "it won't just be South Carolina that revolts. The whole South will be united against the North."

This answer seemed to satisfy Lucas, but for Sarah it only sparked a question.

"Would Virginia join this theoretical Southern revolution?" she asked.

"Naturally," the Judge replied.

"But if I may," Sarah said. "It seems to me that most Virginians are very loyal to the Union. Meaning they want North and South to get along for the greater good, so to speak."

Henry's cheeks were flushed red with drunkenness. "You don't know what you're talking about," he muttered.

Stung by Henry's rebuke, Sarah bowed her head and kept quiet.

The Judge gave his son an admonishing look. "Her question is valid," the Judge said. Now he turned back to Sarah. "Valid, though I must say misguided. Sarah, my rose, you've evidently heard too many of your daddy's speeches. Of course Virginians are all Unionists at heart. We are Americans, aren't we? But then again, what *is* the Union? It's quite clear to me that it is an agreement, an alliance if you will, between a collection of sovereign American states. The Federal government derives its power from the *states* which prop it up. After all, it was the states who revolted against the British. Without the states, there would be no Union at all.

"But in the North, they'd rather see the Union become an all-powerful institution capable of exerting tremendous power over all the states. They think the United States ought to spoken of not in the plural *are*, but in the singular *is*. They'd rather see a hegemonic government that derives its power directly from the common people, meaning all those immigrants and negrophiles up in Yankeeland. Their ranks far outnumber our own here in the South, but why should that make their opinions more important? After all, our Constitution was designed to protect minorities like ourselves.

"Here in Virginia, and across the South, we understand that the notion of states' rights provides a natural buffer that protects our fragile democracy from the whims of the unwashed majority. With no slaves to work their fields and factories, the Yankees invited all those immigrants to their shores, expecting cheap labor with no fuss. Now the fools are awash with millions of godless miscreants who can't speak English and care nothing of American values. The Yankees look to the South — and to Virginia especially — and they see that our Christian civilization remains intact. They resent our stability and they want to tear it down so that we become more like them. This is to say, they want to plunge us into chaos for their benefit. Well, we worked hard to build and maintain this civilization of ours, and we won't give it up without a fight. In that regard, Virginians are as likely to revolt against a Republican coup as any other state in the South."

Unsure what to say to all this, Sarah could only sit and nod slowly.

Mrs. Cutler touched her husband's arm and gently chided him. "Be kind to the girl, Tobias. I haven't the slightest clue what you're talking about, and I imagine Sarah doesn't either. Washington is a man's world, and that's as it should be."

The Judge sighed. "And yet what happens in Washington affects everything *everywhere*, including here in our own home," he said. "You'd do well to remember that, Mrs. Cutler."

As his wife blushed and turned her attention back to her meal, Sarah gleaned the impression that Mrs. Cutler was not actually so deferential to her husband. The old woman knew exactly what her husband was talking about, and maybe knew it better than he did. She was merely pretending to be thick-headed in his presence. She was acting.

We all must play our part.

The Judge looked up at Sarah again. "The blame for this entire crisis rests upon the shoulders of weak-minded men who put their own interests before the interests of their neighbors."

Sarah stared down at her plate. The Judge didn't mention Daddy exactly, but of course that's who he meant.

Ever since they'd gone to Charleston together, the friendship between Daddy and Judge Cutler had chilled, and after Daddy's campaign announcement their last bond had broken. Sarah was keenly aware that the Judge still smarted over Daddy's decision to run for the presidency. Sometimes she heard the Judge talk openly about her father in the harshest of terms: *John Roscoe is a corrupt cheat; John Roscoe is a laughable failure; John Roscoe is a nigger-loving Yankee machinist posing as a Southern gentleman; John Roscoe cares more about his toy trains than his wife and children,* and on and on and on.

Still, what could Sarah possibly say about it? She cleared her throat and made an attempt to defend Daddy, but she didn't know where to begin.

She looked to Henry for support. Would her husband say something — anything? All he had to do was change the subject.

But Henry only sat back, his red-rimmed eyes bleary with drunkenness, and waited for a servant to refill his glass. The servant was a plump young woman, and Henry made little effort to hide his admiration of her rear end.

Frustration and anger seeped into Sarah's thoughts. Her headache became much worse, but suddenly she felt stabs of pain in her abdomen. Butterflies scraped the walls of her stomach and she felt she might be sick all over the table.

But Sarah swallowed hard and remained in her seat.

The meal wore on, and Henry and Glanton became steadily more drunk. Finally, their venison arrived long after the others had finished dessert. At the smell of the meat, Sarah's stomach flip-flopped and she could bear the pain no longer. She stood up and asked for Henry's permission to leave the table. For the first time she considered this ritual not a pleasant tradition but a wearisome exercise, and she was already walking out of the room when Henry slurred his distracted assent.

As Sarah departed the dining room, she fought to maintain stately composure. But as soon as she was out of sight, she rushed down the hallway and up the stairs to the privacy of her bedroom.

After dinner, the men retired to the study to smoke cigars, drink brandy, and talk. It was unfortunate that the study lay directly under Sarah's bedroom, for she could hear the men's muffled voices and laughter long into the night. She could hear Henry's laughter ring loudest of all, and the sound enraged her such that she was soon sweating through her nightdress.

How could her own husband just sit back and let his father tear Daddy's reputation apart? Whatever the Judge thought of Daddy, Daddy was *Henry's father-in-law*. Didn't that mean anything to him? Worse, Henry seemed to enjoy disparaging the Roscoe name.

These thoughts and many more stewed in her mind as she lay in bed. Henry would know she was angry with him — she'd *tell* him, all right. But oh, there'd be no need for any of this if only Daddy was a *normal* sort of person. If only Daddy had just gotten along with the Judge and Mr. Breckinridge, perhaps the Cutlers and the other First Families would not be so resentful. If only Daddy had not taken his work so seriously all those years, perhaps he would not have gotten sick.

Sarah tossed and turned. Her thoughts went back to Henry and she became angry again, and despite how much she tried to wish her anger away it would not dissipate.

Sarah then decided that tomorrow, she would rise early and insist that one of the coach drivers take her away from Arcadia. She'd spend the whole day beyond the plantation borders. Maybe she'd go into Mayfair, or perhaps across the Valley to Clarendon. Henry would go mad not knowing where his wife was. Oh, she couldn't wait to see the look on Henry's face when he discovered that his wife was missing! It would serve him right, the little—

There were heavy footsteps in the hallway outside. The bedroom door flew open and a shaft of light stabbed the dark and Sarah flinched as the door slammed against the far wall. Henry, staggering drunk, shut the door with a bang and suddenly it was dark again, darker than before. She heard his musty breath in the blackness, his shoes clopping along the floor. He was laughing softly about some brilliant joke that had made Glanton and 'the boys' downstairs roar with laughter.

There was a smell on Henry that Sarah couldn't quite put her finger on, something musky and sweet.

"My duchess," Henry slurred in the darkness. "My duchess..."

Henry never told Sarah about his nightly activities, and she had learned not to ask. She suspected it usually involved drinking and smoking and riding horses. It was apparently a man's right to do whatever the hell he wanted with his time, and a woman's duty to wait around until her man came calling.

Tonight, however, Sarah decided she'd have none of it. She rolled over and pretended she was asleep. She didn't want a man who neglected to defend her honor. She nestled against the sheets and tried to ignore the sounds of him undressing.

The bed creaked and she felt Henry's weight beside her. And then, suddenly, he was on top of her. She felt his freezing cold hands pulling up her nightdress and pinch the skin of her buttocks. Her surprise delayed her thoughts and movements, but finally she unfroze and tried to move away from him.

"Henry, stop," she said at last, but it didn't stop. Now he was turning her over on her back and pushing her legs apart. She pulled her legs back in, squeezed them close together like a child tucked into the womb. "*Stop*," she hissed. "Not tonight."

It was quiet for a long time, and she started to believe that Henry had relented. Maybe her defiance had struck a chord in him, and maybe he was getting ready to apologize and explain himself.

But then, with a loud grunt, Henry took her knees one in each palm and forced them apart. Her joints popped and she whimpered with pain. His body pressed against hers and she felt him hot down there, but she didn't want it — not tonight, not like this.

"I said *stop*!" she shouted — loud enough, she hoped, to shame him off her.

Still, he didn't stop. Like some brutish, unthinking animal, he would not stop.

And so, Sarah went limp. She lay there like a doll with tears in her eyes and let Henry have his way with her. And all the while, she heard Mrs. Cutler's voice echo in her ears:

We all must play our part.

Henry finished quickly, mercifully, predictably. Then he rolled over and was asleep within moments, and Sarah lay awake. She stared at the ceiling, breathless, sensing her body grow numb, feeling nothing of the euphoria of her first few sleepless weeks of marriage. Looking over, she realized she barely recognized the man who lay beside her. He had changed so much, and in just a few short months. Could it be that he'd always been like this, and had only now taken off some kind of mask? Was it even possible for a person to *pretend* for such a long time?

We all must play our part.

And what was her part? Why, to finish her family quilt of course. All those children and grandchildren wouldn't just spring out of holes in the ground, after all.

Her part was to put her own needs aside and accept her husband. To accept him, in whatever way he preferred to give himself. To try again, and again, and again, until Henry had his son and the Cutlers had their legacy. It was Daddy's legacy too, she realized. And hadn't she always told herself that this — *all this* — was what she'd always wanted?

Sarah wanted to climb out of bed and get away from Henry. She wanted to sleep somewhere else tonight. But when she tried to get up, she found she didn't have the strength to move. Instead she lay back, sleepless, locked in place with nothing to do but *think*. She lay like that until dawn, until finally the duchess of Arcadia drifted into a restless sleep.

"Now repeat after me. Ready?"

"Yes, ma'am."

Pointing at the words written on a slate so that Tattie could follow along, Sarah tilted her chin high and began:

Moses supposes his toeses are roses;
Moses supposes erroneously,
For nobody's toeses are roses or posies,
As Moses supposes his toeses to be.

When she finished, Sarah smiled and curtsied while Tattie offered polite applause.

"Now you try," Sarah said, gesturing forward. "Come on, up you get. Stand before the class so everyone can see you."

The 'class,' hastily assembled that morning within Sarah's bedroom, was made up of a selection of dolls and plush toys that Sarah had brought over from Clarendon, as well as Mother's portrait propped up on a chair.

For the past several weeks, Sarah had met Tattie once a day for lessons in diction and elocution. Of course she knew it was forbidden to teach slaves how to read, but Sarah was determined to make Arcadia's slaves not only the best behaved help in the Valley, but also the most refined. Everyone at Arcadia had their personal project — Henry the cotton crop, Mrs. Cutler her garden and horses, Lucas his sermons — so why couldn't Sarah have something of her own to work on? At the very least, it would be a distraction from loneliness.

All Sarah's life, she had considered Clarendon the epicenter of boredom and loneliness. Coming to Arcadia, she anticipated a vibrant new world of fêtes and parties, of music and poetry in salons, and most importantly she looked forward to demonstrations of boundless love by Henry. The truth was that Arcadia did host more than its fair share of social gatherings — so many in fact that Sarah soon became drained and overwhelmed, and took to making up excuses for why she could not attend tomorrow's tea with Mrs. Cutler's cousins or next week's luncheon with the governor. She simply needed to be *alone* by times, but even then she found little respite; she would continue to hear a chorus of muffled voices through the walls.

Curious, wasn't it? That she yearned to be around others, and yet also craved time alone. When she had too much of one, she would wish for the other, and the vicious cycle would repeat!

The worst part about having constant visitors was that Henry was under as much pressure as Sarah was to be a good host. Henry was often taken away by male guests to go hunt turkeys or waterfowl, and in the evenings the guests always wanted to smoke and drink into the early hours. Now that harvest time was approaching again, Sarah barely saw Henry at all during the day, and only rarely at night.

And truth be told, Sarah began to meet the nights she spent with Henry with a sort of grim stoicism. Their bouts of lovemaking, previously so passionate, were now few and far between, and it seemed Henry always had to get drunk first. Afterward he would ramble, his whiskey breath blowing in her face, about their 'little duke.' He began to ask the same questions again and again. Had there been any change inside her? Could she feel anything, or should they try again? How many times would it take until she was sure, until *he* could be sure? How much longer until—

"Ma'am?"

Sarah blinked, and she found herself back in her bedroom with Tattie.

"Yes?"

"You were saying, ma'am. About the lesson."

Sarah shook her head a little to clear her mind. "Of course," she said. "The lesson, yes. Now remember, Tattie..."

Here, Sarah paused again, feeling suddenly out of breath. She reached for a handkerchief on a nearby table and dabbed the sweat from her forehead. She felt clammy, and her back was slick with cold sweat. She could feel a churning in her stomach and tried her best to ignore it, but her best wasn't working.

Tattie watched her with a look of growing concern. "Are you feelin all right, ma'am?"

"Oh, of course," Sarah replied, pushing a smile across dry lips. She swallowed a lump in her throat and tasted something salty. "I'm very fine. Now smarten up for the class, Tattie. Feet together, shoulders back, chin up, eyes forward. Ready? Repeat after me. *Moses supposes his toeses are roses...*"

Tattie stared forward with a fixed gaze, as if she was trying to bore holes into the opposite wall. "Moses…Moses supposes…"

"*…his toeses are roses…*"

"…his toeses are roses…"

"Very good," Sarah said. She pointed at the next line. "And?"

Tattie hung her head and took a deep breath.

"What's the matter?" Sarah said. "Have you forgotten the next line already? Oh, dear girl. Well, it's fine. Something to work on. In the meantime, repeat after—"

"Moses supposes his toeses are roses," Tattie said, setting her gaze forward. "Moses supposes erroneously, for nobody's toeses are roses or posies, as Moses supposes his toeses to be."

Sarah was rightly flabbergasted by Tattie's performance. Her voice had been strong and resonant, her enunciation perfect.

"That's…that was…very good, Tattie."

Tattie hung her head. "Thank you, ma'am."

Sarah's mind raced as she tried to think of *some* sort of criticism. She could not simply praise the girl and let her think she'd mastered one of the lessons so easily.

"Let's try it again," Sarah said. "This time, pay special attention to the word *erroneously*. I think you may have slipped in there somewhere."

Tattie turned to Sarah. "Ma'am?"

"Yes, Tattie."

"I'd like to keep goin with the lessons, ma'am…"

"You mean you'd like to continue?"

"Yes, ma'am. Only, could we try a different kind of lesson, ma'am?"

Sarah shrugged. "This one seems fine enough to me. What, is it too challenging for you? You want something easier? I mean, this is as childish as nursery rhymes get, but I suppose…"

"It's not that, ma'am," Tattie said. She looked to be gathering her courage to speak her mind, but in the meantime she only looked down and swept a foot idly across the floor.

"Well if you want to speak up," Sarah said, lifting Tattie's chin, "then speak up. Do as I've been teaching you. Feet together, shoulders back, that's it. Now, tell me, what's the matter?"

Tattie drew a deep breath. "It's just that…well, there ain't no easy way to say this, ma'am."

Sarah maintained a tight-lipped smile and resisted the urge to correct Tattie's manner of speaking. "Go on."

As she spoke, tears began to form in the corners of Tattie's eyes. "It's *Moses*, ma'am. There was a Moses here at Arcadia. He was a runaway, ma'am. A *damn, dirty, no-good-nigger runaway*, ma'am. None of us niggers know what happened to im when they caught im, but we gots an idea and we know it's the *right* idea, ma'am." Tattie's lower lip quivered, and her voice threatened to cut out. Still, she managed to croak: "Moses was my brother, ma'am."

Sarah felt her smile curdle behind her own lips. She swallowed and tasted acid, as if a surge of bile had snuck up her throat.

"I see," Sarah said, coughing to clear her throat. "Well, I suppose that even though Moses was a..."

"A damn, dirty, no-good-nigger—"

"Runaway, yes," Sarah said. "Even though Moses was a runaway, he was still your brother. Sisters and brothers must love each other always, yes?"

Tattie bit her lip and looked away. "Yes, ma'am."

Sarah felt her shoulders drooping, and realizing this she forced herself to stand upright. She thought to say something more to Tattie, maybe to say that she was sorry if she'd caused Tattie any distress. She even thought to reach out and hug Tattie, to try and comfort her somehow. But thinking of it more, she decided against all of it. It was better to keep a certain distance between oneself and the help. It was better for everyone that way.

"That will be all for today, Tattie. You are dismissed."

Tattie bowed. "Thank you, ma'am." With that, the girl turned and made for the door. Her light footsteps receded down the hall.

Sarah turned and looked toward the morning sunlight filtering through the windows. Despite the cheeriness of the light, still warm despite it being the first week of October, Sarah could not shake off a chill that had gripped her out of nowhere.

Moses. Tattie, and Moses. Sarah could see the resemblance now, in her mind's eye. At least, she thought she could. In truth she had never seen Moses before until *that night*, and even then it had been so dark—

And they'd beaten him to a pulp. Henry, and the others.

Sarah felt a sudden headrush and let out a low groan. Her vision dulled, and she found her bed just in time before her legs gave out.

"Ma'am?"

It was Tattie's voice...footsteps returning up the hall, getting closer.

"*Ma'am?*"

When Sarah opened her eyes again, she found herself on the bed staring up at the ceiling. Tattie's face appeared, her eyes quivering with worry. Sarah felt Tattie's hand slide into her grasp and squeeze.

"Ma'am? Ma'am, are you—"

"*No,*" Sarah said. "If you're about to ask if I'm all right, the answer is *no*."

She closed her eyes and pushed her tongue against the roof of her mouth as nausea frothed inside her. After what felt like an eternity, the wave passed on. Heaving a breath, tasting salt on her tongue, she looked up at Tattie and saw that the girl was examining her with a nurse's eye.

"What is it?" Sarah said.

"If I may," Tattie said. "Ma'am, has you been throwin up some mornins?"

Sarah shook her head. "That's none of your business." Suddenly she grimaced, realizing just how much she sounded like Cousin Isabella. With a heavy sigh, she murmured, "Yes, I have been. Mornings and evenings both. And it's been more frequent than usual."

"Usual?" A cloud of concern passed over Tattie's face. She knelt down beside Sarah and reached out to Sarah with both hands. "Ma'am, would you mind?" She gestured, indicating a desire to touch Sarah's belly.

Sarah felt cold fingers of fear. Negroes weren't supposed to touch their betters. "What are you doing?" she hissed, her body going tense.

Tattie held her hands out where Sarah could see them. "I ain't gonna do nothin unless you say it's all right," she said. "I'm only young, but I birthed however many babies in my short time."

Sarah felt a sudden wave of tiredness. What was it Tattie had just said. *Babies?*

"I don't know the number on account I can't count," Tattie said, "but Lord knows it's more than one. I reckon I helped bring my fair share of young ones into the world." Slowly, the girl reached out again, her fingertips reaching underneath the folds of Sarah's dress.

Sarah winced at the touch of Tattie's fingers and was about to cry out, *"Don't touch me!"* — but for whatever reason she kept her mouth shut and waited.

Slowly, Tattie pressed her dry fingers against Sarah's belly. Her fingers moved diligently, now examining a different area. Her fingers were gentle, her touch exploratory and somehow intensely comforting.

"Ma'am," Tattie said, withdrawing her hands. "I reckon you may be with child, ma'am."

Sarah was still recovering from the shock of this statement when she saw that Tattie's face glowed with a happy smile. Suddenly, the realization fixed in Sarah's mind.

She was going to have a... *baby?*

"Are you sure?" she breathed, incredulous. "You can't be sure. There's no way you can be sure by just, well, by just touching around and..."

"I ain't never sure until the bump shows," Tattie admitted. "Even then, there's the chance — well...best not to talk about any of that. Bad spirits might be listenin." Tattie reached out and took Sarah's hand, and despite her instinct to pull away Sarah was thankful for the girl's touch. "Dr. Harper ought to take a look. He'll know for sure if it's a little angel."

"But why must it be like this?" Sarah asked. "I feel absolutely awful."

Tattie shook her head. "I don't know, ma'am. Most girls get a little sick at first. I learned the touch from the older mothers. They was the ones who told me when I was with child. For all the times after, well, I suppose I just *knew*."

Sarah felt another pitching wave of nausea, and this time she felt certain she would be sick. She rolled over on her side and retched, but nothing came this time.

Tattie made to get up. "I'll fetch some water—"

"*No*," Sarah said, gripping Tattie's hand. "Stay with me awhile, Tattie. Until the pain passes."

"There ain't supposed to be no pain, ma'am. Not until the time comes."

"Well, you know what I mean," Sarah said. "It all feels so, so *new*, it just..."

"You sure there ain't no pain, ma'am?"

Sarah heaved a great sigh. "Nothing I can't handle, no. In the meantime, I suppose I'll just suffer."

She laughed now, and Tattie laughed with her. Taking another deep breath, Sarah squeezed Tattie's hand tighter.

"So you've done this before, Tattie?"

Tattie nodded. "A few times, ma'am. I promise you, it ain't all like this. Most times it's real nice. Soon enough you feel him kickin. Oh, it don't hurt, he be playin. And it gets that sometimes, if you put you hand in the right place, you can feel the little heartbeat."

Sarah sighed and shivered. The nausea seemed to have passed, for now, and she felt a wash of calm. "That sounds...very nice, in fact."

Tattie smiled. "It is, ma'am. I don't know what it's really like when the time comes. I reckon there's pain then, but I couldn't say how much. Marse Cutler prefers Dr. Harper to cut Arcadia babies out of the mama's belly. Says it keeps us from attachin ourselves to the little angels. Each of mine was sold away when I was still on the mend. I don't think about em as often as I maybe should, but Reverend Lucas says that's on account of my being a wicked nigger. Although I do get thinkin of em sometimes, wonderin if they happy and servin they people nice and good..."

Sarah could no longer hear Tattie, and was indeed unable to hear anything beyond the voice of jubilation in her own head. She was going to have a baby! What was nine months from today? Oh, she was going to have a sweet, beautiful child — *Henry's* child.

Just wait until she told him. Oh, the look that would fill his eyes! No more would Henry ignore her. No more could he demonstrate his impatience with her and show such callous disregard. No more would he *take* her, instead of making love to her. Henry would love her again in so many ways. After all, she was not just his wife anymore, but the mother of his children. Already she began to recharacterize all the events of recent weeks: her life with the Cutlers really wasn't so dull and predictable, but exceptionally fulfilling; making love with Henry was always a tender, thrilling experience; life at an exquisite, historic plantation like Arcadia really was all that she had ever dreamed of.

A baby, oh praise be to the Lord! Would it be a girl or boy? Whoever it was, they would be hers and Henry's, together. A family of their own. A family that did not know pain or loss or humiliation like the Roscoes had. Hers would be a family in which everyone belonged *to* each other, *with* each other.

"I have to tell Henry!" she gasped, trying to get up from the bed. "I have to go down and—"

"You gotta *rest*," Tattie said. "Lay down a few minutes. When you feelin better, we'll go."

Sarah closed her eyes and settled back. Her hair was wet from sweat, and she felt a hot throbbing in her temple. As she lay there, her memory drifted back far in time. When she was a young girl and took ill, Mae Jane would stay up with her all night. Mae Jane would sit by Sarah's bed and rub Sarah's back and sing in a low voice until she fell asleep. More than anything, Sarah wanted Mae Jane's touch now.

A mother's touch.

"Tattie," Sarah said. "Would you...Could you...sing for me, Tattie? Hum something for me, rather. A lullaby, if you know one."

Tattie smiled down at her, but tears suddenly threatened the girl's eyes. With an obliging nod, the girl moistened her lips. Softly, she began to hum a lullaby. Though it was not a melody Sarah could remember hearing before, it sounded somehow familiar, as if she'd known it all her life.

A baby. Bless the Lord, for He is good, she was going to have a baby.

Closing her eyes, feeling herself lulled to sleep by Tattie's sweet, resonant voice, Sarah contemplated the marvel of a new life slumbering within her somewhere. In that moment, she floated on the epiphany of a previously unknown kinship with Mae Jane, and even Cousin Isabella — and maybe even Tattie too, a mother of sorts several times over. And more than at any other moment in her life, Sarah felt closer to her own mother.

Sarah breathed a pleasured sigh. She drew her legs up, and it was as if she herself were a baby again, and with the lullaby in her ears she soon drifted off into a happy, contented sleep.

Chapter 28
THE LEDGER

The Potomac River shimmered like sheet metal in the late October sunshine. On the Maryland side, lumbering along a length of B&O Railroad track, came an aged three-car locomotive festooned with flags and streamers. Each of its cars was painted a different color (red, white, and blue), and each bore huge letters reading LIBERTY & UNION EXPRESS. As the eastbound train passed within sight of Harper's Ferry, a gloomy face looked out from one of the windows and gazed upon the village that had, almost exactly a year ago, been the subject of Union-wide attention and anxiety. Now, the sleepy riverside town had since resumed its slumber.

The first time Ben Freeman had been on a train, during the Charleston trip back in the springtime, the novelty of bowling along at thirty miles an hour, as fast as steam could carry him, had been enthralling. But now that he'd lived and slept on a hard-backed bench for the greater part of six weeks, Ben considered himself sufficiently disillusioned regarding the realities of life on the campaign trail.

The past summer at Clarendon had been endless, but certainly not in a good way. In the weeks after the disaster at the North Branch Mine, dark rumors spread throughout the Valley and beyond the Branches. A 'valued source' told the *Mayfair First Witness* that many warnings about potential gas explosions at the mine had been disclosed, on several occasions, to the mine's owners, meaning the Roscoe family. Jem Roscoe in particular became a lightning rod for public outrage. When Jem tried to attend the mass funeral for the twenty-three dead miners, he was driven from the cemetery by an angry mob that followed him back to Clarendon and tore down the stone bastions at the front gate before setting upon the rubble with hammers.

While Clarendon was cut off by a veritable siege, there was not much for Ben to do but help Mama keep the place. With Sarah gone to the South Branch the house was quieter, but Tom's return from school brought some life back to the place. Meanwhile, Jem lost himself to guilt and despair. Once, Jem went out to try and reconcile with Audrey Blake, but he returned later with a bloody face (no doubt thanks to Ezra) and an unquenching thirst for any liquor he could get his hands on.

One day, Mama quietly asked Ben to hide the Colonel's trophy weapons, including the old dueling pistols, lest Jem get any 'bad ideas.'

The weeks of hot weather wore on, and Ben's boredom was broken only by news from Senator Roscoe's campaign, which came mostly in the form of newspaper reports and the odd letter from the Senator himself. Toward the middle of September, one such letter explained that the campaign would soon finish a recent tour through the northwest states (where the Senator was attempting to poach voters from both Stephen Douglas and Abraham Lincoln). The Senator's campaign was bound next for Washington City, where it would make camp and await the final weeks of the campaign. The Senator wrote, as he had done several times already during the campaign, that it would 'do this old heart good' to have his family with him. He invited the Roscoes, and the Freemans too, to travel north to meet his train and join him for the final stretch of the national contest.

In the end, only Ben and Jem accepted the call. Both yearned to escape Mayfair, and Clarendon in particular, and not for entirely dissimilar reasons.

As he gazed upon the broad Potomac through the train window, Ben listened as, at the front of the car, the Senator and some fifteen campaign advisors (to the man hired mercenaries handpicked for their ability to stuff ballot boxes) engaged in a strategy meeting.

"The essential message of our campaign is that of Henry Clay," the Senator said to the bored, dour-faced men around him. "Clay was a Kentuckian; he looked North and South and saw only one nation, and he saw the West as our shared destiny. Unionism is the meat of our offering, gentlemen. For the trimmings and flourishes, our poetry and pomp, we turn to Daniel Webster's rousing oratory. And for the fire in our bellies, the raw fighting spirit essential to victory over Democrats and Republicans alike, we call upon the fire-eating ghost of John C. Calhoun of South Carolina. These were the Compromisers, gentlemen, what we used to call the Great Triumvirate. Together, these three men kept the disparate sections of the Union together for the better part of thirty years. Now that they are dead and gone, it's up to us — up to *our Party* — to carry on their legacy. The Union Party, not the Republicans or the Democrats, is the rightful heir to the spirit of American compromise."

To all this, the Senator's advisors only looked into their hands or at the passing views of the countryside. No one, Ben observed, thought to mention that the original triumvirates of the Roman Republic had collapsed, resulting in a dictator seizing the whole kit and kaboodle. Certainly the campaign's hired guns had no interest in the dead dealings of dead men, and they cared not at all for discussions of political philosophy, except to identify a laundry list of policies which might attract more votes to their camp.

"Senator Roscoe raises excellent points," said the campaign manager, a Yankee named Welles. "We must ask ourselves, who is our voter? He is a patriot; that goes without saying. He is a devout Christian, but not a Catholic. He was born in the time of Jefferson and is distrustful of large government. He detests Jews and immigrants, especially Polacks and Irishmen. Germans he can put up with, but again they must be Protestants, and they must speak English. He admires the industrious and despises the shamelessly needy. He abhors abolitionists and Southern nationalists alike, though he may still transact business with both groups. He believes Americans ought to settle the Indian lands between Mississippi and California. He is open to another conquest of Mexico if it will solve the slavery question, but he will not suffer losing his sons nor his workers in order to win it. Our voter believes there ought to be no changes to the Constitution, no new laws favoring any one group or section, and that government remain limited and decentralized. Our voter demands *preservation* of the Republic, and that is all."

"The Union *as it is*," the Senator insisted. "The Constitution *as it is*."

Together, the advisors chorused: *The Union as it is, the Constitution as it is.*

Ben turned wearily away from the scene and looked out the window to study the thinning auburn leaves of passing trees.

All through September and now into October, the Liberty & Union Express had toured around the so-called Border States, visiting cities in Virginia, Kentucky, and Tennessee. There had been a short stint through New York and Pennsylvania, but the Union Party had found few supporters in the larger cities. Not even Richmond, Virginia's capital city, had been receptive to the Senator's speeches.

Cities. The Senator was so focused on visiting *cities* that he insisted on rolling right through small towns and wayside villages (like Harper's Ferry) without stopping, even though it was near these smaller centers that most voters lived. If there was one thing Ben had learned about America in his many weeks of travel, it was that it was not exclusively the land of urban sprawl he thought it was. Most books and newspapers described the United States as a place of ivory towers built next to slums, with millions of people crawling over each other like ants. And maybe in some places that was true. But for most people, in most places across the Union, 'America' was nothing more than one's humble little town, with a church at one end and a tavern at the other. Most people, in most places, lived on hardscrabble farms that made the nearest crossroads village look like a bonafide metropolis. These people could be easily called 'Southerners' or 'Northerners', much as pundits and politicians liked to describe them as such. They were simply *people*, trying to make ends meet as best they could, thanking God for small mercies, wondering what the weather might bring tomorrow and what the harvest might yield next season. The truth was that most folks didn't give a damn about slaves and Yankees and tariffs and immigrants and the Supreme Court and all the bullshit that some yammering fools insisted was so important.

To put it another way, a tiny, wayside place like the Mayfair Valley was America in miniature. There were countless such microcosms all across the Union, and to fully appreciate the complexity of one was to have at least a grasping knowledge of the whole. But John Roscoe, he didn't seem to understand that. He had spent as little time in the Valley as he could, believing it to be only a means to an end. Faced with the prospect of having to retire from Washington and live out his remaining days in Mayfair as a private citizen, he had somehow concocted the insane idea to run for *president*. But how could a man govern a country if he did not understand it, nor even care to try?

But maybe the old man understood more than Ben was giving him credit for. The old man knew history, and he knew politics. He knew how to count votes to pass or kill legislation. He knew where the bodies were buried. John Roscoe knew *men*: their weaknesses, their failings, what kept them up at night, and he knew how to squeeze them. Was this enough?

Ben remembered the newspaper in his lap and started to leaf through it again. It was a copy of the *Washington Star*, one of the Union's most widely read publications. In the funny pages, there was a cartoon depicting John Roscoe as an ostrich with his head buried in the sand, while all around him the other candidates grappled in a cloud of cartoon violence. Stamped on the ostrich's fan-tailed buttocks was the oft-repeated slogan: *The Union as it is, the Constitution as it is.*

Meanwhile, it had been fascinating to follow the evolving treatment of Abraham Lincoln by the Union's largest newspapers. At first, few papers mentioned him at all. Months ago, the idea of a backwoods westerner (Lincoln was from Illinois, but of Kentucky origin), might become the Republican nominee was altogether laughable. After Lincoln in fact became the nominee, the pundits claimed with confidence that the Republican upstart would be eclipsed by the larger-than-life personalities of John Breckinridge and Stephen Douglas. After all, how could a country lawyer compete against the current vice president, not to mention the most famous (or infamous, depending on who was giving the opinion) politician in the Union? Some even claimed that John Roscoe, with one hand extending North and the other South, would turn out to be the dark horse of the 1860 campaign.

But if the content of the *Star* was any indication of the national mood, Ben decided he'd bet money on a Lincoln victory. The man's name was mentioned on almost every page, sometimes as the butt of crass, cutting rebukes and sometimes as the subject of weepy treatises lauding the man as some kind of messiah-like figure. Southerners wrote of Lincoln as a gangly-armed gorilla, while many Northern opinion pieces praised the so-called 'railsplitter' (for Lincoln was apparently a woodcutter in his youth). Ben recalled seeing a painted mural in New York City that depicted Lincoln brandishing an axe before a gnarled willow tree labeled SLAVERY, said tree festooned with tiny negroes hanging from its branches. On the same day, Ben had read *The New York Times'* endorsement of Lincoln for president.

Ben heard a loud *pop* and looked over to see the Senator's advisors pouring glasses of champagne and making loud, teary-eyed toasts to one another. Shaking his head, Ben sighed and looked out the window again.

"You think it's all a big crock, don't you?"

Ben turned and looked over at Jem Roscoe, who was slumped over on a bench across the aisle. Jem had a bottle of gin in hand (for he'd long ago given up the tedium of pouring his drinks into glasses). With a giddy grin, Jem nodded toward his father, who was beaming at the passionate commendations of one brown-noser after another. Sitting upright, Jem leaned over and offered the bottle to Ben.

"Here. This will help you enjoy the ride."

Ben shook his head. "No, thanks."

Jem gave a *suit yourself* shrug and drank, and then he settled back on his bench. Ben felt Jem's eyes watching him a long while.

"Why is it you're here, Ben?"

Ben wasn't sure how to answer that question, nor was he exactly sure what the question meant. While he thought about it, he folded his collection of newspapers together and set them down beside him.

"I suppose I'm here to help write some of your father's campaign speeches. That's what he asked me to do, at least."

"He's got plenty of help," Jem said, nodding toward the advisors and campaign staffers. "I count more than a dozen leeches busy sucking him dry. When we get to Washington, they'll all come crawling out of the woodwork. But you're not one of *them*, meaning you have a mind of your own. So again I ask, what the hell are you doing here?"

Ben shrugged. "Maybe I could ask you the same question."

Jem laughed, but there was no joy in it. "That makes two of us," he said. After a while, he shook his head. "All my life, I always wanted to be *part* of something. To work with others to overcome some challenge, build something better, find a new way. You know, to be there at the beginning, right in the middle, and see the thing through to…well, wherever the end might be. Never anything too difficult, of course." He held up his bottle as an example. "I enjoy life's simple pleasures far too much to take on an excess of hardships."

Ben laughed. Jem laughed with him, and this time his laugh was real.

"I always took you for the lone fox rather than part of the hunting pack," Ben said. "It surprises me that you feel you need the company of others to feel whole."

"You forget I'm a twin," Jem said, grinning. "Besides, it was always JJ who had the tougher time making friends. I always had it easy in that regard, until recently."

Ben nodded. "I suppose you're right there. Still…"

Jem cocked an eyebrow. "Still what? You're surprised I'm sitting here on daddy's choo-choo, and not JJ?"

"Maybe a little," Ben said.

"Again, that makes two of us," Jem said. "I suppose the answer has something to do with attempted murder. But anyway, what was I saying? Some vague claptrap bullshit about finding a new way..."

"To be part of something," Ben said.

Jem snapped his fingers. "Ah, there it is. To be part of something. A cause, a community. And well, here I am. *The Union as it is, the Constitution as it is*, and all that. And I must tell you, Ben, this is all as blissfully boring as I'd hoped it would be. What's more, there's nobody calling for my head on a pike."

Ben turned and looked out at the world passing by. "I wonder sometimes. Is it enough to merely be part of something? Wouldn't it be better to feel you're part of the *right* something?"

Jem took a swig from the bottle. "Who the hell can say they feel that? I mean, truly?" He thought about it a little longer. "Maybe it feels right for a day, or even a great many days. But sooner or later, you feel yourself looking elsewhere, or else you get careless. Maybe you're forced out, for reasons you didn't want or expect." Slowly, Jem's gaze drew off elsewhere. "Most of us would sooner just feel we belong *anywhere*, so long as it's somewhere."

Ben looked at Jem. "If you don't mind my asking," he said. "Audrey Blake. Has she...have you—?"

"I'd rather not talk about that," Jem said, his voice muted.

Ben nodded awkwardly and looked down at the floorboards running along the aisle. He watched pebbles and little pieces of dirt dance on the shaking, shuddering floor.

"I've been thinking of going back home," Ben said quietly.

Jem sat up and looked at him. "Oh?"

"Yes," Ben said. He nodded toward the Senator and his cheery staffers. "I don't know if I'm doing any good here. I'm not doing any good at all."

"Because you're not drunk," Jem said.

"Maybe," Ben said. "Or maybe it's because I don't believe in it."

"In what?"

"This. Any of it."

Jem shrugged. "It's not a matter of belief. It's a matter of making all those poor saps out there believe *us*. At least, that's what those men over there tell me."

"But that's exactly what I mean," Ben said. "I don't believe *that*."

Jem laughed. "Well, then I suppose you need to find yourself a new line of work. You'd make a good preacher, maybe."

Ben nodded morosely. "Maybe."

Jem watched Ben for a long while. Some part of the old Jem cut through the red fog of drunkenness. "Speak to me now, Ben. Haven't you been writing Father's campaign speeches? They've been good speeches, some of his best. There's honor in doing good work. Not many men are capable of good work. Most can't even bother to show up."

"I don't write anything I don't mean," Ben said.

Jem nodded. "And isn't there something *right* in that? Can't you take a little piece of something right for yourself out of all this goddamn mess?"

Ben shook his head. "What's true on paper doesn't always ring true when it's spoken aloud. Words can be shaped, meanings twisted. And in the end, for those men down the aisle, it's not about the truth at all. It's about votes. To my mind, the votes ought to follow truth, not the other way around."

Jem smiled. "Seems you suffer the same curse as all us romantics," he said. "You're hopelessly lost somewhere between how things should be and how they are."

Jem's eyes landed on his father. He tilted the bottle and drank, but his gaze never wavered.

"The truth is, this is a circus train full of clowns who don't know their time on stage has already come and gone. Still, I want to see where it's going. Call it morbid curiosity, or simply my wanting to escape the shame of what happened down the North Branch. Maybe it even comes down to a sense of loyalty."

"Loyalty?" Ben echoed.

Jem nodded. "Sometimes I hate the bastard for all he's done, and for all he hasn't. Mother can barely bring herself to look at him. Sarah's long since realized 'Daddy' doesn't make the world go round, and Tom's coming to terms with that too. Bayard, well, I think he's always been terrified of the old man. And JJ...well, you know JJ.

"But the fact remains, he's Father, *my* father. And I have to admire the old man a little, you know? He's out here, fighting with one hand tied behind his back and a clock ticking in his head. I've never done much to curry his favor — that was always JJ. But now, I can't help but feel I owe it to Father to stand with him. Maybe it's because there isn't much solid ground for me to stand on anymore. But maybe it's because I can't bear the thought of him being alone through all this, alone to the end..."

"You're a good son," Ben said.

Jem snorted. "That's a stretch. But you know? I'll take it." Jem drank again. "If you really want my opinion on what you should do, Ben..."

"I do," Ben said.

Jem turned to him. "Everybody has their reasons for staying or going. But if you're looking for a sense of *right* in all this, you should jump ship first chance you get."

Ben listened and pondered these things. He opened his mouth and was just starting to form the words *Come with me* on his lips when suddenly the train shuddered. Brakes hissed, and the train began to slow to a crawl.

Ben turned and looked out the window. Where before there had been green foliage and farmhouses sitting atop long pastures, now there were clusters of weathered shacks and warehouses, and countless wagons and carriages churning muddy streets. A station platform slid into view, and Ben read the name of their destination, almost mythic in his mind, scrawled plainly on a simple hand-painted sign:

DISTRICT OF COLUMBIA

❧

The campaign staffer pushed the attic door open and stepped into a murky semi-darkness. "And here's yours," he mumbled.

Suitcase in hand, Ben looked around the cramped attic on the third floor of the Senator's Washington townhouse. The air was thick with dust and stale memories. Past the tiny cot in the corner were heaps of junk looked ready to pitch over at the slightest touch. In the furthest corner stood a great bulky monolith covered with a discolored white sheet. Ben felt himself drawn to the mysterious shape as if by some sort of magnet, until finally he stood next to it with the sheet clutched in his hands and—

"*Don't touch that*. Mr. Welles' orders."

Ben dropped the sheet and turned around to face the staffer. The man, a Yankee barely in his twenties, made no secret of his disgust and annoyance at having to show Ben around his new living quarters. Already the man was descending the attic stairs to the main floors below.

"The speech is at eight o'clock, at Ford's across the street," the staffer said over his shoulder. "You can be there or not, I don't care."

Ben made a face at the back of the staffer's balding head. Alone now, Ben went over to his cot and lay down. It felt good to stretch out on a mattress, thin as it was. He stared up at the ceiling for a while, watching a cloud of dust settle around him. He sneezed once, twice, three times, and then he got up from the cot and went to the tiny hexagonal window that looked out onto 10th Street. From here he saw people and carriages bustling up and down the street. Eager for some fresh air, Ben decided to go down and have a cigar.

Ben went down to the second floor. Looking up the hallway, Ben saw the Senator through the half-closed door of the master bedroom. There were half a dozen senior staffers in there, including the campaign manager Mr. Welles. While the Senator was dressing for the speech he would deliver later that evening, staffers were peppering him with notes and questions.

Ben poked his head into a corner room, where Jem was still settling in.

"Fancy a smoke?"

Jem was thankful for a distraction from unpacking. Together, they went down to the first floor. They passed by the kitchen and three parlors — every room was occupied by campaign staffers and various hangers-on — and stepped out into the brisk air of an October evening.

A large horse-drawn omnibus was rolling down 10th Street. Ben's eyes followed its path, and then he settled upon a grand brickwork building with a roof that gleamed brilliant orange against a canvas of gray thunderheads. The inscription on the nearest stone bastion read: FORD'S ATHENEUM.

"Do you have any idea where we are?" Ben asked.

"Washington," was Jem's answer.

Ben lit a cigar and started down the street. "Fancy a walk with your smoke?"

Jem sighed. "I'd rather sit down in a saloon somewhere, to tell you the truth."

They descended 10th Street, and Ben counted the numbers of shops and homes as they went (the Senator's townhouse was Number 514). At the corner of 10th and E, they kept wandering south.

"All the street names are letters and numbers," Jem said. "Not very creative, were they?"

By and by they landed at the street's terminus, and here they looked upon a broad thoroughfare called Pennsylvania Avenue. From here, the whole of Washington was laid out for them.

Horse-drawn omnibuses rolled by, carrying commuters to and fro. Slaves walked with their masters and mistresses, and some hurried about on their owner's business with identification placards hung around their necks. Gangs of white laborers sidled down the dirt sidewalks after a long day's work. All slaves, whether they were dressed in rags or the finest suits and gowns their masters could afford, were compelled to step out of the white man's path and trod the muddy refuse trenches dug into the streets.

Across the bustling Avenue was a canal that fed into the broad Potomac, and beyond that was a stretch of woodlands and pastures where cattle grazed. Here and there could be seen the tops of buildings, some of them styled like Greek temples and others looking like castles picked up from Europe and dropped here in the New World.

Recalling a map of Washington he'd once studied in a book, Ben started to recognize the features of the city around him. "Look," he said, pointing. "There's the grounds of the Smithsonian Botanical Garden. There's the National Museum, the city gasworks, and that must be the Washington Armory. Over there is the Treasury Building I'd guess, and beyond that would be the White House, except we can't see it from here. And look, that clump of stone and scaffolding over there has got to be the Washington Monument. They started building it, oh, twelve years ago I'd say, but it was over budget almost from the beginning. Nobody's laid a new stone in five years."

Jem followed Ben's gaze and gestures, but it was clear that he gleaned a far lesser impression of the city than Ben did. "And how is it you know all these things?"

Ben shrugged. "I like to read, is all."

Looking to the northeast, Jem's eyes lit up. Pointing, he said, "I can at least tell you what *that* is."

Ben turned and saw the Capitol Building for the first time. The looming structure, home to the House of Representatives, the Senate, and the Supreme Court too, was the beating heart of the Union. Ben had thought the Capitol might be smaller than he imagined, but in fact it was much larger. Its long façade shimmered white in the October sun, though many sections were obscured by skeletal scaffolding. An ambitious project was underway to build a magnificent dome atop the Capitol, but the project managers were as embattled as those struggling to complete the Washington Monument. The dome was not set to be completed until 1865, which seemed to Ben an awfully long time away.

"Beautiful, isn't it?" Ben breathed.

Before the Capitol was a flat, tree-lined pasture where a large herd of cattle was grazing and groaning. As Ben and Jem watched the herd, a bull mounted a cow while two approving farmers looked on. In another corner of the field, a group of slaves were busy forking cow patties into a wagon.

"It's something all right," Jem said. "I wonder, when all the bigshots debate the future of the Union, do they look out the window for inspiration?"

Ben laughed with Jem, but he could not take his eyes off the unfinished dome of the Capitol. He wondered what it would be like to wander inside its hallowed halls, to look upon the sprawling House of Representatives in heated session, or to witness the stern, sober deliberations of the Senate. Of course, blacks were not permitted in the Capitol without a chaperone, and even then entry was never guaranteed. Though slaves had built the houses of government, their access to them was severely restricted.

Jem pointed his thumb back up 10th Street. "It's getting late."

"Right," Ben said, nodding. "We should be heading back."

He watched Jem start up the street. Ben lingered a moment longer to study the Capitol, its proud facades obscured by ugly scaffolding. He tried to imagine the building finished, complete with glittering dome and the Stars and Stripes fluttering over the city. But try as he did, Ben couldn't picture it.

"You coming?" Jem called.

"Coming," Ben said, and he turned his back to the Capitol and followed Jem back the way they came.

The interior of Ford's Atheneum loomed a tall three levels, but its grandeur was intimate. Looking up, Ben wondered if it was the billowing thunderhead of cigar smoke that made this so. Gaslight fixtures lined the walls, and three huge candelabras hung from the ceiling. Great hulking spotlights, powered by candlelight and large mirrors, cut arcs through the smoke and beamed upon blood red curtains.

There was a full house tonight for the Senator's speech. This being the last week of October, most assumed this would be John Roscoe's last public appearance before the election on November 6th. All the seats were occupied, but this being a political fundraiser many more bodies were permitted to sit and stand in the aisles (provided they paid the hefty admission fee). It was among this crowd that Ben now stood with Jem, who crossed his arms and tapped his feet in an agitated sort of way.

"Nervous?" Ben asked.

Jem nodded. "Sick with it. I'm not even going up there, and I feel a rock in my stomach."

Crashing cymbals split the dull roar like a thundercrack, and then a sweeping overture drowned out every conversation.

Ben peered up at the box seats that lined the galleries. There were many famous personages here tonight, including much of the Union Party faithful. Sitting in the president's box was Governor Sam Houston of Texas, together with the esteemed Kentucky senator John Crittenden. In the next box was the dour Senator John Bell of Tennessee. Rumor had it that Bell had once been a top contender for the Party's leadership — until John Roscoe became the candidate, of course.

Beside Bell was the Party's pick for vice president, Edward Everett of Massachusetts. Everett was the one man in the Party who was not a slave-owner — the one man save for John Roscoe himself, at least. Incidentally, it was well known aboard the 'Liberty & Union Express' that Everett and the Senator shared a vicious distrust of the other. Still, as the overture crashed in a heap and the red curtain was jerked upwards, Everett applauded as politely as the rest.

And there under the spotlight, was the man of the hour. A hush of silence, thickened by the sudden absence of the orchestra's music, filled the air.

Ben tried to imagine what the Atheneum must feel like from the Senator's perspective, blinded by god lights, squinting out at an empty, rustling, breathy blackness. No wonder Jem had a rock in his stomach; Ben felt one too, and it was working its way through his insides. It was one thing to write a few words on paper, but to *deliver* them?

And that was exactly what the Senator was about to do. Public performance seemed to be the only time the urgent flame of living shone out from him. At least, it was the only time the old man exhibited something of a soul. It was as if all John Roscoe's time of living before and after TONIGHT'S REMARKS was time he would rather not live through, for living *through* something meant suffering it or being bored by it. Onstage, the Senator seemed twenty years younger. There was a *belief* in his eyes that seemed to speak to every heart.

But still, a quiet voice within Ben whispered its reminder. Precious few of these other people (there were something like six hundred in attendance tonight), could fathom what John Roscoe was like *off* stage. Precious few had ever stood under the cold, unfeeling spotlight of his gaze. As far as anyone else was concerned, based on the broad, beaming smile on the Senator's face, John Roscoe was a gentleman they knew, and a gentleman who understood them.

"My friends," the Senator began. "In two short weeks, the people of our United States will elect one of four individuals its chief executive. This executive, standing at the vanguard of our Union, will face momentous issues such as have never been encountered before. We have a divided Congress; a flailing economy riven by sectional tariffs; a spineless judiciary; longstanding oversights in immigration, taxation, and foreign policy; not to mention the twin snake heads of secession and abolitionism. Note that I did not name the issue of *slavery*, friends. I suppose in that regard you may now pencil at least one tally mark in your diaries, though I can assure you that number will remain the same."

A polite laugh rippled through the smoke before another great, smoky silence swallowed it whole.

"Secession and abolitionism," the Senator said, placing his hands upon the sides of the podium. Even from Ben's vantage point, he could see the old man's white knuckles straining against the boards, his arms quivering. "These two rival causes of our time have little in common except that they both refute and reject, in practice and in principle, the spirit of a people's Union.

"This place we call America is not a realm of despots or kings, and it is altogether a better place because of that. Yet have we become sluggish in our modern times, and permitted ourselves to take our hard-won, hard-kept democracy for granted? Is it so naively pat and simplistic to still believe that America is, truly, a domain of the common people? Rich and poor, Christian and pagan, Democrat and Republican, we have all agreed to shelter in a single house with the Constitution as our roof. We agree that the shared burden of maintaining this house, especially the unity of its occupants, is our best chance to preserve peace and promote prosperity for all. So what can we say to those resentful factions tucked away in broom closets who claim to speak for the whole house? What are we to do with those vain few who would see the whole structure burned to the ground so that they may demand or coerce the construction of a new shelter, one built to *their* specifications? I say, it is a people's right and responsibility to send these pretenders out the door, where they can lord over the elements in the state of nature they so prefer. Let them coerce the rain. Let them condemn the sun. Let them revolt against the air they breathe."

Applause thundered. While Ben clapped along politely, he watched as much of the audience shot to their feet with wild cheers, their eyes wide with servile adoration of the man on stage. Ben laughed under his breath, and he wanted to get Jem's attention so they could share in the moment together. But when he turned to Jem, he saw that Jem was applauding just as fiercely as the others.

"I've often claimed that *compromise* is the beating heart of democracy," the Senator said. "It seems that, in recent times, the act of extending the olive branch has become unfashionable. Pundits have determined that to consider alternative points of view is a waste of time. Indeed, compromise has become synonymous with weakness. Nowadays, every man and his goat has an opinion, every newspaper and institution has an interest, and some men are too quick to lament the supposed trampling of their constitutional rights even while they shirk every responsibility required of a free citizen. It is all too rare that a public representative feels safe to vote and act according to his conscience. As our Union threatens to break apart, what are we to do? Shall we dig in our feet and hasten our Republic's demise, or shall we determine to come together in bonds of fellowship?"

More applause, and Ben found himself clapping along with the rest of the audience. But while the Senator's speech went on, Ben's eyes began to wander. His gaze rolled over the gray, thinning heads of the audience, until at last, far across the main floor, Ben thought he recognized someone.

...JJ?

JJ, or at least someone Ben *thought* was JJ, stood under the shadows of the far galleries. The figure stood erect, and he wore a military uniform and close-cropped hair. But there was such a crush of bodies, and it was so dark there under the awning, that Ben could not identify the figure with any certainty. But somehow, Ben knew that it was JJ standing there, watching the Senator's speech with intense focus.

Ben blinked and shook his head, and he told himself he had to be imagining things. Still, he had to be sure. He turned and touched Jem's arm.

"What is it?" Jem whispered, distracted.

Ben pointed across the orchestra, but then he saw that the figure was gone, disappeared into the crowd. Maybe the figure had never been there in the first place.

Jem shrugged and shot Ben a look of mild annoyance, and now he turned back to the Senator's speech.

After a long moment's confusion, Ben felt the hairs on the back of his neck stand up. JJ *was* here, lurking somewhere in the crowd, perhaps snaking his way closer to the stage. Could he have a weapon on him? Had he come here tonight to see to unfinished business? For God's sake, shouldn't Ben try to warn everyone?

But what could be done? He was wedged within a twitching mass of hundreds. If he shouted out some shrill warning, he might inspire a mass panic or stampede.

Would that be better or worse than witnessing an assassination here at Ford's Atheneum?

"Let me say something about my opponents," the Senator went on, "for they seem to have a great deal to say about me. But who are these so-called challengers, really? The Republican candidate has no commensurate experience in national leadership, save for a brief and ineffectual term in the House many years ago. Elect Lincoln, and what you'll really be doing is giving power to William Seward and other abolitionist radicals, who will rule from behind the throne. Would such a president lead us in the direction of unity?"

One cue, the crowd sounded their disapproval of the idea.

"Of course, there are others who intend to rule from behind the throne. One might think Vice President Breckenridge would make a capable chief executive, but who is the gleeful engineer who drives the Southern Democrats' train? It is William Yancey, a self-proclaimed Southern nationalist and disunionist who mocks our federal institutions. Would such a president lead us in the direction of unity?"

Once again the crowd shouted the idea down as a travesty.

"Indeed," the Senator said. "That leaves only the embattled Stephen A. Douglas, who sees American democracy, to borrow from Hobbes, as a war of all against all. Senator Douglas craves personal *kudos* above all else. Power is his only principle, and he has made public and private declarations that he will crush any and all dissenters. He will not compromise, and he will not seek a reconciliation between North and South. So I ask you once again, my friends, would such a president lead us in the direction of unity?"

While the crowd frothed and roiled, Ben's eyes found JJ in the crowd once more. JJ was indeed moving toward the stage, his unblinking eyes fixed on the Senator, and as he drew closer JJ opened the coat of his uniform and reached inside.

Ben's heart leapt into his throat. He opened his mouth to shout his best warning, but suddenly he was pushed aside by a heavy figure who barreled through the crowd. It was a young, pock-faced man who pointed two accusing fingers toward the stage.

"*CUR!*" the young man shouted, amid gasps from the crowd. "*We're not asleep anymore! Stand up, American brothers! Stand against the tyranny of the slave power!*"

With that, the protester pitched a glass bottle at the man on stage. The bottle soared through the air and missed the Senator by inches, and it shattered on the floor behind him.

Amid the ensuing pandemonium, Ben was pushed aside once again, this time by Jem, who lunged at the protester. While the crowd hissed and roared, the protester shook off grabbing hands and continued to holler his frantic message. A blade flashed in the darkness and nearly cut Jem's face open. Screams of panic sounded, but the next instant Jem snatched the protester's wrist and disarmed him while other men in the crowd pummeled the young man's kidneys.

Across the main floor, another protester revealed himself. This man threw not a bottle but a rotten onion, and this time the missile struck the Senator and sprayed him in foul juices. While others in the crowd grabbed him and dragged him outside, this second protester shouted, *"John Roscoe is a nigger lover!"*

Even as Mr. Welles and other staffers rushed the stage to guide the Senator to safety, a third dissenter stood up in the crowd.

"Southern traitors in our midst!"

To this, yet another new voice roared: *"Says the goddamn Yankee! Show yourself, you son of a bitch, and I'll show you how we treat traitors down in Pensacola!"*

And then the mountain came down. The crowd exploded: some roaring with indignation, others hurling jibes. Still more protesters leaped up, and Union Party supporters plunged forward to do battle with them. Tiny eddies of violence became one swallowing Charybdis, and Ben resisted the insane urge to laugh.

A breathless Jem found Ben in the crowd. "Come on," he said over the shouting. "Let's get backstage."

They moved slowly against the flow of people pushing their way to the exits. At last, they reached the doors leading backstage, which had been barred by staffers and police constables. After speaking with one of the constables, Jem and Ben were permitted to pass backstage.

The corridors backstage were dark, twisting, mazelike. Suddenly Ben remembered JJ, and the panicked idea struck him that they might bump into JJ here in the darkness. Had JJ been part of the protest?

They found the Senator tucked away in a dressing room, where Mr. Welles and several other staffers were busy cleaning rotten onion from his suit. The Senator was pale and sweating, and breathing heavily. Blood dribbled from the corner of his mouth, indicating he had just suffered a violent coughing fit. Jem whipped out a handkerchief and gingerly wiped the blood from his father's mouth.

"That was an excellent speech, Father," Jem said. "Very rousing, very true. Pay no mind to those Black Republican lowlifes out there."

Recalling the shouts of 'nigger-lover', Ben shook his head. "They weren't Republicans."

"One of them was waving a flag with Lincoln's face stamped on it," Jem said. "I should say they were Republicans all right."

"Maybe they were Democrat plants," Mr. Welles said. "A gift from Stephen Douglas."

"Or Breckinridge," a staffer said.

Agitated, the Senator slapped away the hands that were touching him. "Get the hell off me!"

"We should leave," Jem said. "There might be more commotion outside."

"We have a coach waiting," Welles said. "But where to go? We can't let you go home yet. Five-Fourteen is just across the street."

"Willard's," the Senator huffed. "Take us to the Willard Hotel. I could use a drink."

"Yes, sir." Welles turned and snapped his fingers, and the small army of staffers began to move out.

The Senator was led out of the dressing room and through the winding backstage corridors. Jem grabbed the Senator's overcoat, which had been left behind, and moved to follow. Thinking of JJ lurking somewhere, Ben put a hand on Jem's shoulder.

"Jem, I need to talk to you—"

"It'll have to wait," Jem said curtly. "I'll go with Father to Willard's. You'll be fine, yes? Get yourself back to 514, and lock the door. We'll return in good time."

Ben thought to insist, but for whatever reason, he didn't. Maybe it was the wild look in Jem's eyes that stopped him. Jem wore the look of a caged wildcat, and he seemed prepared to lash out at anybody, even Ben himself.

"Right," Ben said. "You go. I'll stay back."

Ben staggered into the darkness of the Senator's townhouse and shut the door behind him. All at once the sounds of the unrest outside were muffled. After locking the door, Ben leaned heavily against the frame and caught his breath. His brow ached from where a stranger in the street had struck him, but he knew he had been lucky. A brawl had opened in the street outside Ford's Atheneum, which was just now being broken up by constables on horseback.

The Senator and his entourage were off to the Willard Hotel. They would not return until the commotion on 10th Street calmed down, which probably wouldn't happen for several hours.

The Willard Hotel housed perhaps the most luxurious smoking room in Washington. Certainly the Willard was a *who's-who* sort of place, where the lobby was host to games of chance and intrigue by senators, generals, bureaucrats, and would-be political players. Ben briefly considered walking his way across town to try his luck at the door, but he knew it would be pointless. No *maître d'* of any of Washington's fine establishments, and certainly not at the Willard Hotel, would let someone like him through the door. That wasn't feeling sorry for himself; it was just plain fact.

It was getting dark outside, and already dark within the empty townhouse. Ben's blood was still pumping hot, so there was no chance he would sleep. Lighting an oil lamp in the hallway, Ben decided he would spend a little time exploring 514.

At first glance, there was nothing extravagant about the place. Where Clarendon was a palace of excess, this narrow burrow was rather spartan. Of course, the effect was diminished somewhat by the occupation of slovenly campaign staffers, who seemed to be engaged in a game of who could build the largest rubbish pile. Half-smoked cigars lay crushed on tabletops, stationery papered all the chairs and chesterfields, and stacks of newspapers balanced atop uneaten lunches from three days ago.

"Mama would have a fit," Ben whispered to nobody, and he laughed softly in the pleasant darkness.

Down a long hallway was a humble kitchen that led out to a mud yard. There was an outhouse there, together with a cramped building that had to be a stables of some kind. Peering out the door, Ben spied a sag-bellied cat watching him.

Suddenly, Ben thought about his 'room' up in the attic. There was that hulking thing under the white sheet that might be worth investigating. Otherwise, maybe he would find some books up there (certainly there seemed to be none here on the main floor). And yes, a little reading at the end of a long, troublesome day sounded like just the ticket.

Ben took the shadowed stairs slowly. As he reached a landing halfway up, the light revealed a sneering face right next to him. Ben reeled, frightened, but it was only a stone bust that stared back at him.

Only a statue. He had to laugh at himself for that.

The stone visage he looked at belonged to Colonel Spencer, or so Ben first thought. The face had a Roman nose to set the standard for all others, except somewhere in time the nose had broken off, whether by accident or by vandalism. The stone man's unseeing eyes were huge and focused eternally on the horizon. Its lips were carved open, with a slit for an open mouth, as if the man was in the rapture of something grand. It was now that Ben wondered whether he could still trust his memory of his former master's likeness. There were so many paintings of the Colonel back at Clarendon, but none of the portraits looked alike. And when he tried to picture the Colonel now, he could only see the back of the man's head under a floppy Panama hat.

Could it be that the statue was of John Roscoe himself? Somehow, the stone face exuded the Senator's essence. Still, the closer Ben looked, the less sure he was of the idea. The Senator was a vain man, but Ben did not seriously believe he would commission a bust of himself. The stone man could be anyone, even an old half-remembered hero who had never really existed.

Ben continued upstairs to the attic. Setting the lamp down, he rummaged about a few cases and boxes in search of reading material. He searched a suitcase and found nothing but old linens, and the next box he searched was filled with tiny metal letters of the kind typesetters use. Pulling out an old trunk, Ben discovered heaps of dry, yellow paper within.

Old memoirs? A diary? Ben felt a finger of shame drive down his throat. He certainly did not want to pry into someone's life. That was especially the case if these letters belonged to the Senator.

But no, the papers seemed to contain nothing intimate. Any letters he found were pieces of official correspondence with banks and legal firms, and many bore the personal letterheads of senators. Stuffed below these pages was a leather book, which Ben hoped might be an encyclopedia of some kind. Instead, when he opened to a random page he saw the book was a ledger of the kind used in transactions. Scrawled within the top margin was a name:

JOYOUS LATIMER, NEGRO SALES

The finger sliding down Ben's throat became a fist, as if someone had plunged their hand down his esophagus to pluck out his stomach. He shut the book and looked closer at the front cover. There, pressed into the leather, was a symbol of twin eagles, their talons and beaks locked in mortal battle.

Clarendon. The book was from *Clarendon.*

Ben opened to the same page as before. Tracing down the page, Ben read the contents of the ledger.

ITEM	DESCRIPTION	CONSIDERATION	NAME	DATE
'Celi'	*40 yrs (approx), and child*	*$300*	*J. Cready, Frankfort KY*	9/1/40
'Phibe'	*40 yrs, no children*	*$135*	*P.M. Thompson, NO LA*	9/1/40
'Polly'	*16 yrs, likely*	*$400*	*P.M. Thompson, NO LA*	9/1/40
Jackson Spencer†	*50 yrs, hand*	*$100*	*T. Merrick, Mayfair VA*	9/1/40
'Moses'	*15 yrs, likely, bright*	*$800*	*T. Cutler, Mayfair VA*	9/1/40
George Spencer†	*20-30 yrs, hand & ginner*	*$775*	*W. Ellison, Charleston SC*	9/1/40
Deborah Spencer†	*3-5 yrs, sickly*	*$75*	*Rachel Felton, Athens GA*	9/1/40
Walter Spencer†	*0-3 yrs, c'pox recovery*	*$125*	*Rachel Felton, Athens GA*	9/1/40
'Andie'	*14 yrs, fair complexion, virgin*	*$700*	*Q. Barnwell, Franklin TN*	9/1/40

For Ben, the full weight of what he read did not hit him all at once. Somehow he lost himself in the details, noting how tiny crosses marked those bearing the Colonel's surname, possibly suggesting they were baptized with Christian names. The other names were noted in quotations, endearing monikers like those given to family pets.

Ben scanned down the page, his eyes searching for a date of sale that wasn't the First of September 1840. Finding none — after *thirty pages of names* — Ben tried to think back to that day and couldn't picture it. It was after Daddy was sold away, that he was sure of. And probably it was after the Colonel had died. But what was one day twenty years ago compared to another? He had been a child back then, and in the intervening years he'd done his best to forget as much of those times as he possibly could. Still, he knew he had to have at least *some* memory of such a large auction, what Mama and the others had called a *leaving*. These ledger lines represented a truly massive exodus of people. As far as Ben could remember, the only great leaving he knew was when John Roscoe, ever the quiet critic of slavery, manumitted all of Clarendon's as soon as he assumed the deed of the estate...

The ledger trembled in Ben's hands. Squinting and blinking, Ben tried to convince himself he was only seeing things. He read and re-read the signature again and again. It was a fake, or else some cruel trick. It had to be...

Son of a bitch.

There, under the last item, was a signature: *John M. Roscoe*.

Crouched in the darkness, Ben sat very still for a long while. He ran his thumb over the dried ink to make sure it was real, and then only for something to do while his thoughts ran headless in circles.

A hasty summation of the Consideration column — just less than five hundred names, with an average price of, what, $350? — counted almost two hundred thousand dollars in profits. Enough to give Clarendon's longtime overseers handsome compensation on their way out the door. Enough to dig a mine shaft into the heart of the North Branch. Enough to launch a political career.

Suddenly, an idea thrust its way into Ben's mind. He tore through the ledger again, his eyes reading faster than ever before, and he swept from page to page in a frantic search.

Joby. Was there a Joby listed here somewhere?

And just how much had Daddy been worth?

Ben found no record of his father. He was lost somewhere beyond the margins of the ledger, as if he had never existed in the first place.

Ben did not know how long he sat there slumped over, head down, the ledger clutched against his chest. He thought at several times to take the ledger down to the yard outside and set the fucking thing on fire, but he could not bring himself to move an inch.

Suddenly, from downstairs, Ben heard the click of a latch. The front door opened, and floating up to him came voices and shuffling footsteps. He heard Jem's clear-ringing voice for sure, and there also, murmuring in a lower register...

Ben stared at John Roscoe's signature a final time before he shut the ledger, tucked the book under his shoulder, and stood up. He kicked the open trunk into the darkness, watched dull-eyed as a groaning tower of junk collapsed in a heap. Leaving the oil lamp on the table, Ben descended the darkened stairs with heavy feet.

He found Jem and the Senator in the front parlor. The Senator was leaning back on a chesterfield, a cigar clamped between his teeth. Jem stood before an upright piano in the corner, glass of gin in hand, and with the other he keyed a discordant melody.

When Ben entered the parlor, the Senator's face brightened. "Ah, Ben! Come join us, my boy. We're in the throes of celebration."

"Throes of war, you mean," Jem said. He turned away from the piano, and Ben saw that half of Jem's face was red and raw. "Some bastard outside Ford's took a swipe at me with a belt," he went on. "A goddamn *belt*! Can you believe it? I would have strangled the Republican son of a bitch with his own weapon if the crowd hadn't swallowed him up."

The Senator puffed clouds of smoke. "Tonight tells us one thing. They're agitated, every one of my opponents — especially Stephen. They know I'm catching up, that it's not just the Border States who are listening. Who knows, Stephen might have planted those hecklers at the Atheneum, just like Mr. Welles said."

Jem shook his head. "Those men could have *killed* you, Father. Maybe it was only bottles and onions in the theater, but outside it was rocks and knives. Where in God's name were the city constables? I don't care if those criminals are Yankee Republicans or Yancey's boys, their assault on you is an assault on everything we stand for."

Jem went to the window and peered out from behind the curtains. "Is the Federal government going to do nothing to protect a man in high public office? No doubt the Feds were behind it somehow. President Buchanan doesn't trust you, and he'd sooner see you gone. You ought to write to Governor Wise, Father, and rouse the home guard for your protection. If only I'd known all this was waiting for us, I might have brought our pistols from home..."

Ben remained there in the middle of the floor. He remembered that shadowy man back at Ford's, the man he thought had been JJ.

But now Ben's thoughts returned to the ledger tucked under his arm. *That* was what mattered right now — not the twins and not the goddamn campaign, and certainly not the old liar's last kick at the fucking can. He thought only about the name Moses in the ledger, and about the other four hundred and sixty-three names too.

"How was Willard's?" Ben asked, his throat tight.

Jem drained his glass and began to pour another. "Oh, fine. We had dinner. What about you, Ben, did you eat?"

Ben clenched his jaw. "I wasn't hungry."

Ben felt the Senator's eyes on him. The old man was watching him, had noticed the change in him. With a smile creeping across his lips, the Senator said, "Won't you sit down with us, Ben? It's been a day."

Ben let out a long breath. "It certainly has. But I'd rather remain standing."

"Suit yourself." The Senator put his feet up and ashed his cigar on the floor. "Jeremiah?"

Jem looked up from the hearth, where he was presently building a fire. "Yes, sir?"

"A pillow for my feet, Jeremiah."

Jem abandoned his project and went to a nearby sofa, and he returned with a throw pillow. His father lifted up his feet and Jem slid the pillow underneath, and the feet came down to rest again. Watching all this, Ben felt his stomach churn. The ledger under his arm weighed a hundred pounds.

The Senator nodded at the ledger. "What's that you've got there, Ben? More speeches for me, I hope." He laughed. "Don't tell me it's more letters to Justice Taney about that damn Dred Scott."

Ben said nothing in response. Instead he stepped forward and offered the ledger out to the old man.

The Senator's smile hung on its hinges. "But what is it?" he asked, his humor fading. "I've far too much to *read* at all times, Ben. Can't you just give a summary? And be concise."

Ben offered the ledger again. "There's not much I can say about it, Senator. Open the book, if you please. I rather think it speaks for itself."

Jem turned to Ben, the fire poker still in his grasp. "What is it, Ben? Message from one of the other campaigns?"

The Senator took the ledger at last, and he rested it upon his lap. Ben watched as the old man drew a long drag, and with the other hand he opened the ledger to the first page. He read the contents slowly, his eyes dragging left to right, but then Ben saw it — the blink, and then the conscious pulling down of a mask of ignorance.

"And what is all this supposed to mean?"

Ben stared back at him, stone-faced. "Turn to the last page."

The Senator sighed and shook his head, as if vaguely bemused. "Why should I—?"

"*Turn to the last page*," Ben hissed.

Jem took a sharp breath. "Easy does it there, Ben. Just what's the matter? What's got you uppity?"

Ben ignored Jem, though he wanted nothing more than to tell him to shut up. The last page of the ledger was open on the Senator's lap, and Ben pointed down at it.

"Read the last two entries."

The Senator stared at Ben a moment longer, his gaze lidded, before he relented and looked down at the page. His eyes did not linger there long before they flickered up to Ben once more.

"Read it," Ben breathed. "Read it out loud, so Jem might hear."

"Hear *what?*" Jem said. "What's with all the damn theatrics?"

The Senator shook his head. Leaning forward, he dropped the ledger on the small table before him. "I'm not going to read it."

"Then I will," Ben said, his mouth bone dry. "There are two names there. Mae

Jane, Benjamin. No last name. How is it Mama's described? *Likely, faithful; three hundred dollars*. And Ben: *six, perhaps seven years, sickly; two hundred fifty dollars*. Both mother and son were purchased together via Joyous Latimer, Negro Sales by one Tobias Cutler of Mayfair, Virginia. But then, do you see? Someone crossed out the names. As it turned out, Mama and I weren't for sale. Still, it's good to know what we are really and truly *worth* to a man like you."

The Senator stared icily up at Ben while cigar smoke wreathed around his nostrils.

Jem reached down for the ledger on the table, but the Senator snarled and rapped Jem across the knuckles with his cane. Jem drew back and nursed his hand, and the ledger lay unread. Lifting one of his feet, the Senator shut the ledger.

"There are almost five hundred names in there," Ben said. "Less two, of course. And all these years, I really did believe the story of John Roscoe, the Great Liberator. John Roscoe, the self-made man of action, who feels for the plight of the downtrodden, and who seeks to institute slow but meaningful changes from within — my God, what a man to believe in! What a lodestar in which to place one's deepest faith. If I'm being honest, I even believed some of the things you said tonight. The way you spoke on stage at the Atheneum, Senator, I know *you* believed it all."

"Because it's the truth," the Senator replied.

Ben tried to swallow the hot lump that had formed in his throat, but he could not. "No," he croaked, shaking his head. He pointed at the open ledger. "That's the truth, right there. And you've been lying about it for twenty years. Not even Lady Isabella knows. Not even your own children."

The Senator shrugged and smoked. "Withholding elements of the truth is not the same as lying. What would you have preferred I do? Climb atop the North Branch and shout to the world that I, too, had sullied myself with slavery? The Colonel had gambled away the Spencer family's future — the *Roscoe* family's future too. Bankers were coming to take Clarendon, to take everything. If you really think you would have acted any differently, Ben, you would be lying to yourself. Those who asked for their freedom — like your mother — were granted it. For some others, a difficult choice had to be made."

Ben threw a bitter laugh on the floor. "Difficult. I'm sure."

In his mind's eye, Ben could remember that day of the great leaving. He could still see all those people walking down the tree-lined path at Clarendon, many about to leave the grounds for the first time in their lives. He remembered them wearing happy faces and singing, and many were weeping. But could he trust that memory? Maybe they had been *told* they were walking to their freedom, when in fact they were being led up to Harper's Ferry to be shackled and shoved into the holds of steamboats. Others would soon be dragged back to Mayfair and sold across the Valley to plantations along the South Branch. Did any of those people guess what was really happening to them? Had any thought to try and escape? Did any of them make an attempt later? And what had they thought of him, little Ben, unknowingly waving at them and laughing goodbye?

Suddenly, Ben's mind returned to the parlor within the Senator's townhouse. The Senator was droning on about something, and as the old man spoke, it took everything for Ben not to lunge and strike him.

"...and what's more, you should speak with that colored supporter of mine," the Senator was saying. "He's from, where is it, Jeremiah — Annapolis? Somewhere. He's an ex-slave like yourself, but who now owns slaves of his own. He turned the system around to work in his favor, and there he is, as much a planter as Clay Claiborne. If you want to talk about social progress, Ben, there's a fine example of how to—"

"What about my father?" Ben said.

The Senator paused. "I beg your pardon?"

"*My father*," Ben said. "Joby. The man who was castrated like a fucking animal while you stood there and watched—"

"*Christ*, Ben," Jem said. "Will you just stop all this?"

"Shut up," Ben hissed. "You open your mouth again, Jem, and I'll shut it for you." He turned to look at the Senator once again. "There's no record of my father. What happened to him?"

The old man shrugged. "I don't know."

"*What happened to him*."

"I tell you, *I-don't-know*!" the Senator growled. "That was back in the Colonel's time. God rest his soul, my father-in-law wasn't much of a record-keeper. So what else do you want me to goddamn say about it?"

Ben shook his head. "There's nothing more to say." He went to the table and snatched up the ledger. "Nothing," he said, "except that you can no longer pretend you're some high-minded idealist — not anymore. You always say that nothing good may happen before its proper time. Well, now is the time when the contents of this little ledger is going to blow your whole campaign wide open. I'm going to take this to the newspapers, and I'm going to tell them *everything*."

The Senator laughed. "Oh, you hear that, Jeremiah? Ben's going to go the newspapers."

"Whatever happens," Ben said, "it won't be half what you deserve."

"Try it," the Senator said, seemingly bored with the whole conversation. "You'll find it's a big world out there, Ben, and it doesn't give a damn about what anyone deserves."

Ben wanted to stay. He wanted to root himself there and shout at the old man until he was hoarse. He wanted to unleash all the hateful vitriol that had been churning inside him for hours now. It took everything for him to turn on his heels and make for the door.

Jem blocked his path. He was not angry or mocking, and in fact there was a deep sadness in his eyes. Still, it was clear that Jem was not simply going to let Ben pass by.

"If you walk out that door," Jem warned, "you're a traitor to this family."

Ben looked long into Jem's eyes. There was something of the old Jem there, and maybe always would be. But something had changed, maybe since the accident on the Branch, and certainly since Jem had joined his father's campaign. It was clear enough to Ben that Jem Roscoe, that rootless maverick, had finally found his cause.

"Traitor to the family?" Ben echoed. "Like JJ, you mean?"

Jem stood unmoving, his expression stonelike.

Ben gestured back at the Senator. "Meanwhile, you've allowed yourself to become his lapdog. So tell me, Jem, what's worse: being a traitor to others, or to yourself?"

Having said this, Ben shouldered Jem aside. He more than half expected Jem to grab him from behind, and his body was tensed for a brutal fight. But he made it to the townhouse's foyer unimpeded, and he was through the door and standing outside in the cool late October air before he realized exactly what he was doing.

From inside, Ben now heard the Senator's voice calling to him.

"Don't be a fool, Ben! You would abandon our great cause in the hour of victory? Why must you insist on condemning the past when we could discuss the future? Don't you understand, we are going to *win* this election? Lincoln and Breckinridge will split the radical vote, and Douglas has been declawed. Soon enough it will be over — soon enough we can *begin*. Finally, I can get to work on all those great ideas we discussed: ideas of liberty and opportunity and justice. Now that we possess the necessary power, now that the *proper time* has finally arrived, we can shape a legacy which will stand the test of time. Now is the time where—"

Ben slammed the door shut behind him, and he heard no more from John Roscoe.

Ben shivered. There was a chill fog in the air, and the streets were wet. A city lamplighter was coming up the street, lighting gas-lamps as he went. Shining from within windows were the warm glows of candles and kerosene lamps, and as the night air felt its way down his spine Ben realized he had left without his trunk, without clothes, without even his overcoat.

But really, what did such things matter? He had some money with him, enough for a train ticket, at least. And he had the ledger — *that* was worth more than anything.

Ben turned up 10th Street, heading in the direction of the lighted streets. It was of course dangerous for a man like him to walk about the streets of Washington alone at night. He'd heard enough stories of Washington freedmen who were kidnapped and sold into slavery that his mind sharpened to the sights and sounds of the night. Still, Ben felt a lightness in his step. He looked up at the gas-lamps and thought them beautiful, their glowing pattern hinting at some sort of predestined pathway.

John Roscoe was a man who claimed he didn't believe in destiny, and maybe he was right about that. In recent time, Ben himself had come to seriously doubt the idea that there was any deeper meaning to the confused, chaotic ways of the world. Still, as he walked alone through the quiet streets of Washington, with the living record of so many people — *his* people — tucked under his arm, Ben could not help but feel that the gas-lamps were leading him somewhere meaningful, somewhere he was destined to reach.

In less than two weeks, on November 6th, the United States would elect a new president.

Chapter 29

THE RAILSPLITTER ASCENDANT

Fireworks exploded over the Willard Hotel. Huge columns of orange fire streaked through the night sky. The air was colored a sickly gray by a choking cloud of powder smoke and showering sparks. Though it was by now well after midnight, cannons boomed and bells tolled. No one, it seemed, wanted to let this historic day pass into the next without a celebration of some kind. Or a fight.

Clutched in peoples' hands, their pages ravaged by eye and mind and tearing grasp, the papers' front-page stories of the hour were the newest reports from Washington, and those wired in from every major newspaper east of the Mississippi.

It was just before midnight on November 6th. To the shock and disbelief of the Union, the announcement came that Abraham Lincoln would be the 16th President of the United States.

JJ Roscoe stalked down Pennsylvania Avenue, his face flashing and darkening in the flare of Roman candles. He moved quickly, eager to avoid the impending clash of Republican revelers and Democrat protesters. His destination was the Willard. Being so close to the White House, the Willard was often host to congressmen, visiting governors, former presidents, heads of state, even monarchs.

Tonight, the Willard was host to drunks, scoundrels, and lowlifes of all stripes.

JJ paused outside the hotel and peered through the windows. The hotel bar was the site of a great and terrible debauchery. Men from all four presidential campaigns were singing, drinking, buying prostitutes by the minute for hourly prices, and showering praise and insults on each other in the same breath. There was a lineup out the door, with a supposed four hour wait for a table. Though JJ was joining a previously booked reservation, he used this opportunity to get some fresh air and take the pulse of a city descending into chaos.

The wind flung scattered newspapers about. JJ caught the headlines in brief flashes. Northern papers had exultant lines: SWEEPING REPUBLICAN VICTORY and THE RAILSPLITTER ASCENDANT!

Southern papers were more apocalyptic in tone: IMPEACHMENT OR WAR! and BRECKINRIDGE VOWS TO FIGHT ELECTION FRAUD and SHAM REPUBLICAN VICTORY REIGNITES SECESSION DEBATE.

JJ lit a cigar and puffed on it. The sound of heavy boots echoed up the street. Stamping into view came an army of chanting men dressed in oil-cloth capes and hoods. They carried torches and American flags embroidered with the visage of Lincoln. Others in their ranks carried banners painted with a single, unblinking eye.

An old man standing near JJ chewed his pipe and said, to no one in particular, "Wide Awakes."

For months now, the cause of the 'Wide Awakes' had seized the attention of young men all across the Union, especially in the Northern states. The organization's radical, single-minded devotion to the Republican Party, combined with its militant structure, was endlessly appealing to American youths who sought to plant themselves firmly against the old, conservative ideas that their parents held with such dogmatic reverence. As he studied the young men tramping about with divine purpose in each step, JJ couldn't help but laugh. If only they weren't Republicans, the Wide Awakes' romantic idiocy was just the kind of thing that would appeal to Jem.

"Devil's spawn," another man nearby hissed. "They're a gang of Satan-worshipers, I tell you. Just look at that ghastly eyeball they idolize. What in God's name does it even mean?"

Just then a hooded man broke ranks and stepped up to the door of the Willard. "Hear this, old men!" he shouted in a shrill voice for all to hear. "We are the youth of this country! We are fervent in our belief and steadfast in our cause. We are swept up, as you shall be, by the Republican tide of good government, good leadership, and su-preme *good* for all."

"And *we* are sick and tired of your screeching!" the old pipe-chewer cried. "Come back when your voice drops, little girl."

The other men at the door laughed aloud. JJ smiled and smoked.

If the Wide Awake felt any emotion at the insult, his black hood concealed it. His voice rang out, louder than before: "This country is changing. We young Republicans intend to drive that change forward, and claim a new America for ourselves."

"You mean claim it for your nigger friends," the pipe-chewer said.

The Wide Awake said, "Your Union is dead, you old and fearful man. Ours is the future." With that, he turned and joined his comrades as a thousand voices rang out:

Ain't you glad you joined the Republicans—
Joined the Republicans—
Joined the Republicans—
Ain't you glad you joined the Republicans
Down in Illinois?

The old man spat. "Goddamn kids."

A gunshot rang out. A large group of Democratic protesters had appeared a hundred yards down 14th Street. Some broke ranks to hurl rocks at the Wide Awakes while others smashed nearby storefront windows with clubs. In one voice they cried for an official recount, Lincoln's head on a pike, and, at the very least, a good and honest street fight. In answer, the Wide Awakes brandished bats and clubs they had concealed under their capes and tramped off to meet their enemy with throaty cheers.

JJ stepped into the Willard. Before the second set of doors, he passed a young *maître d'* who hailed him.

"I'm sorry, sir. We're full tonight."

"No matter," JJ said. "I'm meeting someone."

Before the *maître d'* could say anything, JJ turned and passed into the lobby. He hit a wall of cigar smoke and could barely make out the shape of a long bar stretching across a wide, high-ceilinged room flanked with columns. Through the haze, he spied billiards tables and sofa sets and several tables occupied by gangs of men.

JJ felt a hand close on his arm, and the *maître d'* pulled JJ over to one side.

"I recognize you," the man whispered urgently. "Please, don't go where I can't find you. What's your name?"

JJ blinked. "What?"

The *maître d'* leaned in to whisper into JJ's ear. He felt the man's lips brush lightly against his skin, making the hairs on his neck stand up straight. "There's an old storeroom at the end of the hall on the second floor. No one ever goes there, and it locks from the inside. I'll meet you there in an hour. Understand? One hour. But I won't open the door unless I know you're alone. So what's your name? Mine is—*Hey*!"

JJ pinned the *maître d'* against the wall and yanked one of the man's arms behind his back. He growled into the man's ear, "I don't want to know your fucking name, you pox degenerate. Touch me like that again — *look* at me like that again — and I'll be obliged to have a word with the hotel manager about you and what you like to do in that storeroom. Understood?"

The man whimpered and hung his head.

JJ pulled the man's arm back, threatening to tear it from its socket. "*Understood?*"

"Yes — *yes*! For God's sake, *yes*."

JJ let the *maître d'* go. The smoke screen within the lobby had obscured this altercation to most curious onlookers. The *maître d'* hurried away, leaving JJ alone to check himself in a nearby mirror. In the reflection, JJ saw the old pipe-chewer staring in at him from a nearby window. JJ turned and shot the man a dark glare before he plunged into the smoky lobby and made straight for the bar.

JJ was doing well in Washington, or at least as well as could be expected of a junior officer. The only problem was that his commanding officer was a desk jockey, and that made JJ one too.

As the summer waned, JJ began to crave for some dramatic crisis where he could show his quality. Instead, his days were spent following the presidential campaign, and in particular the progress of Father's bid for the White House. He knew Father visited Washington often, and usually frequented the Willard Hotel, but JJ had never been able to glimpse him across the smoky barroom. JJ had gone to one of Father's stump speeches at Ford's Atheneum, but nerves overwhelmed him and he decided to flee. He had made straight for the nearest saloon and ordered himself a drink, and then another. It did not take long for him to get roaring drunk, a sensation he decided he quite enjoyed.

The hot summer and dry autumn of 1860 had been a lonely time for JJ. He slowly discovered, to great surprise and rather sincere dismay, that there were certain men who took eager notice of him. They seemed to register a certain look in his eyes, or noted the way he carried himself, or maybe they were drawn to the pungent cologne he wore. Some were bachelors and others were married, some were old and others were his own age. In all cases, despite whatever thrilling sensations flared within him thanks to such meaningful attention, JJ spurned any hushed encounter that might even be remotely considered an advance. He determined to stamp down that thrilling feeling whenever it came to him, to banish any and all lurid thoughts that popped into his head, and to go about his business by day or night with a cool, steely disposition that warned off all interested glances. Evidently, he had let his guard down tonight, for the Willard Hotel's *maître d'* had glimpsed whatever it was he was hiding behind the veil.

But unfortunately for the *maître d'*, JJ had learned a few months ago that sometimes it wasn't enough to rebuff the eager suggestions of strangers. Sometimes it was necessary to break bones, and thus prove to himself time and again that Father's opinion of his firstborn son had been horribly wrong: JJ Roscoe was not and never would be *that kind of man*.

Tonight, within the Willard Hotel lobby, US Army officers roamed about in the midst of a wild hurricane. They were captains, majors, colonels, and here and there a general or two. These officers spoke in hushed voices with men of disparate political factions, but they bought drinks for only members of the Republican Party. The Republicans, after all, would be the ones making special appointments in the War Department for the foreseeable future.

JJ worked his jaw (it had developed an audible *click* ever since his ricochet wound healed), and meandered across the room.

A man looked up as JJ passed and flashed him a look not unlike the *maître d'* had given him moments earlier. JJ stared the stranger down with a face of stone. Another man looked up, his eyes were merely curious, not suggestive. More men regarded JJ, and he felt their eyes pick him apart piece by piece: the second lieutenant's insignia, the nascent mustache only just beginning to darken on his upper lip, the way JJ seemed not to recognize any face he looked upon. JJ decided his entire manner must scream 'junior officer, probable Democrat, without prospects.'

Stepping up to the bar, JJ put a nickel down and ordered a mint julep.

"Jem?" a voice called. "Jem Roscoe, is it?"

JJ turned and looked into the eyes of a young man. He was a staff clerk of some kind, probably with one of the campaigns. Instantly the man's eyes shifted from a look of happy recognition to crippling doubt.

"You...you're not...you're not with John Roscoe's campaign, are you?"

"No," JJ replied haughtily. "What the fuck do you want?"

Embarrassed, the man gave a little bow. "My mistake," he said, and he fled the bar.

JJ watched him go. For a moment he thought to follow the man, to put a fist in his face and demand to know just what he meant about asking for *Jem* Roscoe. Was Jem in Washington now? Had he become one of Father's cronies? But of course he had. The question was, would Jem be at the Willard later? JJ's body trembled at the thought. And here he was, with a revolver and saber attached to his belt...

JJ's drink arrived. He downed it in one gulp and ordered another.

"Roscoe! It's good to see you."

JJ took a breath of grim resolve and turned around. Who had mistaken him for his brother this time?

Instead, he looked up at the faces of two fellow graduates from the Point. There was Osborne on his left, Cready on his right. Cready was the first to extend his hand.

"Pleasure as always, *Lieutenant*."

Cready was wearing his second lieutenant's insignia on his dress uniform just like JJ and was waiting for JJ to notice.

JJ formed a carefully constructed smile on his lips. He took Cready's hand, then Osborne's. "Good to see you, gents." He only half meant it, but at least it was something to say.

They looked out at the party and Cready sneezed. Cready was a sickly man and his nose dripped like a faucet gummed with calcium. He blew his nose noisily. "The world's going to hell, isn't it?" he said under the tent of his handkerchief.

JJ nodded. "Seems that way."

Cready blew his nose again and pushed his wet handkerchief in his pocket. "Think they'll loot the White House?" It was a question Cready seemed to have already asked several men that night, always expecting interesting answers but having gleaned no satisfying responses thus far.

Osborne, meanwhile, had heard Cready's question one too many times. "Why don't you take a walk over there if you're so goddamn curious? Report back on the color of the First Lady's bloomers."

Cready fell silent, but when JJ looked at him he smiled and shrugged it off, as if the two of them silently agreed that Osborne didn't have a sense of humor anyway.

The sounds of the street battle outside began to overtake the sounds of the party. Men stood up from their tables and went to the windows to gaze out at the melee.

JJ looked at Osborne and noted with biting jealousy that the man wore the gold insignia of a first lieutenant. Just how the hell had he gotten promoted in just a few short months? JJ had also heard a rumor that Dodson Ramseur had been promoted to captain. *Captain*!

"Think anyone's going to kill somebody out there?" JJ asked.

Osborne shrugged. "Wouldn't be election night if they didn't."

The hotel door opened and three haggard men stepped inside to escape the melee without. With them came the frantic sounds of the street battle: police whistles shrieking, men shouting, others screaming, clubs and fists hitting bodies, bodies hitting the ground. All conversation suspended for a moment and all ears fixed on the sounds of violence. But presently the door swung shut again, and the screams and war-cries were muffled. A beet-faced hotel manager snapped his fingers and waved his arms frantically. Presently a collection of beautiful ladies from upstairs came down to entertain the guests with smiles and busting bosoms. Soon enough the old drunks returned to their merriment, and the hotel manager appeared satisfied.

Osborne's eyes followed the girls hungrily. "Ought to find ourselves some company tonight," he said with a wide grin. "The whole city's celebrating, one way or another. Look there, Roscoe. That brunette has her eyes on you now, but she'll soon have them on me."

JJ's julep finally arrived. He put the glass to his lips and looked through the large windows to the street beyond. Rather than quash the violence, policemen and soldiers had taken opposite sides in the conflict and were just now turning their weapons on each other. In the midst of it all, a man shuffled out of the melee, pulled down his trousers, and defecated in the street.

"Isn't it just beautiful?" Osborne said. "That's democracy for you. Right there."

JJ watched all this with a glazed expression. He registered surprise only when he brought his julep glass to his lips and found it dry.

"Let me get that for you," Osborne said. He poured whiskey from a bottle into JJ's mint-garnished glass, and now he raised the bottle in a toast. "To the president."

The trio drank.

Having finished yet another drink, JJ stared at the bottom of the glass. He tried to remember when the fog of drunkenness had settled into his mind.

"Who do you think Lincoln will name to his cabinet?" Cready asked.

JJ shrugged. "Who cares?"

Osborne whistled and grinned knowingly. "Not pleased with the outcome, eh, Roscoe?"

"I'll tell you who won't be pleased," Cready said. "My relations in Kentucky. Wife's side. Her daddy would roll in his grave if he knew a nigger-lover like Lincoln was living in the big-house. He took it hard enough when Sadie came up to Maine to marry me."

"Lincoln's no savior for the slaves," JJ said. "He thinks slavery's a sort of disease rotting the Union from the inside out, and no arguments there. But he opposes negro equality as much as every other man in the Union. And what does he propose to do? Ship four million people off to Liberia or some damn place. The idea is asinine." Finally, he turned to Osborne. "I'm *not* pleased with the outcome, to answer your question."

JJ felt Cready's wet breath over his shoulder. "You wanted your daddy to win, didn't you? Oh, I certainly wish he'd made a bigger splash. The Border States made their voices heard, so to speak."

Osborne flashed a knowing smile. "So to speak. Quite the scandal the *Star* cooked up about ol' JR, don't you think?"

JJ shrugged. "What, that story about him selling my grandfather's slaves?" He shook his head. "Nothing but the empty accusations of a crank. Though I must say, if it were true, I wouldn't be surprised in the least."

"You mean you didn't plant that story?" Osborne said.

JJ bristled. "Of course not. Why would I? Whoever fed that drivel to the *Star* probably thought they could bring the man down in one fell swoop. Well, the world simply doesn't work that way."

Cready nodded. "I just wish more folks had the guts to vote for the alternative. Most people think they have to go Democrat or Republican now, in order to make their vote count. I say the more choices, the better."

"To hell with your protest votes," JJ spat. "They don't amount to a goddamn thing."

"You're wrong there," Osborne said. "It was the splitting of votes that helped Lincoln win. Only forty percent of the country voted for him, but the Electoral College put him over the top." He laughed. "That's democracy for you."

Cready said, "Who *were* you cheering for, Roscoe?"

"I don't suppose I was cheering for anyone," JJ said. "In fact, I find the whole business of 'cheering' for elected officials rather crass. It cheapens the whole thing."

Osborne grinned. "Not much for presidents, are you?"

JJ shrugged. "I rather prefer kings and queens."

Cready leaned into JJ. "Surely you must have *voted.*"

JJ gritted his teeth. "Of course I did."

Osborne nodded with knowing certainty. "Roscoe's still a Democrat at heart. I'll bet he voted for Douglas. Ah, but poor old Steve couldn't make a go of it this time either, thus ending a long life of campaign failures." Osborne drank. "And *you* talk about a protest vote, Roscoe. This wasn't the right election for Douglas' kind of foolishness. Him going against the slave powers and all? Against Buchanan? No Democrat worth his salt wanted to be associated with that traitor. If you ask me, Douglas got exactly what he deserved."

Cready shrugged. "I'll be fine with the Republicans. I like old Abe myself. He's done good things."

JJ turned on him. "Oh yes? Tell me three good things he's done."

Cready fretted under JJ's stare. "I'm sure he's done at least three. Used to split rail fences, they say. Held the axe with one arm, they say."

"You base your entire opinion of a man on myths? Stories that, if true, don't have a single thing to do with his qualifications to hold the highest office in the country?"

Cready squirmed. "I'm sure he's done more. I can't rightly say what they might be at this time. I'd need a newspaper in front of me."

JJ shook his head. "You let the goddamn newspapers do all your thinking for you. Why, tomorrow's headlines in Boston will be 'Hallelujah, God be gracious, Lincoln is our chosen one.' Down in New Orleans they'll read 'The sky is falling — gather your loved ones and pray, goddamn you, for the Endtimes is come.' I swear to Christ, it's all a fucking circus."

Osborne laughed. "So young, and yet so bitter."

Cready's brow furrowed with contemplation. "No, this election is different than you're suggesting, Roscoe. Much, much different."

"Explain it then," JJ muttered.

Cready shook his head. "I don't know exactly. But things won't be the same. They *can't* be the same. I don't know if it's that something's broken. But something's surely gone missing."

JJ sighed. "I need another drink."

Osborne refilled his glass, and they drank in silence. After a time, Osborne winked at Cready. Loudly, he said, "Say, Roscoe. I heard your unit was transferred recently. Mind telling us where you're off to next?"

JJ's stomach flipped. In fact, he'd come here tonight to drink until he forgot all about *that* little piece of news. Major Anderson had just received orders of transfer, and being his adjutant, that meant JJ was going with him.

"I don't want to talk about it."

Osborne took out a cigar and lit it. "It's just that I expect myself and Cready to be wearing cavalry lace as soon as the war gets going. *If* the war gets going, of which I still have doubts. Although with Lincoln in the hot seat, you know all you Southrons are going to start a war sooner or later. It's in your blood, for Christ's sake. Do you think you'll ride cavalry for Virginia, Roscoe?"

JJ stiffened with indignation. He waited for Osborne to shut up, but Osborne kept jawing.

"I heard old Beauregard was mustering all the Southern boys to his cause around graduation time. Dod Ramseur's keen on overthrowing the government tomorrow, if only they'd let him. In any case, me and Cready will be up in the saddle lopping off secesh heads. But what about you, Roscoe? Are you still in the infantry?" Osborne laughed. "Oh, don't tell me you're going to spend the entire war pushing paper behind a—"

Glasses and bottles flew as JJ snatched Osborne by the collar and pinned him against the bar. The lively conversations around them died. Eyes were staring. Through his periphery, JJ saw the *maître d'* staring gob-smacked. Meanwhile, outside the Willard, the brawl between the Wide Awakes and Southern Democrats raged on.

Osborne struggled lamely against JJ's strength. "Take it easy, old boy. Take it easy."

JJ felt suddenly dizzy. He saw two Osbornes before him, and now four. Oh, to hell with it. JJ released the man and braced against the bar. He snatched up Osborne's bottle of whiskey and poured himself a stiff drink.

Keenly aware of staring eyes, Cready stood up and pulled on his overcoat. "Let's get some air, shall we?"

Osborne ran his hands through his hair and shot JJ a callous glare. "Yes," he said, smoothing his uniform down. "Let's do that."

They went outside. A wet November wind clung to their faces and hands, and it penetrated their clothes. By now, the street battle had gasped to a finish. Broken teeth glinted in the light of the streetlamps. A fallen flag with Lincoln's face stitched upon it lay trampled to tatters. Down the street, silhouetted by the streetlamp in the gathering fog, a sobbing woman clutched the broken form of a man.

JJ teetered on the cobblestones, feeling suddenly queasy. He doubled over.

"He's about ready to spew," Cready groaned.

Instead, JJ stood upright again and produced a bottle of gin from inside his jacket.

"Where'd you get that?!" Cready exclaimed.

"Fast fingers," Osborne laughed. He led them on. "You never cease to make me wonder, Roscoe. Let's go before the barkeep catches up."

They turned away and ventured south down 14th Street.

"Where are we going?" Cready huffed.

"The place of a lady I know," Osborne said. "I think we could all use a little horizontal refreshment. What do you say, Roscoe?"

JJ tipped the bottle to his lips and drank. Osborne shrugged and carried on. He and Cready paced side by side, with JJ trailing behind.

"Fort Moultrie," JJ muttered at last.

Ahead, Osborne and Cready slowed. Cready looked back, squinting against the harsh wind. "*Moultrie?*"

JJ cradled the gin bottle in the crook of his arm and stuffed his frozen hands in his pockets. "Charleston."

"Charleston?" Osborne echoed. "*Lord.*" He fell back to walk alongside JJ. "They're really sending you down to babysit a rock in the middle of that secesh loonyland?"

JJ nodded and spat. "Of all the goddamn backwater posts, that's where they send me."

"That's too bad," Cready said. "We were sure you'd be cavalry. You were the best damn rider in our whole year."

JJ nodded again to let that be the end of it.

But Cready pressed on with blind enthusiasm. "We were sure you'd be with Robert Lee down in Texas. Or maybe Sidney Johnston and the 2nd Cavalry way out in California. Those are fine units, those. We were sure of it, weren't we, Oz?"

"That's enough, Joe," Osborne said.

"Oh, right. Well..."

JJ scowled at the drizzle that fell around them. "I was sure of it too..."

But instead here he was, five whole months out of the Point and still a lowly second lieutenant without a command. Even Osborne had his first lieutenant's bars, and with his political connections Cready was bound to get them soon enough. If the rumors were true and there was some kind of war coming, Cready and Osborne's stars were bound to shoot even brighter. The wind was changing across the Union, and with the changing wind came a change of the guard. The old Democrats and Unionists like Father were on their way out. JJ would never bask in the unfettered, glorious nepotism here in Washington. But Cready and Osborne were Republicans, the former agreeably and the latter opportunistically so. Now that there was to be a new Republican government, the bureaucrats would of course surround themselves with Republican army officers.

"Charleston," Osborne said again. For the first time that night, Osborne did not speak in his usual assured, patronizing way. For the first time there was a semblance of worry in his voice. Perhaps deeper than that, his voice betrayed a sense of fear. "Are they really expecting the Southrons to attack the coastal forts?"

JJ looked up at Osborne. In many ways Osborne was very much like him: ambitious, calculating, with the wealth and charm and will to get whatever he wanted. Osborne liked to play the role of good-time-Charlie, but was in fact absorbed in observation, analysis, strategy. And though JJ would never dare admit it, he had learned many things from Osborne. In their pursuit of achievement JJ and Osborne shared a kind of kinship, but indulging any potential friendship was dangerous. Osborne was a threat, which meant he could never be a friend. Still, JJ knew he must be *friendly*. Even if Osborne didn't have JJ's friendship, he certainly had an element of begrudging respect.

It was this respect that inspired JJ's answer, spoken in a low voice to Osborne directly.

"General Scott is increasing the Charleston garrison under orders of President Buchanan," he said. "If any of the states are going to rise up against the government, the brass believes it will happen in South Carolina first. The idea is a show of strength to make them think twice."

Osborne nodded slowly. "You might find yourself drawing against fellow Southerners, Roscoe. Maybe against Virginia too, against your own people. Will you be ready for it?"

JJ took the gin bottle back from Cready. "They aren't my people," he said in a low voice. He took a long drink and wiped his mouth with his sleeve. "They haven't been my people for a long time."

❧

Though it was not widely known to the public, there was a townhouse at 514 10th Street (just across from Ford's Atheneum) owned by Senator John Roscoe. The townhouse was just one of a series of identical homes built with narrow windows and intricate molding along the eaves. At 514, the Maryland brownstone facade was painted a bright red. The striking color often caught eyes as walkers and drivers marshaled up and down the street each day and night. But what caught many eyes that gray morning of November 7th was a broken window on the second floor. Someone had hurled a rock through the glass pane.

Not many witnesses came forward to speak with harried city constables when they came prowling around shortly after daybreak. The city had sustained far more overnight property damage in other neighborhoods, and there were people with cloven heads lying dead in the alleys. But the local commissioner knew who lived at 514 and promptly ordered an investigation. Thus, two creaking antiques calling themselves policemen went out into the gray morning to ask the neighbors who broke the window, which was as good as asking the window itself.

But one witness, a gray-haired black man recently freed and made homeless upon the death of his ancient childless master, shuffled forward to brave the bully sticks and make his report.

While trying to sleep on a stoop, the old freeman had seen a young white man, alone and dressed in an army uniform, and very visibly drunk, stumbling down the street. The drunk man had stopped deliberately in front of 514. The man had cried out for someone (the witness forgot the name) and then the man searched the potholes in the street for chunks of stone. Finding one suitable, the man righted himself and pulled back to throw. The first rock went wide and bounced harmlessly off the red stone wall. The second rock missed too. Finally the man took the empty bottle in his hand and hurled it, and the bottle smashed out the top right window on the second floor. The drunk man offered a strangled battle cry. As the sky lightened with approaching dawn, he proceeded to carry on down the street laughing like a madman. All the while, he sang:

Ain't you glad you joined the Republicans?
Ain't YOU glad you joined the Republicans!
Ain't-ya-fuckin-glad-ya-joined-the-fuckin-Re-pub-li-cans
DOWN — IN — ILLL —A —NOYYYYYYY

CHAPTER 30

CROWN OF THORNS

THAT AUTUMN WAS QUIET AT CLARENDON. Mae Jane spent most of her days trying to fill her time with all manner of autumn projects: whitewashing, pickling, salting, candle-making, and anything else that kept her hands busy. The big-house was otherwise silent, except for the soft trilling of Bayard's piano-playing and the dusty swish of Isabella's skirts as she paced about her darkened study.

Tom had returned to his downstate school in September, and she murmured prayers for the boy every night. He hadn't been right since late in the summer, ever since his dog Tipper had run off. Lord bless that creature, he'd probably been eaten by coyotes. Tom was understandably distraught, and he soon became violent and withdrawn. One day he even lashed out at Bayard for no apparent reason, almost breaking his brother's arm in two.

Mae Jane had thought about appealing to Mr. John to let Tom stay in the Valley for school, where she could keep a closer eye on him. Miss Blake was supposed to be a wonderful teacher, much better than that old coot Mr. Braxton had been anyway. And for a boy Tom's age, it wasn't right to send him away to suffer heartbreak far from home. Mae Jane feared that he might end up in a bad sort of way.

A bad way...like JJ perhaps? Of course Mae Jane would never say as much out loud, but inside she felt it. Oh, Lord help her, she felt it. Prolonged detachment turned lonely boys into dangerous men.

Still, there wasn't anything Mae Jane could do for Tom. Mr. John was away on his campaign, and in any case he probably would have insisted that Tom go down to Lynchburg.

Ben and Mr. Jem were traveling with Mr. John, and Mae Jane prayed for the three of them together. In particular, she prayed for Ben. Her boy had developed a burning sense of outrage that was difficult for him to conceal, and during the summer he even stopped saying his prayers. Mae Jane was convinced the whole thing promised trouble. She'd seen it happen to plenty of other folks: the withdrawal from others, the abandonment of responsibilities, even the refusal to acknowledge a God suddenly deemed cruel and unjust for creating blacks as slaves of whites. Mae Jane hoped that some time away would be good for Ben, that it would set his head straight.

The Cutlers didn't visit much anymore (not that they were particularly social in the first place). Mae Jane missed Sarah greatly, especially since learning that Sarah was with child. Sarah was already showing, and she looked to be, to Mae Jane's eye at least, the happiest that she had ever been. For her part, Mae Jane could not wait until she could meet the child.

September and October passed without incident, and soon it was November. This, Mae Jane knew, was the month that would decide a great many things. Like, for instance, whether she would soon have to manage the Roscoe family's move from one big white house in Mayfair to another in Washington. Whenever she felt herself overwhelmed by the prospect, she reminded herself to relax and remain patient, that tomorrow never arrived before today. Still, these reassurances were of little comfort.

On the night of the election, Mae Jane woke up from a vivid nightmare. She had hoped that such terrible dreams would become fewer in number as she aged, but she continued to wake up in a cold sweat most nights. Only rarely were the dreams about the old days anymore. Lately, she'd been dreaming of waking up to discover that Clarendon was on fire, and all the doors and windows were blocked from the outside. She could hear Lady Isabella screaming from within the east wing study, but the door was jammed. As panic sunk in, Mae Jane decided to plunge through billowing smoke to find Bayard, and as she wandered through the haze she could smell the tarry black smoke poisoning her lungs. She heard a loud *crack,* and just as she craned her head up to see a burning beam come crashing down she was torn from the dream and—

"*Lord*...Lord have mercy...Jesus have mercy..."

Shivering, Mae Jane sat up in the darkness and sniffed the air (just in case there really *was* a whiff of smoke). She flinched when she heard the sudden clang of the doorknocker. For a moment, she wondered whether she had slipped into some other kind of dream-world. But still the doorknocker pounded. Visitors, at this hour?

Wrapping herself up, she shuffled through the cold, empty halls until she came to the grand foyer. She unlocked the door and opened it, and there upon the doorstep was—

"*Ben!*"

Ben was coughing and shaking. He had lost weight, and the light in his eyes that she loved so much had turned dull and glassy. Dried vomit stained one shoulder. Unable to carry his trunk any longer, he let it drop at his side.

"I left," Ben had said to her, his voice weak and raspy. "I couldn't take it anymore, and I left." Sheepishly he added, "Mama, I...I'm ashamed. I took to drinking, Mama, and I...well, I had too much to drink."

Mae Jane helped her boy to bed, and she tucked him in like he was still a little boy. She stroked his head while he slept. Ben woke up the next morning with chills and a wet rattle in his lungs, and he did not get up again for a week. Pneumonia was her guess, and she didn't need Dr. Harper's approval to be sure of it. Thankfully, she knew a thing or two about treating the disease. Upright position, head back, boiling tea with crushed herbs, sunlight, as much as could be found this time of year, and time.

And a healthy dose of prayer, too. She'd spent enough sleepless nights at children's bedsides, feeling helpless while the Devil tried to drown those tiny lungs, to know that sickness couldn't be defeated without God's grace. Medicine alone wasn't enough.

Despite the aches and chills that gnawed at his body, Ben was still able to share some news from the road. The new president was someone named Abraham Lincoln, a man Mae Jane had never even heard of. Then again, she supposed she hadn't heard of the last half-dozen presidents either. She'd only recently associated the name 'Buchanan' with what folks in the old days called a 'bad egg.' The story went that the divide between Yankees and Southerners had worsened under Mr. Buchanan due to his tendency to ignore the fact that there was a divide in the first place.

Then again, wasn't that what Mr. John had promised in his own campaign? That he'd 'do nothing' about the disagreements between North and South? Far be it from her to comment on something so alien to her as politicking, but it was Mae Jane's hunch that folks tended to prefer leaders who promised to do something, *anything*, rather than nothing.

Still, upon hearing that Lincoln was neither a Virginian nor a Democrat like Mr. John, Mae Jane decided she didn't like the president-elect and never would. Shaking her head, she sighed. "What in Lord's name they doin namin a Yankee they president? I got sense enough to know that ain't gonna solve nothin."

Ben laughed, though his laughter was thick and gurgling. "He's not a Yankee, Mama. He's from Illinois."

"Same difference, ain't it?"

Ben said earnestly, "He's going to end slavery, Mama, for good. Well, he *might*. There's ample cause to be pessimistic about the man's intentions. But I have faith he will do the right thing. Lord knows, enough men have said they'll do something and remain content to sit on their hands."

"Mhm. Oh? Oh, that's nice, child." She stood up and tucked him in, and thought to get ready for bed herself. "Now, no more talkin, Benny. You just rest. Another night and day, and then you might be fit to take a walk."

Ben had looked at her then. There was a deep pain in his eyes, a sort of suffering she had seen in plenty of other faces in her time, but never in Ben.

"Mama," he said. "Mama, I need to tell you somethin. It's about Mr. John, Mama. It's...it's about *Daddy*, Mama..."

Mae Jane put her hands together and pulled at her fingers. Joby's face flashed in her mind's eye before she blinked it away. She quieted her quickened breath and steeled herself as much as she could manage. The way Ben was looking at her, his news could hardly be *good*. She planted her feet on the creaking floorboards, as if she expected the earth to split open and swallow her up.

She'd denied Ben a long time. About his daddy, she meant. For years now, any time the boy tried to talk about Joby, Mae Jane refused or else pretended she hadn't heard his questions. Maybe it was because it was all too painful, or maybe she was just scared. Wasn't it Carlotta-George who once scolded her for being a pushover, that her skin wasn't really black but in fact a cowardly yellow? When faced with a difficult or uncomfortable situation, it had always been easier to walk away. Better yet, it had been easier to not get anywhere close to the thing in the first place.

Taking a deep breath, Mae Jane sat down at Ben's bedside again.

"You tell me, child. Whatever it is you got to tell, I's here." She reached out and took his hand. "I's *listenin*."

There were tears in Ben's eyes. He looked up at her for a long while, not saying anything, somehow saying it all with just a look. Taking her weathered hand closer, Ben kissed it softly.

"It's nothing, Mama."

She shook her head. "No, child. You can *tell* me. I'm ready, child, whatever it is you—"

"I know, Mama." He tried a smile then. "I know, and I appreciate it. I just...the more I think on it, I don't think it would do any good, my telling you. I might sit on it a little while longer."

She nodded and squeezed his hand. "Well, that's up to you," she said. Now she offered a wry smile. "Just watch you don't sit on it too long, child. You might end up like me: old and crotchety."

They shared a quiet laugh together, though Mae Jane could tell that Ben was pretending to be better than he was. Soon enough Ben went to sleep, and Mae Jane spent the night praying on his behalf.

November stretched on, and there was no news from Mr. John in Washington. As the days and weeks rolled by, Ben seemed to be turning a corner. The rattle in his chest was fainter now, less sludge-like. Soon he was up and walking, and even able to help with some chores again.

Mae Jane soon found herself slipping into another quiet sort of routine. She liked routine, always having something to do. She liked getting up early and getting to it, knowing she could expect more of the same tomorrow. Some folks called that a dull life; she called it good living.

And so, when toward months' end a boy from the telegraph company really arrived with a message from Washington, Mae Jane stared at the yellow envelope for a long time. She knew the letter had to be from Mr. John. Somehow, she knew that as soon as she opened it, as soon as she gave it to Ben to read, everything would change.

Besides the usual handwritten information, a word was stamped upon the envelope. She didn't know what the word was, but the red ink was dark like blood.

"It says 'Urgent,'" Ben said when Mae Jane gave him the envelope.

Mae Jane took a deep breath and steeled herself. There would be no ignoring this one, no chance to look the other way.

"Go on," she said.

Ben opened the telegram and read it. "It's from Jem," he said. "*Father badly ill stop. En route home, one or two days travel stop. Have doctor and reverend waiting stop.*"

And that was it. That was the message. Stunned, Mae Jane sat back and felt her heart tighten in her chest.

Have doctor and reverend waiting.

Ben said, "You think it's—?"

"Yes," she said. "Yes, I think it is. It's Mr. John's time."

Ben read the telegram again. The paper clutched in his fingers trembled, as if Ben were resisting the urge to tear it to pieces. "Maybe it's just another scare," he said. "Maybe it's...maybe it's not so bad after all."

Mae Jane nodded slowly, trying to grasp the new reality that had thrust itself to the forefront of everything. Maybe Ben was right. Maybe this was just another scare, just another stretch of bad days that some doctor who didn't know Mr. John had misread as *the end*. After all, the old man had taken as many bad turns over the years to set him right-way forward again.

But somehow, she couldn't shake the idea that this really was the last of it.

"No," she said, her voice barely above a whisper. "This time feels different. I don't think it'll be long now. I don't think it'll be long at all."

❧

Late the next night, a black coach came rumbling past Clarendon's ruined gate and up the sodden clay path. The front door flew open and a flurry of sleet blew inside on a gust of wind. Mr. Jem, wearing whiskers on his cheeks and worry in his red, sleep-deprived eyes, dropped down from the coach to direct two porters, who carried Mr. John into Clarendon upon a stretcher.

When Mae Jane saw the pallid, corpselike gray of Mr. John's face, she felt an icy claw clutch her chest. The poor man was too weak to speak nor even open his eyes, and his breathing was thick and gurgling, as if some fluid had congealed in his lungs.

They settled Mr. John in a parlor on the main floor called the sunroom, so-called for its wall of large, south-facing windows. Dr. Harper was already waiting there, his instruments ready. Reverend Lucas Cutler sent a telegram expressing his regrets that he would be 'delayed', but the message did not specify when he would ultimately arrive.

As Dr. Harper began his examination, Mae Jane saw Ben watching from the corner wearing a sullen expression. She sent him off to fetch rags and hot water, and Ben looked thankful for an excuse to leave the room.

While Harper moved his stethoscope across Mr. John's bare sunken chest, Jem explained all that had happened in the last few weeks.

"We were at a celebration ball the night of the election," Jem said. "Rather, I suppose it was more of a concession ball than anything. Father seemed fine then, as fine as a man could be given the circumstances. We came back to 10th Street late, and though it was very cold in the place I lit a fire and thought little more of it. Father went up to sleep and I wasn't far behind him. It was only when city constables knocked on the door the next morning that I realized someone had hurled a rock through Father's bedroom window while we had been gone. The heavy curtains had blanketed the broken glass, but the chill in the room was deep. I had the window fixed right away, but even afterward Father insisted on sleeping in that same room."

Harper looked up at Jem with a touch of anger in his eyes. "And you *let* him? The man has tuberculosis, and you let him sleep next to a drafty window in November?"

A scowl flared across Jem's face, but he did his best to master it. "When my father insists on something," he muttered, "it's the wiser move to adhere to his wishes."

Harper continued to listen to the old man's breathing, his mustache tick-tocking as he moved his stethoscope about. "Are you sure Senator Roscoe didn't insist, knowing that this would be the end result?"

"*Please*, Doctor," Mae Jane said sharply. "Our Mr. John don't got a death wish, if that's what you suggestin."

Jem shook his head morosely. "Even with a large fire in the hearth and blankets heaped upon the bed, it was enough. Just those few hours, that sudden cold snap before dawn…it was enough."

Suddenly, Jem roared with anger and struck out at a nearby table covered in trinkets, sending most of them crashing to the floor.

"Christ, it's *murder*! The constables said it was some crazed Republican nut singing songs. An assassin, no doubt!"

"*Calm down*," Harper growled. "None of that shouting does your father any good."

Mae Jane went up to Jem and put a soothing hand on his back. Turning around, Jem embraced her and began to weep quietly.

Harper looked up again. "So all this was three weeks ago. Why am I seeing him only now?"

Jem looked up from Mae Jane's shoulder and wiped tears from his eyes. "He...he was getting better. Father was sick for several days, bedridden, but then...it seemed to me he was turning a corner. I had three doctors come see him, and they all thought the same."

Here, Jem left Mae Jane's side and crossed to the bed on which Mr. John lay. Kneeling down low, he hunched his neck and back so that he could look into his father's face. He studied it a long while, as if noticing for the first time the shape and character of his father's features.

Jem said, "He seemed to be getting better, and the next week he really *was*. Father was moving about, talking about writing memoirs or some such nonsense. I'd never seen him so lively, so full of zeal. He was like how he was *before*, meaning before his diagnosis. Oh, you should have seen him, Mae Jane. He was like a little boy, running about the place, talking incessantly about his plans for this, his plans for that. He talked no more about railroads but about newspapers. He said he would buy the *Mayfair First Witness*, then all the papers in Virginia, then all the papers in the major cities. He said that the search for *truth* would be the new Roscoe family legacy. But then, one day, three days ago now, he was late in rising. I thought he was only sleeping in a little, but by noon there was still no sign of him. I went up to his bedroom and I...I found him like this."

Harper drew a long breath. He pinched a point of one of Mr. John's cheeks and counted the seconds until blood returned there. "I would not have advised moving him," the doctor said. "A hard journey whether by train or Virginia roads, even in good weather, and so cold..."

"I had to take him home," Jem declared. "Clarendon is his home. If he's going to..."

Jem's voice trailed off for a moment. When he found it again, it was stronger.

"If he's going to *die*, then it's better he die here at home. With family."

Harper shrugged and nodded, and Mae Jane blessed herself.

Having finished his examination, Harper stood up and placed his stethoscope back in its leather case. "All to be done tonight. Hot broth for breakfast tomorrow, Ms. Freeman. Keep him upright, comfortable. And pray, for his sake and yours."

Jem stood up from his father's bedside. "You mean there's...there's nothing you can—?"

"What?" Harper said. "You want me to put leaches on his skin? Let the blood and bad humors drain out?"

Jem clenched his fists. "I want you to take this matter *seriously*, Ira. Don't you know who this man is? Don't you know what this man has done for the Valley, for this country?"

"I do know, and I do take the matter seriously," Harper replied. "And as I say, president or pauper, there's nothing more to be done for this man tonight."

Jem looked away, glowering.

Harper addressed Mae Jane directly. "Will you be so kind as to walk me to the door, Ms. Freeman?"

Mae Jane looked to Jem, and Jem gave a slow nod. She went to a table nearby and picked up the doctor's hat, meaning to carry it.

"This way, Doctor."

As they walked down the hall, Mae Jane side by side with the young doctor, Jem trailing several steps behind, Harper explained the situation to the best degree he could manage. There was no sense in speaking around the thing. This was indeed the end, or rather the beginning of the end. The only work to be done now was to stave off the inevitable for as long as possible. Still, a battle against consumption, however nobly fought, always ended but one way.

Somehow, in the midst of all this, Mae Jane noted a marked change in the young Dr. Harper since the last time she had seen him. He was more confident, but at the same time less concerned with manners and appearances. There was a bewildered sense of calm about him, as if he'd finally learned enough to know he didn't know very much at all. This somehow made the man seem wise, and probably he had become just that. Mae Jane had no inkling what had brought about such a change, or when, but there it was.

As they passed into the grand foyer, they were interrupted by Lady Isabella, who was presently coming down the staircase. It felt to Mae Jane as if the old woman had been waiting there in order to time her appearance.

"Ah, there you are, Doctor," the Lady of Clarendon said. "Oh, now just where are you running off to? I want to speak with you, boy. It's about my prescription..."

"*Please*, Mother," Jem said testily. He turned back to Harper. "Continue, Doctor."

Harper now addressed all of them together, including Isabella.

"He'll awake from time to time. He'll be able to talk awhile, but never for long, and you should not make him strain. In the days to come, his breathing will become more difficult. You'll hear a sort of wetness in his voice. Once he's so weak that he can no longer speak, he won't be able to cough up the fluid in his lungs. And if he can't cough, he soon won't be able to breathe. Then, the dying will really begin."

Jem stared at the far wall with a blank expression. "How long?"

"Months are out of the question," Harper replied. "Maybe a few weeks." Nodding, he seemed to settle on this answer. "Two or three weeks. Before Christmas, I suspect."

Mae Jane let out a quiet groan. Two weeks. A stretch of time that felt like both a year and a day. Too long and cruel a time to suffer, and too short a time for a man to finish all the parts of his life that were yet unfinished.

Jem nodded slowly. "I see..."

Mae Jane swallowed the hot lump that had lodged itself in her throat. "Well," she whispered, feeling her whole body go numb. "I suppose we gotta thank God for however long we got, right? Some folks drop dead at they dinner table. Some folks die in they sleep without a chance to say goodbye. We still got a little time with Mr. John. Lord bless us, we still got a little time to—"

"No," Jem said. "There's not enough, not nearly enough. If only we had *more time* to—"

"We've had plenty of time, I should think," Lady Isabella said curtly. Turning to Harper, she pursed her lips in a curious smile. "Thank you, Doctor, for your services. *Adieu*."

Harper nodded gravely and swung the front door open and stepped outside.

For a strangled moment, Mae Jane stood staring at the floor while being very aware that Jem and Lady Isabella were on either side of her, with no one speaking or acknowledging each other. It was all Mae Jane could do to propel herself through the door after Dr. Harper before the silence suffocated her.

Outside on the veranda, Mae Jane watched as the young doctor turned to her. His face lit up with recognition.

"Ah, my hat. Thank you."

It was only then that Mae Jane realized she was still holding Harper's hat. She handed it over and watched as Harper placed the hat on his head. He looked about to say something grand, but then only turned and stepped out into the soft-falling December snow. Mae Jane watched as the young doctor clambered atop his shaggy horse and started down the sodden path toward Clarendon's ruined gate and the Valley beyond.

When Mae Jane came back inside, she saw Lady Isabella halfway up the stairs. Turning, she caught the last glimpse of a shadowed Jem as he disappeared around the corner and out of sight. Looking at Isabella again, she saw that the Lady was nearly to the top of the staircase.

"Bella?"

The Lady paused, but only long enough to pass a glare over her shoulder. "I thought I already made myself clear on this point, Mae Jane. You are to address me properly *at all times*. If not, I'll be obliged to see to your correction, freedman or not."

Mae Jane sighed. "Bella, we ain't got much time." She advanced to the foot of the stairs and looked up at the Lady. "Why don't I take you down there now, hm? To go see Mr. John. Why don't we go down there together, me and you? We can sit with you husband awhile. He wants to see you, Lady, I know he does." Slowly, Mae Jane started up the steps. "And you, Bella, if there's anythin you feel you wanna say—"

"*I've nothing to say to that man*," Isabella hissed. Her face, the whole of it flushed red, had become like an open, bleeding sore. So hideous was the look she gave that Mae Jane had to shut her eyes and bow her head. Grimacing, she listened as the Lady's heavy footsteps and hurried swish of her skirts receded down the hallway. Far down the east wing, the door to Isabella's study slammed shut.

When Mae Jane opened her eyes again, she found herself alone on the staircase. Turning, she achingly trudged down the stairs one at a time, like a bedraggled debutante wearing a dirty apron over heavy broadcloth, making her debut to a ball attended by no one.

❧

As November became December, the days shortened and the nights of anxiety grew longer. With each latening dawn, the news from beyond the Branches became darker.

Ben became obsessed with scouring the newspapers for reports of protests and riots in the cities, together with rumors of bands of highwaymen roaming country roads. Mae Jane did her best to ignore all such doom and gloom goings-on and tried to keep her hands busy.

Mr. John had been lucid once or twice in recent weeks, but only for short periods of time. Here and there, Mae Jane had been able to speak with the old man for a few minutes. Each of these times, she wondered whether this might be *the last time*.

One evening, while a heavy snow was falling outside the sunroom's frosted windows, Mae Jane sat alone with Mr. John. By candlelight, they shared reminisces of Clarendon in the old times. Mostly, it was Mae Jane who did the telling while Mr. John listened. Mae Jane focused on the happier stories — stories of laughter and song and celebration — but even these seemed to conjure a deep pain in the old man's eyes that Mae Jane had never seen before.

"We don't gotta talk bout any of that if you ain't feel like it, Mr. John."

For a long moment, the old man stared at the candle at his bedside. Its meager light reflected in the wet darks of his eyes.

"I feel I need to ask you if you think I'm a good man," Mr. John said, his voice very weak. "But the truth is, Mae Jane, the answer I want is hidden there in the question. The *real* answer...well, I think I know what the real answer is, and I fear it. Maybe...maybe I'm ashamed by it."

Mae Jane shook her head. "No, Mr. John, *no*. It's natural, I s'ppose, you feelin such a way when things is...well, when things is near the end. Everybody done feel like that, I reckon. Even Jesus doubted himself near the end, in the garden before dawn. You only in the garden, Mr. John."

The old man continued to study the candle's tiny flame. "He knows the truth," he whispered. "Your Ben. He knows who I really am. *What* I really am."

Here, Mae Jane too looked at the candle, and she studied the flame as it danced in the ether. She pondered for a moment the idea that she and Mr. John were looking at the very same thing, only from two different vantage points. Two perspectives, two sets of conclusions to draw, and yet the flame burned the same.

"Maybe he knows part of it," Mae Jane said. "Maybe Ben's got a page or two from your book, and maybe them pages tell a lot. But they can't tell the whole story of a soul. You look in the mirror a hundred years, or you try to put together all the things you ever said or did, and still you ain't gonna know who you is — not really. They's still so much the heart don't let out, still so much hidden in dreams. And if we can't know ourselves, how in the Lord's name do we expect to know anybody else? How dare we claim we got the full-painted picture of somebody, when all we got for ourselves is a hand sketch?"

Mr. John said nothing. Mae Jane watched his wheezing chest rise and fall, rise and fall.

Mae Jane said, "I know I thanked you many times for what you done for me and Ben all them years ago. As I say, I don't got the full picture of you, Mr. John. All I know is, when a young mother came to you fearin what lay beyond them Branches, what lay even beyond that broken gate yonder...you *listened*, Mr. John. You listened, and you acted. In that moment, you did the right thing, and did it for its own sake. So maybe you got a hundred, a thousand reasons for feelin that you a bad man. Maybe they's ten thousand reasons, I don't know. But they's at least two reasons I can give you, two reasons to believe you got some *good* in you heart. Who's to say how it all stacks up in the end?"

A curious smile was set on the old man's lips. "You think too much of me, Mae Jane."

Mae Jane gave a soft laugh. "Well. Maybe that's just my nature."

Slowly, Mr. John turned his head to the doorway. Suddenly, the old man's eyes lit up with recognition, and it was as if the deathly shroud that hung over him was lifted and cast aside. Mae Jane could think of no other term to describe it: the old man was *glowing*.

"Jonathan," he rasped. "Jonathan, is that...?"

Confused, Mae Jane looked to the door. "Jon Jacob?" she said, incredulous. But seeing the doorway empty, she shook her head. "No, Mr. John, there ain't nobody..."

Slowly, the realization of what the old man meant dawned on her. She saw the quivering fear in his yellowish gaze, the yearning hope that gleamed there. So much else about the man was gray and spent, like watching a tree give the last of its leaves, but the hope in Mr. John's eyes — the hope for JJ — still kept the flame of life burning within him.

The old man stared up at the ceiling, seeing something far past it.

"Jonathan..."

Outside the windows, the winter wind groaned and wailed. Mae Jane reached out and took the old man's hand. She felt his pulse, very weak, ebbing. Looking down at the old man, she gave an assuring nod and whispered to him.

"JJ's comin, Mr. John. Your boy's comin. I know it."

The old man closed his eyes and shook his head. When his eyes opened again, they welled with tears.

"No…no…"

She squeezed his hand tighter. "He *is*," she whispered. "You wanna see JJ? You wanna see you boy, talk to him awhile?"

The old man shook his head slowly, weakly.

Mae Jane found a handkerchief and gently wiped the old man's tears away. "Well as it just so happens, I wasn't fibbin when I said he's on the way. We sent for JJ a few days ago, Mr. John. And guess what? He wrote back sayin he's comin home. Oh, ain't it wonderful, Mr. John? With Thomas back a few days ago, and now with Jon Jacob home in a few days more, we'll all be together again. We'll all be a family again, Mr. John, just like we's supposed to be. Ain't that gonna be fine?"

Mr. John nodded again, and the shroud of fear lifted from his eyes. The old man gave a peaceful, contented smile. His breathing quieted and his eyes became heavy.

"Now you get some rest," Mae Jane said quietly. She stood up and smoothed down her dress and apron. "It's time I leave you be. You ring if you need anythin, Mr. John?"

But Mr. John was already fast asleep.

Mae Jane stood there a long while wringing her hands and making sure that Mr. John's chest continued to rise and fall. At last she managed to turn herself around and leave the room.

Mae Jane moved slowly through Clarendon's hallways, same as she'd done ten thousand times before. But more than ever, she felt a crushing weight press down on her shoulders, making her back scream and her knees wobble. She wanted nothing more than to collapse there in a heap and say nothing more, do nothing more.

Oh *laws*, why had she said all those wicked things?

Mae Jane entered the library slowly. Within the library, the Roscoe family had gathered together to discuss all that was to come. Sarah and Henry Cutler were there too, though as Mae Jane entered she heard Henry explaining to Jem that they would not be staying long.

Despite the gloomy nature of the gathering, Henry was in fine spirits; he even wore a fine, blue-ribboned cockade pinned to his lapel. Ben stood in the corner, his head bowed. Bayard sat beside Sarah, who stroked the boy's hair with one hand and kept the other over her bulging belly. Tom was home too, called early from Lynchburg Academy. When he arrived a few days earlier, Mae Jane could tell the boy had not been eating much while away at school. He had a haunted look in his eyes, which became even more hollowed out whenever he spent any time at his father's bedside.

Mae Jane walked over and joined Tom, who stood by the fire. She put a comforting hand on his shoulder, but she felt him stiffen up. Slowly, she pulled her hand away. At times like this, some people craved touch while others preferred to be invisible.

As Mae Jane went to a nearby chair and sat down, she listened absentmindedly as Jem and Henry discussed various goings-on. Jem was distracted, only half paying attention, but Henry spoke with an air of keen interest and authority.

"In the wake of the niggerphile's election, more and more of us are now calling for a complete separation between North and South," Henry said. "There's an expectation — not an unfounded one — that Lincoln is going to declare abolition as soon as he takes office, and maybe send troops down to enforce his new laws. Daddy says we need to act *before* that happens."

"Where is Lady Isabella?" Mae Jane asked. "She didn't come down?"

Henry turned and glowered at Mae Jane for interrupting.

In answer to the question, Jem shook his head slowly. "Mother is...she's mourning in her own way, I suppose."

"Or celebrating," Sarah murmured.

Henry laughed quietly. "One day I'd like to know the whole sad tale about those two. What was it that did them in? Was the old man too busy chasing skirts in Washington?"

If this had been intended as a joke, it fizzled. The air in the library was thick with silence, broken only by the dry snap of Ben striking a match and lighting one of his hand-rolled cigars.

Jem looked down at the glass of bourbon in his hand. He'd in fact been paying it little attention all this time. He asked, maybe only to make conversation, about the status of the compromise.

Henry furrowed his brow. "Compromise? What compromise?"

"Before he took ill, Father said something about his friend John Crittenden organizing a committee," Jem said. "Mr. Crittenden is assembling thirteen senators — Democrats and Republicans — to draft some means of compromise to table before Congress. Father was invited to the discussions, but then..."

Henry shook his head. "It's too late for talk. South Carolina's state legislature has already convened a debate on secession. I hear that, any day now, they'll be ready to take it to a vote. And we all know what the result will be."

Jem nodded slowly as the news sunk in. "Secession? So...we're really there."

"We're really there," Henry said, grinning. "How about a toast to the Southern nation?" He quickly drank his own toast without waiting for Jem. Perking up with an idea, Henry set his empty glass down and reached into his breast pocket. "That reminds me, Jem. I've brought something for you..."

Henry produced a strand of blue ribbon as if he was a magician pulling an endless string of colored garments from his pocket. But now Henry tied the ribbon into a tight knot, forming a cockade much like his own, and this he offered to Jem.

"It's a symbol of solidarity," Henry said. "To show support for the people of South Carolina. If I may?"

Jem shrugged, and Henry stepped forward to pin the cockade to Jem's breast.

As he fixed the ribbons, Henry said, "Daddy took the Stars and Stripes down from the flagpole at Arcadia, and now we're flying the palmetto flag. After all, what does Old Glory mean to us anymore? Its essence has been corrupted by Huns and Quakers up in Yankeeland. There! Look at you. A noble Southern knight. You see, Sarah-darling? Somehow your brother's become even more handsome than before."

"Take that off," Ben muttered from the corner.

All heads, including Mae Jane's, turned to look at Ben, who glared at the cockade through a screen of cigar smoke.

With a grin spreading along his lips, Henry turned to address Ben directly. "I do beg your pardon, Mr. Freeman. You were saying?"

"The cause of secession goes against everything your father stands for," Ben said, ignoring Henry completely and speaking only to Jem. "At least, it goes against everything he *claimed* to stand for."

Henry chuckled and shook his head. "How you put up with this boy's uppity nonsense, Jem, I'll never figure out. He can't even stomach a little hot-blooded patriotism."

"It's not patriotism," Ben said. "It's the furthest thing from it. It's a mockery."

"*Pshaw!*" Mae Jane said. For God's sake, now was no time for arguing about something so stupid as politics. There was a man dying in the other room! When, if ever, would her Ben learn? "You don't mean that, Mr. Freeman. You ain't got a lick of sense in you, and there you is runnin you mouth. Mr. Cutler here knows right."

Henry beamed a smile at Mae Jane, but it made her skin crawl. "You should listen to your mother," Henry said.

Ben glared at Mae Jane. He shook his head with disgust and disbelief. "You're defending *him* now?"

"I ain't defendin nobody," Mae Jane said. She gestured vaguely toward the sunroom down the hall. "Mr. John's in there. He needs us — all-us, together. And here you is, tryin to get a row outta somebody? Tryin to attack you own *family*?"

Ben's mouth dropped open and his jaw went slack. Mae Jane knew she'd struck a nerve.

Meanwhile, Jem examined the blue cockade on his chest. Reaching up, he stroked the ribbons thoughtfully. "Maybe secession isn't what you think it is, Ben. All sorts of crazy folk came out of the woodwork during the campaign. One of them — no doubt a Republican, no doubt a man calling himself a patriot — smashed a rock through Father's window, and now look what's happened. Secession? There are worse paths to tread. Tyranny, for starters, and tyranny begins with apathy. Well, maybe secession is nothing more than a means of saying, '*Go to hell!*' to every smug bastard who thinks he knows which way the world's going to turn next. Maybe the folks down in Charleston aren't talking about just one issue. Maybe secession is a means to bite the sleeping horse, to try and get this country to come to its senses again."

"It's more than that," Ben said. "It's *less* than that, and you know it. Jem, your father campaigned against abolitionism and secession both. He said both sides were shouting past each other. He said—"

"You called him a liar," Jem said sharply. "Right before you spat at his feet, you called my father a liar."

Ben went very quiet. "I did," he said at last. "And I meant it."

"I'm sure you did," Jem said. "Lord knows, the man in that room is no paragon. But at least he spent his life believing *in* something, rather than let himself succumb to petty resentment."

"Is that what you think this is?" Ben said.

"Only weak men are content to condemn and criticize from the sidelines," Jem said. "Weak men go crying to newspapers about matters they don't understand. They think themselves heroes, they think themselves Truth personified, but in fact it's all rank and utter vanity."

Ben said nothing, but he and Jem scowled at each other with barely concealed contempt.

"It's for men of action to *do something* with the time we have," Jem said. "Father was content to sit on the fence on a great many issues, because for his generation that was the best course to keep. Now, the ground is shifting under our feet, and it's up to our generation to do something about it. There are some folks who are trying to rip down the fence along with everyone on it. I'd say Henry here, and men like him, are only trying to get clear before the wreckage comes down on top of them."

Ben shook his head. "If you throw in with the secessionists, you'll be nothing but a goddamn traitor."

"You *shut up*," Mae Jane hissed. "You shut up this instant, Mr. Freeman!"

Ben scowled at her. "For Christ's sake, leave me be."

"Both you gotta stop it," Mae Jane said, clutching her hands to her head. "It's all gotta *stop*!"

But it was no use. Suddenly the library became like a battlefield. Jem and Henry piled accusations upon Ben while Ben hurled charges back at them. Bayard cowered against Sarah while Sarah implored everyone to calm down, but her voice was drowned out by the uproar. Meanwhile, Tom proceeded to pick up a fire poker and thrash it absentmindedly against the hard stone of the hearth — *thwack-thwack-thwack* — as if keeping time with the chaos.

At last, Mae Jane could take no more.

"Mr. John asked to see him."

At first, no one heard her. The shouting continued, and Mae Jane was compelled to speak up again, louder:

"He wants to see JJ."

Finally, there was silence. All heads turned to her. Tom's arm, still holding the poker, was suspended in mid-swing. Within the cavernous library, the only sound was the muffled crackle and snap of the fire.

Jem stared at Mae Jane and blinked. "He...he wants to see...?"

Mae Jane nodded gravely. "That's right."

All around, the realization slowly sank in. But when no one responded, Mae Jane felt it her duty to press the case.

"I'll send Jon Jacob a letter," she said. "I don't know where he might be, but I figure the soldier-folks will get it to him somehow. That'll take weeks, which means we ain't got much time. I'll need Benny's help with the writin, but I can do the thinkin myself. The letter will be from me. I ain't got no bad blood with JJ, and I don't think he got any with me. Whatever we may got, we can work through it sooner than you-all can. But first things first, he gotta come back and see his daddy, and together they can try to set things straight before the end. It's the right thing, and you-all know it."

Silence pressed down on all present. Mae Jane waited for someone to say something, anything.

"JJ's not going to come back," Jem said.

Mae Jane shook her head. "You don't know that, Mr. Jem. Not for sure."

"I *know it*," Jem said, and with that he started for the liquor cabinet across the room. "And besides, I wouldn't let the bastard come within a mile of this place. He'd be more likely to take one of those guns"—and he pointed at the Colonel's dueling pistols hanging over the mantle—"and shoot Father dead as soon as try to reconcile." Jem poured himself a fresh bourbon, one so full that it spilled over the top of the glass. With a trembling hand, he took up the glass and downed its contents in a single gulp. "If JJ tries to set foot in Clarendon again," Jem said, "I'll...I'll kill him."

Ben threw a bitter laugh on the floor. "This goddamn family..."

Reeling, Jem turned on Ben and scowled at him. "What the fuck did you just say?"

Mae Jane made a thunderclap with her hands. "*Stop it*," she hissed. "Lord help me, I won't say it again."

Before anyone could hurl another insult at another, Mae Jane planted her feet and addressed everyone at once. Each face she looked at was worn by grief, etched with exhaustion.

"I just can't believe you-all. Here we got a chance to make things right, a chance to make this family *whole* again before it's too late. And you just gonna sit there and...what? Bicker about nonsense? Feel sorry for youselves? *Pretend* you ain't gonna feel sorry, sooner or later? That poor man in there is dyin, and he asked for his son. Who you think you is to deny him that?"

Again, she was met with silence. Mae Jane's heart crept up her throat. It was loon insane, what she was doing right now, talking down to these Roscoes like they were children. They would have every right to terminate her on the spot and throw her out into the cold — she and Ben both. After that, there would be no stopping the likes of Henry Cutler and his cronies from finding them and doing whatever they wanted with them. Indeed, Henry's current expression, twisted with disgust that the Roscoes permitted such outbursts from their negroes, suggested he was thinking much along the same lines. Still, so far as Mae Jane was concerned, sometimes it was necessary to throw one's weight around. And though she was thin as a needle, Mae Jane had throwing weight aplenty.

She studied their faces in the thick quiet. Scowling, Jem shook his head and poured himself another drink. Pale and tired, Bayard lay with his head on Sarah's shoulder. Tom was disconnected, his vacant eyes staring somewhere unknowable. Henry Cutler wore a similarly blank expression that gave Mae Jane nothing, not that his input mattered much to her anyhow. Sarah kept her hands resting on the humble bulge of her belly, as if trying to comfort the little one inside her. Mae Jane finally succeeded in catching the girl's gaze and holding it. Though she said nothing, Sarah's eyes communicated her silent approval.

"Very well," Mae Jane said, her voice raw. She turned now to Ben. "Will you help me write that letter, Mr. Freeman?"

Ben only stared at the floor and smoked the last of his cigar. Having spent it, he crushed the cigar in a nearby ashtray and left the library without a word.

After watching Ben go, Mae Jane looked around at the Roscoes and Cutlers. She thought to say something, but nothing came to her. She felt her pulse pound in her throat, in her brow, and she felt an unthinking, frothing rage inside her. Turning, she picked up her skirts and hurried after her son.

Out in the hallway, Mae Jane saw that Ben was nearly around the next corner. She called for him in a sharp voice, though she more than half expected him to ignore her and keep going. Instead Ben stopped and waited, his shoulders tensed as if itching for a fight.

Mae Jane bit her tongue as she moved up the hallway, her skirts swishing along the floor, but when she at last stood before her son (well out of earshot of the library, she hoped), she let fly her full fury.

"Just what the hell's wrong with you? I never thought no son of mine would start no stupid row while a man's on his deathbed next door."

Ben was stunned into silence. He hung his head. "Mama, I—"

"You *look* at you mama when you speak to her, child."

When Ben did look up, his eyes were clouded with resentment. "I'm leaving, Mama. I'm leaving the Valley. Maybe I'll go tonight."

Mae Jane shook her head with disbelief. "Sam Hill, child. You can't just *leave* 'cause you eyes is misty. The man in there is *dyin*, and you really got the nerve to—"

"It's going to happen, Mama. Sooner or later. And I'd rather not be here for the funeral."

"Listen to youself!" she growled. "This ain't no discussion. You stayin put, and you doin as I tell you. We here to serve, and so we gonna serve. Besides, you think a nigger like you can take a stroll up the road any time he damn well please? It's too dangerous out there."

Ben stepped forward and took her hands into his. "That's why I want you to come with me, Mama. We could both leave together. There's nothing tying us here to Clarendon anymore, or at least, there soon won't be. And if this secession talk is real — if it's really happening — then we won't be safe even here. Maybe we'll go to Washington, or maybe we'll push on. We'll go North to New York, or maybe Boston."

She burst out laughing — not because of any of it was funny, but only to keep herself from slapping her boy across the face.

"I don't care a lick about New York and Boston, child. I told you before, this is *home*. It ain't safe noplace else."

"It's never been safe!" Ben hissed. "Not here, not anywhere. I figure, better to try the uncertainty of *out there* than stay *here*, where we know there's nothing to hope for." He pushed her hands away. "But what do you want to do? Hole up in here and never leave? You want your son to shut himself away from the world, just like you did? Oh yes, we can remain the happy slaves who play dress-up for the Roscoes."

"You take that back!" Mae Jane seethed. "We *ain't* slaves, and we ain't been such for—"

"We might as well be," Ben said. "The way you crawl over to Lady Isabella whenever she needs a foot-stool, the way you spoke up for Cutler in there just now. *Cutler*, of all goddamn people! But oh, you're the good, wise nigger-mammy. Well, maybe you've been playing make-believe so long you think it's real. But maybe you just forgot those people in there don't give a damn about us. You forgot that the man we're supposedly weeping about tried to *sell us* like we were animals. You forgot—"

"I ain't forgot *one moment*!" Mae Jane shouted, her voice shrill. "You never forget the feel of the whip on you back. Then again, you wouldn't know that feelin at all, would you? That's 'cause *I* was there to stand in its way, there to shield you when the blows came. There ain't *one moment* I forgot what's been done to us, child, to *all-us*. But what, you think that all this has been about *you*?"

Instead of her son standing there, Mae Jane imagined it was Joby. Joby, who loved her, but only when she spoke about things that he wanted to speak about. Red with rage, she threw out her hands and pushed against Ben with all her might. Her son was strong and could have resisted, but he didn't. Somehow this submission just enraged her all the more.

"You think you the one who's gonna make everythin right?" she shouted. "You think *you* the one? Ha! You and every uppity nigger I ever known. You know what happens to them big-heads, child? Oh but I'm sure you *already* know, big-head you is. But just once, let you stupid nigger of a mama tell it to you anyway. Just once, you let you stupid mama feel like she got a big head too, hm? There ain't no fightin against nature. There ain't no fightin against they world. You keep goin the way you goin, you gonna end up just another dead nigger, like that Cutler one they hanged last year. What you call *forgettin* I call *survivin*. But it seems I didn't raise a survivor. No, sir. I'm sorry to say, all I did was raise a no-sense nigger with a big mouth who maybe wishes he was dead. Laws, ain't that somethin to be proud of?"

Ben glared at her and said nothing. There were tears in his eyes that refused to fall.

"You got nothin to say now, huh?" Mae Jane said with a mocking laugh. "Nigger what uses all them big words, now you got nothin to say? You wanna say anythin, you go to Mr. John's side and you pray to God that He don't make Mr. John suffer any more than he got to. You go in that room and you *pray*, child."

Wearing a look of abject disgust, Ben stepped away from her.

"Daddy would be ashamed of you," he muttered. "The people who tortured him, who stood by while it happened, who *continue* to do nothing — somehow you still think the world of them." He shook his head slowly, pitying her. "They took everything from you, they give you nothing, and still you kiss their feet."

With that, Ben turned and disappeared around the corner. Stunned, Mae Jane stood watching the empty space where he had been. She could do nothing now but open her mouth and toss one hoarse jibe after another at the far wall, hoping her words would yet reach him and wound him somehow. But finally she fell silent, exhausted, with her own venomous accusations echoing in her ears.

All she could do now was hang her head and put her dry, cracked hands together, and with one hand she began to trace the outline of the other, one finger following the weathered skin of her thumb and the soft flesh between her fingers and the furrowed lines of her palm.

"...Mae Jane?"

Wearily, she turned around. Tom was standing there, his hands at his sides. The boy seemed older than she'd ever seen him look before, as if he'd aged years in just a few short months.

"I'll help you," Tom said to her. His voice threatened to give out, but then he swallowed and gave a firm nod of reassurance. "I'll help you write your letter to JJ."

Mae Jane opened her mouth to say something, but no words came. Instead she reached out and took Tom into her arms. She closed her eyes and held the boy close against her.

She did not know how long they stood there together, but when Mae Jane opened her eyes again and looked toward the nearest window, she saw that the snow falling outside was heavier now, becoming before her eyes a smoking white tempest. It was as if the squall had caught sight of Mae Jane and howled at her, delighted by its own tremendous power. For her part, Mae Jane only stood and stared back, meeting the madness outside with a tired resignation.

Chapter 31
RIVER OF JORDAN

Near dawn a few days later, a weary, sleepless Mae Jane approached the door of the east wing study. Standing there, she gathered her courage in the darkness of the hallway. Taking a deep breath, she knocked softly on the door.

A muffled voice from inside: "Who is it?"

"Mae Jane, ma'am. May I come in?"

There was no answer from within, but Mae Jane opened the door anyway. The door was almost shut before she remembered to lift the handle so the latch would click silently into place. Turning around, she peered into the thick darkness of the study.

The embers of a low fire burned in the hearth, and within the glow Mae Jane saw the familiar shape of Isabella standing before a large oil pastoral of Clarendon, with Colonel Spencer and his wife Anna standing in the foreground amid their pack of hounds.

"The hour is late, Mae Jane," Isabella said. "What is it you want?"

Mae Jane wrung her hands together. She shuffled forward, acutely aware of a knotted pain coiled around her heart.

"Ma'am. It's...I think it's time, ma'am."

Isabella seemed not to have heard her; she continued to examine the huge painting on the wall. "I thought I heard Dr. Harper's voice from downstairs," Isabella said at last. "Was he here again? Did he deliver more of my medicine?"

Mae Jane shook her head wearily. "No, ma'am. The doctor seen Mr. John, and he...well, I don't think he's comin back. Not until..."

"Pity," Isabella said, though it wasn't clear what she was referring to. With a sigh, the Lady of Clarendon turned and swept across the floor. At the large table across the study, she picked up a brown medicine bottle. Mae Jane knew without thinking that it was Mother Bailey's. Taking up a silver spoon, Isabella tipped the bottle and carefully measured out a brimming spoonful of gelatinous yellow liquid.

Mae Jane stepped forward. She felt hot sweat on her brow, felt cold and clammy all over, indeed felt sick to her stomach. She wanted nothing more than to stagger over to the sofa and sit down. Oh but *laws*, when had she become such a sit-around?

Her heart was fine, *she* was fine. Just a touch of fever, and nothing more.

"If you've nothing to say," Isabella said, "then you shouldn't be in here bothering me. I've important business to attend to."

Mae Jane watched as Isabella plunged the spoonful of medicine down her throat. The woman's lips closed around the spoon's edge, and Mae Jane could almost hear the dull scraping of teeth against metal.

"Ma'am, did you hear me? Mr. John, he's near the end. I sent for the Cutlers. The boys are downstairs now sayin they goodbyes. It's…it's *time*, Bella."

Isabella pursed her lips to soak up the last drops as she withdrew the spoon again. She swallowed and closed her eyes, and she shuddered and let out a faint sigh. When Isabella opened her eyes again, her mind was lost somewhere in a pleasurable fog. Suddenly, Isabella burst out in girlish giggling.

"Oh, Mae Jane," she said, with a slow shake of her head. "Mae Jane, *sister*, do you remember—?" She stopped as another fit of giggles took hold of her. "Do you remember it, Mae Jane, the day we got into Daddy's dandelion wine? We were only, what, twelve years old? Oh, I still remember, such a *scolding* we got. I was surprised Daddy didn't tie me to the whipping post for that. And I was even more surprised he didn't end up selling you away like he'd threatened to do."

"*Bella*," Mae Jane said, trying to be firm but remain calm. "We ain't got much time."

Mae Jane stepped up next to Isabella and looked into the woman's eyes, which were waxen and saucer-like. Somehow, she knew that getting through to Isabella would be impossible. The real Isabella was gone — vanished, or else hidden away — and she would not be back until the medicine wore off, until the vacant-minded, yellow-eyed monster before her had retreated back into the recesses of a dark somewhere.

Still, Mae Jane yearned to speak with the real Isabella. She hoped that somehow, her words might get through. Lord knew, Mae Jane wasn't getting through to anybody in recent days. Not Mr. Jem or the other Roscoes, and certainly not with Ben.

Looking at Isabella again, Mae Jane pushed across her lips the biggest smile she could manage. It felt unnatural, and she was sure it must look so too, but she could think of nothing else to do. Nothing else to do but put on a face, a mask, and play whatever part was required.

"Why don't I take you down there now, Bella, hm? Why don't we go down there together, me and you? We can sit with Mr. John. We can sit with him, and we can talk bout whatever you—"

"*I already told you*," Isabella snarled, "*I don't want to see him*."

Mae Jane's smile froze on her lips. It remained there a while after, though her eyes had already gone glassy. Meanwhile, Isabella began to pace about before her, her accusing gestures bloodying the canvas of the air.

"For God's sake, is all this not yet over? After all, who is John Roscoe to me? A *machinist*. A pretender. A petty gambler who won a fine hand once — and only once — and who thinks himself a luminary because of it..."

Mae Jane heard all these things, but she realized she was no longer listening. All she could think was—

Nothing else to do.

"Must it be my duty to kiss this stranger goodbye?" Isabella said. "Just as it was my duty to stand and watch him desecrate my father's house? Well, I would do it — I would kiss him, if only his soul would finally up and *leave*. Oh, with such a guarantee, I'd give my beloved husband everything. Certainly he took from me whatever he wanted..."

Mae Jane watched Isabella's noiseless lips form meaningless shapes, the variations piling up one atop the other, unceasing. Mae Jane felt sweat run from her brow and into her eyes, where they stung and blinded her.

Nothing else to do.

A man was dying, a house was broken. A family had forgotten itself, and maybe never knew itself to begin with.

And still the Lady kept on, and kept on, and kept on.

Because there was *nothing else to do.*

Isabella laughed in Mae Jane's face. "You were always a puppy for your 'Mr. John', weren't you, Mae Jane? You were as smitten with him as were my sisters, once upon a time. You were jealous of Cousin Sarah, then jealous of me. Is that why you insisted on staying behind when all the others were sent away? Surely you didn't stay on *my* account, despite all I've done for you. I've been an unfailing friend to you for so many years, but now you can do naught but scurry around barking moral objections into my ear. You dare tell me how I ought to think, how I ought to feel, and all within my father's house? You want me to go down there with you, Mae Jane? Well, let us go. Let us go down there and stuff my beloved, usurping husband in a wheelbarrow, and let us cart him outside to the edge of the property and—*oh*!"

Mae Jane cuffed Isabella hard across the face. She'd struck the woman before she even felt the urge to do so — that's how fast it had happened, how unthinking it had been.

Except, no. She *had* thought to do it. And she *had* warned herself against it, even dismissed the notion as vile and cruel. But then she hit her mistress anyway. And maybe Mae Jane did it because she was tired, or because she was sick. Maybe she was just sick of a different sort, sick of hearing the same old drivel. Or maybe it was because Mae Jane heard Ben's voice cut through the anger she felt boiling inside her.

They took everything from you, they give you nothing, and yet you still kiss their feet.

Nothing else to do.

Stunned, Mae Jane watched as blood ran from Isabella's nose. The blood was the darkest red she had ever seen, indeed almost black. Isabella's face was a rictus of pain and shock, but even now she opened her mouth wide as if to scream some familiar, trusted insult. But in fact, Isabella said nothing. The woman remained silent, cowed by the bloodshot determination in Mae Jane's eyes, the sincere promise of another strike — harder this time — with more blows to come if necessary.

As her fury dissipated, Mae Jane looked down at her hand. The skin of her palm was angry, and she saw the beginnings of a welt that emanated heat and pain. She felt the first fingers of shame creep down her spine. But she would not apologize — *no*, she would not. Set against an entire life spent under Isabella Spencer's shadow, a girlhood spent with a knotted leash around her neck, feeling the splinters pricking her skin...no, Mae Jane was sorry for nothing. Nothing, she supposed, except—

"I's sorry only for stayin quiet all this time," Mae Jane said. "Sorry for always keepin my head down, for doin what don't feel right just because my 'betters' tell me it gotta be so. Sorry for answerin every time you ring the bell, *because* you ring it. Maybe I just wanted to feel useful. Maybe I just wanted a place in all this. A place in somethin small, somethin I could understand. The truth is, I don't understand much anymore. And maybe I never did."

A wave of dizziness washed over her, and Mae Jane decided she could not bear to stand any longer. Turning, she made for the sofa nearby. Once she had collapsed there on the plush seat, a heap of the Lady's dresses underneath her, Mae Jane put her head in her hands and let out a low, despairing groan.

"Nothing else to do...nothing else to do..."

With her hands over her eyes, Mae Jane could see nothing but black. It was comfortable here in the world of unseeing. To unsee was to unknow, and to unknow was to unthink. And somehow, everything felt easier that way. When nothing and everything made no sense, *had* no sense, it was somehow easier to comprehend.

"...Mae Jane?"

It was Lady Isabella's voice, and Mae Jane heard within it a rare note of concern. Still, she decided to ignore the Lady outright. For God's sake, Mae Jane didn't even know why she'd come up here in the first place. What else had she expected to happen? Just more bitching and moaning, just more *yes, ma'am* and *right away, ma'am*, same as it ever was.

Nothing else to do, and that's just the way it go.

"Mae Jane, are you all right?"

The only answer was to laugh. Mae Jane felt a fool for laughing, but no sooner had it started than the laugh became a cry, and she felt a fool for that too. But there was nothing to do but close her eyes and let her choking tears wrack her body, and try to imagine her own clutching hands were those of Evie or Carlotta-George.

Laws, was this what it was like to go mad?

"No," Mae Jane managed at last, her voice thick and halting. "No, Bella, I ain't all right. I ain't no ways good at all."

Slowly, Mae Jane loosened her hands from around her eyes and let some light seep in. When she finally drew her hands away and looked up at Isabella, she saw that the Lady stood beside her. Isabella looked down at Mae Jane, but without her usual patronizing stare. This time, Isabella's expression was one of genuine concern and compassion. Her nose had stopped bleeding, though a thin line of red ran down from her nostril to rest upon her upper lip. Within Isabella's eyes was a chastened self-awareness, a waking empathy that had been asleep for too long.

"I'm sorry, Mae Jane," Isabella whispered. Slowly, she sat down beside Mae Jane. She reached out to touch her shoulder. "I'm sorry for—"

"*Don't*," Mae Jane growled, and she slapped Isabella's hand away. "What, you think you can 'pologize for *everythin*? You just gonna say you sorry for *everythin*, and that's gonna be that? It ain't gonna work, Bella. Maybe I's still the help, but I can hit back. I can hit back now, and hit hard."

In another time, Isabella might have lost herself to unthinking fury at being swatted away like a pest. But instead, the Lady of Clarendon hung her head and became very still. And looking upon Isabella's sorrow, which to her eye was the truest, most dejected misery she had ever seen, Mae Jane knew that she ought to feel pity for the woman. She knew that she ought to feel a matching sense of compassion, knew she ought to feel the urge to forgive. That was Jesus' way, the Christian way. But still, in this moment Mae Jane refused it — all of it. For so many years, she had denied her anger against her Bella — against Clarendon, against the world. She had stamped it all down for so long, and now she wanted nothing more than to unleash the full force of it, to let the gales of hatred scream until they had blown themselves out. Seeing the dawning, quivering change in Isabella's eyes just now, seeing the light of another's revelation, Mae Jane's first instinct was to deny it, to cover it in darkness until she herself had the chance to scream and shout and wail to her heart's content. Maybe she would even strike Isabella again. After all, how many times had Isabella struck *her*? Yes, maybe the heartless old woman deserved another cuff, and a swift backhander to follow. Wouldn't that be only fair? Wouldn't that be justice of the kind Ben always talked about? For Mae Jane to have suffered such mockery and derision for so long, to have spent her girlhood playing with a girl who kept a rope around her neck like a dog, was it not *right* to meet such evils on their own terms?

But then again, where did all of that lead? Where would it all end?

"You think you the only one who feels as you do," Mae Jane said, her voice thick. "You lookin up at them paintins, wishin you was inside them somehow, wishin you was back in times before. Well, I feel it too, Bella, Lord knows. Most days I wish I was back too, back to times when I at least felt like I knew what was comin next.

Maybe times before wasn't perfect, but at least you knew em for what they was. But with tomorrow, with all that not knowin that lays ahead, you can't help feel that time's just gonna bring on somethin worse — worse than ever. And I'm tired, Bella. I'm *tired* and I…I just don't know. I *never* knew, much as I liked to think I did."

Isabella said nothing. Slowly, the woman leaned over and rested her head against Mae Jane's chest. Mae Jane tensed up, and her instinct was to push Isabella off. But instead she sat back and drew a deep breath, and she listened to Isabella's own quiet breathing.

Against Mae Jane's shoulder, Isabella murmured, "I never treated you well, Mae Jane. I never deserved you for a friend. Certainly not for a sister."

Mae Jane said nothing. She tried to swallow the hot lump in her throat, to no avail.

"I'd like to be a friend to you now," Isabella said. "I'd like to *try*, if…if it's not too late."

Trembling, Isabella turned into Mae Jane and embraced her. The two women sat there holding each other, Isabella clutching, Mae Jane rubbing her hands along Isabella's back in wide, sweeping circles. They sat there a long time, an endless time, each feeling the breath of the other.

By and by, Mae Jane turned her head to the study's windows and realized that there was a faint strip of light beyond the heavy curtains. Dawn was coming soon.

Mr. John's time was coming, and it was now so very near.

"I'll go down," Isabella said, as if the same thought had been on her mind. "I'll go down and see John."

Lifting her head, Isabella looked into Mae Jane's eyes. Their faces were very close, so close that the Lady's eyes filled the whole of Mae Jane's vision. Within those eyes, Mae Jane saw something of the old Isabella. But no, it wasn't the old Bella at all, but maybe the true Bella, the one who sometimes revealed herself to Mae Jane in quiet moments. The Bella who really had been like a sister — *was* a sister. A sister like Evie.

"Will you come down with me, Mae Jane? Will you…will you walk with me?"

Slowly, Mae Jane nodded. "Yes, Bella. I'll walk with you."

❧

The quickening dawn washed the world in golden light. The twin shadows of Mae Jane and Lady Isabella darkened the hallways of the east wing, then stretched up the walls of the grand foyer as they descended the staircase there, taking one slow step at a time. As they passed before the door of the sunroom, Mae Jane sensed encroaching death in the air. Quietly, she offered to go with Isabella to Mr. John's deathbed.

Isabella's gaze was far away, somewhere back in time. "You've said goodbye to him?"

Mae Jane nodded. "For my part. But I could sit with you, if you wanted."

Isabella considered this, and deeply. But at length, she shook her head and set a look of determination on her face. "No," she said. "I thank you, Mae Jane, but…it's been some time since John and I were alone together."

Mae Jane squeezed Isabella's hand and nodded. She opened the door and stepped aside, leaving the way open. The Lady of Clarendon looked into the death-room and, lifting her chin and taking a breath, she crossed the threshold.

Mae Jane looked into the sunroom only long enough to see the Lady standing before the bed where Mr. John lay. The whole room was bathed in morning light, and despite the dark, heavy gown the Lady wore she looked like an angel watching over the mortal man next to her. Slowly, Isabella sat down in a chair at the bedside. After a long while, the woman reached out and touched her husband's hand.

Quietly, Mae Jane shut the door.

Outside, fresh snow was falling against a bright sun and blue winter sky: a 'sun-snow' she'd heard folks call it in times past. Though the cold made her bones ache, Mae Jane felt the sudden desire to step out on the veranda and breathe in the brisk December air.

The air outside was chill, but at least there was no wind. Creamy drops of snow, light and effervescent as they were in the piercing morning light, drifted down on tiny eddies of winter's breath. Mae Jane began to trace a slow, directionless path down the veranda. As she neared the corner that would open toward the lawn and the worn slave shacks and the willow grove beyond, she heard a curious sound of metal crunching against something hard. She wondered whether it was Ben chopping wood, but the sound suggested otherwise.

Someone was digging at the ground.

Mae Jane turned the corner, and there she paused. Looking out, she saw Jem Roscoe hard at work with a spade in his hands and a shallow scar of broken earth at his feet. The idle thought crossed Mae Jane's mind that it might not be possible to dig a fresh grave this late in December, and that arrangements might have to be made to store Mr. John's body until the warmth of springtime, as they did in some places in the North.

Jem had dressed in layers, but by now he had discarded most of them. The boy drove the spade down again and again, a pale, single-minded resolve etched into his face as he dug and dug, but the blade bit only small chunks out of the frozen earth. Despite Jem's energy and strength, every strike at the earth brought him no closer to finishing his father's grave. At last Jem was compelled to stop and catch his breath, his chest heaving, and the grave no more than a divot.

Once more, Mae Jane felt a swollen pain around her heart. Putting a hand over her chest, she tried to quiet her pounding pulse. She closed her eyes and winced at the twinging strands of nerves stretching from the eyelids to the roots of her brain. She thought to pray and tried to, but no string of words came to mind. Instead she could only stand there, alone, feeling the sun's light but none of its warmth.

Mae Jane opened her eyes when she heard a door open far down the veranda. Turning her head, she watched in stunned silence as her Ben trudged across the snow-dusted lawn. Ben carried a spade over his shoulder, and before long he reached the site of Mr. John's grave. For a long while, Ben and Jem stood there staring at each other in silence. And then, movement at last. Without a word, Jem brought his spade up and struck at the earth for the hundredth time, and now Ben began to dig alongside him. The two said nothing to each other, but they worked together in a methodical fashion that soon produced a gash in the earth, now a hole, and now the walls of a grave.

While she watched the digging, the memory of a song came back to Mae Jane. As a child, she'd taken special note of weddings, wakes, and funerals — the aspects of life that were like islands of memory rising from a roiling sea of timeless monotony. Whenever one of Clarendon's servants died, whether by natural causes or otherwise, the Colonel allowed the other servants to hold a service for the departed. Mae Jane remembered how everyone would gather close to the body while an ancient woman, whom everyone understood had been touched by God, led them in song after song. Mae Jane could still hear that shaky, warbling voice on the summer air, now joined by a soft chorus of throaty voices choked with emotion. Hearing all those voices in her mind, Mae Jane began to sing quietly:

Oh, the good old chariot passing by
One more river to cross
She jarred the earth an' shook the sky
One more river to cross
The good old chariot passing by

Oh, wasn't that a wide river
River of Jordan, Lord,
Wide river
There's one more river to cross

By and by, Mae Jane turned away from the hopeful sight of Ben and Jem working together again. Retracing her steps, she stepped back into Clarendon's welcome warmth. Just as she shut the cold out and turned around, she saw Lady Isabella emerging from the sunroom with tears running down her cheeks.

Isabella cleared her throat to speak, though Mae Jane already knew what she was going to say.

"He's gone," Isabella whispered. "My poor John, he's..."

"With the Lord now," Mae Jane said.

Isabella nodded slowly. She kept nodding, and nodding still, as if the more she did the easier it would be to accept the truth. When fresh tears overtook her, the Lady held her arms wide. Without another thought, Mae Jane stepped forward and took her Bella into her arms. They stood wrapped together in the morning light, each woman leaning against the other for comfort, each standing strong to support the other. And though Mae Jane knew she could never prove it, though she knew it would be no good to try and explain it out loud, she felt an invisible weight begin to lift from her shoulders, felt the pressure around her heart begin to subside, felt the dark fog in her mind begin to clear, as if the soft, golden light of this new day had touched something beyond earthly flesh and mortal bone.

Chapter 32
EVENING AND MORNING

Jem peered past the gust of his icy breath and watched the last stragglers of Father's funeral cortège join the throng of mourners that had gathered within Clarendon's willow grove. Soft-falling December snow drifted down to rest upon the body in its open casket, and the snow filled up the open grave next to it. Drawing a handkerchief, Jem leaned down and gently wiped the snow from the body's ashen face.

Jem studied the grave, noticing the roots and rocks that jutted out from its earthen walls. A mound of dry earth had been transported to Clarendon for use in the burial, though the soil was yellow rather than the red-tinged dirt that was native to Clarendon. Then again, Jem supposed it was all the same now. Dirt was dirt.

Reverend Lucas Cutler finished his sermon, a rather gloomy speech about Jonah fleeing from God on a ship bound for 'a land where God did not exist.' Then God, all-knowing and all-powerful, conjured a great storm and sent a great leviathan to consume Jonah as punishment for his transgressions. Rather puzzlingly, the boy reverend ended the sermon there, leaving Jonah trapped in the belly of a monstrous whale seemingly for all eternity.

The congregation said together, "Amen," and the service was over.

More snow had fallen, and the body's eyelashes were white. Some present observed with morbid fascination that snowflakes did not melt on the ice-cold skin of the deceased. Still, Jem was moved to wipe his father's face clean once more—

One final time

—but a group of men had already closed the coffin and were presently nailing it shut. One of the men hammered his thumb and let out a yowl before continuing, red-faced. And just like that, the body was encased in darkness and the world saw no more of the visage of John M. Roscoe.

Sarah put her face in her hands and sobbed while Henry Cutler placed a firm, comforting hand on her pregnant belly. The rest of the Cutler family looked on, with Tobias Cutler taking his place before the crowd as the leading dignitary present.

Off to the side, Mae Jane stood holding a confused Bayard's hand, and she wept against the shoulder of Ben, who fought to keep himself from crying.

Tom stared down at the snow collecting on the tips of his shoes. Jem reached down and put his arm around Tom's shoulder. Tom looked up at him and tried a brave smile, but he didn't make it halfway before he broke down. Holding him close, Jem watched as a group of men lowered the coffin down using ropes. One of the ropes snapped, or else the men holding it were careless, for the coffin dropped with a sudden *crunch* that made the crowd gasp.

Jem started forward, but two men had already jumped into the grave to lift the coffin up and set the rope in place again. Jem's heart twisted at the sight of this. He wanted to cry *desecration* and leap forward and accost the men for their insult, but he had neither the energy nor the inclination. And really, what did it mean for a man to step first in another's grave? Jem and Ben had done this very thing when they were busy digging it out.

When the coffin was in its place and the ropes were withdrawn, Mother stepped forward. She took up a handful of yellow dirt from the larger pile. Her face was dry and hard-set as she raised her arm out over the grave and let the dirt go, first in a slow trickle like an hourglass, now releasing all of it at once. She flicked her fingers out and then wiped her palms together, and when her hands were finally clean she stepped back.

Mourners stepped forward, some to count the shivering wreaths standing nearby, others to drop clods of cold earth upon the coffin's lacquered wood. Heads of families extended their hands to Jem, and Jem accepted each gesture with the same jerking head-nod and murmur of appreciation. Jem received many whispered compliments about the blue secession cockade he wore on the lapel of his jacket. Then, the mourners braced themselves against the wind and began a slow procession away from the grave, which was hurriedly filled and mounded by four spades.

Some of the people departed in their carriages, and some went up to Clarendon to carry on the business of living with refreshments in hand. Mae Jane was soon obliged to depart, and wiping her eyes she went up to Clarendon to serve the people gathering there. By and by, the Cutlers left to join the other First Families, who had already gone. Sarah kissed each of her brothers, and she took a moment to squeeze Mother's hand. Mother, it seemed, was quietly grateful for the gesture. Sarah passed by Ben, but they only looked away from each other.

And slowly, the Roscoe family left the graveside too. First went Mother leading Bayard, then Ben and Tom. Jem decided to stay behind a moment longer, so that he could…

So that he could what? Say goodbye? What the hell did that even mean? He knew that every morning he woke up from now on, he would first think to look out the window and stare at the fresh mound of earth. He would stare at it until the fresh mound became an old mound, until grass grew up and it became indiscernible from any other patch of yard except that it lay before a new gravestone. He would stare at this place until one day he stopped looking for it, until he walked past it without a second thought. He would stare at this place until it became alien to him (more alien than it was now, anyway), and he would think of it only on certain important days of the year, because the current of life went on and he would be swept up with it. And then came the end, for himself, he meant. Was there a real *goodbye, Father* hidden somewhere within that long stretch of time?

Or was this really it?

Jem looked down at the mound of earth. He felt the instinct to dig it all up again, by hand if necessary, and tear the nailed coffin open so that he could look upon Father's face for just a little while longer. But he knew it wasn't Father in there, but a lifeless body that resembled Father, and even then it no longer looked much like him.

Just then, something made Jem look up. And looking up, he saw her there, her hair white against the snow-tipped trees.

Audrey.

She was looking at him, and indeed had been for some time. She stood apart from a large group of young Valley folks, most of them come out to see the funeral of 'JR' for the social outing, rather than to pay their respects. She carried a yearning sorrow on her face, and there was a deep wish in her eyes.

Jem started forward, but her eyes warned him away — regretfully, ruefully, but firmly. Behind her the crowd of young folks began to depart on their horses and in coaches and carriages, most of them probably bound for the Curtis House Tavern down in Mayfair. And as the milling crowd began to thin, Jem saw Ezra Blake standing amidst a familiar gang of Valley toughs, most of them men from the North Branch Mine. They were turned away from the scene of the funeral, busy looking out at the Valley from a new vantage point.

Jem could only look into Audrey's eyes again, and seeing the tear-filled warning within them, Jem finally understood.

This was it. This had to be it. His father's soul was lost to the ether, and hers would be kept forever apart from his own.

But no. Slowly, Audrey put her hand over her heart. She held it there, squeezing, and she nodded. Somehow, Jem understood.

Me. Audrey.

She made a pillow with her hands and rested her cheek upon it. Half a dozen possible meanings came to mind before Jem realized...

Tonight.

Jem nodded to her. He wanted to run to her anyway, to take her by the hand and flee together if they had to. But for now Jem stayed where he was, at his father's graveside, and watched as she turned to go.

Tonight.

Snow began to fall heavier all around Jem and the mound of earth. Soon enough, the ground would be blanketed in white.

It was now that Jem saw there was a large, ugly rock protruding from the mound. Stooping, he pulled the rock out and tossed it away. He patted the earth with his hand, shaping it, until it was as if he had never touched it.

And the snow continued to fall.

❧

No moon shone on the Blake house crouched in the overgrown field. There were no lights from within, or at least none that Jem could see. The squat goat barn stood hunched and silent in the dark. Jem's focus was fixed on the lean-to set against the house, sheltered from prevailing winds on the south side. There, between the cracks in the board, he guessed at the sallow light of a candle flickering within.

He knew Audrey would be there.

Jem stood up from the thickets and made ready to cross the open field. A loud voice in his head delivered its final warning, urging him to turn around and go home. Had he gone completely insane? Everett Blake or his son Ezra would shoot him dead if they saw him, and still he was so willing to enter the lion's den?

But somehow, none of that mattered. He had to see Audrey.

As he rode Greenbrier through the chill of the night, Jem tried to think of what he would say to Audrey when he first saw her. Everyone else in the Valley blamed Jem and the Roscoe family for the North Branch disaster, and maybe with good cause. Why shouldn't Audrey feel the same way, especially when her brothers Jonah and Charlie were among the dead? Why shouldn't she harden her heart to a man whom so many others considered a monster at worst, and a sniveling coward at best?

But then, if she felt such a way, why had she come to Father's funeral? She had looked at him (not *through* him, as he feared), and she had said much without speaking a word.

Tonight.

Jem tied Greenbrier to a snow-covered tree farther back in the woods where the colt would not be seen or heard. But something about the stillness of the night was unnerving. Hunched down at the edge of the Blake property, he studied the light shining from within the lean-to. It was the dead of night of course, so it was curious that a candle should be lit at all. Jem wondered whether he might be walking into a trap of some kind. He waited to hear the sudden baying of a hound and the *click* of a shotgun's hammer, to turn his head and spy the glint of a barrel just before Ezra Blake blew a hole through his head. Maybe each step he took toward the Blake farm was just another step closer to unwitting suicide.

Jem tried to put these thoughts out of his mind. He drew a sharp breath.

It was time to go.

Keeping low, Jem made his way along the Blake property. He knew Audrey lived in the lean-to beside the house, though he had never entered the space himself. He was aware of the cruel jokes circulating the Valley about the roof over Audrey Blake's head; specifically, that it made sense that a family of mud-eaters kept its only woman in a pigsty. But Jem knew the simple truth of it, for Audrey had told him as much. Her father had built the lean-to for his only daughter after her mother died so that Audrey might have a place of her own, a 'woman's haven' as she called it. And looking at it now, Jem surmised that the lean-to was the product of more care and craftsmanship than had ever been put into the original structure. Someday when the Blake house finally rotted out and collapsed, the sturdy lean-to might remain standing for a hundred years or more.

Jem stood before the Blake house. He was close now, close enough to reach out and touch the rough knots on the stacked timbers. Close enough that if the Blake men heard him and found him out, they'd shoot him dead and then shoot him again for good measure. It was their right, after all. Here was a trespasser, a predator lurking outside a young girl's door. It wouldn't matter if either he or Audrey pleaded their shared case. If caught, Jem was a dead man.

Jem put his hand on the screen door of the lean-to and paused. A gray blanket of some kind hung there, blocking any sight of what might be on the other side of the door. He could not risk the sound of knocking, imagining a sleeping dog's ears perking up. Instead, he pushed against the flimsy pine door just enough that he could slide inside, all the while wincing at the door's low groaning. He held his hand to catch between the jamb and the door as it closed. He pulled his fingers out one at a time until the door graced the jamb with a whisper. He took a breath and turned and saw that he was alone in a pool of candlelight.

Vanilla. That was what the small room smelled of. The smell of a dollop of fresh ice cream. Instead of filling Jem's senses it seemed to clear them out, flushing all thought from his mind and leaving him in a state of pleasurable shock, like stepping outside on a winter's day to breathe in the chilled fragrance of snow and pines. It was Audrey's scent, the taste of her pale white skin riddled with goosebumps on a cold night.

Jem glanced at the small, neat bed where she slept before looking away. Whatever his relationship with Audrey was (or had been), it was improper to gawk at the place a woman slept. There was a small coal stove with a blackened kettle atop it, and next to it was a spinning wheel with a bucket of yarn beside it. Around the room were books of various titles and volumes. Audrey's father had no money to buy books even if he had the interest or ability to read them, so Jem reasoned the books must be from the schoolhouse. They were scattered about here and there, all dog-eared and at varying stages of completion.

But no Audrey.

Jem slipped outside into the cold night air once more. He listened to the wind for a long moment and finally decided it was time to go home. But when Jem heard the noises coming from within the barn, he turned and started walking toward it. They were the low groaning sounds of an animal in distress. Jem wondered whether he ought to stamp his curiosity down and just turn away for home, but he had barely begun to formulate the idea when—

The barn door suddenly swung open. Jem shut his eyes tight.

Slowly, Jem risked opening but one eye. He expected to see the shocked mug of Ezra Blake twisting into a face of blind rage. Instead, Jem saw Audrey standing there, bright and glowing in the moonlight against the yawning blackness of the barn interior.

"Audrey," Jem croaked. Finally, he found his voice again. "Audrey, I..."

She rushed forward and embraced him. They drew ever closer, squeezing ever tighter, and Jem felt a shudder of relief. The simple touch of her was, well, he finally felt *right* again, after feeling so empty for so many months.

Audrey whispered against his shoulder, "Your father...Jem, I'm so sorry..."

Jem shook his head. "It's all right."

When she pulled back, there were the beginnings of tears in her eyes. There was also a touch of fear. "There's not much time," she said.

"Time?" he echoed. "Time for what?"

"Will you help me?"

"Help you? Yes, of course."

Audrey turned and picked up an empty bucket from nearby.

"Will you fetch some water for me, please?"

Jem could only gawk at her, stupefied. Finally, he turned and looked back at the rusty water pump standing in the field, and then he looked at Audrey again. From within the barn came the sound of some wailing animal. It had to be one of the many goats the Blakes tended.

Audrey stepped toward him and pushed the bucket into his hands. "Please, be quick about it!" she whispered hoarsely. "Meet me back in the barn and shut the door behind you. And mind you don't make any noise."

With that, she turned and disappeared into the barn. Jem stood in the field holding the bucket for a long moment, still trying to make sense of what was happening. He hurried to the pump and filled the bucket to the brim with icy water. He looked toward the darkened Blake house and listened to confirm that nothing stirred within. Then he picked up the bucket and carried it toward the barn.

The interior of the barn was lit by a single kerosene lantern. Jem shut the door behind him and was immediately greeted by dozens of curious goat snouts. Roosters and hens clucked in the corner, and a barn cat watched him with wide, unblinking eyes. A juvenile goat dipped her head toward the bucket and began to drink greedily until Jem lifted the bucket out of reach.

Jem pushed through the crowd of goats until he stood beside Audrey. She knelt down beside a nanny goat that lay in a pile of hay. The nanny was restless and she licked anxiously at the palm of Audrey's hand, now and then bleating while Audrey hushed her and sang lullabies. The nanny's rectangular eyes popped out of their sockets and one eye followed Jem as he approached.

"She's in labor," Jem breathed.

"It won't be long," Audrey said. "Set the water there."

Jem listened to the nanny's guttural groanings. He looked toward the goat's rear and saw something like a bloody red sausage sticking out from her rectum. Jem paled and swallowed hard.

"That doesn't look so good," he said. Awestruck, he reached out to prod the malformation.

"Don't touch that!" Audrey hissed, slapping his hand away. "She's prolapsed, but she's about to kid any moment now. We'll see to it when she's finished."

A dozen questions flashed in Jem's mind, but just then he felt a wet snuffling against his hand. The other goats, ever curious, pressed upon the nanny. Furious and frightened, the nanny rose with a start. Audrey and Jem fell back and watched as the nanny reared on her hind legs and bleated angrily. The other goats scattered in fear. The nanny settled and remained standing. Her whole swollen body began to twitch and shudder, and she let out several pitiful groans. Then the nanny dropped down and rolled on her side.

"Contractions," Audrey said. "It's about to happen. Help me with her. We need to get her upright again."

Jem followed Audrey's every instruction; his main task was to keep the other goats away from the nanny. For a long moment Jem forgot all about this task and simply marveled at Audrey as if caught in a trance. He watched Audrey pet the old nanny and sing a soothing lullaby, watched her massage the goat's swollen underside as much as the creature would allow. Audrey frequently inspected the nanny's rectum with a discerning, experienced eye. Finally, sensing that the nanny's moment had come, Audrey pushed herself back and created a soft bed of hay underneath the nanny's dripping rear. The nanny, maintaining the kind of stoicism only animals can demonstrate, now began to push.

Jem's mouth fell open as he watched a miniature head and four hoofed legs drop out of the nanny's womb. Audrey sighed and caught the tiny kid in the bed of hay. Meanwhile the quivering nanny collapsed with relief and turned around to inspect her progeny. Audrey pulled back to give the mother her space with her baby, but she could not resist cooing with pleasure at the little newborn. Seeing all this, Jem's heart sang. He forgot all about the other goats, and presently several rushed up to inspect the newest member of their community.

The nanny licked her shivering kid, whose hairy body was slicked with blood and feces. Audrey cupped water into her hands and doused the kid like she was a baptizing priestess, and the nanny continued licking all the while. Finally, Audrey looked up at Jem with a beaming smile.

"Isn't she wonderful?"

Jem stared at her, his eyes filled with wonder. "I'll say."

The nanny struggled upright again. Another kid was coming. Two more came, in fact, both just as tiny and precious as the first. In between births, the mother paused to clean each kid. The newborns, blind and barely able to stand, groped and writhed toward their mother's udders. But just as the suckling babies began to feed, the nanny pushed herself upright once more.

"One more," Audrey said. "She'll have one more."

"Tough goat," Jem said with a laugh.

The joke was lost on Audrey. She inspected the nanny's rectum and sagging belly with fearful concern. "Oh no," she murmured. "Oh no, no, no. . ."

Jem knelt down beside her. "What's wrong? What's—"

"He's malpresented," Audrey said. "The legs are about to come out, but not the head. The head will pull back along his spine, and when the contractions are strongest..."

She broke off and pressed her fingers along the nanny's belly. The nanny groaned and kicked at Audrey's chest.

"I'm sorry, girl, I'm sorry..."

Feeling helpless, Jem stroked the top of the old nanny's head. "What can we do?"

"Whatever we can," Audrey said. "The rest is up to God."

Jem nodded. But did God give a damn about goats? He supposed now wasn't the time for such questions.

Audrey put her hands on the nanny's belly until she found the outline of the kid within her womb. The nanny bucked and bleated and kicked violently at Audrey.

"Hold her," Audrey said. "Hold her. She doesn't understand."

Jem wrapped his arms around the nanny's neck and forelegs, holding her firmly but careful not to pin her down. The nanny struggled pitifully, and his instincts screamed at him to let the poor thing go. But he held on, and he watched over his shoulder as Audrey massaged the nanny's distended bag. Audrey's face was grim and intently focused on the task at hand.

The nanny bucked again, but then suddenly her fighting spirit left her as the contractions began again. Audrey went to the goat's rear and heaved an anxious breath of anticipation. Slowly, Jem let go of the old nanny and inched back. Now it was up to nature, up to God, up to forces greater and deeper than any human effort. He sat beside Audrey and watched with astonishment as the nanny delivered her fourth and final kid. There were the forelegs, now the hind...

...and what about the head?

Jem heard Audrey take in a sharp breath.

Finally, there it was. A tiny, beautiful head emerged from the nanny's open womb. The kid plopped down into the bed of hay and let out a squeak of displeasure.

Teary-eyed and trembling, Audrey sighed with relief and threw herself into Jem's arms. Jem regained his balance and embraced her and they laughed together. Then Audrey crawled over to the nanny goat, who was busy licking her little runt, and she wrapped her arms around the mother's neck. She kissed the nanny a dozen times on the head and rubbed her cheek against the goat's bristling face. Somehow Jem detected in the old goat's square eyes a loving affection for her mistress, and he laughed seeing the two of them nuzzle each other like the oldest of friends. In that moment, Jem loved Audrey Blake more than ever.

"You know," Jem said, "my sister may have need for a midwife soon."

Audrey laughed and shook her head. "I only know barn animals, I'm afraid."

Jem laughed with her, but slowly his smile faded when he realized that the world outside the barn was getting brighter. A new day had arrived already, and he'd spent the whole night with Audrey and the goats. He swallowed hard, trying to gather his thoughts and courage for what he needed to say.

"Audrey. I came to see you because—"

"I know," she said. "I'm sorry, Jem. I didn't think she would kid tonight of all nights. I was hoping to spend more time, just me and you."

Jem's chest tightened. "It's not that. It's *me* who's sorry, Audrey. For everything. You have every right to blame me, and to...to hate me."

She reached out and took his hand. "Oh, Jem. How could I hate you?"

Her hands were small, warm to the touch. Jem moved his thumb along the palm of her hand.

"All the same, I'd understand if you did," he murmured. "The others say—"

"I don't care what the others say," Audrey said. "All those boys down the mine, and Jonah and Charlie — none of it was your fault. I wish to God none of it had happened, but still it *wasn't your fault*. What's more, you went down there. You tried to get them out, but...there wasn't anything else you or anyone else could have done." She squeezed his hands and looked into his eyes. "You're a good man, Jem Roscoe."

Jem hung his head. "Maybe. But no matter how much I try to tell myself that, I don't know if I'll ever believe it."

"Believe me then," she said. There were tears in her eyes now, the ones she'd been trying all this time to fight off. "I tried to come to you after. I did try, Jem, you must believe me. Daddy, he got sick after the boys died. He stopped eating, stopped sleeping. It came to be that my teacher's salary was all we had to live on. And Ezra, he said Jonah and Charlie would be ashamed of me if I tried to see you. He said he'd do terrible things to you if he saw us together, and I just couldn't let that happen on my account."

Jem pulled her into his arms and held her. He felt her hot tears through his shirt. His own tears stung his eyes and dribbled down his cheeks.

Speaking against his chest, she said, "Maybe I did try to put you out of my mind, Jem. Maybe I did try to convince myself it was for the best. But I…I couldn't, and I can't. And seeing you today, at your father's funeral…" She burrowed into him. "I don't know what to do, Jem. I *don't know what to do…*"

He kissed her and whispered, "I love you." She kissed him back. Breathless, her lips touching his, she whispered the same and kissed him again.

Outside, a dog barked and a door slammed.

"Audie!" a gruff voice cried. "Hey, Audie!"

It was Ezra.

Jem's blood turned cold. Meanwhile, Audrey was already at the barn door. Just as she began to open it, Jem put a hand on her arm.

"Don't," he said. "Maybe I could—"

"Don't be a fool," she whispered, and gently but firmly pushed him aside. Audrey opened the door and was suddenly bathed in morning light. She stepped outside and shut the door behind her, and the barn was once again dark and quiet save for the snuffling of the goats. While he clung to the shadows, Jem listened as Audrey exchanged quiet words with her brother out in the barnyard.

A few minutes later, the barn door opened and Audrey returned, alone.

"You should go," she whispered as she shut the door.

Jem nodded. "That's a good idea. But, Audrey—"

"Ezra's around," she said. "Daddy won't be up for a while yet, but the dogs are out. I'll feed them, keep them busy so you'll have a chance to—"

From outside came a loud crash, the yelp of a dog, and a savage voice: "Fucking mutt…"

"We can't linger," Audrey said. "I'll keep the dogs busy. You slip out and you go, and you keep going. And don't you dare come back here again, Jem Roscoe. I was a fool for trying to bring you here. It's not safe for you, and what's more—"

"Dixon's Mill," Jem said.

"Pardon?"

"Dixon's Mill," Jem repeated. "The storehouse. Sugar Dave gave me a key. It's dry there, warm. We'll be safe." Jem took her hands in his. "You think you can get away? You think you can get away tonight, at candle-lighting?"

Audrey looked fearfully toward the barn door, and what lay beyond. "I'll try," she said, her voice tight with fear. But now she took a deep breath, and her resolve strengthened. "Yes," she affirmed. "I'll meet you there, Jem. Tonight."

He leaned down and kissed her. He could have stayed there forever, but now

Audrey drew back. She placed her hands on either side of his head and looked into his eyes.

"You need to go, Jem. You need to leave me be, *please*."

He smiled at her. "I will. But only for a little while."

Audrey nodded. And at last, she smiled back at him.

"Yes, my love. Only for a little while."

❧

Pale light seeped into the winter sky from the eastern horizon, as if an invisible hand were painting the dawn over the dried black ink of night. Jem had no desire to sleep. How *could* he, with Audrey's face still seared in his vision, and her kiss still warm on his lips? And so, instead Jem fetched Greenbrier and decided he'd ride around the Valley before returning home. Doing so was no small feat, but he knew he had time.

It was December 20th, 1860, and Jem Roscoe had all the time in the world.

Jem ascended the West Cut, the wind-blasted ridge that formed the western border of the Valley. There was no road here, but the riding was easy, relatively speaking. Down in the dense forests of the Valley itself the roads wound through the undergrowth. As the crow flew, a rider could pass from one Branch to the other much faster by taking either of the Cuts.

Jem turned to the late December sun and felt its fragile warmth on his cold cheeks. He imagined Audrey riding beside him, or better yet, riding with him atop Greenbrier. When it was warmer, they would ride down into the Valley and go swimming at the creek near Dixon's Mill. Afterward they would lay in the grass and talk together for hours. They would talk about anything and everything, and in fact Jem would be content to simply lay back and listen to Audrey's voice and not utter a word.

And what of tonight?

Tonight, he and Audrey would finally be together again. Finally, they would have the time to speak together, to make up for lost time, to say all the things that had gone unsaid for so long.

Jem felt a return of boyish giddiness. He began to compose terrible love poems in his head. He looked out at his surroundings without his usual dour sense of disappointment. Instead he gazed in awe at the rough-hewn beauty of the snow-capped North Branch, and he marveled at the rugged majesty of the Valley's crescent moon shape. The humble sprawl of Mayfair, which he used to so easily dismiss as a one-horse nowhere, now appeared to him an enchanting place of possibility.

For so long a time, Jem Roscoe had dreamed of nothing more than leaving Mayfair behind forever, so long and good riddance. As the second son, he had believed it his destiny to be wanderer, to remain staunchly irreverent to his father's ambitions for the Roscoe family. When the current of life took him elsewhere, he had fought against it. But with Father gone, and with no one else to preserve the Roscoe legacy, the awareness of what Jem had to do — what he felt he *must do* — came into sharp relief.

And now, looking out at the shimming Mayfair Valley, his spirit attuned to that curious instinct of the deep connectivity of all things, with almost every thought fixed upon the beauty and grace and joy that was Audrey Blake and the blissful promise of building a life with her *here*, Jem Roscoe began to look upon his humble one-horse nowhere with a feeling very near to contentment.

When the bell of the Mayfair First Church tolled the first time, Jem reckoned it had to be a call for Sunday service. But when the bell sounded again, Jem remembered it wasn't Sunday yet. Still, the bell went on knelling with frantic energy, until Jem was compelled to sit Greenbrier and listen and watch.

Down in the Valley below, moving like ants upon patches of white snow, the people of Mayfair flocked into the rutted streets. All were moving, some running, toward the First Church, where a great crowd was gathering. They looked up at the tower, toward the sound of the tolling bell, as if it were signaling the hour of deliverance, or doom.

Agitated by the incessant knelling, Greenbrier gave a start. Jem hushed him, but he could feel the colt's nervousness in his own clenching heart. Maybe it was keen instinct, or maybe it was just unthinking foolishness, but Jem had to know what had happened. He nudged Greenbrier's sides and started in the direction of Mayfair. As he drew ever closer, he still could not tell whether the bells extolled joy, or whether something, somewhere, had gone terribly, terribly wrong.

Chapter 33

A POINT OF HONOR

"Atten-*tion!*"

Some four score raw recruits splashed to a sluggish halt and grimaced against the driving December rain. Even in tropical South Carolina, the rain this time of year was cold enough to kill a grown man with pneumonia.

Rain drummed on the visor of JJ Roscoe's forage cap as he strolled up and down the ranks correcting posture and identifying infractions. Even in a soaking downpour he had a sharp eye for loose threads, dirty collars, missing buttons, unlaced boots.

One man broke attention to scratch his buttocks. Another attempted to hold a chest-rattling sneeze and instead exploded, and now the others around him began to point and laugh at the great string of green snot drooping from the man's flooded nostrils.

JJ gritted his teeth. These lickfinger fools were the pride of the Union? The last vestige of American democracy standing against a traitorous Charleston mob?

JJ reached for a powerful voice within himself and threw his head back.

"*You men*...are the garrison of the last Federal fortress in the state of South Carolina."

JJ watched steam rise up from the drenched shoulders of the men standing like hunchbacks. These were not soldiers. They were farm boys, blacksmiths, carpenters, grocery clerks. Some were prisoners sent here under hard labor sentences. In any case, the men that were here were the men JJ had. He pointed at the low earthen walls separating tiny Fort Moultrie from the gray world beyond.

"Last night, South Carolina enacted an ordinance of secession. For the uneducated, that means South Carolina has decided to split from the Union. You-all heard the bells and cheering, and you saw the fireworks too. But make no mistake: those people across the harbor are nothing more than traitors. The people of South Carolina have illegally declared themselves a free people in opposition to the United States. Beyond those walls, gentlemen, are rebels. They are not soldiers, they are not patriots. Again I say they are *traitors*, and they stand ready to storm this fortress at the slightest provocation, for they now consider us foreign invaders. It is my responsibility, and your duty, to put down any attempt to seize the ground upon which we stand. For if you fail, the rebels will show no mercy. Offer yourself as a prisoner, and they will shoot you like a dog — provided I don't shoot you down first."

The soldiers' eyes widened with fear. JJ paced up and down the line.

"I will instruct you in the ways of war. I will teach you to march, to shoot, to kill."

Someone sneezed just then, and JJ turned on the sound like a fox. He stepped up to the sneezing man, a scrawny private named—

"—Daniel Hough, sir," the private replied in a high, girlish voice. "Tipperary."

JJ squinted at the man through the pelting rain. "What the fuck is Tipperary, Private?"

The private wiped the snot away, but his nose continued to run in the rain. "It's a place, sir. In Ireland, sir."

Well, that explained the lilt in the boy's voice, but not his swarthy skin and dark hair. Weren't all Irishmen supposed to be redheads?

"You don't look Irish to me, Private Hough. You look like a mulatto."

"I'm Irish, sir, honest. Me ma had red hair and the like."

JJ glared down at the sopping wet Irishman, who was still wiping his nose. "I don't care where the hell you're from, Private. You're an American now, and a soldier. Act like one."

Hough snorted back phlegm. "Yessir!"

JJ turned and paced down the line, brooding. Across the parade ground, something caught his eye. Warm light out shone from a warped window slicked with rain, and standing inside was the blurry blue shape of a man.

Major Anderson.

The major was beckoning him inside. Seeing this, JJ nodded and turned back to address his men one final time.

"Fall out for your assigned work details, gentlemen. *Dismissed*!"

The men scattered, showing more spirit in their escape than at any point during the drill. JJ met Private Hough's watery eyes, looked past him, and examined the gathering darkness above the fort. A tropical storm was on the way, very late in the season. As thunder pealed somewhere offshore, JJ recalled the sound of fireworks that boomed all through the previous night.

Last night, December 20th, JJ had been on night watch. As he roamed the ramparts of Fort Moultrie, he could not help but feel a strange churning in his stomach. The disturbing sensation that gripped him was more than simply feeling *not right*; he felt utterly *wrong*, as if the blood flowing through his veins had become black bile, or the breaths he drew were in fact noxious fumes. And though JJ despised any notion of *intuition*, he could not help but feel that something, somewhere, had gone terribly wrong.

For some reason, he thought about Father.

Just then, blinding lights had flashed in the sky. A terrific *boom* roared over the water as the city of Charleston exploded with jubilation. Bells pealed from every church steeple, cannons thundered, muskets and pistols cracked. The cheering of the South Carolinian people, rejoicing freedom and liberty, rang out loudest of all.

"They must be celebrating Christmas early," one of the men said.

As the night stretched on, the rooftops and towers glowed with bonfires and flaring Roman candles, and the night air was filled with fireworks and joyful voices singing together. South Carolina had declared its independence and severed all ties with the United States. From the walls of Fort Moultrie, the gaunt-faced garrison looked on at the celebrating city with pits hardening in their stomachs.

An hour after the commotion began, a breathless soldier of the garrison stumbled back to Moultrie. He had been enjoying a two-day leave in Charleston to woo a local girl when the announcement of secession came. The man described wild-eyed Charlestonians passing around blue secession cockades and sticking palmetto leaves in their hats. Flags bearing the Stars and Stripes were set aflame, while blue flags bearing a white palmetto tree and crescent moon were hoisted from every high place.

"And they're dancin like colored minstrels," the man gasped. A corporal gave the man a shot of liquor and the man continued. Companies of militia stalked Charleston's streets, the man said, and they had stormed the gates of Castle Pinckney in the city center and took its tiny garrison prisoner. Already, a convention of Carolinian politicians and renegade US Army officers were organizing to discuss what should be done about the two remaining Federal forts in the immediate area, which were now considered foreign installations on sovereign Carolina soil.

"I escaped just in time," the eyewitness said, "but I seen hundreds of men board steamers with orders to capture or sink any Federal vessels in the harbor. And they're sendin soldiers to scout the walls here."

"Stop calling them soldiers," JJ had said to the man. "They're rebels, and nothing more."

The disturbing news had badly shaken the men of Fort Moultrie, and JJ even heard rumors of men considering desertion. Many were themselves Southerners, with no particular affection for the incoming 'Black Republican' government.

All the same, JJ drove the men out of bed early the next morning and drilled them all day long. Tired soldiers did not run off, especially not with rebels prowling the woods beyond Moultrie's walls, and especially not after JJ explained that the rebels would shoot prisoners on sight. As far as JJ was concerned, the garrison's loyalty was no longer a problem.

But as for Major Anderson — now *there* was a different problem altogether.

Before stepping into the commander's quarters, JJ removed his cap and shook the rain from his boots and poncho. Entering, JJ immediately went rigid and saluted a frail man wearing the insignia of a major.

"Dammit, man, shut the door. You'll let the warm out."

JJ closed the door behind him.

Major Robert Anderson was, in a word, unremarkable. He was of average height, plain to look at, and looked out at the world through large eyes set in deep, knobby holes. He wore his thinning gray hair in a tight comb-over. He was what young soldiers like JJ called one of the Old Breed: born to heroes of the Revolution and raised with unwavering devotion to the Union. He bore on stooped shoulders the Old World weights of chivalry and nobility, and was rooted in place by stale notions of honor and self-sacrifice. A native of Kentucky, Anderson's love of the South was, so he said, exceeded only by his love of the Union. JJ wondered if his was even patriotic love at all, but rather some kind of automatic, unthinking compliance to higher authority.

Anderson sat down at a solid old desk in the corner near the fireplace. He beckoned for JJ to sit in the chair across. Finally seated before the fire, JJ appreciated its warmth. But while his eyes were fixed on Anderson, the major stared blankly at the flames.

"How are the men?" Anderson asked, speaking in a Kentucky drawl.

JJ searched for the right word. "Pliable," he offered.

Anderson continued to stare at the fire, as if deep in thought.

"One thing," JJ said. "The men are complaining about the mail. The last delivery was more than a month ago. They are expecting tokens from family, Christmas cards."

Anderson scoffed. "Christmas cards..." His eyes sharpened. "Do you think they're ready? For action, I mean."

JJ sat up straight. *Action?*

"None of them have ever fired a shot in anger," JJ said. He paused as he tried to guess the true nature of the question. "But they will be ready, sir. It will take some time, but I'll whip them into fighting shape."

A bitter smile spread across Anderson's wrinkled lips. "President Buchanan told me I'd have crack troops under my command. *Cracked* troops." He looked up at JJ. "It may surprise you, Roscoe, but I've seen much worse. I commanded an artillery battery at Veracruz, and compared to those damn fools this lot is the Praetorian Guard. I only care if they can fire the guns."

"I'll have them ready, sir."

A long moment of silence passed, broken only by the crackling of the fire. Outside, a lone bugler gurgled the evening mess call. The fire reflected in Anderson's unblinking eyes, red-rimmed and distant. JJ saw that Anderson clutched a letter in his hands.

JJ cleared his throat. Anderson looked at him with surprise, as if he'd forgotten JJ was still there.

"May I speak freely, sir?"

Anderson grunted his assent, and his eyes returned to the fire.

"I've had time to reconnoiter the defenses of Fort Moultrie," JJ said. "Sir, it's my estimation that Moultrie is absolutely indefensible to a land attack. It's not a question of *if* an enemy force could overrun our defenses, but *when*. The ramparts are low and easily scaled, and we are surrounded by sand hills, which are perfect nests for sharpshooters. Castle Pinckney in Charleston is lost to us, and to try to retake it would be suicide. The rebels will come here next. Therefore, sir, I recommend we abandon Fort Moultrie and consolidate our men and guns on the island of Fort Sumter before they occupy the harbor."

Anderson perked up. "Abandon Fort Moultrie? Retreat?"

JJ clenched his jaw. A career officer of the Old Breed, even this middling major, would sooner put a bullet in his brain than abandon his post. JJ considered his next words carefully.

"Forgive me, sir, if I misspoke. Not retreat. A strategic consolidation. A grouping of every man under your command. Fort Sumter has guns, sir, and good ones. We could wire Washington for resupply and reinforcements. From the island we dominate not just Charleston Harbor, but the shipping lanes leading into it. No vessel can enter or leave without first passing by Sumter. When the rebellion here turns violent, we could blockade the city's sea routes and—"

"You mean *if* the rebellion turns violent," Anderson said.

"Sir..."

Anderson shook his head. "This is still a political situation, Roscoe, not a military one. I will not surrender any Federal ground. That would only embolden the knaves further."

JJ twitched. He sat upright in his chair, squared his shoulders, and abandoned any platitudes.

"If I may, Major: you surrender nothing. There is no enemy — not yet. But if we occupy Sumter now, we will be in the best position to defend ourselves against possible attack. At the moment of violence, the people of Charleston will sail out and occupy Sumter under our noses, and then they will turn its guns upon Moultrie and pound us to pieces at their leisure."

As Anderson listened to all this, his pale face suddenly flushed a furious red. The old man leaped to his feet, his cheeks swollen with anger.

"Goddammit, man, don't you realize I've thought of all that?!"

JJ remained unshaken. Instead he stared at the major, his own frustration concealed behind glass eyes. JJ stood up to match Anderson's height.

"If you've already thought of it, sir, then I wonder why the commanding officer hasn't already issued the order to move the garrison. Sir."

Anderson glared at JJ defiantly. "There's little doubting your intellect, Roscoe, or your ambition. Beauregard told me everything I needed to know about you. But you want to know what will hold you back? You think yourself the smartest man in the room, and this makes you resentful. Somebody somewhere must have done you a terrible disservice, because you seem to hold the entire world in utter disregard."

For a brief moment, JJ looked away.

"How can you expect to lead men when you are incapable of following?" Anderson said.

JJ looked up at the major again. He reminded himself to maintain a sense of calm deference, if only for show.

"Just as my superiors demand greatness from me, sir, I expect greatness from them." Here, JJ gestured beyond the rain-slicked window at the blurry shapes toiling in the mud outside. "A soldier has a duty to obey his commander, certainly, but he has no duty to respect him. Soldiers respect men of decisive action, and a commander must earn that respect."

"Says the boy six months out of West Point," the major said with a laugh. "So what, you don't respect me? You look at me and think, what, that I'm just some old dog who never learned any good tricks in the first place?"

"I did not say that, sir."

Anderson laughed again. "No, of course you didn't." Slowly, the old man's laugh ebbed away as he looked down at the letter still clutched in his hands. Suddenly, he thrust the letter toward JJ.

"What do you and your brilliant mind make of this then?"

JJ took the letter. "From the War Department, sir?"

"From Washington, yes. Go on."

JJ unfolded the letter. He glanced at the major once, then turned his eyes on the note and read aloud:

"*Major Anderson. In your verbal instructions, you were directed to hold possession of the forts in the harbor of Charleston, and, if attacked, to defend yourself to the last extremity. Under these instructions, you might infer that you are required to make a vain and useless sacrifice of your own life and the lives of the men under your command, upon a mere point of honor. This is far from President Buchanan's intentions. You are to exercise sound military discretion on this subject.*

"*It is neither expected nor desired that you should expose your own life or that of your men in a hopeless conflict in defense of these forts. If they are invested or attacked by a force so superior that resistance would, in your judgment, be a useless waste of life, it will be your duty to yield to necessity, and make the best terms in your power.*

"*This will be the conduct of an honorable, brave, and humane officer, and you will be fully justified in such an action.*"

JJ lowered the letter and met Anderson's gaze.

Anderson finished the rest of the letter from memory: "*These orders are strictly confidential, and not to be communicated even to the officers under your command, without close necessity."*

JJ shook his head with disbelief. "I don't understand it, sir."

"Buchanan will not send food or ammunition," Anderson replied. "He will not send reinforcements. Instead, I have orders to strengthen the forts — dig ditches, build fences, move the guns to and fro."

JJ shook his head again. "For what? So the Carolinians can waltz in here and take it all whenever they wish? That letter says it all, sir. The president doesn't want us to defend the harbor forts. He wants us to hand everything over to *them*."

JJ folded the letter on the creases. His mind whirred.

"The Secretary of War is a known secessionist, sir. Buchanan's cabinet is full of them, and there are just as many secessionist in the House and Senate too. They mean to hand the keys of all the coastal forts, from Virginia to Texas, over to the rebels before Lincoln's inauguration."

Anderson waved him off. "I don't like you, Roscoe, and I have briefed you on our situation only after great reflection. As such, I won't suffer any traitorous talk. Secessionists in the administration? Good God, is that all your *brilliant* mind can conjure?"

"Sir..."

Anderson folded his hands behind his back and walked to the fire. He stood before the hearth and stared down at the flames. "I don't know how much longer this charade can go on," he said. There was a long pause. "I don't know much longer *I* can go on."

For some reason, JJ heard Father's voice come back to him from some distant memory he thought he had stamped down.

I haven't the time to be pedantic. What I have to say, I will simply say.

Anderson hung his head. There was a deep melancholy in his eyes.

"With every passing day we stay here, every day we defy them, more flock to their banner. They have a new flag, Roscoe. You see the blue flag with the single star? It is only a matter of time before they declare a new government, write a new constitution. They will soon organize a new army. It is a new America, at once the same and yet wholly different. Meanwhile, the old Union withers on the vine, crushed by the weight of its own contradictions.

"Our country is dying, Roscoe. Have you ever seen rats on a sinking ship? Faced with the same fate, people are no different. They will abandon each other, and perhaps consume each other. It will happen here first. And one by one, the other states will leave and join South Carolina. The Deep South first, but then Tennessee, Virginia, perhaps even my Kentucky. And even if a Southern man still bears love for the Union of his fathers, how can that man remain loyal to a Union he no longer recognizes, or feel love for a country that is suddenly foreign and hostile? That man Lincoln isn't my president, and he never shall be. So how can I stand up for strangers and stand against my own community? How can a man stand against his friends and family? His homeland?"

JJ's voice hardened. "With respect, sir," he said sternly, "you told me just now you won't hear traitorous talk from me. I advise you to heed your own advice."

Anderson turned to face him, and there were angry tears in his eyes.

"You claim to know much about what it takes to be a leader of men, Roscoe. Well, an officer has his duty. An officer has honor. Commitment to service, commitment to his flag. I won't serve under any new flag, no matter what I believe. I was born under the Stars and Stripes, and I'll go to my grave wrapped in them. Can you say the same?"

"Of course," JJ said. "I've never once doubted my loyalty to the Union."

Anderson tossed a bitter laugh at his feet and shook his head. "Oh, *well*. If only we could all be as upstanding as you are, Roscoe."

While Anderson turned back to the fire and became lost in his thoughts, JJ looked down at the War Department letter one last time. Suddenly, an idea came to mind. Approaching Anderson, he stretched out his hand and offered the letter back.

"Forts."

Anderson scrunched his brows. "I beg your pardon? Forts?"

"*Forts*." JJ offered the letter again until Anderson took it from him. "President Buchanan orders against engaging in a 'hopeless defense of the *forts*.' He says nothing about continuing to defend a single fortress."

Anderson opened the letter and read it quickly, then looked at JJ again. "You're reaching, Lieutenant."

JJ now stood eye to eye with Anderson. For the first time in that interview he spoke softly, assuming at last the role of quiet confidant, offering the considerate counsel he knew Anderson was so desperate to have.

"Fort Sumter is our best chance for survival, sir. No, it's our *only* chance. If we stay here, the Carolinians will force our hand sooner or later. And when we react, they will cut us down like animals. We'll end up dead or in chains working alongside their negroes. But if we move the garrison to Sumter, we stand the best chance of outlasting them, and if need be, outfighting them. We can hold until relieved. And if we do that, then even if the moon should plunge into the sea, we will know we have done our duty."

Anderson hung his head and sighed. "I told you, I cannot willfully abandon my post."

JJ shook his head. "But we abandon nothing, Major. If we keep our men here at Moultrie while leaving Sumter undefended, the situation is the same. Better then to transfer your command to the stronger point of defense. Once there, we hold until relieved."

Anderson was quiet, brooding. For a strained moment, his face was full of doubt and anxiety. The old man looked away and stared at the fire, the same as he'd done countless times already. When finally he turned back to JJ again, his expression had shifted from one of despair to one of determined action.

"You're certain this action can be undertaken?"

"Beyond certain, sir."

Anderson nodded. "The Charlestonians cannot know. Once they catch wind of what we're up to — if they spot us out there on the water en route to Sumter..."

"We move under cover of darkness," JJ said.

Anderson nodded again. "Agreed. When can we be ready?"

JJ thought about it, and a smile crept across his lips. "There will be no moon cover from now until Christmas Day. I think we'll be ready to move just in time for the holidays, sir."

❧

Thick fog rolled across Charleston Harbor. Near midnight, the low clouds creeped in and scattered the moonlight, then billowed up and blocked it completely. The beams of search lanterns from prowling steamers could not pierce the gloom.

In the safety of the shadows, the men of Fort Moultrie moved about like ghosts on the parapets, hurrying but not rushing to make their final preparations. As a last measure, the carpenters turned their saws on the massive flagpole anchoring the parade grounds. As the saws bit at the husky pinewood, the Stars and Stripes was lowered, carefully folded, and placed under the arm of Major Anderson, who cradled the flag like it was a newborn child.

The boats waited on the beach. JJ conducted a final inspection, murmuring orders to shift the weight of men and supplies either fore or aft, and hushing the men when their hoarse, excited whispers carried on the wind.

Anderson joined them now, his face taut and grim. He seemed to be in pain, no doubt already regretting leaving his post. But the major had made his decision, and JJ had assured him that it was the right decision to make. It was a mile sail from the shores of Moultrie to the island fortress called Sumter. If they were lucky, and if the elements cooperated, they could slip across the harbor undetected. Besides, it was Christmas Eve. How many secessionists could be prowling around tonight?

From inside Moultrie, a sharp blast snapped the still quiet. Now came a splintering sound followed by a tremendous groan. In the inky darkness, the men squinted and watched the great flagpole topple down to crash on Moultrie's battlements. There it splintered and the pieces crashed down on either side of the wall.

A man said aloud, "Merry Christmas, you secesh bastards."

There was soft laughter from the men. Now came the wild scampering of several cloaked figures racing from Moultrie's yawning front gate to join the waiting boats. The carpenters-turned-saboteurs had done their duty. The men on the boats congratulated them with low cheers and handshakes. Anderson called their work beautiful. Then he nodded to JJ.

JJ removed his forage cap. "Hats off. Remove your jackets. No lights, nothing shines." The men dressed down and draped their blue uniforms over their muskets to conceal the glint of their bayonets. Their breath misted in the chilly December air.

"Row tight, row steady," JJ said. "All together now."

Fort Sumter dominated Charleston Harbor atop a sandbar of seventy thousand tons of granite. The granite was from New England, a fact to which most Charleston citizens were oblivious, or else willfully ignorant. JJ decided it was only the mistaken belief that Fort Sumter, named after a hero of the Revolution, stood on hallowed South Carolina soil that had so far prevented its seizure by Charlestonians. But he suspected the seceshes *would* try to seize it, and soon.

But for now, the way to Sumter lay open.

Shaped as a truncated pentagon, Fort Sumter was designed to house nearly seven hundred men and over one hundred heavy guns. Sumter had sixty guns lining the battlements, though few among the garrison knew how to fire them. But at least they would be sheltered. Though Sumter's barracks was still under construction, its walls were high and several inches thick.

As the convoy of rowboats neared Sumter, JJ scanned the battlements for signs of life and saw nothing. There seemed to be no light emitting from within the fortress walls. That was good. If the fortress was deserted, it would be simple enough to—

"*Steamer!*"

All heads turned starboard. Emerging from the gloom was a long white steamship plowing through the icy black water like a monstrous whale, and for a brief moment JJ thought he might indeed be witnessing the passing of some great leviathan. There were gaslights on the bow and a great spotlight burning holes through the fog, and there were deckhands leaning over the gunwales peering into the gloom.

Here were eighty-five men suspended in the water, their oars pulled in, drifting in the current. JJ watched the steamer's spotlight carve slices out of the fog. It really did seem like the all-seeing eye of some terrible sea monster.

The spotlight was nearly upon them. But just now a man on the steamer's port side called aloud, the spotlight jerked away, and it lighted upon a patch of fog far away. Maybe the deckhand had seen a rock or a seal in the water and mistook it for a man. Whatever it was, it didn't matter.

It was time to move, and Fort Sumter lay just a few hundred yards away.

JJ gave a stern nod to the men and they dipped their oars again for the final push.

❧

Christmas Day dawned clear over Charleston, with the night sky brightening to a vibrant blue. But as the people of the city rose from their beds and looked out their windows, they saw dark clouds drifting up from the South. The currents from the southern seas brought thankfully few storms this time of year, but it seemed to most that there would be a mess of weather that would land sometime before the New Year. In the meantime, a blue-sky Christmas, with a warmer breeze than Charleston had known in weeks, seemed a providential gift.

The people of Charleston dressed and greeted their kin at their hearths, and there they shared quiet mornings of simple Christmas pleasures and intimate family traditions. When the bells began to ring, not many paid them much heed. But then, the incessant ringing became too much, and the people of Charleston stepped outdoors to complain together in the streets.

And then, spreading like wildfire, came the dark tidings which the bells were signaling.

The news spread slowly at first, then at a pace too fast for even the *Charleston Mercury* printers to beat. The sentries atop Castle Pinckney were perhaps the first to see it, but the beggars along the Battery were the first to send urgent messages through the streets. Young orphans raced down alleyways and snaked their way through fenced yards, some delivering the message personally and with great solemnity to each doorstep, others obnoxiously calling out the news for whole neighborhoods to hear:

"*The Yankees have taken Sumter! The Yankees have taken Sumter!*"

Now the pealing bells were justified in their clamor. The quiet of that tropical Christmas morning fell away as the people of Charleston rushed up to their highest windows and strained to see across the vast harbor. Those who reached the edges of the piers and those with looking-glasses trained their eyes upon the rumored sight with gasps of shock:

The Stars and Stripes, proud and defiant, rippled atop Fort Sumter's flagpole.

The Yankees had taken Sumter!

Though distant and apparently easy to miss, when pointed out to an observer the sight suddenly dominated the landscape. Prideful Charleston, with the fires of secession's celebration still smoldering and with its blue palmetto flag flying from every pole and window, a cityscape pure in its revolutionary spirit, was now besmudged by the brazen, ugly stain of the Federal flag flying in open mockery of the newborn South Carolina nation.

That Christmas Day saw the number of Charleston's militia service signatures skyrocket like never before. The recruiting offices, makeshift as they were, were overrun with volunteers. Even members of the city council signed their names and became officers. Men were given uniforms, boots, and rifled muskets that had been seized from the city's Federal armory. Citizen soldiers fell into loose ranks in large parades marching through the streets, and though clumsy and uncoordinated the men stepped together with unified spirit and purpose. The people of Charleston watched their brave men march off into the hills in the slow afternoon, and before Christmas dinner they saw smoke rising from the battlements of Fort Moultrie. A new flagpole was erected next to where the Federals had splintered the original, and by sunset the palmetto flag flew proudly in the sea breeze, a goading challenger to the Yankee flag flying in the harbor.

With renewed fervor the people of Charleston cheered and lit fires and rang the bells. A dazzled correspondent for the *Charleston Mercury* wandered through crowded streets where people sang joyously. That night, he submitted the following in scrawled shorthand for the next day's print:

> *The people of Charleston rejoice unto Heaven! And there is good reason for such joy and virtue: our Savior is reborn this day, as is our solemn revolution of freedom. Let us sing with the hosts of the Lord this Christmas Day: Hark! Hark! Glory to the newborn King, glory to the sovereign Republic of South Carolina — death and all Hell's wrath to the Northern invader — and God bless this free and holy city of Charleston.*

III

STARS IN THEIR COURSES

JANUARY – JULY 1861

From the heavens the stars fought,
in their courses they fought against their enemy.

Judges 5:20

Chapter 34
THE TIMES

The New Year came, and the New Year went.

There were rumblings from beyond the Branches. Folks spoke of a great anxiety spreading from town to town like whooping cough. Meanwhile, cynics huffed at the suggestion that the whole secession matter was of any great concern. Even still, a slow-creeping dread penetrated the Mayfair Valley. Minds were gnawed by foretold nightmares, and fearful hearts clenched to bursting. People took to looking out their darkened windows day and night, as if keeping a sullen, uneasy watch for *it*.

And when *it* finally came, it came very quickly.

The so-called Crittenden Compromise — a last-ditch bipartisan effort to coax South Carolina back into the Union — was soundly defeated in Congress in early January. Before the vote, President-elect Lincoln published a statement condemning the compromise for its many concessions to the South, namely, its commitment to expand the institution of slavery while forbidding any future amendments that might endanger 'Southern traditions.' Facing overwhelming opposition from the new Republican majority, the compromise died on the House floor with barely a whimper.

Then, on January 9th, the dominos began to fall. The State of Mississippi, following its South Carolina sister, enacted an ordinance of secession. Within days of this news, Mississippi's favored son Jefferson Davis stood up to address the United States Senate. The floor and the galleries were packed with lawmakers and citizens alike, all eager to hear the esteemed gentleman's case.

Davis was a hero from the Mexican War, and had been Secretary of War in a previous administration. Through the past year, newspapers had written favorably of Davis for his status as a firm moderate. He was not an out-and-out Fire Eater like William Yancey, but nor was he a double-tongued pushover. Davis would *fight*, whether in the halls of government or if need be on the field of battle, to preserve American democracy.

With the electoral failure of the ineffectual John Breckinridge back in November, and with a growing number of people already convinced that Abraham Lincoln would be an abject failure as president, there were many in both the North and

South who believed that Jefferson Davis could sweep to national victory in 1864. There were even some who entertained the idea that Lincoln's election might be overturned, and that a coalition of Democrats and conservative Republicans would install Davis as a bonafide 'healing president.' Jefferson Davis, many said, might be the Republic's true chosen one, the man to finally end divisions within the Union.

Of course, the Republicans refused such an idea outright. Any act by a 'coalition', they said, would be no more than a traitorous *coup d'état*. It was not that the Republicans had unshakeable faith in Lincoln, for many in that party were doubtful of the man's abilities, but the Republicans nevertheless held the White House and were determined to keep it.

All this served as the context within and against which Jefferson Davis made his farewell speech to the Senate, indeed to the United States as a whole. The speech was addressed to the Senate's president, a dour-faced Breckinridge. Davis announced his immediate and permanent resignation, much to the consternation of many present. Davis was retiring, he said, and committing himself to private life. In his speech, he spoke in defense of secession, including his personal reasons for leaving his post.

"It is known to senators who have served with me here, that I have for many years advocated, as an essential attribute of state sovereignty, the right of a state to secede from the Union. Secession is to be justified upon the basis that the states are sovereign. There was a time when none denied it. I hope the time may come again, when a better comprehension of the theory of our government, and the inalienable rights of the people of the states, will prevent anyone from denying that each state is a sovereign. I therefore say I concur in the action of the people of Mississippi, believing it to be necessary and proper, and should have been bound by their action if my belief had been otherwise."

Davis went on to explain that there was no mention of slavery in the Declaration of Independence, partly because Thomas Jefferson and the others who penned it were not concerned with negroes, but by the overwhelming threat of the English Crown. The idea that 'All men are created equal' was further clarified, Davis went on to say, by the Constitution's three-fifths clause regarding negroes. The implication, of course, was that negroes were not men at all, and therefore were not and could never be, equal. Davis suggested the Constitution, being the document which was drafted, vetted, and agreed upon by representatives from each and all of the United States, naturally superseded the Declaration in every respect, and particularly with respect to the omission of slavery.

"We of the South therefore recur to the compact which binds the states together," Davis said. "We recur to the principles upon which our government was founded; and when you deny them, and when you deny us the right to withdraw from a government which threatens to be destructive of our rights, we tread in the path of our fathers when we proclaim our independence. This is done, not in hostility to others; not to injure any section of the country, not even for our own pecuniary benefit, but from the high and solemn motive of defending and protecting the rights we inherited, and which it is our duty to transmit unshorn to our children."

Thus, Davis. The supreme Southern gentleman left Washington the very same day. Whatever the pundits wished or claimed, Davis had abandoned the idea of becoming president in 1864, or in any other year for that matter. When Davis left, so too did the other Mississippi senators, and all of her House representatives too.

After Mississippi's departure, Florida enacted an ordinance of secession on the 10th of January, and Alabama went out the very next day. Upon hearing the news, an extravagant secession soirée was thrown at the Montgomery, Alabama home of one William Yancey, who set off fireworks in a Fourth of July-style celebration. That same night in Montgomery, the customshouses, post offices, mints, and armories — all Federal institutions — were looted and some of the buildings burned.

Back on the Senate floor, John Roscoe's desk had remained empty since November. Now in just a few short days in January, more bodies disappeared from more desks until close to only half the senators remained.

The American people called for a leader to make sense of the chaos and confusion. In his last annual message to Congress, the embattled President James Buchanan blamed the North, and the Republican Party specifically, for "incessant and violent agitation of the slavery question." He suggested the incoming administration ought to accept the South's demand for a 13th Amendment that prohibited any and all threats against the institution of slavery. Asked what he would do about the secessionists themselves, Buchanan balked and said the Federal government had no power to "coerce a state into submission which is attempting to withdraw."

Whether Buchanan was right or wrong, the South was emboldened by his passivity. Georgia abandoned the Union on January 19th, followed by Louisiana on the 26th. By February, the newspapers reported that Texas was gone too. More Southern senators and representatives resigned from their posts in Washington, quitting en masse and leaving the Federal government hamstrung with only weeks until Abraham Lincoln's inauguration. Reports circulated that there were secessionists in Buchanan's cabinet, and that the incumbent Secretary of War was secretly sending Federal arms to Southern leaders.

The newborn Southern republics now had an important decision to make. Would they remain isolated as independent nation-states, or would they come together to create a new American confederation? Since most Southern nationalists recognized the necessity for solidarity in the face of the overwhelming power of the 'Yankee government', representatives from the seceded states decided to meet in Montgomery. And though back in 1775-76 it had taken the second Continental Congress well over a year of debate and deliberation before it declared American independence, the creation of the Confederate States of America unfolded in a matter of weeks.

With blistering speed, the 'New America' (or rather, 'America-As-It-Should-Have-Been') adopted a new constitution for itself. It was almost a carbon copy of the original 1789 Constitution, amendments and all. Of course, among the changes was the addition of one important line:

"...the institution of negro slavery as it now exists in the Confederate States, shall be recognized and protected by Congress."

In mid-February, officials of the newborn Confederacy coaxed Jefferson Davis out of retirement and made him its first president. Davis had not been elected, but rather selected by an esteemed group of gentlemen including William Yancey and one Tobias Cutler, who had resigned from the House in February. Despite Cutler's departure, the Commonwealth of Virginia yet remained within the Union.

The decision to make Jefferson Davis provisional president of a new American nation seemed to make good sense. After all, Breckinridge was ill and William Yancey had spurned the idea of becoming president, apparently preferring to remain a 'man of ideas.' Yankees were threatening from all sides — even from the Atlantic, where rumors held they were landing ashore roving gangs of blacks in order to sow distrust and rebellion among tidewater slave populations. A strong leader was needed *now*, to take concerted action *now*. This was no time for damn bureaucracy and election campaigns. The presidential post was provisional, supposedly for a period of months until the citizenry elected an official president. And so, Jefferson Davis took the job believing he would be a transitionary figure. Still, most newspapers reported that Davis had enough popular support to win an eventual election, and thus serve in his official capacity as president for a full six-year term.

William Yancey's cold feet regarding the national spotlight did not stop him from inserting himself into the middle of Davis' inauguration ceremony. After Davis swore his oath of allegiance under the portico of the Capitol Building in Montgomery, Alabama, the Prince of Fire Eaters rushed forward, grabbed Davis' hand, and thrust it into the air. To the watching crowd, Yancey roared:

"*The man and the hour have met!*"

All across the South, people were jubilant. The anxiety of the dark winter lifted. The tensions which people had held in their chests and had worn upon furrowed brows were finally released in states of cathartic euphoria.

Even as perky January snow sunk down under freezing February rain, and as the March winds froze everything to ice that was harder than rock, the Southern people — the *Confederate people*, folks reminded each other — danced at wild celebratory balls. Militia companies paraded the streets of Southern cities and towns and backwater villages, singing songs and burning the Stars and Stripes, now derided as the 'Yankee flag.'

In Mayfair, as elsewhere, the excitement was somewhat dampened by the lingering sentiment of what folks called 'Unionism', which some others claimed was synonymous with 'Yankeeism.' In Virginia, enough people were still fond of the Stars and Stripes, even if they hated the Republicans who had taken over the government. A Southern Confederacy was a fine idea, but wasn't the Union worth saving? Surely the whole idea of the Confederacy was little more than an extravagant bluff, with the ultimate object being to reform the Federal government?

Virginia, after all, hadn't seceded (at least not yet). Even after Jefferson Davis' inauguration down in Montgomery, the Commonwealth remained in the Union along with the other Border States: North Carolina, Tennessee, Arkansas, Missouri, Kentucky, Maryland, and Delaware. Folks in these places expected that, soon enough, tempers would calm and good sense would prevail.

Still, floating through the air came whispered conspiracies and fearful admissions, thickened with the loud assertions of braggarts. There were chuckling denials from self-assured gentlemen who claimed to have been around long enough to know that this latest crisis would fade away in time, just like all crises of the past. In the meantime, most folks were too busy raising families, cutting firewood, seeing to their livestock, and repairing equipment in time for spring planting to worry about Yankees or secession or any of that drivel.

In Washington, a fractured Union welcomed a new president under a light drizzle of March rain. Standing before the unfinished dome of the Capitol (a sight held by many to be a symbol of the stillborn fate of American democracy), Abraham Lincoln took the oath of office in a muted ceremony where the soaking fog muffled even the most ardent applause. The first reactions to Mr. Lincoln's inaugural address were less than enthusiastic, with most pundits ignoring the speech's content and remarking only that the president's voice was raspier and of a higher pitch than they had anticipated.

"I hold that in contemplation of universal law," Mr. Lincoln said, "and of the Constitution, the Union of these states is perpetual. Perpetuity is implied, if not expressed, in the fundamental law of all national governments. It is safe to assert that no government proper ever had a provision in its organic law for its own termination.

"If the United States be not a government proper, but an association of states in a contract — can it, as a contract, be peaceably unmade, by less than all the parties who made it? One party to a contract may violate it — break it, so to speak; but does it not require all to lawfully rescind it?"

While the new president delivered his address, thunder rumbled over the fields of Virginia across the Potomac. As it was later learned, the thunder was in fact a battery of Rebel cannon engaged in target practice.

"The president," Lincoln went on, "derives all his authority from the people, and they have referred none upon him to fix terms for the separation of the states. The people themselves can do this if also they choose; but the executive, as such, has nothing to do with it. His duty is to administer the present government, as it came to his hands, and to transmit it, unimpaired by him, to his successor.

"By the frame of the government under which we live, this same people have wisely given their public servants but little power for mischief; and have, with equal wisdom, provided for the return of that little to their own hands at very short intervals. While the people retain their virtue and vigilance, no administration, by any extreme of wickedness or folly, can very seriously injure the government in the short space of four years."

And yet, already in print shops across the Union, newspaper editors aligned against Mr. Lincoln were setting type for admonishments and condemnations of the new president's impending acts of tyranny. Of course Lincoln would injure the government, these editors said, and he would do so, as did all cowardly despots, 'in the name of the people.'

Toward the end of his speech the new president took up a Janus-like posture, with one face a gaunt grimace steeling itself for a fight, and the other face inhabiting a soft, conciliatory appeal to reason.

"In *your* hands, my dissatisfied fellow countrymen, and not in mine, is the momentous issue of civil war. The government will not assail *you*. You can have no conflict without being yourselves the aggressors. *You* have no oath registered in Heaven to destroy the government, while *I* shall have the most solemn one to 'preserve, protect, and defend it.'

"I am loath to close. We are not enemies, but friends. We must not be enemies. Though passion may have strained, it must not break our bonds of affection. The mystic chords of memory, stretching from every battlefield and patriot grave to every living heart and hearth-stone all over this broad land, will yet swell the chorus of the Union, when again touched, as surely they will be, by the better angels of our nature."

The truth was, few people in the North or South wanted a war, and certainly didn't want one on behalf of 'darkies.' Many in the North groaned at Lincoln's speech. Southerners were merely exercising their rights, weren't they? Why had Lincoln even *mentioned* the term 'war', if he had not intended to sow further division between neighbors?

Meanwhile, Southerners were certain that, if war came, the Yankees wouldn't put up much of a fight. After all, the North was a nation of mechanics and desk-bound clerks, not cavalier warriors. Why, a gang of Southern schoolchildren would surely whip any force that Mr. Lincoln and his fellow ingrates could muster! The confident assured their neighbors that, should there be a civil war between North and South, "A lady's thimble will hold all the blood that will be shed."

And in the North, those bellicose hawks who suggested the South ought to be taught a lesson were chastised and humiliated by their peers. All through March, abolitionist newspaper offices were fire-bombed by angry neighbors.

But as further news trickled up from the breakaway states that Southern nationalists had, in the name of their newfound Confederacy, looted millions of dollars from Federal mints, seized Federal forts and countless stockpiles of weapons, and declared themselves independent from a 'sick nation of negro-loving degenerates', the people of the North became outraged. The South's actions, despite President Davis' insistence that Southerners merely wanted to be 'left alone', seemed hardly conciliatory.

All these fears and predictions, declarations and condemnations, soon coalesced into a single question, repeated by newspapers and laymen alike:

What should be done with Fort Sumter down in South Carolina?

❧

Major Robert Anderson, the commander of Federal troops in Charleston, quickly shot to fame in late December when, soon after South Carolina's secession announcement and the ensuing seizure of Federal property, Anderson abandoned the indefensible Fort Moultrie and moved his command to Fort Sumter in the middle of Charleston Harbor. Almost immediately, militiamen from Charleston stormed Moultrie while rebel steamships surrounded Sumter like vultures around starving prey.

In the weeks that followed, Fort Sumter became for many a symbol of Union resilience in the face of existential threat. For many others, particularly in Charleston, Sumter represented a similar existential threat, this one a dagger pointed at the underbelly of the newborn Confederate States.

Back in January, when Buchanan was still president, his administration had attempted to reinforce the besieged Fort Sumter with a force of some two hundred troops. When the relief ship arrived in Charleston Harbor, however, the South Carolinians opened fire and drove the ship back to open sea. This might have been the opening salvo of civil war, except Sumter's garrison chose not to return fire. In the weeks that followed, news arrived that Sumter's garrison was running desperately low on supplies, particularly food.

The siege of Sumter remained unbroken all through the final hours of Buchanan's presidency, and the responsibility for resolving the crisis soon passed into Mr. Lincoln's hands on March 4th. In the meantime, the Sumter situation had become a Gordian knot of the worst kind. To withdraw the garrison and abandon the fort might appease the eight remaining slave-holding states who had not yet thrown in their lot with the Confederacy, but it would just as likely demoralize the Northern people. Evacuation meant recognizing the Confederacy's sovereignty and independence; effectively, to give up Sumter meant giving up the Union.

Outraged by what many considered Southern aggression, the people of the North began to organize themselves. Militia companies mustered on factory floors and in humble farm towns, with all eyes turning southward. Loud voices declared there was no such thing as the 'Confederacy' — those people down there were damn *rebels*, and nothing more. And yes, maybe the seceshes really ought to be taught a lesson after all, one they wouldn't soon forget.

Steadily increasing in number were the predictions — always impassioned, though rarely nuanced. Whims and opinions popped into minds from the subconscious ether and were cemented without question as rock-solid fact. Warnings of a particular kind, previously buried in the back pages of newspapers, began their slow march toward the front page.

War was coming. A war between the states.

Civil war.

About this same time, tucked away in obscure corners of obscure science journals, came reports of a newly-discovered celestial object. A huge comet had appeared in the northwestern sky, near the constellation of Sirius. With each passing day, the comet became brighter. By April it was visible to the naked eye.

The comet was a brilliant white mass with a fan-like tail that stretched across a quarter of the sky. To some observers, the comet seemed to be diving straight for the earth itself. As the spring earth bloomed and blossomed with all the colors of life, so also the comet brightened until it could be seen even in the daytime. Newspapers, whenever they were not obsessed with apocalyptic predictions, took to calling the object the 'Great Comet of 1861.'

To gaze up at the Great Comet conjured in one's heart all the ominous feelings that could not be so easily described in newspaper columns or whispered conversations. For even as some rejoiced and claimed the heavenly body was a sign of God's approval of their 'side,' so others deemed the comet a sinister omen, a wink from the eye of Lucifer. Where some saw a glimmer of Christ's vindication and salvation, others saw the spear of Ares hurtling toward earth, and still others braced against the pulsing fire and brimstone which Yahweh had used to obliterate Sodom and Gomorrah.

As the Great Comet streaked across the sky, and as the hungry garrison of Fort Sumter went down to half-rations, the question remained: what would Mr. Lincoln and Mr. Davis do? Surely the president in Washington would not cede victory to rebels, nor let nearly a hundred men starve to death. And surely the *other* president, the man in Montgomery, would not condemn those same men, some of whom were fellow Southerners, to death, all to prove some theoretical point of government? Surely the two presidents could arrange some sort of compromise?

"No," Mr. Davis declared to his supporters. "The time for compromise has passed. The South is determined to maintain her position, and make all who oppose her smell Southern powder and feel Southern steel."

To this ultimatum, friends of Mr. Lincoln pointed to the president's previously published statement: "If you undertake to destroy the Union, it will be our duty to deal with you as old John Brown has been dealt with. We shall do our duty."

Overhead, oblivious to the hopeful prayers, solemn predictions, and earnest declarations of Man, the white comet continued to plow silently through the still waters of the uncaring cosmos.

Chapter 35

THE COMET

"Oh, *look*, Henry! There it is!"

"Where? I don't see it."

"There! There, the bright one."

"Where?"

It was a cold night in late March, still rather wintry despite claims that spring had arrived, and the stars in the night sky were crystal clear. Sarah reached out and took Henry's hand, and she pointed his index finger toward a black patch of sky in the northwest. Barely visible, but visible nonetheless, was a white mass with a fan-like tail.

"*That's it?*" Henry said, unimpressed.

Sarah could not take her eyes off the point of white light above, and she couldn't stop smiling.

"That's it," she whispered.

As a hobby, astronomy had never once crossed Sarah's mind before. But with the baby on the way, she'd taken up the habit of consulting the heavens for guidance. She consulted the Gospels too, of course. But somehow the night sky gave her a deeper comfort, in that it asked no questions and insisted no answers.

The longer Sarah looked at the comet, the easier it became to trace its faded tail, which in fact stretched across a quarter of the sky. To her eye, the comet seemed to be diving straight for the earth itself. She shivered at the thought, but of course the reports in the newspapers had given no cause for alarm. The winking light above seemed too harmless and pleasant, like a tiny ship plowing noiselessly through still, black waters.

For a full week in April, front page reports in the *First Witness* described the comet's discovery and character. These articles were a welcome distraction from ad nauseum predictions of civil war and the so-called 'Charleston Crisis' happening somewhere down in the Carolinas.

The most Sarah knew about the cosmic visitor was that an Englishman (not Sir Halley) had discovered a 'comet', apparently some sort of flying rock, and the telegraph wire carried his findings all over continental Europe and the Americas.

But the comet, bright as it was, had appeared to Valley folks long before any official sighting was announced. In fact, Sarah first heard of the comet when Henry mentioned that some object in the sky was agitating the field hands and causing them to sing songs of God's deliverance. According to the newspapers, the comet would glow even brighter in a month's time, and brighter still in the summer, until by summer's end the comet would pass on to some distant corner of the heavens.

Believing the comet to promise tidings of great joy about the baby, Sarah managed to rouse Henry in the dark of one early morning to look upon the heavenly sight.

"The papers say that in another month or so, we'll be able to see the comet even during daytime. Isn't that wonderful, Henry? It's like a shooting star's big brother. Like the Star of Bethlehem, or something."

"I'm fucking freezing," Henry said, pulling up his collar. "Let's get inside, Sarah."

Such activities as stargazing were not to Henry's liking. He preferred riding and wrestling and dice games, and all those things were fine enough. Still, as husband and wife they never spoke (if they spoke at all) about anything that didn't have something to do with Henry himself. In fact, she considered herself fortunate to have managed to rouse him out of bed at all tonight.

Sarah rose up on her toes, remembering girlhood ballet classes that had finished too soon for her to realize, and she kissed Henry on the cheek.

"You go back to bed, darling. I'll be along in a moment."

Henry nodded and turned to go, but a thought stopped him. "It's cold tonight," he said, "and you're underdressed."

Sarah was touched by his concern. She could not deny that Henry had become more doting and affectionate in recent months.

"I'll only be out another minute," she said.

"I mean it about *him*, Sarah."

"Oh, he'll be fine too." They'd taken to calling the baby *he*, since Henry wanted a son more than anything. (But if Sarah was being honest with herself, she was secretly hoping for a girl.)

Henry was too tired to push his case further. With a quiet grunt, he turned and went inside. After he'd gone, she finally felt her shoulders relax.

Standing with her neck craned upward, Sarah slid her hand up her nightdress (a scandalous gesture were anyone to see it, but she knew she was alone) and touched a hand to her belly. Her fingers were icicles on warm, goosebumped flesh. She hoped to feel *her* moving around inside her, as if the little one might be stirred by the starry wonders in her mother's vision.

"Wake up, little one. I could describe the stars for you."

Sarah remembered the first time the baby had kicked. She had been sitting in one of Arcadia's drawing rooms reading a copy of Godey's Fashion Magazine hidden behind a large Bible. It was about twenty-five weeks into her pregnancy, according to the timeline that she and Dr. Harper had settled on. The kick hadn't hurt, but it had surprised her. She felt a bulge in her lower abdomen, and then another bump somewhere in her ribs. She laughed and decided the little one had to be dancing. Her next instinct was to cry out for Henry, or maybe for Tattie, so that she would not be alone during this joyous moment. But then she only sat still for a while and counted the kicks as they came, and she realized that she wasn't alone at all. She wept in that moment, but they were quiet tears of bliss. She began to whisper softly to the little one and, though she considered herself nothing of a singer, sang half-remembered lullabies that Mae Jane used to murmur to her. The little one's kicking increased at the sound of her voice, but after a time she settled down and went to sleep.

Tonight, with the comet shining down, Sarah felt again for movement. She could feel none, and hadn't felt anything since before lunchtime. Still, she supposed that was normal. More than likely, the little one (already a night owl) was only resting up to spend the rest of the night kicking at Sarah's belly. Sometimes, even when the spirited bumps and flip-flops rendered Sarah sleepless, she would touch her hands to her belly and hum those same lullabies until she herself fell asleep with a smile on her face.

There was a strange hardness in her belly, but she considered it had to be due to the cold. Despite these assurances, she could not shake off the idea that the little one had never been this quiet, not for this long.

Sarah counseled herself against undue panic. She neglected to tell Henry, certain he would only dismiss her concerns as 'hysteria.' And if she really tried hard enough — like now, looking up at the comet — she could almost forget her worry.

Still, she could not ignore the change in her belly. What was normally plush and soft was now undeniably hard. She hadn't eaten much since supper, enduring a sour taste in her throat in the meantime.

Sarah willed the little one to stretch, to move in the slightest way, just so she knew.

"Wake up, little one," she whispered, rubbing in slow circles. "Won't you wake up, little one? Don't you want me to describe the stars for you?"

She waited for an answer, but none came.

Sleeping. Only sleeping.

"A night owl no more," Sarah said, trying a shaky laugh. "Morning is the best time, you'll see. Waking with the sun is like, well...there's nothing quite like it. Still, with a view like this one above us..."

She kept rubbing, but the little one did not stir. Sarah pressed down on her belly, as if giving a hug.

"Goodnight, little one. See you with the sun."

Sarah stared up at the white comet for a moment longer. She whispered a silent prayer to it, and to all the heavenly host. She admitted (and Lord knew) she wasn't the most devout Christian wife in the Valley, but she declared her intention then and there that she would raise the little one in the light of the Gospels. Maybe, by doing so, she herself would draw closer to the Lord.

Sarah returned to bed, thankful for the warmth of the blankets. Henry was already fast asleep. For herself, sleep was a long time coming. She tried to remember those lullabies, but she could remember none of the melodies. And when Sarah at last drifted off, her face was set in a pained grimace.

❧

When Sarah awoke, she knew instinctively that something was wrong.

Sarah pushed away the sheets and lifted up the folds of her nightdress. She put her hands to her belly, and what she felt shocked her. Her belly had hardened as if to stone, and still she felt no sliding or kicking from within. Just now she felt a cramping, grinding pain begin somewhere deep inside, but it was more like a—

Lord. Sarah winced at a sudden stab of pain. It was gone before she could guess at it, but then another flare of pain cut off her breath. Her hands felt all around, but she no longer knew what to feel for. Dr. Harper and Mrs. Cutler had said something about contractions, but of course it was far too early for any of that. She still had almost half her pregnancy until the baby was due. Suddenly, a single idea expelled all other thoughts.

Out. She needed to get the baby *out.*

But that was good. That was a good instinct. That had to mean the baby was coming, didn't it? Of course babies came whenever they wished, and most of the time they came well. Still, she knew there was an early that was much too early. Couldn't she somehow convince the little one to keep warm inside a little while longer?

More stabs of pain answered the question. *Out.* She needed to get the baby out. For the little one's sake, and for her own too.

"Henry..."

He stirred, still only half awake.

"Henry, there's something wrong."

An eye cracked open, now two. "You sick again? Not another mess. The chamber pot..."

Sarah's breath sharpened. "Not that. It's something else."

Henry sat up on his elbow. He wore a look of annoyance at being disturbed. "Well I can't tell you what it is you're feeling, Sarah, if you don't describe for me exactly what's—"

"*Please*, Henry. I…I think I need the doctor. I *need* the doctor, Henry-darling."

Henry leaped out of bed as if he had just discovered a snake between them. He glared down at Sarah with a look that suggested he was about to chastise her. Just who did she think she was with all this attention-seeking? But Henry must have seen something in the wild, primeval expression that overtook Sarah then, for he turned immediately for the door. Throwing it open, he was met by a shocked footman carrying fresh linens, whose frozen arm was raised to knock.

"*Call the doctor*," Henry growled.

The footman, a quivering boy of barely twelve, turned and started off at a stiff walk. Henry hurled a fox hunter's yelp at the boy's back, and this sent the boy careening down the hallway as fast as he could run.

Henry stood in the doorway, breathing hard, looking up and down the hall with his hands on his sides. From the bed, past the bleary streams of sweat running into her eyes, Sarah could see her husband's mind working.

Henry entered the bedroom again, but only long enough to pull on a robe. His face wore a look of pale detachment. Without a word, without even a second glance at Sarah on the bed, Henry turned and left the room once more, turning in the direction of his private dressing room down the hall. Sarah heard Henry scream at someone, and now came the quick patter of feet. Just as Sarah felt she could no longer focus her eyes on the door, she saw Tattie turn the corner.

"Miss Sarah? Miss Sarah, you got a fever? *Oh*, Lord…"

Sarah reached out for Tattie's hand.

"I'm frightened, Tattie. I don't know what's—"

Tattie was at her side the next instant, holding her hand. "Hush now, Miss Sarah. It'll be all right, you see. It'll be all right. I'm here with you now. You ain't alone."

Sarah could barely keep her eyes open, could barely think past the grinding pain from within, and the stabs that streaked out from her abdomen. She thought suddenly of Mother and saw her standing over her, her face kind and her skin colored with flecks of paint. Sarah thought of dying just like Mother had, and she decided she had to live long enough to help the little one *get out* before the Lord took her. She thought with despair of the little one — her daughter — growing up without knowing how much Sarah already loved her. She thought of her daughter knowing her only through portraits, and how her daughter would miss her and maybe even quietly resent her for not being around.

"You ain't alone, Miss Sarah."

Sarah reeled, but Tattie hushed her again. Sarah felt Tattie's hands on her belly and winced at her touch. But before another moment had passed an overwhelming wave of exhaustion took hold, and Sarah's vision folded together, and she knew no more.

It was no fairytale dream that Sarah woke to, though she could hear spring bird-song outside her bedroom window, which had been cracked a little to let fresh air inside. There was a stubborn woodpecker off somewhere, and even the chirrup of robins. Sunlight winked in past lace curtains, and somehow Sarah knew it was morning light, which meant she'd been asleep for more than an entire day.

For the longest time, Sarah felt she could not move at all. It was as if she'd lost every part of her body except for her head. Slowly she became aware of the base of her neck, and moving around she felt a terrible stiffness. Her throat was parched, and it hurt to swallow. A numbing headache coursed through her skull and—

And what about the pain in her belly?

Sarah reached her hands down. The hardness was gone, but...

But now her belly was very tender to touch and it was...well, she could describe it in no other way but *mushy*. The bump had deflated somehow, the skin there shrunken and wrinkled. Lingering pain emanated like waves of heat. She moved her hands down where her white flesh had turned purple. She winced as she touched her vulva next, feeling a raw openness and—

"No, my God...*Please*, my God..."

Unable to move, and too weak to call out, she lay bedridden most of the morning. In thinking back, she tried to remember sensations of pain in the night. She could not tell whether or not the screaming and pushing had been part of a dream, a nightmare. She could remember vague visions of Mother, and of Father too, and even of Cousin Isabella, but all of their faces had somehow looked so much like that of Dr. Harper.

Fear and thirst gnawed at her, and Sarah kept herself lucid only by the desperate hope that the little one had been delivered. Yes, the little one had to be sleeping soundly in another room somewhere. She imagined Tattie was there looking after her, and thinking of that she felt a little better.

Much better.

It was midday and the sun had shifted beyond the windows when a soft knock came on the door. The door opened slowly, and then Dr. Harper entered, with Henry coming in behind. Henry was dressed in his work clothes and riding boots, as if he'd just returned from his rounds about the plantation fields. Henry turned and beckoned for someone, and then two servants (one was Tattie) hurried inside to open the curtains and shut out the cold.

"You're awake, Mrs. Cutler," Harper said. "We thought it best to let you rest awhile."

Harper offered a smile that was easy to see through, while Henry's expression was vacant, vaguely grim. In that moment, the tide of Sarah's hope turned toward the creeping onset of despair.

Tattie drew forward with a pitcher of water and a bowl of dried peaches. Coming very close to Sarah's face, she gave Sarah a meaningful look of…no, it could not be sympathy.

Sympathy?! Sarah wanted to scream out. She felt the instinct to grab Tattie's hand to keep her close, but she could not find the strength. Maybe feeling a cold glare from Henry, Tattie stood up and retreated from Sarah's bedside.

But no, maybe not sympathy. Maybe only empathy. Compassion. There was a *difference* between these things, of course.

But where was the joy? Where was the spirit of thankfulness? Had new life not just come into the world, and safely? Had God not just granted Sarah and Henry Cutler with a beautiful child?

Dr. Harper cleared his throat. "There's no easy way to say this," he said, "so I suppose I ought to just go ahead and say it…"

Propped up in bed, Sarah sat and listened calmly as Harper abandoned all attempts at euphemism. He explained in the most clinical language he knew that the baby was stillborn, that God had taken the little one even before she had a chance to come into the world.

"*She?*" Sarah echoed. "You said *she*, Doctor?"

Harper stared at her a moment, dumbstruck. "Yes," he said, nodding at last. "Yes, it was a…ahem, a girl, ma'am."

Henry put his hands on his sides and stared down at the floor.

Sarah looked at her husband. "Henry…"

His gaze shifted up to her, but he would not look her in the eye.

Sarah reached out to him. "Henry, will you…?"

Henry looked all around, as if searching desperately for some means of distraction. Turning around, he blew a sharp whistle at the sight of Tattie and the other servant standing in the far corner of the room.

"What the fuck are you still doing here?" he snarled at the girls. "*Get gone*."

The servants bowed their heads and hurried outside. Sarah caught a brief, sorrowful look from Tattie before the girl disappeared. Sarah wished to call her back, but she could not manage to speak up.

Sarah closed her eyes and reached down to her belly again. For the briefest of moments she almost thought she might feel it round and bulging and healthy again, and this sensation would cause her to wake up from whatever terrible dream into which she had strayed. She waited to feel the little one kick, but there was nothing. When Sarah opened her eyes again, they welled with tears.

Henry shifted from one foot to the other. "I'll send Mother in to sit with you awhile," he murmured. "She knows the ways of these things. She'll be more comfort."

"Please, Henry," Sarah said through sobs. "Won't you stay? Please stay?"

Henry only stared at Dr. Harper, who hung his head and said nothing. Then Henry sniffed and approached Sarah's bedside. He pecked her once on the forehead and stood up again. Sarah reached out for him, but he turned away before she could touch him.

"My wife deserves the greatest quality care," Henry muttered to Harper.

"Of course," Harper replied.

Then Henry was gone, his riding boots clamping along the floor and down the hallway.

For a long while, Dr. Harper stood apart from Sarah in silence. In seeking some way to cut through the quiet, Harper produced a handkerchief and offered it to Sarah. Sarah took it, but she did not bother to wipe her eyes or nose.

"Was it me, Ira? Was it...was it some *failure* of mine that—?"

"Nothing of the sort," Harper said. He removed his half-moon glasses and wiped at them while blinking away tears of his own. He set his glasses on his nose again. "There's no blame to lay anywhere, Mrs. Cutler. It was an act of God, and nothing more."

An act of God. And just the night before Sarah had pledged to be more faithful, to raise the little one in God's light. What sort of cruel, damnable trick was that?

Harper insisted on pouring a glass of water for Sarah. As he did so, Harper continued in his explanation of her case. She had indeed delivered sometime in the last twenty-four hours, and in the process she had lost a great deal of blood. The bedsheets had been changed twice, but she was to expect more contraction-like pain, more blood, and certainly she would have to deliver the afterbirth. It might disturb her, the sight of it, but he assured her that there was nothing to—

"Can I see her?"

Harper swallowed. "You...you want to...?"

"I want to see her, Doctor. My daughter."

Harper gulped again several times until he found his voice. "I'm afraid...I'm afraid that's not possible, Mrs. Cutler."

Sarah shook her head with disbelief and a touch of anger. "What do you mean it's *not possible?*"

Again Harper struggled to answer right away. "Your husband," he managed at last. "Mr. Cutler, he...he ordered the child to be buried. You must understand, he thought it best not to wait. Not with the child being so small and so...frail, you might say. I assure you every care was taken, Mrs. Cutler. She was swaddled, and covered, and the reverend your brother-in-law blessed the child. Then it — she — was laid to rest." He offered his best smile, as if it might help matters. "It was an earnest affair, not as somber as you might imagine." Then, realizing what he was saying, the young doctor bit his tongue and went quiet for a time.

"I...I am very sorry, Sarah."

Sarah stared out the window, though she saw nothing but circles. She thought she would feel the sudden grip of hysteria, of torrential heartbreak, that her steady crying would break down into disconsolate sobbing. Instead, she felt her tears begin to dry on her cheeks. She felt nothing now but a numb absence.

Already buried?! No chance to say goodbye? Sarah wished for Henry to be here again, if only that she could scream at him. Whose goddamn idea had it really been to bury the child? Had it been the brilliance of Mrs. Cutler — the *real* Mrs. Cutler? Meanwhile, no thought had been given to the child's mother. But how was that even possible? These were Christian folk, the kindest and most devout people Sarah had ever known. And still no thought, not the *slightest* consideration?! No thought that a mother might wish to…?

Sarah looked up and saw Dr. Harper standing there, a dejected look on his face.

"Thank you, Ira," she murmured. "For everything."

Harper hung his head. "I only wish there was something more I could have done. I only wish—"

"No, Ira," Sarah said. "You said it yourself, there's no one to blame. Certainly no one can blame you. I thank you for coming when you did, and for your counsel."

Harper nodded and mumbled something inaudible, and then he excused himself. "I'll be back shortly," he said. "I'll be able to guide you through the next stages, help you pass the remnants." Looking to bite his tongue again, Harper turned and left the bedroom without saying anything more.

And then the door was closed, and all the sounds of the world were shut out. And for the first time in so many weeks, ever since she'd first felt the little one announce herself with a sprightly little kick, Sarah felt really and truly alone.

She *was* alone.

Sarah lay back down to touch her disfigured belly. There was nothing to do now but wait for the final contractions, for the afterbirth, for more blood.

But not for the little one. The little one was gone.

Already buried. Already *cold in the ground.*

And gone without a touch. No embrace from Mother, and no chance for Mother to say goodbye.

Sarah tried to cry again, but she could not withstand the pangs of pain all down her abdomen. Besides, she was too dehydrated for her burning eyes to make tears.

Slowly, she reached for the glass of water beside her. With her hand trembling as if from palsy, Sarah put the glass to her lips and drank. She had never tasted anything so good in her life, but she took no pleasure from the glass.

She wondered whether she might take pleasure in anything anymore.

Already buried. Already cold in the ground…

Sarah reached to set the glass down on the bedside table, but she missed the ledge and the glass fell and shattered on the floor. She did not care. She sat back to feel the sensation of the water she'd drank trickle down into her empty, rumbling stomach. Her body was desperately weak, and it had become demanding. But for now, eating was the last thing on Sarah Cutler's mind. Right now, there was only the waiting.

The waiting, with nothing to hope for.

Chapter 36

ALL NIGHT FOREVER

An eerie silence hung in the still night air. There was only the faint sound of the massive Stars and Stripes banner rippling in a gusting ocean breeze. Under its moonlit shadow, the men of Fort Sumter stood hard and silent like statues, but there was a defiant gleam in their eyes.

There was fear also.

Standing upon the battlements, JJ peered at the twinkling lights of Charleston across the harbor. Much of the sleeping city was obscured by a thick fog rolling across the water.

JJ turned his gaze skyward. He looked up at the great comet and its ghostly light. As he watched the comet, guessing at its trajectory, he thought back over a long winter of waiting.

For the men of Fort Sumter, the first three months of 1861 had been characterized by equal parts debilitating boredom and dark foreboding. Day after day, the sentries stood limply upon the walls, gazing out at the gallant Confederate steamers that constantly patrolled the harbor. The men thought of a mascot for the Confederates: 'Johnny Rebel.' Over time, the men came to refer to the Confederates not just as rebels, but as *the Rebels*.

The Rebels, though enforcing a veritable siege of Sumter since Christmas Day, had at least been gracious enough to send a small dory to the Fort's jetty to deliver newspapers from across the Union. The Rebels watched gleefully as the men of Sumter read the chilling reports of secession, culminating in the inauguration of President Jefferson Davis and the secession of Texas. The newborn Confederacy now numbered seven states unified against the government in Washington.

As February progressed, news arrived that Federal fortresses across the South had been seized by Confederate militiamen. It soon became clear that Fort Sumter was the last remaining holdout, and only because its isolated position in the middle of Charleston Harbor made it nigh unassailable.

March arrived, and with it the newspaper accounts of Lincoln's inaugural address. JJ was rather unimpressed with the speech. At times Lincoln sounded like a groveling sycophant. Wherever the president's so-called 'better angels' were, they were not here in Charleston.

Isolated from the mainland for over three months now, the men of Fort Sumter began to turn against each other. JJ had to break up a dinnertime brawl by thrusting himself into the fray. Afterward, while the entire garrison watched, JJ personally gave ten lashes each to the two ringleaders. He overheard one of the onlookers, a man from New England, snicker and joke that of course the Virginian had a natural inclination to the whip. JJ whipped that man too, and whipped him hard.

In the second week of March, a grim reality of the siege revealed itself. The Fort's quartermaster sheepishly reported to JJ one night that food stocks were running dangerously low.

"I thought they resupplied this place before we left Moultrie," JJ said.

The quartermaster shook his head. "Only enough for a couple months, and we're well past that now. The waterfront is shut to us, the sea lanes too."

JJ maintained a stony look while he chewed on this information. "And how long can we hold out?"

"A month. Maybe less. Probably less. I'm sorry, sir."

One month. That meant that by mid-April, Sumter might become the site of a bloody mutiny. And JJ had a pretty good idea whose throat some of the men, still nursing the wounds on their backs, would try to cut first.

"Don't be sorry," JJ had said, standing up. "Just don't let word of this get around. If it does, we'll have a goddamn riot on our hands."

JJ immediately relayed the report to Major Anderson. The garrison commander dashed off a letter to the War Department. Without an urgent resupply, Anderson explained that he would be forced to surrender Sumter to the Rebels.

Anderson ordered JJ to pass the letter to the Rebels when the next delivery boat arrived.

"But, Major," JJ said. "What if the Rebels read your letter? I don't doubt they tear open every envelope that comes in and out of this place."

"Their eyes are welcome," Anderson had replied. The old man was aloof, rather detached, as if he was too busy thinking of his home and family back in Kentucky. "If their knowledge of our situation expedites negotiations with Washington, all the better. I won't command a garrison of starved corpses."

JJ clenched his jaw. "Might I remind you, sir, of our duty to hold out to the last man. Our duty is to keep the flag flying, no matter the cost."

Anderson looked at him with a blank stare. "We are not at war, Lieutenant. A situation like this ought to be left to the politicians. Now do as I say, and get that letter out on the next transport."

As JJ left that meeting, he decided to keep a close eye on Anderson. He prepared himself for the possibility that, should the Kentuckian try to surrender Sumter to the Rebels without direct orders from Washington, the only way to keep the Fort out of enemy hands — and JJ now openly referred to the Rebels as 'the enemy' — might be to inspire a mutiny of his own. Would the men of the garrison choose to starve to death as patriots, or swallow a shameful surrender in order to live into old age?

Food rations were cut, then cut again, and still the stocks dwindled. As blustery March became dreary April, steamship activity in the harbor increased. Evidently the Rebels were aware of Fort Sumter's plight and were on constant lookout for possible resupply attempts. When Rebel mailmen brought new correspondence to the Sumter men on April 1st, they also brought news that Rebel forces in Charleston had a new commander.

"General Beauregard sends his regards," one of the mailmen said to JJ.

JJ blinked. *General* Beauregard? Why, the man had only been a colonel when JJ last saw him at West Point. Probably the Creole had resigned his post when Louisiana seceded, and now he'd taken up a convenient new posting with the Confederacy.

"A shorter ladder to climb down here," JJ murmured with a grin.

The mailman squinted at him. "Whatsay?"

"Nothing," JJ said. He passed Anderson's letter over to the mailman and took possession of a large mailbag. The men would be thankful to have letters from home, which had been piling up in Charleston for over three months.

"And one for you," the mailman said, handing over a sealed letter. "You're Roscoe, ain't you? That's who this one's for."

JJ did not answer the man, but he did take the letter. Looking at it, he saw that the envelope was from Clarendon.

Suddenly, the air split open with the sound of cannonfire across the mouth of the harbor. The Rebel cannoneers fired salvos of practice shots into the waters just off Sumter.

JJ scanned the harbor from right to left. The Rebels were triangulating fire from three areas: from the former base at Fort Moultrie, and from a floating battery of cannons mounted on barges in the harbor, and finally from Cummings Point, a breakwater that stretched into the Atlantic and pointed an accusing finger back at Sumter. The message from the gunners was clear: should there be any fighting, the Rebels had plenty of firepower to reduce Sumter to rubble.

The Rebel mailman grinned. "Laws, I surely wouldn't want to be stuck on this rock when all that starts up."

JJ gave the man a cold smile. "Then you'd better be moving along, then."

The mailman sneered and ordered his comrades back into their dory.

That night, sitting alone in his private quarters, JJ carefully opened the letter from Clarendon. It was dated from mid-December, which felt like a thousand years ago. The letter was from Mae Jane, written in a shaky, childish cursive that

JJ guessed had to be Tom's writing. As he read the letter by candlelight, JJ could almost hear Mae Jane's raspy voice in his ears.

Your father is dying, and he wants to see you.

Upon reading those words, JJ sat back in his chair and stared at the low-burning fire in the corner for…how long? Minutes, hours? He read and re-read the letter again, and each time the words seemed less real. How could it be that just a few words, strung together in such a way, could cause one's heart to twist into knots? The invisible wounds that JJ thought had long since scarred over were suddenly opened again, bleeding worse than ever before. Each time he breathed, the wounds seemed to widen and deepen, the pain numbing all other sensations.

For several days, JJ hid himself in his quarters and saw no one. When he was certain that no eavesdropping ear was listening in, JJ tried to weep. He tried to let out all that he had so carefully repressed for so many months, for so many years, but to his dismay JJ found that he could not weep. Somehow, his body would not produce the tears he yearned to shed.

It had been over three months since Mae Jane's letter was penned. *Three months*! Three months where JJ had gone on living, completely unaware that Father was dying, that he was now dead.

But…but what if Father yet lived? Mae Jane had only said the old man *was* dying. Could it be that there was still time?

All the same, JJ somehow felt certain that Father really was gone. Maybe, in his own way, JJ had sensed a shift in the wind, a change in his own spirit. And those dreams he had been having lately, about he and Father walking through the grove at Clarendon, perhaps those were not merely idle fantasies but visions of mystical import.

He wants to see you.

JJ attempted a score of responses to Mae Jane's letter, but he ended up discarding each of them. And really, what could possibly be said? Even if he could escape Sumter and slip around the Rebels (which was impossible), he was far too late for his homecoming to do any good.

And the more JJ thought about it, the more his sorrow became tinged with anger and hurt. Father *wanted* to see him? Not a question or a request, but an order — an expectation. Even on his deathbed, the man was full of demands. Did anyone really expect JJ to drop everything and come running to the side of the man who had humiliated him, who had robbed him of his birthright, who had condemned him as a faithless degenerate?

Of course, JJ tried to rationalize as best he could. The words in the letter were Mae Jane's words, not Father's. And part of JJ wanted to believe that Father had in fact uttered, in the zealous manner of the dying, some low, rasping appeal to God to permit a reunion between father and son: a penultimate pardoning of the prodigal son, a final reconciliation, an end to suffering and the beginning of a new era where JJ would honor Father's memory.

Oh, but for Christ's sake, how many times had JJ gone down this road before? How many times had he convinced himself that Father's forgiveness was near, let alone *real?* JJ's place as Father's favored child had in fact been contingent — he'd only been too young, too enthralled with the man, to realize it. The love that JJ felt for Father was true, but now he understood that Father's love for him — indeed for everyone the old man claimed to care about — was transactional, entangled with countless conditions. To love John Roscoe was to sign a contract of the soul, terms of which were eternally binding to one party but which the other could infringe as needed.

He wants to see you.

Oh, yes? Well, to hell with whatever Father wants or wanted. The old man was *gone,* and that was all there was to it. As Father rejected JJ in life, so JJ would reject Father in death.

❧

Yawning, circling his shoulders to get the blood moving, JJ started off on another patrol. As he turned up Sumter's east wall, he passed the shivering figure of a young sentry. Suddenly, the sentry let out a hoarse whistle. JJ perked up and hurried back to the sentry. It was the little Irishman, Private—

"Hough, sir. From Tipperary."

"Yes, yes. What did you see, Private?"

"Seceshes coming, sir," Hough said. "Down there on the water."

Alert, JJ scanned the water below. Emerging through the fog was a long, dark boat with four shadowy figures aboard. The figures braced against the cold sea spray and huddled under blankets. The spectral form of the helmsman could have been Charon guiding damned souls along the Styx. Somewhere distant, the lonely toll of a bell echoed across the harbor.

JJ turned to Hough. "Inform Major Anderson the enemy party has returned."

Hough's eyes were glazed with fear. "*Enemy,* sir?"

"*Now,* Private."

Hough scurried off.

JJ watched the men in the boat below. The Rebels had offered Major Anderson the opportunity to surrender many times over the last few months, and especially over the last several days. Fortunately, Major Anderson had so far been resolute in his refusals.

On the Rebel boat, one of the seated figures looked up. He spotted JJ, stood up shakily, and saluted with his hat. JJ remained motionless and defiant, not caring to return the salute as was custom. The Rebel in the boat slowly replaced his hat and sat down again to murmur with his comrades.

Minutes later, JJ stood on the jetty with Major Anderson and six armed men. The Rebel boat slid toward the jetty and two Sumter men stepped forward to take the ropes. The Rebels, eager to be ashore again and out of the chop, gratefully accepted the help. There was unity in their combined effort, almost like they were all still countrymen. But JJ entertained no such illusions; he stayed where he was and offered no help.

Low-hanging fog shrouded their boots upon the jetty. The waves, obscured by the mist, roared with terrible fury. The Rebels staggered onto the jetty platform like drunks. All of them were pale and quivering from seasickness. They wore fine gray uniforms of a unique design, with loose seams and wide breasts. Shining brass buttons framed their chests in heart shapes. Ornamental designs embroidered their wide sleeves, and fine white gloves completed the look. Compared with the elegant dress of the enemy, the Sumter men were now keenly aware of their own plain, frumpy blue uniforms.

The ranking officer of the Rebel party, an aging Charleston gentleman named Chesnut, had dark bags under eyes that had suffered a week of sleepless nights. Chesnut and Anderson saluted each other. With Chesnut were two young adjutants, with the helmsman standing back from the group to watch the boat.

Major Anderson removed his hat and bowed to the Rebels, a chivalric gesture that made JJ want to roll his eyes.

"Colonel Chesnut," Anderson said. "It's good to see you again, despite the circumstances."

Chesnut had a letter in his hand. "Major, I have an urgent message."

Anderson gestured at the fort. "Please, gentlemen, let's step inside out of the cold."

The Rebels were not exactly impressed with Sumter's condition. JJ read on Chesnut's face a questioning look, as if the man was truly baffled that two mighty nations might go to war over *this*, a pile of rocks sinking into the ocean. Symbol of Federal oppression or not, the Rebels did not appear to envy the men living in drafty, half-built living quarters perched on the frothing Atlantic.

They gathered in Anderson's quarters. This space at least had a large hearth with a roaring fire. The adjutants went immediately to the fire, no doubt thankful for its warmth. Their dark shadows loomed large against the orange glow of the stone walls. Chesnut stood before Anderson's desk at rapt attention. He was an older man, a handsome Fire Eater who now fancied himself a military leader, and the blonde hair on his aquiline head was only just beginning to gray. His eyes were large, but of no discernible color, intense with a glint of humor. His lips, taut and bloodless, stretched in a patronizing smile.

"Major," Chesnut said in a distinct South Carolina drawl, "I have a message from General Beauregard."

Anderson glanced at JJ, who stood by the door, then looked back at the Rebels.

"You gentlemen may not know this," the major said with a small smile. "General Beauregard was my *student* at West Point. And what subject did I teach him? Artillery. Specifically, the science of reducing enemy fortresses to rubble. It's a strange irony that I should stare down the barrel of his guns now, or maybe it's a great cosmic joke made at my expense."

Chesnut sniffed. "We are aware of General Beauregard's relationship with you, Major," he said flatly. Chestnut now glanced at JJ with a tight-lipped smile. "The general sends his regards, Lieutenant. I understand you know each other well from your time at West Point."

"Tell the general he is a traitor," JJ replied coldly. "Tell him that I look forward to seeing him hang."

The Rebels' faces paled with shock, and promptly reddened with hateful indignation. Anderson turned and fired a silent glare at JJ, who remained stone-faced.

Chesnut's mouth formed a mocking grin. "I suppose I reserve the right to extend your greetings to the general in slightly more friendly terms," he said. Now he turned to Anderson and gestured at the letter. "The message *is* urgent, Major. Time is of the essence."

Before opening the letter, Anderson paused. "Have you gentlemen read its contents?"

The adjutants only looked to Chesnut, who replied, "No, sir. We would never betray our general's confidence, sir."

Anderson opened the letter. "Then, given the peculiar situation we all find ourselves in, I think it right if I read the general's words aloud."

Chesnut and his adjutants nodded.

Clearing his throat, Anderson read: "*Dear sir. Some days ago, your Secretary of War notified Confederate States officials in Charleston that a peaceful attempt would be made to supply Fort Sumter by sea. The supplies would be restricted to provisions only, with no other effort to throw in men or arms.*"

JJ saw the flush of relief on Anderson's face. So, the garrison would not be starved out after all — provided the Rebels didn't fire on the supply ship as they had fired on others. If supplies could reach Sumter, the fort could hold out several weeks or maybe months longer. Maybe indefinitely.

As Anderson read on, however, his face slowly turned pale.

"*I regret to inform you, however, that Confederate States authorities recently intercepted a Navy Department message to the captain of the warship USS* Powhatan. *The contents of that message, signed by the Secretary of the Navy and with reference to a direct order from President Lincoln, authorize the* Powhatan *to open fire upon Confederate forces should any attempt be made to block the resupply of Fort Sumter.*"

Major Anderson looked up from the letter with quiet despair.

"What is this supposed to mean?"

Chesnut flashed a smirk of vindication. "I think the meaning of such a message is very clear. Your president is maneuvering the Confederacy toward a declaration of war."

"It says no such thing," JJ growled. "Telling a man to defend himself if he is attacked is not an act of—"

"This kind of backdoor treachery," Chesnut said, "might be expected of a country lawyer. But a president? An *American* president? Your man Lincoln has the nerve to attempt Fort Sumter's resupply, even after President Davis has repeatedly called for the fort's *surrender*. The land on which we stand is sovereign South Carolina soil, which makes it Confederate soil, which means you and your men are trespassers, Major. What's more, that secret letter between Lincoln and the Navy Department proves that your administration is planning hostilities against us, even when official correspondence assures peaceful action." Chesnut sniffed. "If this sort of double-tongued talk is the future of United States foreign policy, gentlemen, then thank God for the Southern Confederacy."

JJ exploded, "Foreign policy?!"

"*Enough*," Anderson barked at JJ. With a flustered sigh, he turned back to Chesnut. "Colonel, with respect. If I may speak for President Lincoln, the president believes he cannot negotiate with the Confederate States of America because the Federal government does not *recognize* the Confederate States' existence. As far as the president is concerned, there is no 'President Davis.' This is a matter between President Lincoln and Governor Pickens of South Carolina."

Chesnut laughed. "I assure you, Major, the Confederacy does in fact exist. President Davis was heretofore pleased to accept the promise of Fort Sumter's surrender with terms decidedly in your favor. You would have been able to salute your flag and retire with honor and dignity, Major. But now, faced as we are with the prospect of hostile warships forcing their way into Charleston Harbor..."

Chesnut was no longer indignant; rather, his face softened for the first time. A great sorrow weighed on his every word as he spoke.

"Gentlemen, the president recognizes that our newborn country has been forced into a corner. We do not intend to be suffocated there. This, tonight, is our breakout."

JJ scoffed, "Say the men who have besieged a Federal fort."

Major Anderson reached out and took Chesnut's hand into his own. "Colonel, I beseech you and your comrades against any rash action. I give you my personal guarantee that the only cargo on those ships is food and water for my men. Nothing more."

Grimacing, Chestnut pulled his hand free of Anderson's grasp. "I have another message," he said. "This shall be the final communication." Chesnut squared his shoulders and delivered the news verbatim, like a judge reading a death sentence:

"By authority of General Beauregard, Commander of the Provisional Forces of the Confederate States, we have the honor to notify you that his batteries will open fire on Fort Sumter in one hour's time."

Anderson's mouth fell open. He began to babble a host of excuses.

"Orders can sometimes be bungled, Colonel Chesnut. Miscommunications abound in the War Department. If I may speak for President Lincoln again, I do believe he will peacefully—"

"And I speak for the general," Chesnut said, "who speaks for President Davis. The Confederacy intends to drive foreign invaders from our American soil."

The colonel regarded the surrounding four walls with an air of finality. Each man present now understood the gravity of the situation.

"I am sorry, gentlemen. Our government will fire upon you this day. The president will accept no terms except unconditional surrender of Fort Sumter and the recognition of Southern independence."

"This is madness!" Anderson exploded, his face aflame. "Tell Beauregard to stand down. Tell him to stand down and accept reason."

"I'm sorry," Chesnut said. "Note the time. It is three o'clock in the morning, April 12th. At four o'clock, our batteries will proceed to open fire—"

"*Twelve hours,*" Anderson insisted. "Give me twelve hours and we will—"

JJ spat on the floor with disgust. "For the love of God, Major. If it's war these fanatics want, then it's war we'll give them. If these traitors want to fire upon their own flag, let them do it, and let history judge them accordingly."

Anderson roared, "*Lieutenant—*"

"I regret," JJ continued, speaking over Anderson, "that such idiocy and warmongering has brought us here. You are honorable men, Colonel Chesnut, or at least your fancy uniforms suggest as much. I only wish you had an honorable cause to fight for."

JJ looked at the Rebel adjutants, who watched the unfolding scene with grave masks of marble. Chesnut looked ready to pull out his pistol and start the war right there. JJ goaded him with a haughty smile. Well, let him try it. The old secesh would be the first to taste the steel of JJ's saber — the same one that had brought low John Brown.

Chesnut said, "On the contrary, Lieutenant; history will not be kind to *you.* I gather from your accent you are a Virginian, hm? You stand here, a Virginian trespassing on South Carolina soil, a fellow Southerner working to oppress his own people. Well, a man who does not defend his homeland against the forces of oppression is no man at all."

JJ snarled, "And neither is the man who betrays his country."

"That is quite enough!" Anderson said, shaking with fury. "We are all Americans here, are we not? Are we not still countrymen? Are we not still brothers?"

It was quiet. The dying fire in the hearth crackled once and went out.

Chesnut turned to Anderson. "I think it would be best, Major, if my men and I returned to our boat."

Anderson acquiesced, and together Rebel and defender alike left the warm comfort of the major's quarters. They trudged back to the jetty without a word spoken between anyone. As they crossed the parade grounds, JJ looked up at the Stars and Stripes flying high over Sumter, its rippling canvas set against a black starry night. And there, to the northwest, was the comet continuing its silent voyage.

At the jetty, Chesnut's aides climbed down to their boat. The old colonel turned and shook Major Anderson's hand.

"If we never meet in this world again," Anderson said, "God grant that we may meet in the next."

"The Lord smiles on the blessed South," Chesnut said. "I am certain of our victory, Major." He looked up with a melancholy stare at Sumter's walls. "But I do hope the Lord saves grace enough for you and your men."

JJ watched all these gentlemanly proceedings with a grimace. This sort of knights-in-shining-armor posturing was excruciating to watch. Soon enough, the Rebels pushed off and began to row through the whitecaps toward Charleston. Slowly, JJ drew up beside Anderson and watched as the Rebels disappeared into the gloom.

"Roscoe?"

JJ turned to Anderson. "Yes, sir?"

"If you ever speak out of turn like that again," Anderson said, "I *will* have you flogged to within an inch of your miserable goddamn life. Is that understood?"

JJ looked out at the angry sea. "Yes, sir."

"Report on our ammunition supply."

"In a word, sir? Nonexistent. We're severely low on shells and even lower on gunpowder. I would estimate we can return fire for twenty-four hours, maybe more. Maybe less."

"Well, well," Anderson said. "Now you may go down in a blaze of glory like the one you've apparently always dreamed of. Meanwhile, the whole country will be plunged into a ghastly civil war. And over what? To what end?"

JJ glanced up at the comet overhead, as if it might have some say in the matter.

"To make things right," JJ offered.

Anderson laughed. It was an odd sound at this hour, in these circumstances. "You're a damn good soldier, Roscoe, but I can see right through you. I know who you really are. *What* you really are. I have no doubt this war will be a boon for your career. But what will it do to your humanity?"

Having said this, the major turned and walked toward the fort entrance.

Midway, he paused and called back through the wind:

"Congratulations, Lieutenant. Now you have your war."

"*INCOMING!*"

A screaming 10-inch mortar shell exploded over Fort Sumter, casting a blinding sheet of lightning that slashed through the darkness of night. Red hot shrapnel rained down on the men scrambling across Sumter's grounds.

A mule tied to a post in the courtyard was struck in the head and collapsed dead on the ground. The Irish private named Hough paused to watch blood gush out of the gaping hole in the poor animal's head. JJ rushed up and grabbed him by the collar and hauled him to the ground.

"Cover, goddammit!"

Frantic calls went up and down the battlements. No casualties, the reply came, but Sumter's chapel was on fire. JJ ordered five men there to fight the flames, but his voice was lost as shells screamed down from every direction. They came from Fort Moultrie on the right, and over on the left from Fort Johnson far on the other side of Charleston Harbor. Now the Rebel batteries boomed from Cummings Point.

JJ watched with awe the parabolic rise and fall of Rebel shells and rockets. Fort Sumter was designed to withstand a naval siege, with its walls sloped so as to deflect shells from man-o'-wars firing at sea level. But the Rebel batteries stationed at Sumter's sister forts were lobbing shells in high arcs over the walls. Cannonballs tore at the soft earth of the parade ground, and they splintered the fort's wooden buildings like they were piles of matchsticks.

In the face of overwhelming fire atop the battlements, someone — JJ knew it must have been Major Anderson — gave the order to abandon the walls. As JJ watched with shock and growing rage, the defenders scrambled down to seek refuge in the yard below.

What the hell were they doing?! Return fire, goddammit. Return fire!

The constant flurry of shells slashed through the barracks buildings, spraying fire in all directions. JJ had all but blinked when suddenly the mess hall was consumed by flames.

Too fast. It was all happening too fast!

It was now a choice of whether to return fire or put out the wild flames that threatened to consume Sumter whole and fry its garrison like shrimp in a pan. The defenders formed lines to pass along buckets of seawater to douse the flames. Others tried to smother the fires with their jackets and shoveled sand on the embers. All but six guns were abandoned, with some of the abandoned cannons still primed for firing.

JJ, his uniform singed by fire and his face already caked with black soot, raced to

Major Anderson's quarters. He found the old man pacing about before an empty fireplace. A dusty bottle of Kentucky bourbon stood unopened on the major's desk.

"Major," JJ gasped. "We need to get the men back atop the battlements and return fire, sir. The top guns are the only ones with the range to do real damage."

Anderson shook his head. "It's a firestorm out there, Roscoe. As you said, we don't have the ammunition. We don't have the men." He collapsed in his chair and gripped his hands together. "And we don't have the time."

"The resupply will come, sir," JJ insisted. "If that letter the Rebels had speaks the truth, then the Navy will force its way into the harbor to help us. Until then, we need to return fire."

Anderson put a hand over his face. A vacant, unseeing eye stared beyond the web of his fingers. "They really did it. The bastards really did it. War. It's war. Here, in America, *between ourselves*. How many will die? How many will—"

"*Major*. Do you have orders?"

Anderson perked up as they heard shouts from the men fighting the fires along the parade ground outside. The major folded his arms and tucked his chin against his chest. "I can't put a six-man battery at each gun when they're firing at us from every side of the harbor..."

JJ's mind hummed while Anderson spoke. Suddenly, the solution came to him.

"All I need is five men," JJ said. "Five men plus myself to man a gun on the Cummings Point side. That's where the fire is fiercest." JJ's eyes glittered as the plan came to life in his mind. "I pre-sighted those guns myself, sir. All we need do is load and pull the firing pins. The rest of the men can stay below on the first level. Those walls are twelve feet thick; the Rebels can pound them all week and not make a dent. We'll send teams of men to fire the first level guns to distract the Rebels and kick up gusts of smoke. Meanwhile, my team will knock out their guns at Cummings Point, then we'll turn to Moultrie. We'll take out each battery piecemeal, one by one." He held Anderson's gaze. "Do I have your permission to act, sir?"

"You never seemed to respect my rank before," Anderson said haughtily. "Always inserting yourself into my decisions, forcing my hand." The old man was absent-mindedly examining the bottle of bourbon. At the sound of another loud crash, he looked up with fear. "We're stuck here like fish in a barrel. Sumter will fall, sooner or later. We'll either be overrun, or we'll be burned to a crisp."

JJ advanced on Anderson's desk and looked the old man straight in the eyes. "But that's not now, sir," JJ said. "Right now, we can still fight."

A shriek pierced the air and then a thundering crash sounded overhead. All at once the contents of the major's quarters were hurled about by the force of the shockwave. Both men went to the floor as the walls and floorboards shook and splintered. The whole world groaned with primeval fury, as if an earthquake had released some ancient and terrible monster from the depths.

Trembling amidst the wreckage, JJ murmured, "That was close..."

Anderson coughed and wiped the dust from his uniform. In a shaky voice, he said, "You're confident you can destroy those guns, Roscoe?"

JJ stood up and nodded eagerly. "And the whole goddamn Rebel army if I have to."

Anderson chewed on this in silence. At length, he nodded. "We'll fire one round every six minutes," he said, seeming to do swift calculations in his head. "Yes, six minutes should do to ration our rounds and keep up that smoke screen you need. When you find the range, hammer them with everything we've got."

Anderson reached for the bourbon. He uncorked the bottle and set two small glasses on the desk. "But the priority is to save the buildings within the fort. I want men dousing those flames. Teams of ten to each fire." Anderson poured two shots of bourbon and offered one to JJ. "And pray for some goddamn rain, Roscoe."

JJ accepted the bourbon. "Yes, sir."

The two men nodded to each other, then gulped the bourbon down. JJ barely registered the flames that down his throat. He slammed the glass down on the table, gave Anderson a sharp salute, and then he ran out to meet a world on fire.

❧

What can be said of war? In a word, it is real. It is proof against any skepticism of Man's mortal existence or the truth of his suffering. It vindicates both the rational and the empirical by destroying both. While the rest of Man's world is a shadowbox of posturings and vicarious experience, war hurls him back to his time among beasts and roots him there in the primeval. As the scattered bones of our ancestors attest, war is natural, some say inevitable. Man made war against man before either found God. To know war is to yearn for peace; to forget war is to crave and clamor for it.

For the men of Fort Sumter, cowering together as the heavens rained down pillars of fire like on the Day of Judgment, war was confusion and unrelenting bafflement. Many a man wished to climb atop the battlements if only to *see what was going on*, a wish that promised death to any who indulged it. For the men of Sumter, war stank of spent gunpowder and woodsmoke and watery bowels.

And for JJ Roscoe, war was beautiful.

Red parabolas of death streaked over and past Sumter's walls, and each time JJ wished they landed closer so he could see and feel the explosions. In the dark of night, most of the cannonballs hurtling down were almost invisible when they struck the parade grounds, pelting the earth there like so many black, murderous raindrops. Gangs of firemen were forced to retreat within the safety of the walls, but there the smoke from the fires and from the guns was so suffocating that many men lay down and went to sleep in the midst of the barrage.

JJ felt the strange urge to run across the field to the other side, to somehow weave his way through the murderous deluge of iron, but he knew that to do that was to run through rain and not get wet. Meanwhile, all the scattered fires within the fort became one all-consuming fire, a cleansing fire that compelled believer and nonbeliever alike to pray for rain — *real* rain, for a bonafide tempest to douse the flames and drown the Rebs and carry each man back to the safety of his own front porch.

By dawn the first day, the fires burned so hot that JJ felt he must tear his clothes off or be baked in them. None of the buildings in the parade grounds were unscathed, and most had been reduced to piles of blackened sticks atop chalky gray dust. And still the guns of April pounded, the deafening clang and whizzing rattle of iron upon iron unceasing all that day and into the next night. It became so loud that the gun crews, with blood pouring from their ears, no longer bothered shouting at each other, but only worked with silent precision, each man perfect in his specialized task and tuned to the rhythm of his comrades.

Another night stretched on endlessly, and still the fires raged. The men ate their last meal, for all the contents of the kitchens were hastily thrown together into whatever cooking vessels had not been destroyed in the barrage. Supper was cooked over the burning embers of Sumter's chapel and served with the grim notice that there was no more food and precious little water remaining. While the men ate, they exchanged rumors that Major Anderson was planning to surrender the fort by the next day, Sunday morning.

For JJ, even he had concluded that surrender was inevitable. The guns were almost out of shot, and soon there would be no water to drink or fight the fires. The garrison would not last another day and night, on and on, *ad infinitum*. Instead the Rebels would find the scorched bodies of the men of Sumter, all of them arrayed neatly around the Stars and Stripes (still flying despite being torn to shreds by shrapnel) like they were part of some apocalyptic cult.

And JJ knew he'd be lying to himself if he said that no part of him wished to die in battle. A small part of him (and in fact it was no small part at all, but a rather sizeable one) urged him to find some available crisis, even if he had to conjure one himself, so that he could throw himself upon it and give himself to Oblivion. He wished for a man to be wounded upon the field so that he could rush out and save him, and be killed himself in the attempt. He wished to see the Stars and Stripes come toppling down from its mast, so that he could haul the giant flag over his shoulders and race up the steps to the battlements and let Old Glory unfurl while every Rebel battery trained its sights upon him. JJ imagined his death would somehow end the battle, would indeed end the war before it even had a chance to begin. The Rebels, observing the awesome sacrifice of their valiant foe, would be compelled to lay down their arms and fight no more. The men of Fort Sumter would say afterward that, yes, JJ Roscoe had been the bravest man of the battle, and that they happy few would not have lived to tell the tale were it not for their proud lieutenant's gallantry. JJ believed that when news of his patriotic death reached Clarendon, the Roscoes would bow their heads in shame and utter their sorrowful acknowledgements that yes, JJ had really been the best of them and that no, they were not deserving of their association with him, but that yes, they would honor and revere their proud JJ forevermore, would say no more that 'this man was John Roscoe's son' but that 'this other man was JJ Roscoe's father.' He imagined the people of Mayfair, overcome with remorse over their past treatment of their favored son, gathering together to remove the statue of Thomas Jefferson in the town square and erect a new statue of JJ in its place. He imagined all the neighbors and familiar faces of his youth shining with tears of pride and sorrow. He could even see, in some distant age hence, visitors waiting in line to tour Clarendon, now designated by the Federal government as a national historic site: the birthplace of Jonathan J. Roscoe, the man who gave everything for the Union. All others in the Roscoe family — Jem especially — would be remembered only in footnotes; trivial names to be glazed over when American schoolchildren learned the official history. But only JJ's name would be etched into the plaques and cornerstones and monuments which commemorated the Hero of Fort Sumter's ultimate, vindicating sacrifice.

All that, JJ knew, would be very fine. Very fine indeed.

Still, though these daydreams warmed JJ's blood against the cold terror of the Rebel bombardment, he knew they were all lies. He knew there was only one person whom he wished might weep over his body, and that person was himself dead. There was no point in JJ sacrificing himself for anything anymore, for he did not believe the regretful, broken-hearted weeping of anyone but Father would provide a fair trade for his own life and future. After all, there was too much for JJ to do. There was too much to accomplish. There was a *war* on, after all, and it needed to be won. There were too many opportunities to seize, too many chances to eclipse the light of Father and take his place as a great man of the century. Indeed, JJ believed some future persons would speak of John Roscoe not as some notable figure, but give him only the passive description of 'father of *JJ Roscoe*, one of the great American heroes.' If Father was one of the myriad winking stars above, indistinguishable from all the rest, then JJ would be the streaking Great Comet whose brilliance commanded the awe of untold millions the world over.

And all that, to JJ, seemed like a just cause well worth living for.

When the first light of dawn arrived, JJ watched as a handful of men crawled up to the battlements and hoisted a dirty white flag. Soon enough, the booming guns went silent at last.

Slowly, moving like ghosts in a world of gray ash, the battered and deafened defenders of Fort Sumter gathered on the parade grounds. They were defeated, officially so, but their spirits remained unbroken. Though shaken, they offered smiles of acknowledgement and encouragement to each other. They had fought as bravely as men could, and indeed had given the Rebels a fever-pitched fight that stretched over forty-eight hours into Sunday morning. That made today the 14th of April.

Miraculously, not a single defender had been killed. Very few had been wounded, and none seriously. In fact, the only listed casualty on JJ's report, hastily scrawled out as he watched Rebel ships approaching in the grim dawn, was the old mule killed by the opening salvo.

JJ recognized little Daniel Hough among the men. The young Irishman was shivering with shock. Looking around, JJ saw that a shell had splintered the proud flagpole during the fighting. The tattered Stars and Stripes, torn ragged by shrapnel, lay in the dust. JJ and three others removed the flag from the pole and folded it. JJ tucked the flag under his arm. It was heavy and cumbersome, but JJ carried it with solemn pride.

Now that the guns were silent, it was eerily quiet. JJ remembered the pre-battle stillness from two nights ago. Could the battle, or even the war itself, really have begun and ended so quickly?

A sentry announced the arrival of the victorious Rebels. They came over in long rowboats, and behind them their steamers plowed the chop. Those defenders not still fighting the fires, now a battle as futile as the one against the Rebels had been, trudged through the gate to wait for the Rebels on the jetty platform.

"Let it burn," a sergeant said to the boys around him. "Let the seceshes have the ashes."

As JJ stepped out into the full breeze of the harbor, he saw a world bathed in the pale light of a steely white sun. Far across the harbor, the bells of Charleston rang in jubilation. Squinting, JJ could just make out the palmetto and Stars and Bars banners flying from every pole and steeple in the city. The breeze was strong, and it carried with it the sound of forty thousand people reveling in the streets, all making toasts to victory and independence. Meanwhile, the small Rebel armada drifted toward Sumter in silence.

A dapper gentleman in a general's uniform stood on the prow of the lead boat. A hand was thrust into the breast of his coat in the image of Washington crossing the Delaware, or perhaps in emulation of the conquering Napoleon. As the boat neared, JJ finally recognized the man. He wore a light touch of makeup to mask the wrinkles of age, and his hair and mustache was trimmed in the French style and dyed jet black. It was General (previously *Colonel*) Beauregard, the former Superintendent of West Point.

Beauregard saluted the defenders. "Major Anderson! May we come ashore?"

Anderson called back, "You may do whatever you damn well please."

The Sumter men helped tie the Rebel boats to the jetty. This time the Rebels had not arrived to parley, but to accept a formal surrender. Beauregard stepped onto the aged jetty suspended over the frothing, windswept ocean. The general offered a tight salute to Anderson, who made sure his returning salute was tighter. Now the two men shook hands.

"It's good to see you again, Robert," Beauregard said. "Only I wish it were under better circumstances."

Anderson looked up at the smoking battlements. "Well, it was a good show," he said. "Did you suffer any casualties?"

"No, thank God."

"Thank God indeed."

Beauregard turned to the smug, smiling Colonel Chesnut, who brought forward a case of cigars. Beauregard clipped a cigar and offered it to Anderson, who accepted it together with a light from an adjutant's match. Together the Rebel general and Federal major smoked and chatted about old times at West Point. Meanwhile, the sea wind whipped at JJ's face. He saw Chesnut grinning at him and scowled back.

Eventually, all that remained for discussion was the business at hand. Beauregard asked, "Do you surrender your flag and guns to me?"

"Well, I suppose shooting you here and now would be unbecoming of an officer."

JJ smiled at that. Frail though he was, Anderson had finally grown some teeth in the last forty-eight hours. Beauregard recognized this too and offered a small laugh. He excused himself while Chesnut, holding a stamped dispatch, whispered in his ear. Beauregard listened carefully, frowned, and then snatched the dispatch from Chesnut's hands. After reading the dispatch he looked at the colonel in disbelief, but Chesnut nodded.

At last, Beauregard turned stiffly to Anderson. "It appears that your convoy of resupply ships arrived *without* their armed escort."

Anderson shrugged. "Your president's spies must have been misinformed. In any case, perhaps it would have been more practicable to have postponed the opening of hostilities until you ascertained for yourself the threat upon Charleston."

Beauregard bristled. "I followed my orders, like a good soldier."

Anderson sighed and offered a relenting nod. "Yes, I suppose you did."

"Well?" Beauregard said. "Your flag and guns, Major. Do you surrender?"

The major took the folded flag from JJ and gripped it close to his chest and closed his eyes, as if praying. JJ and the other soldiers on both sides, and Beauregard also, watched motionless and ready.

"Robert, please understand me," Beauregard said. "You are a gentleman of Kentucky. There are many men on my staff from your state, and it's expected that Kentucky will soon add her star to the banner of the Confederacy. If ever you have an opportunity to join the righteous cause against tyranny, sir, this is your hour. I would be honored to have you join my staff." Beauregard now turned to JJ for the first time. "I would also be prepared to extend this offer to certain officers under your command." The general smiled. "After all, we are all patriots here."

Anderson remained still, with his eyes closed. It took everything for JJ not to respond to Beauregard himself, took everything for him to hold his tongue and keep himself from drawing his saber and cutting the damn Creole and the smug bastard Chesnut down until the Rebels shot him dead.

But before JJ could do anything, Major Anderson heaved a loud sigh. "General Beauregard, I surrender my guns to you. I cannot surrender my flag, for I will continue to serve under it."

JJ smiled and held his head high.

Beauregard's nostrils flared, and he was silent for a long, angry moment. Then his dark eyes softened. He ran his fingers over his moustache in a contemplative manner.

"Very well, Major. We'll be gracious victors today, and every day to come. We will ferry you and your men — and your flag — to a steamer in the harbor. There, you-all shall wait until your president's convoy arrives to take you home. Where you belong."

Beauregard looked at JJ once more, and maybe he noted JJ's defiant glare.

"I needn't remind you," Beauregard continued, "that if there is any show of resistance, or if your president's ships fire upon my men, I will not hesitate to blow you-all from the water. Now, is there anything you request before your departure?"

"Water," Anderson said without thinking. "Food and water for my men."

"You shall have it."

Anderson thought more on the offer. "And a gunned salute," he added. "To honor my country." Now he indicated the men in Federal blue around him. "To honor *our* country. Fifty rounds is my request."

Beauregard was quiet for a time. Finally, he nodded. "Very well. Fifty rounds."

Anderson turned to JJ. "Lieutenant?"

JJ saluted Anderson. "Major." With that, he turned his back to the Rebels and started up the jetty.

Beauregard said loudly: "Major Anderson, your executive officer refuses to salute a ranking officer. Will he not turn and show me the customary respect?"

Hearing this, JJ turned back to face Beauregard. Through his periphery, he caught a curious look from Anderson. JJ expected Anderson to warn him away from a confrontation, but instead Anderson gave JJ a small nod of approval.

Emboldened, JJ looked squarely at Beauregard and Chesnut.

"I don't salute traitors, General," JJ said. He pointed at the Stars and Stripes tucked under Anderson's arm. "The only patriots here are the men who risked their lives for that flag. The men who fired upon it will be forever reviled as enemies of liberty."

Beauregard offered the thinnest of smiles. "How naive you are, Lieutenant." The general folded his hands behind his back. "I was very sorry to hear of your father's passing. But it's pointless to think you are defending the Union that he loved so dearly. That old Union, I'm sorry to say, died along with your father. And that flag under the major's arm has been corrupted by evil men who would see an entire civilization go up in flames."

JJ shook his head. "You're wrong, General. It's true: your civilization, such as it is, will burn. But don't fool yourself. You just lit the match by your own hand."

Minutes later, the Federal guns at Fort Sumter fired for the last time.

JJ directed the salute from the battlements while Major Anderson and the Rebels watched from the jetty. From his position, JJ heard the enemy cheering from the city and the gun batteries along the coast. The faint pop of firing pistols and muskets sounded from Charleston, but most of these sounds were drowned out by the pounding of Sumter's guns. As JJ listened to the enemy's cheers, whistles, and gunshots, hot rage quickened his pulse.

Ahead, Private Daniel Hough struggled to keep up with the steady firing. The veteran cannoneers pushed him aside and shouldered his share of the heavy work until the Irishman was relegated to standing and watching.

"Hough!" JJ shouted furiously. He would have no man standing idle during the ceremony.

The Irishman scampered over. JJ yelled over the thundering guns, "Get down to the magazine and fetch more powder."

Hough's eyes were wide with fear and red with smoke. He flinched with each cannon blast. He was dazed, uncomprehending. "Might I return to the barracks instead, sir? There's a fire near the magazine, and I heard the boys say it might—"

JJ grabbed Hough by the collar and shook him violently. "Nobody is shooting at you anymore, Private," he snarled. He pushed Hough away from him.

Hough cowered like a beat dog. Without another word, the boy hurried down the steps to the magazine across the parade ground below.

JJ watched Hough go, then turned back to oversee the salute. He counted twenty-five rounds fired. Halfway there. The cannoneers had found their rhythm and were now working together like an oiled machine.

"We could have held out longer," JJ breathed to himself. The boom of the cannons drowned out his voice, but he continued to whisper aloud. "Fifty rounds, for God's sake. Fifty rounds that could have leveled Moultrie and Cummings Point, and maybe—"

A deafening explosion rocked the fortress. Men screamed and hollered as hot shrapnel came raining down to split open flesh and rock. The ground shook, and JJ reached for his Colt. He peered over the battlements down at the jetty below, but the Rebels had not taken up arms against them. In fact, they had scattered with hands covering their heads just like the Federals.

Whirling about, JJ saw black plumes of smoke rising from a fresh blast inside the fort.

"Hold your fire!" JJ hollered. The call echoed down the line.

Sumter's guns fell silent once more. JJ holstered his revolver and hurried down to the courtyard. Across the parade grounds, black smoke billowed black against the hazy sky.

The ammunition magazine had blown.

Men were already gathering there and calling for others to help. Six men lay on the smoking ground. Five squirmed about moaning in pain, their bodies charred and with their skin peeling off from the intense heat of the blast.

"Put out those fires!" JJ cried to the men who gawked at the wounded. "And ferry those munitions away from here. Move!"

As JJ drew closer, he saw that the sixth man lay in pieces. He had been all but vaporized in the blast. A spreading pool of blood stained the dirt and soaked the charred timbers around the body.

For a moment, JJ's air of command left him. He asked, in barely a whisper, "What happened here?"

"Pile of cartridges went up in flames, sir," a man reported. "They were lit somehow, by somebody unawares. Maybe a cannon fuse, maybe a cigar."

JJ felt Major Anderson at his shoulder. The major pointed at the boy in pieces. "Someone identify that man." The old major's voice trembled, and suddenly he turned away, red with shame. "Oh, damn it all..."

"It's Private Hough, sir," a sergeant said. "New recruit."

JJ was stunned. He stooped down to confirm for himself that the dead boy was indeed little David Hough from Tipperary. He turned away and tried to take a deep breath of air, but all he could smell was the stench of scorched flesh. This time, he felt no sense of power or vigor in the presence of death. He only felt a creeping, sweaty chill in his bones that felt like shame.

Anderson wasted no time. "Get our boys to the infirmary, Sergeant, or whatever is left of it." He still clutched the Stars and Stripes in his hands. As the men carried the wounded away, Anderson handed the flag to JJ. "Roscoe?"

JJ looked at Anderson for a long, quiet moment. Then he understood.

Taking the flag into his hands, JJ knelt before the body of Daniel Hough. Unfurling the flag, JJ draped it like a shroud over the boy's remains.

"He died as we all should die," Anderson said to the men around. "He died as a true American patriot." With that, Anderson saluted the bloody mess of ragged limbs. "Bury this man here in the yard, Sergeant. This is good soil for a patriot's grave."

A hastily assembled grave detail stepped forward with grim faces. The other men drifted away to await the ships that would take them on the long journey home. But little Daniel Hough would remain here at Sumter in an unmarked grave, so many thousands of miles from home.

As the digging began, JJ stared at the Stars and Stripes draped over the body. He wondered about a man's name, and how it exists to be remembered only for the briefest span of time, and how maybe the purpose of a man's physical life was to extend the life of his name — his *legacy* — for as long as he could. No man lived forever, but perhaps a name could. Alexander, Caesar, Bonaparte...

Roscoe.

But for little Daniel Hough, it seemed he would be forgotten among the untold billions of history's nameless dead. And in that quiet moment, JJ Roscoe promised to God — no, he promised to *himself* — that he would not suffer the same fate.

In the center of the flag, a spot of blood appeared. At first faint, it now began to spread until the whole of the Stars and Stripes was colored a dark crimson.

Chapter 37

LIBERTY & UNION

Ben leaned forward so the drumming rain fell away from the brim of his hat. It was dark all around, and a cold rain had whipped up since he passed beyond Berryville earlier that day. Though he'd left Clarendon on Wednesday the 10th, the coach had splintered a wheel just outside Winchester. Thankfully a local farmer helped Ben repair the wheel and hadn't asked too many questions, but by the time Ben started off again it was the wee hours of Friday morning. After the storm set in, Ben lost his way. His sincere lack of direction was underlined by his stubbornness, and Ben had driven blind through the tempest all Friday afternoon and night with only one thought on his mind: he had to get to Washington.

From somewhere, a voice cut through the downpour: "*HALT*!"

Now the same cry sounded again from somewhere in the thickets. Now a flash in the dark and an ear-splitting gunshot. Ben tore at the reins and slowed Mabel and the coach. As he did this, he cursed himself for not just bolting the hell out of there. Here he was, a black man driving a horse and coach that could not possibly be his, and flying like a bat out of hell. The optics of his situation, as Senator Roscoe might have put it, were distinctly unfavorable.

Ben watched swinging lanterns float up from the gloom. He decided he wasn't just crazy for stopping but also stupid, damn stupid. He looked into the nearest light and saw a bearded man squinting up at him.

"What's the holdup?" Ben called, doing his best to sound authoritative.

It wasn't a wise choice. The man facing him did not say anything, but his unblinking eyes spoke plenty. They were the eyes of a predator who had spotted a lone and isolated quarry.

Nervously, Ben said, "This is a Federal road. You can't block my passage."

The man's eyes widened. "Federal road?" He looked at his companions knowingly. Now he leaned over and spat a stream of black tobacco into the rain. He turned his eyes up to Ben again and said, "This is the Commonwealth of *Virginia*, boy, and we's defenders of the common good. Federal government ain't got no authority here except what we give it."

The rain was falling harder now, and Ben could barely see anything past the rainwater flowing from his hat brim. But he did see that any man who didn't hold a lantern held a musket in hand, and the men with lanterns carried pistols in their belts. Maybe it was wiser that he hadn't bolted after all; they might have shot him down, thinking him some kind of runaway or criminal. Of course, they might just decide to do that anyway — or worse.

The first man noticed Ben's watchful eyes and continued smiling, holding his gaze, as if his stare might hold Ben frozen forever. The man put his hands on Mabel's bit and admired her, cooing to her softly. Still looking at the horse, the man said, "Where you goin all in a hurry, boy?"

"My name is Benjam—"

"I didn't ask your goddamn name. I asked where you was goin."

Again Ben looked around at the weapons, spied fingers brushing triggers. He watched the leader's breath mist in the night and felt a wet finger run down his spine.

"Washington," Ben said. "I'm going to 514 10th Street. Senator John Roscoe lives there. *Lived* there." When this was met with no response, Ben said, "He was my master."

"Roscoe?" The militia captain turned to his comrades, exchanging curious expressions. "You say he's a senator?"

"*Was*, yes. From Mayfair."

"I hadn't heard he died," a voice said from the darkness.

"Roscoe?" another voice said. "I voted for him, election before last. He was a good man."

"He's a son of a bitch," another groaned.

"Shut up," the captain growled to the group. "I tell y'all to shoot, you shoot. Beyond that, y'all don't do or say a goddamn thing without my say-so."

Ben's pulse pounded as he scanned the darkened faces surrounding him. Despite the drenching rain, Ben could still pick out the blue secession cockades the men wore tied to their sleeves and around their necks.

"I'm coming from Mayfair, southwest of here," Ben said. "That's Senator Roscoe's home district, and his family is there. They sent me to Washington to collect some of the family's personal effects and to settle the Senator's estate."

"Settle his what now?"

"His estate," Ben repeated. "I've been charged with looking after his affairs. I'm to meet with John Roscoe's attorney, help him close all outstanding business, so to speak. I must go there, work quickly, and come back. What with all the trouble down in South Carolina, the Roscoe family thought it pertinent to take care of everything sooner rather than—"

"He sounds funny, cap'n," one of the men said.

Ben's eyes darted around. He braced for one of the men to yank the reins from his hands and pull him down into the mud. The bored, gaunt-eyed men looked to be craving some kind of sport.

"Naw," the captain said with a shrug. "Just a learned nigger. I seen their kind before. Don't let him irritate you, Charlie." He squinted up at Ben once again. "What'd you say your name was?"

"Benjamin." Thinking it might improve his case, he added, "Benjamin *Roscoe*, sir."

The captain nodded and chewed on the name. "Roscoe. You got papers sayin as such?"

Ben swallowed. No, he had no damn papers. There was nothing to indicate whether he and Mama were slave or free, living or dead, or whether they had ever existed in the first place. If he couldn't produce some kind of official paper, it would be nothing for these defenders of the 'common good' to hang Ben as a suspected runaway.

Thunder peeled and the captain looked up as the steady rain became a torrent. He shook his head and turned away. "Nah, forget it. Boys, let him go and let's get outta this piss." The captain waved Ben on. "This one may be a nigger, but he's tellin the truth. G'won, boy, get. But you see you get back from Wash City soon. The border could close any day now. G'won."

Trembling, Ben said, "Yes, sir, thank you, sir."

The militiamen stepped back and made way for Ben to ride on. He looked ahead at the darkened road stretching on through the fog. He looked down at the captain.

"This *is* the road to Washington, isn't it?"

The captain pointed. "Six miles up you take the Leesburg road on your left. Keep Ashburn on your right and you make it just fine."

A man standing nearby smiled at Ben with mock cheer. "Godspeed, nigger."

Ben nodded stiffly and started off through the rain. As the coach rolled on he waited for the call of *Hey boys watch this!*, waited for the bullet to strike him before he heard the thundercrack of the shot. Leaning forward, he drove Mabel faster and the old mare seemed as eager to get away as he did. He did not look back until he had gone several miles; only then did he turn briefly and stare back into the impenetrable gloom.

Facing forward once more, with darkness surrounding him, Ben slashed the reins and urged Mabel on into the visionless night.

Ben arrived in Washington late on Friday, April 12th, late enough to be considered early. The streets were alive with crushing crowds in states of severe agitation. Several times, Ben was compelled to backtrack and wind his way past roadblocks and throngs of people in order to reach 10th Street. Ben heard the startling sound of windows shattered and smelled the acrid stench of housefires in his nostrils. Washington was alive with unrest and foreboding. Exactly why this was the case, Ben wasn't sure. He'd been on the road almost two days.

John Roscoe's lawyer, a man named Bartholomew, had traveled down to Mayfair earlier in the year to settle the old man's estate. But the last piece of the puzzle, the sale of the Senator's Washington townhouse, was able to proceed only recently. Bartholomew's associates placed the townhouse on the market, and after several fitful months it sold for well under asking price. (Apparently no one wanted to move to the Union's capital when it was becoming increasingly likely that Washington might no longer be the capital of anything.) And before the deed and keys were handed to the new owner, Ben had the weekend to collect whatever personal effects he could carry from the Senator's townhouse. The rest would be removed and sold at auction.

After Ben returned to Mayfair, there was of course the North Branch Mine to see about. The mine had been closed for almost an entire year by now. What with the Senator pouring all his resources into his 1860 presidential campaign, there had been no financing available to repair the mine or even clear out the rubble. In the spring, Lady Isabella had convinced Jem to sell the mine in order to eliminate the Senator's debts. Jem, who had once been a heartfelt advocate for the North Branch as a beacon of social progress, agreed without protest or enthusiasm.

Once campaign debts were paid — *if* indeed the sale of the mine and the townhouse and auction items were enough — then the Roscoes might be flush once more. Humbled, certainly, but not destitute. But though everyone seemed so focused on the dollars and cents of the situation, without the omniscient presence of John Roscoe to guide the family, Ben could not help but wonder:

What the hell were the Roscoes going to do now?

Ben had an idea what *he* was going to do, at least. Gather whatever trinkets he could, take them back to Clarendon, and then pull Mama aboard the coach and leave — *for good.*

The murky light of dawn stretched down 10th Street. The coach rolled past Ford's Atheneum and reached Number 514 across the street. Ben maneuvered the coach down the back alley and led Mabel into the small stable. He fed Mabel and got her settled in a bed of fresh straw. Crossing to the front door of the Senator's townhouse, Ben knocked and waited for an answer. When none came, he rang the bell. Still there was no answer. Taking out the Senator's key, Ben moved it toward the lock and—

The door swung open and ripped the key from Ben's fingers.

Bending low, Ben picked up the key from the ground. Looking up, he stared into the face of a small red-haired woman of about thirty. She was elegantly dressed and looked supremely uncomfortable because of it, and her hair was six directions astray. Her cheeks were red and puffy from crying. The woman regarded Ben with quiet fear and spoke in a sharp tone.

"Well who the hell are you supposed to be?" she snapped. She had a thick accent that Ben didn't recognize. "We don't want whatever your massa's selling."

Ben removed his hat. "Uh, h-hello." In a subtle way he checked the number over the door. "My name is Ben Freeman. I'm looking for—"

"You must be with the movers," the woman said.

Ben blinked. "*Movers?*" He fumbled with his hat in his hands. "Uh, no, ma'am. I'm sorry but I'm...Do you...*live* here?"

The woman huffed a sigh. "I used to."

Ben nodded slowly. "This house is owned — *was* owned — by Senator John Roscoe."

"I know who owns it," she said. "Johnny gave me a key, you know."

Ben smiled with pursed lips. *Johnny?*

"Yes," he said. Looking down, he saw that the young woman wore a ring on her finger and—

Engagement ring?!

But no, wrong finger. Still, it was a fine ring nonetheless, though the woman pulled it at incessantly as if it gave here severe discomfort. Her whole body moved in jerking motions like that of a bird.

"You must be one of Johnny's men," the woman said.

Ben nodded. "Yes, ma'am. My name is—"

"You already told me your name. Come inside. *Oh*! Look. There's the movers' coach."

They both looked up the street toward a rickety wagon drawn by two sickly horses. Three boys clambered down and proceeded up the steps. They pushed straight past Ben and went directly inside the townhouse.

"They were here yesterday and the day before," the woman explained. "This morning should see the last of my things out of here. Now *be quick about it*, boys. My train leaves in just two hours."

From within the townhouse there came the sounds of creaking boards and shuffling boots and "One-two-*three*!" followed by wheezing grunts. Two boys emerged carrying a large writing desk between them. Stepping into the doorway once more, the woman looked out at Ben and beckoned him inside.

"Come out of the cold, Mr. Freeland."

"Thank you."

Ben stepped inside. Meanwhile, the third moving boy passed by with a load of fine dishes rattling in their case.

"Do be careful with that!" the woman quipped to the boy. "I don't want to pay you for a fine job and then get to Philadelphia and open everything up and find that all my things are broken and shattered. I'm not *stupid*, you know."

"Yes, ma'am."

Ben stared after the boy a moment before he turned to the woman. "I'm afraid I didn't catch your name, ma'am."

"*Miss,*" she said. "Miss Francine Robson. You, sir, may call me Miss Robson."

"Miss Robson."

"Yes."

"I thought I recognized some of Isabella Spencer's china poking out of that box, Miss Robson."

Miss Robson smiled. "Oh, yes. It's a very fine set. She has good taste, that woman does."

"Indeed," Ben said. He cleared his throat. "It's just that, well, I believe that china belongs to Senator Roscoe's family."

Miss Robson shrugged. "Johnny's son said I could have it."

Johnny's son. Jem, perhaps? It had to be.

"I see..."

"I came to visit one night, back last November," Miss Robson explained. "I hadn't seen Johnny for *weeks*. He had guests here, so he told me, and he'd put me up in a hotel in the meantime. Well, I got terribly bored and decided to surprise him. But when I arrived, Johnny was lying sick over there on the chesterfield. His son was there with him, taking care of him. Oh, the boy was *very* handsome! Looked so much like Johnny, only much younger. A coach had just arrived to take Johnny back to his home in wherever-it's-called..."

"Mayfair."

"Mayfair, yes. My beloved Johnny was white as a sheet and his son Jeremiah didn't look much better. I think I must have surprised them, but that didn't call for the son to be so, well, he was so *rude*. He must have thought I was some kind of *maid*. I explained I was there to get some money from Johnny, money for shopping of course, and this Jeremiah just told me to take whatever the hell I wanted from the place so long as I stopped blocking the door. They left and I stayed behind, waiting for Johnny to come back. Oh, he takes these sorts of spells from time to time. Sometimes I would wake up and see blood on his pillow. Doctors take him away, but he always comes back. This time, however, he didn't come back."

Ben nodded slowly, barely registering the things the woman was saying. He wondered if he was going to be the one to tell Miss Robson that her beloved Johnny was—

"I know he's dead," she said, as if she'd heard his question aloud. "I can read the papers you know. I'm not stupid."

"Of course not," Ben said. "If you knew the Senator well, I'm sorry for your—"

"He knew *me*," she replied, "but I wouldn't say I knew him. Not beyond what he *wanted* me to know. Johnny was strange like that."

Ben nodded. "I understand what you mean."

Miss Robson looked about the place wistfully. "I thought about staying, but I figured that sooner or later someone like you would show up to take all this away. I'm not taking everything; only things of sentimental value." As she said this, Miss Robson caught Ben staring at two of the moving boys carrying a huge Persian rug outside, and so she added, "Johnny bought that for me last Christmas."

Ben nodded. "I see." Unsure of what to do or where to stand, he gestured vaguely toward the stairs. "Do you mind if I take a walk around?"

Miss Robson shrugged. "Make yourself at home. The boys here will be done in just a few minutes." As Ben started to climb the stairs, she started after him with a note of urgency in her voice. "Everything I'm taking belongs to me, you know. You'll have no right coming after me for anything later on. I know my rights; I'm not stupid, you know."

Wearily, Ben agreed. In truth, he didn't give a damn about any of the furniture and trinkets in the townhouse. It would mean fewer things for himself to lug out.

As Ben trudged up the endless steps, he remarked that it was strange to be back in the Senator's townhouse without the Senator and his entourage present. Months ago, this place had been crawling with campaign staffers and yes-men.

It was dark upstairs; all the bedroom doors had been shut. Ben opened the door to one of the bedrooms, which had been used as an office during the campaign. The room was completely empty; Miss Robson had even taken the window curtains.

Ben wondered for a while about Miss Robson. Who was she? How had she come to know John Roscoe, and how had she become his lover? There was something *off* about the woman that Ben couldn't quite put his finger on. Her strangled, agitated temperament seemed to indicate a deeper part of her core nature. Somehow it made sense that the Senator had attracted such a fragile person to dwell within his aura, and under his thumb.

Ben wondered also about the Senator, whether his personality had ever changed when in the company of Miss Robson. Had he been a different sort of John Roscoe when in the company of this woman? Ben supposed that, whatever the answers to these questions were, they would remain unknown.

He opened the door to the Senator's bedroom and listened to it yawn open. It seemed no one, not Miss Robson nor even a housekeeper, had stepped foot inside this room for several months. He stared at the old man's desk for a long while, studying the newspapers strewn about, the dried-up inkwell, the unfinished letters and telegrams and speeches. An unfinished life now finished, for better or for worse.

Though he sometimes wanted to feel relief at the old man's passing, Ben couldn't feel anything beyond the numb chill of the realization that such a *presence* was suddenly and conspicuously absent from his world. The big, looming figure of John Roscoe had faded away like a shadow in the dusk, but from time to time Ben felt the man's shadow fall over him once again, as if some part of him yet lived beyond the grave.

"Stop thinking about it," Ben told himself. "You'll be back home soon enough, and you'll see for yourself that same hole in the ground where he's buried. You'll see the terminal point of every idea and ambition any person could ever have. You'll see the place where your own dreams will end up someday."

Ben stoked a small fire in the hearth. It was quiet down below; Ben guessed the movers had finished their work. Ben was bone-weary, but he felt compelled to go down and speak again with Miss Robson. He trudged back downstairs, but when he reached the landing he realized that the house was empty, silent. The movers had gone, and so had Francine Robson. All that was left of her was a square envelope that had been slid under the door. Ben opened the envelope and found another house key inside.

And so, Ben went back upstairs. He had much work to do, and he wished he had thought to hire those moving boys to help him. But before he could work, he knew he needed sleep.

Back in the Senator's bedroom, the fire was hot and crackling. Ben peeled off his soaking wet clothes and draped them to dry. He coughed and spat goopy phlegm into a handkerchief, and he thought briefly about the pneumonia he'd fought back in the fall.

At the window, he looked out at the quickening gray light of the new morning. His hand traced the corners of a new pane of glass that had been installed there. Looking out, he tried to imagine a faceless man holding a rock down on the street below.

Ben drew the curtains and got under the covers of the bed. He shivered there for some time, his body exhausted but his mind restless. Eventually, sleep overcame him.

❧

After what felt like only a short rest, Ben woke up. He heard the sounds of city life outside the window. Beyond the curtains, it appeared to be sunset. He'd slept most of the day away.

Ben lay in bed, thinking. He hadn't slept well; he'd dreamed fitfully about Mama. They hadn't spoken much since the Senator died, and when Ben left for Washington he'd given only a hurried, distant goodbye. He decided to attempt some kind of clearing of the air as soon as he got back home to Clarendon, to try and make things right with Mama again. With everything going on, it was no use carrying on alone.

But oh, why wouldn't Mama listen to him? Why couldn't she see the Valley — and life at Clarendon — for what it was? Why didn't she want to leave? Instead of lingering in Mayfair, they might stay here in Washington together, or push on farther north.

But maybe staying in Mayfair just made more sense to Mama. Maybe she was just trying to protect herself, and trying to protect Ben too. Maybe she didn't insist on staying out of any weakness, even if Ben wasn't convinced it was an act of strength either. With the Senator gone, maybe life at Clarendon would improve. Perhaps the shadows would lift from the dark corners. The more Ben considered this possibility, however, the more he doubted it. A perpetual cloud of sickness shrouded Clarendon; it had been there long before John Roscoe, and it seemed it would remain for a long time to come.

Pulling on an old housecoat and slippers, Ben wandered through the townhouse in the twilight. As he moved about, Ben suddenly heard church bells tolling the commencement of Sunday morning services.

Sunday morning? But that didn't make any sense at all. That would mean he'd slept a full day and night, over twenty-four hours. But as he looked out the window, he realized that the light in the sky was growing, not receding. Somehow he'd slept all day and night Saturday, and here he was feeling he still needed a few good hours more.

But he knew he had to make contact with the lawyer named Bartholomew. There was work to be done here, after all.

For whatever reason, Ben made his way up to the large attic on the third floor. It was here, after all, where he'd found the evidence that John Roscoe had lied when he said he'd freed all of Colonel Spencer's slaves all those years ago. Probably the space was still crammed with knick-knacks.

Up in the attic, Ben inched past tottering towers of junk. He recognized in the furthest corner a great bulky shape covered with a discolored white sheet. He had forgotten all about the mysterious shape, but now he felt drawn to it as if by magnetism. At last, he stood before it with the sheet clutched in his hands.

With one great sweep Ben lifted the sheet and pulled it away, revealing a monstrous cast iron machine of wheels and pistons and arms and cylinders. Looking at the sheet in his hands, Ben saw it was marked with smears and splotches of black ink. And slotted into the base of the machine itself was a wooden board into which were set tiny metal letters of varying shapes and sizes.

It was a printing press.

Ben hadn't the slightest idea how to operate a printing press, but his intuition guided him. He spied a foot pedal that seemed to turn the great iron wheel, which itself looked to power the rest of the machine. Setting a foot upon the pedal, Ben pressed down. Nothing happened; the pedal depressed but there was no movement, not even a sound of gears touching together. After some guessing, Ben put a hand on the iron wheel and pushed against it. Slowly it began to spin, and then as Ben stepped upon the pedal the wheel moved faster and faster. And there, just as he surmised, the other parts of the machine came to life: two arms lifted up, rolling a cylinder against a flat pan of dried ink; and at the same time a slot opened up like a gaping mouth with a board for a tongue. Down in the machine's throat Ben saw a case of letters set backwards, right to left. As the wheel spun the tongue retracted, the mouth closed shut, and the inked roller came down and flattened against the tongue. Then the mouth and tongue opened once more.

Beside the machine were stacks of yellow paper. Ben reached for a sheet and waited for the mouth to open wide again. He placed the sheet of paper upon the tongue and watched, fascinated, as the machine swallowed the paper and the inked roller together. After a few seconds, with the great wheel still spinning, the mouth opened again and the tongue offered the same paper as before — except now the blank sheet had become a printed handbill.

Ben withdrew the paper just as the mouth snapped shut again. Ben took good note of that, for he guessed it would be nothing for the fast-running iron mouth to mash a straying finger to pulp. Taking up the handbill, Ben breathed a heavy sigh as he looked upon its printed contents. The ink was dry and cracked, and Ben had inserted the sheet at a crooked angle, but the effect was nonetheless marvelous to look upon. Printed on the paper were the words:

LIBERTY & UNION!

Elect John M. Roscoe Your President
No to Black Republicanism
No to Southern Secession
No to Foreigners, Catholics, Jews,
and Women's Suffrage
Yes to a Man of the People in 1860!

It was, of course, one of the Senator's campaign flyers. Just months ago, this piece of paper had been a valuable asset to the old man's campaign. Now it was a historical document, and one that Ben supposed would go rightfully undocumented and unnoticed. Looking around the room, he saw there were stacks of printed handbills tied with string. There had to be thousands of them, with thousands of blank sheets of paper ready for printing. Whoever had worked the printing press for the Senator had not finished the job, or just as likely the election's outcome had rendered the job pointless.

Tucked in the corner was a standing desk with dozens of tiny shelves built like a honeycomb network. In each of the shelves were tiny letters molded in iron and plaster. With one scoop, Ben held in his palm several dozen tiny ornaments shaped in the letter *E*.

Stunned, his mind racing, Ben dropped the iron letters back where he found them. The full weight of his discovery now dawned on him. Here was a one-man printing press, the same kind used by independent country newspapers like the *Mayfair First Witness*. And here, all laid out, were the letters with which Ben could print anything: a handbill, a magazine, a newspaper, even a novel. The process of setting type seemed as foreign to him as learning a new language, but he was certain he could figure it out quickly enough.

All he would need to get started was fresh ink.

But how to get the press home? Was he really going to lug such a contraption all the way back to Mayfair? If he took the press, that would leave precious little room for other items — items the Roscoe family probably cared about. But then again, Miss Robson had stripped the place almost bare. And besides, what did the Roscoes need any more junk for?

Yes, Ben decided to take the press and the honeycomb desk with it. He hadn't yet decided what he would actually *do* with the press, but he told himself he'd figure that out later. First, he needed to find an extra set of hands to help him with the lifting.

Intent on going out, hoping he might find some kind-looking person in search of honest work, Ben began to dress. He could still hear the curious tolling of bells outside, which was strange. Still, his racing mind took little notice.

Ben's clothes were still wet from rain, so he opened the Senator's closet. The old man's scent filled his nostrils. Ben had never really considered John Roscoe's *smell* before, but here it was: a heady spice that was as much a part of every shirt and jacket as the woven stitches that held them together. The old man's clothes were ill-fitting, but they would do for now.

Ben dressed and went down to the first floor. He wandered into the kitchen and found the shelves empty (for evidently the pantry's contents had belonged to Miss Robson as well).

Ben reached into his pocket and withdrew his coin purse. He had precious little money, and for a moment he wondered whether he really ought to spend it hiring a laborer to move some hunk of wood and iron, or just buy some bread to eat and forget his fantasy altogether.

Why was he so enthralled with the idea of playing with a printing press when the real purpose of his journey to Washington still loomed large? His time here was intended to be brief and productive. The press was a damn pig of a thing. It had to weigh at least five hundred pounds anyway, and in any case it was not Ben's to take. The press would have to go to auction, just like everything else.

And yet, Ben could not help but wonder. *If* he could somehow transport the press to Clarendon, who would know the difference? And really, would anyone even care? It was not a heap of gold doubloons but a squeaking, clanking knot of metal gears and pipes. And if it really mattered so much to Ben to *own* the thing, why, he could simply pay a fair price into John Roscoe's estate. That would settle the matter for good. And once back at Clarendon, free from his duties to the Senator, Ben would have all the time in the world to tinker with the press.

Just how many negro newspapermen were there in the Union? Just how many papers were printed *by* blacks, *for* blacks? Just how many new voices would the world now hear, their ideas and hopes and prayers and convictions printed on black ink by Ben Freeman's own hand? No longer would he be voiceless, no longer would he be unheard or unseen.

Ben stopped at the mirror in the foyer before the front door. He paused there for a long moment to consider his reflection.

"Extra, extra!" Ben cried to the man in the mirror. "Read your daily *Liberty & Union*! It's real news delivered at the right time. Don't forget, gentlemen, your daily dose of reason: *Liberty & Union*!"

He laughed softly to himself. That really wasn't a bad name for the paper, now that he thought about it.

From outside, the *bang* of a gunshot rang out. Ben flinched, then flinched again when he heard another *bang* followed by the sharp whizz of a ricochet.

His whole body clenched, Ben strained to listen.

The commotion outside did not sound like a gunfight or riot, but perhaps a… could it be a celebration? Suddenly there came the sound of vibrant cheering and throaty voices singing together. Then came the church bells again, tolling not for Sunday services now but to share some kind of urgent message.

His curiosity piqued, Ben went downstairs and stepped out onto the street.

Down on the corner of 10th and E Street, a swelling crowd was herded and corralled by a company of newsboys. Ben watched from the front steps of 514 as other people hurried out of homes and cafes and storefronts to join the crowd. Almost in a trance, Ben started toward the gathering crowd at the corner.

Commanding the attention of all was a company of small boys with stacks of fresh newspapers tucked under their arms. The crowd tossed pennies at the boys and snatched papers from their tiny hands. The people talked excitedly, some cheering for Lincoln, others hurrahing for Jeff Davis.

"*War*!" the newsboys called. "Lincoln calls war! The Confed'rates respond. Read it here, read it quick!"

Blocked from buying a paper by the mindless jostling of the crowd, Ben stepped back and surveyed the scene. To his left, he saw a young black boy sitting atop the street gutter, with a couple spare newspapers clutched to his chest. He'd been clocked in the nose by someone, maybe a rival newsboy or an overzealous customer. The boy held his nose and watched with dark fascination as drops of his blood splashed into the city bilgewater that ran down the gutter. Maybe feeling Ben's shadow pass over him, the boy looked up and regarded Ben's clothes.

"Who you belong to?" the boy asked. He had a thick accent that suggested he was from bayou country, maybe Louisiana or Mississippi.

"My own self," Ben said. He offered a penny for one of the boy's newspapers. "And you?"

The boy shrugged. "Ringo sells whatever massa tells."

Ben nodded and took a paper from the boy who called himself Ringo. He unfolded the front page and looked at the headline. It was a single word, in bold type, and it took up over half the page.

WAR!

Shocked at the word on the page, Ben forgot how to speak. He wandered away from the newsboy named Ringo without thinking to thank him, nor with any thought in mind whatsoever. His mind, his sense of self, all of it was gone.

"Christ — watch it, nigger!"

Ben shrank back from the pair of city constables. He'd stepped on one of the constable's shining black shoes. Immediately the two men grabbed Ben and pinned him against a brick wall.

"We oughta whup you, boy," one of the constables growled. "You step on a white man's shoes again and you'll damn well pay for it, monkey."

Ben froze and waited for the constables to lash out again or move on. After spitting in Ben's face, they moved on.

It was some time before Ben caught his breath and found the strength to move again. He stooped and picked up the newspaper that had been torn in the scuffle. As he walked on, Ben read about the firing on Fort Sumter.

Sumter. The island fortress he'd seen down in Charleston. Last year's Democratic National Convention felt like a thousand years ago, and the country in which it had taken place now seemed as distant and foreign as China.

The Confederate States — 'Secessionist Rebels' according to the newspaper — had launched an attack upon Fort Sumter just before dawn on Friday. Here it was Sunday morning, and according to reports wired up to Washington from jubilant Charleston journalists, Fort Sumter's defenders had surrendered at daybreak, just a few hours ago.

The paper in Ben's hands also made clear what President Lincoln was prepared to do in response. The next story detailed the president's call for 75,000 volunteers to march on Charleston. The story styled the insurrection in South Carolina and elsewhere as 'the Rebellion, the test of our time.' The Rebels had or were in the process of seizing state and Federal armories, factories, post offices, railways, banks, hospitals, and converting everything to the cause of the new Southern nation. Lincoln's call for troops was, in his own words on page two, an 'effort to maintain the honor, the integrity, and the existence of our national Union, and the perpetuity of popular government; and to redress wrongs already long endured.'

The next story shared the telegraphed responses of several state governors. The first reply, from the Governor of Virginia, hit Ben like a gut punch:

I have only to say that the militia of Virginia will not be furnished to the powers at Washington for any such use or purpose as they have in view.
Mr. Lincoln's object is to subjugate the Southern states, and a requisition made upon me for such an object — an object, in my judgment, not within the purview of the Constitution — will not be complied with. You have chosen to inaugurate civil war, and having done so, we will meet it in a spirit as determined as the administration has exhibited toward the South.

Ben lowered the newspaper and clutched his chest. So it had really happened. Virginia was gone — seceded!

The militiamen from the night before had been right: the border between Washington and Virginia would close soon, if it hadn't already. Virginia, the Union's brightest star, was destined to become a war zone. Much of the state lay in the line of fire between Richmond and Washington, and it was here Ben suspected the great majority of Federal and Rebel forces would fight and die. The war might rage from coast to coast, consuming as it did all the states from Texas to Maine, but Virginia would most certainly be turned to ashes.

Taking up the newspaper again, Ben forced himself to continue reading. The other Border States had followed Virginia's example. Kentucky, North Carolina, Tennessee, Arkansas, Missouri, all condemned Lincoln's call for troops as a 'gross usurpation of power' and refused to support the 'unholy crusade.'

But what about Maryland? If Maryland joined the Confederacy, then the District of Columbia would be cut off and surrounded by secessionists. All the newspaper had about Maryland was a fractured, unconfirmed report about deadly riots in Baltimore, a rumor that Federal troops had shot protesters after several soldiers had been stoned to death by a hostile crowd.

Ben dropped the paper to his side at last. Looking around, he saw that Washington was quickly descending into chaos. Rich and poor alike were frantically packing carts and wagons with their families and all their earthly possessions. Some rode hard northward while others abandoned bewildered slaves, leaving them in charge of their townhouses and property. Still others cursed the 'nigger-lover in the Executive Mansion' and ordered their slaves to follow on foot as they turned their wagons south.

"I must get home!" a man nearby shouted, voicing the reaction of untold thousands who stalked the streets of Washington in a daze similar to Ben's.

"Home better be north!" another man replied with a sneer. "Ain't nobody gettin across the Potomac this night, nor any time from now 'til the end."

It finally dawned on Ben. Washington too might become a war zone. Why, Virginia was just across the river! The Potomac was wide, but not so wide that shells could not be lobbed across to set the whole city ablaze. A Rebel army might already be on the march to besiege and destroy the city. Would Lincoln's volunteer troops arrive in time? *Were* there any volunteers on the way?

Ben checked the paper again. He saw no patriotic declarations by the Northern governors, no promises by Northern militias — no word from the Northern states at all. There was no hope in the headlines, only panic and despair. Was there really no solidarity in the face of open rebellion?

Ben flinched at a shotgun blast that shattered the dull roar of panic. An old woman had shot a lame horse in the street, screaming, "Lest the Rebels take her!"

As he reached the steps of the Senator's townhouse, Ben looked up 10th Street as scores of doors were flung open, through which fled panicked people burdened with whatever valuables they could carry. Down the street, a crowd of teenaged toughs gathered to burn Lincoln in effigy. Southern supporters exuded brash confidence to anyone who would listen, suggesting Lincoln was weak and that Jeff Davis would soon arrive in Washington to seize power. Before the theatre called Ford's Atheneum, a young girl was nearly run over by a speeding cart bound for the Maryland countryside.

Ben felt weak with despair. Had everyone given up on their new president already? Had everyone given up on the Union itself, and all without a fight?

Ben thought suddenly of Mama. Oh, Mama. She was still at Clarendon, still doting on Lady Isabella and the Roscoes. Still unaware, or only dimly so, of the mortal danger that was now swelling around her like a poisonous cloud.

Federal armies might descend on Mayfair within weeks, maybe days. The Shenandoah Valley was like a grassy highway leading from the shores of the Potomac straight down to the border with North Carolina. If any Federal army was bound for Charleston, it would likely strike for the Shenandoah River and follow it downstate to southern Virginia and the Carolinas. Might Mama have a chance to slip northward against the southbound flow of soldiers?

But there was little doubting that the people of Mayfair, and all Virginians with them, would rise up in revolution at the first sign of 'foreign' invaders. Very likely Jem would rise up with them and take up arms against his own country, and in the same violent action pledge his allegiance to a new American nation. If there was a place where the coming fury might be fiercest, it would be on the rugged hills and rolling pastures surrounding Mayfair.

And Mama, poor Mama. She would be caught in the middle of it all!

Ben took out the townhouse key and locked the front door. He passed around the corner and down the alleyway toward the shared stables at the back of the lot. The old mare Mabel was agitated by all the screaming and singing and gunfire, and Ben brushed her and spoke to her soothingly. This meditative process gave him a few more minutes to think about his next steps.

He would go to Clarendon. Yes, he would go back to Mayfair, but only long enough to pull Mama aboard the coach and turn northward. They would find somewhere to live far away from the warzone, and there Ben would find some means of earning a living. With so many men about to go off to war, surely there would job openings of some kind. The Roscoes could come too if they wished, though somehow Ben knew the family would never leave Clarendon.

And what of Sarah? Well, Ben could not concern himself with Sarah any longer. It was not his place to do so, and in truth it never had been. In any case she was a Cutler now; she'd thrown her lot in with the First Families. However things turned out, she would never stand on the same side of the dividing line as Ben. Maybe he had too long deluded himself to ever think she would. Sarah was the wife of *Henry Cutler* now, and there was nothing redeemable in that fact. No, the Sarah Roscoe he used to know was now Sarah Cutler, daughter of the Confederacy.

Ben guided Mabel and the coach into the street once more. There was no time to pack, no time to do anything more than *go*. Climbing aboard the coach, he urged Mabel toward the bridges and causeways that spanned the Potomac. The closer he got to the river, the more fearful he became. Families and the elderly had either already fled or had shut themselves indoors, and now there were only gangs of men and women roaming the streets with violence gleaming in their eyes. Ben did his best to keep his head down and drive quickly — but not too quickly, lest he draw undue attention from those idly firing their pistols into the sky.

It was a long drive to the bridges that spanned the Potomac. Soon the streets became snarled with wagons and horses and foot traffic. It seemed thousands of people had the same idea as Ben. He slowed the coach and waited, but then the crowd pressed in tighter and tighter, flowing around the coach and jostling for position. And all the while, the people murmured together or else cried aloud:

— *What's taking so long?*

— *There's been an accident.*

— *No accident. The Rebels have burned the bridges.*

— *They've closed the border. No one in or out of Virginia!*

— *Why would they close the border? Who closed it? This is a free country.*

— *It's all a lie, I tell you. A lie! There is only one enemy, friends: the government!*

— *This man speaks the truth! A great conspiracy. The rich send the poor to fight!*

— *Pass it on: The border is closing. Rebels are camped across the river!*

— *Pass it on: The border is closed. Rebels are attacking the city!*

— *Pass it on: The border closed yesterday. Rebels have seized the White House!*

Ben fought the urge to panic. So the crossings to Virginia were blocked, whether by Rebels or the snarl of human traffic he couldn't be sure. In any case, it didn't matter now. But was the border closed everywhere? He thought to strike north and west into Maryland and pass over the Potomac at Harper's Ferry or some other crossing. But would he meet similar blockades there too? And what if Maryland joined the Confederacy as he journeyed along its roads? Suddenly he would be a foreign national in enemy territory.

Oh, Mama. How was he to get her away from Clarendon? Away from Mayfair?

Ben tried to turn the coach around. He decided to head north and try his luck at Harper's Ferry. There was no use fighting against the whole city to get across. Out in the country, he'd have a better chance at slipping across the border and—

"*Get that nigger*!" a man shouted from below. "This is all the darkies' fault!"

"Take his wagon!" another cried.

Yet another screamed: "I want his horse!"

Before Ben could identify the people shouting at him, a burly, wild-eyed man climbed upon the coach and slid down the driver's bench. The man boxed Ben's ears with crushing force and pushed him back. Dazed, Ben toppled from the bench into the arms of the waiting crowd. Some hands moved to break his fall and support his head, while others flailed down in a flurry of blows. Finally Ben collapsed onto the street, and just in time he pulled his legs out of the path of the huge coach wheels as they rolled forward.

The coach thief was presently joined by another atop the bench. Three or four others, eager to escape Washington, climbed aboard the back of the coach and tossed trunks inside and reached out to pull friends and family up. The chassis groaned under the weight of some fifteen people scrambling about like rats on a sinking ship, kicking and pushing others away, and old Mabel strained to pull the crushing weight. The thief brought up a great stick and pummeled Mabel's backside, screaming at the old mare to go faster, faster, faster.

Dazed and furious, Ben blinked and tried to focus his blurry vision. He staggered toward the departing coach, moving to intercept and lash out at the thieving driver. Before he could get far at all, a gang of strangers threw him down and kicked at him. For whatever reason they abandoned him almost as suddenly as they'd set upon him, possibly because he neglected to put up a fight.

The street became quiet again. Ben, his insides smashed to pulp, groaned from the pain and crawled through the muck toward the wooden planks of the sidewalk.

An old woman stepped forward and helped Ben to his feet. "I'm sorry," she said.

"Thank you," he wheezed.

"For your horse," she said. "No one ever steals a horse to give them extra helpings of hay."

Ben hung his head and nodded. It was impossible to catch up to the coach now, futile to fight against the insanity of the crowd, the madness of a people at war. Mabel was on her own now.

And the poor thing couldn't possibly know what was happening to her.

Then again, Ben didn't have a clue either. He wandered like a ghost through the terror-stricken city, the sickening smell of gunpowder and housefires filling his nostrils, the clamor of street battles and looting and the shrill shriek of police whistles piercing his ears. Somehow, he remembered John Roscoe's familiar refrain:

Nothing good may happen before its proper time.

Nothing good. Nothing *good?!* This was not *good.* This was madness.

And there, heard somewhere over the clamoring chaos, Ben heard a little girl singing in a sweet voice, like a dove crying over the din of battle. Looking up, Ben saw her: a dirty, frail, black orphan in tattered rags standing next to an ash heap. As she stared out at the insanity that surrounded her, her song continued unbroken:

The Lord my soul will soon prepare
For never-ending peace,
Where everlasting pleasures roll
And praises never cease

I am bound for the promised land,
Bound for the promised land;
Oh, who will come and go with me,
I am bound for the promised land

Chapter 38

"HE HATH LOOSED THE FATEFUL LIGHTNING..."

THERE WAS NEVER SUCH A CROWD in Mayfair before or since that proud April day.

"Hurrah for Jeff Davis!" the people cried. "Hurrah for the Southern Confederacy!"

Among the crowd were old fathers, mothers, wives, children, sweethearts, and complete strangers who had come to see the brave boys of the Mayfair off on the adventure of war and glory and certain victory. Many present declared that this day — April 17th, 1861 — would be enshrined in the annals of history as Mayfair's happiest and proudest day.

'The War of Northern Aggression' had finally arrived, and Virginia had finally made a decision regarding which side of the fence it would occupy. Weeks earlier, a secession vote held in the state legislature had failed, and it seemed that the jewel of the Union would remain loyal to the Stars and Stripes. But in the wake of hostilities at Fort Sumter, and upon hearing Mr. Lincoln's call for a vast army to attack South Carolina, the people of Virginia sounded their outrage. In Richmond, a second secession vote was quickly called for, and this one passed. Though many representatives of the Commonwealth's far northwestern counties (which included Mayfair) had once again voted against secession, citing that region's fondness for the Federal Union and apathy towards the institution of slavery, a large majority in the legislature (most of them slave-owners) decided that the whole of Virginia would nevertheless join the Southern Confederacy. More states were expected to follow Virginia's example.

No sooner had Virginia seceded did messengers fly to all distant corners of the Commonwealth to share the good news and rally local militia companies to muster. And though some men in the mountain counties of Virginia's northwest spurned the invitation to 'go Rebel' and instead traveled to join Federal troops organizing in Ohio, down in Mayfair the people were much more inclined to following Richmond's example. In Mayfair, situated as it was on the borders of the greater Shenandoah, and perhaps owing to the influence of the First Families, the people were thrilled at the prospect of being part of the Confederacy. For so long, the Union had represented little more than a distant, alienating symbol of arbitrary power, of wastefulness and despair, a thing to be despised just like a previous generation had despised King George's England.

But the Confederacy — now *there* was something to be proud of! With so much talk of Southern liberty and independence and God-given rights, how could anyone resist the opportunity to help forge a new democratic nation? America had been reborn, and this time it would be built the *right* way, laid down to look how it was originally envisioned, shaped for the benefit of future generations.

In Mayfair's main square, a clumsy band of old-timers played marching songs, and they strained to be heard above the din of the cheering crowd. Drums rolled, fifes piped, fiddles sang, and banjo strings danced. And over it all sounded the steady crunch of boots on gravel while deep voices sang in triumphant unison:

I'll place my knapsack on my back
My rifle on my shoulder
I'll march away to the firing line
And kill that Yankee soldier!
And kill that Yankee soldier!
I'll march away to the firing line
And kill that Yankee soldier!

The ranks of Mayfair's militia company had swelled to over a hundred and fifty boys and men. Some were clothed in their traditional blue uniforms, but many had traded the 'Yankee blue' for new gray uniforms hastily sewn by the mothers of Mayfair. The newest recruits, who had pledged themselves to the Confederate cause just minutes ago, tramped about wearing the clothes they had pulled on earlier that morning.

Julep flowed in rivers. Young girls presented wreaths of flowers to shy-faced soldiers. Promises of marriage were made, and some couples were married on the spot by an obliging Reverend Cutler. Aged fathers, who had never heard a kind word from their own fathers, took their uniformed sons aside and fumbled through heartfelt admissions of love and pride.

The middle-aged planter John-Lee Merrick created a scene when, in a fit of chivalric fancy, he picked up his young fiancé and swung her around, only to stumble and land both of them in the dirt. Percy Claiborne disappeared into a barn pulling a young, bewildered farmgirl by the hand and emerged minutes later alone, sweating, combing his hair and smoothing down his fine uniform. George Hunt was meanwhile chased into the street by the village tanner, who had discovered Hunt in bed with his daughter.

The village trickster Jimmy Stanton was held up by a collection of neighbors who offered him a gargantuan apple pie. Apparently someone had dared Jimmy that he couldn't eat the pie all in one sitting, for Jimmy was presently shoveling handfuls into his pudgy cheeks to great fanfare.

Gales of laughter rang out when folks saw Ed Ripley marching to war with two squawking roosters tucked under his arms. With thousands of men milling about in an army camp, Ripley charged, there was a small fortune to be made in cock fights.

Meanwhile, Sugar Dave Dixon showed off a new six-shooter revolver. "It's a gift from my daddy," Dave said, smiling from ear to ear. "Ain't she a beauty?"

The eminent Clay Claiborne rode into the square atop a magnificent white horse. Reflections of hundreds of happy, exuberant faces shone in the horse's glistening, night black eyes. Claiborne sat the horse in front of the worn statue of Thomas Jefferson that stood in the shade of Mayfair's courthouse and held up a white-gloved hand. There was too much frantic energy about Mayfair for there to be complete silence. But over the dull roar of the crowd, Claiborne's booming voice could yet be heard.

"*Ladies and gentlemen*. Today, your men ride out to meet the Yankee invader!"

The crowd roared and cheered.

"I am honored," Claiborne went on, "to have been elected the leader of Mayfair's proud militia. As captain, together with my son Percy as second-in-command, I will lead your men against the unwashed Black Republican hordes. We will claim victory for ourselves, or we will die in the attempt!"

Proud voices shouted in agreement. A young boy — Billy Clements, some noted it was — raced up the courthouse steps and unfurled a giant flag that, when the spring breeze snapped it taut, threatened to carry the boy into the sky. Stretching across the flag was a broad white bar bordered by two red stripes, and sewn into the blue rectangular canton was a circle of seven white stars. In the middle of the circle was an eighth star, larger than the rest and added just that morning, which represented the Commonwealth of Virginia's place among the nascent Confederate States. Seeing their new national flag, the Stars and Bars, for the first time, the people of Mayfair began to weep with joy.

"Look at her, the beauty!" Claiborne cried, and he doffed his hat and saluted the flag. All at once the other militiamen joined him, and even the men, women, and children gathered there saluted their flag or else held their hands over their chests. Those who saluted the flag, and looked around at their friends and neighbors doing the same, were touched by a sense of fate and unfolding destiny, as if all their lives had been leading to this singular point of providential promise. There was exultation in the knowledge that, soon enough, more stars would be added to the flag. In light of 'King Lincoln's' mustering of Yankee hordes, newspapers were already reporting that Arkansas was preparing to secede, and Tennessee and North Carolina were expected to 'go Rebel' at any time.

Having paid his respects to the Stars and Bars, Claiborne replaced his hat.

"And now, ladies and gentlemen, a word from our former county judge, and soon to be the newest member of the Senate of the Confederate States: Tobias Cutler!"

The crowd fawned as Judge Cutler stepped up to a hastily constructed podium underneath the statue of Jefferson. While Claiborne had exuded the happy spirit of expedition-bound adventurer, Cutler instead wore an expression of sober seriousness. The crowd quieted as the Judge reached up and gestured toward the stone face of Thomas Jefferson, with its skeptical gaze fixed on some distant point, its shrewd mouth held tight by pursed lips.

"It is said," Cutler said, throwing his head back with an orator's flourish, "that the sculptor modeled this statue of President Thomas Jefferson off a bust of Cato the Younger. As a senator, Cato was the last pillar of the Roman Republic who stood against the populist dictates of Caesar and the mob that propped him up."

Enthralled, the people of Mayfair gave Cutler their full attention. Some of the old-timers reflected that Cutler's manner of speaking, including the way he placed a fist upon his hip, reminded them of how old John Roscoe used to deliver his speeches.

"I was but a boy," Cutler continued, "when Thomas Jefferson was president, some sixty years ago. But even as a boy, I recognized that here was a man who stood *for* something noble, and who stood *against* something treacherous. Here was a man who championed the United States as a confederacy of sovereign states working in concert, but never lashed together like chain gang inmates. Jefferson stood for the rights of those states to self-determine, and for the right of every American — no matter his class or station — to build for himself a temple of freedom without fear of government obstruction. He stood *against* a centralized power structure, where democracy would be most prone to the diseases of corruption, greed, and the dictates of mob rule. Today, we know that the old Union is dead, held hostage for so long by self-serving, would-be tyrants. Today, we give thanks that Jefferson's democracy has been finally and fully realized down in Dixieland. Today, we here are citizens of the Confederate States of America!"

Here, the people of the Valley erupted in fresh applause. Hailed by so many adoring voices, Cutler dropped his grave earnestness and allowed himself a bright smile.

"Well, boys!" Cutler cried, waving a hand to the boy-soldiers lined up in the square. "I think we can all learn a lot from men like Thomas Jefferson."

The boys thrust their weapons into the air and cheered: *HURRAH*!

"And men like Andrew Jackson!"

— *HURRAH*!

"And men like *President* Jefferson Davis!"

—*HURRAH*!

"And I need not mention to *all our citizens*," Cutler went on, addressing the entire assembly once more. "Your noble boys here, they aren't going off to fight for themselves. They aren't going off to fight for me, or for any man who happens to own a negro or two. No, ladies and gentlemen, you proud mothers and fathers of the Confederacy: Captain Claiborne and his *men* are off to meet the foreign invader because that invader seeks to destroy *your* homes, your families, your property, and your future. It is for *our mutual protection* that the men of Mayfair march today. They march to preserve our God-given rights and liberties. Today, I call upon each of you here to march alongside them. May we all march together, under the light of God's grace, and take back what belongs to us. I promise you, ladies and gentlemen, we are going to fight like hell!"

The people of Mayfair cheered again, and not a few fainted from fits of euphoria. The bands struck up new tunes, and now the people began to dance in the streets. During all these events, the boy-soldiers continued to sing:

Before the South shall bow her head,
Before the tyrants harm us,
I'll give my all to the Southern cause
And die in the Southern army
And die in the Southern army
I'll give my all to the Southern cause
And die in the Southern army

It was about this time that, at the northern end of town, a lone straggler wandered down the main road from the North Branch. He was dressed in a new gray uniform, its buttons shining the same as the rest, and he carried on his belt a sheathed cavalry saber. He led a bright-eyed colt and fed it crabapples as they walked. He entered Mayfair with an apprehension that with each step forward gave way to a look of solemn determination. Many in the Valley had looked upon this face many times before, and in those times before they'd seen a face that was flushed with cherub-like cheer, eyes alight with humor and wit, a spirit that exuded reckless abandon. Now, the face revealed a self-aware maturation, a dawning of something that, if not wisdom, was at least not foolishness. Before, Valley folks had looked upon the haughty face of a boy, *the boy who had everything*, and many had resented him for that. Now, those same folks looked upon the face of a man, a man who had lost much. And though resentment was slow to wane in the Valley as it is everywhere, there were some who watched the straggler march into Mayfair that day with the sense that Jem Roscoe, with his straight back and set jaw and unassuming gaze, cut a rather fine figure as a soldier.

A fine figure indeed.

❧

Before leaving Clarendon that morning, Jem had lain fresh-picked flowers over his father's grave, which was already sprouting new grass. After whispering a prayer and a wish for Father to watch over him, Jem had finished the last of his preparations.

He had risen early, intending to get on the road while it was still damp with dew and before the sun turned the dirt into red dust. Within Clarendon, he bid farewell to Mother and Mae Jane and Bayard.

Mother was surprisingly tender in saying her goodbyes, and she even whispered that Jem, standing proud in his new gray uniform, looked just like Colonel Spencer. Mother even urged Jem to take the Colonel's saber with him, so that its blade might gleam on the battlefield once more.

"All this is worth defending," Mother said to Jem. She smiled at him then, and he realized it was the first time she'd seen her smile like that in, laws, it was months. Maybe years.

With her hands, Mother indicated the whole of the estate. "Your father and I may have disagreed as to the character of Clarendon's legacy, and to its future, but we were united in the belief that such a legacy must nevertheless be preserved. I know your father would be proud of you, Jeremiah. *I* am proud, certainly."

Hearing these things, Jem embraced his mother and held her close. It had been years since they had touched each other in such a way, and Jem only wished that Father was still alive to see it, to hear Mother's affirmations. He could not understand what had changed in his mother's attitude, not just toward Father but toward seemingly the whole world. It was as if Mother had discovered the true depths of her love for Father only after he'd died. In recent months Mother appeared healthier, acted in a kinder way toward the family and the Freemans, and she was apparently reducing the intake of her medicine. All of these were good things, but somehow Jem still worried about Mother. He worried that her change was not a shift, but something of a lull.

In any case, he could not deny how his spirit soared at feeling true affection in his mother's touch. It was almost enough to sow doubt in his mind over whether he actually wanted to leave home or not. Part of him wished to remain home so he could spend more time with Mother, so that he could ask her about her life, about the Colonel and Father and the good old times, the times when there was peace and Clarendon flourished. Jem had been dreaming lately of such times, times that he knew only from stories. He found himself wishing to live in such times again, when one's place in life was known and certain, and when there was no President Lincoln warning Virginians and other Southerners to keep quiet while he sent tens of thousands of soldiers down to rampage through the Carolinas.

Well, maybe such times could be reclaimed. Maybe it was still possible for

Southerners to determine their own path, and do so separately from the Northerners if necessary. And maybe Jem's ideas about a Southern enlightenment, about homegrown solutions to homegrown problems, could finally take root. Meanwhile there were plenty of folks, not just Northerners but people like Ben (and probably JJ too) who believed, as Mr. Lincoln did, that America must "become all one thing, or all the other." But did it really have to be that way? What was it that made Yankees the arbiters of the righteous?

After the South's honor was restored, after Mayfair was made safe from invasion, maybe a place like the North Branch Mine could be reopened. And maybe the First Families didn't have to be the antagonists in such a situation, but helpful allies. Why, just a few weeks ago Henry Cutler had even offered to staff the mine with some of his hands, which would surely help to clear the last of the rubble and get operations going again. In this way, the mine would be ready for when the Valley's yeomen returned after the war was over, as folks expected would happen in a few months' time. And in the meantime, the hands of the Cutlers and the other First Families would reinvigorate not just the North Branch Mine, but the whole of the Valley's economy. It would be like what Father used to say about compromise. To merely condemn those who disagreed with you was to effect no solutions, solve no problems. Slavery was of course distasteful, but it was presently necessary. Besides, everyone in Mayfair — Henry Cutler included — knew that slavery would fade away in the long run. But in order to move forward, one had to share the road a little.

After all, nothing good may happen before its proper time.

"Now you look after youself," Mae Jane said.

Mother had remained inside while Jem, Bayard, and their mammy stepped out into the early morning air. They now stood on the path before Clarendon. Jem held Greenbrier's reins and tugged at the collar of his uniform, which was already itching him like mad.

Without a word, Mae Jane reached up and adjusted Jem's collar with rough tugs and twists. Though she made a show of fussing with his appearance, she wouldn't look Jem in the eye. When she caught him trying to read her, she pushed onto him a flat, vaguely accusatory, "What's the matter?"

"The matter?" Jem said. He shrugged. "I...don't rightly know."

Mae Jane flashed her brow, as if the response didn't surprise her. She proceeded to reach for a large knapsack on the veranda steps that had been expertly packed but hopelessly overstuffed with provisions and preserves, including many of Jem's favorites. As she passed the dead weight to Jem, she said, "This'll be enough to get you wherever needs gettin to."

Remaining quiet, Jem tried to read her again. The old mammy gave him nothing.

"You'll give my best to Tom," Jem said.

"Sure."

"And Sarah too. Tell her I'm sorry again about her baby. We'll make it so that she can raise more proud Cutlers in peace, right?"

"Sure."

Jem wasn't sure what else to say, but still he did not feel it was yet time to go. He glanced over at Bayard, who smiled up at him with wide-eyed adoration. Once again Jem felt right in his purpose. He was going off to war — it was a *just war* — and there was no reason to feel confused just when he was about to step off.

"So there you go," Mae Jane said curtly. "That's it." When Jem lingered still longer, she became exasperated. "You good to walk to the gate yonder, or do you need you mammy to help you?"

Jem wasn't sure whether to laugh or not. "I'll be fine, Mae Jane. It's just—"

"It's just what?" she said.

Jem went quiet again while his mind groped for something to say.

"I'm doing this for all of us," he said. "I'm doing this for Clarendon."

Mae Jane closed her eyes a moment. They fluttered there, as if she'd gone to sleep. When she opened her eyes again, she looked Jem in the eye. Then came a smile, broad and shining, and almost real. But that last feature was all Jem noticed, all that he remembered later.

Almost real.

"You doin this for Clarendon, Mr. Jem, that's right. And we's all behind you."

Jem didn't feel he had a smile in him, but he pushed one across his face anyway. For a moment they stood there just smiling at each other, a black mammy and a boy in gray. After a long silence, Jem felt he must burst out laughing at the absurdity of the moment or else go insane.

"I can't help feel it, Mae Jane, but I do. I feel your heart's in me — in Jem Roscoe, in who *I* am. But as for what I'm doing, I…I feel from you only shame." He shook his head. "I don't want to shame you, Mae Jane."

A long moment of quiet passed, as if Mae Jane were thinking of something to say. But at last she looked up again and said, "You doin this for *Clarendon*, Mr. Jem. We's all *real* proud."

He didn't believe her of course, and he wasn't sure she believed herself either.

Still, what was there to do? Jem could only pull up his knapsack and reach again for Greenbrier's reins and turn toward the far gate. Mae Jane walked slowly alongside him, and Bayard dropped down from the veranda to trail behind.

Jem knew he ought not look back, but he did anyway. Mother was upstairs, looking down from an open window. Jem knew Sarah and the Cutlers would be in Mayfair with the rest of the Valley. It fully dawned on him that *the rest of the Valley* really did mean exactly that. The whole of Mayfair would be gathered in one place to see off their soldiers. Almost everybody Jem had ever known would be there.

Almost everybody.

"Now you mind you don't fall in with sinners," Mae Jane said. "Lord knows when they's a gang a boys, they's some what start all the trouble, and they's some what can't do nothin but go along."

"I'll mind them, Mae Jane."

"You ain't the *goin along* kind, Jem."

"No, Mae Jane."

They continued to trudge forward. Jem thought to ask Mae Jane about Ben, who had left for Washington more than a week ago and hadn't been heard from since, but he didn't raise any questions.

When they reached the gate, they held another mournful silence. Nothing was said between them, though there were a thousand threads of possible conversations hanging down like streamers from the tree branches, ready to be plucked. When he could bear it no longer, Jem turned and looked toward the main road that would lead through the Valley. He drew a long breath.

"Well...I suppose I should—"

He was only half turned around when Mae Jane stepped forward and embraced him. It was fast, over before he barely knew it had happened, but still he felt a loving sincerity in the old woman's touch. She gave a final squeeze, a mother's squeeze, before she drew back and clasped her hands together.

"God bless you, Jem. God keep you."

Jem's eyes were suddenly misty, but he knew it wouldn't do for a soldier to cry. Jem nodded to her (it was all he seemed able to do in that moment) and started off. He waved a final goodbye to Bayard before he turned, content not to look back this time, and trudged down the sloping road.

"Jem."

It was a call, not a question. When Jem turned around, he saw the old mammy standing there before Clarendon's broken gate holding Bayard's hand. There was no happy smile on either of their faces. There was only Mae Jane's knowing consternation and little Bayard's ignorant contentment.

"You bring Jon Jacob home safe," Mae Jane said. She let these words sink in a moment longer before repeating herself. "You fetch you brother, and you get youselves on home."

Jem stood there in the middle of the road, no longer sure which way to turn. His first instinct was to calmly explain to Mae Jane that truth be told, he had no idea what he would do if he encountered JJ across the battlefield. Jem thought to tell Mae Jane that, faced with such a situation as his own brother pointing a gun at him (again), Jem would do nothing else than his duty. He wanted to say that if JJ insisted on wearing the Federal uniform, if JJ joined the ranks of those men marching down to subjugate Mayfair and a thousand small towns like it, well, then maybe that meant JJ wasn't interested in 'getting himself on home.' And brother or not, if they met face to face, Jem decided he would not be the first to yield.

"This war gonna destroy many families," Mae Jane said. "It's gonna turn them against each other. But it don't gotta be like that for you. It don't gotta be like that for *us*."

All Jem could do was nod and say, "I'll make it right." He paused and thought to say something more, but nothing else came to mind. "I'll make it right," he said again, and then he turned and led Greenbrier down the road toward Mayfair.

As he turned down Mayfair's main street with a hand on Greenbrier's bridle, Jem was mobbed with well-wishers. Old ladies from church embraced him with tears streaming down their age-etched cheeks. Young girls kissed him and draped circles of flowers over proud Greenbrier's bulging neck muscles.

Beautiful Pippa Claiborne, who had barely spoken more than ten words to Jem before, and though she had just the previous night said yes to a last-minute marriage proposal from Sam Hanley, kissed Jem violently on the lips and whispered that she would pray for him. Stunned, Jem pulled away and mumbled an awkward goodbye before fleeing from Pippa's groping grasp.

Tough old men broke down with tears of joy and lined up to shake Jem's hand. Bewildered, Jem thanked the gentlemen for their encouragement. Indeed he found himself waiting for a fist or open hand to strike him, for someone to spit in his eye and mutter some nasty remark about the North Branch, but none of these things happened. The people of Mayfair saw Jem in his gray coat and they were proud of what they saw. Children looked up at Jem and his proud warhorse with wonder and admiration in their eyes.

"Jem!" a voice cried. "Hey there, Jem!"

Looking up, Jem saw Sugar Dave rush over to him with a giddy laugh.

"Laws, ain't this a crusher!"

Jem nodded. "I'll say."

A rogue hand reached out from the crowd and pinched the flab of Jem's cheek hard until Jem yowled. A grinning George Hunt appeared with six bottles of liquor tucked under one arm. "Spoils of war!" he cried. "Somebody raided the Curtis House and started passing these around. Here, take one!"

A husband and wife went about pouring cups of iced julep from a massive jug. Jem and the others received theirs gratefully and clicked their cups together. The julep — bourbon, sugar, mint leaves, crushed ice — soothed Jem's jitters.

Sugar Dave sniffed the air. "Is that…barbecue?"

Jem smelled it too. "Over yonder I think. Must be in the yard at the Evans' place."

Hunt was already on the scent. "I'll be back," he called over his shoulder. "You fellas want anything?"

Ed Ripley and Sugar Dave hollered their orders, but Jem shook his head. "I'm all right."

"May not get real home cooking for a good spell," Sugar Dave warned.

Jem patted his knapsack, the one which Mae Jane had stayed up all night packing for him. "I've got a few things here," he said.

Sugar Dave grabbed Ripley and they pushed their way through the crowd in pursuit of Hunt. "Shucks, anytime's a good time for barbecue. Wait up, Georgie!"

If I must die for my home and land
My spirit will not falter
Upon my country's altar
Upon my country's altar
Oh, here's my heart and here's my hand
Upon my country's altar

Jem wandered about the commotion, reminding himself to stop and bask in the unbridled joy of the moment. But he could think of nothing else just now except finding Audrey. He had stopped by the Blake farm on his way down the North Branch, but the farm had been deserted. Audrey and her father had to be among the crowd to say goodbye to their Ezra.

Jem searched for Audrey, but he saw only a thousand variations of red-faced, bellowing, fervent people of Mayfair wishing their boys off to war. At last he saw Ezra Blake standing in an ill-fitting gray uniform, a scowl set on his face. But still, Jem saw no sign of Audrey.

Cheers soared into the air as Judge Cutler finished his rousing speech. Attention returned once more to Captain Claiborne, who rose up in his stirrups and pointed down the street. "First we march east to Winchester to organize with militia from the other counties," he said. "And after Winchester, we march *north* — to Washington!"

Jem wondered if anyone realized that Claiborne was pointing not east or north, but west. It didn't matter in any case, for the crowd's energy swelled to a fever pitch. Now came the frantic activity of hugging, kissing, and the uttering of revelations. Solemn fathers and their youngest sons stepped up to pry sobbing, clutching mothers away from their handsome soldier boys. Sweethearts embraced, professing but none seriously believing that this might be the last time their lips would meet.

And at last, a smiling Clay Claiborne shook hands with Tobias Cutler before turning his horse away from the statue of Jefferson and started off down the road. Seeing their captain go, the proud boys of the militia company turned to follow. As they began to form ranks and march off, they were hailed by countless voices:

—G'won, boys! G'won now and kill them sumbitches!

—Hail, Virginia! Glory be to God!

—Y'all bring back a Yankee scalp or three, y'hear?

—Have at em! Do your duty!

—I'm pregnant, Bill. I'm pregnant!

—Do us proud, fellas! For Mayfair!

—Give it your all, boys! We's behind you.

—Look smart, gents, and give em what-for!

Jem fell into line beside a giddy George Hunt, together with Ed Ripley and Sugar Dave. As he marched along, Jem's eyes searched the crowd in a final, desperate attempt to—

"Hello, Jem."

Jem's stomach flipped. Slowly, he turned around and saw her.

Audrey Blake stood in a dark dress, as one might wear in mourning. Indeed, she had tears in her eyes. Several attempts of speech formed on her trembling lips, but she could say nothing more.

Uttering an awkward groan, Ripley abandoned the scene instantly. With a knowing look, Hunt tapped Sugar Dave on the shoulder. "We'd best be off, Davey. Good day to you, Miss Blake."

Timidly, Sugar Dave reached out and took Greenbrier's reins from Jem's grasp. "Let me lead him awhile," Dave murmured to Jem. He offered Audrey a shy smile before he pushed on through the crowd with Greenbrier in tow.

Audrey watched the boys go. "They're good friends to you," she said.

Jem nodded. "They are," he said, his mouth dry. "I'm lucky to have them."

From here, he wasn't sure what to say next. He felt the current of the crowd pushing them downstream, but he refused to let the moment slip away. Taking her hand boldly, Jem led Audrey out of the flow. They ducked into an alleyway beside Dance & Franklin's General. There, shaded from the sun and prying gazes, Jem looked long into Audrey's eyes.

"Will you write to me?"

"Of course I will," she said. "But only if you—"

"Every day," he said breathlessly. "I'll write so often you'll be sick of hearing from me."

She laughed. "That'll never be the case."

Some loud braggarts cheered nearby. Audrey looked out at the happy celebrations with a drawn expression. "This is all a very happy thing, at least." She looked at Jem again, and her face turned red when she smiled. "And you-all look mighty dashing."

Jem likewise blushed. "Well, it sure is a fine occasion."

A shadow passed over Audrey's smile. "I only hope our cause is just."

Jem laughed. "Of course it's just. What could make you think otherwise?"

She shrugged and offered a new smile. "I only mean that I hope the war ends soon. I only hope that everyone comes back safe."

A long moment of silence passed between them, silence that was filled with loud cheering and screaming and chanting of songs all around them. Several drunkards pushed their way between them going up the alley, and it was some time before they stood alone together once more.

"I made something for you," Audrey said. "For your trip."

She produced a homemade pouch of blue cloth. It was embroidered with roses and thorny vines of golden thread that shimmered in the daylight. The opening was fastened with a button, and attached to the button was an ornamental knot of the same gold string with tassels on each end. She opened the bag. As Jem's eyes took in the wondrous gift, his nostrils twinged with the sweet, earthy fragrance that could only be one thing.

"Tobacco," Audrey said. "It's from Wyolah Hall." Then she added hastily, "The Claibornes gave Daddy a whole barrel as a present last season, is why I have it. I didn't want to accept it. You know I think nothing of Percy. But Daddy and Ezra smoke, and so…Anyway, I figured you would appreciate good tobacco." She lowered her eyes and winced with shame. "Some of the other girls are giving their boys photo-graph portraits of themselves. I can't afford one, Jem, otherwise I—"

"This is perfect," Jem said. He beamed at her. "It's wonderful."

She glowed. "Really?"

"Really," he said. "Thank you, Audrey. Thank you very much."

She offered the tobacco bag, and as she gave it to him their fingers touched. Jem's hand moved over hers and held it firmly, gently. Slowly, they drew closer. The mobbing crowd seemed miles distant, and it was as if Jem and Audrey stood together in a quiet glade, or in the sun-washed clearing by Dixon's Mill that they knew so well. Jem wished more than anything to take Audrey back there now.

Audrey kissed him.

After the kiss, Jem tried to say something — anything — but his voice was caught in his throat. Was it too late to change his mind? Was it too late to fall out of line, to disappear somewhere until the militia company had moved off, and to remain behind with Audrey? Who cared if anyone called him a damn coward. He and Audrey could build a cabin somewhere in the Valley — somewhere quiet, where they would never be disturbed by anyone. Maybe that clearing would do just fine. They would be happy there, sharing days of love and simple pleasures.

Was it too late for these things? Was the cause of war *so* just that he could not choose any other path?

From the street, drums rolled and pipes whistled. A great cheer went up, and now the last of the Mavericks were marching off.

It was time to go.

"I love you, Audrey."

"I love you, Jem."

They embraced again. He felt her hot tears mix with his own, and for a long moment they pressed together as one being, heedless to any raised eyebrows or mocking laughter. But no one called out any scandal, for all present were too busy sobbing and shouting and dancing together to pay them any notice.

Hand in hand, Jem and Audrey passed out onto the street once more. They slipped into the stream of marching boys in gray. As Jem was about to turn around and give Audrey one last kiss of farewell, her hand was suddenly torn from his grasp.

Pushed forward by the crowd, Jem turned and watched as he was borne farther away from Audrey. He reached out, but he could not touch her. They bid a secret and wordless goodbye within the long look that passed between them. Then someone unfurled a great flag bearing the Stars and Bars, and its bulk stretched and whipped in a sudden gust and covered Audrey's face, blocking everything from Jem's view but the full vision of patriotic fervor.

A moment later when the gust subsided and the flag ebbed low again, Audrey Blake was gone.

The Mayfair boys turned northeast, bound for the unknown wilds beyond the Branches.

And out there, lurking somewhere, was the hated Federal army.

Sweat and teardrops fell upon Jem's dusty boots, which rose up and pounded the dirt down again in quick succession — left, left, left-right-left. When Jem looked up again, he saw that he was now surrounded on all sides by his neighbors. Many of them had been miners at the North Branch. But whatever and whoever they had been *before* didn't matter, for *now* they were all soldiers.

As the soldiers departed Mayfair, the sounds of drums and pipes and cheering voices faded. The sun had passed the meridian and was racing away to the west. Ahead lay nothing but the quiet stillness of the country, and in a few hours' time, the cheerless dark of night.

Every man and boy stared forward with a defiant sadness written on their faces, their jaws tight but their eyes quivering with emotion. To rouse themselves, the Mayfair Valley boys coughed to clear the lumps of homesickness from their throats. Together, they began to sing, louder and louder still:

If I must die for my home and land
My spirit will not falter
Oh, here's my heart and here's my hand
Upon my country's altar

Chapter 39

"...OF HIS TERRIBLE SWIFT SWORD"

While he waited to be called onstage, JJ Roscoe decided to polish the buttons on his uniform a third time. Concealed from the public within the thin-walled shelter of a huge pavilion, he could hear the hurricane roar of the crowd in his ears, could feel the thud of their tramping feet in his chest. Touching the canvas wall, he could not tell if the tent was pitched in the middle of New York City's Union Square (where he knew it ought to be), or if it stood amid a stampeding herd of buffalo on the western plains. Punctuating the roar of the crowd were the brass blasts of countless marching bands, their discordant melodies clashing in mid-air. Heard amid the fervent cries of "*All for the Union!*" were the sounds of more entrepreneurial-minded patriots who were busy selling wares, hot food, tiny Stars and Stripes to wave aloft, anything to turn a dime.

JJ looked around the great pavilion. He recognized most of the wide-eyed men who had served at Fort Sumter, who were now turned together in small circles discussing their universal bewilderment at their present situation. Some looked far more terrified at the prospect of leaving the tent than they had been when cannonballs were exploding all around them just three nights earlier.

The tent also held another two or three dozen men who appeared to have no reason to be there but were nevertheless determined to look important. Some of them were white-haired, round-bellied officers in uniform, and others were white-haired, round-bellied politicians and businessmen in dark suits. Every breast was festooned with cockades colored red, white, and blue. Tiny orphans, members of a children's chorus, wore outfits made from repurposed flags, with white stars on blue trousers and coats striped red and white. The children ran about the place while exasperated nuns tried to corral them just as dogs minded a flock of sheep.

A circus. All of it, a damn circus.

'The War of the Rebellion' was just a few days old. JJ and the defenders of Fort Sumter had spent much of this time aboard a steamship bearing them away from Charleston toward friendly territory. In the meantime, the Rebels had blockaded the Potomac, which made it impossible to disembark in Washington. Instead, the steamer chugged northward and finally docked in New York City.

JJ had stepped off the gangplank at Manhattan's southern docks to find that the entire Union had become war mad. The national flag flew from every flagpole and windowsill. People ran about the streets wearing flags as cloaks and capes. There were bloody riots in the streets, for in fact New York had been sympathetic to the cause of secession during the first months of 1861. The owners of textile factories, whose vast sums of wealth depended on regular shipments of Southern cotton, had once railed against the Lincoln administration for needlessly dividing the country. Much of the city's immigrant population, especially the Irish, considered the Confederacy a place where all negroes (including Northern freedmen) ought to be fenced in and left to rot. But now that the Rebels had fired upon the Stars and Stripes, public opinion in the city had turned firmly against the South and its allies.

Considering President Lincoln's call for 75,000 militiamen to put down the Rebellion, the mayor of New York hurried to organize a great rally at Union Square, which stood at the confluence of Bowery Street and Bloomingdale Avenue. The point of the rally was to celebrate the 'heroes of Fort Sumter' and to whip up support for the war. While said heroes were concealed within the thin walls of hastily constructed pavilions, reports began to trickle in that over a hundred thousand people were milling about the Square.

A *hundred thousand people*! The number beggared belief. JJ had never heard of so many people gathering in one place ever before. But judging from the tempestuous roar of voices from all around, he determined the reports had to be true.

From the stage outside came the piercing oratory of New York's mayor, Fernando Wood:

"It is not only my duty to support the Constitution, but also to support the Union, the government, the laws, and the flag. And in the discharge of that duty, I care not what past political associations may be severed. I am willing to give up all past prejudices and sympathies, if they conflict with the honor and interest of my country in this great crisis. Today, we are *all* Democrats. Today, we are *all* Republicans. Today, we are all *Americans*!"

The crowd cheered and bellowed. Several men within the tent clapped their hands over their ears to stopper the noise. For himself, JJ didn't mind the crowd noises so much. His ears were still ringing from the days-long cannonade at Fort Sumter.

"First time in New York, Lieutenant?"

JJ turned to the voice and looked into the proud, handsome face of a young brigadier general. (JJ could tell the man was a general by the single star on each of his shoulders.) The general's crisp new uniform was taut against his broad, barrel-shaped chest. He was the picture of manliness: strong jawline, piercing brown eyes, fine dark hair set in a precise combover, and a healthy mustache with not a single hair out of place. For a long moment, JJ was stunned and, if he was being honest with himself, rather smitten.

Goddammit, he would think no more of it. He knew he must stamp down such vile thoughts and—

"I've been to Manhattan many times, General," JJ said. He snapped his boots together and raised his hand to salute. "It's a fine city."

The general smiled at JJ's show of respect, but he did not return the salute; instead, he stretched out a large hand. "No need for that, Lieutenant. You are the man of the hour, after all." The general spoke in a vibrant baritone. "We should all be showering you with our praises. Your name is Roscoe, isn't it?"

JJ nodded and shook the man's hand. "Yes, sir. Jonathan Roscoe. I served under Major Anderson at Fort—"

"Of course you did," the young general said, as if he'd already known the answer to that question, and every question he might ask next. "What's more, I heard a rumor that old Anderson was ready to give into the Rebels until you convinced him to fire back."

JJ wasn't sure what to say. He looked across the pavilion to where 'old Anderson' now stood, the guest of honor flanked by wizened officers and politicians. Just now, Anderson was hastily slurping down a tray of oysters to distract himself from such bewildering circumstances. The bloody, torn, and singed Stars and Stripes, the flag that had flown over Sumter, was cradled on the major's lap. The old man kept a hand on the flag, as if he expected someone to try and snatch it from him.

"Well," JJ said at last, "I suppose every man's faith must be tested, sooner or later."

The young general grinned. "You are your father's son."

JJ concealed a grimace at the mention of 'father.' He pushed a smile across his lips. "Might I inquire your name, General?"

"McClellan," the man replied with a cheery smile, as if his own name tasted delicious on his lips. "George McClellan. Did your father ever mention me?"

JJ tried to remember, but the word *father* rattled him again. "Perhaps he did," JJ said at length. "Speaking honestly, General, I cannot remember. In fact, my father died a few months—"

"Yes, yes, tragic," McClellan replied.

The young general spoke brusquely; already JJ had detected in the man a habit for interrupting others. Still, JJ could not help but marvel at the man's magnetic presence.

"You know," McClellan went on, "I nearly went into business with John Roscoe. This time last year, I was President of the Illinois Central Railroad. Your father and I both wanted to build the transcontinental railroad. The powers that be weren't about to cut that baby in two, so to speak, and in the end the contract was promised to my ICR. But that was back in the days of reason, before the election and the resulting secession crisis. There won't be any railroad now — not until the war ends. *If* it ends. I fear we've trespassed upon some terrible, alternate course of history, Jon.

May I call you Jon?"

"Absolutely, sir," JJ said, even though he knew the general was not asking him but telling him. He tried to think of what to say next, but his words did not come easily. It was strange to feel so, well, *under the influence* of a man like McClellan, who seemed to be three, four, five steps ahead of himself. Of course, JJ normally considered himself the commanding party in any conversation, able to steer others where he wanted to go. But against the young general, he was no match. McClellan's manner of speaking reminded JJ of Father. But while Father's domineering attitude had exhausted him, JJ found himself looking upon the young general with wonder and interest.

But not *that* kind of interest. For God's sake, no more of that.

At length, JJ settled on an opinion. "I believe we'll make everything right again, sir, and quickly. Whatever ambitions we held before the war, we'll realize them tenfold after the Rebels capitulate."

McClellan offered a knowing smile. "A fine outlook. You're a West Point man, aren't you, Jon?"

"Yes, sir."

McClellan nodded, still smiling. "Then you know something of the relationship between the army and politics." Suddenly, McClellan's smile disappeared. He leaned closer in the manner of a conspirator. "As such I want to make one thing very clear, Jon. Look around you. See all those civilians in dark suits? See all those beady eyes, watchful eyes? It's not just the Rebs who are the enemy. After all, this war of ours will not be won by politicians and their machinations. It will be won by soldiers who fight battles."

JJ nodded. "I agree wholeheartedly, sir."

McClellan stood upright again; the dark light of conspiracy had vanished from his eyes. "So," he said. "Now that you've cut your teeth against the Rebs, where is it you see yourself going next?"

JJ was quiet for a time. "Well, to be honest, General, I hadn't much thought of it. I was assigned to be Major Anderson's adjutant, so I expect that—"

"Anderson's out," McClellan said flatly.

JJ blinked. "*Out?*"

"To pasture," McClellan added with a grin. He put an arm around JJ and squeezed him in a friendly way. JJ was very aware of the tight press of the man's muscles.

"Come now, Jon, and take a good look at the old man. He's almost as old as the Union itself. He served his country well and now he deserves a good, long rest. Out with the old, in with the new — that's what I say. I'm only thirty-three, and here I am already a brigadier. How old are you, Jon?"

"I'll be twenty-two in July."

"Twenty-two! Oh, to be young again." McClellan winked at him. "But here, do you see any gray hairs on this head of mine? No, and you won't for a long while yet. And I assure you it's not because I douse my hair with black dye like that damn Beauregard. My, I cannot wait to teach that old Creole a lesson."

JJ nodded, feeling his chest tighten at the mention of his former superintendent. "I feel much the same, sir."

"I'll serve that French-tongued nancy his just desserts," McClellan said. "And Lee too. All of them."

JJ furrowed his brow. "You mean Colonel Lee, sir? Robert Lee?"

"The very same," McClellan said. "What, didn't you hear? The administration offered Lee a major general's post, and Lee *turned them down*. He said he couldn't draw his sword against his native country, meaning Virginia. Now Lee has slipped across the Potomac to muster Rebel forces near the Shenandoah. Any day, a rabble of buckskins may march on Washington."

As if to emphasize this news, the crowd outside threw up a great halloo. JJ turned his head to the sound, imagining Robert Lee leading a mob of angry Virginians — with Jem among them — toward the gates of Washington.

"As it turns out, Virginia is my destination as well," McClellan said. "Though I'm not going there to join Lee, but rather to crush him. What's more, my army will support the Unionist population in the region. After all, most of Virginia's western counties voted *against* secession during the secession debate. Their legislature was fractured, but the Rebel snakes found a way to enact the secession ordinance in any case. Still, there are rumblings that there is a convention about to assemble up in the town of Wheeling, near the Ohio border. A group of delegates intend to declare a *new* Virginia, a breakaway state that is loyal to the Union."

A new Virginia? JJ thought about the rugged mountain country to which McClellan referred. North of the Mayfair Valley, high in the hardscrabble western reaches of Virginia, there were relatively few plantations and even fewer slaves, certainly when compared to the lush, rolling farmlands of the state's Piedmont and Tidewater regions. It made sense that the western counties had rejected Virginia's secession ordinance, and were in effect seceding from secession. After all, why would people who had little to no affection for slavery throw in their lot with the Confederacy? Some of course would still go with Virginia, citing loyalty to their state, but just as many would balk at the idea of supporting a bloody rebellion.

Of course, there was Mayfair itself to consider. Mayfair bordered the mountain counties, but it still enjoyed a vibrant slave economy. Would the people of Mayfair reject the whims of Richmond and join the breakaway state, the *new* Virginia? Or would they choose to defend the Confederacy to the last man?

The answer, JJ knew, was not so simple. But if the First Families had anything to say about it — the wealthy clans of Cutler, Claiborne, Merrick, and all the others

— then most able-bodied men in Mayfair would fight tooth and nail against the 'damn Yankees' they claimed to hate so much.

McClellan now looked at JJ as if seeing him for the first time.

"You're a native Virginian, aren't you, Jon? Of course you are, being Roscoe's son. You must know the land well. Like the back of your hand, as the saying goes."

JJ nodded slowly. "I know it very well, in fact." Quieter, he added: "I know the people well too."

"Excellent," McClellan said. "Of course, it's the locals I'm most interested in. We must win the hearts and minds of the Southern people, Jon, for it's the wives and sisters and mothers and the like who will convince their wayward Johnny Rebels to lay down their arms and go home. However, should they refuse to surrender, we must of course do our duty."

JJ nodded again. But inwardly, he thought once more about his brother. For God's sake, Jem never gave up on anything — not a wrestling match, not an argument, not even a coin toss. How readily would Jem just 'give up' when Federal troops came marching down the North Branch?

Then again, why should JJ give a damn about Jem any longer? Why should he give a damn about anyone at Clarendon, or in Mayfair for that matter? Had any member of his family stood up for him that fateful night almost two years ago? Not even Ben Freeman had come to his aid. All of them had lived under the shadow of John Roscoe, and probably they still did even while the man lay six feet underground. The Roscoe legacy was a lie, a fiction, a put-on. The official aim of the war was to restore the old Union, but JJ was now of the mind that there were some things that were unworthy of restoration, unworthy of preservation. There were some things — maybe even some people — who would have to be sacrificed.

McClellan seemed to try to read JJ's expression. Fearing the general would see too much, *sense* too much, JJ looked away.

McClellan had apparently seen enough. Pointedly, he asked, "What about you, Jon? Are you willing to draw your sword against your own state? Against your own family?"

JJ chewed on that question for a long while. Beauregard — that smug bastard — had asked him such a question, a long time ago now. And JJ had been asking himself the same question almost every day since. He had a scar on his cheek from Jem's bullet, a wound in his heart that refused to heal, and somehow JJ knew he would not feel right again until justice was delivered. And if Jem really was Father's favored son, if Jem really was the heir to the corruption that was the Roscoe legacy, then JJ knew he would not rest until his brother submitted to him and accepted the shame of defeat.

And what if Jem did not submit? What if he refused to bow his head?

Well, the truth was that JJ had *already* drawn his sword, and if compelled to use it he would not hesitate.

Against your own family?

Yes, of course. In all things, at all times, JJ Roscoe would do his duty.

Looking at McClellan again, JJ said, "They aren't my family, sir. They're Rebels, and nothing more."

McClellan nodded and gave a small smile. "I couldn't have said it better myself, Jon. I could use a company commander like you in Virginia."

JJ blinked. Had he heard that right?

"Company—?"

"Commander, yes," McClellan said. "You can work out the details with my adjutant Marcy later — there he is just over there. Now don't misunderstand me, Jon, I brown my nose for no man. But like Bonaparte, I recognize that a superior officer's greatness depends on the capability of his subordinates. And you, Jon, I think might be quite capable indeed."

JJ shivered. "Thank you, sir. I…I do appreciate it, sir."

"Prove this one compliment correct," McClellan said with a smile, "and there will surely be more to follow."

From outside the tent, the roar of the crowd reached a fever pitch as Mayor Wood invited the heroes of Fort Sumter onto the stage. JJ watched as Major Anderson, the tattered flag still clutched to his side, led the rest of the garrison out of the pavilion in single-file. Behind them trailed the hangers-on: officers, politicians, and other dignitaries who yearned for the love of the crowd.

"You'd best catch up," McClellan said. "Enjoy your time in the spotlight."

JJ held back a moment. "You're not coming out, sir?"

McClellan listened to the sounds of the crowd for a moment before shaking his head. "My time on the stage is coming," he said, a note of pleasure in his voice. "Every man who craves the people's favor must be able to tell when they cheer with him, and when they cheer *for* him. Wouldn't you agree, Jon?"

JJ nodded. "I would, General."

With that, he offered McClellan a sharp salute. The young general returned the salute with a knowing wink and grin, and this sent JJ off with a lightness in his step that he had not known for a long time. He saw the inviting gray light of the world beyond the slit of the pavilion door. The people beyond this threshold would not know him as JJ Roscoe, the senator's son. They would not know him as JJ Roscoe, the sinful degenerate. The people out there, innumerable and nameless, would know him only as JJ Roscoe, HERO.

And so, taking a deep breath, JJ pushed through the tent flaps and stepped into the blinding light of recognition to meet a deluge of adoration and feverish applause.

Chapter 40

TRAITORS & PATRIOTS

Ben walked alone down a busy Washington street. It was late at night, but looking around one wouldn't think the city was on the brink of invasion. Gangs of thugs calling themselves soldiers roamed about in rumpled, liquor-sodden uniforms. The army hadn't paid them yet, but they were busy blowing the last of the money their mothers had given to them upon leaving the family homestead.

"Hey, fella!" a drunk soldier hailed.

Ben knew better than to stop, but he did anyway.

"Hey, fella!" the soldier said again. He tramped up to Ben along with three or four buddies. They looked at Ben with great earnestness, as if all their fervent hopes now rested on his shoulders. They were tall, but none looked to be older than Tom. What were all these kids doing in uniform?

The soldier became suddenly bashful. His drunken friends murmured and pushed him forward. The youthful soldier assumed an air of command, a tea-sipping general in a private's uniform.

"Now listen here, little fella, my comrades and I are searchin for adventuresses of a first-rate kind."

Ben blinked. "Excuse me?"

"Strumpets!" one of the other soldiers said.

"You know, peaches and cream?" the third called, and then he burst out laughing.

"You mean crumpets," the fourth said.

"Now we don't want negro girls," the first soldier said loudly, piling attention on himself once more. "Begging your pardon, but that just ain't right. And we don't want none of them diseased Irish whores."

"What we want is Orientals!"

"Fuck that."

"I surely will. I don't discriminate."

"You call yourself a Christian?"

"I ain't Christian. I'm Methodist."

Ben shook his head and began to back away. "I'm sorry, gentlemen. I don't think I have what you're looking for."

The soldier sidestepped to block Ben's path. "Then what *do* you have?"

Ben looked over his shoulder at the other soldiers and put the pieces together. There was a game in play, and the grinning youth standing before him was vying to be the winner. He craved the adulation and congratulatory handshakes of his comrades; sex with an 'adventuress' was only secondary, but of course there would be stories to share about that too.

Warning bells sounded in Ben's mind. He took another slow step backward. The soldiers looked hungry, and the kind of hunger Ben saw in their eyes made men impulsive and mean. It would be nothing for these good boys to take a few socks at Ben if he said or looked at them the wrong way.

But now, Ben stopped and rooted himself. The opportunity to run away had long since come and gone. To turn and flee now would only inspire in these boys some kind of predatory instinct. The only thing that could help Ben now was reason. He just hoped these drunken boy-soldiers had the capacity for it.

"I have an idea of what you're looking for," Ben said calmly, speaking in a low voice to the leader. "But I can't help you. I'm sorry."

The boy's eyes glassed over upon hearing these words. Suddenly it was as if Ben was invisible to him.

"Good luck to you," Ben said, and with that he turned and started to walk away. He strived to appear casual in his pace, but in his head he counted the steps until he could turn the corner.

"Damn darkie!" one of the soldiers shouted wrathfully. "You too good for my money, you rotten nigger?"

Ben pushed on through the streets. He determined it was well past time to turn back for home, but he had no intention of retracing his steps. As he ventured blindly block to block, the city around him became a ghostly metropolis, with few signs of life anywhere. Washington was disconsolate, internally roiling with despair and outwardly facing down annihilation with grim determination.

Ever since he'd been stranded in Washington in the wake of Fort Sumter's fall, Ben had lived a nocturnal existence. He hid inside John Roscoe's townhouse through the day, venturing out only at night. He'd bought some printer's ink from a shop whose owner was hastily packing up to head north. But the printing press itself remained an enigma. There was nothing to write about — nothing that wasn't already in every other paper, and no one had time to read the papers anyway. Washington was in the grip of mass panic, with widespread looting and lawlessness. It soon became too dangerous to go out at night, but nevertheless Ben needed food. The pantry shelves at 514 had been stripped bare when Miss Robson vacated the place, and already there were rumors that food stocks in the capital were dangerously close to running out. After arming himself with a knife, Ben hit the street in search of a grocer who would sell to negroes.

Ben gathered all the news he could about what was happening across the Union. President Lincoln's call for 75,000 troops to put down the Rebellion had inspired secessionists in Virginia's state legislature to throw in their lot with the Confederacy. Arkansas and North Carolina were gone shortly after, and then Tennessee went dark in late May. Though Ben tried to send letters back to Clarendon, workers for the Postal Service refused to venture across the Potomac.

Rumors filtered up from Virginia that many thousands of buckskins were marshaling for war. Militia companies were hastily formed into loose conglomerations of troops branded the 'Confederate States Army.'

From Washington's heights, Ben could see hundreds of campfires burning just across the Potomac's far shore. Everyone in Washington understood that the campfires were not those of Union troops, but an unknown mass of armed Rebels. It seemed that all Jefferson Davis had to do was give the order for those Rebels to seize the bridges over the Potomac, and then take Washington itself.

Though news reports suggested young men all over the Union were signing up for war, very few of Lincoln's requested 75,000 had yet arrived in the capital. Certainly there were not enough defenders to put up much of a fight against the Rebels, who had somehow organized an army seemingly overnight. All this time, Washington remained isolated and undefended. Long lines of expectant refugees began to pour out of the city heading in all directions.

Ben imagined President Lincoln, alone in the White House, spending all day and night looking up Pennsylvania Avenue, watching for his armies to come to the rescue of the capital. Dark rumors suggested that Lincoln had a loaded pistol in his desk, and would surely use it when despair overwhelmed him. Ben never took much stock in gossip, but the idea seemed too plausible to rule out.

Were the people of the Northern states ready to defend their national government? Did they even believe the national government was worthy of sacrifice? How many soldiers would sign up for service, not out of a sense of moral duty, but simply so he could 'whip dirty rednecks' and chase down 'adventuresses' while on leave — just for that once-in-a-lifetime thrill that war was supposed to provide?

Did the Union stand behind its president? Millions had voted Lincoln into office to be sure, but millions more had voted *against* him. Now that the whole country was poised to tip over into bloody ruin, would people search for a scapegoat? And how many lives would be lost in the witch hunt to follow? The back pages of papers hinted at hangings of 'suspicious persons' (often black men, Ben knew) in cities and county burgs all over the North. There were reports of lynchings in the *North*, with plenty of unrest between neighbors to suggest Maine was as likely to wage war against Massachusetts as against Mississippi. The haughty arrogance of the secessionists had peeled back the layers of civility all over the Union, and in the North the people responded to the idea of coming catastrophe by setting their own houses on fire.

And if Washington fell, it was all over. Many people would surely die. Lincoln would likely be ejected from office, or worse. And then what? Maybe the Rebels would seize control of the Federal government. Maybe a new ragdoll president would be installed while the Confederacy continued to build its new government. And that would mean the Union — the Constitution, the Republic, the very ideas of consensual government and the peaceful transition of power — would all be cast aside. If Washington fell, there would be a new precedent, a new and violent normal. Slaves would be kept in the cotton fields not just with chains and whips, but with standing armies. If Washington fell, the United States' experiment of peaceful, representative democracy would cease to exist. If ordinary people gave up, their capital's capitulation would be a foregone conclusion.

In order to survive, Washington needed a symbol of hope. The Union needed hope, and a reason to believe.

But where the hell would such a symbol come from? Who in God's name could provide a reason to believe in anything these days, let alone suggest it as *the* reason for saving the Union? And here was Ben Freeman, small, insignificant mote of dust that he was, tinkering with metal letters on a piece of wood, thinking he might somehow change tomorrow for the better.

At dawn (it was only then that he realized he had been walking all night) Ben stopped within sight of the half-built dome of the Capitol Building and lit a cigar. He puffed quietly and looked upon the silhouette of the dome standing against purple clouds.

Turning his head, Ben looked toward the Potomac River. As he smoked, he observed the thousand tiny firelights in the darkness, each Rebel campfire blazing like the red cherry of his cigar.

Two drunk men staggered up out of the darkness, both reeking of the night's end-of-the-world revelry. They stopped short beside Ben, their eyes fixed on the same unnerving sight across the Potomac.

The first man looked bored to tears. "You think the seceshes are about done with their tantrum?"

The other wheezed, in the casually explosive manner of a man who is more than half-deaf: "Goddamn Republicans. *I* voted for Steve Douglas. I *told* folks what would happen otherwise. If they only thought like me, this big goatfuck would have never happened."

They turned away, glancing at Ben as one might look at a street pigeon pecking in the dirt. The first man spat absentmindedly in Ben's direction before turning back to his friend.

"Yeah, if only we all thought like you, Arnie. We'd all be better off."

"Whatsay?"

"I said, we'd all be better off."

"What?"

The two men carried on down the street. Ben watched them go, but something the first man said continued to rattle in his mind like a stone in a galvanized bucket.

Douglas. Stephen Douglas.

Thanks to several Democrat-leaning newspapers with national syndication, the Little Giant had been in and out of the national spotlight ever since the election. Even after the failure of the Crittenden Compromise back in January, Douglas had worked feverishly to prevent Congress from imploding. Rumor had it that Douglas had concocted an idea for a new invasion of Mexico, with the intent of taking even more land than the United States had won back in '48. This new territory would be used, of course, to expand slavery southward.

Whether such an outlandish idea was seriously considered or not, the secessionists had in any case rebuffed Douglas and his allies. Still, Douglas persisted. After South Carolina and the Deep South states went out of the Union, Douglas had attempted to organize a bipartisan Peace Conference. In the end, the meeting intended to heal wounds between North and South was one attended by very few Southerners, most of whom had no power or position within the new Confederate government. By the time of the Fort Sumter crisis and the commencement of war, Stephen Douglas had disappeared from the public eye.

But maybe...just maybe...

Ben had good reason to believe the Little Giant was still in Washington, but it was unlikely he would remain in the city much longer. With the Rebels just across the river, many of the Union's politicians had already skipped town.

Ben took a final look at the Rebel campfires before he pressed his thumb against the cherry of his cigar and snuffed out the red flame. Tucking the cigar in his pocket, he turned and hurried up the street, and he refused to look back at the enemy over his shoulder.

❧

"Maybe you ought to come back again in a few weeks," the butler said, eyeing Ben suspiciously from behind the huge oak door. The butler was a black man of about fifty, trimly dressed. He spoke with the prim voice of an Englishman, an effect that was strange to Ben's ears. "Senator Douglas is not feeling well."

"Please," Ben said. "I need to speak with Senator Douglas. There's business—"

"Whose business?"

Ben removed his hat. "My own business."

The blinking butler went momentarily speechless. "Negro callers are not permitted on these premises."

"I am not a caller, sir. I'm...I'm an associate of Mr. Douglas."

The butler stifled a laugh. "I do beg your pardon, sir, but Mr. Douglas does not associate with people of... *your persuasion*, sir."

The butler turned his head as, from inside, a weak voice groaned the butler's name. The warbling voice had to belong to someone very ill, perhaps dying. For a brief, anguished moment, Ben imagined he was listening to John Roscoe.

The butler, turning away to answer the master of the house, inadvertently let the door yawn open. Ben seized his opportunity to open it wider, and he slid gracefully inside. The butler glared at Ben and hauled the door open wide again.

"Get out!" the butler said urgently. "Get out this instant, or I'll hail the—"

"He's sick," Ben said, almost as a question. "Consumption?"

This remark gave the butler pause. "No," he said, shaking his head. "Typhoid."

Ben cast his eyes to the floor. "I'm sorry."

The butler looked to the shadowed staircase down the hall, now back at Ben. He dropped his accent and spoke plainly. "It's bad, *real* bad. He don't wanna see nobody."

Ben looked around the foyer. The Douglas home was spartan, showcasing no exquisite paintings or fancy wallpaper, and only the simplest furniture arranged in a utilitarian fashion. Douglas was a wealthy man, but apparently quite frugal. From the kitchen somewhere within came the smell of fresh-baked bread, with more loaves on the way. Ben's stomach grumbled, and he realized he hadn't eaten in almost two days. The thought occurred to him that the loaves might not be for the occupants of the house, but for funeral guests.

"I know Senator Douglas only a little," Ben said to the butler. "We don't know each other enough to be friends. But I'd like to be one to him now."

The butler stared at Ben for a long while. Whatever he read in Ben's eyes, he eventually sighed and nodded.

"He's upstairs. This way."

The second floor was even less lavish than the first. The hall was quite dark, but a shaft of gray sunlight from a high window illuminated a framed pencil drawing hanging on the wall. The drawing depicted a sprawling western town surrounded by flat, fertile farmland. The inscription below read JACKSONVILLE, ILLINOIS.

They entered a large study off the hall. Though it was late May, a huge fire roared in the hearth. The rest of the room was empty. At the far end near the windows, an iron staircase wound up to a third floor. The butler paused at its base and craned his neck upward.

"Senator Douglas, sir? A Mr. — what's your name?"

"Ben Freeman."

"A Mr. Freeman is here to see you, sir."

"*Who?*" the reply came. It was faint and hoarse, not at all like the exuberant Little

Giant whose voice had boomed throughout Charleston's Institute Hall a year and a half ago.

Ben stood with the butler. "It's Ben Freeman, sir," he called. Though he thought against it, he added, "John Roscoe's man."

A gargling laugh floated down. "Roscoe's *black* man, is it?"

Ben glanced at the butler, who stared blankly back at him.

"Yes, sir," Ben said..

Douglas' warbling voice floated down: "Come on up, Mr. Freeman."

Ben nodded to the butler and started up the staircase. Upon reaching the top, he found himself standing in a circular room, like a castle's turret, overlooking much of Georgetown, Washington, and the Potomac River beyond. Stephen Douglas sat in a chair with a large afghan over his lap. The Little Giant was pale, his eyes hollow and his cheeks sunken.

"Good morning, Senator," Ben said.

Douglas smiled weakly. "Hello, Mr. Freeman. You look a fright. Have you slept? I have to say, I'm surprised to see you. I would have thought the Roscoe family would have you on the tightest of leashes given all that's happening."

Before Ben could begin to explain, Douglas turned and pointed out the window.

"Look," Douglas said. He indicated the myriad pillars of smoke that drifted across the morning sky. "They're so close you can hear them singing. Listen. Do you hear that? I had the staff open the window there for me. Sounds like *Dixie* is a favorite. For God's sake, I've been hearing that song everywhere. They'll be singing it in church ere long."

From this vantage point, Ben counted many hundreds more campfires than he had seen even a few hours earlier. Could the Rebel army have *grown* overnight? But then, it wasn't at all a ridiculous notion. It was now startlingly clear that the Rebels were getting ready for a big push across the Potomac.

And meanwhile, the boys of Washington's garrison were busy at the brothels.

Douglas reached for a crumpled newspaper and tossed it into the nearby fireplace, which was smaller than the one downstairs but no less lively. "I read a story in the *Star* this morning. Our good friend Tobias Cutler had a few wonderfully doltish quotes. I'd read them to you, but the fire's getting low."

"Judge Cutler?" In truth, Ben hadn't thought about that bastard in a long while. There had been too much else to think about.

Douglas nodded. "He was part of the convention that passed Virginia's ordinance of secession. Of course he was there; he had to be seen leading the charge. *Senator* Cutler, I suppose he is now." Douglas gazed at the smoke across the river. "I suppose it was wrong of me to think that Virginians were *unconditional* Unionists. It doesn't matter that you birthed the Republic's greatest presidents. You lot are all still Southerners, after all."

"There are many Virginians who will fight for the Union," Ben said. "The Roscoes..."

Ben's voice fell away. He remembered the Senator. He remembered Jem, and Sarah, and almost everyone he knew in Mayfair. Who in the Valley did not consider themselves a Virginian first, an American second? After all, most considered themselves nothing but 'Valley folk' to begin with.

Well, at least there was JJ. Wherever he was, JJ would defend the Union. Still, Ben supposed it was more likely that JJ would fight chiefly to improve his own station rather than out of any patriotic impulse.

Looking at Douglas, seeing the weary expression etched into his face, Ben thought about the Senator once more.

"I suppose you know about John Roscoe," Ben murmured.

Douglas was quiet for a long time. He clenched and unclenched his hands like a cat kneading a blanket. "I was sorry I could not attend the funeral. Truly, I was. I was here in Washington with Senator Crittenden and the others trying to cobble together some damnable eleventh-hour compromise. Even Jeff Davis was there, though I knew that *he knew* it was all in vain." Douglas shrugged and tried to laugh it all off, but he only succeeded in letting out a quiet whimper. "Well, a lot of good it did us. A lot of good it did me. Meanwhile, there goes John."

Ben hung his head. Though he could not comprehend the full depth of the pain in Douglas' voice, he could at least grasp at it. Douglas and the Senator had been intimate friends for decades. Meanwhile, Ben had known John Roscoe as a sort of father figure. Ben wondered about the differences in those relationships, about the different John Roscoes that both he and Douglas had known. Who had known the *real* John Roscoe? And how many times was a person's true essence divided among the people one knew, the confidences one kept, the vulnerabilities one permitted others to see?

"It's unfortunate how it all ended between us," Douglas said. "Still, there's no taking any of it back now. You'll soon find yourself at an age, Mr. Freeman, when life stops giving and death starts taking. It's not so bad, knowing that you yourself will die. It's the realization that soon enough there won't be anyone else around who remembers you. And what does the wind recall of a man?"

Ben put a hand on a nearby chair. "May I sit, sir?"

Douglas mumbled some version of a response, and Ben sat down. They sat in silence together for a long while.

"You say you're not frightened of death?" Ben asked at length.

Douglas shrugged. "It's impossible to fear what I do not understand."

Ben permitted himself a wry laugh. "I know a lot of folks who would disagree with that."

"So do I," Douglas said. "What did John say about it when you asked him?"

"I never had the chance to ask," Ben said. "Maybe it's more accurate to say, when I had the chance to say something, I said nothing."

Douglas looked out the window once more, but not at the Rebels; his gaze seemed to look somewhere inward.

"My doctor said late June — *this* June, and only if I'm stubborn. But I'm not that stubborn. Not anymore." Douglas smiled, but there were tears in his eyes. "It might be any day. I hope it's a Friday." Suddenly, the Little Giant gave a violent shake of his head. "But no more of this! I was a young man once, you know, and nothing bores a young man more than listening to an old man wail about his impending doom."

Ben smiled. "I don't mind at all, sir."

"On the bright side," Douglas said, "my demise seems altogether preferable compared to the fate which will hang around poor Mr. Lincoln's neck. He'll be the one tarred and feathered in history books for presiding over the downfall of American democracy. No, thank you. I'll accept my destiny of obscurity with whatever dignity I have left, thank you very much."

Ben shifted in his chair. "I suppose there's some silver lining to that, sir, for what it's worth."

Douglas grinned. "Certainly there is, and it's worth a great deal to me."

Suddenly, Douglas coughed sharply. Ben heard the familiar chest rattle that had pained John Roscoe for so many years. Douglas sat up wheezing, and after a while he managed a shallow breath.

"So what is it you've come to see me about, Mr. Freeman?"

Ben was quiet for a long moment. "Well, sir, I suppose it's…if it's not too silly to mention it…it's hope that's brought me here. The hope of a fool, maybe."

"You'll eventually get over that," Douglas said.

Ben sat up straight in his chair. "I…I have an idea for a story."

Douglas sighed. "Come now, Mr. Freeman. Don't tell me you think yourself an American Voltaire. Haven't you heard what the English have been saying for a hundred years? We have no culture here, and we never shall."

Ben laughed. "Nothing like that, sir. But I have an idea for a story all the same. A *news* story, if you understand me."

"Ah, a journalist," Douglas grumbled. To make a point, he snatched up another bundle of newspapers and tossed them to the hungry fireplace. "You see what I'm doing, Mr. Freeman? You see what happens to all those *ideas* for all those *stories*? Fuel for warming the bones of a dying man. And these worthless scraps aren't even capable of doing that much for very long. I'd be better off wiping my rear with them. Well, let's hear the damn thing, whatever it is."

"I haven't quite thought it all through yet," Ben said. "But it starts with a village. A village, and the people who live in it. This village is tucked away somewhere in the mountains. And one day, the people look up from their various goings-on, and they see a man — one of their own — stranded on the commons. He stands alone, surrounded by a pack of wolves. But no one ventures out to help the man. They don't have the courage to risk their own lives to save him. They hold quiet assurances that *someone else* will take their place. And because no one steps forward, the wolves can take their time—"

"That's not news," Douglas grumbled. "That's a parable, Mr. Freeman, and a poor one."

Ben shrugged. "I suppose I was just trying to—"

"Trying to what? Make rational sense from a rabid dog's barking? No one in Washington understands secession, no one understands these *wolves* you allude to. The Rebellion is positively baffling in its absurdity. What started out as a small group of self-interested racketeers has grown to capture the hearts and minds of *millions*. Do you understand the implications of this, Mr. Freeman? *Millions* of people are now working in concert to tear down the pillars of their own government, while at the same time those original fraudsters are busy erecting the shoddy foundations of a new government which — I am calling it now — shall prove to be even more hostile to the liberties of its citizens than any crackpot idea the Republicans might cook up in the meantime. The Rebels, fearing the government will take away their slaves, have declared *war* on that same government — *their* government. In the end, by firing upon the American flag, Yancey and Jeff Davis and all those selfish fools will fulfill their own dreaded prophecy."

"Only if the government survives," Ben warned. "Only if the Union can defeat the Rebels."

Douglas dabbed his greasy forehead with a handkerchief. "John Roscoe and I are an old breed of men — *were* an old breed. Our time passed long before we realized it was gone. I might have retired ten years ago and been much happier for it. At least I could say that as the country went mad, I had nothing to do with its demise."

Ben shrugged. "Maybe it's not too late to save it."

Douglas laughed and shook his head. "I've failed too many times at trivial matters to believe any one man can save *the Union*, Mr. Freeman. Perhaps when I was your age I thought such a thing possible. But as time marches on, and as the wrinkles of age deepen, a man starts to realize certain things. Only a select few ever achieve the fame and recognition we all think is destined to be ours. And that recognition is never what we wanted it to be. It's clear to me now that, for all my years of work, for all my sleepless nights..."

Here, Douglas pointed out at the Rebel camp.

"...*that* is my legacy. It's not what I wanted, certainly not. But now, even if I'm not content to die, at least I'm looking forward to it. And death will come soon, according to my doctor. Did I tell you already? June, if I'm stubborn."

Ben stood up and went to the window. He stared down at the Rebel fires across the river, but now he looked up and glared at the reflection of Douglas in the glass.

"With respect, sir, this isn't about you. This isn't about anyone's goddamn *legacy*. If John Roscoe had one failing — and there were many contenders — it was the vanity you now describe. He was concerned, obsessed even, with his legacy. It was his obsession for high, unblemished status that leached away his love for his own children. It was his insatiable desire for *more* that compelled him to trade in his conscience at the slightest whiff of power and influence. It was his craving to be universally admired and respected — and *right*, in all things — that caused him to lose every friend he ever had. It was his need to have no one believe he ever did anything wrong, at the expense of never doing anything at all."

Hearing all this, Douglas said nothing. He looked down into his lap and pulled distractedly at a loose thread in the afghan.

"An entire nation cannot be saved by one person, it's true," Ben said. "You will not be the one; I will not be the one. Lincoln will not be the one. There are no gods among us. If Christ is dead and risen, or God forbid there *is* no Christ, then there is nobody here to save us except ourselves. The *people* can save our Union, Senator. The American people, united, can save their country from those who seek to claim it only for themselves. What *one* — any*one* — can do, and do now, is to be the first to stand up and rally others to defend their neighbor."

Douglas offered a thin smile. "Back to your wolves on the commons idea. Well, let's for a moment imagine you're onto something. Tell me, Mr. Free-man, what has America ever done for *you*, for *your* people? Sure, maybe the Spaniards took you here — that's not our fault. But *we* kept you here. We beat you, raped you, degraded you. Evidently we would rather kill each other than let you walk free. Were I in your position, I might be inclined to let the Union burn to ashes and sail off to Liberia or some damn place. Your hero, Frederick Douglass, has openly called to 'let the Union perish.' So why should you care whether this country is saved?"

Ben thought about that question for a long while. It was a good question, and one to which he did not have an immediate answer.

"This is my home," Ben offered at last. He pointed southward across the Potomac, indicating the broad land beyond it. "Virginia — Mayfair — that's my home there. It's where I was born, the place that shaped who I am. And no matter what any pasty-faced son of a bitch out there says to the contrary, I'm an American. I'm a man, a human being, and I know it's right to fight for the little good that remains in this world. There won't be any world left to rebuild if we give up the pittance we have."

"So what will you do?" Douglas said mirthlessly. "Write your little stories?"

Ben gave a defiant nod. "The army won't let negroes fight, even though this fight could be and ought to be *ours*, as much as yours. So what can I do? If all I can do is use my mind, put pen to paper, share messages of hope and faith in the cause, then that is what I will do."

Here, Ben pulled out his battered notebook and held it up for Douglas to see.

"Even the loudest shout is too weak to be heard more than a mile away. But the printed word can travel anywhere, and it can meet any mind where it is at the very moment of comprehension. When people look at me, they see a nigger. But maybe if they can read my words, they will finally hear me. And maybe, in time, they'll start to see me."

The Little Giant was quiet for a long time. Finally, he gave a quiet laugh and shook his head. His laugh drifted away in a tired sigh.

"You really are a rare specimen, Mr. Freeman. You are a rare specimen indeed. So, you'll write some parables and call them articles, hm?"

Ben shook his head. "No parables, sir. No fictions, no myths. Only facts. For instance, I'll be covering your upcoming meeting with President Lincoln."

Douglas was still smiling, but the mocking light in his eyes had dimmed.

"Meeting?" Douglas echoed. "What meeting? There is no meeting."

"I'll write about your upcoming visit to the White House," Ben went on. "I'll write about how the Union's chief Democrat, seeing a nation in tatters, was the first to step out and speak up in support of President Lincoln's stance against the Rebellion. I'll record word for word, sir, your call for patriotic Americans to stand against the wolves that threaten our democracy."

Douglas sighed and glared down into his lap. "So let me understand this correctly. You're going to write an article about Stephen Douglas trudging over to the White House to grovel before his most bitter political rival, all in the hopes that it will somehow inspire notions of compassion and unity among the American people?"

Ben nodded. "In so many words."

Douglas shook his head. "Putting aside the immense naivety of your entire endeavor, Mr. Freeman, there is one problem that sticks in my craw. You are fabricating a news story, creating a human drama out of thin air. In my time, we called that yellow journalism."

"It's only yellow if the story isn't true," Ben said. "In the end, the story isn't about you or Lincoln. It's not about Democrats or Republicans. It's about standing up for what's right."

Douglas nodded toward the campfires across the river. "You realize those poor fools over there think they're doing the same thing? They feel their actions are right, and they'll die to prove it. Who can say who *is* right?"

Ben smiled as a pleasant memory of home came to mind. "My mama says something about how all things come out in the wash eventually," he said. "The Rebels are on the record, and so we've got to go on the record too. The verdict of who's right will be decided in time."

Douglas watched Ben for a long, quiet moment. Douglas blinked, and he might have burst out laughing again, but he didn't. In that moment, Ben knew his idea had lodged itself in the Little Giant's mind. The seed was ready to germinate.

As a last effort, Douglas waved Ben off with an irritable grunt. "I've retired from public life, Mr. Freeman. John Roscoe didn't have the time to enjoy his retirement, God rest his soul. My wife arrives tomorrow, and I intend to leave with her for Illinois to enjoy whatever time I have left."

Ben thought to press his case further. He thought to spell out for Douglas exactly why he was right, and that Douglas ought to listen to him. He even thought to explain to Douglas that he had the chance to finally do the thing that John Roscoe had never been able or willing to do: to craft a *true* American compromise. But really, what good would any of that hardheadedness do? Ben had tried such a strategy before, a thousand times, with only rare instances of success. Perhaps there was something to Jem's idea that a free-thinking man deserved to draw his own conclusions, rather than have someone else tell him how to think. And so, Ben remained quiet.

"What, you're just going to give up?" Douglas said.

Ben shook his head. "No, sir. I only ask for your consideration. Nothing more."

"Consideration?" Douglas heaved a sigh of protest. "It's not as if Lincoln would want to see me anyway. He's liable to slap me in chains, just like he's been arresting dissidents without charges up in Baltimore. Did you hear about *that* little story? Our own president has suspended *habeas corpus* and is throwing suspected traitors in jail without charges or hope for a trial. Rather than pledge my friendship and support, I'm in fact more likely to accuse the man of being a tyrant. It's a silly notion, Mr. Freeman, an *insane* notion, to suggest that I might actually..."

Douglas' voice drifted off. His sallow gaze became fixed once more on the Rebel campfires across the Potomac. Ben could almost read the questions on the Little Giant's face as if they were stamped there in red ink. What would it mean to the American people to finally see two bitter rivals meet in the center aisle and join together in a common cause? How would it strengthen the Union to have Democrats and Republicans finally set aside, if only for a little while, the games of power and intrigue that had done so much to bring the country to the brink of disaster?

The seed of Ben's idea finally began to take root. Ben watched as Douglas' face contorted with the strain of internal debate, shifting between a defiant grimace and a final sigh of resignation.

"Well," Douglas said at last, "all that damn smoke across the river ruins my sunsets anyway. Can't a dying man enjoy one more decent dusk before he's taken from this world? Fine, Mr. Freeman. We'll embark on your fool's odyssey. I'll have the staff send a telegram. Besides, of course Abe will want to see me — I'm the only friend the poor bastard has in this godforsaken place!"

Ben could not help but smile. "That's fine, sir. That's very fine."

Douglas wagged his finger at Ben. "But I demand to say whatever I damn well please, Mr. Freeman, and you will quote me *verbatim*. I won't allow myself to be censured. And please, don't make me sound like that moron Tobias Cutler. For God's sake, I want to sound intelligible!"

❧

Stephen Douglas did in fact meet with President Lincoln, on a humid morning in late May 1861 while angry storm clouds rolled in from the south. In his last appearance before the public, the Little Giant's coach rolled up to the south portico of the White House. Douglas was ushered inside while Ben was permitted only to walk the grounds. Ben had not counted on gaining permission to enter the Executive Mansion; even with a Republican in charge, there were no blacks permitted within the White House unless they were the help.

Still, Ben could not help but feel a sense of disappointment. There had been a spark of hope, maybe a deluded one, that some secretary might whisk him inside to stand before the 'railsplitter' president. He'd held at least a glimmer of hope that he might be able to make his case to Lincoln personally, and explain to the president about why the war against the South ought to be fought. The war couldn't simply be about putting the Union back together again. The war had to *create* something: a new kind of Union, with equality under the law as its foundation.

"And don't try to assuage me with promises of compromise," Ben wished he could say. "I was raised up by a so-called man of compromise, but in the end he did nothing but compromise the ideas and values that make our Union great. Having fired the first shot, the Rebels have launched a war upon *us*, Mr. President. Ours is a just war, and there are oppressed people living under the thumb of the enemy. If the enemy can be conquered, and I think they can, then part of our victory will be in the breaking of chains. But if you make premature peace, or if you take only half-measures against the institution of slavery, then by what principle can you return the newly freed back into bondage? Mr. President, this *must* be a war for freedom."

But as Ben murmured this imaginary conversation under his breath, he soon grew tired of being his own audience. With his hands clasped behind his back, Ben walked about the grounds in silence.

About an hour later, Douglas emerged from the White House to address a meager band of correspondents that had gathered together. Most of them represented faraway prairie papers with no national circulation. Douglas had done his best to tip off newsmen from the big papers like the *Washington Star* and *The New York Times*, but evidently a private meeting between Douglas and the president had not been deemed newsworthy when there was so much else going on.

Ben stood well apart from this tiny group, having withstood curious glances and contemptuous glares from other correspondents. As Douglas took his position on the south portico, Ben took out his notebook.

Ben detected a hint of disappointment on the Little Giant's pallid face as he looked out at the depressing size of the crowd. No doubt Douglas had envisioned a much larger audience for what would be his last speech. What good was a final bow with no standing ovation to inspire it?

But as Ben well knew and hoped, 'the wire' would take Stephen Douglas' last speech national. There was a telegraph office a half block from the White House, and minutes after Douglas' speech concluded the office would be filled with breathless, red-faced correspondents jockeying to submit orders for the tapper. With enough papers printing the story, the *Star* and the *Times* would carry it too. Eventually, even the Rebels down in Richmond and Atlanta would read Douglas' words. Ben knew that his original idea, that of printing his first 'exclusive' for the *Liberty & Union* newspaper, was a vanity that no longer mattered. What mattered was that the message of unity spread far and wide. What mattered was that the story of Douglas and Lincoln's newfound friendship was *true*. Ben had lost faith in a great many things in recent time, but he yet believed that the truth spoke for itself.

After all, everything came out in the wash eventually.

"Today," Douglas began, his voice projecting some of its former resonance, "I pledged to President Lincoln, using whatever prestige I still have within the Democratic Party, a spirit of friendship and cooperation between Democrats and Republicans. I also pledged my personal support to the president, together with the faith and belief of all Americans. In his inaugural address back in March, the president presented an offering of peace and reconciliation to secessionist sympathizers. They eagerly spurned it, and worse, they fired upon the flag of our national Union. That is the highest of crimes, and one that cannot go unpunished."

A correspondent called out, "And what of Lincoln's 75,000 invaders?"

"What *of* them?" another man laughed. "They're nowhere to be seen!"

Still another voice cried, "Do you support the North's planned invasion of the South, sir? Do you support civil war, sir? Do you support Americans killing Americans to prop up a tyrant's whims?"

"I support the call for troops, yes," Douglas answered emphatically. "You gentlemen do realize this country is under *attack*, yes? You do realize those campfires across the river are not *our* soldiers, but those of Mr. Davis? Of course I support the president's call for patriots to step forward. What's more, I said to him just a few minutes ago: 'Seventy-five thousand is not nearly enough, Mr. President. You ought to have called for *two hundred thousand* to put the secesh bastards in their place!'"

Ben smiled. The other correspondents laughed together, though a few grumbled and spat on the ground.

"But I wish to address that last question further," Douglas continued. "I know of no sane man who could 'support war' except to see a war brought to an end, and quickly. And this, I remind you, is not in principle a war of *North* versus *South*. This is not a war between states, and certainly not between sovereign nations. Rather it is a war between *the United States* and certain insurrectionists intent on overthrowing their own government. The Confederate States do not actually exist, neither legally nor empirically. Mississippi remains Mississippi, and Virginia is still Virginia. The force opposing the United States is not a sovereign people, but only a mass of angry Americans who have been misled and misdirected by corrupt men of tremendous power. Is it tyranny for a people's government to defend itself against the whims of *real* tyrants?"

This was met with low murmurings from the correspondents, some in favor, some in violent disagreement. Over it all, Douglas stood proud and unmoved. The Little Giant's eyes scanned the small crowd until they found Ben off to the side. Here, Douglas smiled. Now he seemed to rise in stature, and rosy color returned to his pale cheeks. He appeared once more as the bulldog Ben had met in Charleston the spring before.

"I've known Mr. Lincoln a longer time than any of you gentlemen have, and indeed longer than the country has. He'll come out all right, and we will all stand by him. 'Liberty and Union' is our rallying cry, gentlemen. We here today call ourselves Americans for no reasons relating to race or creed or association, but only because we hold certain truths in our minds. Liberty and Union, gentlemen: the inalienable right to the former, and the responsibility to uphold the latter for the well-being of ourselves and all we hold dear. That is the contract we sign by participating in this experiment we call the United States. Those selfish souls who would destroy our democracy for selfish means — those shriveled minds who believe a 'right' is something intended only for *me* and never for *thee* — do not deserve to call themselves Americans."

Ben felt an urgent swelling in his chest. His next breath was deeper and fuller and fresher than any he'd known in a long time. Looking around, he saw small cracks in the cynical masks of some of the correspondents. As they scribbled notes in their own journals, Ben felt the pinch of anxiety lift from his shoulders.

"And here I say to you," Douglas said. "All of America, together, stands with our national government against the Rebellion. If we are to safeguard our democracy and restore peace, we shall only do so as one Union, as one people. Alone, one person cannot save an entire nation. But alone, one person may stand up and rally his neighbors, and thus make the cause of *one* indistinguishable from the cause of *all*."

Later that night, in the attic of 514 10th Street, Ben pulled the sheet off the printing press and gazed upon the massive contraption. For a long moment he stared at it, dumbstruck, wondering if he was really about to commit himself to the work that lay ahead. Other newspapers were already doing the same thing, and doing it better, faster. But somehow, none of that mattered.

Ben reached for the first page on the stack of papers beside him, and he set to work.

He had the handwritten draft of his article — his very first article — laid out on the table with paperweights. The first step was to open up the press and withdraw the letter tray, and conduct the tedious disassembly of Senator Roscoe's old campaign handbill word by word, letter by letter. Ben had only a vague notion of what he was doing, but he let his instincts guide him.

Many hours later, Ben was still only halfway finished installing the tiny metal letters in their proper order. He had a masthead, and a headline, but still no story.

LIBERTY & UNION

An Independent Newspaper for the New American
Washington, D.C. - May 31st, 1861 - Issue No. 1

TRAITORS & PATRIOTS:
AMERICANS STAND UNITED AGAINST THE REBELLION

Ben had made countless frustrating mistakes along the way, and at one point had knocked an entire tray of precious letters onto the floor. Seeing how much work was left to be done, and feeling the weight of sleepless exhaustion pulling him down, Ben sat back and lit a cigar.

As he smoked, fresh doubts began to creep into his mind. What was the point of publishing a one-off, one-page newspaper with only one article, when there were already so many thousands of daily newspapers all across the Union? If the *Star* or the *Times* had caught a whiff of the Douglas story in the hours since the Little Giant's speech, then they would publish long before Ben had a hope of even assembling his letter tray. For God's sake, people were probably reading the story already.

But the more Ben thought about it, the more he realized the folly of his doubts. This wasn't about being *first*, or about claiming arbitrary points against some other newspaper. This wasn't about himself or the *Liberty & Union* at all. The idea was to change the tune of the funeral dirge the country had been moaning for so many long months, for so many *years*. A change was coming, and this story, Ben hoped, was just the first dancing pebble of a great rockslide. This first story might be important, in its own humble way, for just that reason: for being the first of many to follow.

Suddenly, Ben heard the sound of shouting and gunfire from outside. He turned and listened, and his heart leapt into his mouth.

The Rebels were coming. The attack on Washington had begun!

Or had it? As well as gunfire, Ben heard cheering. He supposed that Southern sympathizers might be cheering on the Rebels they so admired, but somehow that didn't seem possible. Standing up, Ben went downstairs and entered the Senator's bedroom, where a door opened out to a small balcony overlooking 10th Street.

In the open air of the warm night, Ben heard the heavy rhythm of boots echoing like rolling thunder.

Could it be?

Ben looked south down 10th Street toward the broad expanse of Pennsylvania Avenue. There, far down the street, he saw the swift, blurry movement of many bodies marching past. They were soldiers in blue marching in step under the glow of torches, moving with whatever loose cohesion could be impressed in just a few days of training. But as the undisciplined mass of uniformed boys came on, the sound of drums and pipes and trumpets filled the air with dignified, marshal jubilation.

Union soldiers!

Ben raced downstairs and burst out the front door of the townhouse. Together with countless others, he hustled down the street toward the corner, and there he looked up Pennsylvania Avenue. The sight stole his breath, and he staggered backward in awe.

As hundreds of soldiers passed by, cheering and waving banners aloft, hundreds and thousands more came up behind them. Darkened windows all along the Avenue lit up with candles and lamps, and presently some onlookers unfurled American flags and let them fly in the night breeze. In exchange, the soldiers saluted the rippling flags and threw up great cheers to the sky announcing their places of origin:

— *Bangor, Maine, all for the Union!*

— *Columbus, Ohio, all for the Union!*

— *New York, New York, all for the Union!*

And on and on. Dazed men, women, and children stepped out into the streets to watch the soldiers march on by, and over the thundering of bootsteps the people began to shower praise upon Washington's saviors. More people spilled out of their homes and filled the streets, and instead of abject panic the city came alive with exultation and triumph.

Washington had been delivered.

Ben could have stood there all night watching the grand procession, but immediately he was struck with the urgent need to finish his work. Turning away, he raced back up 10th Street toward 514. He leapt up the stairs and found himself before the old printing press once more, and with the rhythm of boots thundering in his ears Ben resumed his work at a feverish pace.

Only a short time later, Ben installed the letter tray into the chaser and locked it in place. He changed the ink, and finally he was ready to print. He pushed against the iron wheel and pumped the foot pedal, and the press' yawning mouth opened wide. Ben inserted a blank page into the maw and watched as the press swallowed it up for a brief moment before spitting it back out. Inked onto the page were tiny black shapes and symbols arranged in neat rows.

With trembling fingers, Ben snatched up the page and marveled at it. He read the shining, black-inked copy once, twice, a third time. He felt a swell of pride each time he reached the final section:

"The president and I share the same opinion," Senator Douglas said to the crowd, bringing his final statements to a close. "It is not the Southern people, but their masters — and I use that term with its every definition in mind — who ought to be punished. But this is a war, gentlemen, make no mistake about that. And in this war, there are but two sides. Every man must be for the United States, or against it. There can be no neutrals; only traitors and patriots."

"It's ready," Ben whispered to himself. "As ready as it's going to be."

Liberty & Union Issue No. 1 was indeed ready, but Ben's work was not yet finished. With one final admiring glance, Ben set the first copy aside. There was no time for slumbering in self-satisfaction.

Taking up another blank sheet, Ben pumped the press to life once more. And as Ben found his rhythm, as the stack of printed copies became two, then ten, then twenty-five, then a hundred, the throbbing thrum of the press became indistinguishable from the steady tramp of soldiers' boots marching down Pennsylvania Avenue.

CHAPTER 41

GONE FOR A SOLDIER

THE WAR BETWEEN THE STATES, as the *Mayfair First Witness* had taken to calling it, was in full swing by the end of May. Every morning at the breakfast table, Sarah Cutler ate quietly while her father-in-law read the day's news reports aloud.

"President Davis and his administration are finally settled in Richmond," Judge Cutler said.

At first, no one answered. Certainly Sarah wasn't going to try. Lately she did her best to remain invisible as much as she could. She spoke only when directly spoken to. She avoided Henry whenever she could, except for family meals.

From across the table, Henry scowled. "Why would we move the capital to within a hundred miles of Washington? It's damn stupid."

"We're better off running the country here in Virginia than way down in Montgomery," his father replied. "When *that man* is deposed, Davis will need to move quickly to seize Washington and the government offices there."

That man. It was forbidden to utter Abraham Lincoln's name at Arcadia.

"Except the Federals have invaded Virginia," Henry replied coldly. "They're occupying the counties north and west of here, and the coloreds of all the surrounding country are flocking to them like liberators. Pretty soon the Yankees might arrive here in the Valley."

The Judge shook his head. "Have faith, Henry. God is on our side. And with God, we'll soon have the support of the British Empire as well. President Davis is searching for representatives to seek official recognition from Her Majesty's Parliament. The British economy depends heavily on our cotton. Without stable trade with the South, they face recession or worse. If the British recognize the Confederacy as a sovereign nation, they can trade openly with us. What's more, they may lend us military assistance against the Federals."

Mrs. Lucretia Cutler breezed into the room still wearing her horse-riding outfit from her routine early morning ride. The men of the family stood up and waited until the Lady of Arcadia sat down at the table.

"You are shining this morning, my dear," the Judge said.

"Thank you, Mr. Cutler." Niceties were quickly dispensed with; now Mrs. Cutler was all business. "You'll be pleased to know the Mayfair Women's Society has just mailed an additional three hundred homemade uniforms to the camps around Winchester."

"How fine," the Judge said.

With a nod toward Sarah, Mrs. Cutler added, "The younger Mrs. Cutler was strong enough to overcome her recent ill health." (This was the Cutlers' euphemism for the loss of the baby, an event which they refused to speak about.) "Sarah was instrumental in garnering support from all our new war brides in the Valley."

Turning the page of his newspaper, the Judge smiled. "How fine, how fine."

Sarah smiled at her mother-in-law, but only to be polite. In truth, she had come to loathe the woman. Oh, but was loathe too strong a word? On the other hand, perhaps the word was not strong enough.

It was Mrs. Cutler who had buried Sarah's stillborn child without giving Sarah a chance to say goodbye, without a chance of even *looking* upon the poor thing. It was a day after Sarah passed the bloody afterbirth that Mrs. Cutler breezed into Sarah's bedroom on the pretense that she 'missed' her daughter-in-law.

"It's a terrible thing, what happened," Mrs. Cutler had said. "And both of you so young and vibrant. But of course, you'll have nothing to worry about regarding the social aspects of this situation, my dear. All the Valley will be made to know the truth, which is really no uncommon thing. There will be no whiff of scandal, I assure you. All reputations will stand."

Sarah had only listened to this with a blank face. A child was dead, and Sarah herself might have died. But her own husband had visited her only twice, and acted as if he was doing Sarah a favor both times. And here was Henry's mother thinking only about *reputations*.

"Poor girl," Mrs. Cutler said. "Your case reminds me of your mother, may she rest in peace. You know my Tobias once had an eye for Sarah Carter? Every man in Mayfair did back in those days. Still, I worked my charms, as any woman ought to do."

Sitting numb in her bed, her body still bruised and raw from the delivery, Sarah had only pretended to listen to the rest of Mrs. Cutler's self-absorbed stories.

This morning at the breakfast table, Sarah pretended to listen once again. She only perked up when, from down the table, Lucas Cutler said, "The Valley is virtually empty of men. They're all gone off to defend their womenfolk. These days it's almost strange to see a young man still wandering about Mayfair."

Henry scowled at his brother. "Will you quit it with your damn insinuations?"

Lucas was baffled. "Insinuations? Just what are you talking about, dear brother?"

"You know *exactly* what I'm talking about," Henry growled. "Your sermon the other day, remember? I thought you would drop the whole recruitment drive nonsense after most men in the Valley volunteered for the militia, but every week you jaw about how more men must sign up. 'There are cowards hiding among my Father's flock, oh Lord. Why do I see so many young men sitting here in God's house when God has already called them out to become Christian soldiers?'"

Lucas smiled and touched the cross around his neck. "It pleases me that you actually listened to my sermon for once, Henry."

Henry gave a mighty roar and swept his arm across the table, sending dishes and cutlery flying. Leaping to his feet, he cried, "You might as well have called *me* a coward in front of the entire congregation!"

This remark brought a long, pregnant silence over the table. Sarah looked to Henry, who regarded his younger brother with trembling disdain. Meanwhile the Judge and Mrs. Cutler made no effort to respond, turning instead to bark orders for the help to clean up the mess on the table and floor.

While an army of servants stepped forward to clear away shattered dishes and wipe down the table, Sarah watched Henry closely. She began to wonder exactly what she had once seen in the man that was so wonderful.

"Don't breathe in my fucking face," Henry growled to one of the servants working next to him.

"Yessuh, Marse Henry, suh," the boy replied.

The boy proceeded to gather up a heap of broken dishes into his arms. Sensing an opportunity, Henry stuck out his foot and then pushed the boy back. The boy careened backwards and toppled to the floor, and the broken shards he clutched shattered into even smaller pieces all around him.

While Henry grinned at the destruction, Sarah grimaced at her husband and slowly shook her head.

The disturbance was enough to make the Judge look up from his newspaper and glare down at the boy on the floor. "When did we start breeding such thick-headed ingrates? *Solomon*!"

The ancient butler Solomon stepped forward. "Yessuh."

The Judge pointed down at the boy, whose palms were peppered white by tiny shards of china. "I don't want that boy in my dining room ever again. You hear?"

"Yessuh, Marse Tobe." Solomon gave a meaningful click of his tongue, and a team of servants rushed silently forward to whisk the boy away and carry on with the cleanup.

The Judge cleared his throat with a low rumble and resumed his news announcements. The old man insisted on reading every news report aloud, as if he himself was the source of all the world's knowledge.

"Colonel Thomas Jackson has seized the Federal armory at Harper's Ferry," he said. "Can you believe it? Not two years ago, John Brown and his fanatics tried to take the armory in the name of Black Republicanism. Now *we* have taken it in the name of liberty. Can you believe it, Henry?"

Henry heaved a sigh and sat down again, a sulking look on his face. "How fucking wonderful. Tell me more news from beyond the Branches, Father. It won't help our hands work any faster."

The Judge and Mrs. Cutler exchanged joyless, thin-lipped smiles, but made no condemnations of Henry's rudeness and foul language.

Meanwhile, Sarah glanced sidelong at her brother-in-law. Lucas was calmly finishing his breakfast of a single piece of toast dipped in raw egg. It was the only meal the boy-reverend ate all day.

Before she had fully thought it through, Sarah said aloud, "It must be hard, Henry, being one of the only young men in the Valley who can't fight."

Another silence swept over the table, this one painful to bear. Sarah's heart went into her throat, but she swallowed it down and made no attempt to dismiss what she'd just said. Henry's expression did not change, but she detected in his eyes a fiery indignation. Somehow, seeing his reaction made her shiver with satisfaction.

"I *can* fight, wife," Henry muttered darkly.

Sarah focused on her breakfast and pretended she hadn't heard him. She looked up again with a feigned look of surprise. "Oh, what's that, Henry-dear? You were saying something?"

Henry was positively seething. "It's not that I *can't* fight, but that it's simply not—"

"Not possible for you to risk losing this year's cotton crop just to fight some Yankees," Lucas finished for his brother. "Oh yes, we've heard you say it before, Henry. You're very concerned about the yields this year, *very* concerned. It's just, such an excuse hasn't stopped almost every other man in the Valley, rich or poor, from signing up to fight."

Henry's eyes narrowed and his expression darkened as he looked from Sarah to Lucas, Lucas to Sarah. "What's this about?" he demanded. "Are the two of you up to something? Trying to guilt me into going off to war?"

"Guilt has nothing to do with it," Lucas said. "It's more a question of duty, I should think."

"My duty is to provide for this family," Henry growled. "It's not just cotton I have to worry about anymore, but that damn coal mine too." Having said this, he turned to the Judge. "It's a fine time to get us tied up with the Roscoe venture up the North Branch."

"It's a fine opportunity to diversify," the Judge replied.

"It's a distraction," Henry muttered. "It's cotton that's king, and darkies are going for twice the price they used to. Meanwhile you want us to throw our property down a hole in the ground to cough their lungs out, and for what? A coal mine in Mayfair is as pointless now as it was ten years ago."

Sarah looked up at Henry. "I know my brother Jeremiah certainly appreciates what you're doing for the family, darling."

"Oh, I'm sure he does," Henry said with a scowl. "Leave the Cutlers to clean up the mess he made. If John Roscoe was still alive, I'd tell the both of them to go piss up a rope."

Sarah bit her tongue and said nothing.

It was Lucas who spoke up next. "The war is expected to be finished by midsummer," the boy-reverend said. "There will be a dustup outside Washington, victory will go to one side or the other — ours, more than likely — and that will be that. Lincoln will capitulate and the boys will come home to great fanfare."

"And well deserved recognition," Sarah added.

Henry leveled a cold stare at her. "The more you speak, woman, the less inclined I am to treat you charitably."

Sarah shook her head and maintained a polite, obliging smile. "Please, Henry, *darling*, I would never question your valor and courage. I was only remarking that it must be, well, rather trying to see your friends go off while you remain behind. I know that for my brother Jem, he just couldn't stand to be left behind and—"

"We don't care to hear about your brother," Henry muttered.

Though she felt like spitting in his face, Sarah instead bowed her head. "No, of course not, dear."

The Cutlers went on eating, but Sarah knew that her remarks were still buzzing in Henry's ears like a cloud of hornets. Her husband's face presently contorted into shapes of rage and disgust and self-doubt, his cheeks draining of color all the while, until finally he looked as though he might be sick.

"So what if I *did* go?" Henry burst at last. He shot accusing looks all around the table, even at his parents. "What if I *did* join the army in Winchester? Am I not the head planter here at Arcadia? Who will look after the place while I'm gone? Father, you'll be away in Richmond with the Confederate Congress. So we would leave almost a thousand servants in the care of, whom? The women? The bulls would ravage and kill them all before the next full moon."

The Judge eyed Henry over the top of his newspaper. "Rather too graphic a description for my taste," he said. "You should not say such things in front of your wife, dear boy."

"Or your mother," Mrs. Cutler said, rather unimpressed. "Now, where is my darling princess Penelope?"

Sarah felt a breath of wind beside her as Tattie stepped forward. "She's takin her lessons in the garden this morn, Madam Cutler."

"Fetch her for me, Tattie."

"Yes, ma'am."

As Tattie turned to go, Sarah caught eyes with the girl. They traded silent looks, Tattie's nervous and inquiring (about how Sarah was holding up, no doubt), while Sarah's look was reassuring though maybe not entirely convincing. Of course they could speak of nothing here. There would be plenty of time for that later when they were alone during Tattie's lessons (which lately hadn't been lessons at all, but merely chances for the two to speak freely together in private, woman to woman). As Tattie departed, Sarah realized that Henry had been watching her, had no doubt noticed the lingering looks between his wife and a slave girl. But rather than say anything, Henry instead watched Tattie go, his eyes following the swish of the girl's dress.

"The women and negroes would be under *my* care," Lucas said stiffly. "With Father gone to Richmond, and you leading our proud armies in the field, Henry, the honor would be mine to oversee Arcadia's expansion."

"Expansion?" Henry said with a haughty laugh.

"Indeed." Lucas sipped a cup of black coffee, the one luxury he permitted himself each day. "After all, someone must stay behind to beat swords into plowshares. I think our negroes ought to have a church of their own in which to worship the Lord."

Henry bristled. "And just how do you expect us to pay for your new church, baby brother?"

Suddenly, Sarah giggled. She stopped herself, but not before Henry turned on her with another thinly veiled scowl.

"What is it this time?"

"I'm sorry," Sarah said, covering her mouth. "It's just a memory. My brother, well, you know my brother JJ. He used to call Jem 'baby brother' all the time. Jem would get positively incensed and start a fight, and then—"

"Again, we don't care," Henry muttered.

Sarah looked to her in-laws for support. Still wearing the ghosts of smiles on their faces, the Judge and Mrs. Cutler only looked down at their plates and remained quiet.

"*I* care, in fact," Lucas said, and he offered an encouraging smile to Sarah. "Older brothers believe they are superior simply because they are older. But unfortunately for them, the length of one's teeth is not correlated with wisdom."

Sarah returned Lucas' smile to be polite, but she was careful not to look Lucas in the eye. Though she couldn't put her finger on it, something about the boy-reverend was unnerving. Whenever she looked at him too long, her skin began to crawl. Maybe it was in the way Lucas smiled, and how his eyes seemed to mask too many secrets, like dark shadows moving just below the surface of still water.

Judge Cutler resumed his daily report. "Finally! Arkansas ratified their secession ordinance yesterday. I expect Congress will welcome their delegation by week's end."

Sarah closed her eyes and wished she was anywhere else.

"And what of Tennessee?" Lucas asked.

"And Kentucky?" Mrs. Cutler added, with a note of hopeful concern in her voice.

The Judge wore a troubled look. "Tennessee's put the secession question to a public referendum. Lord, I have faith in democracy, but such faith certainly isn't blind. The Federals will try to spoil that vote somehow. The only legitimate result will be the one that binds Tennessee to the Confederate cause. As for Kentucky, they're still dragging its heels. There are too many bleeding heart Unionists there." Reading on, the Judge shook his head with dismay. "And still more news from those fools up in Wheeling. Goddamn those traitors."

Sarah recalled the name *Wheeling*, the mountainous city in the far west of Virginia. A few weeks ago, a group of men calling themselves the Restored Government of Virginia had recently convened under the protection of Federal troops. The Restored Government stood in opposition to the Virginia General Assembly which, having voted successfully for secession back in April, was now firmly pro-Confederate.

The Unionists in Wheeling were currently debating how to form an independent state to be called 'West Virginia.' The proposed state had widespread support among Virginia's western counties, where slave plantations were few and far between. The proposed borders extended as far southeast as Harper's Ferry. Some folks, the Judge in particular, feared that the Mayfair Valley might be cut in half, and thus Mayfair would be at the center of fierce back-and-forth fighting until the war ended.

"It would mean ruin for us all," the Judge concluded. "Meanwhile, it's looking like *that man* will soon make a move on Richmond. That dustup Lucas mentioned will soon be upon us."

Sarah glanced up at the painted portrait of Jefferson Davis that hung over the fireplace. That same space had featured the portrait of the incumbent president ever since the days of Washington, or so Judge Cutler said. After the portrait of President Buchanan was removed in March, up went the portrait of President Davis. Mrs. Cutler often remarked that one day, the portrait of 'President Cutler' would hang there over the fireplace. Sarah could not imagine it.

Henry cleared his throat. "I'm riding to join the army this Sunday," he announced.

Shocked, Sarah looked up at Henry and gasped, "Really?"

Henry glowered at her and muttered, "Really."

Instinctively, Sarah tried to pull on a mask of abject sorrow. Both her question and expression had been almost hopeful in tone, and Henry had seen right through it.

The Judge slowly folded his newspaper together. The old man's face had turned pale. "Henry, my boy, no. Surely you're only being sore? Lucas didn't mean anything he said, did you, Lucas? You can't be *serious*, Henry, surely."

Henry shrugged. "Why not? We'll be finished planting in a few days." He cast a meaningful side-eye toward his brother. "If we're going to whip the Feds as everyone expects, I'll be back well before harvesting time. And whatever *expansions* are required, I can see to them myself."

The Judge blinked. "But…but who will look after the negroes?"

Lucas sighed. "As I've just said, Father, I will—"

"Horace and a few hired hands will stay behind," Henry replied, speaking over his brother. "Horace won't be happy about keeping back, but he'll do as I say."

In her mind's eye, Sarah saw Henry riding off to war atop his horse. She saw him receding into the distance, a small figure becoming smaller and smaller before disappearing. And as she imagined Henry gone away for some unknown length of time, a sense of great joy awakened within her. But as soon as she felt such happiness, she became ashamed of it. Just what kind of wife, even one mistreated, should crave that a war might take her husband away from her? She recalled seeing those teenaged widows in black, all of them shut away in stuffy parlors at parties. Oh Lord, whatever Arcadia's woes, let her not join *their* solemn company.

"There are plenty of men already off fighting," Judge Cutler said. He reached out to Henry and offered his hand with a grave, pleading look. "I urge you, my boy, *don't go*. Let the other fathers mourn their sons. Our cause is glorious, to be sure, but it is not worth—"

"It is God's cause," Lucas affirmed, "and I am proud of Henry for answering the call."

"As am I," Sarah said.

In the silence that followed, she bowed her head and prepared herself for some nasty retort from Henry. But when the silence persisted, she looked up at Henry. He looked small and afraid and on the verge of tears. Seeing this, she offered him the most loving, reassuring smile she could manage (which in that moment was not very much, but it looked convincing enough).

"Though my heart breaks at the prospect of your leaving, Henry, I do adore you for your decision. You are doing a very noble thing, a brave thing. You are defending your country and your home. You are safeguarding a brighter future for our children."

At the mention of *children*, the Cutlers all blushed and looked into their laps.

"We've been married almost a year now," Sarah said. "Do you remember what you said to me on our wedding day, Henry? I remember it well. You said that you wished you didn't have to live through such evil times, but that you believed you had the strength to overcome the coming crisis and rise above it. You said you would meet whatever may come, for the sake of the unborn."

Henry began to tremble in his chair. The vindictive bully that had sat there moments before was gone, and in his place sat a quivering boy. Unable to bear the situation any longer, Henry muttered something under his breath, pushed back from the table, and abandoned the dining room.

The Cutlers continued their breakfast in stilted silence. The Judge glared at Lucas with bitter contempt before hiding himself behind his newspaper once more.

Sarah felt the weight of Mrs. Cutler's stare on her, and she could read blame in the old woman's eyes. Rather than shy away, Sarah lifted her chin and met her mother-in-law's gaze with a smile until Mrs. Cutler was obliged to look away.

Penelope soon entered the dining room, skipping along without a care in the world. The Judge and Mrs. Cutler welcomed their daughter and showered idle praises upon her, and Mrs. Cutler snapped her fingers at the servants and ordered her daughter's every whim to be catered to, post-haste. Watching all this, Sarah felt a measure of envy over Penelope's innocence. She realized it had not been so long ago that she herself had been so wide-eyed and impressionable.

What could be said of Sarah now? She was getting older and more bitter by the day, like another Cousin Isabella in the making. How soon until her envy of Penelope's youthful promise devolved into resentment?

And how soon until Sarah, like Cousin Isabella, came to loathe her own husband? Had she already unwittingly slipped into such a mindset now? Hadn't she just goaded her husband into signing up for war?

Sarah became aware that Lucas was staring at her. Looking up, she saw that Lucas offered a knowing smile. Suddenly, whatever appetite Sarah still had deserted her, and promptly she stood up and excused herself from the table.

❧

On the day her husband left for war, Sarah Cutler felt a lightness in her heart that she knew she ought to be ashamed about. Still, as she watched Henry prepare to depart, she did not know whether to laugh or cry.

She looked out at the spectacle laid out before her. The whole of Arcadia's servants had come out to see their young master off. Nearly a thousand black men, women, and children — the sheer number of them was staggering to look upon — stood before the big-house with their hats in their hands. They watched in formal silence as Henry shook hands first with Horace Glanton, now Lucas, and now with his father. Judge Cutler reached out and took his son into a tearful embrace.

Henry approached Sarah next. He leaned down to kiss her, but for whatever reason she turned her cheek. It was a subtle move, but Henry certainly took notice. Still, he did not become angry or mocking, and instead he kissed Sarah's cheek and touched her hand with great tenderness.

"I love you, Sarah. Think better of me while I'm gone."

Suddenly, Sarah began to doubt her resolve. Was she really so giddy at the prospect of her husband riding off to war, and possibly to his death? Even as she whispered a flat-toned, "I love you," back to Henry, she tried to rationalize that yes, Henry's leaving would be the best thing for their marriage. Sarah needed time to heal, and perhaps Henry needed time out in the world to grow up.

But as Henry turned away at last, Sarah could not help but feel that she had betrayed her husband somehow, was *in the act* of betraying him. Perhaps it was she who needed to grow up, she who needed to realize that, whatever problems they had as a married couple (and Lord knew there were many), ignoring them or delaying them would do nothing but deepen the resentments that were already starting to form.

Henry went to kiss his mother's hand. Mrs. Cutler wailed with a mother's despair. Sarah looked at the old woman with a quiet bewilderment. How was it that Sarah herself was not overcome with sickening anguish? After all, she was Henry's wife. His true love. At least, that's what she called herself.

Sarah felt a soft touch on her fingers. Little Penelope reached up and took Sarah's hand in her own, and the sweet girl smiled up at her with adoration. Sarah smiled back, and here for the first time she felt a hitch of raw emotion. Her lips quivered, and her eyes glistened with tears. But looking out at Henry again, who was just now mounting his horse, the urge to cry died without fanfare. Sarah remained dry-eyed and stone-faced, uncertain of what to feel or exactly how much she ought to feel about anything in the first place.

Had she really come to loathe Henry? Had she really come to *hate* her husband?

No, of course not. She was only hurt by him, and Henry, he wouldn't *listen*...

But for pity's sake, what of *marriage*? What of love and loyalty, of faithfulness?

Judge Cutler stepped up to Henry astride his horse and looked out at all the servants gathered around.

"You folk," the Judge began, suddenly pausing as emotion caught in his throat. When he looked up again, tears rolled down his cheeks. "You folk ought to be *thankful*. Look here at my boy. My proud, noble boy is riding off to war to keep you-all safe and free under our protection."

The slaves stared in silence.

As Sarah watched, a shiver ran down the length of her spine. Oh, she refused to be a failure, in marriage or in anything else. She refused to become like Cousin Isabella, to let her marriage wither until her love shrunk to a decaying husk. Why must she give up on Henry so soon? They were married only a single *year*, after all, and there was a lifetime yet to live. A man like Henry was difficult to change, but she had to believe that he *could* change.

What was more, Sarah could not bear the idea of giving up on Henry himself. Even as she looked at him now, Sarah felt the quiet stirrings of hope. He'd hurt her — *terribly*, and in more ways than one. But she'd lived. She'd overcome the dark hours. Their *marriage* had overcome. It *would* overcome, if only given enough time. If only she could remain strong for her husband.

The ugliness was not permanent — it couldn't be. That much she knew had to be true. No evil ever lasted in the world, but could eventually be softened and washed away, like fine sand in the surf. The darkness in a man's heart needed loving care from his wife, and he needed time and space to heal, and yes, sometimes that meant the caregiver would be hurt. But it was *worth it,* because over time Henry's evil would release from him as a piercing splinter retracted from flesh.

But did she really believe all that?

The answer, she supposed, wasn't quite so simple. There were some things in life that depended on nothing but *faith.*

Still speaking to the assembly of slaves, Judge Cutler said, "As he departs on his journey to defeat the monstrous Yankee invader, I want you to show your master the respect and gratitude he deserves. God bless him."

Arcadia's servants answered in unison: *God bless Marse Henry.*

Henry didn't let on about his own feelings regarding the whole matter. He maintained a stoic expression through the proceedings, and rather looked like he wished the whole thing would hurry along.

Henry turned his horse and started down the path toward the main road. Arcadia's servants turned and followed him en masse, and they began to cheer and applaud and whistle. Their energy was at first dour and languid, but maybe seeing the Cutler men with whips and weapons in hand the servants' spirit became a joyous fanfare.

Henry stopped to turn his horse round and round in the dirt, the same trick that had once delighted Sarah so long ago, and the servants laughed and cheered as his horse danced. As if he too recalled their courtship, Henry looked at Sarah. Despite the distance between them, she could see quite clearly the warm smile on his lips.

And despite herself, despite *everything,* Sarah smiled back at him.

Oh, God bless Master Henry.

"Wait!" Sarah cried. "Wait for me, Henry!"

She picked up her skirts and hurried after him. The slaves parted for her like a human Red Sea, and they gazed upon her with awe and wonder. When Sarah finally reached Henry's side, she reached up to him. And Henry, taking Sarah's hand, leaned over far in his saddle. They kissed, and suddenly Sarah was transported back in time to their days of courtship (which seemed like so many years ago now). The slaves cheered and sang while their young master and mistress demonstrated their love. And indeed, Sarah did feel a rekindled love surge through her, and she determined never to stop kissing Henry, never to let go.

But let go they finally did, Henry's hand lingering to grace Sarah's cheek. She saw tears in his eyes — true tears, the kind Henry hated to show anyone, including Sarah. And with that, Henry called out to his horse and turned away, and then he went galloping down the path with ferocious energy. Small black children chased the clouds of dust in a hopeless pursuit of horse and master. When the dust settled at last, Henry was gone.

Sarah watched the space where Henry had been, still feeling the sensation of his lips on hers. Her darling Henry was gone for a soldier, and she missed him already.

The whole of Arcadia stood silent in the late morning heat. Judge Cutler, who watched the road for a long time until no sight nor sound could be made of his son, finally turned to face the congregated servants once more. He opened his mouth wide to give some other speech, but just then his emotions overtook him and he instead put his head into his hands. Seeing this, Lucas Cutler gave a firm nod to Horace Glanton, the head overseer.

Glanton uncoiled his bullwhip and threw back his head. "Niggers: *back to work*!"

Chapter 42

REVEILLE

From the riverbank, Jem saw her there in the moonlit water: a pale figure with silver hair blazing chill white. Steam rose up from the water's surface — steam from body heat. She turned and looked back at him, and that was all the motivation he needed.

The chill of the water would have given him pause at any other time but this one. He couldn't remember when he had removed his clothes, but he was naked now. He waded in, slowly but deliberately. He splashed his chest and arms and kicked his feet up and cut through the silken water in a single stroke until he tread water before her.

"Stand up," she said.

He let his feet float down and they sank into the riverbed. The mud was greasy but somehow warm, and he felt a shiver run up his spine. Their breath misted in the early morning air, two clouds rising and dissipating and coming together like a tempest in miniature. She drifted toward him and finally he felt her skin on his. He pulled her closer and they shivered against each other.

Jem's blood pumped hot. He could not say anything. His mind, meanwhile, was insistent: *Don't say anything.*

Audrey swept an arm out into the river. A vision of night stars nuzzled into the water's surface winked and bobbed in the wake of her motion. He saw those same stars and the white linen moon reflected in her eyes, and now he even saw himself there in two beads of darkness crowned with green ivy.

Though their bodies were like ice, Jem felt a growing warmth. He pushed his body against hers. He lifted her up in his arms and she clutched at him. Her hand guided him and suddenly he felt her own warmth in the cool rippling, and they both sighed and trembled. They moved together as the river around them flowed silken and silent. Somewhere in the distance, Jem heard the faint call of heavenly trumpets.

Sighing louder now, Audrey whispered to him: "Jem…oh, Jem…"

And then, he heard the voice louder in his ears: "…Jem…Jem…"

"*Jem?* Wake up, Jem. Wake up!"

Suddenly, his eyes cracked open.

Audrey was gone, her angelic face replaced by that of Sugar Dave Dixon wearing a look of grave concern. Suddenly, Jem realized he was back in his tent, back at the army camp outside Winchester. The heavenly sound of trumpets was just the brassy call of the camp bugler sounding *reveille*, the signal to wake.

With a heavy sigh, Jem closed his eyes.

"Shit..."

The bugle kept blowing. Across the tent, George Hunt lumbered to his feet. "I'm up, dammit! That boy sounds like a drowning duck."

Hunt threw the tent flaps open, and a slash of searing light drove spikes into Jem's eyes. The flap mercifully closed again. Outside, Hunt shuffled about hacking phlegm. After a moment, there came the sound of streaming urine.

Jem groaned, exhausted. It felt like he had only just put his head down to sleep, his whole body spent from the previous day's hard drilling. But now it was all about to begin again.

"Hey, Jem."

Jem wiped the sleep from his eyes. "Yeah, Davey."

"You were talkin in your sleep."

"Was I? Just a dream, I guess."

"Good one?"

Just then, Jem felt the wetness around his crotch. Goddammit.

"Well," he mumbled, "it certainly felt real."

Morning light carved through the tent as George Hunt opened the flap from outside. "Maybe they're going to surprise us with breakfast," he called in. "A *real* breakfast. Fat bacon, a dozen eggs per man, fresh bread with cream, sausages the size of my pecker..."

Sugar Dave peered out at the world beyond the tent. "No luck. Some of the companies are forming up in full dress."

Ed Ripley sat up in the far corner of the tent. He had been murmuring prayers under his breath this whole time until Dave's question roused him. "Well I'll be cussed," he murmured. "It's Sunday. They ain't supposed to drill us on Sunday. I thought Colonel Jackson was supposed to be a God-fearin man."

Clutching his blanket against his waist, Jem crawled over and looked out at the world. The sky was slowly changing from inky black to indigo to a grayish blue. Silhouettes of uniformed boys moved hurriedly across the painted canvas of morning light. Sergeants were barking orders to form ranks.

Jem withdrew from the tent flap and sat on his bedroll again. He tried to remember the details of his dream, but they were fading too quickly.

Ripley threw back the covers of his bedroll and pulled his boots over two bare feet. "They ain't rousing a worshipful man on a Sunday. I'm gonna tell that pompous Tidewater bastard Lowery it ain't sanctified."

Lieutenant Franklin Lowery was the company's executive officer and chief drillmaster. He'd been sent to Winchester as part of a contingent of professional regulars who had recently resigned their US Army posts to serve the cause of the Confederate States. It was Lowery's job to get the Mayfair boys in fighting shape in time for the 'big dustup', which was set to happen any day now.

Jem looked up at Ripley. "You're really going to talk to Lowery about it?"

"Not just that," Ripley said. "I'm gonna tell him exactly what's on my mind, and then I'm gonna tell him exactly where he can go."

Later, in front of the full company, Ripley attempted just this. But he had no sooner begun his protestations to Lieutenant Lowery than the officer's face colored purple with an unholy fury.

"I don't give a goddamn what you think!" Lowery snarled. "I saw plenty of shitstains like you down in Mexico get their heads replaced with cannonballs, and all on account of them *thinking* instead of following orders. Form up for the roll, Private, or I *will* yank those buck teeth out of your fucking face."

Shocked, Ripley nodded meekly. "Yessir. Right away, sir."

Ripley rejoined the formation under a hail of whistles and catcalls.

When Ripley had returned, Jem leaned over to him and whispered, "You forgot to tell him where to go."

"Hush it."

The company stood in formation. They were a hundred and thirty-five all told, mostly boys from Mayfair and some others from the surrounding villages of Capon Bridge, Berryville, and Mountain Falls.

Jem had learned the organization quite quickly. Fiftyish men made a platoon, and two or three platoons made a company. Ten companies made a regiment, five regiments made a brigade. Three brigades made a division, and two divisions made a corps. Put two corps together and you had an army. Put all the armies together and you had *the Army*, the Confederate States Army (CSA).

Or something like that, anyway.

As far as Jem understood, the only unit of any consequence was the regiment, which numbered about a thousand men. The Mayfair boys' regiment was the 2nd Virginia Infantry. The regiment's number had caused a terrific scandal when the boys first heard it. Why were they the *2nd* and not the *1st*? Couldn't they change their number? The boys were consoled somewhat by the knowledge that they were at least part of the *1st Brigade*, a unit of four thousand men under the command of a Virginian colonel named Thomas Jackson.

Jem had yet to see Colonel Jackson for himself, though common knowledge held that he was an ex-instructor at the Virginia Military Institute, and a Mexican fighter to boot. Apparently Jackson was also a man of the Old Testament, as vengeful as Hammurabi. But if the colonel was anything like Lieutenant Lowery—

"ATTEN-*TION*!"

Jem abandoned his train of thought and stood erect, silent and statue-like.

Lieutenant Lowery was a stickler for form and cleanliness. He wove through the ranks inspecting the boys one by one, pointing out infractions as he saw them. Few men escaped the morning roll without being called out for having dirty fingernails or bad posture or a loose thread on his shirtsleeve. Marching front and center once more, Lowery said in a booming voice:

"The company commander would like a word."

Here, Captain Claiborne stepped forward. Old Clay was really in his element as a soldier, this time the leader of a real *company* of uniformed soldiers, not just a rabble of country militiamen. Claiborne's boyish giddiness in the pomp and circumstance of army drilling was perhaps endearing, but it did not exactly inspire much confidence.

"Good morning, boys."

—*Good morning, Captain*!

Claiborne flashed a broad grin. "The bigwigs are in town, gentlemen. General Joseph E. Johnston and his staff arrived here yesterday evening from Richmond. I've just received word from Colonel Jackson that there is to be a grand review for the general this afternoon. While the rest of the brigade marches, our regiment will form up for musket drills and firing practice. I remind you that the general and his staff will be watching you *closely*. I want all you men polished up and on your best behavior, and for God's sake hit your targets. Is that understood?"

—*Yes, Captain*.

"Very good!" Claiborne stepped back with a nod of encouragement. "In other news, here's something that should interest you boys. To help instill a little good feeling among the men, and to inspire a hard-fighting, Yankee-killing spirit in all of you, there is to be a regimental boxing tournament following today's drilling. Companies will put forward the names of two men who will fight for the honor of representing their company in a regimental contest next week. The week after that, the regimental winner will fight others in the brigade."

Still holding ranks, the men turned their heads together and babbled excitedly.

"*Eyes forward*!" Lowery bellowed, and instantly the company went silent once more.

Claiborne placed his hands behind his back and assumed the stern look of a chastising father. "The fights are to be clean, both inside and outside the ring. There is to be *no drinking* during the fights, and *no gambling* of any sort. Is that understood?"

Almost as one body, the company grimaced. No booze? No *betting*? But the boys were slowly becoming soldiers, and a soldier's life is chock full of disappointments. The company sounded its begrudging understanding.

To the full view of everyone, Claiborne now offered a knowing wink. "Those are the official orders from on high. But *discretion* is the better part of valor. You understand what I mean by discretion, don't you, boys?"

Lowery's head snapped to Claiborne, and the lieutenant's eyes dulled with derision. But the damage had already been done: the realization of Claiborne's true meaning swept through the boys like a wave. The rules would be enforced all right, but only if there was reason to go looking for rulebreakers.

"And now," Claiborne said, "I leave you in the very capable hands of Mr. Lowery. Thank you, boys."

—*Thank you, Captain*!

The boys turned together and started to chatter about their great luck when Lowery, determined to whip the Mayfair boys into shape despite a soft-hearted captain, stepped forward with a martial air.

"On the drill ground in sixty seconds — with arms. Company, *fall out*!"

The boys turned and raced back to retrieve their weapons stacked together near the tents. As the boys pushed and clambered over each other to snatch up a musket, all conversations were dominated at the prospect of THE FIGHT. Who would fight? Who would clobber all?

George Hunt, meanwhile, clicked his tongue with open disgust. "Drill, drill, drill. I swear, they must think our close-order drill is gonna make the Yankees shit themselves so bad they just squat on home."

"It ain't right," Ripley insisted. "This is the Lord's day."

"It's the *Confederate Army's* day," Lowery shouted from the rear. Evidently the lieutenant had the ears of a fox. "It's the CSA's day today, and it'll be the CSA's day tomorrow, and the next day, and the next day. And I promise you, gentlemen: you fuck up for me today, there'll be no pussy-footed boxing match for you. *One minute*, gentlemen! Fall in, on the double!"

❧

Four weeks prior, just days after mustering in Mayfair's main square, Jem and the Mayfair boys entered the camps around Winchester for the first time. Then, the 'Confederate States Army' had been more like a mob of men in a patchwork of obsolete uniforms and plain working clothes. Only one in five boys had a rifled musket; the others carried old flintlocks and shotguns, squirrel guns and hobby bows. Sam Hanley even carried a broadsword, a dull family heirloom that took two hands to wield.

Most boys were given uniforms, new CSA issue, stiff and woolen and gray and handsome. When the uniforms ran out, others were given homespun militia rags of various shapes and sizes that were dyed butternut brown to create some vague sense of uniformity. The vast majority of boys came threadbare and barefoot, some not owning shoes and others thinking them unnecessary for hunting Yankees in the dry brush and open fields around Washington.

Every door in the handsome and sizable town of Winchester was opened wide to the boys, and every day without fail the citizens lined the streets to cheer for them. Already, the boys felt like war heroes. The Mayfair boys also soon realized just how *country* they really were. For years they had believed Mayfair was a metropolis, but now they were faced with some twenty thousand strange and adoring faces. Upon entering Winchester the first time, Sugar Dave exclaimed, "I do believe I seen more folk in one day than a whole lifetime in the Valley."

The Mayfair boys met Winchester boys, and they met Kernstown boys, Berryville and Stephensburg boys, and soon they would meet the boys from Harper's Ferry who, according to wild rumors, had dug up John Brown's body at Charles Town and were any day expected to parade into Winchester with the corpse set aflame, a banner of rage and vindication to surely staunch the bravest of the Yankee rabble.

Whatever Jem and the Mayfair boys thought of comrades carrying burning bodies, to say nothing of what it might smell like, the meeting at Winchester had a festive atmosphere. Worlds were colliding, and the energy for fistfights and gambling was as intoxicating as the liquor the boys drank and the food they gorged on. But pervading any festive atmosphere was an existential purpose, a need to *do something*. The men began to ask questions: Who was really in charge anyway, and why weren't they *doing something*? Weren't there damned Yankees afoot?

The self-appointed 'officers', all high-horse members of the planter gentry from the surrounding counties, certainly believed they were doing something. These captains and lieutenants, Clay Claiborne included, convened a large meeting in Winchester's largest saloon, barring entry to 'enlisted yeomen' and reserving the best liquors for themselves. It was during this meeting that companies were officially organized. The Mayfair boys were slotted as L Company, 2nd Virginia Infantry Regiment.

Slowly, a sense of unity began to permeate. Soon enough the boys from Mayfair became friendly with the boys from Berryville and elsewhere. Even if the desire to get out and fight Yankee scum was all-consuming, the growing bond between the militia groups was something the boys took to nurturing.

After only a few short days of fun, the 'regulars' arrived on horseback. These men were bonafide commissioned officers from places like Lynchburg and Richmond, some educated at West Point and others at the Virginia Military Institute. They were men who had until very recently fought under the Stars and Stripes, and they were none too impressed by the rabble of wannabe soldiers that greeted them. The animosity and distrust was for the most part mutual. Most of these old husks appeared too long in the tooth to the Mayfair boys, being creaking antiques of thirty years or older.

One of these young Napoleons was ordered to serve as L Company's executive officer. Franklin Lowery, hailing from Hampton Roads in the Tidewater, was said to be of very good First Family stock. His features were sharp and wolflike, and rumors told of Lowery's inability to smile; some suggested it was an actual medical diagnosis. Lowery was sharp and capable, but not even he could make up for Clay Claiborne's supreme lack of military acumen. Lowery tried his best to maintain composure while instructing a hapless Claiborne in the delivery of a proper salute. Watching Claiborne's stubborn clumsiness opposite Lowery's growing frustration, the Mayfair boys snickered and winked at each other.

Within the regiment, each company had the opportunity to name itself. A variety of names were put forward for L Company: the Valley Boys, Claiborne's Comanches, the Berryville Bastards. But to the boys of Mayfair, making up a super-majority, there was only one company name that would do. From beginning to end the boys would be the Mayfair Mavericks. That name won the company vote by a stunning margin, and for weeks afterward the boys tipped their forage caps and addressed each other as, "Mav'rick." Even those boys not from Mayfair itself took pride in the name.

Lowery and the regulars were keen on whipping the raw recruits into fighting shape. Part of this process involved stripping the boys of all the comforts of home. Jem and the other Mavericks awoke one morning to discover the trunks and suitcases that they had lugged all the way from the Valley (and which contained any number of trinkets, foodstuffs, and jars of preserves) were burning in a great bonfire. Animal companions, including pet dogs and cats and even Ripley's chickens, were 're-homed' to the citizens of Winchester or else driven off into the dark forests surrounding the camp.

Not even Greenbrier was spared. The plucky colt was confiscated so that he could serve elsewhere, either as a cavalry mount or a work horse. With eyes blazing, Jem clutched his musket and swore to kill Lowery if he so much as looked at his beloved colt, but Sugar Dave and George Hunt talked Jem down from that tree. Heartbroken, Jem could do nothing but say goodbye to Greenbrier. He embraced the colt's sinewy neck and broke down crying when Greenbrier gnawed at his knuckles in search of crabapples. Wiping away his tears, Jem watched helpless as an orderly took Greenbrier away by the halter.

And the drilling went on.

May marched into June. Colonel Jackson was promoted to General Jackson, and meanwhile the ranks of the brigade grew day by day, week by week. Before long the brigade was compelled to abandon the town limits of Winchester and make a new camp in the hills far away from town. There was another reason for this move, particularly that too many boys shirked camp duties in order to spend time frolicking in town. Orders came down that leaving camp was now impossible without an official pass. To desert one's post became a capital offense.

"What the hell is that supposed to mean?" George Hunt had asked.

Lieutenant Lowery's reply was matter of fact: it meant death by firing squad.

The seriousness of this order was made all too clear to the boys when a young private from G Company, just a boy of fifteen, decided one night he'd had enough of army life and started off for home. His disappearance might have gone entirely unnoticed, except that when he left the boy was supposed to be on sentry duty. The boy was found, promptly court-martialed and, with the laws as they were, sentenced to death. This sparked an uproar and hundreds of boys threatened to desert, until finally General Jackson commuted the sentence. The sentry boy was assigned to the miserable task of latrine duty "...until the war is won, or until Doomsday," Jackson said, "whichever comes first." Jackson also sent word down to the company commanders that, in the future, any and all deserters would be executed by firing squad.

And the drilling (and more drilling) went on.

As the brigade's ranks swelled, the boys learned of a phenomenon known as the 'army camp cough.' It began each morning before *reveille* at daybreak. The early risers wandered around camp like specters in the night, hacking into their palms and wiping runny noses. At *reveille*, thousands of cramped boys rose at once and stretched stiff bones that cracked like the sound of axes chipping at old trees. They groaned and coughed together like an entire forest being felled at once.

Upon waking, the boys had a few minutes to whip up a hasty breakfast over the cooking fires, provided they could start them. From dawn to dusk the boys drilled, drilled, and drilled. They marched in open ranks and they marched in closed ranks. They presented and shouldered arms until they began to perform the actions in their dreams as they slept. They route-stepped and counter-columned and marked time and marched by the flanks, and only sometimes did the boys understand what they were doing. By nightfall the boys collapsed around the campfires and cooked up whatever rations they could manage, and they spent the precious hours until 'lights out' talking and smoking and cussing and playing cards.

One evening, after the day's drilling had finally ended, Jem sat around the campfire with his friends. He held his right foot into the firelight to examine a stretch of painful blisters running along his heel.

"Our boots'll be worn out before we so much as sniff a Yankee," Sugar Dave said.

There was some activity a few fires down. Looking up, Jem peered through the smoky darkness. Down the way he saw a group of boys greeting a newcomer. Squinting, Jem finally recognized who it was.

"Well I'll be goddamned."

It was Henry Cutler.

Biting his cheek against the pain, Jem pulled his boots on and stood up. Wearing a broad smile, he limped over to Henry surrounded by other fellows. "Make way there, boys," Jem called. "Make way, if you please. That's my brother-in-law, don't you know."

Henry stood in the center of a circle that included Percy Claiborne and a host of noncoms. Jem listened as Henry took the boys on a crass geographic tour of the vulva when the sickening realization hit Jem that Henry was talking about *Sarah*. Jem forced a nauseous smile and waited for Henry to finish his lewd accounts of the marital bed. Finally sensing an opening, Jem stepped forward.

"Hiya, Henry," he said, offering his hand. "Great to have you with us, brother."

The South Branch boys turned and looked at Jem with half-lidded gazes, as if a rat had crawled into their presence. Henry smiled at Jem, but it looked more like an embarrassed grimace.

"I've just made Cutler a sergeant," Percy Claiborne announced with a sneer. "It ain't right for *private soldiers* to fraternize with men of higher rank."

Jem ignored Percy and instead flashed a wink at Henry. "First day here and you've already made sergeant. I suppose you know just where the dog likes the scratch, huh?" Jem's hand twitched; he still held it out, waiting for a handshake.

Percy glared at Jem and said coldly, "That will be all, *Private*."

Finally, Henry stepped forward. "That's all fine, Percy," he said, and he took Jem's hand and shook it. He made eye contact for only a brief moment. "Nice to see you again, Jem."

That might have been that, for Henry had already turned back to carry on with his friends. Still smiling, Jem took another step forward and caught Henry's attention once more.

"And how's the missus?" Jem asked, thinking it an innocent inquiry.

The boys standing around snickered at the question. Henry blushed a little and shrugged. To every ear that would listen he said: "Oh, you boys know she's been well cared for."

The air filled with cheers and catcalls. Sam Hanley stuck his fingers in his mouth and made a shrieking whistle like a steam engine. The boys laughed together and pushed against Henry, ribbing and cajoling. But though the others laughed with Henry, Jem realized he was only laughing at himself. He found himself steadily pushed back by overeager bodies, and finally he was forced away out of the circle entirely. Disheartened, Jem walked backward with his eyes still on Henry. He tripped over something in the darkness and splayed out on all fours, but no one seemed to notice. Picking himself up, Jem turned and trudged back to his tent.

Days later, news went around that Sergeant Charlie Borden had woken up with a fever. He was admitted to the camp hospital by nightfall, and it wasn't a week before he was dead. Typhoid, the regimental doctor said. Suddenly the idea of the 'army camp cough' lost its humor, and instead it became a grim reminder that the chances of contracting one disease or another increased exponentially with each passing day.

"And it makes sense, doesn't it?" George Hunt said one night as they sat around the campfire feeling morose. "Most of these boys have never been off the farm in their lives. Now they come to a place where there's five thousand men shitting and pissing at their feet, and here we all are sleeping in it, and eating around it. When you live like a pig, boys, you're bound to die like one."

A few days after Charlie Borden died, a gruesome bout of dysentery drained poor Sam Hanley until someone found him sitting up dead near one of the latrines. The sudden death of a healthy highborn terrified the wealthy South Branch boys, and Jem knew he'd be lying if he said it didn't scare him too. He started to boil his drinking water.

In the third week of June, a fever struck down Henry Cutler.

Jem visited Henry in a Presbyterian church in Winchester, which was being used as a hospital for the sick. The pews and floors were thick with boys suffering from all manner of ailments. Henry lay frozen on a pew under a blanket, his hands clutched around his abdomen, his sallow face a rictus of terrible pain. When Henry opened his eyes, Jem saw they were spotted yellow. They spoke little before a nurse shooed Jem away. The nurse assured Jem that Henry's condition was not as serious as the others. "He just needs rest," the nurse explained, "but he won't get no rest with hangers-on like you buzzing around him."

The next day, the decaying bodies of Charlie Borden, Sam Hanley, and seventeen other Valley boys were sent home by horse and wagon. None of the nineteen were victims of bullets; all of them were struck down by typhoid from rancid pork and beef, typhus from fleas, influenza and pneumonia from other boys coughing around them. It was what some of the regulars like Lowery darkly referred to as 'the culling,' suggesting that such deaths were a matter of course in army life. Panic set in when unfounded rumors exploded that the 1st Brigade's overflowing latrines had leached into the river where the boys swam and took their drinking water.

Henry Cutler was sent home with another wagonload of Mayfair boys. They were not dead — not yet, anyway. Jem bid Henry a solemn goodbye and wished him good luck. He requested a leave of furlough to escort Henry home safely, and maybe to linger a day or two in order to visit Audrey. He craved Audrey's touch and the sound of her voice, and he missed his family, and with each passing day the pangs of longing increased.

Lieutenant Lowery denied Jem's request. "There's a war on, Private. We all need to learn to live with homesickness."

As the days of drudgery wore on, and as each new case of illness was counted, the festive atmosphere of camp life darkened. The boys got used to boiling gray river water before drinking it. Some went so far as to drink only the steam they collected off the boiling. All the while, the hard drilling continued. In each boy, the desire to escape the putrefied stillness of camp and get into the damn war became more urgent than ever before.

And the drilling (and still more drilling) went on, and on, and on.

"*FIRE!*"

Jem squeezed the trigger and the hammer shot forward. The hammer crushed the cap. The sparked flame surged through the nipple into the barrel where it set off the powder charge.

Down the range, the scarecrows arranged as targets exploded in gusts of smoke and straw.

The bullets the Mavericks fired were 'minnie balls', half-inch lead slugs that rattled down the barrel before exploding from the muzzle. The Springfield rifled musket was accurate up to 250 yards, but its minnie ball projectile was still lethal at over half a mile.

The sobering physics of the minnie ball was described to the boys by a loud and dispassionate Lieutenant Lowery. Steps apart from the target, a minnie could sever a leg at the knee, completely rip off an arm at the elbow, and fully decapitate a man. The minnie was prone to mushrooming, which meant a gutshot was a death sentence.

As the smoke cleared from the firing range, Jem watched with horrified fascination as the straw guts of one of the scarecrows burst aflame.

Lowery stood behind Jem and said flatly, "Good work, Roscoe. You just blew a hole in that Fed's stomach the size of a watermelon. Watch he doesn't do the same to you."

Jem swallowed hard and set to reloading.

"Reload and prepare to fire!" Lowery called. "*Reload*, goddammit! Those Yankee sons of bitches have just fired a volley and killed the man on either side of you. When are you piss-proud idiots going to return the favor? *Reload*!"

Later, after the Mavericks had finished at the firing range, there were great discussions as to who would fight in the company boxing match that evening. Candidates were offered and withdrawn and offered again, and the debates raged on. Slowly, however, a consensus started to build.

"*Not a chance*," Jem protested when the news reached him. "Not a chance in hell!"

"You can't back out," George Hunt said solemnly. "Your name's on the list."

"List? What list? I didn't put my name on any damn list!"

"Somebody wrote it," Hunt said. "Captain Claiborne's seen it too. He says it's all set."

"All set?!" Jem could not believe what he was hearing. "They really think I'm going to trade fists with Ezra Blake?"

Sugar Dave, who was sitting nearby at a small cooking fire, shook his head sorrowfully. "Nobody thinks you're gonna trade. They think you're gonna take every lump he throws at you."

"You're gonna get whipped, is what they say," Ed Ripley added.

Dismayed, Jem went off to find the dreaded list his friends talked about. As it turned out, there really was a list of fighters and Jem's name really was on it. Several other contenders had been listed, but their names had been systematically crossed out until only 'E. Blake' and 'Roscoe' remained. The fight was scheduled for dusk.

Jem wandered about camp in a frantic state of mind. Already the sun was waning in the sky. Watchful eyes followed him everywhere he went, and trailing after him came all manner of jokes, condemnations, and dark predictions as to his fate. Jem's first instinct was to approach some higher authority. Lowery might put a stop to the charade, or maybe Captain Claiborne. Then again, Jem had no faith that Lowery would intercede on his behalf, and he knew just how much his jolly old company commander was predisposed against him.

Turning down a nearby street (a term used for the rows between lines of tents), Jem froze when he saw Ezra Blake crouched near a cooking fire. Blake, wearing a corporal's double chevrons on the sleeve of his uniform, was flanked on all sides by a thuggish gang of privates who looked over at Jem with lidded gazes. Whatever theory Jem had been formulating (that he could reason with Ezra Blake, and that perhaps they could announce a joint agreement calling off the fight), died without a whimper. Jem watched Blake bite a hunk of pork sidemeat, chew, and spit a large bone into the fire before Jem turned and trudged away, certain that his cause of self-preservation was now hopeless.

Jem returned to his own mess, sat down, and stared vacantly at the fire. There was no way to know whether he'd been selected as part of some conspiracy, whether the impending bone-crushing agony was some sort of revenge for what had happened up at the North Branch. In the end, he supposed it didn't really matter what the reason was. The fight was set.

Two years ago, when he had brashly agreed to a pistol duel with Percy Claiborne, Jem had felt nothing like the fear that gnawed at him now. The fear came later when JJ had impressed upon Jem just how easily a sober Percy would have gunned him down. The cold realization of death's nearness sank deeper when Jem saw Percy's mangled ear for the first time. And then, while plunging below the North Branch Mine after the collapse, Jem had kept his numbing fear in check only by focusing on the systematic, step-by-step search for survivors.

For most of Jem's life, the concept of Death had been an abstract theory, something that happened to old people. But ever since Jem had tasted the bitterness of several close calls, and since observing the wasting death of his father (who had been old, certainly, but still young enough that others claimed he *died young*), and now that he'd seen Death's invisible hand cut down almost two dozen boys his own age, Jem understood the theory was *fact*, the only fact that mattered. Of course, Jem told himself he was deluding himself to think that Ezra Blake would actually try to *kill him* that night. But then again, the possibility was not nearly as outrageous as he knew it ought to be.

So what could be done about it? Jem didn't have a clue, and so he burst out laughing at the absurdity of his situation.

"Poor Jem," Ripley said from across the fire. "He's gone loon-crazy."

George Hunt gnawed on a dry biscuit. "Oh, he's always been like this, Rip. You just only seen him on his good days."

"*Pshaw*!" Sugar Dave cried, and he shot to his feet. "I'm sick of this." He turned on Jem with a fire blazing in his eyes. "You just gonna give up before the fight's even started? You just gonna walk up and let him thrash you? You think anybody wants to see that?"

"I reckon there's every fellow in the company wants to see that," Hunt observed wanly. "Excepting us three, of course."

"George?"

"Yes, Davey."

"Shut up."

"Yes, Davey."

"Now," Sugar Dave said, and he squared Jem's shoulders. Jem's gaze lingered elsewhere, his mind lost in thought, and Dave slapped him across the face. "There. You fresh? Now listen to me, Jemmo. Laws, don't this bring back memories? Who you fightin *this* time? But now listen: there's a fact you know, and that is there's no way you can fight Blake square and win. So, you don't fight square."

Hunt spat. "What's he gotta do? Dress in feathers and squawk? That ain't no plan."

"Back when the redcoats were muckin about in the South," Sugar Dave said, "the rebels couldn't ever beat em in a square fight. So instead the rebels, all the militia boys like us, we ran into the hills like we was scared. We made it look like we were goners when we weren't. We dragged the redcoats all over the damn place, wore em out, waited for em to get tired and make a mistake. That's when we turned around and hit em, drove em back all the way to the coast, and that's why we still speak American today."

"Fine lesson, professor," Hunt said. "So, what? Our boy's gotta run for his life?"

Sugar Dave shook his head. "That ain't what I'm sayin."

"Then what is you sayin?" Ripley called.

"Wait," Jem said suddenly. Looking at Sugar Dave, he nodded slowly, as his mind began to formulate a strategy. "He's saying I have to wear Ezra down. Get close to him that he'll swing, but keep far enough away that I won't catch a paw. When he gets tired, he'll make a mistake."

"Right," Dave said, looking proud of himself. "And when he does, that's when you whip him."

Hunt bit his lip and shook his head. "Or he *won't* make a mistake, and he'll snap you like a dry match." He shrugged. "Listen, I'm just trying to outline all possibilities here."

"It ain't much of a hope," Ripley said, nodding to Jem and Dave, "but it's a hope."

"A loon-crazy hope is what it is," Jem admitted with a quiet laugh.

"It's a plan," Sugar Dave said. He and Jem shared a warm, affirming smile. Then, without warning, Dave lunged and tried to slap Jem across the face a second time. Jem was ready for it this time, and he dodged the blow and side-stepped out of reach.

"Not bad," Hunt said. Looking up, he nodded toward the crowd of Mavericks gathering near the parade grounds. The hulking figure of Ezra Blake was already there, standing a full head taller than all the others. "But I might point out, fellas, that our opponent's built like a brick shithouse, and he moves like one too. It ain't gonna be easy wearing him down."

"Won't be easy wearing the Yankees down either, despite what everybody says," Sugar Dave said. "But we all agreed it's worth a try, ain't it? Ain't this here worth a try?"

Jem laughed, and he felt a little better — less like getting a head start on digging his own grave, at least.

"I wish I had your optimism, Davey."

"Oh, you got it," Sugar Dave said with a wink. "I just gave it to you."

❧

As the sun began to set, the Mavericks formed a square. Some held torches in the fading light, while others were certain that the fight would be finished long before full darkness set in.

The combatants were stripped to the waist. Some noted that Roscoe was surprisingly well-built, but there had already been enough comparisons to David and Goliath that very few wagers were withdrawn or renegotiated. Without question, Ezra Blake was the favorite.

Percy Claiborne was to serve as the fight's referee, and he looked supremely pleased to have the best view of the impending action. When all the men of the company were assembled and the combatants waited at opposite corners of the makeshift ring, Percy took his position in the center.

"Gentlemen, to me!"

Taking a deep breath, Jem started forward. His first few steps were heaviest of all, as if he slogged through drying mud. At last he stood before Blake, who towered a full head taller than he. Only too late did Jem realize he was positioned in direct view of the setting sun. Jem squinted past the blinding sunlight and looked at Percy, but when he saw the smug, knowing expression on Percy's face he realized there was no point in saying anything about it.

"Shake hands!"

Jem offered his hand first, together with a final conciliatory look that he hoped would appeal to whatever sense of reason might exist in Ezra Blake's mind.

"Go on," Percy said to Blake. "Shake hands!"

Begrudgingly, Blake stuck out his mitt; it swallowed Jem's hand whole. Jem felt the bones in his hand crack and crumble as if he'd just thrust his hand into some industrial machine. He could read Blake's eyes scanning his own for signs of pain and anguish, but Jem channeled all the strength he had to refuse so much as a twitch of his brow.

"Take your stance!"

Blake finally let go. The huge man settled back into a ready stance, his trunk-like arms forming an impenetrable wall of flesh and bone.

Trying his best to ignore the screaming pain in his right hand — his *good* hand, for God's sake — Jem crouched down and brought up his fists to cover his face.

Percy looked from Jem to Blake, Blake to Jem. "No biting, kicking, or scratching. The last man standing is the winner." Throwing back his head, Percy called: "Gentlemen! You may commence fighting… *NOW*!"

A deafening chorus of shouts filled Jem's ears, and as he saw Ezra Blake lumber forward he wondered whether it might be easier to just kneel down and wait for the inevitable. Taking a sharp breath, Jem gathered together whatever courage he had left in him. As he strode forward to meet his adversary, he repeated the same string of words in his head:

Wear him—watch him—whip him

Wear him—watch him—whip him

Wear him—watch him—JESUS—!

He'd strayed too close to the killer bear, and a paw came swiping down. Jem evaded the blow just in time, but he felt a literal *woosh* of air as Blake's right fist sailed past his head. There was no time to recover, for Blake now hurled his left. Jem leaped aside and watched Blake stagger, the weight of his own punches dragging him forward.

Jem looked to his friends standing at the perimeter. They were all shouting something at him, but amid the incessant howling of the crowd he couldn't make out anything they were saying. He thought he heard Sugar Dave shout, "*Left!*"

Left. Blake's first punch had been right, so that had to be his dominant hand. If Jem had to take a punch, he'd let it be the left. *Watch the right, take the left* became another phrase Jem repeated under his breath as he circled around Blake, his entire world reduced to the sliver of space between his two braced arms. Blake jabbed and Jem dodged it easily, but when he backstepped he suddenly knocked into someone's foot and went barreling to the ground.

Tripped!

Jem looked up at Percy Claiborne, whose smug grin vanished when cries of *FOUL!* sounded from the crowd.

"Shut up!" Percy shouted back. "No foul, no foul!" He kicked at Jem, urging him to get back on his feet and continue the fight.

Jem picked himself up just as Blake lunged for him. Blake tried a right hook and swung wide. Jem's hungry eyes locked on Blake's kidneys — exposed for the briefest of seconds — and he lunged in for a strike of his own. But just as he committed, he heard George Hunt's voice streak over the crowd:

"His *left*, goddammit — *watch* his left!"

Too late, Jem saw that the right had been a fake. Blake's left rushed up and boxed Jem in the ear. Jem staggered, his vision suddenly blurry. Somehow, he was able to sense Blake closing the gap and dove out of reach at the last second.

The first round was fast. The second was endless. By the opening of the third, Jem felt his body growing heavier while Blake showed no signs of flagging — even after Jem landed three shots to Blake's rock-hard belly. The two-minute rounds would count up and up endlessly until one of the fighters was knocked out.

Or killed.

Jem had done well to protect his face so far, but just then Blake chinned him with a right uppercut. Fighting to maintain a face of stone (for if he showed the slightest wince, Blake would lunge for the kill), Jem wagged his head and ducked out of reach. Keeping close to the perimeter, he bounced on the balls of his feet.

"Quit yer dancin!" a voice from behind bellowed.

A set of hands from the crowd pushed Jem from behind and nearly knocked him to the ground. Indignant cries of *FOUL!* sounded from all around, and the crowd could not resist leaping upon the culprit (not a referee this time) to bludgeon him. Though many in the crowd were convinced Ezra Blake would soon break every bone in Jem Roscoe's body, they nevertheless demanded to see it done in a fair fight.

Wear him—watch him—whip him

Whip him?! Who in God's name was Jem kidding? Blake was a monster!

And yet, Jem could now see that Blake *was* starting to tire. The big brute was sucking in ragged gasps of air like he was an injured buffalo.

Wear him—watch him—WHIP HIM!

Deciding to bring some of the fight back to Blake, Jem advanced in a flurry of fast steps. Blake was caught sleeping and Jem landed one, two, three hard jabs on Blake's nose. The last jab triggered a gush of blood from Blake's nostrils.

A hush went up from the crowd, punctuated by a few cheers. Blake staggered back and groaned like a felled tree, and Jem was gripped by an insane hope that maybe, just maybe, he'd done enough. But no sooner did Jem begin to tremble at the prospect of possible victory did Blake steady himself and flash his blood-stained teeth in a knowing grin. Seeing this, the crowd hooted and bellowed.

Jem's best had been given, the last of his energy spent, and now Ezra Blake was going to close up shop.

When the first blow landed, Jem felt as if his brain had been dislodged from his skull. When the second struck, the mashed contents of his brain sloshed about in their confines. Jem no longer heard anything except the sound of his own labored breathing. He watched helplessly as Blake's third blow rushed up to greet him, and just before impact Jem had a vision of Audrey smiling at him.

The next thing Jem knew, he was on the ground looking up at a darkening sky. His body jerked and twitched as if he was controlled by an inept puppeteer. He felt the sensation of his head and shoulders being lifted up by invisible hands, even as he wanted nothing more than to sink deeper between individual blades of grass.

Ezra Blake thrust his bloody fists in the air, and this gesture was met by resounding cheers. Now came laughter, scattered applause, and a few grunts of *That's-a-boy, Ez* and *Showed im, Blake*. Even while Blake staggered about, grinning at his victory, most of the Mavericks turned immediately away from the makeshift ring to argue over the settlement of their wagers.

Only a few caught the first glimpse of Jem Roscoe getting up again.

Jem moved slowly, cautiously, feeling a hundred-pound weight tied to his neck. His fingers felt their way out in front of him, and now he pressed his palms down and pushed up from the ground. He drew up on his knees, and now he looked to be worshiping Blake's feet. But Jem kept moving, kept rising, until at last he'd managed to plant himself squarely upright. By now every head had turned back to look upon him. All eyes — even those of Ezra Blake — stared at Jem in stunned disbelief.

Blake's surprise did not linger long. Sizing up the punch-drunk Jem, Blake's eyes narrowed.

"You got nothin to prove, Roscoe. You got nothin worth provin."

Jem didn't reply. He spat two teeth and a gout of blood on the ground, and he ran his tongue over the empty spaces in his gums. He gritted his teeth against the searing pain and lifted his chin as high and proud as he could manage. He stared back at Blake with a quiet determination to stand his ground. From all around, voices in the crowd murmured together.

There was a flash of unthinking fury in Blake's eyes, and then Jem saw one of Blake's curled fists fly forward once again. The world went black, and Jem felt the vague sensation that he was flying. The crowd caught Jem's flailing arms and prevented him from collapsing. George Hunt and the others were there next instant, propping Jem up and looking into his eyes for some sign of consciousness.

"Jem? Jem, can you hear me? *Jesus*."

"Can he walk?" Ripley asked.

"He can't *stand*," Sugar Dave said.

"Lay him down," another man said. "His head's broke."

Jem felt hands pushing him down, felt a hand cupping his head, and he wanted to sink down again. God, he wanted to lay down more than anything. He yearned to just let go and let darkness take him.

"Them first two was for my brothers," Blake called. "But that one was just for me."

His senses submerged, Jem barely heard the ensuing laughter and catcalls. Again the others pushed him down to the ground, urging him to rest.

"It's done, Jemmo. It's done. You did good, but it's done."

Somehow, some part of Jem demanded resistance. Some force deep within him willed his legs to root themselves. Groggily, he pushed the others away and shrugged off their protests.

Jem fixed his bleary vision upon Blake, who was massaging his ballooning knuckles with a satisfied smile. When Blake looked at Jem and saw him still standing upright, the crooked smile curdled.

Again?!

Wheezing, barely able to stand up any longer, Jem staggered forward until he planted himself before Blake once more, as if offering himself in some kind of strange sacrifice.

Again.

With a growl, Blake snatched Jem by the throat and pulled a fist back to deliver the final, skull-crushing blow.

"That's enough, Blake."

It was Lowery, who stepped forward from the crowd wearing a dour grimace. Flashing a glare at Percy Claiborne, Lowery muttered, "You just going to stand there and let a man be killed?"

Claiborne shrugged and skulked away.

Lowery walked up to Blake and put a hand on the giant's heaving shoulder. "You got him, Blake. We all saw it. You're the bigger man, the better man. We know it."

Blake still held Jem in a death grip, his free fist shaking with anticipation. Staring back at Blake with swollen, bloodshot eyes that stung with sweat and blood, Jem resigned himself to his fate. He closed his eyes and waited for the final killing blow.

The blow, however, never came. Suddenly Jem could breathe again, and he realized that Blake had let him go. When Jem opened his eyes again, he saw Blake turn and push his way through the exalting crowd to the company street beyond. The victor, it seemed, no longer had any interest in staying to bask in his triumph. The crowd parted for him as he went, and when the circle closed it was as if Blake had never been there.

Still, there was plenty evidence of Blake's work — most of it was dripping from Jem's mouth and nostrils. Jem suddenly lost his footing and pitched back, and Hunt and the others caught him again.

Many Mavericks now stepped forward to get a closer look at Jem. Some of them were congratulatory, assuring Jem that he was, if nothing else, 'one tough sumbitch.' Some gazes from the crowd were vindictive, as if they believed the thrashing ought to continue. Others were neutral, their eyes acknowledging justice served. Many were simply astounded that anyone could actually remain standing after suffering such a decking from Ezra Blake.

"Let's get him out of here," Sugar Dave murmured to the others.

They tried to make Jem walk, but once again he pushed them back.

"I can do it," he insisted. "I can walk. I can..."

Planting his feet, Jem felt a little steadier now. He tried a ginger step forward, now another. As he took yet another step, the man closest him moved quietly aside. This inspired two others to move, and still more, until the sea of soldiers parted and a clear path lay open.

Feeling a surge of strength despite a swimming head, Jem kept putting one foot in front of the other. When his knees buckled and he nearly went down, several hands caught him and held him upright. The hands did not belong only to Sugar Dave or Ripley or Hunt, but to other boys in the company who moments before had cheered each time Jem was knocked down. These hands now held Jem up and guided him forward.

"Easy does it," one of the boys said. "We got you, brother."

Jem realized that some of the boys and men guiding him were miners from the North Branch. Jem couldn't be sure of their opinions of him, but at least they didn't appear to be opinions of hate or loathing. Maybe there was some sort of understanding in their eyes, a recognition of some kind. Maybe there was even encouragement, and some small measure of quiet admiration.

Easy does it. We got you, brother.

Feeling steadier now, Jem held his head high and started forward once more.

Chapter 43
BLUEBELLIES

Tom should have been thrilled when the Lynchburg Academy closed up earlier than expected. Of course, he would have been more thrilled to have enlisted along with the older pupils. But being too young to enlist (he would only turn fourteen in July), Tom was sent home along with the other 'babies'.

It was rather strange being back at Clarendon with so much going on beyond the Branches. Jem was gone off to war, and Ben Freeman had apparently run off somewhere. There was grass covering the area around Father's headstone out in the willow grove.

Much to his surprise, Tom found himself spending more time with Mother. No longer did she confine herself to the east wing study, though she continued to retreat there from time to time. With the weather being so fine, Mother routinely asked Mae Jane to set dinner outside so that the family might lunch in the warm shade of the veranda. Mother doted on Bayard, and she began to ask questions of Tom that she had never asked before: what his opinion was regarding one subject or another, or what he planned to do that afternoon, or what he wanted for his birthday later in July. Tom mumbled his way through unconvincing answers, and at first he expected Mother to only pretend to listen as Father always had. But in fact, Mother was a keen listener, and in time Tom felt comfortable enough to initiate conversations of his own.

So far as Tom could tell, Mother looked far better than he ever remembered. The past few months had been a slow process of recuperation, though from what Tom couldn't be exactly sure. Maybe it had something to do with Mother's medicine, or more precisely the fact that she no longer took it. That strange, familiar fog had since lifted from her eyes, and she no longer slurred her words, and there was a sense that a *person* occupied her mind where before there had been only the essence of someone. There were times, however, when Tom caught glimpses of the toll that Mother's convalescence had taken upon her. Now and then Mother would reel with a sudden headache and clutch her head, and there were some stretches of days where she could not rise from bed. Tom worried for his mother during these times, but he was comforted by the idea that Mae Jane was there beside Mother, ready to care for her. Mae Jane was always there for everyone.

Sarah visited home often, and Tom found it easier to speak with her. No longer did they bicker and quarrel, but actually shared in fine conversations together. Tom had some vague notion that his sister had lost her baby months ago, but he did not dare ask about it.

Summer began early in the Valley that year, for with the war on the children of Mayfair were called to help with fieldwork on their family farms. Of course Tom had no such responsibilities, and so he and Bayard spent much of their time exploring forested dells carved into the North Branch. For obvious reasons, Tom made sure to avoid the northeastern slope, where he and Tipper had gone hunting last summer.

"What do you say we go down to Mayfair?" Tom said to Bayard.

Bayard nodded his agreement, and the brothers started off.

As he and Bayard walked down the dirt road together, Tom breathed in the full fragrance of June. This was his favorite month, the month where everything was at its greenest. He recalled a word from a spelling bee several weeks back. *Zenith*. June, at least in Tom's estimation, was when the beauty and possibility of any given year was at its zenith.

At intervals the boys turned off the road to investigate shallow gullies. Flower smells, trapped in the stagnant air, nearly overpowered him. Like a naturalist he traced his fingertips over the tops of mushrooms that had sprouted from clumps of dead leaves. Underneath it all he could almost detect a vibrant energy, a thriving undercurrent of new life ready to burst forth.

Down in Mayfair, Tom noticed just how quiet the town had become. The usual hustle and bustle of the place was gone, replaced by the slow meanderings of white-haired men who were too old to fight, together with slaves running errands for their masters. Women stood at the counters of most of the shops, and women and girls made up most of the shoppers too.

There were rumors that Yankees were sniffing about in the western counties near the Valley, though Tom didn't put much stock in what grownups said anymore. He'd learned that grownups tended to lie just as much as children did, sometimes more often. Even Mae Jane was a liar, like when she made up that story about Tipper still being alive and living a good life somewhere in the wild, as if Tom didn't already know the truth. It didn't matter to Tom if his old mammy was only trying to make him feel better; a lie was a lie.

But back to Yankees. Despite Tom's distrust of its accuracy, the notion that there might be Yankees prowling around just a few miles away was disconcerting. Jem and the rest of the Valley's militia would still be away in Winchester, too far away to lend any assistance on short notice. If any Yankees invaded Mayfair, the only resistance would be Tom, Bayard, and, well, not much else.

Tom and Bayard found their way into Dance & Franklin's, where Tom used some of the money Mae Jane gave him to buy some penny candies for himself and Bayard. Though Tom ate one of the candies, he gave the rest to Bayard. Candy didn't do much for him anymore, in the same way that his toy soldiers no longer excited him. Tom had reached the sad age when he looked upon his toys, which had once given him so much joy, like they were the strange artifacts of some long-dead civilization.

As he and Bayard at last turned for home, Tom recognized Penelope Cutler standing under the shade of a distant tree talking with an older boy. The older boy had said something funny and Penelope was laughing, and for whatever reason Tom remembered how Jem and Miss Blake had looked under that giant jacaranda tree back — when was that, last summer? No, the autumn before.

"We're getting old," Tom remarked to Bayard, but Bayard did not respond.

Tom glanced toward Penelope and the boy one final time before he and Bayard turned their backs and started toward the North Branch. Tom felt a heaviness in his chest, but then again, what of it? Penelope was the sister of his brother-in-law. Didn't that make her his cousin or something like that? Something-something once- or twice-removed, perhaps? Tom didn't know how any of that lineage nonsense worked. But all the same, no matter what the family tree was supposed to look like, Tom's heart dragged with his feet.

From toys to girls. Laws, what next?

It wasn't long before the familiar path home began to wind its way up the North Branch. They passed low, cramped farm houses overlooking weed-infested fields. Tom knew the next bend in the road would take them past the Clements farm, and he began to wonder about his friend Billy again.

Former friend. He and Billy hadn't spoken a word to each other since last summer.

The brothers rounded the bend. Then, almost as if Tom's thoughts had conjured his friend from a puff of smoke, he saw Billy sitting on the rail fence that lined his family's property. Billy looked to be waiting for someone.

"Waiting for *you*," Billy called. His face was dirty, and his shirt was soaked through with the sweat of a long day's labor.

"Us?" Tom said. He almost looked over his shoulder to see if there were others coming up behind.

Tom and Bayard stopped in the road and stared at Billy. Billy was sinewy and tall, a little taller than Tom now but not by much. He wore a hopeful smile on his face, and Tom's instinct was to smile back. But then he remembered how Billy had abandoned him the summer before, and the tiny smile on his lips curdled. Tom put his arm around Bayard's shoulder.

"What is it you want?"

Billy jumped down from the fence and stepped forward sheepishly. "I seen you fellas pass down into the Valley. And I thought...well, I was wonderin if I could walk with you fellas back up the mountain."

Tom looked at Bayard, then back at Billy. "You don't have chores?"

Billy shrugged. "Daddy's drinkin. He says he don't want me doin nothin when he gets drinkin. He'll sleep a while. We'll work again come dark."

Tom looked up and down the road. "What about Ira Smith? What about Joe Merrick and all those others?" After a moment, Tom added pointedly, "All your *pals*."

Billy kicked the rocks at his feet and shook his head. "They's...well...I don't hang around with them no more. They reckoned I'm just a dumb farmhand who couldn't keep up with their fancy-dan ways. Maybe they reckon right, I don't know."

There was a long moment of silence broken only by the sound of birds overhead. Tom tried to maintain a stony expression, but he couldn't keep it up. Finally, his mask broke and he beamed a wry smile at Billy.

"You can walk with us, *if* you can keep up."

Billy grinned — it was a thankful grin — and stepped eagerly into line with Tom and Bayard.

The three boys traced a meandering path up the North Branch. There was much to catch up about, and much else to talk about. It had been well over a year since they'd spent any time together, and in some ways it was like getting to know a new person. Billy's voice was deeper, and he had sickly patches of whiskers growing on his cheeks.

"Now that the war's on, Daddy wants me to go back to school," Billy said. "He thinks it'll keep me outta trouble. Keep me from runnin off and signin up."

"It's already summer. School's let out for the year."

Billy laughed. "Then I reckon there's plenty of time for gettin into trouble before the fall."

As they walked, their conversation took a more serious turn. Billy apologized to Tom for shutting him out the year before. It was the other boys who didn't like Tom for one reason or another, and Billy had wanted to impress them. "At the time, I thought impressin em was the only thing that mattered. But I was wrong, Tommy. Dead wrong. And I'm sorry for it."

Tom just shrugged and played the whole thing off as if he hadn't thought twice about it. Inwardly, he felt a great sense of relief. He almost choked on tears that came out of nowhere, but he promptly stamped them down because crying was for sissies and sodomites.

"Partners?" Tom said, offering his hand to Billy.

"Partners," Billy said, and they shook. As their hands were clasped, Billy clarified: "*Brothers*."

Tom looked at Bayard, who had raced ahead to chase crickets in the dust.

Bayard was Tom's brother — his *true* brother by blood — but at the same time Tom knew there were some things he couldn't talk about with Bayard. The same went for Jem and JJ and even Ben Freeman. It was as if all the Roscoe brothers were really more like strangers who just happened to look the same, and who shared the same parents. But the *sameness* they shared was somehow repellent, an obstacle with no easy bypass. Tom remembered that Mae Jane had once said something about love being a choice. A person had to *choose* his family, and keep on choosing. Otherwise, not even the case of being twins was enough to keep two people together.

But Billy — Billy was different. He wasn't Tom's brother, and somehow that made their connection all the stronger.

"Brothers," Tom agreed, and they walked on together.

"I was sorry to hear about your daddy," Billy went on. He nodded toward Bayard. "Both of you."

"That's fine," Tom said. "Mae Jane says he's in a better place now."

"Yeah. I was sorry to hear about Tipper too, your dog."

Tom nodded. "Thanks." They walked on a little while before Tom asked, "You believe in Heaven?"

"I don't know," Billy said. "Sounds nice."

"Yeah."

They walked on together, each boy with his hands in his pockets.

"I was sorry too," Tom said after a time. "I heard your daddy's new wife up and ran off."

Billy kicked at stones in the road. "Yeah. I miss her cooking."

"Your daddy gonna get a gun and go after her?"

Billy shrugged. "It's his right. But no, I don't think he got the heart for it."

They went farther up the mountain toward Clarendon. They could hear the sounds of the North Branch Mine (there were Cutler slaves working there now, Tom remembered) and they could see the smoke billowing up from the camp. As the three walked toward Clarendon, they discussed plans to build a wooden ship — not a boat, but a *ship* — and sail it down the Sleepy Creek.

"Your mama gonna send you back to that city school in the fall?" Billy asked.

"I don't know," Tom said. "With the war on, most of those schools are shut down."

And then, just like every other conversation did these days, their talk became consumed by a discussion of the war.

"I just don't know why there hasn't been a big fight yet," Billy said. "It's been two months already. What are they waitin for?"

"Didn't you hear about Big Bethel last week?" Tom said. "I heard the Rebs and Feds had a bonafide dustup."

"Really?!" Billy cried excitedly. "Did we win? Did we whip em?"

Tom shrugged. "A little bit, I think. But the Feds haven't quit yet."

Billy went quiet. "Well. You think it'll be over before we can sign up?"

Tom raised his eyebrows. "They won't take us until we're eighteen. Seventeen, if they're really desperate. Will the war last that long? That's a mighty long time. No, I reckon there's no way we get in. Not unless we lie, or grow like beanstalks."

"Heard they're takin on drummer boys as young as ten," Billy said. "Bay here is almost that, and we's well over."

"I don't want to get stuck banging a damn drum," Tom said.

They turned up the road toward the pile of rubble that marked Clarendon's front gate. The year before, just after the mine collapse, vandals had toppled one of the pillars. Its twin had been smashed to half its size, but it still stood defiantly. The iron gate lay rusting in the ditch.

"What do you want to do?" Tom asked.

Billy shrugged. "I don't feel like building nothing just yet. How about we play War?"

Tom's spirits soared at the idea. Maybe toys no longer excited him, but games of imagination, of play-acting and make-believe — he was sure he'd never want to stop playing games like that. They were just too damn fun.

"Hold on," Tom said. "I'll be right back!"

After a few minutes, Tom returned to the gate with the long rifle slung over his shoulder and the Colonel's dueling pistols in his hands. He'd made sure they were all unloaded, and he made a show of pulling all three triggers to prove it. Billy and Bayard each took a pistol while of course Tom reserved the long rifle for himself. Laughing, the boys launched themselves into a desperate scenario where they were hardened frontiersmen circled by imaginary redskins. Next, Tom promoted himself General of the Confederacy and threw his troops into battle against the Yankees.

"Fight for your freedom, men!" Tom cried. "Freedom! *Freedom*!"

Suddenly, Tom's ears perked up. At first, he thought he was just hearing sounds from the North Branch Mine. But there, floating on the wind, came a sound that was totally unfamiliar.

"You hear that?"

Billy had just blown off the head of the Yankee general. "Hear what?"

Tom listened harder...and there it was again.

Drums.

Drums rolling a slow cadence, and heavy boots — hundreds of them, thousands of them maybe — marching in step.

And marching this way.

"*Soldiers*!" Tom cried.

Billy strained to listen. "What? I don't hear nothin."

With a shout, Tom turned up the main road heading north. That's where the sounds were coming from. "There's soldiers coming, Billy. I can hear them! Drums and boots, hear it? Drums and boots!"

But were the soldiers Yankees, or were they Rebels?

Maybe Jem and the militia boys had already whipped the Feds outside Washington and were returning home in triumph. Tom ran as fast as he could toward the bend about a half-mile up the road, but suddenly he thought better of this impulse. If the soldiers were Yankees, there was no telling what they might think of a 'damn Rebel' running toward them with a rifle in his hands. Just as Billy and Bayard came up behind, breathing hard, Tom turned back and pointed toward Clarendon's front gate.

"There! We'll climb the pillar and keep a look-out."

They raced back. The sound of drums and marching feet was louder now, and Tom could feel the pounding beat in his chest. He climbed up the broken pillar and looked to the north. Any moment now, he might spot the vanguard coming around...

And there they were!

Soldiers in blue came marching down the road. Tom squinted, scanning the approaching soldiers for some indication of their loyalty. Blue uniforms didn't necessarily mean they were Feds. Maybe six or seven Confederate regiments had already passed through Mayfair over the last few weeks, and not a few of them wore blue uniforms stolen from government armories and storehouses across Virginia.

How the opposing armies were supposed to know which men in blue to shoot at was a question Tom hadn't been able to answer until just now, for rounding the corner came a color party brandishing regimental flags together with a huge, glorious Stars and Stripes banner. Even though Tom knew that he was now supposed to hate that flag, he could not help but feel a swell of pride in his chest upon seeing its vibrant colors rippling in the wind.

"Yankees," Tom breathed with awe and wonder. Instinctively, he changed his tone and growled, "*Damn Yankees.*"

Most of the soldiers looked to be young boys just a few years older than himself and Billy, and they marched with a timid clumsiness that suggested they hadn't been soldiers for very long at all. Their heads faced forward but their fearful eyes darted back and forth, looking out for Rebel partisans hidden in the brush. Upon seeing the three boys watching them, several soldiers broke ranks and hustled forward. They leveled their rifled muskets at the boys and stood ready to fire.

"Drop those weapons!" a bluebelly shouted. "*Drop em!*"

Atop the broken pillar, Tom felt no fear. He lowered the Colonel's long rifle to his side and placed his other hand over his brow in a smart salute. Billy and Bayard stuck their pistols into their trousers and watched in awe.

The marching soldiers laughed at Tom's show. The riflemen lowered their weapons and hastily rejoined the column. As the soldiers passed by the boys, their bayonets glittering in the sunlight, several of them shouted out.

"Lookee here, boys. We got the Johnny Reb Junior Club!"

"Where the Rebs at, boys? Where they hidin at?"

"Hey, boys, you got any chickens to spare?"

"A handful of eggs is fine, boys—"

"An armful! An armful of eggs!"

"Be good to us now. Eggs, hm? Be good about it. We ain't et in days."

"You tell your daddy to come home now so's we can all get back. You hear it?"

"Hey-ho, Virginny. Can you tell us the way to Carolinny?"

The soldiers laughed and sang and carried on down the road.

Tom, Billy, and Bayard gazed at the marching column with wide smiles of wonder, but their smiles quickly vanished when a rock sailed by Tom's head. Another rock whizzed past, whistling in his ear, and Tom fearfully clambered down as a voice shouted from the blue mass.

"*Fuck you*, secesh!" a voice snarled, followed by gales of laughter.

"Y'all gonna walk right past them Rebs?" another cried. "Them guns could be loaded!"

Breathless, Tom grabbed Bayard and dove behind the stone column. Billy caught a rock in the shoulder and let out a yelp, and then he went down on all fours for cover.

"Run for the house!" Tom shouted to Billy, pointing down the path toward Clarendon.

With Bayard's hand in his, Tom stood up. He made to run, but instead he plowed smack into the belly of a fat and bearded man with stripes on his sleeves. The fat man reached out and snatched the long rifle from Tom's grasp while three grinning soldiers lunged for Billy and Bayard. While they grappled, other soldiers started eagerly down the path toward Clarendon.

"Let's see if they's any Southern belles in there!"

"To hell with the gals. Let's find us some of them eggs."

Frantic, Tom called out to the soldiers, "*Hey*! You can't go down there!" He started after them, but a meaty hand held him firm. Turning, he looked up into the face of the fat sergeant.

"Hush now," the sergeant said. He looked at Tom with a friendly, disarming smile that suggested only the noblest of intentions, but there was something in the man's eyes that made Tom's skin crawl. "You understand, son, it's our job to secure victuals for this here regiment. You'd be doing your country a grand service by opening your stores to us, son."

Without a second thought, Tom raised his arm to strike the sergeant. The man caught the blow easily, so the best Tom could do was stomp down hard on the man's boot and yank himself free. While the sergeant yowled, Tom turned and saw that Billy and Bayard had been pinned to the ground by soldiers.

"Run, Tommy!" Billy shouted.

Tom tried, but in his urgency he tripped over his own feet and toppled to the ground. From his place in the dirt, he could see the passing faces of soldiers gawking at him before the fat sergeant stepped forward and filled his vision.

"Teach you to strike a man in uniform, you fucking secesh…"

The sergeant reached down. For a split second Tom had a horrifying vision of an undead monster opening its dripping maw to bite a chunk out of his leg, and this made him thrash with renewed vigor. He slithered on the ground and grabbed the sergeant's leg and decided to pre-empt the biting by plunging his own teeth into the sergeant's fat ankle. With a savage cry, the sergeant tore his leg free and then brought the butt of the Colonel's long rifle down. There was a blinding flash of pain and then Tom's world went black for a time — a few seconds or a few minutes, he couldn't be sure.

When Tom opened his eyes again, his ears registered shouting on the other side of the gate. He saw three blurry versions of the fat sergeant scramble to his feet while a vaguely familiar voice snarled:

"…exactly your purpose in beating a young boy into the dirt, Sergeant?"

Blinking, Tom tried to focus. He looked up at the sergeant, who stood at attention before a tall shadow. Tom felt a warm wetness running from his mouth and he reached up and took his hand away red with blood. When he looked up at the tall shadow, he was amazed to see Jem staring down at him.

—No, not Jem…

JJ!

Still not yet believing what he was seeing — *who* he was seeing — Tom closed his eyes and lay his head back.

"You probably knocked the boy braindead," JJ muttered. "We are here to defeat the Rebels, Sergeant. We are not here to loot homes and terrorize the locals. Certainly we are not here to kill young boys."

The sergeant grumbled moodily, "Yes, sir."

"Call those men back, Sergeant. If they so much as pluck a blade of grass from that property yonder, I'll have them all shot."

"Yes, sir. You, men! Let them other boys go."

Tom heard the crunch of bootsteps moving away, but he continued to lie still. He saw red through the membranes of his closed eyes, but presently they darkened as a shadow passed overhead.

"Get up, Tom."

When Tom opened his eyes, he looked up at JJ once more. JJ held the long rifle in one hand, and the other was stretched out to help him up. Tom took JJ's hand

and got to his feet. Something within him spurred him to reach out and embrace his brother, because of course that's what a loving brother would do. But for whatever reason, Tom hesitated. It wasn't that he didn't want to embrace JJ; he was simply too scared to try.

Tom looked JJ up and down. His brother was dressed in a fine new uniform laced with gold trim, and this one fit him perfectly. A gold bar was sewn into each side of his collar. JJ must have noted Tom's interest in his insignia, for he reached up and touched his collar.

"That's right," he said, full of pride. "I've been *Lieutenant* Roscoe — officially so — for a year now."

Tom squinted at him. "But why are you in a Fed uniform?"

JJ's smile soured. "I've always worn the uniform of our country," he said, "and I've never had the intention or inclination to wear anything else."

Tom shook his head. "But Virginia ain't Union anymore."

"*Isn't,*" JJ corrected. "And as a matter of fact, it is. All the so-called Confederate States are still legally part of the Union. Anyone wearing the Confederate uniform is in league with an illegitimate government, a gang of criminals. Anyone in gray is a traitor. Remember that, Tom."

"Funny," Tom said. "Mother says the bluebellies are the traitors."

"Oh yes? And when have you ever believed anything Mother says?" JJ reached out and brushed the dirt from Tom's clothes. "Laws, you're an absolute mess." JJ looked over at Bayard, who was shaking with fright. "Are either of you hurt?"

Bayard shook his head slowly.

"And what the hell are you doing playing with these?" JJ growled, shaking the long rifle in his hands. He ordered the Colonel's pistols brought to him at once. "You're going to put all these back where they belong, and they're going to *stay there,* understand? You run around like this, you're liable to get shot. Just what the hell—"

"Jem's gone off to fight," Tom blurted.

JJ said nothing. Tom's news didn't exactly seem to shock him, so Tom went on.

"He and all the Mayfair boys signed up. They marched off—"

"Who is that?" JJ said. He was pointing at Billy Clements, who was nursing a bloody nose. One of his eyes was swollen shut.

Tom explained who Billy was. He finished by adding, "He's my friend."

"Clements," JJ said. "Your father's Josiah Clements, yes? He's still at home?"

Billy nodded. "Yessir."

"Good. You best run to him then. It's not safe to be out and about right now. Tell your neighbors to lay low a few days until we clear any Rebels out of town."

Billy snapped an eager salute. "Yessir!" He looked briefly at Tom and said, "Be seeing you, Tommy." And with that, Billy ran off down the road. The column of bluebellies jeered him as he went.

Tom turned to JJ once again. "Did you hear me? I said Jem's gone. He and everybody else left weeks ago—"

"I know. Keep your damn voice down, Tom, for God's sake."

Tom was eager to know: "Is there going to be a big commotion?"

JJ regarded the destroyed gate, but he didn't ask about it. Instead he turned and watched the long column of soldiers march by. "I imagine there will be something big happening soon, yes. That's why I'm here: to keep the peace here in the Valley." Looking at Tom again, JJ asked, "Where did Jem and the others go?"

Tom shrugged. He had no idea, truly. "North, probably."

"I mean *where*."

"Winchester, maybe."

"Are you lying to me?"

"No."

"No, *sir*."

"No, sir."

JJ worked his jaw. He nodded toward the house. "Is Mother home?"

Tom nodded. "And Mae Jane." Suddenly, a realization slammed into Tom's chest. Before he knew what was happening, his throat was thick with emotion. "JJ, it's Father. He's..."

"I know."

Tom blinked. "You know?"

"Show me his grave," JJ said, a look of solemn determination on his face. "I'd like to pay the old man a visit."

While the bluebellies marched down into the Valley, their heavy boots clomping in step, JJ slung the long rifle over his shoulder and started toward Clarendon.

Tom and Bayard looked at each other. Then they followed their brother down the path.

❧

The three brothers stood at their father's grave in the willow grove behind Clarendon. JJ stared at the headstone, but Tom and Bayard stared at JJ. His expression betrayed no emotion that Tom could easily read. He himself was still trying to process the fact that JJ was standing there before him after all this time, after all that had happened.

Slowly, JJ reached out his hand and touched Father's headstone. Tom imagined the chill sensation against JJ's fingers, for he knew the feel of the cold rock himself.

"When did he die?" JJ asked. "What day, I mean. The letters didn't say."

Tom had to search his mind for the answer. "December. Seventeenth of December."

JJ nodded. He closed his eyes and hung his head, and Tom could do nothing but study his brother standing before their father's grave like a forlorn sentinel.

But when JJ opened his eyes again, they were cold and wrathful. He stepped back from the headstone and coughed up yellow phlegm and spat upon the stone's face. Tom watched, shocked, as saliva oozed across the name *John Methuselah Roscoe*.

"Goodbye, Father," JJ said stiffly. His voice croaked, as if he might suddenly burst into tears.

Suddenly, Bayard let out a guttural scream and ran at JJ with clenched fists. He was no match for JJ, who held him back with ease until Bayard's thrashing subsided. With tears in his eyes, Bayard tore away and ran for the house. Tom looked far across the lawn and saw Mae Jane there under the shade of the veranda, watching. Bayard ran to Mae Jane and the old mammy took the boy into her arms.

"I think Bay loved him the most," Tom said, looking after Bayard. "He knew Father the least of all of us, but he loved him the most."

JJ shrugged. "None of us knew him. Whatever love each of us felt for him, it was a lie. We just didn't know it."

Tom watched JJ and tried to decide if his brother was right. He was certainly being truthful in what he said, but was JJ *right?* That was what Tom couldn't figure out. And looking at the marred headstone again, his best attempt at an answer was to step forward and kneel down. With his sleeve, he did his best to wipe away the spittle. There was an audible *click* in his bad shoulder as it moved in its socket. Standing up again to observe his work, Tom was dismayed to see that he'd only made the splotch of dark wet bigger. He murmured an anxious apology to Father and God both, knowing they were one and the same now. He heard JJ walking away and hurried to catch up with him.

As they walked through the yard, JJ said, "The place looks a lot better than the last time I was home. The weeds are gone, the hedges cut back."

Tom nodded. "Henry's nig — I mean, his *servants* — they come by now and then to tend the grass and such. Mother says Clarendon's never looked better. Not since the old times. Henry says he wants the whole extended family to look respectable, starting with their land."

JJ stared in tight-lipped silence at the fresh flowerbeds and the newly-whitewashed walls of the house. Behind his unblinking eyes, his mind seemed to be running at a feverish pace. "The whole extended family," he said scornfully.

"That's what the man said," Tom replied. "I like Henry well enough. He's nice to me, Bayard too. Say, JJ, how long are you going to be home? How long are those bluebellies going to be in Mayfair?"

JJ ignored Tom's questions. They stepped up to the cool shade of the veranda. Mae Jane and Bayard had already gone. JJ produced a hand-rolled cigar from his pocket and stuck it between his lips. He struck a match against one of the columns and puffed thoughtfully on his cigar. As he did so, his eyes went up to the summit of the North Branch.

"There's smoke from the mine."

Tom turned and pointed. "Henry's got his colored folks up there too. They're clearing the rubble from the mine. Jem reckons it will be up and running again by the time the war's over."

JJ squinted through his cigar smoke. "Rubble? What are you talking about?"

Tom explained all that happened up at the North Branch Mine. At least, he explained all that he himself knew. When he finished his telling, he watched as JJ's head began to shake slowly back and forth.

"Twenty-three men dead?"

Tom nodded. "That's right."

Hearing that, JJ spat at his feet. Tom thought to remind JJ that it was an abject wrong for a Southerner to spit on the floor of his own house, even on the veranda, but he said nothing.

JJ's eyes were fixed on the puffing chimneys of the mine. "And now the Cutlers have control of everything. That's what you're saying, isn't it? Father took on too much debt from his campaign, and now Jem's given control of our inheritance to the Cutler family?"

Tom shrugged. "That's my understanding of it. You'd best ask Mother if you want the full story."

"I don't need to ask her," JJ said. "I know enough already."

Nervously, Tom asked, "You gonna get…angry?"

A look of surprise, and almost something like amusement, flashed in JJ's eyes. He turned to Tom and blew a ring of smoke. "Angry how?"

Tom didn't want to have to describe it in any more detail than he already had. "Angry like…like how you were the last time."

JJ puffed on his cigar as if the question required deep consideration. When he looked up at Tom again, JJ offered a smile — the first he'd given since arriving home. "No, Tom," JJ said. "I won't get angry again. Things at Clarendon are different now. They *will* be different." Taking in the fresh character of the house and grounds once more, JJ gave a satisfied nod. "The Cutlers have done a fine job with the place, and it gives me some ideas. Ideas for *change*, Tom. The Valley will soon change, and Clarendon will change with it." JJ looked down at Tom again. "What do you say, Tom? Would you like to help me make some changes around here?"

Tom wanted to say yes, but he could not deny that his first instinct warned otherwise.

"What sorts of changes do you mean?"

"All good changes," JJ said. "Progressive changes, of the kind that are long overdue. You see all those little holes in the ground, where all those weeds were uprooted? That's the change I mean. An *uprooting* is in order, all across the Valley. A plucking out of the old, and a planting of something new."

Hearing all this, Tom could only shrug. "I suppose that sounds nice enough."

"It'll be very nice indeed," JJ said. "Finally, Clarendon will become what it was always supposed to be. Our family will become what it was always supposed to be. There's a sickness that lives here in Mayfair, Tom, and it infects all of us. But just like a weed can be uprooted, so the sickness can be dispelled. This war promises very good things for the right sort of people, Tom."

Tom nodded in vague agreement. "Mhm. And we're the right sort of people, right, JJ?"

"Of course," JJ said. He dropped his spent cigar and crushed it under his heel. "I've many ideas for our family's future. Bold ideas — ideas that Father could have never dreamed of, nor courageous enough to try. But first, the sickness of the Valley must be cured. That's what the war is all about, Tom. It's a means of cleansing ourselves, a way to make things *right* again." JJ took a final look up at the North Branch. "And when it's over, we can finally begin."

"Begin what?" Tom asked.

JJ turned to Tom and offered another smile. "When you're older, maybe we'll go into business together. We'll start drilling for oil, I should think, or invest in steel production. Father's railroad was a project of personal vanity. And after the tracks are laid, then what? But those other ventures, they'll shape the country for centuries to come. Our work will become indispensable to the growth that will transform every city and country village when the war is over. Whatever we do, the Roscoe brothers will be dominant — the undeniable top men of our field, answerable to no one else. Seems a fine thing to me, at least. Would you like to be part of all that, Tom? Would you like to climb those heights with me, and stand atop the summit together?"

Tom shrugged. "Sure, I guess. But what about the coal mine?"

JJ shook his head. "We need to think bigger than the Valley. It's a wide world out there, Tom, but already pieces of it are being snatched up by others. We'll need to move quickly if we're to claim enough for ourselves."

"*Roscoe Brothers*," Tom said. "That could be our company name, in fancy writing and everything."

JJ nodded and laughed. "A fine name, I should say."

Tom's eyes lit up. "And we'll write our initials beneath the name! Yours, mine, Bayard's too, and Jem of course..."

JJ's laugh faded at the mention of *Jem*, and so too did Tom's voice. Tom saw JJ's jaw clench up tight, watched as the vibrant green of his eyes shifted to a cloudy gray — like how Father's eyes used to look when he was angry. But rather than say anything more about the subject, JJ abruptly turned and went inside the house.

Tom lingered a moment longer on the veranda. He was unsure whether he wanted to follow JJ inside or not. And the more he thought about it, the less sure he was that he had any interest in the ideas that JJ had talked about.

By and by, Tom went to the door and stepped inside. He wandered down the hallway and passed by the doors that led into the great ballroom. Usually the doors to the ballroom were shut, but right now they were open and Tom peered inside. Within the expanse stood JJ, a silhouette in the fading light of the afternoon.

Tom looked at the empty, echoing vastness of the ballroom floor, the cloth-covered furniture pieces that stood like ghosts in every corner, the sensual curve of the staircase leading up to the second floor, where the walls were dominated by a collection of dusty oil paintings. Rather than a family home, Clarendon looked more like one of those museums that city folks visited.

But within JJ's eyes, it seemed that the ballroom was not dark and empty but filled with people and lit with hundreds, thousands of candles set along the walls and upon the cobwebbed chandeliers on high. Within the gleam of JJ's eyes, Tom could almost see the ballroom as it had looked when he was very young, back in a time he could scarcely remember. And looking at his brother reliving memories of such a time, Tom thought that he saw a smile of genuine happiness spread across JJ's lips. It was a smile of BEFORE, back when Clarendon was a place of music and light — back when the light had not just reflected in JJ's eyes, but shone out of them.

Tom felt a creeping sensation crawl down his back and realized that he had been spying too long. It felt strange to watch his brother unmoor himself to the present and set himself adrift in the past. Stepping away from the door, Tom turned and padded quietly down the hallway, and he left JJ there alone in the expanse of his memory, still trying to recapture what was lost.

❧

Later, with the deep orange light of the evening painting their faces and clothes and tinting even the shadows in the corners of the room, the Roscoe family sat down to supper. They were a part of the family, anyhow.

Tom and Bayard sat in their usual places. Mae Jane sat beside Mother, and across from them was Sarah, who had arrived at Clarendon earlier that evening. Henry was not with her, for he'd gone off to join the war a few weeks earlier. The places where Jem and Ben usually sat were empty.

JJ's chair was vacant too, for JJ now occupied Father's old chair at the head of the table. Sitting in his uniform, he looked like a young Napoleon. The impression was magnified by the large goblet of wine that JJ continually paused to refill. Tom wondered why he didn't simply drink from the bottle, for in space of an hour JJ had emptied one bottle and was halfway through a second.

"I could get you a third bottle," Mae Jane offered. "I'd have to go down the cellar is the only thing. I didn't know you was much of a drinker, Jon Jacob."

JJ shrugged and gave a quiet laugh. "I've become rather fond of it, in fact. Call it the soldier's curse. But no need for another bottle, Mae Jane. Not yet, anyhow."

The meal went on quietly, with the only sounds the light scraping of cutlery and the chewing of food. Tom could not help but feel that the teeth of all present were set on edge — all except for JJ, of course. In fact, it was JJ who was the source of the quiet discomfort, his watchful gaze that seemed to hold everyone hostage in their chairs.

At length, JJ gazed down the line of candles upon the table and looked at Sarah. "Dear sister, it's been so long. You've been keeping well?"

Sarah would not look JJ in the eye, but instead nodded stiffly. "Well enough, thank you," she replied in a formal tone. She ate and said nothing more.

In fact, to Tom's eye at least, Sarah did not look well at all. She was pale and drained, and some strands of her raven hair had turned gray. Her eyes tended to dart around the room, in particular toward the door, as if she expected someone to burst inside at any moment.

"I was very sorry to hear about your...late unpleasantness," JJ said. "With your baby and all, I mean."

Sarah went very still in the midst of chewing. Reflections of candles quivered in her eyes. She swallowed hard and stared down at her plate. "I thank you for your concern, brother. The Lord works in mysterious ways."

"I suppose He does," JJ said. "Henry must have been particularly heartbroken."

"Naturally," Sarah replied. She coughed to clear her throat. "If it pleases you, brother, I'd rather not speak about it."

"Of course," JJ said, and for a time the dining room was silent.

Tom looked from JJ to Sarah and back again. JJ's eyes were narrow and watchful, missing nothing. Tom was reminded of Father's ability to read minds and uncover truths with just his eyes, and it seemed that JJ had inherited some of that talent.

"You seem on edge, dear sister."

"Edge?" Sarah echoed. "I'm afraid I don't know what you mean."

JJ offered a knowing grin. "Is it the color of my uniform?"

They were interrupted when Mother cleared her throat loudly and continued eating without a word. JJ smiled at Mother, but behind his eyes was a glint of disdain. Presently JJ turned his smile upon Sarah once more.

"I only hope, dear sister, that I'm not making you uncomfortable..."

"Why on earth would you be making me uncomfortable, Jonathan?" Sarah said. She was trying to sound pleasant, but instead her voice was hoarse and on the verge of cracking. "I came here tonight in order to see you, after all."

JJ smiled. "You're right," he said, and he sat back in his chair, satisfied. Remembering the wine bottle on the table, he picked it up and offered it to Sarah. "How about a drink for you? A toast to our cheerful reunion?"

Sarah shook her head. "No, thank you."

JJ made a dramatic display of surprise, though his eyes remained watchful. "Oh? Why ever not? A drop of wine is a harmless vice when properly measured." (Even as he said this, he began to slur his words.) "What, are you and Henry expecting again already?"

Sarah let out a long, shaky breath. "No, we are not. I'd simply rather not drink. It doesn't agree with me."

JJ gave a suit-yourself shrug and proceeded to refill his own glass yet again. "That's unfortunate for you. But speaking of Henry, how is he? I feel I haven't spoken to him since, oh, it would be years ago now. If only I'd known the last time I was home how important he would become to this family, I might have said more than a few words to him at Wyolah Hall. That's where the two of you met, yes?"

Sarah gave a curt nod. "It's where our courtship began, yes."

Tom watched as a smile spread slowly across JJ's lips. JJ seemed to sense Sarah's increasing discomfort. But rather than turn away from it, he looked keen on exploiting her agitation.

"It was a whirlwind romance, as I understand," JJ said.

"We were very happy together," Sarah said.

JJ blinked. "*Were?*"

"*Are,*" Sarah corrected. "We *are* very happy."

"I'm glad to hear it," JJ said with a smile. "And yet, happy as you both are together, your husband decided not to accompany you tonight?"

Sarah delayed her answer by drinking from a glass of water. Now she dabbed her lips with a napkin and proceeded to fold the napkin back into its original pattern.

JJ's smile twitched. "You need time to think about where your husband is?"

Still Sarah did not answer, and instead looked down at her plate. For Tom's part, he couldn't understand why JJ was pressing their sister as he was, and why he continued to make remarks about Henry. After all, what had Sarah and the Cutlers ever done to JJ? But there was a yellow gleam in JJ's eyes, a searching light that set Tom's teeth on edge. It was as if his brother was a cat looking for helpless mice to play with. Maybe there was no deeper point to JJ's prodding of Sarah except that he had somehow determined her to be the most vulnerable person in the room — or else she was the strongest person, and it made sense to go after her first.

But to what end? Just what the hell was JJ on about anyway?

"Come now, Sarah," JJ said. "It's impolite to refuse an honest answer to an honest question."

Sarah's composure collapsed, and she glared up at JJ with venom in her eyes. "You speak of honesty? Why don't you just come out and say whatever it is you're going to say, Jonathan? Why play these games? You know that Henry's gone to the war. You know Jem's gone too, along with almost every other able-bodied man in the Valley. And you know full well which side they fight for."

JJ held his palms out and expressed a look of innocence. "There's no need to get angry, dear sister. Can we not forget the war for one night? I've been away so long, you see, and I'm only trying to catch up on the latest news."

"Then perhaps you'd like to know what your soldiers are doing down in Mayfair," Sarah said with a scowl. "Since they arrived, they've caused nothing but mischief. They wander into sundry stores and take whatever they please without paying. They've occupied the Curtis House Tavern and have already drunk it dry. Your men are sleeping in the church — in the *First Church of Mayfair*, Jonathan — and their muddy boots are soiling the pews. When I drove through town this evening to get here, your men blocked my coach and harassed my driver. If your goal is to ingratiate yourselves with the people of Mayfair, you're doing a very poor job of it."

JJ nodded. "I understand your concerns," he said. "But you would do well to understand a few things yourself, dear sister. The men under my command are not Virginians, and they are not Southerners. They are not, as we might say, genteel. They are from Ohio and Pennsylvania, and they are admittedly more of the rough-and-tumble type."

"They are brigands," Sarah said. "If Henry were here, he would have been forced to defend my honor given how they insulted me."

JJ shook his head. "Not a wise choice, one man taking on so many." He paused to drain his wine glass and refill it again. "But you'll be pleased to know, my men won't be staying in Mayfair proper more than a night. Tomorrow, we'll move to occupy the North Branch Mine."

"The mine?" Sarah echoed. "What good is that place to you?"

"From atop the North Branch, we can keep watch over the surrounding country for miles in every direction," JJ said. "If the Rebels try to move troops through the Shenandoah, they won't be able to do so discreetly."

Sarah shook her head with disgust. "So you and your Yankee brigands plan on staying for a long while then?"

"Until the war is over," JJ said, looking very satisfied. "Or until my orders dictate otherwise."

Sarah stabbed at her food with her cutlery. "At the beck and call of your Yankee masters, are you?"

JJ laughed. "That's an interesting charge coming from you, Mrs. Cutler."

Sarah's gaze hardened. "Everyone in Mayfair knows what we're fighting for. But what are *you* fighting for, Jonathan? Yourself? My Henry's gone off to protect our home and neighbors. He's gone off to fight back against corrupt politicians and criminals. He's gone to defend our family — *my family*."

JJ laughed again. "And don't forget your 'property', dear sister."

Sarah cried, "It's all the same thing! Haven't the Freemans been family to us here at Clarendon? Likewise, Arcadia's negroes are part and parcel of the Cutler family. We care for them, and they care for us. The circumstances are decidedly better than that which the Yankees and abolitionists would seek to impose."

"And there it is," JJ said. "I couldn't have said it better myself." JJ shoveled a heaping forkful into his mouth. As he chewed, he said, "I must say, I'm impressed with you, dear sister. We always knew your destiny was to marry some rich bigwig, most likely a planter. But I for one never thought you'd take to the whole self-righteous charade so quickly, and so completely!" He swallowed. "My, you play the part of slave mistress so well. You've memorized all the lines to the point you're starting to believe them. Tell me, have you taken up the whip too?"

"Enough with that," Mae Jane growled, speaking up for the first time. The old mammy gave a nod of recognition to Mother before turning back to admonish JJ. "I beg you pardon, Lady Isabella, everybody, but this mean kinda talk won't stand. Not in this here house. Not in John Roscoe's house."

Through gritted teeth, JJ muttered, "This isn't *his* house anymore."

Mother cleared her throat. "No," she said, speaking up for the first time. "But Clarendon is still mine. You'd do well to remember, Jonathan, this was the Spencer house before it was the Roscoe house."

"But the Roscoe house it remains," JJ said. "You'd do well to remember yourself, Mother, that your precious son Jeremiah is a traitor to his country. And by joining up with the Rebels, Jem has forfeited his claim to Father's inheritance. I'd have no trouble proving any of this in court, I can assure you."

Mother looked down her nose at JJ. "If Jeremiah has forfeited anything — which he hasn't — then Clarendon will go to Thomas after I'm gone. And after Thomas, everything goes to Bayard."

"They are children," JJ replied.

"Indeed, and they are *my* children," Mother said. "That's more than I can say for you."

JJ laughed. "Your words can't hurt me, Mother. Maybe once upon a time they did, when I was young and knew no better. But now my eyes are open. I can see quite clearly what kind of man Father really was, what kind of woman you really are, what kind of place Clarendon really is. And it sickens me, Mother, to think that I once desired to be a part of it all."

Sarah groaned with dismay. "You're a bitter boy become a bitter man, JJ. You think you can hide behind supposedly righteous causes and accuse your own family of villainy. You think that by serving the 'right side', you can act in any way that pleases you and still remain virtuous. You can even send your soldiers to desecrate churches and harass your neighbors, and consider all of it justified."

"You see?" Mother said to JJ. "Now you even have the Carter girl and I agreeing with each other."

"Indeed," Sarah said. "The only sickening aspect of this conversation is your willingness to trade your family and honor for political gain."

JJ scoffed. "And what could I possibly owe to the *family* that cast me out like a leper? What do I owe to Father, who spent his entire life engaged in the very hypocrisy you claim I perpetrate? You're all lost in the same delusion that our Valley society is great and grand and worthy of preservation. You refuse to believe that the winds of change are blowing. Some of the changes will be violent, but all are necessary."

"Necessary for what?" Mae Jane said. "There ain't no war that's *gotta* be fought, even for good reasons. Seems you set on fixin what ain't broke, Jon Jacob."

"Oh, it's certainly broken," JJ said. "You of all people ought to know that best, Mae Jane. You've all been living among the wreckage so long you can't see it. But you're right in one aspect, Mae Jane. I'm going to fix it, make things right again. It will begin here in Mayfair, but it will not end here."

"So, what?" Sarah snapped, directing a cold glare back at JJ. "Are you going to kill your own brother when you meet him out there? Is that what you mean by 'fixing it'? Well, there will be a whole lot more than just Jem you'll meet out there, you know. Are you really going to kill all your old school friends? Your neighbors, their fathers and sons and brothers? Husbands? Will you bleed the whole Valley dry before you're satisfied that some score has been settled?"

"I'll follow orders," JJ said. "Whatever my duty requires, I'll do what needs doing."

The others hid their eyes from JJ, until there was only Tom who remained looking at his brother. The touch of gray in JJ's green eyes had finally won out; JJ looked more like Father than ever.

"Even murder?" Tom asked, unable to remain quiet any longer. "If your duty required it, would you do such a thing?" Even after he finished speaking, he couldn't be sure whether he'd meant to ask a question or pose a challenge.

Turning to Tom, JJ smiled and shook his head. "Of course not, Tom. Who do you think I am? I don't have murder in my heart." Here, a shadow passed over JJ's face. "But don't you forget, baby brother, that this is war. And in the fog of war, some words of peacetime lose their meaning and relevance."

And that might have been that. The Roscoe family, such as it was, might have gone on eating in a raw, uncomfortable silence, with each member finally pushing back from the table and offering lame excuses for their departure, and nothing more of substance would be spoken between any of them. The rest of the evening might have unfolded that way, were it not for Tom.

"I feel sorry for you, JJ," Tom said.

Stunned, the others could do nothing but look over and gape at Tom. Each tried to discern whether they'd heard his statement right. Sarah and Mother even looked to each other for some kind of shared understanding.

Meanwhile, Tom's remark wiped the lingering smile off JJ's face. The last remnant of mocking glee vanished and JJ sat stunned. But he allowed himself to be taken aback only a mere moment before his expression darkened with the demand for an explanation regarding Tom's choice of words. Still, before JJ could utter a word, Tom pushed on.

"I don't know what it used to be like between you and Father," Tom said. "I'm not even sure I know what it's like…what it *was* like…between Father and myself. But I'm sorry for whatever happened between you two that night, that October before last. I'm sorry for it, as much as I can be sorry for the doings of somebody else. And I'm sorry for whatever Jem may have done to you, or for what he didn't do. Maybe nothing anyone said or did that night as very noble. But as it is, Jem thinks he's doing something noble now. A lot of folks in Mayfair think it's noble, what they're doing. You say we're all wrong for thinking how we do, and maybe you're right about it. But I feel sorry for you all the same. Maybe Father burned a bridge to you once, a long time ago. But in the meantime you've been burning all the rest from your side. Maybe you're afraid, and that's why you do it; I don't rightly know. All I know is that we're all sitting down here together, and you're way over there in the high seat. But even though you've wanted to sit in that chair for so long, you look awful lonely up there."

Incredulous, the others looked down into their laps. Only Mae Jane kept an eye on Tom, and when Tom met his old mammy's gaze, he saw that she wore a look of quiet pride.

JJ sat back with a pale look of shock stamped on his face. Without a word, he drained his glass in one extended, painful-looking gulp. When JJ caught his breath, he pushed a purple smile across his lips and began to laugh. It was a quiet titter at first, now getting louder, brasher.

"The philosophies of children," JJ said. He waved Tom off. "You think I want your pity, baby brother? Look here, Mother: you raised another fool."

Tom shot to his feet and stepped away from the table. He said, "May I be excused," but it was a statement, not a question.

JJ's smile vanished. He pointed down at Tom's empty seat. "No, you may not. For God's sake, sit down. We're all enjoying a nice supper, aren't we? A perfect meal in our perfect home in our perfect Mayfair Valley…"

Tom rolled his eyes and turned to go. But as he took his first steps, he heard the sudden screech of a chair against the floor and now the pounding rush of feet. Tom turned back to the sound, but no sooner had he done so than JJ lunged into view with a ferocious scowl on his face. A flash of red pain stole Tom's next breath, and he staggered back clutching the side of his face where JJ had struck him.

Next instant, amid gasps and admonishments, the other chairs around the table screeched. Within moments Tom felt the comforting touch of many hands. Squinting past the bleary veil of tears, Tom looked up at the concerned faces of Sarah and Mother and Mae Jane, with Bayard peering around Mae Jane's skirts. Though Tom felt like crying (for the burning pain in his cheek and the blood trickling from his nose certainly seemed to justify a good wail), he refused to break down. Even while Sarah turned to unleash a flurry of hateful accusations against JJ, and while Mother and Mae Jane brought up a handkerchief to stanch the blood from his nose, Tom remained calm and level-headed.

"He's fine," JJ groaned. "Nothing but a friendly tap so far as soldiers are concerned."

"He's a boy!" Sarah cried. "You think yourself big and mighty for striking a boy?" Having said this Sarah lunged with a hand raised, as if to strike JJ herself.

JJ easily caught Sarah's wrist and squeezed until she cried out. Wearing a blank expression, he pushed her limp hand away and gestured toward the door.

"Go on, all of you," JJ said. "Get out, and leave me in peace."

Mother was the first to move. She reached for Bayard's hand and led him outside. Next went Sarah, lingering only long enough to deliver a final hateful glare at JJ before turning her back on him.

Tom remained behind with Mae Jane. As she led him to the door, Mae Jane let go of the handkerchief while Tom held it in place. They crossed the threshold, but here Tom halted.

"We should go, Mr. Thomas," Mae Jane murmured. She glanced at JJ and shook her head. "He ain't worth it."

After giving Mae Jane a look of understanding, Tom proceeded to turn around and look upon JJ. His brother had taken his seat again at the head of the table, the lone guest at a feast for ghosts. For a brief moment, Tom thought back to that October night when the whole family had been together here in the dining room. Tom remembered how, for the briefest of moments, the air had been charged with quiet joy and laughter, and the candles on the table had burned brighter.

JJ looked up and sneered at him. "What are you gloating about?" he said. "Fucking little wretch. Come here and I'll really set your head straight."

Tom's next instinct was to rush forward, grab the nearest knife, and with a bellow plunge it deep into JJ's shrunken heart. But the fantasy, such as it was, melted away when he felt the warmth of Mae Jane's arm over his shoulder. He heard her whisper into his ear to *Come away, come away*, and without protest he let her guide him out of the room. But just before the dining room door groaned shut, Tom looked over his shoulder and saw JJ hunched over a meal that had long gone cold while the candles on the table cast his huge, monstrous shadow upon the far wall.

Chapter 44
THE CONVALESCENT

Just a few days following the disastrous reunion with JJ at Clarendon, Sarah Cutler began to hear rumors of dead bodies returning from Winchester atop slow-rolling wagons. The bodies were those of Mayfair boys to be sure, though Sarah did not know any of them personally. The common understanding was that the army camp had become a cesspool that incubated diseases of all kinds. Among the South Branch gentry, nervous minds were assuaged by the fact that the dead were only mud-eaters, who tended to be of sickly health even at the best of times.

But the real shock came when the body of Sam Hanley arrived on the South Branch. A great wail went up from all the First Families. Apparently, poor Sam's face was so puffed up that his own mother didn't recognize him. And though Sarah tried to deny it, she could not help but feel that something terrible had happened concerning Henry.

In the first days following her husband's departure for war, Sarah had spent much of her time thinking about Henry and praying for him. She withdrew from Mrs. Cutler's social gatherings, preferring to be alone for much of the day. She postponed Tattie's elocution lessons, and then postponed them again. Sarah found the grave of her little one (it was unmarked, but she inferred its location by the tufts of new grass over a tiny mound of earth in a far corner of the estate), and she spent many hours sitting on a blanket beside it. At first she wept beside the grave, grieving her little one and missing Henry. As the days passed, she found herself weeping only for her little one and the life her daughter might have lived.

And as days became weeks, there were times when Sarah did not weep, but instead felt the wash of the sun and listened to birdsong and the drone of insects. In such stretches of stillness, she came to forget where she was. Indeed she forgot *who* she was, and *when*. She felt she could touch eternity as fingertips tracing the surface of still water. And each time she emerged from these trancelike moments, she felt a softening in her shoulders, a lifting in her soul. Sometimes darkness crept back into her thoughts, and she wept again for her little one. But with each coming day, as the blackness behind closed eyelids reddened with each rising sun, Sarah began to awaken with a smile on her lips once more.

Sarah wandered the lush, pristine grounds of Arcadia as if looking upon the plantation for the very first time. She no longer felt restricted to the four walls of the big-house, for Henry was no longer around to bark at her to remain inside. Henry was of course fearful that the Cutlers' field hands would see Sarah's beauty and become lustful, but Sarah discovered she could walk from one end of the estate to the other without the slightest apprehension. After reconnecting with Tattie, Sarah invited the girl to walk the grounds with her, and Tattie always obliged. Once or twice Tattie offered to show Sarah the shacks where she and the other servants lived, but Sarah politely declined. She knew it was better to keep hidden what ought not be seen.

After all, there was much to see beyond the grounds of Arcadia. Sarah no longer felt bound to the plantation itself, but felt she could now journey down into the Valley whenever she pleased. Often she was escorted by Tattie and her man Kofi, who drove the coach up and down the streets of Mayfair. Even with Yankee soldiers in the Valley, the sleepy town was as peaceful as ever. If Sarah wanted to browse Dance & Franklin's she could, and without needing Henry's permission. If she wanted to visit the seamstress' shop she could, without permission. If she wanted to visit Clarendon far across the Valley she could, without permission.

And speaking of Clarendon, Sarah had recently discovered a sublime affection for the old place. Perhaps it had something to do with the fact that Sarah had lately been spending more time with Cousin Isabella (whom she no longer referred to as *that woman*). At first, Sarah had been more than apprehensive about spending any more time with the Lady of Clarendon than she needed to. But after taking tea with the old woman one day, and after hearing Isabella fumble her way through a sort of apology for her many years of 'unpleasantness,' Sarah slowly began to let her guard down.

With Mae Jane's help, Cousin Isabella was trying to wean herself off her medicine. Sometimes her jumbled thoughts and slurred stories still felt apart halfway through the telling. Sometimes the old woman reverted to her old snappish ways, and other times she flew into inexplicable rages. But it was clear to Sarah that Isabella *was* improving, day by day, much the same as she herself was improving.

But was *improvement* really the right word for what Sarah felt? Her husband was gone to war after all, and at any moment he might be killed in battle without her realizing it. How, in his absence, could she possibly feel the sensation of healing, as if she was a convalescent in the midst of a slow but certain recovery? Thinking of this only brought dark thoughts back into her mind, and so she did her best not to think about it.

Instead, Sarah focused on listening to Lady Isabella's stories of the old days: about the glittering balls the Colonel used to host, and of the petty feuds between debutantes that made both women squeal with laughter. Isabella told a story of the time that President Jackson visited the Valley and made a speech within Clarendon's ballroom. Isabella even talked about Mother — Sarah Carter — and the day she first came to the Valley. It seemed that, at one point, Isabella and Mother had once been closer than friends. They'd been like sisters, in fact.

And the more she listened to Cousin Isabella, the more Sarah came to appreciate that *that woman* was just that, a woman. A human being like any other, host to every flaw and failing in the book. She had only tried to make sense of each day as it passed her by, just like everyone else in the world. In the moments when it was quiet and the craving for her medicine was briefly forgotten, Isabella embodied a silent strength — a sort of grit that Sarah could not help but admire, and wish to emulate.

And the woman had noble traits too. Sarah came to appreciate Isabella's strength, what she'd heard others call grit. The woman's incessant wailing and complaining was little more than play-acting, a cry for attention that she'd learned as a means of holding power over others. But when it was quiet and her mind was clear, Isabella was a different sort of person altogether.

Life in the Valley went on, the same as it ever was, and the longer Henry was away the lighter her steps became. Free from the darkness of his shadow, Sarah could simply be herself, and think and say and do as she pleased. In practice she did nothing revolutionary, but within her mind it was as if the colors of the world had suddenly become fuller, brighter. Even when the first of the soldiers' bodies came into the Valley, Sarah Cutler's renaissance continued with all the promise of even better days to come.

But once Sam Hanley's body returned to the Valley, premonitions about Henry took hold of Sarah's mind and would not let go. And then, about a week after poor Sam was laid to rest, another wagon arrived in Mayfair driven by a Confederate orderly. Henry lay on a stretcher in the wagon among several bodies, their faces bloated with gray tongues lolling out of blistered mouths. Sarah had to remind herself to thank God for the qualifying fact that, alone among the wagon's passengers, Henry was still alive.

Henry was unconscious when he was finally brought to Arcadia. When Sarah saw him lying in his sickbed, she was certain she looked upon a dying man. He was so pale, his lips blue, and he'd lost patches of hair from his head. His body, shriveled by disease, was constantly drenched in sweat no matter how many times the servants cleaned him. He shivered and trembled even while he slept.

"Typhus," was Dr. Harper's diagnosis. He spoke as if delivering a death sentence.

And a death sentence it had been, this disease and others, for so many other Valley boys.

Judge Cutler soon returned to the Valley, despite reports that there was an outstanding Federal warrant for his arrest and the general belief that 'the Yankee sodomizer' JJ Roscoe had returned to exact his craven revenge upon the people of the Valley.

"What can Roscoe and the Yankees do?" the Judge said to anyone who would listen. "They claim to police American soil. As such, they are beholden to the old laws of the dead Union. If they try to barge in here and kidnap me, well, I've got my pistol on my belt. No one shall prevent me from seeing my son."

Day and night the Cutlers maintained a silent vigil while Henry's body fought a great battle. And all this time, Sarah never left Henry's side. She ate only when he did, and he never ate. He slept a great deal, but she didn't dare doze off for fear that he might slip away when she wasn't paying attention.

Weeks passed, and late June became July. Sarah heard rumors that small groups of Arcadia's field hands were running away and gathering slaves from other plantations to join the Yankees across the Valley, but she paid no attention to anything outside Henry's bedroom. Instead Sarah uttered fervent prayers to God that her husband would recover. But sometimes, Sarah found herself praying for God to end Henry's suffering quickly. She asked for her husband's soul to be taken, and soon.

Why did she pray for this? Was it so that Henry would not wake up vomiting, or have to suffer the shame of soiling his bed again? Or was it because she wanted God to release her from her holy vows? Was it because she *wanted* Henry to die, in the same way she had looked forward to his departure to the war?

"I pray that his death be painless," she said under her breath, not daring to speak any louder just in case Henry might be able to hear. "I pray that Henry passes peacefully, with no more discomfort. And I pray that his soul will go to a better place, and that he will be reunited with all his loved ones who have gone before him."

Sarah stopped short of praying that she and Henry would be reunited in the afterlife. But in any case, her prayers were met by silence and nothing more. And as the weeks stretched on, there was never any answer to her prayers. Sarah wondered if God had even heard her cries, or whether He cared to listen. Though her conscience accused her of blasphemy, she began to doubt whether He even existed to listen to her in the first place.

"But if you really are there, then please, take Henry soon and without pain..."

Sarah found herself thinking more and more about the teenaged widows who frequented South Branch balls, always cordoned off in side-parlors with the older widows. If it was Sarah's fate to join that group of women, then she decided she was ready for it. She did not go so far as to compare widowhood with continuing to live with Henry, but in effect this was exactly what she had in mind. Oh, but certainly she would mourn Henry, and for many years. The next few years were sure to be somber, and of course she would spurn any advances that might come her way. After all, she was Sarah Cutler; even as a married woman she'd turned countless heads at all the balls and soirées and luncheons she and Henry had hosted or attended over the past year. She was growing older, yes, but youth was still on her side. And it was not an uncommon thing for a man, especially some exotic stranger from beyond the Branches, to search for a wife among the South Branch widows. Why else were the widows always so finely, if rather mutely, dressed? It helped matters that black happened to be a color which suited Sarah's skin tone quite nicely, and…

Oh, for God's sake, what was wrong with her? Here was Henry, her beloved husband, laying mere inches from death's door, and here was his heartless wife already plotting her new life as, what, a painted strumpet? For shame. Sarah ceased all personal appeals to God and instead focused on reciting the Lord's Prayer over and over, until she became entranced by her own steady incantations.

There came one day which Sarah was certain was Henry's last. Somehow, she *knew* the end had come. She felt it somewhere inside her, the same as she'd felt when she knew something was wrong with the baby. An intuition, maybe. Kneeling at Henry's bedside, stroking his hair, Sarah knew that her husband's time was near.

Henry lay very still, and he gave not the slightest movement or twitch. His breathing had slowed such that Sarah could no longer tell if he was taking in any air. She reached out and felt his pulse, and with a gasp she realized it was fading, growing fainter.

But then Henry's eyes suddenly fluttered, and Sarah felt his pace quicken against the press of her fingers. His eyes opened slowly, sluggishly, and it was as if her own touch had brought Henry back from the brink — if only for a short while. When Henry woke up at last, he smiled at her and whispered:

"Sarah-darling…"

Sarah was dumbstruck. Henry hadn't smiled at her like that for many months — not since she still had the baby inside her. It was such a perfect, blessed moment in which Sarah felt truly *seen*, and in which she could see the truth of Henry behind his eyes — the beautiful truth of his inner self that he kept so closely guarded within him. Sarah did believe that, somewhere beneath Henry's brutish qualities and talent for mockery, there was a pure and childlike essence within him. After all, she would not have married Henry if she had not first seen a glimpse of this inherent goodness. Such an essence, she believed, was God's love: the breath of life which He gave to each of his creations. And for Sarah, looking upon the naked light of love in Henry's eyes, she felt all her lingering resentments fade and dissolve. She sensed that she looked not just upon her beloved Henry's body, but was presently gazing through a window into his soul.

But so convinced was Sarah that she at last looked upon Henry's true essence, that she realized that their final moments together had arrived and were presently slipping away. In short, there was not much time, too little time. Whatever she wanted to say to Henry, whatever she *had* to say, she had to say it now.

Sarah took one of Henry's hands into her own. As she did this, his eyes fluttered and closed again. Already he was losing strength, but he still had enough to squeeze her hand ever so slightly. Sarah knew that he could hear her, and that he was listening.

"I forgive you, Henry. For everything. What utter trifles everything seems to be now, after all that's happened, but I forgive you nonetheless for whatever pain you caused me. But do not fret, darling, for I assure you that most of the pain I felt was only imagined pain, a woman's sort of pain. What's more, Henry, I ask your forgiveness for my own failings, for I know I have many. I haven't always been a good wife to you. I know that losing the baby was my fault, all my fault..."

But wait. Did she really believe everything she was saying, especially about 'imagined pain' and the baby? Thinking about it more, of course she hadn't meant all that, at least not in a literal sense. And besides, she wasn't at all sure that she forgave Henry for what had happened surrounding the stillbirth. Henry had bolted from her sickbed as soon as he was able to get away, and he had stayed away. Her husband had been more attentive of his mother's whims than the needs of his own wife, even after Sarah had almost died on the birthing bed. Sarah began to ask herself in an accusing tone, would *Henry* have knelt by her bedside for this long? Would *Henry* have uttered so many fervent prayers for the return of his health? Would *Henry* have been kept away by worry and concern for her, comforted only by the unfailing hope that she might yet pull through?

The answer to all the questions, she knew, was an emphatic *NO*. Henry had not been there for her during a time when she needed him more than ever before. Henry hadn't been there for Sarah at any other time for that matter, unless of course he had something to gain. And this man presumed to still call himself her *husband?*

But Lord, what was she thinking? What was she saying? The man before her *was* her husband, and he was *dying*. What did it matter who was right or wrong anymore? It wasn't worth holding a grudge against a dying man, and certainly not against the love of her life. Grudges only destroyed the person who held them. Just look at what had happened to JJ, or Cousin Isabella.

Henry's hand went limp. Looking down, Sarah realized he was...dead?

But no, only asleep. Henry had fallen asleep, and there was a smile on his lips.

Sarah drew a series of long, deep breaths and watched her husband sleep. And then she made a decision. If Henry really was going to die soon, then she would make peace with him before he passed. If there was anything she *had* to do, it was this.

"I'm sorry, Henry. I'm sorry for holding anger and contempt for you. I'm sorry for cursing your name, for Lord knows I have. And before I lose you — oh, Henry, darling, I do not want to lose you! — just know that I love you. More than anything, more than life itself, I *love you*, Henry Cutler. I pray that God delivers you back into my arms. If He does, I will serve you, in body and in spirit, to my dying day. I will serve you, Henry, and I will raise our children to adore you. *Our* children, Henry. They will be strong as you are strong, and they will survive as you survive. Henry, darling, please come back to me. Come back to me so that we may start over, so that we may start again. Please, Henry, I beg of you."

Feeling not the strength to say anything more, Sarah leaned forward and kissed Henry on his lips, and on each of his eyes, and upon his forehead too.

There was a daybed across the floor from Henry's bed. The hour was late, and there would be no servants knocking until first light. Sarah drifted over to the daybed and stood there a long moment, wavering. She thought to whisper a final prayer for Henry, but then she lay down and fell asleep before her head met the pillow. She had no dreams until the last hour before dawn, when she dreamt of a cemetery burial under a hot sun.

❧

The next day, Sarah was reading aloud a passage from Luke when Henry woke up.

She thought she was imagining things at first. She glanced over the top of the page and saw his form lying there on the bed, except this time his eyes were open. Henry began to look around, blinking slowly, his reasoning mind not yet conscious. Very slowly his vision drank in the world, and presently the familiar rhomboid glint in Henry's eyes glimmered once more.

Frozen in her chair, Sarah watched her husband make the final turn away from death's door. And in that moment — a moment which Sarah would deny to herself for the rest of her life — she felt her heart drop into her stomach. She next instant she was at Henry's side, squeezing his hand and speaking to him.

Yes, Henry was really there. He was really *here*, where just last night Sarah had dreamt possible lives where Henry was gone and she touched the cold stone of the grave marker and felt a sensation of, well, was it to right to call it *calm?* But thinking of it more, she couldn't remember exactly whose name she had read on the stone. Maybe it had been HENRY CUTLER, or JOHN ROSCOE, or maybe there hadn't been a name there at all.

Looking up at the sun-washed ceiling, Henry opened his mouth to speak.

"I'm here, Henry," Sarah said, squeezing his hand tighter. "I'm here, darling. We're here, together."

The help was called, and soon enough servants were rushing through the broad halls of Arcadia delivering the joyous news. The whole house was soon a site of quiet pandemonium as the Cutler family stepped through their doors and hurried to Henry's bedroom.

Mrs. Cutler was there first, and she all but shoved Sarah away as she dropped to

Henry's bedside. Henry recognized his mother, and while he could not yet speak he held a loving smile. When Judge Cutler entered the room last, Lucas and Penelope stepped away from Henry's bedside so that the good father could look upon his great son. Noting the pride and unconditional affection with which Henry's parents looked upon him, Sarah felt pangs of jealousy that were as confusing as they were painful.

Before long, Henry proved able to speak. His voice was weak, but he said he felt a little better. He drank water, and he did not soil the bed. He drank more, and he ate solid food. Dr. Harper called, and when he arrived he expressed his astonishment at Henry's recovery. He said that Henry would be a few more weeks in convalescing, but that it seemed the worst had passed.

The Cutler family rejoiced, and Sarah joined them in their fervent celebrations. But all the while, she shivered under a dark cloud. She had been so *sure* that Henry would die. And maybe she'd counted on it. But when the day came that she watched two slaves help Henry out of bed and guide him across the bedroom with the assistance of a cane, Sarah went numb even as she pushed a happy smile across her face.

At the end of the hall, Henry turned around and made his way back. Watching her husband pick his way toward her with his cane, looking so much like Daddy as he limped on three legs, Sarah found herself urging him on along with everyone else. She laughed with the others because she didn't know what else to do. And when Henry finally reached her, exhausted and drenched in sweat from the effort, he looked at her with a giddy grin.

"I'm back, my love. I'm back."

Out of nowhere, bile surged up Sarah's throat. She did not let on, but instead remained a beaming source of adoration. Swallowing the raw, acid taste down, Sarah reached out to her husband — her darling, loving husband — and kissed him.

Chapter 45
CONTRABAND

Standing high atop the North Branch, JJ Roscoe and six Federal cannons frowned on the Mayfair Valley down below.

It was a grim, hungover morning and the whole sky was the color of ash and yellow bourbon. Little Mayfair lay far below, still asleep, but the machinery in JJ's head cranked on despite the nauseating headache that leeched at his skull. He'd drank far too much last night, or perhaps he hadn't drunk enough.

JJ's company was a unit of wide-eyed volunteers from Ohio's corn belt. Most of the men under his command were first-generation Germans, which in JJ's mind made them little better than Irishmen. Not trusting immigrants to do the job, he had trained the sights of the guns himself while the cannoneers looked on in gloomy silence. Two guns covered the approach up the mountain while the remaining four guns pointed toward Mayfair itself. The town was of course too far out of range, but JJ had worked out the distance so that, if necessity demanded, his men could roll the guns close enough to shell the town's main square. He would spare the courthouse if he could, if only because it would make a suitable headquarters once he occupied the town. And besides, the post office attached to the courthouse was Federal property.

JJ found a wooden chair outside the old log cabin at the North Branch Mine and sat down to gaze across the Valley. After JJ's men had ascended the North Branch, they seized the mine and all its buildings and equipment. The mine's slave workers and their overseers were evicted and pushed downhill, where they began a bewildered march back across the Valley toward Arcadia. JJ had no doubt that one of the Cutlers (maybe even Sarah herself) would soon visit him to deliver a vehement protest. In fact, he was rather looking forward to it.

Standing near to JJ, supposedly at attention, was the first sergeant who ran his company. The first sergeant, an ex-police constable from Cincinnati, scratched his buttocks and groaned.

The coffee JJ set to his lips was thin and tasteless. Peering over the brim of the cup, his eyes suspended behind the fog of steam, he was aware of the irony that, after all this time, he at last occupied the place he'd dreamed of as a child. For years, sitting here had been all JJ wanted. But now he was in command of a hundred and fifty strangers from the foreign Northwest, all trained to kill, all with enough guns and ammunition to lay his hometown to waste five times over.

JJ chewed on all this, as well as the realization that the man who had most recently occupied this cabin was Jem, who had run off to war with seemingly every other goddamn fool in Mayfair below the age of thirty-five. But the impulse to 'go Rebel' was strong in Mayfair. Already, JJ's soldiers were turning back 'patriotic' fifty year-olds at the Valley's borders. It was JJ's idea to insist that such men be released from custody only after swearing the Oath of Allegiance to the United States.

JJ's thoughts drifted to Jem. Christ, what was his brother thinking? The stupidity of his joining the Confederacy was baffling, almost hilarious. Then again, Jem had always adored the underdog. But if Father was alive, the old man would tear Jem to pieces for signing up with insurrectionists. If only Father was alive, he would see JJ in blue defending the Stars and Stripes, and he would be proud. The pride would be JJ's again, and Jem's star would finally go dim, as used to be the case.

But of course, Father wasn't alive — he was gone. And though JJ could not bring himself to admire the idea, he had to admit that Jem had always been one for lost causes.

Sweating in the humid morning air, JJ turned his attention away from Jem and back to his watery coffee. Some whiskey would give it a kick at least. He reached for the bottle on the table. Hair of the dog. He poured, and kept pouring.

The celebration at New York's Union Square had been a royal lay-down. For almost two days, JJ and every other man in blue had been the toast of every hole in the wall in the city. And ever since arriving with General McClellan's expedition in Virginia two weeks ago, JJ had secured for himself a steady supply of whiskey siphoned from his company's rations, which included two ounces daily for every soldier. (Incidentally, most of the Germans under his command were teetotalers.)

The fog of drunkenness did nothing to dull JJ's talent for command, but thankfully it did stifle certain nagging internal voices. After all, what use was empathy or compassion to a leader of men at war? Officers made their reputation by their boldness, tenacity, and yes, sometimes their ruthlessness. Every great military leader who had ever lived had adhered to similar convictions, from Caesar to Bonaparte to, yes, even young General George McClellan.

So far, JJ's time in Virginia had dragged. He had not seen General McClellan since he arrived in the western counties, nor did he expect to. The general was somewhere to the southwest, mopping up from a claimed victory over the Rebels there. The commander of the Ohio regiment in which JJ served distrusted JJ because he was a Virginian, and so his company was held away from the action and consigned to 'liberation' duty.

But in fact, liberation was exactly the kind of work that interested JJ. At the head of his company, he had successfully liberated six villages and towns dotting the mountain plateaus. It was fate, or rather necessity, that had brought JJ back to Mayfair itself. Apparently, a brigade of Rebels under Jackson was marshaling somewhere near Winchester, due northeast of Mayfair. Soon after taking command of his company, JJ was ordered to detach from the regiment and occupy a strategic position that overlooked the wider Shenandoah. That position, of course, was the North Branch of the Mayfair Valley.

And now, here JJ was. But though he wanted to savor the bittersweet satisfaction of his return, wanted to gloat a little longer over that headstone back at Clarendon, JJ could think of nothing but McClellan.

How to win George McClellan's favour?

The young Pennsylvanian was already being hailed in newspapers as the 'Young Napoleon' for his trouncing of the Rebels, first at Philippi in June and later at Cheat Mountain. It was well known even among junior officers like JJ that McClellan surrounded himself with a loyal circle of staff officers who were like his Praetorian Guard.

For JJ to be a member of McClellan's inner circle would be a step towards gaining a better command, a *broader* command. His own regiment, maybe, or perhaps a brigade. With enough force behind him, JJ could really show the powers that be what he was made of. And as McClellan's star rose, so would JJ's — until one day, JJ knew his star would rise yet higher, eclipsing all.

"Lieutenant, sir?"

Torn from his daydreams, JJ turned in his chair. His executive officer, a flabby second lieutenant from Columbus, was staring at him with a sheepish look.

"Lieutenant, I, er, I wish..."

JJ scowled at the man's — the boy's — apparent lack of backbone. Didn't he know there was a goddamn *war* on? Oh, wouldn't JJ have liked to see a measly fellow like this stand up against the cutting gaze of John Roscoe.

"Speak up, Lieutenant, for God's sake."

"Er, *yes*, Lieutenant. Forgive me. I wish to give my morning report, sir."

It was sometimes confusing, with both of them being lieutenants. But since JJ was now a *first* and the flabby man (what was his name again?) only a *second*, JJ held the privilege of rank.

JJ sipped his coffee and the whiskey he'd just poured in stung his lips. That was better.

"Go ahead, Lieutenant."

"Duty to report, sir, the trenches aren't yet finished, sir. The men say they can't dig into the cliffs. They say there's nowhere to dig at all."

The first sergeant, still standing nearby, called in a booming voice, "Tell me who the troublemakers are and I'll deal with em."

After some pause, the flabby lieutenant continued. "Without earthworks of some kind, sir, the cannons are exposed. The men are—"

"Vulnerable, yes, I get it," JJ said. He set the coffee cup down beside his chair and stood up. He knew how important it was to show unflinching assertiveness in the presence of subordinates. "These goddamn Germans don't know how to push a broom, let alone dig."

"They don't know an honest day's work, sir," the first sergeant muttered in agreement.

"The men simply need stronger direction, sir," the lieutenant countered.

The sergeant grimaced, making his lack of respect for the lieutenant abundantly clear. "That so? Maybe I'll direct em with my bootheel."

JJ scanned the mountainside in the hazy morning light. His men were clumped together in tight groups — juicy targets for Rebel sharpshooters — and while one or two picked halfheartedly at the ground with spades, most stood around smoking and talking. Apparently, the men thought they were on some kind of holiday. Breakfast was supposed to be finished, but many were still cooking bacon and boiling coffee. JJ shook his head. These men weren't soldiers. They weren't even fit to dig goddamn holes in the ground. Why was it that the higher-ups had once again placed him in charge of a bunch of mule drivers?

In an instant, a voice in his head gave the answer: *Because they think you're a dirty secesh in disguise, that's why.*

"On your orders, sir," the lieutenant said.

JJ worked his jaw, felt the familiar snap of the bone in his cheek from where the hot lead of Jem's shot had split it open. "I heard gunshots before dawn," he said. "Five shots. What's the report from the picket line?"

The lieutenant filed through his reports — chickenscratch he'd scribbled on scraps of paper to remind himself of important details. "Fairly quiet, sir. I posted pickets all around our perimeter as you ordered. A man every ten yards, as you ordered. There was some firing near a…let's see…near a stone quarry this morning. Southeast of here, sir. The men gave chase but lost the culprits in the woods."

"Culprits? What did they do?"

"They, well…someone urinated in the men's boots while they slept."

The first sergeant slapped his pot belly and roared with laughter. He shut up immediately when JJ shot a glare in his direction.

JJ turned his glare to the Valley, and in particular the distant roof of Clarendon, which he could see down the mountainside. For some reason, he thought of Tom and that friend of his sneaking around and causing mischief.

The lieutenant finished his report. "When our men discovered the miscreants, they shot at them and they ran off. That was before dawn, as you said, sir."

JJ nodded grimly. "The Rebels must be testing our strength. Searching for weak points. Either that, or it was a bunch of kids making fools of us." He wondered again about Tom, but in the same instant he decided his next order.

"Send the word down, Lieutenant. Half rations until the work is done. The men can eat after they've dug those trenches. And I want them *deep*, Lieutenant. Take Sergeant Wilson with you to properly motivate the men."

The lieutenant saluted stiffly. "Half rations. Yes, sir."

The first sergeant hesitated, then turned back and removed his cap. "Half rations. Does that include company staff, sir?"

"Half rations for *everyone*," JJ said, "including the company commander."

A shadow fell over the first sergeant's face. "Yessir."

Watching his subordinates slink away, JJ sat down again and brooded. There was incompetence everywhere, and it was dangerous. There would always be incompetence, especially before the men were hardened by battle. If incompetence were allowed to linger, it would soon fester like a disease.

Yes, bloodshed was the only way to make true soldiers of men. JJ himself knew he'd been changed forever after living through the all-too-brief fury of John Brown's Raid. Even now, he felt himself growing soft. Combat was the only way to cull the weak and clear the fog of peace from men's minds. Better to be the viper than the mouse. And better yet to be the eagle than the viper.

JJ's stomach growled. Oh, to hell with it all. He snatched up his cup of coffee and polished it off. He sat back and watched as dark clouds rolled in from the east. His thoughts drifted to the reports from other sectors.

Lincoln's top field general, a man named McDowell, was apparently marshaling a great army around Washington for a strong push on Richmond. Meanwhile most of the Rebels were gathering around Manassas, just thirty miles south of Washington. The two armies would likely clash somewhere near there, and JJ fumed at not being part of the big show. Here he was, a hero of Sumter, stuck babysitting his sleepy hometown during what the papers were calling the Mountain Campaign. Company commander or not, he was now convinced that someone somewhere had it out for him.

Then again, hadn't McClellan *asked* JJ to join him? Hadn't the Young Napoleon seemed to reach down with a providential hand and pluck JJ out of obscurity? Didn't any of that matter?

Well, of course it mattered. But it wasn't enough. If only he'd known that the fighting in the mountains would in fact be a sideshow of the big show, he would have happily remained in Washington. At least then he might have a chance of being part of the dustup.

Despite these thoughts, or maybe because of them, JJ reminded himself that the initiative never seized itself. Aloud, he murmured one of Father's old sayings:

"Nothing is given; it must be taken."

What would Father have thought of all this? North versus South? Brother versus brother? More than likely, Father would have found some way to capitalize on the moment's anger, confusion, and bouts of bitter violence for his own gain.

JJ heard a commotion down the mountain. Soldiers were crying out and running about with their rifles ready.

JJ sat up. Probably it was some indignant citizen of Mayfair come to complain about his men trampling their flowerbed or some such nonsense.

But then JJ saw a lone figure coming up the mountain path, and it was no rich planter's son at all.

The stranger was a black man in rags.

Soldiers in blue rushed to intercept the black man, and there was a great deal of nervous shouting. The soldiers pointed their rifles at the intruder, but their doubtful faces looked at JJ for direction. JJ stood up and descended the path.

"What's going on here?"

JJ did not recognize the black man, but he did recognize the style of brand on the side of the man's neck.

The flabby lieutenant ran up breathless and saluted JJ. "This, ahem…this *negroid*…he wants protection, sir."

JJ paused a moment. Had he heard that right?

"I said, sir, that this negroid individual wants—"

"I heard what you *said*." JJ glared at the lieutenant. "Pickets all around the mountain, you say? A man every ten yards?" He pointed at the black stranger and spoke through gritted teeth. "And you let this one get all the way up the main goddamn road?"

The lieutenant looked away with a twitching grimace but gave no answer. JJ turned to his first sergeant, but the fat man only stared at his boots.

Turning back to the black man, JJ addressed him directly. "State your business."

The man removed his hat and looked down at the dirt. He was afraid of looking a white man in the eye.

"Name's Abel," the man said. "I come from the Cutler farm yonder." He paused and eyed JJ curiously. There was a hint of recognition, then caution. "I thought I done saw you a few weeks ago, back when the other white boys in gray up and left."

"That was someone else," JJ replied coolly. "Now tell me. What is it you want, Mr. Abel?"

Abel wagged his head. "I don't want for nothin, sir. Just free passage over the mountain." Presently the man thought about his answer a little more. "But free passage won't get me far without water. Some food too, if you can spare. Don't need to be hot or nothin, just somethin."

Among the faces of his men, JJ saw a mix of expressions: amusement, contempt, disgust, pity, apathy.

"And I ask you don't send me back to my marse," Abel said. "And if he come lookin for me, I beg you don't tell him where I gone."

JJ offered a thin smile. "First you say you want nothing. Now you're asking for a great many things."

The first sergeant stepped up and shoved at Abel. "G'won, boy. Get the hell away from here!"

Abel staggered back from the blow, but he stepped forward again and rooted himself. The first sergeant whistled sharply and advanced on Abel with the butt of his rifle.

"Skat! We don't want no trouble, nigger."

"Shut up," JJ growled at the man. His order sapped the energy from the first sergeant's voice and body. The man's arms drooped, and his rifle went to his side.

JJ stepped forward and studied Abel carefully, and Abel seemed to read his mind in return.

"I heard yous was comin," Abel said, his voice barely above a whisper. "And when I seen yous comin up the mountain I thought, *I gotta try*. Lord save me, I gotta try. So I hid out while the others was chained up and brought down the mountain. My brother, his wife and baby, they wouldn't hide with me; they was taken away. But I had to stay and find out. This, what yous doin, it never been done before. The Lord Jesus sent yous here. I knows it in my heart."

Before Abel could say anything more, the first sergeant stepped forward again. "God didn't send us here to help *you*." He spoke now to the other soldiers standing nearby. "I'm a constable back in Cincinnati. We used to catch fellas like this one all the time. One darkie come up from Kentucky, begged around for help and passage to Canada. Some old man and his old lady hid the boy in their attic. Well, me and my partner found this nigger right quick, and the department telegraphed his owner, who come up to collect him. The nigger went back to the whipping post in Kentucky, and the old man who helped him went to jail for breaking the Fugitive Slave Law. That's justice, I say."

The lieutenant nodded along, even though the idea of agreeing with the first sergeant seemed to pain him. "Wilson is right, sir," the lieutenant said to JJ. "If we take in this…ahem, this *man*, sir, more are bound to show up. And then their owners will demand their return, and possibly compensation. The local population might rise up against us, and then we'd have more than Rebels to worry about."

The first sergeant grunted, "We came here to win the war, not play abolitionist."

The enlisted men nodded and mumbled in gruff agreement.

But Abel, unbroken, pleaded only to JJ. "Please, sir. I won't be no trouble. I can go. Or I can stay and work for you. Anythin you need done, I get it done. I don't need nothin. Just don't send me back." Emotion finally got the better of the man. His eyes welled and a tear rolled down his shining black cheek. Choked with feeling, he said again, in a thin croak, "I'd ruther die than go back."

"*Back* is where you belong, nigger," the first sergeant growled.

And now, all eyes turned to JJ for an answer.

The machine in JJ's mind whirred faster than it ever had before. Now here was a new dilemma. The United States was still a land of slavery, even while most of the slave states were in open rebellion. As far as the official narrative was concerned, the Union was still intact; the Republic was still *one country*; the Confederacy did not legally exist. As such, the 'war' was really just a matter of putting down certain citizens under arms. In the meantime, it was expected and required that all United States laws be enforced *everywhere* in the Union, including in the seceded states. One of the laws to be enforced was the Fugitive Slave Law, which called for all citizens to help recapture runaway slaves and return them to their masters. Legally, JJ was required to return this man Abel back to his owners, the Cutler family.

But JJ Roscoe also knew an opportunity when he saw one.

"What services do you provide for your master?" JJ asked. "Describe them for us in detail."

Abel blinked, for a moment not seeming to understand. But then he spoke quickly and clearly. "Me and my brother is field hands. But lately Marse Lucas been hirin us to work down this-here mine diggin for coal. We dig coal for the Confed'racy, see. Every week we load up all them freight cars on the train down the station, and it gets shipped off every which way. The soldiers tryna build a railroad down to Charlottesville, see, so they can bring they big guns up north for the big show."

JJ nodded as he took all this in. So the North Branch Mine was no longer a private enterprise in service of private interests. The coal down below was being shipped off to support the Rebel war effort.

"And Judge Cutler," JJ said. "He's a former United States congressman, yes? What does he do now?"

Abel shrugged. "Still a politics man, sir."

"Does he own the mine? Does your marse own the North Branch?"

Abel shrugged again. "Maybe a piece of it, sir, I don't rightly know. Here I was thinkin *you* still owned it. You family, I mean."

"The Roscoe family."

"Yes, sir. That's you, ain't you?"

JJ's jaw tightened as his mind became clear. This was it!

"The man who owns this mine is a Rebel soldier," JJ said. "And the man is presently engaged in a conspiracy with one Judge Cutler to use slave labor to supply an illegal insurrection against the United States." Here, JJ looked at his lieutenant. "*Write this down*, quickly."

The flabby lieutenant rifled through his pockets for extra scraps of paper. He took out a tiny knife-sharpened pencil and looked up at JJ, who dictated:

"To General George McClellan, Commander, West Virginia Theatre."

The lieutenant blinked. "The *general*, sir? Don't you mean to write to the regimental commander?"

"This is an unprecedented situation," JJ replied. "As such, I must bypass the regular chain of command. *Write*, Lieutenant, and stop asking questions."

The lieutenant nodded and set his pencil to paper.

JJ gathered his thoughts. "I have taken into my possession several negro slaves as contraband of war," he said. "It is this officer's opinion that the property of Rebels, no matter what kind of property, can and should be confiscated by the national authority if the property is used *against* the national authority. The slaves in question are owned by a man engaged in armed rebellion against the Federal government. Accordingly, the slaves are illegal contraband. We will hold them and use them, if anything so the Rebels cannot. I welcome your opinion on this matter. Yours, respectfully, Lieutenant Jonathan James Roscoe."

The first sergeant shook his head. "We can't have a darkie livin with us in camp."

"And there's only *one* slave," the lieutenant added. "Your order mentioned—"

"The order stands as given," JJ said.

Abel wiped fresh tears away. Spreading his arms wide, he reached out to JJ. "Oh, *thank you*, sir."

JJ evaded the man's embrace. "You said there are others like you? Others who wish to get away from your marse?"

"Yessir. Oh indeed, sir."

JJ nodded. "Then go back and gather them all. And get your brother's wife and child too. They will be quite safe here with us. But for God's sake be quiet about it, man. Don't go getting yourself killed. Until you reach our lines, we can do nothing to help you."

The lieutenant had just finished scrawling the note to McClellan. "Sir, I really must protest. The general will not approve."

"Are you the general?" JJ countered. After a long silence, he answered his own question. "No, you're not. So perhaps you need this spelled out to you, Lieutenant. By sheltering this man and any others, we are denying the enemy a valuable resource. This man before us is exactly why the Rebels are Rebels. They are clearly using their slaves to power their violent efforts against the government. It is therefore a military necessity that we impede this in any way possible."

The first sergeant cut in: "But it ain't right, sir."

"I am not interested in what is *right*," JJ snapped. "I am interested in crushing the Rebellion. If you two gentlemen thought of that more often, you might both inspire more fortitude among the enlisted men."

The lieutenant and sergeant mumbled together: "Yes, sir."

JJ looked at Abel. "You have a strong back?"

"Yessir. I been workin my whole life, if that's what you mean."

JJ nodded. "Then you'll get a shovel too. You may be free when you return, but Abel won't be idle. Maybe you can show these Ohio boys how real men work."

Abel bowed and left with an expression of bewilderment on his face.

JJ watched the man go and then, ignoring the glowering gazes of his men, he turned and started back up the mountainside.

Within the darkened cabin, JJ sat in a pool of amber kerosene light. He studied a map of western Virginia and noted the locations of battles and skirmishes. Philippi, Rich Mountain, Corrick's Ford. General McClellan was pushing the Rebels back across the state's mountain counties. The embattled Rebel commander, JJ noted with a smile of vindictive pleasure, was the old hero of Harper's Ferry himself, Colonel — now *General* — Robert E. Lee.

But JJ knew well enough that his own situation was not exactly promising. Scouts reported that Thomas Jackson's force of Rebels had slipped away from Winchester. Could they be moving on Washington itself? Meanwhile, there was nothing to stop the Rebels from attacking JJ here on the North Branch before rolling right across the Mayfair Valley to land right in McClellan's rear in the northwest mountain country around Morgantown.

Earlier that night, JJ had received a note from McClellan stating that the general was expected to arrive in Mayfair any day now. Having sent Lee and other Rebel commanders back on their heels, McClellan's plan was to seek out Jackson's force and trap it against the banks of the Potomac River, and there destroy it.

JJ wanted to be prepared for McClellan's arrival. The commanding general was young and ambitious and a real rising star. There was only one way out of obscurity here on the North Branch, and that was to make a good impression with McClellan. JJ studied the map, trying to trace out the fastest routes across the Shenandoah. The Rebels had torn up the railroads in an attempt to slow Federal movements, but JJ was determined to offer McClellan a bold plan of attack that would catch the haughty Rebels sleeping.

As he pored over roads and rivers and elevation guides and tiny villages dotting the paper landscape, JJ realized that wherever they found Jackson, Jem was likely to be there too with a rifle in his hands. Just as that thought came to mind, a heavy knock sounded at the door. A moment later the fat face of the first sergeant appeared.

"Visitor for you, Lieutenant."

"Who is it?" JJ barked.

The sergeant replied, "Local preacher, sir. Young fella."

Young preacher? JJ's expression darkened. That could only be one person.

"Send him in, Sergeant."

JJ stood up and folded the map and reports together, placing all of them back in his map case. A few moments later, Lucas Cutler entered the cabin dressed all in black.

JJ crossed the floor and extended his hand. "It's been a long time, Reverend."

Lucas' grasp was cold and clammy. "A long time indeed," the boy-reverend replied. "I understand you are *Lieutenant* Roscoe these days."

"Indeed I am. Please, take a seat. Drink?"

"No libations for me. Coffee, if you have any."

Later, after setting two steaming cups of watery coffee down on the table, JJ sat down across from Lucas. The two men endured a long silence.

At length, Lucas cleared his throat. "I suppose you're wondering why I'm here."

JJ poured whiskey into his coffee and made no show of hiding it. "I have an idea."

Lucas seemed to relax a little. "I suppose I should come right out with my request then."

"First let me say," JJ said. "The North Branch Mine has been connected with certain individuals in open rebellion against the United States of America. As such, the mine will remain closed until further notice, with no one permitted in or out without my authorization. That much isn't going to change, Reverend."

Lucas took a deep breath. "Though your closure of the mine is unquestionably illegal, this place is not my concern. Not tonight. Rather, I am here to kindly ask you to return my daddy's negroes." He looked around the cabin, as if the very people he sought might be hiding in the dark corners. "I've had nearly twenty run off in just the last two days. They are a fearful, superstitious breed as you know, and I believe the sight of your Yankees has simply wound them up beyond comprehension. May I see them?"

JJ smiled and ignored the question. "How is my darling sister?"

"She's well," Lucas said, and that was all the information he seemed willing to part with.

"I dined with her a short while ago," JJ said. "With my whole family, in fact, save my treasonous brother."

Lucas maintained the wisp of a polite smile. "How very nice."

"But enough about my family," JJ said. "How are your parents, Reverend?"

"They are well."

"And Henry? How is my favorite brother-in-law?"

A shadow passed over Lucas Cutler's face. "My brother was very ill," he said. "*Is* very ill, I should say, for he is still not himself. He caught something at camp, I'm afraid."

"Oh, I'm sorry to hear that." JJ grinned. "What sort of venereal disease is it?"

"Typhus," Lucas said pointedly. "We think."

JJ slurped his drink. "Oh, dear me. How unfortunate."

Lucas sniffed and sat upright in his chair. "I must ask your forgiveness, for I intend to speak frankly. I know you despise me, for some reason."

"Despise you?" JJ said, furrowing his brow. "Nonsense. I must tell you, Reverend: *despise* is a strong word." JJ offered an innocent smile. "And besides, if it turned out I did despise you for some reason, it would surely be a good one."

The boy-reverend permitted himself a quiet chuckle. "Quite right. But as it stands, I am here tonight on the business of God."

JJ shrugged. "As opposed to your own?"

Lucas smiled again, though his teeth were clenched such that his gums were white.

"You don't really care for those darkies you've stolen, do you?" Lucas said. "You're the son of John Roscoe after all. The secrets of Clarendon are well known in Mayfair — *all of them*. Your father was not nearly the defender of the downtrodden that he claimed to be. I just hope you yourself haven't become some softhearted Black Republican deep down. Have you become a warring abolitionist in the spirit of John Brown?"

JJ stiffened. "I was there to watch Brown hang, Reverend. And, God forgive me, I might have enjoyed myself."

"Then we understand each other," Lucas said. "Brown was a traitor to Virginia."

"He was a traitor to the United States," JJ corrected. "I had hoped his trial, despite its taking place in a kangaroo court, would have been enough to dissuade others from plotting insurrection against the laws of this land. Evidently Brown was just another sorry sop in a long line of misguided fools with guns in their hands and delusions of grandeur in their shrunken skulls."

"So you are not an abolitionist," Lucas said. "You can understand it's important I know the kind of person I'm speaking with."

"I'm a Christian," JJ said. "Isn't that enough?"

The boy-reverend offered a thin smile. "Oblige me, would you?"

JJ nodded. "Abolition is an idea," he said with a dismissive air. "It's an idea the same as giving the vote to women or the Irish is an idea, the same as secession is an idea. The supremacy of the white race over all others is an idea. Ideas may be considered, some rejected, and others accepted, but few ever become enshrined as law. We reserve such laws for ideas we might consider universal, ideas which touch upon the essence of human nature. And as such, the rule of law stands paramount over everything. Isn't that how the Founders structured our democracy in the beginning? To make it next to impossible for any mere whim to become law? Therefore, ideas in and of themselves are not my official concern. I wear this uniform not to espouse ideas, but to uphold the laws of the United States."

Lucas' eyes brightened at the prospect of a rebuttal. "But here it is, JJ—"

"Lieutenant."

"Here it is, Lieutenant. The Fugitive Slave Law. For decades now, Northerners have been smuggling Southern property across state lines. That law — a *federal* law — exists to curb such illegal activity, and to punish transgressors. Slaves that escape *must* be returned to their masters, or else. Anyone who aids or abets a fugitive slave is themselves a criminal. You might soon find yourself in the same chains that John Brown wore, and for what? Because you sought some kind of revenge against your former neighbors?"

JJ cocked an eyebrow. "Why on earth would I want revenge against the people of Mayfair?"

Lucas shrugged. "There are other *ideas* that stand outside the law, which one might call criminal. The idea of two men loving each other, for instance." Lucas held a lidded gaze at JJ for a long moment. "You might be, how should I put it, *intimate* with such ideas, Lieutenant. But these ideas are not only dangerous for one's soul. They might destroy a man's reputation."

"Or a young boy's life," JJ said flatly.

Lucas tried his coffee and set it down again. "Too hot for me yet," he said with a smile.

"Your argument about the Slave Law is moot," JJ said. "If a man's property — a gun, a horse, a negro slave — is being used in the course of rebellion against the United States, then I have the right to confiscate such property."

Lucas shook his head. "My daddy shall produce legal precedents that refute that claim."

JJ nodded his head at the mention of the elder Cutler. "And how is your old man, anyway? I imagine the Judge is in Richmond these days?"

"He is," Lucas said, with a measure of pride. "There is much work to be done in the Senate."

"Ah yes," JJ said, and his grin stretched wider. "The Senate. *Congress*. Interesting times we live in, to witness two separate Americas operating within a hundred miles of each other. But the task of nation-building is complex, uncertain work at the best of times, and you-all have the added challenge of starting almost completely from scratch. You need banks, you need armies, you need a judiciary. But most of all, you need your mail delivered on time. North or South, we're all very particular about the punctuality of our postmen, aren't we?"

Lucas played with the gold rings on his hand. "Yes, yes, I suppose we are." He continued to toy with his rings until he realized JJ was watching him, and now he placed his hands flat on the table.

JJ drank from his coffee cup. "You don't seem so well yourself, Reverend. Have you taken ill? The same ailment as your brother, perhaps?"

Lucas shook his head. "It's the heat." He took out a handkerchief and dabbed his forehead gingerly. "Yesterday's sermon was particularly draining."

"I can well imagine," JJ said. He smiled. "I'm sorry I wasn't able to attend. Lots of screaming and thrashing, I bet. I remember people coming from miles around to see the famous boy-reverend's energetic appeals to 'the power and glory of God.'"

Lucas blushed. "My people are desperate for reassurance in these dark times."

"And how about you, Reverend? Who is reassuring you in these dark times?"

The response was automatic: "The word of God, of course."

JJ nodded. "Of course. And God, did He tell you to come up here to reclaim your property?"

Lucas tried his coffee again. He smiled. "That's very good."

"Thank you."

Lucas set his cup down again. "I listen to my heart. And through me, God's will is and shall be done. His will shall always be done while I have the power to act on His behalf. That's just how I live my life."

JJ gave a sardonic grin. "Oh, of course. And what right does a man have to question how another man lives his life?"

Lucas matched JJ's grin, but it soon faded again. "I feel I must impress upon you the urgency of my request," he said. "My father's negroes are creatures of corruption. If left to wallow in sin for too long, their domesticity will degrade in short order. Once wild, they will—"

"We ought to discuss something else," JJ said, and he intended this to be the end of it.

For a long moment, the boy-reverend was very quiet. When he looked up at JJ again, he said, "My brother will be well soon, you know. You might come to long for my congenial tone whenever it is Henry rides up here demanding to know where his negroes are being kept."

JJ maintained a firm jaw. "A civilian may make no demands of an officer, Reverend. An officer has no duty to listen to anyone except a superior. The higher the rank, the fewer the voices that may question him. Call it a privilege; I call it good order."

"Whatever you wish to call it, this is theft," Lucas said. "This is the aiding and abetting of fugitives. This is—"

"*Let me be clear,*" JJ interrupted. "Your negroes will remain here, with me."

Lucas simply stared at JJ, and JJ stared back. They sat together in silence for a long while. Finally, Lucas stirred again.

"Then allow me to make myself just as clear," the boy-reverend said. "Virginia may be in rebellion against your Black Republican government, but until the war ends every Confederate citizen can yet claim he is still a *United States* citizen. It would be nothing for me, as a citizen, to lodge a formal complaint with your superiors. Your company is attached to what you men of war call a *regiment*, yes? The 37th Ohio Infantry, if I understand correctly?"

JJ kept his jaw tight. "That is correct."

Lucas smiled. "Then, considering the chain of command, I really don't have to consult with you at all on the matter of my negroes. After all, you're only a company commander."

JJ felt hot bile surge up his throat. He swallowed it down.

"You are only a company commander," Lucas repeated, "and you are going *against* orders, not to mention the laws of the country you claim to serve." Here, Lucas furrowed his brow, as if he was thinking deeply about something. "I wonder *what other laws* you might have broken, or perhaps you're breaking them still. To eschew the laws of God will surely bring about eternal damnation, of that there is no question. But in *this* world, to break the laws of man carries serious enough consequences. If you are not careful, *JJ*..."

Lucas paused, waiting for JJ to correct him. This time, JJ remained silent.

Smiling, Lucas continued. "If you are not careful, you might find yourself at the center of an investigation into your private conduct. And given your talent for soldiering, it would be an awful shame to see you stripped of even this lowly post. Worse, it would be a shame to see you imprisoned for your...questionable morals."

The boy-reverend stopped there, and the point was made.

In the silence that followed, JJ calmly pulled a cigar case from his pocket and opened it. He took his time selecting a cigar. He placed one between his lips, and he fished through his pockets for his matchbox. He struck a match and held it against the cigar and puffed. Now he looked at Lucas with a note of surprise, as if just realizing he was there.

"You don't mind if I smoke, do you, Reverend?"

"Of course not."

"And you, do you smoke?"

"No, thank you."

JJ sat back in his chair and smoked. He lifted his legs and placed his boots on the table, one atop the other. "What is it you said a few minutes ago? That God's will shall always be done while you have the power to act on His behalf?"

Lucas wore a look of quiet relish. "That's right."

JJ puffed rings of smoke and watched them float in the air.

"Do you remember, Reverend, a particularly festive evening at Clarendon? This is years ago now, some sort of fundraising ball for a friend of my father's. But if memory serves me right, at some point you found yourself on the second floor of my parents' home. You were only looking to get away from the party for a while, or maybe you had some other reason in mind. You were wandering, perhaps searching. And upon opening the door to one of the bedrooms, you found two boys in the darkness. The boys were locked in a rather...delicate situation. I should know, for one of the boys was me. And I seem to remember asking you — begging you, rather, and on my knees no less — to speak nothing of what you saw."

JJ watched as the smug grin on Lucas Cutler's face vanished.

With a nonchalant shrug, JJ carried on. "It was all just a childish mistake after all," he said. "It was no great sinful conspiracy. Just...boys being boys. Or perhaps there was in fact something more profound. Perhaps you interrupted a true and honest expression of something *good*."

"Blasphemy," Lucas said automatically.

JJ smiled. "Perhaps it was. Or perhaps you were confused, Reverend. Confused and mistaken. Perhaps you simply could not bear to witness to such an affront to 'God's will' and say nothing. You knew you *had* to speak up, to expose those boys in that room as satanic sinners, and only then would God's will be done."

Trying a fresh smile, Lucas began: "JJ. I want to—"

"Lieutenant."

Lucas swallowed. "*Lieutenant*." The first hints of strain began to show on the boy-reverend's face. "I assure you, I did not tell anyone what I saw. I assure you that—"

"You told *someone*," JJ said. The cigar's red cherry flared as he took a long, pleasurable drag. "Specifically, you told your story to the man who needed to hear it most." Chalky smoke billowed from JJ's mouth and nostrils, and he smiled at Lucas through the hazy screen. "Did I see that the First Church has a belltower now? Why, when I left for West Point years ago, the church was a rather modest structure. Now, I daresay its elegance might rival the cathedrals of Europe."

Lucas shifted in his seat. "Your father deserved to hear about what you—"

"And *your* father," JJ said. "He needed to hear it too, I suppose? Or perhaps you'd already whispered the rumor in his ear, and he sent you upstairs that night to find evidence, to catch the alleged culprits red-handed, as it were. Of course, it makes perfect sense to me. What better way to throw a hound off your own scent?"

Lucas scowled at him. "You dare call me a filthy *sodomite—?*"

"I didn't call you anything," JJ said. He squinted at Lucas, as if trying to read something hidden in the boy-reverend's face. "But if you *were* anything like me, I would have known. And you would have known too, a long time ago. But you are indeed hiding something, Reverend, that's plain to see. You are hiding aspects of your, what did you call it just now, private conduct? Still, I can't quite guess at the nature of *your* forbidden fruit. Although I must say, it must be quite a temptation to command a church filled with young women gripped by the passions of the holy spirit, all of them so lonely while their husbands and sweethearts are away fighting..."

Grunting, Lucas stood up and turned for the door. "I won't sit here and suffer these accusations—"

"*Sit down*," JJ ordered. The power and violence in his voice compelled the boy-reverend to freeze and sit down once again.

"You seem to forget," JJ said, "that when you discovered Richard Harper and I together that night, you were not alone. Clutched in your arms was the new wife of one of your family's overseers. A Mrs. Horace Glanton, I believe? I understand Mrs. Glanton is very devout, no doubt thanks in large part to your attention and guidance. Perhaps you were searching for a place in which you could pray together in private."

Something like panic began to shine in Lucas Cutler's eyes. "You have to understand," he said breathlessly. "I swore to your father that I would keep silent. And I *did* keep silent."

"For a price," JJ added sharply. Taking a deep breath, he relaxed a little. "The Cutler family was given much for their cooperation. A belltower for your church, a Congressional seat for your father. But what did my own father receive in return? The Roscoe family's reputation was still soiled by rumors. I've always wondered how, since you swore silence, those horrible rumors about Richard Harper and myself could still have spread so far and wide?"

The question lingered in the air with JJ's cigar smoke. JJ looked at the spent stub of his cigar and shrugged.

"But I suppose the answer doesn't matter much anymore." JJ reached across the table and tapped his ashes into Lucas' coffee. "None of it matters. Our dear friend Richard is dead now, after all. And besides, we must accept that it was all God's will."

They both watched gray ashes swirl on the coffee's greasy surface.

When Lucas looked up again, his meekness had vanished. A smile crept across his lips, and he stared at JJ with unblinking eyes.

"You must think yourself very clever."

JJ shrugged. "What I think is of no consequence," he replied. "There are but three facts to note in our present case. The first is that your father and brother are criminals in open rebellion against American democracy. The second is that I have every right to confiscate your 'property' — the human beings you hold in chains at Arcadia — to prevent their labors from aiding criminal activities."

Scowling, Lucas said, "And the third?"

"You've threatened me with blackmail, suggesting my *intimate* secret might destroy my reputation with the army," JJ said. "Except you forget you already played that card, and you played it a long time ago. You might have succeeded in destroying JJ Roscoe the boy, but there is a JJ Roscoe sitting here now whom you cannot touch."

Lucas laughed and shook his head. "So you really *do* think yourself very clever. Except you are hopelessly misguided. This war you're waging is not a war over slavery. You are a slave yourself, in service to the machine of a Yankee empire." The boy-reverend placed a hand over his heart. "*We* are fighting to forge a new nation, a clean and pure Christian society. We wish only to be left alone." Now Lucas snatched up his coffee cup and held it aloft. "*You* and your mongrel dogs outside are fighting to suppress your fellow citizens in support of a corrupt, dogmatic regime. If you are looking for some kind of moral authority over me, you will find none. Our Father will bar you from the gates of Heaven, just as your earthly father barred you from the gates of Clarendon. And therefore, the next time you see me, I promise that you *will* return my daddy's negroes to my custody. And in the meantime..."

Lucas set the coffee cup to his lips and drained it, cigar ashes and all. Setting the cup down empty, he stood up and politely pushed his chair against the table.

"I thank you for the pleasant discussion, *Lieutenant*."

JJ smiled. The bastard was good.

He stood up and walked with Lucas to the door. They stepped out to the porch and JJ watched as Lucas unhitched his horse and climbed into the saddle.

"I fear this will be a long and bloody war," Lucas said solemnly.

"It may be so," JJ said. "And what of it, Reverend? Should all of Mayfair's boys die in battle, your brother among them, would you put on the uniform and take up their fight?"

Atop his horse, Lucas Cutler smiled. There were ashes in his teeth.

"I'm already wearing a uniform," Lucas answered, and he touched his collar. "I am a soldier of God."

With that, the boy-reverend turned and rode off into the dark night.

LIBERTY & UNION

An Independent Newspaper for
the New American
Washington, D.C. – July 20, 1861 -
Issue No. 6

ON TO RICHMOND!
THE GREAT CONTEST OF OUR TIME

Today dawned atmospheric in Washington, with the smell of sixty thousand cooking fires and the collective groan of men and beasts of burden starting the long march to war. Soldiers of the Union, together with the people who lined the streets to see them off, chanted, "ON TO RICHMOND!" as General McDowell's vast column of troops moved toward Dixie's Land. Before the sun sets on the Sabbath tomorrow, two great armies will join in battle.

Following in the wake of the army are the people themselves. And these witnesses are not just from Washington City, not only bigwigs and politicians and giddy correspondents, but are indeed persons from all walks of life and from all corners of the Union. Rather than listen to the thud of the guns from miles away, they have chosen to follow their army on its march, and to see for themselves what shall happen to our country.

I disagree with those who claim that this battle, and this war more generally, shall answer all of the deep, fundamental questions that trouble us and which divide us. In particular, some in Washington anticipate victory as a license to subjugate the so-called South according to the whims of the so-called North. Some desire, in short, to push another man down the path to righteousness. But should our final aim — the aim of peace beyond war — be not to dictate the morality of other men, but only to invite them to walk alongside us, even if indeed they choose separate paths forward?

In and of itself, this war shall not decide the dreaded SLAVERY QUESTION, nor will it determine the nature of our soul. All this war will decide is whether the soul of America remains whole: whether a people can maintain their country and government — these United States, with all its institutions, scars, virtues, and hypocrisies — in which all citizens North, South, East, and West may continue the fraught, uncertain, but noble and humble work in achieving consensus over fundamental principles. We may one day rid ourselves of slavery and other injustices, but we can do none of these things if the country fails.

Wrongs can be made right, but in the meantime we must commit no wrongs out of self-righteousness. If and when the Rebels are beaten in a fair fight, they must not be made to feel ashamed in defeat. I do not say this lightly, for even in a fairly recent time my sincerest hope was to see every Rebel traitor hang from the highest tree. But what, in the end, would this solve? We would make martyrs of misguided souls, and the wheel of hate would keep turning. If there must be war, let it end quickly and decisively. But let me be clear: though this great contest may end in any number of ways, it can yield but one outcome which God and our own descendants might feel is just. The coming peace may indeed prove more treacherous than the fury of war.

There was a time when I felt a deep resentment for this country. As a child, I learned of the leviathan called America as one learns of the vastness of the Creator. And yet I could not help but hate this idea of America, this place of immense beauty and cheerful purpose which yet gave freedom for one section of men to dominate another. While men robbed my father of his dignity, and for all I know his life, America took no notice. God took no action against that crime and countless others, and certainly His human creations were content to turn the other cheek and 'look away, Dixieland.' When my faith in men I believed to be virtuous returned only disillusionment and heartbreak, I did indeed wish for someone to put this nation to the flames. I prayed for someone, God if it must be, to bring this rotten roof down and scatter the ashes.

Gone is the Union of our forefathers. Gone is the Union of John Roscoe, the so-called Great Liberator, who can be said to be neither a great man nor even a very good man — but only a mortal man, with a capacity for goodness the same as myself, the same as any other. Gone is the Union of William Yancey, whose only ambition was personal aggrandizement and his only ability that of driving wedges between neighbors. Gone is the Union of Stephen A. Douglas, who died in early June after pledging Democratic Party support for President Lincoln, thus finally trading self-importance and party for the good of his country.

From the old comes the new. Yet to come is the Union of We the People: a people who are naked and fearful under a white comet, who seek both shelter and a renewal of that cheerful purpose which once made us great. To come is the Union which I and four million souls like me shall finally join, not because another section permits it but because there is a higher law which commands in whispers to every beating heart across this broad land. To come is the Union in which we all shall be proud to live.

But it is not for us to sit back and idly wait for the promised land to be delivered to us. Nothing is given; it must be taken. Rather, it must be tended and cultivated, and the roads and canals and cities of that promised land must be built by our own hands. Its greater purpose must be decided through fair and honest consensus, and always with an ear open to opposition. We cannot be so fearful of hasty action that we do nothing at all; we cannot be so blind in our belief that we will know when the 'proper time' has finally arrived in which to finally, at last and possibly too late, do the right thing. The time to do the right thing is always now.

If you are scornful of such ideas as legacy, as I myself once was — if you are doubtful of this nation's foundations, contemptuous of its sins — then may God help each of us to see the necessity of delivering the Union from this terrible trial. We have seen time and time again over the course of human history, that to tear down old structures in favor of proposed paradises only condemns us to a vicious cycle of vengeance and cynicism. Indeed it is the nature of all things to decay over time, and some structures are better left to rot. But what of the Union itself? Must the whole of it be cast into some cleansing fire? Maybe I thought as much once, but I think this way no longer. In this respect, I must extend some measure of gratitude to men like John Roscoe, who by seeking to preserve 'the Union as it is, and the Constitution as it is,' had at least uncovered part of the right answer.

What is required to save our Union — not just today, but in all the days to come — is the honest effort by every man, woman, and child to balance preservation with transformation, to temper opposition with compromise. We must dig in our heels while at the same time extend our hand in friendship and understanding. These are not naïve whims, but simple actions that are within our personal control. Our national salvation depends on neither stubborn stasis nor radical revolution, but upon our individual and collective willingness to engage continually in the fraught, frustrating, and plodding evolution of our democracy. We already have the tools and materials to shore up our walls and foundations, and with which to build amending additions to our house such that it may provide sufficient shelter to all. In an older time, a vain and prideful people built the Tower of Babel in order to bring Man closer to God. Today, let us make the humble pledge to build an earthly shelter such that we may bring Man closer to Man.

Must brothers spill each other's blood in order to build this better, more perfect Union? Is there any such thing as a good and necessary war that ought be fought? The answer to such a question may never be decided beyond all measure of doubt. But if we living today allow our divided house to collapse, future generations will condemn us forever. If our house falls, it will not be due to the actions of any one section, but rather to the uncaring apathy of all. As such, I myself cannot hide behind fanciful words on paper. If I, Benjamin Freeman (that unqualified though committed editor of this publication), cannot take up a rifle, I will yet go out to bear witness to the Union's fate, for better or for worse.

Today, I look out at the fields and farmland south of Washington, and I realize it is already hallowed ground. I will go out today, and I invite others with me, not to indulge in the bloody spectacle of battle but to witness a slow dying and a hopeful rebirth. Hopeful, because victory is not yet certain. Through the crucible of civil war we may win peace. But when the guns fall silent at last, as I hope and pray they will, we must be ready to earn that peace for ourselves, for each other, and for all.

Chapter 46

THE STONE WALL

Jem Roscoe woke before *reveille*. In truth he hadn't slept much at all. He lay on the ground looking up at the clear morning sky, and for a long moment he wondered whether he might be dead. He willed his body to move, and stiffly he sat up and looked around.

It was very quiet. All around him lay the men of the regiment, most still asleep, all looking like a field of corpses in the gray light of dawn.

This was it: the big push on Washington. The Mavericks, together with the 2nd Virginia Infantry and the rest of General Jackson's 1st Brigade, had broken camp at Winchester over a week ago. Word came down that the Federals were marching out of Washington in force. "On to Richmond!" was the Yankee battle cry, while for the Confederates it was "Washington by Sundown!"

Jem and the Mavericks had marched cross-country until they came to a railroad town, and from there piled aboard a creaking locomotive and rode southeast as fast as steam could carry them. Finally they disembarked at a sleepy village called Manassas, about thirty miles south of Washington. Confederate troops in the area, so recently encamped on the southern bank of the Potomac, had fallen back to a trickling creek called Bull Run. The newborn Confederacy was now poised to make its first — and perhaps final — stand against the invader here, amid rolling farm country lost in a summer slumber.

Jem put his hands down and felt the cool grass between his fingers. When he lifted his hands again, there were fistfuls of torn grass and earth clutched in his grasp.

"What day is it?" Jem asked the world.

Ed Ripley was the first to answer: "Twenty-first of July." As a grumbling afterthought, he added, "The Lord's day, no less."

It soon became stifling hot. Sickly pale mists reeled against sunlight, and the dissipating remnants of predawn fog retreated south and west. The way north, to *the North*, lay open.

And there they went: mounted messengers, adjutants, chiefs of staff, and staff officers pounding the earth to muck. Many riders had passed through camp all night, and the sound of drumming hooves had become to Jem like a lullaby. But there were more riders now, and their faces were grim and urgent.

Beside Jem, George Hunt stirred awake and groaned aloud. "Goddamn cavalry makin another goddamn predawn parade?"

Jem watched horsemen hand letters to stiff-necked majors and colonels, exchange uncertain salutes, and ride off to the next officer with copies of the same message in hand.

"This is it," Jem said.

Hunt sat up. "What do you mean?"

"The big show," Jem said. "The dustup."

Beside them, Sugar Dave sat bolt upright. "Has it started yet?"

Beyond the camp, down the hills stretching to a little stream below, the wind sighed along lush green pastures. There were cattle fattening in the fields. Blue smoke rose from stone chimneys here and there across the chuckling stream waters. The whole scene was peaceful, pastoral, undisturbed save for the clumps of berry bushes that had been picked bare by soldiers.

By now most men had guessed that today was 'the day,' and they proceeded to gather their belongings and shoulder their packs. They had cooked three days' rations the night before, with orders to keep this morning's breakfast light. For most that meant gnawing on a strip of salt beef or hard cracker and preparing hasty cups of coffee over cooling campfire embers.

In the meantime, the men had a chance to swap rumors. The night had been full of them. There was chatter of a Federal assault across the Bull Run down at Blackburn's Ford, which lay a scarce half mile away from the 2nd Regiment's position in defilade below a broad hill.

Ragged, bleary-eyed men wandered about camp with strange accents. They told stories of bluebellies streaming across the river in the predawn darkness, only to be mowed down by Mississippi bullets like wheat under the scythe. But then why, some of the Mavericks called back, weren't the Mississippians chasing the Yankees back into Washington? And why had no one heard any noises of battle during the night? The answers came that there *had* been battle noises, and all of them very loud, but that the dells and valleys around Manassas were shaped such that they played tricks on men's ears.

"You won't see em or hear em until y'all right on top of em," one of the strangers said.

The Mavericks put their heads together to try and make sense of this new information. If the rumors were true, then the Federal bluebellies were trying to ford the river and outflank the Confederate Army while it was still fixed on the main road to Washington. At any moment, the bluebellies might appear on the slope of the wooded hill and cut into the 2nd's flanks with bayonets. Other rumors told of Confederate brigadiers sending men east to a place called McLean's Ford to hit the Yankee right and attempt a breakthrough.

Jem knew better than to trust much from these story-swappings. Men were as likely to make up tall tales for attention than share any honest truths. But with this being the morning of the big show, each of the rumors seemed equally plausible.

Based on the rumors, Jem determined the Federals were moving right to outflank the Confederate left. It was a fundamental strategy, and one which he remembered well from Colonel Spencer's war stories. If an attacker could hit the defender in his side or rear, the effect was like sending a rival boxer back on his heels with a surprise jab before delivering the knockout hook. As he chewed on this analogy, Jem stuck his fingers into his mouth to feel out the spaces where Ezra Blake had knocked out some of his teeth.

If the Confederates were themselves planning to move right and outflank the Federal left, as the rumors seemed to suggest, then both armies would end up chasing the tail of the other. Jem pictured the Mavericks splashing over the Bull Run at one ford while, a mile upriver to the west, the Yankees thundered across at the very same time. Round and round they would go, with phantoms racing ahead and bullets nipping at their heels. Ashes, ashes, we all fall down.

Bleak breakfast discussions continued. Someone noted that there were no birds in the sky, no woodland beasts shuffling along the edges of the brush. Someone else answered that of course there were no animals about; they could smell Death in the air, and knew well enough when to hide away.

Jem looked over at a nearby fire. Ezra Blake was crouched there, looking at the hard crackers in his palm and examining them for weevils. Blake took a bite, and there was a sharp *crunch* and Blake yowled in pain. The heavy silence of the camp was broken with—

"*Christ Jesus!*"

The men sitting around chuckled, and Blake cursed them next.

Jem stood up and walked over to Blake. He offered his cup of coffee to him. "Here. Soak it."

Blake ignored him. "Fuckin tooth…"

Jem offered the coffee again. "Soak it. It's easier to eat that way."

Blake scowled up at him. "Whenever I want your advice I'll ask for it, shitbird."

Saying nothing, Jem pulled his arm back and drained the last of his coffee. Meanwhile, Blake spat blood and hurled the crackers into the ashes of the fire with an angry roar.

The moment was split by thunder — *cannonfire!* — and Jem's heart leapt into his throat as all eyes went to the sky. The ground began to shake, as if the very earth might split open.

The concussion hit them next instant. The guns sucked the oxygen from the air so that Blake's voice was ripped from his throat by the vacuum.

As the gunfire rolled, Ed Ripley gasped, "On our left."

Jem realized he was holding his breath. He remembered to breathe and then gulped for air. He tasted gunpowder on his tongue.

Nearby, Jimmy Stanton examined his half-shaven face in a dirty looking glass. He'd cut his cheek open when the guns started. "Left?" he said. "Thought we was going right. That's what them 'Bama boys said."

"*Rider!*" someone cried. "Rider approaching!"

They looked. A messenger galloped toward them on a black horse. Captain Claiborne, his usual jollity replaced with dour anxiety, approached on foot and returned the messenger's salute. The messenger, a pimple-pocked lieutenant, handed a dispatch to Claiborne, wished him Godspeed, and then spurred his horse on to the next company.

The men watched their captain in anxious silence. They did not need to wait long. Claiborne's eyes flickered across the brief message. He dropped the message — Jem watched the paper fly away in the summer breeze — and then the captain's eyes found Lieutenant Lowery. The captain's gaze flashed with determination, and maybe a glint of terror also.

"Lieutenant Lowery, order the men to break camp and form ranks." Now to the whole company he shouted: "*Now's our chance, boys*! The Feds have turned our left flank. Let's get up there and give em hell!"

The Mavericks cheered, and now they moved very quickly. They doused the fires and broke down tents and shouldered their packs. Jem paused for a moment to watch the clouds of black smoke rising from the treetops far to the west. The Federals were over there, just across the next few hills. Thousands of them — and maybe JJ was with them.

The Mavericks loaded wagons with everything except their rifles, ammunition, and water. The horses kicked up dust as the teamsters drove off to the rear. "We'll be back to collect the dead," the lead teamster said aloud. Then they were off.

George Hunt squinted as he watched them go. "Well, that doesn't inspire much confidence."

Claiborne called the march and the Mavericks were off with another grand cheer. Jem found himself marching with George Hunt and the others on one side, and Ezra Blake on the other. The drums rattled and the regimental band played *Dixie*.

As they marched, Jem's bowels turned to water and his mouth went dry. He reached for his canteen and cursed. He'd forgotten to fill up the night before. Perhaps they would march along the Bull Run and he could break ranks for just a moment to fill his canteen. The guns answered this question with steady and ferocious booming.

"That's just across the river," Sugar Dave said nervously.

"Maybe we're whippin em already," Ripley offered. "Yanks are probably already runnin back to Washington."

Lowery walked alongside them with his pistol in hand. "Stay in formation."

The Mavericks marched on. The guns boomed louder until Jem was certain the thick of the fighting must be just over the crest of the next smoking hill. But once they reached the top, he saw yet another deserted pasture, and another hill beyond.

Other companies and regiments had joined them now. Jem saw men in gray stretched out as far as his eyes could see, all marching forward together with grim determination. The sounds of the various marching bands crashed together. But drowning out all of it was the steady roar of cannon, the thumping of untold thousands of feet, the sliding of leather and chink of metal.

Jem turned to Hunt. "George..."

"Yes, Jem, I'll look after your little Audie if you get it."

"Water. Can I steal a drink?"

"Steal two." Hunt passed his canteen over. Jem drank greedily. Still wanting more, he ruefully passed it back. Hunt tied the canteen to his belt again and looked over at him. "How are you keeping, Jemmo?"

Jem nodded. "I'm all right."

Hunt's eyes stared right through him. "You look like dogshit."

Ezra Blake called back, "Aw, that's just how he always looks."

From down the line came the order: "Company, *halt*!"

The Mayfair boys listened and watched. The next hill reached into the sky above them. It formed an almost perfect dome, sloped a little there on the right, tilting up on the left, and beyond it was a sky painted a startling blue. The hill was the meeting place of Earth and Heaven, a sight of great and quiet beauty now disrupted by the black smoke billowing into the air, by the sounds of clashing iron and hoarse shrieking and guttural death gasps.

The Mavericks looked at each other uneasily, for the world just beyond the ridgeline sounded like the Book of Revelation. Atop the crest was a farmhouse that had once been handsome, but was now a raging ball of orange flames.

Ezra Blake was the first to pull himself together. "Doesn't sound so bad," he said with forced assurance. "Eh, boys? Sounds like a fuckin church picnic."

As Blake spoke, there came over the din of battle the splintering of wood, and the roof of the burning farmhouse collapsed. Silhouette figures appeared at the ridgeline, and they shuffled toward the Mavericks like they were animated corpses.

Word came down the line: "It's us. Fourth Carolina, pass it on."

It appeared to Jem more than a regiment, but maybe an entire brigade engaged in a sluggish retreat. It seemed to take forever for the shambling mass of Carolinians to reach them, but at last the host of ghoulish husks staggered past the stunned Mavericks. The men's uniforms had been torn to strips, and blood ran from every ear. The soldiers were led by a glaze-eyed colonel trying to steady his blood-spattered horse, which shied and started as cannonshot streaked through the air overhead.

One ragged member of this shambling mass had a wide, insane grin stamped on his face. He broke ranks — what ranks there were — and happened to step toward a pale-faced Ed Ripley.

"Have ya seen it?"

It took everything for Ripley not to quake when he answered, "Seen what?"

The ragged man burst out laughing in Ripley's face. "The elephant! Great big one, a real sight to see! G'won, just over that hill yonder, boys."

"Ignore him," George Hunt muttered. "Man's gone loon crazy."

"*Find the elephant*!" the ragged man shouted with another giddy burst of laughter. Even as he laughed, the man could not stop his terror-stricken eyes from flickering toward the roiling smoke and chaos beyond the ridgeline. "Don't worry, boys. The elephant's right there. Ya can't miss it!"

A shadow fell over the ragged man, and he looked up to see Lieutenant Lowery looming over him. Lowery knocked the man flat and proceeded to kick at him like he was beating a bad dog.

"Damn fucking clown," Lowery seethed. "Get out of here! Go on now, back!"

The ragged man leaped to his feet and staggered toward the rear. The Mavericks laughed at him, and they laughed louder still when Lowery landed a final kick square on the man's rear to spur him forward.

The boys' laughter faded when they heard a whining cannonball soar overhead. The missile found its target: a caisson of artillery shells pulled by six horses, positioned a few hundred yards from where Jem and the others stood. All at once the caisson, horses, and two men driving the wagon disappeared in an angry gust of orange flame. Neither the horses nor the men had time to scream before they were consumed. Fingers of fire shot into the sky, followed by bleeding pillars of choking black smoke. A split second later, a shock of sound collapsed the air and ruptured the eardrums of every man for a half-mile around.

With his head splitting, Jem reached up and touched his ears and felt blood trickling down. He took off his forage cap and ran sweaty fingers through his hair. He took hard, shallow breaths. The bottom of his trousers were wet and stinking. Unable to control his bowels from numbing fear, they started to leak out of him. He squeezed his buttocks tight and waited for a sudden stab of indigestion to pass.

Horses thundered somewhere in the rear. Jem turned his head and saw a group of officers on horseback ride down the line. They were led by a bearded, wild-eyed man wearing a mangy blue uniform and dirty cadet cap. As he rode closer, Jem saw he wore the stripes of a brigadier general. The general was busy gnashing a lemon with his teeth and sucking at the juice through holes in its yellow skin.

Thomas Jackson.

"I want you men to advance!" Jackson called as he rode along. "Advance with the wrath of God hot in your blood. Don't take counsel of your fear, men. By the grace of the God of Battles, we will whip our enemy and send their ranks streaming back to their holes. Draw the sword, boys, and throw away the scabbard."

It was talk right out of Shakespeare, or maybe the Old Testament, and this was exactly what Jackson intended. The wild-eyed general thundered past Jem and the Mayfair boys. Down the line, before another company, he began again. "I want you men to advance! Advance with the wrath of God hot in your blood. Don't take counsel of your fear..."

The Mavericks spread into a wide formation two men deep and began to march forward at Claiborne's command. As they approached the burning house and the gunfire and screaming, inching closer toward the great baptism of fire that waited for them over the crest of the green, peaceful hill, the tang of gunpowder intensified in the heavy air and the men gasped for breath with swollen tongues lolling out of cracked mouths. And the July sun poured down its stifling heat all the while. The thought invaded Jem's mind that it was a fine day to go swimming at the quarry back home, and he suddenly felt the urge to turn and run.

Wiping the sweat from stinging eyes, Jem now saw a mass of soldiers appear at the top of the hill just as the Mavericks neared its crest. These soldiers were engaged in no shuffling retreat — they were running pell-mell in a mad frenzy. Instinctively, Jem brought his rifle up but Ezra Blake pushed it down.

"Hold it!" Blake cried. "Them's ours."

And now Jem saw: the running soldiers were indeed Confederates in gray. They dashed down the hill throwing their rifles and packs away, their open coats flapping behind them. As the men fled they shouted, "Betrayed! *Betrayed*!"

Alarm gripped Jem's heart. Betrayed? Betrayed by whom? But before he had time to consider possible answers, the fleeing men were upon them. The Mavericks hailed the men and grabbed at them, but the men did not linger to give any news. Instead they reeled and screamed, their eyes white and wild with primal fear, and they tore away and ran as fast as their legs could carry them.

Captain Claiborne saw these retreating men and cursed loudly. "Never mind them, boys! Mayfair men do not retreat!"

The boys repeated their captain's cry up and down the line: *Mayfair men do not retreat*!

Jem cried out in fear as he heard a stray bullet fly past. His body began to shake, and it shook so violently he thought he would be sick. He bent his head to the ground. Perhaps if he didn't look up, he would not be frightened. Looking down toward his boots he saw craters of charred earth, bloody bandages, packs and rifles thrown aside in panic. Now he saw for the first time a man killed by a bullet. He was a boy in gray, and he lay crumpled on the hillside, his neck twisted at a vicious angle. He wore a blue cockade emblazoned with a gilded palmetto button. The boy was — *had been* — a South Carolinian, and he had been shot in the back.

Green with nausea, Captain Claiborne stepped over the dead boy. "Mayfair men do *not* retreat!" he shouted again, his voice thick. "Other men may run away, but Mayfair men do not. We run headlong into battle! *Advance*, men. *Advance*!"

"Oh, would he *shut up*," Blake hissed through gritted teeth. And despite his terror, Jem burst out laughing at Blake's remark. Blake took notice of this, and he permitted himself a quiet laugh too.

At last, the Mavericks crested the hill and passed beyond the burning farmhouse that had become like a raging bonfire. And now they could see 'the elephant' that the ragged soldier had raved about. They could see the hellish battle playing out before them like miniature toys on a kitchen table.

A few hundred yards below them, a colossal tide of men in blue crashed down on thin lines of men in gray. Blue and gray waves swelled and collided and fell back, with bodies left in the wake and pastures consumed by fire and the entire field bathed in black smoke. The air was thick with the stench of sunbaked death.

Blue uniformed troops cheered together, and wave after wave crashed into the beleaguered Confederate line. Exhausted and terrified, hundreds of men in gray broke and scattered. The trumpeting sounds of retreat were cut viciously short as bullets tore through the lungs of the buglers. Jem watched his comrades from Louisiana and Virginia race back up the hill, many falling to bullets and shells splitting their exposed backs.

As the retreating men reached the safety of the Mavericks' line, Captain Claiborne broke ranks and ran ahead. He snarled at the men and hit them with the flat of his saber. The familiar jolly red shine of Claiborne's cheeks was gone. He was under the microscope as it were; the main subject of field glasses held by calculating colonels and generals. Claiborne was no longer the jovial good-time host of his famous balls and barbecues. The veneer of his station and respectability had been stripped away by desperation, by fear, by the nauseating anxiety to *impress*. The only way 'good ol' Clay' knew how to gain prestige now was with bitter savagery. He hurled a young boy down and kicked him in the stomach.

"Turn back, you cowards! Take a rifle! Turn back or I'll shoot you myself!"

Jem saw the faces of the fleeing men. Their faces were contorted in grotesque expressions of absolute terror. Jem caught Ezra Blake's eye beside him, looking cool and calm. For whatever reason, Blake gave Jem a somber, knowing nod. A shiver streaked down Jem's spine.

Rifles cracked and a stream of bullets whizzed overhead. Jem was paralyzed with the blink-of-an-eye savagery as several Mavericks dropped to their knees with geysers of blood spouting from wounds in their necks and chests.

"The captain's been hit!"

In the fury, Clay Claiborne had taken a minnie ball to the hand. His son Percy rushed over with a bandage in hand. Grunting and groaning, the father stomped about and fought with his son over the best way to dress the wound. Percy, his lower lip quivering, tried to wrap a bandage with shaking hands. His father waved him off angrily, desperate to get back to impressing the generals whom he knew had to be studying him from afar. But at that moment, another bullet struck Clay Claiborne in the heart and he collapsed dead.

As his father's body slumped against him and dropped to the ground like a stone, Percy was left with the bloody bandage still clutched in his hands. His face, frozen in horror, was splattered with his father's blood. Shivering, he dropped the now useless bandage and put his hands to his face.

And then Percy Claiborne screamed.

The Mayfair boys cowered and the line wavered. Who would command? Who *could*? Lieutenant Lowery was raving like a madman in front of the line, but no one came forward to stand with him. Some of the sergeants barked at the men to push forward, but several others were already edging toward the rear. The boys around Jem wailed and begged for someone to call a retreat.

Suddenly, the blue tide of Federals shook their rifles, slashed the air with gleaming bayonets, and rushed cheering up the hill, drunk with the thrill of the chase. They clambered over the bodies of young boys from Alabama, Mississippi, Louisiana, and South Carolina. Through the gunsmoke, Jem watched with horror as some of the wounded were bayoneted and trampled.

Seeing Death racing toward them, the Mayfair boys turned and made their own calls for retreat. They screamed for their comrades to have sense, for God's sake, and all at once they broke ranks and ran. For the last two months, Claiborne and Lowery had worked to mold the Mayfair Mavericks into a unit that would think as one fearless mind, act as one tireless body. But here, at the critical moment, all that training seemed to be for naught. The boys of the Valley were too free-spirited, too independently-minded. And now, with bullets nipping their heels, the Mavericks turned away and fled to save themselves. In the retreat of so many individuals, they did almost appear as one cohesive whole, a solid mass numbed by surreal horror.

All the while, Percy Claiborne continued to wail and scream.

Boys pushed Jem aside as they ran, dropping rifles and hats so they could run unburdened. Jem wondered why he continued to stand there frozen, why he was not compelled to turn and run after his comrades. He wanted to — God knew he wanted to. He saw Ezra Blake standing close beside him on the right, Sugar Dave Dixon on his left. Not far away was George Hunt, and farther down the line Ed Ripley. There were others too, all continuing to stand firm.

Jem felt a spark of relief flame in a heart chilled by fear. He was not alone. His friends stood with him. Though many had fled, a few stout hearts remained for the fight.

Up ahead, in the open field between the oncoming Federals and the hemorrhaging Confederate line, Percy Claiborne knelt cradling his dead father's head in his lap.

Breathing a quiet *Goddammit,* Jem broke from the line and raced ahead. Sugar Dave and the others shouted at him, but the concussion of the guns sucked their voices from the air.

Jem pumped his legs and finally reached Percy Claiborne's side. He hauled the boy to his feet. Percy fought against him like an animal, but he was weak with grief. Jem dragged the boy with him, finding a rifle and thrusting it into his hands, and he pushed Percy back to rejoin the line.

The bluebellies surged up the hill, but they appeared to be tiring. Lieutenant Lowery called the remaining Mavericks to walk slowly and steadily backwards, eyes and bayonets forward. Inch by inch, the wavering line passed back below the crest of the hill and out of sight of the Federals.

"Form a wall and here we stand!" Lowery shouted. "When they come over the top, we'll give them a welcoming surprise!"

Hearing the sound of pounding hooves, Jem craned his neck to catch a glimpse of the returning General Jackson and his aides as they thundered behind the line and implored the men to stay their ground.

"Hold fast, men of the South!" Jackson cried in a deep baritone drawl. "What's happened here?"

Lieutenant Lowery waited for a whining shell to pass. "The company commander is dead, General. Shot through the heart."

Jackson listened intently and nodded. "Very commendable. Very commendable indeed." Then the general whipped himself out of the saddle and dismounted. Jackson was not a large man, but his spirit was such that he seemed taller than any man around him. He called to the retreating men, "*Hold fast*! You are Virginia boys and you fight on Virginian soil. This is your home, the Lord Jesus Christ is your God, and I am your general. I am proud—"

Federal shells screamed. The line took three hits. Hot shrapnel sliced through dozens of screaming men. Jem watched with white shock as six Mavericks — boys he knew, old schoolmates and North Branch miners and good old boys — fell to the ground in ragged pieces. Frantic voices again called for a retreat, but again Jackson shouted over them.

"I am proud of each and every one of you. You have my eternal gratitude." Jackson raised his voice louder. "*Hold fast, you men of Virginia*! We have the Lord as our shield. Those traitors will soon appear atop that hill. And when they break upon us, we shall turn them round and give them the bayonet!"

A tremendous cheer went up and down the thin line. It was unlike anything Jem had ever heard in his life. A cry of unity, a defiant insult hurled at approaching Death. All around him, Jem felt the presence of sheepish comrades returning to the line. Many of those who had retreated had decided to come back. Jem felt his spirits rise. His heart was still encased in ice, but he felt the warm trickle of hot blood thaw his fear.

The line would hold.

From beyond the crest of the hill, the Federals let out a great cheer.

"*Here they come!*" Blake shouted.

When the first of the Federal troops appeared on the horizon and crested the domed hill, the boys in gray launched a salvo of jeers at them. The blue wave had lost strength in its extended charge, growing sluggish in its struggle up the long, unending climb under withering fire. As the Confederate cheers rang out across the smoking hill, the bluecoats looked down and faltered. But the vanguard were at the front of a stampede, and the crush of the pounding herd forced them down the hill to meet their destiny, whatever it would be.

For most, that destiny was to be a bullet. The call now went up the Confederate line:

"*MAKE READY!*"

Jem dropped his musket into firing position. The sight at the end of the barrel was crooked and hammered out of shape. He let his instincts aim for him. Ahead, the Federals raced closer.

Twenty yards and closing. Rifles popped from close range. More men around Jem fell to the ground, gored by bullets and shrapnel.

Jem became aware that Sugar Dave was shouting something at him. Jem turned to answer him. The next instant, a shrieking bullet caught Sugar Dave's throat and unleashed a gout of blood and ragged flesh. Another weak heartbeat's worth of blood trickled out from the hole in Sugar Dave's throat and then he was dead.

In a dying reflex, Dave's finger squeezed his musket's trigger. The musket fired into the air like the gunshot before a race. The sharp crack struck the company of Mavericks like a lightning bolt. Some boys fired instinctively, and others threatened to break to the finish line, which was anywhere but here.

"*HOLD FIRE!*" Lowery screamed.

From behind the line, General Jackson shouted: "*Do not fire until you see the whites of their Yankee eyes!*"

Sugar Dave's limp body collapsed against Jem. Taking his friend in his arms, Jem lowered him to rest in the blood-soaked grass. He stared horrified at Dave's neck and chin, which had been raked and gored by hot metal. The boy's wide, innocent eyes were glazed and lightless.

"Oh, Davey. Davey, God..."

"*AIM!*"

"Up, Jem!" George Hunt shouted. Tears were streaming down his cheeks. "Up for Davey!"

Jem struggled to stand again, but his feet were caught under Dave's weight.

"FIRE!"

Jem's eardrums split open as a hundred muskets cracked at once. He gagged on the sharp tang of iron on his tongue. Gunsmoke plunged into his lungs. Less than ten yards away, several of the bluecoats sprinting toward him suddenly toppled and fell, many cut legless, headless, or completely in two. Smoke shrouded the carnage like a blanket of rippling death.

But still the Federals came on, pouring up and over the hill. Jem searched the ground for his rifle, for any weapon he could find. Ahead, several figures in blue staggered forward. They were nearly on top of him. They saw him through narrowing eyes that were filled with rage and terror.

Lowery screamed, "Fire at will!"

At last, Jem found a Colt revolver holstered against Sugar Dave's belt. From somewhere in time, Dave's voice echoed in Jem's ringing ears:

A gift from my daddy.

Jem pulled the revolver free, cocked it, and fired point blank into the face of a boy with lush blonde hair under a blue cap. The face disappeared in a burst of flesh and brains and the body it commanded dropped lifeless.

Jem emptied the revolver into the smoke. Then he picked up a rifle and stabbed blindly at the smoke with its attached bayonet. He felt a shudder and heard a guttural scream, and he squeezed off a blind shot before pulling the bayonet back to find it slicked red with blood.

When the shell hit near his feet, the explosion split the earth and sent Jem sailing through the air. The ground, covered in mangled corpses, rushed to meet him. The impact knocked the wind from his lungs, and he gasped like a river trout writhing on dry land. The screams of battle around him somehow sounded like children laughing — laughing at the absurd sight of some flopping, choking fish with its eyes bulging wide, a laughter unable to comprehend the creature's writhing, unspeakable agony.

Jem clutched his chest. He tried in vain to breathe—

Breathe!

Feeling the world drain away, Jem shut his eyes tight and thought of Audrey.

❧

When Jem finally came to, he was staring into a pair of fierce, glittering blue eyes.

"On your feet, soldier!"

General Jackson hauled him up by the collar. The general stooped, dusted off Jem's forage cap, and slapped it on his head.

"There. Yourself again."

Jackson pushed Jem back to rejoin the line and stalked behind as the line reformed. Bewildered, Jem watched the general sink his teeth deep into a bright yellow lemon. Just how many of those damn things did the man have in his pocket?

Jem checked himself for wounds. He patted his arms, chest, legs, and groin. Everything was where it was supposed to be, and for a moment Jem stood stunned. Then there was an earth-shattering hammering — another volley of musket fire. Jem ducked as bullets whizzed by, slashed the ground, and punched holes through the boys around him. He pried a rifle free from a dead man's clutches and hurried over to join the main line. The line was thin, ragged, but holding.

"*Steady*, boys." That was Lieutenant Lowery, his saber held high. "Steady. Reload!"

Jem checked his rifle and realized it hadn't been fired even once. Its previous owner had been killed before even getting off a single shot. Jem peered through the smoke. The sharp crack of rifles punctuated the screams from either side.

"*Aim*!"

Jem dropped to one knee to steady himself. The Federals came on again, looking ghoulish in soot-covered uniforms. This was the final wave set to break upon the shoreline — it had to be.

Jem became suddenly aware of the muscles in his back. They were tense, cramped. He straightened and exhaled deeply, let his posture soften and relax, allowed his mind and vision to clear.

He found his target.

"*Fire*!"

Jem squeezed and the musket bucked. Not five yards away, the Federals seemed to all drop dead at once. Those lucky enough to survive the hellfire broke ranks and fled down the hill, screaming for a general retreat.

Someone shouted wildly and Jem's eyes darted to their left flank. He blinked and tried to shake the mirage from his eyes, but what he saw was really there, really happening. Hundreds of horses and riders in gray pounded across the woodland. Many of the fleeing Federals were trampled down under-hoof.

"Jeb Stuart!" someone cried.

"That's Jeb *goddamn* Stuart!" another shouted.

Jem squinted. Jeb Stuart? Who the hell was that?

"Lookit, he's got a peacock feather in his cap!"

The men cheered as the gray horsemen came on. The Confederate cavalry had arrived to win the day.

"Look at those fuckin gloryhounds!" Ezra Blake shouted. "They're stealin our fight, the bastards!"

It is a strange thing to hear men laugh at a joke in the midst of bloody carnage, but that is what the Mavericks did. And everything that happened next Jem could scarcely recall later, for it happened very quickly.

General Jackson drew his saber with a shrill slicing sound that commanded attention from the boys like a dog whistle might enrapture a pack of hounds.

"Let's give 'em hell, boys! *Yell like furies!*"

At the same instant, the boys became just like that pack of hounds. Rather, they became wolves and foxes and coyotes — the hunted turned loose upon the hunters. They dropped low, and from their throats came a guttural scowling and snarling, baying and barking, howling, whining, and roaring. The Mavericks now had one terrifying voice of rage and bloodlust.

Together the Mayfair boys sprinted after the retreating Federals, firing and reloading as they went. They rolled over bodies in blue, unflinching against the hail of bullets and metal balls. A man to Jem's left dropped, made legless from a cannonball skipping up the hill like a stone on water. Two men on the right fell to rifle fire. But amid the chase, Jem's fear melted away. At the top of his lungs Jem cried *VIRGINIA!* with the others.

Up ahead, a color bearer drove the Stars and Bars through the melee. Bullets tore strips of cloth from the flag, but the bearer heaved the flagpole and signaled the charge. At that moment, a desperate deluge of Federal gunfire raked the Confederate line. The flag pitched and dipped, and finally it toppled to the ground while flames rolled over the cloth. The Mavericks, and the gray lines on either side, wavered and shrank away from the feeding frenzy just ahead. Only one of them pushed forward.

Jem Roscoe ran for the colors.

He ran, not sure whether he was actually willing his body onward or if it was some unknown force that guided him. But he committed, and soon he stood over the dying color bearer and wrenched the flagpole from his defiant hands. As he pulled, Jem caught a glimpse of the man's eyes looking out from blackened flesh, and they signaled to him some unspoken message that would yet shake Jem for months to come, would send him spinning out of his dreams in a cold sweat. But then the dying man's eyes and message were gone, and Jem was running full tilt into the hailstorm. He gripped the flagpole and gritted his teeth.

The wind was strong, and the colors went taut and flew against him. A great, shaking energy surged from the spike atop the pole down to sting Jem's white knuckles. He gripped harder and heaved the pole, and now his bulging arms commanded the colors with all his strength. He drew the flag right, now left, and right again, as hard and as fast as he could. His arms were drained but kept on pumping with some phantom strength.

The boys of Mayfair watched the colors dance and dip for a long moment, blinking not because of the misty sting of gunpowder but because their disbelieving eyes were trained on crazy Jem Roscoe hurling himself up the hill and over it, he and the flag wreathed in smoke. Before their very eyes, the silhouette of the running boy transformed into the shape of a man, and the burning red clouds beyond cast a titan's shadow along the bleeding, smoking hill in his wake.

And so with great cheers, squalls, and roars, their chests burning hotter than they'd ever know again in their lives, however brief some would be, the Mayfair boys raced to join their new color bearer, to cross themselves over the threshold from which he beckoned. They raced to become men, and their Rebel yell echoed down the hillside.

The flag snarled in the savage wind and seemed to carry Jem up into the air until he was flying over the earth. And when at last he stepped down to the ground again, the battlefield — the whole world — belonged to the Mayfair Mavericks.

Seeing the bluebellies turn and flee at last, watching the boys in gray take the field, Jem planted the colors in the blood-soaked ground. Heaving for breath, he looked up at the tatters of the flag flying in the wind. Jem put a hand to his smoking chest and felt the pulsing fire within him burn, burn, burn.

And far overhead, the tranquil blue sky appeared as cheerfully indifferent as it ever had in all the ages of the world.

❧

Later, Jem wandered about the smoking battlefield. Though he did not admit as much to himself, he was looking for JJ.

It was very quiet. The smoke was clearing. Jem's nostrils flared, stung by the stench of burning flesh. There were dead men everywhere. Dead *boys*, mostly, and whether they were clad in blue or gray didn't matter anymore. Jem guessed that many of them had come from hardworking farm families. The boys would be missed come harvest time, and in all the times to come. They had mothers who upon hearing the tragic news would lose all joy in life, never to be whole again. They had fathers who would soon spend their waking hours lost in a fog, their sleeping hours wasted by the guilt of signing the enlistment papers.

Jem looked down at his blackened hands. He knew for sure that he'd killed at least one man — a boy — earlier that day. The boy had had blonde hair…or had it been brown? Blue eyes, or maybe green. But no, they were definitely blue. Those eyes had looked right at him, fixed upon his soul, right before the bullet from Jem's hand blew the life out of them.

Jem imagined going to the home of the boy he'd killed. He imagined standing on the doorstep with his forage cap in his hands. He saw the mother and father opening the door, and he could see how their faces fell when their meager, impossible hope — the hope that their beloved boy was alive and had come home — was dashed forever. And Jem imagined speaking to them, trying to explain to them why it was their boy who had to die, why Jem had been forced to kill him. He was only following orders, you see, and everything was happening so quickly. Why, your boy might have killed Jem first if he had the chance. Would that have been any better for them, knowing their son was a killer? He could almost hear their whispered response, that they'd rather have a killer son than no son at all, before the door was shut in Jem's face.

But Jem had performed his duty, the duty of all soldiers.

Just like the dead boy had.

And just like Sugar Dave Dixon too.

Jem tried to turn away from the dead boys and found there was no escape from them. He gagged, staggered, fell to his knees. For a time, the world was lost and everything went black.

The field belonged to the South. That was a certainty. For most of the day, the Mayfair Mavericks and the rest of Virginia's 1st Brigade held the hill against wave after wave of Federal troops while General Jackson strolled behind them, urging his boys on. There was no question that the Federals outnumbered the Confederates, but when Jeb Stuart's cavalry arrived to save the day, the Federals had turned and fled. Jem's heartbeat quickened when he remembered the Mayfair boys' war cries echoing in his still-ringing ears.

The air stank of sweet death. The grass all around was covered with mounds of smoking bodies and torn limbs adrift in rivers of blood. The flies gathered in clouds through the smoke. They were settling down to lay their eggs. Soon the maggots would come.

Thunder pealed somewhere distant. A hard rain was coming soon. Jem wondered if they could bury all the bodies before they started to rot and become larvae nests. He waited for some sign from above, some indication that the souls of all these dead men all around him were ascending to a better place. Maybe he could go with them and forget about everything he'd seen today.

But no angels came, and there was no heavenly singing. The clouds of late July rolled on as they always had. Somewhere, somehow, the birds that had been so silent that morning began to sing again.

Jem felt eyes on the back of his head. He turned to see Ezra Blake staring at him.

"So you made it too," Blake murmured.

Jem nodded. He realized he hadn't seen Blake for hours, not since they'd routed the Federals. That felt like an eternity ago. He looked around for the rest of their company. "Any of the others?"

"Your pal Hunt made it."

Jem sighed with relief. "Thank God. Have you seen Ripley?"

Blake grunted that he had. He gestured across the field. "He got pinched in the arm but he made it. Lowery in the neck, he's all right. But Alden, Young, Rawlins, all gone." Blake examined the carnage without expression. Suddenly, he remembered: "And Tommy Burke, he's dead too." It was like he was reading a grocery list. He finished by saying, "We tore them to goddamn pieces."

"They tore us something awful in return," Jem replied. He said quietly, "Dave Dixon—"

"I know," Blake said. "I seen it."

Jem heard a low groaning from somewhere. Peering through the drifting smoke, he saw a young boy propped up against a pile of ragged bodies. A marching drum lay smashed at his side. The boy's leg had been torn clean off. His blood had mixed with the blood of a hundred others in a dark red pond. Jem waded through the pond saw that the boy wore a blue uniform.

Blake noticed too. Without a word, he strode over and raised his rifle like a club. Jem lunged and caught Blake's arms before he crested the swing. His arms nearly broke under Blake's brute strength.

"Wait!" Jem cried, straining to hold. "It's finished, Ezra. Let it be."

Blake stared at him, bug-eyed and breathing hard. Slowly, he lowered his rifle and turned away.

Jem was left looking down at the wounded Yankee. He bent down on one knee to get a closer look. The boy before him certainly wasn't JJ. And really, what hope did he think he had of finding JJ in all this mess? Maybe it was for the best he hadn't found his brother, because Jem had no idea what he would do if he ever did.

"Everything's all right now," Jem said to the Yankee. "No one will hurt you."

The boy's lip quivered and his eyes were fearful. He was still waiting for a knife or a bullet.

Jem studied the boy's dirty face. He was very young. Jem thought first of Tom, and then he thought of the other Yankee boy he'd shot earlier that day. Jem squeezed his eyes shut and tried to banish the thought from his mind.

"What's your name?" the boy asked in a weak voice. His face was whiter than even a few moments ago. He was fading.

"Jeremiah," Jem said. "I'm from Virginia. What's yours?"

He waited. The boy was trying to say something. Blood bubbled at the corner of his mouth, and he tried to blink away the tears welling in his eyes. But when his eyes opened again, they were unseeing, glazed with death, hot tears already cooling in his eye ducts. Jem waited longer, maybe out of hope but more out of desperation. But the boy was dead, and to Jem he would remain nameless.

Blake returned. "Shoulda let me do it."

Jem sighed and stood up. "What's the point?"

Blake's answer was to spit on the drummer boy's body.

There was frantic movement and shouting behind them. An ecstatic George Hunt rushed up to join them.

"*Jackson's being hailed a hero*!" Hunt shouted. He was still deaf from the noise of battle. Jem and Blake failed to respond immediately, and so he shouted louder, *"Jackson's being hailed a hero! You hear me? I said, Jackson's being—"*

Blake slapped him across the face.

Hunt went instantly red with fury. *"Hey, now what's the idea?!"*

"Stop shouting."

"*What?!*"

"I said *stop fucking shouting!*"

Hunt fell silent. He'd finally heard and understood. Then, quieter: "General Jackson's being hailed—"

"Goddammit, we heard you the first time."

Jem stood and looked away from the dead drummer boy. "What's this all about, George?"

Hunt plunged a finger into one of his ears. "Word round is Jackson's brigade — that's *us*, mind you — stopped the Yankees single-handedly." He beamed with pride. "Joe Johnston and all the top generals called us Virginians 'the Stone Wall.' We held the line until the others could fetch their pigs from the sty, so to speak."

"So to speak," Blake said contemptuously. "Seems we's the only fuckin saps who can tie our boots in this goddamn circus. You see how many other companies turned tail and ran while we held em back?"

"So what now?" Jem asked Hunt.

Hunt smiled. "The newspapers are gonna make 'Stonewall' Jackson famous, that's what. If that don't earn a drink for his boys, I don't know what will."

"Famous?" Blake echoed. "Well, how bout that."

Jem turned and watched as a line of ambulance carts rumbled forward. It was time for the victors of the battle to count and collect the dead of both sides.

"Yeah," Jem said grimly. "How about that."

All together, the Mavericks piled identifiable bodies into the ambulance carts, which would transport them to the trains. Bodies that couldn't be identified, or were in too rough shape to be moved, were to be buried on the spot.

"Stack the bodies to make room," Lieutenant Lowery ordered gruffly. Seeing the strained faces of his men, his expression softened a little. "If you can. And load the wounded at the front."

Lieutenant Lowery, now acting company commander, tallied the dead. A ricochet wound in his neck had made him irritable, and the loss of forty-five dead and wounded — nearly half the company, including Captain Claiborne — had shaken his resolve.

Jem found Ed Ripley standing over the body of Sugar Dave Dixon. An ambulance waited nearby. Slowly, Ripley knelt and shut the miller's boy's eyes. Ripley then removed some of Dave's personal belongings to send home. One of the items was a group photograph of their tent mess — Jem, Dave, Ripley, and Hunt —

taken back in the late spring in Winchester. Ripley handed the photograph, folded and creased, to Jem, who looked at it for a long moment. Everyone in the photo wore a mean, warlike grimace except for Sugar Dave. Old Davey was smiling, his eyes bright and full of eager excitement, and his Colt revolver was gripped in his hand as if he was a baby-faced gunslinger. For the buttermilk-drinking boy who had never hurt a fly, who had never fired a shot in anger, the war — and everything else — was over.

Jem shuddered under the threat of tears. He bit them back and stuffed the photograph into his jacket.

"I'll help," Hunt said, and he joined Jem and Ripley over Dave's body.

Jem stooped low and nodded to the others, and they took hold of the boy's hands and feet.

"Let's get him up," Jem said. "Ready? One, two, three..."

Chapter 47
CHOICES

From the Valley below, JJ looked up as pockets of orange flame consumed swathes of evergreens atop the North Branch. He studied the gaping black mouth of the North Branch Mine, the deforested mountainside, the slag heaps, the stacks of timber logs piled ten men thick and five men high. His gaze fixed on the tiny speck that was the mine's main office, the finishing school of his father's ambitions and the birthplace of his own. His eyes followed the choking black smoke as it rolled over the mountaintop and drifted into the blue summer sky.

Down in Mayfair, still asleep on a Sunday morning, drums rolled a slow cadence. Cruel bayonet blades reflected in shop windows while heavy boots crunched the gravel of abandoned streets. The Federal vanguard began to assemble barricades at the courthouse as curious townspeople, drawn by the stench of smoke up on the Branch, looked upon the Yankees and their wordless machinations with expressions of wonder, denial, and hatred. Behind the vanguard came a long column of soldiers winding down the mountainside like a giant blue snake, with hundreds of bayonets glinting in the sun like so many scales.

General McClellan and his army had arrived in the Mayfair Valley.

The men marched briskly but their heads swiveled, eyes darting around, alert for danger. They were volunteers on mere three-month contracts, and while their hearts swelled with bravado, they were not keen on being massacred like rumors told of the armies near Washington. *Sensible* was the watchword, repeated loudly by the company sergeants:

"Look sensible, boys! This is secesh country!"

JJ looked all around. Secesh country. *His* country. Now, foreign soil.

Sitting a black Saddler in the main square opposite the courthouse, JJ saw in his mind's eye the great gathering that must have taken place there just a few months ago, when all of Mayfair had seen their brave boys off to war. JJ imagined Jem among those boys, looking happy and proud in a new gray uniform. JJ's heart tightened in his chest, but he promptly swallowed down any emotion and spurred his horse forward.

JJ had offered the estate of Clarendon to General McClellan in order to draw battle plans. No doubt the Young Napoleon's intent was to use Mayfair as a doorway into the wider Shenandoah, and from there march toward Richmond and link up with the larger army marching south from Washington.

The Rebels, of course, might already be on their way west to intercept McClellan's contingent. There were, after all, rumors on the wire about a general engagement in the fields south of Washington, though no one could make sense of the garbled reports. But if the Rebel army hit McClellan with as large a force as his top aides suggested, it would take nothing for the Rebels to roll back this tiny force of men all the way up Virginia's northwestern tip. And if the Rebels made it that far, they might seize Wheeling and arrest the Restored Government assembled there. The hope of either restoring Virginia to the Union, or else of creating a West Virginia that stood against the Confederacy, would be lost.

And so, the orders came down: McClellan would plant himself here in Mayfair as long as was needed, and if the Rebels attacked they would be funneled into the Valley which would become like a deathtrap for them. In the meantime, the railroad line leading to the Valley (the one John Roscoe had built years before) was to be wrecked. The North Branch Mine was also ordered for destruction, with McClellan aiming to starve the Rebels of precious fuel. Further orders specified that civilians and other property were to be left untouched, but protesters and Rebel sympathizers would be arrested. Anyone who took up arms against United States troops would be summarily shot.

JJ trotted up the street, eyeing his reflection in the windows of Father's old congressional office and various shops and sundry stores. The front windows of Dance & Franklin's General had been shattered by looters in the night, and now two soldiers stood sentry while a group of young slave boys picked up shards of glass from the street.

JJ passed outlying homes until there were only wooded thickets on either side of the road. He passed companies of men who cheered his skill at jumping a stone wall. His horse snorted and shifted uneasily at the approaching smell of burning, but JJ dug his spurs and urged her across the bridge over Sleepy Creek.

At Clarendon, which shone a brilliant white under the hot sun, soldiers were busy erecting a blockade where the ruined front gate had once stood. JJ passed through the picket line and rode hard down the main path. Soldiers and officers milled about on the veranda, talking and smoking and eating sandwiches. JJ dismounted before the house and tossed the reins to a black orderly.

JJ entered Clarendon to find the house filled with cigar smoke and lively debates. The library was now host to fifty staff officers in blue poring over maps and drinking tall glasses of Father's private liquor stock.

As JJ stood observing his surroundings, a deep voice sounded behind him:

"Welcome home, Lieutenant."

JJ turned and saluted General McClellan. "Thank you, sir."

McClellan wrinkled his nose at the pervading smell of smoke. "I sense your mission's been accomplished, Jon."

"It is, General. I've set a controlled fire to collapse the mine. It won't do the Rebels any good anymore."

McClellan nodded and went to the window. "I suppose it won't do us any good either. The War Department seems to have forgotten its soldiers travel on trains too, and those trains need coal. But with the Rebels seizing every railyard in Virginia..." The general stared out at the plumes of black smoke rising from the North Branch. He sipped at a glass of Father's bourbon and smiled at the pleasure of its taste. "Still, a shame to destroy your inheritance. Such is war, I suppose."

JJ nodded. "Yes, sir."

McClellan offered a knowing smile and started toward the hallway. "Take a walk with me, Jon, won't you?"

"Of course, sir."

JJ fell into step with the general. He did his best to ignore the jealous, petulant stares of the other officers present. It was well known that McClellan surrounded himself with staff officers whose loyalty edged toward the fanatical. JJ knew such an inner circle would be tough to crack.

McClellan announced he wanted some fresh air. JJ knew the way and led him down to a set of French doors that opened out to the veranda.

Outside in the open air, McClellan stopped to smell the flowers blooming from one of Mae Jane's many garden boxes perched along the veranda. The general leaned in very close to sniff, so close that he disturbed a honeybee nestled in the pollen. The bee shot upward with an angry buzz that caused the general to leap back in fright. Soon the bee, confused and forgetful, flew off somewhere. McClellan righted himself and, seeing JJ watching him, quickly smoothed down his hair and uniform and cleared his throat.

"I thought it was a wasp."

"Yes, sir," JJ said. "I suppose that's the trouble with beautiful flowers. They attract all sorts of pests."

McClellan smiled and turned down the veranda toward the south end. "You've done fine work here in...where is this...Mayfair? You've done fine work here in Mayfair, Jon."

"Thank you, General."

"Really, I mean it. As I've said before, I've no reason to brown my nose for you. But there is no question you are a fine soldier, and still so young. You might yet prove to be the best of all of us."

Hearing this praise, JJ's pulse throbbed and his heart performed a somersault. "I do appreciate it, sir. Very much so, sir."

JJ expected the general to continue praising him, or else to bring JJ into his confidence somehow. But instead, the general's face became troubled.

"You make a fine soldier, but I wonder if you'd be better suited as a politician. An *abolitionist* politician, for that matter. Maybe a Republican."

JJ's pride turned to ashes in his mouth. "I'm afraid I don't understand, sir. I'm a Democrat, have been my whole life."

McClellan shrugged. "Your decision to let a band of negroes camp out on the back lawn of this estate suggests otherwise."

Ah, so that was it.

"Sir, is this about my decision to—?"

"Yes it is," McClellan replied stiffly. "This is about your decision to steal Southern property."

JJ blinked. "*Steal?* Sir, those negroes came to me inspired by their own delusions. They came freely..." He drifted off, and thought about his next words carefully. "Even if they did not come to me freely per se, they did come to me of their own free will."

"Details, Lieutenant, these are details — not truths. This way to the garden?"

JJ gestured forward. "After you, sir."

They descended the veranda steps and traced a slow path through the garden and the willow grove beyond. Childhood memories of treading this same path with Father — of circling the grove countless times, with minutes becoming hours — they all came flooding back to JJ in an instant. It took all his strength to stamp them down, to push them back into the lockbox from which they'd sprung.

"Are you feeling all right, Jon?"

"Yes, sir," JJ said, turning his head. "Just a touch of something, is all. Maybe it's all the flowers."

McClellan gave a low grunt and continued his line of thought. "The truth is," he said, "you can't go around freeing and anointing negroes like you're the Pope of Rome. You can't do it, and I can't let you do it, because President Lincoln won't allow it. Republican hack or not, he's already shown he has the sand to sack a man like General Frémont for trying the very same thing over in Missouri."

"Sir?"

"Just what I said, Jon. An officer who outranks both of us tried the very same stunt out west, and now he's gone. Why? Because this is no time for altruism. Freeing slaves presents a score of problems, starting first with logistics. How do you feed them? Where do they sleep, what do they do with their time? We are soldiers, not brothers of some holy order. You've got those darkies penned up like sheep, but are you going to protect them from the wolves forever?

"And beyond the work of soldiers, there is the question of secession. Fine enough to rob a Virginian of his slaves when Virginia is already at war with the Union. But what will the people of Maryland say? Or the people of Kentucky? Those states are still pledged to the Union cause, but what will happen when they learn that Union soldiers are actively stealing their neighbors' property? By giving a few blacks their freedom, you might inadvertently add more stars to the Confederate banner. And all the resulting deaths would be on your hands."

JJ listened with a bowed head. There was no denying that McClellan's logic was sharp.

The young general sniffed. "While George McClellan is in command of Union troops, I will give that lanky ape in the White House no cause for giving me the boot. What's more, I will uphold the laws of the Union. Today, the laws of the Union include the Fugitive Slave Law. We are compelled by law to return runaways to their rightful owners."

JJ took a deep breath. The general's logic was indeed sharp, but did it weigh all considerations?

"With respect, General. My decision to shelter the enemy's...*property*, if we must call them that...was made out of necessity. By taking away their chattel slaves, we take away their industry. We pull out the rotting platform upon which the Rebels stand, sir. Without slaves to power their economy, their means to make war will collapse by next summer."

McClellan nodded. "Your decision, from a soldier's perspective, was a good one. But civilians do not think like soldiers. Politicians especially do not think like soldiers. Were the politicians willing to get out of soldiers' way, I might have made the decision myself." Here, McClellan gave a great belly laugh. "Although I must say, I would never have promised the negroes their *freedom*. For God's sake, that is a cruel joke you played, Jon."

JJ pretended to laugh along, but in truth he was busy thinking about Abel, the brave slave who had gathered over a dozen slaves from the South Branch and led them across the Valley. When they arrived, JJ opened Clarendon's slave cabins for them to live in, and gave them food and water, and placed them under guard lest any slave-catchers try to kidnap them. Indeed he had hoped McClellan might help him arrange to send the slaves somewhere north, far from the Valley.

"Yes, sir," JJ said, still laughing. "That's just my sense of humor, sir."

"A sick sense," the general agreed. "At war's end, those poor wretches would be heartbroken to learn that their saviors in blue would only turn them back to their masters. They are a selfish race of men, Jon, those negroes. They really think this war is about *them*."

JJ maintained a laughing smile. "As I said, General, they came to me with their own delusions."

"Indeed," McClellan said. "Well, the bungling of the slave question will rest on Lincoln's shoulders." The young general's eyes now turned inward, and his face darkened. "And it's my estimation that our president is a stupid, weak-willed man — and there he is, in charge of everything!" He shook his head with another laugh, but suddenly he looked up at JJ as if JJ himself had uttered such slander. "What, do you resent your general for mocking the commander in chief?"

JJ shook his head. "Not at all, sir. In fact, I'm rather inclined to agree."

They rounded the last turn along the garden path, and now they stood before Father's gravesite. Once again, JJ's mind flooded with vicious emotions coursing at breakneck speed, and if he had been alone he might have collapsed upon his knees. Knowing McClellan was now watching him closely, JJ bit his tongue behind clamped lips and maintained an outward show of calm, collected stillness.

McClellan looked toward Father's headstone. "I didn't know John Roscoe as well as I might have liked, but I know he was a good Democrat. Like me, he believed the best course of action is to preserve and maintain. Were you very close with him?"

JJ's lips moved, but the croaking voice that answered did not feel like his own.

"Yes. Once."

McClellan asked no more questions about Father. "Politics is a noble pursuit," the general said, returning to an earlier point in their conversation. "It is the men who practice politics for personal gain — those are the men we should be wary of. Oh, I've seen it already, Jon, even when I was raising troops in Pennsylvania. I witnessed congressmen demanding field commissions, governors demanding whole armies to lead, committees of bloodsucking backbenchers obstructing every provision of military necessity while quarreling about trivialities. We aren't six months into the war and it's already become a sham, a circus event. Gone are the days when a soldier could perform his duties without a politician breathing down his neck. There are too many compromises."

Still staring at Father's grave, JJ pondered all this before speaking up again.

"Perhaps it's time to do away with compromise," JJ said. "My father was ambitious, but his goals were always curbed by the whims of other men. Perhaps, instead of propping up dealmakers and compromisers, it's time to put men of real conviction in power. The Union has reached a crisis point, General, and only decisive action can stop it. The purest, most effective decisions are often made by a single intellect. An intellect like yours, General, if I might be so bold to say."

McClellan smiled. "Don't tempt me, Lieutenant. The Romans said as much to Caesar once upon a time." He smoothed the ends of his mustache. "You say you have great ambitions, Jon. Are they really so very great?"

JJ saw that McClellan was staring at him intently. He returned the stare squarely, unblinking.

"Yes, sir. Absolutely, sir. As I said, I'm a decision-maker. I assess a situation, I weigh the possibilities, and I take action to effect a solution. And if I'm speaking honestly, sir, my abilities have caused me some strain with a roster of superior officers."

McClellan laughed. "I know they have. And you should know, I don't take insubordination lightly. But I also know a good man when I see one, and I think you're sharp enough to know that however loud you may bark at me, I can always bark louder. That said, I think — and looking at you presently I feel quite assured — that there won't be any strain between you and I. In fact, I should think a commander ought to welcome such a freethinking spirit, and daresay encourage it. Let the banner fly freely in the wind, as it were. Strategy is mine to dictate, but the tactics shall be yours to execute. Any act, at any cost, to win the war. Wouldn't you agree?"

JJ beamed. "Yes, sir."

Now, placing a muscled hand on JJ's shoulder, McClellan drew JJ in very close until JJ could almost taste the whiskey on the general's lips.

"Those negroes will be sent back to their masters, Jon. I mean they'll be sent back today. No one in Washington will hear a word about it. No careers need be ruined by one little mistake. All this will become just another of Johnny Reb's rumors. But I *will* return those slaves, Jon, and then we'll all get back to soldiering."

JJ stared into his general's eyes. He thought again about the slaves who had come to him. Abel and the others wanted nothing more than safe passage out of the Valley, and from there to be left alone to make their own way.

JJ thought about arguing his case further, but decided against it. When a man like McClellan made up his mind, it was made up. And probably the general was doing JJ a favor by shielding him from the machinations of all those power-hungry bureaucrats in Washington, who just like the Jacobins of revolutionary France were desperate to make public examples out of anyone who stepped out of line.

McClellan's eyes hardened. "I trust you agree with my decision, Lieutenant?"

And so JJ, who had never shied away from the challenges of other superiors like Beauregard and Anderson, nonetheless hung his head before the Young Napoleon.

"Yes, sir. Of course, sir."

McClellan's eyes shone. He pulled back, his face brightening again. "Good man," he said, and he slapped JJ on the back.

They were interrupted by roaring halloos coming from the front of the house. Confounded, McClellan turned and abandoned the willow grove. JJ remained standing before Father's gravestone for a moment longer. Feeling another wave of emotion rearing its head, preparing to crash down, JJ turned his back on the stone and fled from the garden as fast as he could.

McClellan led the way to the front veranda, and there JJ saw mounted messengers riding hard up the path toward them. As McClellan stepped forward, the officers and men lounging about the veranda stood up and saluted their young general.

One of the approaching horsemen, a middle-aged colonel with a fine-combed beard, dismounted and hurried over to McClellan. "Urgent message from Washington, General."

JJ watched the general's face as he read the telegram. McClellan's bright expression faded to a dark frown, and his shining eyes clouded to dull glass.

"Christ Almighty. It's as bad as I feared."

McClellan looked up at the men standing nearby, who watched their general with bated breath.

"It was a massacre," McClellan said. "That damn fool McDowell has been routed by the Rebel commanders Johnston and Beauregard."

JJ's eye twitched at the mention of Beauregard. Christ, that damn Creole got around, didn't he?

"The nation's army has been defeated on the banks of the Bull Run River near Manassas," McClellan went on. "Even as we speak, the Rebel army might be moving to surround and besiege Washington."

The officers shook their heads in stunned disbelief.

The colonel who delivered the message was as shocked as anyone. "It doesn't make any sense, sir," the man said. "The Rebel army is an unorganized rabble. Some of them fight without shoes!"

McClellan scratched his chin. "And I suppose they fight very well without them too. I suspect McDowell didn't take the necessary precautions. He didn't scout the terrain, likely underestimated the enemy's numbers and reinforcements. Well, in any case it all proved overwhelming for him, as if that should come as any surprise. *Custer*!"

A bright-faced lieutenant hopped forward. "Yes, sir!"

"Ready my horse. And alert the balance of my staff. We ride for Washington at once."

"Yes, sir, General, sir!"

Stunned, JJ stared at McClellan. "*Washington*, sir? But what about the campaign to secure western Virginia? Is Mayfair to be abandoned?"

It was a question written on the faces of the other officers present. Looking around, McClellan took a deep breath. The dark worry on his face faded, and his smile returned. "I abandon nothing. The defense of the Restored Government is now the responsibility of Colonel Rosecrans here," he said.

The bearded colonel whitened with shock. "...Sir?"

To the whole assembly of men, McClellan now cried, "That's right, gentlemen. The War Department might be inept, but they wouldn't waste a telegram telling me something I already know. The Battle of the Bull Run is lost, but the war goes on. And meanwhile, I will go to *Washington* to take command of the nation's armies. Provided there is still a force of troops there to lead, I will lead them to final victory."

Hearing this, the staff officers broke into wild cheering and applause.

The colonel named Rosecrans stepped forward, and McClellan passed the telegram over to him. "It's all there, Rosey, my friend. You are to command this theater from now on. I'm off to the viper's nest by personal request of the president, who has apparently heard news of our successes here in Virginia."

Rosecrans yet retained a look of shock. "Lincoln's giving McDowell the boot?"

McClellan grinned. "And placing me in command of the Army of the Potomac, that's right."

JJ, for his part, was dumbstruck. The Army of the Potomac! McClellan would now be the man who would lead the Union's largest army.

But where would JJ be when the next great and probably deciding clash finally came? The end of the whole war might pass him by before autumn ended. Would he still be here in Mayfair, the commander of an obscure mountain garrison that saw no action and captured no glory?

"So what do you think, Jon?"

Dazed, JJ turned to McClellan. "I beg your pardon, sir?"

"*Custer*!"

From a distance: "Sir?"

McClellan pointed dramatically at JJ's chest. "I want you to count this man in my escort. Find him a billet when we arrive in the capital."

"Yes, General!"

Looking at JJ again, McClellan turned his pointed finger into an offering hand. "I invite you to join my staff in Washington, Jon. This army has far too many soft bellies for my liking. I could use a man like you. An ally." The young general smiled. "Dare I say, a friend. But I must warn you: I expect unwavering loyalty from my friends. Can I count on your loyalty, *Captain*?"

Captain? Did McClellan just say—

Captain?!

Beaming, JJ took McClellan's hand with strength and vigor. The general's grip clenched down like the jaws of a gator, as if to drive his point home. Awestruck, JJ whispered, "It would be a…a supreme honor…to serve you, General."

McClellan released his grip with a broad smile. "Just see that you don't let me down, Captain."

Turning, the general gave a bow to the assembled officers as they cheered him again.

"This is our time, gentlemen!" McClellan cried. "The old guard is marching away into history, and now is the time for a new generation to take its place. The country has called for a savior, and that savior is me. Ride at my side, and you will have your share of glory. Now, gentlemen, is the season of victory!"

Tears of pride welled in JJ's eyes as he shouted at the top of his lungs with the others:

—*THE SEASON OF VICTORY*!

Trembling with excitement regarding General McClellan's invitation, *Captain* JJ Roscoe (he was already calling himself that, even though his promotion was not yet official) burst into Clarendon's east wing study with great energy.

JJ looked around the darkened room. Mae Jane was at the window with tears in her eyes, for there were soldiers rifling through her prized vegetable garden down below. Little Bayard lay on the floor playing with toy soldiers. Mother was seated at a desk, a pen in her hands and reams of stationery before her. Upon JJ's entering, all eyes looked up at him.

All except for those of one.

"Where's Tom?" JJ asked.

"You tell us somethin first," Mae Jane said, turning away from the window. "You tell us when it is we's allowed outta here. When are them soldiers gonna leave so's we can get back to livin our lives? When do we get our house back?"

"You need to get Tom back in here, and keep him here," JJ said. "If he steps out of line, someone's bound to think him a Rebel and act accordingly. When I'm gone, there won't be anyone around to give him preferential treatment."

"Gone?" Mother echoed. "What do you mean, after you're gone?"

JJ looked at Mother, then stared down at the letters she was writing. "If you divulge any information about Federal troop movements in the Valley area, you could be arrested as a spy."

Mother offered a blank stare. "You really think your own mother would do such a thing?"

JJ scoffed. "In this family? Yes, I do."

"It's a letter to my sister in Atlanta," Mother said. "You must remember Auntie Cordelia?"

JJ grimaced. "Just make sure to keep military matters out of your correspondence," he said. "I say that for your sake and not my own, of course."

Mother returned to her writing. "Oh, of course."

Mae Jane wrung her hands together. "Tell us," she said. "You leavin Clarendon again, and so soon?"

"Today," JJ replied, and he puffed his chest out wide. "You'll be happy to know I'm going away to Washington as a member of General McClellan's staff. McClellan is now Chief of the Army, you know. He'll be the one to lead us to victory over the Rebels, and I'll be right there with him. I've come up here to say goodbye to everyone."

He expected, or rather hoped, to hear sudden and sincere congratulations from Mother and Mae Jane. Instead, Mae Jane offered no response except to look toward the window and stare down at the soldiers uprooting the last of her vegetables.

Mother, for her part, merely turned back to her letters. "Then I guess this is goodbye, Jonathan."

JJ gave a cheerless laugh. "Really? That's it? That's all you're going to say?"

Mother looked up again and shrugged. "You said you came up here to say goodbye. I take it you've done so, and now so have I."

"No well-wishes?" JJ said. "No words of encouragement, or even congratulations?"

Again Mother shrugged. "Tell me the words you wish to hear, and I'll say them."

"But you won't mean them."

"I cannot mean what I don't believe," Mother said. "Our family is tied to Clarendon — to what Clarendon *represents* — in a deeper way than I think you realize. This land is ours, and has been for almost two hundred and fifty years. The blood of nine generations is mixed with the soil at our feet. This place is our *home*, and it is our duty to preserve it for those who will come after us."

"This place is cursed," JJ said. "The soil at our feet was stolen, and later on it was tended by people in chains. I could not see the sickness of Mayfair while I grew up here. But after I left and came back, all was laid bare to me. This whole Valley is like an open wound — a gash cut into the green, good earth — and it's been festering in the sun for many long years." Here, JJ's eyes narrowed at his mother. "You, and every other fool who calls themselves Southerner first, American second, is under the same delusion. The glorious past you yearned for never existed in the first place. There was only ever sorrow and heartbreak."

Mother shook her head. "If such a past never existed, then why are you trying so hard to destroy it? I'm not yet an old woman, Jonathan, but I'm old enough to realize that there is nothing in this world that is entirely good or altogether evil. All that might be said is that the color of the past is painted according to the palette of the present time."

JJ sneered at her. "How trite. Isabella Spencer, the philosopher."

"*Jon Jacob*," Mae Jane said huskily from the corner. "This is you mother, child."

"Is that so?" JJ said. "You were more a mother to me than she was, Mae Jane. You were the true mother to all of us. I still remember walking into the nursery and seeing baby Tom at your breast. Jem didn't believe me, but I knew what I saw. And I recall the stunning realization that, if you nursed Tom, you had nursed the rest of us too." Here, JJ's slitted eyes looked from Mae Jane to Mother. "You nourished the Roscoe children because our *real* mother had poisoned her own milk with that filth she calls medicine."

Mother sat up straight. "I don't take my medicine anymore. And I'll soon be cured of a need for it."

"*Cured?* Oh, you'll never be cured of that disease, Mother — just like I'll never be cured of the so-called disease of the soul which afflicts me, according to you and Father at least. That poison is part of you, no matter how hard you try to stamp it down or bottle it up."

Mae Jane shook her head. "You ain't got no *disease*, Jon Jacob. You ain't got no affliction. But what you do got is hate in you heart, and maybe that's worse. You see enemies everywhere, even among you own family. Now maybe you got good reason for feelin that hate awhile, but tell me, what good's it done for you lately? It's got hold of you like that medicine had a hold of you mother. She's fightin her fight, and it's a hard fight, but God bless her she's *winnin*. You too got what it takes to overcome, to win you own battle. But you can't do it alone, Jon Jacob."

JJ ignored Mae Jane and flashed a smirk at Mother. "So you've really turned the corner, dear Mother? Life has begun anew for you? I suppose congratulations are in order, but forgive me if I say I really don't care."

Tears glistened in Mother's eyes, and for a moment JJ wondered whether he'd gone too far. But thinking of it more, *no*, there was still much more to say. Much more that *deserved* to be said. Mother had said far more to him in the last few minutes than she had said in many years. What did it matter that a cold heart was beginning to thaw, and at so convenient a time? It was too late for Mother to change, just as it had been too late for Father to call JJ to his deathbed. It was too late for the Roscoes, for Clarendon, for all of it.

"This is a house of traitors," JJ growled. "Father was supposed to serve his family and country and served only himself. Jem has rebelled against his flag in some impulse of honor-keeping which he doesn't understand, and which is in fact built on a lie. Sarah has married into a covetous family of secessionists. Tom will grow up to be a failure in your eyes, Mother, just like the rest of us — provided he doesn't get himself killed in the meantime. And as for Bayard..."

Hearing his name, Bayard looked up at JJ. The boy watched him, his eyes unblinking.

"Well," JJ said, a little softer now, "just what can be said of little Bayard?"

Mae Jane reached down and softly squeezed Bayard's shoulder. "He's the best of us," she said. "Bay here is the best of all-us."

JJ's throat tightened again. "The best of us?" he muttered. "He's an idiot. Let's finally call a spade a spade, shall we? *Id-i-ot*. He's the crooked capstone that sits atop this whole rotten structure. He's the future of this family, which is to say, there's no future at all. He can't even understand a fucking word I'm saying right now. Do you, Bayard? Do you understand, dear brother, that you're nothing but a mush-brained fool? Do you understand—?"

"*That's enough*!" Mae Jane hissed, and she went down on her knees beside Bayard. Trembling with fear, Bayard turned and buried his face against Mae Jane's chest. The old mammy glared up at JJ. "Shame on you, Jon Jacob, *shame on you*. What'd this boy ever do you? Ain't he you brother? Ain't you and he share the same blood?"

"Oh, spare me," JJ said. He turned to Mother once more. "But here we see the true Roscoe legacy, and the Spencer legacy wrapped up with it. A crumbling mansion on a weed-choked hilltop. All of the old man's dreams and ambitions gone up in smoke. A brace of traitorous fools, a slave-whipping whore, and a blithering idiot to boot. Oh, and let us not forget the star-child who was promised the brightest of all futures, but who was later dispensed with at the first sign of disappointment. Quite a brood you and Father produced, Mother. Quite a brood indeed."

Very slowly, Mother rose to her feet. She clasped her hands together, and her head was slightly bowed. But her eyes remained fixed on JJ, and they did not look away even once as she spoke to him.

"You are right to be angry, Jonathan," she said. "You are right to feel betrayed. I was never much of a mother to you, or to any of my children. I don't think God intended for me to be a mother, or a wife for that matter. But I bent to the whims of people whom I cared about: the Colonel and my mother, and my sisters, and my perfect Cousin Sarah, and eventually my beloved husband. Indeed I came to care a great deal about the opinions of others, especially veritable strangers who knew the real *me* not at all. It's as if I wanted to appear for each person exactly as I believed they saw me, which is to say, I was a different Isabella to everyone I met.

"Well, a person can only pull on so many faces, can only break up their soul into so many pieces, before they forget which faces and pieces are real and which are imagined. And in time, an actor who is trapped onstage comes to resent her audience, especially those closest to her."

Here, Mother paused to glance at Mae Jane, and they shared a quiet look together before she turned to JJ once more.

"It may seem convenient to you that I blamed all my woes upon my husband, your father. And I can finally admit, it *was* convenient. Your father embodied all the real and imagined expectations which pressed down my shoulders, and I did *hate* him for trapping me. Now I realize I was only trapping myself. For so many years I took solace in remembering some distant time in which I was still *myself*. For the last twenty years, I've lived every present moment lost in the past, wishing I might stay there. Because if only I could go back, I might have made a different choice. I might have spurned the marriage which the Colonel arranged for me. I might have refuted the doctor's insistence I take medicine for my 'hysteria'. I might have taken greater notice and care of my babies, of my family. I might have spoken up in your defense four years ago, Jonathan, when your father branded you a liability to our family's future. Instead, I remained silent and convinced myself to be ashamed of you."

Listening to all this, JJ felt a raw soreness in his throat. He tried to swallow and found he could not.

"I might have made any number of different choices," Mother said, "and thus unlock all those doors that are now shut to me." Here, Mother paused. The tears welling in her eyes now began to roll down her cheeks. "I don't mean to make excuses, Jonathan. The choices I made, even those times I chose to say and do nothing, they are now etched in stone somewhere. I am reminded of how I once believed my own parents failed my sisters and I, and in such egregious ways. I swore I'd never make the same mistakes as they did…but look where we are. And maybe that's the nature of parents and children, and the nature of souls more generally. Everyone wearing masks, speaking past each other, too afraid to come together lest we lose ourselves in part or in whole. Maybe it's been like that a long while, and maybe it'll keep on being like this for a long time to come. I can't rightly speak to any of that.

"All I can speak to, or else try, is to say that forgiving someone for the pain they caused doesn't mean they never did you wrong in the first place. It doesn't mean that nothing needs to change. It doesn't mean that all your suffering will end here and now, because Lord knows there's plenty to go around. But maybe, by giving in a little, we can at least look to help each other instead of drawing the knife the first chance we get. Maybe we can open our eyes to some measure of love for the other — and for *ourselves* — however meager it might be, and choose to nurture it. Because it's easy enough to keep wandering through the world so blinded and numbed by pain and resentment that you can't help but create more sorrow. It's much more difficult to make a different sort of choice. If it means anything to you, Jonathan, I'm starting to appreciate that such a choice might indeed be worth all the trouble."

In the silence that followed, JJ trembled. He bit the inside of his cheek until blood flowed, and when the pain screamed in his head he finally began to feel right again. And looking at Mother, who had slowly drawn closer to him as she'd spoken, JJ pushed his quivering lips into a hateful sneer.

"After all that's been said and done, you seriously ask for my forgiveness?"

Mother wore a look of deep sorrow. "No," she said. "I cannot ask such a thing for my sake, nor for your father's. But I do ask it for Jem's sake, for your siblings. For the sake of your family. You think the love you used to know is nothing but a lie, but I swear to you, Jonathan, it was real. It still is. And what's more, it can come back. It can grow and flourish. But whether you accept it or not, and whether you reciprocate…well, those will be your choices to make."

An endless stretch of time seemed to pass, and JJ could almost see strips of light move across the floor as the sun shifted position. His shoulders were hunched, the muscles in his neck corded almost to bursting. He willed himself to move, tried to turn away and put one foot in front of the other, but he was rooted to the floorboards.

Maintaining a face of stone, JJ clamped ever harder on the inside of his cheek.

He fought the instinct to throw out his arms and embrace Mother, to collapse against her in tears so that they might weep together — for each other, for Father and the family, for everything. JJ felt hot blood pooling in his mouth and he continued to bite down until he thought he might pass out from the pain. When finally he could stand it no longer, he let go, and a surge of relief washed over him. And with the relief came a sharp clarity, an instinct from the ether that demanded obedience.

No. The time and need for forgiveness was gone — dead and gone, and there was no good reason to bring it back. What need did Captain Jonathan Jacob Roscoe have for whims of sentimentality when he was a rising star, destined to become like that bristling white comet which now shone overhead even in the daytime? *Choices* had nothing to do with it. An arrow could only point in one direction.

JJ swallowed the blood in his mouth. He tasted his warm iron, and he shivered at the pleasure of it.

"You ought to start taking your medicine again, Mother," JJ said. "Better to distract yourself from the pain you feel, and the pain you've caused." He gestured toward the four walls surrounding them, toward Clarendon and the whole world beyond. "Whatever meager wisdom you might proclaim, you've lost all of this. It's gone, and your medicine is all you have now."

For a long while, the study was silent. Slowly, Mother took a small step back.

"Then I suppose this really is goodbye," she said.

JJ nodded stiffly. "I suppose it is."

And with that, JJ turned and quit the study. He did not linger to look a final time upon Bayard or Mae Jane, but instead passed through the door and out into the hallway. It was only when he heard Mae Jane call his name that he paused and turned around.

The old mammy stood there in the doorway. A scowl of fury was set upon her face, but then she closed her eyes a long moment and allowed the anger to pass. When Mae Jane opened her eyes again, she drew a deep breath and formed a sad smile on her lips.

"I pity you, Jon Jacob, I truly do. Because for all the shiny buttons on you fancy uniform…my boy, you grown to be an ugly man."

Having said this, Mae Jane closed the door on him, and the latch clicked softly into place.

JJ felt the pangs of a gnawing emptiness, but he could not discern their origin. He put his hands up to his eyes and found them still dry. And so, smoothing down his uniform, JJ turned and hurried downstairs.

Men hurried about Clarendon packing up General McClellan's headquarters. JJ saw one or two men pocketing trinkets and other house valuables, but he said nothing. What use did he have for any such things? To hell with Clarendon. To hell with Mother, and to hell with Mae Jane and all the rest of them. The old shack could burn — the whole *Valley* could burn, for all he cared. When he left with General McClellan today, JJ knew in his heart that it really would be the last time he ever set foot in Mayfair. That was a promise he intended to keep.

But first, JJ was going to claim something that was rightfully his.

Ever since he was a boy, his grandfather the Colonel had promised his weapons to his grandsons. As firstborn, first pick went to JJ. He had a saber of his own, of course, but it was nothing like the Colonel's blade, which had been blooded countless times. JJ imagined himself drawing the Colonel's saber, with the dueling eagles on the hilt, and pointing it toward a mass of Rebels as he sounded the charge toward final victory…

JJ entered the library, which so far had been spared from thievery and pilfering. He paused briefly to look up at the vaunted ceiling, to gaze upon the hole he had made there. And he lingered to run a hand over the smooth, lacquered surface of Father's desk. Now turning to gaze upon the bear-sized hearth, JJ looked for the Colonel's saber and realized it wasn't there.

Stolen!

For God's sake, *Jem*! That had to be the answer. Jem had taken the Colonel's sword like a thief in the night. He had no respect for tradition, despite his claims to the contrary. Now that goddamn fool was traipsing about in a goddamn Rebel uniform with JJ's goddamn birthright attached to his goddamn belt!

Breathing hard, his pulse pounding, JJ strode forward and snatched up both of the Colonel's flintlock pistols hanging over the mantle. Each bore the same sigil, the same image of dueling eagles. A chill ran down JJ's spine with the realization that Jem had used one of these pistols when he shot at him. That had been a lifetime ago, but as JJ clenched his jaw and heard the now-familiar *snap* of the scar tissue there, the sensations of that fateful night returned to him. He gripped the pistols and felt his heart race faster. Oh, just wait until he got within range of Jem with one of these beauties. One well-aimed shot could rip a man's head off, or just about. At the proper time, JJ would reclaim the Colonel's saber. After all, it was his property, his by right.

JJ pushed the pistols into his belt. Looking up again, he was suddenly struck by what should have been so obvious before.

Something else of the Colonel's was also missing.

The long rifle.

Gritting his teeth, JJ muttered his brother's name under his breath.

Chapter 48
AMBUSCADE!

"Tommy?"

"Shh!"

Tom watched the blue soldiers tramp through the streets of Mayfair. He gripped the Colonel's long rifle in both hands.

Beside him, Billy Clements whispered, "You know where the Yankees are going?"

From their tree-covered vantage point above the unfinished railroad tracks, Tom and Billy could see the back doors of houses and shops along Mayfair's main street. The street turned up to the crossroads, and here they saw bluebellies marching in the open. A group of horsemen wearing sloped hats were gathered there watching the soldiers. By Tom's estimation the horsemen were ready to move out.

Tom shook his head. "I don't know for sure. East to Winchester, maybe. I heard some of them say us Rebs are holed up outside Washington somewhere."

"They gonna try to smoke em out?" Billy asked. "Just like they done to your daddy's mining camp?"

Tom propped himself up with an elbow and looked back up the North Branch, where black smoke curled over distant trees. The sight of it filled him with an unthinking rage, and he knew that JJ had to be responsible somehow. "They might try something like that," Tom said, and he turned back to face the soldiers. "But I ain't waiting around to find out. Come on."

They crawled forward on their hands and knees through the brush. They stopped again a few yards closer to a rock overhang near the railroad tracks. Tom sat up and began to clean and check the long rifle.

"It ain't right, what they did," Billy said. "But your brother's with em. See? You gonna shoot at your own brother?"

Hearing the sound of pounding hooves, Tom turned and saw another group of horsemen approaching the town from the main road. Just as Billy said, he spotted JJ riding among them. JJ looked distracted, angry about something.

Tom said, "No, I ain't shooting at him." Now he pointed at the horseman beside JJ, a barrel-chested man with a mustache who rode high in the saddle. "You see that piss-proud dandy there on the big black horse? The one with that funny hat?"

"Looks like he got a stick up his ass."

"Which makes him the best target," Tom said. "He looks like a general, don't he? You can end a war in a day if you kill a general. I'll bet you two whole dollars that's a bonafide general right there."

Billy took a deep breath as the weight of the situation settled on his chest. "I ain't too sure about this, Tommy. There's a lot of soldiers down there, and they ain't gonna be so happy you pinged their general. Besides, I don't got two whole dollars anyhow."

"Pshaw, I don't want your money," Tom said. "Don't worry, Bill, they'll be like chickens with their heads cut off after the big fella goes down. You'll see."

"Your brother's a Yankee. You think he'll come after you?"

Tom scowled at Billy. "My brother ain't a goddamn Yankee. He's just confused is all. Confused and angry."

"Easy, Tommy. Just a question."

"Well, we don't have time for questions." Tom rose up on his haunches and took up the long rifle. "With the general gone, all those bluebellies will pack up and high-tail it. JJ too. Or maybe he'll finally come to his senses."

Billy didn't move. "Why don't we just shoot him from here? The dandy general, I mean."

Tom leaned over and spat, because the heroes in the dime novels he read always spat before they were about to say something profound. "Because this block of wood don't shoot that far, stupid. Now come on, let's go!"

They ran with bent knees, keeping low along the rock cliff until they found a soft earth embankment to slide down. Standing upon the railroad tracks, they could see men in blue on three sides. All of them were too far away to notice or care what two young boys were up to, and even if they did, the musket the boys carried might as well be a toy gun. Billy had better eyes than Tom did, and he was the one who counted twenty horsemen readying their mounts for a long ride.

They crouched low and moved across the tracks and reached a decaying picket fence on the other side. Hogs snorted in the mud on the other side of the narrow fence. Tom felt a hot wet stink blow on his hand in the grass, and in any other circumstances would have laughed and waited for the pig's curious snout to push through the break in the pickets. But there was a war happening, for God's sake, and so Tom moved on with the grim determination of a suicidal Comanche brave. He then realized that it was a shame he and Billy hadn't colored their faces with warpaint.

They passed a second yard overgrown with weeds and they paused behind the fence as the back door groaned open. Two sets of heavy boots clopped down the back steps and clumped into the yard. The shuffling sounds of a woman's dress followed. "Please, you can't!" the woman cried. "They're all we got. All we got..."

The boots of the soldiers stepped so close to Tom and Billy that Billy whimpered and looked ready to cry out in surrender. Tom fired a warning glare at him and put a finger to his lips. There was the screech of a latch and then some squawking and ruffling of feathers. One of the soldiers said in a dry accent, "We ain't takin but two hens each, ma'am. We got papers tellin us we're in our rights to do this."

"My husband will be back from the war soon. He'll lodge a complaint."

The second soldier laughed. "That right? That astoundin revelation supposed to make us feel scared-like? Well, your inbred husband gonna have a lark chasin down four chickens in the middle of this whole goddamn mess. Christ."

"Don't you swear at me, stranger."

"Lady, we'll *swear* at you all we want. We'll take everythin you rednecks got. We'll turn you ass side up in the dirt and play husband if we want to. Give me a reason and I *swear* I'll pry your fuckin tongue out myself."

Behind the fence, Billy pulled on Tom's sleeve. "Shoot these bastards, Tommy."

Tom shook his head: *Not yet.*

They pushed on. It wasn't much farther until they reached the last house on the street. Tom took a quick look around before he leaped over the fence and landed softly in the mushy green yard. Billy came next. They moved up through the yard in bare feet, their dirty toes squeezing warm blades of grass. As they reached the back facade Tom stood up and braced himself against the worn plank siding.

"Get behind me."

Billy positioned himself behind Tom. Slowly, they inched along the wall until there was no more wall to cover. Here at the corner Tom peered around and saw the horsemen gathered together in the street. The general in the hat was speaking to JJ in low tones. There was a hustle of activity around them, and now it was very clear that all the soldiers were preparing to leave. A bearded officer was shouting orders at all the soldiers on foot.

Meanwhile, the general said something to JJ and JJ laughed. Tom studied JJ's smile and realized for the first time that though JJ and Jem were identical twins, they in fact looked very different. It was something in the way they smiled. Jem's smile was ever bright and true, naturally crooked, with one cheek dimpled and the other drooping. Lately, Tom had noticed that Mother's smile was crooked too, as was his own.

JJ's smile, on the other hand, seemed almost too practiced, too mechanical, too *perfect*. It was the kind of smile that suggested there was no real laughter behind those bloodless lips, no real joy within those gleaming eyes. There was little more there than the same cold, calculating intellect that Father's eyes had possessed.

Tom had loaded the long rifle up in the woods, but he checked again to make sure. He turned back to Billy and pointed beyond, across the yard, across the railway tracks, up the embankment and into the heavy woods stretching up on the mountainside.

"We've got one shot. Soon as it's done, we run. Jump that fence, climb that hill, into the woods. We split up. They can't catch two of us. We'll meet at the quarry. And no matter *what,* we don't look back. We don't turn back. You with me?"

Billy was staring pale-faced at the ground, so Tom gripped the boy's shirt collar.

"Are you with me, Bill? Partner?" He tried again. "Brother?"

Billy shivered with fear. Despite this, he offered his best and bravest smile.

"I'm with you, brother."

They spat into their palms and shook, and Tom felt a deep stirring in his heart. Presently he cocked the musket and there was a soft click, the dry rasp of ancient history coming back to life. Tom brought the long rifle up in both hands and slid around the corner and leveled the barrel until he could look down the iron sight.

From somewhere in his mind, Tom heard Jem's voice whisper to him: *You may not have a second chance, Tom. You'll have only one shot, so you must make it count.*

Suddenly, Tom saw a vision of Tipper in his mind's eye. His poor dog, looking up at him, willing his boy to do something to end his suffering. And what had Tom done? He'd lost his nerve, and he'd abandoned his dog to die alone.

You will need to do what needs doing, and you can't allow yourself another thought about it.

Tom aimed carefully, and at last he found his target.

The trigger was loose. As soon as Tom's finger brushed it there came a sudden explosion of sparks followed by a sucking gust of smoke. The long rifle kicked and bruised Tom's shoulder, but for a split second he didn't know whether he'd actually fired the rifle or if the old thing had simply blown up in his hands. But in the same instant, a horse screamed and men cried out and Tom stared into the smoke of his own making with a drawn look of shock.

"Did you get him?" Billy asked, breathless.

The smoke cleared enough for Tom to see a black shape writhing in the smoke. An ungodly scream pierced the air, which stank of gunpowder.

Frantic cries went up from the soldiers: "*Rebels! The Rebels shot General McClellan*!"

Over the shouting in the street, Tom heard the quick patter of feet. From somewhere nearby he heard Billy's voice again:

"*Away,* Tom! Chrissakes!"

Tom's eyes locked on two bluebellies who had spotted him. The next instant he looked over his shoulder and saw Billy fleeing across the yard as fast as his toothpick legs could carry him. Tom let the long rifle drop to the earth at his feet. He stared down at the rifle long enough for only the briefest of reconsiderations before he turned and raced for the fence. He jumped it with the breath of the bluebellies hot on his neck. They cursed and slashed with their bayonets at the place where Tom had been. One of their muskets went off and the cracking explosion made blood run from Tom's ears.

Another gasping bluebelly appeared out of nowhere, and Tom knew he didn't have the space to outrun him. He tried anyway, but he felt a rough hand grab at his bucking shoulders. Tom turned, in the same instant reaching for his whittling knife in his pocket, but he caught a sucking punch against his front teeth and was knocked almost comatose.

When Tom blinked and opened his eyes again, he was on his back, his breath blown out of his lungs. He knew he was a goner, a prisoner at best and a dead man — *boy* — at worst.

The scowling bluebelly loomed overhead, but suddenly a pinewood board came swinging up and cracked the man in the mouth. The pinewood did an uglier job than could any hand of man; the bluebelly lay face down in a spreading pool of blood and didn't get up again.

Billy's face suddenly filled Tom's field of vision. There wasn't any time to say anything, but Tom would later think of a thousand things he could have said. Billy just dropped the board and hauled Tom to his feet while more bluebellies shouted at them to halt. They instead ran off, sprinting side by side, making for the thickets up the East Cut.

Tom winced as the sharp shale pieces along the unfinished railroad jabbed at the soles of his feet. He and Billy scurried up the embankment, much steeper to climb up than it had been to slide down. Their fingers and nails clawed frantically at the earth.

Tom heard shouts and the rattle of boots on shale. At last they reached the top of the embankment and looked down. Bluebellies were racing toward them from all sides, and just now some of them halted and leveled their muskets and fired. Tom watched the sparking muzzle flashes and little gasps of smoke from their weapons like it was a fireworks show.

The first ricochets brought reality crashing down on Tom again. Bullets tore at the earth around his feet and several trees became decorated with yellow wounds where the bullets stripped fleshy bark as a whip flays skin.

"Split up!" Tom cried to Billy. "The plan!"

Instantly Billy tore away and darted off on a separate path up the ridge. Tom watched him run a moment before he turned and saw more breathless bluebellies staggering toward him. He gave a whoop and a holler and decided he was invincible. Standing defiant on the outcrop, he shouted down:

"Come and get me, you Yankee bastards!"

Then he went racing along the cliff face, shouting and laughing with glee as bullets whined and ricocheted around him.

"I'm the ghost of Davy Crockett! Go to hell, Yankees! I'm going to California!"

A shrill scream from somewhere up the Cut killed Tom's laughter in his throat. Looking ahead, he saw Billy poised against the blue summer sky with arms outstretched. The boy tottered under an unseen weight, and now Tom saw the blood gushing from his elbow, and then he watched Billy drop down the embankment and out of sight.

Without thinking, Tom ran for Billy with a wild shout. But just now he saw blue caps and grim faces appear over the ridge. More bullets whined overhead. Tom leaped over a fallen log as a bullet shunked into the old wood and sprayed his feet and forelegs with needlelike splinters. Crying at the sudden pain, Tom staggered up and started forward again. He made the cover of some thickets and kept moving on a diagonal path up the Cut.

He could still hear the sound of soldiers rushing after him.

Only now did Tom Roscoe's giddy joy leave him, and he began to feel cold and afraid.

"There he is! Gut the damn Rebel!"

After cresting the East Cut, Tom clambered down the trail that led to the quarry. Behind him, a gang of gasping bluebellies followed in close pursuit.

Tom's springing feet flew at a faster pace than what his pursuers could maintain, but he was quickly running out of ground. Once he made it to the quarry, he would be exposed on all sides.

He tripped over a gnarled root and fell face-first into the dust. He came up coughing, blinded by sand and grit. He heard pounding boots and haggard breathing close behind. Staggering upright, Tom nearly toppled again as a bullet whizzed by and went ricocheting off a nearby rock.

Forcing his eyes open against the grains that scratched his eyes, Tom searched in panic for a means of escape. Up ahead, the Promontory's silhouette loomed against the shining sun like a black obelisk.

Pumping his legs, Tom sprang for the heights. He felt, rather than saw, that one of the younger bluebellies had surged forward with the aid of a second wind, and his outstretched hand threatened to clamp down on Tom's shoulder.

Ahead, the Promontory stretched out into a cloudless sky.

There was no time to think; no time to be afraid. Tom ran for the open sky and barely had time to glimpse the edge of the world falling away before he hurled himself into the blue expanse with a savage cry. Suspended in mid-air, he wheeled about so he could look into the face of his closest pursuer. The bluebelly saw the sudden drop rushing up and skidded to a halt with a scream. Tom grinned at the bluebelly — the soldier was a boy little older than Tom himself — before the full force of gravity brought Tom plummeting down to the glassy surface of the quarry lake below.

Tom plunged into darkness, cold and wet and with a terrific pressure that suddenly collapsed upon his eardrums. Tom felt himself drifting ever downward. He opened his eyes and took in the otherworldly green glow of the quarry lake. For a brief moment, Tom forgot all about the bluebelly general and Billy and the soldiers who had shot at him.

The realization now dawned on him: *he'd jumped the Promontory*! Tom let out a great underwater cheer that generated a cluster of bubbles. He opened his mouth and drank in some of the cool water, and the rite of passage was complete.

Suddenly he heard the whooshing sound of bullets hitting the water and saw tiny streams of bubbles plowing in the missiles' wake. Still Tom drifted down, though his lungs began to protest. Fear began to settle in, and then panic. Oh, if only he'd taken a deeper breath!

His toes graced the greasy lake bottom. Something squirmed nearby and Tom thought of the eels that prowled the muddy floor. He pushed off and began to swim away from where he believed the Promontory to be. If he could make it clear across the quarry lake, if he could swim behind one of the rocks that protruded from the opposite shore, if he could hide behind such obstacles until the bluebellies gave up their search…

But his lungs began to burst from insufferable pain and pressure. He looked up and saw the sun glinting off the water's surface so far above. Too far above. He would never make it back up there, and there was still such a distance to cover. He felt his strength drain from him with each laborious stroke, but still he strained on, farther on, a little farther on.

High atop the Promontory, five soldiers stared down at the quarry lake and tried to catch their breath.

"Is he drowned?" one of the soldiers asked.

"He hit the water like a brick."

"He's fish food."

"Pshaw. This rock ain't high enough to kill a goat."

"Then why don't you jump in after him?"

"I ain't the one who lost him."

"There! Hey, look!"

"What?"

"Never mind. Thought I seen bubbles. Try shootin the water again."

"I ain't wastin another minnie ball on this bullshit."

"We got the one of em. I say we go back and report this other fella drowned."

"But we don't know that for certain. There could be Rebs hiding all over these ridges."

"Then I ain't about to die chasin after a damn kid. Let's go."

"Aye, let's go. *You* can tell the company commander it was your idea to give up the search."

"Roscoe? That sumbitch's probably a secesh himself. You know he's a Virginian? This is *his* home-damn-town. Prob'ly got hisself a whole whack of hillbilly cousins holed up in that ridgeline."

The other soldiers guffawed and turned back for Mayfair.

Just as the soldiers abandoned the Promontory, a shape broke the surface of the water across the far end of the quarry lake. Tom surged up, gasping for air. Frantic, he immediately plunged down again for fear of being seen or heard. Slowly, he swam until he found the cover of a large rock and quietly surfaced again. Clutching the slippery face of the rock, he peered around the edge and looked up at the Promontory. The top of the quarry was deserted. Tom strained to listen and, hearing nothing, determined that the soldiers had in fact given up their search.

But now came a new series of problems. How was he going to make it across the Valley without being seen? Were there still soldiers at Clarendon? What if Mother, Mae Jane, and the others were being held captive? What if they gave Tom away should he come to them in secret? And if the Valley was no longer safe, where could he possibly go? All these questions and more plagued Tom as he drew himself out of the water and crept up the winding path toward the top of the quarry.

And what about Billy? No, no, poor Billy. Was he dead? Would the bluebellies torture him? Oh, but of course they would, and of course Billy would refuse to say anything. Billy was a Johnny Reb, after all. But how long could he hold out? And then came the greatest question of all, how would Tom save him?

At last, Tom stood atop the quarry. He crouched down low, fearful that lingering soldiers might spot him. As he devised a hasty rescue plan in his head, Tom suddenly heard a wail that chilled his blood. The wail was echoed by another, then another, and still more until a chorus of screaming and sobbing and shouting. Standing upright, Tom peered across the Valley.

The wailing was coming from Mayfair.

Chapter 49
THE SHAPE OF THINGS TO COME

JJ CURSED LOUDLY, drew his revolver, and pulled the trigger.

Nothing happened. His ears still ached from the shrill screaming that pierced the air. He cocked the hammer and fired again. Nothing.

"First Sergeant!"

The fat first sergeant stepped forward and handed his own revolver to JJ, who cocked the hammer and pointed it at McClellan's screaming, writhing horse and put a bullet through its brain. The horse's quaking hooves went still in the dirt and the dust began to settle. Though the world went mercifully silent, JJ's ears yet rang from the beast's screams.

JJ checked the revolver and handed it back to the sergeant.

A pale and wide-eyed General McClellan sat on the porch of the Curtis House Tavern across the street. A group of men circled the general showering care and concern. JJ was about to join McClellan and ask after the general himself when several soldiers stepped forward to report.

JJ raised his eyebrows in surprise. "You found one of the Rebels?"

"Yessir. They're bringing him up now."

"And we found this, sir. Looks like the weapon the scoundrels used, sir."

JJ accepted the Colonel's long rifle with silent shock. Gripping the old musket in his hands, he studied the wood grain and the sigil of the twin eagles on the stock. He closed his eyes for a long moment and felt a deep and painful ache within, but he kicked the ache down and kept kicking until he no longer felt it stirring. He opened his eyes again.

"Did you capture him alive?" JJ asked, his throat choked by the dust in the air.

In answer, two soldiers carried the would-be assassin forward and threw him in the dirt before JJ's feet. The sobbing boy yelped and clutched at his arm, which had been torn from its socket and shattered at the elbow. The only thing JJ knew about the boy was that he was not Tom, and for that he breathed a deep sigh of relief.

JJ handed the long rifle to one of the men and crouched down on his knees until he was face to face with the wounded boy. Even with medical attention, the boy would likely lose his arm. When JJ said this to the boy, coolly explaining that the army doctor could saw off the boy's arm and that he would be a cripple the rest of his life but that he would *live*, the boy only cried and said nothing.

JJ was very close to the boy now. "What's your name?"

"B-Billy—C-Clem-ments..."

JJ put a hand on the boy's smooth chin and held it firm so that he could look directly into the boy's eyes. "Where's my brother?" he whispered. "Where's Tom?"

Billy Clements closed his eyes and wept. JJ let go and stared down into the dust and listened to the boy cry.

All around, the people of Mayfair had crept out from their locked doors and hiding holes and they stood several yards away blocked by the soldiers. The people saw Billy and cried out, "The Clements boy!" and sent children running off to the Clements farm.

The people hailed the bluebellied officers with urgent promises. Josiah Clements would pay the Yankee general for his horse. Hell, the whole town would chip in. The little fellow Billy didn't mean anything by it — he was simply playing a game that got out of hand. For God's sake, let the boy go!

"*That's enough*!" McClellan roared.

The street went silent. The young general snapped his fingers, and an orderly brought a fresh horse forward. Lifting his chin high, McClellan pulled on his riding gloves and mounted up a second time.

JJ stood and held the new horse's bridle. In a low tone through gritted teeth, McClellan said, "Captain Roscoe, these townsfolk have witnessed an act of terror planned and perpetrated by a Rebel criminal. I'll leave the act of justice to you."

JJ blinked. "Justice, General? But...but, sir, he's just a boy and—"

"I gave you an order, Captain," McClellan snapped. "I expect you to *adhere*."

JJ bowed his head. "Yes, General."

McClellan glared out at the townsfolk, who stared back at him with lidded gazes. To JJ he said, "Catch up with my escort when you are finished. We ride for Harper's Ferry, and from there to Washington."

JJ nodded solemnly. "By your leave, General."

McClellan turned to his retinue and muttered, "Away from this godforsaken place."

After the Young Napoleon departed and the soldiers continued their march out of Mayfair, JJ remained standing in the street with a group of men surrounding little Billy Clements. Though the men said nothing, he saw clearly the singular idea in their eyes:

Kill the goddamn Rebel.

JJ looked at the Colonel's long rifle and thought of Tom, of the terrible thing he'd done. He looked at the dead horse. Stupid, stupid boy. Now JJ looked at Billy Clements bleeding in the dirt. Many of Mayfair's people were watching Billy too.

Many more were watching JJ himself.

I expect you to adhere. That was something Father might have said, once upon a time.

JJ studied the onlookers carefully. He recognized many of them, knew most of their names. They were old farmers and shopkeepers and blacksmiths and planters. They were young girls and old mothers alike, and old men who hadn't gone off to fight. Among them were slave-keepers and slave-catchers. Only now did he realize that, just as all these individuals had formed a company of backdrop characters to the scenes of JJ's early life, so he himself had been a background character in the separate and distinct lives of each person he now looked upon.

Was he really going to become the villain for all these people?

I'll leave the act of justice to you.

Kill the Rebel.

As JJ looked out at the faces of his neighbors, he saw in their eyes the fresh-kindled flames of hatred. The people of Mayfair no longer looked upon the firstborn Roscoe boy, their neighbor, a local boy who'd always done the Valley proud. They saw nothing but a cold-hearted traitor in a fancy uniform, a sinful degenerate who now symbolized a corrupt Federal autocracy. The collective fire of the Valley folks was not yet fully ablaze, but soon enough it would be powerful enough to burn down everything that stood in its path. If there were any in Mayfair who still looked upon JJ and his comrades as countrymen, those minds would very soon be irrevocably changed. Once JJ and his bluebellies carried out the 'act of justice' that McClellan had ordered, they would no longer be considered countrymen, but loathsome invaders who deserved slow deaths.

But then again, why should JJ treat them any differently? How quickly had the people of Mayfair turned him into a laughingstock when those horrible rumors spread across the Valley? How many of these faces he looked upon now had sullied his honor for years, mocked him even after he brought glory to the Valley after capturing John Brown? And how many of these people present, who now called for mercy, had cheered on their boys in gray with giddy bloodlust?

Looking out at all the hateful stares, JJ realized that he no longer felt weakened by shame. No longer did he quake from the awful consideration of what others might think of him. He was *Captain JJ Roscoe* after all, the Hero of Harper's Ferry and Fort Sumter both — a rising star, and soon to be, he believed, a household name.

Kill the Rebel.

JJ's mind was now finally clear, and his decision had been made. "That tree," he said, pointing to a nearby sycamore. "First Sergeant, hang the traitor there."

A collective wail went up from the people of Mayfair.

JJ whirled to face them again. "Why do you cry out?" he shouted, his eyes piercing and vindictive. "You people have made war upon your own country. You people have *asked* for death and destruction. And here in Mayfair we hang uppity troublemakers from trees all the time, don't we?" He pointed up at the North Branch, where the mine continued to burn. "This is what happens when you declare war on your own country." Now he pointed at the dead horse in the street. "*This* is what happens." And now he pointed a trembling finger toward the white-faced Billy Clements. "*This* is what happens!"

One woman fell to her knees and began to sob. The elderly clutched at each other for strength and the very young watched everything from behind their mothers' skirts. Billy Clements seemed almost relieved at the idea that the excruciating pain in his arm would soon pass.

It took ten minutes and three frustrated attempts for JJ's men to tie an acceptable noose. In that time, Josiah Clements arrived and tried to break through the wall of the soldiers in order to reach his son.

"Have mercy!" he cried. "For God's sake, Jon Roscoe, have mercy!"

The soldiers held the man back. When he flailed at them, they pushed him down. When he became enraged and kicked at them, they beat him down and cracked his head with the butts of their rifles until he lay still.

Two men carried the limp form of Billy Clements forward and set him upright on his knees. The first sergeant slipped the noose over the boy's head and tightened it. Five men took position behind the boy, and together they grasped a long length of rope slung across the top of a high bough. The first sergeant and the five men stopped and waited for JJ to give the order.

JJ searched for something to say. He looked out at the people of Mayfair and felt their hateful glares bore into him. Squaring his shoulders to the crowd, he announced:

"By the authority of George McClellan, General in Chief, United States Army, this man is hereby accused, tried, and convicted as a traitor against the United States of America. This man is hereby accused, tried, and convicted of attempted murder—"

"This *boy*!" a woman cried out.

JJ's gaze whipped to Audrey Blake, who stood among the people with sorrow in her eyes, her whole body trembling with fear and revulsion. "Billy's just a *child* for God's sake."

"And it was just a goddamn horse!" a man roared. "Gov'ment get you another one."

"Roscoe!" another man cried. "Jonathan Roscoe, ain't it? You ain't like this, Jon Roscoe."

"Sure he is. He always been like this. *Traitor*!"

"Let the boy go! He ain't done nothing!"

"Ought to hang you instead, you goddamn soddy!"

Over all these cries and outbursts and jeers, JJ bellowed: "*This man is hereby sentenced to death, and will be punished in accordance with military law.*"

Trembling, with blood running down from his scalp, Josiah Clements looked up at JJ. For a brief moment, JJ thought his resolve might crumble then and there. Seeing the despair and desperation in the father's eyes, and how the man strained to reach his son, JJ waited for the angel on his right shoulder to whisper in his ear and tell him to stop, to stop everything at once, to live and let live.

But no voice spoke up. And indeed JJ Roscoe felt no creeping guilt, no sense of remorse.

In fact, he couldn't feel a thing.

"Sergeant," JJ said. "Carry out the sentence."

The first sergeant nodded to the five men holding the rope. Together, they all heaved on it at once. Billy Clements was lifted up like a marionette upon a string, and as he was hauled up his dangling arm danced limply in the air, swaying in time with writhing legs. There were tears on the boy's face, and tears on the face of his father, and tears on the faces of all the people, and tears even on the faces of the soldiers who held the hanging rope taut.

JJ had watched John Brown hang. Back then, the act of hanging had been a curiosity, a moment of justice, and JJ had not looked away. This time, however, JJ chose to stare up at the North Branch. He studied the columns of smoke rising up from the place that had once seemed to him like a princely seat of power. But though he could avert his gaze, JJ could not shut out the sounds of the Clements boy gasping and croaking, the ripping sound of twine rope sliding against the tree bark, and the high bough groaning under weighted pressure. JJ could not shut out the wails of the people and the pitiful, heartbreaking sobs of the boy's father.

Now the first sergeant stepped forward and wrapped his arms around the boy. "There, there, boy," he said. "There, there." With that, the big man gripped the boy in a bear hug and squatted down, and with all his weight he hauled down with a loud cry. Billy Clement's neck snapped like a dry branch, and the last of the boy's tears drained from lifeless eyes.

Josiah Clements threw his hands out with a gargling scream before he slumped forward and clawed at the dirt, as if groveling before an altar. All the while he moaned, "My boy...my boy...my boy..."

The father's moans were met by a deafening silence.

JJ's eyes found Audrey Blake once again. He thought to go to her, but the look in her eyes stayed him. There was more than sorrow in her eyes now; there was hate also. Scowling at JJ, Audrey leaned forward and spat at his feet. This defiant gesture was repeated by dozens of others, until the ground at JJ's feet was wet.

JJ called for his horse.

Mounting up, JJ made ready to ride out. The first sergeant approached and gestured at JJ's uniform. Looking down, JJ saw that some spittle had landed on his uniform. With a handkerchief, JJ polished his buttons until they shone again. Satisfied, he dropped the rag on the ground and rode away.

JJ rode hard out of the Mayfair Valley, taking the same path upon the Capon Bridge Road that he had taken all those years ago, when he first set off in exile from home. He did not pause to look back — or maybe he didn't dare to.

It was not until JJ rejoined McClellan's column that he allowed himself a moment to think. He thought of the way the wounded horse's eyes had rolled white just before a bullet ripped through its brain. He thought of the Clements boy's neck breaking with such an audible *snap*. He thought about Audrey Blake and the horror and loathing in her eyes. He thought of the hateful glares from all the people who had once been his neighbors, and how seeing them weep had made him feel...well, he could not deny that even now he felt blood running hot in his veins.

The people of Mayfair, with their self-righteous devotion to conformity, would suffer as they'd made others suffer. The people of the *South* would suffer as they'd made others suffer. Finally, the oppressor would become the oppressed. And it was right that such people should suffer.

But despite the humming thrill of vengeance — no, it was *justice* — that reverberated in his bones as he rode for Washington, JJ trembled when he heard Mae Jane's voice echo in his ears.

You grown to be an ugly man.

And despite his best efforts, despite his talent for banishing emotion, the painful tears that stung his eyes would not cease. He dropped back from the column so that the others would not see. Oh, what had happened to his dry eyes? He could not wipe the tears away fast enough.

Captain JJ Roscoe rode blindly down the road toward his destiny. And all the while Mae Jane's voice echoed:

My boy, you grown to be an ugly man.

As night began to fall over Washington, the people of the Union's capital waited with bated breath for news from Virginia.

Some newspapers had already published triumphant reports that the Union Army had been victorious, and was just now chasing the Rebels back to Richmond. But when panic-stricken horses carried speeding carriages and wagons across the Potomac causeways, and as feverish spectators of the battle began to return, first in a trickle and then as a hording mass, a great hush fell over the city. Soldiers in blue were seen running for their lives amidst the sprawl. Soon after came the ordered columns made of up men who no longer had the heart to fight but could still quick-march in ranks, and these columns were nudged together by nervous brigadiers and colonels who were busy trying to calm their shellshocked mounts. Trumpets sounded while blood-splattered, soot-blackened men marched, but even the peppiest bugle tunes sounded mournful. After a time the stragglers came on, with the boom of the guns echoing behind them. Many of these were walking wounded, some nursing only scratches while others held shot-out eyes in place or clutched at elbows and forearms that had been shattered by minnie balls. Many stragglers shuffled and staggered, their faces gray like those of the dead. Among this final sorry mass trudged Ben Freeman, erstwhile Editor-in-Chief of the *Liberty & Union*.

After crossing the Potomac causeways, Ben made it as far as the National Mall before he collapsed from exhaustion. The Mall was not the grassy monument that the Founders had envisioned it to be, but rather a village commons where countless head of cattle grazed behind rail fences, where free negroes lived in shack villages in the swampier depressions of the pasture, where preachers delivered sermons in white tents and where all manner of people sold their wares, from fruits and leather-makings to slaves. Someone had torn down the fence, resulting in an exodus of panicked cattle that poured into the streets of Washington, causing confusion and traffic snarls and washing the whole scene with absurdity.

Slumped on the grass, Ben looked up at the sky. A bright and happy blue was beginning to cloud over with gray thunderheads that soon turned black. When the rain finally came, Ben was almost relieved. He turned his face up to the sky and let the rain wash the blood from the gash over his brow.

Ben had not been injured on the battlefield, or at least not by any Rebel soldier. Many thousands from the capital had gone out to the southern fields in a show of solidarity (though some admittedly went only for the spectacle, while still others went only to be *seen* to go). Ben had gone out, as the latest issue of *Liberty & Union* proclaimed, because he felt he must. If he was really going to call himself a 'newsman,' he knew he had to prove himself by drawing as near to danger as possible in order to record the happenings. After all, Ben knew nothing of journalism except that the first duty of an honest journalist had to be to go out into the world and bear witness.

Well, he'd borne witness all right. Ben had crossed south over the Potomac in a great shuffle of people, and his first thought was to duck down a side road and follow it until he reached a broader thoroughfare leading to Mayfair, and Mama. But the crowd was pressed together and it moved like a river over rapids, and Ben was swept toward a series of high hills overlooking the battlefield.

And there, all laid out like toys on a tabletop, was the great contest. Except Ben found himself routinely distracted from the roar and smoke of battle by the spectators who sat on picnic blankets across the hills. There were congressmen and their wives, and Ben saw colonels and generals shaking hands with these dignitaries while their backs were turned away from the battle. Looking down the other side of the hills, Ben studied faces in the crowd. There were families sitting together, the children wide-eyed as if they were watching a circus show. Other children had already grown bored of the sight and were playing together at the bottom of the hill, even as murmuring voices suggested that 'those whizzing sounds in the air overhead' were in fact stray bullets. There were whispers that someone far to the left (some said it was a city councilor from Baltimore) had been killed by a bullet that ricocheted off a rock.

Ben watched as orderlies served a sumptuous lunch to still more colonels and generals who watched the battle with the keen eyes of sports gamblers, though they issued no orders and instead talked amongst themselves.

There were other correspondents moving about on the ridge, and Ben tried at first to follow them in order to be appear competent and purposeful like they were. He held his notebook to his chest and listened intently while a correspondent interviewed a man about what was 'going on', until the correspondent turned and barked at Ben to 'crawl in a fucking hole,' and Ben moved on.

The picnic stretched into the afternoon, and Ben became mesmerized by the sight of a flaming farmhouse on the far opposite hill. Two swarms of men, one in blue and the other in a brownish gray, fought for control of the farmhouse and the hill it commanded. The house changed hands several times, until finally the Union men drove the Rebels from the hill and kept chasing them until they passed out of sight over the ridgeline. A great cheer went up from the watching crowd, and Ben felt his heart swell with joy. The country had been delivered!

But then, beyond the ridgeline, there suddenly came a blast of cannon and gunfire together with the voices of ten thousand men all sounding in one bloodcurdling scream. Pillars of smoke burst upon the horizon, and then the Union men came streaming back down the hill in a flight of panic and dismay. Spectators gasped and talked together in nervous, excited circles, until they finally spotted hundreds of Rebel cavalry racing across the valley, aiming to coral the unthinking mass of wild-eyed bluebellies as if they were sheep. While a great cheer sounded from the Rebel ranks high atop the opposite hill, Ben felt his joy turn to ashes in his mouth.

Some warned that the fleeing troops were about to overtake the spectators' hill. These warnings went unheeded, for the people were rooted by the spectacle of horror playing out before them. Only when a flaming artillery caisson driven by a man and horse on fire shot up the hill and plowed a murderous path through the crowd did the entire mass of people turn and flee. Rebel cavalrymen raced ahead, whooping and hollering and firing shots into the air rather than at the crowd. The cavalrymen encircled the coaches of the congressmen and their wives, who had been the first and fastest to flee the battlefield, and many dull-eyed representatives of the

Federal government were placed in chains and carried south on horseback. When civilians drew pistols and fired at the enemy, Rebel horsemen shot and ran their sabers through them.

Ben had not been among the first to flee, but certainly he was not among the last. Even as he turned to flee with so many others, he thought of what he had written just the day before. Hadn't he proclaimed that, should he stumble upon an opportunity to take up arms against the Rebellion, he would take it? Well, wasn't this just such an opportunity? Ben thought to turn around and look for a weapon to fight with, but the bullets that whined past his ears reduced him to terror-stricken inaction, and he knew that if he stopped running now he would only drop to the ground and lay there frozen.

Even as they fled together, the crowd began to turn against each other. In the chaos, some men became thieves and predators, and soon enough pistol shots rang out between civilian neighbors. Bodies collided, hands became fists and walking sticks became clubs, and any remaining threads of solidarity were cut loose. It was in this madness that Ben heard a savage cry in his mangled ear. He turned his head just in time to catch the sharp end of a spade thrown by a soldier in blue whose eyes saw nothing around him but bloodthirsty Rebel phantoms. The spade cut Ben's brow open and he dropped like a stone, and while blood ran into his eyes he was picked up bodily and hauled forward. Panicking, Ben tried to fight against the hands that held him.

"Don't fight us, brother, we're tryin to help," a young man's voice replied.

"We's all gettin the hell outta here," another man said.

"Take this," the first man said, and he pushed a handkerchief over Ben's bleeding brow.

With the help of the two men, Ben staggered back to Washington along with several thousand stragglers, all of whom wore looks suggesting they'd had their fill of war after just one go, and they wanted no more part in it. Ben regained his feet and sense of balance, and he soon drifted away from the two young men. He thought to ask their names and maybe walk with them awhile, but when he turned to speak to them they'd passed on. Ben felt his heart twist at the realization that he hadn't even thanked the men — boys, really — for helping him. He thanked them now, and then turned toward the Mall.

And here Ben had remained for an hour or more, clutching the blood-soaked handkerchief against his brow and welcoming the deluge that began just as the sun slipped past the western horizon. Darkness came quickly now, ushered in closer by the black storm clouds. And all this time, the soldiers of the United States Army continued to trudge past, and their ordered lines disintegrated as men fled to distant corners of the city to rest, to weep, to pray, to die, to buy comfort from whores, and to stare down at their hands and trace the quivering contours of their palms.

While he shivered in the rain, Ben watched thousands of ragged, soot-covered soldiers shuffle by, their faces set in innumerable variations of shock, anger, and confusion. On came the wagon trains, and upon the wagons were the writhing wounded while others ferried the silent dead. Ben watched as an old soldier lay down on the grass of the Mall and turned his thirsty mouth to the sky. But it was too late, and he expired with his mouth open to drink in drops. The rain filled the man's breathless lungs until the water began to spill from the corners of purple lips now turning white.

A failure, all of it. Ben felt such a way not only for himself, but for the whole Union — the whole damn everything. Ben had not the strength to cry, nor do anything but bear sullen witness to the beginning of the end.

As he watched so many forlorn, dejected faces pass by, Ben withdrew into himself. The pelting rain seemed to rust him to the spot, and he became certain he would never move again. His thoughts were only of tragedy and despair. The south — and *the South* — was shut to him. *Home* was shut to him, and Mama too. Should he have slipped away when he had the chance? Well, it was too late to think about any of that now. He was stuck in Washington once more, with nothing to comfort him except for a damned hunk of wood and metal and ink. And what comfort could possibly exist for him in the world soon coming?

The Union was in its last death throes. The democratic experiment had ended in abject failure, with despotism, sickness, and hunger sure to follow. Any tiny, flickering hope there might have been to fulfill ideals of freedom and liberty for all had been snuffed out by an endless, soulless night that was only just now descending over the whole of the continent.

They'd won. Men like Tobias Cutler — like Jefferson Davis and William Yancey, like the Clairbornes and the Hanleys and the Merricks, and countless others like them — had everything now, including a stunning victory over the Federal army.

Men like John Roscoe and Stephen Douglas, by their inaction and obstinacy and their preference of political expediency over doing the right thing, had opened the door for the slave-masters and their ultimatum of slavery or secession. And all the people of Mayfair, and of every village across the South — people like Jem Roscoe — they'd eagerly put the torch to everything the Founders had built — thrilled, if nothing else, by the prospect of being part of something *important*.

Ben sensed movement beside him. Looking over, he saw a young black boy sit down beside him. The boy was vaguely familiar. Looking at him a moment longer, Ben finally recognized him as the newsboy who had given him the news about the attack on Fort Sumter back in April.

As if to confirm this, the boy said, "I read you newspaper."

Ben blinked. "...Pardon me?"

"I read you newspaper," the boy echoed. He brought up a clenched fist in which he held a crumpled broadside. "Seen you tryin to pass these out to folks in the street."

The boy flattened the paper against his thigh, careful not to rip its already torn edges. Ben read the words *Liberty & Union* upon the mud-splattered page and felt a pang of nausea.

"Oh, it ain't *that* bad," the boy said. He held the page out in the gathering dark, even as the rain soaked the paper through. "Only thing is, it's only one page long — two sides. You gotta have at least two pages and four sides to call it a newspaper." The boy scanned the article again. "And you should write less bout you youself think, more about what other folks says and does. Folks don't like to be preached at. They like the stories. That's why they buy em."

Ben nodded wearily. "I appreciate the advice. But I don't know if I'll be printing another issue any time soon."

"No?" The boy wore a genuine look of surprise. "Why not?"

Ben shrugged. "So many voices on the wind. Who should care to hear mine?"

Now it was the boy's turn to shrug. "That's a reason. But it ain't about just you though, is it?" He nodded toward the line of blue specters marching with their heads bent in shame, and at the solemn people who trudged alongside their shattered army. "Ain't it about them too? Ain't it about all-us?"

Ben turned and looked at the boy as if seeing him for the first time.

"Your name's Ringo, isn't it?"

Though the boy had no hat, he tipped an imaginary one with a bright grin. "Ringo, yessir, that's right."

Ben held out his hand. "Will you help me up, Ringo?"

Ringo sprang to his feet and took Ben's hand. Ben groaned and got upright. He looked across the Mall, past the equestrian statue of George Washington toward the unfinished dome of the Capitol. The Senator's townhouse was a long way off.

"We've got a walk ahead of us," Ben said.

Ringo shrugged. "I'll walk with you. I ain't got nothin but time. Massa's busy printin his next issue."

Ben started forward, moving very slowly at first. There was a hot, grinding pain his head, as if someone was sharpening a dull blade against his skull. "I wonder what your master thinks of all these goings-on."

"Oh, he says Jeff Davis'll be in the White House by tomorrow noon," Ringo said. "He thinks that Mr. Lincoln gonna be strung up and hanged before the week's out, whether by the Rebs or by his own Republicans. That's Massa's top headline. I reckon the rest of it will be more of the same."

Ben managed a weak laugh. "That's all rather disconcerting news."

"It's what sells," Ringo said.

As they wandered through the mist and rain, Ben looked around at the columns of men slithering through the arteries and alleyways of the city like so many blue snakes, their dripping bayonets glinting under the gas lamps like innumerable silver scales.

Darkness had finally arrived.

"*All night*," Ben murmured, his voice lost in the rain. "For the slave, for everyone. All night, forever."

Ringo shook his head. "I ain't so sure about that," he said. "Darkness come, sure, but darkness goes."

They stepped out of the way as a wagon full of wounded men raced up the street. Shivering in the rain, Ben pulled his coat tight. With a grim smile on his face, he and Ringo walked side by side with the battered survivors of Bull Run into the unknown mists of the dark evening.

"How much do you earn, Ringo? How much do you collect per paper?"

Ringo told him what he earned.

"I'll pay you better," Ben said, and reaching into his pocket he pulled out a fistful of coins. "Would you help me hand out my next batch of papers? I could maybe use your help printing them too."

The boy shrugged. "Sounds like more work for more money, but more money don't matter to Ringo. All the money goes to Massa anyway."

"But I'm sure your master would be pleased that you're earning him more than usual," Ben said. "Or maybe you give him the same amount you do now, and keep the extra for yourself."

Ringo chewed on this for a long while. "I want it all up front."

"Half," Ben countered.

"All."

"Half."

"Deal," Ringo said, and he snatched the money from Ben's hand. As he counted the change and handed back the difference, Ringo mused, "You don't got a lick of sense about you, nigger."

Ben laughed. "I guess you'll just have to trust me."

"Trust you? Sure, I trust you. I trust you one crazy nigger."

Ben laughed again. He began to feel a growing warmth inside himself. He stepped faster, with steady determination.

"You're right," Ben said after a time. "About what you said earlier. Folks can't hang their hats on abstract philosophies, and they won't listen to preachings and bitter condemnations. Especially these men here, the ones who have to do the fighting. They need a reason to pick themselves up from the muck and go after the Rebs again tomorrow. *We*, all of us, need a cause to believe in, a cause to unite us. Because it's not enough to stand *against* something, not enough to just put the Rebellion down and get back to whatever it is we were doing yesterday. Otherwise, this war won't ever end. We need to stand *for* something, to give folks a reason to believe that tomorrow can be better — *will be* better."

Ringo said, "Them's nice words, but that still ain't no story, and it sure ain't no headline." The boy looked down at the change he still clutched in his hand, as if he was considering giving it all back.

"All right," Ben said. Looking around them, he gazed upon the abandoned monuments and dilapidated boarding houses of a riven nation's broken capital. Over the sounds of wagons and shuffling boots and dying whispers and moans of pain, Ben heard the faint crying of a tiny infant.

"How about this," Ben said. "*The Cause: A New Birth of Freedom.*"

Ringo shrugged. "Freedom, hey? Fine. Folks like that word. I suppose it's a headline, that. Whether it's any good, only time'll tell. So what's the story, crazy man?"

Ben thought about it.

The story? Well, it might be about anything, about anyone. Looking around at all the faces in the street, Ben gazed upon the full spectrum of human emotion. There was despair and disconsolation, numb horror and hopelessness. But here and there, twinkling in the murk like stars shining against the immense canvas of blackest night, were expressions of plucky defiance, and of stiff-lipped determination, and, miraculously, of smiling gratitude, and a fast-spreading reassurance that the coming night need not cover all, and it need not last forever.

"Did you hear me, crazy man?" Ringo said. "I said, what's the story?"

Ben looked at Ringo, and he gave a little smile. "I'm working on it." He put his arm around the boy, and they walked on together through the rain. "*We*," he corrected. "We are working on it."

Some thirty miles away, in the darkened fields around Manassas, the victorious Mayfair Mavericks pulled their coats and bedrolls overhead to keep the rain off while they squatted around campfires and nursed tall cups of libations confiscated from Federal wagon trains.

Ever the entrepreneur, George Hunt toured from mess to mess with dozens of jugs and bottles quivering within a wooden crate.

"Shine, dear fellows! I've got shine. Gin for you, sir? Rum? How's about some of ol Mama Todd-Lincoln's vanilla rum, yes? Talk into my good ear; the other was shot off by a Vermont schoolmarm. Yes, yes to the rum? Splendid! You can pay young Master Ripley beside me, sir. And you, sir. A Winfield Scott Special: aged brandy for your troubles. That'll be…oh, a special drink demands a special price doesn't it? How much do you have? A little more and…*sir*, God love you, it's been a pleasure doing business with you. *Listen up*, dear fellows! Courtesy of his bluebellied eminence General Irwin

McDowell: anti-fogmatics for the anti-Yankee algerine anti-Christs! Something like that and a jar of cherries to boot. One at a time, dear fellows, one at a time. And remember that the good general expects his dues, good men. For alas, Mr. Lincoln just cut poor Irwin's salary to ribbons, just as we ribboned his men on the battlefield. Can you blame the poor fool, dear fellows? He's only an honest Yankee trying to earn honest pay. This *is* America, after all, dear fellows!"

While the victors and day-old veterans were gripped in drunken revelry, Jem Roscoe drank a cup of hot coffee. He paused periodically to swish coffee around and spit out fine grains of black gunpowder.

Jem cradled Sugar Dave Dixon's personal effects: unmailed letters home, a pocket Bible, newspaper scraps about the war. Gingerly, Jem touched the group photograph and tried to caress Dave's face printed there.

Beside Jem, Ezra Blake poked at the dying fire absentmindedly with his musket's ramrod. After they met during the battle's aftermath, Jem and Blake had stuck together, though they hadn't spoken to each other for several hours. Each was locked within his own mind, each trying to make sense of what he had witnessed throughout that long day.

"I suppose you'll be wantin to see her," Blake said suddenly.

Jem looked up. "What's that?"

Blake shrugged. "I said, you'll be wanting to see her. Whenever it is we get back."

Jem stared at Blake across the fire. "You mean…"

Blake spat into the flames. "Yeah."

Jem set his coffee down and cleared his throat. He chose his words carefully, not for fear but out of a respect that had been slow-building over the whole day.

"You should know, Ezra," he began, before drifting off briefly. Across the darkened field a great hulloo went up, with men from some other regiment cheering and laughing together. Jem waited for the excitement to die down again.

"I love her," Jem said to Blake. "And she…she loves me. I'm not afraid to say it to you. It's not some idle thing. It's more than that. It's as true as—"

Blake grunted his understanding. He looked supremely uncomfortable.

Jem scratched his chin and breathed a long sigh. "Anyway. I don't believe I ever had a responsibility to ask your permission for anything. *Her* permission, certainly. And when the time is right, I ought to ask for your father's blessing. But never permission. Something like this, it's between the two people involved and no one else."

The fire crackled in the rain, which was starting to lessen. Blake gave no response.

Jem said, "However…Perhaps we were wrong to keep it such a secret. I was wrong. In my defense, I figured secrecy was our only chance of being together. But now I realize. If it really isn't an idle thing, if it's really to last, then the endeavor is bigger than the two of us — meaning Audrey and myself. What I mean is, there's family to consider."

Blake pushed tobacco into his mouth and chewed on it noisily. Jem watched the campfire flicker in each of the big man's eyes. At length, Blake looked up and met Jem's gaze. After a long moment, Blake nodded and awkwardly grunted something inaudible, though undoubtedly cordial.

Jem managed a grin. "My thoughts exactly."

Here, the two men laughed. Jem now offered his hand, and Blake reached out to accept the gesture with a meaty shake. Then they turned their eyes back to the fire and continued to sit in contented silence.

By and by, Hunt and Ripley returned with their spoils. "Forty-five dollars," Hunt exclaimed. "*Forty-five dollars*!"

"Hush," Ripley warned. "You think the officers won't take heed of your boasting? They're liable to confiscate everythin we got."

"The officers were our best customers," Hunt replied. He dropped his crate to the ground and lay down beside it. "What shall we do with our earnings, boys? We're rich! Name anything in the world and I'll buy it for you. No, whatever you want, I'll buy *two*. What'll it be, Blake?"

Blake reached into the crate and pulled out the last unsold bottle. It was champagne. "How's about you go out there and get us a real drink."

"And somethin to eat from the company cook," Ripley said. "I'm mighty peckish."

Jem looked up at the night sky. The rainclouds were moving off, and here and there he could see a clear sky beyond. He saw the Great Comet overhead, still ploughing silently through the darkness.

"We ought to send some money back to Davey's parents," Jem said.

The mention of Sugar Dave silenced the others. Hunt's grin faded, and Ripley set to picking out tufts of grass from the earth. Blake opened the champagne bottle with a dull *pop* and poured several measures out onto the fire, raising up white smoke in the process. Blake took a swig of the champagne before he passed it around to the others. Each drank in succession, with Jem taking the bottle last. After a silent prayer for Sugar Dave, Jem tipped the bottle back and drank.

A shadowy figure moving between the campfires stepped into the light. It was Lieutenant Lowery.

"We're moving out at first light," he said. "The supply trains aren't coming, so cook whatever rations you can find. I hear there's a stack of dead Feds yonder that way that haven't been picked through yet. You might find luck there."

"Moving out where?" Ripley asked. He hastily amended his question with an obliging, "*Sir.*"

Lowery shook his head. "I don't know. That's tomorrow's news. This here is today's."

Hunt sat up. "Have you heard anything about the Yankee surrender, sir?"

"Surrender? What surrender?"

"The Yankee surrender, sir. There's talk all over camp. Lincoln invited President Davis to Washington this evening. They're hashing out terms as we speak, and likely they've already finished. The war's all set to be over at midnight, sir. You haven't heard anything about it?"

"I don't know anything about that," Lowery replied gruffly. "All I know is we're moving out at first light. Spread the word to any others you see."

"Maybe old Stoney Jackson's taking us back to Winchester," Hunt said. "Sure, back to Winchester to get decommissioned and all that. Then we'll all tramp down to Mayfair and have a real drink. Didn't we say we'd do it, boys? We whipped the Yankees good and proper, and now they'll think twice about crossing a Southern man again!"

Lowery shook his head. "There's a hundred thousand Feds in Washington tonight." The lieutenant spoke now with a lashing tongue. "They're whipped and ashamed and damn well pissed off, and they're hot for another crack at Johnny Reb. You really thought this was all going to end with just one big thunderclap?"

The accusation robbed George Hunt of whatever he intended to say next, and now it was silent all around the fire. An air of forlorn dejection hung low like a chilling mist, pinning all of their spirits to the ground. Jem watched how Lowery fidgeted. The lieutenant knew even more than he was letting on.

Lowery adjusted his cap. "We all signed up to do our duty," he said. "No matter how long it takes."

At this, Ripley squinted up at him. "But we only signed up for three months, sir. Our time's up in September. Are we gonna have another spat before then?"

Lowery stared into the fire for a long while. "We may, Ripley. There might be another big fight before enlistments are up. There might be many more big fights, worse than today." He coughed sharply and cleared his throat. "And if the Feds have as much grit as I suspect they do, we might have to keep fighting until Christmas. Maybe into the next winter."

This realization lodged itself in Jem's throat like a chicken bone. He coughed harshly and pounded his chest. He tried to cough again and found he could not, and with the panic of a choking man he felt up and down his throat and chest with his fingers. But there was no alien object stuck in his craw, and finally Jem remembered how to breathe once more.

Still, the painful realization lingered. He would not be able to see Audrey for many more weeks now. Maybe months. The possibility that it might be a *year* or more until she was in his arms again was too horrible an idea to be even remotely considered.

But Jem considered it all the same. At least, he tried to.

Blake laughed. "*Pshaw*. Yankees can't keep up the fight that long. Look how they turned tail and ran today! Don't you worry, boys. We'll be back home by harvest time at the latest."

Lowery remained stone-faced. "As I said, all of that's tomorrow's news. Tonight, you've got your orders. See they get done."

Jem and the others chorused in low voices, "*Yessir.*"

After Lowery moved off to the next campfire, the others began to trade a number of conflicting theories and hypotheses. George Hunt explained aspects of grand strategy to Ripley as if he was General Beauregard himself. Ripley contended that once the Feds in Washington took stock of their losses, they'd send an emissary out to negotiate peace terms. The CSA's continued presence on the field at Manassas was simply a show of force and nothing more.

Meanwhile, Blake assured the others, himself, the fire, and the stars above that there was no way in hell he was staying with the army past September. "Don't matter whether the war's still on or not," he said. "I done my part, and my part is done. I got a farm to look after, and my daddy ain't gettin no younger."

During all these discussions, Jem lay back and watched the silent comet skim along the sea of stars. He looked upon the white-fired tail with quiet foreboding. The comet was dimmer tonight, its sheen less striking, its hue less brilliant. Earlier in the evening, Jem had heard another man explain to his messmates that a fellow who knew another fellow who knew an amateur astronomer in another brigade said that the comet would soon fade from sight in just another few weeks. By autumn, the comet would be gone, still ploughing its inevitable course toward some distant corner of the cosmos.

Though Jem knew he shouldn't place much stock in omens, he couldn't help but ponder the significance of such an event. The comet had first appeared early in the new year, just after the dawn of the Confederacy and before the guns had sounded at Fort Sumter. And all during the happy months of May and June, the comet had seemed to foretell of a great victory to come. Now, at last, such a victory had been won and the departing comet's purpose had been served. If the comet would soon disappear, did that mean that God was still on the side of the Confederacy?

Feeling sudden exhaustion drape over him like a warm blanket, Jem soon fell asleep. But whether because the sounds of gunfire and cannon blasts and men's death-screams yet rang in his ears, or because he dreamed of wading through a cold, eternal darkness where no light shone, Jem awoke in the middle of the night with a savage cry of fright. Suddenly, he heard another voice cry out in the darkness:

"*Goddamn nigger!*"

Sleeping men awoke and heads turned to the sound of a great commotion at the next fire over. Percy Claiborne, clutching a club of some kind, was beating one of his slaves with vicious energy.

"Teach you to drink white man's liquor!" Percy shouted. These, together with his first outcry, were the first words the boy had spoken since his father had been killed on the field earlier that day.

The young slave shrieked for mercy. There was no sign that the boy had touched any liquor, but Percy continued to shout accusations while he brought his club down again and again. Several men stood up to intercede, but they kept their distance when they saw the crazed look in Percy's eyes. The beating went on and on until the club dropped from Percy's shaking hand and he collapsed, weeping and moaning for his father, for Mayfair, for home, for BEFORE. The men formed a circle around Percy and wrapped him up in a blanket. One of the Mavericks inspected the crumpled form of the slave boy. Looking toward the others, the man gave a slow, solemn shake of his head.

Jem looked upon all this without moving, his mind barely comprehending the murky figures moving about in the darkness. Realizing he still lay on the smoking battlefield of Manassas which reeked of death, and knowing that the dawn and the bugles of *reveille* would come all too soon, Jem closed his eyes and tried to sleep again. This time, however, sleep would not come to him.

Jem Roscoe lay awake all through the rest of the night, his bleary eyes staring up at the winking, uncaring stars of the abyss that stared back. And when the creeping fingers of dawn finally stretched over the horizon, when the bugles of *reveille* finally announced another cycle of the world's slow and ceaseless turning, and with Jem pondering that the same quiet summer dawn was just now lighting upon the humble Mayfair Valley, so close and yet so impossibly far away, Jem pulled his blanket over his eyes and, safely ignorant in the fabricated darkness, wondered whether he had made a terrible mistake.

❧

After she put Bayard to bed, Mae Jane went into the east wing study to speak with the Lady of Clarendon. Not finding Isabella there, Mae Jane went downstairs and traced a path through the maze of drawing rooms and parlors. Inwardly, Mae Jane hoped to discover Tom lounging about in one of the rooms, but he was nowhere to be found either. Ever since she heard the distant gunshots and wailing voices from Mayfair, Mae Jane had been restless with fear for Tom's safety. And despite everything JJ had said earlier that day, Mae Jane nevertheless found herself praying for him too. Lord knew, that boy needed all the prayers he could get.

Mae Jane found Isabella in the sunroom sitting in a chair beside the made-up bed where Mr. John had died so many months ago.

"Lady Spencer? Bella?"

The woman's back was turned to Mae Jane, and she had a hand on the bed as if she was touching someone under the covers.

When no answer came, Mae Jane whispered, "Bella? Bella, are you…?"

Slowly, the Lady's head lifted and she turned to look at Mae Jane. Her eyes were red and glossy, and her lips were stained a familiar color like that of iodine. In an instant Mae Jane realized what Isabella had done, and now the Lady confirmed it with a slow shake of her head.

"I took my medicine, Mae Jane," she whispered, her speech thick and sluggish. "I found my Mother Bailey's again, and I realized just how badly I needed it." The Lady of Clarendon turned and hid her face. "I've lost them, Mae Jane. All of them. Except maybe I never had them in the first place. If I did, I was too blind to see it."

Mae Jane went very quiet, very still. Slowly, she reached down and touched Isabella's shoulder, and she squeezed softly.

"You ain't lost everybody," Mae Jane said. She looked her oldest tormentor, her oldest friend, in the eyes. "We still got each other, hm? And there's little Bay upstairs. Miss Sarah, she's right across the Valley. Tom'll be back in good time, I know it. And Jem'll be home soon too, you see. All this ruckus will stop right quick and he'll be back. Maybe he can talk some sense into you Jonathan, hm? Maybe they'll make things right together, those boys."

Mae Jane didn't know if she really believed that last part, but right now she had to, for Isabella's sake.

Isabella looked at Mae Jane with cold fear in her eyes. "Did you hear all that screaming coming from town, Mae Jane? Do you think…do you think it was…?"

"I don't know who it was," Mae Jane replied, and she truly didn't. "I don't know *what* it was neither. Coulda been a pig they slaughtered in the courthouse square. But never you mind all that, ma'am. There ain't no cause for worry. No cause at all."

Except that was a lie. There was plenty of cause for worry.

Oh, Tom. Wherever that child was, God bless him and keep him. And please, bring him home soon.

"I think I'd like to see John tomorrow," Isabella said.

Mae Jane became very quiet.

"You mean…?"

"Yes," Isabella said, nodding. She blinked, and the fog of Mother Bailey's Quieting Syrup cleared from her eyes a little. "I'd like to talk with Bayard awhile about his father. You're right, I think. That boy understands more than we give him credit for." Isabella nodded slowly. "Yes, I'd like to visit John, and pray for him. I'd like to ask him to pray for us, wherever he may be."

Mae Jane bowed her head. "Of course, Bella."

"Would you like to walk with us tomorrow, Mae Jane?"

"I'd like that very much, Bella."

Isabella reached down and gently patted the top sheet, as if saying goodnight to the person in the bed. Slowly, the Lady of Clarendon rose to her feet. Mae Jane stood up with her.

"It's late," Isabella said. "I think I'll retire. You'll let me know when Thomas comes back, won't you?"

"Of course," Mae Jane said. A question then came to mind. "Shall I make up the bed in the study for you?"

"No, thank you," Isabella said. "I should like to sleep in my bedroom tonight. I sleep better in there."

Mae Jane nodded. "That's very fine, ma'am."

She helped Isabella to her feet. Isabella kissed Mae Jane on the cheek and departed, and Mae Jane turned and watched the Lady of Clarendon disappear around the corner, the skirts of her dress swish-swishing after her.

After cleaning up, Mae Jane decided to retire herself. She made her way slowly to the pantry apartment she shared with Ben — used to share with him, anyhow.

Upon a small table, she found the letter that she had been writing to her son. Though she had no idea how to read, and still less how to write, she had asked Tom a few weeks ago to teach her how to do these very things. The boy had tried his best, but he was no teacher. He had offered to simply write the letter for her, but she couldn't do that. "I need to write it my own self," she told him. "My boy needs to hear his own mama's voice when he reads them words."

Oh, Ben. Mae Jane had not heard from her boy since he left for Washington on the eve of the war's beginning. No letters had arrived, but Mae Jane refused to believe this was because Ben had been somehow killed or captured. Few letters came to the Valley at all now, except those sent from other places in the Confederacy (and even those kinds of deliveries were few and far between). Washington and all destinations north of the Potomac River were closed to Mayfair now, and maybe forever. Of course, she realized this made the writing of her own letter next to pointless. But maybe, once she finished her letter, it might somehow make its way through. Some letters always had a way of getting through. And maybe, someday, Ben would receive the letter and read it, and he would know that his Mama loved him very much.

Maybe someday.

Mae Jane put the unfinished letter down and decided she needed some air. Even though the Yankee soldiers were gone, their cigar smoke still lingered all throughout Clarendon, and the acrid stench did not agree with her. Crossing from the pantry into the kitchens, she went to one of the doors leading out to the veranda. Stepping outside into the balmy air of the late July night — an awfully *long* July it had been, and still was — Mae Jane found that she could breathe easier.

The departing soldiers, with their horses and wagons, had torn up the lawn. JJ had warned the other bluebellies against plundering Mae Jane's garden, but as soon as that big general McSomething showed up JJ changed his mind and the damn Yankees had ravaged her garden worse than a family of rabbits. Most of the kitchens had been looted, and even some of Mr. John's prized paintings had been confiscated. Mae Jane had protested, of course she had. How could the men of the Union

Army desecrate the home of a man who had defended the Union his entire life?

Mae Jane looked toward the sky. She'd been doing a great deal of stargazing as late, finding it as much comforting as it was mystifying.

The stars dotted the sky like a jeweled crown. And there, way above, was the familiar sight of the white-tailed comet. But looking closer now, Mae Jane noticed there was something different about the comet. It was fainter in the sky, and farther away than when she'd last marked it. While all the other stars in the sky appeared to be fixed, this brightest star of all seemed to be receding into the distance, slipping across whatever counted for a horizon in the heavens. To Mae Jane, the disappearing comet might be a sign of death, or else just another sign of the general hopelessness that had infected the Valley, and seemingly everywhere beyond the Branches too.

Lord, where was Tom? Where had he gone? She considered bundling herself up and going out to search for him. Where she'd begin her search, she had no idea. And what if Tom had gotten into trouble with the Yankees? What if the screaming down in Mayfair...

Wretched anxiety gripped Mae Jane's heart. Clutching her chest, she feared the sudden onset of a heart attack, what Carlotta-George called a 'scrunching'. Mae Jane remembered she had once seen an old uncle drop dead when she was a girl. For a moment, she welcomed such a fate. No more suffering, no more pain. No more asking questions of God, only to have them all go unanswered.

"He'll be all right, that Thomas," she whispered to herself, though maybe it wasn't her own voice that spoke to her. "You see, Mae Jane. You gonna wake up tomorrow and he'll be asleep in his bed. And Bella, she's finally mending. It'll take time, Lord, but she will make it. And Ben, my poor Benny, he'll be back to his mama soon. Us Freemans and the Roscoes, we'll be all right maybe. Someday, we'll all be together again. Maybe someday..."

Looking up at the sky's black canvas, and watching the comet fade away almost before her very eyes, Mae Jane felt the twisting pressure in her chest finally unclench and relax. It was very dark out there, wherever *out there* was, and she suspected it was cold too.

But no matter how dark or cold it became *here*, Mae Jane wondered whether there might always be a little flame shivering somewhere inside herself.

Maybe the fire was tiny, insignificant, just as one of those specks of light *out there* was tiny and insignificant. But the light was there nonetheless, and it was shining. It was there inside her, and would be forever so, a bright spot where once there had only been darkness.

It was still dark when Tom finally woke up outside Manassas.

He was still hidden aboard the rumbling freight train, tucked away behind supply crates and great mounds of bagged flour. He had already encountered one railroad bull outside Winchester, and the singularly unpleasant experience of losing a tooth to the big bastard's fist had taught Tom a valuable lesson about jumping trains: find an escape route first, a good hiding spot second.

Tom's stomach had stopped growling, though a peculiar numbness had long settled in. He had not eaten for two, maybe three days. However long since he and Billy had killed that…well, he didn't want to think about any of that right now.

Suffice it to say, after running out of Mayfair, Tom had kept running. He ventured south into the Shenandoah, and he hadn't stopped until he made it to a rail town called Strasberg. Yankee patrols occupied the train station, and so Tom decided to try his luck by pushing northeast on foot.

Two full days and nights had passed in the meantime, and the only sustenance Tom had was to drink water from brooks and streams. Once he had stopped to pick berries from a bush and had wasted two precious hours squatting in pain beside a tree.

He followed the rail tracks and kept hidden in the brush, and in this manner he caught a slow train (nearly losing a leg under the wheels in the process) just outside a village called Front Royal. That train had borne him here to Manassas Junction, where Jem and the Confederate Army was supposed to be.

But upon reaching Manassas and scurrying down from the train before he was discovered, Tom realized that he was not the only person with the idea of finding the Confederate Army. There were hundreds, *thousands*, of people swarming the countryside. Some were looking for missing loved ones, others for work, and all were looking for something to eat and drink. Taking note of all the gray uniforms milling about, Tom picked out the kindest-looking face and offered the man a sharp salute.

"I ain't no officer, boy. I'm a sergeant, and I ain't in the business of minding the likes of you."

"I need to find my brother," Tom explained.

"You ain't about to find nobody," the man replied. "Son, if you go tramping up to any army camp, they're liable to hang you as a spy. That is, if they don't shoot you on sight first."

Tom shook his head. "But the Yankees, they've taken our town! They're thieving, killing. I need to find my brother, rustle up a hundred men — a *thousand* men — and go back and—"

"Son, you sound like a patriot. But you don't got a lick of sense. You got a mother?"

"Yes."

"Yes, *sir*."

"Yes, sir."

"Fine. Then go back to your mother, son. Go back now, before I make you taste this boot."

Well, damn. Tom tried to speak with other soldiers and officers, but those who didn't ignore him outright only turned on him with threatening scowls and foul oaths. Tom was soon relegated to stalking the battlefield. There were corpses everywhere, but Tom did not dare approach them. And as Tom trudged about, exhausted and hungry, one question gnawed at his mind and stomach.

Where the hell was he supposed to go now?

Not east, not north, and certainly not back to Mayfair. Tom was a wanted criminal now, just like Robin Hood. He would have to wait out JJ and the other bluebelly sons of bitches until they either left Mayfair or until the Valley was retaken by Jem and the Confederates. Still, Tom missed his family and the warmth of his bed and the sleepy contentment that followed one of Mae Jane's wonderful meals.

And what about Billy?

Billy had been badly hurt, that much Tom knew for certain. But maybe he'd be all right. Billy was a tough son of a gun, and of course JJ knew he was Tom's friend. JJ would look after Billy as much as he could. Tom had to believe that his brother was still decent, still good at heart. After all, JJ was a Roscoe.

Despite the pangs of hunger and homesickness, Tom reminded himself that he hadn't felt this *good* since before Tipper had died, meaning he hadn't felt such marvelous wonder at the workings of the world. Following the ever-unfolding road, and meeting so many strange people — it felt as if the last two days contained as many happenings as he might encounter in two months back in the Valley. Whenever Tom kept his feet moving, any sad memory of what he'd left behind was distracted by the novelty of something new waiting just around the bend. And so, after consulting the great white comet shining overhead, with its knot of white light streaming westward, Tom decided to follow its course by land.

"West," Tom murmured. "West to California at last! I'll get rich, and quick too, with all that gold to find in all those hills. I'll send money back home, with instructions to get Billy out of whatever stockade they're keeping him in. If they won't let him out, I'll *buy* him out. No Yankee would ever say no to a bribe!"

The fastest way west, Tom knew, was actually south down the Mississippi. From New Orleans, he might gain passage on a ship that would sail way down past Brazil and around Cape Horn, and from there steam up the Pacific coast to San Francisco. And from there, he would strike for the gold-capped peaks of the Sierra Nevadas. He'd get rich all right, and lickety-split too.

But would he do all this in time? What if rescuing Billy and the rest of the Valley couldn't wait that long?

And what about the Yankees? Tom had heard rumors among the crowds around Manassas that the Federals were organizing a naval blockade that would block access to every port in the South. The idea, so the rumors went, was for the Feds to starve and strangle the Confederacy into submission.

So what else could be done? Well, of course Tom could strike west by heading *due west* via the railroads. Hadn't such an idea been Father's dream all along? Well, there was no railroad that would take him all the way to California, but Tom knew there was one that would at least get him as far as St. Louis, and maybe Kansas City beyond.

And from there, who knew?

"I'll go," Tom said. "I'll go, and I'll get strong. I'll rally a boodle of folks to help me. And when I come back, I'll save them. I'll save all of them."

Bolstered by these convictions, Tom turned and made his way back toward Manassas Junction. There were trains there heading out in all directions. Tom slunk about, keeping to the shadows lest any soldiers or laborers spot him. He found a train heading west by way of Lynchburg, and Tom smiled at the thought of riding past the Lynchburg Academy and blowing a raspberry at its frowning walls. If he wished for the Yankees to burn anything down, his first choice would be that sorry place.

Tom marked his chosen train and proceeded to follow the tracks along their south-southwest path, keeping to the trees until he was far out of sight of the platform. Here he waited until the train rumbled to life and started its slow-roll down the line. The train was already roaring by the time it screeched past Tom, and it seemed to him to be moving much too fast to jump safely aboard. He wondered whether he ought to just wait to catch another train.

Tom craned his neck to the sky to utter a prayer to the comet overhead, but he found the sky obscured by dark clouds. Instead he wished for the spirits of Kit Carson and Davy Crockett and all his heroes to lend courage to him. And feeling the warmth of this newfound courage, he shook his head and shrugged off his fear.

"You leaped the Promontory, Tom. You're a Rebel, goddammit, and you're a Roscoe too. Now it's time you act like it."

The train was almost past him now, and soon it would be gone, his opportunity lost. Tom closed his eyes and drew a deep, calming breath. His eyes opened again and narrowed with resolve. Bending low, his body coiled like a spring, Tom Roscoe made ready to jump.

"One…two…*three!*"

CHAPTER 50
CROWN OF GLORY

IT WAS DARKEST NIGHT, with dawn still so far off, when Henry finally came back to bed.

Sarah had been awake all night, unable to sleep. She didn't know if she was kept awake by the pulsating pain in her tongue and jaw from where Henry had cracked her earlier that day, or whether it was because seething anger for Henry had her heart beating a fast and incessant rhythm, her pulse pounding in her ears like syncopating drums.

Throughout the last weeks of July, even as Henry slowly convalesced from typhus, Sarah had doted upon him. As he recovered, Henry was very attentive in return. He looked upon Sarah as he once had in the early days. (*Early days. For God's sake, she was just over a year married and here she was already thinking of* OLD TIMES *as if she was an old woman.*) Henry asked Sarah about how she was keeping — not how his plantation or his family were keeping, but how *she* was keeping. It had been a long time since Henry had asked a question like that. And for the days that followed, Sarah found herself hoping and praying that her husband might have finally changed for the better. Henry might finally become the man she had seen that first enchanted night at Wyolah Hall so long ago, the man whom he had promised to become when they spoke their vows together.

And yet, that familiar doubting voice gnawed at Sarah's thoughts and gouged invisible talons into the soft spots between her ribs. Who in God's name did she think she was to expect to *change* anyone? Didn't she have a particular duty — a wife's duty — to fulfill? God had commanded Eve to serve Adam, after all. So she ought to serve Henry, for the good of the family.

For a long time she had thought the voice belonged to Cousin Isabella, but lately she hadn't heard the Lady's voice at all. The voice in her head had changed, what Lucas Cutler called *transmogrified*. No longer was it the biting voice of the wicked stepmother that tortured her, but the voice of Sarah herself.

Henry sometimes hit Sarah when they made love (encounters which Sarah decidedly had not missed while Henry was away at war). And even though terror gripped her heart each time Henry's violence flared, so earnest was his animalistic passion that she had always tried to convince herself that the blows were only part of a strange sort of affection. Something primeval, protective.

For the good of the family.

But the more Sarah tried to convince herself, the less certain she believed any of it.

Never before had Henry hit her in the fullness of daylight, and away from the bedroom, and certainly not without at least the pretense of loving passion. But that is exactly what he did earlier that morning in the garden, where Mr. and Mrs. Cutler sat together in the sun, Henry reading newspapers and Sarah working diligently on the family quilt, trying to ignore the sweat dampening her brow under her broad sunhat.

"I *missed* it!" Henry shouted without warning. He stood up from his chair and kicked it away.

Sarah flinched and jabbed herself with one of her needles, but she ignored the injury and instead directed all of her attention on Henry. "Oh, darling, what's wrong? What's happened?"

Henry's eyes had turned black. "They whipped them. There at Manassas, just days ago. And I *missed it*. The battle, the victory, the parades, *all of it*. My war was a sea of tents covered by the stench of ten thousand men flatulating like fucking mules. Now the war will soon be over — Lincoln hanged, and all the boys come home like proud heroes."

Henry began to pace around the garden with his head in his hands. Whenever Sarah caught glimpses of his face, she saw a rictus of shame and loathing that made her fear for Henry's state of mind.

"You know what some bitch gave to me in town yesterday?" Henry muttered. "She walked right up to me, looked me right in the eye, and she gave me a white feather. She branded me a goddamn coward in front of the entire Valley. I could have shot her on the spot. I at least should have belted her is what I should have done. The fucking mud-eating bitch..."

"But you *served*, Henry," Sarah said. She abandoned her work on her quilt and hurried to Henry's side. She put her hand on his shoulder and tried to soothe him. "You served your country, Henry. You were struck down, darling. It was an act of God. There was nothing you could do about it." When Henry resisted her touch, she only reached for him again. She squeezed at him, tried to turn him around so she could look into his eyes. "Darling, you are a hero like all the others. You can still hold your head up high. You can be proud of your sacrifice to the—"

He roared and struck her across the face with the back of his hand.

The blow sent Sarah flying. She tripped over the overturned chair and collapsed, and her head smashed against the brick pathway. Servants rushed over from their hiding places and called her name, knelt beside her to inspect her condition. Sarah lay dazed, unable to move, for several long minutes. She'd bitten through part of her tongue, and a screaming pain consumed her. When she rolled over, she winced at another terrific pain that streaked down her neck. Slowly, with the servants' help, Sarah pulled herself upright and looked around the garden for Henry.

But Henry was gone.

That evening, as she got ready for bed, Sarah heard a knock on her door. Henry had visited her bedroom every night for the last week or so, and tonight he probably expected nothing different. For Sarah, as she examined her swollen tongue and studied the misshapen bruise on her jaw, she knew that what Henry expected was certainly not what he was going to get.

Not tonight. And maybe not for a long time to come.

Sarah hurried to bed and lay down and went very still as if asleep. The door opened and Henry stepped inside and, probably noting that the candles in the bedroom were still lit and fluttering as if a great wind had just passed through the space, spoke to Sarah as if she was still awake.

"Sarah, I think you ought to listen to me."

Sarah shut her eyes tight and wished herself anyplace but here. She lay still and listened. What else could she do?

"I went too far this morning," Henry said. "Sometimes a man must correct his wife, but this wasn't that. What I did...I hesitate to call it *wrong*, but...but it was unnecessary. Yes, it was unnecessary. I can admit it, you see? I am taking personal responsibility for my actions."

Gingerly, Sarah tested her swollen tongue against her teeth, and through the smarting pain she maintained a stony silence.

"I know this hasn't been easy for you, Sarah, this life of ours. It hasn't been easy for either of us. Mother's told me how you left the plantation grounds often when I was away. But have I ever once pestered you about it? I am a trusting person, Sarah, but you test the limits of that trust. And maybe...maybe part of that anger came out today."

Still Sarah said nothing. She lay there and listened.

"But maybe there's something else at work. Something else on my mind, I mean. When you lost my child, I felt somehow...betrayed. I felt as if you'd given to me something so wonderful, but then like a squaw you took it back. I know I should not blame you, but I did. And so maybe...maybe there was a slow-building resentment I did not appreciate until just now."

Slowly, Sarah shut her eyes tight and wished herself anywhere else.

"And you did not see what I saw in the war, Sarah. Though I did not fight at Manassas, I did *see* war. I saw things that you could never understand, never even begin to comprehend. You are not only a husband's wife now, Sarah, but the wife of a veteran. The debilitating effects of war can linger with some veterans. Sometimes

I lash out, and I cannot say I will ever stop. Correction comes naturally to me. But with you, Sarah-darling, it's never to hurt. You are never the object of my anger. It's simply me lashing out against, well, against *everything*."

Hearing this, Sarah did not know whether to laugh or scream. But the next thing she knew, she felt a weight land on the bed and heard the bed groan, and then she felt Henry's warmth touch her and felt his warm breath tingle her neck while a shiver ran down her spine. Though it was dark in the room, she could still see a fading lightness in the evening sky beyond the windows.

"Oh, Sarah," Henry whispered. "Oh, Sarah, I don't know why I do such things."

She glared at the far wall as she felt him harden between her legs.

Henry was quiet for a long moment. Waiting for her to say something, maybe, or else to move.

"I love you, Sarah. I love you so much. And I've been thinking, darling. I've been thinking about our family. In all the time I was away, I could think of nothing but our children. I could see them in my dreams at night. I saw *our* children, Sarah, and they were the most beautiful angels you could ever imagine. And for so long, I've been away from you, thinking only of returning to you…returning to *this*…"

He kissed her neck once, twice, over and over. His hands swept down the curves of her body. She felt her own warmth reveal itself down there. She wanted him, wanted all of him, and as she started to turn into him she—

No.

No. For God's sake, no! What in God's name was wrong with her? *No, no, no*!

She lay very still, like a stone.

Henry stopped. He rolled her over. "What's wrong? Are you feeling all right?"

She swallowed. It took every effort to answer him. "No, darling. I'm afraid I don't feel very well tonight…"

Henry did not hear her, or else he hadn't cared to listen. "Oh, but won't you care for me, Sarah-darling? I need your *care*, darling."

Slowly, she rolled over and looked at him. There was an expectant grin on his eyes, the knowing look he gave when he knew she was his to take, his to shape in any way he pleased. But looking back at Henry's crooked smile, her own gaze hardened with conviction. No, she wasn't going to give him her 'care'. She wasn't even going to acknowledge him. She was simply going to roll over on her side and try to get some sleep.

Henry's grin faded, and the light in his eyes began to dim.

"You should answer me when I talk to you, Sarah."

Sarah swallowed and mumbled something.

"Say again, darling?" Henry said, his teeth clenched. "You must speak up."

Finally, Sarah found her voice. "I won't."

He blinked. "Won't *what*? What won't you do, Sarah-darling?"

She swallowed again, but somehow her breath remained even, measured. She felt, well, she felt calm, despite everything.

"I won't answer you, Henry, if I don't feel like speaking. I won't do what you say anymore just because you say it. I won't touch you if I don't wish to. This is not to say I'll never do any of these things again, but they must be on shared terms or not at all. I won't be a plaything, and I won't be your property, something for you to *take* whenever you wish. Whatever you want for me, whatever you want *from* me, you will only get it if I *give* it to you."

Henry froze in place. His caressing hands now felt like clutching vises. Breathless, Sarah waited for Henry to say something, or maybe to strike out at her. But instead, Henry slowly slithered away from her and got up from the bed.

As Henry's boots made for the bedroom door and the latch clicked open, Sarah rolled over in the bed and called:

"I do love you, Henry. Forever."

Henry paused at the threshold, and he lingered long enough that he could have echoed Sarah's words twice or three times over. During this time, Sarah wondered if she herself had really meant what she said about loving him forever. In any case, Henry gave no response. He only shut the door loudly behind him, and his bootsteps decayed down the hall.

In the hours since Henry had gone, Sarah had been unable to sleep. She lay awake feeling the minutes and hours crawl past as if they were tiny ants carrying morsels across a windowsill. And all the while, Sarah's tongue throbbed and her jaw ached and her heart had twisted itself up into a Gordian knot that choked her breath. Only when it was very close to dawn did Sarah finally feel sleep dull all these edges, and she felt her feet float up, and she readied to let go completely.

Just then, she heard heavy footsteps — *boot*steps — thudding up the hall. The bedroom doorknob rattled and the door swung open with a creaking whine, and then Sarah heard it close again. For a long moment she lay gripped by fear, unsure just who or what had entered her room. But then she heard Henry's musty breath in the darkness, and she smelled the stench of moonshine on his breath. No doubt Henry had been out drinking 'headsplitters' with Horace Glanton and the rest of the plantation's overseers.

Weight landed on the bed and the bed groaned the same as it had earlier, but this time Henry's body pressed freezing cold against Sarah's skin. In the pitch blackness, his hands began to reach for her. She felt wet, comatose kisses on her cheek, his lips sucking on her nose, his lips moving over hers. She did not kiss Henry back, but tried to keep her mouth closed. As far as she was concerned, Henry was drunk and she was asleep, and determined to remain so.

"Sarah," Henry whispered. He bit her ear. "*Sarah*...it's time to wake up, darling..."

"*Ow*! Henry, that hurts—"

He stopped her with his mouth. He pushed his tongue like an invasive worm down her throat. His teeth gnashed against hers and she reeled in pain, but before she could protest his lips had locked over hers and his whole body was crushing down, down, down. She pushed against him, and she began to panic when her strength wasn't enough to hold Henry back. All she could think to do was to use her teeth to bite down as hard as she could and—

"Fucking Christ!" Henry roared, and he leaped away. "You fucking bit me!"

Sarah clutched at the covers and pulled them over her. "I'm sorry, Henry. I—"

"You bitch. You fucking bitch, you fucking bit me."

"I only nipped you, Henry."

"...You *what?*"

"I...I bit you, Henry. I needed you to stop. You were hurting me. You...you *hurt* me."

It was pitch black in the bedroom, but somehow she could see his eyes suspended over her like two spheres of glassy volcanic rock. The longer she looked into those eyes the colder she felt, but she did not dare look away.

Henry said nothing. Though she did not dare entertain the hope more than a moment, she wondered if her words had somehow finally sunken in. Maybe Henry was in fact stunned and shamed by his own monstrous behavior.

But then she felt Henry's hands on her, and she knew the horrible truth. While he hiked up her nightdress and pushed himself against her, his musty breath spoke into her ear with great urgency:

"Our family, Sarah. Tonight...Our baby...Christ, I want you..."

While Sarah winced at Henry's touch, her mind clouded with poisonous thoughts. *Our baby*. She wanted to strike out at Henry and ask him exactly who he meant when he said *'our baby'*. The baby she had carried and delivered after so many months, and whom Henry had not even wished to bless or name when he ordered 'it' buried? For Sarah, 'it' had been a beautiful little girl, a heavenly potential too pure for the brutal actuality of this ugly world. But Henry, he was content to forget the child had ever existed.

Just as she had earlier that evening, Sarah stiffened up as if she had been turned to stone. But this time, Henry did not notice, or else did not care. He took her anyway, and though her flesh crawled she let him do it. What the hell else was she going to do? Run downstairs and grab a knife from the kitchens?

He finished quickly as he always did, a small mercy Sarah could usually count on, but as he neared his climax he gave a breathy laugh and wrapped both hands around her neck.

She couldn't breathe.

His body grinded against hers, harder and faster. There was no way he could not see the bulging terror in her eyes, but maybe Henry didn't care. He was moaning and laughing to himself, and still his hands squeezed tighter around her throat.

She couldn't breathe.

He stabbed her again and again, thrusting deep into her, and he felt like a hot knife carving her insides, and she wasn't sure whether the warm stickiness oozing deep within herself was blood or—

She couldn't breathe!

She reached up and made a claw with her fingernails and dared herself to strike at him, but at that moment Henry's body hitched and convulsed and he let out a great sigh of pleasure. She felt his hardness break inside her and felt his warmth spreading for a long, still moment.

It felt like years before Sarah deemed it safe to move again. Even so, she lay there in the quiet dark until she heard Henry snoring peacefully. Slowly, carefully, she reached down and inspected herself with her fingers. The sheets underneath her buttocks were soaked, and when she brought her fingers up she saw they were covered in blood. A scraping rawness in her groin promised a night of sleepless pain. The tender pain of her wedding night had been nothing like this. Horseplay aside, Henry had never been violent before now. He'd never *attacked...*

For the good of the family.

The difference, she realized, was that she'd never felt afraid before. Not like now.

She thought about leaving. She thought about getting up from the bed and padding away to some other bedroom, somewhere safe. Or maybe she'd go somewhere else. Clarendon, maybe. She needed time to process what had happened. She needed time to make sense of what her husband, her darling Henry, had done to her.

But of course she knew she'd stay. The voice in her head told her as much. She would stay—

For the good of the family.

Henry snored as Sarah imagined elephants might snore, and she knew he would not wake for some time to come. At one point Henry rolled to his side and wrapped an arm around her waist. Though her heart leapt into her throat immediately following this, she soon sank against Henry's warmth. Despite everything, that siren-like voice in her head told her that *this was where she belonged*, and that *husbands never hit their wives without a good reason*. It was her responsibility to reflect on her failings, and try to do better. This was just another part of the wife's duty. After all, every soul had to know its place.

When she remembered herself, Sarah peeled away from Henry's grasp and shivered with revulsion. She tried to make herself fall asleep, but she could not quiet her racing heart. In her head, Sarah heard the incessant, high-pitched screaming of a teakettle that had been forgotten on the stove. She shivered in a cold sweat but loathed the idea of sharing the covers with Henry another night.

This was not love. This was not what she had dreamed of since she was a little girl. Lord, this was a *nightmare*. She wondered whether it was possible for her to retrace her steps back in time, so that she might change her present course, so that she might live forever in a time BEFORE.

Very slowly, Sarah became aware that the darkness of the world around her was lightening. There were colors fading up in the eastern sky through the windows.

Dawn was coming. At last, a new day.

But would it be the same as the day before? And the one before that? And the one before that?

Every soul knows its place.

All at once the bitter pangs of dread and despair and shame consumed her. Tears welled in her eyes, and Sarah buried her face in her hands and wept in choked silence. She wanted to scream but knew she could not, and somehow this made her want to shriek all the louder.

The darkness of the bedroom, the stillness of Arcadia's hallways and drawing rooms — none of it cared about her. Sarah finally realized that there were no caring spirits watching over her. God had to be an impassive non-thing. The flecked oil painting of Mother was just that, a flecked oil painting that just so happened to capture the essence — and maybe only a fictional essence at that — of a woman Sarah had never even met. There was nothing here at Arcadia but an emptiness in which to carry out a meaningless existence, nothing in the Valley but *Nothing*, a void over which she was suspended like a marionette, with the strings ready to let go at any moment.

Sarah felt herself sink deeper into her bed, felt four plush walls rise up like the confines of a coffin.

But just then, from somewhere, as if floating out of a dream, Sarah heard...well, what was it she heard exactly?

A voice?

Yes. A faint voice outside, and it was...

The voice was *singing*.

At first, Sarah thought of the lullabies that Mae Jane used to sing to her and her brothers. She felt herself slip into a half-dream of her childhood, and she saw Mae Jane's loving smile and heard the old woman's melodic voice. And thinking of this, the chill began to lift from Sarah's bones.

But wait. As she listened, she heard many voices singing together as one, and she realized she was not dreaming at all. Still, she could not make out the words of the song.

Sarah rose from the bed, unable to bear laying next to Henry any longer. Standing in her nightgown, she padded barefoot across the creaking floor until she stood before a large window. The view looked east, and she could anticipate the sun's fast-approaching arrival over the distant Blue Ridge mountains. High above, circles of stars still shone in the part of the sky where night lingered. Though the Great

Comet had faded, Sarah could still make out the shining light of Venus and the dim outline of the Big Dipper. She was astonished at the sight of bulbous pink clouds awaiting the new sun's birth. She'd seen many sunrises before, but something about this one quieted her racing heart and stilled her breathing. A halo of light was rising in the east, and above it rested a starry crown suspended in a fading cosmic blue.

Sarah looked down and saw that the window was closed. Her instincts made her press her palms against the glass, and with both hands she pushed up until the window slid open. Myriad sensations hit her at once: the coolness of the morning air, the smell of summer pine and tobacco and pungent violets, and the clear-ringing sound of many deep voices floating in the ether. Their song drifted over Arcadia's cotton fields, and it curled around moss-covered trees, and it seemed to pass right through Sarah's shivering body and touch some part of her that lay deep within. As the voices sang, Sarah's weeping began to ebb.

We are climbing Jacob's Ladder,
We are climbing Jacob's Ladder,
Soldiers of the cross

Every rung goes higher, higher,
Every rung goes higher, higher,
Soldiers of the cross

Keep on climbing, we will make it,
Keep on climbing, we will make it,
Soldiers of the cross

The sun had not yet fully risen, yet Sarah realized Arcadia's field hands were already hard at work. And looking down now, she could see many people down there among the pink-white rows of the cotton fields. To Sarah's quiet astonishment, she realized that there were no overseers stalking about the fields supervising the hands, for all the overseers were still asleep. And yet, the field hands were out together, working side by side with purposeful energy. And their voices, they were so *joyful*. Sarah had noted many times before the rather sorrowful sound of the field hands' voices, and how, when working under the lash of whips during the heat of the day, the people sang with an earnestness that suggested their choruses were simply a strategy of keeping themselves sane.

But this morning, the voices sang with a passion that reached for bliss. In these precious few moments, the people were together as one, and it was almost as if they could forget they were slaves — almost as if they were singing together back in a distant time and place, back to a faraway home in an ancient BEFORE when the pink-white fields of Arcadia were seen only in the nightmares of village shamans.

Sarah had been here at Arcadia for well over a year now, but she had rarely looked upon the field workers until now. She had learned, from her very first day, to always look *past* Arcadia's servants, to look *through* them. She had learned to pretend the people weren't even there.

But they were here now, all spread out before her, and Sarah felt the inexplicable urge to be down there working alongside them. She knew the people were trapped here at Arcadia by Henry and his family — *her* family — and she knew she herself was trapped here in the darkened bedroom. But surely she was not trapped in the literal sense. For pity's sake, it was not as if there were chains around her feet...

While Sarah listened to the voices, she listened also for the sound of rattling chains. But though she strained, she could hear nothing of the sort. Of course, she'd forgotten that at Arcadia, the Cutlers did not need to put their slaves in chains. Those who were bound to Arcadia never ran away.

After all, every soul knows its place.

Sarah Cutler — *Roscoe* — could hear the people's voices clearer than ever now. There was a rhythm to the voices, as if the very earth was speaking through them. And though the baritones and tenors of men filled the air, the voices of the women rang clearest and purest of all.

Children, do you want your freedom?
Children, do you want your freedom?
Children, do you want your freedom?

Standing at the confines of her window, watching the silhouettes under the rising sun and feeling the first warmth of dawn, Sarah wept again. But this time, she did not weep only for herself. Tears rolled down her cheeks, but she forgot her pain. She forgot her loathing, her hopelessness. She could no longer hear the cruel voice in her head that poisoned her thoughts with bitter counsel. Indeed, she could not hear herself at all.

Sarah heard only those voices on the wind and the precious music they made. And for perhaps the first time in her life, she listened.

Printed in Great Britain
by Amazon

27767820R00443